The Stories of
RAY BRADBURY

with an introduction by the author

THIS IS A BORZOI BOOK
PUBLISHED BY ALFRED A. KNOPF, INC.

LIBRARY OF CONGRESS CATALOGING IN PUBLICATION DATA
Bradbury, Ray [date]
The Stories of Ray Bradbury
I. Title.
PZ3.B72453St   1980   [PS3503.R167]   813' .54   80-7655
ISBN 0-394-51335-5

Manufactured in the United States of America
First Edition

And this one, with love,
for Nancy Nicolas and Robert Gottlieb,
whose arguments about favorites
put this book together

Contents

Drunk, and in Charge
of a Bicycle

an introduction by Ray Bradbury

In 1953 I wrote an article for *The Nation* defending my work as a science-fiction writer, even though that label only applied to perhaps one third of my output each year.

A few weeks later, in late May, a letter arrived from Italy. On the back of the envelope, in a spidery hand, I read these words:

> B. Berenson
> I Tatti, Settignano
> Firenze, Italia

I turned to my wife and said, "My God, this can't be from *the* Berenson, can it, the great art historian?!"

"Open it," said my wife.

I did, and read:

Dear Mr. Bradbury:

In 89 years of life, this is the first fan letter I have written. It is to tell you that I have just read your article in *The Nation*—"Day After Tomorrow." It is the first time I have encountered the statement by an artist in any field, that to work creatively he must put flesh into it, and enjoy it as a lark, or as a fascinating adventure.

How different from the workers in the heavy industry that professional writing has become!

If you ever touch Florence, come to see me.

Sincerely yours. B. BERENSON.

Thus, at the age of thirty-three, I had my way of seeing, writing and living approved of by a man who became a second father to me.

I needed that approval. We all need someone higher, wiser, older to tell us we're not crazy after all, that what we're doing is all right. All right, hell, *fine!*

But it is easy to doubt yourself, because you look around at a community of notions held by other writers, other intellectuals, and they make you blush with guilt. Writing is supposed to be difficult, agonizing, a dreadful exercise, a terrible occupation.

But, you see, my stories have led me through my life. They shout, I follow. They run up and bite me on the leg—I respond by writing down everything that goes on during the bite. When I finish, the idea lets go, and runs off.

That is the kind of life I've had. Drunk, and in charge of a bicycle, as an Irish police report once put it. Drunk with life, that is, and not knowing where off to next. But you're on your way before dawn. And the trip? Exactly one half terror, exactly one half exhilaration.

When I was three my mother snuck me in and out of movies two or three times a week. My first film was Lon Chaney in *The Hunchback of Notre Dame.* I suffered permanent curvature of the spine *and* of my imagination that day a long time ago in 1923. From that hour on, I knew a kindred and wonderfully grotesque compatriot of the dark when I saw one. I ran off to see all the Chaney films again and again to be deliciously frightened. The Phantom of the Opera stood astride my life with his scarlet cape. And when it wasn't the Phantom it was the terrible hand that gestured from behind the bookcase in *The Cat and the Canary*, bidding me to come find more darkness hid in books.

I was in love, then, with monsters and skeletons and circuses and carnivals and dinosaurs and, at last, the red planet, Mars.

From these primitive bricks I have built a life and a career. By my staying in love with all of these amazing things, all of the good things in my existence have come about.

In other words, I was *not* embarrassed at circuses. Some people are. Circuses are loud, vulgar, and smell in the sun. By the time many people are fourteen or fifteen, they have been divested of their loves, their ancient and intuitive tastes, one by one, until when they reach maturity there is no fun left, no zest, no gusto, no flavor. Others have criticized, and they have criticized themselves, into embarrassment. When the circus pulls in at five of a dark cold summer morn, and the calliope sounds, they do not rise and run, they turn in their sleep, and life passes by.

I did rise and run. I learned that I was right and everyone else wrong when I was nine. Buck Rogers arrived on scene that year, and it was instant love. I collected the daily strips, and was madness maddened by them. Friends criticized. Friends made fun. I tore up the Buck Rogers strips. For a month I walked through my fourth-grade classes, stunned and empty. One day I burst into tears, wondering what devastation had happened to me. The answer was: Buck Rogers. He was gone, and life simply wasn't worth living. The next thought was: Those are not my friends, the ones who got me to tear the strips apart and so tear my own life down the middle; those are my enemies.

I went back to collecting Buck Rogers. My life has been happy ever since. For that was the beginning of my writing science fiction. Since then, I have never listened to anyone who criticized my taste in space-travel, sideshows or gorillas. When such occurs, I pack up my dinosaurs and leave the room.

For, you see, it is all mulch. If I hadn't stuffed my eyes and stuffed my head with all of the above for a lifetime, when it came round to word-associating myself into story ideas, I would have brought up a ton of ciphers and a half-ton of zeros.

"The Veldt," collected herein, is a prime example of what goes on in a headful of images, myths, toys. Back some thirty years ago I sat down to my typewriter one day and wrote these words: "The Playroom." Playroom where? The Past? No. The Present? Hardly. The Future? Yes! Well, then, what would a Playroom in some future year be like? I began typing, word-associating around the Room. Such a Playroom must have wall-to-wall television in each wall, and in the ceiling. Walking into such an environment, a child could shout: River Nile! Sphinx! Pyramids! and they would appear, surrounding him, in full color, full sound, and, why not? glorious warm scents and smells and odors, pick one, for the nose!

All this came to me in a few seconds of fast typing. I knew the Room, now I must put characters in the Room. I typed out a character named George, brought him into a future-time kitchen, where his wife turned and said:

"George, I wish you'd look at the Playroom. I think it's broken—"

George and his wife go down the hall. I follow them, typing madly, not knowing what will happen next. They open the door of the Playroom and step in.

Africa. Hot sun. Vultures. Dead meats. Lions.

Two hours later the lions leaped out of the walls of the Playroom and devoured George and his wife, while their TV-dominated children sat by and sipped tea.

End of word-association. End of story. The whole thing complete and almost ready to send out, an explosion of idea, in something like 120 minutes.

The lions in that room, where did they come from?

From the lions I found in the books in the town library when I was ten. From the lions I saw in the real circuses when I was five. From the lion that prowled in Lon Chaney's film *He Who Gets Slapped* in 1924!

1924! you say, with immense doubt. Yes, 1924. I didn't see the Chaney film again until a year ago. As soon as it flashed on the screen I knew that that was where my lions in "The Veldt" came from. They had been hiding out, waiting, given shelter by my intuitive self, all these years.

For I am that special freak, the man with the child inside who remembers all. I remember the day and the hour I was born. I remember being circumcised on the second day after my birth. I remember suckling at my mother's breast.

Years later I asked my mother about the circumcision. I had information that couldn't have been told me, there would be no reason to tell a child, especially in those still-Victorian times. Was I circumcised somewhere away from the lying-in hospital? I was. My father took me to the doctor's office. I remember the doctor. I remember the scalpel.

I wrote the story "The Small Assassin" twenty-six years later. It tells of a baby born with all its senses operative, filled with terror at being thrust out into a cold world, and taking revenge on its parents by crawling secretly about at night and at last destroying them.

When did it all really begin? The writing, that is. Everything came together in the summer and fall and early winter of 1932. By that time I was stuffed full of Buck Rogers, the novels of Edgar Rice Burroughs, and the night-time radio serial *Chandu the Magician*. Chandu said magic and the psychic summons and the Far East and strange places which made me sit down every night and from memory write out the scripts of each show.

But the whole conglomeration of magic and myths and falling downstairs with brontosaurs only to arise with La of Opar, was shaken into a pattern by one man, Mr. Electrico.

He arrived with a seedy two-bit carnival, The Dill Brothers Combined Shows, during Labor Day weekend of 1932, when I was twelve. Every night for three nights, Mr. Electrico sat in his electric chair, being fired with ten billion volts of pure blue sizzling power. Reaching out into the audience, his eyes flaming, his white hair standing on end, sparks leaping between his smiling teeth, he brushed an Excalibur sword over the heads of the children, knighting them with fire. When he came to me, he tapped me on both shoulders and then the tip of my nose. The lightning jumped into me. Mr. Electrico cried: *"Live forever!"*

I decided that was the greatest idea I had ever heard. I went to see Mr. Electrico the next day, with the excuse that a nickel magic trick I had purchased from him wasn't in working order. He fixed it, and toured me around the tents, shouting at each, "Clean up your language," before we entered to meet the dwarfs, acrobats, fat women, and Illustrated Men waiting there.

We walked down to sit by Lake Michigan where Mr. Electrico spoke his small philosophies and I talked my big ones. Why he put up with me, I'll never know. But he listened, or it seemed he listened, maybe because he was far from home, maybe because he had a son somewhere in the world, or had no son at all and wanted one. Anyway he was a defrocked Presbyterian minister, he said, and lived down in Cairo, Illinois, and I could write him there, any time I wished.

Finally he gave me some special news.

"We've met before," he said. "You were my best friend in France in 1918, and you died in my arms in the battle of the Ardennes forest that year. And here you are, born again, in a new body, with a new name. Welcome back!"

I staggered away from that encounter with Mr. Electrico wonderfully uplifted by two gifts: the gift of having lived once before (and of being told about it) . . . and the gift of trying somehow to live forever.

A few weeks later I started writing my first short stories about the planet Mars. From that time to this, I have never stopped. God bless Mr. Electrico, the catalyst, wherever he is.

If I consider every aspect of all the above, my beginnings almost inevitably had to be in the attic. From the time I was twelve until I was twenty-two or -three, I wrote stories long after midnight—unconventional stories of ghosts and haunts and things in jars that I had seen in sour armpit carnivals, of friends lost to the tides in lakes, and of consorts of three in the morning, those souls who had to fly in the dark in order not to be shot in the sun.

It took me many years to write myself down out of the attic, where I had to make do with my own eventual mortality (a teenager's preoccupation), make it to the living room, then out to the lawn and sunlight where the dandelions had come up, ready for wine.

Getting out on the front lawn with my Fourth of July relatives gave me not only my Green Town, Illinois, stories, it also shoved me off toward Mars, following Edgar Rice Burroughs' and John Carter's advice, taking my childhood luggage, my uncles, aunts, my mom, dad, and brother with me. When I arrived on Mars I found them, in fact, waiting for me, or Martians who looked like them, pretending me into a grave. The Green Town stories that found their way into an accidental novel titled *Dandelion Wine* and the Red Planet stories that blundered into another accidental novel called *The Martian Chronicles* were written, alternately, during the same years that I ran to the rainbarrel outside my grandparents' house to dip out all the memories, the myths, the word-associations of other years.

Along the way, I also re-created my relatives as vampires who inhabited a town similar to the one in *Dandelion Wine*, dark first cousin to the town on Mars where the Third Expedition expired. So, I had my life three ways, as town explorer, space-traveler, and wanderer with Count Dracula's American cousins.

I realize I haven't talked half enough, as yet, about one variety of creature you will find stalking this collection, rising here in nightmares to founder there in loneliness and despair: dinosaurs. From the time I was seventeen until I was thirty-two, I wrote some half-dozen dinosaur stories.

One night when my wife and I were walking along the beach in Venice, California, where we lived in a thirty-dollar-a-month newlyweds' apartment, we came upon the bones of the Venice Pier and the struts, tracks, and ties of the ancient roller-coaster collapsed on the sand and being eaten by the sea.

"What's that dinosaur doing lying here on the beach?" I said.

My wife, very wisely, had no answer.

The answer came the next night when, summoned from sleep by a voice calling, I rose up, listened, and heard the lonely voice of the Santa Monica bay fog horn blowing over and over and over again.

Of course! I thought. The dinosaur heard that lighthouse fog horn blowing, thought it was another dinosaur arisen from the deep past, came swimming in for a loving confrontation, discovered it was only a fog horn, and died of a broken heart there on the shore.

I leaped from bed, wrote the story, and sent it to the *Saturday Evening Post* that week, where it appeared soon after under the title "The Beast from 20,000 Fathoms." That story, titled "The Fog Horn" in this collection, became a film two years later.

The story was read by John Huston in 1953, who promptly called to ask if I would like to write the screenplay for his film *Moby Dick*. I accepted, and moved from one beast to the next.

Because of *Moby Dick*, I reexamined the life of Melville and Jules Verne, compared their mad captains in an essay written to reintroduce a new translation of *20,000 Leagues Beneath the Sea*, which, read by the 1964 New York World's Fair people, put me in charge of conceptualizing the entire upper floor of the United States Pavilion.

Because of the Pavilion, the Disney organization hired me to help plan the dreams that went into Spaceship Earth, part of Epcot, a permanent world's fair, now building to open in 1982. In that one building, I have crammed a history of mankind, coming and going back and forth in time, then plunging into our wild future in space.

Including dinosaurs.

All of my activities, all of my growing, all of my new jobs and new loves, caused and created by that original primitive love of the beasts I saw when I was five and dearly cherished when I was twenty and twenty-nine and thirty.

Look around among these stories and you will probably find only one or two that actually happened to me. I have resisted, most of my life, being given assignments to go somewhere and "sponge up" the local color, the natives, the look and feel of the land. I learned long ago that I am not seeing directly, that my subconscious is doing most of the "sponging" and it will be years before any usable impressions surface.

As a young man I lived in a tenement in the Chicano section of Los Angeles. Most of my Latino stories were written years after I had moved from the tenement, with one terrifying, on-the-spot, exception. In late 1945, with World War II freshly over, a friend of mine asked me to accompany him to Mexico City in an old beat-up Ford V-8. I reminded him of the vow of poverty that circumstances had forced on me. He rebutted by calling me a coward, wondering why I didn't rev up my courage and send out three or four stories which I had hidden away. Reason for the hiding: the stories had been rejected once or twice by various magazines. Pummeled by my friend, I dusted the stories off and mailed them out, under the pseudonym William Elliott. Why the pseudonym? Because I feared that some Manhattan editors might have seen the name Bradbury on the covers of *Weird Tales* and would be prejudiced against this "pulp" writer.

I mailed off three short stories to three different magazines, in the second week of August 1945. On August 20, I sold one story to *Charm*, on August 21, I sold a story to *Mademoiselle*, and on August 22, my twenty-fifth birthday, I sold a story to *Collier's*. The total monies amounted to $1,000, which would be like having $10,000 arrive in the mail today.

I was rich. Or so close to it I was dumbfounded. It was a turning point in my life, of course, and I hastened to write to the editors of those three magazines confessing my true name.

All three stories were listed in *The Best American Short Stories of 1946* by Martha Foley, and one of them was published in Herschel Brickell's O. Henry Memorial Award *Prize Stories* the following year.

That money took me to Mexico, to Guanajuato, and the mummies in the catacombs. The experience so wounded and terrified me, I could hardly wait to flee Mexico. I had nightmares about dying and having to remain in the halls of the dead with those propped and wired bodies. In order to purge my terror, instantly, I wrote "The Next in Line." One of the few times that an experience yielded results almost on the spot.

Enough of Mexico. What about Ireland?

There is every kind of Irish story here because after living in Dublin for six months I saw that most of the Irish I met had a variety of ways of making do with that dreadful beast Reality. You can run into it head-on, which is a dire business, or you can skirt around it, give it a poke, dance for it, make up a song, write you a tale, prolong the gab, fill up the flask. Each partakes of Irish cliché, but each, in the foul weather and the foundered politics, is true.

I got to know every beggar in the streets of Dublin, the ones near O'Connell's Bridge with maniac pianolas grinding more coffee than tunes and the ones who loaned out a single baby among a whole tribe of rainsoaked mendicants, so you saw the babe one hour at the top of Grafton Street and the next by the Royal Hibernian Hotel, and at midnight down by the river, but I never thought I would write of them. Then the need to howl and give an angry weep made me rear up one night and write "McGillahee's Brat" out of terrible suspicions and the begging of a rainwalking ghost that had to be laid. I visited some of the old burnt-out estates of the great Irish landowners, and heard tales of one "burning" that had not quite come off, and so wrote "The Terrible Conflagration up at the Place."

"The Anthem Sprinters," another Irish encounter, wrote itself down years later when, one rainy night, I recalled the countless times my wife and I had sprinted out of Dublin cinemas, dashing for the exit, knocking children and old folks to left and right, in order to make it to the exit before the National Anthem was played.

But how did I begin? Starting in Mr. Electrico's year, I wrote a thousand words a day. For ten years I wrote at least one short story a week, somehow guessing that a day would finally come when I truly got out of the way and let it happen.

The day came in 1942 when I wrote "The Lake." Ten years of doing everything wrong suddenly became the right idea, the right scene, the right characters, the right day, the right creative time. I wrote the story sitting outside, with my typewriter, on the lawn. At the end of an hour the story was finished, the hair on the back of my neck was standing up, and I was in tears. I knew I had written the first really good story of my life.

All during my early twenties I had the following schedule. On Monday morning I wrote the first draft of a new story. On Tuesday I did a second draft. On Wednesday a third. On Thursday a fourth. On Friday a fifth. And on Saturday at noon I mailed out the sixth and final draft to New York. Sunday? I thought about all the wild ideas scrambling for my attention, waiting under the attic lid, confident at last that, because of "The Lake," I would soon let them out.

If this all sounds mechanical, it wasn't. My ideas drove me to it, you see. The more I did, the more I wanted to do. You grow ravenous. You run fevers. You know exhilarations. You can't sleep at night, because your beast-creature ideas want out and turn you in your bed. It is a grand way to live.

There was another reason to write so much: I was being paid twenty to forty dollars a story, by the pulp magazines. High on the hog was hardly my way of life. I had to sell at least one story, or better two, each month in order to survive my hot-dog, hamburger, trolley-car-fare life.

In 1944 I sold some forty stories, but my total income for the year was only $800.

It suddenly strikes me that there is much in this collection I haven't commented on yet. "The Black Ferris" is of interest here because early one autumn twenty-three years ago it changed itself from a short short story into a screenplay and then into a novel, *Something Wicked This Way Comes*.

"The Day It Rained Forever" was another word-association I handed myself one afternoon, thinking about hot suns, deserts, and harps that could change the weather.

"The Leave-Taking" is the true story of my great-grandmother who nailed shingles on rooftops well into her seventies, then took herself up to bed when I was three and said farewell to everyone and went to sleep.

"Calling Mexico" sprang into being because I visited a friend of mine one afternoon in the summer of 1946 and, as I entered the room, he handed me the telephone and said, "Listen." I listened and heard the sounds of Mexico City coming from two thousand miles away. I went home and wrote about my telephone experience to a friend in Paris. Halfway through my letter, the letter turned into the story, which went off in the mail that day.

"Skeleton" happened because I went to my doctor when I was twenty-two, complaining that my neck, my throat, felt strange. I touched all around the tendons and muscles of my neck. The doctor did likewise and said, "You know what you're suffering from?"

"What?"

"A bad case," he said, "of discovery of the larynx. We all discover, at one time or another, various tendons, various bones, in our bodies we never noticed before. That's you. Take an aspirin and go home."

I went home, feeling my elbows, my ankles, my ribs, my throat, and my medulla oblongata.

"Skeleton," a contest between a man and his hidden bones, wrote itself that night.

"The Picasso Summer" was the result of my walking on the shoreline with friends and my wife one late afternoon. I picked up a Popsicle stick, drew pictures in the sand and said: "Wouldn't it be awful, if you'd wanted to own a Picasso all your life, and suddenly bumped into him here, drawing mythological beasts in the sand . . . your very own Picasso 'etching' right in front of you. . . . "

I finished the story, about Picasso on the beach, at two in the morning.

Hemingway. "The Parrot Who Met Papa." One night in 1952 I drove across Los Angeles with friends to invade the printing plant where *Life* was publishing their issue with Hemingway's *Old Man and the Sea* in it. We grabbed copies, hot off the press, sat in the nearest bar, and talked about Papa, Finca Vigía, Cuba, and, somehow, a parrot who had lived in that bar and talked to Hemingway every night. I went home, made a notation about the parrot, and put it away for sixteen years. Prowling my file folders in 1968 I came upon just the note for a title: "The Parrot Who Met Papa."

My God, I thought, Papa's been dead eight years. If that parrot is still around, remembers Hemingway, can speak with his voice, he's worth millions. And what if someone kidnapped the parrot, held it for ransom?

"The Haunting of the New" happened because John Godley, Lord Kilbracken, wrote me from Ireland describing his visit to a house that had burned and been replaced, stone by stone, brick by brick, in imitation of the original. Within half a day of reading Kilbracken's postcard, I had first-drafted the tale.

Enough now. There you have it. Here are one hundred stories from almost forty years of my life, containing half the damning truths I suspected at midnight, and half of the saving truths I re-found next noon. If anything is taught here, it is simply the charting of the life of someone who started out to somewhere—and went. I have not so much thought my way through life as done things and found what it was and who I was after the doing. Each tale was a way of finding selves. Each self found each day slightly different from the one found twenty-four hours earlier.

It all started that autumn day in 1932 when Mr. Electrico gave me the two gifts. I don't know if I believe in previous lives, I'm not sure I can live forever. But that young boy believed in both and I have let him have his head. He has written my stories and books for me. He runs the Ouija Board and says Aye or Nay to submerged truths or half-truths. He is the skin through which, by osmosis, all the stuffs pass and put themselves on paper. I have trusted his passions, his fears, and his joys. He has, as a result, rarely failed me. When it is a long damp November in my soul, and I think too much and perceive too little, I know it is high time to get back to that boy with the tennis shoes, the high fevers, the multitudinous joys, and the terrible nightmares. I'm not sure where he leaves off and I start. But I'm proud of the tandem team. What else can I do but wish him well, and at the same time acknowledge and wish two other people well? In the same month that I married my wife Marguerite, I became affiliated with my literary representative and closest friend, Don Congdon. Maggie typed and criticized my stories, Don criticized and sold the results. With the two of them as teammates these past thirty-three years, how could I have failed? We are the Connemara Lightfoots, the Queen's Own Evaders. And we're still sprinting for that exit.

Here are the stories. Turn the page.

The Stories of
RAY BRADBURY

The Night

You are a child in a small town. You are, to be exact, eight years old, and it is growing late at night. Late for you, accustomed to bedding in at nine or nine-thirty; once in a while perhaps begging Mom or Dad to let you stay up later to hear Sam and Henry on that strange radio that is popular in this year of 1927. But most of the time you are in bed and snug at this time of night.

It is a warm summer evening. You live in a small house on a small street in the outer part of town where there are few street lights. There is only one store open, about a block away: Mrs. Singer's. In the hot evening Mother has been ironing the Monday wash and you have been intermittently begging for ice cream and staring into the dark.

You and your mother are all alone at home in the warm darkness of summer. Finally, just before it is time for Mrs. Singer to close her store, Mother relents and tells you:

"Run get a pint of ice cream and be sure she packs it tight."

You ask if you can get a scoop of chocolate ice cream on top, because you don't like vanilla, and Mother agrees. You clutch the money and run barefooted over the warm evening cement sidewalk, under the apple trees and oak trees, toward the store. The town is so quiet and far off, you can only hear the crickets sounding in the spaces beyond the hot indigo trees that hold back the stars.

Your bare feet slap the pavement, you cross the street and find Mrs. Singer moving ponderously about her store, singing Yiddish melodies.

"Pint ice cream?" she says. "Chocolate on top? Yes!"

You watch her fumble the metal top off the ice-cream freezer and manipulate the scoop, packing the cardboard pint chock full with "chocolate on top, yes!" You give the money, receive the chill, icy pack, and rubbing it across your brow and cheek, laughing, you thump barefootedly homeward. Behind you, the lights of the lonely little store blink out and there is only a street light shimmering on the corner, and the whole city seems to be going to sleep. . . .

Opening the screen door you find Mom still ironing. She looks hot and irritated, but she smiles just the same.

"When will Dad be home from lodge-meeting?" you ask.

"About eleven-thirty or twelve," Mother replies. She takes the ice cream to the kitchen, divides it. Giving you your special portion of chocolate, she dishes out some for herself and the rest is put away, "For Skipper and your father when they come."

Skipper is your brother. He is your older brother. He's twelve and healthy, red-faced, hawk-nosed, tawny-haired, broad-shouldered for his years, and always running. He is allowed to stay up later than you. Not much later, but enough to make him feel it is worthwhile having been born first. He is over on the other side of town this evening to a game of kick-the-can and will be home soon. He and the kids have been yelling, kicking, running for hours, having fun. Soon he will come clomping in, smelling of sweat and green grass on his knees where he fell, and smelling very much in all ways like Skipper; which is natural.

You sit enjoying the ice cream. You are at the core of the deep quiet summer night. Your mother and yourself and the night all around this small house on this small street. You lick each spoon of ice cream thoroughly before digging for another, and Mom puts her ironing board away and the hot iron in its case, and she sits in the armchair by the phonograph, eating her dessert and saying, "My lands, it was a hot day today. It's still hot. Earth soaks up all the heat and lets it out at night. It'll be soggy sleeping."

You both sit there listening to the summer silence. The dark is pressed down by every window and door, there is no sound because the radio needs a new battery, and you have played all the Knickerbocker Quartet records and Al Jolson and Two Black Crows records to exhaustion; so you just sit on the hardwood floor by the door and look out into the dark dark dark, pressing your nose against the screen until the flesh of its tip is molded into small dark squares.

"I wonder where your brother is?" Mother says after a while. Her spoon scrapes on the dish. "He should be home by now. It's almost nine-thirty."

"He'll be here," you say, knowing very well that he will be.

You follow Mom out to wash the dishes. Each sound, each rattle of spoon or dish is amplified in the baked evening. Silently, you go to the living room, remove the couch cushions and, together, yank it open and extend it down into the double bed that it secretly is. Mother makes the bed, punching pillows neatly to flump them up for your head. Then, as you are unbuttoning your shirt, she says:

"Wait awhile, Doug."

"Why?"

"Because. I say so."

"You look funny, Mom."

Mom sits down a moment, then stands up, goes to the door, and calls. You listen to her calling and calling Skipper, Skipper, Skiiiiiiiiperrrrrrrr over and over. Her calling goes out into the summer warm dark and never comes back. The echoes pay no attention.

Skipper. Skipper. Skipper.

Skipper!

And as you sit on the floor a coldness that is not ice cream and not winter, and not part of summer's heat, goes through you. You notice Mom's eyes sliding, blinking; the way she stands undecided and is nervous. All of these things.

She opens the screen door. Stepping out into the night she walks down the steps and down the front sidewalk under the lilac bush. You listen to her moving feet.

She calls again. Silence.

She calls twice more. You sit in the room. Any moment now Skipper will reply, from down the long long narrow street:

"All right, Mom! All right, Mother! Hey!"

But he doesn't answer. And for two minutes you sit looking at the made-up bed, the silent radio, the silent phonograph, at the chandelier with its crystal bobbins gleaming quietly, at the rug with the scarlet and purple curlicues on it. You stub your toe on the bed purposely to see if it hurts. It does.

Whining, the screen door opens, and Mother says:

"Come on, Shorts. We'll take a walk."

"Where to?"

"Just down the block. Come on. Better put your shoes on, though. You'll catch cold."

"No, I won't. I'll be all right."

You take her hand. Together you walk down St. James Street. You smell roses in blossom, fallen apples lying crushed and odorous in the deep grass. Underfoot, the concrete is still warm, and the crickets are sounding louder against the darkening dark. You reach a corner, turn, and walk toward the ravine.

Off somewhere, a car goes by, flashing its lights in the distance. There is such a complete lack of life, light, and activity. Here and there, back off from where you are walking toward the ravine, you see faint squares of light where people are still up. But most of the houses, darkened, are sleeping already, and there are a few lightless places where the occupants of a dwelling sit talking low dark talk on their front porches. You hear a porch swing squeaking as you walk near.

"I wish your father was home," says Mother. Her large hand tightens around your small one. "Just wait'll I get that boy. I'll spank him within an inch of his life."

A razor strop hangs in the kitchen for this. You think of it, remember when Dad has doubled and flourished it with muscled control over your frantic limbs. You doubt Mother will carry out her promise.

Now you have walked another block and are standing by the holy black silhouette of the German Baptist Church at the corner of Chapel Street and Glen Rock. In back of the church a hundred yards away, the ravine begins. You can smell it. It has a dark sewer, rotten foliage, thick green odor. It is a wide ravine that cuts and twists across the town, a jungle by day, a place to let alone at night, Mother has often declared.

You should feel encouraged by the nearness of the German Baptist Church, but you are not—because the building is not illumined, is cold and useless as a pile of ruins on the ravine edge.

You are only eight years old, you know little of death, fear, or dread. Death is the waxen effigy in the coffin when you were six and Grandfather passed away—looking like a great fallen vulture in his casket, silent, withdrawn, no more to tell you how to be a good boy, no more to comment succinctly on politics. Death is your little sister one morning when you awaken at the age of seven, look into her crib and see her staring up at you with a blind blue, fixed and frozen stare until the men come with a small wicker basket to take her away. Death is when you stand by her high chair four weeks later and suddenly realize she'll never be in it again, laughing and crying, and make you jealous of her because she was born. That is death.

But this is more than death. This summer night wading deep in time and stars and warm eternity. It is an essence of all the things you will ever feel or see or hear in your life again, being brought steadily home to you all at once.

Leaving the sidewalk, you walk along a trodden, pebbled, weed-fringed path to the ravine's edge. Crickets, in loud full drumming chorus now, are shouting to quiver the dead. You follow obediently behind brave, fine, tall Mother who is defender of all the universe. You feel braveness because she goes before, and you hang back a trifle for a moment, and then hurry on, too. Together, then, you approach, reach, and pause at the very edge of civilization.

The ravine.

Here and now, down there in that pit of jungled blackness is suddenly all the evil you will ever know. Evil you will never understand. All of the nameless things are there. Later, when you have grown you'll be given names to label them with. Meaningless syllables to describe the waiting nothingness. Down there in the huddled shadow, among thick trees and trailed vines, lives the odor of decay. Here, at this spot, civilization ceases, reason ends, and a universal evil takes over.

You realize you are alone. You and your mother. Her hand trembles.

Her hand *trembles*.

Your belief in your private world is shattered. You feel Mother tremble. Why? Is she, too, doubtful? But she is bigger, stronger, more intelligent than yourself, isn't she? Does she, too, feel that intangible menace, that groping out of darkness, that crouching malignancy down below? Is there, then, no strength in growing up? no solace in being an adult? no sanctuary in life? no flesh citadel strong enough to withstand the scrabbling assault of midnights? Doubts flush you. Ice cream lives again in your throat, stomach, spine and limbs; you are instantly cold as a wind out of December-gone.

You realize that all men are like this. That each person is to himself one alone. One oneness, a unit in a society, but always afraid. Like here, standing. If you should scream now, if you should holler for help, would it matter?

You are so close to the ravine now that in the instant of your scream, in the interval between someone hearing it and running to find you, much could happen.

Blackness could come swiftly, swallowing; and in one titanically freezing moment all would be concluded. Long before dawn, long before police with flashlights might probe the disturbed pathway, long before men with trembling brains could rustle down the pebbles to your help. Even if they were within five hundred yards of you now, and help *certainly* is, in three seconds a dark tide could rise to take all eight years of life away from you and—

The essential impact of life's loneliness crushes your beginning-to-tremble body. Mother is alone, too. She cannot look to the sanctity of marriage, the protection of her family's love, she cannot look to the United States Constitution or the City Police, she cannot look anywhere, in this very instant, save into her heart, and there she'll find nothing but uncontrollable repugnance and a will to fear. In this instant it is an individual problem seeking an individual solution. You must accept being alone and work on from there.

You swallow hard, cling to her. Oh Lord, don't let her die, please, you think. Don't do anything to us. Father will be coming home from lodge-meeting in an hour and if the house is empty. . . ?

Mother advances down the path into the primeval jungle. Your voice trembles. "Mom. Skip's all right. Skip's all right. He's all right. Skip's all right."

Mother's voice is strained, high. "He always comes through here. I tell him not to, but those darned kids, they come through here anyway. Some night he'll come through and never come out again—"

Never come out again. That could mean anything. Tramps. Criminals. Darkness. Accident. Most of all—death.

Alone in the universe.

There are a million small towns like this all over the world. Each as dark, as lonely, each as removed, as full of shuddering and wonder. The reedy playing of minor-key violins is the small towns' music, with no lights but many shadows. Oh the vast swelling loneliness of them. The secret damp ravines of them. Life is a horror lived in them at night, when at all sides sanity, marriage, children, happiness, are threatened by an ogre called Death.

Mother raises her voice into the dark.

"Skip! Skipper!" she calls. "Skip! Skipper!"

Suddenly, both of you realize there is something wrong. Something very wrong. You listen intently and realize what it is.

The crickets have stopped chirping.

Silence is complete.

Never in your life a silence like this one. One so utterly complete. Why should the crickets cease? Why? What reason? They have never stopped ever before. Not ever.

Unless. Unless—

Something is going to happen.

It is as if the whole ravine is tensing, bunching together its black fibers, drawing in power from all about sleeping countrysides, for miles and miles. From dew-sodden forests and dells and rolling hills where dogs tilt heads to moons, from all around the great silence is sucked into one center, and you at the core of it. In ten seconds now, something will happen, something will happen. The crickets keep their truce, the stars are so low you can almost brush the tinsel. There are swarms of them, hot and sharp.

Growing, growing, the silence. Growing, growing, the tenseness. Oh it's so dark, so far away from everything. Oh God!

And then, way way off across the ravine:

"Okay, Mom! Coming, Mother!"

And again:

"Hi, Mom! Coming, Mom!"

And then the quick scuttering of tennis shoes padding down through the pit of the ravine as three kids come dashing, giggling. Your brother Skipper, Chuck Redman, and Augie Bartz. Running, giggling.

The stars suck up like the stung antennae of ten million snails.

The crickets sing!

The darkness pulls back, startled, shocked, angry. Pulls back, losing its appetite at being so rudely interrupted as it prepared to feed. As the dark retreats like a wave on a shore, three kids pile out of it, laughing.

"Hi, Mom! Hi, Shorts! Hey!"

It smells like Skipper all right. Sweat and grass and his oiled leather baseball glove.

"Young man, you're going to get a licking," declares Mother. She puts away her fear instantly. You know she will never tell anybody of it, ever. It will be in her heart though, for all time, as it is in your heart, for all time.

You walk home to bed in the late summer night. You are glad Skipper is alive. Very glad. For a moment there you thought—

Far off in the dim moonlit country, over a viaduct and down a valley, a train goes rushing along and it whistles like a lost metal thing, nameless and running. You go to bed, shivering, beside your brother, listening to that train whistle, and thinking of a cousin who lived way out in the country where that train is now; a cousin who died of pneumonia late at night years and years ago. . . . You smell the sweat of Skip beside you. It is magic. You stop trembling. You hear footsteps outside the house on the sidewalk, as Mother is turning out the lights. A man clears his throat in a way you recognize.

Mom says, "That's your father."

It is.

"Go away," she said, not even looking at him. "I can't work with you gawking."

"Allhallows Eve, Ellen; just think!" he said, trying to be friendly.

"Hunh!" She put some fingernail clippings in a small white sack, labeled them. "What can it mean to you? What do you know of it? It'll scare hell out of you. Go back to bed."

His cheeks burned. "I'm needed to polish and work and help serve."

"If you don't go, you'll find a dozen raw oysters in your bed tomorrow," said Ellen, matter-of-factly. "Good-by, Timothy."

In his anger, rushing downstairs, he bumped into Laura.

"Watch where you're going!" she shrieked from clenched teeth.

She swept away. He ran to the open cellar door, smelled the channel of moist earthy air rising from below. "Father?"

"It's about time," Father shouted up the steps. "Hurry down, or they'll be here before we're ready!"

Timothy hesitated only long enough to hear the million other sounds in the house. Brothers came and went like trains in a station, talking and arguing. If you stood in one spot long enough the entire household passed with their pale hands full of things. Leonard with his little black medical case, Samuel with his large, dusty ebon-bound book under his arm, bearing more black crape, and Bion excursioning to the car outside and bringing in many more gallons of liquid.

Father stopped polishing to give Timothy a rag and a scowl. He thumped the huge mahogany box. "Come on, shine this up, so we can start on another. Sleep your life away."

While waxing the surface, Timothy looked inside.

"Uncle Einar's a big man, isn't he, Papa?"

"Unh."

"How big is he?"

"The size of the box'll tell you."

"I was only asking. Seven feet tall?"

"You talk a lot."

About nine o'clock Timothy went out into the October weather. For two hours in the now-warm, now-cold wind he walked the meadows collecting toadstools and spiders. His heart began to beat with anticipation again. How many relatives had Mother said would come? Seventy? One hundred? He passed a farmhouse. If only you knew what was happening at our house, he said to the glowing windows. He climbed a hill and looked at the town, miles away, settling into sleep, the town-hall clock, high and round, white in the distance. The town did not know, either. He brought home many jars of toadstools and spiders.

In the little chapel belowstairs a brief ceremony was celebrated. It was like all the other rituals over the years, with Father chanting the dark lines, Mother's beautiful white ivory hands moving in the reverse blessings, and all the children gathered except Cecy, who lay upstairs in bed. But Cecy was present. You saw her peering, now from Bion's eyes, now Samuel's, now Mother's, and you felt a movement and now she was in you, fleetingly, and gone.

Timothy prayed to the Dark One with a tightened stomach. "Please, please, help me grow up, help me be like my sisters and brothers. Don't let me be different. If only I could put the hair in the plastic images as Ellen does, or make people fall in love with me as Laura does with people, or read strange books as Sam does, or work in a respected job like Leonard and Bion do. Or even raise a family one day, as Mother and Father have done. . . . "

At midnight a storm hammered the house. Lightning struck outside in amazing, snow-white bolts. There was a sound of an approaching, probing, sucking tornado, funneling and nuzzling the moist night earth. Then the front door, blasted half off its hinges, hung stiff and discarded, and in trooped Grandmama and Grandpapa, all the way from the old country!

From then on people arrived each hour. There was a flutter at the side window, a rap on the front porch, a knock at the back. There were fey noises from the cellar; autumn wind piped down the chimney throat, chanting. Mother filled the large crystal punch bowl with a scarlet fluid poured from the jugs Bion had carried home. Father swept from room to room lighting more tapers. Laura and Ellen hammered up more wolfsbane. And Timothy stood amidst this wild excitement, no expression to his face, his hands trembling at his sides, gazing now here, now there. Banging of doors, laughter, the sound of liquid pouring, darkness, sound of wind, the webbed thunder of wings, the padding of feet, the welcoming bursts of talk at the entrances, the transparent rattlings of casements, the shadows passing, coming, going, wavering.

"Well, well, and *this* must be Timothy!"

"What?"

A chilly hand took his hand. A long hairy face leaned down over him. "A good lad, a fine lad," said the stranger.

"Timothy," said his mother. "This is Uncle Jason."

"Hello, Uncle Jason."

"And over here—" Mother drifted Uncle Jason away. Uncle Jason peered back at Timothy over his caped shoulder, and winked.

Timothy stood alone.

From off a thousand miles in the candled darkness, he heard a high fluting voice; that was Ellen. "And my brothers, they *are* clever. Can you guess their occupations, Aunt Morgiana?"

"I have no idea."

"They operate the undertaking establishment in town."

"What!" A gasp.

"Yes!" Shrill laughter. "Isn't that priceless!"

Timothy stood very still.

A pause in the laughter. "They bring home sustenance for Mama, Papa and all of us," said Laura. "Except, of course, Timothy. . . ."

An uneasy silence. Uncle Jason's voice demanded, "Well? Come now. What about Timothy?"

"Oh, Laura, your tongue," said Mother.

Laura went on with it. Timothy shut his eyes. "Timothy doesn't—well—doesn't *like* blood. He's delicate."

"He'll learn," said Mother. "He'll learn," she said very firmly. "He's my son, and he'll learn. He's only fourteen."

"But I was raised on the stuff," said Uncle Jason, his voice passing from one room on into another. The wind played the trees outside like harps. A little rain spatted on the windows—"raised on the stuff," passing away into faintness.

Timothy bit his lips and opened his eyes.

"Well, it was all my fault." Mother was showing them into the kitchen now. "I tried forcing him. You can't force children, you only make them sick, and then they never get a taste for things. Look at Bion, now, he was thirteen before he . . ."

"I understand," murmured Uncle Jason. "Timothy will come around."

"I'm sure he will," said Mother, defiantly.

Candle flames quivered as shadows crossed and recrossed the dozen musty rooms. Timothy was cold. He smelled the hot tallow in his nostrils and instinctively he grabbed at a candle and walked with it around and about the house, pretending to straighten the crape.

"*Timothy*," someone whispered behind a patterned wall, hissing and sizzling and sighing the words, "*Timothy is afraid of the dark.*"

Leonard's voice. Hateful Leonard!

"I like the candle, that's all," said Timothy in a reproachful whisper.

More lightning, more thunder. Cascades of roaring laughter. Bangings and clickings and shouts and rustles of clothing. Clammy fog swept through the front door. Out of the fog, settling his wings, stalked a tall man.

"Uncle Einar!"

Timothy propelled himself on his thin legs, straight through the fog, under the green webbing shadows. He threw himself across Einar's arms. Einar lifted him.

"You've wings, Timothy!" He tossed the boy light as thistles. "Wings, Timothy: fly!" Faces wheeled under. Darkness rotated. The house blew away. Timothy felt breezelike. He flapped his arms. Einar's fingers caught and threw him once more to the ceiling. The ceiling rushed down like a charred wall. "Fly, Timothy!" shouted Einar, loud and deep. "Fly with wings! Wings!"

He felt an exquisite ecstasy in his shoulder blades, as if roots grew, burst to explode and blossom into new, moist membrane. He babbled wild stuff; again Einar hurled him high.

The autumn wind broke in a tide on the house, rain crashed down, shaking the beams, causing chandeliers to tilt their enraged candle lights. And the one hundred relatives peered out from every black, enchanted room, circling inward, all shapes and sizes, to where Einar balanced the child like a baton in the roaring spaces.

"Enough!" shouted Einar, at last.

Timothy, deposited on the floor timbers, exaltedly, exhaustedly fell against Uncle Einar, sobbing happily. "Uncle, uncle, uncle!"

"Was it good, flying? Eh, Timothy?" said Uncle Einar, bending down, patting Timothy's head. "Good, good."

It was coming toward dawn. Most had arrived and were ready to bed down for the daylight, sleep motionlessly with no sound until the following sunset, when they would shout out of their mahogany boxes for the revelry.

Uncle Einar, followed by dozens of others, moved toward the cellar. Mother directed them downward to the crowded row on row of highly polished boxes. Einar, his wings like sea-green tarpaulins tented behind him, moved with a curious whistling down the passageway; where his wings touched they made a sound of drumheads gently beaten.

Upstairs, Timothy lay wearily thinking, trying to like the darkness. There was so much you could do in darkness that people couldn't criticize you for, because they never saw you. He *did* like the night, but it was a qualified liking: sometimes there was so much night he cried out in rebellion.

In the cellar, mahogany doors sealed downward, drawn in by pale hands. In corners, certain relatives circled three times to lie, heads on paws, eyelids shut. The sun rose. There was a sleeping.

Sunset. The revel exploded like a bat nest struck full, shrieking out, fluttering, spreading. Box doors banged wide. Steps rushed up from cellar damp. More late guests, kicking on front and back portals, were admitted.

It rained, and sodden visitors laid their capes, their water-pelleted hats, their sprinkled veils upon Timothy who bore them to a closet. The rooms were crowd-packed. The laughter of one cousin, shot from one room, angled off the wall of another, ricocheted, banked, and returned to Timothy's ears from a fourth room, accurate and cynical.

A mouse ran across the floor.

"I know you, Niece Leibersrouter!" exclaimed Father, around him but not to him. The dozens of towering people pressed in against him, elbowed him, ignored him.

Finally, he turned and slipped away up the stairs.

He called softly. "Cecy. Where are you now, Cecy?"

She waited a long while before answering. "In the Imperial Valley," she murmured faintly. "Beside the Salton Sea, near the mud pots and the steam and the quiet. I'm inside a farmer's wife. I'm sitting on a front porch. I can make her move if I want, or do anything or think anything. The sun's going down."

"What's it like, Cecy?"

"You can hear the mud pots hissing," she said, slowly, as if speaking in a church. "Little gray heads of steam push up the mud like bald men rising in the thick syrup, head first, out in the boiling channels. The gray heads rip like rubber fabric, collapse with noises like wet lips moving. And feathery plumes of steam escape from the ripped tissue. And there is a smell of deep sulphurous burning and old times. The dinosaur has been abroiling here ten million years."

"Is he done yet, Cecy?"

The mouse spiraled three women's feet and vanished into a corner. Moments later a beautiful woman rose up out of nothing and stood in the corner, smiling her white smile at them all.

Something huddled against the flooded pane of the kitchen window. It sighed and wept and tapped continually, pressed against the glass, but Timothy could make nothing of it, he saw nothing. In imagination he was outside staring in. The rain was on him, the wind at him, and the taper-dotted darkness inside was inviting. Waltzes were being danced; tall thin figures pirouetted to outlandish music. Stars of light flickered off lifted bottles; small clods of earth crumbled from casques, and a spider fell and went silently legging over the floor.

Timothy shivered. He was inside the house again. Mother was calling him to run here, run there, help, serve, out to the kitchen now, fetch this, fetch that, bring the plates, heap the food—on and on—the party happened.

"Yes, he's done. Quite done." Cecy's calm sleeper's lips turned up. The languid words fell slowly from her shaping mouth. "Inside this woman's skull I am, looking out, watching the sea that does not move, and is so quiet it makes you afraid. I sit on the porch and wait for my husband to come home. Occasionally, a fish leaps, falls back, starlight edging it. The valley, the sea, the few cars, the wooden porch, my rocking chair, myself, the silence."

"What now, Cecy?"

"I'm getting up from my rocking chair," she said.

"Yes?"

"I'm walking off the porch, toward the mud pots. Planes fly over, like primordial birds. Then it is quiet, so quiet."

"How long will you stay inside her, Cecy?"

"Until I've listened and looked and felt enough: until I've changed her life some way. I'm walking off the porch and along the wooden boards. My feet knock on the planks, tiredly, slowly."

"And now?"

"Now the sulphur fumes are all around me. I stare at the bubbles as they break and smooth. A bird darts by my temple, shrieking. Suddenly I am in the bird and fly away! And as I fly, inside my new small glass-bead eyes I see a woman below me, on a boardwalk, take one two three steps forward into the mud pots. I hear a sound as of a boulder plunged into molten depths. I keep flying, circle back. I see a white hand, like a spider, wriggle and disappear into the gray lava pool. The lava seals over. Now I'm flying home, swift, swift, swift!"

Something clapped hard against the window. Timothy started.

Cecy flicked her eyes wide, bright, full, happy, exhilarated.

"Now I'm *home*!" she said.

After a pause, Timothy ventured, "The Homecoming's on. And everybody's here."

"Then why are you upstairs?" She took his hand. "Well, ask me." She smiled slyly. "Ask me what you came to ask."

"I didn't come to ask anything," he said. "Well, almost nothing. Well—oh, Cecy!" It came from him in one long rapid flow. "I want to do something at the party to make them look at me, something to make me good as them, something to make me belong, but there's nothing I can do and I feel funny and, well, I thought you might . . . "

"I might," she said, closing her eyes, smiling inwardly. "Stand up straight. Stand very still." He obeyed. "Now, shut your eyes and blank out your thought."

He stood very straight and thought of nothing, or at least thought of thinking nothing.

She sighed. "Shall we go downstairs now, Timothy?" Like a hand into a glove, Cecy was within him.

"Look everybody!" Timothy held the glass of warm red liquid. He held up the glass so that the whole house turned to watch him. Aunts, uncles, cousins, brothers, sisters!

He drank it straight down.

He jerked a hand at his sister Laura. He held her gaze, whispering to her in a subtle voice that kept her silent, frozen. He felt tall as the trees as he walked to her. The party now slowed. It waited on all sides of him, watching. From all the room doors the faces peered. They were not laughing. Mother's face was astonished. Dad looked bewildered, but pleased and getting prouder every instant.

He nipped Laura, gently, over the neck vein. The candle flames swayed drunkenly. The wind climbed around on the roof outside. The relatives stared from all the doors. He popped toadstools into his mouth, swallowed, then beat his arms against his flanks and circled. "Look, Uncle Einar! I can fly, at last!" Beat went his hands. Up and down pumped his feet. The faces flashed past him.

At the top of the stairs, flapping, he heard his mother cry, "Stop, Timothy!" far below. "Hey!" shouted Timothy, and leaped off the top of the well, thrashing.

Halfway down, the wings he thought he owned dissolved. He screamed. Uncle Einar caught him.

Timothy flailed whitely in the receiving arms. A voice burst out of his lips, unbidden. "This is Cecy! This is Cecy! Come see me, all of you, upstairs, first room on the left!" Followed by a long trill of high laughter. Timothy tried to cut it off with his tongue.

Everybody was laughing. Einar set him down. Running through the crowding blackness as the relatives flowed upstairs toward Cecy's room to congratulate her, Timothy banged the front door open.

"Cecy, I hate you, I hate you!"

By the sycamore tree, in deep shadow, Timothy spewed out his dinner, sobbed bitterly and thrashed in a pile of autumn leaves. Then he lay still. From his blouse pocket, from the protection of the matchbox he used for his retreat, the spider crawled forth. Spid walked along Timothy's arm. Spid explored up his neck to his ear and climbed in the ear to tickle it. Timothy shook his head. "Don't, Spid. Don't."

The feathery touch of a tentative feeler probing his eardrum set Timothy shivering. "Don't, Spid!" He sobbed somewhat less.

The spider traveled down his cheek, took a station under the boy's nose, looked up into the nostrils as if to seek the brain, and then clambered softly up over the rim of the nose to sit, to squat there peering at Timothy with green-gem eyes until Timothy filled with ridiculous laughter. "Go away, Spid!"

Timothy sat up, rustling the leaves. The land was very bright with the moon. In the house he could hear the faint ribaldry as Mirror, Mirror was played. Celebrants shouted, dimly muffled, as they tried to identify those of themselves whose reflections did not, had not ever, appeared in a glass.

"Timothy." Uncle Einar's wings spread and twitched and came in with a sound like kettledrums. Timothy felt himself plucked up like a thimble and set upon Einar's shoulder. "Don't feel badly, Nephew Timothy. Each to his own, each in his own way. How much better things are for you. How rich. The world's dead for us. We've seen so much of it, believe me. Life's best to those who live the least of it. It's worth more per ounce, Timothy, remember that."

The rest of the black morning, from midnight on, Uncle Einar led him about the house, from room to room, weaving and singing. A horde of late arrivals set the entire hilarity off afresh. Great-great-great-great and a thousand more great-greats Grandmother was there, wrapped in Egyptian cerements. She said not a word, but lay straight as a burnt ironing board against the wall, her eye hollows cupping a distant, wise, silent glimmering. At the breakfast, at four in the morning, one-thousand-odd-greats Grandmama was stiffly seated at the head of the longest table.

The numerous young cousins caroused at the crystal punch bowl. Their shiny olive-pit eyes, their conical, devilish faces and curly bronze hair hovered over the drinking table, their hard-soft, half-girl half-boy bodies wrestling against each other as they got unpleasantly, sullenly drunk. The wind got higher, the stars burned with fiery intensity, the noises redoubled, the dances quickened, the drinking became more positive. To Timothy there were thousands of things to hear and watch. The many darknesses roiled, bubbled, the many faces passed and repassed. . . .

"Listen!"

The party held its breath. Far away the town clock struck its chimes, saying six o'clock. The party was ending. In time to the rhythm of the striking clock, their one hundred voices began to sing songs that were four hundred years old, songs Timothy could not know. Arms twined, circling slowly, they sang, and somewhere in the cold distance of morning the town clock finished out its chimes and quieted.

Timothy sang. He knew no words, no tune, yet the words and tune came round and high and good. And he gazed at the closed door at the top of the stairs.

"Thanks, Cecy," he whispered. "You're forgiven. Thanks."

Then he just relaxed and let the words move, with Cecy's voice, free from his lips.

Good-bys were said, there was a great rustling. Mother and Father stood at the door to shake hands and kiss each departing relative in turn. The sky beyond the open door colored in the east. A cold wind entered. And Timothy felt himself seized and settled in one body after another, felt Cecy press him into Uncle Fry's head so he stared from the wrinkled leather face, then leaped in a flurry of leaves up over the house and awakening hills. . . .

Then, loping down a dirt path, he felt his red eyes burning, his fur pelt rimed with morning, as inside Cousin William he panted through a hollow and dissolved away. . . .

Like a pebble in Uncle Einar's mouth, Timothy flew in a webbed thunder, filling the sky. And then he was back, for all time, in his own body.

In the growing dawn, the last few were embracing and crying and thinking how the world was becoming less a place for them. There had been a time when they had met every year, but now decades passed with no reconciliation. "Don't forget," someone cried, "we meet in Salem in 1970!"

Salem. Timothy's numbed mind turned the words over. Salem, 1970. And there would be Uncle Fry and a thousand-times-great Grandmother in her withered cerements, and Mother and Father and Ellen and Laura and Cecy and all the rest. But would he be there? Could he be certain of staying alive until then?

With one last withering blast, away they all went, so many scarves, so many fluttery mammals, so many sere leaves, so many whining and clustering noises, so many midnights and insanities and dreams.

Mother shut the door. Laura picked up a broom. "No," said Mother. "We'll clean tonight. Now we need sleep." And the family vanished down cellar and upstairs. And Timothy moved in the crape-littered hall, his head down. Passing a party mirror, he saw the pale mortality of his face all cold and trembling.

"Timothy," said Mother.

She came to touch her hand on his face. "Son," she said, "we love you. Remember that. We all love you. No matter how different you are, no matter if you leave us one day." She kissed his cheek. "And if and when you die, your bones will lie undisturbed, we'll see to that. You'll lie at ease forever, and I'll come visit every Allhallows Eve and tuck you in the more secure."

The house was silent. Far away the wind went over a hill with its last cargo of dark bats, echoing, chittering.

Timothy walked up the steps, one by one, crying to himself all the way.

Uncle Einar

"It will take only a minute," said Uncle Einar's sweet wife.

"I refuse," he said. "And that takes but a *second*."

"I've worked all morning," she said, holding to her slender back, "and you won't help? It's drumming for a rain."

"Let it rain," he cried, morosely. "I'll not be pierced by lightning just to air your clothes."

"But you're so quick at it."

"Again, I refuse." His vast tarpaulin wings hummed nervously behind his indignant back.

She gave him a slender rope on which were tied four dozen fresh-washed clothes. He turned it in his fingers with distaste. "So it's come to this," he muttered, bitterly. "To this, to this, to this." He almost wept angry and acid tears.

"Don't cry; you'll wet them down again," she said. "Jump up, now, run them about."

"Run them about." His voice was hollow, deep, and terribly wounded. "I say: let it thunder, let it pour!"

"If it was a nice, sunny day I wouldn't ask," she said, reasonably. "All my washing gone for nothing if you don't. They'll hang about the house—"

That *did* it. Above all, he hated clothes flagged and festooned so a man had to creep under on the way across a room. He jumped up. His vast green wings boomed. "Only so far as the pasture fence!"

Whirl: up he jumped, his wings chewed and loved the cool air. Before you'd say Uncle Einar Has Green Wings he sailed low across his farmland, trailing the clothes in a vast fluttering loop through the pounding concussion and backwash of his wings!

"Catch!"

Back from the trip, he sailed the clothes, dry as popcorn, down on a series of clean blankets she'd spread for their landing.

"Thank you!" she cried.

"Gahh!" he shouted, and flew off under the apple tree to brood.

Uncle Einar's beautiful silklike wings hung like sea-green sails behind him, and whirred and whispered from his shoulders when he sneezed or turned swiftly. He was one of the few in the Family whose talent was visible. All his dark cousins and nephews and brothers hid in small towns across the world, did unseen mental things or things with witch-fingers and white teeth, or blew down the sky like fire-leaves, or loped in forests like moon-silvered wolves. They lived comparatively safe from normal humans. Not so a man with great green wings.

Not that he hated his wings. Far from it! In his youth he'd always flown nights, because nights were rare times for winged men! Daylight held dangers, always had, always would; but nights, ah, nights, he had sailed over islands of cloud and seas of summer sky. With no danger to himself. It had been a rich, full soaring, an exhilaration.

But now he could not fly at night.

On his way home to some high mountain pass in Europe after a Homecoming among Family members in Mellin Town, Illinois (some years ago) he had drunk too much rich crimson wine. "I'll be all right," he had told himself, vaguely, as he beat his long way under the morning stars, over the moon-dreaming country hills beyond Mellin Town. And then—crack out of the sky—

A high-tension tower.

Like a netted duck! A great sizzle! His face blown black by a blue sparkler of wire, he fended off the electricity with a terrific back-jumping percussion of his wings, and fell.

His hitting the moonlit meadow under the tower made a noise like a large telephone book dropped from the sky.

Early the next morning, his dew-sodden wings shaking violently, he stood up. It was still dark. There was a faint bandage of dawn stretched across the east. Soon the bandage would stain and all flight would be restricted. There was nothing to do but take refuge in the forest and wait out the day in the deepest thicket until another night gave his wings a hidden motion in the sky.

In this fashion he met his wife.

During the day, which was warm for November first in Illinois country,

pretty young Brunilla Wexley was out to udder a lost cow, for she carried a
silver pail in one hand as she sidled through thickets and pleaded cleverly to the
unseen cow to please return home or burst her gut with unplucked milk. The
fact that the cow would have most certainly come home when her teats needed
pulling did not concern Brunilla Wexley. It was a sweet excuse for forest-
journeying, thistle-blowing, and flower-chewing; all of which Brunilla was
doing as she stumbled upon Uncle Einar.

Asleep near a bush, he seemed a man under a green shelter.

"Oh," said Brunilla, with a fever. "A man. In a camp-tent."

Uncle Einar awoke. The camp-tent spread like a large green fan behind
him.

"Oh," said Brunilla, the cow-searcher. "A man with wings."

That was how she took it. She was startled, yes, but she had never been
hurt in her life, so she wasn't afraid of anyone, and it was a fancy thing to see a
winged man and she was proud to meet him. She began to talk. In an hour they
were old friends, and in two hours she'd quite forgotten his wings were there.
And he somehow confessed how he happened to be in this wood.

"Yes, I noticed you looked banged around," she said. "That right wing
looks very bad. You'd best let me take you home and fix it. You won't be able to
fly all the way to Europe on it, anyway. And who wants to live in Europe these
days?"

He thanked her, but he didn't quite see how he could accept.

"But I live alone," she said. "For, as you see, I'm quite ugly."

He insisted she was not.

"How kind of you," she said. "But I am, there's no fooling myself. My folks
are dead, I've a farm, a big one, all to myself, quite far from Mellin Town, and
I'm in need of talking company."

But wasn't she afraid of him? he asked.

"Proud and jealous would be more near it," she said. "*May* I?" And she
stroked his large green membraned veils with careful envy. He shuddered at the
touch and put his tongue between his teeth.

So there was nothing for it but that he come to her house for medicaments
and ointments, and my! what a burn across his face, beneath his eyes! "Lucky
you weren't blinded," she said. "How'd it happen?"

"Well . . ." he said, and they were at her farm, hardly noticing they'd
walked a mile, looking at each other.

A day passed, and another, and he thanked her at her door and said he must
be going, he much appreciated the ointment, the care, the lodging. It was
twilight and between now, six o'clock, and five the next morning, he must cross
an ocean and a continent. "Thank you; good-by," he said, and started to fly off
in the dusk and crashed right into a maple tree.

"Oh!" she screamed, and ran to his unconscious body.

When he waked the next hour he knew he'd fly no more in the dark again ever; his delicate night-perception was gone. The winged telepathy that had warned him where towers, trees, houses and hills stood across his path, the fine clear vision and sensibility that had guided him through mazes of forest, cliff, and cloud, all were burnt forever by that strike across his face, that blue electric fry and sizzle.

"How?" he moaned softly. "How can I go to Europe? If I flew by day, I'd be seen and—miserable joke—maybe shot down! Or kept for a zoo perhaps, what a life *that'd* be! Brunilla, tell me, what shall I do?"

"Oh," she whispered, looking at her hands. "We'll think of something. . . . "

They were married.

The Family came for the wedding. In a great autumnal avalanche of maple, sycamore, oak, elm leaf, they hissed and rustled, fell in a shower of horse-chestnut, thumped like winter apples on the earth, with an over-all scent of farewell-summer on the wind they made in their rushing. The ceremony? The ceremony was brief as a black candle lit, blown out, and smoke left still on the air. Its briefness, darkness, upside-down and backward quality escaped Brunilla, who only listened to the great tide of Uncle Einar's wings faintly murmuring above them as they finished out the rite. And as for Uncle Einar, the wound across his nose was almost healed and, holding Brunilla's arm, he felt Europe grow faint and melt away in the distance.

He didn't have to see very well to fly straight up, or come straight down. It was only natural that on this night of their wedding he take Brunilla in his arms and fly right up into the sky.

A farmer, five miles over, glanced at a low cloud at midnight, saw faint glows and crackles.

"Heat lightning," he observed, and went to bed.

They didn't come down till morning, with the dew.

The marriage took. She had only to look at him, and it lifted her to think she was the only woman in the world married to a winged man. "Who else could say it?" she asked her mirror. And the answer was: "No one!"

He, on the other hand, found great beauty behind her face, great kindness and understanding. He made some changes in his diet to fit her thinking, and was careful with his wings about the house; knocked porcelains and broken lamps were nerve-scrapers, he stayed away from them. He changed his sleeping habits, since he couldn't fly nights now anyhow. And she in turn fixed chairs so they were comfortable for his wings, put extra padding here or took it out there, and the things she said were the things he loved her for. "We're in our cocoons, all of us. See how ugly I am?" she said. "But one day I'll break out, spread wings as fine and handsome as you."

"You broke out long ago," he said.

She thought it over. "Yes," she had to admit. "I know just which day it was, too. In the woods when I looked for a cow and found a tent!" They laughed, and with him holding her she felt so beautiful she knew their marriage had slipped her from her ugliness, like a bright sword from its case.

They had children. At first there was fear, all on his part, that they'd be winged.

"Nonsense, I'd love it!" she said. "Keep them out from under foot."

"Then," he exclaimed, "they'd be in your *hair*!"

"Ow!" she cried.

Four children were born, three boys and a girl, who, for their energy, seemed to have wings. They popped up like toadstools in a few years, and on hot summer days asked their father to sit under the apple tree and fan them with his cooling wings and tell them wild starlit tales of island clouds and ocean skies and textures of mist and wind and how a star tastes melting in your mouth, and how to drink cold mountain air, and how it feels to be a pebble dropped from Mt. Everest, turning to a green bloom, flowering your wings just before you strike bottom!

This was his marriage.

And today, six years later, here sat Uncle Einar, here he was, festering under the apple tree, grown impatient and unkind; not because this was his desire, but because after the long wait, he was still unable to fly the wild night sky; his extra sense had never returned. Here he sat despondently, nothing more than a summer sun-parasol, green and discarded, abandoned for the season by the reckless vacationers who once sought the refuge of its translucent shadow. Was he to sit here forever, afraid to fly by day because someone might see him? Was his only flight to be as a drier of clothes for his wife, or a fanner of children on hot August noons? His one occupation had *always* been flying Family errands, quicker than storms. A boomerang, he'd whickled over hills and valleys and like a thistle, landed. He had always had money; the Family had good use for their winged man! But now? Bitterness! His wings jittered and whisked the air and made a captive thunder.

"Papa," said little Meg.

The children stood looking at his thought-dark face.

"Papa," said Ronald. "Make more thunder!"

"It's a cold March day, there'll soon be rain and plenty of thunder," said Uncle Einar.

"Will you come watch us?" asked Michael.

"Run on, run on! Let Papa brood!"

He was shut of love, the children of love, and the love of children. He thought only of heavens, skies, horizons, infinities, by night or day, lit by star, moon, or sun, cloudy or clear, but always it was skies and heavens and horizons that ran ahead of you forever when you soared. Yet here he was, sculling the pasture, kept low for fear of being seen.

Misery in a deep well!

"Papa, come watch us; it's March!" cried Meg. "And we're going to the Hill with all the kids from town!"

Uncle Einar grunted. "What hill is that?"

"The Kite Hill, of course!" they all sang together.

Now he looked at them.

Each held a large paper kite, their faces sweating with anticipation and an animal glowing. In their small fingers were balls of white twine. From the kites, colored red and blue and yellow and green, hung caudal appendages of cotton and silk strips.

"We'll fly our kites!" said Ronald. "Won't you come?"

"No," he said, sadly. "I mustn't be seen by anyone or there'd be trouble."

"You could hide and watch from the woods," said Meg. "We made the kites ourselves. Just because we know how."

"How do you know?"

"You're our father!" was the instant cry. "That's why!"

He looked at his children for a long while. He sighed. "A kite festival, is it?"

"Yes, sir!"

"I'm going to win," said Meg.

"No, *I'm*!" Michael contradicted.

"Me, *me*!" piped Stephen.

"God up the chimney!" roared Uncle Einar, leaping high with a deafening kettledrum of wings. "Children! Children, I love you dearly!"

"Father, what's wrong?" said Michael, backing off.

"Nothing, nothing, nothing!" chanted Einar. He flexed his wings to their greatest propulsion and plundering. Whoom! they slammed like cymbals. The children fell flat in the backwash! "I have it, I *have* it! I'm free again! Fire in the flue! Feather on the wind! Brunilla!" Einar called to the house. His wife appeared. "I'm free!" he called, flushed and tall, on his toes. "Listen, Brunilla, I don't need the night any more! I can fly by day! I don't need the night! I'll fly *every* day and *any* day of the year from now on!—but, God, I waste time, talking. Look!"

And as the worried members of his family watched, he seized the cotton tail from one of the little kites, tied it to his belt behind, grabbed the twine ball, held one end in his teeth, gave the other end to his children, and up, up into the air he flew, away into the March wind!

And across the meadows and over the farms his children ran, letting out string to the daylit sky, bubbling and stumbling, and Brunilla stood back in the farmyard and waved and laughed to see what was happening; and her children marched to the far Kite Hill and stood, the four of them, holding the twine in their eager, proud fingers, each tugging and directing and pulling. And the children from Mellin Town came running with *their* small kites to let up on the wind, and they saw the great green kite leap and hover in the sky and exclaimed:

"Oh, oh, what a kite! What a kite! Oh, I wish I'd a kite like that! Where, where did you *get* it!"

"Our father made it!" cried Meg and Michael and Stephen and Ronald, and gave an exultant pull on the twine and the humming, thundering kite in the sky dipped and soared and made a great and magical exclamation mark across a cloud!

The Traveler

Father looked into Cecy's room just before dawn. She lay upon her bed. He shook his head uncomprehendingly and waved at her.

"Now, if you can tell me what good she does, lying there," he said, "I'll eat the crape on my mahogany box. Sleeping all night, eating breakfast, and then lying on top her bed all day."

"Oh, but she's so helpful," explained Mother, leading him down the hall away from Cecy's slumbering pale figure. "Why, she's one of the most adjustable members of the Family. What good are your brothers? Most of them sleep all day and do nothing. At least Cecy is *active*."

They went downstairs through the scent of black candles; the black crape on the banister, left over from the Homecoming some months ago and untouched, whispering as they passed. Father unloosened his tie, exhaustedly. "Well, we work nights," he said. "Can we help it if we're—as you put it—old-fashioned?"

"Of course not. Everyone in the Family can't be modern." She opened the cellar door; they moved down into darkness arm in arm. She looked over at his round white face, smiling. "It's really very lucky I don't have to sleep *at all*. If you were married to a night-sleeper, think what a marriage it would be! Each of us to our own. None of us the same. All wild. That's how the Family goes. Sometimes we get one like Cecy, all mind; and then there are those like Uncle Einar, all wing; and then again we have one like Timothy, all even and calm and normal. Then there's you, sleeping days. And me, awake all and all of my life. So Cecy shouldn't be too much for you to understand. She helps me a million ways each day. She sends her mind down to the green-grocer's for me, to see what he sells. She puts her mind inside the butcher. That saves me a long trip if he's fresh out of good cuts. She warns me when gossips are coming to visit and talk away the afternoon. And, well, there are six hundred other things—!"

They paused in the cellar near a large empty mahogany box. He settled himself into it, still not convinced. "But if she'd only contribute more," he said. "I'm afraid I'll have to ask her to find some sort of work."

"Sleep on it," she said to him. "Think it over. You may change your mind by sunset."

She was closing the lid down on him. "Well," he said, thoughtfully. The lid closed.

"Good morning, dear," she said.

"Good morning," he said, muffled, enclosed, within the box.

The sun rose. She hurried upstairs to make breakfast.

Cecy Elliott was the one who Traveled. She seemed an ordinary eighteen-year-old. But then none of the Family looked like what they were. There was naught of the fang, the foul, the worm or wind-witch to them. They lived in small towns and on farms across the world, simply, closely re-aligning and adapting their talents to the demands and laws of a changing world.

Cecy Elliott awoke. She glided down through the house, humming. "Good morning, Mother!" She walked down to the cellar to recheck each of the large mahogany boxes, to dust them, to be certain each was tightly sealed. "Father," she said, polishing one box. "Cousin Esther," she said, examining another, "here on a visit. And—" she rapped at a third, "Grandfather Elliott." There was a rustle inside like a piece of papyrus. "It's a strange, cross-bred family," she mused, climbing to the kitchen again. "Night-siphoners and flume-fearers, some awake, like Mother, twenty-five hours out of twenty-four; some asleep, like me, fifty-nine minutes out of sixty. Different species of sleep."

She ate breakfast. In the middle of her apricot dish she saw her mother's stare. She laid the spoon down. Cecy said, "Father'll change his mind. I'll show him how fine I can be to have around. I'm family insurance; he doesn't understand. You wait."

Mother said, "You were inside me a while ago when I argued with Father?"

"Yes."

"I thought I felt you looking out my eyes," the mother nodded.

Cecy finished and went up to bed. She folded down the blankets and clean cool sheets, then laid herself out atop the covers, shut her eyes, rested her thin white fingers on her small bosom, nodded her slight, exquisitely sculptured head back against her thick gathering of chestnut hair.

She started to Travel.

Her mind slipped from the room, over the flowered yard, the fields, the green hills, over the ancient drowsy streets of Mellin Town, into the wind and past the moist depression of the ravine. All day she would fly and meander. Her mind would pop into dogs, sit there, and she would feel the bristly feels of dogs, taste ripe bones, sniff tangy-urined trees. She'd hear as a dog heard. She forgot human construction completely. She'd have a dog frame. It was more than telepathy, up one flue and down another. This was complete separation from one body environment into another. It was entrance into tree-nozzling dogs, men, old maids, birds, children at hopscotch, lovers on their morning beds, into workers asweat with shoveling, into unborn babies' pink, dream-small brains.

Where would she go today? She made her decision, and went!

When her mother tiptoed a moment later to peek into the room, she saw Cecy's body on the bed, the chest not moving, the face quiet. Cecy was gone already. Mother nodded and smiled.

The morning passed. Leonard, Bion and Sam went off to their work, as did Laura and the manicuring sister; and Timothy was dispatched to school. The house quieted. At noontime the only sound was made by Cecy Elliott's three young girl-cousins playing Tisket Tasket Coffin Casket in the back yard. There were always extra cousins or uncles or grand-nephews and night-nieces about the place; they came and went; water out a faucet, down a drain.

The cousins stopped their play when the tall loud man banged on the front door and marched straight in when Mother answered.

"That was Uncle Jonn!" said the littlest girl, breathless.

"The one we hate?" asked the second.

"What's he want?" cried the third. "He looked mad!"

"*We're* mad at *him*, that's what," explained the second, proudly. "For what he did to the Family sixty years ago, and seventy years ago and twenty years ago."

"Listen!" They listened. "He's run upstairs!"

"Sounds like he's cryin'."

"Do grown-ups cry?"

"Sure, silly!"

"He's in Cecy's room! Shoutin'. Laughin'. Prayin'. Cryin'. He sounds mad, and sad, and fraidy-cat, all together!"

The littlest one made tears, herself. She ran to the cellar door. "Wake up! Oh, down there, wake up! You in the boxes! Uncle Jonn's here and he might have a cedar stake with him! I don't want a cedar stake in my chest! Wake up!"

"Shh," hissed the biggest girl. "He hasn't a stake! You can't wake the Boxed People, anyhow. Listen!"

Their heads tilted, their eyes glistened upward, waiting.

"Get off the bed!" commanded Mother, in the doorway.

Uncle Jonn bent over Cecy's slumbering body. His lips were misshaped. There was a wild, fey and maddened focus to his green eyes.

"Am I too late?" he demanded, hoarsely, sobbing. "Is she gone?"

"Hours ago!" snapped Mother. "Are you blind? She might not be back for days. Sometimes she lies there a week. I don't have to feed the body, she finds sustenance from whatever or whoever she's in. Get away from her!"

Uncle Jonn stiffened, one knee pressed on the springs.

"Why couldn't she wait?" he wanted to know, frantically, looking at her, his hands feeling her silent pulse again and again.

"You heard me!" Mother moved forward curtly. "She's not to be touched. She's got to be left as she is. So if she comes home she can get back in her body exactly right."

Uncle Jonn turned his head. His long hard red face was pocked and senseless, deep black grooves crowded the tired eyes.

"Where'd she go? I've *got* to find her."

Mother talked like a slap in the face. "I don't know. She has favorite places. You might find her in a child running along a trail in the ravine. Or swinging on a grape vine. Or you might find her in a crayfish under a rock in the creek, looking up at you. Or she might be playing chess inside an old man in the court-house square. You know as well as I she can be anywhere." A wry look came to Mother's mouth. "She might be vertical inside me now, looking out at you, laughing, and not telling you. This might be her talking and having fun. And you wouldn't know it."

"Why—" He swung heavily around, like a huge pivoted boulder. His big hands came up, wanting to grab something. "If I *thought*—"

Mother talked on, casual quiet. "Of course she's *not* in me, here. And if she was there'd be no way to tell." Her eyes gleamed with a delicate malice. She stood tall and graceful, looking upon him with no fear. "Now, suppose you explain what you want with her?"

He seemed to be listening to a distant bell, tolling. He shook his head, angrily, to clear it. Then he growled. "Something . . . inside me . . . " He broke off. He leaned over the cold, sleeping body. "Cecy! Come back, you hear! You can come back if you want!"

The wind blew softly through the high willows outside the sundrifted windows. The bed creaked under his shifted weight. The distant bell tolled again and he was listening to it, but Mother could not hear it. Only he heard the drowsy summer-day sounds of it, far far away. His mouth opened obscurely:

"I've a thing for her to do to me. For the past month I've been kind of going—insane. I get funny thoughts. I was going to take a train to the big city and talk to a psychiatrist but he wouldn't help. I know that Cecy can enter my head and exorcise those fears I have. She can suck them out like a vacuum cleaner, if she wants to help me. She's the only one can scrape away the filth and cobwebs and make me new again. That's why I need her, you understand?" he said, in a tight, expectant voice. He licked his lips. "She's *got* to help me!"

"After all you've done to the Family?" said Mother.

"I did nothing to the Family!"

"The story goes," said Mother, "that in bad times, when you needed money, you were paid a hundred dollars for each of the Family you pointed out to the law to be staked through the heart."

"That's unfair!" he said, wavering like a man hit in the stomach. "You can't prove that. You lie!"

"Nevertheless, I don't think Cecy'd want to help you. The Family wouldn't want it."

"Family, Family!" He stomped the floor like a huge, brutal child. "Damn the Family! I won't go insane on their account! I need help, God damn it, and I'll get it!"

Mother faced him, her face reserved, her hands crossed over her bosom.

He lowered his voice, looking at her with a kind of evil shyness, not meeting her eyes. "Listen to me, Mrs. Elliott," he said. "And you, too, Cecy," he said to the sleeper. "If you're there," he added. "Listen to this." He looked at the wall clock ticking on the far, sun-drenched wall. "If Cecy isn't back here by six o'clock tonight, ready to help clean out my mind and make me sane, I'll—I'll go to the police." He drew himself up. "I've got a list of Elliotts who live on farms all around and inside Mellin Town. The police can cut enough new cedar stakes in an hour to drive through a dozen Elliott hearts." He stopped, wiped the sweat off his face. He stood, listening.

The distant bell began to toll again.

He had heard it for weeks. There was no bell, but he could hear it ringing. It rang now, near, far, close, away. Nobody else could hear it save himself.

He shook his head. He shouted to cover the sound of those bells, shouted at Mrs. Elliott. "You heard me?"

He hitched up his trousers, tightened the buckle clasp with a jerk, walked past Mother to the door.

"Yes," she said. "I heard. But even I can't call Cecy back if she doesn't want to come. She'll arrive eventually. Be patient. Don't go running off to the police—"

He cut her. "I can't wait. This thing of mine, this noise in my head's gone on eight weeks now! I can't stand it much longer!" He scowled at the clock. "I'm going. I'll try to find Cecy in town. If I don't get her by six—well, you know what a cedar stake's like. . . . "

His heavy shoes pounded away down the hall, fading down the stairs, out of the house. When the noises were all gone, the mother turned and looked, earnestly, painfully, down upon the sleeper.

"Cecy," she called, softly, insistently. "Cecy, come home!"

There was no word from the body. Cecy lay there, not moving, for as long as her mother waited.

Uncle Jonn walked through the fresh open country and into the streets of Mellin Town, looking for Cecy in every child that licked an ice-pop and in every little white dog that padded by on its way to some eagerly anticipated nowhere.

The town spread out like a fancy graveyard. Nothing more than a few monuments, really—edifices to lost arts and pastimes. It was a great meadow of elms and deodars and hackmatack trees, laid out with wooden walks you could haul into your barn at night if the hollow sound of walking people irked you. There were tall old maiden houses, lean and narrow and wisely wan, in which were spectacles of colored glass, upon which the thinned golden hair of age-old bird nests sprouted. There was a drug shop full of quaint wire-rung soda-fountain stools with plywood bottoms, and the memorious clear sharp odor that used to be in drug stores but never is any more. And there was a barber emporium with a red-ribboned pillar twisting around inside a chrysalis of glass in front of it. And there was a grocery that was all fruity shadow and dusty boxes and the smell of an old Armenian woman, which was like the odor of a rusty penny. The town lay under the deodar and mellow-leaf trees, in no hurry, and somewhere in the town was Cecy, the one who Traveled.

Uncle Jonn stopped, bought himself a bottle of Orange Crush, drank it, wiped his face with his handkerchief, his eyes jumping up and down, like little kids skipping rope. I'm afraid, he thought. I'm afraid.

He saw a code of birds strung dot-dash on the high telephone wires. Was Cecy up there laughing at him out of sharp bird eyes, shuffling her feathers, singing at him? He suspicioned the cigar-store Indian. But there was no animation in that cold, carved, tobacco-brown image.

Distantly, like on a sleepy Sunday morning, he heard the bells ringing in a valley of his head. He was stone blind. He stood in blackness. White, tortured faces drifted through his inturned vision.

"Cecy!" he cried, to everything, everywhere. "I know you can help me! Shake me like a tree! Cecy!"

The blindness passed. He was bathed in a cold sweating that didn't stop, but ran like a syrup.

"I know you can help," he said. "I saw you help Cousin Marianne years ago. Ten years ago, wasn't it?" He stood, concentrating.

Marianne had been a girl shy as a mole, her hair twisted like roots on her round ball of head. Marianne had hung in her skirt like a clapper in a bell, never ringing when she walked; just swithering along, one heel after another. She gazed at weeds and the sidewalk under her toes, she looked at your chin if she saw you at all—and never got as far as your eyes. Her mother despaired of Marianne's ever marrying or succeeding.

It was up to Cecy, then. Cecy went into Marianne like fist into glove.

Marianne jumped, ran, yelled, glinted her yellow eyes. Marianne flickered her skirts, unbraided her hair and let it hang in a shimmery veil on her half-nude shoulders. Marianne giggled and rang like a gay clapper in the tolling bell of her dress. Marianne squeezed her face into many attitudes of coyness, merriment, intelligence, maternal bliss, and love.

The boys raced after Marianne. Marianne got married.

Cecy withdrew.

Marianne had hysterics; her *spine* was gone!

She lay like a limp corset all one day. But the habit was in her now. Some of Cecy had stayed on like a fossil imprint on soft shale rock; and Marianne began tracing the habits and thinking them over and remembering what it was like to have Cecy inside her, and pretty soon she was running and shouting and giggling all by herself; a corset animated, as it were, by a memory!

Marianne had lived joyously thereafter.

Standing with the cigar-store Indian for conversation, Uncle Jonn now shook his head violently. Dozens of bright bubbles floated in his eyeballs, each with tiny, slanted, microscopic eyes staring in, in at his brain.

What if he never found Cecy? What if the plain winds had borne her all the way to Elgin? Wasn't that where she dearly loved to bide her time, in the asylum for the insane, touching their minds, holding and turning their confetti thoughts?

Far-flung in the afternoon distance a great metal whistle sighed and echoed, steam shuffled as a train cut across valley trestles, over cool rivers through ripe cornfields, into tunnels like finger into thimble, under arches of shimmering walnut trees. Jonn stood, afraid. What if Cecy was in the cabin of the engineer's head, now? She loved riding the monster engines across country far as she could stretch the contact. Yank the whistle rope until it screamed across sleeping night land or drowsy day country.

He walked along a shady street. Out of the corners of his eyes he thought he saw an old woman, wrinkled as a dried fig, naked as a thistle-seed, floating among the branches of a hawthorn tree, a cedar stake driven into her breast.

Somebody screamed!

Something thumped his head. A blackbird, soaring skyward, took a lock of his hair with it!

He shook his fist at the bird, heaved a rock. "Scare me, will you!" he yelled. Breathing rawly, he saw the bird circle behind him to sit on a limb waiting another chance to dive for hair.

He turned slyly from the bird.

He heard the whirring sound.

He jumped about, grabbed up. "Cecy!"

He had the bird! It fluttered, squalled in his hands.

"Cecy!" he called, looking into his caged fingers at the wild black creature. The bird drew blood with its bill.

"Cecy, I'll crush you if you don't help me!"

The bird shrieked and cut him.

He closed his fingers tight, tight, tight.

He walked away from where he finally dropped the dead bird and did not look back at it, even once.

He walked down into the ravine that ran through the very center of Mellin Town. What's happening now? he wondered. Has Cecy's mother phoned people? Are the Elliotts afraid? He swayed drunkenly, great lakes of sweat bursting out under his armpits. Well, let *them* be afraid awhile. He was tired of being afraid. He'd look just a little longer for Cecy and then go to the police!

On the creek bank, he laughed to think of the Elliotts scurrying madly, trying to find some way around him. There was no way. They'd have to make Cecy help him. They couldn't afford to let good old Uncle Jonn die insane, no, sir.

B-B-shot eyes lay deep in the water, staring roundly up at him.

On blazing hot summer noons, Cecy had often entered into the soft-shelled grayness of the mandibled heads of crayfish. She had often peeked out from the black egg eyes upon their sensitive filamentary stalks and felt the creek sluice by her, steadily, and in fluid veils of coolness and captured light. Breathing out and in the particles of stuff that floated in water, holding her horny, lichened claws before her like some elegant salad utensils, swollen and scissor-sharp. She watched the giant strides of boy feet progressing toward her through the creek bottom, heard the faint, water-thickened shout of boys searching for crayfish, jabbing their pale fingers down, tumbling rocks aside, clutching and tossing frantic flippery animals into open metal cans where scores of other crayfish scuttled like a basket of waste-paper come to life.

She watched pale stalks of boy legs poise over her rock, saw the nude loin-shadows of boy thrown on the sandy muck of the creek floor, saw the suspenseful hand hovered, heard the suggestive whisper of a boy who's spied a prize beneath a stone. Then, as the hand plunged, the stone rolled, Cecy flirted the borrowed fan of her inhabited body, kicked back in a little sand explosion and vanished downstream.

On to another rock she went to sit fanning the sand, holding her claws before her, proud of them, her tiny glass-bulb eyes glowing black as creek-water filled her bubbling mouth, cool, cool, cool. . . .

The realization that Cecy might be this close at hand, in any live thing, drove Uncle Jonn to a mad fury. In any squirrel or chipmunk, in a disease germ, even, on his aching body, Cecy might be existing. She could even enter amoebas. . . .

On some sweltering summer noons, Cecy would live in an amoeba, darting, vacillating, deep in the old tired philosophical dark waters of a kitchen well. On days when the world high over her, above the unstirred water, was a dreaming nightmare of heat printed on each object of the land, she'd lie somnolent, quivering and cool and distant, settling in the well-throat. Up above, trees were like images burned in green fire. Birds were like bronze stamps you inked and punched on your brain. Houses steamed like manure sheds. When a door slammed it was like a rifle shot. The only good sound on a simmering day was the asthmatic suction of well water drawn up into a porcelain cup, there to be inhaled through an old skelatinous woman's porcelain teeth. Overhead, Cecy could hear the brittle clap of the old woman's shoes, the sighing voice of the old woman baked in the August sun. And, lying lowermost and cool, sighting up up through the dim echoing tunnel of well, Cecy heard the iron suction of the pump handle pressed energetically by the sweating old lady; and water, amoeba, Cecy and all rose up the throat of the well in sudden cool disgorgement out into the cup, over which waited sun-withered lips. Then, and only then, did Cecy withdraw, just as the lips came down to sip, the cup tilted, and porcelain met porcelain. . . .

Jonn stumbled, fell flat into the creek water!

He didn't rise, but sat dripping stupidly.

Then he began crashing rocks over, shouting, seizing upon and losing crayfish, cursing. The bells rang louder in his ears. And now, one by one, a procession of bodies that couldn't exist, but seemed to be real, floated by on the water. Worm-white bodies, turned on their backs, drifting like loose marionettes. As they passed, the tide bobbed their heads so their faces rolled over, revealing the features of the typical Elliott family member.

He began to weep, sitting there in the water. He had wanted Cecy's help, but now how could he expect to deserve it, acting a fool, cursing her, hating her, threatening her and the Family?

He stood up, shaking himself. He walked out of the creek and up the hill. There was only one thing to do now. Plead with individual members of the Family. Ask them to intercede for him. Have them ask Cecy to come home, quickly.

In the undertaking parlor on Court Street, the door opened. The undertaker, a short, well-tonsored man with a mustache and sensitively thin hands, looked up. His face fell.

"Oh, it's *you*, Uncle Jonn," he said.

"Nephew Bion," said Jonn, still wet from the creek, "I need your help. Have you seen Cecy?"

"Seen her?" said Bion Elliott. He leaned against the marble table where he was working on a body. He laughed. "God, don't ask me *that*!" he snorted. "Look at me, close. Do you know me?"

Jonn bristled. "You're Bion Elliott, Cecy's brother, of course!"

"Wrong." The undertaker shook his head. "I'm Cousin Ralph, the butcher! Yes, the *butcher*." He tapped his head. "Here, inside, where it counts, I'm Ralph. I was working in my refrigerator a moment ago over at the butcher shop when suddenly Cecy was inside me. She borrowed my mind, like a cup of sugar. And brought me over here just now and sifted me down into Bion's body. Poor Bion! What a joke!"

"You're—you're *not* Bion!"

"No, ah, no, dear Uncle Jonn. Cecy probably put Bion in *my* body! You see the joke? A meat-cutter exchanged for a meat-cutter! A dealer in cold-cuts traded for another of the same!" He quaked with laughter. "Ah, that Cecy, what a child!" He wiped happy tears from his face. "I've stood here for five minutes wondering what to do. You know something? Undertaking isn't hard. Not much harder than fixing pot roasts. Oh, Bion'll be mad. His professional integrity. Cecy'll probably trade us back, later. Bion never was one to take a joke on himself!"

Jonn looked confused. "Even *you* can't control Cecy?"

"God, no. She does what she does. We're helpless."

Jonn wandered toward the door. "Got to find her somehow," he mumbled. "If she can do this to you, think how she'd help me if she wanted. . . . " The bells rang louder in his ears. From the side of his eyes he saw a movement. He whirled and gasped.

The body on the table had a cedar stake driven through it.

"So long," said the undertaker to the slammed door. He listened to the sound of Jonn's running feet, fading.

The man who staggered into the police station at five that afternoon was barely able to stand up. His voice was a whisper and he retched as if he'd taken poison. He didn't look like Uncle Jonn any more. The bells rang all the time, all the time, and he saw people walking behind him with staked chests, who vanished whenever he turned to look.

The sheriff looked up from reading a magazine, wiped his brown mustache with the back of one clawlike hand, took his feet down off a battered desk and waited for Uncle Jonn to speak.

"I want to report a family that lives here," whispered Uncle Jonn, his eyes half-shut. "A wicked family, living under false pretenses."

The sheriff cleared his throat. "What's the family's name?"

Uncle Jonn stopped. "What?"

The sheriff repeated it. "What's the family's name?"

"Your voice," said Jonn.

"What about my voice?" said the sheriff.

"Sounds familiar," said Jonn. "Like—"

"Who?" asked the sheriff.

"Like Cecy's mother! That's who you sound like!"

"Do I?" asked the sheriff.

"That's who you are inside! Cecy changed you, too, like she changed Ralph and Bion! I can't report the Family to you, now, then! It wouldn't do any good!"

"Guess it wouldn't," remarked the sheriff, implacably.

"The Family's gotten around me!" wailed Uncle Jonn.

"Seems that way," said the sheriff, wetting a pencil on his tongue, starting on a fresh crossword puzzle. "Well, good day to you, Jonn Elliott."

"Unh?"

"I said 'Good day.' "

"Good day." Jonn stood by the desk, listening. "Do you—do you *hear* anything?"

The sheriff listened. "Crickets?"

"No."

"Frogs?"

"No," said Uncle Jonn. "Bells. Just bells. Holy church bells. The kind of bells a man like me can't stand to hear. Holy church bells."

The sheriff listened. "No. Can't say as I hear 'em. Say, be careful of that door there; it slams."

The door to Cecy's room was knocked open. A moment later, Uncle Jonn was inside, moving across the floor. The silent body of Cecy lay on the bed, not moving. Behind him, as Jonn seized Cecy's hand, her mother appeared.

She ran to him, struck him on head and shoulders till he fell back from Cecy. The world swelled with bell sounds. His vision blacked out. He groped at the mother, biting his lips, releasing them in gasps, eyes streaming.

"Please, please tell her to come back," he said. "I'm sorry. I don't want to hurt anyone any more."

The mother shouted through the clamor of bells. "Go downstairs and wait for her there!"

"I can't hear you," he cried, louder. "My head." He held his hands to his ears. "So loud. So loud I can't stand it." He rocked on his heels. "If only I knew where Cecy was—"

Quite simply, he drew out a folded pocket knife, unfolded it. "I can't go on—" he said. And before the mother moved he fell to the floor, the knife in his heart, blood running from his lips, his shoes looking senseless one atop the other, one eye shut, the other wide and white.

The mother bent down to him. "Dead," she whispered, finally. "So," she murmured, unbelievingly, rising up, stepping away from the blood. "So he's dead at last." She glanced around, fearfully, cried aloud.

"Cecy, Cecy, come home, child, I need you!"

A silence, while sunlight faded from the room.

"Cecy, come home, child!"

The dead man's lips moved. A high clear voice sprang from them.

"Here! I've been here for days! I'm the fear he had in him; and he never guessed. Tell Father what I've done. Maybe he'll think me worthy now...."

The dead man's lips stopped. A moment later, Cecy's body on the bed stiffened like a stocking with a leg thrust suddenly into it, inhabited again.

"Supper, Mother," said Cecy, rising from bed.

The Lake

They cut the sky down to my size and threw it over the Michigan lake, put some kids yelling on yellow sand with bouncing balls, a gull or two, a criticizing parent, and me breaking out of a wet wave, finding this world very bleary and moist.

I ran up on the beach.

Mama swabbed me with a furry towel. "Stand there and dry," she said.

I stood there, watching the sun take away the water beads on my arms. I replaced them with goose-pimples.

"My, there's a wind," said Mama. "Put on your sweater."

"Wait'll I watch my goose-bumps," I said.

"Harold," said Mama.

I put the sweater on and watched the waves come up and fall down on the beach. But not clumsily. On purpose, with a green sort of elegance. Even a drunken man could not collapse with such elegance as those waves.

It was September. In the last days when things are getting sad for no reason. The beach was so long and lonely with only about six people on it. The kids quit bouncing the ball because somehow the wind made them sad, too, whistling the way it did, and the kids sat down and felt autumn come along the endless shore.

All of the hot-dog stands were boarded up with strips of golden planking, sealing in all the mustard, onion, meat odors of the long, joyful summer. It was like nailing summer into a series of coffins. One by one the places slammed their covers down, padlocked their doors, and the wind came and touched the sand, blowing away all of the million footprints of July and August. It got so that now, in September, there was nothing but the mark of my rubber tennis shoes and Donald and Delaus Schabold's feet, down by the water curve.

Sand blew up in curtains on the sidewalks, and the merry-go-round was hidden with canvas, all of the horses frozen in mid-air on their brass poles, showing teeth, galloping on. With only the wind for music, slipping through canvas.

I stood there. Everyone else was in school. I was not. Tomorrow I would be on my way west across the United States on a train. Mom and I had come to the beach for one last brief moment.

There was something about the loneliness that made me want to get away by myself. "Mama, I want to run up the beach a ways," I said.

"All right, but hurry back, and don't go near the water."

I ran. Sand spun under me and the wind lifted me. You know how it is, running, arms out so you feel veils from your fingers, caused by wind. Like wings.

Mama withdrew into the distance, sitting. Soon she was only a brown speck and I was all alone.

Being alone is a newness to a twelve-year-old child. He is so used to people about. The only way he can be alone is in his mind. There are so many real people around, telling children what and how to do, that a boy has to run off down a beach, even if it's only in his head, to get by himself in his own world, with his own miniature values.

So now I was really alone.

I went down to the water and let it cool up to my stomach. Always before, with the crowd, I hadn't dared to look, to come to this spot and search around in the water and call a certain name. But now—

Water is like a magician. Sawing you in half. It feels as if you were cut half in two, part of you, the lower part, sugar, melting, dissolving away. Cool water, and once in a while a very elegantly stumbling wave that falls with a flourish of lace.

I called her name. A dozen times I called it.

"Tally! Tally! Oh, Tally!"

Funny, but you really expect answers to your calling when you are young. You feel that whatever you may think can be real. And sometimes maybe that is not so wrong.

I thought of Tally, swimming out into the water last May, with her pigtails trailing, blonde. She went laughing, and the sun was on her small twelve-year-old shoulders. I thought of the water settling quiet, of the life-guard leaping into it, of Tally's mother screaming, and of how Tally never came out. . . .

The life-guard tried to persuade her to come out, but she did not. He came back with only bits of water-weed in his big-knuckled fingers, and Tally was gone. She would not sit across from me at school any longer, or chase indoor balls on the brick streets on summer nights. She had gone too far out, and the lake would not let her return.

And now in the lonely autumn when the sky was huge and the water was huge and the beach was so very long, I had come down for the last time, alone.

I called her name over and over. Tally, oh, Tally!

The wind blew so very softly over my ears, the way wind blows over the mouths of sea-shells to set them whispering. The water rose, embraced my chest, then my knees, up and down, one way and another, sucking under my heels.

"Tally! Come back, Tally!"

I was only twelve. But I know how much I loved her. It was that love that comes before all significance of body and morals. It was that love that is no more bad than wind and sea and sand lying side by side forever. It was made of all the warm long days together at the beach, and the humming quiet days of droning education at the school. All the long autumn days of the years past when I had carried her books home from school.

Tally!

I called her name for the last time. I shivered. I felt water on my face and did not know how it got there. The waves had not splashed that high.

Turning, I retreated to the sand and stood there for half an hour, hoping for one glimpse, one sign, one little bit of Tally to remember. Then, I knelt and built a sand-castle, shaping it fine, building it as Tally and I had often built so many of them. But this time, I only built half of it. Then I got up.

"Tally, if you hear me, come in and build the rest."

I walked off toward that faraway speck that was Mama. The water came in, blended the sand-castle circle by circle, mashing it down little by little into the original smoothness.

Silently, I walked along the shore.

Far away, a merry-go-round jangled faintly, but it was only the wind.

The next day, I went away on the train.

A train has a poor memory; it soon puts all behind it. It forgets the cornlands of Illinois, the rivers of childhood, the bridges, the lakes, the valleys, the cottages, the hurts and the joys. It spreads them out behind and they drop back of a horizon.

I lengthened my bones, put flesh on them, changed my young mind for an older one, threw away clothes as they no longer fitted, shifted from grammar to high school, to college books, to law books. And then there was a young woman in Sacramento. I knew her for a time, and we were married.

I continued my law study. By the time I was twenty-two, I had almost forgotten what the East was like.

Margaret suggested that our delayed honeymoon be taken back in that direction.

Like a memory, a train works both ways. A train can bring rushing back all those things you left behind so many years before.

Lake Bluff, population ten thousand, came up over the sky. Margaret looked so handsome in her fine new clothes. She watched me as I felt my old world gather me back into its living. She held my arm as the train slid into Bluff Station and our baggage was escorted out.

So many years, and the things they do to people's faces and bodies. When we walked through the town together I saw no one I recognized. There were faces with echoes in them. Echoes of hikes on ravine trails. Faces with small laughter in them from closed grammar schools and swinging on metal-linked swings and going up and down on teeter-totters. But I didn't speak. I walked and looked and filled up inside with all those memories, like leaves stacked for autumn burning.

We stayed on two weeks in all, revisiting all the places together. The days were happy. I thought I loved Margaret well. At least I thought I did.

It was on one of the last days that we walked down by the shore. It was not quite as late in the year as that day so many years before, but the first evidences of desertion were coming upon the beach. People were thinning out, several of the hot dog stands had been shuttered and nailed, and the wind, as always, waited there to sing for us.

I almost saw Mama sitting on the sand as she used to sit. I had that feeling again of wanting to be alone. But I could not force myself to speak of this to Margaret. I only held on to her and waited.

It got late in the day. Most of the children had gone home and only a few men and women remained basking in the windy sun.

The life-guard boat pulled up on the shore. The life-guard stepped out of it, slowly, with something in his arms.

I froze there. I held my breath and I felt small, only twelve years old, very little, very infinitesimal and afraid. The wind howled. I could not see Margaret. I could see only the beach, the life-guard slowly emerging from the boat with a gray sack in his hands, not very heavy, and his face almost as gray and lined.

"Stay here, Margaret," I said. I don't know why I said it.

"But, why?"

"Just stay here, that's all—"

I walked slowly down the sand to where the life-guard stood. He looked at me.

"What is it?" I asked.

The life-guard kept looking at me for a long time and he couldn't speak. He put the gray sack down on the sand, and water whispered wet up around it and went back.

"What is it?" I insisted.

"She's dead," said the life-guard quietly.

I waited.

"Funny," he said, softly. "Funniest thing I ever saw. She's been dead. A long time."

I repeated his words.

He nodded. "Ten years, I'd say. There haven't been any children drowned here *this* year. There were twelve children drowned here since 1933, but we recovered all of them before a few hours had passed. All except one, I remember. This body here, why it must be ten years in the water. It's not—pleasant."

I stared at the gray sack in his arms. "Open it," I said. I don't know why I said it. The wind was louder.

He fumbled with the sack. "The way I know it's a little girl, is because she's still wearing a locket. There's nothing much else to tell by—"

"Hurry, man, *open it*!" I cried.

"I better not do that," he said. Then perhaps he saw the way my face must have looked. "She was such a *little* girl—"

He opened it only part way. That was enough.

The beach was deserted. There was only the sky and the wind and the water and the autumn coming on lonely. I looked down at her there.

I said something over and over. A name. The life-guard looked at me. "Where did you find her?" I asked.

"Down the beach, that way, in the shallow water. It's a long long time for her, ain't it?"

I shook my head.

"Yes, it is. Oh God, yes it is."

I thought: People grow. I have grown. But she has not changed. She is still small. She is still young. Death does not permit growth or change. She still has golden hair. She will be forever young and I will love her forever, oh God, I will love her forever.

The life-guard tied up the sack again.

Down the beach, a few moments later, I walked by myself. I stopped, and looked down at something. This is where the life-guard found her, I said to myself.

There, at the water's edge, lay a sand-castle, only half-built. Just like Tally and I used to build them. She half and I half.

I looked at it. I knelt beside the sand-castle and saw the little prints of feet coming in from the lake and going back out to the lake again and not ever returning.

Then—I knew.

"I'll help you to finish it," I said.

I did. I built the rest of it up very slowly, then I arose and turned away and walked off, so as not to watch it crumble in the waves, as all things crumble.

I walked back up the beach to where a strange woman named Margaret was waiting for me, smiling. . . .

The Coffin

There was any amount of banging and hammering for a number of days; deliveries of metal parts and oddments which Mr. Charles Braling took into his little workshop with a feverish anxiety. He was a dying man, a badly dying man, and he seemed to be in a great hurry, between racking coughs and spittlings, to piece together one last invention.

"What are you doing?" inquired his younger brother, Richard Braling. He had listened with increasing difficulty and much curiosity for a number of days to that banging and rattling about, and now he stuck his head through the work-room door.

"Go far far away and let me alone," said Charles Braling, who was seventy, trembly and wet-lipped most of the time. He trembled nails into place and trembled a hammer down with a weak blow upon a large timber and then struck a small metal ribbon down into an intricate machine, and, all in all, was having a carnival of labor.

Richard looked on, bitter-eyed, for a long moment. There was a hatred between them. It had gone on for some years and now was neither any better nor any worse for the fact that Charlie was dying. Richard was delighted to know of the impending death, if he thought of it at all. But all this busy fervor of his old brothers stimulated him.

"Pray tell," he said, not moving from the door.

"If you must know," snarled old Charles, fitting in an odd thingumabob on the box before him, "I'll be dead in another week and I'm—I'm building my own coffin!"

"A coffin, my dear Charlie. That doesn't *look* like a coffin. A coffin isn't that complex. Come on now, what are you up to?"

"I tell you it's a coffin! An odd coffin, yes, but nevertheless," the old man shivered his fingers around in the large box, "—nevertheless a coffin!"

"But it would be easier to buy one."

"Not one like this! You couldn't buy one like this anyplace, ever. Oh, it'll be a real fine coffin, all right."

"You're obviously lying." Richard moved forward. "Why, that coffin is a good twelve feet long. Six feet longer than normal size!"

"Oh, yes?" The old man laughed quietly.

"And that transparent top; who ever heard of a coffin lid you can see through? What good is a transparent lid to a corpse?"

"Oh, just never you mind at all," sang the old man heartily. "La!" And he went humming and hammering about the shop.

"This coffin is terribly thick," shouted the young brother over the din. "Why, it must be five feet thick; how utterly unnecessary!"

"I only wish I might live to patent this amazing coffin," said old Charlie. "It would be a god-send to all the poor peoples of the world. Think how it would eliminate the expenses of most funerals. Oh, but, of course, you don't know how it would do that, do you? How silly of me. Well, I shan't tell you. If this coffin could be mass-produced—expensive at first, naturally—but then when you finally got them made in vast quantities, gah, but the money people would save."

"To hell with you!" And the younger brother stormed out of the shop.

It had been an unpleasant life. Young Richard had always been such a bounder he never had two coins to clink together at one time; all of his money had come from old brother Charlie, who had the indecency to remind him of it at all times. Richard spent many hours with his hobbies; he dearly loved piling up bottles with French wine labels, in the garden. "I like the way they glint," he often said, sitting and sipping, sipping and sitting. He was the only man in the county who could hold the longest gray ash on a fifty-cent cigar for the longest recorded time. And he knew how to hold his hands so his diamonds jangled in the light. But he had not bought the wine, the diamonds, the cigars—no! They were all gifts. He was never allowed to buy anything himself. It was always brought to him and given to him. He had to ask for everything, even writing paper. He considered himself quite a martyr to have put up with taking things from that rickety old brother for so long a time. Everything Charlie ever laid his hand to turned to money; everything Richard had ever tried in the way of a leisurely career had failed.

And now, here was this old mole of a Charlie whacking out a new invention which would probably bring Charlie additional specie long after his bones were slotted in the earth!

Well, two weeks passed.

One morning, the old brother toddled upstairs and stole the insides out of the electric phonograph. Another morning he raided the gardener's greenhouse. Still another time he received a delivery from a medical company. It was all young Richard could do to sit and hold his long gray cigar ash steady while these murmuring excursions took place.

"I'm finished!" cried old Charlie on the fourteenth morning, and dropped dead.

Richard finished out his cigar, and, without showing his inner excitement, he laid down his cigar with its fine long whitish ash, two inches long, a real record, and arose.

He walked to the window and watched the sunlight playfully glittering among the fat beetlelike champagne bottles in the garden.

He looked toward the top of the stairs where old dear brother Charlie lay peacefully sprawled against the banister. Then he walked to the phone and perfunctorily dialed a number.

"Hello, Green Lawn Mortuary? This is the Braling residence. Will you send around a wicker, please? Yes. For brother Charlie. Yes. Thank you. Thank you."

As the mortuary people were taking brother Charles out in their wicker they received instructions. "Ordinary casket," said young Richard. "No funeral service. Put him in a pine coffin. He would have preferred it that way— simple. Good-by."

"Now!" said Richard, rubbing his hands together. "We shall see about this 'coffin' built by dear Charlie. I do not suppose he will realize he is not being buried in his 'special' box. Ah."

He entered the downstairs shop.

The coffin sat before some wide-flung French windows, the lid shut, complete and neat, all put together like the fine innards of a Swiss watch. It was vast, and it rested upon a long long table with rollers beneath for easy maneuvering.

The coffin interior, as he peered through the glass lid, was six feet long. There must be a good three feet of false body at both head and foot of the coffin, then. Three feet at each end which, covered by secret panels that he must find some way of opening, might very well reveal—exactly what?

Money, of course. It would be just like Charlie to suck his riches into his grave with himself, leaving Richard with not a cent to buy a bottle with. The old bastard!

He raised the glass lid and felt about, but found no hidden buttons. There was a small sign studiously inked on white paper, thumbtacked to the side of the satin-lined box. It said:

THE BRALING ECONOMY CASKET. Copyright, April, 1946. Simple to operate. Can be used again and again by morticians and families with an eye to the future.

Richard snorted thinly. Who did Charlie think he was fooling?
There was more writing:

DIRECTIONS: SIMPLY PLACE BODY IN COFFIN—

What a fool thing to say. Put body in coffin! Naturally! How else would one go about it? He peered intently and finished out the directions:

SIMPLY PLACE BODY IN COFFIN—AND MUSIC WILL START.

"It can't be—" Richard gaped at the sign. "Don't tell me all this work has been for a—" He went to the open door of the shop, walked out upon the tiled terrace and called to the gardener in his greenhouse. "Rogers!" The gardener stuck his head out. "What time is it?" asked Richard. "Twelve o'clock, sir," replied Rogers. "Well, at twelve-fifteen, you come up here and check to see if everything is all right, Rogers," said Richard. "Yes, sir," said the gardener. Richard turned and went back into the shop. "We'll find out—" he said, quietly.

There would be no harm in lying in the box, testing it. He noticed small ventilating holes in the sides. Even if the lid were closed down there'd be air. And Rogers would be up in a moment or two. SIMPLY PLACE BODY IN COFFIN— AND MUSIC WILL START. Really, how naive of old Charlie! Richard hoisted himself up.

He was like a man getting into a bathtub. He felt naked and watched over. He put one shiny shoe into the coffin and crooked his knee and eased himself up and made some little remark to nobody in particular, then he put in his other knee and foot and crouched there, as if undecided about the temperature of the bath-water. Edging himself about, chuckling softly, he lay down, pretending to himself (for it was fun pretending) that he was dead, that people were dropping tears on him, that candles were fuming and illuminating and that the world was stopped in mid-stride because of his passing. He put on a long pale expression, shut his eyes, holding back the laughter in himself behind pressed, quivering lips. He folded his hands and decided they felt waxen and cold.

Whirr. Spung! Something whispered inside the box-wall. *Spung!*

The lid slammed down on him!

From outside, if one had just come into the room, one would have imagined a wild man was kicking, pounding, blathering, and shrieking inside a closet! There was a sound of a body dancing and cavorting. There was a thudding of flesh and fists. There was a squeaking and a kind of wind from a frightened man's lungs. There was a rustling like paper and a shrilling as of many pipes simultaneously played. Then there was a real fine scream. Then— silence.

Richard Braling lay in the coffin and relaxed. He let loose all his muscles. He began to chuckle. The smell of the box was not unpleasant. Through the little perforations he drew more than enough air to live on, comfortably. He need only push gently up with his hands, with none of this kicking and screaming, and the lid would open. One must be calm. He flexed his arms.

The lid was locked.

Well, still there was no danger. Rogers would be up in a minute or two. There was nothing to fear.

The music began to play.

It seemed to come from somewhere inside the head of the coffin. It was green music. Organ music, very slow and melancholy, typical of Gothic arches and long black tapers. It smelled of earth and whispers. It echoed high between stone walls. It was so sad that one almost cried listening to it. It was music of potted plants and crimson and blue stained-glass windows. It was late sun at twilight and a cold wind blowing. It was a dawn with only fog and a faraway fog horn moaning.

"Charlie, Charlie, Charlie, you old fool you! So this is your odd coffin!" Tears of laughter welled into Richard's eyes. "Nothing more than a coffin which plays its own dirge. Oh, my sainted grandma!"

He lay and listened critically, for it was beautiful music and there was nothing he could do until Rogers came up and let him out. His eyes roved aimlessly, his fingers tapped soft little rhythms on the satin cushions. He crossed his legs idly. Through the glass lid he saw sunlight shooting through the French windows, dust particles dancing on it. It was a lovely blue day.

The sermon began.

The organ music quieted and a gentle voice said:

"We are gathered together, those who loved and those who knew the deceased, to give him our homage and our due—"

"Charlie, bless you, that's *your* voice!" Richard was delighted. "A mechanical funeral, by God. Organ music and lecture. And Charlie giving his own oration for himself!"

The soft voice said, "We who knew and loved him are grieved at the passing of—"

"What was *that?*" Richard raised himself, startled. He didn't quite believe what he had heard. He repeated it to himself just the way he had heard it:

"We who knew and loved him are grieved at the passing of Richard Braling."

That's what the voice had said.

"Richard Braling," said the man in the coffin. "Why, *I'm* Richard Braling."

A slip of the tongue, naturally. Merely a slip. Charlie had meant to say "Charles" Braling. Certainly. Yes. Of course. Yes. Certainly. Yes. Naturally. Yes.

"Richard was a fine man," said the voice, talking on. "We shall see no finer in our time."

"My name again!"

Richard began to move about uneasily in the coffin.

Why didn't Rogers come?

It was hardly a mistake, using that name twice. Richard Braling. Richard Braling. We are gathered here. We shall miss— We are grieved. No finer man. No finer in our time. We are gathered here. The deceased. Richard Braling. *Richard* Braling.

Whirrrr. Spung!

Flowers! Six dozen bright blue, red, yellow, sun-brilliant flowers leaped up from behind the coffin on concealed springs!

The sweet odor of fresh-cut flowers filled the coffin. The flowers swayed gently before his amazed vision, tapping silently on the glass lid. Others sprang up until the coffin was banked with petals and color and sweet odors. Gardenias and dahlias and daffodils, trembling and shining.

"Rogers!"

The sermon continued.

"—Richard Braling, in his life, was a connoisseur of great and good things—"

The music sighed, rose and fell, distantly.

"Richard Braling savored of life, as one savors of a rare wine, holding it upon the lips—"

A small panel in the side of the box flipped open. A swift bright metal arm snatched out. A needle stabbed Richard in the thorax, not very deeply. He screamed. The needle shot him full of a colored liquor before he could seize it. Then it popped back into a receptacle and the panel snapped shut.

"Rogers!"

A growing numbness. Suddenly he could not move his fingers or his arms or turn his head. His legs were cold and limp.

"Richard Braling loved beautiful things. Music. Flowers," said the voice.

"Rogers!"

This time he did not scream it. He could only think it. His tongue was motionless in his anaesthetized mouth.

Another panel opened. Metal forceps issued forth on steel arms. His left wrist was pierced by a huge sucking needle.

His blood was being drained from his body.

He heard a little pump working somewhere.

"—Richard Braling will be missed among us—"

The organ sobbed and murmured.

The flowers looked down upon him, nodding their bright-petalled heads.

Six candles, black and slender, rose up out of hidden receptacles, and stood behind the flowers, flickering and glowing.

Another pump started to work. While his blood drained out one side of his body, his right wrist was punctured, held, a needle shoved into it, and the second pump began to force formaldehyde into him.

Pump, pause, *pump*, pause, *pump*, pause, *pump*, pause.

The coffin moved.

A small motor popped and chugged. The room drifted by on either side of him. Little wheels revolved. No pallbearers were necessary. The flowers swayed as the casket moved gently out upon the terrace under a blue clear sky.

Pump, pause. *Pump*, pause.

"Richard Braling will be missed—"

Sweet soft music.

Pump, pause.

"Ah, sweet mystery of life, at last—" Singing.

"Braling, the gourmet—"

"Ah, at last I have the secret of it all—"

Staring, staring, his eyes egg-blind, at the little card out of the corners of his eyes:

THE BRALING ECONOMY CASKET. . . .

DIRECTIONS: SIMPLY PLACE BODY IN COFFIN—AND MUSIC WILL START.

A tree swung by overhead. The coffin rolled gently through the garden, behind some bushes, carrying the voice and the music with it.

"Now it is the time when we must consign this part of this man to the earth—"

Little shining spades leaped out of the sides of the casket.

They began to dig.

He saw the spades toss up dirt. The coffin settled. Bumped, settled, dug, bumped and settled, dug, bumped and settled again.

Pulse, pause, *pulse*, pause. *Pump*, pause, *pulse*, *pump*, pause.

"Ashes to ashes, dust to dust—"

The flowers shook and jolted. The box was deep. The music played.

The last thing Richard Braling saw was the spading arms of the Braling Economy Casket reaching up and pulling the hole in after it.

"Richard Braling, Richard Braling, Richard Braling, Richard Braling, Richard Braling . . ."

The record was stuck.

Nobody minded. Nobody was listening.

The Crowd

Mr. Spallner put his hands over his face.

There was the feeling of movement in space, the beautifully tortured scream, the impact and tumbling of the car with wall, through wall, over and down like a toy, and him hurled out of it. Then—silence.

The crowd came running. Faintly, where he lay, he heard them running. He could tell their ages and their sizes by the sound of their numerous feet over the summer grass and on the lined pavement, and over the asphalt street; and picking through the cluttered bricks to where his car hung half into the night sky, still spinning its wheels with a senseless centrifuge.

Where the crowd came from he didn't know. He struggled to remain aware and then the crowd faces hemmed in upon him, hung over like the large glowing leaves of down-bent trees. They were a ring of shifting, compressing, changing faces over him, looking down, looking down, reading the time of his life or death by his face, making his face into a moon-dial, where the moon cast a shadow from his nose out upon his cheek to tell the time of breathing or not breathing any more ever.

How swiftly a crowd comes, he thought, like the iris of an eye compressing in out of nowhere.

A siren. A police voice. Movement. Blood trickled from his lips and he was being moved into an ambulance. Someone said, "Is he dead?" And someone else said, "No, he's not dead." And a third person said, "He won't die, he's not going to die." And he saw the faces of the crowd beyond him in the night, and he knew by their expressions that he wouldn't die. And that was strange. He saw a man's face, thin, bright, pale; the man swallowed and bit his lips, very sick. There was a small woman, too, with red hair and too much red on her cheeks and lips. And a little boy with a freckled face. Others' faces. An old man with a wrinkled upper lip, an old woman, with a mole upon her chin. They had all come from—where? Houses, cars, alleys, from the immediate and the accident-shocked world. Out of alleys and out of hotels and out of streetcars and seemingly out of nothing they came.

The crowd looked at him and he looked back at them and did not like them at all. There was a vast wrongness to them. He couldn't put his finger on it. They were far worse than this machine-made thing that happened to him now.

The ambulance doors slammed. Through the windows he saw the crowd looking in, looking in. That crowd that always came so fast, so strangely fast, to form a circle, to peer down, to probe, to gawk, to question, to point, to disturb, to spoil the privacy of a man's agony by their frank curiosity.

The ambulance drove off. He sank back and their faces still stared into his face, even with his eyes shut.

The car wheels spun in his mind for days. One wheel, four wheels, spinning, spinning, and whirring, around and around.

He knew it was wrong. Something wrong with the wheels and the whole accident and the running of feet and the curiosity. The crowd faces mixed and spun into the wild rotation of the wheels.

He awoke.

Sunlight, a hospital room, a hand taking his pulse.

"How do you feel?" asked the doctor.

The wheels faded away. Mr. Spallner looked around.

"Fine—I guess."

He tried to find words. About the accident. "Doctor?"

"Yes?"

"That crowd—was it last night?"

"Two days ago. You've been here since Thursday. You're all right, though. You're doing fine. Don't try and get up."

"That crowd. Something about wheels, too. Do accidents make people, well, a—little off?"

"Temporarily, sometimes."

He lay staring up at the doctor. "Does it hurt your time sense?"

"Panic sometimes does."

"Makes a minute seem like an hour, or maybe an hour seem like a minute?"

"Yes."

"Let me tell you then." He felt the bed under him, the sunlight on his face. "You'll think I'm crazy. I was driving too fast, I know. I'm sorry now. I jumped the curb and hit that wall. I was hurt and numb, I know, but I still remember things. Mostly—the crowd." He waited a moment and then decided to go on, for he suddenly knew what it was that bothered him. "The crowd got there too quickly. Thirty seconds after the smash they were all standing over me and staring at me . . . it's not right they should run that fast, so late at night. . . ."

"You only think it was thirty seconds," said the doctor. "It was probably three or four minutes. Your senses—"

"Yeah, I know—my senses, the accident. But I was conscious! I remember one thing that puts it all together and makes it funny, God, so damned funny. The wheels of my car, upside down. The wheels were still spinning when the crowd got there!"

The doctor smiled.

The man in bed went on. "I'm positive! The wheels were spinning and spinning fast—the front wheels! Wheels don't spin very long, friction cuts them down. And these were really spinning!"

"You're confused," said the doctor.

"I'm not confused. That street was empty. Not a soul in sight. And then the accident and the wheels still spinning and all those faces over me, quick, in no time. And the way they looked down at me, I *knew* I wouldn't die. . . ."

"Simple shock," said the doctor, walking away into the sunlight.

They released him from the hospital two weeks later. He rode home in a taxi. People had come to visit him during his two weeks on his back, and to all of them he had told his story, the accident, the spinning wheels, the crowd. They had all laughed with him concerning it, and passed it off.

He leaned forward and tapped on the taxi window.

"What's wrong?"

The cabbie looked back. "Sorry, boss. This is one helluva town to drive in. Got an accident up ahead. Want me to detour?"

"Yes. No. No! Wait. Go ahead. Let's—let's take a look."

The cab moved forward, honking.

"Funny damn thing," said the cabbie. "Hey, *you*! Get that fleatrap out the way!" Quieter, "Funny thing—more damn people. Nosy people."

Mr. Spallner looked down and watched his fingers tremble on his knee. "You noticed that, too?"

"Sure," said the cabbie. "All the time. There's always a crowd. You'd think it was their own mother got killed."

"They come running awfully fast," said the man in the back of the cab.

"Same way with a fire or an explosion. Nobody around. Boom. Lotsa people around. I dunno."

"Ever seen an accident—at night?"

The cabbie nodded. "Sure. Don't make no difference. There's always a crowd."

The wreck came in view. A body lay on the pavement. You knew there was a body even if you couldn't see it. Because of the crowd. The crowd with its back toward him as he sat in the rear of the cab. With its back toward him. He opened the window and almost started to yell. But he didn't have the nerve. If he yelled they might turn around.

And he was afraid to see their faces.

"I seem to have a penchant for accidents," he said, in his office. It was late afternoon. His friend sat across the desk from him, listening. "I got out of the hospital this morning and first thing on the way home, we detoured around a wreck."

"Things run in cycles," said Morgan.

"Let me tell you about my accident."

"I've heard it. Heard it all."

"But it was funny, you must admit."

"I must admit. Now how about a drink?"

They talked on for half an hour or more. All the while they talked, at the back of Spallner's brain a small watch ticked, a watch that never needed winding. It was the memory of a few little things. Wheels and faces.

At about five-thirty there was a hard metal noise in the street. Morgan nodded and looked out and down. "What'd I tell you? Cycles. A truck and a cream-colored Cadillac. Yes, yes."

Spallner walked to the window. He was very cold and as he stood there, he looked at his watch, at the small minute hand. One two three four five seconds—people running—eight nine ten eleven twelve—from all over, people came running—fifteen sixteen seventeen eighteen seconds—more people, more cars, more horns blowing. Curiously distant, Spallner looked upon the scene as an explosion in reverse, the fragments of the detonation sucked back to the point of impulsion. Nineteen, twenty, twenty-one seconds and the crowd was there. Spallner made a gesture down at them, wordless.

The crowd had gathered so fast.

He saw a woman's body a moment before the crowd swallowed it up.

Morgan said, "You look lousy. Here. Finish your drink."

"I'm all right, I'm all right. Let me alone. I'm all right. Can you see those people? Can you see any of them? I wish we could see them closer."

Morgan cried out, "Where in hell are you going?"

Spallner was out the door, Morgan after him, and down the stairs, as rapidly as possible. "Come along, and hurry."

"Take it easy, you're not a well man!"

They walked out on to the street. Spallner pushed his way forward. He thought he saw a red-haired woman with too much red color on her cheeks and lips.

"There!" He turned wildly to Morgan. "Did you see her?"

"See *who*?"

"Damn it; she's gone. The crowd closed in!"

The crowd was all around, breathing and looking and shuffling and mixing and mumbling and getting in the way when he tried to shove through. Evidently the red-haired woman had seen him coming and run off.

He saw another familiar face! A little freckled boy. But there are many freckled boys in the world. And, anyway, it was no use; before Spallner reached him, this little boy ran away and vanished among the people.

"Is she dead?" a voice asked. "Is she dead?"

"She's dying," someone else replied. "She'll be dead before the ambulance arrives. They shouldn't have moved her. They shouldn't have moved her."

All the crowd faces—familiar, yet unfamiliar, bending over, looking down, looking down.

"Hey, mister, stop pushing."

"Who you shovin', buddy?"

Spallner came back out, and Morgan caught hold of him before he fell. "You damned fool. You're still sick. Why in hell'd you have to come down here?" Morgan demanded.

"I don't know, I really don't. They moved her, Morgan, someone moved her. You should never move a traffic victim. It kills them. It kills them."

"Yeah. That's the way with people. The idiots."

Spallner arranged the newspaper clippings carefully.

Morgan looked at them. "What's the idea? Ever since your accident you think every traffic scramble is part of you. What are these?"

"Clippings of motor-car crackups, and photos. Look at them. Not at the cars," said Spallner, "but at the crowds around the cars." He pointed. "Here. Compare this photo of a wreck in the Wilshire District with one in Westwood. No resemblance. But now take this Westwood picture and align it with one taken in the Westwood District ten years ago." Again he motioned. "This woman is in both pictures."

"Coincidence. The woman happened to be there once in 1936, again in 1946."

"A coincidence once, maybe. But twelve times over a period of ten years, when the accidents occurred as much as three miles from one another, no. Here." He dealt out a dozen photographs. "She's in *all* of these!"

"Maybe she's perverted."

"She's more than that. How does she *happen* to be there so quickly after each accident? And why does she wear the same clothes in pictures taken over a period of a decade?"

"I'll be damned, so she does."

"And, last of all, why was she standing over *me* the night of my accident, two weeks ago?"

They had a drink. Morgan went over the files. "What'd you do, hire a clipping service while you were in the hospital to go back through the newspapers for you?" Spallner nodded. Morgan sipped his drink. It was getting late. The street lights were coming on in the streets below the office. "What does all this add up to?"

"I don't know," said Spallner, "except that there's a universal law about accidents. *Crowds gather.* They always gather. And like you and me, people have wondered year after year, why they gathered so quickly, and how? I know the answer. Here it is!"

He flung the clippings down. "It frightens me."

"These people—mightn't they be thrill-hunters, perverted sensationalists with a carnal lust for blood and morbidity?"

Spallner shrugged. "Does that explain their being at all the accidents? Notice, they stick to certain territories. A Brentwood accident will bring out one group. A Huntington Park another. But there's a norm for faces, a certain percentage appear at each wreck."

Morgan said, "They're not *all* the same faces, are they?"

"Naturally not. Accidents draw normal people, too, in the course of time. But these, I find, are always the *first* ones there."

"Who are they? What do they want? You keep hinting and never telling. Good Lord, you must have some idea. You've scared yourself and now you've got me jumping."

"I've tried getting to them, but someone always trips me up, I'm always too late. They slip into the crowd and vanish. The crowd seems to offer protection to some of its members. They see me coming."

"Sounds like some sort of clique."

"They have one thing in common, they always show up together. At a fire or an explosion or on the sidelines of a war, at any public demonstration of this thing called death. Vultures, hyenas, or saints, I don't know which they are, I just don't know. But I'm going to the police with it, this evening. It's gone on long enough. One of them shifted that woman's body today. They shouldn't have touched her. It killed her."

He placed the clippings in a briefcase. Morgan got up and slipped into his coat. Spallner clicked the briefcase shut. "Or, I just happened to think . . . "

"What?"

"Maybe they *wanted* her dead."

"Why?"

"Who knows. Come along?"

"Sorry. It's late. See you tomorrow. Luck." They went out together. "Give my regards to the cops. Think they'll believe you?"

"Oh, they'll believe me all right. Good night."

Spallner took it slow driving downtown.

"I want to get there," he told himself, "alive."

He was rather shocked, but not surprised, somehow, when the truck came rolling out of an alley straight at him. He was just congratulating himself on his keen sense of observation and talking out what he would say to the police in his mind, when the truck smashed into his car. It wasn't really his car, that was the disheartening thing about it. In a preoccupied mood he was tossed first this way and then that way, while he thought, What a shame, Morgan has gone and lent me his extra car for a few days until my other car is fixed, and now here I go again. The windshield hammered back into his face. He was forced back and forth in several lightning jerks. Then all motion stopped and all noise stopped and only pain filled him up.

He heard their feet running and running and running. He fumbled with the car door. It clicked. He fell out upon the pavement drunkenly and lay, ear to the asphalt, listening to them coming. It was like a great rainstorm, with many drops, heavy and light and medium, touching the earth. He waited a few seconds and listened to their coming and their arrival. Then, weakly, expectantly, he rolled his head up and looked.

The crowd was there.

He could smell their breaths, the mingled odors of many people sucking and sucking on the air a man needs to live by. They crowded and jostled and sucked and sucked all the air up from around his gasping face until he tried to tell them to move back, they were making him live in a vacuum. His head was bleeding very badly. He tried to move and he realized something was wrong with his spine. He hadn't felt much at the impact, but his spine was hurt. He didn't dare move.

He couldn't speak. Opening his mouth, nothing came out but a gagging.

Someone said, "Give me a hand. We'll roll him over and lift him into a more comfortable position."

Spallner's brain burst apart.

No! Don't move me!

"We'll move him," said the voice, casually.

You idiots, you'll kill me, don't!

But he could not say any of this out loud. He could only think it.

Hands took hold of him. They started to lift him. He cried out and nausea choked him up. They straightened him out into a ramrod of agony. Two men did it. One of them was thin, bright, pale, alert, a young man. The other man was very old and had a wrinkled upper lip.

He had seen their faces before.

A familiar voice said, "Is—is he dead?"

Another voice, a memorable voice, responded, "No. Not yet. But he will be dead before the ambulance arrives."

It was all a very silly, mad plot. Like every accident. He squealed hysterically at the solid wall of faces. They were all around him, these judges and jurors with the faces he had seen before. Through his pain he counted their faces.

The freckled boy. The old man with the wrinkled upper lip.

The red-haired, red-cheeked woman. An old woman with a mole on her chin.

I know what you're here for, he thought. You're here just as you're at all accidents. To make certain the right ones live and the right ones die. That's why you lifted me. You knew it would kill. You knew I'd live if you left me alone.

And that's the way it's been since time began, when crowds gather. You murder much easier, this way. Your alibi is very simple; you didn't know it was dangerous to move a hurt man. You didn't mean to hurt him.

He looked at them, above him, and he was curious as a man under deep water looking up at people on a bridge. Who are you? Where do you come from and how do you get here so soon? You're the crowd that's always in the way, using up good air that a dying man's lungs are in need of, using up space he should be using to lie in, alone. Tramping on people to make sure they die, that's you. I know *all* of you.

It was like a polite monologue. They said nothing. Faces. The old man. The red-haired woman.

Someone picked up his briefcase. "Whose is this?"

It's mine! It's evidence against all of you!

Eyes, inverted over him. Shiny eyes under tousled hair or under hats.

Faces.

Somewhere—a siren. The ambulance was coming.

But, looking at the faces, the construction, the cast, the form of the faces, Spallner saw it was too late. He read it in their faces. They *knew*.

He tried to speak. A little bit got out:

"It—looks like I'll—be joining up with you. I—guess I'll be a member of your—group—now."

He closed his eyes then, and waited for the coroner.

The Scythe

Quite suddenly there was no more road. It ran down the valley like any other road, between slopes of barren, stony ground and live oak trees, and then past a broad field of wheat standing alone in the wilderness. It came up beside the small white house that belonged to the wheat field and then just faded out, as though there was no more use for it.

It didn't matter much, because just there the last of the gas was gone. Drew Erickson braked the ancient car to a stop and sat there, not speaking, staring at his big, rough farmer's hands.

Molly spoke, without moving where she lay in the corner beside him. "We must of took the wrong fork back yonder."

Drew nodded.

Molly's lips were almost as white as her face. Only they were dry, where her skin was damp with sweat. Her voice was flat with no expression in it.

"Drew," she said. "Drew, what are we a-goin' to do now?"

Drew stared at his hands. A farmer's hands, with the farm blown out from under them by the dry, hungry wind that never got enough good loam to eat.

The kids in the back seat woke up and pried themselves out of the dusty litter of bundles and bedding. They poked their heads over the back of the seat and said:

"What are we stoppin' for, Pa? Are we gonna eat now, Pa? Pa, we're awful hungry. Can we eat now, Pa?"

Drew closed his eyes. He hated the sight of his hands.

Molly's fingers touched his wrist. Very light, very soft. "Drew, maybe in the house there they'd spare us somethin' to eat?"

A white line showed around his mouth. "Beggin'," he said harshly. "Ain't none of us ever begged before. Ain't none of us ever goin' to."

Molly's hand tightened on his wrist. He turned and saw her eyes. He saw the eyes of Susie and little Drew, looking at him. Slowly all the stiffness went out of his neck and his back. His face got loose and blank, shapeless like a thing that has been beaten too hard and too long. He got out of the car and went up the path to the house. He walked uncertainly, like a man who is sick, or nearly blind.

The door of the house was open. Drew knocked three times. There was nothing inside but silence, and a white window curtain moving in the slow, hot air.

He knew it before he went in. He knew there was death in the house. It was that kind of silence.

He went through a small, clean living room and down a little hall. He wasn't thinking anything. He was past thinking. He was going toward the kitchen, unquestioning, like an animal.

Then he looked through an open door and saw the dead man.

He was an old man, lying out on a clean white bed. He hadn't been dead long; not long enough to lose the last quiet look of peace. He must have known he was going to die, because he wore his grave clothes—an old black suit, brushed and neat, and a clean white shirt and a black tie.

A scythe leaned against the wall beside the bed. Between the old man's hands there was a blade of wheat, still fresh. A ripe blade, golden and heavy in the tassel.

Drew went into the bedroom, walking soft. There was a coldness on him. He took off his broken, dusty hat and stood by the bed, looking down.

The paper lay open on the pillow beside the old man's head. It was meant to be read. Maybe a request for burial, or to call a relative. Drew scowled over the words, moving his pale, dry lips.

To him who stands beside me at my death bed:

Being of sound mind, and alone in the world as it has been decreed, I, John Buhr, do give and bequeath this farm, with all pertaining to it, to the man who is to come. Whatever his name or origin shall be, it will not matter. The farm is his, and the wheat; the scythe, and the task ordained thereto. Let him take them freely, and without question—and remember that I, John Buhr, am only the giver, not the ordainer. To which I set my hand and seal this third day of April, 1938.

[Signed]   *John Buhr.* Kyrie eleison!

Drew walked back through the house and opened the screen door. He said, "Molly, you come in. Kids, you stay in the car."

Molly came inside. He took her to the bedroom. She looked at the will, the scythe, the wheat field moving in a hot wind outside the window. Her white face tightened up and she bit her lips and held on to him. "It's too good to be true. There must be some trick to it."

Drew said, "Our luck's changin', that's all. We'll have work to do, stuff to eat, somethin' over our heads to keep rain off." He touched the scythe. It gleamed like a half-moon. Words were scratched on its blade: WHO WIELDS ME— WIELDS THE WORLD! It didn't mean much to him, right at that moment.

"Drew," Molly asked, staring at the old man's clasped hands, "why—why's he holdin' that wheat-stalk so hard in his fingers?"

Just then the heavy silence was broken by the sound of the kids scrambling up the front porch. Molly gasped.

They lived in the house. They buried the old man on a hill and said some words over him, and came back down and swept the house and unloaded the car and had something to eat, because there was food, lots of it, in the kitchen; and they did nothing for three days but fix the house and look at the land and lie in the good beds, and then look at one another in surprise that all this was happening this way, and their stomachs were full and there was even a cigar for him to smoke in the evenings.

There was a small barn behind the house and in the barn a bull and three cows; and there was a well-house, a spring-house, under some big trees that kept it cool. And inside the well-house were big sides of beef and bacon and pork and mutton, enough to feed a family five times their size for a year, two years, maybe three. There was a churn and a box of cheese there, and big metal cans for the milk.

On the fourth morning Drew Erickson lay in bed looking at the scythe, and he knew it was time for him to work because there was ripe grain in the long field; he had seen it with his eyes, and he did not want to get soft. Three days' sitting were enough for any man. He roused himself in the first fresh smell of dawn and took the scythe and held it before him as he walked out into the field. He held it up in his hands and swung it down.

It was a big field of grain. Too big for one man to tend, and yet one man had tended it.

At the end of the first day of work, he walked in with the scythe riding his shoulder quietly, and there was a look on his face of a puzzled man. It was a wheat field the like of which he had never seen. It ripened only in separate clusters, each set off from the others. Wheat shouldn't do that. He didn't tell Molly. Nor did he tell her the other things about the field. About how, for instance, the wheat rotted within a few hours after he cut it down. Wheat shouldn't do that, either. He was not greatly worried. After all, there was food at hand.

The next morning the wheat he had left rotting, cut down, had taken hold and come up again in little green sprouts, with tiny roots, all born again.

Drew Erickson rubbed his chin, wondered what and why and how it acted that way, and what good it would be to him—he couldn't sell it. A couple of times during the day he walked far up in the hills to where the old man's grave was, just to be sure the old man was there, maybe with some notion he might get an idea there about the field. He looked down and saw how much land he owned. The wheat stretched three miles in one direction toward the mountains, and was about two acres wide, patches of it in seedlings, patches of it golden, patches of it green, patches of it fresh-cut by his hand. But the old man said nothing concerning this; there were a lot of stones and dirt in his face now. The grave was in the sun and the wind and silence. So Drew Erickson walked back down to use the scythe, curious, enjoying it because it seemed important. He didn't know just why, but it was. Very, very important.

He couldn't just let the wheat stand. There were always new patches of it ripened, and in his figuring out loud to no one in particular he said, "If I cut the wheat for the next ten years, just as it ripens up, I don't think I'll pass the same spot twice. Such a damn big field." He shook his head. "That wheat ripens just *so*. Never too much of it so I can't cut all the ripe stuff each day. That leaves nothin' but green grain. And the next mornin', sure enough, another patch of ripe stuff. . . . "

It was damned foolish to cut the grain when it rotted as quick as it fell. At the end of the week he decided to let it go a few days.

He lay in bed late, just listening to the silence in the house that wasn't anything like death silence, but a silence of things living well and happily.

He got up, dressed, and ate his breakfast slowly. He wasn't going to work. He went out to milk the cows, stood on the porch smoking a cigarette, walked about the back yard a little and then came back in and asked Molly what he had gone out to do.

"Milk the cows," she said.

"Oh, yes," he said, and went out again. He found the cows waiting and full, and milked them and put the milk cans in the spring-house, but thought of other things. The wheat. The scythe.

All through the morning he sat on the back porch rolling cigarettes. He made a toy boat for little Drew and one for Susie, and then he churned some of the milk into butter and drew off the buttermilk, but the sun was in his head, aching. It burned there. He wasn't hungry for lunch. He kept looking at the wheat and the wind bending and tipping and ruffling it. His arms flexed, his fingers, resting on his knee as he sat again on the porch, made a kind of grip in the empty air, itching. The pads of his palms itched and burned. He stood up and wiped his hands on his pants and sat down and tried to roll another cigarette and got mad at the mixings and threw it all away with a muttering. He had a feeling as if a third arm had been cut off of him, or he had lost something of himself. It had to do with his hands and his arms.

He heard the wind whisper in the field.

By one o'clock he was going in and out of the house, getting underfoot, thinking about digging an irrigation ditch, but all the time really thinking about the wheat and how ripe and beautiful it was, aching to be cut.

"Damn it to hell!"

He strode into the bedroom, took the scythe down off its wall-pegs. He stood holding it. He felt cool. His hands stopped itching. His head didn't ache. The third arm was returned to him. He was intact again.

It was instinct. Illogical as lightning striking and not hurting. Each day the grain must be cut. It had to be cut. Why? Well, it just did, that was all. He laughed at the scythe in his big hands. Then, whistling, he took it out to the ripe and waiting field and did the work. He thought himself a little mad. Hell, it was an ordinary-enough wheat field, really, wasn't it? Almost.

The days loped away like gentle horses.

Drew Erickson began to understand his work as a sort of dry ache and hunger and need. Things built in his head.

One noon, Susie and little Drew giggled and played with the scythe while their father lunched in the kitchen. He heard them. He came out and took it away from them. He didn't yell at them. He just looked very concerned and locked the scythe up after that, when it wasn't being used.

He never missed a day, scything.

Up. Down. Up, down, and across. Back and up and down and across. Cutting. Up. Down.

Up.

Think about the old man and the wheat in his hands when he died.

Down.

Think about this dead land, with wheat living on it.

Up.

Think about the crazy patterns of ripe and green wheat, the way it grows!

Down.

Think about . . .

The wheat whirled in a full yellow tide at his ankles. The sky blackened. Drew Erickson dropped the scythe and bent over to hold his stomach, his eyes running blindly. The world reeled.

"I've killed somebody!" he gasped, choking, holding to his chest, falling to his knees beside the blade. "I've killed a lot—"

The sky revolved like a blue merry-go-round at the county fair in Kansas. But no music. Only a ringing in his ears.

Molly was sitting at the blue kitchen table peeling potatoes when he blundered into the kitchen, dragging the scythe behind him.

"Molly!"

She swam around in the wet of his eyes.

She sat there, her hands fallen open, waiting for him to finally get it out.

"Get the things packed!" he said, looking at the floor.

"Why?"

"We're leavin'," he said, dully.

"We're leavin'?" she said.

"That old man. You know what he did here? It's the wheat, Molly, and this scythe. Every time you use the scythe on the wheat a thousand people die. You cut across them and—"

Molly got up and put the knife down and the potatoes to one side and said, understandingly, "We traveled a lot and haven't eaten good until the last month here, and you been workin' every day and you're tired—"

"I hear voices, sad voices, out there. In the wheat," he said. "Tellin' me to stop. Tellin' me not to kill them!"

"Drew!"

He didn't hear her. "The field grows crooked, wild, like a crazy thing. I didn't tell you. But it's wrong."

She stared at him. His eyes were blue glass, nothing else.

"You think I'm crazy," he said, "but wait 'til I tell you. Oh, God, Molly, help me; I just killed my mother!"

"Stop it!" she said firmly.

"I cut down one stalk of wheat and I killed her. I felt her dyin', that's how I found out just now—"

"Drew!" Her voice was like a crack across the face, angry and afraid now. "Shut up!"

He mumbled. "Oh—Molly—"

The scythe dropped from his hands, clamored on the floor. She picked it up with a snap of anger and set it in one corner. "Ten years I been with you," she said. "Sometimes we had nothin' but dust and prayers in our mouths. Now, all this good luck sudden, and you can't bear up under it!"

She brought the Bible from the living room.

She rustled its pages over. They sounded like the wheat rustling in a small, slow wind. "You sit down and listen," she said.

A sound came in from the sunshine. The kids, laughing in the shade of the large live oak beside the house.

She read from the Bible, looking up now and again to see what was happening to Drew's face.

She read from the Bible each day after that. The following Wednesday, a week later, when Drew walked down to the distant town to see if there was any General Delivery mail, there was a letter.

He came home looking two hundred years old.

He held the letter out to Molly and told her what it said in a cold, uneven voice.

"Mother passed away—one o'clock Tuesday afternoon—her heart—"

All that Drew Erickson had to say was, "Get the kids in the car, load it up with food. We're goin' on to California."

"Drew—" said his wife, holding the letter.

"You know yourself," he said, "this is poor grain land. Yet look how ripe it grows. I ain't told you all the things. It ripens in patches, a little each day. It ain't right. And when I cut it, it rots! And next mornin' it comes up without any help, growin' again! Last Tuesday, a week ago, when I cut the grain it was like rippin' my own flesh. I heard somebody scream. It sounded just like— And now, today, this letter."

She said, "We're stayin' here."

"Molly."

"We're stayin' here, where we're sure of eatin' and sleepin' and livin' decent and livin' long. I'm not starvin' my children down again, ever!"

The sky was blue through the windows. The sun slanted in, touching half of Molly's calm face, shining one eye bright blue. Four or five water drops hung and fell from the kitchen faucet slowly, shining, before Drew sighed. The sigh was husky and resigned and tired. He nodded, looking away. "All right," he said. "We'll stay."

He picked up the scythe weakly. The words on the metal leaped up with a sharp glitter.

WHO WIELDS ME—WIELDS THE WORLD!

"We'll stay. . . . "

Next morning he walked to the old man's grave. There was a single fresh sprout of wheat growing in the center of it. The same sprout, reborn, that the old man had held in his hands weeks before.

He talked to the old man, getting no answers.

"You worked the field all your life because you *had* to, and one day you came across your own life growin' there. You knew it was yours. You cut it. And you went home, put on your grave clothes, and your heart gave out and you died. That's how it was, wasn't it? And you passed the land on to me, and when I die, I'm supposed to hand it over to someone else."

Drew's voice had awe in it. "How long a time has this been goin' on? With nobody knowin' about this field and its use except the man with the scythe. . . ?"

Quite suddenly he felt very old. The valley seemed ancient, mummified, secretive, dried and bent and powerful. When the Indians danced on the prairie it had been here, this field. The same sky, the same wind, the same wheat. And, before the Indians? Some Cro-Magnon, gnarled and shag-haired, wielding a crude wooden scythe, perhaps, prowling down through the living wheat. . . .

Drew returned to work. Up, down. Up, down. Obsessed with the idea of being the wielder of *the* scythe. He, himself! It burst upon him in a mad, wild surge of strength and horror.

Up! WHO WIELDS ME! Down! WIELDS THE WORLD!

He had to accept the job with some sort of philosophy. It was simply his way of getting food and housing for his family. They deserved eating and living decent, he thought, after all these years.

Up and down. Each grain a life he neatly cut into two pieces. If he planned it carefully—he looked at the wheat—why, he and Molly and the kids could live forever!

Once he found the place where the grain grew that was Molly and Susie and little Drew he would never cut it.

And then, like a signal, it came, quietly.

Right there, before him.

Another sweep of the scythe and he'd cut them away.

Molly, Drew, Susie. It was certain. Trembling, he knelt and looked at the few grains of wheat. They glowed at his touch.

He groaned with relief. What if he had cut them down, never guessing? He blew out his breath and got up and took the scythe and stood back away from the wheat and stood for a long while looking down.

Molly thought it awfully strange when he came home early and kissed her on the cheek, for no reason at all.

At dinner, Molly said, "You quit early today? Does—does the wheat still spoil when it falls?"

He nodded and took more meat.

She said, "You ought to write to the Agriculture people and have them come look at it."

"No," he said.

"I was just suggestin'," she said.

His eyes dilated. "I got to stay here all my life. Can't nobody else mess with that wheat; they wouldn't know where to cut and not to cut. They might cut the wrong parts."

"What wrong parts?"

"Nothin'," he said, chewing slowly. "Nothin' at all."

He slapped his fork down, hard. "Who knows *what* they might want to do! Those gover'ment men! They might even—might even want to plow the whole field under!"

Molly nodded. "That's just what it needs," she said. "And start all over again, with new seed."

He didn't finish eating. "I'm not writin' any gover'ment, and I'm not handin' this field over to no stranger to cut, and that's that!" he said, and the screen door banged behind him.

He detoured around that place where the lives of his children and his wife grew up in the sun, and used his scythe on the far end of the field where he knew he would make no mistakes.

But he no longer liked the work. At the end of an hour he knew he had brought death to three of his old, loved friends in Missouri. He read their names on the cut grain and couldn't go on.

He locked the scythe in the cellar and put the key away. He was done with the reaping, done for good and all.

He smoked his pipe in the evening on the front porch, and told the kids stories to hear them laugh. But they didn't laugh much. They seemed withdrawn, tired and funny, like they weren't his children any more.

Molly complained of a headache, dragged around the house a little, went to bed early, and fell into a deep sleep. That was funny, too. Molly always stayed up late and was full of vinegar.

The wheat field rippled with moonlight on it, making it into a sea.

It wanted cutting. Certain parts needed cutting *now*. Drew Erickson sat, swallowing quietly, trying not to look at it.

What'd happen to the world if he never went in the field again? What'd happen to people ripe for death, who waited the coming of the scythe?

He'd wait and see.

Molly was breathing softly when he blew out the oil lamp and got to bed. He couldn't sleep. He heard the wind in the wheat, felt the hunger to do the work in his arms and fingers.

In the middle of the night he found himself walking in the field, the scythe in his hands. Walking like a crazy man, walking and afraid, half-awake. He didn't remember unlocking the cellar door, getting the scythe, but here he was in the moonlight, walking in the grain.

Among these grains there were many who were old, weary, wanting so very much to sleep. The long, quiet, moonless sleep.

The scythe held him, grew into his palms, forced him to walk.

Somehow, struggling, he got free of it. He threw it down, ran off into the wheat, where he stopped and went down on his knees.

"I don't want to kill any more," he said. "If I work with the scythe I'll have to kill Molly and the kids. Don't ask me to do that!"

The stars only sat in the sky, shining.

Behind him, he heard a dull, thumping sound.

Something shot up over the hill into the sky. It was like a living thing, with arms of red color, licking at the stars. Sparks fell into his face. The thick, hot odor of fire came with it.

The house!

Crying out, he got sluggishly, hopelessly, to his feet, looking at the big fire.

The little white house with the live oaks was roaring up in one savage bloom of fire. Heat rolled over the hill and he swam in it and went down in it, stumbling, drowning over his head.

By the time he got down the hill there was not a shingle, bolt or threshold of it that wasn't alive with flame. It made blistering, crackling, fumbling noises.

No one screamed inside. No one ran around or shouted.

He yelled in the yard. "Molly! Susie! Drew!"

He got no answer. He ran close in until his eyebrows withered and his skin crawled hot like paper burning, crisping, curling up in tight little curls.

"Molly! Susie!"

The fire settled contentedly down to feed. Drew ran around the house a dozen times, all alone, trying to find a way in. Then he sat where the fire roasted his body and waited until all the walls had sunken down with fluttering crashes, until the last ceiling bent, blanketing the floors with molten plaster and scorched lathing. Until the flames died and smoke coughed up, and the new day came slowly; and there was nothing but embering ashes and an acid smoldering.

Disregarding the heat fanning from the leveled frames, Drew walked into the ruin. It was still too dark to see much. Red light glowed on his sweating throat. He stood like a stranger in a new and different land. Here—the kitchen. Charred tables, chairs, the iron stove, the cupboards. Here—the hall. Here the parlor and then over there was the bedroom where—

Where Molly was still alive.

She slept among fallen timbers and angry-colored pieces of wire spring and metal.

She slept as if nothing had happened. Her small white hands lay at her sides, flaked with sparks. Her calm face slept with a flaming lath across one cheek.

Drew stopped and didn't believe it. In the ruin of her smoking bedroom she lay on a glittering bed of sparks, her skin intact, her breast rising, falling, taking air.

"Molly!"

Alive and sleeping after the fire, after the walls had roared down, after ceilings had collapsed upon her and flame had lived all about her.

His shoes smoked as he pushed through piles of fuming litter. It could have seared his feet off at the ankles, he wouldn't have known.

"Molly . . ."

He bent over her. She didn't move or hear him, and she didn't speak. She wasn't dead. She wasn't alive. She just lay there with the fire surrounding her and not touching her, not harming her in any way. Her cotton nightgown was streaked with ashes, but not burnt. Her brown hair was pillowed on a tumble of red-hot coals.

He touched her cheek, and it was cold, cold in the middle of hell. Tiny breaths trembled her half-smiling lips.

The children were there, too. Behind a veil of smoke he made out two smaller figures huddled in the ashes sleeping.

He carried all three of them out to the edge of the wheat field.

"Molly. Molly, wake up! Kids! Kids, wake up!"

They breathed and didn't move and went on sleeping.

"Kids, wake up! Your mother is—"

Dead? No, not dead. But—

He shook the kids as if they were to blame. They paid no attention; they were busy with their dreams. He put them back down and stood over them, his face cut with lines.

He knew why they'd slept through the fire and continued to sleep now. He knew why Molly just lay there, never wanting to laugh again.

The power of the wheat and the scythe.

Their lives, supposed to end yesterday, May 30, 1938, had been prolonged simply because he refused to cut the grain. They should have died in the fire. That's the way it was meant to *be*. But since he had not used the scythe, nothing could hurt them. A house had flamed and fallen and still they lived, caught halfway, not dead, not alive. Simply—waiting. And all over the world thousands more just like them, victims of accidents, fires, disease, suicide, waited, slept just like Molly and her children slept. Not able to die, not able to live. All because a man was afraid of harvesting the ripe grain. All because one man thought he could stop working with a scythe and never work with that scythe again.

He looked down upon the children. The job had to be done every day and every day with never a stopping but going on, with never a pause, but always the harvesting, forever and forever and forever.

All right, he thought. All right. I'll use the scythe.

He didn't say good-by to his family. He turned with a slow-feeding anger and found the scythe and walked rapidly, then he began to trot, then he ran with long jolting strides into the field, raving, feeling the hunger in his arms, as the wheat whipped and flailed his legs. He pounded through it, shouting. He stopped.

"Molly!" he cried, and raised the blade and swung it down.

"Susie!" he cried. "Drew!" And swung the blade down again.

Somebody screamed. He didn't turn to look at the fire-ruined house.

And then, sobbing wildly, he rose above the grain again and again and hewed to left and right and to left and to right and to left and to right. Over and over and over! Slicing out huge scars in green wheat and ripe wheat, with no selection and no care, cursing, over and over, swearing, laughing, the blade swinging up in the sun and falling in the sun with a singing whistle! Down!

Bombs shattered London, Moscow, Tokyo.

The blade swung insanely.

And the kilns of Belsen and Buchenwald took fire.

The blade sang, crimson wet.

And mushrooms vomited out blind suns at White Sands, Hiroshima, Bikini, and up, through, and in continental Siberian skies.

The grain wept in a green rain, falling.

Korea, Indo-China, Egypt, India trembled; Asia stirred, Africa woke in the night. . . .

And the blade went on rising, crashing, severing, with the fury and the rage of a man who has lost and lost so much that he no longer cares what he does to the world.

Just a few short miles off the main highway, down a rough dirt road that leads to nowhere, just a few short miles from a highway jammed with traffic bound for California.

Once in a while during the long years a jalopy gets off the main highway, pulls up steaming in front of the charred ruin of a little white house at the end of the dirt road, to ask instructions from the farmer they see just beyond, the one who works insanely, wildly, without ever stopping, night and day, in the endless fields of wheat.

But they get no help and no answer. The farmer in the field is too busy, even after all these years; too busy slashing and chopping the green wheat instead of the ripe.

And Drew Erickson moves on with his scythe, with the light of blind suns and a look of white fire in his never-sleeping eyes, on and on and on. . . .

There Was an Old Woman

"No, there's no lief arguin'. I got my mind fixed. Run along with your silly wicker basket. Land, where you ever get notions like that? You just skit out of here; don't bother me, I got my tattin' and knittin' to do, and no never minds about tall, dark gentlemen with fangled ideas."

The tall, dark young man stood quietly, not moving. Aunt Tildy hurried on with her talk.

"You *heard* what I said! If you got a mind to talk to me, well, you can talk, but meantime I hope you don't mind if I pour myself coffee. There. If you'd been more polite, I'd offer you some, but you jump in here high and mighty and you never rapped on the door or nothin'. You think you *own* the place."

Aunt Tildy fussed with her lap. "Now, you made me lose count! I'm makin' myself a comforter. These winters get on mighty chill, and it ain't fittin' for a lady with bones like rice-paper to be settin' in a drafty old house without warmin' herself."

The tall, dark man sat down.

"That's an antique chair, so be gentle," warned Aunt Tildy. "Start again, tell me things you got to tell, I'll listen respectful. But keep your voice in your shoes and stop starin' at me with funny lights in your eyes. Land, it gives me the collywobbles."

The bone-porcelain, flowered clock on the mantel finished chiming three. Out in the hall, grouped around the wicker basket, four men waited, quietly, as if they were frozen.

"Now, about that wicker basket," said Aunt Tildy. "It's past six feet long, and by the look, it ain't laundry. And those four men you walked in with, you don't need them to carry that basket—why, it's light as thistles. Eh?"

The dark young man was leaning forward on the antique chair. Something in his face suggested the basket wouldn't be so light after a while.

"Pshaw," Aunt Tildy mused. "Where've I seen a wicker like that before? Seems it was only a couple years ago. Seems to me—oh! Now I remember. It was when Mrs. Dwyer passed away next door."

Aunt Tildy set her coffee cup down, sternly. "So *that's* what you're up to? I thought you were workin' to sell me somethin'. You just set there until my little Emily trounces home from college this afternoon! I wrote her a note last week. Not admittin', of course, that I wasn't feelin' quite ripe and pert, but sort of hintin' I want to see her again, it's been a good many weeks. Her livin' in New York and all. Almost like my own daughter, Emily is.

"Now, she'll take care of you, young man. She'll shoo you out'n this parlor so quick it'll—"

The dark young man looked at Aunt Tildy as if she were tired.

"No, I'm *not!*" she snapped.

He weaved back and forth on the chair, half shutting his eyes, resting himself. O, wouldn't she like to rest, too? he seemed to murmur. Rest, rest, nice rest. . . .

"Great sons of Goshen on the Gilberry Dike! I got a hundred comforters, two hundred sweaters and six hundred potholders in these fingers, no matter they're skinny! You run off, come back when I'm done, maybe I'll talk to you." Aunt Tildy shifted subjects. "Let me tell you about Emily, my sweet, fair child."

Aunt Tildy nodded thoughtfully. Emily, with hair like yellow corn tassels, just as soft and fine.

"I well remember the day her mother died, twenty years ago, leavin' Emily to my house. That's why I'm mad at you and your wickers and such goin's-on. Who ever heard of people dyin' for any good cause? Young man, I don't *like* it. Why, I remember—"

Aunt Tildy paused; a brief pain of memory touched her heart. Twenty-five years back, her father's voice trembled in the late afternoon:

"Tildy," he whispered, "what you goin' to *do* in life? The way you act, men don't walk much with you. You kiss and skedaddle. Why don't you settle down, marry, raise children?"

"Papa," Tildy shouted back at him, "I like laughin' and playin' and singin'. I'm not the marryin' kind. I can't find a man with my philosophy, Papa."

"What 'philosophy's' that?"

"That death is ridiculous! It run off with Mama when we needed her most. You call *that* intelligent?"

Papa's eyes got wet and gray and bleak. "You're always right, Tildy. But what can we do? Death comes to everybody."

"Fight!" she cried. "Strike it below the belt! Don't *believe* in it!"

"Can't be done," said Papa sadly. "We all stand alone in the world."

"There's got to be a change sometime, Papa. I'm startin' my own philosophy here and now! Why, it's silly people live a couple years and are shoved like wet seeds in a hole; but nothin' sprouts. What good do they do? Lay there a million years, helpin' no one. Most of them fine, nice, neat people, or at least tryin'."

But Papa wasn't listening. He bleached out, faded away, like a photo left lying in the sun. She tried to talk him out of it, but he passed on, anyway. She spun about and ran. She couldn't stay on once he was cold, for his coldness denied her philosophy. She didn't attend his burial. She didn't do anything but set up this antique shop on the front of an old house and live alone for years, that is, until Emily came. Tildy didn't want to take the girl in. Why? Because Emily believed in dying. But her mother was an old friend and Tildy had promised help.

"Emily," continued Aunt Tildy, to the man in black, "was the first to live in this house with me in all the years. I never got married. I feared the idea of livin' with a man twenty-thirty years and then have him up and die on me. It'd shake my convictions like a house of cards. I shied off from the world. I screamed at people if they so much as mentioned death."

The young man listened patiently, politely. Then he lifted his hand. He seemed to know everything, with the dark, cold shining of his eyes, before she opened her mouth. He knew about her and World War II, when she shut off her radio forever and stopped the newspapers and beat a man's head with an umbrella, driving him from her shop when he insisted on describing the invasion beaches and the long, slow tides of the dead drifting under the silent urgings of the moon.

Yes, the dark young man smiled from the antique rocker, he knew how Aunt Tildy had stuck to her nice old phonograph records. Harry Lauder singing "Roamin' in the Gloamin'," Madame Schumann-Heink and lullabies. With no interruptions, no foreign calamities, murders, poisonings, auto accidents, suicides. Music stayed the same each day, every day. So the years ran, while Aunt Tildy tried to teach Emily her philosophy. But Emily's mind was fixed on mortality. She respected Aunt Tildy's way of thinking, however, and never mentioned— eternity.

All this the young man knew.

Aunt Tildy sniffed. "How do you know all those things? Well, if you think you can talk me into that silly wicker basket, you're way off the trestle. You lay hands on me, I'll spit right *in* your face!"

The young man smiled. Aunt Tildy sniffed again.

"Don't simper like a sick dog. I'm too old to be made love at. That's all twisted dry, like an old tube of paint, and left behind in the years."

There was a noise. The mantel clock chimed three. Aunt Tildy flashed her eyes to it. Strange. Hadn't it chimed three o'clock just five minutes ago? She liked the bone-white clock with gold angels dangling naked about its numeraled face and its tone like cathedral bells, soft and far away.

"Are you just goin' to *sit* there, young man?"

He was.

"Then, you won't mind if I take a little cat nap. Now, don't you stir off that chair. Don't come creepin' around me. Just goin' to close my eyes for a spell. That's right. That's right. . . . "

Nice and quiet and restful time of day. Silence. Just the clock ticking away, busy as termites in wood. Just the old room smelling of polished mahogany and oiled leather in the Morris chair, and books sitting stiff on the shelves. So nice. Nice. . . .

"You aren't gettin' up from the chair, are you, mister? Better not. I got one eye open for you. Yes, indeed I have. Yes, I have. Oh. Ah, hmmmm."

So feathery. So drowsy. So deep. Under water, almost. Oh, so nice.

Who's that movin' around in the dark with my eyes closed?

Who's that kissin' my cheek? You, Emily? No. No. Guess it was my thoughts. Only—dreamin'. Land, yes, that's it. Driftin' off, off, off. . . .

Ah? What say? Oh!

"Wait while I put on my glasses. There!"

The clock chimed three again. Shame, old clock, now, shame. Have to have you fixed.

The young man in the dark suit stood near the door. Aunt Tildy nodded.

"You leavin' so soon, young man? Had to give up, didn't you? Couldn't convince me; no, I'm mule-stubborn. Never get me free of this house, so don't bother comin' back to try!"

The young man bowed with slow dignity.

He had no intention of coming again, ever.

"Fine," declared Aunt Tildy. "I always told Papa I'd win! Why, I'll knit in this window the next thousand years. They'll have to chew the boards down around me to get me out."

The dark young man twinkled his eyes.

"Quit lookin' like the cat that ate the bird," cried Aunt Tildy. "Get that old fool wicker away!"

The four men trod heavily out the front door. Tildy studied the way they handled an empty basket, yet staggered with its weight.

"Here, now!" She rose in tremulous indignation. "Did you steal my antiques? My books? The clocks? What you got in that wicker?"

The dark young man whistled jauntily, turning his back to her, walking along behind the four staggering men. At the door he pointed to the wicker, offered its lid to Aunt Tildy. In pantomime he wondered if she would like to open it and gaze inside.

"Curious? Me? Pshaw, no. Get out!" cried Aunt Tildy.

The dark young man tapped a hat onto his head, saluted her crisply.

"Good-by!" Aunt Tildy slammed the door.

There, there. That was better. Gone. Darned fool men with their maggoty ideas. No never minds about the wicker. If they stole something, she didn't care, long as they let her alone.

"Look." Aunt Tildy smiled. "Here comes Emily, home from college. About time. Lovely girl. See how she walks. But, land, she looks pale and funny today, walkin' so slow. I wonder why. Looks worried, she does. Poor girl. I'll just fix some coffee and a tray of cakes."

Emily tapped up the front steps. Aunt Tildy, rustling around, could hear the slow, deliberate steps. What *ailed* the girl? Didn't sound like she had no more spunk than a flue-lizard. The front door swung wide. Emily stood in the hall, holding to the brass doorknob.

"Emily?" called Aunt Tildy.

Emily shuffled into the parlor, head down.

"Emily! I been waitin' for you! There was the darndest fool men here with a wicker. Tryin' to sell me somethin' I didn't want. Glad you're home. Makes it right cozy—"

Aunt Tildy realized that for a full minute Emily had been staring.

"Emily, what's wrong? Stop starin'. Here, I'll bring you a cup of coffee. There!

"Emily, why you backin' away from me?

"Emily, stop screamin', child. Don't scream, Emily! Don't! You keep screamin' that way, you go crazy. Emily, get up off the floor, get away from that wall! Emily! Stop cringin', child. I won't hurt you!

"Land, if it ain't one thing it's another.

"Emily, what's *wrong*, child . . . ?"

Emily groaned through her hands over her face.

"Child, child," whispered Aunt Tildy. "Here, sip this water. Sip it, Emily, that's it."

Emily widened her eyes, saw something, then shut them, quivering, pulling into herself. "Aunt Tildy, Aunt Tildy, Aunt—"

"Stop that!" Tildy slapped her. "What *ails* you?"

Emily forced herself to look up again.

She thrust her fingers out. They vanished inside Aunt Tildy.

"What fool notion!" cried Tildy. "Take your hand away! Take it, I say!"

Emily dropped aside, jerked her head, the golden hair shaking into shiny temblors. "You're not here, Aunt Tildy. I'm dreaming. You're dead!"

"Hush, baby."

"You *can't* be here."

"Land of Goshen, Emily—"

She took Emily's hand. It passed clean through her. Instantly, Aunt Tildy raised straight up, stomping her foot.

"Why, why!" she cried angrily. "That—fibber! That sneak-thief!" Her thin hands knotted to wiry, hard, pale fists. "That dark, dark fiend; he stole it! He toted it away, he did, oh he did, he did! Why, I—" Wrath steamed in her. Her pale blue eyes were fire. She sputtered into an indignant silence. Then she turned to Emily. "Child, get up! I need you!"

Emily lay, quivering.

"Part of me's here!" declared Aunt Tildy. "By the Lord Harry, what's left will have to do, for a bit. Fetch my bonnet!"

Emily confessed. "I'm scared."

"Certainly, oh, certainly not of *me?*"

"Yes."

"Why, I'm no spook! You known me most of your life! Now's no time to snivel-sop. Fetch up on your heels or I'll slap you crack across your nose!"

Emily rose, in sobs, stood like something cornered, trying to decide which direction to bolt in.

"Where's your car, Emily?"

"Down at the garage—ma'am."

"Good!" Aunt Tildy hustled her through the front door. "Now—" Her sharp eyes poked up and down the streets. "Which way's the mortuary?"

Emily held to the step rail, fumbling down. "What're you going to do, Aunt Tildy?"

"Do?" cried Aunt Tildy, tottering after her, jowls shaking in a thin, pale fury. "Why, get my body back, of course! Get my body back! Go on!"

The car roared, Emily clenched to the steering wheel, staring straight ahead at the curved, rain-wet streets. Aunt Tildy shook her parasol.

"Hurry, child, hurry, before they squirt juices in my body and dice and cube it the way them persnickety morticians have a habit of doin'. They cut and sew it so it ain't no good to no one!"

"Oh, Auntie, Auntie, let me go, don't make me drive! It won't do any good, no good at all," sighed the girl.

"Here we are." Emily pulled to the curb, and collapsed over the wheel, but Aunt Tildy had already popped from the car and trotted with mincing skirt up the mortuary drive, around behind to where the shiny black hearse was unloading a wicker basket.

"You!" She directed her attack at one of the four men with the wicker. "Put that down!"

The four men looked up.

One said, "Step aside, lady. We're doing our job."

"That's my body tucked in there!" She brandished the parasol.

"That I wouldn't know anything about," said a second man. "Please don't block traffic, madam. This thing is heavy."

"Sir!" she cried, wounded. "I'll have you know I weigh only one hundred and ten pounds."

He looked at her casually. "I'm not interested in your heft, lady. I'm due home for supper. My wife'll kill me if I'm late."

The four of them moved on, Aunt Tildy in pursuit, down a hall, into a preparations room.

A white-smocked man awaited the wicker's arrival with a rather pleased smile on his long, eager-looking face. Aunt Tildy didn't care for the avidity of that face, or the entire personality of the man. The basket was deposited, the four men wandered off.

The man in the white smock glanced at Auntie and said:

"Madam, this is no fit place for a gentlewoman."

"Well," she said, gratified, "glad you feel that way. It's exactly what I tried to tell that dark-clothed young man!"

The mortician puzzled. "What dark-clothed young man is that?"

"The one that came puddlin' around my house, that's who."

"No one of that description works for us."

"No matter. As you just so intelligently stated, this is no place for a lady. I don't want me here. I want me home cookin' ham for Sunday visitors, it's near Easter. I got Emily to feed, sweaters to knit, clocks to wind—"

"You are quite philosophical, and philanthropical, no doubt of it, madam, but I have work. A body has arrived." This last, he said with apparent relish, and a winnowing of his knives, tubes, jars, and instruments.

Tildy bristled. "You put so much as a fingerprint on that body, and I'll—"

He laid her aside like a little old moth. "George," he called with a suave gentleness, "escort this lady out, please."

Aunt Tildy glared at the approaching George.

"Show me your backside, goin' the other way!"

George took her wrists. "This way, please."

Tildy extricated herself. Easily. Her flesh sort of—slipped. It even amazed Tildy. Such an unexpected talent to develop at this late day.

"See?" she said, pleased with her ability. "You can't budge me. I want my body back!"

The mortician opened the wicker lid casually. Then, in a recurrent series of scrutinies he realized the body inside was . . . it seemed . . . could it be? . . . maybe . . . yes . . . no . . . no . . . it just *couldn't* be, but . . . "Ah," he exhaled, abruptly. He turned. His eyes were wide, then they narrowed.

"Madam," he said, cautiously. "This lady here is—a—relative—of yours?"

"A very dear relation. Be careful of her."

"A sister, perhaps?" He grasped at a straw of dwindling logic, hopefully.

"No, you fool. Me, do you hear? *Me!*"

The mortician considered the idea. "No," he said. "Things like this don't happen." He fumbled with his tools. "George, get help from the others. I can't work with a crank present."

The four men returned. Aunt Tildy crossed her arms in defiance. "Won't budge!" she cried, as she was moved like a pawn on a chessboard, from preparations room to slumber room, to hall, to waiting chamber, to funeral parlor, where she threw herself down on a chair in the very center of the vestibule. There were pews going back into gray silence, and a smell of flowers.

"Please, ma'am," said one of the men. "That's where the body rests for the service tomorrow."

"I'm sittin' right plumb here until I get what I want."

She sat, pale fingers fussing with the lace at her throat, jaw set, one high-buttoned shoe tapping with irritation. If a man got in whopping distance, she gave him a parasol whop. And when they touched her, now, she remembered to—slip away.

Mr. Carrington, Mortuary President, heard the disturbance in his office and came toddling down the aisle to investigate. "Here, here," he whispered to everyone, finger to mouth. "More respect, more respect. What is this? Oh, madam, may I help you?"

She looked him up and down. "You may."

"How may I be of service, please?"

"Go in that room back there," directed Aunt Tildy.

"Yee-ess."

"And tell that eager young investigator to quit fiddlin' with my body. I'm a maiden lady. My moles, birthmarks, scars, and other bric-a-brac, includin' the turn of my ankle, are my own secret. I don't want him pryin' and probin', cuttin', or hurtin' it any way."

This was vague to Mr. Carrington, who hadn't correlated bodies yet. He looked at her in blank helplessness.

"He's got me in there on his table, like a pigeon ready to be drawn and stuffed!" she told him.

Mr. Carrington hustled off to check. After fifteen minutes of waiting silence and horrified arguing, comparing notes with the mortician behind closed doors, Carrington returned, three shades whiter.

Carrington dropped his glasses, picked them up. "You're making it difficult for us."

"*I* am?" raged Aunt Tildy. "Saint Vitus in the mornin'! Looky here, Mister Blood and Bones or whatever, you tell that—"

"We're already draining the blood from the—"

"What!"

"Yes, yes, I assure you, yes. So, you just go away, now; there's nothing to be done." He laughed nervously. "Our mortician is also performing a brief autopsy to determine cause of death."

Auntie jumped to her feet, burning.

"He can't do that! Only coroners are allowed to do that!"

"Well, we sometimes allow a little—"

"March straight in and tell that Cut-'em-up to pump all that fine New England blue blood right back into that fine-skinned body, and if he's taken anything out, for him to attach it back in so it'll function proper, and then turn that body, fresh as paint, into my keepin'. You hear!"

"There's nothing I can do. Nothing."

"Tell you *what*. I'm settin' here for the next two hundred years. You listenin'? And every time any of your customers come by, I'll spit ectoplasm right squirt up their nostrils!"

Carrington groped that thought around his weakening mind and emitted a groan. "You'd ruin our business. You wouldn't do that."

Auntie smiled. "*Wouldn't* I?"

Carrington ran up the dark aisle. In the distance you could hear him dialing a phone over and over again. Half an hour later cars roared up in front of the mortuary. Three vice-presidents of the mortuary came down the aisle with their hysterical president.

"What seems to be the trouble?"

Auntie told them with a few well-chosen infernalities.

They held a conference, meanwhile notifying the mortician to discontinue his homework, at least until such time as an agreement was reached. . . . The mortician walked from his chamber and stood smiling amiably, smoking a big black cigar.

Auntie stared at the cigar.

"Where'd you put the *ashes?*" she cried, in horror.

The mortician only grinned imperturbably and puffed.

The conference broke up.

"Madam, in all fairness, you wouldn't force us out on the street to continue our services, would you?"

Auntie scanned the vultures. "Oh, I wouldn't mind at all."

Carrington wiped sweat from his jowls. "You can have your body back."

"Ha!" shouted Auntie. Then, with caution: "Intact?"

"Intact."

"No formaldehyde?"

"No formaldehyde."

"Blood in it?"

"Blood, my God, yes, blood, if only you'll take it and go!"

A prim nod. "Fair enough. Fix 'er up. It's a deal."

Carrington snapped his fingers at the mortician. "Don't *stand* there, you mental incompetent. Fix it up!"

"And be careful with that cigar!" said the old woman.

"Easy, easy," said Aunt Tildy. "Put the wicker on the floor where I can step in it."

She didn't look at the body much. Her only comment was, "Natural-lookin'." She let herself fall back into the wicker.

A biting sensation of arctic coldness gripped her, followed by an unlikely nausea and a giddy whorling. She was two drops of matter fusing, water trying to seep into concrete. Slow to do. Hard. Like a butterfly trying to squirm back into a discarded husk of flinty chrysalis!

The vice-presidents watched Aunt Tildy with apprehension. Mr. Carrington wrung his fingers and tried to assist with boosting and pushing moves of his hands and arms. The mortician, frankly skeptical, watched with idle, amused eyes.

Seeping into cold, long granite. Seeping into a frozen and ancient statue. Squeezing all the way.

"Come alive, damn ye!" shouted Aunt Tildy to herself. "Raise up a bit."

The body half-rose, rustling in the dry wicker.

"Fold your legs, woman!"

The body grabbled up, blindly groping.

"See!" shouted Aunt Tildy.

Light entered the webbed blind eyes.

"Feel!" urged Aunt Tildy.

The body felt the warmth of the room, the sudden reality of the preparations table on which to lean, panting.

"Move!"

The body took a creaking, slow step.

"Hear!" she snapped.

The noises of the place came into the dull ears. The harsh, expectant breath of the mortician, shaken; the whimpering Mr. Carrington; her own crackling voice.

"Walk!" she said.

The body walked.

"Think!" she said.

The old brain thought.

"Speak!" she said.

The body spoke, bowing to the morticians:

"Much obliged. Thank you."

"Now," she said, finally, "cry!"

And she began to cry tears of utter happiness.

And now, any afternoon about four, if you want to visit Aunt Tildy, you just walk around to her antique shop and rap. There's a big, black funeral wreath on the door. Don't mind that! Aunt Tildy left it there; that's how her humor runs. You rap on the door. It's double-barred and triple-locked, and when you rap her voice shrills out at you.

"Is that the man in black?"

And you laugh and say, No, no, it's only me, Aunt Tildy.

And she laughs and says, "Come on in, quick!" and she whips the door open and slams it shut behind, so no man in black can ever slip in with you. Then she sets you down and pours your coffee and shows you her latest knitted sweater. She's not as fast as she used to be, and can't see as good, but she gets on.

"And if you're 'specially good," Aunt Tildy declares, setting her coffee cup to one side, "I'll give you a little treat."

"What's that?" visitors will ask.

"This," says Auntie, pleased with her little uniqueness, her little joke.

Then with modest moves of her fingers she will unfasten the white lace at her neck and chest and for a brief moment show what lies beneath.

The long blue scar where the autopsy was neatly sewn together.

"Not bad sewin' for a man," she allows. "Oh, some more coffee? *There!*"

There Will Come Soft Rains

In the living room the voice-clock sang, *Tick-tock, seven o'clock, time to get up, time to get up, seven o'clock!* as if it were afraid that nobody would. The morning house lay empty. The clock ticked on, repeating and repeating its sounds into the emptiness. *Seven-nine, breakfast time, seven-nine!*

In the kitchen the breakfast stove gave a hissing sigh and ejected from its warm interior eight pieces of perfectly browned toast, eight eggs sunnyside up, sixteen slices of bacon, two coffees, and two cool glasses of milk.

"Today is August 4, 2026," said a second voice from the kitchen ceiling, "in the city of Allendale, California." It repeated the date three times for memory's sake. "Today is Mr. Featherstone's birthday. Today is the anniversary of Tilita's marriage. Insurance is payable, as are the water, gas, and light bills."

Somewhere in the walls, relays clicked, memory tapes glided under electric eyes.

Eight-one, tick-tock, eight-one o'clock, off to school, off to work, run, run, eight-one! But no doors slammed, no carpets took the soft tread of rubber heels. It was raining outside. The weather box on the front door sang quietly: "Rain, rain, go away; rubbers, raincoats for today . . ." And the rain tapped on the empty house, echoing.

Outside, the garage chimed and lifted its door to reveal the waiting car. After a long wait the door swung down again.

At eight-thirty the eggs were shriveled and the toast was like stone. An aluminum wedge scraped them into the sink, where hot water whirled them down a metal throat which digested and flushed them away to the distant sea. The dirty dishes were dropped into a hot washer and emerged twinkling dry.

Nine-fifteen, sang the clock, *time to clean*.

Out of warrens in the wall, tiny robot mice darted. The rooms were acrawl with the small cleaning animals, all rubber and metal. They thudded against chairs, whirling their mustached runners, kneading the rug nap, sucking gently at hidden dust. Then, like mysterious invaders, they popped into their burrows. Their pink electric eyes faded. The house was clean.

Ten o'clock. The sun came out from behind the rain. The house stood alone in a city of rubble and ashes. This was the one house left standing. At night the ruined city gave off a radioactive glow which could be seen for miles.

Ten-fifteen. The garden sprinklers whirled up in golden founts, filling the soft morning air with scatterings of brightness. The water pelted windowpanes, running down the charred west side where the house had been burned evenly free of its white paint. The entire west face of the house was black, save for five places. Here the silhouette in paint of a man mowing a lawn. Here, as in a photograph, a woman bent to pick flowers. Still farther over, their images burned on wood in one titanic instant, a small boy, hands flung into the air; higher up, the image of a thrown ball, and opposite him a girl, hands raised to catch a ball which never came down.

The five spots of paint—the man, the woman, the children, the ball— remained. The rest was a thin charcoaled layer.

The gentle sprinkler rain filled the garden with falling light.

Until this day, how well the house had kept its peace. How carefully it had inquired, "Who goes there? What's the password?" and, getting no answer from lonely foxes and whining cats, it had shut up its windows and drawn shades in an old-maidenly preoccupation with self-protection which bordered on a mechanical paranoia.

It quivered at each sound, the house did. If a sparrow brushed a window, the shade snapped up. The bird, startled, flew off! No, not even a bird must touch the house!

The house was an altar with ten thousand attendants, big, small, servicing, attending, in choirs. But the gods had gone away, and the ritual of the religion continued senselessly, uselessly.

Twelve noon.

A dog whined, shivering, on the front porch.

The front door recognized the dog voice and opened. The dog, once huge and fleshy, but now gone to bone and covered with sores, moved in and through the house, tracking mud. Behind it whirred angry mice, angry at having to pick up mud, angry at inconvenience.

For not a leaf fragment blew under the door but what the wall panels flipped open and the copper scrap rats flashed swiftly out. The offending dust, hair, or paper, seized in miniature steel jaws, was raced back to the burrows.

There, down tubes which fed into the cellar, it was dropped into the sighing vent of an incinerator which sat like evil Baal in a dark corner.

The dog ran upstairs, hysterically yelping to each door, at last realizing, as the house realized, that only silence was here.

It sniffed the air and scratched the kitchen door. Behind the door, the stove was making pancakes which filled the house with a rich baked odor and the scent of maple syrup.

The dog frothed at the mouth, lying at the door, sniffing, its eyes turned to fire. It ran wildly in circles, biting at its tail, spun in a frenzy, and died. It lay in the parlor for an hour.

Two o'clock, sang a voice.

Delicately sensing decay at last, the regiments of mice hummed out as softly as blown gray leaves in an electrical wind.

Two-fifteen.

The dog was gone.

In the cellar, the incinerator glowed suddenly and a whirl of sparks leaped up the chimney.

Two thirty-five.

Bridge tables sprouted from patio walls. Playing cards fluttered onto pads in a shower of pips. Martinis manifested on an oaken bench with egg-salad sandwiches. Music played.

But the tables were silent and the cards untouched.

At four o'clock the tables folded like great butterflies back through the paneled walls.

Four-thirty.

The nursery walls glowed.

Animals took shape: yellow giraffes, blue lions, pink antelopes, lilac panthers cavorting in crystal substance. The walls were glass. They looked out upon color and fantasy. Hidden films clocked through well-oiled sprockets, and the walls lived. The nursery floor was woven to resemble a crisp, cereal meadow. Over this ran aluminum roaches and iron crickets, and in the hot still air butterflies of delicate red tissue wavered among the sharp aromas of animal spoors! There was the sound like a great matted yellow hive of bees within a dark bellows, the lazy bumble of a purring lion. And there was the patter of okapi feet and the murmur of a fresh jungle rain, like other hoofs, falling upon the summer-starched grass. Now the walls dissolved into distances of parched weed, mile on mile, and warm endless sky. The animals drew away into thorn brakes and water holes.

It was the children's hour.

Five o'clock. The bath filled with clear hot water.

Six, seven, eight o'clock. The dinner dishes manipulated like magic tricks, and in the study a *click*. In the metal stand opposite the hearth where a fire now blazed up warmly, a cigar popped out, half an inch of soft gray ash on it, smoking, waiting.

Nine o'clock. The beds warmed their hidden circuits, for nights were cool here.

Nine-five. A voice spoke from the study ceiling:

"Mrs. McClellan, which poem would you like this evening?"

The house was silent.

The voice said at last, "Since you express no preference, I shall select a poem at random." Quiet music rose to back the voice. "Sara Teasdale. As I recall, your favorite. . . .

> *There will come soft rains and the smell of the ground,*
> *And swallows circling with their shimmering sound;*
>
> *And frogs in the pools singing at night,*
> *And wild plum trees in tremulous white;*
>
> *Robins will wear their feathery fire,*
> *Whistling their whims on a low fence-wire;*
>
> *And not one will know of the war, not one*
> *Will care at last when it is done.*
>
> *Not one would mind, neither bird nor tree,*
> *If mankind perished utterly;*
>
> *And Spring herself, when she woke at dawn*
> *Would scarcely know that we were gone.*

The fire burned on the stone hearth and the cigar fell away into a mound of quiet ash on its tray. The empty chairs faced each other between the silent walls, and the music played.

At ten o'clock the house began to die.

The wind blew. A falling tree bough crashed through the kitchen window. Cleaning solvent, bottled, shattered over the stove. The room was ablaze in an instant!

"Fire!" screamed a voice. The house lights flashed, water pumps shot water from the ceilings. But the solvent spread on the linoleum, licking, eating, under the kitchen door, while the voices took it up in chorus: "Fire, fire, fire!"

The house tried to save itself. Doors sprang tightly shut, but the windows were broken by the heat and the wind blew and sucked upon the fire.

The house gave ground as the fire in ten billion angry sparks moved with flaming ease from room to room and then up the stairs. While scurrying water rats squeaked from the walls, pistoled their water, and ran for more. And the wall sprays let down showers of mechanical rain.

But too late. Somewhere, sighing, a pump shrugged to a stop. The quenching rain ceased. The reserve water supply which had filled baths and washed dishes for many quiet days was gone.

The fire crackled up the stairs. It fed upon Picassos and Matisses in the upper halls, like delicacies, baking off the oily flesh, tenderly crisping the canvases into black shavings.

Now the fire lay in beds, stood in windows, changed the colors of drapes!

And then, reinforcements.

From attic trapdoors, blind robot faces peered down with faucet mouths gushing green chemical.

The fire backed off, as even an elephant must at the sight of a dead snake. Now there were twenty snakes whipping over the floor, killing the fire with a clear cold venom of green froth.

But the fire was clever. It had sent flame outside the house, up through the attic to the pumps there. An explosion! The attic brain which directed the pumps was shattered into bronze shrapnel on the beams.

The fire rushed back into every closet and felt of the clothes hung there.

The house shuddered, oak bone on bone, its bared skeleton cringing from the heat, its wire, its nerves revealed as if a surgeon had torn the skin off to let the red veins and capillaries quiver in the scalded air. Help, help! Fire! Run, run! Heat snapped mirrors like the first brittle winter ice. And the voices wailed, Fire, fire, run, run, like a tragic nursery rhyme, a dozen voices, high, low, like children dying in a forest, alone, alone. And the voices fading as the wires popped their sheathings like hot chestnuts. One, two, three, four, five voices died.

In the nursery the jungle burned. Blue lions roared, purple giraffes bounded off. The panthers ran in circles, changing color, and ten million animals, running before the fire, vanished off toward a distant steaming river. . . .

Ten more voices died. In the last instant under the fire avalanche, other choruses, oblivious, could be heard announcing the time, playing music, cutting the lawn by remote-control mower, or setting an umbrella frantically out and in, the slamming and opening front door, a thousand things happening, like a clock shop when each clock strikes the hour insanely before or after the other, a scene of maniac confusion, yet unity; singing, screaming, a few last cleaning mice darting bravely out to carry the horrid ashes away! And one voice, with sublime disregard for the situation, read poetry aloud in the fiery study, until all the film spools burned, until all the wires withered and the circuits cracked.

The fire burst the house and let it slam flat down, puffing out skirts of spark and smoke.

In the kitchen, an instant before the rain of fire and timber, the stove could be seen making breakfasts at a psychopathic rate, ten dozen eggs, six loaves of toast, twenty dozen bacon strips, which, eaten by fire, started the stove working again, hysterically hissing!

The crash. The attic smashing into kitchen and parlor. The parlor into cellar, cellar into sub-cellar. Deep freeze, armchair, film tapes, circuits, beds, and all like skeletons thrown in a cluttered mound deep under.

Smoke and silence. A great quantity of smoke.

Dawn showed faintly in the east. Among the ruins, one wall stood alone. Within the wall, a last voice said, over and over again and again, even as the sun rose to shine upon the heaped rubble and steam:

"Today is August 5, 2026, today is August 5, 2026, today is . . . "

Mars Is Heaven

The ship came down from space. It came from the stars and the black velocities, and the shining movements, and the silent gulfs of space. It was a new ship; it had fire in its body and men in its metal cells, and it moved with a clean silence, fiery and warm. In it were seventeen men, including a captain. The crowd at the Ohio field had shouted and waved their hands up into the sunlight, and the rocket had bloomed out great flowers of heat and color and run away into space on the *third* voyage to Mars!

Now it was decelerating with metal efficiency in the upper Martian atmospheres. It was still a thing of beauty and strength. It had moved in the midnight waters of space like a pale sea leviathan; it had passed the ancient Moon and thrown itself onward into one nothingness following another. The men within it had been battered, thrown about, sickened, made well again, each in his turn. One man had died, but now the remaining sixteen, with their eyes clear in their heads and their faces pressed to the thick glass ports, watched Mars swing up under them.

"Mars!" cried Navigator Lustig.

"Good old Mars!" said Samuel Hinkston, archaeologist.

"Well," said Captain John Black.

The rocket landed on a lawn of green grass. Outside, upon this lawn, stood an iron deer. Further up on the green stood a tall brown Victorian house, quiet in the sunlight, all covered with scrolls and rococo, its windows made of blue and pink and yellow and green colored glass. Upon the porch were hairy geraniums and an old swing which was hooked into the porch ceiling and which now swung back and forth, back and forth, in a little breeze. At the summit of the house was a cupola with diamond leaded-glass windows and a dunce-cap roof! Through the front window you could see a piece of music titled "Beautiful Ohio" sitting on the music rest.

Around the rocket in four directions spread the little town, green and motionless in the Martian spring. There were white houses and red brick ones, and tall elm trees blowing in the wind, and tall maples and horse chestnuts. And church steeples with golden bells silent in them.

The rocket men looked out and saw this. Then they looked at one another and then they looked out again. They held to each other's elbows, suddenly unable to breathe, it seemed. Their faces grew pale.

"I'll be damned," whispered Lustig, rubbing his face with his numb fingers. "I'll be damned."

"It just can't be," said Samuel Hinkston.

"Lord," said Captain John Black.

There was a call from the chemist. "Sir, the atmosphere is thin for breathing. But there's enough oxygen. It's safe."

"Then we'll go out," said Lustig.

"Hold on," said Captain John Black. "How do we know what this is?"

"It's a small town with thin but breathable air in it, sir."

"And it's a small town the like of Earth towns," said Hinkston, the archaeologist. "Incredible. It can't be, but it *is*."

Captain John Black looked at him idly. "Do you think that the civilizations of two planets can progress at the same rate and evolve in the same way, Hinkston?"

"I wouldn't have thought so, sir."

Captain Black stood by the port. "Look out there. The geraniums. A specialized plant. That specific variety has only been known on Earth for fifty years. Think of the thousands of years it takes to evolve plants. Then tell me if it is logical that the Martians should have: one, leaded-glass windows; two, cupolas; three, porch swings; four, an instrument that looks like a piano and probably *is* a piano; and five, if you look closely through this telescopic lens here, is it logical that a Martian composer would have published a piece of music titled, strangely enough, 'Beautiful Ohio'? All of which means that we have an Ohio River on Mars!"

"Captain Williams, of course!" cried Hinkston.

"What?"

"Captain Williams and his crew of three men! Or Nathaniel York and his partner. That would explain it!"

"That would explain absolutely nothing. As far as we've been able to figure, the York expedition exploded the day it reached Mars, killing York and his partner. As for Williams and his three men, their ship exploded the second day after their arrival. At least the pulsations from their radios ceased at that time, so we figure that if the men were alive after that they'd have contacted us. And anyway, the York expedition was only a year ago, while Captain Williams and his men landed here some time during last August. Theorizing that they are still alive, could they, even with the help of a brilliant Martian race, have built such a town as this and *aged* it in so short a time? Look at that town out there; why, it's been standing here for the last seventy years. Look at the wood on the porch newel; look at the trees, a century old, all of them! No, this isn't York's work or Williams'. It's something else. I don't like it. And I'm not leaving the ship until I know what it is."

"For that matter," said Lustig, nodding, "Williams and his men, as well as York, landed on the *opposite* side of Mars. We were very careful to land on *this* side."

"An excellent point. Just in case a hostile local tribe of Martians killed off York and Williams, we have instructions to land in a further region, to forestall a recurrence of such a disaster. So here we are, as far as we know, in a land that Williams and York never saw."

"Damn it," said Hinkston, "I want to get out into this town, sir, with your permission. It may be there *are* similar thought patterns, civilization graphs on every planet in our sun system. We may be on the threshold of the greatest psychological and metaphysical discovery of our age!"

"I'm willing to wait a moment," said Captain John Black.

"It may be, sir, that we're looking upon a phenomenon that, for the first time, would absolutely prove the existence of God, sir."

"There are many people who are of good faith without such proof, Mr. Hinkston."

"I'm one myself, sir. But certainly a town like this could not occur without divine intervention. The *detail*. It fills me with such feelings that I don't know whether to laugh or cry."

"Do neither, then, until we know what we're up against."

"Up against?" Lustig broke in. "Against nothing, Captain. It's a good, quiet green town, a lot like the old-fashioned one I was born in. I like the looks of it."

"When were you born, Lustig?"

"Nineteen fifty, sir."

"And you, Hinkston?"

"Nineteen fifty-five, sir. Grinnell, Iowa. And this looks like home to me."

"Hinkston, Lustig, I could be either of your fathers. I'm just eighty years old. Born in 1920 in Illinois, and through the grace of God and a science that, in the last fifty years, knows how to make *some* old men young again, here I am on Mars, not any more tired than the rest of you, but infinitely more suspicious. This town out here looks very peaceful and cool, and so much like Green Bluff, Illinois, that it frightens me. It's too *much* like Green Bluff." He turned to the radioman. "Radio Earth. Tell them we've landed. That's all. Tell them we'll radio a full report tomorrow."

"Yes, sir."

Captain Black looked out the rocket port with his face that should have been the face of a man eighty but seemed like the face of a man in his fortieth year. "Tell you what we'll do, Lustig; you and I and Hinkston'll look the town over. The other men'll stay aboard. If anything happens they can get the hell out. A loss of three men's better than a whole ship. If something bad happens, our crew can warn the next rocket. That's Captain Wilder's rocket, I think, due to be ready to take off next Christmas. If there's something hostile about Mars we certainly want the next rocket to be well armed."

"So are we. We've got a regular arsenal with us."

"Tell the men to stand by the guns then. Come on, Lustig, Hinkston."

The three men walked together down through the levels of the ship.

It was a beautiful spring day. A robin sat on a blossoming apple tree and sang continuously. Showers of petal snow sifted down when the wind touched the green branches, and the blossom scent drifted upon the air. Somewhere in the town someone was playing the piano and the music came and went, came and went, softly, drowsily. The song was "Beautiful Dreamer." Somewhere else a phonograph, scratchy and faded, was hissing out a record of "Roamin' in the Gloamin'," sung by Harry Lauder.

The three men stood outside the ship. They sucked and gasped at the thin, thin air and moved slowly so as not to tire themselves.

Now the phonograph record being played was:

> *Oh, give me a June night*
> *The moonlight and you . . .*

Lustig began to tremble. Samuel Hinkston did likewise.

The sky was serene and quiet, and somewhere a stream of water ran through the cool caverns and tree shadings of a ravine. Somewhere a horse and wagon trotted and rolled by, bumping.

"Sir," said Samuel Hinkston, "it must be, it *has* to be, that rocket travel to Mars began in the years before the First World War!"

"No."

"How else can you explain these houses, the iron deer, the pianos, the music?" Hinkston took the captain's elbow persuasively and looked into the captain's face. "Say that there were people in the year 1905 who hated war and got together with some scientists in secret and built a rocket and came out here to Mars—"

"No, no, Hinkston."

"Why not? The world was a different world in 1905; they could have kept it a secret much more easily."

"But a complex thing like a rocket, no, you couldn't keep it secret."

"And they came up here to live, and naturally the houses they built were similar to Earth houses because they brought the culture with them."

"And they've lived here all these years?" said the captain.

"In peace and quiet, yes. Maybe they made a few trips, enough to bring enough people here for one small town, and then stopped for fear of being discovered. That's why this town seems so old-fashioned. I don't see a thing, myself, older than the year 1927, do you? Or maybe, sir, rocket travel is older than we think. Perhaps it started in some part of the world centuries ago and was kept secret by the small number of men who came to Mars with only occasional visits to Earth over the centuries."

"You make it sound almost reasonable."

"It has to be. We've the proof here before us; all we have to do is find some people and verify it."

Their boots were deadened of all sound in the thick green grass. It smelled from a fresh mowing. In spite of himself, Captain John Black felt a great peace come over him. It had been thirty years since he had been in a small town, and the buzzing of spring bees on the air lulled and quieted him, and the fresh look of things was a balm to the soul.

They set foot upon the porch. Hollow echoes sounded from under the boards as they walked to the screen door. Inside they could see a bead curtain hung across the hall entry, and a crystal chandelier and a Maxfield Parrish painting framed on one wall over a comfortable Morris chair. The house smelled old, and of the attic, and infinitely comfortable. You could hear the tinkle of ice in a lemonade pitcher. In a distant kitchen, because of the heat of the day, someone was preparing a cold lunch. Someone was humming under her breath, high and sweet.

Captain John Black rang the bell.

Footsteps, dainty and thin, came along the hall, and a kind-faced lady of some forty years, dressed in the sort of dress you might expect in the year 1909, peered out at them.

"Can I help you?" she asked.

"Beg your pardon," said Captain Black uncertainly. "But we're looking for—that is, could you help us—" He stopped. She looked out at him with dark, wondering eyes.

"If you're selling something—" she began.

"No, wait!" he cried. "What town is this?"

She looked him up and down. "What do you mean, what town is it? How could you be in a town and not know the name?"

The captain looked as if he wanted to go sit under a shady apple tree. "We're strangers here. We want to know how this town got here and how you got here."

"Are you census takers?"

"No."

"Everyone knows," she said, "this town was built in 1868. Is this a game?"

"No, not a game!" cried the captain. "We're from Earth."

"Out of the *ground*, do you mean?" she wondered.

"No, we came from the third planet, Earth, in a ship. And we've landed here on the fourth planet, Mars—"

"This," explained the woman, as if she were addressing a child, "is Green Bluff, Illinois, on the continent of America, surrounded by the Atlantic and Pacific oceans, on a place called the world, or, sometimes, the Earth. Go away now. Good-by."

She trotted down the hall, running her fingers through the beaded curtains.

The three men looked at one another.

"Let's knock the screen door in," said Lustig.

"We can't do that. This is private property. Good God!"

They went to sit down on the porch step.

"Did it ever strike you, Hinkston, that perhaps we got ourselves somehow, in some way, off track, and by accident came back and landed on Earth?"

"How could we have done that?"

"I don't know, I don't know. Oh God, let me think."

Hinkston said, "But we checked every mile of the way. Our chronometers said so many miles. We went past the Moon and out into space, and here we are. I'm *positive* we're on Mars."

Lustig said, "But suppose, by accident, in space, in time, we got lost in the dimensions and landed on an Earth that is thirty or forty years ago."

"Oh, go away, Lustig!"

Lustig went to the door, rang the bell, and called into the cool dim rooms: "What year is this?"

"Nineteen twenty-six, of course," said the lady, sitting in a rocking chair, taking a sip of her lemonade.

"Did you hear that?" Lustig turned wildly to the others. "Nineteen twenty-six! We *have* gone back in time! This *is* Earth!"

Lustig sat down, and the three men let the wonder and terror of the thought afflict them. Their hands stirred fitfully on their knees. The captain said, "I didn't ask for a thing like this. It scares the hell out of me. How can a thing like this happen? I wish we'd brought Einstein with us."

"Will anyone in this town believe us?" said Hinkston. "Are we playing with something dangerous? Time, I mean. Shouldn't we just take off and go home?"

"No. Not until we try another house."

They walked three houses down to a little white cottage under an oak tree. "I like to be as logical as I can be," said the captain. "And I don't believe we've put our finger on it yet. Suppose, Hinkston, as you originally suggested, that rocket travel occurred years ago? And when the Earth people lived here a number of years they began to get homesick for Earth. First a mild neurosis about it, then a full-fledged psychosis. Then threatened insanity. What would you do as a psychiatrist if faced with such a problem?"

Hinkston thought. "Well, I think I'd rearrange the civilization on Mars so it resembled Earth more and more each day. If there was any way of reproducing every plant, every road, and every lake, and even an ocean, I'd do so. Then by some vast crowd hypnosis I'd convince everyone in a town this size that this really *was* Earth, not Mars at all."

"Good enough, Hinkston. I think we're on the right track now. That woman in that house back there just *thinks* she's living on Earth. It protects her sanity. She and all the others in this town are the patients of the greatest experiment in migration and hypnosis you will ever lay eyes on in your life."

"That's *it*, sir!" cried Lustig.

"Right!" said Hinkston.

"Well." The captain sighed. "Now we've got somewhere. I feel better. It's all a bit more logical. That talk about time and going back and forth and traveling through time turns my stomach upside down. But *this* way—" The captain smiled. "Well, well, it looks as if we'll be fairly popular here."

"Or will we?" said Lustig. "After all, like the Pilgrims, these people came here to escape Earth. Maybe they won't be too happy to see us. Maybe they'll try to drive us out or kill us."

"We have superior weapons. This next house now. Up we go."

But they had hardly crossed the lawn when Lustig stopped and looked off across the town, down the quiet, dreaming afternoon street. "Sir," he said.

"What is it, Lustig?"

"Oh, sir, sir, what I *see*—" said Lustig, and he began to cry. His fingers came up, twisting and shaking, and his face was all wonder and joy and incredulity. He sounded as if at any moment he might go quite insane with happiness. He looked down the street and began to run, stumbling awkwardly, falling, picking himself up, and running on. "Look, look!"

"Don't let him get away!" The captain broke into a run.

Now Lustig was running swiftly, shouting. He turned into a yard halfway down the shady street and leaped up upon the porch of a large green house with an iron rooster on the roof.

He was beating at the door, hollering and crying, when Hinkston and the captain ran up behind him. They were all gasping and wheezing, exhausted from their run in the thin air. "Grandma! Grandpa!" cried Lustig.

Two old people stood in the doorway.

"David!" their voices piped, and they rushed out to embrace and pat him on the back and move around him. "David, oh, David, it's been so many years! How you've grown, boy; how big you are, boy. Oh, David boy, how are you?"

"Grandma, Grandpa!" sobbed David Lustig. "You look fine, fine!" He held them, turned them, kissed them, hugged them, cried on them, held them out again, blinking at the little old people. The sun was in the sky, the wind blew, the grass was green, the screen door stood wide.

"Come in, boy, come in. There's iced tea for you, fresh, lots of it!"

"I've got friends here." Lustig turned and waved at the captain and Hinkston frantically, laughing. "Captain, come on up."

"Howdy," said the old people. "Come in. Any friends of David's are our friends too. Don't stand there!"

In the living room of the old house it was cool, and a grandfather clock ticked high and long and bronzed in one corner. There were soft pillows on large couches and walls filled with books and a rug cut in a thick rose pattern, and iced tea in the hand, sweating, and cool on the thirsty tongue.

"Here's to our health." Grandma tipped her glass to her porcelain teeth.

"How long you been here, Grandma?" said Lustig.

"Ever since we died," she said tartly.

"Ever since you what?" Captain John Black set down his glass.

"Oh yes." Lustig nodded. "They've been dead thirty years."

"And you sit there calmly!" shouted the captain.

"Tush." The old woman winked glitteringly. "Who are you to question what happens? Here we are. What's life, anyway? Who does what for why and where? All we know is here we are, alive again, and no questions asked. A second chance." She toddled over and held out her thin wrist. "Feel." The captain felt. "Solid, ain't it?" she asked. He nodded. "Well, then," she said triumphantly, "why go around questioning?"

"Well," said the captain, "it's simply that we never thought we'd find a thing like this on Mars."

"And now you've found it. I dare say there's lots on every planet that'll show you God's infinite ways."

"Is this Heaven?" asked Hinkston.

"Nonsense, no. It's a world and we get a second chance. Nobody told us why. But then nobody told us why we were on Earth, either. That other Earth, I mean. The one you came from. How do we know there wasn't *another* before *that* one?"

"A good question," said the captain.

Lustig kept smiling at his grandparents. "Gosh, it's good to see you. Gosh, it's good."

The captain stood up and slapped his hand on his leg in a casual fashion. "We've got to be going. Thank you for the drinks."

"You'll be back, of course," said the old people. "For supper tonight?"

"We'll try to make it, thanks. There's so much to be done. My men are waiting for me back at the rocket and—"

He stopped. He looked toward the door, startled.

Far away in the sunlight there was a sound of voices, a shouting and a great hello.

"What's that?" asked Hinkston.

"We'll soon find out." And Captain John Black was out the front door abruptly, running across the green lawn into the street of the Martian town.

He stood looking at the rocket. The ports were open and his crew was streaming out, waving their hands. A crowd of people had gathered, and in and through and among these people the members of the crew were hurrying, talking, laughing, shaking hands. People did little dances. People swarmed. The rocket lay empty and abandoned.

A brass band exploded in the sunlight, flinging off a gay tune from upraised tubas and trumpets. There was a bang of drums and a shrill of fifes. Little girls with golden hair jumped up and down. Little boys shouted, "Hooray!" Fat men passed around ten-cent cigars. The town mayor made a speech. Then each member of the crew, with a mother on one arm, a father or sister on the other, was spirited off down the street into little cottages or big mansions.

"Stop!" cried Captain Black.

The doors slammed shut.

The heat rose in the clear spring sky, and all was silent. The brass band banged off around a corner, leaving the rocket to shine and dazzle alone in the sunlight.

"Abandoned!" said the captain. "They abandoned the ship, they did! I'll have their skins, by God! They had orders!"

"Sir," said Lustig, "don't be too hard on them. Those were all old relatives and friends."

"That's no excuse!"

"Think how they felt, Captain, seeing familiar faces outside the ship!"

"They had their orders, damn it!"

"But how would you have felt, Captain?"

"I would have obeyed orders—" The captain's mouth remained open.

Striding along the sidewalk under the Martian sun, tall, smiling, eyes amazingly clear and blue, came a young man of some twenty-six years. "John!" the man called out, and broke into a trot.

"What?" Captain John Black swayed.

"John, you old son of a bitch!"

The man ran up and gripped his hand and slapped him on the back.

"It's you," said Captain Black.

"Of course, who'd you *think* it was?"

"Edward!" The captain appealed now to Lustig and Hinkston, holding the stranger's hand. "This is my brother Edward. Ed, meet my men, Lustig, Hinkston! My brother!"

They tugged at each other's hands and arms and then finally embraced. "Ed!" "John, you bum, you!" "You're looking fine, Ed, but, Ed, what *is* this? You haven't changed over the years. You died, I remember, when you were twenty-six and I was nineteen. Good God, so many years ago, and here you are and, Lord, what goes on?"

"Mom's waiting," said Edward Black, grinning.

"Mom?"

"And Dad too."

"Dad?" The captain almost fell as if he had been hit by a mighty weapon. He walked stiffly and without co-ordination. "Mom and Dad alive? Where?"

"At the old house on Oak Knoll Avenue."

"The old house." The captain stared in delighted amaze. "Did you hear that, Lustig, Hinkston?"

Hinkston was gone. He had seen his own house down the street and was running for it. Lustig was laughing. "You see, Captain, what happened to everyone on the rocket? They couldn't help themselves."

"Yes. Yes." The captain shut his eyes. "When I open my eyes you'll be gone." He blinked. "You're still there. God, Ed, but you look *fine*!"

"Come on, lunch's waiting. I told Mom."

Lustig said, "Sir, I'll be with my grandfolks if you need me."

"What? Oh, fine, Lustig. Later, then."

Edward seized his arm and marched him. "There's the house. Remember it?"

"Hell! Bet I can beat you to the front porch!"

They ran. The trees roared over Captain Black's head; the earth roared under his feet. He saw the golden figure of Edward Black pull ahead of him in the amazing dream of reality. He saw the house rush forward, the screen door swing wide. "Beat you!" cried Edward. "I'm an old man," panted the captain, "and you're still young. But then, you *always* beat me, I remember!"

In the doorway, Mom, pink, plump, and bright. Behind her, pepper-gray, Dad, his pipe in his hand.

"Mom, Dad!"

He ran up the steps like a child to meet them.

It was a fine long afternoon. They finished a late lunch and they sat in the parlor and he told them all about his rocket and they nodded and smiled upon him and Mother was just the same and Dad bit the end off a cigar and lighted it thoughtfully in his old fashion. There was a big turkey dinner at night and time flowing on. When the drumsticks were sucked clean and lay brittle upon the plates, the captain leaned back and exhaled his deep satisfaction. Night was in all the trees and coloring the sky, and the lamps were halos of pink light in the gentle house. From all the other houses down the street came sounds of music, pianos playing, doors slamming.

Mom put a record on the Victrola, and she and Captain John Black had a dance. She was wearing the same perfume he remembered from the summer when she and Dad had been killed in the train accident. She was very real in his arms as they danced lightly to the music. "It's not every day," she said, "you get a second chance to live."

"I'll wake in the morning," said the captain. "And I'll be in my rocket, in space, and all this will be gone."

"No, don't think that," she cried softly. "Don't question. God's good to us. Let's be happy."

"Sorry, Mom."

The record ended in a circular hissing.

"You're tired, Son." Dad pointed with his pipe. "Your old bedroom's waiting for you, brass bed and all."

"But I should report my men in."

"Why?"

"Why? Well, I don't know. No reason, I guess. No, none at all. They're all eating or in bed. A good night's sleep won't hurt them."

"Good night, Son." Mom kissed his cheek. "It's good to have you home."

"It's good to *be* home."

He left the land of cigar smoke and perfume and books and gentle light and ascended the stairs, talking, talking with Edward. Edward pushed a door open, and there was the yellow brass bed and the old semaphore banners from college and a very musty raccoon coat which he stroked with muted affection. "It's too much," said the captain. "I'm numb and I'm tired. Too much has happened today. I feel as if I'd been out in a pounding rain for forty-eight hours without an umbrella or a coat. I'm soaked to the skin with emotion."

Edward slapped wide the snowy linens and flounced the pillows. He slid the window up and let the night-blooming jasmine float in. There was moonlight and the sound of distant dancing and whispering.

"So this is Mars," said the captain, undressing.

"This is it." Edward undressed in idle, leisurely moves, drawing his shirt off over his head, revealing golden shoulders and the good muscular neck.

The lights were out; they were in bed, side by side, as in the days how many decades ago? The captain lolled and was nourished by the scent of jasmine pushing the lace curtains in upon the dark air of the room. Among the trees, upon a lawn, someone had cranked up a portable phonograph and now it was playing softly, "Always."

The thought of Marilyn came to his mind.

"Is Marilyn here?"

His brother, lying straight out in the moonlight from the window, waited and then said, "Yes. She's out of town. But she'll be here in the morning."

The captain shut his eyes. "I want to see Marilyn very much."

The room was square and quiet except for their breathing.

"Good night, Ed."

A pause. "Good night, John."

He lay peacefully, letting his thoughts float. For the first time the stress of the day was moved aside; he could think logically now. It had all been emotion. The bands playing, the familiar faces. But now . . .

How? he wondered. How was all this made? And why? For what purpose? Out of the goodness of some divine intervention? Was God, then, really that thoughtful of his children? How and why and what for?

He considered the various theories advanced in the first heat of the afternoon by Hinkston and Lustig. He let all kinds of new theories drop in lazy pebbles down through his mind, turning, throwing out dull flashes of light. Mom. Dad. Edward. Mars. Earth. Mars. Martians.

Who had lived here a thousand years ago on Mars? Martians? Or had this always been the way it was today?

Martians. He repeated the word idly, inwardly.

He laughed out loud almost. He had the most ridiculous theory quite suddenly. It gave him a kind of chill. It was really nothing to consider, of course. Highly improbable. Silly. Forget it. Ridiculous.

But, he thought, just *suppose* . . . Just suppose, now, that there were Martians living on Mars and they saw our ship coming and saw us inside our ship and hated us. Suppose, now, just for the hell of it, that they wanted to destroy us, as invaders, as unwanted ones, and they wanted to do it in a very clever way, so that we would be taken off guard. Well, what would the best weapon be that a Martian could use against Earth Men with atomic weapons?

The answer was interesting. Telepathy, hypnosis, memory, and imagination.

Suppose all of these houses aren't real at all, this bed not real, but only figments of my own imagination, given substance by telepathy and hypnosis through the Martians, thought Captain John Black. Suppose these houses are really some *other* shape, a Martian shape, but, by playing on my desires and wants, these Martians have made this seem like my old home town, my old house, to lull me out of my suspicions. What better way to fool a man, using his own mother and father as bait?

And this town, so old, from the year 1926, long before *any* of my men were born. From a year when I was six years old and there *were* records of Harry Lauder, and Maxfield Parrish paintings *still* hanging, and bead curtains, and "Beautiful Ohio," and turn-of-the-century architecture. What if the Martians took the memories of a town *exclusively* from *my* mind? They say childhood memories are the clearest. And after they built the town from *my* mind, they populated it with the most-loved people from all the minds of the people on the rocket!

And suppose those two people in the next room, asleep, are not my mother and father at all. But two Martians, incredibly brilliant, with the ability to keep me under this dreaming hypnosis all of the time.

And that brass band today? What a startlingly wonderful plan it would be.

First, fool Lustig, then Hinkston, then gather a crowd; and all the men in the rocket, seeing mothers, aunts, uncles, sweethearts, dead ten, twenty years ago, naturally, disregarding orders, rush out and abandon ship. What more natural? What more unsuspecting? What more simple? A man doesn't ask too many questions when his mother is suddenly brought back to life; he's much too happy. And here we all are tonight, in various houses, in various beds, with no weapons to protect us, and the rocket lies in the moonlight, empty. And wouldn't it be horrible and terrifying to discover that all of this was part of some great clever plan by the Martians to divide and conquer us, and kill us? Sometime during the night, perhaps, my brother here on this bed will change form, melt, shift, and become another thing, a terrible thing, a Martian. It would be very simple for him just to turn over in bed and put a knife into my heart. And in all those other houses down the street, a dozen other brothers or fathers suddenly melting away and taking knives and doing things to the unsuspecting, sleeping men of Earth. . . .

His hands were shaking under the covers. His body was cold. Suddenly it was not a theory. Suddenly he was very afraid.

He lifted himself in bed and listened. The night was very quiet. The music had stopped. The wind had died. His brother lay sleeping beside him.

Carefully he lifted the covers, rolled them back. He slipped from bed and was walking softly across the room when his brother's voice said, "Where are you going?"

"What?"

His brother's voice was quite cold. "I said, where do you think you're going?"

"For a drink of water."

"But you're not thirsty."

"Yes, yes, I am."

"No, you're not."

Captain John Black broke and ran across the room. He screamed. He screamed twice.

He never reached the door.

In the morning the brass band played a mournful dirge. From every house in the street came little solemn processions bearing long boxes, and along the sun-filled street, weeping, came the grandmas and mothers and sisters and brothers and uncles and fathers, walking to the churchyard, where there were new holes freshly dug and new tombstones installed. Sixteen holes in all, and sixteen tombstones.

The mayor made a little sad speech, his face sometimes looking like the mayor, sometimes looking like something else.

Mother and Father Black were there, with Brother Edward, and they cried, their faces melting now from a familiar face into something else.

Grandpa and Grandma Lustig were there, weeping, their faces shifting like wax, shimmering as all things shimmer on a hot day.

The coffins were lowered. Someone murmured about "the unexpected and sudden deaths of sixteen fine men during the night—"

Earth pounded down on the coffin lids.

The brass band, playing "Columbia, the Gem of the Ocean," marched and slammed back into town, and everyone took the day off.

The Silent Towns

There was a little white silent town on the edge of the dead Martian sea. The town was empty. No one moved in it. Lonely lights burned in the stores all day. The shop doors were wide, as if people had run off without using their keys. Magazines, brought from Earth on the silver rocket a month before, fluttered, untouched, burning brown, on wire racks fronting the silent drugstores.

The town was dead. Its beds were empty and cold. The only sound was the power hum of electric lines and dynamos, still alive, all by themselves. Water ran in forgotten bathtubs, poured out into living rooms, onto porches, and down through little garden plots to feed neglected flowers. In the dark theaters, gum under the many seats began to harden with tooth impressions still in it.

Across town was a rocket port. You could still smell the hard, scorched smell where the last rocket blasted off when it went back to Earth. If you dropped a dime in the telescope and pointed it at Earth, perhaps you could see the big war happening there. Perhaps you could see New York explode. Maybe London could be seen, covered with a new kind of fog. Perhaps then it might be understood why this small Martian town is abandoned. How quick was the evacuation? Walk in any store, bang the NO SALE key. Cash drawers jump out, all bright and jingly with coins. That war on Earth must be very bad. . . .

Along the empty avenues of this town, now, whistling softly, kicking a tin can ahead of him in deepest concentration, came a tall, thin man. His eyes glowed with a dark, quiet look of loneliness. He moved his bony hands in his pockets, which were tinkling with new dimes. Occasionally he tossed a dime to the ground. He laughed temperately, doing this, and walked on, sprinkling bright dimes everywhere.

His name was Walter Gripp. He had a placer mine and a remote shack far up in the blue Martian hills and he walked to town once every two weeks to see if he could marry a quiet and intelligent woman. Over the years he had always returned to his shack, alone and disappointed. A week ago, arriving in town, he had found it this way!

That day he had been so surprised that he rushed to a delicatessen, flung wide a case, and ordered a triple-decker beef sandwich.

"Coming up!" he cried, a towel on his arm.

He flourished meats and bread baked the day before, dusted a table, invited himself to sit, and ate until he had to go find a soda fountain, where he ordered a bicarbonate. The druggist, being one Walter Gripp, was astoundingly polite and fizzed one right up for him!

He stuffed his jeans with money, all he could find. He loaded a boy's wagon with ten-dollar bills and ran lickety-split through town. Reaching the suburbs, he suddenly realized how shamefully silly he was. He didn't need money. He rode the ten-dollar bills back to where he'd found them, counted a dollar from his own wallet to pay for the sandwiches, dropped it in the delicatessen till, and added a quarter tip.

That night he enjoyed a hot Turkish bath, a succulent filet carpeted with delicate mushrooms, imported dry sherry, and strawberries in wine. He fitted himself for a new blue flannel suit, and a rich gray Homburg which balanced oddly atop his gaunt head. He slid money into a juke box which played "That Old Gang of Mine." He dropped nickels in twenty boxes all over town. The lonely streets and the night were full of the sad music of "That Old Gang of Mine" as he walked, tall and thin and alone, his new shoes clumping softly, his cold hands in his pockets.

But that was a week past. He slept in a good house on Mars Avenue, rose mornings at nine, bathed, and idled to town for ham and eggs. No morning passed that he didn't freeze a ton of meats, vegetables, and lemon cream pies, enough to last ten years, until the rockets came back from Earth, if they ever came.

Now, tonight, he drifted up and down, seeing the wax women in every colorful shop window, pink and beautiful. For the first time he knew how dead the town was. He drew a glass of beer and sobbed gently.

"Why," he said, "I'm all *alone*."

He entered the Elite Theater to show himself a film, to distract his mind from his isolation. The theater was hollow, empty, like a tomb with phantoms crawling gray and black on the vast screen. Shivering, he hurried from the haunted place.

Having decided to return home, he was striking down the middle of a side street, almost running, when he heard the phone.

He listened.

"Phone ringing in someone's house."

He proceeded briskly.

"Someone should answer that phone," he mused.

He sat on a curb to pick a rock from his shoe, idly.

"Someone!" he screamed, leaping. "Me! Good Lord, what's wrong with me!" he shrieked. He whirled. Which house? That one!

He raced over the lawn, up the steps, into the house, down a dark hall.

He yanked up the receiver.

"Hello!" he cried.

Buzzzzzzzz.

"Hello, hello!"

They had hung up.

"Hello!" he shouted, and banged the phone. "You stupid idiot!" he cried to himself. "Sitting on that curb, you fool! Oh, you damned and awful fool!" He squeezed the phone. "Come on, ring again! Come *on*!"

He had never thought there might be others left on Mars. In the entire week he had seen no one. He had figured that all other towns were as empty as this one.

Now, staring at this terrible little black phone, he trembled. Interlocking dial systems connected every town on Mars. From which of the thirty cities had the call come?

He didn't know.

He waited. He wandered to the strange kitchen, thawed some iced huckleberries, ate them disconsolately.

"There wasn't anyone on the other end of that call," he murmured. "Maybe a pole blew down somewhere and the phone rang by itself."

But hadn't he heard a click, which meant someone had hung up far away?

He stood in the hall the rest of the night. "Not because of the phone," he told himself. "I just haven't anything else to do."

He listened to his watch tick.

"She won't phone back," he said. "She won't *ever* call a number that didn't answer. She's probably dialing other houses in town right *now*! And here I sit— Wait a minute!" He laughed. "Why do I keep saying 'she'?"

He blinked. "It could as easily be a 'he,' couldn't it?"

His heart slowed. He felt very cold and hollow.

He wanted very much for it to be a "she."

He walked out of the house and stood in the center of the early, dim morning street.

He listened. Not a sound. No birds. No cars. Only his heart beating. Beat and pause and beat again. His face ached with strain. The wind blew gently, oh so gently, flapping his coat.

"Shh," he whispered. "*Listen.*"

He swayed in a slow circle, turning his head from one silent house to another.

She'll phone more and more numbers, he thought. It must be a woman. Why? Only a woman would call and call. A man wouldn't. A man's independent.

Did I phone anyone? No! Never thought of it. It must be a woman. It *has* to be, by God!

Listen.

Far away, under the stars, a phone rang.

He ran. He stopped to listen. The ringing, soft. He ran a few more steps. Louder. He raced down an alley. Louder still! He passed six houses, six more. Much louder! He chose a house and its door was locked.

The phone rang inside.

"Damn you!" He jerked the doorknob.

The phone screamed.

He heaved a porch chair through the parlor window, leaped in after it.

Before he even touched the phone, it was silent.

He stalked through the house then and broke mirrors, tore down drapes, and kicked in the kitchen stove.

Finally, exhausted, he picked up the thin directory which listed every phone on Mars. Fifty thousand names.

He started with number one.

Amelia Ames. He dialed her number in New Chicago, one hundred miles over the dead sea.

No answer.

Number two lived in New New York, five thousand miles across the blue mountains.

No answer.

He called three, four, five, six, seven, eight, his fingers jerking, unable to grip the receiver.

A woman's voice answered, "Hello?"

Walter cried back at her, "Hello, oh Lord, hello!"

"This is a recording," recited the woman's voice. "Miss Helen Arasumian is not home. Will you leave a message on the wire spool so she may call you when she returns? Hello? This is a recording. Miss Arasumian is not home. Will you leave a message—"

He hung up.

He sat with his mouth twitching.

On second thought he redialed that number.

"When Miss Helen Arasumian comes home," he said, "tell her to go to hell."

He phoned Mars Junction, New Boston, Arcadia, and Roosevelt City exchanges, theorizing that they would be logical places for persons to dial from; after that he contacted local city halls and other public institutions in each town. He phoned the best hotels. Leave it to a woman to put herself up in luxury.

Suddenly he stopped, clapped his hands sharply together, and laughed. Of course! He checked the directory and dialed a long-distance call through to the biggest beauty parlor in New Texas City. If ever there was a place where a woman would putter around, patting mud packs on her face and sitting under a drier, it would be a velvet-soft, diamond-gem beauty parlor!

The phone rang. Someone at the other end lifted the receiver.

A woman's voice said, "Hello?"

"If this is a recording," announced Walter Gripp, "I'll come over and blow the place up."

"This isn't a record," said the woman's voice. "Hello! Oh, hello, there *is* someone alive! Where *are* you?" She gave a delighted scream.

Walter almost collapsed. "*You!*" He stood up jerkily, eyes wild. "Good Lord, what luck, what's your name?"

"Genevieve Selsor!" She wept into the receiver. "Oh, I'm so glad to hear from you, whoever you are!"

"Walter Gripp!"

"Walter, hello, Walter!"

"Hello, Genevieve!"

"Walter. It's such a nice name. Walter, Walter!"

"Thank you."

"Walter, where *are* you?"

Her voice was so kind and sweet and fine. He held the phone tight to his ear so she could whisper sweetly into it. He felt his feet drift off the floor. His cheeks burned.

"I'm in Marlin Village," he said. "I—"

Buzz.

"Hello?" he said.

Buzz.

He jiggled the hook. Nothing.

Somewhere a wind had blown down a pole. As quickly as she had come, Genevieve Selsor was gone.

He dialed, but the line was dead.

"I know where she is, anyway." He ran out of the house. The sun was rising as he backed a beetle-car from the stranger's garage, filled its back seat with food from the house, and set out at eighty miles an hour down the highway, heading for New Texas City.

A thousand miles, he thought. Genevieve Selsor, sit tight, you'll hear from me!

He honked his horn on every turn out of town.

At sunset, after an impossible day of driving, he pulled to the roadside, kicked off his tight shoes, laid himself out in the seat, and slid the gray Homburg over his weary eyes. His breathing became slow and regular. The wind blew and the stars shone gently upon him in the new dusk. The Martian mountains lay all around, millions of years old. Starlight glittered on the spires of a little Martian town, no bigger than a game of chess, in the blue hills.

He lay in the half-place between awakeness and dreams. He whispered. Genevieve. *Oh, Genevieve, sweet Genevieve*, he sang softly, *the years may come, the years may go. But Genevieve, sweet Genevieve*... There was a warmth in him. He heard her quiet sweet cool voice sighing. *Hello, oh, hello, Walter! This is no record. Where are you, Walter, where are you?*

He sighed, putting up a hand to touch her in the moonlight. Long dark hair shaking in the wind; beautiful, it was. And her lips like red peppermints. And her cheeks like fresh-cut wet roses. And her body like a clear vaporous mist, while her soft cool sweet voice crooned to him once more the words to the old sad song, *Oh, Genevieve, sweet Genevieve, the years may come, the years may go* ...

He slept.

He reached New Texas City at midnight.

He halted before the Deluxe Beauty Salon, yelling.

He expected her to rush out, all perfume, all laughter.

Nothing happened.

"She's asleep." He walked to the door. "Here I am!" he called. "Hello, Genevieve!"

The town lay in double moonlit silence. Somewhere a wind flapped a canvas awning.

He swung the glass door wide and stepped in.

"Hey!" He laughed uneasily. "Don't hide! I know you're here!"

He searched every booth.

He found a tiny handkerchief on the floor. It smelled so good he almost lost his balance. "Genevieve," he said.

He drove the car through the empty streets but saw nothing. "If this is a practical joke ... "

He slowed the car. "Wait a minute. We were cut off. Maybe *she* drove to Marlin Village while I was driving here! She probably took the old Sea Road. We missed each other during the day. How'd she know I'd come get her? I didn't say I would. And she was so afraid when the phone died that she rushed to Marlin Village to find me! And here I am, by God, what a fool I am!"

Giving the horn a blow, he shot out of town.

He drove all night. He thought, What if she isn't in Marlin Village waiting, when I arrive?

He wouldn't think of that. She *must* be there. And he would run up and hold her and perhaps even kiss her, once, on the lips.

Genevieve, sweet Genevieve, he whistled, stepping it up to one hundred miles an hour.

Marlin Village was quiet at dawn. Yellow lights were still burning in several stores, and a juke box that had played steadily for one hundred hours finally, with a crackle of electricity, ceased, making the silence complete. The sun warmed the streets and warmed the cold and vacant sky.

Walter turned down Main Street, the car lights still on, honking the horn a double toot, six times at one corner, six times at another. He peered at the store names. His face was white and tired, and his hands slid on the sweaty steering wheel.

"Genevieve!" he called in the empty street.

The door to a beauty salon opened.

"Genevieve!" He stopped the car.

Genevieve Selsor stood in the open door of the salon as he ran across the street. A box of cream chocolates lay open in her arms. Her fingers, cuddling it, were plump and pallid. Her face, as she stepped into the light, was round and thick, and her eyes were like two immense eggs stuck into a white mess of bread dough. Her legs were as big around as the stumps of trees, and she moved with an ungainly shuffle. Her hair was an indiscriminate shade of brown that had been made and remade, it appeared, as a nest for birds. She had no lips at all and compensated this by stenciling on a large red, greasy mouth that now popped open in delight, now shut in sudden alarm. She had plucked her brows to thin antenna lines.

Walter stopped. His smile dissolved. He stood looking at her.

She dropped her candy box to the sidewalk.

"Are you—Genevieve Selsor?" His ears rang.

"Are you Walter Griff?" she asked.

"Gripp."

"Gripp," she corrected herself.

"How do you do," he said with a restrained voice.

"How do you do." She shook his hand.

Her fingers were sticky with chocolate.

"Well," said Walter Gripp.

"What?" asked Genevieve Selsor.

"I just said, 'Well,'" said Walter.

"Oh."

It was nine o'clock at night. They had spent the day picnicking, and for supper he had prepared a filet mignon which she didn't like because it was too rare, so he broiled it some more and it was too much broiled or fried or something. He laughed and said, "We'll see a movie!" She said okay and put her chocolaty fingers on his elbow. But all she wanted to see was a fifty-year-old film of Clark Gable. "Doesn't he just kill you?" She giggled. "Doesn't he *kill* you, now?" The film ended. "Run it off again," she commanded. "Again?" he asked. "Again," she said. And when he returned she snuggled up and put her paws all over him. "You're not quite what I expected, but you're nice," she admitted. "Thanks," he said, swallowing. "Oh, that Gable," she said, and pinched his leg.

"Ouch," he said.

After the film they went shopping down the silent streets. She broke a window and put on the brightest dress she could find. Dumping a perfume bottle on her hair, she resembled a drowned sheep dog. "How old are you?" he inquired. "Guess." Dripping, she led him down the street. "Oh, thirty," he said. "Well," she announced stiffly, "I'm only twenty-seven, so there!

"Here's another candy store!" she said. "Honest, I've led the life of Riley since everything exploded. I never liked my folks, they were fools. They left for Earth two months ago. I was supposed to follow on the last rocket, but I stayed on; you know why?"

"Why?"

"Because everyone picked on me. So I stayed where I could throw perfume on myself all day and drink ten thousand malts and eat candy without people saying, 'Oh, that's full of calories!' So here I *am*!"

"Here you are." Walter shut his eyes.

"It's getting late," she said, looking at him.

"Yes."

"I'm tired," she said.

"Funny. I'm wide awake."

"Oh," she said.

"I feel like staying up all night," he said. "Say, there's a good record at Mike's. Come on, I'll play it for you."

"I'm tired." She glanced up at him with sly, bright eyes.

"I'm very alert," he said. "Strange."

"Come back to the beauty shop," she said. "I want to show you something."

She took him in through the glass door and walked him over to a large white box. "When I drove from Texas City," she said, "I brought this with me." She untied the pink ribbon. "I thought: Well, here I am, the only lady on Mars, and here is the only man, and, well . . . " She lifted the lid and folded back crisp layers of whispery pink tissue paper. She gave it a pat. "There."

Walter Gripp stared.

"What is it?" he asked, beginning to tremble.

"Don't you know, silly? It's all lace and all white and all fine and everything."

"No, I don't know what it is."

"It's a wedding dress, silly!"

"Is it?" His voice cracked.

He shut his eyes. Her voice was still soft and cool and sweet, as it had been on the phone. But when he opened his eyes and looked at her . . .

He backed up. "How nice," he said.

"Isn't it?"

"Genevieve." He glanced at the door.

"Yes?"

"Genevieve, I've something to tell you."

"Yes?" She drifted toward him, the perfume smell thick about her round white face.

"The thing I have to say to you is . . . " he said.

"Yes?"

"Good-by!"

And he was out the door and into his car before she could scream.

She ran and stood on the curb as he swung the car about.

"Walter Griff, come back here!" she wailed, flinging up her arms.

"Gripp," he corrected her.

"Gripp!" she shouted.

The car whirled away down the silent street, regardless of her stompings and shriekings. The exhaust from it fluttered the white dress she crumpled in her plump hands, and the stars shone bright, and the car vanished out onto the desert and away into blackness.

He drove all night and all day for three nights and days. Once he thought he saw a car following, and he broke into a shivering sweat and took another highway, cutting off across the lonely Martian world, past little dead cities, and he drove and drove for a week and a day, until he had put ten thousand miles between himself and Marlin Village. Then he pulled into a small town named Holtville Springs, where there were some tiny stores he could light up at night and restaurants to sit in, ordering meals. And he's lived there ever since, with two deep freezes packed with food to last him one hundred years, and enough cigars to last ten thousand days, and a good bed with a soft mattress.

And when once in a while over the long years the phone rings—he doesn't answer.

The Earth Men

Whoever was knocking at the door didn't want to stop.

Mrs. Ttt threw the door open. "Well?"

"You speak *English*!" The man standing there was astounded.

"I speak what I speak," she said.

"It's wonderful *English*!" The man was in uniform. There were three men with him, in a great hurry, all smiling, all dirty.

"What do you want?" demanded Mrs. Ttt.

"You are a *Martian*!" The man smiled. "The word is not familiar to you, certainly. It's an Earth expression." He nodded at his men. "We are from Earth. I'm Captain Williams. We've landed on Mars within the hour. Here we are, the *Second* Expedition! There was a First Expedition, but we don't know what happened to it. But here we are, anyway. And you are the first Martian we've met!"

"Martian?" Her eyebrows went up.

"What I mean to say is, you live on the fourth planet from the sun. Correct?"

"Elementary," she snapped, eying them.

"And we"—he pressed his chubby pink hand to his chest—"we are from Earth. Right, men?"

"Right, sir!" A chorus.

"This is the planet Tyrr," she said, "if you want to use the proper name."

"Tyrr, Tyrr." The captain laughed exhaustedly. "What a *fine* name! But, my good woman, how is it you speak such perfect English?"

"I'm not speaking, I'm thinking," she said. "Telepathy! Good day!" And she slammed the door.

A moment later there was that dreadful man knocking again.

She whipped the door open. "What now?" she wondered.

The man was still there, trying to smile, looking bewildered. He put out his hands. "I don't think you *understand*—"

"What?" she snapped.

The man gazed at her in surprise. "We're from *Earth*!"

"I haven't time," she said. "I've a lot of cooking today and there's cleaning and sewing and all. You evidently wish to see Mr. Ttt; he's upstairs in his study."

"Yes," said the Earth Man confusedly, blinking. "By all means, let us see Mr. Ttt."

"He's busy." She slammed the door again.

This time the knock on the door was most impertinently loud.

"See here!" cried the man when the door was thrust open again. He jumped in as if to surprise her. "This is no way to treat visitors!"

"All over my clean floor!" she cried. "Mud! Get out! If you come in my house, wash your boots first."

The man looked in dismay at his muddy boots. "This," he said, "is no time for trivialities. I think," he said, "we should be celebrating." He looked at her for a long time, as if looking might make her understand.

"If you've made my crystal buns fall in the oven," she exclaimed, "I'll hit you with a piece of wood!" She peered into a little hot oven. She came back, red, steamy-faced. Her eyes were sharp yellow, her skin was soft brown, she was thin and quick as an insect. Her voice was metallic and sharp. "Wait here. I'll see if I can let you have a moment with Mr. Ttt. What was your business?"

The man swore luridly, as if she'd hit his hand with a hammer. "Tell him we're from Earth and it's never been done before!"

"What hasn't?" She put her brown hand up. "Never mind. I'll be back."

The sound of her feet fluttered through the stone house.

Outside, the immense blue Martian sky was hot and still as warm deep sea water. The Martian desert lay broiling like a prehistoric mud pot, waves of heat rising and shimmering. There was a small rocket ship reclining upon a hilltop nearby. Large footprints came from the rocket to the door of this stone house.

Now there was a sound of quarreling voices upstairs. The men within the door stared at one another, shifting on their boots, twiddling their fingers, and holding onto their hip belts. A man's voice shouted upstairs. The woman's voice replied. After fifteen minutes the Earth Men began walking in and out the kitchen door, with nothing to do.

"Cigarette?" said one of the men.

Somebody got out a pack and they lit up. They puffed slow streams of pale white smoke. They adjusted their uniforms, fixed their collars. The voices upstairs continued to mutter and chant. The leader of the men looked at his watch.

"Twenty-five minutes," he said. "I wonder what they're up to up there." He went to a window and looked out.

"Hot day," said one of the men.

"Yeah," said someone else in the slow warm time of early afternoon. The voices had faded to a murmur and were now silent. There was not a sound in the house. All the men could hear was their own breathing.

An hour of silence passed. "I hope we didn't cause any trouble," said the captain. He went and peered into the living room.

Mrs. Ttt was there, watering some flowers that grew in the center of the room.

"I knew I had forgotten something," she said when she saw the captain. She walked out to the kitchen. "I'm sorry." She handed him a slip of paper. "Mr. Ttt is much too busy." She turned to her cooking. "Anyway, it's not Mr. Ttt you want to see; it's Mr. Aaa. Take that paper over to the next farm, by the blue canal, and Mr. Aaa'll advise you about whatever it is you want to know."

"We don't want to know anything," objected the captain, pouting out his thick lips. "We already *know* it."

"You have the paper, what more do you want?" she asked him straight off. And she would say no more.

"Well," said the captain, reluctant to go. He stood as if waiting for something. He looked like a child staring at an empty Christmas tree. "Well," he said again. "Come on, men."

The four men stepped out into the hot silent day.

Half an hour later, Mr. Aaa, seated in his library sipping a bit of electric fire from a metal cup, heard the voices outside in the stone causeway. He leaned over the window sill and gazed at the four uniformed men who squinted up at him.

"Are you Mr. Aaa?" they called.

"I am."

"Mr. Ttt sent us to see you!" shouted the captain.

"Why did he do that?" asked Mr. Aaa.

"He was busy!"

"Well, that's a shame," said Mr. Aaa sarcastically. "Does he think I have nothing else to do but entertain people he's too busy to bother with?"

"That's not the important thing, sir," shouted the captain.

"Well, it is to me. I have much reading to do. Mr. Ttt is inconsiderate. This is not the first time he has been this thoughtless of me. Stop waving your hands, sir, until I finish. And pay attention. People usually listen to me when I talk. And you'll listen courteously or I won't talk at all."

Uneasily the four men in the court shifted and opened their mouths, and once the captain, the veins on his face bulging, showed a few little tears in his eyes.

"Now," lectured Mr. Aaa, "do you think it fair of Mr. Ttt to be so ill-mannered?"

The four men gazed up through the heat. The captain said, "We're from Earth!"

"I think it very ungentlemanly of him," brooded Mr. Aaa.

"A rocket ship. We came in it. Over there!"

"Not the first time Ttt's been unreasonable, you know."

"All the way from Earth."

"Why, for half a mind, I'd call him up and tell him off."

"Just the four of us; myself and these three men, my crew."

"I'll call him up, yes, that's what I'll do!"

"Earth. Rocket. Men. Trip. Space."

"Call him and give him a good lashing!" cried Mr. Aaa. He vanished like a puppet from a stage. For a minute there were angry voices back and forth over some weird mechanism or other. Below, the captain and his crew glanced longingly back at their pretty rocket ship lying on the hillside, so sweet and lovely and fine.

Mr. Aaa jerked up in the window, wildly triumphant. "Challenged him to a duel, by the gods! A duel!"

"Mr. Aaa—" the captain started all over again, quietly.

"I'll shoot him dead, do you hear!"

"Mr. Aaa, I'd like to *tell* you. We came sixty million miles."

Mr. Aaa regarded the captain for the first time. "Where'd you say you were from?"

The captain flashed a white smile. Aside to his men he whispered, "*Now* we're getting someplace!" To Mr. Aaa he called, "We traveled sixty million miles. From Earth!"

Mr. Aaa yawned. "That's only *fifty* million miles this time of year." He picked up a frightful-looking weapon. "Well, I have to go now. Just take that silly note, though I don't know what good it'll do you, and go over that hill into the little town of Iopr and tell Mr. Iii all about it. *He's* the man you want to see. Not Mr. Ttt, he's an idiot; I'm going to kill him. Not me, because you're not in my line of work."

"Line of work, line of work!" bleated the captain. "Do you have to be in a certain line of work to welcome Earth Men!"

"Don't be silly, everyone knows *that*!" Mr. Aaa rushed downstairs. "Good-by!" And down the causeway he raced, like a pair of wild calipers.

The four travelers stood shocked. Finally the captain said, "We'll find someone yet who'll listen to us."

"Maybe we could go out and come in again," said one of the men in a dreary voice. "Maybe we should take off and land again. Give them time to organize a party."

"That might be a good idea," murmured the tired captain.

The little town was full of people drifting in and out of doors, saying hello to one another, wearing golden masks and blue masks and crimson masks for pleasant variety, masks with silver lips and bronze eyebrows, masks that smiled or masks that frowned, according to the owners' dispositions.

The four men, wet from their long walk, paused and asked a little girl where Mr. Iii's house was.

"There." The child nodded her head.

The captain got eagerly, carefully down on one knee, looking into her sweet young face. "Little girl, I want to talk to you."

He seated her on his knee and folded her small brown hands neatly in his own big ones, as if ready for a bedtime story which he was shaping in his mind slowly and with a great patient happiness in details.

"Well, here's how it is, little girl. Six months ago another rocket came to Mars. There was a man named York in it, and his assistant. Whatever happened to them, we don't know. Maybe they crashed. They came in a rocket. So did we. You should see it! A *big* rocket! So we're the *Second* Expedition, following up the First. And we came all the way from Earth. . . . "

The little girl disengaged one hand without thinking about it, and clapped an expressionless golden mask over her face. Then she pulled forth a golden spider toy and dropped it to the ground while the captain talked on. The toy spider climbed back up to her knee obediently, while she speculated upon it coolly through the slits of her emotionless mask and the captain shook her gently and urged his story upon her.

"We're Earth Men," he said. "Do you believe me?"

"Yes." The little girl peeped at the way she was wiggling her toes in the dust.

"Fine." The captain pinched her arm, a little bit with joviality, a little bit with meanness to get her to look at him. "We built our own rocket ship. Do you believe *that*?"

The little girl dug in her nose with a finger. "Yes."

"And—take your finger out of your nose, little girl—*I* am the captain, and—"

"Never before in history has anybody come across space in a big rocket ship," recited the little creature, eyes shut.

"Wonderful! How did you know?"

"Oh, telepathy." She wiped a casual finger on her knee.

"Well, aren't you just *ever* so excited?" cried the captain. "Aren't you glad?"

"You just better go see Mr. Iii right away." She dropped her toy to the ground. "Mr. Iii will like talking to you." She ran off, with the toy spider scuttling obediently after her.

The captain squatted there looking after her with his hand out. His eyes were watery in his head. He looked at his empty hands. His mouth hung open. The other three men stood with their shadows under them. They spat on the stone street. . . .

Mr. Iii answered his door. He was on his way to a lecture, but he had a minute, if they would hurry inside and tell him what they desired. . . .

"A little attention," said the captain, red-eyed and tired. "We're from Earth, we have a rocket, there are four of us, crew and captain, we're exhausted, we're hungry, we'd like a place to sleep. We'd like someone to give us the key to the city or something like that, and we'd like somebody to shake our hands and say 'Hooray' and say 'Congratulations, old man!' That about sums it up."

Mr. Iii was a tall, vaporous, thin man with thick blind blue crystals over his yellowish eyes. He bent over his desk and brooded upon some papers, glancing now and again with extreme penetration at his guests.

"Well, I haven't the forms with me here, I don't *think*." He rummaged through the desk drawers. "Now, where *did* I put the forms?" He mused. "Somewhere. Somewhere. Oh, *here* we are! Now!" He handed the papers over crisply. "You'll have to sign these papers, of course."

"Do we have to go through all this rigmarole?"

Mr. Iii gave him a thick glassy look. "You say you're from Earth, don't you? Well, then there's nothing for it but you sign."

The captain wrote his name. "Do you want my crew to sign also?"

Mr. Iii looked at the captain, looked at the three others, and burst into a shout of derision. "*Them* sign! Ho! How marvelous! Them, oh, *them* sign!" Tears sprang from his eyes. He slapped his knee and bent to let his laughter jerk out of his gaping mouth. He held himself up with the desk. "*Them* sign!"

The four men scowled. "What's funny?"

"*Them* sign!" sighed Mr. Iii, weak with hilarity. "So very funny. I'll have to tell Mr. Xxx about this!" He examined the filled-out form, still laughing. "Everything seems to be in order." He nodded. "Even the agreement for euthanasia if final decision on such a step is necessary." He chuckled.

"Agreement for *what?*"

"Don't talk. I have something for you. Here. Take this key."

The captain flushed. "It's a great honor."

"Not the key to the city, you fool!" snapped Mr. Iii. "Just a key to the House. Go down that corridor, unlock the big door, and go inside and shut the door tight. You can spend the night there. In the morning I'll send Mr. Xxx to see you."

Dubiously the captain took the key in hand. He stood looking at the floor. His men did not move. They seemed to be emptied of all their blood and their rocket fever. They were drained dry.

"What is it? What's wrong?" inquired Mr. Iii. "What are you waiting for? What do you want?" He came and peered up into the captain's face, stooping. "Out with it, you!"

"I don't suppose you could even—" suggested the captain. "I mean, that is, try to, or think about . . ." He hesitated. "We've worked hard, we've come a long way, and maybe you could just shake our hands and say 'Well done!' do you—think?" His voice faded.

Mr. Iii stuck out his hand stiffly. "Congratulations!" He smiled a cold smile. "Congratulations." He turned away. "I must go now. Use that key."

Without noticing them again, as if they had melted down through the floor, Mr. Iii moved about the room packing a little manuscript case with papers. He was in the room another five minutes but never again addressed the solemn quartet that stood with heads down, their heavy legs sagging, the light dwindling from their eyes. When Mr. Iii went out the door he was busy looking at his fingernails. . . .

They straggled along the corridor in the dull, silent afternoon light. They came to a large burnished silver door, and the silver key opened it. They entered, shut the door, and turned.

They were in a vast sunlit hall. Men and women sat at tables and stood in conversing groups. At the sound of the door they regarded the four uniformed men.

One Martian stepped forward, bowing. "I am Mr. Uuu," he said.

"And I am Captain Jonathan Williams, of New York City, on Earth," said the captain without emphasis.

Immediately the hall exploded!

The rafters trembled with shouts and cries. The people, rushing forward, waved and shrieked happily, knocking down tables, swarming, rollicking, seizing the four Earth Men, lifting them swiftly to their shoulders. They charged about the hall six times, six times making a full and wonderful circuit of the room, jumping, bounding, singing.

The Earth Men were so stunned that they rode the toppling shoulders for a full minute before they began to laugh and shout at each other:

"Hey! This is more *like* it!"

"This is the life! Boy! Yay! Yow! Whoopee!"

They winked tremendously at each other. They flung up their hands to clap the air. "Hey!"

"Hooray!" said the crowd.

They set the Earth Men on a table. The shouting died.

The captain almost broke into tears. "Thank you. It's good, it's good."

"Tell us about yourselves," suggested Mr. Uuu.

The captain cleared his throat.

The audience ohed and ahed as the captain talked. He introduced his crew; each made a small speech and was embarrassed by the thunderous applause.

Mr. Uuu clapped the captain's shoulder. "It's good to see another man from Earth. I am from Earth also."

"How was that again?"

"There are many of us here from Earth."

"You? From Earth?" The captain stared. "But is that possible? Did you come by rocket? Has space travel been going on for centuries?" His voice was disappointed. "What—what country are you from?"

"Tuiereol. I came by the spirit of my body, years ago."

"Tuiereol." The captain mouthed the word. "I don't know that country. What's this about spirit of body?"

"And Miss Rrr over here, she's from Earth, too, *aren't* you, Miss Rrr?"

Miss Rrr nodded and laughed strangely.

"And so is Mr. Www and Mr. Qqq and Mr. Vvv!"

"I'm from Jupiter," declared one man, preening himself.

"I'm from Saturn," said another, eyes glinting slyly.

"Jupiter, Saturn," murmured the captain, blinking.

It was very quiet now; the people stood around and sat at the tables which were strangely empty for banquet tables. Their yellow eyes were glowing, and there were dark shadows under their cheekbones. The captain noticed for the first time that there were no windows; the light seemed to permeate the walls. There was only one door. The captain winced. "This is confusing. Where on Earth is this Tuiereol? Is it near America?"

"What is America?"

"You never heard of America! You say you're from Earth and yet you don't know!"

Mr. Uuu drew himself up angrily. "Earth is a place of seas and nothing but seas. There is no land. I am from Earth, and know."

"Wait a minute." The captain sat back. "You look like a regular Martian. Yellow eyes. Brown skin."

"Earth is a place of all *jungle*," said Miss Rrr proudly. "I am from Orri, on Earth, a civilization built of silver!"

Now the captain turned his head from and then to Mr. Uuu and then to Mr. Www and Mr. Zzz and Mr. Nnn and Mr. Hhh and Mr. Bbb. He saw their yellow eyes waxing and waning in the light, focusing and unfocusing. He began to shiver. Finally he turned to his men and regarded them somberly.

"Do you realize what this is?"

"What, sir?"

"This is no celebration," replied the captain tiredly. "This is no banquet. These aren't government representatives. This is no surprise party. Look at their eyes. Listen to them!"

Nobody breathed. There was only a soft white move of eyes in the close room.

"Now I understand"—the captain's voice was far away—"why everyone gave us notes and passed us on, one from the other, until we met Mr. Iii, who sent us down a corridor with a key to open a door and shut a door. And here we are. . . ."

"Where are we, sir?"

The captain exhaled. "In an insane asylum."

It was night. The large hall lay quiet and dimly illumined by hidden light sources in the transparent walls. The four Earth Men sat around a wooden table, their bleak heads bent over their whispers. On the floors, men and women lay huddled. There were little stirs in the dark corners, solitary men or women gesturing their hands. Every half-hour one of the captain's men would try the silver door and return to the table. "Nothing doing, sir. We're locked in proper."

"They think we're really insane, sir?"

"Quite. That's why there was no hullabaloo to welcome us. They merely tolerated what, to them, must be a constantly recurring psychotic condition." He gestured at the dark sleeping shapes all about them. "Paranoids, every single one! What a welcome they gave us! For a moment there"—a little fire rose and died in his eyes—"I thought we were getting our true reception. All the yelling and singing and speeches. Pretty nice, wasn't it—while it lasted?"

"How long will they keep us here, sir?"

"Until we prove we're not psychotics."

"That should be easy."

"I *hope* so."

"You don't sound very certain, sir."

"I'm not. Look in that corner."

A man squatted alone in darkness. Out of his mouth issued a blue flame which turned into the round shape of a small naked woman. It flourished on the air softly in vapors of cobalt light, whispering and sighing.

The captain nodded at another corner. A woman stood there, changing. First she was embedded in a crystal pillar, then she melted into a golden statue, finally a staff of polished cedar, and back to a woman.

All through the midnight hall people were juggling thin violet flames, shifting, changing, for nighttime was the time of change and affliction.

"Magicians, sorcerers," whispered one of the Earth Men.

"No, hallucination. They pass their insanity over into us so that we see their hallucinations too. Telepathy. Autosuggestion and telepathy."

"Is that what worries you, sir?"

"Yes. If hallucinations can appear this 'real' to us, to anyone, if hallucinations are catching and almost believable, it's no wonder they mistook us for psychotics. If that man can produce little blue fire women and that woman there melt into a pillar, how natural if normal Martians think *we* produce our rocket ship with *our* minds."

"Oh," said his men in the shadows.

Around them, in the vast hall, flames leaped blue, flared, evaporated. Little demons of red sand ran between the teeth of sleeping men. Women became oily snakes. There was a smell of reptiles and animals.

In the morning everyone stood around looking fresh, happy, and normal. There were no flames or demons in the room. The captain and his men waited by the silver door, hoping it would open.

Mr. Xxx arrived after about four hours. They had a suspicion that he had waited outside the door, peering in at them for at least three hours before he stepped in, beckoned, and led them to his small office.

He was a jovial, smiling man, if one could believe the mask he wore, for upon it was painted not one smile, but three. Behind it, his voice was the voice of a not so smiling psychologist. "What seems to be the trouble?"

"You think we're insane, and we're not," said the captain.

"Contrarily, I do not think *all* of you are insane." The psychologist pointed a little wand at the captain. "No. Just you, sir. The others are secondary hallucinations."

The captain slapped his knee. "So *that's* it! That's why Mr. Iii laughed when I suggested my men sign the papers too!"

"Yes, Mr. Iii told me." The psychologist laughed out of the carved, smiling mouth. "A good joke. Where was I? Secondary hallucinations, yes. Women come to me with snakes crawling from their ears. When I cure them, the snakes vanish."

"We'll be glad to be cured. Go right ahead."

Mr. Xxx seemed surprised. "Unusual. Not many people want to be cured. The cure is drastic, you know."

"Cure ahead! I'm confident you'll find we're all sane."

"Let me check your papers to be sure they're in order for a 'cure.'" He checked a file. "Yes. You know, such cases as yours need special 'curing.' The people in that hall are simpler forms. But once you've gone this far, I must point out, with primary, secondary, auditory, olfactory, and labial hallucinations, as well as tactile and optical fantasies, it is pretty bad business. We have to resort to euthanasia."

The captain leaped up with a roar. "Look here, we've stood quite enough! Test us, tap our knees, check our hearts, exercise us, ask questions!"

"You are free to speak."

The captain raved for an hour. The psychologist listened.

"Incredible," he mused. "Most detailed dream fantasy I've ever heard."

"God damn it, we'll show you the rocket ship!" screamed the captain.

"I'd like to see it. Can you manifest it in this room?"

"Oh, certainly. It's in that file of yours, under *R*."

Mr. Xxx peered seriously into his file. He went "Tsk" and shut the file solemnly. "Why did you tell me to look? The rocket isn't there."

"Of course not, you idiot! I was joking. Does an insane man joke?"

"You find some odd senses of humor. Now, take me out to your rocket. I wish to see it."

It was noon. The day was very hot when they reached the rocket.

"So." The psychologist walked up to the ship and tapped it. It gonged softly. "May I go inside?" he asked slyly.

"You may."

Mr. Xxx stepped in and was gone for a long time.

"Of all the silly, exasperating things." The captain chewed a cigar as he waited. "For two cents I'd go back home and tell people not to bother with Mars. What a suspicious bunch of louts."

"I gather that a good number of their population are insane, sir. That seems to be their main reason for doubting."

"Nevertheless, this is all so damned irritating."

The psychologist emerged from the ship after half an hour of prowling, tapping, listening, smelling, tasting.

"*Now* do you believe!" shouted the captain, as if he were deaf.

The psychologist shut his eyes and scratched his nose. "This is the most incredible example of sensual hallucination and hypnotic suggestion I've ever encountered. I went through your 'rocket,' as you call it." He tapped the hull. "I hear it. Auditory fantasy." He drew a breath. "I smell it. Olfactory hallucination, induced by sensual telepathy." He kissed the ship. "I taste it. Labial fantasy!"

He shook the captain's hand. "May I congratulate you? You are a psychotic genius! You have done a most complete job! The task of projecting your psychotic image life into the mind of another via telepathy and keeping the hallucinations from becoming sensually weaker is almost impossible. Those people in the House usually concentrate on visuals or, at the most, visuals and auditory fantasies combined. You have balanced the whole conglomeration! Your insanity is beautifully complete!"

"My insanity." The captain was pale.

"Yes, yes, what a lovely insanity. Metal, rubber, gravitizers, foods, clothing, fuel, weapons, ladders, nuts, bolts, spoons. Ten thousand separate items I checked on your vessel. Never have I seen such a complexity. There were even *shadows* under the bunks and under *everything*! Such concentration of will! And everything, no matter how or when tested, had a smell, a solidity, a taste, a sound! Let me embrace you!"

He stood back at last. "I'll write this into my greatest monograph! I'll speak of it at the Martian Academy next month! *Look* at you! Why, you've even changed your eye color from yellow to blue, your skin to pink from brown. And those clothes, and your hands having five fingers instead of six! Biological metamorphosis through psychological imbalance! And your three friends—"

He took out a little gun. "Incurable, of course. You poor, wonderful man. You will be happier dead. Have you any last words?"

"Stop, for God's sake! Don't shoot!"

"You sad creature. I shall put you out of this misery which has driven you to imagine this rocket and these three men. It will be most engrossing to watch your friends and your rocket vanish once I have killed you. I will write a neat paper on the dissolvement of neurotic images from what I perceive here today."

"I'm from Earth! My name is Jonathan Williams, and these—"

"Yes, I know," soothed Mr. Xxx, and fired his gun.

The captain fell with a bullet in his heart. The other three men screamed.

Mr. Xxx stared at them. "You continue to exist? This is superb! Hallucinations with time and spatial persistence!" He pointed the gun at them. "Well, I'll scare you into dissolving."

"No!" cried the three men.

"An auditory appeal, even with the patient dead," observed Mr. Xxx as he shot the three men down.

They lay on the sand, intact, not moving.

He kicked them. Then he rapped on the ship.

"*It* persists! *They* persist!" He fired his gun again and again at the bodies. Then he stood back. The smiling mask dropped from his face.

Slowly the little psychologist's face changed. His jaw sagged. The gun dropped from his fingers. His eyes were dull and vacant. He put his hands up and turned in a blind circle. He fumbled at the bodies, saliva filling his mouth.

"Hallucinations," he mumbled frantically. "Taste. Sight. Smell. Sound. Feeling." He waved his hands. His eyes bulged. His mouth began to give off a faint froth.

"Go away!" he shouted at the bodies. "Go away!" he screamed at the ship. He examined his trembling hands. "Contaminated," he whispered wildly. "Carried over into me. Telepathy. Hypnosis. Now *I'm* insane. Now *I'm* contaminated. Hallucinations in all their sensual forms." He stopped and searched around with his numb hands for the gun. "Only one cure. Only one way to make them go away, vanish."

A shot rang out. Mr. Xxx fell.

The four bodies lay in the sun. Mr. Xxx lay where he fell.

The rocket reclined on the little sunny hill and didn't vanish.

When the town people found the rocket at sunset they wondered what it was. Nobody knew, so it was sold to a junkman and hauled off to be broken up for scrap metal.

That night it rained all night. The next day was fair and warm.

The Off Season

Sam Parkhill motioned with the broom, sweeping away the blue Martian sand.

"Here we are," he said. "Yes, sir, look at that!" He pointed. "Look at that sign. SAM'S HOT DOGS! Ain't that beautiful, Elma?"

"Sure, Sam," said his wife.

"Boy, what a change for me. If the boys from the Fourth Expedition could see me now. Am I glad to be in business myself while all the rest of them guys're off soldiering around still. We'll make thousands, Elma, thousands."

His wife looked at him for a long time, not speaking. "Whatever happened to Captain Wilder?" she asked finally. "That captain that killed that guy who thought he was going to kill off every other Earth Man, what was his name?"

"Spender, that nut. He was too damn particular. Oh, Captain Wilder? He's off on a rocket to Jupiter, I hear. They kicked him upstairs. I think he was a little batty abouts Mars too. Touchy, you know. He'll be back down from Jupiter and Pluto in about twenty years if he's lucky. That's what he gets for shooting off his mouth. And while he's freezing to death, look at me, look at this place!"

This was a crossroads where two dead highways came and went in darkness. Here Sam Parkhill had flung up this riveted aluminum structure, garish with white light, trembling with juke-box melody.

He stooped to fix a border of broken glass he had placed on the footpath. He had broken the glass from some old Martian buildings in the hills. "Best hot dogs on two worlds! First man on Mars with a hot-dog stand! The best onions and chili and mustard! You can't say I'm not alert. Here's the main highways, over there is the dead city and the mineral deposits. Those trucks from Earth

Settlement 101 will have to pass here twenty-four hours a day! Do I know my locations, or don't I?"

His wife looked at her fingernails.

"You think those ten thousand new-type work rockets will come through to Mars?" she said at last.

"In a month," he said loudly. "Why you look so funny?"

"I don't trust those Earth people," she said. "I'll believe it when I see them ten thousand rockets arrive with the one hundred thousand Mexicans and Chinese on them."

"Customers." He lingered on the word. "One hundred thousand hungry people."

"If," said his wife slowly, watching the sky, "there's no atomic war. I don't trust no atom bombs. There's so many of them on Earth now, you never can tell."

"Ah," said Sam, and went on sweeping.

From the corners of his eyes he caught a blue flicker. Something floated in the air gently behind him. He heard his wife say, "Sam. A friend of yours to see you."

Sam whirled to see the mask seemingly floating in the wind.

"So you're back again!" And Sam held his broom like a weapon.

The mask nodded. It was cut from pale blue glass and was fitted above a thin neck, under which were blowing loose robes of thin yellow silk. From the silk two mesh silver hands appeared. The mask mouth was a slot from which musical sounds issued now as the robes, the mask, the hands increased to a height, decreased.

"Mr. Parkhill, I've come back to speak to you again," the voice said from behind the mask.

"I thought I told you I don't want you near here!" cried Sam. "Go on, I'll give you the Disease!"

"I've already had the Disease," said the voice. "I was one of the few survivors. I was sick a long time."

"Go on and hide in the hills, that's where you belong, that's where you've been. Why you come on down and bother *me*? Now, all of a sudden. Twice in one day."

"We mean you no harm."

"But I mean you harm!" said Sam, backing up. "I don't like strangers. I don't like Martians. I never seen one before. It ain't natural. All these years you guys hide, and all of a sudden you pick on me. Leave me alone."

"We come for an important reason," said the blue mask.

"If it's about this land, it's mine. I built this hot-dog stand with my own hands."

"In a way it *is* about the land."

"Look here," said Sam. "I'm from New York City. Where I come from there's ten million others just like me. You Martians are a couple dozen left, got no cities, you wander around in the hills, no leaders, no laws, and now you come tell me about this land. Well, the old got to give way to the new. That's the law of give and take. I got a gun here. After you left this morning I got it out and loaded it."

"We Martians are telepathic," said the cold blue mask. "We are in contact with one of your towns across the dead sea. Have you listened on your radio?"

"My radio's busted."

"Then you don't know. There's big news. It concerns Earth—"

A silver hand gestured. A bronze tube appeared in it.

"Let me show you this."

"A gun," cried Sam Parkhill.

An instant later he had yanked his own gun from his hip holster and fired into the mist, the robe, the blue mask.

The mask sustained itself a moment. Then, like a small circus tent pulling up its stakes and dropping soft fold on fold, the silks rustled, the mask descended, the silver claws tinkled on the stone path. The mask lay on a small huddle of silent white bones and material.

Sam stood gasping.

His wife swayed over the huddled pile.

"That's no weapon," she said, bending down. She picked up the bronze tube. "He was going to show you a message. It's all written out in snake-script, all the blue snakes. I can't read it. Can you?"

"No, that Martian picture writing, it wasn't anything. Let it go!" Sam glanced hastily around. "There may be others! We've got to get him out of sight. Get the shovel!"

"What're you going to do?"

"Bury him, of course!"

"You shouldn't have shot him."

"It was a mistake. Quick!"

Silently she fetched him the shovel.

At eight o'clock he was back sweeping the front of the hot-dog stand self-consciously. His wife stood, arms folded, in the bright doorway.

"I'm sorry what happened," he said. He looked at her, then away. "You know it was purely the circumstances of Fate."

"Yes," said his wife.

"I hated like hell to see him take out that weapon."

"What weapon?"

"Well, I thought it was one! I'm sorry, I'm sorry! How many times do I say it!"

"Ssh," said Elma, putting one finger to her lips. "Ssh."

"I don't care," he said. "I got the whole Earth Settlements, Inc., back of me!" He snorted. "These Martians won't dare—"

"Look," said Elma.

He looked out onto the dead sea bottom. He dropped his broom. He picked it up and his mouth was open, a little free drop of saliva flew on the air, and he was suddenly shivering.

"Elma, Elma, Elma!" he said.

"Here they come," said Elma.

Across the ancient sea floor a dozen tall, blue-sailed Martian sand ships floated, like blue ghosts, like blue smoke.

"Sand ships! But there aren't any more, Elma, no more sand ships."

"Those seem to be sand ships," she said.

"But the authorities confiscated all of them! They broke them up, sold some at auction! I'm the only one in this whole damn territory's got one and knows how to run one."

"Not any more," she said, nodding at the sea.

"Come on, let's get out of here!"

"Why?" she asked slowly, fascinated with the Martian vessels.

"They'll kill me! Get in our truck, quick!"

Elma didn't move.

He had to drag her around back of the stand where the two machines stood, his truck, which he had used steadily until a month ago, and the old Martian sand ship which he had bid for at auction, smiling, and which, during the last three weeks, he had used to carry supplies back and forth over the glassy sea floor. He looked at his truck now and remembered. The engine was out on the ground; he had been puttering with it for two days.

"The truck don't seem to be in running condition," said Elma.

"The sand ship. Get in!"

"And let you drive me in a sand ship? Oh no."

"Get in! I can do it!"

He shoved her in, jumped in behind her, and flapped the tiller, let the cobalt sail up to take the evening wind.

The stars were bright and the blue Martian ships were skimming across the whispering sands. At first his own ship would not move, then he remembered the sand anchor and yanked it in.

"There!"

The wind hurled the sand ship keening over the dead sea bottom, over long-buried crystals, past upended pillars, past deserted docks of marble and brass, past dead white chess cities, past purple foothills, into distance. The figures of the Martian ships receded and then began to pace Sam's ship.

"Guess I showed them, by God!" cried Sam. "I'll report to the Rocket Corporation. They'll give me protection! I'm pretty quick."

"They could have stopped you if they wanted," Elma said tiredly. "They just didn't bother."

He laughed. "Come off it. Why should they let me get off? No, they weren't quick enough, is all."

"Weren't they?" Elma nodded behind him.

He did not turn. He felt a cold wind blowing. He was afraid to turn. He felt something in the seat behind him, something as frail as your breath on a cold morning, something as blue as hickory-wood smoke at twilight, something like old white lace, something like a snowfall, something like the icy rime of winter on the brittle sedge.

There was a sound as of a thin plate of glass broken—laughter. Then silence. He turned.

The young woman sat at the tiller bench quietly. Her wrists were thin as icicles, her eyes as clear as the moons and as large, steady and white. The wind blew at her and, like an image on cold water, she rippled, silk standing out from her frail body in tatters of blue rain.

"Go back," she said.

"No." Sam was quivering, the fine, delicate fear-quivering of a hornet suspended in the air, undecided between fear and hate. "Get off my ship!"

"This isn't your ship," said the vision. "It's old as our world. It sailed the sand seas ten thousand years ago when the seas were whispered away and the docks were empty, and you came and took it, stole it. Now turn it around, go back to the crossroad place. We have need to talk with you. Something important has happened."

"Get off my ship!" said Sam. He took a gun from his holster with a creak of leather. He pointed it carefully. "Jump off before I count three or—"

"Don't!" cried the girl. "I won't hurt you. Neither will the others. We came in peace!"

"One," said Sam.

"Sam!" said Elma.

"Listen to me," said the girl.

"Two," said Sam firmly, cocking the gun trigger.

"Sam!" cried Elma.

"Three," said Sam.

"We only—" said the girl.

The gun went off.

In the sunlight, snow melts, crystals evaporate into a steam, into nothing. In the firelight, vapors dance and vanish. In the core of a volcano, fragile things burst and disappear. The girl, in the gunfire, in the heat, in the concussion, folded like a soft scarf, melted like a crystal figurine. What was left of her, ice, snowflake, smoke, blew away in the wind. The tiller seat was empty.

Sam holstered his gun and did not look at his wife.

"Sam," she said after a minute more of traveling, whispering over the moon-colored sea of sand, "stop the ship."

He looked at her and his face was pale. "No, you don't. Not after all this time, you're not pulling out on me."

She looked at his hand on his gun. "I believe you would" she said. "You actually would."

He jerked his head from side to side, hand tight on the tiller bar. "Elma, this is crazy. We'll be in town in a minute, we'll be okay!"

"Yes," said his wife, lying back cold in the ship.

"Elma, listen to me."

"There's nothing to hear, Sam."

"Elma!"

They were passing a little white chess city, and in his frustration, in his rage, he sent six bullets crashing among the crystal towers. The city dissolved in a shower of ancient glass and splintered quartz. It fell away like carved soap, shattered. It was no more. He laughed and fired again, and one last tower, one last chess piece, took fire, ignited, and in blue flinders went up to the stars.

"I'll show them! I'll show everybody!"

"Go ahead, show us, Sam." She lay in the shadows.

"Here comes another city!" Sam reloaded his gun. "Watch me fix it!"

The blue phantom ships loomed up behind them, drawing steadily apace. He did not see them at first. He was only aware of a whistling and a high windy screaming, as of steel on sand, and it was the sound of the sharp razor prows of the sand ships preening the sea bottoms, their red pennants, blue pennants unfurled. In the blue light ships were blue dark images, masked men, men with silvery faces, men with blue stars for eyes, men with carved golden ears, men with tinfoil cheeks and ruby-studded lips, men with arms folded, men following him, Martian men.

One, two, three. Sam counted. The Martian ships closed in.

"Elma, Elma, I can't hold them all off!"

Elma did not speak or rise from where she had slumped.

Sam fired his gun eight times. One of the sand ships fell apart, the sail, the emerald body, the bronze hull points, the moon-white tiller, and all the separate images in it. The masked men, all of them, dug into the sand and separated out into orange and then smoke-flame.

But the other ships closed in.

"I'm outnumbered, Elma!" he cried. "They'll kill me!"

He threw out the anchor. It was no use. The sail fluttered down, folding unto itself, sighing. The ship stopped. The wind stopped. Travel stopped. Mars stood still as the majestic vessels of the Martians drew around and hesitated over him.

"Earth Man," a voice called from a high seat somewhere. A silverine mask moved. Ruby-rimmed lips glittered with the words.

"I didn't do anything!" Sam looked at all the faces, one hundred in all, that surrounded him. There weren't many Martians left on Mars—one hundred, one hundred and fifty, all told. And most of them were here now, on the dead seas, in their resurrected ships, by their dead chess cities, one of which had just fallen like some fragile vase hit by a pebble. The silverine masks glinted.

"It was all a mistake," he pleaded, standing out of his ship, his wife slumped behind him in the deeps of the hold, like a dead woman. "I came to

Mars like any honest enterprising businessman. I took some surplus material from a rocket that crashed and I built me the finest little stand you ever saw right there on that land by the crossroads—you know where it is. You've got to admit it's a good job of building." Sam laughed, staring around. "And that Martian—I know he was a friend of yours—came. His death was an accident, I assure you. All I wanted to do was have a hot-dog stand, the only one on Mars, the first and most important one. You understand how it is? I was going to serve the best darned hot dogs there, with chili and onions and orange juice."

The silver masks did not move. They burned in the moonlight. Yellow eyes shone upon Sam. He felt his stomach clench in, wither, become a rock. He threw his gun in the sand.

"I give up."

"Pick up your gun," said the Martians in chorus.

"What?"

"Your gun." A jeweled hand waved from the prow of a blue ship. "Pick it up. Put it away."

Unbelieving, he picked up the gun.

"Now," said the voice, "turn your ship and go back to your stand."

"Now?"

"Now," said the voice. "We will not harm you. You ran away before we were able to explain. Come."

Now the great ships turned as lightly as moon thistles. Their wing-sails flapped with a sound of soft applause on the air. The masks were coruscating, turning, firing the shadows.

"Elma!" Sam tumbled into the ship. "Get up, Elma. We're going back." He was excited. He almost gibbered with relief. "They aren't going to hurt me, kill me, Elma. Get up, honey, get up."

"What—what?" Elma blinked around and slowly, as the ship was sent into the wind again, she helped herself, as in a dream, back up to a seat and slumped there like a sack of stones, saying no more.

The sand slid under the ship. In half an hour they were back at the crossroads, the ships planted, all of them out of the ships.

The Leader stood before Sam and Elma, his mask beaten of polished bronze, the eyes only empty slits of endless blue-black, the mouth a slot out of which words drifted into the wind.

"Ready your stand," said the voice. A diamond-gloved hand waved. "Prepare the viands, prepare the foods, prepare the strange wines, for tonight is indeed a great night!"

"You mean," said Sam, "you'll let me stay on here?"

"Yes."

"You're not mad at me?"

The mask was rigid and carved and cold and sightless.

"Prepare your place of food," said the voice softly. "And take this."

"What is it?"

Sam blinked at the silver-foil scroll that was handed him, upon which, in hieroglyph, snake figures danced.

"It is the land grant to all of the territory from the silver mountains to the blue hills, from the dead salt sea there to the distant valleys of moonstone and emerald," said the Leader.

"M-mine?" said Sam, incredulous.

"Yours."

"One hundred thousand miles of territory?"

"Yours."

"Did you hear that, Elma?"

Elma was sitting on the ground, leaning against the aluminum hot-dog stand, eyes shut.

"But why, why—why are you giving me all this?" asked Sam, trying to look into the metal slots of the eyes.

"That is not all. Here." Six other scrolls were produced. The names were declared, the territories announced.

"Why, that's half of Mars! I own half of Mars!" Sam rattled the scrolls in his fists. He shook them at Elma, insane with laughing. "Elma, did you hear?"

"I heard," said Elma, looking at the sky.

She seemed to be watching for something. She was becoming a little more alert now.

"Thank you, oh, thank you," said Sam to the bronze mask.

"Tonight is the night," said the mask. "You must be ready."

"I will be. What is it—a surprise? Are the rockets coming through earlier than we thought, a month earlier from Earth? All ten thousand rockets, bringing the settlers, the miners, the workers and their wives, all hundred thousand of them? Won't that be swell, Elma? You see, I told you. I told you, that town there won't always have just one thousand people in it. There'll be fifty thousand more coming, and the month after that a hundred thousand more, and by the end of the year five million Earth Men. And me with the only hot-dog stand staked out on the busiest highway to the mines!"

The mask floated on the wind. "We leave you. Prepare. The land is yours."

In the blowing moonlight, like metal petals of some ancient flower, like blue plumes, like cobalt butterflies immense and quiet, the old ships turned and moved over the shifting sands, the masks beaming and glittering, until the last shine, the last blue color, was lost among the hills.

"Elma, why did they do it? Why didn't they kill me? Don't they know anything? What's wrong with them? Elma, do you understand?" He shook her shoulder. "I own half of Mars!"

She watched the night sky, waiting.

"Come on," he said. "We've got to get the place fixed. All the hot dogs boiling, the buns warm, the chili cooking, the onions peeled and diced, the relish laid out, the napkins in the clips, the place spotless! Hey!" He did a little wild dance, kicking his heels. "Oh boy, I'm happy; yes, sir, I'm happy," he sang, off key. "This is my lucky day!"

He boiled the hot dogs, cut the buns, sliced the onions in a frenzy.

"Just think, that Martian said a surprise. That can only mean one thing, Elma. Those hundred thousand people coming in ahead of schedule, tonight, of all nights! We'll be flooded! We'll work long hours for days, what with tourists riding around seeing things, Elma. Think of the money!"

He went out and looked at the sky. He didn't see anything.

"In a minute, maybe," he said, snuffing the cool air gratefully, arms up, beating his chest. "Ah!"

Elma said nothing. She peeled potatoes for French fries quietly, her eyes always on the sky.

"Sam," she said half an hour later. "There it is. Look."

He looked and saw it.

Earth.

It rose full and green, like a fine-cut stone, above the hills.

"Good old Earth," he whispered lovingly. "Good old wonderful Earth. Send me your hungry and your starved. Something, something—how does that poem go? Send me your hungry, old Earth. Here's Sam Parkhill, his hot dogs all boiled, his chili cooking, everything neat as a pin. Come on, you Earth, send me your rockets!"

He went out to look at his place. There it sat, perfect as a fresh-laid egg on the dead sea bottom, the only nucleus of light and warmth in hundreds of miles of lonely wasteland. It was like a heart beating alone in a great dark body. He felt almost sorrowful with pride, gazing at it with wet eyes.

"It sure makes you humble," he said among the cooking odors of wieners, warm buns, rich butter. "Step up," he invited the various stars in the sky. "Who'll be the first to buy?"

"Sam," said Elma.

Earth changed in the black sky.

It caught fire.

Part of it seemed to come apart in a million pieces, as if a gigantic jigsaw had exploded. It burned with an unholy dripping glare for a minute, three times normal size, then dwindled.

"What was that?" Sam looked at the green fire in the sky.

"Earth," said Elma, holding her hands together.

"That can't be Earth, that's not Earth! No, that ain't Earth! It can't be."

"You mean it couldn't be Earth," said Elma, looking at him. "That just isn't Earth. No, that's not Earth; is that what you mean?"

"Not Earth—oh no, it *couldn't* be," he wailed.

He stood there, his hands at his sides, his mouth open, his eyes wide and dull, not moving.

"Sam." She called his name. For the first time in days her eyes were bright. "Sam?"

He looked up at the sky.

"Well," she said. She glanced around for a minute or so in silence. Then briskly she flapped a wet towel over her arm. "Switch on more lights, turn up the music, open the doors. There'll be another batch of customers along in about a million years. Gotta be ready, yes, sir."

Sam did not move.

"What a swell spot for a hot-dog stand," she said. She reached over and picked a toothpick out of a jar and put it between her front teeth. "Let you in on a little secret, Sam," she whispered, leaning toward him. "This looks like it's going to be an off season."

The Million-Year Picnic

Somehow the idea was brought up by Mom that perhaps the whole family would enjoy a fishing trip. But they weren't Mom's words; Timothy knew that. They were Dad's words, and Mom used them for him somehow.

Dad shuffled his feet in a clutter of Martian pebbles and agreed. So immediately there was a tumult and a shouting, and very quickly the camp was tucked into capsules and containers, Mom slipped into traveling jumpers and blouse, Dad stuffed his pipe full with trembling hands, his eyes on the Martian sky, and the three boys piled yelling into the motorboat, none of them really keeping an eye on Mom and Dad, except Timothy.

Dad pushed a stud. The water boat sent a humming sound up into the sky. The water shook back and the boat nosed ahead, and the family cried, "Hurrah!"

Timothy sat in the back of the boat with Dad, his small fingers atop Dad's hairy ones, watching the canal twist, leaving the crumbled place behind where they had landed in their small family rocket all the way from Earth. He remembered the night before they left Earth, the hustling and hurrying, the rocket that Dad had found somewhere, somehow, and the talk of a vacation on Mars. A long way to go for a vacation, but Timothy said nothing because of his younger brothers. They came to Mars and now, first thing, or so they said, they were going fishing.

Dad had a funny look in his eyes as the boat went up-canal. A look that Timothy couldn't figure. It was made of strong light and maybe a sort of relief. It made the deep wrinkles laugh instead of worry or cry.

So there went the cooling rocket, around a bend, gone.

"How far are we going?" Robert splashed his hand. It looked like a small crab jumping in the violet water.

Dad exhaled. "A million years."

"Gee," said Robert.

"Look, kids." Mother pointed one soft long arm. "There's a dead city."

They looked with fervent anticipation, and the dead city lay dead for them alone, drowsing in a hot silence of summer made on Mars by a Martian weatherman.

And Dad looked as if he was pleased that it was dead.

It was a futile spread of pink rocks sleeping on a rise of sand, a few tumbled pillars, one lonely shrine, and then the sweep of sand again. Nothing else for miles. A white desert around the canal and a blue desert over it.

Just then a bird flew up. Like a stone thrown across a blue pond, hitting, falling deep, and vanishing.

Dad got a frightened look when he saw it. "I thought it was a rocket."

Timothy looked at the deep ocean sky, trying to see Earth and the war and the ruined cities and the men killing each other since the day he was born. But he saw nothing. The war was as removed and far off as two flies battling to the death in the arch of a great high and silent cathedral. And just as senseless.

William Thomas wiped his forehead and felt the touch of his son's hand on his arm, like a young tarantula, thrilled. He beamed at his son. "How goes it, Timmy?"

"Fine, Dad."

Timothy hadn't quite figured out what was ticking inside the vast adult mechanism beside him. The man with the immense hawk nose, sunburnt, peeling—and the hot blue eyes like agate marbles you play with after school in summer back on Earth, and the long thick columnar legs in the loose riding breeches.

"What are you looking at so hard, Dad?"

"I was looking for Earthian logic, common sense, good government, peace, and responsibility."

"All that up there?"

"No. I didn't find it. It's not there any more. Maybe it'll never be there again. Maybe we fooled ourselves that it was ever there."

"Huh?"

"See the fish," said Dad, pointing.

There rose a soprano clamor from all three boys as they rocked the boat in arching their tender necks to see. They *oohed* and *ahed*. A silver ring fish floated by them, undulating, and closing like an iris, instantly, around food particles, to assimilate them.

Dad looked at it. His voice was deep and quiet.

"Just like war. War swims along, sees food, contracts. A moment later— Earth is gone."

"William," said Mom.

"Sorry," said Dad.

They sat still and felt the canal water rush cool, swift, and glassy. The only sound was the motor hum, the glide of water, the sun expanding the air.

"When do we see the Martians?" cried Michael.

"Quite soon, perhaps," said Father. "Maybe tonight."

"Oh, but the Martians are a dead race now," said Mom.

"No, they're not. I'll show you some Martians, all right," Dad said presently.

Timothy scowled at that but said nothing. Everything was odd now. Vacations and fishing and looks between people.

The other boys were already engaged making shelves of their small hands and peering under them toward the seven-foot stone banks of the canal, watching for Martians.

"What do they look like?" demanded Michael.

"You'll know them when you see them." Dad sort of laughed, and Timothy saw a pulse beating time in his cheek.

Mother was slender and soft, with a woven plait of spun-gold hair over her head in a tiara, and eyes the color of the deep cool canal water where it ran in shadow, almost purple, with flecks of amber caught in it. You could see her thoughts swimming around in her eyes, like fish—some bright, some dark, some fast, quick, some slow and easy, and sometimes, like when she looked up where Earth was, being nothing but color and nothing else. She sat in the boat's prow, one hand resting on the side lip, the other on the lap of her dark blue breeches, and a line of sunburnt soft neck showing where her blouse opened like a white flower.

She kept looking ahead to see what was there, and, not being able to see it clearly enough, she looked backward toward her husband, and through his eyes, reflected then, she saw what was ahead; and since he added part of himself to this reflection, a determined firmness, her face relaxed and she accepted it and she turned back, knowing suddenly what to look for.

Timothy looked too. But all he saw was a straight pencil line of canal going violet through a wide shallow valley penned by low, eroded hills, and on until it fell over the sky's edge. And this canal went on and on, through cities that would have rattled like beetles in a dry skull if you shook them. A hundred or two hundred cities dreaming hot summer-day dreams and cool summer-night dreams . . .

They had come millions of miles for this outing—to fish. But there had been a gun on the rocket. This was a vacation. But why all the food, more than enough to last them years and years, left hidden back there near the rocket?

Vacation. Just behind the veil of the vacation was not a soft face of laughter, but something hard and bony and perhaps terrifying. Timothy could not lift the veil, and the two other boys were busy being ten and eight years old, respectively.

"No Martians yet. Nuts." Robert put his V-shaped chin on his hands and glared at the canal.

Dad had brought an atomic radio along, strapped to his wrist. It functioned on an old-fashioned principle: you held it against the bones near your ear and it vibrated singing or talking to you. Dad listened to it now. His face looked like one of those fallen Martian cities, caved in, sucked dry, almost dead.

Then he gave it to Mom to listen. Her lips dropped open.

"What—" Timothy started to question, but never finished what he wished to say.

For at that moment there were two titanic, marrow-jolting explosions that grew upon themselves, followed by a half-dozen minor concussions.

Jerking his head up, Dad notched the boat speed higher immediately. The boat leaped and jounced and spanked. This shook Robert out of his funk and elicited yelps of frightened but ecstatic joy from Michael, who clung to Mom's legs and watched the water pour by his nose in a wet torrent.

Dad swerved the boat, cut speed, and ducked the craft into a little branch canal and under an ancient, crumbling stone wharf that smelled of crab flesh. The boat rammed the wharf hard enough to throw them all forward, but no one was hurt, and Dad was already twisted to see if the ripples on the canal were enough to map their route into hiding. Water lines went across, lapped the stones, and rippled back to meet each other, settling, to be dappled by the sun. It all went away.

Dad listened. So did everybody.

Dad's breathing echoed like fists beating against the cold wet wharf stones. In the shadow, Mom's cat eyes just watched Father for some clue to what next.

Dad relaxed and blew out a breath, laughing at himself.

"The rocket, of course. I'm getting jumpy. The rocket."

Michael said, "What happened, Dad, what happened?"

"Oh, we just blew up our rocket, is all," said Timothy, trying to sound matter-of-fact. "I've heard rockets blown up before. Ours just blew."

"Why did we blow up our rocket?" asked Michael. "Huh, Dad?"

"It's part of the game, silly!" said Timothy.

"A game!" Michael and Robert loved the word.

"Dad fixed it so it would blow up and no one'd know where we landed or went! In case they ever came looking, see?"

"Oh boy, a secret!"

"Scared by my own rocket," admitted Dad to Mom. "I am nervous. It's silly to think there'll ever *be* any more rockets. Except *one*, perhaps, if Edwards and his wife get through with *their* ship."

He put his tiny radio to his ear again. After two minutes he dropped his hand as you would drop a rag.

"It's over at last," he said to Mom. "The radio just went off the atomic beam. Every other world station's gone. They dwindled down to a couple in the last few years. Now the air's completely silent. It'll probably remain silent."

"For how long?" asked Robert.

"Maybe—your great-grandchildren will hear it again," said Dad. He just sat there, and the children were caught in the center of his awe and defeat and resignation and acceptance.

Finally he put the boat out into the canal again, and they continued in the direction in which they had originally started.

It was getting late. Already the sun was down the sky, and a series of dead cities lay ahead of them.

Dad talked very quietly and gently to his sons. Many times in the past he had been brisk, distant, removed from them, but now he patted them on the head with just a word and they felt it.

"Mike, pick a city."

"What, Dad?"

"Pick a city, Son. Any one of these cities we pass."

"All right," said Michael. "How do I pick?"

"Pick the one you like the most. You, too, Robert and Tim. Pick the city you like best."

"I want a city with Martians in it," said Michael.

"You'll have that," said Dad. "I promise." His lips were for the children, but his eyes were for Mom.

They passed six cities in twenty minutes. Dad didn't say anything more about the explosions; he seemed much more interested in having fun with his sons, keeping them happy, than anything else.

Michael liked the first city they passed, but this was vetoed because everyone doubted quick first judgments. The second city nobody liked. It was an Earth Man's settlement, built of wood and already rotting into sawdust. Timothy liked the third city because it was large. The fourth and fifth were too small and the sixth brought acclaim from everyone, including Mother, who joined in the Gees, Goshes, and Look-at-thats!

There were fifty or sixty huge structures still standing, streets were dusty but paved, and you could see one or two old centrifugal fountains still pulsing wetly in the plazas. That was the only life—water leaping in the late sunlight.

"This is the city," said everybody.

Steering the boat to a wharf, Dad jumped out.

"Here we are. This is ours. This is where we live from now on!"

"From now on?" Michael was incredulous. He stood up, looking, and then turned to blink back at where the rocket used to be. "What about the rocket? What about Minnesota?"

"Here," said Dad.

He touched the small radio to Michael's blond head. "Listen."

Michael listened.

"Nothing," he said.

"That's right. Nothing. Nothing at all any more. No more Minneapolis, no more rockets, no more Earth."

Michael considered the lethal revelation and began to sob little dry sobs.

"Wait a moment," said Dad the next instant. "I'm giving you a lot more in exchange, Mike!"

"What?" Michael held off the tears, curious, but quite ready to continue in case Dad's further revelation was as disconcerting as the original.

"I'm giving you this city, Mike. It's yours."

"Mine?"

"For you and Robert and Timothy, all three of you, to own for yourselves."

Timothy bounded from the boat. "Look, guys, all for *us*! All of *that*!" He was playing the game with Dad, playing it large and playing it well. Later, after it was all over and things had settled, he could go off by himself and cry for ten minutes. But now it was still a game, still a family outing, and the other kids must be kept playing.

Mike jumped out with Robert. They helped Mom.

"Be careful of your sister," said Dad, and nobody knew what he meant until later.

They hurried into the great pink-stoned city, whispering among themselves, because dead cities have a way of making you want to whisper, to watch the sun go down.

"In about five days," said Dad quietly, "I'll go back down to where our rocket was and collect the food hidden in the ruins there and bring it here; and I'll hunt for Bert Edwards and his wife and daughters there."

"Daughters?" asked Timothy. "How many?"

"Four."

"I can see that'll cause trouble later." Mom nodded slowly.

"Girls." Michael made a face like an ancient Martian stone image. "Girls."

"Are they coming in a rocket, too?"

"Yes. If they make it. Family rockets are made for travel to the Moon, not Mars. We were lucky we got through."

"Where did you get the rocket?" whispered Timothy, for the other boys were running ahead.

"I saved it. I saved it for twenty years, Tim. I had it hidden away, hoping I'd never have to use it. I suppose I should have given it to the government for the war, but I kept thinking about Mars. . . . "

"And a picnic!"

"Right. This is between you and me. When I saw everything was finishing on Earth, after I'd waited until the last moment, I packed us up. Bert Edwards had a ship hidden, too, but we decided it would be safer to take off separately, in case anyone tried to shoot us down."

"Why'd you blow up the rocket, Dad?"

"So we can't go back, ever. And so if any of those evil men ever come to Mars they won't know we're here."

"Is that why you look up all the time?"

"Yes, it's silly. They won't follow us, ever. They haven't anything to follow with. I'm being too careful, is all."

Michael came running back. "Is this really *our* city, Dad?"

"The whole darn planet belongs to us, kids. The whole darn planet."

They stood there, King of the Hill, Top of the Heap, Ruler of All They Surveyed, Unimpeachable Monarchs and Presidents, trying to understand what it meant to own a world and how big a world really was.

Night came quickly in the thin atmosphere, and Dad left them in the square by the pulsing fountain, went down to the boat, and came walking back carrying a stack of paper in his big hands.

He laid the papers in a clutter in an old courtyard and set them afire. To keep warm, they crouched around the blaze and laughed, and Timothy saw the little letters leap like frightened animals when the flames touched and engulfed them. The papers crinkled like an old man's skin, and the cremation surrounded innumerable words:

"GOVERNMENT BONDS; Business Graph, 1999; Religious Prejudice: An Essay; The Science of Logistics; Problems of the Pan-American Unity; Stock Report for July 3, 1998; The War Digest . . . "

Dad had insisted on bringing these papers for this purpose. He sat there and fed them into the fire, one by one, with satisfaction, and told his children what it all meant.

"It's time I told you a few things. I don't suppose it was fair, keeping so much from you. I don't know if you'll understand, but I have to talk, even if only part of it gets over to you."

He dropped a leaf in the fire.

"I'm burning a way of life, just like that way of life is being burned clean of Earth right now. Forgive me if I talk like a politician. I am, after all, a former state governor, and I was honest and they hated me for it. Life on Earth never settled down to doing anything very good. Science ran too far ahead of us too quickly, and the people got lost in a mechanical wilderness, like children making over pretty things, gadgets, helicopters, rockets; emphasizing the wrong items, emphasizing machines instead of how to run the machines. Wars got bigger and bigger and finally killed Earth. That's what the silent radio means. That's what we ran away from.

"We were lucky. There aren't any more rockets left. It's time you knew this isn't a fishing trip at all. I put off telling you. Earth is gone. Interplanetary travel won't be back for centuries, maybe never. But that way of life proved itself wrong and strangled itself with its own hands. You're young. I'll tell you this again every day until it sinks in."

He paused to feed more papers to the fire.

"Now we're alone. We and a handful of others who'll land in a few days. Enough to start over. Enough to turn away from all that back on Earth and strike out on a new line—"

The fire leaped up to emphasize his talking. And then all the papers were gone except one. All the laws and beliefs of Earth were burnt into small hot ashes which soon would be carried off in a wind.

Timothy looked at the last thing that Dad tossed in the fire. It was a map of the World, and it wrinkled and distorted itself hotly and went—flimpf—and was gone like a warm, black butterfly. Timothy turned away.

"Now I'm going to show you the Martians," said Dad. "Come on, all of you. Here, Alice." He took her hand.

Michael was crying loudly, and Dad picked him up and carried him, and they walked down through the ruins toward the canal.

The canal. Where tomorrow or the next day their future wives would come up in a boat, small laughing girls now, with their father and mother.

The night came down around them, and there were stars. But Timothy couldn't find Earth. It had already set. That was something to think about.

A night bird called among the ruins as they walked. Dad said, "Your mother and I will try to teach you. Perhaps we'll fail. I hope not. We've had a good lot to see and learn from. We planned this trip years ago, before you were born. Even if there hadn't been a war we would have come to Mars, I think, to live and form our own standard of living. It would have been another century before Mars would have been really poisoned by the Earth civilization. Now, of course—"

They reached the canal. It was long and straight and cool and wet and reflective in the night.

"I've always wanted to see a Martian," said Michael. "Where are they, Dad? You promised."

"There they are," said Dad, and he shifted Michael on his shoulder and pointed straight down.

The Martians were there. Timothy began to shiver.

The Martians were there—in the canal—reflected in the water. Timothy and Michael and Robert and Mom and Dad.

The Martians stared back up at them for a long, long silent time from the rippling water. . . .

The Fox and the Forest

There were fireworks the very first night, things that you should be afraid of perhaps, for they might remind you of other more horrible things, but these were beautiful, rockets that ascended into the ancient soft air of Mexico and shook the stars apart in blue and white fragments. Everything was good and sweet, the air was that blend of the dead and the living, of the rains and the dusts, of the incense from the church, and the brass smell of the tuba on the bandstand which pulsed out vast rhythms of "La Paloma." The church doors were thrown wide and it seemed as if a giant yellow constellation had fallen from the October sky and lay breathing fire upon the church walls; a million candles sent their color and fumes about. Newer and better fireworks scurried like tight-rope walking comets across the cool-tiled square, banged against adobe café walls, then rushed on hot wires to bash the high church tower, in which boys' naked feet alone could be seen kicking and re-kicking, clanging and tilting and re-tilting the monster bells into monstrous music. A flaming bull blundered about the plaza chasing laughing men and screaming children.

"The year is 1938," said William Travis, standing by his wife on the edge of the yelling crowd, smiling. "A good year."

The bull rushed upon them. Ducking, the couple ran, with fire balls pelting them, past the music and riot, the church, the band, under the stars, clutching each other, laughing. The bull passed, carried lightly on the shoulders of a charging Mexican, a framework of bamboo and sulphurous gunpowder.

"I've never enjoyed myself so much in my life." Susan Travis had stopped for her breath.

"It's amazing," said William.

"It will go on, won't it?"

"All night."

"No, I mean our trip."

He frowned and patted his breast pocket. "I've enough traveler's checks for a lifetime. Enjoy yourself. Forget it. They'll never find us."

"Never?"

"Never."

Now someone was setting off giant crackers, hurling them from the great bell-tolling tower of the church in a sputter of smoke, while the crowd below fell back under the threat and the crackers exploded in wonderful concussions among their dancing feet and flailing bodies. A wondrous smell of frying tortillas hung all about, and in the cafés men sat at tables looking out, mugs of beer in their brown hands.

The bull was dead. The fire was out of the bamboo tubes and he was expended. The laborer lifted the framework from his shoulders. Little boys clustered to touch the magnificent papier-mâché head, the real horns.

"Let's examine the bull," said William.

As they walked past the café entrance Susan saw the man looking out at them, a white man in a salt-white suit, with a blue tie and blue shirt, and a thin, sunburned face. His hair was blond and straight and his eyes were blue, and he watched them as they walked.

She would never have noticed him if it had not been for the bottles at his immaculate elbow; a fat bottle of crème de menthe, a clear bottle of vermouth, a flagon of cognac, and seven other bottles of assorted liqueurs, and, at his finger tips, ten small half-filled glasses from which, without taking his eyes off the street, he sipped, occasionally squinting, pressing his thin mouth shut upon the savor. In his free hand a thin Havana cigar smoked, and on a chair stood twenty cartons of Turkish cigarettes, six boxes of cigars, and some packaged colognes.

"Bill—" whispered Susan.

"Take it easy," he said. "He's nobody."

"I saw him in the plaza this morning."

"Don't look back, keep walking. Examine the papier-mâché bull here. That's it, ask questions."

"Do you think he's from the Searchers?"

"They couldn't follow us!"

"They might!"

"What a nice bull," said William to the man who owned it.

"He couldn't have followed us back through two hundred years, could he?"

"Watch yourself, for God's sake," said William.

She swayed. He crushed her elbow tightly, steering her away.

"Don't faint." He smiled, to make it look good. "You'll be all right. Let's go right in that café, drink in front of him, so if he is what we think he is, he won't suspect."

"No, I couldn't."

"We've *got* to. Come on now. And so I said to David, that's ridiculous!" This last in a loud voice as they went up the café steps.

We are here, thought Susan. Who are we? Where are we going? What do we fear? Start at the beginning, she told herself, holding to her sanity, as she felt the adobe floor underfoot.

My name is Ann Kristen; my husband's name is Roger. We were born in the year A.D. 2155. And we lived in a world that was evil. A world that was like a great black ship pulling away from the shore of sanity and civilization, roaring its black horn in the night, taking two billion people with it, whether they wanted to go or not, to death, to fall over the edge of the earth and the sea into radioactive flame and madness.

They walked into the café. The man was staring at them.

A phone rang.

The phone startled Susan. She remembered a phone ringing two hundred years in the future, on that blue April morning in 2155, and herself answering it.

"Ann, this is Rene! Have you heard? I mean about Travel in Time, Incorporated? Trips to Rome in 21 B.C., trips to Napoleon's Waterloo—any time, any place!"

"Rene, you're joking."

"No. Clinton Smith left this morning for Philadelphia in 1776. Travel in Time, Inc., arranges everything. Costs money. But, *think*—to actually see the burning of Rome, Kubla Khan, Moses and the Red Sea! You've probably got an ad in your tube mail now."

She had opened the suction mail tube and there was the metal foil advertisement:

ROME AND THE BORGIAS!
THE WRIGHT BROTHERS AT KITTY HAWK!

Travel in Time, Inc., can costume you, put you in a crowd during the assassination of Lincoln or Caesar! We guarantee to teach you any language you need to move freely in any civilization, in any year, without friction. Latin, Greek, ancient American colloquial. Take your vacation in *Time* as well as Place!

Rene's voice was buzzing on the phone. "Tom and I leave for 1492 tomorrow. They're arranging for Tom to sail with Columbus. Isn't it amazing!"

"Yes," murmured Ann, stunned. "What does the Government say about this Time Machine company?"

"Oh, the police have an eye on it. Afraid people might evade the draft, run off and hide in the Past. Everyone has to leave a security bond behind, his house and belongings, to guarantee return. After all, the war's on."

"Yes, the war," murmured Ann. "The war."

Standing there, holding the phone, she had thought, Here is the chance my husband and I have talked and prayed over for so many years. We don't like this world of 2155. We want to run away from his work at the bomb factory, I from my position with disease-culture units. Perhaps there is a chance for us to escape, to run for centuries into a wild country of years where they will never find and bring us back to burn our books, censor our thoughts, scald our minds with fear, march us, scream at us with radios . . .

They were in Mexico in the year 1938.

She looked at the stained café wall.

Good workers for the Future State were allowed vacations into the Past to escape fatigue. And so she and her husband had moved back into 1938, a room in New York City, and enjoyed the theaters and the Statue of Liberty which still stood green in the harbor. And on the third day they had changed their clothes, their names, and had flown off to hide in Mexico!

"It *must* be him," whispered Susan, looking at the stranger seated at the table. "Those cigarettes, the cigars, the liquor. They give him away. Remember our first night in the Past?"

A month ago, their first night in New York, before their flight, drinking all the strange drinks, savoring and buying odd foods, perfumes, cigarettes of ten dozen rare brands, for they were rare in the Future, where war was everything. So they had made fools of themselves, rushing in and out of stores, salons, tobacconists, going up to their room to get wonderfully ill.

And now here was this stranger doing likewise, doing a thing that only a man from the Future would do who had been starved for liquors and cigarettes for many years.

Susan and William sat and ordered a drink.

The stranger was examining their clothes, their hair, their jewelry—the way they walked and sat.

"Sit easily," said William under his breath. "Look as if you've worn this clothing style all your life."

"We should never have tried to escape."

"My God!" said William. "He's coming over. Let me do the talking."

The stranger bowed before them. There was the faintest tap of heels knocking together. Susan stiffened. That military sound!—unmistakable as that certain ugly rap on your door at midnight.

"Mr. Roger Kristen," said the stranger, "you did not pull up your pant legs when you sat down."

William froze. He looked at his hands lying on either leg, innocently. Susan's heart was beating swiftly.

"You've got the wrong person," said William quickly. "My name's not Krisler."

"*Kristen*," corrected the stranger.

"I'm William Travis," said William. "And I don't see what my pant legs have to do with you."

"Sorry." The stranger pulled up a chair. "Let us say I thought I knew you because you did *not* pull your trousers up. *Everyone* does. If they don't, the trousers bag quickly. I am a long way from home, Mr.—Travis, and in need of company. My name is Simms."

"Mr. Simms, we appreciate your loneliness, but we're tired. We're leaving for Acapulco tomorrow."

"A charming spot. I was just there, looking for some friends of mine. They are somewhere. I shall find them yet. Oh, is the lady a bit sick?"

"Good night, Mr. Simms."

They started out the door, William holding Susan's arm firmly. They did not look back when Mr. Simms called, "Oh, just one other thing." He paused and then slowly spoke the words:

"A.D. 2155."

Susan shut her eyes and felt the earth falter under her. She kept going, into the fiery plaza, seeing nothing.

They locked the door of their hotel room. And then she was crying and they were standing in the dark, and the room tilted under them. Far away firecrackers exploded, and there was laughter in the plaza.

"What a damned, loud nerve," said William. "Him sitting there, looking us up and down like animals, smoking his damn cigarettes, drinking his drinks. I should have killed him then!" His voice was nearly hysterical. "He even had the nerve to use his real name to us. The Chief of the Searchers. And the thing about my pant legs. My God, I should have pulled them up when I sat. It's an automatic gesture of this day and age. When I didn't do it, it set me off from the others; it made *him* think, Here's a man who never wore pants, a man used to breech uniforms and future styles. I could kill myself for giving us away!"

"No, no, it was my walk—these high heels—that did it. Our haircuts—so new, so fresh. Everything about us odd and uneasy."

He turned on the light. "He's still testing us. He's not positive of us—not completely. We can't run out on him, then. We can't make him certain. We'll go to Acapulco leisurely."

"Maybe he *is* sure of us, but is just playing."

"I wouldn't put it past him. He's got all the time in the world. He can dally here if he wants, and bring us back to the Future sixty seconds after we left it. He might keep us wondering for days, laughing at us."

Susan sat on the bed, wiping the tears from her face, smelling the old smell of charcoal and incense.

"They won't make a scene, will they?"

"They won't dare. They'll have to get us alone to put us in that Time Machine and send us back."

"There's a solution then," she said. "We'll never be alone; we'll always be in crowds. We'll make a million friends, visit markets, sleep in the Official Palaces in each town, pay the Chief of Police to guard us until we find a way to kill Simms and escape, disguise ourselves in new clothes, perhaps as Mexicans."

Footsteps sounded outside their locked door.

They turned out the light and undressed in silence. The footsteps went away. A door closed.

Susan stood by the window looking down at the plaza in the darkness. "So that building there is a church?"

"Yes."

"I've often wondered what a church looked like. It's been so long since anyone saw one. Can we visit it tomorrow?"

"Of course. Come to bed."

They lay in the dark room.

Half an hour later their phone rang. She lifted the receiver.

"Hello?"

"The rabbits may hide in the forest," said a voice, "but a fox can always find them."

She replaced the receiver and lay back straight and cold in the bed.

Outside, in the year 1938, a man played three tunes upon a guitar, one following another.

During the night she put her hand out and almost touched the year 2155. She felt her fingers slide over cool space of time, as over a corrugated surface, and she heard the insistent thump of marching feet, a million bands playing a million military tunes, and she saw the fifty thousand rows of disease cultures in their aseptic glass tubes, her hand reaching out to them at her work in that huge factory in the Future; the tubes of leprosy, bubonic, typhoid, tuberculosis, and then the great explosion. She saw her hand burned to a wrinkled plum, felt it recoil from a concussion so immense that the world was lifted and let fall and all the buildings broke and people hemorrhaged and lay silent. Great volcanoes, machines, winds, avalanches slid down to silence and she awoke, sobbing, in the bed, in Mexico, many years away. . . .

In the early morning, drugged with the single hour's sleep they had finally been able to obtain, they awoke to the sound of loud automobiles in the street. Susan peered down from the iron balcony at a small crowd of eight people only now emerging, chattering, yelling, from trucks and cars with red lettering on them. A crowd of Mexicans had followed the trucks.

"*Qué pasa?*" Susan called to a little boy.

The boy replied.

Susan turned back to her husband. "An American motion-picture company, here on location."

"Sounds interesting." William was in the shower. "Let's watch them. I don't think we'd better leave today. We'll try to lull Simms. Watch the films being made. They say the primitive film-making was something. Get our minds off ourselves."

Ourselves, thought Susan. For a moment in the bright sun, she had forgotten that somewhere in the hotel, waiting, was a man smoking a thousand cigarettes, it seemed. She saw the eight loud happy Americans below and wanted to call to them: "Save me, hide me, help me! Color my hair, my eyes; clothe me in strange clothes. I need your help. I'm from the year 2155!"

But the words stayed in her throat. The functionaries of Travel in Time,

Inc., were not foolish. In your brain, before you left on your trip, they placed a psychological bloc. You could tell no one your true time or birthplace, nor could you reveal any of the Future to those in the Past. The Past and the Future must be protected from each other. Only with this psychological bloc were people allowed to travel unguarded through the ages. The Future must be protected from any change brought about by her people traveling in the Past. Even if she wanted to with all her heart, she could not tell any of those happy people below in the plaza who she was, or what her predicament had become.

"What about breakfast?" said William.

Breakfast was being served in the immense dining room. Ham and eggs for everyone. The place was full of tourists. The film people entered, all eight of them—six men and two women, giggling, shoving chairs about. And Susan sat near them, feeling the warmth and protection they offered, even when Mr. Simms came down the lobby stairs, smoking his Turkish cigarette with great intensity. He nodded at them from a distance, and Susan nodded back, smiling, because he couldn't do anything to them here, in front of eight film people and twenty other tourists.

"Those actors," said William. "Perhaps I could hire two of them, say it was a joke, dress them in our clothes, have them drive off in our car when Simms is in such a spot where he can't see their faces. If two people pretending to be us could lure him off for a few hours, we might make it to Mexico City. It'd take him years to find us there!"

"Hey!"

A fat man, with liquor on his breath, leaned on their table.

"American tourists!" he cried. "I'm so sick of seeing Mexicans, I could kiss you!" He shook their hands. "Come on, eat with us. Misery loves company. I'm Misery, this is Miss Gloom, and Mr. and Mrs. Do-We-Hate-Mexico! We all hate it. But we're here for some preliminary shots for a damn film. The rest of the crew arrives tomorrow. My name's Joe Melton. I'm a director. And if this ain't a hell of a country! Funerals in the streets, people dying. Come on, move over. Join the party; cheer us up!"

Susan and William were both laughing.

"Am I funny?" Mr. Melton asked the immediate world.

"Wonderful!" Susan moved over.

Mr. Simms was glaring across the dining room at them.

She made a face at him.

Mr. Simms advanced among the tables.

"Mr. and Mrs. Travis," he called. "I thought we were breakfasting together, alone."

"Sorry," said William.

"Sit down, pal," said Mr. Melton. "Any friend of theirs is a pal of mine."

Mr. Simms sat. The film people talked loudly, and while they talked, Mr. Simms said quietly, "I hope you slept well."

"Did you?"

"I'm not used to spring mattresses," replied Mr. Simms wryly. "But there are compensations. I stayed up half the night trying new cigarettes and foods. Odd, fascinating. A whole new spectrum of sensation, these ancient vices."

"We don't know what you're talking about," said Susan.

"Always the play acting," Simms laughed. "It's no use. Nor is this strategem of crowds. I'll get you alone soon enough. I'm immensely patient."

"Say," Mr. Melton broke in, his face flushed, "is this guy giving you any trouble?"

"It's all right."

"Say the word and I'll give him the bum's rush."

Melton turned back to yell at his associates. In the laughter, Mr. Simms went on: "Let us come to the point. It took me a month of tracing you through towns and cities to find you, and all of yesterday to be sure of you. If you come with me quietly, I might be able to get you off with no punishment, if you agree to go back to work on the hydrogen-plus bomb."

"Science this guy talks at breakfast!" observed Mr. Melton, half listening.

Simms went on, imperturbably. "Think it over. You can't escape. If you kill me, others will follow you."

"We don't know what you're talking about."

"Stop it!" cried Simms irritably. "Use your intelligence! You know we can't let you get away with this escape. Other people in the year 2155 might get the same idea and do what you've done. We need people."

"To fight your wars," said William at last.

"Bill!"

"It's all right, Susan. We'll talk on his terms now. We can't escape."

"Excellent," said Simms. "Really, you've both been incredibly romantic, running away from your responsibilities."

"Running away from horror."

"Nonsense. Only a war."

"What are you guys talking about?" asked Mr. Melton.

Susan wanted to tell him. But you could only speak in generalities. The psychological bloc in your mind allowed that. Generalities, such as Simms and William were now discussing.

"Only the war," said William. "Half the world dead of leprosy bombs!"

"Nevertheless," Simms pointed out, "the inhabitants of the Future resent you two hiding on a tropical isle, as it were, while they drop off the cliff into hell. Death loves death, not life. Dying people love to know that others die with them. It is a comfort to learn you are not alone in the kiln, in the grave. I am the guardian of their collective resentment against you two."

"Look at the guardian of resentments!" said Mr. Melton to his companions

"The longer you keep me waiting, the harder it will go for you. We need you on the bomb project, Mr. Travis. Return now—no torture. Later, we'll force you to work, and after you've finished the bomb, we'll try a number of complicated new devices on you, sir."

"I've a proposition," said William. "I'll come back with you if my wife stays here alive, safe, away from that war."

Mr. Simms considered it. "All right. Meet me in the plaza in ten minutes. Pick me up in your car. Drive me to a deserted country spot. I'll have the Travel Machine pick us up there."

"Bill!" Susan held his arm tightly.

"Don't argue." He looked over at her. "It's settled." To Simms: "One thing. Last night you could have gotten in our room and kidnaped us. Why didn't you?"

"Shall we say that I was enjoying myself?" replied Mr. Simms languidly, sucking his new cigar. "I hate giving up this wonderful atmosphere, this sun, this vacation. I regret leaving behind the wine and the cigarettes. Oh, how I regret it. The plaza then, in ten minutes. Your wife will be protected and may stay here as long as she wishes. Say your good-bys."

Mr. Simms arose and walked out.

"There goes Mr. Big Talk!" yelled Mr. Melton at the departing gentleman. He turned and looked at Susan. "Hey. Someone's crying. Breakfast's no time for people to cry. Now *is* it?"

At nine-fifteen Susan stood on the balcony of their room, gazing down at the plaza. Mr. Simms was seated there, his neat legs crossed, on a delicate bronze bench. Biting the tip from a cigar, he lit it tenderly.

Susan heard the throb of a motor, and far up the street, out of a garage and down the cobbled hill, slowly, came William in his car.

The car picked up speed. Thirty, now forty, now fifty miles an hour. Chickens scattered before it.

Mr. Simms took off his white panama hat and mopped his pink forehead, put his hat back on, and then saw the car.

It was rushing sixty miles an hour, straight on for the plaza.

"William!" screamed Susan.

The car hit the low plaza curb, thundering; it jumped up, sped across the tiles toward the green bench where Mr. Simms now dropped his cigar, shrieked, flailed his hands, and was hit by the car. His body flew up and up in the air, and down and down, crazily, into the street.

On the far side of the plaza, one front wheel broken, the car stopped. People were running.

Susan went in and closed the balcony doors.

They came down the Official Palace steps together, arm in arm, their faces pale, at twelve noon.

"*Adiós, señor,*" said the Mayor behind them. "*Señora.*"

They stood in the plaza where the crowd was pointing at the blood.

"Will they want to see you again?" asked Susan.

"No, we went over and over it. It was an accident. I lost control of the car. I wept for them. God knows I had to get my relief out somewhere. I *felt* like weeping. I hated to kill him. I've never wanted to do anything like that in my life."

"They won't prosecute you?"

"They talked about it, but no. I talked faster. They believe me. It was an accident. It's over."

"Where will we go? Mexico City? Uruapan?"

"The car's in the repair shop. It'll be ready at four this afternoon. Then we'll get the hell out."

"Will we be followed? Was Simms working alone?"

"I don't know. We'll have a little head start on them, I think."

The film people were coming out of the hotel as they approached. Mr. Melton hurried up, scowling. "Hey I heard what happened. Too bad. Everything okay now? Want to get your minds off it? We're doing some preliminary shots up the street. You want to watch, you're welcome. Come on, do you good."

They went.

They stood on the cobbled street while the film camera was being set up. Susan looked at the road leading down and away, and the highway going to Acapulco and the sea, past pyramids and ruins and little adobe towns with yellow walls, blue walls, purple walls, and flaming bougainvillea, and she thought, We shall take the roads, travel in clusters and crowds, in markets, in lobbies, bribe police to sleep near, keep double locks, but always the crowds, never alone again, always afraid the next person who passes may be another Simms. Never knowing if we've tricked and lost the Searchers. And always up ahead, in the Future, they'll wait for us to be brought back, waiting with their bombs to burn us and disease to rot us, and their police to tell us to roll over, turn around, jump through the hoop! And so we'll keep running through the forest, and we'll never ever stop or sleep well again in our lives.

A crowd gathered to watch the film being made. And Susan watched the crowd and the streets.

"Seen anyone suspicious?"

"No. What time is it?"

"Three o'clock. The car should be almost ready."

The test film was finished at three forty-five. They all walked down to the hotel, talking. William paused at the garage. "The car'll be ready at six," he said, coming out, worried.

"But no later than that?"

"It'll be ready, don't worry."

In the hotel lobby they looked around for other men traveling alone, men who resembled Mr. Simms, men with new haircuts and too much cigarette smoke and cologne smell about them, but the lobby was empty. Going up the stairs, Mr. Melton said, "Well, it's been a long hard day. Who'd like to put a header on it? You folks? Martini? Beer?"

"Maybe one."

The whole crowd pushed into Mr. Melton's room and the drinking began.

"Watch the time," said William.

Time, thought Susan. If only they had time. All she wanted was to sit in the plaza all of a long bright day in October, with not a worry or a thought, with the sun on her face and arms, her eyes closed, smiling at the warmth, and never move. Just sleep in the Mexican sun, and sleep warmly and easily and slowly and happily for many, many days. . . .

Mr. Melton opened the champagne.

"To a very beautiful lady, lovely enough for films," he said, toasting Susan. "I might even give you a test."

She laughed.

"I mean it," said Melton. "You're very nice. I could make you a movie star."

"And take me to Hollywood?" cried Susan.

"Get the hell out of Mexico, sure!"

Susan glanced at William and he lifted an eyebrow and nodded. It would be a change of scene, clothing, locale, name, perhaps; and they would be traveling with eight other people, a good shield against any interference from the Future.

"It sounds wonderful," said Susan.

She was feeling the champagne now. The afternoon was slipping by; the party was whirling about her. She felt safe and good and alive and truly happy for the first time in many years.

"What kind of film would my wife be good for?" asked William, refilling his glass.

Melton appraised Susan. The party stopped laughing and listened.

"Well, I'd like to do a story of suspense," said Melton. "A story of a man and wife, like yourselves."

"Go on."

"Sort of a war story, maybe," said the director, examining the color of his drink against the sunlight.

Susan and William waited.

"A story about a man and wife, who live in a little house on a little street in the year 2155, maybe," said Melton. "This is ad lib, understand. But this man and wife are faced with a terrible war, super-plus hydrogen bombs, censorship, death in that year, and—here's the gimmick—they escape into the Past, followed by a man who they think is evil, but who is only trying to show them what their duty is."

William dropped his glass to the floor.

Mr. Melton continued: "And this couple take refuge with a group of film people whom they learn to trust. Safety in numbers, they say to themselves."

Susan felt herself slip down into a chair. Everyone was watching the director. He took a little sip of champagne. "Ah, that's fine. Well, this man and woman, it seems, don't realize how important they are to the Future. The man, especially, is the keystone to a new bomb metal. So the Searchers, let's call them, spare no trouble or expense to find, capture, and take home the man and wife, once they get them totally alone, in a hotel room, where no one can see. Strategy. The Searchers work alone, or in groups of eight. One trick or another will do it. Don't you think it would make a wonderful film, Susan? Don't you, Bill?" He finished his drink.

Susan sat with her eyes straight ahead of her.

"Have a drink?" said Mr. Melton.

William's gun was out and fired three times, and one of the men fell, and the others ran forward. Susan screamed. A hand was clamped to her mouth. Now the gun was on the floor and William was struggling, held.

Mr. Melton said, "Please," standing there where he had stood, blood showing on his fingers. "Let's not make matters worse."

Someone pounded on the hall door.

"Let me in!"

"The manager," said Mr. Melton dryly. He jerked his head. "Everyone, let's move!"

"Let me in! I'll call the police!"

Susan and William looked at each other quickly, and then at the door.

"The manager wishes to come in," said Mr. Melton. "Quick!"

A camera was carried forward. From it shot a blue light which encompassed the room instantly. It widened out and the people of the party vanished, one by one.

"Quickly!"

Outside the window, in the instant before she vanished, Susan saw the green land and the purple and yellow and blue and crimson walls and the cobbles flowing down like a river, a man upon a burro riding into the warm hills, a boy drinking Orange Crush, she could feel the sweet liquid in her throat, a man standing under a cool plaza tree with a guitar, she could feel her hand upon the strings, and, far away, the sea, the blue and tender sea, she could feel it roll her over and take her in.

And then she was gone. Her husband was gone.

The door burst wide open. The manager and his staff rushed in.

The room was empty.

"But they were just here! I saw them come in, and now—gone!" cried the manager. "The windows are covered with iron grating. They couldn't get out that way!"

In the late afternoon the priest was summoned and they opened the room again and aired it out, and had him sprinkle holy water through each corner and give it his blessing.

"What shall we do with these?" asked the charwoman.

She pointed to the closet, where there were 67 bottles of Chartreuse, cognac, crème de cacao, absinthe, vermouth, tequila, 106 cartons of Turkish cigarettes, and 198 yellow boxes of fifty-cent pure Havana-filler cigars. . . .

Kaleidoscope

The first concussion cut the rocket up the side with a giant can opener. The men were thrown into space like a dozen wriggling silverfish. They were scattered into a dark sea; and the ship, in a million pieces, went on, a meteor swarm seeking a lost sun.

"Barkley, Barkley, where are you?"

The sound of voices calling like lost children on a cold night.

"Woode, Woode!"

"Captain!"

"Hollis, Hollis, this is Stone."

"Stone, this is Hollis. Where are you?"

"I don't know. How can I? Which way is up? I'm falling. Good God, I'm falling."

They fell. They fell as pebbles fall down wells. They were scattered as jackstones are scattered from a gigantic throw. And now instead of men there were only voices—all kinds of voices, disembodied and impassioned, in varying degrees of terror and resignation.

"We're going away from each other."

This was true. Hollis, swinging head over heels, knew this was true. He knew it with a vague acceptance. They were parting to go their separate ways, and nothing could bring them back. They were wearing their sealed-tight space suits with the glass tubes over their pale faces, but they hadn't had time to lock on their force units. With them they could be small lifeboats in space, saving themselves, saving others, collecting together, finding each other until they were an island of men with some plan. But without the force units snapped to their shoulders they were meteors, senseless, each going to a separate and irrevocable fate.

A period of perhaps ten minutes elapsed while the first terror died and a metallic calm took its place. Space began to weave its strange voices in and out, on a great dark loom, crossing, recrossing, making a final pattern.

"Stone to Hollis. How long can we talk by phone?"

"It depends on how fast you're going your way and I'm going mine."

"An hour, I make it."

"That should do it," said Hollis, abstracted and quiet.

"What happened?" asked Hollis a minute later.

"The rocket blew up, that's all. Rockets do blow up."

"Which way are you going?"

"It looks like I'll hit the Moon."

"It's Earth for me. Back to old Mother Earth at ten thousand miles per hour. I'll burn like a match." Hollis thought of it with a queer abstraction of mind. He seemed to be removed from his body, watching it fall down and down through space, as objective as he had been in regard to the first falling snowflakes of a winter season long gone.

The others were silent, thinking of the destiny that had brought them to this, falling, falling, and nothing they could do to change it. Even the captain was quiet, for there was no command or plan he knew that could put things back together again.

"Oh, it's a long way down. Oh, it's a long way down, a long, long, long way down," said a voice. "I don't want to die, I don't want to die, it's a long way down."

"Who's that?"

"I don't know."

"Stimson, I think. Stimson, is that you?"

"It's a long, long way and I don't like it. Oh, God, I don't like it."

"Stimson, this is Hollis. Stimson, you hear me?"

A pause while they fell separate from one another.

"Stimson?"

"Yes." He replied at last.

"Stimson, take it easy; we're all in the same fix."

"I don't want to be here. I want to be somewhere else."

"There's a chance we'll be found."

"I must be, I must be," said Stimson. "I don't believe this; I don't believe any of this is happening."

"It's a bad dream," said someone.

"Shut up!" said Hollis.

"Come and make me," said the voice. It was Applegate. He laughed easily, with a similar objectivity. "Come and shut me up."

Hollis for the first time felt the impossibility of his position. A great anger filled him, for he wanted more than anything at this moment to be able to do something to Applegate. He had wanted for many years to do something and now it was too late. Applegate was only a telephonic voice.

Falling, falling, falling . . .

Now, as if they had discovered the horror, two of the men began to scream. In a nightmare Hollis saw one of them float by, very near, screaming and screaming.

"Stop it!" The man was almost at his fingertips, screaming insanely. He would never stop. He would go on screaming for a million miles, as long as he was in radio range, disturbing all of them, making it impossible for them to talk to one another.

Hollis reached out. It was best this way. He made the extra effort and touched the man. He grasped the man's ankle and pulled himself up along the body until he reached the head. The man screamed and clawed frantically, like a drowning swimmer. The screaming filled the universe.

One way or the other, thought Hollis. The Moon or Earth or meteors will kill him, so why not now?

He smashed the man's glass mask with his iron fist. The screaming stopped. He pushed off from the body and let it spin away on its own course, falling.

Falling, falling down space Hollis and the rest of them went in the long, endless dropping and whirling of silence.

"Hollis, you still there?"

Hollis did not speak, but felt the rush of heat in his face.

"This is Applegate again."

"All right, Applegate."

"Let's talk. We haven't anything else to do."

The captain cut in. "That's enough of that. We've got to figure a way out of this."

"Captain, why don't you shut up?" said Applegate.

"What!"

"You heard me, Captain. Don't pull your rank on me, you're ten thousand miles away by now, and let's not kid ourselves. As Stimson puts it, it's a long way down."

"See here, Applegate!"

"Can it. This is a mutiny of one. I haven't a damn thing to lose. Your ship was a bad ship and you were a bad captain and I hope you break when you hit the Moon."

"I'm ordering you to stop!"

"Go on, order me again." Applegate smiled across ten thousand miles. The captain was silent. Applegate continued, "Where were we, Hollis? Oh yes, I remember. I hate you too. But you know that. You've known it for a long time."

Hollis clenched his fists, helplessly.

"I want to tell you something," said Applegate. "Make you happy. I was the one who blackballed you with the Rocket Company five years ago."

A meteor flashed by. Hollis looked down and his left hand was gone. Blood spurted. Suddenly there was no air in his suit. He had enough air in his lungs to move his right hand over and twist a knob at his left elbow, tightening the joint and sealing the leak. It had happened so quickly that he was not surprised. Nothing surprised him any more. The air in the suit came back to normal in an instant now that the leak was sealed. And the blood that had flowed so swiftly was pressured as he fastened the knob yet tighter, until it made a tourniquet.

All of this took place in a terrible silence on his part. And the other men chatted. That one man, Lespere, went on and on with his talk about his wife on Mars, his wife on Venus, his wife on Jupiter, his money, his wondrous times, his drunkenness, his gambling, his happiness. On and on, while they all fell. Lespere reminisced on the past, happy, while he fell to his death.

It was so very odd. Space, thousands of miles of space, and these voices vibrating in the center of it. No one visible at all, and only the radio waves quivering and trying to quicken other men into emotion.

"Are you angry, Hollis?"

"No." And he was not. The abstraction had returned and he was a thing of dull concrete, forever falling nowhere.

"You wanted to get to the top all your life, Hollis. You always wondered what happened. I put the black mark on you just before I was tossed out myself."

"That isn't important," said Hollis. And it was not. It was gone. When life is over it is like a flicker of bright film, an instant on the screen, all of its prejudices and passions condensed and illumined for an instant on space, and before you could cry out, "There was a happy day, there a bad one, there an evil face, there a good one," the film burned to a cinder, the screen went dark.

From this outer edge of his life, looking back, there was only one remorse, and that was only that he wished to go on living. Did all dying people feel this way, as if they had never lived? Did life seem that short, indeed, over and done before you took a breath? Did it seem this abrupt and impossible to everyone, or only to himself, here, now, with a few hours left to him for thought and deliberation?

One of the other men, Lespere, was talking. "Well, I had me a good time: I had a wife on Mars, Venus, and Jupiter. Each of them had money and treated me swell. I got drunk and once I gambled away twenty thousand dollars."

But you're here now, thought Hollis. I didn't have any of those things. When I was living I was jealous of you, Lespere; when I had another day ahead of me I envied you your women and your good times. Women frightened me and I went into space, always wanting them and jealous of you for having them, and money, and as much happiness as you could have in your own wild way. But now, falling here, with everything over, I'm not jealous of you any more, because it's over for you as it is for me, and right now it's like it never was. Hollis craned his face forward and shouted into the telephone.

"It's all over, Lespere!"

Silence.

"It's just as if it never was, Lespere!"

"Who's that?" Lespere's faltering voice.

"This is Hollis."

He was being mean. He felt the meanness, the senseless meanness of dying. Applegate had hurt him; now he wanted to hurt another. Applegate and space had both wounded him.

"You're out here, Lespere. It's all over. It's just as if it had never happened, isn't it?"

"No."

"When anything's over, it's just like it never happened. Where's your life any better than mine, now? Now is what counts. Is it any better? Is it?"

"Yes, it's better!"

"How!"

"Because I got my thoughts, I remember!" cried Lespere, far away, indignant, holding his memories to his chest with both hands.

And he was right. With a feeling of cold water rushing through his head and body, Hollis knew he was right. There were differences between memories and dreams. He had only dreams of things he had wanted to do, while Lespere had memories of things done and accomplished. And this knowledge began to pull Hollis apart, with a slow, quivering precision.

"What good does it do you?" he cried to Lespere. "Now? When a thing's over it's not good any more. You're no better off than I."

"I'm resting easy," said Lespere. "I've had my turn. I'm not getting mean at the end, like you."

"Mean?" Hollis turned the word on his tongue. He had never been mean, as long as he could remember, in his life. He had never dared to be mean. He must have saved it all of these years for such a time as this. "Mean." He rolled the word into the back of his mind. He felt tears start into his eyes and roll down his face. Someone must have heard his gasping voice.

"Take it easy, Hollis."

It was, of course, ridiculous. Only a minute before he had been giving advice to others, to Stimson; he had felt a braveness which he had thought to be the genuine thing, and now he knew that it had been nothing but shock and the objectivity possible in shock. Now he was trying to pack a lifetime of suppressed emotion into an interval of minutes.

"I know how you feel, Hollis," said Lespere, now twenty thousand miles away, his voice fading. "I don't take it personally."

But aren't we equal? he wondered. Lespere and I? Here, now? If a thing's over, it's done, and what good is it? You die anyway. But he knew he was rationalizing, for it was like trying to tell the difference between a live man and a corpse. There was a spark in one, and not in the other—an aura, a mysterious element.

So it was with Lespere and himself; Lespere had lived a good full life, and it made him a different man now, and he, Hollis, had been as good as dead for many years. They came to death by separate paths and, in all likelihood, if there were kinds of death, their kinds would be as different as night from day. The quality of death, like that of life, must be of an infinite variety, and if one has already died once, then what was there to look for in dying for good and all, as he was now?

It was a second later that he discovered his right foot was cut sheer away. It almost made him laugh. The air was gone from his suit again. He bent quickly, and there was blood, and the meteor had taken flesh and suit away to the ankle. Oh, death in space was most humorous. It cut you away, piece by piece, like a black and invisible butcher. He tightened the valve at the knee, his head whirling into pain, fighting to remain aware, and with the valve tightened, the blood retained, the air kept, he straightened up and went on falling, falling, for that was all there was left to do.

"Hollis?"

Hollis nodded sleepily, tired of waiting for death.

"This is Applegate again," said the voice.

"Yes."

"I've had time to think. I listened to you. This isn't good. It makes us bad. This is a bad way to die. It brings all the bile out. You listening, Hollis?"

"Yes."

"I lied. A minute ago. I lied. I didn't blackball you. I don't know why I said that. Guess I wanted to hurt you. You seemed the one to hurt. We've always fought. Guess I'm getting old fast and repenting fast. I guess listening to you be mean made me ashamed. Whatever the reason, I want you to know I was an idiot too. There's not an ounce of truth in what I said. To hell with you."

Hollis felt his heart begin to work again. It seemed as if it hadn't worked for five minutes, but now all of his limbs began to take color and warmth. The shock was over, and the successive shocks of anger and terror and loneliness were passing. He felt like a man emerging from a cold shower in the morning, ready for breakfast and a new day.

"Thanks, Applegate."

"Don't mention it. Up your nose, you bastard."

"Hey," said Stone.

"What?" Hollis called across space; for Stone, of all of them, was a good friend.

"I've got myself into a meteor swarm, some little asteroids."

"Meteors?"

"I think it's the Myrmidone cluster that goes out past Mars and in toward

Earth once every five years. I'm right in the middle. It's like a big kaleidoscope. You get all kinds of colors and shapes and sizes. God, it's beautiful, all that metal."

Silence.

"I'm going with them," said Stone. "They're taking me off with them. I'll be damned." He laughed.

Hollis looked to see, but saw nothing. There were only the great diamonds and sapphires and emerald mists and velvet inks of space, with God's voice mingling among the crystal fires. There was a kind of wonder and imagination in the thought of Stone going off in the meteor swarm, out past Mars for years and coming in toward Earth every five years, passing in and out of the planet's ken for the next million centuries. Stone and the Myrmidone cluster eternal and unending, shifting and shaping like the kaleidoscope colors when you were a child and held the long tube to the sun and gave it a twirl.

"So long, Hollis." Stone's voice, very faint now. "So long."

"Good luck," shouted Hollis across thirty thousand miles.

"Don't be funny," said Stone, and was gone.

The stars closed in.

Now all the voices were fading, each on his own trajectory, some to Mars, others into farthest space. And Hollis himself . . . He looked down. He, of all the others, was going back to Earth alone.

"So long."

"Take it easy."

"So long, Hollis." That was Applegate.

The many good-bys. The short farewells. And now the great loose brain was disintegrating. The components of the brain which had worked so beautifully and efficiently in the skull case of the rocket ship firing through space were dying one by one; the meaning of their life together was falling apart. And as a body dies when the brain ceases functioning, so the spirit of the ship and their long time together and what they meant to one another was dying. Applegate was now no more than a finger blown from the parent body, no longer to be despised and worked against. The brain was exploded, and the senseless, useless fragments of it were far scattered. The voices faded and now all of space was silent. Hollis was alone, falling.

They were all alone. Their voices had died like echoes of the words of God spoken and vibrating in the starred deep. There went the captain to the Moon; there Stone with the meteor swarm; there Stimson; there Applegate toward Pluto; there Smith and Turner and Underwood and all the rest, the shards of the kaleidoscope that had formed a thinking pattern for so long, hurled apart.

And I? thought Hollis. What can I do? Is there anything I can do now to make up for a terrible and empty life? If only I could do one good thing to make up for the meanness I collected all these years and didn't even know was in me! But there's no one here but myself and how can you do good all alone? You can't. Tomorrow night I'll hit Earth's atmosphere.

I'll burn, he thought, and be scattered in ashes all over the continental lands.

I'll be put to use. Just a little bit, but ashes are ashes and they'll add to the land.

He fell swiftly, like a bullet, like a pebble, like an iron weight, objective, objective all of the time now, not sad or happy or anything, but only wishing he could do a good thing now that everything was gone, a good thing for just himself to know about.

When I hit the atmosphere, I'll burn like a meteor.

"I wonder," he said, "if anyone'll see me?"

The small boy on the country road looked up and screamed. "Look, Mom, look! A falling star!"

The blazing white star fell down the sky of dusk in Illinois.

"Make a wish," said his mother. "Make a wish."

The Rocket Man

The electrical fireflies were hovering above Mother's dark hair to light her path. She stood in her bedroom door looking out at me as I passed in the silent hall. "You *will* help me keep him here this time, won't you?" she asked.

"I guess so," I said.

"Please." The fireflies cast moving bits of light on her white face. "This time he mustn't go away again."

"All right," I said, after standing there a moment. "But it won't do any good; its's no use."

She went away, and the fireflies, on their electric circuits, fluttered after her like an errant constellation, showing her how to walk in darkness. I heard her say, faintly, "We've got to try, anyway."

Other fireflies followed me to my room. When the weight of my body cut a circuit in the bed, the fireflies winked out. It was midnight, and my mother and I waited, our rooms separated by darkness, in bed. The bed began to rock me and sing to me. I touched a switch; the singing and rocking stopped. I didn't want to sleep. I didn't want to sleep at all.

This night was no different from a thousand others in our time. We would wake nights and feel the cool air turn hot, feel the fire in the wind, or see the walls burned a bright color for an instant, and then we knew *his* rocket was over our house—his rocket, and the oak trees swaying from the concussion. And I would lie there, eyes wide, panting, and Mother in her room. Her voice would come to me over the interroom radio:

"Did you feel it?"

And I would answer, "That was him, all right."

That was my father's ship passing over our town, a small town where space rockets never came, and we would lie awake for the next two hours, thinking. "Now Dad's landed in Springfield, now he's on the tarmac, now he is signing the papers, now he's in the helicopter, now he's over the river, now the hills, now he's settling the helicopter in at the little airport at Green Village here. . . ." And the night would be half over when, in our separate cool beds, Mother and I would be listening, listening. "Now he's walking down Bell Street. He always walks . . . never takes a cab . . . now across the park, now turning the corner of Oakhurst and *now* . . . "

I lifted my head from my pillow. Far down the street, coming closer and closer, smartly, quickly, briskly—footsteps. Now turning in at our house, up the porch steps. And we were both smiling in the cool darkness, Mom and I, when we heard the front door open in recognition, speak a quiet word of welcome, and shut, downstairs. . . .

Three hours later I turned the brass knob to their room quietly, holding my breath, balancing in a darkness as big as the space between the planets, my hand out to reach the small black case at the foot of my parents' sleeping bed. Taking it, I ran silently to my room, thinking, He won't tell me, he doesn't want me to *know*.

And from the opened case spilled his black uniform, like a black nebula, stars glittering here or there, distantly, in the material. I kneaded the dark stuff in my warm hands; I smelled the planet Mars, an iron smell, and the planet Venus, a green ivy smell, and the planet Mercury, a scent of sulphur and fire; and I could smell the milky Moon and the hardness of stars. I pushed the uniform into a centrifuge machine I'd built in my ninth-grade shop that year, set it whirling. Soon a fine powder precipitated into a retort. This I slid under a microscope. And while my parents slept unaware, and while our house was asleep, all the automatic bakers and servers and robot cleaners in an electric slumber, I stared down upon brilliant motes of meteor dust, comet tail, and loam from far Jupiter glistening like worlds themselves which drew me down the tube a billion miles into space, at terrific accelerations.

At dawn, exhausted with my journey and fearful of discovery, I returned the boxed uniform to their sleeping room.

Then I slept, only to waken at the sound of the horn of the dry-cleaning car which stopped in the yard below. They took the black uniform box with them. It's good I didn't wait, I thought. For the uniform would be back in an hour, clean of all its destiny and travel.

I slept again, with the little vial of magical dust in my pajama pocket, over my beating heart.

When I came downstairs, there was Dad at the breakfast table, biting into his toast. "Sleep good, Doug?" he said, as if he had been here all the time, and hadn't been gone for three months.

"All right," I said.

"Toast?"

He pressed a button and the breakfast table made me four pieces, golden brown.

I remember my father that afternoon, digging and digging in the garden, like an animal after something, it seemed. There he was with his long dark arms moving swiftly, planting, tamping, fixing, cutting, pruning, his dark face always down to the soil, his eyes always down to what he was doing, never up to the sky, never looking at me, or Mother, even, unless we knelt with him to feel the earth soak up through the overalls at our knees, to put our hands into the black dirt and not look at the bright, crazy sky. Then he would glance to either side, to Mother or me, and give us a gentle wink, and go on, bent down, face down, the sky staring at his back.

That night we sat on the mechanical porch swing which swung us and blew a wind upon us and sang to us. It was summer and moonlight and we had lemonade to drink, and we held the cold glasses in our hands, and Dad read the stereo-newspapers inserted into the special hat you put on your head and which turned the microscopic page in front of the magnifying lens if you blinked three times in succession. Dad smoked cigarettes and told me about how it was when he was a boy in the year 1997. After a while he said, as he had always said, "Why aren't you out playing kick-the-can, Doug?"

I didn't say anything, but Mom said, "He does, on nights when you're not here."

Dad looked at me and then, for the first time that day, at the sky. Mother always watched him when he glanced at the stars. The first day and night when he got home he wouldn't look at the sky much. I thought about him gardening and gardening so furiously, his face almost driven into the earth. But the second night he looked at the stars a little more. Mother wasn't afraid of the sky in the day so much, but it was the night stars that she wanted to turn off, and sometimes I could almost see her reaching for a switch in her mind, but never finding it. And by the third night maybe Dad'd be out here on the porch until way after we were all ready for bed, and then I'd hear Mom call him in, almost like she called me from the street at times. And then I would hear Dad fitting the electric-eye door lock in place, with a sigh. And the next morning at breakfast I'd glance down and see his little black case near his feet as he buttered his toast and Mother slept late.

"Well, be seeing you, Doug," he'd say, and we'd shake hands.

"In about three months?"

"Right."

And he'd walk away down the street, not taking a helicopter or beetle or bus, just walking with his uniform hidden in his small underarm case; he didn't want anyone to think he was vain about being a Rocket Man.

Mother would come out to eat breakfast, one piece of dry toast, about an hour later.

But now it was tonight, the first night, the good night, and he wasn't looking at the stars much at all.

"Let's go to the television carnival," I said.

"Fine," said Dad.

Mother smiled at me.

And we rushed off to town in a helicopter and took Dad through a thousand exhibits, to keep his face and head down with us and not looking anywhere else. And as we laughed at the funny things and looked serious at the serious ones, I thought, My father goes to Saturn and Neptune and Pluto, but he never brings me presents. Other boys' fathers who go into space bring back bits of ore from Callisto and hunks of black meteor or blue sand. But I have to get my own collection, trading from other boys, the Martian rocks and Mercurian sands which filled my room, but about which Dad would never comment.

On occasion, I remembered, he brought something for Mother. He planted some Martian sunflowers once in our yard, but after he was gone a month and the sunflowers grew large, Mom ran out one day and cut them all down.

Without thinking, as we paused at one of the three-dimensional exhibits, I asked Dad the question I always asked:

"What's it like, out in space?"

Mother shot me a frightened glance. It was too late.

Dad stood there for a full half-minute trying to find an answer, then he shrugged.

"It's the best thing in a lifetime of best things." Then he caught himself. "Oh, it's really nothing at all. Routine. You wouldn't like it." He looked at me, apprehensively.

"But you always go back."

"Habit."

"Where're you going next?"

"I haven't decided yet. I'll think it over."

He always thought it over. In those days rocket pilots were rare and he could pick and choose, work when he liked. On the third night of his homecoming you could see him picking and choosing among the stars.

"Come on," said Mother, "let's go home."

It was still early when we got home. I wanted Dad to put on his uniform. I shouldn't have asked—it always made Mother unhappy—but I could not help myself. I kept at him, though he had always refused. I had never seen him in it, and at last he said, "Oh, all right."

We waited in the parlor while he went upstairs in the air flue. Mother looked at me dully, as if she couldn't believe that her own son could do this to her. I glanced away. "I'm sorry," I said.

"You're not helping at all," she said. "At all."

There was a whisper in the air flue a moment later.

"Here I am," said Dad quietly.

We looked at him in his uniform.

It was glossy black with silver buttons and silver rims to the heels of the black boots, and it looked as if someone had cut the arms and legs and body from a dark nebula, with little faint stars glowing through it. It fit as close as a glove fits to a slender long hand, and it smelled like cool air and metal and space. It smelled of fire and time.

Father stood, smiling awkwardly, in the center of the room.

"Turn around," said Mother.

Her eyes were remote, looking at him.

When he was gone, she never talked of him. She never said anything about anything but the weather or the condition of my neck and the need of a washcloth for it, or the fact that she didn't sleep nights. Once she said the light was too strong at night.

"But there's no moon this week," I said.

"There's starlight," she said.

I went to the store and bought her some darker, greener shades. As I lay in bed at night, I could hear her pull them down tight to the bottom of the windows. It made a long rustling noise.

Once I tried to mow the lawn.

"No." Mom stood in the door. "Put the mower away."

So the grass went three months at a time without cutting. Dad cut it when he came home.

She wouldn't let me do anything else either, like repairing the electrical breakfast maker or the mechanical book reader. She saved everything up, as if for Christmas. And then I would see Dad hammering or tinkering, and always smiling at his work, and Mother smiled over him, happy.

No, she never talked of him when he was gone. And as for Dad, he never did anything to make a contact across the millions of miles. He said once, "If I called you, I'd want to be with you. I wouldn't be happy."

Once Dad said to me, "Your mother treats me, sometimes, as if I weren't here—as if I were invisible."

I had seen her do it. She would look just beyond him, over his shoulder, at his chin or hands, but never into his eyes. If she did look at his eyes, her eyes were covered with a film, like an animal going to sleep. She said yes at the right times, and smiled, but always a half second later than expected.

"I'm not there for her," said Dad.

But other days she would be there and he would be there for her, and they would hold hands and walk around the block, or take rides, with Mom's hair flying like a girl's behind her, and she would cut off all the mechanical devices in the kitchen and bake him incredible cakes and pies and cookies, looking deep into his face, her smile a real smile. But at the end of such days when he was there to her, she would always cry. And Dad would stand helpless, gazing about the room as if to find the answer, but never finding it.

Dad turned slowly, in his uniform, for us to see.

"Turn around again," said Mom.

The next morning Dad came rushing into the house with handfuls of tickets. Pink rocket tickets for California, blue tickets for Mexico.

"Come on!" he said. "We'll buy disposable clothes and burn them when they're soiled. Look, we take the noon rocket to L.A., the two-o'clock helicopter to Santa Barbara, the nine o'clock plane to Ensenada, sleep overnight!"

And we went to California and up and down the Pacific Coast for a day and a half, settling at last on the sands of Malibu to cook wieners at night. Dad was always listening or singing or watching things on all sides of him, holding on to things as if the world were a centrifuge going so swiftly that he might be flung off away from us at any instant.

The last afternoon at Malibu Mom was up in the hotel room. Dad lay on the sand beside me for a long time in the hot sun. "Ah," he sighed, "this is it." His eyes were gently closed; he lay on his back, drinking the sun. "You *miss* this," he said.

He meant "on the rocket," of course. But he never said "the rocket" or mentioned the rocket and all the things you couldn't have on the rocket. You couldn't have a salt wind on the rocket or a blue sky or a yellow sun or Mom's cooking. You couldn't talk to your fourteen-year-old boy on a rocket.

"Let's hear it," he said at last.

And I knew that now we would talk, as we had always talked, for three hours straight. All afternoon we would murmur back and forth in the lazy sun about my school grades, how high I could jump, how fast I could swim.

Dad nodded each time I spoke and smiled and slapped my chest lightly in approval. We talked. We did not talk of rockets or space, but we talked of Mexico, where we had driven once in an ancient car, and of the butterflies we had caught in the rain forests of green warm Mexico at noon, seeing the hundred butterflies sucked to our radiator, dying there, beating their blue and crimson wings, twitching, beautiful, and sad. We talked of such things instead of the things I wanted to talk about. And he listened to me. That was the thing he did, as if he was trying to fill himself up with all the sound he could hear. He listened to the wind and the falling ocean and my voice, always with a rapt attention, a concentration that almost excluded physical bodies themselves and kept only the sounds. He shut his eyes to listen. I would see him listening to the lawn mower as he cut the grass by hand instead of using the remote-control device, and I would see him smelling the cut grass as it sprayed up at him behind the mower in a green fount.

"Doug," he said, about five in the afternoon, as we were picking up our towels and heading back along the beach near the surf, "I want you to promise me something."

"What?"

"Don't ever be a Rocket Man."

I stopped.

"I mean it," he said. "Because when you're out there you want to be here, and when you're here you want to be out there. Don't start that. Don't let it get hold of you."

"But—"

"You don't know what it is. Every time I'm out there I think, If I ever get back to Earth I'll stay there; I'll never go out again. But I go out, and I guess I'll always go out."

"I've thought about being a Rocket Man for a long time," I said.

He didn't hear me. "I *try* to stay here. Last Saturday when I got home I started trying so damned hard to *stay* here."

I remembered him in the garden, sweating, and all the traveling and doing and listening, and I knew that he did this to convince himself that the sea and the towns and the land and his family were the only real things and the good things. But I knew where he would be tonight: looking at the jewelry in Orion from our front porch.

"Promise me you won't be like me," he said.

I hesitated awhile. "Okay," I said.

He shook my hand. "Good boy," he said.

The dinner was fine that night. Mom had run about the kitchen with handfuls of cinnamon and dough and pots and pans tinkling, and now a great turkey fumed on the table, with dressing, cranberry sauce, peas, and pumpkin pie.

"In the middle of August?" said Dad, amazed.

"You won't be here for Thanksgiving."

"So I won't."

He sniffed it. He lifted each lid from each tureen and let the flavor steam over his sunburned face. He said "Ah" to each. He looked at the room and his hands. He gazed at the pictures on the wall, the chairs, the table, me, and Mom. He cleared his throat. I saw him make up his mind. "Lilly?"

"Yes?" Mom looked across her table which she had set like a wonderful silver trap, a miraculous gravy pit in which, like a struggling beast of the past caught in a tar pool, her husband might at last be caught and held, gazing out through a jail of wishbones, safe forever. Her eyes sparkled.

"Lilly," said Dad.

Go on, I thought crazily. Say it quick: say you'll stay home this time, for good, and never go away; say it!

Just then a passing helicopter jarred the room and the windowpane shook with a crystal sound. Dad glanced at the window.

The blue stars of evening were there, and the red planet Mars was rising in the East.

Dad looked at Mars a full minute. Then he put his hand out blindly toward me. "May I have some peas," he said.

"Excuse me," said Mother. "I'm going to get some bread."

She rushed out into the kitchen.

"But there's bread on the table," I said.

Dad didn't look at me as he began his meal.

I couldn't sleep that night. I came downstairs at one in the morning and the moonlight was like ice on all the housetops, and dew glittered in a snow field on our grass. I stood in the doorway in my pajamas, feeling the warm night wind, and then I knew that Dad was sitting in the mechanical porch swing, gliding gently. I could see his profile tilted back, and he was watching the stars wheel over the sky. His eyes were like gray crystal there, the Moon in each one.

I went out and sat beside him.

We glided awhile in the swing.

At last I said, "How many ways are there to die in space?"

"A million."

"Name some."

"The meteors hit you. The air goes out of your rocket. Or comets take you along with them. Concussion. Strangulation. Explosion. Centrifugal force. Too much acceleration. Too little. The heat, the cold, the sun, the Moon, the stars, the planets, the asteroids, the planetoids, radiation . . ."

"And do they bury you?"

"They never find you."

"Where do you go?"

"A billion miles away. Traveling graves, they call them. You become a meteor or a planetoid traveling forever through space."

I said nothing.

"One thing," he said later, "it's quick in space. Death. It's over like that.

You don't linger. Most of the time you don't even know it. You're dead and that's it."

We went up to bed.

It was morning.

Standing in the doorway, Dad listened to the yellow canary singing in its golden cage.

"Well, I've decided," he said. "Next time I come home, I'm home to stay."

"Dad!" I said.

"Tell your mother that when she gets up," he said.

"You *mean* it!"

He nodded gravely. "See you in about three months."

And there he went off down the street, carrying his uniform in its secret box, whistling and looking at the tall green trees and picking chinaberries off the chinaberry bush as he brushed by, tossing them ahead of him as he walked away into the bright shade of early morning. . . .

I asked Mother about a few things that morning after Father had been gone a number of hours. "Dad said that sometimes you don't act as if you hear or see him," I said.

And then she explained everything to me quietly.

"When he went off into space ten years ago, I said to myself, He's dead. Or as good as dead. So think of him dead. And when he comes back, three or four times a year, it's not him at all, it's only a pleasant little memory or a dream. And if a memory stops or a dream stops, it can't hurt half as much. So most of the time I think of him dead—"

"But other times—"

"Other times I can't help myself. I bake pies and treat him as if he were alive, and then it hurts. No, it's better to think he hasn't been here for ten years and I'll never see him again. It doesn't hurt as much."

"Didn't he say next time he'd settle down?"

She shook her head slowly. "No, he's dead. I'm very sure of that."

"He'll come alive again, then," I said.

"Ten years ago," said Mother, "I thought, What if he dies on Venus? Then we'll never be able to see Venus again. What if he dies on Mars? We'll never be able to look at Mars again, all red in the sky, without wanting to go in and lock the door. Or what if he died on Jupiter or Saturn or Neptune? On those nights when those planets were high in the sky, we wouldn't want to have anything to do with the stars."

"I guess not," I said.

The message came the next day.

The messenger gave it to me and I read it standing on the porch. The sun was setting. Mom stood in the screen door behind me, watching me fold the message and put it in my pocket.

"Mom," I said.

"Don't tell me anything I don't already know," she said.

She didn't cry.

Well, it wasn't Mars, and it wasn't Venus, and it wasn't Jupiter or Saturn that killed him. We wouldn't have to think of him every time Jupiter or Saturn or Mars lit up the evening sky.

This was different.

His ship had fallen into the sun.

And the sun was big and fiery and merciless, and it was always in the sky and you couldn't get away from it.

So for a long time after my father died my mother slept through the days and wouldn't go out. We had breakfast at midnight and lunch at three in the morning, and dinner at the cold dim hour of 6 A.M. We went to all-night shows and went to bed at sunrise.

And, for a long while, the only days we ever went out to walk were the days when it was raining and there was no sun.

Marionettes, Inc.

They walked slowly down the street at about ten in the evening, talking calmly. They were both about thirty-five, both eminently sober.

"But why so early?" said Smith.

"Because," said Braling.

"Your first night out in years and you go home at ten o'clock."

"Nerves, I suppose."

"What I wonder *is* how you ever managed it. I've been trying to get you out for ten years for a quiet drink. And now, on the one night, you insist on turning in early."

"Mustn't crowd my luck," said Braling.

"What did you do, put sleeping powder in your wife's coffee?"

"No, that would be unethical. You'll see soon enough."

They turned a corner. "Honestly, Braling, I hate to say this, but you *have* been patient with her. You may not admit it to me, but marriage has been awful for you, hasn't it?"

"I wouldn't say that."

"It's got around, anyway, here and there, how she got you to marry her. That time back in 1979 when you were going to Rio—"

"Dear Rio. I never *did* see it after all my plans."

"And how she tore her clothes and rumpled her hair and threatened to call the police unless you married her."

"She always was nervous, Smith, understand."

"It was more than unfair. You didn't love her. You told her as much, didn't you?"

"I recall that I was quite firm on the subject."

"But you married her anyhow."

"I had my business to think of, as well as my mother and father. A thing like that would have killed them."

"And it's been ten years."

"Yes," said Braling, his gray eyes steady. "But I think perhaps it might change now. I think what I've waited for has come about. Look here."

He drew forth a long blue ticket.

"Why, it's a ticket for Rio on the Thursday rocket!"

"Yes, I'm finally going to make it."

"But how wonderful! You *do* deserve it! But won't *she* object? Cause trouble?"

Braling smiled nervously. "She won't know I'm gone. I'll be back in a month and no one the wiser, except you."

Smith sighed. "I wish I were going with you."

"Poor Smith, *your* marriage hasn't exactly been roses, has it?"

"Not exactly, married to a woman who overdoes it. I mean, after all, when you've been married ten years, you don't expect a woman to sit on your lap for two hours every evening, call you at work twelve times a day and talk baby talk. And it seems to me that in the last month she's gotten worse. I wonder if perhaps she isn't a little simple-minded?"

"Ah, Smith, always the conservative. Well, here's my house. Now, would you like to know my secret? How I made it out this evening?"

"Will you really tell?"

"Look up, there!" said Braling.

They both stared up through the dark air.

In the window above them, on the second floor, a shade was raised. A man about thirty-five years old, with a touch of gray at either temple, sad gray eyes, and a small thin mustache looked down at them.

"Why, that's *you*!" cried Smith.

"Sh-h-h, not so loud!" Braling waved upward. The man in the window gestured significantly and vanished.

"I must be insane," said Smith.

"Hold on a moment."

They waited.

The street door of the apartment opened and the tall spare gentleman with the mustache and the grieved eyes came out to meet them.

"Hello, Braling," he said.

"Hello, Braling," said Braling.

They were identical.

Smith stared. "Is this your twin brother? I never knew—"

"No, no," said Braling quietly. "Bend close. Put your ear to Braling Two's chest."

Smith hesitated and then leaned forward to place his head against the uncomplaining ribs.

Tick-tick-tick-tick-tick-tick-tick-tick.

"Oh no! It *can't* be!"

"It is."

"Let me listen again."

Tick-tick-tick-tick-tick-tick-tick-tick.

Smith staggered back and fluttered his eyelids, appalled. He reached out and touched the warm hands and the cheeks of the thing.

"Where'd you get him?"

"Isn't he excellently fashioned?"

"Incredible. Where?"

"Give the man your card, Braling Two."

Braling Two did a magic trick and produced a white card:

> MARIONETTES, INC.
> Duplicate self or friends; new humanoid plastic 1990
> models, guaranteed against all physical wear. From
> $7,600 to our $15,000 de luxe model.

"No," said Smith.

"Yes," said Braling.

"Naturally," said Braling Two.

"How long has this gone on?"

"I've had him for a month. I keep him in the cellar in a toolbox. My wife never goes downstairs, and I have the only lock and key to that box. Tonight I said I wished to take a walk to buy a cigar. I went down cellar and took Braling Two out of his box and sent him back up to sit with my wife while I came on out to see you, Smith."

"Wonderful! He even *smells* like you: Bond Street and Melachrinos!"

"It may be splitting hairs, but I think it highly ethical. After all, what my wife wants most of all is *me*. This marionette *is* me to the hairiest detail. I've been home all evening. I shall be home with her for the next month. In the meantime another gentleman will be in Rio after ten years of waiting. When I return from Rio, Braling Two here will go back in his box."

Smith thought that over a minute or two. "Will he walk around without sustenance for a month?" he finally asked.

"For six months if necessary. And he's built to do everything—eat, sleep, perspire—everything, natural as natural is. You'll take good care of my wife, won't you, Braling Two?"

"Your wife is rather nice," said Braling Two. "I've grown rather fond of her."

Smith was beginning to tremble. "How long has Marionettes, Inc., been in business?"

"Secretly, for two years."

"Could I—I mean, is there a possibility—" Smith took his friend's elbow earnestly. "Can you tell me where I can get one, a robot, a marionette, for myself? You *will* give me the address, won't you?"

"Here you are."

Smith took the card and turned it round and round. "Thank you," he said. "You don't know what this means. Just a little respite. A night or so, once a month even. My wife loves me so much she can't bear to have me gone an hour. I love her dearly, you know, but remember the old poem: 'Love will fly if held too lightly, love will die if held too tightly.' I just want her to relax her grip a little bit."

"You're lucky, at least, that your wife loves you. Hate's my problem. Not so easy."

"Oh, Nettie loves me madly. It will be my task to make her love me comfortably."

"Good luck to you, Smith. Do drop around while I'm in Rio. It will seem strange, if you suddenly stop calling by, to my wife. You're to treat Braling Two, here, just like me."

"Right! Good-by. And thank you."

Smith went smiling down the street. Braling and Braling Two turned and walked into the apartment hall.

On the crosstown bus Smith whistled softly, turning the white card in his fingers:

> Clients must be pledged to secrecy, for while an act is
> pending in Congress to legalize Marionettes, Inc., it
> is still a felony, if caught, to use one.

"Well," said Smith.

> Clients must have a mold made of their body and a
> color index check of their eyes, lips, hair, skin, etc.
> Clients must expect to wait for two months until
> their model is finished.

Not so long, thought Smith. Two months from now my ribs will have a chance to mend from the crushing they've taken. Two months from now my hand will heal from being so constantly held. Two months from now my bruised underlip will begin to reshape itself. I don't mean to sound *ungrateful.* . . . He flipped the card over.

> Marionettes, Inc., is two years old and has a fine record of satisfied customers behind it. Our motto is "No Strings Attached." Address: 43 South Wesley Drive.

The bus pulled to his stop; he alighted, and while humming up the stairs he thought, Nettie and I have fifteen thousand in our joint bank account. I'll just slip eight thousand out as a business venture, you might say. The marionette will probably pay back my money, with interest, in many ways. Nettie needn't know. He unlocked the door and in a minute was in the bedroom. There lay Nettie, pale, huge, and piously asleep.

"Dear Nettie." He was almost overwhelmed with remorse at her innocent face there in the semidarkness. "If you were awake you would smother me with kisses and coo in my ear. Really, you make me feel like a criminal. You have been such a good, loving wife. Sometimes it is impossible for me to believe you married me instead of that Bud Chapman you once liked. It seems that in the last month you have loved me more wildly than *ever* before."

Tears came to his eyes. Suddenly he wished to kiss her, confess his love, tear up the card, forget the whole business. But as he moved to do this, his hand ached and his ribs cracked and groaned. He stopped, with a pained look in his eyes, and turned away. He moved out into the hall and through the dark rooms. Humming, he opened the kidney desk in the library and filched the bankbook. "Just take eight thousand dollars is all," he said. "No more than that." He stopped. "Wait a minute."

He rechecked the bankbook frantically. "Hold on here!" he cried. "Ten thousand dollars is missing!" He leaped up. "There's only five thousand left! What's she done? What's Nettie done with it? More hats, more clothes, more perfume! Or, wait—I know! She bought that little house on the Hudson she's been talking about for months, without so much as a by your leave!"

He stormed into the bedroom, righteous and indignant. What did she mean, taking their money like this? He bent over her. "Nettie!" he shouted. "Nettie, wake up!"

She did not stir. "What've you done with my money!" he bellowed.

She stirred fitfully. The light from the street flushed over her beautiful cheeks.

There was something about her. His heart throbbed violently. His tongue dried. He shivered. His knees suddenly turned to water. He collapsed. "Nettie, Nettie!" he cried. "What've you done with my money!"

And then, the horrid thought. And then the terror and the loneliness engulfed him. And then the fever and disillusionment. For, without desiring to do so, he bent forward and yet forward again until his fevered ear was resting

firmly and irrevocably upon her round pink bosom. "Nettie!" he cried.
Tick-tick-tick-tick-tick-tick-tick-tick-tick-tick-tick.

As Smith walked away down the avenue in the night, Braling and Braling Two turned in at the door to the apartment. "I'm glad he'll be happy too," said Braling.

"Yes," said Braling Two abstractedly.

"Well, it's the cellar box for you, B-Two." Braling guided the other creature's elbow down the stairs to the cellar.

"That's what I want to talk to you about," said Braling Two, as they reached the concrete floor and walked across it. "The cellar. I don't like it. I don't like that toolbox."

"I'll try and fix up something more comfortable."

"Marionettes are made to move, not lie still. How would you like to lie in a box most of the time?"

"Well—"

"You wouldn't like it at all. I keep running. There's no way to shut me off. I'm perfectly alive and I have feelings."

"It'll only be a few days now. I'll be off to Rio and you won't have to stay in the box. You can live upstairs."

Braling Two gestured irritably. "And when you come back from having a good time, back in the box I go."

Braling said, "They didn't tell me at the marionette shop that I'd get a difficult specimen."

"There's a lot they don't know about us," said Braling Two. "We're pretty new. And we're sensitive. I hate the idea of you going off and laughing and lying in the sun in Rio while we're stuck here in the cold."

"But I've wanted that trip all my life," said Braling quietly.

He squinted his eyes and could see the sea and the mountains and the yellow sand. The sound of the waves was good to his inward mind. The sun was fine on his bared shoulders. The wine was most excellent.

"*I'll* never get to go to Rio," said the other man. "Have you thought of that?"

"No, I—"

"And another thing. Your wife."

"What about her?" asked Braling, beginning to edge toward the door.

"I've grown quite fond of her."

"I'm glad you're enjoying your employment." Braling licked his lips nervously.

"I'm afraid you don't understand. I think—I'm in love with her."

Braling took another step and froze. "You're *what?*"

"And I've been thinking," said Braling Two, "how nice it is in Rio and how I'll never get there, and I've thought about your wife and—I think we could be very happy."

"Th-that's nice." Braling strolled as casually as he could to the cellar door. "You won't mind waiting a moment, will you? I have to make a phone call."

"To whom?" Braling Two frowned.

"No one important."

"To Marionettes, Incorporated? To tell them to come get me?"

"No, no—nothing like that!" He tried to rush out the door.

A metal-firm grip seized his wrists. "Don't run!"

"Take your hands off!"

"No."

"Did my wife put you up to this?"

"No."

"Did she guess? Did she talk to you? Does she know? Is *that* it?" He screamed. A hand clapped over his mouth.

"You'll never know, will you?" Braling Two smiled delicately. "You'll never know."

Braling struggled. "She *must* have guessed; she *must* have affected you!"

Braling Two said, "I'm going to put you in the box, lock it, and lose the key. Then I'll buy another Rio ticket for your wife."

"Now, now, wait a minute. Hold on. Don't be rash. Let's talk this over!"

"Good-by, Braling."

Braling stiffened. "What do you mean, 'good-by'?"

Ten minutes later Mrs. Braling awoke. She put her hand to her cheek. Someone had just kissed it. She shivered and looked up. "Why—you haven't done that in years," she murmured.

"We'll see what we can do about that," someone said.

No Particular Night
or Morning

He had smoked a packet of cigarettes in two hours.

"How far out in space are we?"

"A billion miles."

"A billion miles from where?" said Hitchcock.

"It all depends," said Clemens, not smoking at all. "A billion miles from home, you might say."

"Then say it."

"Home. Earth. New York. Chicago. Wherever you were from."

"I don't even remember," said Hitchcock. "I don't even believe there is an Earth now, do you?"

"Yes," said Clemens. "I dreamt about it this morning."

"There is no morning in space."

"During the night then."

"It's always night," said Hitchcock quietly. "Which night do you mean?"

"Shut up," said Clemens irritably. "Let me finish."

Hitchcock lit another cigarette. His hand did not shake, but it looked as if, inside the sunburned flesh, it might be tremoring all to itself, a small tremor in each hand and a large invisible tremor in his body. The two men sat on the observation corridor floor, looking out at the stars. Clemens's eyes flashed, but Hitchcock's eyes focused on nothing; they were blank and puzzled.

"I woke up at 0500 hours myself," said Hitchcock, as if he were talking to his right hand. "And I heard myself screaming, 'Where am I? where am I?' And the answer was 'Nowhere!' And I said, 'Where've I been?' And I said, 'Earth!' 'What's Earth?' I wondered. 'Where I was born,' I said. But it was nothing and worse than nothing. I don't believe in anything I can't see or hear or touch. I can't see Earth, so why should I believe in it? It's safer this way, not to believe."

"There's Earth." Clemens pointed, smiling. "That point of light there."

"That's not Earth; that's our sun. You can't see Earth from here."

"I can see it. I have a good memory."

"It's not the *same*, you fool," said Hitchcock suddenly. There was a touch of anger in his voice. "I mean *see* it. I've always been that way. When I'm in Boston, New York is dead. When I'm in New York, Boston is dead. When I don't *see* a man for a day, he's dead. When he comes walking down the street, my God, it's a resurrection. I do a dance, almost, I'm so glad to see him. I used to, anyway. I don't dance any more. I just look. And when the man walks off, he's dead again."

Clemens laughed. "It's simply that your mind works on a primitive level. You can't hold on to things. You've got no imagination, Hitchcock, old man. You've got to learn to hold on."

"Why should I hold on to things I can't use?" said Hitchcock, his eyes wide, still staring into space. "I'm practical. If Earth isn't here for me to walk on, you want me to walk on a memory? That *hurts*. Memories, as my father once said, are porcupines. To hell with them! Stay away from them. They make you unhappy. They ruin your work. They make you cry."

"I'm walking on Earth right now," said Clemens, squinting to himself, blowing smoke.

"You're kicking porcupines. Later in the day you won't be able to eat lunch, and you'll wonder why," said Hitchcock in a dead voice. "And it'll be because you've got a footful of quills aching in you. To hell with it! If I can't drink it, pinch it, punch it, or lie on it, then I say drop it in the sun. I'm dead to Earth. It's dead to me. There's no one in New York weeping for me tonight. Shove New York. There isn't any season here; winter and summer are gone. So is spring, and autumn. It isn't any particular night or morning; it's space and space. The only thing right now is you and me and this rocket ship. And the only thing I'm positive of is *me*. That's all of it."

Clemens ignored this. "I'm putting a dime in the phone slot right now," he said, pantomiming it with a slow smile. "And calling my girl in Evanston. Hello, Barbara!"

The rocket sailed on through space.

The lunch bell rang at 1305 hours. The men ran by on soft rubber sneakers and sat at the cushioned tables.

Clemens wasn't hungry.

"See, what did I tell you!" said Hitchcock. "You and your damned porcupines! Leave them alone, like I told you. Look at me, shoveling away food." He said this with a mechanical, slow, and unhumorous voice. "Watch me." He put a big piece of pie in his mouth and felt it with his tongue. He looked at the pie on his plate as if to see the texture. He moved it with his fork. He felt the fork handle. He mashed the lemon filling and watched it jet up between the tines. Then he touched a bottle of milk all over and poured out half a quart into a glass, listening to it. He looked at the milk as if to make it whiter. He drank the milk so swiftly that he couldn't have tasted it. He had eaten his entire lunch in a few minutes, cramming it in feverishly, and now he looked around for more, but it was gone. He gazed out the window of the rocket, blankly. "Those aren't real either," he said.

"What?" asked Clemens.

"The stars. Who's ever touched one? I can see them, sure, but what's the use of seeing a thing that's a million or a billion miles away? Anything that far off isn't worth bothering with."

"Why did you come on this trip?" asked Clemens suddenly.

Hitchcock peered into his amazingly empty milk glass and clenched it tight, then relaxed his hand and clenched it again. "I don't know." He ran his tongue on the glass rim. "I just had to, is all. How do you know why you do anything in this life?"

"You liked the idea of space travel? Going places?"

"I don't know. Yes. No. It wasn't going places. It was being between." Hitchcock for the first time tried to focus his eyes upon something, but it was so nebulous and far off that his eyes couldn't make the adjustment, though he worked his face and hands. "Mostly it was space. So much space. I liked the idea of nothing on top, nothing on the bottom, and a lot of nothing in between, and me in the middle of the nothing."

"I never heard it put that way before."

"*I* just put it that way; I hope you listened."

Hitchcock took out his cigarettes and lit up and began to suck and blow smoke, again and again.

Clemens said, "What sort of childhood did you have, Hitchcock?"

"I was never young. Whoever I was then is dead. That's more of your quills. I don't want a hideful, thanks. I've always figured it that you die each day and each day is a box, you see, all numbered and neat; but never go back and lift the lids, because you've died a couple of thousand times in your life, and that's a lot of corpses, each dead a different way, each with a worse expression. Each of those days is a different you, somebody you don't know or understand or want to understand."

"You're cutting yourself off, that way."

"Why should I have anything to do with that younger Hitchcock? He was a fool, and he was yanked around and taken advantage of and used. His father was no good, and he was glad when his mother died, because she was the same. Should I go back and see his face on that day and gloat over it? He was a fool."

"We're all fools," said Clemens, "all the time. It's just we're a different kind each day. We think, I'm not a fool today. I've learned my lesson. I was a fool yesterday but not this morning. Then tomorrow we find out that, yes, we were a fool today too. I think the only way we can grow and get on in this world is to accept the fact that we're not perfect and live accordingly."

"I don't want to remember imperfect things," said Hitchcock. "I can't shake hands with that younger Hitchcock, can I? Where is he? Can you find him for me? He's dead, so to hell with him! I won't shape what I do tomorrow by some lousy thing I did yesterday."

"You've got it wrong."

"Let me have it then." Hitchcock sat, finished with his meal, looking out the port. The other men glanced at him.

"Do meteors exist?" asked Hitchcock.

"You know damn well they do."

"In our radar machines—yes, as streaks of light in space. No, I don't believe in anything that doesn't exist and act in my presence. Sometimes"—he nodded at the men finishing their food—"sometimes I don't believe in anyone or anything but me." He sat up. "Is there an upstairs to this ship?"

"Yes."

"I've got to see it immediately."

"Don't get excited."

"You wait here; I'll be right back." Hitchcock walked out swiftly. The other men sat nibbling their food slowly. A moment passed. One of the men raised his head. "How long's this been going on? I mean Hitchcock."

"Just today."

"He acted funny the other day too."

"Yes, but it's worse today."

"Has anyone told the psychiatrist?"

"We thought he'd come out of it. Everyone has a little touch of space the first time out. I've had it. You get wildly philosophical, then frightened. You break into a sweat, then you doubt your parentage, you don't believe in Earth, you get drunk, wake up with a hang-over, and that's it."

"But Hitchcock don't get drunk," said someone. "I wish he would."

"How'd he ever get past the examining board?"

"How'd we all get past? They need men. Space scares the hell out of most people. So the board lets a lot of borderlines through."

"That man isn't a borderline," said someone. "He's a fall-off-a-cliff-and-no-bottom-to-hit."

They waited for five minutes. Hitchcock didn't come back.

Clemens finally got up and went out and climbed the circular stair to the flight deck above. Hitchcock was there, touching the wall tenderly.

"It's here," he said.

"Of course it is."

"I was afraid it might not be." Hitchcock peered at Clemens. "And you're alive."

"I have been for a long time."

"No," said Hitchcock. "Now, just now, this *instant*, while you're here with me, you're alive. A moment ago you weren't anything."

"I was to me," said the other.

"That's not important. You weren't here with me," said Hitchcock. "Only that's important. Is the crew down below?"

"Yes."

"Can you prove it?"

"Look, Hitchcock, you'd better see Dr. Edwards. I think you need a little servicing."

"No, I'm all right. Who's the doctor, anyway? Can you prove he's on this ship?"

"I can. All I have to do is call him."

"No. I mean, standing here, in this instant, you can't prove he's here, can you?"

"Not without moving, I can't."

"You see. You have no mental evidence. That's what I want, a mental evidence I can *feel*. I don't want physical evidence, proof you have to go out and drag in. I want evidence that you can carry in your mind and always touch and smell and feel. But there's no way to do that. In order to believe in a thing you've got to carry it with you. You can't carry the Earth, or a man, in your pocket. I want a way to do that, carry things with me always, so I can believe in them. How clumsy to have to go to all the trouble of going out and bringing in something terribly physical to prove something. I hate physical things because they can be left behind and it becomes impossible to believe in them."

"Those are the rules of the game."

"I want to change them. Wouldn't it be fine if we could prove things with our mind, and know for certain that things are always in their place? I'd like to know what a place is *like* when I'm *not there*. I'd like to be *sure*."

"That's not possible."

"You know," said Hitchcock, "I first got the idea of coming out into space about five years ago. About the time I lost my job. Did you know I wanted to be a writer? Oh yes, one of those men who always talk about writing but rarely write. And too much temper. So I lost my good job and left the editorial business and couldn't get another job and went on down hill. Then my wife died. You see, nothing stays where you put it—you can't trust material things. I had to put my boy in an aunt's trust, and things got worse; then one day I had a story published with my name on it, but it wasn't me."

"I don't get you."

Hitchcock's face was pale and sweating.

"I can only say that I looked at the page with my name under the title. By Joseph Hitchcock. But it was some other man. There was no way to *prove*—actually *prove*, *really* prove—that that man was me. The story was familiar—I knew I had written it—but that name on the paper still was not me. It was a symbol, a name. It was alien. And then I realized that even if I did become successful at writing, it would never mean a thing to me, because I couldn't identify myself with that name. It would be soot and ashes. So I didn't write any more. I was never sure, anyway, that the stories I had in my desk a few days later were mine, though I remembered typing them. There was always that gap of proof. That gap between doing and having done. What is done is dead and is not proof, for it is not an action. Only actions are important. And pieces of paper were remains of actions done and over and now unseen. The proof of doing was over and done. Nothing but memory remained, and I didn't trust my memory. Could I actually *prove* I'd written these stories? No. Can *any* author? I mean *proof*. I mean action as proof. No. Not really. Not unless someone sits in the room while you type, and then maybe you're doing it from memory. And once a thing is accomplished there is no proof, only memory. So then I began to find gaps between everything. I doubted I was married or had a child or ever had a job in my life. I doubted that I had been born in Illinois and had a drunken father and swinish mother. I couldn't prove anything. Oh yes, people could say, 'You are thus-and-so and such-and-such,' but that was nothing."

"You should get your mind off stuff like that," said Clemens.

"I can't. All the gaps and spaces. And that's how I got to thinking about the stars. I thought how I'd like to be in a rocket ship in space, in nothing, in *nothing*, going on into nothing with just a thin something, a thin eggshell of metal holding me, going on away from all the somethings with gaps in them that couldn't prove themselves. I knew then that the only happiness for me was space. When I get to Aldebaran II I'll sign up to return on the five-year journey to Earth and so go back and forth like a shuttlecock all the rest of my life."

"Have you talked about this to the psychiatrist?"

"So he could try to mortar up the gaps for me, fill in the gulfs with noise and warm water and words and hands touching me, and all that? No, thanks." Hitchcock stopped. "I'm getting worse, aren't I? I thought so. This morning when I woke up I thought, I'm getting worse. Or is it better?" He paused again and cocked an eye at Clemens. "Are you there? Are you *really* there? Go on, prove it."

Clemens slapped him on the arm, hard.

"Yes," said Hitchcock, rubbing his arm, looking at it very thoroughly, wonderingly, massaging it. "You were there. For a brief fraction of an instant. But I wonder if you are—*now*."

"See you later," said Clemens. He was on his way to find the doctor. He walked away.

A bell rang. Two bells, three bells rang. The ship rocked as if a hand had slapped it. There was a sucking sound, the sound of a vacuum cleaner turned on. Clemens heard the screams and felt the air thin. The air hissed away about his ears. Suddenly there was nothing in his nose or lungs. He stumbled and then the hissing stopped.

He heard someone cry, "A meteor!" Another said, "It's patched!" And this was true. The ship's emergency spider, running over the outside of the hull, had slapped a hot patch on the hole in the metal and welded it tight.

Someone was talking and talking and then beginning to shout at a distance. Clemens ran along the corridor through the freshening, thickening air. As he turned in at a bulkhead he saw the hole in the steel wall, freshly sealed; he saw the meteor fragments lying about the room like bits of a toy. He saw the captain and the members of the crew and a man lying on the floor. It was Hitchcock. His eyes were closed and he was crying. "It tried to kill me," he said, over and over. "It tried to kill me." They got him on his feet. "It can't do that," said Hitchcock. "That's not how it should be. Things like that can't happen, can they? It came in after *me*. Why did it do that?"

"All right, all right, Hitchcock," said the captain.

The doctor was bandaging a small cut on Hitchcock's arm. Hitchcock looked up, his face pale, and saw Clemens there looking at him. "It tried to *kill* me," he said.

"I know," said Clemens.

Seventeen hours passed. The ship moved on in space.

Clemens stepped through a bulkhead and waited. The psychiatrist and the captain were there. Hitchcock sat on the floor with his legs drawn up to his chest, arms wrapped tight about them.

"Hitchcock," said the captain.

No answer.

"Hitchcock, listen to me," said the psychiatrist.

They turned to Clemens. "You're his friend?"

"Yes."

"Do you want to help us?"

"If I can."

"It was that damned meteor," said the captain. "This might not have happened if it hadn't been for that."

"It would've come anyway, sooner or later," said the doctor. To Clemens: "You might talk to him."

Clemens walked quietly over and crouched by Hitchcock and began to shake his arm gently, calling in a low voice, "Hey there, Hitchcock."

No reply.

"Hey, it's me. Me, Clemens," said Clemens. "Look, I'm here." He gave the arm a little slap. He massaged the rigid neck, gently, and the back of the bent-down head. He glanced at the psychiatrist, who sighed very softly. The captain shrugged.

"Shock treatment, Doctor?"

The psychiatrist nodded. "We'll start within the hour."

Yes, thought Clemens, shock treatment. Play a dozen jazz records for him, wave a bottle of fresh green chlorophyll and dandelions under his nose, put grass under his feet, squirt Chanel on the air, cut his hair, clip his fingernails, bring him a woman, shout, bang and crash at him, fry him with electricity, fill the gap and the gulf, but where's your proof? You can't keep proving to him forever. You can't entertain a baby with rattles and sirens all night every night for the next thirty years. Sometime you've got to stop. When you do that, he's lost again. That is, if he pays any attention to you at all.

"Hitchcock!" he cried, as loud as he could, almost frantically, as if he himself were falling over a cliff. "It's me. It's your pal! Hey!"

Clemens turned and walked away out of the silent room.

Twelve hours later another alarm bell rang.

After all of the running had died down, the captain explained: "Hitchcock snapped out of it for a minute or so. He was alone. He climbed into a space suit. He opened an airlock. Then he walked out into space—alone."

Clemens blinked through the immense glass port, where there was a blur of stars and distant blackness. "He's out there now?"

"Yes. A million miles behind us. We'd never find him. First time I knew he was outside the ship was when his helmet radio came in on our control-room beam. I heard him talking to himself."

"What did he say?"

"Something like 'No more space ship now. Never was any. No people. No people in all the universe. Never were any. No plants. No stars.' That's what he said. And then he said something about his hands and feet and legs. 'No hands,' he said. 'I haven't any hands any more. Never had any. No feet. Never had any.

Can't prove it. No body. Never had any. No lips. No face. No head. Nothing. Only space. Only space. Only the gap."

The men turned quietly to look from the glass port out into the remote and cold stars.

Space, thought Clemens. The space that Hitchcock loved so well. Space, with nothing on top, nothing on the bottom, a lot of empty nothings between, and Hitchcock falling in the middle of the nothing, on his way to no particular night and no particular morning. . . .

The City

The city waited twenty thousand years.

The planet moved through space and the flowers of the fields grew up and fell away, and still the city waited; and the rivers of the planet rose and waned and turned to dust. Still the city waited. The winds that had been young and wild grew old and serene, and the clouds of the sky that had been ripped and torn were left alone to drift in idle whitenesses. Still the city waited.

The city waited with its windows and its black obsidian walls and its sky towers and its unpennanted turrets, with its untrod streets and its untouched doorknobs, with not a scrap of paper or a fingerprint upon it. The city waited while the planet arced in space, following its orbit about a blue-white sun, and the seasons passed from ice to fire and back to ice and then to green fields and yellow summer meadows.

It was on a summer afternoon in the middle of the twenty thousandth year that the city ceased waiting.

In the sky a rocket appeared.

The rocket soared over, turned, came back, and landed in the shale meadow fifty yards from the obsidian wall.

There were booted footsteps in the thin grass and calling voices from men within the rocket to men without.

"Ready?"

"All right, men. Careful! Into the city. Jensen, you and Hutchinson patrol ahead. Keep a sharp eye."

The city opened secret nostrils in its black walls and a steady suction vent deep in the body of the city drew storms of air back through channels, through thistle filters and dust collectors, to a fine and tremblingly delicate series of coils and webs which glowed with silver light. Again and again the immense suctions occurred; again and again the odors from the meadow were borne upon warm winds into the city.

"Fire odor, the scent of a fallen meteor, hot metal. A ship has come from another world. The brass smell, the dusty fire smell of burned powder, sulphur, and rocket brimstone."

This information, stamped on tapes which sprocketed into slots, slid down through yellow cogs into further machines.

Click-chakk-chakk-chakk.

A calculator made the sound of a metronome. Five, six, seven, eight, nine. Nine men! An instantaneous typewriter inked this message on tape which slithered and vanished.

Clickety-click-chakk-chakk.

The city awaited the soft tread of their rubberoid boots.

The great city nostrils dilated again.

The smell of butter. In the city air, from the stalking men, faintly, the aura which wafted to the great Nose broke down into memories of milk, cheese, ice cream, butter, the effluvia of a dairy economy.

Click-click.

"Careful, men!"

"Jones, get your gun out. Don't be a fool!"

"The city's dead; why worry?"

"You can't tell."

Now, at the barking talk, the Ears awoke. After centuries of listening to winds that blew small and faint, of hearing leaves strip from trees and grass grow softly in the time of melting snows, now the Ears oiled themselves in a self-lubrication, drew taut, great drums upon which the heartbeat of the invaders might pummel and thud delicately as the tremor of a gnat's wing. The Ears listened and the Nose siphoned up great chambers of odor.

The perspiration of frightened men arose. There were islands of sweat under their arms, and sweat in their hands as they held their guns.

The Nose sifted and worried this air, like a connoisseur busy with an ancient vintage.

Chikk-chikk-chakk-click.

Information rotated down on parallel check tapes. Perspiration; chlorides such-and-such percent; sulphates so-and-so; urea nitrogen, ammonia nitrogen, *thus*: creatinine, sugar, lactic acid, *there!*

Bells rang. Small totals jumped up.

The Nose whispered, expelling the tested air. The great Ears listened:

"I think we should go back to the rocket, Captain."

"I give the orders, Mr. Smith!"

"Yes, sir."

"You, up there! Patrol! *See* anything?"

"Nothing, sir. Looks like it's been dead a long time!"

"You see, Smith? Nothing to fear."

"I don't like it. I don't know why. You ever feel you've seen a place before? Well, this city's too familiar."

"Nonsense. This planetary system's billions of miles from Earth; we couldn't possibly've been here ever before. Ours is the only light-year rocket in existence."

"That's how I feel, anyway, sir. I think we should get out."

The footsteps faltered. There was only the sound of the intruder's breath on the still air.

The Ear heard and quickened. Rotors glided, liquids glittered in small creeks through valves and blowers. A formula and a concoction—one followed another. Moments later, responding to the summons of the Ear and Nose, through giant holes in the city walls a fresh vapor blew out over the invaders.

"Smell *that*, Smith? Ahh. Green grass. Ever smell anything better? By God, I just like to stand here and smell it."

Invisible chlorophyll blew among the standing men.

"*Ahh!*"

The footsteps continued.

"Nothing wrong with *that*, eh, Smith? Come on!"

The Ear and Nose relaxed a billionth of a fraction. The countermove had succeeded. The pawns were proceeding forward.

Now the cloudy Eyes of the city moved out of fog and mist.

"Captain, the windows!"

"What?"

"Those house windows, there! I saw them move!"

"*I* didn't see it."

"They shifted. They changed color. From dark to light."

"Look like ordinary square windows to me."

Blurred objects focused. In the mechanical ravines of the city oiled shafts plunged, balance wheels dipped over into green oil pools. The window frames flexed. The windows gleamed.

Below, in the street, walked two men, a patrol, followed, at a safe interval, by seven more. Their uniforms were white, their faces as pink as if they had been slapped; their eyes were blue. They walked upright, upon hind legs, carrying metal weapons. Their feet were booted. They were males, with eyes, ears, mouths, noses.

The windows trembled. The windows thinned. They dilated imperceptibly, like the irises of numberless eyes.

"I tell you, Captain, it's the windows!"

"Get along."

"I'm going back, sir."

"What?"

"I'm going back to the rocket."

"Mr. Smith!"

"I'm not falling into any trap!"

"Afraid of an empty city?"

The others laughed, uneasily.

"Go on, laugh!"

The street was stone-cobbled, each stone three inches wide, six inches long. With a move unrecognizable as such, the street settled. It weighed the invaders.

In a machine cellar a red wand touched a numeral: 178 pounds . . . 210, 154, 201, 198—each man weighed, registered and the record spooled down into a correlative darkness.

Now the city was fully awake!

Now the vents sucked and blew air, the tobacco odor from the invaders' mouths, the green soap scent from their hands. Even their eyeballs had a delicate odor. The city detected it, and this information formed totals which scurried down to total other totals. The crystal windows glittered, the Ear tautened and skinned the drum of its hearing tight, tighter—all of the senses of the city swarming like a fall of unseen snow, counting the respiration and the dim hidden heartbeats of the men, listening, watching, tasting.

For the streets were like tongues, and where the men passed, the taste of their heels ebbed down through stone pores to be calculated on litmus. This chemical totality, so subtly collected, was appended to the now increasing sums waiting the final calculation among the whirling wheels and whispering spokes.

Footsteps. Running.

"Come back! Smith!"

"No, blast you!"

"Get him, men!"

Footsteps rushing.

A final test. The city, having listened, watched, tasted, felt, weighed, and balanced, must perform a final task.

A trap flung wide in the street. The captain, unseen by the others, running, vanished.

Hung by his feet, a razor drawn across his throat, another down his chest, his carcass instantly emptied of its entrails, exposed upon a table under the street, in a hidden cell, the captain died. Great crystal microscopes stared at the red twines of muscle; bodiless fingers probed the still-pulsing heart. The flaps of his sliced skin were pinned to the table while hands shifted parts of his body like a quick and curious player of chess, using the red pawns and the red pieces.

Above on the street the men ran. Smith ran, men shouted. Smith shouted, and below in this curious room blood flowed into capsules, was shaken, spun, shoved on smear slides under further microscopes, counts made, temperatures taken, heart cut in seventeen sections, liver and kidneys expertly halved. Brain was drilled and scooped from bone socket, nerves pulled forth like the dead wires of a switchboard, muscles plucked for elasticity, while in the electric subterrene of the city the Mind at last totaled out its grandest total and all of the machinery ground to a monstrous and momentary halt.

The total.

These are men. These are men from a far world, a certain planet, and they have certain eyes, certain ears, and they walk upon legs in a specified way and carry weapons and think and fight, and they have particular hearts and all such organs as are recorded from long ago.

Above, men ran down the street toward the rocket.

Smith ran.

The total.

These are our enemies. These are the ones we have waited for twenty thousand years to see again. These are the men upon whom we waited to visit revenge. Everything totals. These are the men of a planet called Earth, who declared war upon Taollan twenty thousand years ago, who kept us in slavery and ruined us and destroyed us with a great disease. Then they went off to live in another galaxy to escape that disease which they visited upon us after ransacking our world. They have forgotten that war and that time, and they have forgotten us. But we have not forgotten them. These are our enemies. This is certain. Our waiting is done.

"Smith, come back!"

Quickly. Upon the red table, with the spread-eagled captain's body empty, new hands began a flight of motion. Into the wet interior were placed organs of copper, brass, silver, aluminum, rubber and silk; spiders spun gold web which was stung into the skin; a heart was attached, and into the skull case was fitted a platinum brain which hummed and fluttered small sparkles of blue fire, and the wires led down through the body to the arms and legs. In a moment the body was sewn tight, the incisions waxed, healed at neck and throat and about the skull—perfect, fresh, new.

The captain sat up and flexed his arms.

"Stop!"

On the street the captain reappeared, raised his gun and fired.

Smith fell, a bullet in his heart.

The other men turned.

The captain ran to them.

"That fool! Afraid of a city!"

They looked at the body of Smith at their feet.

They looked at their captain, and their eyes widened and narrowed.

"Listen to me," said the captain. "I have something important to tell you."

Now the city, which had weighed and tasted and smelled them, which had used all its powers save one, prepared to use its final ability, the power of speech. It did not speak with the rage and hostility of its massed walls or towers, nor with the bulk of its cobbled avenues and fortresses of machinery. It spoke with the quiet voice of one man.

"I am no longer your captain," he said. "Nor am I a man."

The men moved back.

"I am the city," he said, and smiled.

"I've waited two hundred centuries," he said. "I've waited for the sons of the sons of the sons to return."

"Captain, sir!"

"Let me continue. Who built me? The city. The men who died built me. The old race who once lived here. The people whom the Earth Men left to die of a terrible disease, a form of leprosy with no cure. And the men of that old race, dreaming of the day when Earth Men might return, built this city, and the name of this city was and is Revenge, upon the Planet of Darkness, near the shore of the Sea of Centuries, by the Mountains of the Dead; all very poetic. This city was to be a balancing machine, a litmus, an antenna to test all future space travelers. In twenty thousand years only two other rockets landed here. One from a distant galaxy called Ennt, and the inhabitants of that craft were tested, weighed, found wanting, and let free, unscathed, from the city. As were the visitors in the second ship. But today! At long last, you've come! The revenge will be carried out to the last detail. Those men have been dead two hundred centuries, but they left a city here to welcome you."

"Captain, sir, you're not feeling well. Perhaps you'd better come back to the ship, sir."

The city trembled.

The pavements opened and the men fell, screaming. Falling, they saw bright razors flash to meet them!

Time passed. Soon came the call:

"Smith?"

"Here!"

"Jensen?"

"Here!"

"Jones, Hutchinson, Springer?"

"Here!" "Here!" "Here!"

They stood by the door of the rocket.

"We return to Earth immediately."

"Yes, sir!"

The incisions on their necks were invisible, as were their hidden brass hearts and silver organs and the fine golden wire of their nerves. There was a faint electric hum from their heads.

"On the double!"

Nine men hurried the golden bombs of disease culture into the rocket.

"These are to be dropped on Earth."

"Right, sir!"

The rocket valve slammed. The rocket jumped into the sky.

As the thunder faded, the city lay upon the summer meadow. Its glass eyes were dulled over. The Ear relaxed, the great nostril vents stopped, the streets no longer weighed or balanced, and the hidden machinery paused in its bath of oil.

In the sky the rocket dwindled.

Slowly, pleasurably, the city enjoyed the luxury of dying.

The Fire Balloons

Fire exploded over summer night lawns. You saw sparkling faces of uncles and aunts. Skyrockets fell up in the brown shining eyes of cousins on the porch, and the cold charred sticks thumped down in dry meadows far away.

The Very Reverend Father Joseph Daniel Peregrine opened his eyes. What a dream: he and his cousins with their fiery play at his grandfather's ancient Ohio home so many years ago!

He lay listening to the great hollow of the church, the other cells where other Fathers lay. Had they, too, on the eve of the flight of the rocket *Crucifix*, lain with memories of the Fourth of July? Yes. This was like those breathless Independence dawns when you waited for the first concussion and rushed out on the dewy sidewalks, your hands full of loud miracles.

So here they were, the Episcopal Fathers, in the breathing dawn before they pinwheeled off to Mars, leaving their incense through the velvet cathedral of space.

"Should we go at all?" whispered Father Peregrine. "Shouldn't we solve our own sins on Earth? Aren't we running from our lives here?"

He arose, his fleshy body, with its rich look of strawberries, milk, and steak, moving heavily.

"Or is it sloth?" he wondered. "Do I dread the journey?"

He stepped into the needle-spray shower.

"But I shall take you to Mars, body." He addressed himself. "Leaving old sins here. And on to Mars to find *new* sins?" A delightful thought, almost. Sins no one had ever thought of. Oh, he himself had written a little book: *The Problem of Sin on Other Worlds*, ignored as somehow not serious enough by his Episcopal brethren.

Only last night, over a final cigar, he and Father Stone had talked of it.

"On Mars sin might appear as virtue. We must guard against virtuous acts there that, later, might be found to be sins!" said Father Peregrine, beaming. "How exciting! It's been centuries since so much adventure has accompanied the prospect of being a missionary!"

"*I* will recognize sin," said Father Stone bluntly, "*even* on Mars."

"Oh, we priests pride ourselves on being litmus paper, changing color in sin's presence," retorted Father Peregrine, "but what if Martian chemistry is such we do not color *at all*! If there are new senses on Mars, you must admit the possibility of unrecognizable sin."

"If there is no malice aforethought, there is no sin or punishment for same—the Lord assures us that," Father Stone replied.

"On Earth, yes. But perhaps a Martian sin might inform the subconscious of its evil, telepathically, leaving the conscious mind of man free to act, seemingly without malice! What *then*?"

"What *could* there be in the way of new sins?"

Father Peregrine leaned heavily forward. "Adam *alone* did not sin. Add Eve and you add temptation. Add a second man and you make adultery possible. With the addition of sex or people, you add sin. If men were armless they could not strangle with their hands. You would not have that particular sin of murder. Add arms, and you add the possibility of a new violence. Amoebas cannot sin because they reproduce by fission. They do not covet wives or murder each other. Add sex to amoebas, add arms and legs, and you would have murder and adultery. Add an arm or leg or person, or take away each, and you add or subtract possible evil. On Mars, what if there are five new senses, organs, invisible limbs we can't conceive of—then mightn't there be five *new sins*?"

Father Stone gasped. "I think you *enjoy* this sort of thing!"

"I keep my mind alive, Father; just alive, is all."

"Your mind's always juggling, isn't it?—mirrors, torches, plates."

"Yes. Because sometimes the Church seems like those posed circus tableaus where the curtain lifts and men, white, zinc-oxide, talcum-powder statues, freeze to represent abstract Beauty. Very wonderful. But I hope there will always be room for me to dart about among the statues, don't you, Father Stone?"

Father Stone had moved away. "I think we'd better go to bed. In a few hours we'll be jumping up to see your *new* sins, Father Peregrine."

The rocket stood ready for the firing.

The Fathers walked from their devotions in the chilly morning, many a fine priest from New York or Chicago or Los Angeles—the Church was sending its best—walking across town to the frosty field. Walking, Father Peregrine remembered the Bishop's words:

"Father Peregrine, you will captain the missionaries, with Father Stone at your side. Having chosen you for this serious task, I find my reasons deplorably obscure, Father, but your pamphlet on planetary sin did not go unread. You are a flexible man. And Mars is like that uncleaned closet we have neglected for millenniums. Sin has collected there like bric-a-brac. Mars is twice Earth's age and has had double the number of Saturday nights, liquor baths, and eye-poppings at women as naked as white seals. When we open that closet door, things will fall on us. We need a quick, flexible man—one whose mind can dodge. Anyone a little too dogmatic might break in two. I feel you'll be resilient. Father, the job is yours."

The Bishop and the Fathers knelt.

The blessing was said and the rocket given a little shower of holy water. Arising, the Bishop addressed them:

"I know you will go with God, to prepare the Martians for the reception of His Truth. I wish you all a *thoughtful* journey."

They filed past the Bishop, twenty men, robes whispering, to deliver their hands into his kind hands before passing into the cleansed projectile.

"I wonder," said Father Peregrine, at the last moment, "if Mars is Hell? Only waiting for our arrival before it bursts into brimstone and fire."

"Lord, be with us," said Father Stone.

The rocket moved.

Coming out of space was like coming out of the most beautiful cathedral they had ever seen. Touching Mars was like touching the ordinary pavement outside the church five minutes after having *really* known your love for God.

The Fathers stepped gingerly from the steaming rocket and knelt upon Martian sand while Father Peregrine gave thanks.

"Lord, we thank Thee for the journey through Thy rooms. And, Lord, we have reached a new land, so we must have new eyes. We shall hear new sounds and must needs have new ears. And there will be new sins, for which we ask the gift of better and firmer and purer hearts. Amen."

They arose.

And here was Mars like a sea under which they trudged in the guise of submarine biologists, seeking life. Here the territory of hidden sin. Oh, how carefully they must all balance, like gray feathers, in this new element, afraid that walking *itself* might be sinful; or breathing, or simple fasting!

And here was the mayor of First Town come to meet them with outstretched hand. "What can I do for you, Father Peregrine?"

"We'd like to know about the Martians. For only if we know about them can we plan our church intelligently. Are they ten feet tall? We will build large doors. Are their skins blue or red or green? We must know when we put human figures in the stained glass so we may use the right skin color. Are they heavy? We will build sturdy seats for them."

"Father," said the mayor, "I don't think you should worry about the Martians. There are two races. One of them is pretty well dead. A few are in hiding. And the second race—well, they're not quite human."

"Oh?" Father Peregrine's heart quickened.

"They're round luminous globes of light, Father, living in those hills. Man or beast, who can say? But they act intelligently, I hear." The mayor shrugged. "Of course, they're not men, so I don't think you'll care—"

"On the contrary," said Father Peregrine swiftly. "Intelligent, you say?"

"There's a story. A prospector broke his leg in those hills and would have died there. The blue spheres of light came at him. When he woke, he was down on a highway and didn't know how he got there."

"Drunk," said Father Stone.

"That's the story," said the mayor. "Father Peregrine, with most of the Martians dead, and only these blue spheres, I frankly think you'd be better off in First City. Mars is opening up. It's a frontier now, like in the old days on Earth, out West, and in Alaska. Men are pouring up here. There's a couple thousand black Irish mechanics and miners and day laborers in First Town who need saving, because there're too many wicked women came with them, and too much ten-century-old Martian wine—"

Father Peregrine was gazing into the soft blue hills.

Father Stone cleared his throat. "Well, Father?"

Father Peregrine did not hear. "Spheres of blue *fire?*"

"Yes, Father."

"Ah," Father Peregrine sighed.

"Blue balloons." Father Stone shook his head. "A circus!"

Father Peregrine felt his wrists pounding. He saw the little frontier town with raw, fresh-built sin, and he saw the hills, old with the oldest and yet perhaps an even newer (to him) sin.

"Mayor, could your black Irish laborers cook one more day in hellfire?"

"I'd turn and baste them for you, Father."

Father Peregrine nodded to the hills. "Then that's where we'll go."

There was a murmur from everyone.

"It would be so simple," explained Father Peregrine, "to go into town. I prefer to think that if the Lord walked here and people said, 'Here is the beaten path,' He would reply, 'Show me the weeds. I will *make* a path.'"

"But—"

"Father Stone, think how it would weigh upon us if we passed sinners by and did not extend our hands."

"But globes of fire!"

"I imagine man looked funny to other animals when we first appeared. Yet he has a soul, for all his homeliness. Until we prove otherwise, let us assume that these fiery spheres have souls."

"All right," agreed the mayor, "but you'll be back to town."

"We'll see. First, some breakfast. Then you and I, Father Stone, will walk alone into the hills. I don't want to frighten those fiery Martians with machines or crowds. Shall we have breakfast?"

The Fathers ate in silence.

At nightfall Father Peregrine and Father Stone were high in the hills. They stopped and sat upon a rock to enjoy a moment of relaxation and waiting. The Martians had not as yet appeared and they both felt vaguely disappointed.

"I wonder—" Father Peregrine mopped his face. "Do you think if we called 'Hello!' they might answer?"

"Father Peregrine, won't you ever be serious?"

"Not until the good Lord is. Oh, don't look so terribly shocked, please. The Lord is not serious. In fact, it is a little hard to know just what else He is except loving. And love has to do with humor, doesn't it? For you cannot love someone unless you put up with him, can you? And you cannot put up with someone constantly unless you can laugh at him. Isn't that true? And certainly we are ridiculous little animals wallowing in the fudge bowl, and God must love us all the more because we appeal to His humor."

"*I* never thought of God as humorous," said Father Stone.

"The Creator of the platypus, the camel, the ostrich, and man? Oh, come now!" Father Peregrine laughed.

But at this instant, from among the twilight hills, like a series of blue lamps lit to guide their way, came the Martians.

Father Stone saw them first. "Look!"

Father Peregrine turned and the laughter stopped in his mouth.

The round blue globes of fire hovered among the twinkling stars, distantly trembling.

"Monsters!" Father Stone leaped up. But Father Peregrine caught him. "Wait!"

"We should've gone to town!"

"No, listen, look!" pleaded Father Peregrine.

"I'm afraid!"

"Don't be. This is God's work!"

"The devil's!"

"No, now, quiet!" Father Peregrine gentled him and they crouched with the soft blue light on their upturned faces as the fiery orbs drew near.

And again, Independence Night, thought Father Peregrine, tremoring. He felt like a child back in those July Fourth evenings, the sky blowing apart, breaking into powdery stars and burning sound, the concussions jingling house windows like the ice on a thousand thin ponds. The aunts, uncles, cousins crying, "Ah!" as to some celestial physician. The summer sky colors. And the Fire Balloons, lit by an indulgent grandfather, steadied in his massively tender hands. Oh, the memory of those lovely Fire Balloons, softly lighted, warmly billowed bits of tissue, like insect wings, lying like folded wasps in boxes and, last of all, after the day of riot and fury, at long last from their boxes, delicately unfolded, blue, red, white, patriotic—the Fire Balloons! He saw the dim faces of dear relatives long dead and mantled with moss as Grandfather lit the tiny candle and let the warm air breathe up to form the balloon plumply luminous in his hands, a shining vision which they held, reluctant to let it go; for, once released, it was yet another year gone from life, another Fourth, another bit of Beauty vanished. And then up, up, still up through the warm summer night constellations, the Fire Balloons had drifted, while red-white-and-blue eyes followed them, wordless, from family porches. Away into deep Illinois country, over night rivers and sleeping mansions the Fire Balloons dwindled, forever gone. . . .

Father Peregrine felt tears in his eyes. Above him the Martians, not one but a *thousand* whispering Fire Balloons, it seemed, hovered. Any moment he might find his long-dead and blessed grandfather at his elbow, staring up at Beauty.

But it was Father Stone.

"Let's go, please, Father!"

"I must speak to them." Father Peregrine rustled forward, not knowing what to say, for what had he ever said to the Fire Balloons of time past except with his mind: *you are beautiful, you are beautiful*, and that was not enough now. He could only lift his heavy arms and call upward, as he had often wished to call after the enchanted Fire Balloons, "Hello!"

But the fiery spheres only burned like images in a dark mirror. They seemed fixed, gaseous, miraculous, forever.

"We come with God," said Father Peregrine to the sky.

"Silly, silly, silly." Father Stone chewed the back of his hand. "In the name of God, Father Peregrine, stop!"

But now the phosphorescent spheres blew away into the hills. In a moment they were gone.

Father Peregrine called again, and the echo of his last cry shook the hills above. Turning, he saw an avalanche shake out dust, pause, and then, with a thunder of stone wheels, crash down the mountain upon them.

"Look what you've done!" cried Father Stone.

Father Peregrine was almost fascinated, then horrified. He turned, knowing they could run only a few feet before the rocks crushed them into ruins. He had time to whisper, *Oh, Lord!* and the rocks fell!

"Father!"

They were separated like chaff from wheat. There was a blue shimmering of globes, a shift of cold stars, a roar, and then they stood upon a ledge two hundred feet away watching the spot where their bodies should have been buried under tons of stone.

The blue light evaporated.

The two Fathers clutched each other. "What happened?"

"The blue fires lifted us!"

"We ran, *that* was it!"

"No, the globes saved us."

"They couldn't!"

"They *did*."

The sky was empty. There was a feel as if a great bell had just stopped tolling. Reverberations lingered in their teeth and marrow.

"Let's get away from here. You'll have us killed."

"I haven't feared death for a good many years, Father Stone."

"We've proved nothing. Those blue lights ran off at the first cry. It's useless."

"No." Father Peregrine was suffused with a stubborn wonder. "Somehow, they saved us. That proves they have souls."

"It proves only that they *might* have saved us. Everything was confused. We might have escaped, ourselves."

"They are not animals, Father Stone. Animals do not save lives, especially of strangers. There is mercy and compassion here. Perhaps, tomorrow, we may prove more."

"Prove what? How?" Father Stone was immensely tired now; the outrage to his mind and body showed on his stiff face. "Follow them in helicopters, reading chapter and verse? They're not human. They haven't eyes or ears or bodies like ours."

"But I feel something about them," replied Father Peregrine. "I know a great revelation is at hand. They saved us. They *think*. They had a choice; let us live or die. That proves free will!"

Father Stone set to work building a fire, glaring at the sticks in his hands, choking on the gray smoke. "I myself will open a convent for nursling geese, a monastery for sainted swine, and I shall build a miniature apse in a microscope so that paramecium can attend services and tell their beads with their flagella."

"Oh, Father Stone."

"I'm sorry." Father Stone blinked redly across the fire. "But this is like blessing a crocodile before he chews you up. You're risking the entire missionary expedition. We belong in First Town, washing liquor from men's throats and perfume off their hands!"

"Can't you recognize the human in the inhuman?"

"I'd much rather recognize the inhuman in the human."

"But if I prove these things sin, know sin, know a moral life, have free will and intellect, Father Stone?"

"That will take much convincing."

The night grew rapidly cold and they peered into the fire to find their wildest thoughts, while eating biscuits and berries, and soon they were bundled for sleep under the chiming stars. And just before turning over one last time Father Stone, who had been thinking for many minutes to find something to bother Father Peregrine about, stared into the soft pink charcoal bed and said, "No Adam and Eve on Mars. No Original Sin. Maybe the Martians live in a state of God's grace. Then we can go back down to town and start work on the Earth Men."

Father Peregrine reminded himself to say a little prayer for Father Stone, who got so mad and who was now being vindictive, God help him. "Yes, Father Stone, but the Martians killed some of our settlers. That's sinful. There must have been an Original Sin and a Martian Adam and Eve. We'll find them. Men are men, unfortunately, no matter what their shape, and inclined to sin."

But Father Stone was pretending sleep.

Father Peregrine did not shut his eyes.

Of course they couldn't let these Martians go to Hell, could they? With a compromise to their consciences, could they go back to the new colonial towns, those towns so full of sinful gullets and women with scintilla eyes and white oyster bodies rollicking in beds with lonely laborers? Wasn't that the place for the Fathers? Wasn't this trek into the hills merely a personal whim? Was he really thinking of God's Church, or was he quenching the thirst of a spongelike curiosity? Those blue round globes of St. Anthony's fire—how they burned in his mind! What a challenge, to find the man behind the mask, the human behind the inhuman. Wouldn't he be proud if he could say, even to his secret self, that he had converted a rolling huge pool table full of fiery spheres! What a sin of pride! Worth doing penance for! But then one did many prideful things out of Love, and he loved the Lord so much and was so happy at it that he wanted everyone else to be happy too.

The last thing he saw before sleep was the return of the blue fires, like a flight of burning angels silently singing him to his worried rest.

The blue round dreams were still there in the sky when Father Peregrine awoke in the early morning.

Father Stone slept like a stiff bundle, quietly. Father Peregrine watched the Martians floating and watching him. They were human—he *knew* it. But he must prove it or face a dry-mouthed, dry-eyed Bishop telling him kindly to step aside.

But how to prove humanity if they hid in the high vaults of the sky? How to bring them nearer and provide answers to the many questions?

"They saved us from the avalanche."

Father Peregrine arose, moved off among the rocks, and began to climb the nearest hill until he came to a place where a cliff dropped sheerly to a floor two hundred feet below. He was choking from his vigorous climb in the frosty air. He stood, getting his breath.

"If I fell from here, it would surely kill me."

He let a pebble drop. Moments later it clicked on the rocks below.

"The Lord would never forgive me."

He tossed another pebble.

"It wouldn't be suicide, would it, if I did it out of Love . . . ?"

He lifted his gaze to the blue spheres. "But first, another try." He called to them: "Hello, hello!"

The echoes tumbled upon each other, but the blue fires did not blink or move.

He talked to them for five minutes. When he stopped, he peered down and saw Father Stone, still indignantly asleep, below in the little camp.

"I must prove everything." Father Peregrine stepped to the cliff rim. "I am an old man. I am not afraid. Surely the Lord will understand that I am doing this for Him?"

He drew a deep breath. All his life swam through his eyes and he thought, In a moment shall I die? I am afraid that I love living much too much. But I love other things more.

And, thinking thus, he stepped off the cliff.

He fell.

"Fool!" he cried. He tumbled end over end. "You were wrong!" The rocks rushed up at him and he saw himself dashed on them and sent to glory. "Why did I do this thing?" But he knew the answer, and an instant later was calm as he fell. The wind roared around him and the rocks hurtled to meet him.

And then there was a shift of stars, a glimmering of blue light, and he felt himself surrounded by blueness and suspended. A moment later he was deposited, with a gentle bump, upon the rocks, where he sat a full moment, alive, and touching himself, and looking up at those blue lights that had withdrawn instantly.

"You saved me!" he whispered. "You wouldn't let me die. You knew it was wrong."

He rushed over to Father Stone, who still lay quietly asleep. "Father, Father, wake up!" He shook him and brought him round. "Father, they saved me!"

"Who saved you?" Father Stone blinked and sat up.

Father Peregrine related his experience.

"A dream, a nightmare; go back to sleep," said Father Stone irritably. "You and your circus balloons."

"But I was awake!"

"Now, now, Father, calm yourself. There now."

"You don't believe me? Have you a gun? Yes, there, let me have it."

"What are you going to do?" Father Stone handed over the small pistol they had brought along for protection against snakes or other similar and unpredictable animals.

Father Peregrine seized the pistol. "I'll prove it!"

He pointed the pistol at his own hand and fired.

"Stop!"

There was a shimmer of light, and before their eyes the bullet stood upon the air, poised an inch from his open palm. It hung for a moment, surrounded by a blue phosphorescence. Then it fell, hissing, into the dust.

Father Peregrine fired the gun three times—at his hand, at his leg, at his body. The three bullets hovered, glittering, and, like dead insects, fell at their feet.

"You see?" said Father Peregrine, letting his arm fall, and allowing the pistol to drop after the bullets. "They know. They understand. They are not animals. They think and judge and live in a moral climate. What animal would save me from myself like this? There is no animal would do that. Only another man, Father. Now, do you believe?"

Father Stone was watching the sky and the blue lights, and now, silently, he dropped to one knee and picked up the warm bullets and cupped them in his hand. He closed his hand tight.

The sun was rising behind them.

"I think we had better go down to the others and tell them of this and bring them back up here," said Father Peregrine.

By the time the sun was up, they were well on their way back to the rocket.

Father Peregrine drew the round circle in the center of the blackboard.

"This is Christ, the Son of the Father."

He pretended not to hear the other Fathers' sharp intake of breath.

"This is Christ, in all His Glory," he continued.

"It looks like a geometry problem," observed Father Stone.

"A fortunate comparison, for we deal with symbols here. Christ is *no* less Christ, you must admit, in being represented by a circle or a square. For centuries the cross has symbolized His love and agony. So this circle will be the Martian Christ. This is how we shall bring Him to Mars."

The Fathers stirred fretfully and looked at each other.

"You, Brother Mathias, will create, in glass, a replica of this circle, a globe, filled with bright fire. It will stand upon the altar."

"A cheap magic trick," muttered Father Stone.

Father Peregrine went on patiently: "On the contrary. We are giving them God in an understandable image. If Christ had come to us on Earth as an octopus, would we have accepted Him readily?" He spread his hands. "Was it then a cheap magic trick of the Lord's to bring us Christ through Jesus, in man's shape? After we bless the church we build here and sanctify its altar and this symbol, do you think Christ would refuse to inhabit the shape before us? You know in your hearts He would not refuse."

"But the body of a soulless animal!" said Brother Mathias.

"We've already gone over that, many times since we returned this morning, Brother Mathias. These creatures saved us from the avalanche. They realized that self-destruction was sinful, and prevented it, time after time. Therefore we must build a church in the hills, live with them, to find their own special ways of sinning, the alien ways, and help them to discover God."

The Fathers did not seem pleased at the prospect.

"Is it because they are so odd to the eye?" wondered Father Peregrine. "But what is a shape? Only a cup for the blazing soul that God provides us all. If tomorrow I found that sea lions suddenly possessed free will, intellect, knew when not to sin, knew what life was and tempered justice with mercy and life with love, then I would build an undersea cathedral. And if the sparrows should, miraculously, with God's will, gain everlasting souls tomorrow, I would freight a church with helium and take after them, for all souls, in any shape, if they have free will and are aware of their sins, will burn in Hell unless given their rightful communions. I would not let a Martian sphere burn in Hell either, for it is a sphere only in mine eyes. When I close my eyes it stands before me, an intelligence, a love, a soul—and I must not deny it."

"But that glass globe you wish placed on the altar," protested Father Stone.

"Consider the Chinese," replied Father Peregrine imperturbably. "What sort of Christ do Christian Chinese worship? An oriental Christ, naturally. You've all seen oriental Nativity scenes. How is Christ dressed? In Eastern robes. Where does He walk? In Chinese settings of bamboo and misty mountain and crooked tree. His eyelids taper, His cheekbones rise. Each country, each race adds something to Our Lord. I am reminded of the Virgin of Guadalupe, to whom all Mexico pays its love. Her skin? Have you noticed the paintings of her? A dark skin, like that of her worshipers. Is this blasphemy? Not at all. It is not logical that men should accept a God, no matter how real, of another color. I often wonder why our missionaries do well in Africa, with a snow-white Christ. Perhaps because white is a sacred color, in albino, or any other form, to the African tribes. Given time, mightn't Christ darken there too? The form does not matter. Content is everything. We cannot expect these Martians to accept an alien form. We shall give them Christ in their own image."

"There's a flaw in your reasoning, Father," said Father Stone. "Won't the Martians suspect us of hypocrisy? They will realize that *we* don't worship a round, globular Christ, but a man with limbs and a head. How do we explain the difference?"

"By showing there is none. Christ will fill any vessel that is offered. Bodies or globes, He is there, and each will worship the same thing in a different guise. What is more, we must *believe* in this globe we give the Martians. We must believe in a shape which is meaningless to us as to form. This spheroid *will* be Christ. And we must remember that we ourselves, and the shape of our Earth Christ, would be meaningless, ridiculous, a squander of material to these Martians."

Father Peregrine laid aside his chalk. "Now let us go into the hills and build our church."

The Fathers began to pack their equipment.

The church was not a church but an area cleared of rocks, a plateau on one of the low mountains, its soil smoothed and brushed, and an altar established whereon Brother Mathias placed the fiery globe he had constructed.

At the end of six days of work the "church" was ready.

"What shall we do with this?" Father Stone tapped an iron bell they had brought along. "What does a bell mean to *them?*"

"I imagine I brought it for our own comfort," admitted Father Peregrine. "We need a few familiarities. This church seems so little like a church. And we feel somewhat absurd here—even I; for it is something new, this business of converting the creatures of another world. I feel like a ridiculous play actor at times. And then I pray to God to lend me strength."

"Many of the Fathers are unhappy. Some of them joke about all this, Father Peregrine."

"I know. We'll put this bell in a small tower for their comfort, anyway."

"What about the organ?"

"We'll play it at the first service, tomorrow."

"But, the Martians—"

"I know. But again, I suppose, for our own comfort, our own music. Later we may discover theirs."

They arose very early on Sunday morning and moved through the coldness like pale phantoms, rime tinkling on their habits; covered with chimes they were, shaking down showers of silver water.

"I wonder if it *is* Sunday here on Mars?" mused Father Peregrine, but seeing Father Stone wince, he hastened on, "It might be Tuesday or Thursday— who knows? But no matter. My idle fancy. It's Sunday to *us*. Come."

The Fathers walked into the flat wide area of the "church" and knelt, shivering and blue-lipped.

Father Peregrine said a little prayer and put his cold fingers to the organ keys. The music went up like a flight of pretty birds. He touched the keys like a man moving his hands among the weeds of a wild garden, startling up great soarings of Beauty into the hills.

The music calmed the air. It smelled the fresh smell of morning. The music drifted into the mountains and shook down mineral powders in a dusty rain.

The Fathers waited.

"Well, Father Peregrine." Father Stone eyed the empty sky where the sun was rising, furnace-red. "I don't see our friends."

"Let me try again." Father Peregrine was perspiring.

He built an architecture of Bach, stone by exquisite stone, raising a music cathedral so vast that its furthest chancels were in Nineveh, its furthest dome at St. Peter's left hand. The music stayed and did not crash in ruin when it was over, but partook of a series of white clouds and was carried away among other lands.

The sky was still empty.

"They'll come!" But Father Peregrine felt the panic in his chest, very small, growing. "Let us pray. Let us ask them to come. They read minds; they *know*."

The Fathers lowered themselves yet again, in rustlings and whispers. They prayed.

And to the East, out of the icy mountains of seven o'clock on Sunday morning or perhaps Thursday morning or maybe Monday morning on Mars, came the soft fiery globes.

They hovered and sank and filled the area around the shivering priests. "Thank you; oh, thank you, Lord." Father Peregrine shut his eyes tight and played the music, and when it was done he turned and gazed upon his wondrous congregation.

And a voice touched his mind, and the voice said:

"We have come for a little while."

"You may stay," said Father Peregrine.

"For a little while only," said the voice quietly. "We have come to tell you certain things. We should have spoken sooner. But we had hoped that you might go on your way if left alone."

Father Peregrine started to speak, but the voice hushed him.

"We are the Old Ones," the voice said, and it entered him like a blue gaseous flare and burned in the chambers of his head. "We are the old Martians, who left our marble cities and went into the hills, forsaking the material life we had lived. So very long ago we became these things that we now are. Once we were men, with bodies and legs and arms such as yours. The legend has it that one of us, a good man, discovered a way to free man's soul and intellect, to free him of bodily ills and melancholies, of deaths and transfigurations, of ill humors and senilities, and so we took on the look of lightning and blue fire and have lived in the winds and skies and hills forever after that, neither prideful nor arrogant, neither rich nor poor, passionate nor cold. We have lived apart from those we left behind, those other men of this world, and how we came to be has been forgotten, the process lost; but we shall never die, nor do harm. We have put away the sins of the body and live in God's grace. We covet no other property; we have no property. We do not steal, nor kill, nor lust, nor hate. We live in happiness. We cannot reproduce; we do not eat or drink or make war. All the sensualities and childishnesses and sins of the body were stripped away when our bodies were put aside. We have left sin behind, Father Peregrine, and it is burned like the leaves in the autumn, and it is gone like the soiled snow of an evil winter, and it is gone like the sexual flowers of a red-and-yellow spring, and it is gone like the panting nights of hottest summer, and our season is temperate and our clime is rich in thought."

Father Peregrine was standing now, for the voice touched him at such a pitch that it almost shook him from his senses. It was an ecstasy and a fire washing through him.

"We wish to tell you that we appreciate your building this place for us, but we have no need of it, for each of us is a temple unto himself and needs no place wherein to cleanse himself. Forgive us for not coming to you sooner, but we are separate and apart and have talked to no one for ten thousand years, nor have we interfered in any way with the life of this planet. It has come into your mind now that we are the lilies of the field; we toil not, neither do we spin. You are right. And so we suggest that you take the parts of this temple into your own new cities and there cleanse others. For, rest assured, we are happy and at peace."

The Fathers were on their knees in the vast blue light, and Father Peregrine was down, too, and they were weeping, and it did not matter that their time had been wasted; it did not matter to them at all.

The blue spheres murmured and began to rise once more, on a breath of cool air.

"May I"—cried Father Peregrine, not daring to ask, eyes closed—"may I come again, someday, that I may learn from you?"

The blue fires blazed. The air trembled.

Yes. Someday he might come again. Someday.

And then the Fire Balloons blew away and were gone, and he was like a child, on his knees, tears streaming from his eyes, crying to himself, "Come back, come back!" And at any moment Grandfather might lift him and carry him upstairs to his bedroom in a long-gone Illinois town. . . .

They filed down out of the hills at sunset. Looking back, Father Peregrine saw the blue fires burning. No, he thought, we couldn't build a church for the likes of you. You're beauty itself. What church could compete with the fireworks of the pure soul?

Father Stone moved in silence beside him. And at last he spoke:

"The way I see it is there's a Truth on every planet. All parts of the Big Truth. On a certain day they'll all fit together like the pieces of a jigsaw. This has been a shaking experience. I'll never doubt again, Father Peregrine. For this Truth here is as true as Earth's Truth, and they lie side by side. And we'll go on to other worlds, adding the sum of the parts of the Truth until one day the whole Total will stand before us like the light of a new day."

"That's a lot, coming from you, Father Stone."

"I'm sorry now, in a way, we're going down to the town to handle our own kind. Those blue lights now. When they settled about us, and that *voice* . . . " Father Stone shivered.

Father Peregrine reached out to take the other's arm. They walked together.

"And you know," said Father Stone finally, fixing his eyes on Brother Mathias, who strode ahead with the glass sphere tenderly carried in his arms, that glass sphere with the blue phosphorous light glowing forever inside it, "you know, Father Peregrine, that globe there—"

"Yes?"

"It's Him. It *is* Him, after all."

Father Peregrine smiled, and they walked down out of the hills toward the new town.

The Last Night
of the World

"What would you do if you knew that this was the last night of the world?"

"What would I do? You mean seriously?"

"Yes, seriously."

"I don't know. I hadn't thought."

He poured some coffee. In the background the two girls were playing blocks on the parlor rug in the light of the green hurricane lamps. There was an easy, clean aroma of the brewed coffee in the evening air.

"Well, better start thinking about it," he said.

"You don't mean it!"

He nodded.

"A war?"

He shook his head.

"Not the hydrogen or atom bomb?"

"No."

"Or germ warfare?"

"None of those at all," he said, stirring his coffee slowly. "But just, let's say, the closing of a book."

"I don't think I understand."

"No, nor do I, really; it's just a feeling. Sometimes it frightens me, sometimes I'm not frightened at all but at peace." He glanced in at the girls and their yellow hair shining in the lamplight. "I didn't say anything to you. It first happened about four nights ago."

"What?"

"A dream I had. I dreamed that it was all going to be over, and a voice said it was; not any kind of voice I can remember, but a voice anyway, and it said things would stop here on Earth. I didn't think too much about it the next day, but then I went to the office and caught Stan Willis looking out the window in the middle of the afternoon, and I said, A penny for your thoughts, Stan, and he said, I had a dream last night, and before he even told me the dream I knew what it was. I could have told him, but he told me and I listened to him."

"It was the same dream?"

"The same. I told Stan I had dreamed it too. He didn't seem surprised. He relaxed, in fact. Then we started walking through the office, for the hell of it. It wasn't planned. We didn't say, Let's walk around. We just walked on our own, and everywhere we saw people looking at their desks or their hands or out windows. I talked to a few. So did Stan."

"And they all had dreamed?"

"All of them. The same dream, with no difference."

"Do you believe in it?"

"Yes. I've never been more certain."

"And when will it stop? The world, I mean."

"Sometime during the night for us, and then as the night goes on around the world, that'll go too. It'll take twenty-four hours for it all to go."

They sat awhile not touching their coffee. Then they lifted it slowly and drank, looking at each other.

"Do we deserve this?" she said.

"It's not a matter of deserving; it's just that things didn't work out. I notice you didn't even argue about this. Why not?"

"I guess I've a reason," she said.

"The same one everyone at the office had?"

She nodded slowly. "I didn't want to say anything. It happened last night. And the women on the block talked about it, among themselves, today. They dreamed. I thought it was only a coincidence." She picked up the evening paper. "There's nothing in the paper about it."

"Everyone knows, so there's no need."

He sat back in his chair, watching her. "Are you afraid?"

"No. I always thought I would be, but I'm not."

"Where's that spirit called self-preservation they talk so much about?"

"I don't know. You don't get too excited when you feel things are logical. This is logical. Nothing else but this could have happened from the way we've lived."

"We haven't been too bad, have we?"

"No, nor enormously good. I suppose that's the trouble—we haven't been very much of anything except us, while a big part of the world was busy being lots of quite awful things."

The girls were laughing in the parlor.

"I always thought people would be screaming in the streets at a time like this."

"I guess not. You don't scream about the real thing."

"Do you know, I won't miss anything but you and the girls. I never liked cities or my work or anything except you three. I won't miss a thing except perhaps the change in the weather, and a glass of ice water when it's hot, and I might miss sleeping. How can we sit here and talk this way?"

"Because there's nothing else to do."

"That's it, of course; for if there were, we'd be doing it. I suppose this is the first time in the history of the world that everyone has known just what they were going to do during the night."

"I wonder what everyone else will do now, this evening, for the next few hours."

"Go to a show, listen to the radio, watch television, play cards, put the children to bed, go to bed themselves, like always."

"In a way that's something to be proud of—like always."

They sat a moment and then he poured himself another coffee. "Why do you suppose it's tonight?"

"Because."

"Why not some other night in the last century, or five centuries ago, or ten?"

"Maybe because it was never October 19, 1969, ever before in history, and now it is and that's it; because this date means more than any other date ever meant; because it's the year when things are as they are all over the world and that's why it's the end."

"There are bombers on their schedules both ways across the ocean tonight that'll never see land."

"That's part of the reason why."

"Well," he said, getting up, "what shall it be? Wash the dishes?"

They washed the dishes and stacked them away with special neatness. At eight-thirty the girls were put to bed and kissed good night and the little lights by their beds turned on and the door left open just a trifle.

"I wonder," said the husband, coming from the bedroom and glancing back, standing there with his pipe for a moment.

"What?"

"If the door will be shut all the way, or if it'll be left just a little ajar so some light comes in."

"I wonder if the children know."

"No, of course not."

They sat and read the papers and talked and listened to some radio music and then sat together by the fireplace watching the charcoal embers as the clock struck ten-thirty and eleven and eleven-thirty. They thought of all the other people in the world who had spent their evening, each in his own special way.

"Well," he said at last.

He kissed his wife for a long time.

"We've been good for each other, anyway."

"Do you want to cry?" he asked.

"I don't think so."

They moved through the house and turned out the lights and went into the bedroom and stood in the night cool darkness undressing and pushing back the covers. "The sheets are so clean and nice."

"I'm tired."

"We're *all* tired."

They got into bed and lay back.

"Just a moment," she said.

He heard her get out of bed and go into the kitchen. A moment later, she returned. "I left the water running in the kitchen sink," she said.

Something about this was so very funny that he had to laugh.

She laughed with him, knowing what it was that she had done that was funny. They stopped laughing at last and lay in their cool night bed, their hands clasped, their heads together.

"Good night," he said, after a moment.

"Good night," she said.

The Veldt

"George, I wish you'd look at the nursery."

"What's wrong with it?"

"I don't know."

"Well, then."

"I just want you to look at it, is all, or call a psychologist in to look at it."

"What would a psychologist want with a nursery?"

"You know very well what he'd want." His wife paused in the middle of the kitchen and watched the stove busy humming to itself, making supper for four.

"It's just that the nursery is different now than it was."

"All right, let's have a look."

They walked down the hall of their soundproofed Happy-life Home, which had cost them thirty thousand dollars installed, this house which clothed and fed and rocked them to sleep and played and sang and was good to them. Their approach sensitized a switch somewhere and the nursery light flicked on when they came within ten feet of it. Similarly, behind them, in the halls, lights went on and off as they left them behind, with a soft automaticity.

"Well," said George Hadley.

They stood on the thatched floor of the nursery. It was forty feet across by forty feet long and thirty feet high; it had cost half again as much as the rest of the house. "But nothing's too good for our children," George had said.

The nursery was silent. It was empty as a jungle glade at hot high noon. The walls were blank and two-dimensional. Now, as George and Lydia Hadley stood in the center of the room, the walls began to purr and recede into crystalline distance, it seemed, and presently an African veldt appeared, in three dimensions; on all sides, in colors reproduced to the final pebble and bit of straw. The ceiling above them became a deep sky with a hot yellow sun.

George Hadley felt the perspiration start on his brow.

"Let's get out of the sun," he said. "This is a little too real. But I don't see anything wrong."

"Wait a moment, you'll see," said his wife.

Now the hidden odorophonics were beginning to blow a wind of odor at the two people in the middle of the baked veldtland. The hot straw smell of lion grass, the cool green smell of the hidden water hole, the great rusty smell of animals, the smell of dust like a red paprika in the hot air. And now the sounds: the thump of distant antelope feet on grassy sod, the papery rustling of vultures. A shadow passed through the sky. The shadow flickered on George Hadley's upturned, sweating face.

"Filthy creatures," he heard his wife say.

"The vultures."

"You see, there are the lions, far over, that way. Now they're on their way to the water hole. They've just been eating," said Lydia. "I don't know what."

"Some animal." George Hadley put his hand up to shield off the burning light from his squinted eyes. "A zebra or a baby giraffe, maybe."

"Are you sure?" His wife sounded peculiarly tense.

"No, it's a little late to be *sure*," he said, amused. "Nothing over there I can see but cleaned bone, and the vultures dropping for what's left."

"Did you hear that scream?" she asked.

"No."

"About a minute ago?"

"Sorry, no."

The lions were coming. And again George Hadley was filled with admiration for the mechanical genius who had conceived this room. A miracle of efficiency selling for an absurdly low price. Every home should have one. Oh, occasionally they frightened you with their clinical accuracy, they startled you, gave you a twinge, but most of the time what fun for everyone, not only your own son and daughter, but for yourself when you felt like a quick jaunt to a foreign land, a quick change of scenery. Well, here it was!

And here were the lions now, fifteen feet away, so real, so feverishly and startlingly real that you could feel the prickling fur on your hand, and your mouth was stuffed with the dusty upholstery smell of their heated pelts, and the yellow of them was in your eyes like the yellow of an exquisite French tapestry, the yellows of lions and summer grass, and the sound of matted lion lungs exhaling on the silent noontide, and the smell of meat from the panting, dripping mouths.

The lions stood looking at George and Lydia Hadley with terrible green-yellow eyes.

"Watch out!" screamed Lydia.

The lions came running at them.

Lydia bolted and ran. Instinctively, George sprang after her. Outside, in the hall, with the door slammed, he was laughing and she was crying and they both stood appalled at the other's reaction.

"George!"

"Lydia! Oh, my dear poor sweet Lydia!"

"They almost got us!"

"Walls, Lydia, remember; crystal walls, that's all they are. Oh, they look real, I must admit—Africa in your parlor—but it's all dimensional superactionary, supersensitive color film and mental tape film behind glass screens. It's all odorophonics and sonics, Lydia. Here's my handkerchief."

"I'm afraid." She came to him and put her body against him and cried steadily. "Did you see? Did you *feel?* It's too real."

"Now, Lydia . . . "

"You've got to tell Wendy and Peter not to read any more on Africa."

"Of course—of course." He patted her.

"Promise?"

"Sure."

"And lock the nursery for a few days until I get my nerves settled."

"You know how difficult Peter is about that. When I punished him a month ago by locking the nursery for even a few hours—the tantrum he threw! And Wendy too. They *live* for the nursery."

"It's got to be locked, that's all there is to it."

"All right." Reluctantly he locked the huge door. "You've been working too hard. You need a rest."

"I don't know—I don't know," she said, blowing her nose, sitting down in a chair that immediately began to rock and comfort her. "Maybe I don't have enough to do. Maybe I have time to think too much. Why don't we shut the whole house off for a few days and take a vacation?"

"You mean you want to fry my eggs for me?"

"Yes." She nodded.

"And darn my socks?"

"Yes." A frantic, watery-eyed nodding.

"And sweep the house?"

"Yes, yes—oh, yes!"

"But I thought that's why we bought this house, so we wouldn't have to do anything?"

"That's just it. I feel like I don't belong here. The house is wife and mother now and nursemaid. Can I compete with an African veldt? Can I give a bath and scrub the children as efficiently or quickly as the automatic scrub bath can? I cannot. And it isn't just me. It's you. You've been awfully nervous lately."

"I suppose I have been smoking too much."

"You look as if you don't know what to do with yourself in this house, either. You smoke a little more every morning and drink a little more every afternoon and need a little more sedative every night. You're beginning to feel unnecessary too."

"Am I?" He paused and tried to feel into himself to see what was really there.

"Oh, George!" She looked beyond him, at the nursery door. "Those lions can't get out of there, can they?"

He looked at the door and saw it tremble as if something had jumped against it from the other side.

"Of course not," he said.

At dinner they ate alone, for Wendy and Peter were at a special plastic carnival across town and had televised home to say they'd be late, to go ahead eating. So George Hadley, bemused, sat watching the dining-room table produce warm dishes of food from its mechanical interior.

"We forgot the ketchup," he said.

"Sorry," said a small voice within the table, and ketchup appeared.

As for the nursery, thought George Hadley, it won't hurt for the children to be locked out of it awhile. Too much of anything isn't good for anyone. And it was clearly indicated that the children had been spending a little too much time on Africa. That *sun*. He could feel it on his neck, still, like a hot paw. And the *lions*. And the smell of blood. Remarkable how the nursery caught the telepathic emanations of the children's minds and created life to fill their every desire. The children thought lions, and there were lions. The children thought zebras, and there were zebras. Sun—sun. Giraffes—giraffes. Death and death.

That *last*. He chewed tastelessly on the meat that the table had cut for him. Death thoughts. They were awfully young, Wendy and Peter, for death thoughts.

Or, no, you were never too young, really. Long before you knew what death was you were wishing it on someone else. When you were two years old you were shooting people with cap pistols.

But this—the long, hot African veldt—the awful death in the jaws of a lion. And repeated again and again.

"Where are you going?"

He didn't answer Lydia. Preoccupied, he let the lights glow softly on ahead of him, extinguish behind him as he padded to the nursery door. He listened against it. Far away, a lion roared.

He unlocked the door and opened it. Just before he stepped inside, he heard a faraway scream. And then another roar from the lions, which subsided quickly.

He stepped into Africa. How many times in the last year had he opened this door and found Wonderland, Alice, the Mock Turtle, or Aladdin and his Magical Lamp, or Jack Pumpkinhead of Oz, or Dr. Doolittle, or the cow jumping over a very real-appearing moon—all the delightful contraptions of a make-believe world. How often had he seen Pegasus flying in the sky ceiling, or seen fountains of red fireworks, or heard angel voices singing. But now, this yellow hot Africa, this bake oven with murder in the heat. Perhaps Lydia was right. Perhaps they needed a little vacation from the fantasy which was growing a bit too real for ten-year-old children. It was all right to exercise one's mind with gymnastic fantasies, but when the lively child mind settled on *one* pattern . . . ? It seemed that, at a distance, for the past month, he had heard lions roaring, and smelled their strong odor seeping as far away as his study door. But, being busy, he had paid it no attention.

George Hadley stood on the African grassland alone. The lions looked up from their feeding, watching him. The only flaw to the illusion was the open door through which he could see his wife, far down the dark hall, like a framed picture, eating her dinner abstractedly.

"Go away," he said to the lions.

They did not go.

He knew the principle of the room exactly. You sent out your thoughts. Whatever you thought would appear.

"Let's have Aladdin and his lamp," he snapped.

The veldtland remained; the lions remained.

"Come on, room! I demand Aladdin!" he said.

Nothing happened. The lions mumbled in their baked pelts.

"Aladdin!"

He went back to dinner. "The fool room's out of order," he said. "It won't respond."

"Or—"

"Or what?"

"Or it *can't* respond," said Lydia, "because the children have thought about Africa and lions and killing so many days that the room's in a rut."

"Could be."

"Or Peter's set it to remain that way."

"*Set* it?"

"He may have got into the machinery and fixed something."

"Peter doesn't know machinery."

"He's a wise one for ten. That I.Q. of his—"

"Nevertheless—"

"Hello, Mom. Hello, Dad."

The Hadleys turned. Wendy and Peter were coming in the front door, cheeks like peppermint candy, eyes like bright blue agate marbles, a smell of ozone on their jumpers from their trip in the helicopter.

"You're just in time for supper," said both parents.

"We're full of strawberry ice cream and hot dogs," said the children, holding hands. "But we'll sit and watch."

"Yes, come tell us about the nursery," said George Hadley.

The brother and sister blinked at him and then at each other. "Nursery?"

"All about Africa and everything," said the father with false joviality.

"I don't understand," said Peter.

"Your mother and I were just traveling through Africa with rod and reel; Tom Swift and his Electric Lion," said George Hadley.

"There's no Africa in the nursery," said Peter simply.

"Oh, come now, Peter. We know better."

"I don't remember any Africa," said Peter to Wendy. "Do you?"

"No."

"Run see and come tell."

She obeyed.

"Wendy, come back here!" said George Hadley, but she was gone. The house lights followed her like a flock of fireflies. Too late, he realized he had forgotten to lock the nursery door after his last inspection.

"Wendy'll look and come tell us," said Peter.

"She doesn't have to tell *me*. I've seen it."

"I'm sure you're mistaken, Father."

"I'm not, Peter. Come along now."

But Wendy was back. "It's not Africa," she said breathlessly.

"We'll see about this," said George Hadley, and they all walked down the hall together and opened the nursery door.

There was a green, lovely forest, a lovely river, a purple mountain, high voices singing, and Rima, lovely and mysterious, lurking in the trees with colorful flights of butterflies, like animated bouquets, lingering in her long hair. The African veldtland was gone. The lions were gone. Only Rima was here now, singing a song so beautiful that it brought tears to your eyes.

George Hadley looked in at the changed scene. "Go to bed," he said to the children.

They opened their mouths.

"You heard me," he said.

They went off to the air closet, where a wind sucked them like brown leaves up the flue to their slumber rooms.

George Hadley walked through the singing glade and picked up something that lay in the corner near where the lions had been. He walked slowly back to his wife.

"What is that?" she asked.

"An old wallet of mine," he said.

He showed it to her. The smell of hot grass was on it and the smell of a lion. There were drops of saliva on it, it had been chewed, and there were blood smears on both sides.

He closed the nursery door and locked it, tight.

In the middle of the night he was still awake and he knew his wife was awake. "Do you think Wendy changed it?" she said at last, in the dark room.

"Of course."

"Made it from a veldt into a forest and put Rima there instead of lions?"

"Yes."

"Why?"

"I don't know. But it's staying locked until I find out."

"How did your wallet get there?"

"I don't know anything," he said, "except that I'm beginning to be sorry we bought that room for the children. If children are neurotic at all, a room like that—"

"It's supposed to help them work off their neuroses in a healthful way."

"I'm starting to wonder." He stared at the ceiling.

"We've given the children everything they ever wanted. Is this our reward—secrecy, disobedience?"

"Who was it said, 'Children are carpets, they should be stepped on occasionally'! We've never lifted a hand. They're insufferable—let's admit it. They come and go when they like; they treat us as if *we* were offspring. They're spoiled and we're spoiled."

"They've been acting funny ever since you forbade them to take the rocket to New York a few months ago."

"They're not old enough to do that alone, I explained."

"Nevertheless, I've noticed they've been decidedly cool toward us since."

"I think I'll have David McClean come tomorrow morning to have a look at Africa."

"But it's not Africa now, it's Green Mansions country and Rima."

"I have a feeling it'll be Africa again before then."

A moment later they heard the screams.

Two screams. Two people screaming from downstairs. And then a roar of lions.

"Wendy and Peter aren't in their rooms," said his wife.

He lay in his bed with his beating heart. "No," he said. "They've broken into the nursery."

"Those screams—they sound familiar."

"Do they?"

"Yes, awfully."

And although their beds tried very hard, the two adults couldn't be rocked to sleep for another hour. A smell of cats was in the night air.

"Father?" said Peter.

"Yes."

Peter looked at his shoes. He never looked at his father any more, nor at his mother. "You aren't going to lock up the nursery for good, are you?"

"That all depends."

"On what?" snapped Peter.

"On you and your sister. If you intersperse this Africa with a little variety—oh, Sweden perhaps, or Denmark or China—"

"I thought we were free to play as we wished."

"You are, within reasonable bounds."

"What's wrong with Africa, Father?"

"Oh, so now you admit you have been conjuring up Africa, do you?"

"I wouldn't want the nursery locked up," said Peter coldly. "Ever."

"Matter of fact, we're thinking of turning the whole house off for about a month. Live sort of a carefree one-for-all existence."

"That sounds dreadful! Would I have to tie my own shoes instead of letting the shoe tier do it? And brush my own teeth and comb my hair and give myself a bath?"

"It would be fun for a change, don't you think?"

"No, it would be horrid. I didn't like it when you took out the picture painter last month."

"That's because I wanted you to learn to paint all by yourself, Son."

"I don't want to do anything but look and listen and smell; what else *is* there to do?"

"All right, go play in Africa."

"Will you shut off the house sometime soon?"

"We're considering it."

"I don't think you'd better consider it any more, Father."

"I won't have any threats from my son!"

"Very well." And Peter strolled off to the nursery.

"Am I on time?" said David McClean.

"Breakfast?" asked George Hadley.

"Thanks, had some. What's the trouble?"

"David, you're a psychologist."

"I should hope so."

"Well, then, have a look at our nursery. You saw it a year ago when you dropped by; did you notice anything peculiar about it then?"

"Can't say I did; the usual violences, a tendency toward a slight paranoia here or there, usual in children because they feel persecuted by parents constantly, but, oh, really nothing."

They walked down the hall. "I locked the nursery up," explained the father, "and the children broke back into it during the night. I let them stay so they could form the patterns for you to see."

There was a terrible screaming from the nursery.

"There it is," said George Hadley. "See what you make of it."

They walked in on the children without rapping.

The screams had faded. The lions were feeding.

"Run outside a moment, children," said George Hadley. "No, don't change the mental combination. Leave the walls as they are. Get!"

With the children gone, the two men stood studying the lions clustered at a distance, eating with great relish whatever it was they had caught.

"I wish I knew what it was," said George Hadley. "Sometimes I can almost see. Do you think if I brought high-powered binoculars here and—"

David McClean laughed dryly. "Hardly." He turned to study all four walls. "How long has this been going on?"

"A little over a month."

"It certainly doesn't *feel* good."

"I want facts, not feelings."

"My dear George, a psychologist never saw a fact in his life. He only hears about feelings; vague things. This doesn't feel good, I tell you. Trust my hunches and my instincts. I have a nose for something bad. This is very bad. My advice to you is to have the whole damn room torn down and your children brought to me every day during the next year for treatment."

"Is it that bad?"

"I'm afraid so. One of the original uses of these nurseries was so that we could study the patterns left on the walls by the child's mind, study at our leisure, and help the child. In this case, however, the room has become a channel toward—destructive thoughts, instead of a release away from them."

"Didn't you sense this before?"

"I sensed only that you had spoiled your children more than most. And now you're letting them down in some way. What way?"

"I wouldn't let them go to New York."

"What else?"

"I've taken a few machines from the house and threatened them, a month ago, with closing up the nursery unless they did their homework. I did close it for a few days to show I meant business."

"Ah, ha!"

"Does that mean anything?"

"Everything. Where before they had a Santa Claus now they have a Scrooge. Children prefer Santas. You've let this room and this house replace you and your wife in your children's affections. This room is their mother and father, far more important in their lives than their real parents. And now you come along and want to shut it off. No wonder there's hatred here. You can feel it coming out of the sky. Feel that sun. George, you'll have to change your life. Like too many others, you've built it around creature comforts. Why, you'd starve tomorrow if something went wrong in your kitchen. You wouldn't know how to tap an egg. Nevertheless, turn everything off. Start new. It'll take time. But we'll make good children out of bad in a year, wait and see."

"But won't the shock be too much for the children, shutting the room up abruptly, for good?"

"I don't want them going any deeper into this, that's all."

The lions were finished with their red feast.

The lions were standing on the edge of the clearing watching the two men.

"Now *I'm* feeling persecuted," said McClean. "Let's get out of here. I never have cared for these damned rooms. Make me nervous."

"The lions look real, don't they?" said George Hadley. "I don't suppose there's any way—"

"What?"

"—that they could *become* real?"

"Not that I know."

"Some flaw in the machinery, a tampering or something?"

"No."

They went to the door.

"I don't imagine the room will like being turned off," said the father.

"Nothing ever likes to die—even a room."

"I wonder if it hates me for wanting to switch it off?"

"Paranoia is thick around here today," said David McClean. "You can follow it like a spoor. Hello." He bent and picked up a bloody scarf. "This yours?"

"No." George Hadley's face was rigid. "It belongs to Lydia."

They went to the fuse box together and threw the switch that killed the nursery.

The two children were in hysterics. They screamed and pranced and threw things. They yelled and sobbed and swore and jumped at the furniture.

"You can't do that to the nursery, you can't!"

"Now, children."

The children flung themselves onto a couch, weeping.

"George," said Lydia Hadley, "turn on the nursery, just for a few moments. You can't be so abrupt."

"No."

"You can't be so cruel."

"Lydia, it's off, and it stays off. And the whole damn house dies as of here and now. The more I see of the mess we've put ourselves in, the more it sickens me. We've been contemplating our mechanical, electronic navels for too long. My God, how we need a breath of honest air!"

And he marched about the house turning off the voice clocks, the stoves, the heaters, the shoe shiners, the shoe lacers, the body scrubbers and swabbers and massagers, and every other machine he could put his hand to.

The house was full of dead bodies, it seemed. It felt like a mechanical cemetery. So silent. None of the humming hidden energy of machines waiting to function at the tap of a button.

"Don't let them do it!" wailed Peter at the ceiling, as if he was talking to the house, the nursery. "Don't let Father kill everything." He turned to his father. "Oh, I hate you!"

"Insults won't get you anywhere."

"I wish you were dead!"

"We were, for a long while. Now we're going to really start living. Instead of being handled and massaged, we're going to *live*."

Wendy was still crying and Peter joined her again. "Just a moment, just one moment, just another moment of nursery," they wailed.

"Oh, George," said the wife, "it can't hurt."

"All right—all right, if they'll only just shut up. One minute, mind you, and then off forever."

"Daddy, Daddy, Daddy!" sang the children, smiling with wet faces.

"And then we're going on a vacation. David McClean is coming back in half an hour to help us move out and get to the airport. I'm going to dress. You turn the nursery on for a minute, Lydia, just a minute, mind you."

And the three of them went babbling off while he let himself be vacuumed upstairs through the air flue and set about dressing himself. A minute later Lydia appeared.

"I'll be glad when we get away," she sighed.

"Did you leave them in the nursery?"

"I wanted to dress too. Oh, that horrid Africa. What can they see in it?"

"Well, in five minutes we'll be on our way to Iowa. Lord, how did we ever get in this house? What prompted us to buy a nightmare?"

"Pride, money, foolishness."

"I think we'd better get downstairs before those kids get engrossed with those damned beasts again."

Just then they heard the children calling, "Daddy, Mommy, come quick— quick!"

They went downstairs in the air flue and ran down the hall. The children were nowhere in sight. "Wendy? Peter!"

They ran into the nursery. The veldtland was empty save for the lions waiting, looking at them. "Peter, Wendy?"

The door slammed.

"Wendy, Peter!"

George Hadley and his wife whirled and ran back to the door.

"Open the door!" cried George Hadley, trying the knob. "Why, they've locked it from the outside! Peter!" He beat at the door. "Open up!"

He heard Peter's voice outside, against the door.

"Don't let them switch off the nursery and the house," he was saying.

Mr. and Mrs. George Hadley beat at the door. "Now, don't be ridiculous, children. It's time to go. Mr. McClean'll be here in a minute and . . . "

And then they heard the sounds.

The lions on three sides of them, in the yellow veldt grass, padding through the dry straw, rumbling and roaring in their throats.

The lions.

Mr. Hadley looked at his wife and they turned and looked back at the beasts edging slowly forward, crouching, tails stiff.

Mr. and Mrs. Hadley screamed.

And suddenly they realized why those other screams had sounded familiar.

"Well, here I am," said David McClean in the nursery doorway. "Oh, hello." He stared at the two children seated in the center of the open glade eating a little picnic lunch. Beyond them was the water hole and the yellow veldtland; above was the hot sun. He began to perspire. "Where are your father and mother?"

The children looked up and smiled. "Oh, they'll be here directly."

"Good, we must get going." At a distance Mr. McClean saw the lions fighting and clawing and then quieting down to feed in silence under the shady trees.

He squinted at the lions with his hand up to his eyes.

Now the lions were done feeding. They moved to the water hole to drink.

A shadow flickered over Mr. McClean's hot face. Many shadows flickered. The vultures were dropping down the blazing sky.

"A cup of tea?" asked Wendy in the silence.

The Long Rain

The rain continued. It was a hard rain, a perpetual rain, a sweating and steaming rain; it was a mizzle, a downpour, a fountain, a whipping at the eyes, an undertow at the ankles; it was a rain to drown all rains and the memory of rains. It came by the pound and the ton, it hacked at the jungle and cut the trees like scissors and shaved the grass and tunneled the soil and molted the bushes. It shrank men's hands into the hands of wrinkled apes; it rained a solid glassy rain, and it never stopped.

"How much farther, Lieutenant?"

"I don't know. A mile, ten miles, a thousand."

"Aren't you sure?"

"How can I be sure?"

"I don't like this rain. If we only knew how far it is to the Sun Dome, I'd feel better."

"Another hour or two from here."

"You really think so, Lieutenant?"

"Of course."

"Or are you lying to keep us happy?"

"I'm lying to keep you happy. Shut up!"

The two men sat together in the rain. Behind them sat two other men who were wet and tired and slumped like clay that was melting.

The lieutenant looked up. He had a face that once had been brown and now the rain had washed it pale, and the rain had washed the color from his eyes and they were white, as were his teeth, and as was his hair. He was all white. Even his uniform was beginning to turn white, and perhaps a little green with fungus.

The lieutenant felt the rain on his cheeks. "How many million years since the rain stopped raining here on Venus?"

"Don't be crazy," said one of the two other men. "It never stops raining on Venus. It just goes on and on. I've lived here for ten years and I never saw a minute, or even a second, when it wasn't pouring."

"It's like living under water," said the lieutenant, and rose up, shrugging his guns into place. "Well, we'd better get going. We'll find that Sun Dome yet."

"Or we won't find it," said the cynic.

"It's an hour or so."

"Now you're lying to me, Lieutenant."

"No, now I'm lying to myself. This is one of those times when you've got to lie. I can't take much more of this."

They walked down the jungle trail, now and then looking at their compasses. There was no direction anywhere, only what the compass said. There was a gray sky and rain falling and jungle and a path, and, far back behind them somewhere, a rocket in which they had ridden and fallen. A rocket in which lay two of their friends, dead and dripping rain.

They walked in single file, not speaking. They came to a river which lay wide and flat and brown, flowing down to the great Single Sea. The surface of it was stippled in a billion places by the rain.

"All right, Simmons."

The lieutenant nodded and Simmons took a small packet from his back which, with a pressure of hidden chemical, inflated into a large boat. The lieutenant directed the cutting of wood and the quick making of paddles and they set out into the river, paddling swiftly across the smooth surface in the rain.

The lieutenant felt the cold rain on his cheeks and on his neck and on his moving arms. The cold was beginning to seep into his lungs. He felt the rain on his ears, on his eyes, on his legs.

"I didn't sleep last night," he said.

"Who could? Who has? When? How many nights *have* we slept? Thirty nights, thirty days! Who can sleep with rain slamming their head, banging away. . . . I'd give anything for a hat. Anything at all, just so it wouldn't hit my head any more. I get headaches. My head is sore; it hurts all the time."

"I'm sorry I came to China," said one of the others.

"First time I ever heard Venus called China."

"Sure, China. Chinese water cure. Remember the old torture? Rope you against a wall. Drop one drop of water on your head every half hour. You go crazy waiting for the next one. Well, that's Venus, but on a big scale. We're not made for water. You can't sleep, you can't breathe right, and you're crazy from just being soggy. If we'd been ready for a crash, we'd have brought waterproofed uniforms and hats. It's this beating rain on your head gets you, most of all. It's so heavy. It's like BB shot. I don't know how long I can take it."

"Boy, me for the Sun Dome! The man who thought *them* up, thought of something."

They crossed the river, and in crossing they thought of the Sun Dome, somewhere ahead of them, shining in the jungle rain. A yellow house, round and bright as the sun. A house fifteen feet high by one hundred feet in diameter, in which were warmth and quiet and hot food and freedom from rain. And in the center of the Sun Dome, of course, was a sun. A small floating free globe of yellow fire, drifting in a space at the top of the building where you could look at it from where you sat, smoking or reading a book or drinking your hot chocolate crowned with marshmallow dollops. There it would be, the yellow sun, just the size of the Earth sun, and it was warm and continuous, and the rain world of Venus would be forgotten as long as they stayed in that house and idled their time.

The lieutenant turned and looked back at the three men using their oars and gritting their teeth. They were as white as mushrooms, as white as he was. Venus bleached everything away in a few months. Even the jungle was an immense cartoon nightmare, for how could the jungle be green with no sun, with always rain falling and always dusk? The white, white jungle with the pale cheese-colored leaves, and the earth carved of wet Camembert, and the tree boles like immense toadstools—everything black and white. And how often could you see the soil itself? Wasn't it mostly a creek, a stream, a puddle, a pool, a lake, a river, and then, at last, the sea?

"Here we are!"

They leaped out on the farther shore, splashing and sending up showers. The boat was deflated and stored in a cigarette packet. Then, standing on the rainy shore, they tried to light up a few smokes for themselves, and it was five minutes or so before, shuddering, they worked the inverted lighter and, cupping their hands, managed a few drags upon cigarettes that all too quickly were limp and beaten away from their lips by a sudden slap of rain.

They walked on.

"Wait just a moment," said the lieutenant. "I thought I saw something ahead."

"The Sun Dome?"

"I'm not sure. The rain closed in again."

Simmons began to run. "The Sun Dome!"

"Come back, Simmons!"

"The Sun Dome!"

Simmons vanished in the rain. The others ran after him.

They found him in a little clearing, and they stopped and looked at him and what he had discovered.

The rocket ship.

It was lying where they had left it. Somehow they had circled back and were where they had started. In the ruin of the ship green fungus was growing up out of the mouths of the two dead men. As they watched, the fungus took flower, the petals broke away in the rain, and the fungus died.

"How did we do it?"

"An electrical storm must be nearby. Threw our compasses off. That explains it."

"You're right."

"What'll we do now?"

"Start out again."

"Good Lord, we're not any closer to anywhere!"

"Let's try to keep calm about it, Simmons."

"Calm, calm! This rain's driving me wild!"

"We've enough food for another two days if we're careful."

The rain danced on their skin, on their wet uniforms; the rain streamed from their noses and ears, from their fingers and knees. They looked like stone fountains frozen in the jungle, issuing forth water from every pore.

And, as they stood, from a distance they heard a roar.

And the monster came out of the rain.

The monster was supported upon a thousand electric blue legs. It walked swiftly and terribly. It struck down a leg with a driving blow. Everywhere a leg struck a tree fell and burned. Great whiffs of ozone filled the rainy air, and smoke blew away and was broken up by the rain. The monster was a half-mile wide and a mile high and it felt of the ground like a great blind thing. Sometimes, for a moment, it had no legs at all. And then, in an instant, a thousand whips would fall out of its belly, white-blue whips, to sting the jungle.

"There's the electrical storm," said one of the men. "There's the thing ruined our compasses. And it's coming this way."

"Lie down, everyone," said the lieutenant.

"Run!" cried Simmons.

"Don't be a fool. Lie down. It hits the highest points. We may get through unhurt. Lie down about fifty feet from the rocket. It may very well spend its force there and leave us be. Get down!"

The men flopped.

"Is it coming?" they asked each other, after a moment.

"Coming."

"Is it nearer?"

"Two hundred yards off."

"Nearer?"

"Here she is!"

The monster came and stood over them. It dropped down ten blue bolts of lightning which struck the rocket. The rocket flashed like a beaten gong and gave off a metal ringing. The monster let down fifteen more bolts which danced about in a ridiculous pantomime, feeling of the jungle and the watery soil.

"No, no!" One of the men jumped up.

"Get down, you fool!" cried the lieutenant.

"No!"

The lightning struck the rocket another dozen times. The lieutenant turned his head on his arm and saw the blue blazing flashes. He saw trees split and crumple into ruin. He saw the monstrous dark cloud turn like a black disk overhead and hurl down a hundred other poles of electricity.

The man who had leaped up was now running, like someone in a great hall of pillars. He ran and dodged between the pillars and then at last a dozen of the pillars slammed down and there was the sound a fly makes when landing upon the grill wires of an exterminator. The lieutenant remembered this from his childhood on a farm. And there was a smell of a man burned to a cinder.

The lieutenant lowered his head. "Don't look up," he told the others. He was afraid that he too might run at any moment.

The storm above them flashed down another series of bolts and then moved on away. Once again there was only the rain, which rapidly cleared the air of the charred smell, and in a moment the three remaining men were sitting and waiting for the beat of their hearts to subside into quiet once more.

They walked over to the body, thinking that perhaps they could still save the man's life. They couldn't believe that there wasn't some way to help the man. It was the natural act of men who have not accepted death until they have touched it and turned it over and made plans to bury it or leave it there for the jungle to bury in an hour of quick growth.

The body was twisted steel, wrapped in burned leather. It looked like a wax dummy that had been thrown into an incinerator and pulled out after the wax had sunk to the charcoal skeleton. Only the teeth were white, and they shone like a strange white bracelet dropped half through a clenched black fist.

"He shouldn't have jumped up." They said it almost at the same time.

Even as they stood over the body it began to vanish, for the vegetation was edging in upon it, little vines and ivy and creepers, and even flowers for the dead.

At a distance the storm walked off on blue bolts of lightning and was gone.

They crossed a river and a creek and a stream and a dozen other rivers and creeks and streams. Before their eyes rivers appeared, rushing, new rivers, while old rivers changed their courses—rivers the color of mercury, rivers the color of silver and milk.

They came to the sea.

The Single Sea. There was only one continent on Venus. This land was three thousand miles long by a thousand miles wide, and about this island was the Single Sea, which covered the entire raining planet. The Single Sea, which lay upon the pallid shore with little motion. . . .

"This way." The lieutenant nodded south. "I'm sure there are two Sun Domes down that way."

"While they were at it, why didn't they build a hundred more?"

"There're a hundred and twenty of them now, aren't there?"

"One hundred and twenty-six, as of last month. They tried to push a bill through Congress back on Earth a year ago to provide for a couple dozen more, but oh no, you know how *that* is. They'd rather a few men went crazy with the rain."

They started south.

The lieutenant and Simmons and the third man, Pickard, walked in the rain, in the rain that fell heavily and lightly, heavily and lightly; in the rain that poured and hammered and did not stop falling upon the land and the sea and the walking people.

Simmons saw it first. "There it is!"

"There's what?"

"The Sun Dome!"

The lieutenant blinked the water from his eyes and raised his hands to ward off the stinging blows of the rain.

At a distance there was a yellow glow on the edge of the jungle, by the sea. It was, indeed, the Sun Dome.

The men smiled at each other.

"Looks like you were right, Lieutenant."

"Luck."

"Brother, that puts muscle in me, just seeing it. Come on! Last one there's a son-of-a-bitch!" Simmons began to trot. The others automatically fell in with this, gasping, tired, but keeping pace.

"A big pot of coffee for me," panted Simmons, smiling. "And a pan of cinnamon buns, by God! And just lie there and let the old sun hit you. The guy that invented the Sun Domes, he should have got a medal!"

They ran faster. The yellow glow grew brighter.

"Guess a lot of men went crazy before they figured out the cure. Think it'd be obvious! Right off." Simmons panted the words in cadence to his running. "Rain, rain! Years ago. Found a friend. Of mine. Out in the jungle. Wandering around. In the rain. Saying over and over, 'Don't know enough, to come in, outta the rain. Don't know enough, to come in, outta the rain. Don't know enough—' On and on. Like that. Poor crazy bastard."

"Save your breath!"

They ran.

They all laughed. They reached the door of the Sun Dome, laughing.

Simmons yanked the door wide. "Hey!" he yelled. "Bring on the coffee and buns!"

There was no reply.

They stepped through the door.

The Sun Dome was empty and dark. There was no synthetic yellow sun floating in a high gaseous whisper at the center of the blue ceiling. There was no food waiting. It was cold as a vault. And through a thousand holes which had been newly punctured in the ceiling water streamed, the rain fell down, soaking into the thick rugs and the heavy modern furniture and splashing on the glass tables. The jungle was growing up like a moss in the room, on top of the bookcases and the divans. The rain slashed through the holes and fell upon the three men's faces.

Pickard began to laugh quietly.

"Shut up, Pickard!"

"Ye gods, look what's here for us—no food, no sun, nothing. The Venusians—they did it! Of course!"

Simmons nodded, with the rain funneling down on his face. The water ran in his silvered hair and on his white eyebrows. "Every once in a while the Venusians come up out of the sea and attack a Sun Dome. They know if they ruin the Sun Domes they can ruin us."

"But aren't the Sun Domes protected with guns?"

"Sure." Simmons stepped aside to a place that was relatively dry. "But it's been five years since the Venusians tried anything. Defense relaxes. They caught this Dome unaware."

"Where are the bodies?"

"The Venusians took them all down into the sea. I hear they have a delightful way of drowning you. It takes about eight hours to drown the way they work it. Really delightful."

"I bet there isn't any food here at all." Pickard laughed.

The lieutenant frowned at him, nodded at him so Simmons could see. Simmons shook his head and went back to a room at one side of the oval chamber. The kitchen was strewn with soggy loaves of bread, and meat that had grown a faint green fur. Rain came through a hundred holes in the kitchen roof.

"Brilliant." The lieutenant glanced up at the holes. "I don't suppose we can plug up all those holes and get snug here."

"Without food, sir?" Simmons snorted. "I notice the sun machine's torn apart. Our best bet is to make our way to the next Sun Dome. How far is that from here?"

"Not far. As I recall, they built two rather close together here. Perhaps if we waited here, a rescue mission from the other might—"

"It's probably been here and gone already, some days ago. They'll send a crew to repair this place in about six months, when they get the money from Congress. I don't think we'd better wait."

"All right then, we'll eat what's left of our rations and get on to the next Dome."

Pickard said, "If only the rain wouldn't hit my head, just for a few minutes. If I could only remember what it's like not to be bothered." He put his hands on his skull and held it tight. "I remember when I was in school a bully used to sit in back of me and pinch me and pinch me and pinch me every five minutes, all day long. He did that for weeks and months. My arms were sore and black and blue all the time. And I thought I'd go crazy from being pinched. One day I must have gone a little mad from being hurt and hurt, and I turned around and took a metal trisquare I used in mechanical drawing and I almost killed that bastard. I almost cut his lousy head off. I almost took his eye out before they dragged me out of the room, and I kept yelling, 'Why don't he leave me alone? why don't he leave me alone?' Brother!" His hands clenched the bone of his head, shaking, tightening, his eyes shut. "But what do I do *now*? Who do I hit, who do I tell to lay off, stop bothering me, this damn rain, like the pinching, always *on* you, that's all you hear, that's all you feel!"

"We'll be at the other Sun Dome by four this afternoon."

"Sun Dome? Look at this one! What if all the Sun Domes on Venus are gone? What then? What if there are holes in all the ceilings, and the rain coming in!"

"We'll have to chance it."

"I'm tired of chancing it. All I want is a roof and some quiet. I want to be alone."

"That's only eight hours off, if you hold on."

"Don't worry, I'll hold on all right." And Pickard laughed, not looking at them.

"Let's eat," said Simmons, watching him.

They set off down the coast, southward again. After four hours they had to cut inland to go around a river that was a mile wide and so swift it was not navigable by boat. They had to walk inland six miles to a place where the river boiled out of the earth, suddenly, like a mortal wound. In the rain, they walked on solid ground and returned to the sea.

"I've got to sleep," said Pickard at last. He slumped. "Haven't slept in four weeks. Tried, but couldn't. Sleep here."

The sky was getting darker. The night of Venus was setting in and it was so completely black that it was dangerous to move. Simmons and the lieutenant fell to their knees also, and the lieutenant said, "All right, we'll see what we can do. We've tried it before, but I don't know. Sleep doesn't seem one of the things you can get in this weather."

They lay out full, propping their heads up so the water wouldn't come to their mouths, and they closed their eyes. The lieutenant twitched.

He did not sleep.

There were things that crawled on his skin. Things grew upon him in layers. Drops fell and touched other drops and they became streams that trickled over his body, and while these moved down his flesh, the small growths of the forest took root in his clothing. He felt the ivy cling and make a second garment over him; he felt the small flowers bud and open and petal away, and still the rain pattered on his body and on his head. In the luminous night—for the vegetation glowed in the darkness—he could see the other two men outlined, like logs that had fallen and taken upon themselves velvet coverings of grass and flowers. The rain hit his face. He covered his face with his hands. The rain hit his neck. He turned over on his stomach in the mud, on the rubbery plants, and the rain hit his back and hit his legs.

Suddenly he leaped up and began to brush the water from himself. A thousand hands were touching him and he no longer wanted to be touched. He no longer could stand being touched. He floundered and struck something else and knew that it was Simmons, standing up in the rain, sneezing moisture, coughing and choking. And then Pickard was up, shouting, running about.

"Wait a minute, Pickard!"

"Stop it, stop it!" Pickard screamed. He fired off his gun six times at the night sky. In the flashes of powdery illumination they could see armies of raindrops, suspended as in a vast motionless amber, for an instant, hesitating as if shocked by the explosion, fifteen billion droplets, fifteen billion tears, fifteen billion ornaments, jewels standing out against a white velvet viewing board. And then, with the light gone, the drops which had waited to have their pictures taken, which had suspended their downward rush, fell upon them, stinging, in an insect cloud of coldness and pain.

"Stop it! Stop it!"

"Pickard!"

But Pickard was only standing now, alone. When the lieutenant switched on a small hand lamp and played it over Pickard's wet face, the eyes of the man were dilated, and his mouth was open, his face turned up, so the water hit and splashed on his tongue, and hit and drowned the wide eyes, and bubbled in a whispering froth on the nostrils.

"Pickard!"

The man would not reply. He simply stood there for a long while with the bubbles of rain breaking out in his whitened hair and manacles of rain jewels dripping from his wrists and neck.

"Pickard! We're leaving. We're going on. Follow us."

The rain dripped from Pickard's ears.

"Do you hear me, Pickard!"

It was like shouting down a well.

"Pickard!"

"Leave him alone," said Simmons.

"We can't go on without him."

"What'll we do, carry him?" Simmons spat. "He's no good to us or himself. You know what he'll do? He'll just stand here and drown."

"What?"

"You ought to know that by now. Don't you know the story? He'll just stand here with his head up and let the rain come in his nostrils and his mouth. He'll breathe the water."

"No."

"That's how they found General Mendt that time. Sitting on a rock with his head back, breathing the rain. His lungs were full of water."

The lieutenant turned the light back to the unblinking face. Pickard's nostrils gave off a tiny whispering wet sound.

"Pickard!" The lieutenant slapped the face.

"He can't even feel you," said Simmons. "A few days in this rain and you don't have any face or any legs or hands."

The lieutenant looked at his own hand in horror. He could no longer feel it.

"But we can't leave Pickard here."

"I'll show you what we can do." Simmons fired his gun.

Pickard fell into the raining earth.

Simmons said, "Don't move, Lieutenant. I've got my gun ready for you too. Think it over; he would only have stood or sat there and drowned. It's quicker this way."

The lieutenant blinked at the body. "But you killed him."

"Yes, because he'd have killed us by being a burden. You saw his face. Insane."

After a moment the lieutenant nodded. "All right."

They walked off into the rain.

It was dark and their hand lamps threw a beam that pierced the rain for only a few feet. After a half hour they had to stop and sit through the rest of the night, aching with hunger, waiting for the dawn to come; when it did come it was gray and continually raining as before, and they began to walk again.

"We've miscalculated," said Simmons.

"No. Another hour."

"Speak louder. I can't hear you." Simmons stopped and smiled. "By Christ," he said, and touched his ears. "My ears. They've gone out on me. All the rain pouring finally numbed me right down to the bone."

"Can't you hear anything?" said the lieutenant.

"What?" Simmons's eyes were puzzled.

"Nothing. Come on."

"I think I'll wait here. You go on ahead."

"You can't do that."

"I can't hear you. You go on. I'm tired. I don't think the Sun Dome is down this way. And, if it is, it's probably got holes in the roof, like the last one. I think I'll just sit here."

"Get up from there!"

"So long, Lieutenant."

"You can't give up now."

"I've got a gun here that says I'm staying. I just don't give a damn any more. I'm not crazy yet, but I'm the next thing to it. I don't want to go out that way. As soon as you get out of sight I'm going to use this gun on myself."

"Simmons!"

"You said my name. I can read that much off your lips."

"Simmons."

"Look, it's a matter of time. Either I die now or in a few hours. Wait'll you get to that next Dome, if you ever get there, and find rain coming in through the roof. Won't that be nice?"

The lieutenant waited and then splashed off in the rain. He turned and called back once, but Simmons was only sitting there with the gun in his hands, waiting for him to get out of sight. He shook his head and waved the lieutenant on.

The lieutenant didn't even hear the sound of the gun.

He began to eat the flowers as he walked. They stayed down for a time, and weren't poisonous; neither were they particularly sustaining, and he vomited them up, sickly, a minute or so later.

Once he took some leaves and tried to make himself a hat, but he had tried that before; the rain melted the leaves from his head. Once picked, the vegetation rotted quickly and fell away into gray masses in his fingers.

"Another five minutes," he told himself. "Another five minutes and then I'll walk into the sea and keep walking. We weren't made for this; no Earth Man was or ever will be able to take it. Your nerves, your nerves."

He floundered his way through a sea of slush and foliage and came to a small hill.

At a distance there was a faint yellow smudge in the cold veils of water.

The next Sun Dome.

Through the trees, a long round yellow building, far away. For a moment he only stood, swaying, looking at it.

He began to run and then he slowed down, for he was afraid. He didn't call out. What if it's the same one? What if it's the dead Sun Dome, with no sun in it? he thought.

He slipped and fell. Lie here, he thought; it's the wrong one. Lie here. It's no use. Drink all you want.

But he managed to climb to his feet again and crossed several creeks, and the yellow light grew very bright, and he began to run again, his feet crashing into mirrors and glass, his arms flailing at diamonds and precious stones.

He stood before the yellow door. The printed letters over it said THE SUN DOME. He put his numb hand up to feel it. Then he twisted the doorknob and stumbled in.

He stood for a moment looking about. Behind him the rain whirled at the door. Ahead of him, upon a low table, stood a silver pot of hot chocolate, steaming, and a cup, full, with a marshmallow in it. And beside that, on another tray, stood thick sandwiches of rich chicken meat and fresh-cut tomatoes and green onions. And on a rod just before his eyes was a great thick green Turkish towel, and a bin in which to throw wet clothes, and, to his right, a small cubicle in which heat rays might dry you instantly. And upon a chair, a fresh change of uniform, waiting for anyone—himself, or any lost one—to make use of it. And farther over, coffee in steaming copper urns, and a phonograph from which music was playing quietly, and books bound in red and brown leather. And near the books a cot, a soft deep cot upon which one might lie, exposed and bare, to drink in the rays of the one great bright thing which dominated the long room.

He put his hands to his eyes. He saw other men moving toward him, but said nothing to them. He waited, and opened his eyes, and looked. The water from his uniform pooled at his feet, and he felt it drying from his hair and his face and his chest and his arms and his legs.

He was looking at the sun.

It hung in the center of the room, large and yellow and warm. It made not a sound, and there was no sound in the room. The door was shut and the rain only a memory to his tingling body. The sun hung very high in the blue sky of the room, warm, hot, yellow, and very fine.

He walked forward, tearing off his clothes as he went.

The Great Fire

The morning the great fire started, nobody in the house could put it out. It was Mother's niece, Marianne, living with us while her parents were in Europe, who was all aflame. So nobody could smash the little window in the red box at the corner and pull the trigger to bring the gushing hoses and the hatted firemen. Blazing like so much ignited cellophane, Marianne came downstairs, plumped herself with a loud cry or moan at the breakfast table, and refused to eat enough to fill a tooth cavity.

Mother and Father moved away, the warmth in the room being excessive.

"Good morning, Marianne."

"What?" Marianne looked beyond people and spoke vaguely. "Oh, good morning."

"Did you sleep well last night, Marianne?"

But they knew she hadn't slept. Mother gave Marianne a glass of water to drink, and everyone wondered if it would evaporate in her hand. Grandma, from her table chair, surveyed Marianne's fevered eyes. "You're sick, but it's no microbe," she said. "They couldn't find it under a microscope."

"What?" said Marianne.

"Love is godmother to stupidity," said Father detachedly.

"She'll be all right," Mother said to Father. "Girls only seem stupid because when they're in love they can't hear."

"It affects the semicircular canals," said Father. "Making many girls fall right into a fellow's arms. I *know*. I was almost crushed to death once by a falling woman, and let me tell you—"

"Hush." Mother frowned, looking at Marianne.

"She can't hear what we're saying; she's cataleptic right now."

"He's coming to pick her up this morning," whispered Mother to Father, as if Marianne wasn't even in the room. "They're going riding in his jalopy."

Father patted his mouth with a napkin. "Was our daughter like this, Mama?" he wanted to know. "She's been married and gone so long, I've forgotten. I don't recall she was so foolish. One would never know a girl had an ounce of sense at a time like this. That's what fools a man. He says, Oh, what a lovely brainless girl, she loves me, I think I'll marry her. He marries her and wakes up one morning and all the dreaminess is gone out of her and her intellect has returned, unpacked, and is hanging up undies all about the house. The man begins running into ropes and lines. He finds himself on a little desert isle, a little living room alone in the midst of a universe, with a honeycomb that has turned into a bear trap, with a butterfly metamorphosed into a wasp. He then immediately takes up a hobby: stamp collecting, lodge meetings, or—"

"How you *do* run on," cried Mother. "Marianne, tell us about this young man. What was his name again? Was it Isak Van Pelt?"

"What? Oh—Isak, yes." Marianne had been roving about her bed all night, sometimes flipping poetry books and reading incredible lines, sometimes lying flat on her back, sometimes on her tummy looking out at dreaming moonlit country. The smell of jasmine had touched the room all night and the excessive warmth of early spring (the thermometer read fifty-five degrees) had kept her awake. She looked like a dying moth, if anyone had peeked through the keyhole.

This morning she had clapped her hands over her head in the mirror and come to breakfast, remembering just in time to put on a dress.

Grandma laughed quietly all during breakfast. Finally she said, "You must eat, child, you *must*." So Marianne played with her toast and got half a piece down. Just then there was a loud honk outside. That was Isak! In his jalopy!

"Whoop!" cried Marianne, and ran upstairs quickly.

The young Isak Van Pelt was brought in and introduced around.

When Marianne was finally gone, Father sat down, wiping his forehead. "I don't know. This is too much."

"You were the one who suggested she start going out," said Mother.

"And I'm sorry I suggested it," he said. "But she's been visiting us for six months now, and six more months to go. I thought if she met some nice young man—"

"And they were married," husked Grandma darkly, "why, Marianne might move out almost immediately—is *that* it?"

"Well," said Father.

"Well," said Grandma.

"But now it's worse than before," said Father. "She floats around singing with her eyes shut, playing those infernal love records and talking to herself. A man can stand so much. She's getting so she laughs all the time, too. Do eighteen-year-old girls often wind up in the booby hatch?"

"He seems a nice young man," said Mother.

"Yes, we can always pray for that," said Father, taking out a little shot glass.

"Here's to an early marriage."

The second morning Marianne was out of the house like a fireball when first she heard the jalopy horn. There was no time for the young man even to come to the door. Only Grandma saw them roar off together, from the parlor window.

"She almost knocked me down." Father brushed his mustache. "What's *that?* Brained eggs? Well."

In the afternoon, Marianne, home again, drifted about the living room to the phonograph records. The needle hiss filled the house. She played "That Old Black Magic" twenty-one times, going "la la la" as she swam with her eyes closed in the room.

"I'm afraid to go in my own parlor," said Father. "I retired from business to smoke cigars and enjoy living, not to have a limp relative humming about under the parlor chandelier."

"Hush," said Mother.

"This is a crisis," announced Father, "in my life. After all, she's just visiting."

"You know how visiting girls are. Away from home they think they're in Paris, France. She'll be gone in October. It's not so dreadful."

"Let's see," figured Father slowly. "I'll have been buried just about one hundred and thirty days out at Green Lawn Cemetery by then." He got up and threw his paper down into a little white tent on the floor. "By George, Mother, I'm talking to her right *now!*"

He went and stood in the parlor door, peering through it at the waltzing Marianne. "La," she sang to the music.

Clearing his throat, he stepped through.

"Marianne," he said.

"'That old black magic ...'" sang Marianne. "Yes?"

He watched her hands swinging in the air. She gave him a sudden fiery look as she danced by.

"I want to talk to you." He straightened his tie.

"Dah dum dee dum dum dee dum dee dum dum," she sang.

"Did you *hear* me?" he demanded.

"He's *so* nice," she said.

"Evidently."

"Do you know, he bows and opens doors like a doorman and plays a trumpet like Harry James and brought me daisies this morning?"

"I wouldn't doubt."

"His eyes are blue." She looked at the ceiling.

He could find nothing at all on the ceiling to look at.

She kept looking, as she danced, at the ceiling as he came over and stood near her, looking up, but there wasn't a rain spot or a settling crack there, and he sighed, "Marianne."

"And we ate lobster at that river café."

"Lobster. I know, but we don't want you breaking down, getting weak. One day, tomorrow, you must stay home and help your aunt Math make her doilies—"

"Yes, sir." She dreamed around the room with her wings out.

"Did you *hear* me?" he demanded.

"Yes," she whispered. "Yes." Her eyes shut. "Oh yes, yes." Her skirts whished around. "Uncle," she said, her head back, lolling.

"You'll help your aunt with her doilies?" he cried.

"—with her doilies," she murmured.

"There!" He sat down in the kitchen, plucking up the paper. "I guess *I* told her!"

But next morning he was on the edge of his bed when he heard the hot-rod's thunderous muffler and heard Marianne fall downstairs, linger two seconds in the dining room for breakfast, hesitate by the bathroom long enough to consider whether she would be sick, and then the slam of the front door, the sound of the jalopy banging down the street, two people singing off-key in it.

Father put his head in his hands. "Doilies," he said.

"What?" said Mother.

"Dooley's," said Father. "I'm going down to Dooley's for a morning visit."

"But Dooley's isn't open until ten."

"I'll wait," decided Father, eyes shut.

That night and seven other wild nights the porch swing sang a little creaking song, back and forth, back and forth. Father, hiding in the living room, could be seen in fierce relief whenever he drafted his ten-cent cigar and the cherry light illumined his immensely tragic face. The porch swing creaked. He waited for another creak. He heard little butterfly-soft sounds from outside, little palpitations of laughter and sweet nothings in small ears. "My porch," said Father. "My swing," he whispered to his cigar, looking at it. "My house." He listened for another creak. "My God," he said.

He went to the tool shed and appeared on the dark porch with a shiny oil can. "No, don't get up. Don't bother. There, and there." He oiled the swing joints. It was dark. He couldn't see Marianne; he could smell her. The perfume almost knocked him off into the rosebush. He couldn't see her gentleman friend, either. "Good night," he said. He went in and sat down and there was no more creaking. Now all he could hear was something that sounded like the mothlike flutter of Marianne's heart.

"He must be very nice," said Mother in the kitchen door, wiping a dinner dish.

"That's what I'm hoping," whispered Father. "That's why I let them have the porch every night!"

"So many days in a row," said Mother. "A girl doesn't go with a nice young man that many times unless he's serious."

"Maybe he'll propose tonight!" was Father's happy thought.

"Hardly so soon. And she is so young."

"Still," he ruminated, "it might happen. It's *got* to happen, by the Lord Harry."

Grandma chuckled from her corner easy chair. It sounded like someone turning the pages of an ancient book.

"What's so funny?" said Father.

"Wait and see," said Grandma. "Tomorrow."

Father stared at the dark, but Grandma would say no more.

"Well, well," said Father at breakfast. He surveyed his eggs with a kindly, paternal eye. "Well, well, by gosh, last night, on the porch, there was *more whispering*. What's his name? Isak? Well, now, if I'm any judge at all, I think he proposed to Marianne last night; yes, I'm positive of it!"

"It would be nice," said Mother. "A spring marriage. But it's so *soon*."

"Look," said Father with full-mouthed logic. "Marianne's the kind of girl who marries quick and young. We can't stand in her way, can we?"

"For once I think you're right," said Mother. "A marriage would be fine. Spring flowers, and Marianne looking nice in that gown I saw at Haydecker's last week."

They all peered anxiously at the stairs, waiting for Marianne to appear.

"Pardon me," rasped Grandma, sighting up from her morning toast. "But I wouldn't talk of getting rid of Marianne just yet if I were you."

"And why not?"

"Because."

"Because why?"

"I hate to spoil your plans," rustled Grandma, chuckling. She gestured with her little vinegary head. "But while you people were worrying about getting Marianne married, I've been keeping tabs on her. Seven days now I've been watching this young fellow each day he came in his car and honked his horn outside. He must be an actor or a quick-change artist or something."

"What?" asked Father.

"Yep," said Grandma. "Because one day he was a young blond fellow, and next day he was a tall dark fellow, and Wednesday he was a chap with a brown mustache, and Thursday he had wavy red hair, and Friday he was shorter, with a Chevrolet stripped down instead of a Ford."

Mother and Father sat for a moment as if hit with a hammer right behind the left ear.

At last Father, his face exploding with color, shouted, "Do you mean to *say*! You *sat* there, woman, you say; all those men, and you—"

"You were always hiding," snapped Grandma. "So you wouldn't spoil things. If you'd come out in the open you'd have seen the same as I. I never said a word. She'll simmer down. It's just her time of life. Every woman goes through it. It's hard, but they can survive. A new man every day does wonders for a girl's ego!"

"You, you, you, you, *you*!" Father choked on it, eyes wild, throat gorged too big for his collar. He fell back in his chair, exhausted. Mother sat, stunned.

"Good morning, everyone!" Marianne raced downstairs and popped into a chair. Father stared at her.

"You, you, you, you, you," he accused Grandma.

I shall run down the street shouting, thought Father wildly, and break the fire-alarm window and pull the lever and bring the fire engines and the hoses. Or perhaps there will be a late snowstorm and I shall set Marianne out in it to cool.

He did neither. The heat in the room being excessive, according to the wall calendar, everyone moved out onto the cool porch while Marianne sat looking at her orange juice.

The Wilderness

"Oh, the Good Time has come at last—"

It was twilight, and Janice and Leonora packed steadily in their summer house, singing songs, eating little, and holding to each other when necessary. But they never glanced at the window where the night gathered deep and the stars came out bright and cold.

"Listen!" said Janice.

A sound like a steamboat down the river, but it was a rocket in the sky. And beyond that—banjos playing? No, only the summer-night crickets in this year 2003. Ten thousand sounds breathed through the town and the weather. Janice, head bent, listened. Long, long ago, 1849, this very street had breathed the voices of ventriloquists, preachers, fortunetellers, fools, scholars, gamblers, gathered at this selfsame Independence, Missouri. Waiting for the moist earth to bake and the great tidal grasses to come up heavy enough to hold the weight of their carts, their wagons, their indiscriminate destinies, and their dreams.

> *"Oh, the Good Time has come at last,*
> *To Mars we are a-going, sir,*
> *Five Thousand Women in the sky,*
> *That's quite a springtime sowing, sir!"*

"That's an old Wyoming song," said Leonora. "Change the words and it's fine for 2003."

Janice lifted a matchbox of food pills, calculating the totals of things carried in those high-axled, tall-bedded wagons. For each man, each woman, incredible tonnages! Hams, bacon slabs, sugar, salt, flour, dried fruits, "pilot" bread, citric acid, water, ginger, pepper—a list as big as the land! Yet here, today, pills that fit in a wristwatch fed you not from Fort Laramie to Hangtown, but all across a wilderness of stars.

Janice threw wide the closet door and almost screamed. Darkness and night and all the spaces between the stars looked out at her.

Long years ago two things had happened. Her sister had locked her, shrieking, in a closet. And, at a party, playing hide-and-seek, she had run through the kitchen and into a long dark hall. But it wasn't a hall. It was an unlit stairwell, a swallowing blackness. She had run out upon empty air. She had pedaled her feet, screamed, and fallen! Fallen in midnight blackness. Into the cellar. It took a long while, a heartbeat, to fall. And she had smothered in that closet a long, long time without daylight, without friends, no one to hear her screamings. Away from everything, locked in darkness. Falling in darkness. Shrieking!

The two memories.

Now, with the closet door wide, with darkness like a velvet shroud hung before her to be stroked by a trembling hand, with the darkness like a black panther breathing there, looking at her with unlit eyes, the two memories rushed out. Space and a falling. Space and being locked away, screaming. She and Leonora working steadily, packing, being careful not to glance out the window at the frightening Milky Way and the vast emptiness. Only to have the long-familiar closet, with its private night, remind them at last of their destiny.

This was how it would be, out there, sliding toward the stars, in the night, in the great hideous black closet, screaming, but no one to hear. Falling forever among meteor clouds and godless comets. Down the elevator shaft. Down the nightmare coal chute into nothingness.

She screamed. None of it came out of her mouth. It collided upon itself in her chest and head. She screamed. She slammed the closet door! She lay against it! She felt the darkness breathe and yammer at the door and she held it tight, eyes watering. She stood there a long time, until the trembling vanished, watching Leonora work. And the hysteria, thus ignored, drained away and away, and at last was gone. A wristwatch ticked, with a clean sound of normality, in the room.

"Sixty *million* miles." She moved at last to the window as if it were a deep well. "I can't believe that men on Mars, tonight, are building towns, waiting for us."

"The only thing to believe is catching our Rocket tomorrow."

Janice raised a white gown like a ghost in the room.

"Strange, strange. To marry—on another world."

"Let's get to bed."

"No! The call comes at midnight. I couldn't sleep, thinking how to tell Will I've decided to take the Mars Rocket. Oh, Leonora, think of it, my voice traveling sixty million miles on the light-phone to him. I changed my mind so quick—I'm scared!"

"Our *last* night on Earth."

Now they really knew and accepted it; now the knowledge had found them out. They were going away, and they might never come back. They were leaving the town of Independence in the state of Missouri on the continent of North America, surrounded by one ocean which was the Atlantic and another the Pacific, none of which could be put in their traveling cases. They had shrunk from this final knowledge. Now it was facing them. And they were struck numb.

"Our children, they won't be Americans, or Earth people at all. We'll all be Martians, the rest of our lives."

"I don't want to go!" cried Janice suddenly.

The panic froze her.

"I'm afraid! The space, the darkness, the Rocket, the meteors! *Everything* gone! Why should I go out there?"

Leonora took hold of her shoulders and held her close, rocking her. "It's a new world. It's like the old days. The men first and the women after."

"Why, why should I go, tell me!"

"Because," said Leonora at last, quietly, seating her on the bed, "Will is up there."

His name was good to hear. Janice quieted.

"These men make it so hard," said Leonora. "Used to be if a woman ran two hundred miles for a man it was something. Then they made it a thousand miles. And now they put a whole universe between us. But that can't stop us, can it?"

"I'm afraid I'll be a fool on the Rocket."

"I'll be a fool with you." Leonora got up. "Now, let's walk around town, let's see everything one last time."

Janice stared out at the town. "Tomorrow night this'll all be here, but we won't. People'll wake up, eat, work, sleep, wake again, but we won't know it, and they'll never miss us."

Leonora and Janice moved around each other as if they couldn't find the door.

"Come on."

They opened the door, switched off the lights, stepped out, and shut the door behind them.

In the sky there was a great coming-in and coming-in. Vast flowering motions, huge whistlings and whirlings, snowstorms falling. Helicopters, white flakes, dropping quietly. From west and east and north and south the women were arriving, arriving. Through all of the night sky you saw helicopters blizzard down. The hotels were full, private homes were making accommodations, tent cities rose in meadows and pastures like strange, ugly flowers, and the town and the country were warm with more than summer tonight. Warm with women's pink faces and the sunburnt faces of new men watching the sky. Beyond the hills rockets tried their fire, and a sound like a giant organ, all its keys pressed upon at once, shuddered every crystal window and every hidden bone. You felt it in your jaw, your toes, your fingers, a shivering.

Leonora and Janice sat in the drugstore among unfamiliar women.

"You ladies look very pretty, but you sure look sad," said the soda-fountain man.

"Two chocolate malteds." Leonora smiled for both of them, as if Janice were mute.

They gazed at the chocolate drink as if it were a rare museum painting. Malts would be scarce for many years on Mars.

Janice fussed in her purse and took out an envelope reluctantly and laid it on the marble counter.

"This is from Will to me. It came in the Rocket mail two days ago. It was this that made up my mind for me, made me decide to go. I didn't tell you. I want you to see it now. Go ahead, read the note."

Leonora shook the note out of the envelope and read it aloud: *"Dear Janice: this is our house if you decide to come to Mars. Will."*

Leonora tapped the envelope again, and a color photograph dropped out, glistening, on the counter. It was a picture of a house, a dark, mossy, ancient, caramel-brown, comfortable house with red flowers and green cool ferns bordering it, and a disreputably hairy ivy on the porch.

"But, Janice!"

"What?"

"This is a picture of *your* house, here on Earth, here on Elm Street!"

"No. Look close."

And they looked again, together, and on both sides of the comfortable dark house and behind it was scenery that was not Earth scenery. The soil was a strange color of violet, and the grass was the faintest bit red, and the sky glowed like a gray diamond, and a strange crooked tree grew to one side, looking like an old woman with crystals in her white hair.

"That's the house Will's built for me," said Janice, "on Mars. It helps to look at it. All yesterday, when I had the chance, alone, and was most afraid and panicky, I took out this picture and looked at it."

They both gazed at the dark comfortable house sixty million miles away, familiar but unfamiliar, old but new, a yellow light shining in the right front parlor window.

"That man Will," said Leonora, nodding her head, "knows just what he's doing."

They finished their drinks. Outside, a vast warm crowd of strangers wandered by and the "snow" fell steadily in the summer sky.

They bought many silly things to take with them, bags of lemon candy, glossy women's magazines, fragile perfumes; and then they walked out into the town and rented two belted jackets that refused to recognize gravity and imitated only the moth, touched the delicate controls, and felt themselves whispered like white blossom petals over the town. "Anywhere," said Leonora, "anywhere at all."

They let the wind blow them where it would; they let the wind take them through the night of summer apple trees and the night of warm preparation, over the lovely town, over the houses of childhood and other days, over schools and avenues, over creeks and meadows and farms so familiar that each grain of wheat was a golden coin. They blew as leaves must blow before the threat of a fire-wind, with warning whispers and summer lightning crackling among the folded hills. They saw the milk-dust country roads where not so long ago they had drifted in moonlit helicopters in great whorls of sound spiraling down to touch beside cool night streams with the young men who were now gone.

They floated in an immense sigh above a town already made remote by the little space between themselves and the earth, a town receding behind them in a black river and coming up in a tidal wave of lights and color ahead, untouchable and a dream now, already smeared in their eyes with nostalgia, with a panic of memory that began before the thing itself was gone.

Blown quietly, eddying, they gazed secretly at a hundred faces of dear friends they were leaving behind, the lamplit people held and framed by windows which slid by on the wind, it seemed; all of Time breathing them along. There was no tree they did not examine for old confessions of love carved and whittled there, no sidewalk they did not skim across as over fields of mica-snow. For the first time they knew their town was beautiful and the lonely lights and the ancient bricks beautiful, and they both felt their eyes grow large with the beauty of this feast they were giving themselves. All floated upon an evening carrousel, with fitful drifts of music wafting up here and there, and voices calling and murmuring from houses that were whitely haunted by television.

The two women passed like needles, sewing one tree to the next with their perfume. Their eyes were too full, and yet they kept putting away each detail, each shadow, each solitary oak and elm, each passing car upon the small snaking streets below, until not only their eyes but their heads and then their hearts were too full.

I feel like I'm dead, thought Janice, and in the graveyard on a spring night and everything alive but me and everyone moving and ready to go on with life without me. It's like I felt each spring when I was sixteen, passing the graveyard and weeping for them because they were dead and it didn't seem fair, on nights as soft as that, that I was alive. I was guilty of living. And now, here, tonight, I feel they have taken me from the graveyard and let me go above the town just once more to see what it's like to be living, to be a town and a people, before they slam the black door on me again.

Softly, softly, like two white paper lanterns on a night wind, the women moved over their lifetime and their past, and over the meadows where the tent cities glowed and the highways where supply trucks would be clustered and running until dawn. They hovered above it all for a long time.

The courthouse clock was booming eleven forty-five when they came like spider webs floating from the stars, touching on the moonlit pavement before Janice's old house. The city was asleep, and Janice's house waited for them to come in searching for *their* sleep, which was not there.

"Is this *us*, here?" asked Janice. "Janice Smith and Leonora Holmes, in the year 2003?"

"Yes."

Janice licked her lips and stood straight. "I wish it was some other year."

"1492? 1612?" Leonora sighed, and the wind in the trees sighed with her, moving away. "It's always Columbus Day or Plymouth Rock Day, and I'll be darned if I know what we women can do about it."

"Be old maids."

"Or do just what we're doing."

They opened the door of the warm night house, the sounds of the town dying slowly in their ears. As they shut the door, the phone began to ring.

"The call!" cried Janice, running.

Leonora came into the bedroom after her and already Janice had the receiver up and was saying, "Hello, hello!" And the operator in a far city was readying the immense apparatus which would tie two worlds together, and the two women waited, one sitting and pale, the other standing, but just as pale, bent toward her.

There was a long pause, full of stars and time, a waiting pause not unlike the last three years for all of them. And now the moment had arrived, and it was Janice's turn to phone through millions upon millions of miles of meteors and comets, running away from the yellow sun which might boil or burn her words or scorch the meaning from them. But her voice went like a silver needle through everything, in stitches of talking, across the big night, reverberating from the moons of Mars. And then her voice found its way to a man in a room in a city there on another world, five minutes by radio away. And her message was this:

"Hello, Will. This is Janice!"

She swallowed.

"They say I haven't much time. A minute."

She closed her eyes.

"I want to talk slow, but they say talk fast and get it all in. So I want to say—I've decided. I will come up there. I'll go on the Rocket tomorrow. I *will* come up there to you, after all. And I love you. I hope you can hear me. I love you. It's been so long. . . . "

Her voice motioned on its way to that unseen world. Now, with the message sent, the words said, she wanted to call them back, to censor, to rearrange them, to make a prettier sentence, a fairer explanation of her soul. But already the words were hung between planets and if, by some cosmic radiation, they could have been illuminated, caught fire in vaporous wonder there, her love would have lit a dozen worlds and startled the night side of Earth into a premature dawn, she thought. Now the words were not hers at all, they belonged to space, they belonged to no one until they arrived, and they were traveling at one hundred and eighty-six thousand miles a second to their destination.

What will he say to me? What will he say back in *his* minute of time? she wondered. She fussed with and twisted the watch on her wrist, and the light-phone receiver on her ear crackled and space talked to her with electrical jigs and dances and audible auroras.

"Has he answered?" whispered Leonora.

"Shhh!" said Janice, bending, as if sick.

Then his voice came through space.

"I hear him!" cried Janice.

"What does he say?"

The voice called out from Mars and took itself through the places where there was no sunrise or sunset, but always the night with a sun in the middle of the blackness. And somewhere between Mars and Earth everything of the message was lost, perhaps in a sweep of electrical gravity rushing by on the flood tides of a meteor, or interfered with by a rain of silver meteors. In any event, the small words and the unimportant words of the message were washed away. And his voice came through saying only one word:

" . . . love . . . "

After that there was the huge night again and the sound of stars turning and suns whispering to themselves and the sound of her heart, like another world in space, filling her earphones.

"Did you *hear* him?" asked Leonora.

Janice could only nod.

"What did he say, what did he say?" cried Leonora.

But Janice could not tell anyone; it was much too good to tell. She sat listening to that one word again and again, as her memory played it back. She sat listening, while Leonora took the phone away from her without her knowing it and put it down upon its hook.

Then they were in bed and the lights out and the night wind blowing through the rooms a smell of the long journey in darkness and stars, and their voices talking of tomorrow, and the days after tomorrow which would not be days at all, but day-nights of timeless Time; their voices faded away into sleep or wakeful thinking, and Janice lay alone in her bed.

Is this how it was over a century ago, she wondered, when the women, the night before, lay ready for sleep, or not ready, in the small towns of the East, and heard the sound of horses in the night and the creak of the Conestoga wagons ready to go, and the brooding of oxen under the trees, and the cry of children already lonely before their time? All the sounds of arrivals and departures into the deep forests and fields, the blacksmiths working in their own red hells through midnight? And the smell of bacons and hams ready for the journeying, and the heavy feel of the wagons like ships foundering with goods, with water in the wooden kegs to tilt and slop across prairies, and the chickens hysterical in their slung-beneath-the-wagon crates, and the dogs running out to the wilderness ahead and, fearful, running back with a look of empty space in their eyes? Is this, then, how it was so long ago? On the rim of the precipice, on the edge of the cliff of stars? In their time the smell of buffalo, and in our time the smell of the Rocket? Is this, then, how it was?

And she decided, as sleep assumed the dreaming for her, that yes, yes indeed, very much so, irrevocably, this was as it had always been and would forever continue to be.

A Sound of Thunder

The sign on the wall seemed to quaver under a film of sliding warm water. Eckels felt his eyelids blink over his stare, and the sign burned in this momentary darkness:

TIME SAFARI, INC.

SAFARIS TO ANY YEAR IN THE PAST.

YOU NAME THE ANIMAL.

WE TAKE YOU THERE.

YOU SHOOT IT.

A warm phlegm gathered in Eckels' throat; he swallowed and pushed it down. The muscles around his mouth formed a smile as he put his hand slowly out upon the air, and in that hand waved a check for ten thousand dollars at the man behind the desk.

"Does this safari guarantee I come back alive?"

"We guarantee nothing," said the official, "except the dinosaurs." He turned. "This is Mr. Travis, your Safari Guide in the Past. He'll tell you what and where to shoot. If he says no shooting, no shooting. If you disobey instructions, there's a stiff penalty of another ten thousand dollars, plus possible government action, on your return."

Eckels glanced across the vast office at a mass and tangle, a snaking and humming of wires and steel boxes, at an aurora that flickered now orange, now silver, now blue. There was a sound like a gigantic bonfire burning all of Time, all the years and all the parchment calendars, all the hours piled high and set aflame.

A touch of the hand and this burning would, on the instant, beautifully reverse itself. Eckels remembered the wording in the advertisements to the letter. Out of chars and ashes, out of dust and coals, like golden salamanders, the old years, the green years, might leap; roses sweeten the air, white hair turn Irish-black, wrinkles vanish; all, everything fly back to seed, flee death, rush down to their beginnings, suns rise in western skies and set in glorious easts, moons eat themselves opposite to the custom, all and everything cupping one in another like Chinese boxes, rabbits into hats, all and everything returning to the fresh death, the seed death, the green death, to the time before the beginning. A touch of a hand might do it, the merest touch of a hand.

"Hell and damn," Eckels breathed, the light of the Machine on his thin face. "A real Time Machine." He shook his head. "Makes you think. If the election had gone badly yesterday, I might be here now running away from the results. Thank God Keith won. He'll make a fine President of the United States."

"Yes," said the man behind the desk. "We're lucky. If Deutscher had gotten in, we'd have the worst kind of dictatorship. There's an anti-everything man for you, a militarist, anti-Christ, anti-human, anti-intellectual. People called us up, you know, joking but not joking. Said if Deutscher became President they wanted to go live in 1492. Of course it's not our business to conduct Escapes, but to form Safaris. Anyway, Keith's President now. All you got to worry about is—"

"Shooting my dinosaur." Eckels finished it for him.

"A *Tyrannosaurus rex*. The Thunder Lizard, the damndest monster in history. Sign this release. Anything happens to you, we're not responsible. Those dinosaurs are hungry."

Eckels flushed angrily. "Trying to scare me!"

"Frankly, yes. We don't want anyone going who'll panic at the first shot. Six Safari leaders were killed last year, and a dozen hunters. We're here to give you the damndest thrill a *real* hunter ever asked for. Traveling you back sixty million years to bag the biggest damned game in all Time. Your personal check's still there. Tear it up."

Mr. Eckels looked at the check for a long time. His fingers twitched.

"Good luck," said the man behind the desk. "Mr. Travis, he's all yours."

They moved silently across the room, taking their guns with them, toward the Machine, toward the silver metal and the roaring light.

First a day and then a night and then a day and then a night, then it was day-night-day-night-day. A week, a month, a year, a decade. A.D. 2055. A.D. 2019. 1999! 1957! Gone! the Machine roared.

They put on their oxygen helmets and tested the intercoms.

Eckels swayed on the padded seat, his face pale, his jaw stiff. He felt the trembling in his arms and he looked down and found his hands tight on the new rifle. There were four other men in the Machine. Travis, the Safari leader, his assistant, Lesperance, and two other hunters, Billings and Kramer. They sat looking at each other, and the years blazed around them.

"Can these guns get a dinosaur cold?" Eckels felt his mouth saying.

"If you hit them right," said Travis on the helmet radio. "Some dinosaurs have two brains, one in the head, another far down the spinal column. We stay away from those. That's stretching luck. Put your first two shots into the eyes, if you can, blind them, and go back into the brain."

The Machine howled. Time was a film run backward. Suns fled and ten million moons fled after them. "Good God," said Eckels. "Every hunter that ever lived would envy us today. This makes Africa seem like Illinois."

The Machine slowed; its scream fell to a murmur. The Machine stopped.

The sun stopped in the sky.

The fog that had enveloped the Machine blew away and they were in an old time, a very old time indeed, three hunters and two Safari Heads with their blue metal guns across their knees.

"Christ isn't born yet," said Travis. "Moses has not gone to the mountain to talk with God. The Pyramids are still in the earth, waiting to be cut out and put up. *Remember* that. Alexander, Caesar, Napoleon, Hitler—none of them exists."

The men nodded.

"That"—Mr. Travis pointed—"is the jungle of sixty million two thousand and fifty-five years before President Keith."

He indicated a metal path that struck off into green wilderness, over steaming swamp, among giant ferns and palms.

"And that," he said, "is the Path, laid by Time Safari for your use. It floats six inches above the earth. Doesn't touch so much as one grass blade, flower, or tree. It's an anti-gravity metal. Its purpose is to keep you from touching this world of the past in any way. Stay on the Path. Don't go off it. I repeat. *Don't go off.* For *any* reason! If you fall off, there's a penalty. And don't shoot any animal we don't okay."

"Why?" asked Eckels.

They sat in the ancient wilderness. Far birds' cries blew on a wind, and the smell of tar and an old salt sea, moist grasses, and flowers the color of blood.

"We don't want to change the Future. We don't belong here in the Past. The government doesn't *like* us here. We have to pay big graft to keep our franchise. A Time Machine is damn finicky business. Not knowing it, we might kill an important animal, a small bird, a roach, a flower even, thus destroying an important link in a growing species."

"That's not clear," said Eckels.

"All right," Travis continued, "say we accidentally kill one mouse here. That means all the future families of this one particular mouse are destroyed, right?"

"Right."

"And all the families of the families of the families of that one mouse! With a stamp of your foot, you annihilate first one, then a dozen, then a thousand, a million, a *billion* possible mice!"

"So they're dead," said Eckels. "So what?"

"So what?" Travis snorted quietly. "Well, what about the foxes that'll need those mice to survive? For want of ten mice, a fox dies. For want of ten foxes, a lion starves. For want of a lion, all manner of insects, vultures, infinite billions of life forms are thrown into chaos and destruction. Eventually it all boils down to this: fifty-nine million years later, a cave man, one of a dozen on the *entire world*, goes hunting wild boar or saber-tooth tiger for food. But you, friend, have *stepped* on all the tigers in that region. By stepping on *one* single mouse. So the cave man starves. And the cave man, please note, is not just *any* expendable man, no! He is an *entire future nation*. From his loins would have sprung ten sons. From *their* loins one hundred sons, and thus onward to a civilization. Destroy this one man, and you destroy a race, a people, an entire history of life. It is comparable to slaying some of Adam's grandchildren. The stamp of your foot, on one mouse, could start an earthquake, the effects of which could shake our Earth and destinies down through Time, to their very foundations. With the death of that one cave man, a billion others yet unborn are throttled in the womb. Perhaps Rome never rises on its seven hills. Perhaps Europe is forever a dark forest, and only Asia waxes healthy and teeming. Step on a mouse and you crush the Pyramids. Step on a mouse and you leave your print, like a Grand Canyon, across Eternity. Queen Elizabeth might never be born, Washington might not cross the Delaware, there might never be a United States at all. So be careful. Stay on the Path. *Never* step off!"

"I see," said Eckels. "Then it wouldn't pay for us even to touch the *grass*?"

"Correct. Crushing certain plants could add up infinitesimally. A little error here would multiply in sixty million years, all out of proportion. Of course maybe our theory is wrong. Maybe Time *can't* be changed by us. Or maybe it can be changed only in little subtle ways. A dead mouse here makes an insect imbalance there, a population disproportion later, a bad harvest further on, a depression, mass starvation, and, finally, a change in *social* temperament in far-flung countries. Something much more subtle, like that. Perhaps only a soft breath, a whisper, a hair, pollen on the air, such a slight, slight change that unless you looked close you wouldn't see it. Who knows? Who really can say he knows? We don't know. We're guessing. But until we do know for certain whether our messing around in Time *can* make a big roar or a little rustle in History, we're being damned careful. This Machine, this Path, your clothing and bodies, were sterilized, as you know, before the journey. We wear these oxygen helmets so we can't introduce our bacteria into an ancient atmosphere."

"How do we know which animals to shoot?"

"They're marked with red paint," said Travis. "Today, before our journey, we sent Lesperance here back with the Machine. He came to this particular era and followed certain animals."

"Studying them?"

"Right," said Lesperance. "I track them through their entire existence, noting which of them lives longest. Not long. How many times they mate. Not often. Life's short. When I find one that's going to die when a tree falls on him, or one that drowns in a tar pit, I note the exact hour, minute, and second. I shoot a paint bomb. It leaves a red patch on his hide. We can't miss it. Then I correlate our arrival in the Past so that we meet the Monster not more than two minutes before he would have died anyway. This way, we kill only animals with no future, that are never going to mate again. You see how *careful* we are?"

"But if you came back this morning in Time," said Eckels eagerly, "you must've bumped into *us*, our Safari! How did it turn out? Was it successful? Did all of us get through—alive?"

Travis and Lesperance gave each other a look.

"That'd be a paradox," said the latter. "Time doesn't permit that sort of mess—a man meeting himself. When such occasions threaten, Time steps aside. Like an airplane hitting an air pocket. You felt the Machine jump just before we stopped? That was us passing ourselves on the way back to the Future. We saw nothing. There's no way of telling *if* this expedition was a success, *if* we got our Monster, or whether all of us—meaning *you*, Mr. Eckels—got out alive."

Eckels smiled palely.

"Cut that," said Travis sharply. "Everyone on his feet!"

They were ready to leave the Machine.

The jungle was high and the jungle was broad and the jungle was the entire world forever and forever. Sounds like music and sounds like flying tents filled the sky, and those were pterodactyls soaring with cavernous gray wings, gigantic bats out of a delirium and a night fever. Eckels, balanced on the narrow Path, aimed his rifle playfully.

"Stop that!" said Travis. "Don't even aim for fun, damn it! If your gun should go off—"

Eckels flushed. "Where's our *Tyrannosaurus?*"

Lesperance checked his wristwatch. "Up ahead. We'll bisect his trail in sixty seconds. Look for the red paint, for Christ's sake. Don't shoot till we give the word. Stay on the Path. *Stay on the Path!*"

They moved forward in the wind of morning.

"Strange," murmured Eckels. "Up ahead, sixty million years, Election Day over. Keith made President. Everyone celebrating. And here we are, a million years lost, and they don't exist. The things we worried about for months, a lifetime, not even born or thought about yet."

"Safety catches off, everyone!" ordered Travis. "You, first shot, Eckels. Second, Billings. Third, Kramer."

"I've hunted tiger, wild boar, buffalo, elephant, but Jesus, this is *it*," said Eckels. "I'm shaking like a kid."

"Ah," said Travis.

Everyone stopped.

Travis raised his hand. "Ahead," he whispered. "In the mist. There he is. There's His Royal Majesty now."

The jungle was wide and full of twitterings, rustlings, murmurs, and sighs.

Suddenly it all ceased, as if someone had shut a door.

Silence.

A sound of thunder.

Out of the mist, one hundred yards away, came *Tyrannosaurus rex*.

"Jesus God," whispered Eckels.

"Shh!"

It came on great oiled, resilient, striding legs. It towered thirty feet above half of the trees, a great evil god, folding its delicate watchmaker's claws close to its oily reptilian chest. Each lower leg was a piston, a thousand pounds of white bone, sunk in thick ropes of muscle, sheathed over in a gleam of pebbled skin like the mail of a terrible warrior. Each thigh was a ton of meat, ivory, and steel mesh. And from the great breathing cage of the upper body, those two delicate arms dangled out front, arms with hands which might pick up and examine men like toys, while the snake neck coiled. And the head itself, a ton of sculptured stone, lifted easily upon the sky. Its mouth gaped, exposing a fence of teeth like daggers. Its eyes rolled, ostrich eggs, empty of all expression save hunger. It closed its mouth in a death grin. It ran, its pelvic bones crushing aside trees and bushes, its taloned feet clawing damp earth, leaving prints six inches deep wherever it settled its weight. It ran with a gliding ballet step, far too poised and balanced for its ten tons. It moved into a sunlit arena warily, its beautifully reptile hands feeling the air.

"My God!" Eckels twitched his mouth. "It could reach up and grab the Moon."

"Shh!" Travis jerked angrily. "He hasn't seen us yet."

"It can't be killed." Eckels pronounced this verdict quietly, as if there could be no argument. He had weighed the evidence and this was his considered opinion. The rifle in his hands seemed a cap gun. "We were fools to come. This is impossible."

"Shut up!" hissed Travis.

"Nightmare."

"Turn around," commanded Travis. "Walk quietly to the Machine. We'll remit one-half your fee."

"I didn't realize it would be this *big*," said Eckels. "I miscalculated, that's all. And now I want out."

"It *sees* us!"

"There's the red paint on its chest!"

The Thunder Lizard raised itself. Its armored flesh glittered like a thousand green coins. The coins, crusted with slime, steamed. In the slime, tiny insects wriggled, so that the entire body seemed to twitch and undulate, even while the Monster itself did not move. It exhaled. The stink of raw flesh blew down the wilderness.

"Get me out of here," said Eckels. "It was never like this before. I was always sure I'd come through alive. I had good guides, good safaris, and safety. This time, I figured wrong. I've met my match and admit it. This is too much for me to get hold of."

"Don't run," said Lesperance. "Turn around. Hide in the Machine."

"Yes." Eckels seemed to be numb. He looked at his feet as if trying to make them move. He gave a grunt of helplessness.

"Eckels!"

He took a few steps, blinking, shuffling.

"Not *that* way!"

The Monster, at the first motion, lunged forward with a terrible scream. It covered one hundred yards in four seconds. The rifles jerked up and blazed fire. A windstorm from the beast's mouth engulfed them in the stench of slime and old blood. The Monster roared, teeth glittering with sun.

Eckels, not looking back, walked blindly to the edge of the Path, his gun limp in his arms, stepped off the Path, and walked, not knowing it, in the jungle. His feet sank into green moss. His legs moved him, and he felt alone and remote from the events behind.

The rifles cracked again. Their sound was lost in shriek and lizard thunder. The great lever of the reptile's tail swung up, lashed sideways. Trees exploded in clouds of leaf and branch. The Monster twitched its jeweler's hands down to fondle at the men, to twist them in half, to crush them like berries, to cram them into its teeth and its screaming throat. Its boulder-stone eyes leveled with the men. They saw themselves mirrored. They fired at the metallic eyelids and the blazing black iris.

Like a stone idol, like a mountain avalanche, *Tyrannosaurus* fell. Thundering, it clutched trees, pulled them with it. It wrenched and tore the metal Path. The men flung themselves back and away. The body hit, ten tons of cold flesh and stone. The guns fired. The Monster lashed its armored tail, twitched its snake jaws, and lay still. A fount of blood spurted from its throat. Somewhere inside, a sac of fluids burst. Sickening gushes drenched the hunters. They stood, red and glistening.

The thunder faded.

The jungle was silent. After the avalanche, a green peace. After the nightmare, morning.

Billings and Kramer sat on the pathway and threw up. Travis and Lesperance stood with smoking rifles, cursing steadily.

In the Time Machine, on his face, Eckels lay shivering. He had found his way back to the Path, climbed into the Machine.

Travis came walking, glanced at Eckels, took cotton gauze from a metal box, and returned to the others, who were sitting on the Path.

"Clean up."

They wiped the blood from their helmets. They began to curse too. The Monster lay, a hill of solid flesh. Within, you could hear the sighs and murmurs as the furthest chambers of it died, the organs malfunctioning, liquids running a final instant from pocket to sac to spleen, everything shutting off, closing up forever. It was like standing by a wrecked locomotive or a steam shovel at quitting time, all valves being released or levered tight. Bones cracked; the tonnage of its own flesh, off-balance, dead weight, snapped the delicate forearms, caught underneath. The meat settled, quivering.

Another cracking sound. Overhead, a gigantic tree branch broke from its heavy mooring, fell. It crashed upon the dead beast with finality.

"There." Lesperance checked his watch. "Right on time. That's the giant tree that was scheduled to fall and kill this animal originally." He glanced at the two hunters. "You want the trophy picture?"

"What?"

"We can't take a trophy back to the Future. The body has to stay right here where it would have died originally, so the insects, birds, and bacteria can get at it, as they were intended to. Everything in balance. The body stays. But we *can* take a picture of you standing near it."

The two men tried to think, but gave up, shaking their heads.

They let themselves be led along the metal Path. They sank wearily into the Machine cushions. They gazed back at the ruined Monster, the stagnating mound, where already strange reptilian birds and golden insects were busy at the steaming armor.

A sound on the floor of the Time Machine stiffened them. Eckels sat there, shivering.

"I'm sorry," he said at last.

"Get up!" cried Travis.

Eckels got up.

"Go out on that Path alone," said Travis. He had his rifle pointed. "You're not coming back in the Machine. We're leaving you here!"

Lesperance seized Travis's arm. "Wait—"

"Stay out of this!" Travis shook his hand away. "This son of a bitch nearly killed us. But it isn't *that* so much. Hell, no. It's his *shoes*! Look at them! He ran off the Path. My God, that *ruins* us! Christ knows how much we'll forfeit! Tens of thousands of dollars of insurance! We guarantee no one leaves the Path. He left it. Oh, the damn fool! I'll have to report to the government. They might revoke our license to travel. God knows *what* he's done to Time, to History!"

"Take it easy, all he did was kick up some dirt."

"How do we *know*?" cried Travis. "We don't know anything! It's all a damn mystery! Get out there, Eckels!"

Eckels fumbled his shirt. "I'll pay anything. A hundred thousand dollars!"

Travis glared at Eckels' checkbook and spat. "Go out there. The Monster's next to the Path. Stick your arms up to your elbows in his mouth. Then you can come back with us."

"That's unreasonable!"

"The Monster's dead, you yellow bastard. The bullets! The bullets can't be left behind. They don't belong in the Past; they might change something. Here's my knife. Dig them out!"

The jungle was alive again, full of the old tremorings and bird cries. Eckels turned slowly to regard that primeval garbage dump, that hill of nightmares and terror. After a long time, like a sleepwalker, he shuffled out along the Path.

He returned, shuddering, five minutes later, his arms soaked and red to the elbows. He held out his hands. Each held a number of steel bullets. Then he fell. He lay where he fell, not moving.

"You didn't have to make him do that," said Lesperance.

"Didn't I? It's too early to tell." Travis nudged the still body. "He'll live. Next time he won't go hunting game like this. Okay." He jerked his thumb wearily at Lesperance. "Switch on. Let's go home."

1492.   1776.   1812.

They cleaned their hands and faces. Their changed their caking shirts and pants. Eckels was up and around again, not speaking. Travis glared at him for a full ten minutes.

"Don't look at me," cried Eckels. "I haven't done anything."

"Who can tell?"

"Just ran off the Path, that's all, a little mud on my shoes—what do you want me to do—get down and pray?"

"We might need it. I'm warning you, Eckels, I might kill you yet. I've got my gun ready."

"I'm innocent. I've done nothing!"

1999.   2000.   2055.

The Machine stopped.

"Get out," said Travis.

The room was there as they had left it. But not the same as they had left it. The same man sat behind the same desk. But the same man did not quite sit behind the same desk.

Travis looked around swiftly. "Everything okay here?" he snapped.

"Fine. Welcome home!"

Travis did not relax. He seemed to be looking at the very atoms of the air itself, at the way the sun poured through the one high window.

"Okay, Eckels, get out. Don't ever come back."

Eckels could not move.

"You heard me," said Travis. "What're you *staring* at?"

Eckels stood smelling of the air, and there was a thing to the air, a chemical taint so subtle, so slight, that only a faint cry of his subliminal senses warned him it was there. The colors, white, gray, blue, orange, in the wall, in the furniture, in the sky beyond the window, were . . . were . . . And there was a *feel*. His flesh twitched. His hands twitched. He stood drinking the oddness with the pores of his body. Somewhere, someone must have been screaming one of those whistles that only a dog can hear. His body screamed silence in return. Beyond this room, beyond this wall, beyond this man who was not quite the same man seated at this desk that was not quite the same desk . . . lay an entire world of streets and people. What sort of world it was now, there was no telling. He could feel them moving there, beyond the walls, almost, like so many chess pieces blown in a dry wind. . . .

But the immediate thing was the sign painted on the office wall, the same sign he had read earlier today on first entering.

Somehow, the sign had changed:

TYME SEFARI INC.

SEFARIS TU ANY YEER EN THE PAST.

YU NAIM THE ANIMALL.

WEE TAEK YU THAIR.

YU SHOOT ITT.

Eckels felt himself fall into a chair. He fumbled crazily at the thick slime on his boots. He held up a clod of dirt, trembling. "No, it *can't* be. Not a *little* thing like that. No!"

Embedded in the mud, glistening green and gold and black, was a butterfly, very beautiful, and very dead.

"Not a little thing like *that*! Not a butterfly!" cried Eckels.

It fell to the floor, an exquisite thing, a small thing that could upset balances and knock down a line of small dominoes and then big dominoes and then gigantic dominoes, all down the years across Time. Eckels' mind whirled. It *couldn't* change things. Killing one butterfly couldn't be *that* important! Could it?

His face was cold. His mouth trembled, asking: "Who—who won the presidential election yesterday?"

The man behind the desk laughed. "You joking? You know damn well. Deutscher, of course! Who else? Not that damn weakling Keith. We got an iron man now, a man with guts, by God!" The official stopped. "What's wrong?"

Eckels moaned. He dropped to his knees. He scrabbled at the golden butterfly with shaking fingers. "Can't we," he pleaded to the world, to himself, to the officials, to the Machine, "can't we take it *back*, can't we *make* it alive again? Can't we start over? Can't we—"

He did not move. Eyes shut, he waited, shivering. He heard Travis breathe loud in the room; he heard Travis shift his rifle, click the safety catch, and raise the weapon.

There was a sound of thunder.

The Murderer

Music moved with him in the white halls. He passed an office door: "The Merry Widow Waltz." Another door: *Afternoon of a Faun*. A third: "Kiss Me Again." He turned into a cross-corridor: "The Sword Dance" buried him in cymbals, drums, pots, pans, knives, forks, thunder, and tin lightning. All washed away as he hurried through an anteroom where a secretary sat nicely stunned by Beethoven's Fifth. He moved himself before her eyes like a hand; she didn't see him.

His wrist radio buzzed.

"Yes?"

"This is Lee, Dad. Don't forget about my allowance."

"Yes, Son, yes. I'm busy."

"Just didn't want you to forget, Dad," said the wrist radio. Tchaikovsky's *Romeo and Juliet* swarmed about the voice and flushed into the long halls.

The psychiatrist moved in the beehive of offices, in the cross-pollination of themes, Stravinsky mating with Bach, Haydn unsuccessfully repulsing

Rachmaninoff, Schubert slain by Duke Ellington. He nodded to the humming secretaries and the whistling doctors fresh to their morning work. At his office he checked a few papers with his stenographer, who sang under her breath, then phoned the police captain upstairs. A few minutes later a red light blinked, a voice said from the ceiling:

"Prisoner delivered to Interview Chamber Nine."

He unlocked the chamber door, stepped in, heard the door lock behind him.

"Go away," said the prisoner, smiling.

The psychiatrist was shocked by that smile. A very sunny, pleasant warm thing, a thing that shed bright light upon the room. Dawn among the dark hills. High noon at midnight, that smile. The blue eyes sparkled serenely above that display of self-assured dentistry.

"I'm here to help you," said the psychiatrist, frowning. Something was wrong with the room. He had hesitated the moment he entered. He glanced around. The prisoner laughed. "If you're wondering why it's so quiet in here, I just kicked the radio to death."

Violent, thought the doctor.

The prisoner read this thought, smiled, put out a gentle hand. "No, only to machines that yak-yak-yak."

Bits of the wall radio's tubes and wires lay on the gray carpeting. Ignoring these, feeling that smile upon him like a heat lamp, the psychiatrist sat across from his patient in the unusual silence which was like the gathering of a storm.

"You're Mr. Albert Brock, who calls himself The Murderer?"

Brock nodded pleasantly. "Before we start . . . " He moved quietly and quickly to detach the wrist radio from the doctor's arm. He tucked it in his teeth like a walnut, gritted, heard it crack, handed it back to the appalled psychiatrist as if he had done them both a favor. "That's better."

The psychiatrist stared at the ruined machine. "You're running up quite a damage bill."

"I don't care," smiled the patient. "As the old song goes: 'Don't Care What Happens to Me!' " He hummed it.

The psychiatrist said: "Shall we start?"

"Fine. The first victim, or one of the first, was my telephone. Murder most foul. I shoved it in the kitchen Insinkerator! Stopped the disposal unit in mid-swallow. Poor thing strangled to death. After that I shot the television set!"

The psychiatrist said, "Mmm."

"Fired six shots right through the cathode. Made a beautiful tinkling crash, like a dropped chandelier."

"Nice imagery."

"Thanks, I always dreamt of being a writer."

"Suppose you tell me when you first began to hate the telephone."

"It frightened me as a child. Uncle of mine called it the Ghost Machine. Voices without bodies. Scared the living hell out of me. Later in life I was never comfortable. Seemed to me a phone was an impersonal instrument. If it *felt* like it, it let your personality go through its wires. If it didn't *want* to, it just drained your personality away until what slipped through at the other end was some cold fish of a voice, all steel, copper, plastic, no warmth, no reality. It's easy to say the wrong thing on telephones; the telephone changes your meaning on you. First thing you know, you've made an enemy. Then, of course, the telephone's such a *convenient* thing; it just sits there and *demands* you call someone who doesn't want to be called. Friends were always calling, calling, calling me. Hell, I hadn't any time of my own. When it wasn't the telephone it was the television, the radio, the phonograph. When it wasn't the television or radio or the phonograph it was motion pictures at the corner theater, motion pictures projected, with commercials on low-lying cumulus clouds. It doesn't rain rain any more, it rains soapsuds. When it wasn't High-Fly Cloud advertisements, it was music by Mozzek in every restaurant; music and commercials on the busses I rode to work. When it wasn't music, it was interoffice communications, and my horror chamber of a radio wristwatch on which my friends and my wife phoned every five minutes. What is there about such 'conveniences' that makes them so *temptingly* convenient? The average man thinks, Here I am, time on my hands, and there on my wrist is a wrist telephone, so why not just buzz old Joe up, eh? 'Hello, *hello!*' I love my friends, my wife, humanity, very much, but when one minute my wife calls to say, 'Where are you *now*, dear?' and a friend calls and says, 'Got the best off-color joke to tell you. Seems there was a guy—' And a stranger calls and cries out, 'This is the Find-Fax Poll. What gum are you chewing at this very *instant?*' Well!"

"How did you feel during the week?"

"The fuse lit. On the edge of the cliff. That same afternoon I did what I did at the office."

"Which was?"

"I poured a paper cup of water into the intercommunications system."

The psychiatrist wrote on his pad.

"And the system shorted?"

"Beautifully! The Fourth of July on wheels! My God, stenographers ran around looking *lost*! What an uproar!"

"Felt better temporarily, eh?"

"Fine! Then I got the idea at noon of stomping my wrist radio on the sidewalk. A shrill voice was just yelling out of it at me, 'This is People's Poll Number Nine. What did you eat for lunch?' when I kicked the Jesus out of the wrist radio!"

"Felt even *better*, eh?"

"It *grew* on me!" Brock rubbed his hands together. "Why didn't I start a solitary revolution, deliver man from certain 'conveniences'? 'Convenient for who?' I cried. Convenient for friends: 'Hey, Al, thought I'd call you from the locker room out here at Green Hills. Just made a sockdolager hole in one! A hole in one, Al! A *beautiful* day. Having a shot of whiskey now. Thought you'd want to know, Al!' Convenient for my office, so when I'm in the field with my radio car there's no moment when I'm not in touch. *In touch! There's* a slimy phrase. Touch, hell. *Gripped!* Pawed, rather. Mauled and massaged and pounded by FM voices. You can't leave your car without checking in: 'Have stopped to visit gas-station men's room.' 'Okay, Brock, step on it!' 'Brock, what *took* you so long?' 'Sorry, sir.' 'Watch it next time, Brock.' '*Yes*, sir!' So, do you know what I did, Doctor? I bought a quart of French chocolate ice cream and spooned it into the car radio transmitter."

"Was there any *special* reason for selecting French chocolate ice cream to spoon into the broadcasting unit?"

Brock thought about it and smiled. "It's my favorite flavor."

"Oh," said the doctor.

"I figured, hell, what's good enough for me is good enough for the radio transmitter."

"What made you think of spooning *ice cream* into the radio?"

"It was a hot day."

The doctor paused.

"And what happened next?"

"Silence happened next. God, it was *beautiful*. That car radio cackling all day, 'Brock go here, Brock go there, Brock check in, Brock check out, okay Brock, hour lunch, Brock, lunch over, Brock, Brock, Brock.' Well, that silence was like putting ice cream in my ears."

"You seem to like ice cream a lot."

"I just rode around feeling of the silence. It's a big bolt of the nicest, softest flannel ever made. Silence. A whole hour of it. I just sat in my car, smiling, feeling of that flannel with my ears. I felt *drunk* with Freedom!"

"Go on."

"Then I got the idea of the portable diathermy machine. I rented one, took it on the bus going home that night. There sat all the tired commuters with their wrist radios, talking to their wives, saying, 'Now I'm at Forty-third, now I'm at Forty-fourth, here I am at Forty-ninth, now turning at Sixty-first.' One husband cursing, 'Well, get *out* of that bar, damn it, and get home and get dinner started, I'm at Seventieth!' And the transit-system radio playing 'Tales from the Vienna Woods,' a canary singing words about a first-rate wheat cereal. Then—I switched on my diathermy! Static! Interference! All wives cut off from husbands grousing about a hard day at the office. All husbands cut off from wives who had just seen their children break a window! The 'Vienna Woods' chopped down, the canary mangled. *Silence!* A terrible, unexpected silence. The bus inhabitants faced with having to converse with each other. Panic! Sheer, animal panic!"

"The police seized you?"

"The bus *had* to stop. After all, the music *was* being scrambled, husbands and wives *were* out of touch with reality. Pandemonium, riot, and chaos.

Squirrels chattering in cages! A trouble unit arrived, triangulated on me instantly, had me reprimanded, fined, and home, minus my diathermy machine, in jig time."

"Mr. Brock, may I suggest that so far your whole pattern here is not very—practical? If you didn't like transit radios or office radios or car business radios, why didn't you join a fraternity of radio haters, start petitions, get legal and constitutional rulings? After all, this *is* a democracy."

"And I," said Brock, "am that thing best called a minority. I *did* join fraternities, picket, pass petitions, take it to court. Year after year I protested. Everyone laughed. Everyone else *loved* bus radios and commercials. *I* was out of step."

"Then you should have taken it like a good soldier, don't you think? The majority rules."

"But they went too far.If a little music and 'keeping in touch' was charming, they figured a lot would be ten times as charming. I went *wild*! I got home to find my wife hysterical. *Why?* Because she had been completely out of touch with me for half a day. Remember, I did a dance on my wrist radio? Well, that night I laid plans to murder my house."

"Are you *sure* that's how you want me to write it down?"

"That's semantically accurate. Kill it dead. It's one of those talking, singing, humming, weather-reporting, poetry-reading, novel-reciting, jingle-jangling, rockaby-crooning-when-you-go-to-bed houses. A house that screams opera to you in the shower and teaches you Spanish in your sleep. One of those blathering caves where all kinds of electronic Oracles make you feel a trifle larger than a thimble, with stoves that say, 'I'm apricot pie, and I'm *done*,' or 'I'm prime roast beef, so *baste* me!' and other nursery gibberish like that. With beds that rock you to sleep and *shake* you awake. A house that *barely* tolerates humans, I tell you. A front door that barks: 'You've mud on your feet, sir!' And an electronic vacuum hound that snuffles around after you from room to room, inhaling every fingernail or ash you drop. Jesus God, *I* say, Jesus God!"

"Quietly," suggested the psychiatrist.

"Remember that Gilbert and Sullivan song—'I've Got It on My List, It Never Will Be Missed'? All night I listed grievances. Next morning early I bought a pistol. I *purposely* muddied my feet. I stood at our front door. The front door shrilled, 'Dirty feet, muddy feet! Wipe your feet! Please be *neat*!' I shot the damn thing in its keyhole! I ran to the kitchen, where the stove was just whining, 'Turn me *over*!' In the middle of a mechanical omelet I did the stove to death. Oh, how it sizzled and screamed, 'I'm *shorted*!' Then the telephone rang like a spoiled brat. I shoved it down the Insinkerator. I must state here and now I have *nothing* whatever against the Insinkerator; it was an innocent bystander. I feel sorry for it now, a practical device indeed, which never said a word, purred like a sleepy lion most of the time, and digested our leftovers. I'll have it restored. Then I went in and shot the televisor, that insidious beast, that Medusa, which freezes a billion people to stone every night, staring fixedly, that

Siren which called and sang and promised so much and gave, after all, so little, but myself always going back, going back, hoping and waiting until—bang! Like a headless turkey, gobbling, my wife whooped out the front door. The police came. Here I *am!*"

He sat back happily and lit a cigarette.

"And did you realize, in committing these crimes, that the wrist radio, the broadcasting transmitter, the phone, the bus radio, the office intercoms, all were rented or were someone else's property?"

"I would do it all over again, so help me God."

The psychiatrist sat there in the sunshine of that beatific smile.

"You don't want any further help from the Office of Mental Health? You're ready to take the consequences?"

"This is only the beginning," said Mr. Brock. "I'm the vanguard of the small public which is tired of noise and being taken advantage of and pushed around and yelled at, every moment music, every moment in touch with some voice somewhere, do this, do that, quick, quick, now here, now there. You'll *see*. The revolt begins. My name will go down in history!"

"Mmm." The psychiatrist seemed to be thinking.

"It'll take time, of course. It was all so enchanting at first. The very *idea* of these things, the practical uses, was wonderful. They were almost toys, to be played with, but the people got too involved, went too far, and got wrapped up in a pattern of social behavior and couldn't get out, couldn't admit they were *in*, even. So they rationalized their nerves as something else. 'Our modern age,' they said. 'Conditions,' they said. 'High-strung,' they said. But mark my words, the seed has been sown. I got world-wide coverage on TV, radio, films; *there's* an irony for you. That was five days ago. A billion people know about me. Check your financial columns. Any day now. Maybe today. Watch for a sudden spurt, a rise in sales for French chocolate ice cream!"

"I see," said the psychiatrist.

"Can I go back to my nice private cell now, where I can be alone and quiet for six months?"

"Yes," said the psychiatrist quietly.

"Don't worry about me," said Mr. Brock, rising. "I'm just going to sit around for a long time stuffing that nice soft bolt of quiet material in both ears."

"Mmm," said the psychiatrist, going to the door.

"Cheers," said Mr. Brock.

"Yes," said the psychiatrist.

He pressed a code signal on a hidden button, the door opened, he stepped out, the door shut and locked. Alone, he moved in the offices and corridors. The first twenty yards of his walk were accompanied by "Tambourine Chinois." Then it was "Tzigane," Bach's Passacaglia and Fugue in something Minor, "Tiger Rag," "Love Is Like a Cigarette." He took his broken wrist radio from his pocket like a dead praying mantis. He turned in at his office. A bell sounded; a voice came out of the ceiling, "Doctor?"

"Just finished with Brock," said the psychiatrist.

"Diagnosis?"

"Seems completely disoriented, but convivial. Refuses to accept the simplest realities of his environment and work *with* them."

"Prognosis?"

"Indefinite. Left him enjoying a piece of invisible material."

Three phones rang. A duplicate wrist radio in his desk drawer buzzed like a wounded grasshopper. The intercom flashed a pink light and click-clicked. Three phones rang. The drawer buzzed. Music blew in through the open door. The psychiatrist, humming quietly, fitted the new wrist radio to his wrist, flipped the intercom, talked a moment, picked up one telephone, talked, picked up another telephone, talked, picked up the third telephone, talked, touched the wrist-radio button, talked calmly and quietly, his face cool and serene, in the middle of the music and the lights flashing, the phones ringing again, and his hands moving, and his wrist radio buzzing, and the intercoms talking, and voices speaking from the ceiling. And he went on quietly this way through the remainder of a cool, air-conditioned, and long afternoon; telephone, wrist radio, intercom, telephone, wrist radio, intercom, telephone, wrist radio, intercom, telephone, wrist radio, intercom, telephone, wrist radio, intercom, telephone, wrist radio . . .

The April Witch

Into the air, over the valleys, under the stars, above a river, a pond, a road, flew Cecy. Invisible as new spring winds, fresh as the breath of clover rising from twilight fields, she flew. She soared in doves as soft as white ermine, stopped in trees and lived in blossoms, showering away in petals when the breeze blew. She perched in a lime-green frog, cool as mint by a shining pool. She trotted in a brambly dog and barked to hear echoes from the sides of distant barns. She lived in new April grasses, in sweet clear liquids rising from the musky earth.

It's spring, thought Cecy. I'll be in every living thing in the world tonight.

Now she inhabited neat crickets on the tar-pool roads, now prickled in dew on an iron gate. Hers was an adaptably quick mind flowing unseen upon Illinois winds on this one evening of her life when she was just seventeen.

"I want to be in love," she said.

She had said it at supper. And her parents had widened their eyes and stiffened back in their chairs. "Patience," had been their advice. "Remember, you're remarkable. Our whole Family is odd and remarkable. We can't mix or marry with ordinary folk. We'd lose our magical powers if we did. You wouldn't want to lose *your* ability to 'travel' by magic, would you? Then be careful. Be careful!"

But in her high bedroom, Cecy had touched perfume to her throat and stretched out, trembling and apprehensive, on her four-poster, as a moon the color of milk rose over Illinois country, turning rivers to cream and roads to platinum.

"Yes," she sighed. "I'm one of an odd family. We sleep days and fly nights like black kites on the wind. If we want, we can sleep in moles through the winter, in the warm earth. I can live in anything at all—a pebble, a crocus, or a praying mantis. I can leave my plain, bony body behind and send my mind far out for adventure. Now!"

The wind whipped her away over fields and meadows.

She saw the warm spring lights of cottages and farms glowing with twilight colors.

If I can't be in love, myself, because I'm plain and odd, then I'll be in love through someone else, she thought.

Outside a farmhouse in the spring night a dark-haired girl, no more than nineteen, drew up water from a deep stone well. She was singing.

Cecy fell—a green leaf—into the well. She lay in the tender moss of the well, gazing up through dark coolness. Now she quickened in a fluttering, invisible amoeba. Now in a water droplet! At last, within a cold cup, she felt herself lifted to the girl's warm lips. There was a soft night sound of drinking.

Cecy looked out from the girl's eyes.

She entered into the dark head and gazed from the shining eyes at the hands pulling the rough rope. She listened through the shell ears to this girl's world. She smelled a particular universe through these delicate nostrils, felt this special heart beating, beating. Felt this strange tongue move with singing.

Does she know I'm here? thought Cecy.

The girl gasped. She stared into the night meadows.

"Who's there?"

No answer.

"Only the wind," whispered Cecy.

"Only the wind." The girl laughed at herself, but shivered.

It was a good body, this girl's body. It held bones of finest slender ivory hidden and roundly fleshed. This brain was like a pink tea rose, hung in darkness, and there was cider-wine in this mouth. The lips lay firm on the white, white teeth and the brows arched neatly at the world, and the hair blew soft and fine on her milky neck. The pores knit small and close. The nose tilted at the moon and the cheeks glowed like small fires. The body drifted with feather-balances from one motion to another and seemed always singing to itself. Being in this body, this head, was like basking in a hearth fire, living in the purr of a sleeping cat, stirring in warm creek waters that flowed by night to the sea.

I'll like it here, thought Cecy.

"What?" asked the girl, as if she'd heard a voice.

"What's your name?" asked Cecy carefully.

"Ann Leary." The girl twitched. "Now why should I say *that* out loud?"

"Ann, Ann," whispered Cecy. "Ann, you're going to be in love."

As if to answer this, a great roar sprang from the road, a clatter and a ring of wheels on gravel. A tall man drove up in a rig, holding the reins high with his monstrous arms, his smile glowing across the yard.

"Ann!"

"Is that you, Tom?"

"Who else?" Leaping from the rig, he tied the reins to the fence.

"I'm not speaking to you!" Ann whirled, the bucket in her hands slopping.

"No!" cried Cecy.

Ann froze. She looked at the hills and the first spring stars. She stared at the man named Tom. Cecy made her drop the bucket.

"Look what you've done!"

Tom ran up.

"Look what you *made* me do!"

He wiped her shoes with a kerchief, laughing.

"Get away!" She kicked at his hands, but he laughed again, and gazing down on him from miles away, Cecy saw the turn of his head, the size of his skull, the flare of his nose, the shine of his eye, the girth of his shoulder, and the hard strength of his hands doing this delicate thing with the handkerchief. Peering down from the secret attic of this lovely head, Cecy yanked a hidden copper ventriloquist's wire and the pretty mouth popped wide: "Thank you!"

"Oh, so you *have* manners?" The smell of leather on his hands, the smell of the horse rose from his clothes into the tender nostrils, and Cecy, far, far away over night meadows and flowered fields, stirred as with some dream in her bed.

"Not for you, no!" said Ann.

"Hush, speak gently," said Cecy. She moved Ann's fingers out toward Tom's head. Ann snatched them back.

"I've gone mad!"

"You have." He nodded, smiling but bewildered. "Were you going to touch me then?"

"I don't know. Oh, go away!" Her cheeks glowed with pink charcoals.

"Why don't you run? I'm not stopping you." Tom got up. "Have you changed your mind? Will you go to the dance with me tonight? It's special. Tell you why later."

"No," said Ann.

"Yes!" cried Cecy. "I've never danced. I want to dance. I've never worn a long gown, all rustly. I want that. I want to dance all night. I've never known what it's like to be in a woman, dancing; Father and Mother would never permit it. Dogs, cats, locusts, leaves, everything else in the world at one time or another I've known, but never a woman in the spring, never on a night like this. Oh, please—we *must* go to that dance!"

She spread her thought like the fingers of a hand within a new glove.

"Yes," said Ann Leary, "I'll go. I don't know why, but I'll go to the dance with you tonight, Tom."

"Now inside, quick!" cried Cecy. "You must wash, tell your folks, get your gown ready, out with the iron, into your room!"

"Mother," said Ann, "I've changed my mind!"

The rig was galloping off down the pike, the rooms of the farmhouse jumped to life, water was boiling for a bath, the coal stove was heating an iron to press the gown, the mother was rushing about with a fringe of hairpins in her mouth. "What's come over you, Ann? You don't like Tom!"

"That's true." Ann stopped amidst the great fever.

But it's spring! thought Cecy.

"It's spring," said Ann.

And it's a fine night for dancing, thought Cecy.

". . . for dancing," murmured Ann Leary.

Then she was in the tub and the soap creaming on her white seal shoulders, small nests of soap beneath her arms, and the flesh of her warm breasts moving in her hands and Cecy moving the mouth, making the smile, keeping the actions going. There must be no pause, no hesitation, or the entire pantomime might fall in ruins! Ann Leary must be kept moving, doing, acting, wash here, soap there, now out! Rub with a towel! Now perfume and powder!

"You!" Ann caught herself in the mirror, all whiteness and pinkness like lilies and carnations. "*Who* are you tonight?"

"I'm a girl seventeen." Cecy gazed from her violet eyes. "You can't see me. Do you know I'm here?"

Ann Leary shook her head. "I've rented my body to an April witch, for sure."

"*Close*, very close!" laughed Cecy. "Now, on with your dressing."

The luxury of feeling good clothes move over an ample body! And then the halloo outside.

"Ann, Tom's back!"

"Tell him to wait." Ann sat down suddenly. "Tell him I'm not going to that dance."

"What?" said her mother, in the door.

Cecy snapped back into attention. It had been a fatal relaxing, a fatal moment of leaving Ann's body for only an instant. She had heard the distant sound of horses' hoofs and the rig rambling through moonlit spring country. For a second she thought, I'll go find Tom and sit in his head and see what it's like to be in a man of twenty-two on a night like this. And so she had started quickly across a heather field, but now, like a bird to a cage, flew back and rustled and beat about in Ann Leary's head.

"Ann!"

"Tell him to go away!"

"Ann!" Cecy settled down and spread her thoughts.

But Ann had the bit in her mouth now. "No, no, I hate him!"

I shouldn't have left—even for a moment. Cecy poured her mind into the hands of the young girl, into the heart, into the head, softly, softly. *Stand up,* she thought.

Ann stood.

Put on your coat!

Ann put on her coat.

Now, march!

No! thought Ann Leary.

March!

"Ann," said her mother, "don't keep Tom waiting another minute. You get on out there now and no nonsense. What's come over you?"

"Nothing, Mother. Good night. We'll be home late."

Ann and Cecy ran together into the spring evening.

A room full of softly dancing pigeons ruffling their quiet, trailing feathers, a room full of peacocks, a room full of rainbow eyes and lights. And in the center of it, around, around, around, danced Ann Leary.

"Oh, it *is* a fine evening," said Cecy.

"Oh, it's a fine evening," said Ann.

"You're odd," said Tom.

The music whirled them in dimness, in rivers of song; they floated, they bobbed, they sank down, they arose for air, they gasped, they clutched each other like drowning people and whirled on again, in fan motions, in whispers and sighs, to "Beautiful Ohio."

Cecy hummed. Ann's lips parted and the music came out.

"Yes, I'm odd," said Cecy.

"You're not the same," said Tom.

"No, not tonight."

"You're not the Ann Leary I knew."

"No, not at all, at all," whispered Cecy, miles and miles away. "No, not at all," said the moved lips.

"I've the funniest feeling," said Tom.

"About what?"

"About you." He held her back and danced her and looked into her glowing face, watching for something. "Your eyes," he said, "I can't figure it."

"Do you see *me?*" asked Cecy.

"Part of you's here, Ann, and part of you's not." Tom turned her carefully, his face uneasy.

"Yes."

"Why did you come with me?"

"I didn't want to come," said Ann.

"Why, then?"

"Something made me."

"What?"

"I don't know." Ann's voice was faintly hysterical.

"Now, now, hush, hush," whispered Cecy. "Hush, that's it. Around, around."

They whispered and rustled and rose and fell away in the dark room, with the music moving and turning them.

"But you *did* come to the dance," said Tom.

"I did," said Cecy.

"Here." And he danced her lightly out an open door and walked her quietly away from the hall and the music and the people.

They climbed up and sat together in the rig.

"Ann," he said, taking her hands, trembling. "Ann." But the way he said her name it was as if it wasn't her name. He kept glancing into her pale face, and now her eyes were open again. "I used to love you, you know that," he said.

"I know."

"But you've always been fickle and I didn't want to be hurt."

"It's just as well, we're very young," said Ann.

"No, I mean to say, I'm sorry," said Cecy.

"What *do* you mean?" Tom dropped her hands and stiffened.

The night was warm and the smell of the earth shimmered up all about them where they sat, and the fresh trees breathed one leaf against another in a shaking and rustling.

"I don't know," said Ann.

"Oh, but *I* know," said Cecy. "You're tall and you're the finest-looking man in all the world. This is a good evening; this is an evening I'll always remember, being with you." She put out the alien cold hand to find his reluctant hand again and bring it back, and warm it and hold it very tight.

"But," said Tom, blinking, "tonight you're here, you're there. One minute one way, the next minute another. I wanted to take you to the dance tonight for old times' sake. I meant nothing by it when I first asked you. And then, when we were standing at the well, I knew something had changed, really changed, about you. You were different. There was something new and soft, something . . ." He groped for a word. "I don't know, I can't say. The way you looked. Something about your voice. And I know I'm in love with you again."

"No," said Cecy. "With me, with *me*."

"And I'm afraid of being in love with you," he said. "You'll hurt me again."

"I might," said Ann.

No, no, I'd love you with all my heart! thought Cecy. Ann, say it to him, say it for me. Say you'd love him with all your heart.

Ann said nothing.

Tom moved quietly closer and put his hand up to hold her chin. "I'm going away. I've got a job a hundred miles from here. Will you miss me?"

"Yes," said Ann and Cecy.

"May I kiss you good-by, then?"

"Yes," said Cecy before anyone else could speak.

He placed his lips to the strange mouth. He kissed the strange mouth and he was trembling.

Ann sat like a white statue.

"Ann!" said Cecy. "Move your arms, *hold* him!"

She sat like a carved wooden doll in the moonlight.

Again he kissed her lips.

"I do love you," whispered Cecy. "I'm here, it's me you saw in her eyes, it's me, and I love you if she never will."

He moved away and seemed like a man who had run a long distance. He sat beside her. "I don't know what's happening. For a moment there . . ."

"Yes?" asked Cecy.

"For a moment I thought—" He put his hands to his eyes. "Never mind. Shall I take you home now?"

"Please," said Ann Leary.

He clucked to the horse, snapped the reins tiredly, and drove the rig away. They rode in the rustle and slap and motion of the moonlit rig in the still early, only eleven o'clock spring night, with the shining meadows and sweet fields of clover gliding by.

And Cecy, looking at the fields and meadows, thought, It would be worth it, it would be worth everything to be with him from this night on. And she heard her parents' voices again, faintly, "Be careful. You wouldn't want to lose your magical powers, would you—married to a mere mortal? Be careful. You wouldn't want that."

Yes, yes, thought Cecy, even that I'd give up, here and now, if he would have me. I wouldn't need to roam the spring nights then, I wouldn't need to live in birds and dogs and cats and foxes, I'd need only to be with him. Only him. Only him.

The road passed under, whispering.

"Tom," said Ann at last.

"What?" He stared coldly at the road, the horse, the trees, the sky, the stars.

"If you're ever, in years to come, at any time, in Mellin Town, Illinois, a few miles from here, will you do me a favor?"

"Perhaps."

"Will you do me the favor of stopping and seeing a friend of mine?" Ann Leary said this haltingly, awkwardly.

"Why?"

"She's a good friend. I've told her of you. I'll give you her address. Just a moment." When the rig stopped at her farm she drew forth a pencil and paper from her small purse and wrote in the moonlight, pressing the paper to her knee. "There it is. Can you read it?"

He glanced at the paper and nodded bewilderedly.

"Cecy Elliott, 12 Willow Street, Mellin Town, Illinois," he said.

"Will you visit her someday?" asked Ann.

"Someday," he said.

"Promise?"

"What has this to do with us?" he cried savagely. "What do I want with names and papers?" He crumpled the paper into a tight ball and shoved it in his coat.

"Oh, please promise!" begged Cecy.

"... promise ..." said Ann.

"All right, all right, now let me be!" he shouted.

I'm tired, thought Cecy. I can't stay. I have to go home. I'm weakening. I've only the power to stay a few hours out like this in the night, traveling, traveling. But before I go ...

"... before I go," said Ann.

She kissed Tom on the lips.

"This is *me* kissing you," said Cecy.

Tom held her off and looked at Ann Leary and looked deep, deep inside. He said nothing, but his face began to relax slowly, very slowly, and the lines vanished away, and his mouth softened from its hardness, and he looked deep again into the moonlit face held here before him.

Then he put her off the rig and without so much as good night was driving swiftly down the road.

Cecy let go.

Ann Leary, crying out, released from prison, it seemed, raced up the moonlit path to her house and slammed the door.

Cecy lingered for only a little while. In the eyes of a cricket she saw the spring night world. In the eyes of a frog she sat for a lonely moment by a pool. In the eyes of a night bird she looked down from a tall, moon-haunted elm and saw the lights go out in two farmhouses, one here, one a mile away. She thought of herself and her Family, and her strange power, and the fact that no one in the Family could ever marry any one of the people in this vast world out here beyond the hills.

"Tom?" Her weakening mind flew in a night bird under the trees and over deep fields of wild mustard. "Have you still got the paper, Tom? Will you come by someday, some year, sometime, to see me? Will you know me then? Will you look in my face and remember then where it was you saw me last and know that you love me as I love you, with all my heart for all time?"

She paused in the cool night air, a million miles from towns and people, above farms and continents and rivers and hills. "Tom?" Softly.

Tom was asleep. It was deep night; his clothes were hung on chairs or folded neatly over the end of the bed. And in one silent, carefully upflung hand upon the white pillow, by his head, was a small piece of paper with writing on it. Slowly, slowly, a fraction of an inch at a time, his fingers closed down upon and held it tightly. And he did not even stir or notice when a blackbird, faintly, wondrously, beat softly for a moment against the clear moon crystals of the windowpane, then, fluttering quietly, stopped and flew away toward the east, over the sleeping earth.

Invisible Boy

She took the great iron spoon and the mummified frog and gave it a bash and made dust of it, and talked to the dust while she ground it in her stony fists quickly. Her beady gray bird-eyes flickered at the cabin. Each time she looked, a head in the small thin window ducked as if she'd fired off a shotgun.

"Charlie!" cried Old Lady. "You come outa there! I'm fixing a lizard magic to unlock that rusty door! You come out now and I won't make the earth shake or the trees go up in fire or the sun set at high noon!"

The only sound was the warm mountain light on the high turpentine trees, a tufted squirrel chittering around and around on a green-furred log, the ants moving in a fine brown line at Old Lady's bare, blue-veined feet.

"You been starving in there two days, darn you!" she panted, chiming the spoon against a flat rock, causing the plump gray miracle bag to swing at her waist. Sweating sour, she rose and marched at the cabin, bearing the pulverized flesh. "Come out, now!" She flicked a pinch of powder inside the lock. "All right, I'll come get you!" she wheezed.

She spun the knob with one walnut-colored hand, first one way, then the other. "O Lord," she intoned, "fling this door wide!"

When nothing flung, she added yet another philter and held her breath. Her long blue untidy skirt rustled as she peered into her bag of darkness to see if she had any scaly monsters there, any charm finer than the frog she'd killed months ago for such a crisis as this.

She heard Charlie breathing against the door. His folks had pranced off into some Ozark town early this week, leaving him, and he'd run almost six miles to Old Lady for company—she was by way of being an aunt or cousin or some such, and he didn't mind her fashions.

But then, two days ago, Old Lady, having gotten used to the boy around, decided to keep him for convenient company. She pricked her thin shoulder bone, drew out three blood pearls, spat wet over her right elbow, tromped on a crunch-cricket, and at the same instant clawed her left hand at Charlie, crying, "My son you are, you are my son, for all eternity!"

Charlie, bounding like a startled hare, had crashed off into the bush, heading for home.

But Old Lady, skittering quick as a gingham lizard, cornered him in a dead end, and Charlie holed up in this old hermit's cabin and wouldn't come out, no matter how she whammed door, window, or knothole with amber-colored fist or trounced her ritual fires, explaining to him that he was certainly her son *now*, all right.

"Charlie, you *there?*" she asked, cutting holes in the door planks with her bright little slippery eyes.

"I'm all of me here," he replied finally, very tired.

Maybe he would fall out on the ground any moment. She wrestled the knob hopefully. Perhaps a pinch too much frog powder had grated the lock wrong. She always overdid or underdid her miracles, she mused angrily, never doing them just *exact*, Devil take it!

"Charlie, I only wants someone to night-prattle to, someone to warm hands with at the fire. Someone to fetch kindling for me mornings, and fight off the spunks that come creeping of early fogs! I ain't got no fetchings on you for myself, son, just for your company." She smacked her lips. "Tell you what, Charles, you come out and I *teach* you things!"

"What things?" he suspicioned.

"Teach you how to buy cheap, sell high. Catch a snow weasel, cut off its head, carry it warm in your hind pocket. There!"

"Aw," said Charlie.

She made haste. "Teach you to make yourself shotproof. So if anyone bangs at you with a gun, nothing happens."

When Charlie stayed silent, she gave him the secret in a high fluttering whisper. "Dig and stitch mouse-ear roots on Friday during full moon, and wear 'em around your neck in a white silk."

"You're *crazy*," Charlie said.

"Teach you how to stop blood or make animals stand frozen or make blind horses see, all them things I'll teach you! Teach you to cure a swelled-up cow and unbewitch a goat. Show you how to make yourself invisible!"

"Oh," said Charlie.

Old Lady's heart beat like a Salvation tambourine.

The knob turned from the other side.

"You," said Charlie, "are funning me."

"No, I'm not," exclaimed Old Lady. "Oh, Charlie, why, I'll make you like a window, see right through you. Why, child, you'll be surprised!"

"Real invisible?"

"Real invisible!"

"You won't fetch onto me if I walk out?"

"Won't touch a bristle of you, son."

"Well," he drawled reluctantly, "all right."

The door opened. Charlie stood in his bare feet, head down, chin against chest. "Make me invisible," he said.

"First we got to catch us a bat," said Old Lady. "Start lookin'!"

She gave him some jerky beef for his hunger and watched him climb a tree. He went high up and high up and it was nice seeing him there and it was nice having him here and all about after so many years alone with nothing to say good morning to but bird-droppings and silvery snail tracks.

Pretty soon a bat with a broken wing fluttered down out of the tree. Old Lady snatched it up, beating warm and shrieking between its porcelain white teeth, and Charlie dropped down after it, hand upon clenched hand, yelling.

That night, with the moon nibbling at the spiced pine cones, Old Lady extracted a long silver needle from under her wide blue dress. Gumming her excitement and secret anticipation, she sighted up the dead bat and held the cold needle steady-steady.

She had long ago realized that her miracles, despite all perspirations and salts and sulphurs, failed. But she had always dreamt that one day the miracles might start functioning, might spring up in crimson flowers and silver stars to prove that God had forgiven her for her pink body and her pink thoughts and her warm body and her warm thoughts as a young miss. But so far God had made no sign and said no word, but nobody knew this except Old Lady.

"Ready?" she asked Charlie, who crouched cross-kneed, wrapping his pretty legs in long goose-pimpled arms, his mouth open, making teeth. "Ready," he whispered, shivering.

"There!" She plunged the needle deep in the bat's right eye. "So!"

"Oh!" screamed Charlie, wadding up his face.

"Now I wrap it in gingham, and here, put it in your pocket, keep it there, bat and all. Go on!"

He pocketed the charm.

"Charlie!" she shrieked fearfully. "Charlie, where *are* you? I can't *see* you, child!"

"Here!" He jumped so the light ran in red streaks up his body. "I'm here, Old Lady!" He stared wildly at his arms, legs, chest, and toes. "I'm here!"

Her eyes looked as if they were watching a thousand fireflies crisscrossing each other in the wild night air.

"Charlie, oh, you went *fast*! Quick as a hummingbird! Oh, Charlie, come *back* to me!"

"But I'm *here*!" he wailed.

"Where?"

"By the fire, the fire! And—and I can see myself. I'm not invisible at all!"

Old Lady rocked on her lean flanks. "Course *you* can see *you*! Every invisible person knows himself. Otherwise, how could you eat, walk, or get around places? Charlie, touch me. Touch me so I *know* you."

Uneasily he put out a hand.

She pretended to jerk, startled, at his touch. "*Ah!*"

"You mean to say you can't *find* me?" he asked. "Truly?"

"Not the least half-rump of you!"

She found a tree to stare at, and stared at it with shining eyes, careful not to glance at him. "Why, I sure *did* a trick *that* time!" She sighed with wonder. "Whooeee. Quickest invisible I *ever* made! Charlie. Charlie, how you *feel*?"

"Like creek water—all stirred."

"You'll settle."

Then after a pause she added, "Well, what you going to do now, Charlie, since you're invisible?"

All sorts of things shot through his brain, she could tell. Adventures stood up and danced like hell-fire in his eyes, and his mouth, just hanging, told what it meant to be a boy who imagined himself like the mountain winds. In a cold dream he said, "I'll run across wheat fields, climb snow mountains, steal white chickens off'n farms. I'll kick pink pigs when they ain't looking. I'll pinch pretty girls' legs when they sleep, snap their garters in schoolrooms." Charlie looked at Old Lady, and from the shiny tips of her eyes she saw something wicked shape his face. "And other things I'll do, I'll do, I will," he said.

"Don't try nothing on me," warned Old Lady. "I'm brittle as spring ice and I don't take handling." Then: "What about your folks?"

"My folks?"

"You can't fetch yourself home looking like that. Scare the inside ribbons out of them. Your mother'd faint straight back like timber falling. Think they want you about the house to stumble over and your ma have to call you every three minutes, even though you're in the room next her elbow?"

Charlie had not considered it. He sort of simmered down and whispered out a little "Gosh" and felt of his long bones carefully.

"You'll be mighty lonesome. People looking through you like a water glass, people knocking you aside because they didn't reckon you to be underfoot. And women, Charlie, *women*—"

He swallowed. "What about women?"

"No woman will be giving you a second stare. And no woman wants to be kissed by a boy's mouth they can't even *find*!"

Charlie dug his bare toe in the soil contemplatively. He pouted. "Well, I'll stay invisible, anyway, for a spell. I'll have me some fun. I'll just be pretty careful, is all. I'll stay out from in front of wagons and horses and Pa. Pa shoots at the nariest sound." Charlie blinked. "Why, with me invisible, someday Pa might just up and fill me with buckshot, thinkin' I was a hill squirrel in the dooryard. Oh . . ."

Old Lady nodded at a tree. "That's likely."

"Well," he decided slowly, "I'll stay invisible for tonight, and tomorrow you can fix me back all whole again, Old Lady."

"Now if that ain't just like a critter, always wanting to be what he can't be," remarked Old Lady to a beetle on a log.

"What you mean?" said Charlie.

"Why," she explained, "it was real hard work, fixing you up. It'll take a little *time* for it to wear off. Like a coat of paint wears off, boy."

"You!" he cried. "You did this to me! Now you make me back, you make me seeable!"

"Hush," she said. "It'll wear off, a hand or a foot at a time."

"How'll it look, me around the hills with just one hand showing!"

"Like a five-winged bird hopping on the stones and bramble."

"Or a foot showing!"

"Like a small pink rabbit jumping thicket."

"Or my head floating!"

"Like a hairy balloon at the carnival!"

"How long before I'm *whole?*" he asked.

She deliberated that it might pretty well be an entire year.

He groaned. He began to sob and bite his lips and make fists. "You magicked me, you did this, you did this thing to me. Now I won't be able to run home!"

She winked. "But you *can* stay here, child, stay on with me real comfort-like, and I'll keep you fat and saucy."

He flung it out: "You did this on purpose! You mean old hag, you want to keep me here!"

He ran off through the shrubs on the instant.

"Charlie, come back!"

No answer but the pattern of his feet on the soft dark turf, and his wet choking cry which passed swiftly off and away.

She waited and then kindled herself a fire. "He'll be back," she whispered. And thinking inward on herself, she said, "And now I'll have me my company through spring and into late summer. Then, when I'm tired of him and want a silence, I'll send him home."

Charlie returned noiselessly with the first gray of dawn, gliding over the rimed turf to where Old Lady sprawled like a bleached stick before the scattered ashes.

He sat on some creek pebbles and stared at her.

She didn't dare look at him or beyond. He had made no sound, so how could she know he was anywhere about? She couldn't.

He sat there, tear marks on his cheeks.

Pretending to be just waking—but she had found no sleep from one end of the night to the other—Old Lady stood up, grunting and yawning, and turned in a circle to the dawn.

"Charlie?"

Her eyes passed from pines to soil, to sky, to the far hills. She called out his name, over and over again, and she felt like staring plumb straight at him, but she stopped herself. "Charlie? Oh, Charles!" she called, and heard the echoes say the very same.

He sat, beginning to grin a bit, suddenly, knowing he was close to her, yet she must feel alone. Perhaps he felt the growing of a secret power, perhaps he felt secure from the world, certainly he was *pleased* with his invisibility.

She said aloud, "Now where *can* that boy be? If he only made a noise so I could tell just where he is, maybe I'd fry him a breakfast."

She prepared the morning victuals, irritated at his continuous quiet. She sizzled bacon on a hickory stick. "The smell of it will draw his nose," she muttered.

While her back was turned he swiped all the frying bacon and devoured it tastily.

She whirled, crying out, "Lord!"

She eyed the clearing suspiciously. "Charlie, that *you*?"

Charlie wiped his mouth clean on his wrists.

She trotted about the clearing, making like she was trying to locate him. Finally, with a clever thought, acting blind, she headed straight for him, groping. "Charlie, where *are* you?"

A lightning streak, he evaded her, bobbing, ducking.

It took all her will power not to give chase; but you can't chase invisible boys, so she sat down, scowling, sputtering, and tried to fry more bacon. But every fresh strip she cut he would steal bubbling off the fire and run away far. Finally, cheeks burning, she cried, "I know where you are! Right *there*! I hear you run!" She pointed to one side of him, not too accurate. He ran again. "Now you're there!" she shouted. "There, and there!" pointing to all the places he was in the next five minutes. "I hear you press a grass blade, knock a flower, snap a twig. I got fine shell ears, delicate as roses. They can hear the stars moving!"

Silently he galloped off among the pines, his voice trailing back, "Can't hear me when I'm set on a rock. I'll just *set*!"

All day he sat on an observatory rock in the clear wind, motionless and sucking his tongue.

Old Lady gathered wood in the deep forest, feeling his eyes weaseling on her spine. She wanted to babble: "Oh, I see you, I see you! I was only fooling about invisible boys! You're right there!" But she swallowed her gall and gummed it tight.

The following morning he did the spiteful things. He began leaping from behind trees. He made toad-faces, frog-faces, spider-faces at her, clenching down his lips with his fingers, popping his raw eyes, pushing up his nostrils so you could peer in and see his brain thinking.

Once she dropped her kindling. She pretended it was a blue jay startled her.

He made a motion as if to strangle her.

She trembled a little.

He made another move as if to bang her shins and spit on her cheek.

These motions she bore without a lid-flicker or a mouth-twitch.

He stuck out his tongue, making strange bad noises. He wiggled his loose ears so she wanted to laugh, and finally she did laugh and explained it away quickly by saying, "Sat on a salamander! Whew, how it poked!"

By high noon the whole madness boiled to a terrible peak.

For it was at that exact hour that Charlie came racing down the valley stark boy-naked!

Old Lady nearly fell flat with shock!

"Charlie!" she almost cried.

Charlie raced naked up one side of a hill and naked down the other—naked as day, naked as the moon, raw as the sun and a newborn chick, his feet shimmering and rushing like the wings of a low-skimming hummingbird.

Old Lady's tongue locked in her mouth. What could she say? Charlie, go dress? For *shame? Stop* that? *Could* she? Oh, Charlie, Charlie, God! Could she say that now? *Well?*

Upon the big rock, she witnessed him dancing up and down, naked as the day of his birth, stomping bare feet, smacking his hands on his knees and sucking in and out his white stomach like blowing and deflating a circus balloon.

She shut her eyes tight and prayed.

After three hours of this she pleaded, "Charlie, Charlie, come here! I got something to *tell* you!"

Like a fallen leaf he came, dressed again, praise the Lord.

"Charlie," she said, looking at the pine trees, "I see your right toe. *There* it is."

"You do?" he said.

"Yes," she said very sadly. "There it is like a horny toad on the grass. And there, up there's your left ear hanging on the air like a pink butterfly."

Charlie danced. "I'm forming in, I'm forming in!"

Old Lady nodded. "Here comes your ankle!"

"Gimme *both* my feet!" ordered Charlie.

"You got 'em."

"How about my hands?"

"I see one crawling on your knee like a daddy longlegs."

"How about the other one?"

"It's crawling too."

"I got a body?"

"Shaping up fine."

"I'll need my head to go home, Old Lady."

To go home, she thought wearily. "No!" she said, stubborn and angry. "No, you ain't got no head. No head at all," she cried. She'd leave that to the very last. "No head, no head," she insisted.

"No head?" he wailed.

"Yes, oh my God, yes, yes, you got your blamed head!" she snapped, giving up. "Now, fetch me back my bat with the needle in his eye!"

He flung it at her. "Haaaa-yoooo!" His yelling went all up the valley, and long after he had run toward home she heard his echoes, racing.

Then she plucked up her kindling with a great dry weariness and started back toward her shack, sighing, talking. And Charlie followed her all the way, *really* invisible now, so she couldn't see him, just hear him, like a pine cone dropping or a deep underground stream trickling, or a squirrel clambering a bough; and over the fire at twilight she and Charlie sat, him so invisible, and her feeding him bacon he wouldn't take, so she ate it herself, and then she fixed some magic and fell asleep with Charlie, made out of sticks and rags and pebbles, but still warm and her very own son, slumbering and nice in her shaking mother arms . . . and they talked about golden things in drowsy voices until dawn made the fire slowly, slowly wither out. . . .

The Golden Kite,
the Silver Wind

"In the shape of a *pig?*" cried the Mandarin.

"In the shape of a pig," said the messenger, and departed.

"Oh, what an evil day in an evil year," cried the Mandarin. "The town of Kwan-Si, beyond the hill, was very small in my childhood. Now it has grown so large that at last they are building a wall."

"But why should a wall two miles away make my good father sad and angry all within the hour?" asked his daughter quietly.

"They build their wall," said the Mandarin, "in the shape of a pig! Do you see? Our own city wall is built in the shape of an orange. That pig will devour us, greedily!"

"Ah."

They both sat thinking.

Life was full of symbols and omens. Demons lurked everywhere, Death swam in the wetness of an eye, the turn of a gull's wing meant rain, a fan held *so*, the tilt of a roof, and, yes, even a city wall was of immense importance. Travelers and tourists, caravans, musicians, artists, coming upon these two towns, equally judging the portents, would say, "The city shaped like an orange? No! I will enter the city shaped like a pig and prosper, eating all, growing fat with good luck and prosperity!"

The Mandarin wept. "All is lost! These symbols and signs terrify. Our city will come on evil days."

"Then," said the daughter, "call in your stonemasons and temple builders. I will whisper from behind the silken screen and you will know the words."

The old man clapped his hands despairingly. "Ho, stonemasons! Ho, builders of towns and palaces!"

The men who knew marble and granite and onyx and quartz came quickly. The Mandarin faced them most uneasily, himself waiting for a whisper from the silken screen behind his throne. At last the whisper came.

"I have called you here," said the whisper.

"I have called you here," said the Mandarin aloud, "because our city is shaped like an orange, and the vile city of Kwan-Si has this day shaped theirs like a ravenous pig—"

Here the stonemasons groaned and wept. Death rattled his cane in the outer courtyard. Poverty made a sound like a wet cough in the shadows of the room.

"And so," said the whisper, said the Mandarin, "you raisers of walls must go bearing trowels and rocks and change the shape of *our* city!"

The architects and masons gasped. The Mandarin himself gasped at what he had said. The whisper whispered. The Mandarian went on: "And you will change our walls into a club which may beat the pig and drive it off!"

The stonemasons rose up, shouting. Even the Mandarin, delighted at the words from his mouth, applauded, stood down from his throne. "Quick!" he cried. "To work!"

When his men had gone, smiling and bustling, the Mandarin turned with great love to the silken screen. "Daughter," he whispered, "I will embrace you." There was no reply. He stepped around the screen, and she was gone.

Such modesty, he thought. She has slipped away and left me with a triumph, as if it were mine.

The news spread through the city; the Mandarin was acclaimed. Everyone carried stone to the walls. Fireworks were set off and the demons of death and poverty did not linger, as all worked together. At the end of the month the wall had been changed. It was now a mighty bludgeon with which to drive pigs, boars, even lions, far away. The Mandarin slept like a happy fox every night.

"I would like to see the Mandarin of Kwan-Si when the news is learned. Such pandemonium and hysteria; he will likely throw himself from a mountain! A little more of that wine, oh Daughter-who-thinks-like-a-son."

But the pleasure was like a winter flower; it died swiftly. That very afternoon the messenger rushed into the courtroom. "Oh Mandarin, disease, early sorrow, avalanches, grasshopper plagues, and poisoned well water!"

The Mandarin trembled.

"The town of Kwan-Si," said the messenger, "which was built like a pig and which animal we drove away by changing our walls to a mighty stick, has now turned triumph to winter ashes. They have built their city's walls like a great bonfire to burn our stick!"

The Mandarin's heart sickened within him, like an autumn fruit upon the ancient tree. "Oh, gods! Travelers will spurn us. Tradesmen, reading the symbols, will turn from the stick, so easily destroyed, to the fire, which conquers all!"

"No," said a whisper like a snowflake from behind the silken screen.

"No," said the startled Mandarin.

"Tell my stonemasons," said the whisper that was a falling drop of rain, "to build our walls in the shape of a shining lake."

The Mandarin said this aloud, his heart warmed.

"And with this lake of water," said the whisper and the old man, "we will quench the fire and put it out forever!"

The city turned out in joy to learn that once again they had been saved by the magnificent Emperor of ideas. They ran to the walls and built them nearer to this new vision, singing, not as loudly as before, of course, for they were tired, and not as quickly, for since it had taken a month to rebuild the wall the first time, they had had to neglect business and crops and therefore were somewhat weaker and poorer.

There then followed a succession of horrible and wonderful days, one in another like a nest of frightening boxes.

"Oh, Emperor," cried the messenger, "Kwan-Si has rebuilt their walls to resemble a mouth with which to drink all our lake!"

"Then," said the Emperor, standing very close to his silken screen, "build our walls like a needle to sew up that mouth!"

"Emperor!" screamed the messenger. "They make their walls like a sword to break your needle!"

The Emperor held, trembling, to the silken screen. "Then shift the stones to form a scabbard to sheathe that sword!"

"Mercy," wept the messenger the following morn, "they have worked all night and shaped their walls like lightning which will explode and destroy that sheath!"

Sickness spread in the city like a pack of evil dogs. Shops closed. The population, working now steadily for endless months upon the changing of the walls, resembled Death himself, clattering his white bones like musical instruments in the wind. Funerals began to appear in the streets, though it was the middle of summer, a time when all should be tending and harvesting. The Mandarin fell so ill that he had his bed drawn up by the silken screen and there he lay, miserably giving his architectural orders. The voice behind the screen was weak now, too, and faint, like the wind in the eaves.

"Kwan-Si is an eagle. Then our walls must be a net for that eagle. They are a sun to burn our net. Then we build a moon to eclipse their sun!"

Like a rusted machine, the city ground to a halt.

At last the whisper behind the screen cried out:

"In the name of the gods, send for Kwan-Si!"

Upon the last day of summer the Mandarin Kwan-Si, very ill and withered away, was carried into our Mandarin's courtroom by four starving footmen. The two mandarins were propped up, facing each other. Their breaths fluttered like winter winds in their mouths. A voice said:

"Let us put an end to this."

The old men nodded.

"This cannot go on," said the faint voice. "Our people do nothing but rebuild our cities to a different shape every day, every hour. They have no time to hunt, to fish, to love, to be good to their ancestors and their ancestors' children."

"This I admit," said the mandarins of the towns of the Cage, the Moon, the Spear, the Fire, the Sword and this, that, and other things.

"Carry us into the sunlight," said the voice.

The old men were borne out under the sun and up a little hill. In the late summer breeze a few very thin children were flying dragon kites in all the colors of the sun, and frogs and grass, the color of the sea and the color of coins and wheat.

The first Mandarin's daughter stood by his bed.

"See," she said.

"Those are nothing but kites," said the two old men.

"But what is a kite on the ground?" she said. "It is nothing. What does it need to sustain it and make it beautiful and truly spiritual?"

"The wind, of course!" said the others.

"And what do the sky and the wind need to make *them* beautiful?"

"A kite, of course—many kites, to break the monotony, the sameness of the sky. Colored kites, flying!"

"So," said the Mandarin's daughter. "You, Kwan-Si, will make a last rebuilding of your town to resemble nothing more nor less than the wind. And we shall build like a golden kite. The wind will beautify the kite and carry it to wondrous heights. And the kite will break the sameness of the wind's existence and give it purpose and meaning. One without the other is nothing. Together, all will be beauty and co-operation and a long and enduring life."

Whereupon the two mandarins were so overjoyed that they took their first nourishment in days, momentarily were given strength, embraced, and lavished praise upon each other, called the Mandarin's daughter a boy, a man, a stone pillar, a warrior, and a true and unforgettable son. Almost immediately they parted and hurried to their towns, calling out and singing, weakly but happily.

And so, in time, the towns became the Town of the Golden Kite and the Town of the Silver Wind. And harvestings were harvested and business tended again, and the flesh returned, and disease ran off like a frightened jackal. And on every night of the year the inhabitants in the Town of the Kite could hear the good clear wind sustaining them. And those in the Town of the Wind could hear the kite singing, whispering, rising, and beautifying them.

"So be it," said the Mandarin in front of his silken screen.

The Fog Horn

Out there in the cold water, far from land, we waited every night for the coming of the fog, and it came, and we oiled the brass machinery and lit the fog light up in the stone tower. Feeling like two birds in the gray sky, McDunn and I sent the light touching out, red, then white, then red again, to eye the lonely ships. And if they did not see our light, then there was always our Voice, the great deep cry of our Fog Horn shuddering through the rags of mist to startle the gulls away like decks of scattered cards and make the waves turn high and foam.

"It's a lonely life, but you're used to it now, aren't you?" asked McDunn.

"Yes," I said. "You're a good talker, thank the Lord."

"Well, it's your turn on land tomorrow," he said, smiling, "to dance the ladies and drink gin."

"What do you think, McDunn, when I leave you out here alone?"

"On the mysteries of the sea." McDunn lit his pipe. It was a quarter past seven of a cold November evening, the heat on, the light switching its tail in two hundred directions, the Fog Horn bumbling in the high throat of the tower. There wasn't a town for a hundred miles down the coast, just a road which came lonely through dead country to the sea, with few cars on it, a stretch of two miles of cold water out to our rock, and rare few ships.

"The mysteries of the sea," said McDunn thoughtfully. "You know, the ocean's the biggest damned snowflake ever? It rolls and swells a thousand shapes and colors, no two alike. Strange. One night, years ago, I was here alone, when all of the fish of the sea surfaced out there. Something made them swim in and lie in the bay, sort of trembling and staring up at the tower light going red, white, red, white across them so I could see their funny eyes. I turned cold. They were like a big peacock's tail, moving out there until midnight. Then, without so much as a sound, they slipped away, the million of them was gone. I kind of think maybe, in some sort of way, they came all those miles to worship. Strange. But think how the tower must look to them, standing seventy feet above the water, the God-light flashing out from it, and the tower declaring itself with a monster voice. They never came back, those fish, but don't you think for a while they thought they were in the Presence?"

I shivered. I looked out at the long gray lawn of the sea stretching away into nothing and nowhere.

"Oh, the sea's full." McDunn puffed his pipe nervously, blinking. He had been nervous all day and hadn't said why. "For all our engines and so-called submarines, it'll be ten thousand centuries before we set foot on the real bottom of the sunken lands, in the fairy kingdoms there, and know *real* terror. Think of it, it's still the year 300,000 Before Christ down under there. While we've paraded around with trumpets, lopping off each other's countries and heads, they have been living beneath the sea twelve miles deep and cold in a time as old as the beard of a comet."

"Yes, it's an old world."

"Come on. I got something special I been saving up to tell you."

We ascended the eighty steps, talking and taking our time. At the top, McDunn switched off the room lights so there'd be no reflection in the plate glass. The great eye of the light was humming, turning easily in its oiled socket. The Fog Horn was blowing steadily, once every fifteen seconds.

"Sounds like an animal, don't it?" McDunn nodded to himself. "A big lonely animal crying in the night. Sitting here on the edge of ten billion years calling out to the Deeps, I'm here, I'm here, I'm here. And the Deeps *do* answer, yes, they do. You been here now for three months, Johnny, so I better prepare you. About this time of year," he said, studying the murk and fog, "something comes to visit the lighthouse."

"The swarms of fish like you said?"

"No, this is something else. I've put off telling you because you might think I'm daft. But tonight's the latest I can put it off, for if my calendar's marked right from last year, tonight's the night it comes. I won't go into detail, you'll have to see it yourself. Just sit down there. If you want, tomorrow you can pack your duffel and take the motorboat in to land and get your car parked there at the dinghy pier on the cape and drive on back to some little inland town and keep your lights burning nights, I won't question or blame you. It's happened three years now, and this is the only time anyone's been here with me to verify it. You wait and watch."

Half an hour passed with only a few whispers between us. When we grew tired waiting, McDunn began describing some of his ideas to me. He had some theories about the Fog Horn itself.

"One day many years ago a man walked along and stood in the sound of the ocean on a cold sunless shore and said, 'We need a voice to call across the water, to warn ships; I'll make one. I'll make a voice like all of time and all of the fog that ever was; I'll make a voice that is like an empty bed beside you all night long, and like an empty house when you open the door, and like trees in autumn with no leaves. A sound like the birds flying south, crying, and a sound like November wind and the sea on the hard, cold shore. I'll make a sound that's so alone that no one can miss it, that whoever hears it will weep in their souls, and hearths will seem warmer, and being inside will seem better to all who hear it in the distant towns. I'll make me a sound and an apparatus and they'll call it a Fog Horn and whoever hears it will know the sadness of eternity and the briefness of life.'"

The Fog Horn blew.

"I made up that story," said McDunn quietly, "to try to explain why this thing keeps coming back to the lighthouse every year. The Fog Horn calls it, I think, and it comes. . . . "

"But—" I said.

"Sssst!" said McDunn. "There!" He nodded out to the Deeps.

Something was swimming toward the lighthouse tower.

It was a cold night, as I have said; the high tower was cold, the light coming and going, and the Fog Horn calling and calling through the raveling mist. You couldn't see far and you couldn't see plain, but there was the deep sea moving on its way about the night earth, flat and quiet, the color of gray mud, and here were the two of us alone in the high tower, and there, far out at first, was a ripple, followed by a wave, a rising, a bubble, a bit of froth. And then, from the surface of the cold sea came a head, a large head, dark-colored, with immense eyes, and then a neck. And then—not a body—but more neck and more! The head rose a full forty feet above the water on a slender and beautiful dark neck. Only then did the body, like a little island of black coral and shells and crayfish, drip up from the subterranean. There was a flicker of tail. In all, from head to tip of tail, I estimated the monster at ninety or a hundred feet.

I don't know what I said. I said something.

"Steady, boy, steady," whispered McDunn.

"It's impossible!" I said.

"No, Johnny, *we're* impossible. *It's* like it always was ten million years ago. *It* hasn't changed. It's *us* and the land that've changed, become impossible. *Us!*"

It swam slowly and with a great dark majesty out in the icy waters, far away. The fog came and went about it, momentarily erasing its shape. One of the monster eyes caught and held and flashed back our immense light, red, white, red, white, like a disk held high and sending a message in primeval code. It was as silent as the fog through which it swam.

"It's a dinosaur of some sort!" I crouched down, holding to the stair rail.

"Yes, one of the tribe."

"But they died out!"

"No, only hid away in the Deeps. Deep, deep down in the deepest Deeps. Isn't *that* a word now, Johnny, a real word, it says so much: the Deeps. There's all the coldness and darkness and deepness in the world in a word like that."

"What'll we do?"

"Do? We got our job, we can't leave. Besides, we're safer here than in any boat trying to get to land. That thing's as big as a destroyer and almost as swift."

"But here, why does it come *here?*"

The next moment I had my answer.

The Fog Horn blew.

And the monster answered.

A cry came across a million years of water and mist. A cry so anguished and alone that it shuddered in my head and my body. The monster cried out at the tower. The Fog Horn blew. The monster roared again. The Fog Horn blew. The monster opened its great toothed mouth and the sound that came from it was the sound of the Fog Horn itself. Lonely and vast and far away. The sound of isolation, a viewless sea, a cold night, apartness. That was the sound.

"Now," whispered McDunn, "do you know why it comes here?"

I nodded.

"All year long, Johnny, that poor monster there lying far out, a thousand miles at sea, and twenty miles deep maybe, biding its time, perhaps it's a million years old, this one creature. Think of it, waiting a million years; could *you* wait that long? Maybe it's the last of its kind. I sort of think that's true. Anyway, here come men on land and build this lighthouse, five years ago. And set up their Fog Horn and sound it and sound it, out toward the place where you bury yourself in sleep and sea memories of a world where there were thousands like yourself, but now you're alone, all alone in a world not made for you, a world where you have to hide.

"But the sound of the Fog Horn comes and goes, comes and goes, and you stir from the muddy bottom of the Deeps, and your eyes open like the lenses of two-foot cameras and you move, slow, slow, for you have the ocean sea on your shoulders, heavy. But that Fog Horn comes through a thousand miles of water, faint and familiar, and the furnace in your belly stokes up, and you begin to rise, slow, slow. You feed yourself on great slakes of cod and minnow, on rivers of jellyfish, and you rise slow through the autumn months, through September when the fogs started, through October with more fog and the horn still calling you on, and then, late in November, after pressurizing yourself day by day, a few feet higher every hour, you are near the surface and still alive. You've got to go slow; if you surfaced all at once you'd explode. So it takes you all of three months to surface, and then a number of days to swim through the cold waters to the lighthouse. And there you are, out there, in the night, Johnny, the biggest damn monster in creation. And here's the lighthouse calling to you, with a long neck like your neck sticking way up out of the water, and a body like your body, and, most important of all, a voice like your voice. Do you understand now, Johnny, do you understand?"

The Fog Horn blew.

The monster answered.

I saw it all, I knew it all—the million years of waiting alone, for someone to come back who never came back. The million years of isolation at the bottom of the sea, the insanity of time there, while the skies cleared of reptile-birds, the swamps dried on the continental lands, the sloths and saber-tooths had their day and sank in tar pits, and men ran like white ants upon the hills.

The Fog Horn blew.

"Last year," said McDunn, "that creature swam round and round, round and round, all night. Not coming too near, puzzled, I'd say. Afraid, maybe. And a bit angry after coming all this way. But the next day, unexpectedly, the fog lifted, the sun came out fresh, the sky was as blue as a painting. And the monster swam off away from the heat and the silence and didn't come back. I suppose it's been brooding on it for a year now, thinking it over from every which way."

The monster was only a hundred yards off now, it and the Fog Horn crying at each other. As the lights hit them, the monster's eyes were fire and ice, fire and ice.

"That's life for you," said McDunn. "Someone always waiting for someone who never comes home. Always someone loving some thing more than that thing loves them. And after a while you want to destroy whatever that thing is, so it can't hurt you no more."

The monster was rushing at the lighthouse.

The Fog Horn blew.

"Let's see what happens," said McDunn.

He switched the Fog Horn off.

The ensuing minute of silence was so intense that we could hear our hearts pounding in the glassed area of the tower, could hear the slow greased turn of the light.

The monster stopped and froze. Its great lantern eyes blinked. Its mouth gaped. It gave a sort of rumble, like a volcano. It twitched its head this way and that, as if to seek the sounds now dwindled off into the fog. It peered at the lighthouse. It rumbled again. Then its eyes caught fire. It reared up, threshed the water, and rushed at the tower, its eyes filled with angry torment.

"McDunn!" I cried. "Switch on the horn!"

McDunn fumbled with the switch. But even as he flicked it on, the monster was rearing up. I had a glimpse of its gigantic paws, fishskin glittering in webs between the fingerlike projections, clawing at the tower. The huge eye on the right side of its anguished head glittered before me like a caldron into which I might drop, screaming. The tower shook. The Fog Horn cried; the monster cried. It seized the tower and gnashed at the glass, which shattered in upon us.

McDunn seized my arm. "Downstairs!"

The tower rocked, trembled, and started to give. The Fog Horn and the monster roared. We stumbled and half fell down the stairs. "Quick!"

We reached the bottom as the tower buckled down toward us. We ducked under the stairs into the small stone cellar. There were a thousand concussions as the rocks rained down; the Fog Horn stopped abruptly. The monster crashed upon the tower. The tower fell. We knelt together, McDunn and I, holding tight, while our world exploded.

Then it was over, and there was nothing but darkness and the wash of the sea on the raw stones.

That and the other sound.

"Listen," said McDunn quietly. "Listen."

We waited a moment. And then I began to hear it. First a great vacuumed sucking of air, and then the lament, the bewilderment, the loneliness of the great monster, folded over and upon us, above us, so that the sickening reek of its body filled the air, a stone's thickness away from our cellar. The monster gasped and cried. The tower was gone. The light was gone. The thing that had called to it across a million years was gone. And the monster was opening its mouth and sending out great sounds. The sounds of a Fog Horn, again and again. And ships far at sea, not finding the light, not seeing anything, but passing and hearing late that night, must've thought: There it is, the lonely sound, the Lonesome Bay horn. All's well. We've rounded the cape.

And so it went for the rest of that night.

The sun was hot and yellow the next afternoon when the rescuers came out to dig us from our stoned-under cellar.

"It fell apart, is all," said Mr. McDunn gravely. "We had a few bad knocks from the waves and it just crumbled." He pinched my arm.

There was nothing to see. The ocean was calm, the sky blue. The only thing was a great algaic stink from the green matter that covered the fallen tower stones and the shore rocks. Flies buzzed about. The ocean washed empty on the shore.

The next year they built a new lighthouse, but by that time I had a job in the little town and a wife and a good small warm house that glowed yellow on autumn nights, the doors locked, the chimney puffing smoke. As for McDunn, he was master of the new lighthouse, built to his own specifications, out of steel-reinforced concrete. "Just in case," he said.

The new lighthouse was ready in November. I drove down alone one evening late and parked my car and looked across the gray waters and listened to the new horn sounding, once, twice, three, four times a minute far out there, by itself.

The monster?

It never came back.

"It's gone away," said McDunn. "It's gone back to the Deeps. It's learned you can't love anything too much in this world. It's gone into the deepest Deeps to wait another million years. Ah, the poor thing! Waiting out there, and waiting out there, while man comes and goes on this pitiful little planet. Waiting and waiting."

I sat in my car, listening. I couldn't see the lighthouse or the light standing out in Lonesome Bay. I could only hear the Horn, the Horn, the Horn. It sounded like the monster calling.

I sat there wishing there was something I could say.

The Big Black and White Game

The people filled the stands behind the wire screen, waiting. Us kids, dripping from the lake, ran between the white cottages, past the resort hotel, screaming, and sat on the bleachers, making wet bottom marks. The hot sun beat down through the tall oak trees around the baseball diamond. Our fathers and mothers, in golf pants and light summer dresses, scolded us and made us sit still.

We looked toward the hotel and the back door of the vast kitchen, expectantly. A few colored women began walking across the shade-freckled area between, and in ten minutes the far left section of the bleachers was mellow with the color of their fresh-washed faces and arms. After all these years, whenever I think back on it, I can still hear the sounds they made. The sound on the warm air was like a soft moving of dove voices each time they talked among themselves.

Everybody quickened into amusement, laughter rose right up into the clear blue Wisconsin sky, as the kitchen door flung wide and out ran the big and little, the dark and high-yellar uniformed Negro waiters, janitors, bus boys, boatmen, cooks, bottle washers, soda jerks, gardeners, and golf-links tenders. They came capering, showing their fine white teeth, proud of their new red-striped uniforms, their shiny shoes rising and coming down on the green grass as they skirted the bleachers and drifted with lazy speed out on the field, calling to everybody and everything.

Us kids squealed. There was Long Johnson, the lawn-cutting man, and Cavanaugh, the soda-fountain man, and Shorty Smith and Pete Brown and Jiff Miller!

And *there* was Big Poe! Us kids shouted, applauded!

Big Poe was the one who stood so tall by the popcorn machine every night in the million-dollar dance pavilion farther down beyond the hotel on the lake rim. Every night I bought popcorn from Big Poe and he poured lots of butter all over it for me.

I stomped and yelled, "Big Poe! Big Poe!"

And he looked over at me and stretched his lips to bring out his teeth, waved, and shouted a laugh.

And Mama looked to the right, to the left, and back of us with worried eyes and nudged my elbow. "Hush," she said. "Hush."

"Land, land," said the lady next to my mother, fanning herself with a folded paper. "This is quite a day for the colored servants, ain't it? Only time of year they break loose. They look forward all summer to the big Black and White game. But this ain't nothing. You seen their Cakewalk Jamboree?"

"We got tickets for it," said Mother. "For tonight at the pavilion. Cost us a dollar each. That's pretty expensive, I'd say."

"But I always figure," said the woman, "once a year you got to spend. And it's really something to watch them dance. They just naturally got . . . "

"Rhythm," said Mother.

"That's the word," said the lady. "Rhythm. That's what they got. Land, you should see the colored maids up at the hotel. They been buying satin yardage in at the big store in Madison for a month now. And every spare minute they sit sewing and laughing. And I seen some of the feathers they bought for their hats. Mustard and wine ones and blue ones and violet ones. Oh, it'll be a sight!"

"They been airing out their tuxedos," I said. "I saw them hanging on lines behind the hotel all last week!"

"Look at them prance," said Mother. "You'd think they thought they were going to win the game from our men."

The colored men ran back and forth and yelled with their high, fluting voices and their low, lazy interminable voices. Way out in center field you could see the flash of teeth, their upraised naked black arms swinging and beating their sides as they hopped up and down and ran like rabbits, exuberantly.

Big Poe took a double fistful of bats, bundled them on his huge bull shoulder, and strutted along the first-base line, head back, mouth smiling wide open, his tongue moving, singing:

> "—*gonna dance out both of my shoes,*
> *When they play those Jelly Roll Blues;*
> *Tomorrow night at the Dark Town Strutters' Ball!"*

Up went his knees and down and out, swinging the bats like musical batons. A burst of applause and soft laughter came from the left-hand grandstands, where all the young, ripply colored girls with shiny brown eyes sat eager and easy. They made quick motions that were graceful and mellow because, maybe, of their rich coloring. Their laughter was like shy birds; they waved at Big Poe, and one of them with a high voice cried, "Oh, Big Poe! Oh, Big Poe!"

The white section joined politely in the applause as Big Poe finished his cakewalk. "Hey, Big Poe!" I yelled again.

"Stop that, Douglas!" said Mother, straight at me.

Now the white men came running between the trees with their uniforms on. There was a great thunder and shouting and rising up in our grandstand. The white men ran across the green diamond, flashing white.

"Oh, there's Uncle George!" said Mother. "My, doesn't he look nice?" And there was my Uncle George toddling along in his outfit which didn't quite fit because Uncle has a potbelly, and jowls that sit out over any collar he puts on. He was hurrying along, trying to breathe and smile at the same time, lifting up his pudgy little legs. "My, they look *so* nice," enthused Mother.

I sat there, watching their movements. Mother sat beside me, and I think she was comparing and thinking, too, and what she saw amazed and disconcerted her. How easily the dark people had come running first, like those slow-motion deer and buck antelopes in those African moving pictures, like things in dreams. They came like beautiful brown, shiny animals that didn't know they were alive, but lived. And when they ran and put their easy, lazy, timeless legs out and followed them with their big, sprawling arms and loose fingers and smiled in the blowing wind, their expressions didn't say, "Look at *me* run, look at *me* run!" No, not at all. Their faces dreamily said, "Lord, but it's sure nice to run. See the ground swell soft under me? Gosh, I feel good. My muscles are moving like oil on my bones and it's the best pleasure in the world to run." And they ran. There was no purpose to their running but exhilaration and living.

The white men worked at their running as they worked at everything. You felt embarrassed for them because they were alive too much in the wrong way. Always looking from the corners of their eyes to see if you were watching. The Negroes didn't care if you watched or not; they went on living, moving. They were so sure of playing that they didn't have to think about it any more.

"My, but our men look so nice," said my mother, repeating herself rather flatly. She had seen, compared the teams. Inside, she realized how laxly the colored men hung swaying in their uniforms, and how tensely, nervously, the white men were crammed, shoved, and belted into *their* outfits.

I guess the tenseness began then.

I guess everybody saw what was happening. They saw how the white men looked like senators in sun suits. And they admired the graceful unawareness of the colored men. And, as is always the case, that admiration turned to envy, to jealousy, to irritation. It turned to conversation like:

"That's my husband, Tom, on third base. Why doesn't he pick up his feet? He just *stands* there."

"Never you mind, never you mind. He'll pick 'em up when the time comes!"

"That's what *I* say! Now, take my Henry, for instance. Henry mightn't be active all the time, but when there's a crisis—just you *watch* him. Uh—I do wish he'd wave or something, though. Oh, *there*! Hello, Henry!"

"Look at that Jimmie Cosner playing around out there!"

I looked. A medium-sized white man with a freckled face and red hair was clowning on the diamond. He was balancing a bat on his forehead. There was laughter from the white grandstand. But it sounded like the kind of laughter you laugh when you're embarrassed for someone.

"Play ball!" said the umpire.

A coin was flipped. The colored men batted first.

"Darn it," said my mother.

The colored men ran in from the field happily.

Big Poe was first to bat. I cheered. He picked up the bat in one hand like a toothpick and idled over to the plate and laid the bat on his thick shoulder, smiling along its polished surface toward the stands where the colored women sat with their fresh flowery cream dresses stirring over their legs, which hung down between the seat intervals like crisp new sticks of ginger; their hair was all fancily spun and hung over their ears. Big Poe looked in particular at the little, dainty-as-a-chicken-bone shape of his girl friend Katherine. She was the one who made the beds at the hotel and cottages every morning, who tapped on your door like a bird and politely asked if you was done dreaming, 'cause if you was she'd clean away all them old nightmares and bring in a fresh batch—please use them *one* at a time, thank yoah. Big Poe shook his head, looking at her, as if he couldn't believe she was there. Then he turned, one hand balancing the bat, his left hand dangling free at his side, to await the trial pitches. They hissed past, spatted into the open mouth of the catcher's mitt, were hurled back. The umpire grunted. The next pitch was the starter.

Big Poe let the first ball go by him.

"Stee-rike!" announced the umpire. Big Poe winked good-naturedly at the white folks. Bang! "Stee-rike two!" cried the umpire.

The ball came for the third time.

Big Poe was suddenly a greased machine pivoting; the dangling hand swept

up to the butt end of the bat, the bat swiveled, connected with the ball—*Whack!*
The ball shot up into the sky, away down toward the wavering line of oak trees,
down toward the lake, where a white sailboat slid silently by. The crowd yelled,
me loudest! There went Uncle George, running on his stubby, wool-stockinged
legs, getting smaller with distance.

Big Poe stood for a moment watching the ball go. Then he began to run.
He went around the bases, loping, and on the way home from third base he
waved to the colored girls naturally and happily and they waved back, standing
on their seats and shrilling.

Ten minutes later, with the bases loaded and run after run being driven in,
and Big Poe coming to bat again, my mother turned to me. "They're the most
inconsiderate people," she said.

"But that's the game," I said. "They've only got two outs."

"But the score's seven to nothing," my mother protested.

"Well, just you wait until *our* men come to bat," said the lady next to my
mother, waving away a fly with a pale blue-veined hand. "Those Negroes are
too big for their britches."

"Stee-rike two!" said the umpire as Big Poe swung.

"All the past week at the hotel," said the woman next to my mother,
staring out at Big Poe steadily, "the hotel service has been simply terrible.
Those maids don't talk about a thing save the Cakewalk Jamboree, and whenever
you want ice water it takes them half an hour to fetch it, they're so busy
sewing."

"Ball one!" said the umpire.

The woman fussed. "I'll be glad when this week's over, that's what I got to
say," she said.

"Ball two!" said the umpire to Big Poe.

"Are they going to *walk* him?" asked my mother of me. "Are they *crazy?*"
To the woman next to her: "That's right. They been acting funny all week. Last
night I had to tell Big Poe twice to put extra butter on my popcorn. I guess he
was trying to save money or something."

"Ball three!" said the umpire.

The lady next to my mother cried out suddenly and fanned herself furiously
with her newspaper. "Land, I just *thought!* Wouldn't it be awful if they *won* the
game? They *might*, you know. They might do it."

My mother looked at the lake, at the trees, at her hands. "I don't know why
Uncle George had to play. Make a fool of himself. Douglas, you run tell him to
quit right now. It's bad on his heart."

"You're out!" cried the umpire to Big Poe.

"Ah," sighed the grandstand.

The side was retired. Big Poe laid down his bat gently and walked along the
base line. The white men pattered in from the field looking red and irritable,
with big islands of sweat under their armpits. Big Poe looked over at me. I
winked at him. He winked back. Then I knew he wasn't so dumb.

He'd struck out on purpose.

Long Johnson was going to pitch for the colored team.

He ambled out to the rubber, worked his fingers around in his fists to limber them up.

First white man to bat was a man named Kodimer, who sold suits in Chicago all year round.

Long Johnson fed them over the plate with tired, unassuming, controlled accuracy.

Mr. Kodimer chopped. Mr. Kodimer swatted. Finally Mr. Kodimer bunted the ball down the third-base line.

"Out at first base," said the umpire, an Irishman named Mahoney.

Second man up was a young Swede named Moberg. He hit a high fly to center field which was taken by a little plump Negro who didn't look fat because he moved around like a smooth, round glob of mercury.

Third man up was a Milwaukee truck driver. He whammed a line drive to center field. It was good. Except that he tried to stretch it into a two-bagger. When he pulled up at second base, there was Emancipated Smith with a white pellet in his dark, dark hand, waiting.

My mother sank back in her seat, exhaling. "Well, I *never!*"

"It's getting hotter," said the lady elbow-next. "Think I'll go for a stroll by the lake soon. It's too hot to sit and watch a silly game today. Mightn't you come along with me, missus?" she asked Mother.

It went on that way for five innings.

It was eleven to nothing and Big Poe had struck out three times on purpose, and in the last half of the fifth was when Jimmie Cosner came to bat for our side again. He'd been trying all afternoon, clowning, giving directions, telling everybody just where he was going to blast that pill once he got hold of it. He swaggered up toward the plate now, confident and bugle-voiced. He swung six bats in his thin hands, eying them critically with his shiny green little eyes. He chose one, dropped the others, ran to the plate, chopping out little islands of green fresh lawn with his cleated heels. He pushed his cap back on his dusty red hair. "Watch this!" he called out loud to the ladies. "You watch me show these dark boys! Ya-hah!"

Long Johnson on the mound did a slow serpentine windup. It was like a snake on a limb of a tree, uncoiling, suddenly darting at you. Instantly Johnson's hand was in front of him, open, like black fangs, empty. And the white pill slashed across the plate with a sound like a razor.

"Stee-rike!"

Jimmie Cosner put his bat down and stood glaring at the umpire. He said nothing for a long time. Then he spat deliberately near the catcher's foot, took up the yellow maple bat again, and swung it so the sun glinted the rim of it in a nervous halo. He twitched and sidled it on his thin-boned shoulder, and his mouth opened and shut over his long nicotined teeth.

Clap! went the catcher's mitt.

Cosner turned, stared.

The catcher, like a black magician, his white teeth gleaming, opened up his oily glove. There, like a white flower glowing, was the baseball.

"Stee-rike two!" said the umpire, far away in the heat.

Jimmie Cosner laid his bat across the plate and hunched his freckled hands on his hips. "You mean to tell me that was a strike?"

"That's what I said," said the umpire. "Pick up the bat."

"To hit you on the head with," said Cosner sharply.

"Play ball or hit the showers!"

Jimmie Cosner worked his mouth to collect enough saliva to spit, then angrily swallowed it, swore a bitter oath instead. Reaching down, he raised the bat, poised it like a musket on his shoulder.

And here came the ball! It started out small and wound up big in front of him. Powie! An explosion off the yellow bat. The ball spiraled up and up. Jimmie lit out for first base. The ball paused, as if thinking about gravity up there in the sky. A wave came in on the shore of the lake and fell down. The crowd yelled. Jimmie ran. The ball made its decision, came down. A lithe high-yellar was under it, fumbled it. The ball spilled to the turf, was plucked up, hurled to first base.

Jimmie saw he was going to be out. So he jumped feet-first at the base.

Everyone saw his cleats go into Big Poe's ankle. Everybody saw the red blood. Everybody heard the shout, the shriek, saw the heavy clouds of dust rising.

"I'm safe!" protested Jimmie two minutes later.

Big Poe sat on the ground. The entire dark team stood around him. The doctor bent down, probed Big Poe's ankle, saying, "Mmmm," and "Pretty bad. Here." And he swabbed medicine on it and put a white bandage on it.

The umpire gave Cosner the cold-water eye. "Hit the showers!"

"Like hell!" said Cosner. And he stood on that first base, blowing his cheeks out and in, his freckled hands swaying at his side. "I'm safe. I'm staying right here, by God! No nigger put *me* out."

"No," said the umpire. "A white man did. *Me. Get!*"

"He dropped the ball! Look up the rules! I'm safe!"

The umpire and Cosner stood glaring at each other.

Big Poe looked up from having his swollen ankle tended. His voice was thick and gentle and his eyes examined Jimmie Cosner gently.

"Yes, he's safe, Mr. Umpire. Leave him stay. He's safe."

I was standing right there. I heard the whole thing. Me and some other kids had run out on the field to see. My mother kept calling me to come back to the stands.

"Yes, he's safe," said Big Poe again.

All the colored men let out a yell.

"What'sa matter with you, black boy? You get hit in the head?"

"You heard me," replied Big Poe quietly. He looked at the doctor bandaging him. "He's safe. Leave him stay."

The umpire swore.

"Okay, okay. So he's safe!"

The umpire stalked off, his back stiff, his neck red.

Big Poe was helped up. "Better not walk on that," cautioned the doctor.

"I can walk," whispered Big Poe carefully.

"Better not play."

"I can play," said Big Poe gently, certainly, shaking his head, wet streaks drying under his white eyes. "I'll play *good*." He looked no place at all. "I'll play plenty good."

"Oh," said the second-base colored man. It was a funny sound.

All the colored men looked at each other, at Big Poe, then at Jimmie Cosner, at the sky, at the lake, the crowd. They walked off quietly to take their places. Big Poe stood with his bad foot hardly touching the ground, balanced. The doctor argued. But Big Poe waved him away.

"Batter up!" cried the umpire.

We got settled in the stands again. My mother pinched my leg and asked me why I couldn't sit still. It got warmer. Three or four more waves fell on the shore line. Behind the wire screen the ladies fanned their wet faces and the men inched their rumps forward on the wooden planks, held papers over their scowling brows to see Big Poe standing like a redwood tree out there on first base, Jimmie Cosner standing in the immense shade of that dark tree.

Young Moberg came up to bat for our side.

"Come on, Swede, come on, Swede!" was the cry, a lonely cry, like a dry bird, from out on the blazing green turf. It was Jimmie Cosner calling. The grandstand stared at him. The dark heads turned on their moist pivots in the outfield; the black faces came in his direction, looking him over, seeing his thin, nervously arched back. He was the center of the universe.

"Come on, Swede! Let's show these black boys!" laughed Cosner.

He trailed off. There was a complete silence. Only the wind came through the high, glittering trees.

"Come on, Swede, hang one on that old pill. . . . "

Long Johnson, on the pitcher's mound, cocked his head. Slowly, deliberately, he eyed Cosner. A look passed between him and Big Poe, and Jimmie Cosner saw the look and shut up and swallowed, hard.

Long Johnson took his time with his windup.

Cosner took a lead off base.

Long Johnson stopped loading his pitch.

Cosner skipped back to the bag, kissed his hand, and patted the kiss dead center on the plate. Then he looked up and smiled around.

Again the pitcher coiled up his long, hinged arm, curled loving dark fingers on the leather pellet, drew it back and—Cosner danced off first base. Cosner jumped up and down like a monkey. The pitcher did not look at him. The pitcher's eyes watched him secretively, slyly, amusedly, sidewise. Then, snapping his head, the pitcher scared Cosner back to the plate. Cosner stood and jeered.

The third time Long Johnson made as if to pitch, Cosner was far off the plate and running toward second.

Snap went the pitcher's hand. *Bom* went the ball in Big Poe's glove at first base.

Everything was sort of frozen. Just for a second.

There was the sun in the sky, the lake and the boats on it, the grandstands, the pitcher on his mound standing with his hand out and down after tossing the ball; there was Big Poe with the ball in his mighty black hand; there was the infield staring, crouching in at the scene, and there was Jimmie Cosner running, kicking up dirt, the only moving thing in the entire summer world.

Big Poe leaned forward, sighted toward second base, drew back his mighty right hand, and hurled that white baseball straight down along the line until it reached Jimmie Cosner's head.

Next instant, the spell was broken.

Jimmie Cosner lay flat on the burning grass. People boiled out of the grandstands. There was swearing, and women screaming, a clattering of wood as the men rushed down the wooden boards of the bleachers. The colored team ran in from the field. Jimmie Cosner lay there. Big Poe, no expression on his face, limped off the field, pushing white men away from him like clothespins when they tried stopping him. He just picked them up and threw them away.

"Come on, Douglas!" shrieked Mother, grabbing me. "Let's get home! They might have razors! Oh!"

That night, after the near riot of the afternoon, my folks stayed home reading magazines. All the cottages around us were lighted. Everybody was home. Distantly I heard music. I slipped out the back door into the ripe summer-night darkness and ran toward the dance pavilion. All the lights were on, and music played.

But there were no white people at the tables. Nobody had come to the Jamboree.

There were only colored folks. Women in bright red and blue satin gowns and net stockings and soft gloves, with wine-plume hats, and men in glossy tuxedos. The music crashed out, up, down, and around the floor. And laughing and stepping high, flinging their polished shoes out and up in the cakewalk, were Long Johnson and Cavanaugh and Jiff Miller and Pete Brown, and—limping— Big Poe and Katherine, his girl, and all the other lawn-cutters and boatmen and janitors and chambermaids, all on the floor at one time.

It was so dark all around the pavilion; the stars shone in the black sky, and I stood outside, my nose against the window, looking in for a long, long time, silently.

I went to bed without telling anyone what I'd seen.

I just lay in the dark smelling the ripe apples in the dimness and hearing the lake at night and listening to that distant, faint and wonderful music. Just before I slept I heard those last strains again:

"—*gonna dance out both of my shoes,*
When they play those Jelly Roll Blues;
Tomorrow night at the Dark Town Strutters' Ball!"

Embroidery

The dark porch air in the late afternoon was full of needle flashes, like a movement of gathered silver insects in the light. The three women's mouths twitched over their work. Their bodies lay back and then imperceptibly forward, so that the rocking chairs tilted and murmured. Each woman looked to her own hands, as if quite suddenly she had found her heart beating there.

"What time is it?"

"Ten minutes to five."

"Got to get up in a minute and shell those peas for dinner."

"But—" said one of them.

"Oh yes, I forgot. How foolish of me...." The first woman paused, put down her embroidery and needle, and looked through the open porch door, through the warm interior of the quiet house, to the silent kitchen. There upon the table, seeming more like symbols of domesticity than anything she had ever seen in her life, lay the mound of fresh-washed peas in their neat, resilient jackets, waiting for her fingers to bring them into the world.

"Go hull them if it'll make you feel good," said the second woman.

"No," said the first. "I won't. I just won't."

The third woman sighed. She embroidered a rose, a leaf, a daisy on a green field. The embroidery needle rose and vanished.

The second woman was working on the finest, most delicate piece of embroidery of them all, deftly poking, finding, and returning the quick needle upon innumerable journeys. Her quick black glance was on each motion. A flower, a man, a road, a sun, a house; the scene grew under her hand, a miniature beauty, perfect in every threaded detail.

"It seems at times like this that it's always your hands you turn to," she said, and the others nodded enough to make the rockers rock again.

"I believe," said the first lady, "that our souls are in our hands. For we do *everything* to the world with our hands. Sometimes I think we don't use our hands half enough; it's certain we don't use our heads."

They all peered more intently at what their hands were doing. "Yes," said the third lady, "when you look back on a whole lifetime, it seems you don't remember faces so much as hands and what they did."

They recounted to themselves the lids they had lifted, the doors they had opened and shut, the flowers they had picked, the dinners they had made, all with slow or quick fingers, as was their manner or custom. Looking back, you saw a flurry of hands, like a magician's dream, doors popping wide, taps turned, brooms wielded, children spanked. The flutter of pink hands was the only sound; the rest was a dream without voices.

"No supper to fix tonight or tomorrow night or the next night after that," said the third lady.

"No windows to open or shut."

"No coal to shovel in the basement furnace next winter."

"No papers to clip cooking articles out of."

And suddenly they were crying. The tears rolled softly down their faces and fell into the material upon which their fingers twitched.

"This won't help things," said the first lady at last, putting the back of her thumb to each under-eyelid. She looked at her thumb and it was wet.

"Now look what I've done!" cried the second lady, exasperated. The others stopped and peered over. The second lady held out her embroidery. There was the scene, perfect except that while the embroidered yellow sun shone down upon the embroidered green field, and the embroidered brown road curved toward an embroidered pink house, the man standing on the road had something wrong with his face.

"I'll just have to rip out the whole pattern, practically, to fix it right," said the second lady.

"What a shame." They all stared intently at the beautiful scene with the flaw in it.

The second lady began to pick away at the thread with her little deft scissors flashing. The pattern came out thread by thread. She pulled and yanked, almost viciously. The man's face was gone. She continued to seize at the threads.

"What are you *doing*?" asked the other woman.

They leaned and saw what she had done.

The man was gone from the road. She had taken him out entirely.

They said nothing but returned to their own tasks.

"What time is it?" asked someone.

"Five minutes to five."

"Is it supposed to happen at five o'clock?"

"Yes."

"And they're not sure what it'll do to anything, really, when it happens?"

"No, not sure."

"Why didn't we stop them before it got this far and this big?"

"It's twice as big as ever before. No, ten times, maybe a thousand."

"This isn't like the first one or the dozen later ones. This is different. Nobody knows what it might do when it comes."

They waited on the porch in the smell of roses and cut grass. "What time is it now?"

"One minute to five."

The needles flashed silver fire. They swam like a tiny school of metal fish in the darkening summer air.

Far away a mosquito sound. Then something like a tremor of drums. The three women cocked their heads, listening.

"We won't hear anything, will we?"

"They say not."

"Perhaps we're foolish. Perhaps we'll go right on, after five o'clock, shelling peas, opening doors, stirring soups, washing dishes, making lunches, peeling oranges . . ."

"My, how we'll laugh to think we were frightened by an old experiment!" They smiled a moment at each other.

"It's five o'clock."

At these words, hushed, they all busied themselves. Their fingers darted. Their faces were turned down to the motions they made. They made frantic patterns. They made lilacs and grass and trees and houses and rivers in the embroidered cloth. They said nothing, but you could hear their breath in the silent porch air.

Thirty seconds passed.

The second woman sighed finally and began to relax.

"I think I just *will* go shell those peas for supper," she said. "I—"

But she hadn't time even to lift her head. Somewhere, at the side of her vision, she saw the world brighten and catch fire. She kept her head down, for she knew what it was. She didn't look up, nor did the others, and in the last instant their fingers were flying; they didn't glance about to see what was happening to the country, the town, this house, or even this porch. They were only staring down at the design in their flickering hands.

The second woman watched an embroidered flower go. She tried to embroider it back in, but it went, and then the road vanished, and the blades of grass. She watched a fire, in slow motion almost, catch upon the embroidered house and unshingle it, and pull each threaded leaf from the small green tree in the hoop, and she saw the sun itself pulled apart in the design. Then the fire caught upon the moving point of the needle while still it flashed; she watched the fire come along her fingers and arms and body, untwisting the yarn of her being so painstakingly that she could see it in all its devilish beauty, yanking out the pattern from the material at hand. What it was doing to the other women or the furniture or the elm tree in the yard, she never knew. For now, yes now! it was plucking at the white embroidery of her flesh, the pink thread of her cheeks, and at last it found her heart, a soft red rose sewn with fire, and it burned the fresh, embroidered petals away, one by delicate one. . . .

The Golden Apples
of the Sun

"South," said the captain.

"But," said his crew, "there simply *aren't* any directions out here in space."

"When you travel on down toward the sun," replied the captain, "and everything gets yellow and warm and lazy, then you're going in one direction only." He shut his eyes and thought about the smoldering, warm, faraway land, his breath moving gently in his mouth. "South." He nodded slowly to himself. "South."

Their rocket was the *Copa de Oro*, also named the *Prometheus* and the *Icarus*, and their destination in all reality was the blazing noonday sun. In high good spirits they had packed along two thousand sour lemonades and a thousand white-capped beers for this journey to the wide Sahara. And now as the sun boiled up at them they remembered a score of verses and quotations:

"'The golden apples of the sun'?"

"Yeats."

"'Fear no more the heat of the sun'?"

"Shakespeare, of course!"

"*Cup of Gold*? Steinbeck. *The Crock of Gold*? Stephens. And what about the pot of gold at the rainbow's end? *There's* a name for our trajectory, by God. Rainbow!"

"Temperature?"

"One thousand degrees Fahrenheit!"

The captain stared from the huge dark-lensed port, and there indeed was the sun, and to go to that sun and touch it and steal part of it forever away was his quiet and single idea. In this ship were combined the coolly delicate and the coldly practical. Through corridors of ice and milk-frost, ammoniated winter and storming snowflakes blew. Any spark from that vast hearth burning out there beyond the callous hull of this ship, any small firebreath that might seep through would find winter, slumbering here like all the coldest hours of February.

The audio-thermometer murmured in the arctic silence: "Temperature: two thousand degrees!"

Falling, thought the captain, like a snowflake into the lap of June, warm July, and the sweltering dog-mad days of August.

"Three thousand degrees Fahrenheit!"

Under the snow fields engines raced, refrigerants pumped ten thousand miles per hour in rimed boa-constrictor coils.

"Four thousand degrees Fahrenheit."

Noon. Summer. July.

"Five thousand Fahrenheit!"

And at last the captain spoke with all the quietness of the journey in his voice:

"Now, we are touching the sun."

Their eyes, thinking it, were melted gold.

"Seven thousand degrees!"

Strange how a mechanical thermometer could sound excited, though it possessed only an emotionless steel voice.

"What *time* is it?" asked someone.

Everyone had to smile.

For now there was only the sun and the sun and the sun. It was every horizon, it was every direction. It burned the minutes, the seconds, the hourglasses, the clocks; it burned all time and eternity away. It burned the eyelids and the serum of the dark world behind the lids, the retina, the hidden brain; and it burned sleep and the sweet memories of sleep and cool nightfall.

"Watch it!"

"Captain!"

Bretton, the first mate, fell flat to the winter deck. His protective suit whistled where, burst open, his warmness, his oxygen, and his life bloomed out in a frosted steam.

"Quick!"

Inside Bretton's plastic face-mask, milk crystals had already gathered in blind patterns. They bent to see.

"A structural defect in his suit, Captain. Dead."

"Frozen."

They stared at that other thermometer which showed how winter lived in this snowing ship. One thousand degrees below zero. The captain gazed down upon the frosted statue and the twinkling crystals that iced over it as he watched. Irony of the coolest sort, he thought; a man afraid of fire and killed by frost.

The captain turned away. "No time. No time. Let him lie." He felt his tongue move. "Temperature?"

The dials jumped four thousand degrees.

"Look. Will you look? Look."

Their icicle was melting.

The captain jerked his head to look at the ceiling.

As if a motion-picture projector had jammed a single clear memory frame in his head, he found his mind focused ridiculously on a scene whipped out of childhood.

Spring mornings as a boy he had leaned from his bedroom window into the snow-smelling air to see the sun sparkle the last icicle of winter. A dripping of white wine, the blood of cool but warming April fell from that clear crystal blade. Minute by minute, December's weapon grew less dangerous. And then at last the icicle fell with the sound of a single chime to the graveled walk below.

"Auxiliary pump's broken, sir. Refrigeration. We're losing our ice!"

A shower of warm rain shivered down upon them. The captain jerked his head right and left. "Can you see the trouble? Christ, don't stand there, we haven't time!"

The men rushed; the captain bent in the warm rain, cursing, felt his hands run over the cold machine, felt them burrow and search, and while he worked he saw a future which was removed from them by the merest breath. He saw the skin peel from the rocket beehive, men, thus revealed, running, running, mouths shrieking, soundless. Space was a black mossed well where life drowned its roars and terrors. Scream a big scream, but space snuffed it out before it was half up your throat. Men scurried, ants in a flaming matchbox; the ship was dripping lava, gushing steam, nothing!

"Captain?"

The nightmare flicked away.

"Here." He worked in the soft warm rain that fell from the upper decks. He fumbled at the auxiliary pump. "Damn it!" He jerked the feed line. When it came, it'd be the quickest death in the history of dying. One moment, yelling; a warm flash later only the billion billion tons of space-fire would whisper, unheard, in space. Popped like strawberries in a furnace, while their thoughts lingered on the scorched air a long breath after their bodies were charred roast and fluorescent gas.

"Damn!" He stabbed the auxiliary pump with a screwdriver. "Jesus!" He shuddered. The complete annihilation of it. He clamped his eyes tight, teeth tight. God, he thought, we're used to more leisurely dyings, measured in minutes and hours. Even twenty seconds now would be a slow death compared to this hungry idiot thing waiting to eat us!

"Captain, do we pull out or stay?"

"Get the Cup ready. Take over, finish this. Now!"

He turned and put his hand to the working mechanism of the huge Cup; shoved his fingers into the robot Glove. A twitch of his hand here moved a gigantic hand, with gigantic metal fingers, from the bowels of the ship. Now, now, the great metal hand slid out holding the huge *Copa de Oro*, breathless, into the iron furnace, the bodiless body and the fleshless flesh of the sun.

A million years ago, thought the captain, quickly, quickly, as he moved the hand and the Cup, a million years ago a naked man on a lonely northern trail saw lightning strike a tree. And while his clan fled, with bare hands he plucked a limb of fire, broiling the flesh of his fingers, to carry it, running in triumph, shielding it from the rain with his body, to his cave, where he shrieked out a laugh and tossed it full on a mound of leaves and gave his people summer. And the tribe crept at last, trembling, near the fire, and they put out their flinching hands and felt the new season in their cave, this small yellow spot of changing weather, and they, too, at last, nervously, smiled. And the gift of fire was theirs.

"Captain!"

It took all of four seconds for the huge hand to push the empty Cup to the fire. So here we are again, today, on another trail, he thought, reaching for a cup of precious gas and vacuum, a handful of different fire with which to run back up cold space, lighting our way, and take to Earth a gift of fire that might burn forever. Why?

He knew the answer before the question.

Because the atoms we work with our hands, on Earth, are pitiful; the atomic bomb is pitiful and small and our knowledge is pitiful and small, and only the sun really knows what we want to know, and only the sun has the secret. And besides, it's fun, it's a chance, it's a great thing coming here, playing tag, hitting and running. There is no reason, really, except the pride and vanity of little insect men hoping to sting the lion and escape the maw. My God, we'll say, we *did* it! And here is our cup of energy, fire, vibration, call it what you will, that may well power our cities and sail our ships and light our libraries and tan our children and bake our daily breads and simmer the knowledge of our universe for us for a thousand years until it is well done. Here, from this cup, all good men of science and religion: drink! Warm yourselves against the night of ignorance, the long snows of superstition, the cold winds of disbelief, and from the great fear of darkness in each man. So: we stretch out our hand with the beggar's cup. . . .

"Ah."

The Cup dipped into the sun. It scooped up a bit of the flesh of God, the blood of the universe, the blazing thought, the blinding philosophy that set out and mothered a galaxy, that idled and swept planets in their fields and summoned or laid to rest lives and livelihoods.

"Now, *slow*," whispered the captain.

"What'll happen when we pull it inside? That extra heat now, at this time, Captain?"

"God knows."

"Auxiliary pump all repaired, sir."

"Start it!"

The pump leaped on.

"Close the lid of the Cup and inside now, slow, slow."

The beautiful hand outside the ship trembled, a tremendous image of his own gesture, sank with oiled silence into the ship body. The Cup, lid shut, dripped yellow flowers and white stars, slid deep. The audio-thermometer screamed. The refrigerator system kicked; ammoniated fluids banged the walls like blood in the head of a shrieking idiot.

He shut the outer air-lock door.

"Now."

They waited. The ship's pulse ran. The heart of the ship rushed, beat, rushed, the Cup of Gold in it. The cold blood raced around about down through, around about down through.

The captain exhaled slowly.

The ice stopped dripping from the ceiling. It froze again.

"Let's get out of here."

The ship turned and ran.

"Listen!"

The heart of the ship was slowing, slowing. The dials spun on down through the thousands; the needles whirred, invisible. The thermometer voice chanted the change of seasons. They were all thinking now, together: Pull away and away from the fire and the flame, the heat and the melting, the yellow and the white. Go on out now to cool and dark. In twenty hours perhaps they might even dismantle some refrigerators, let winter die. Soon they would move in night so cold it might be necessary to use the ship's new furnace, draw heat from the shielded fire they carried now like an unborn child.

They were going home.

They were going home and there was some little time, even as he tended to the body of Bretton lying in a bank of white winter snow, for the captain to remember a poem he had written many years before:

> *Sometimes I see the sun a burning Tree,*
> *Its golden fruit swung bright in airless air,*
> *Its apples wormed with man and gravity,*
> *Their worship breathing from them everywhere,*
> *As man sees Sun as burning Tree . . .*

The captain sat for a long while by the body, feeling many separate things. I feel sad, he thought, and I feel good, and I feel like a boy coming home from school with a handful of dandelions.

"Well," said the captain, sitting, eyes shut, sighing. "Well, where do we go now, eh, where are we going?" He felt his men sitting or standing all about him, the terror dead in them, their breathing quiet. "When you've gone a long, long way down to the sun and touched it and lingered and jumped around and streaked away from it, where are you going then? When you go away from the heat and the noonday light and the laziness, where do you go?"

His men waited for him to say it out. They waited for him to gather all of the coolness and the whiteness and the welcome and refreshing climate of the word in his mind, and they saw him settle the word, like a bit of ice cream, in his mouth, rolling it gently.

"There's only one direction in space from here on out," he said at last.

They waited. They waited as the ship moved swiftly into cold darkness away from the light.

"North," murmured the captain. "North."

And they all smiled, as if a wind had come up suddenly in the middle of a hot afternoon.

Powerhouse

The horses moved gently to a stop, and the man and his wife gazed down into a dry, sandy valley. The woman sat lost in her saddle; she hadn't spoken for hours, didn't know a good word *to* speak. She was trapped somewhere between the hot, dark pressure of the storm-clouded Arizona sky and the hard, granite pressure of the wind-blasted mountains. A few drops of cool rain fell on her trembling hands.

She looked over at her husband wearily. He sat his dusty horse easily, with a firm quietness. She closed her eyes and thought of how she had been all of these mild years until today. She wanted to laugh at the mirror she was holding up to herself, but there was no way of doing even that; it would be somewhat insane. After all, it might just be the pushing of this dark weather, or the telegram they had taken from the messenger on horseback this morning, or the long journey now to town.

There was still an empty world to cross, and she was cold.

"I'm the lady who was never going to need religion," she said quietly, her eyes shut.

"What?" Berty, her husband, glanced over at her.

"Nothing," she whispered, shaking her head. In all the years, how *certain* she had been. Never, never would she have need of a church. She had heard fine people talk on and on of religion and waxed pews and calla lilies in great bronze buckets and vast bells of churches in which the preacher rang like a clapper. She had heard the shouting kind and the fervent, whispery kind, and they were all the same. Hers was simply not a pew-shaped spine.

"I just never had a reason ever to sit in a church," she had told people. She wasn't vehement about it. She just walked around and lived and moved her hands that were pebble-smooth and pebble-small. Work had polished the nails of those hands with a polish you could never buy in a bottle. The touching of children had made them soft, and the raising of children had made them temperately stern, and the loving of a husband had made them gentle.

And now, death made them tremble.

"Here," said her husband. And the horses dusted down the trail to where an odd brick building stood beside a dry wash. The building was all glazed green windows, blue machinery, red tile, and wires. The wires ran off on high-tension towers to the farthest directions of the desert. She watched them go, silently, and, still held by her thoughts, turned her gaze back to the strange storm-green windows and the burning-colored bricks.

She had never slipped a ribbon in a Bible at a certain significant verse, because though her life in this desert was a life of granite, sun, and the steaming away of the waters of her flesh, there had never been a threat in it to her. Always things had worked out before the necessity had come for sleepless dawns and wrinkles in the forehead. Somehow, the very poisonous things of life had passed her by. Death was a remote storm-rumor beyond the farthest range.

Twenty years had blown in tumbleweeds, away, since she'd come West, worn this lonely trapping man's gold ring, and taken the desert as a third, and constant, partner to their living. None of their four children had ever been fearfully sick or near death. She had never had to get down on her knees except for the scrubbing of an already well-scrubbed floor.

Now all that was ended. Here they were riding toward a remote town because a simple piece of yellow paper had come and said very plainly that her mother was dying.

And she could not imagine it — no matter how she turned her head to see or turned her mind to look in on itself. There were no rungs anywhere to hold to, going either up *or* down, and her mind, like a compass left out in a sudden storm of sand, was suddenly blown free of all its once-clear directions, all points of reference worn away, the needle spinning without purpose, around, around. Even with Berty's arms on her back it wasn't enough. It was like the end of a good play and the beginning of an evil one. Someone she loved was actually going to die. This was impossible!

"I've got to stop," she said, not trusting her voice at all, so she made it sound irritated to cover her fear.

Berty knew her as no irritated woman, so the irritation did not carry over and fill him up. He was a capped jug; the contents there for sure. Rain on the outside didn't stir the brew. He side-ran his horse to her and took her hand gently. "Sure," he said. He squinted at the eastern sky. "Some clouds piling up black there. We'll wait a bit. It might rain. I wouldn't want to get caught in it."

Now she was irritated at her own irritation, one fed upon the other, and she was helpless. But rather than speak and risk the cycle's commencing again, she slumped forward and began to sob, allowing her horse to be led until it stood and tramped its feet softly beside the red brick building.

She slid down like a parcel into his arms, and he held her as she turned in on his shoulder; then he set her down and said, "Don't look like there's people here." He called, "Hey, there!" and looked at the sign on the door: DANGER. BUREAU OF ELECTRIC POWER.

There was a great insect humming all through the air. It sang in a ceaseless, bumbling tone, rising a bit, perhaps falling just a bit, but keeping the same pitch. Like a woman humming between pressed lips as she makes a meal in the warm twilight over a hot stove. They could see no movement within the building; there was only the gigantic humming. It was the sort of noise you would expect the sun-shimmer to make rising from hot railroad ties on a blazing summer day, when there is that flurried silence and you see the air eddy and whorl and ribbon, and expect a sound from the process but get nothing but an arched tautness of the eardrums and the tense quiet.

The humming came up through her heels, into her medium-slim legs, and thence to her body. It moved to her heart and touched it, as the sight of Berty just sitting on a top rail of the corral often did. And then it moved on to her head and slenderest niches in the skull and set up a singing, as love songs and good books had done once on a time.

The humming was everywhere. It was as much a part of the soil as the cactus. It was as much a part of the air as the heat.

"What is it?" she asked, vaguely perplexed, looking at the building.

"I don't know much about it except it's a powerhouse," said Berty. He tried the door. "It's open," he said, surprised. "I wish someone was around." The door swung wide and the pulsing hum came out like a breath of air over them, louder.

They entered together into the solemn, singing place. She held him tightly, arm in arm.

It was a dim undersea place, smooth and clean and polished, as if something or other was always coming through and coming through and nothing ever stayed, but always there was motion and motion, invisible and stirring and never settling. On each side of them as they advanced were what first appeared to be people standing quietly, one after the other, in a double line. But these resolved into round, shell-like machines from which the humming sprang. Each black and gray and green machine gave forth golden cables and lime-colored wires, and there were silver metal pouches with crimson tabs and white lettering, and a pit like a washtub in which something whirled as if rinsing unseen materials at invisible speeds. The centrifuge raced so fast it stood still. Immense snakes of copper looped down from the twilight ceiling, and vertical pipes webbed up from cement floor to fiery brick wall. And the whole of it was as clean as a bolt of green lightning and smelled similarly. There was a crackling, eating sound, a dry rustling as of paper; flickers of blue fire shuttled, snapped, sparked, hissed where wires joined porcelain bobbins and green glass insulation.

Outside, in the real world, it began to rain.

She didn't want to stay in this place; it was no place to stay, with its people that were not people but dim machines and its music like an organ caught and pressed on a low note and a high note. But the rain washed every window and Berty said, "Looks like it'll last. Might have to stay the night here. It's late, anyhow. I'd better get the stuff in."

She said nothing. She wanted to be getting on. Getting on to what thing in what place, there was really no way of knowing. But at least in town she would hold on to the money and buy the tickets and hold them tight in her hand and hold on to a train which would rush and make a great noise, and get off the train, and get on another horse, or get into a car hundreds of miles away and ride again, and stand at last by her dead or alive mother. It all depended on time and breath. There were many places she would pass through, but none of them would offer a thing to her except ground for her feet, air for her nostrils, food for her numb mouth. And these were worse than nothing. Why go to her mother at all, say words, and make gestures? she wondered. What would be the use?

The floor was clean as a solid river under her. When she moved forward on it, it sent echoes cracking back and forth like small, faint gunshots through the room. Any word that was spoken came back as from a granite cavern.

Behind her, she heard Berty setting down the equipment. He spread two gray blankets and put out a little collection of tinned foods.

It was night. The rain still streamed on the high green-glazed windows, rinsing and making patterns of silk that flowed and intermingled in soft clear curtains. There were occasional thunderclaps which fell and broke upon themselves in avalanches of cold rain and wind hitting sand and stone.

Her head lay upon a folded cloth, and no matter how she turned it, the humming of the immense powerhouse worked up through the cloth into her head. She shifted, shut her eyes, and adjusted herself, but it went on and on. She sat up, patted the cloth, lay back down.

But the humming was there.

She knew without looking, by some sense deep in herself, that her husband was awake. There was no year she could remember when she hadn't known. It was some subtle difference in his breathing. It was the absence of sound, rather; no sound of breathing at all, save at long, carefully thought-out intervals. She knew then that he was looking at her in the rainy darkness, concerned with her, taking great care of his breath.

She turned in the darkness. "Berty?"

"Yes?"

"I'm awake too," she said.

"I know," he said.

They lay, she very straight, very rigid, he in a half curl, like a hand relaxed, half bent inward. She traced this dark, easy curve and was filled with incomprehensible wonder.

"Berty," she asked, and paused a long while, "how . . . how are you like you are?"

He waited a moment. "How do you mean?" he said.

"How do you *rest*?" She stopped. It sounded very bad. It sounded so much like an accusation, but it was not, really. She knew him to be a man concerned with all things, a man who could see in darknesses and who was not conceited because of his ability. He was worried for her now, and for her mother's life or death, but he had a way of worrying that seemed indifferent and irresponsible. It was neither of the two. His concern was all in him, deep; but it lay side by side with some faith, some belief that accepted it, made it welcome, and did not fight it. Something in him took hold of the sorrow first, got acquainted with it, knew each of its traceries before passing the message on to all of his waiting body. His body held a faith like a maze, and the sorrow that struck into him was lost and gone before it finally reached where it wanted to hurt him. Sometimes this faith drove her into a senseless anger, from which she recovered quickly, knowing how useless it was to criticize something as contained as a stone in a peach.

"Why didn't I ever catch it from you?" she said at last.

He laughed a little bit, softly. "Catch what?"

"I caught everything else. You shook me up and down in other ways. I didn't know anything but what you taught me." She stopped. It was hard to explain. Their life had been like the warm blood in a person passing through tissues quietly, both ways.

"Everything but religion," she said. "I never caught that from you."

"It's not a catching thing," he said. "Someday you just relax. And there it is."

Relax, she thought. Relax what? The body. But how to relax the mind? Her fingers twitched beside her. Her eyes wandered idly about the vast interior of the powerhouse. The machines stood over her in dark silhouettes with little sparkles crawling on them. The humming-humming-humming crept along her limbs.

Sleepy. Tired. She drowsed. Her eyes lidded and opened and lidded and opened. The humming-humming filled her marrow as if small hummingbirds were suspended in her body and in her head.

She traced the half-seen tubing up and up into the ceiling, and she saw the machines and heard the invisible whirlings. She suddenly became very alert in her drowsiness. Her eyes moved swiftly up and up and then down and across, and the humming-singing of the machines grew louder and louder, and her eyes moved, and her body relaxed; and on the tall, green windows she saw the shadows of the high-tension wires rushing off into the raining night.

Now the humming was in her, her eyes jerked, she felt herself yanked violently upright. She felt seized by a whirling dynamo, around, around in a whirl, out, out, into the heart of whirling invisibilities, fed into, accepted by a thousand copper wires, and shot, in an instant, over the earth!

She was everywhere at once!

Streaking along high monster towers in instants, sizzling between high poles where small glass knobs sat like crystal-green birds holding the wires in their non-conductive beaks, branching in four directions, eight secondary directions, finding towns, hamlets, cities, racing on to farms, ranches, haciendas, she descended gently like a widely filamented spider web upon a thousand square miles of desert!

The earth was suddenly more than many separate things, more than houses, rocks, concrete roads, a horse here or there, a human in a shallow, boulder-topped grave, a prickling of cactus, a town invested with its own light surrounded by night, a million apart things. Suddenly it all had one pattern encompassed and held by the pulsing electric web.

She spilled out swiftly into rooms where life was rising from a slap on a naked child's back, into rooms where life was leaving bodies like the light fading from an electric bulb—the filament glowing, fading, finally colorless. She was in every town, every house, every room, making light-patterns over hundreds of miles of land; seeing, hearing everything, not alone any more, but one of thousands of people, each with his ideas and his faiths.

Her body lay, a lifeless reed, pale and trembling. Her mind, in all its electric tensity, was flung about this way, that, down vast networks of powerhouse tributary.

Everything balanced. In one room she saw life wither; in another, a mile away, she saw wineglasses lifted to the newborn, cigars passed, smiles, handshakes, laughter. She saw the pale, drawn faces of people at white deathbeds, heard how they understood and accepted death, saw their gestures, felt their feelings, and saw that they, too, were lonely in themselves, with no way to get to the world to see the balance, see it as she was seeing it now.

She swallowed. Her eyelids flickered and her throat burned under her upraised fingers.

She was not alone.

The dynamo had whirled and flung her with centrifugal force out along a thousand lines into a million glass capsules screwed into ceilings, plucked into light by a pull of a cord or a twist of a knob or a flick of a switch.

The light could be in *any* room; all that was needed was to touch the switch. All rooms were dark until light came. And here she was, in all of them at once. And she was not alone. Her grief was but one part of a vast grief, her fear only one of countless others. And this grief was only a half thing. There was the other half; of things born, of comfort in the shape of a new child, of food in the warmed body, of colors for the eye and sounds in the awakened ear, and spring wild flowers for the smelling.

Whenever a light blinked out, life threw another switch; rooms were illumined afresh.

She was with those named Clark and those named Gray and the Shaws and Martins and Hanfords, the Fentons, the Drakes, the Shattucks, the Hubbells, and the Smiths. Being alone was not alone, except in the mind. You had all sorts of peekholes in your head. A silly, strange way to put it, perhaps, but there were the holes; the ones to see through and see that the world was there and people in it, as hard put to and uneasy as yourself; and there were the holes for hearing, and the one for speaking out your grief and getting rid of it, and the holes for knowing the changes of season through the scents of summer grain or winter ice or autumn fires. They were there to be used so that one was not alone. Loneliness was a shutting of the eyes. Faith was a simple opening.

The light-net fell upon all the world she had known for twenty years, herself blended with every line. She glowed and pulsed and was gentled in the great easy fabric. It lay across the land, covering each mile like a gentle, warm, and humming blanket. She was everywhere.

In the powerhouse the turbines whirled and hummed and the electric sparks, like little votive candles, jumped and clustered upon bent elbows of electric piping and glass. And the machines stood like saints and choruses, haloed now yellow, now red, now green, and a massed singing beat along the roof hollows and echoed down in endless hymns and chants. Outside, the wind clamored at the brick walls and drenched the glazed windows with rain; inside, she lay upon her small pillow and suddenly began to cry.

Whether it was with understanding, acceptance, joy, resignation, she couldn't know. The singing went on, higher and higher, and she was every-where. She put out her hand, caught hold of her husband, who was still awake, his eyes fixed at the ceiling. Perhaps he had run everywhere, too, in this instant, through the network of light and power. But then, he had always been every-where at once. He felt himself a unit of a whole and therefore he was stable; to her, unity was new and shaking. She felt his arms suddenly around her and she pressed her face into his shoulder for a long while, hard, while the humming and the humming climbed higher, and she cried freely, achingly, against him. . . .

In the morning the desert sky was very clear. They walked from the powerhouse quietly, saddled their horses, cinched on all of the equipment, and mounted.

She settled herself and sat there under the blue sky. And slowly she was aware of her back, and her back was straight, and she looked at her alien hands on the reins, and they had ceased trembling. And she could see the far mountains; there was no blur nor a running-of-color to things. All was solid stone touching stone, and stone touching sand, and sand touching wild flower, and wild flower touching the sky in one continuous clear flow, everything definite and of a piece.

"Wope!" cried Berty, and the horses walked slowly off, away from the brick building, through the cool sweet morning air.

She rode handsomely and she rode well, and in her, like a stone in a peach, was a peacefulness. She called to her husband as they slowed on a rise, "Berty!"

"Yes?"

"Can we . . . " she asked.

"Can we what?" he said, not hearing the first time.

"Can we come here again sometime?" she asked, nodding back toward the powerhouse. "Once in a while? Some Sunday?"

He looked at her and nodded slowly. "I reckon. Yes. Sure. I reckon so."

And as they rode on into town she was humming, humming a strange soft tune, and he glanced over and listened to it, and it was the sound you would expect to hear from sun-warmed railroad ties on a hot summer day when the air rises in a shimmer, flurried and whorling; a sound in one key, one pitch, rising a little, falling a little, humming, humming, but constant, peaceful, and wondrous to hear.

Hail and Farewell

But of course he was going away, there was nothing else to do, the time was up, the clock had run out, and he was going very far away indeed. His suitcase was packed, his shoes were shined, his hair was brushed, he had expressly washed behind his ears, and it remained only for him to go down the stairs, out the front door, and up the street to the small-town station where the train would make a stop for him alone. Then Fox Hill, Illinois, would be left far off in his past. And he would go on, perhaps to Iowa, perhaps to Kansas, perhaps even to California; a small boy, twelve years old, with a birth certificate in his valise to show he had been born forty-three years ago.

"Willie!" called a voice belowstairs.

"Yes!" He hoisted his suitcase. In his bureau mirror he saw a face made of June dandelions and July apples and warm summer-morning milk. There, as always, was his look of the angel and the innocent, which might never, in the years of his life, change.

"Almost time," called the woman's voice.

"All right!" And he went down the stairs, grunting and smiling. In the living room sat Anna and Steve, their clothes painfully neat.

"Here I am!" cried Willie in the parlor door.

Anna looked like she was going to cry. "Oh, good Lord, you can't really be leaving us, can you, Willie?"

"People are beginning to talk," said Willie quietly. "I've been here three years now. But when people begin to talk, I know it's time to put on my shoes and buy a railway ticket."

"It's all so strange. I don't understand. It's so sudden," Anna said. "Willie, we'll miss you."

"I'll write you every Christmas, so help me. Don't you write me."

"It's been a great pleasure and satisfaction," said Steve, sitting there, his words the wrong size in his mouth. "It's a shame it had to stop. It's a shame you had to tell us about yourself. It's an awful shame you can't stay on."

"You're the nicest folks I ever had," said Willie, four feet high, in no need of a shave, the sunlight on his face.

And then Anna *did* cry. "Willie, Willie." And she sat down and looked as if she wanted to hold him but was afraid to hold him now; she looked at him with shock and amazement and her hands empty, not knowing what to do with him now.

"It's not easy to go," said Willie. "You get used to things. You want to stay. But it doesn't work. I tried to stay on once after people began to suspect. 'How horrible!' people said. 'All these years, playing with our innocent children,' they said, 'and us not guessing! Awful!' they said. And finally I had to just leave town one night. It's not easy. You know darned well how much I love both of you. Thanks for three swell years."

They all went to the front door. "Willie, where're you going?"

"I don't know. I just start traveling. When I see a town that looks green and nice, I settle in."

"Will you ever come back?"

"Yes," he said earnestly with his high voice. "In about twenty years it should begin to show in my face. When it does, I'm going to make a grand tour of all the mothers and fathers I've ever had."

They stood on the cool summer porch, reluctant to say the last words. Steve was looking steadily at an elm tree. "How many other folks've you stayed with, Willie? How many adoptions?"

Willie figured it, pleasantly enough. "I guess it's about five towns and five couples and over twenty years gone by since I started my tour."

"Well, we can't holler," said Steve. "Better to've had a son thirty-six months than none whatever."

"Well," said Willie, and kissed Anna quickly, seized at his luggage, and was gone up the street in the green noon light, under the trees, a very young boy indeed, not looking back, running steadily.

The boys were playing on the green park diamond when he came by. He stood a little while among the oak-tree shadows, watching them hurl the white, snowy baseball into the warm summer air, saw the baseball shadow fly like a dark bird over the grass, saw their hands open like mouths to catch this swift piece of summer that now seemed most especially important to hold on to. The boys' voices yelled. The ball lit on the grass near Willie.

Carrying the ball forward from under the shade trees, he thought of the last three years now spent to the penny, and the five years before that, and so on down the line to the year when he was really eleven and twelve and fourteen and the voices saying: "What's wrong with Willie, missus?" "Mrs. B., is Willie late a-growin'?" "Willie, you smokin' *cigars* lately?" The echoes died in summer light and color. His mother's voice: "Willie's twenty-one today!" And a thousand voices saying: "Come back, son, when you're fifteen; *then* maybe we'll give you a job."

He stared at the baseball in his trembling hand, as if it were his life, an interminable ball of years strung around and around and around, but always leading back to his twelfth birthday. He heard the kids walking toward him; he felt them blot out the sun, and they were older, standing around him.

"Willie! Where you goin'?" They kicked his suitcase.

How tall they stood to the sun. In the last few months it seemed the sun had passed a hand above their heads, beckoned, and they were warm metal drawn melting upward; they were golden taffy pulled by an immense gravity to the sky, thirteen, fourteen years old, looking down upon Willie, smiling, but already beginning to neglect him. It had started four months ago:

"Choose up sides! Who wants Willie?"

"Aw, Willie's too little; we don't play with 'kids.' "

And they raced ahead of him, drawn by the moon and the sun and the turning seasons of leaf and wind, and he was twelve years old and not of them any more. And the other voices beginning again on the old, the dreadfully familiar, the cool refrain: "Better feed that boy vitamins, Steve." "Anna, does shortness *run* in your family?" And the cold fist kneading at your heart again and knowing that the roots would have to be pulled up again after so many good years with the "folks."

"Willie, where you goin'?"

He jerked his head. He was back among the towering, shadowing boys who milled around him like giants at a drinking fountain bending down.

"Goin' a few days visitin' a cousin of mine."

"Oh." There was a day, a year ago, when they would have cared very much indeed. But now there was only curiosity for his luggage, their enchantment with trains and trips and far places.

"How about a coupla fast ones?" said Willie.

They looked doubtful, but, considering the circumstances, nodded. He dropped his bag and ran out; the white baseball was up in the sun, away to their burning white figures in the far meadow, up in the sun again, rushing, life coming and going in a pattern. Here, *there*! Mr. and Mrs. Robert Hanlon, Creek Bend, Wisconsin, 1932, the first couple, the first year! Here, there! Henry and Alice Boltz, Limeville, Iowa, 1935! The baseball flying. The Smiths, the Eatons, the Robinsons! 1939! 1945! Husband and wife, husband and wife, husband and wife, no children, no children, no children! A knock on this door, a knock on that.

"Pardon me. My name is William. I wonder if—"

"A sandwich? Come in, sit down. Where you *from*, son?"

The sandwich, a tall glass of cold milk, the smiling, the nodding, the comfortable, leisurely talking.

"Son, you look like you been traveling. You run *off* from somewhere?"

"No."

"Boy, are you an orphan?"

Another glass of milk.

"We always wanted kids. It never worked out. Never knew why. One of those things. Well, well. It's getting late, son. Don't you think you better hit for home?"

"Got no home."

"A boy like you? Not dry behind the ears? Your mother'll be worried."

"Got no home and no folks anywhere in the world. I wonder if—I wonder— could I sleep here tonight?"

"Well, now, son, I don't just *know*. We never considered taking in—" said the husband.

"We got chicken for supper tonight," said the wife, "enough for extras, enough for company. . . . "

And the years turning and flying away, the voices, and the faces, and the people, and always the same first conversations. The voice of Emily Robinson, in her rocking chair, in summer-night darkness, the last night he stayed with her, the night she discovered his secret, her voice saying:

"I look at all the little children's faces going by. And I sometimes think, What a shame, what a shame, that all these flowers have to be cut, all these bright fires have to be put out. What a shame these, all of these you see in schools or running by, have to get tall and unsightly and wrinkle and turn gray or get bald, and finally, all bone and wheeze, be dead and buried off away. When I hear them laugh I can't believe they'll ever go the road I'm going. Yet here they *come*! I still remember Wordsworth's poem: 'When all at once I saw a crowd, A host of golden daffodils; Beside the lake, beneath the trees, Fluttering and dancing in the breeze.' That's how I think of children, cruel as they sometimes are, mean as I know they can be, but not yet showing the meanness around their eyes or *in* their eyes, not yet full of tiredness. They're so eager for everything! I guess that's what I miss most in older folks, the eagerness gone nine times out of ten, the freshness gone, so much of the drive and life down the drain. I like to watch school let out each day. It's like someone threw a bunch of flowers out the school front doors. How does it feel, Willie? How does it feel to be young forever? To look like a silver dime new from the mint? Are you happy? Are you as fine as you *seem?*"

The baseball whizzed from the blue sky, stung his hand like a great pale insect. Nursing it, he heard his memory say:

"I worked with what I had. After my folks died, after I found I couldn't get man's work anywhere, I tried carnivals, but they only laughed. 'Son,' they said, 'you're not a midget, and even if you are, you look like a *boy*! We want midgets with midgets' *faces*! Sorry, son, sorry.' So I left home, started out, thinking: What *was* I? A boy. I looked like a boy, sounded like a boy, so I might as well go on being a boy. No use fighting it. No use screaming. So what could I do? What job was handy? And then one day I saw this man in a restaurant looking at another man's pictures of his children. 'Sure wish I had kids,' he said. 'Sure wish I had kids.' He kept shaking his head. And me sitting a few seats away from him, a hamburger in my hands. I sat there, *frozen*! At that very instant I knew what my job would be for all of the rest of my life. There *was* work for me, after all. Making lonely people happy. Keeping myself busy. Playing forever. I knew I had to play forever. Deliver a few papers, run a few errands, mow a few lawns, maybe. But *hard* work? No. All I had to do was be a mother's son and a father's pride. I turned to the man down the counter from me. 'I beg your pardon,' I said. I *smiled* at him. . . ."

"But, Willie," said Mrs. Emily long ago, "didn't you ever get lonely? Didn't you ever want—*things*—that grownups wanted?"

"I fought that out alone," said Willie. "I'm a boy, I told myself, I'll have to live in a boy's world, read boys' books, play boys' games, cut myself off from everything else. I can't be both. I got to be only one thing—young. And so I played that way. Oh, it wasn't easy. There were times—" He lapsed into silence.

"And the family you lived with, they never knew?"

"No. Telling them would have spoiled everything. I told them I was a runaway; I let them check through official channels, police. Then, when there was no record, let them put in to adopt me. That was best of all; as long as they never guessed. But then, after three years, or five years, they guessed, or a traveling man came through, or a carnival man saw me, and it was over. It always had to end."

"And you're *very* happy and it's *nice* being a child for over forty years?"

"It's a living, as they say. And when you make other people happy, then you're almost happy too. I got my job to do and I do it. And anyway, in a few years now I'll be in my second childhood. All the fevers will be out of me and all the unfulfilled things and most of the dreams. Then I can relax, maybe, and play the role all the way."

He threw the baseball one last time and broke the reverie. Then he was running to seize his luggage. Tom, Bill, Jamie, Bob, Sam—their names moved on his lips. They were embarrassed at his shaking hands.

"After all, Willie, it ain't as if you're going to China or Timbuktu."

"That's right, isn't it?" Willie did not move.

"So long, Willie. See you next week!"

"So long, so long!"

And he was walking off with his suitcase again, looking at the trees, going away from the boys and the street where he had lived, and as he turned the corner a train whistle screamed, and he began to run.

The last thing he saw and heard was a white ball tossed at a high roof, back and forth, back and forth, and two voices crying out as the ball pitched now up, down, and back through the sky, "Annie, annie, over! Annie, annie, over!" like the crying of birds flying off to the far south.

In the early morning, with the smell of the mist and the cold metal, with the iron smell of the train around him and a full night of traveling shaking his bones and his body, and a smell of the sun beyond the horizon, he awoke and looked out upon a small town just arising from sleep. Lights were coming on, soft voices muttered, a red signal bobbed back and forth, back and forth in the cold air. There was that sleeping hush in which echoes are dignified by clarity, in which echoes stand nakedly alone and sharp. A porter moved by, a shadow in shadows.

"Sir," said Willie.

The porter stopped.

"What town's this?" whispered the boy in the dark.

"Valleyville."

"How many people?"

"Ten thousand. Why? This your stop?"

"It looks green." Willie gazed out at the cold morning town for a long time. "It looks nice and quiet," said Willie.

"Son," said the porter, "you know where you *going*?"

"Here," said Willie, and got up quietly in the still, cool, iron-smelling morning, in the train dark, with a rustling and stir.

"I hope you know what you're doing, boy," said the porter.

"Yes, sir," said Willie. "I know what I'm doing." And he was down the dark aisle, luggage lifted after him by the porter, and out in the smoking, steaming-cold, beginning-to-lighten morning. He stood looking up at the porter and the black metal train against the few remaining stars. The train gave a great wailing blast of whistle, the porters cried out all along the line, the cars jolted, and his special porter waved and smiled down at the boy there, the small boy there with the big luggage who shouted up to him, even as the whistle screamed again.

"What?" shouted the porter, hand cupped to ear.

"Wish me luck!" cried Willie.

"Best of luck, son," called the porter, waving, smiling. "Best of luck, boy!"

"Thanks!" said Willie, in the great sound of the train, in the steam and roar.

He watched the black train until it was completely gone away and out of sight. He did not move all the time it was going. He stood quietly, a small boy twelve years old, on the worn wooden platform, and only after three entire minutes did he turn at last to face the empty streets below.

Then, as the sun was rising, he began to walk very fast, so as to keep warm, down into the new town.

The Great Wide World over There

It was a day to be out of bed, to pull curtains and fling open windows. It was a day to make your heart bigger with warm mountain air.

Cora, feeling like a young girl in a wrinkled old dress, sat up in bed.

It was early, the sun barely on the horizon, but already the birds were stirring from the pines and ten billion red ants milled free from their bronze hills by the cabin door. Cora's husband Tom slept like a bear in a snowy hibernation of bedclothes beside her. Will my heart wake him up? she wondered.

And then she knew why this seemed a special day.

"Benjy's coming!"

She imagined him far off, leaping green meadows, fording streams where spring was pushing itself in cool colors of moss and clear water toward the sea. She saw his great shoes dusting and flicking the stony roads and paths. She saw his freckled face high in the sun looking giddily down his long body at his distant hands flying out and back behind him.

Benjy, come on! she thought, opening a window swiftly. Wind blew her hair like a gray spider web about her cold ears. Now Benjy's at Iron Bridge, now at Meadow Pike, now up Creek Path, over Chesley's Field . . .

Somewhere in those Missouri mountains was Benjy. Cora blinked. Those strange high hills beyond which twice a year she and Tom drove their horse and wagon to town, and through which, thirty years ago, she had wanted to run forever, saying, "Oh, Tom, let's just drive and drive until we reach the sea." But Tom had looked at her as if she had slapped his face, and he had turned the wagon around and driven on home, talking to the mare. And if people lived by shores where the sea came like a storm, now louder, now softer, every day, she did not know it. And if there were cities where neons were like pink ice and green mint and red fireworks each evening, she didn't know that either. Her horizon, north, south, east, west, was this valley, and had never been anything else.

But now, today, she thought, Benjy's coming from that world out there; he's seen it, heard it, smelt it; he'll tell me about it. And he can write. She looked at her hands. He'll be here a whole month and teach me. Then I can write out into that world and bring it here to the mailbox I'll make Tom build today. "Get up, Tom! You *hear?*"

She put her hand out to push the bank of sleeping snow.

By nine o'clock the valley was full of grasshoppers flinging themselves through the blue, piney air, while smoke curled into the sky.

Cora, singing into her pots and pans as she polished them, saw her wrinkled face bronzed and freshened in the copper bottoms. Tom was grumbling the sounds of a sleepy bear at his mush breakfast, while her singing moved all about him, like a bird in a cage.

"*Someone's* mighty happy," said a voice.

Cora made herself into a statue. From the corners of her eyes she saw a shadow cross the room.

"Mrs. Brabbam?" asked Cora of her scouring cloth.

"That's who it is!" And there stood the Widow Lady, her gingham dress dragging the warm dust, her letters in her chickeny hand. "Morning! I just been to my mailbox. Got me a real beauty of a letter from my uncle George in Springfield." Mrs. Brabbam fixed Cora with a gaze like a silver needle. "How long since you got a letter from *your* uncle, missus?"

"My uncles are all dead." It was not Cora herself, but her tongue, that lied. When the time came, she knew, it would be her tongue alone that must take communion and confess earthly sinning.

"It's certainly *nice*, getting mail." Mrs. Brabbam waved her letters in a straight flush on the morning air.

Always twisting the knife in the flesh. How many years, thought Cora, had this run on, Mrs. Brabbam and her smily eyes, talking loud of how she got mail; implying that nobody else for miles around could read? Cora bit her lip and almost threw the pot, but set it down, laughing. "I forgot to tell you. My nephew Benjy's coming; his folks are poorly, and he's here for the summer today. He'll teach me to write. And Tom's building us a postal box, aren't you, Tom?"

Mrs. Brabbam clutched her letters. "Well, isn't that fine! You *lucky* lady." And suddenly the door was empty. Mrs. Brabbam was gone.

But Cora was after her. For in that instant she had seen something like a scarecrow, something like a flicker of pure sunlight, something like a brook trout jumping upstream, leap a fence in the yard below. She saw a huge hand wave and birds flush in terror from a crab-apple tree.

Cora was rushing, the world rushing back of her, down the path. "Benjy!"

They ran at each other like partners in a Saturday dance, linked arms, collided, and waltzed, jabbering. "Benjy!"

She glanced swiftly behind his ear.

Yes, *there* was the yellow pencil.

"Benjy, welcome!"

"Why, ma'am!" He held her off at arm's length. "Why, ma'am, you're *crying*."

"Here's my nephew," said Cora.

Tom scowled up from spooning his corn-meal mush.

"Mighty glad," smiled Benjy.

Cora held his arm tight so he couldn't vanish. She felt faint, wanting to sit, stand, run, but she only beat her heart fast and laughed at strange times. Now, in an instant, the far countries were brought near; here was this tall boy, lighting up the room like a pine torch, this boy who had seen cities and seas and been places when things had been better for his parents.

"Benjy, I got peas, corn, bacon, mush, soup, and beans for breakfast."

"Hold on!" said Tom.

"Hush, Tom, the boy's down to the bone with walking." She turned to the boy. "Benjy, tell me all about yourself. You *did* go to school?"

Benjy kicked off his shoes. With one bare foot he traced a word in the hearth ashes.

Tom scowled. "What's it say?"

"It says," said Benjy, "*c* and *o* and *r* and *a*. *Cora*."

"*My* name, Tom, see it! Oh, Benjy, it's good you really write, child. We had one cousin here, long ago, claimed he could spell upside down and backwards. So we fattened him up and he wrote letters and we never got answers. Come to find out he knew just enough spelling to mail letters to the dead-letter office. Lord, Tom knocked two months' worth of vittles out of that boy, batting him up the road with a piece of fence."

They laughed anxiously.

"I write fine," said the serious boy.

"That's all we want to know." She shoved a cut of berry pie at him. "Eat."

By ten-thirty, with the sun riding higher, after watching Benjy devour heaped platters of food, Tom thundered from the cabin, jamming his cap on. "I'm going out, by God, and cut down half the forest!" he said angrily.

But no one heard. Cora was seated in a breathless spell. She was watching the pencil behind Benjy's peach-fuzz ear. She saw him finger it casually, lazily, indifferently. Oh, not so casual, Benjy, she thought. Handle it like a spring robin's egg. She wanted to touch the pencil, but hadn't touched one in years because it made her feel foolish and then angry and then sad. Her hand twitched in her lap.

"You got some paper?" asked Benjy.

"Oh, land, I never thought," she wailed, and the room walls darkened. "What'll we do?"

"Just happens I brought some." He fetched a tablet from his little bag. "You want to write a letter somewhere?"

She smiled outrageously. "I want to write a letter to ... to ... " Her face fell apart. She looked around for someone in the distance. She looked at the mountains in the morning sunshine. She heard the sea rolling off on yellow shores a thousand miles away. The birds were coming north over the valley, on their way to multitudes of cities indifferent to her need at this instant.

"Benjy, why, I never thought until this moment. I don't know anybody in all that world out there. Nobody but my aunt. And if I wrote her it'd make her feel bad, a hundred miles from here, to have to find someone else to read the letter to her. She's got a whale-boned-corset sort of pride. Make her nervous the next ten years, that letter setting in her house on the mantel. No, no letter to her." Cora's eyes moved from the hills and the unseen ocean. "Who then? Where? Someone. I just've got to get me some letters."

"Hold on." Benjy fished a dime magazine from his coat. It had a red cover of an undressed lady screaming away from a green monster. "All sorts of addresses in here."

They leafed the pages together. "What's *this*?" Cora tapped an ad.

" 'Here's your *Power Plus* Free Muscle Chart. Send name, address,' " read Benjy, " 'to Department M-3 for Free Health Map!' "

"And what about *this* one?"

" 'Detectives make secret investigations. Particulars free. Write: G.D.M. Detective School—' "

"Everything's free. Well, Benjy." She looked at the pencil in his hand. He drew up his chair. She watched him turn the pencil in his fingers, making minor adjustments. She saw him bite his tongue softly. She saw him squint his eyes. She held her breath. She bent forward. She squinted her own eyes and clamped her tongue.

Now, now Benjy raised his pencil, licked it, and set it down to the paper.
There it is, thought Cora.
The first words. They formed themselves slowly on the incredible paper.

Dear Power Plus Muscle Company
Sirs, [he wrote] .

The morning blew away on a wind, the morning flowed down the creek, the morning flew off with some ravens, and the sun burned on the cabin roof. Cora didn't turn when she heard a shuffle at the blazing, sun-filled door. Tom was there, but not there; nothing was before her but a series of filled pages, a whispering pencil, and Benjy's careful Palmer Penmanship hand. Cora moved her head around, around, with each *o*, each *l*, with each small hill of an *m*; each tiny dot made her head peck like a chicken; each crossed *t* made her tongue lick across her upper lip.

"It's noon and I'm hungry!" said Tom almost behind her.

But Cora was a statue now, watching the pencil as one watches a snail leaving an exceptional trail across a flat stone in the early morning.

"It's noon!" cried Tom again.

Cora glanced up, stunned.

"Why, it seems only a moment ago we wrote to that Philadelphia Coin Collecting Company, ain't that right, Benjy?" Cora smiled a smile much too dazzling for a woman fifty-five years old. "While you wait for your vittles, Tom, just can't you build that mailbox? Bigger than Mrs. Brabbam's, please?"

"I'll nail up a shoe box."

"Tom Gibbs." She rose pleasantly. Her smile said, Better run, better work, better *do*! "I want a big, pretty mailbox. All white, for Benjy to paint our name on in black spelling. I won't have any shoe box for my very first real letter."

And it was done.

Benjy lettered the finished mailbox: MRS. CORA GIBBS, while Tom stood grumbling behind him.

"What's it say?"

" 'Mr. Tom Gibbs,' " said Benjy quietly, painting.

Tom blinked at it for a minute, quietly, and then said, "I'm *still* hungry. Someone light the fire."

There were no stamps. Cora turned white. Tom was made to hitch up the horse and drive to Green Fork to buy some red ones, a green, and ten pink stamps with dignified gentlemen printed on them. But Cora rode along to be certain Tom didn't hurl these first letters in the creek. When they rode home, the first thing Cora did, face glowing, was poke in the new mailbox.

"You crazy?" said Tom.

"No harm looking."

That afternoon she visited the mailbox six times. On the seventh, a woodchuck jumped out. Tom stood laughing in the door, pounding his knees. Cora chased him out of the house, still laughing.

Then she stood in the window looking down at her mailbox right across from Mrs. Brabbam's. Ten years ago the Widow Lady had plunked her letter box right under Cora's nose, almost, when she could as easily have built it up nearer her own cabin. But it gave Mrs. Brabbam an excuse to float like a flower on a river down the hill path, flip the box wide with a great coughing and rustling, from time to time spying up to see if Cora was watching. Cora always was. When caught, she pretended to sprinkle flowers with an empty watering can, or pick mushrooms in the wrong season.

Next morning Cora was up before the sun had warmed the strawberry patch or the wind had stirred the pines.

Benjy was sitting up in his cot when Cora returned from the mailbox. "Too early," he said. "Postman won't drive by yet."

"*Drive* by?"

"They come in cars this far out."

"Oh." Cora sat down.

"You sick, Aunt Cora?"

"No, no." She blinked. "It's just, I don't recall in twenty years *seeing* no mail truck whistle by here. It just came to me. All this time, I never seen no mailman at all."

"Maybe he comes when you're not around."

"I'm up with the fog spunks, down with the chickens. I never really gave it a thought, of course, but—" She turned to look out the window, up at Mrs. Brabbam's house. "Benjy, I got a kind of sneaking hunch." She stood up and walked straight out of the cabin, down the dust path, Benjy following, across the thin road to Mrs. Brabbam's mailbox. A hush was on the fields and hills. It was so early it made you whisper.

"Don't break the law, Aunt Cora!"

"Shh! Here." She opened the box, put her hand in like someone fumbling in a gopher hole. "And here, and here." She rattled some letters into his cupped hands.

"Why, these been opened already! You open these, Aunt Cora?"

"Child, I never touched them." Her face was stunned. "This is the first time in my life I ever even let my shadow touch this box."

Benjy turned the letters around and around, cocking his head. "Why, Aunt Cora, these letters, they're ten years old!"

"What!" Cora grabbed at them.

"Aunt Cora, that lady's been getting the same mail every day for years. And they're not even addressed to Mrs. Brabbam, they're to some woman named Ortega in Green Fork."

"Ortega, the Mexican grocery woman! All these years," whispered Cora, staring at the worn mail in her hands. "All these years."

They gazed up at Mrs. Brabbam's sleeping house in the cool quiet morning.

"Oh, that sly woman, making a commotion with her letters, making me feel small. All puffed out she was, swishing along, reading her mail."

Mrs. Brabbam's front door opened.

"Put them back, Aunt Cora!"

Cora slammed the mailbox shut with time to spare.

Mrs. Brabbam drifted down the path, stopping here or there, quietly, to peer at the opening wild flowers.

"Morning," she said sweetly.

"Mrs. Brabbam, this is my nephew Benjy."

"How nice." Mrs. Brabbam, with a great swivel of her body, a flourish of her flour-white hands, rapped the mailbox as if to shake the letters loose inside, flipped the lid, and extracted the mail, covering her actions with her back. She made motions, and spun about merrily, winking. "Wonderful! Why, just look at this letter from dear Uncle George!"

"Well, ain't that *nice!*" said Cora.

Then the breathless summer days of waiting. The butterflies jumping orange and blue on the air, the flowers nodding about the cabin, and the hard, constant sound of Benjy's pencil scribbling through the afternoons. Benjy's mouth was always packed with food, and Tom was always stomping in, to find lunch or supper late, cold, or both, or none at all.

Benjy handled the pencil with a delicious spread of his bony hands, lovingly inscribing each vowel and consonant as Cora hovered about him, making up words, rolling them on her tongue, delighted each time she saw them roll out on the paper. But she wasn't learning to write. "It's so much fun watching you write, Benjy. Tomorrow I'll start learning. Now take another letter!"

They worked their way through ads about Asthma, Trusses, and Magic, they joined the Rosicrucians, or at least sent for a free Sealed Book all about the Knowledge that had been damned to oblivion, Secrets from hidden ancient temples and buried sanctuaries. Then there were free packets of Giant Sunflower seeds, and something about HEARTBURN. They had worked back to page 127 of *Quarter Murder Magazine* on a bright summer morning when . . .

"Listen!" said Cora.

They listened.

"A car," said Benjy.

And up the blue hills and through the tall fiery green pines and along the dusty road, mile by mile, came the sound of a car riding along and along, until finally, at the bend, it came full thundering, and in an instant Cora was out the door running, and as she ran she heard and saw and felt many things. First, from the corner of her eye, she saw Mrs. Brabbam gliding down the road from the other direction. Mrs. Brabbam froze when she saw the bright green car boiling on the grade, and there was the whistle of a silver whistle and the old man in the car leaned out just before Cora arrived and said, "Mrs. Gibbs?" "Yes!" she cried. "Mail for you, ma'am," he said, and held it toward her. She put out her hand, then drew it back, remembering. "Oh," she said, "please, would you mind, would you put it, please . . . in my mailbox?" The old man squinted at her, at the mailbox, back at her, and laughed. "Don't mind," he said, and did just that, put the mail in the box.

Mrs. Brabbam stood where she was, not moving, eyes wild. "Any mail for Mrs. Brabbam?" asked Cora.

"That's all." And the car dusted away down the road.

Mrs. Brabbam stood with her hands clenched together. Then, without looking in her own letter box, turned and rustled swiftly up her path, out of sight.

Cora walked around her mailbox twice, not touching it for a long time. "Benjy, I've got me some letters!" She reached in delicately and took them out and turned them over. She put them quietly in his hand. "Read them to me. Is my name on the front?"

"Yes'm." He opened the first letter with due carefulness and read it aloud in the summer morning:

"'Dear Mrs. Gibbs . . .'"

He stopped and let her savor it, her eyes half shut, her mouth moving the words. He repeated it for artistic emphasis and then went on: "'We are sending you our free folder, enclosed, from the Intercontinental Mailing Schools concerning full particulars on how you, too, can take our Correspondence Course in Sanitary Engineering—'"

"Benjy, Benjy, I'm so happy! Start over again!"

"'Dear Mrs. Gibbs,'" he read.

After that the mailbox was never empty. The world came rushing and crowding in, all the places she had never seen or heard about or been to. Travel folders, spicecake recipes, and even a letter from an elderly gentleman who wished for a lady "—fifty years old, gentle disposition, money; object matrimony." Benjy wrote back, "I am already married, but thank you for your kind and thoughtful consideration. Yours truly, Cora Gibbs."

And the letters continued to pour across the hills, coin collectors' catalogues, Dime Novelty books, Magic List Numbers, Arthritis Charts, Flea Killer Samples. The world filled up her letter box, and suddenly she was not alone or remote from people. If a man wrote a form letter to Cora about the Mysteries of Ancient Maya Revealed, he was likely as not to receive three letters from Cora in the next week, budding out their formal meeting into a warm friendship. After one particularly hard day of writing, Benjy was forced to soak his hand in Epsom salts.

By the end of the third week Mrs. Brabbam no longer came down to her mailbox. She didn't even come out the front door of her cabin to get the air, for Cora was always down at the road, leaning out, smiling for the mailman.

All too quickly the summer was at an end, or, at least, that part of the summer that counted most, anyway: Benjy's visit. There was his red bandanna handkerchief on the cabin table, sandwiches folded fresh and oniony in it, tied with a mint sprig to keep it clean to the smell; there on the floor, freshly polished, were his shoes to get into, and there on the chair, with his pencil which had once been long and yellow but was now stubby and chewed, sat Benjy. Cora took hold of his chin and tilted his head, as if she were testing a summer squash of an unfamiliar variety.

"Benjy, I owe you an apology. I don't think I looked at your face once in all this time. Seems I know every wart on your hand, every hangnail, every bump and every crinkle, but I might pass your face in a crowd and miss you."

"It's no face to look at," said Benjy shyly.

"But I'd know that hand in a million hands," Cora said. "Let anyone shake my hand in a dark room, a thousand people, and out of all those I'd say, 'Well, *this* one's Benjy.'" She smiled quietly and walked away to the open door. "I been thinking." She looked up at a distant cabin. "Ain't seen Mrs. Brabbam in weeks. Stays in all the time now. I've got a guilty feeling. I've done a prideful thing, a thing more sinful than she ever done me. I took the bottom out of her life. It was a mean and spiteful thing and I'm ashamed." She gazed up the hill toward that silent, locked place. "Benjy, would you do me one last favor?"

"Yes'm."

"Write a letter for Mrs. Brabbam."

"Ma'am?"

"Yes, write one of those companies for a free chart, a sample, something, and sign Mrs. Brabbam's name."

"All right," said Benjy.

"That way, in a week or a month the postman'll come by and whistle, and I'll tell him to go up to her door, special, and deliver it. And I'll be sure and be out in my front yard where I can see and Mrs. Brabbam can see I see. And I'll wave my letters to her and she'll wave her letters to me, and everybody'll smile."

"Yes'm," said Benjy.

He wrote three letters, licked the envelopes carefully, stuck them in his pocket. "I'll mail them when I get to St. Louis."

"It's been a fine summer," she said.

"It sure has."

"But, Benjy, I didn't learn to write, did I? I was after the letters and made you write late nights, and we were so busy sending labels and getting samples, land, it seemed there wasn't time to learn. And that means . . ."

He knew what it meant. He shook her hand. They stood in the cabin door. "Thanks," she said, "for everything."

Then he was running off. He ran as far as the meadow fence, leaped it easily, and the last she saw of him he was still running, waving the special letters, off into the great world over the hills.

The letters kept coming for some six months after Benjy went away. There would be the postman's little green car and the sharp ice-rimed shout of good morning, or the whistle, as he clapped two or three pink or blue envelopes into that fine mailbox.

And there was that special day when Mrs. Brabbam received her first real letter.

After that the letters were spaced a week apart, then a month, and finally the postman didn't say hello at all, there was no sound of a car coming up that lonely mountain road. First a spider moved into the mailbox, then a sparrow.

And Cora, while the letters still lasted, would clutch them in her bewildered hands, staring at them quietly until the pressure of her face muscles squeezed clear round shiny drops of water from her eyes. She'd hold up one blue envelope. "Who's this from?"

"Don't know," said Tom.

"What's it say?" she wailed.

"Don't know," said Tom.

"What's going on in that world out there, oh, I'll never know, I'll never know now," she said. "And this letter, and this one, and *this*!" She tumbled the stacks and stacks of letters that had come since Benjy ran off. "All the world and all the people and all the happenings, and me not knowing. All that world and people waiting to hear from us, and us not writing, and them not ever writing back!"

And at last the day came when the wind blew the mailbox over. In the mornings again, Cora would stand at the open door of her cabin, brushing her gray hair with a slow brush, not speaking, looking at the hills. And in all the years that followed she never passed the fallen mailbox without stooping aimlessly to fumble inside and take her hand out with nothing in it before she wandered on again into the fields.

The Playground

A thousand times before and after his wife's death Mr. Charles Underhill ignored the Playground on his way to and from his commuters' limited train. He neither liked nor disliked the Playground; he hardly knew it existed.

But only this morning his sister Carol, who had occupied the empty space across the breakfast table from him each day for six months, quietly broached the subject.

"Jim's almost three years old now," she said. "So tomorrow I'm going to start him at the Playground."

"Playground?" said Mr. Underhill.

At his office, he underlined a memorandum with black ink: *Look at Playground*.

That afternoon, the thunder of the train subsiding in his body, Underhill struck up through town on his usual path home, newspaper tucked crisply under arm to prevent reading himself past the park. So it was, at five-ten in the late day, that he came to the cool iron fence and the open gate of the Playground, and stood for a long, long time, frozen there, gazing in at it all. . . .

At first there seemed absolutely nothing whatever to see. And then as he adjusted his attention outward from his usual interior monologue, the scene before him, a gray, blurred television image, came to a slow focus.

Primarily, he was aware of dim voices, faint underwater cries emerging from a series of vague streaks and zigzag lines and shadows. Then, as if someone had kicked the machine, screams jumped at him in full throat, visions leaped clear. Now he saw the children! They were dashing across the Playground meadow, fighting, pummeling, scratching, falling, every wound bleeding or about to bleed or freshly caked over. A dozen cats thrown among sleeping dogs could not have shrieked as loud. With incredible clarity, Mr. Underhill saw the tiniest cuts and scabs on knees and faces.

He weathered the first blast of sound, blinking. His nostrils took over when his eyes and ears retired in panic.

He sniffed the cutting odors of salve, raw adhesive, camphor, and pink Mercurochrome, so strong it lay bitter on his tongue. An iodine wind blew through the steel fence wires which glinted dully in the gray light of the overcast day. The rushing children were hell cut loose in a vast pinball table, colliding, and banging, a totaling of hits and misses, thrusts and plungings to a grand and as yet unforeseen total of brutalities.

And was he mistaken or was the light within the Playground of a peculiar intensity? Every child seemed to possess four shadows: one dark, three faint penumbras which made it strategically impossible to tell which way their swift bodies were racing until they bashed their targets. Yes, the oblique, pressing light made the Playground seem deep, far away, and remote from his touching. Or perhaps it was the hard steel wire fence, not unlike those barriers in zoos, beyond which *anything* might happen.

A pen of misery, thought Underhill. Why do children insist on making life horrible for each other? Oh, the continual torture. He heard himself sigh with immense relief. Thank God, childhood was over and done for him. No more pinchings, bruisings, senseless passions and shattered dreams.

A gust of wind tore the paper from his hand. He ran after it down the Playground steps. Clutching the paper, he retreated hastily. For in that one brief instant, stranded in the Playground's atmosphere, he had felt his hat grow too large, his coat too cumbersome, his belt too loose, his shoes too big; he had felt like a small boy playing businessman in his father's clothes; the gate behind him had loomed impossibly tall, while the sky pressed a huge weight of grayness at his eyes, and the scent of iodine, like a tiger's breath exhaled upon him, blew his hair. He tripped and almost fell, running back.

He stood outside the Playground, like someone who has just emerged, in shock, from a terrible cold sea.

"Hello, Charlie!"

He heard the voice and turned to see who had called him. There on top of a metal slide, a boy of some nine years was waving. "Hello, Charlie. . . !"

Mr. Charles Underhill raised a hand. But I don't *know* that boy, he thought. And why should he call me by my first name?

The boy was smiling high in the misty air, and now, jostled by other yelling children, rushed shrieking down the slide.

Underhill stood bemused by what he saw. Now the Playground was an immense iron industry whose sole products were pain, sadism, and sorrow. If you watched half an hour there wasn't a face in the entire enclosure that didn't wince, cry, redden with anger, pale with fear, one moment or another. Really! Who said Childhood was the best time of life? when in reality it was the most terrible, the most merciless era, the barbaric time when there were no police to protect you, only parents preoccupied with themselves and their taller world. No, if he had his way, he touched the cold fence with one hand, they'd nail a new sign here: TORQUEMADA'S GREEN.

And as for that boy, the one who had called out to him, who was he? There was something familiar there, perhaps in the hidden bones, an echo of some old friend; probably the son of a successfully ulcered father.

So this is the Playground where my son will play, thought Mr. Underhill. So this is it.

Hanging his hat in the hall, checking his lean image in the watery mirror, Underhill felt wintry and tired. When his sister appeared, and his son came tapping on mouse feet, he greeted them with something less than full attention. The boy clambered thinly over him, playing King of the Hill. And the father, fixing his gaze to the end of the cigar he was slowly lighting, finally cleared his throat and said, "I've been thinking about that Playground, Carol."

"I'm taking Jim over tomorrow."

"Not really? *That* Playground?"

His mind rebelled. The smell and look of the place were still vivid. That writhing world with its atmosphere of cuts and beaten noses, the air as full of pain as a dentist's office, and those horrid ticktacktoes and frightening hopscotches under his feet as he picked up his newspaper, horrid and frightening for no reason he could see.

"What's wrong with *that* Playground?" asked Carol.

"Have you seen it?" He paused in confusion. "Damn it, I mean, the children there. It's a Black Hole."

"All the children are from well-to-do families."

"Well, they shove and push like little Gestapos," said Underhill. "It'd be like sending a boy to a flour mill to be crushed into meal by a couple of two-ton grinders! Every time I think of Jim playing in that barbaric pit, I freeze."

"You know very well it's the only convenient park for miles around."

"I don't care about that. All I care is I saw a dozen kinds of bats and clubs and air guns. By the end of the first day, Jim would be in splinters. They'd have him barbecued, with an orange in his mouth."

She was beginning to laugh. "How you exaggerate."

"I'm serious!"

"You can't live Jim's life for him. He has to learn the hard way. He's got to take a little beating and beat others up; boys are like that."

"I don't *like* boys like that."

"It's the happiest time of life."

"Nonsense. I used to look back on childhood with great nostalgia. But now I realize I was a sentimental fool. It was nothing but screaming and running in a nightmare and coming home drenched with terror, from head to foot. If I could possibly save Jim from that, I would."

"That's impractical and, thank God, impossible."

"I won't have him near that place, I tell you. I'll have him grow up a neurotic recluse first."

"Charlie!"

"I will! Those little beasts, you should've seen them. Jim's *my* son, he is;

he's not yours, remember." He felt the boy's thin legs about his shoulders, the boy's delicate fingers rumpling his hair. "I won't have him butchered."

"He'll get it in school. Better to let him take a little shoving about now, when he's three, so he's prepared for it."

"I've thought of that, too." Mr. Underhill held fiercely to his son's ankles which dangled like warm, thin sausages on either lapel. "I might even get a private tutor for him."

"Oh, Charles!"

They did not speak during dinner.

After dinner, he took Jim for a brief walk while his sister was washing the dishes. They strolled past the Playground under the dim street lamps. It was a cooling September night, with the first dry spice of autumn in it. Next week, and the children would be raked in off the fields like so many leaves and set to burning in the schools, using their fire and energy for more constructive purposes. But they would be here after school, ramming about, making projectiles of themselves, crashing and exploding, leaving wakes of misery behind every miniature war.

"Want to go in," said Jim, leaning against the high wire fence, watching the late-playing children beat each other and run.

"No, Jim, you don't want that."

"Play," said Jim, his eyes shining with fascination as he saw a large boy kick a small boy and the small boy kick a smaller boy to even things up.

"Play, Daddy."

"Come along, Jim, you'll never get in that mess if *I* can help it." Underhill tugged the small arm firmly.

"I want to play." Jim was beginning to blubber now. His eyes were melting out of his face and his face was becoming a wrinkled orange of color.

Some of the children heard the crying and glanced over. Underhill had the terrible sense of watching a den of foxes suddenly startled and looking up from the white, hairy ruin of a dead rabbit. The mean yellow-glass eyes, the conical chins, the sharp white teeth, the dreadful wiry hair, the brambly sweaters, the iron-colored hands covered with a day's battle stains. Their breath moved out to him, dark licorice and mint and Juicy Fruit so sickeningly sweet, so combined as to twist his stomach. And over this the hot mustard smell of someone tolerating an early chest cold; the greasy stink of flesh smeared with hot camphorous salves cooking under a flannel sheath. All these cloying and somehow depressing odors of pencils, chalk, grass and slate-board erasers, real or imagined, summoned old memory in an instant. Popcorn mortared their teeth, and green jelly showed in their sucking, blowing nostrils. God! God!

They saw Jim, and he was new to them. They said not a word, but as Jim cried louder and Underhill, by main force, dragged him like a cement bag along the walk, the children followed with their glowing eyes. Underhill felt like pushing his fist at them and crying, "You little beasts, you won't get *my* son!"

And then, with beautiful irrelevance, the boy at the top of the blue metal slide, so high he seemed almost in a mist, far away, the boy with the somehow familiar face, called out to him, waving and waving.

"Hello, Charlie . . . !"

Underhill paused and Jim stopped crying.

"See you later, Charlie . . . !"

And the face of the boy way up there on that high and very lonely slide was suddenly like the face of Thomas Marshall, an old business friend who lived just around the block, but whom he hadn't seen in months.

"See you later, Charlie."

Later, later? What did the fool boy mean?

"I know *you*, Charlie!" called the boy. "Hi!"

"What?" gasped Underhill.

"Tomorrow night, Charlie, hey!" And the boy fell off the slide and lay choking for breath, face like a white cheese from the fall, while children jumped him and tumbled over.

Underhill stood undecided for five seconds or more, until Jim thought to cry again, and then, with the golden fox eyes upon them, in the first chill of autumn, he dragged Jim all the way home.

The next afternoon Mr. Underhill finished at the office early and took the three o'clock train, arriving out in Green Town at three twenty-five, in plenty of time to drink in the brisk rays of the autumnal sun. Strange how one day it is suddenly autumn, he thought. One day it is summer and the next, how could you measure or tell it? Something about the temperature or the smell? Or the sediment of age knocked loose from your bones during the night and circulating in your blood and heart, giving you a slight tremble and a chill? A year older, a year dying, was *that* it?

He walked up toward the Playground, planning the future. It seemed you did more planning in autumn than any other season. This had to do with dying, perhaps. You thought of death and you automatically planned. Well, then, there was to be a tutor for Jim, *that* was positive; none of those horrible schools for him. It would pinch the bank account a bit, but Jim would at least grow up a happy boy. They would pick and choose his friends. Any slam-bang bullies would be thrown out as soon as they so much as touched Jim. And as for this Playground? Completely out of the question!

"Oh hello, Charles."

He looked up suddenly. Before him, at the entrance to the wire enclosure, stood his sister. He noted instantly that she called him Charles, instead of Charlie. Last night's unpleasantness had not quite evaporated. "Carol, what're you doing *here*?"

She flushed guiltily and glanced in through the fence.

"You didn't," he said.

His eyes sought among the scrabbling, running, screaming children. "Do you mean to say . . . ?"

His sister nodded, half amused. "I thought I'd bring him early—"

"Before I got home, so I wouldn't know, is *that* it?"

That was it.

"Good God, Carol, where *is* he?"

"I just came to see."

"You mean you left him there all afternoon?"

"Just for five minutes while I shopped."

"And you *left* him. Good God!" Underhill seized her wrist. "Well, come on, find him, get him out of there!"

They peered in together past the wire to where a dozen boys charged about, girls slapped each other, and a squabbling heap of children took turns at getting off, making a quick run, and crashing one against another.

"That's where he is, I *know* it!" said Underhill.

Just then, across the field, sobbing and wailing, Jim ran, six boys after him. He fell, got up, ran, fell again, shrieking, and the boys behind shot beans through metal blowers.

"I'll stuff those blowers up their noses!" said Underhill. "Run, Jim! Run!"

Jim made it to the gate. Underhill caught him. It was like catching a rumpled, drenched wad of material. Jim's nose was bleeding, his pants were ripped, he was covered with grime.

"*There's* your Playground," said Underhill, on his knees, staring up from his son, holding him, at his sister. "*There* are your sweet, happy innocents, your well-to-do piddling Fascists. Let me catch this boy here again and there'll be hell to pay. Come on, Jim. All right, you little bastards, get back there!" he shouted.

"We didn't do nothing," said the children.

"What's the world coming to?" Mr. Underhill questioned the universe.

"Hi! Charlie!" said the strange boy, standing to one side. He waved casually and smiled.

"Who's that?" asked Carol.

"How in hell do *I* know?" said Underhill.

"Be seeing you, Charlie. So long," called the boy, fading off.

Mr. Underhill marched his sister and his son home.

"Take your hand off my elbow!" said Carol.

He was trembling; absolutely, continually trembling with rage when he got to bed. He had tried some coffee, but nothing stopped it. He wanted to beat their pulpy little brains out, those gross Cruikshank children; yes, that phrase fit them, those fox-fiend, melancholy Cruikshank children, with all the guile and poison and slyness in their cold faces. In the name of all that was decent, what manner of child was this new generation! A bunch of cutters and hangers and bangers, a drove of bleeding, moronic thumbscrewers, with the sewage of neglect running in their veins? He lay violently jerking his head from one side of his hot pillow to the other, and at last got up and lit a cigarette, but it wasn't enough. He and Carol had had a huge battle when they got home. He had yelled at her and she had yelled back, peacock and peahen shrieking in a wilderness where law and order were insanities laughed at and quite forgotten.

He was ashamed. You didn't fight violence with violence, not if you were a gentleman. You talked very calmly. But Carol didn't give you a chance, damn it! She wanted the boy put in a vise and squashed. She wanted him reamed and punctured and given the laying on of hands. To be beaten from playground to kindergarten, to grammar school, to junior high, to high school. If he was lucky, in high school, the beatings and sadisms would refine themselves, the sea of blood and spittle would drain back down the shore of years and Jim would be left upon the edge of maturity, with God knows what outlook to the future, with a desire, perhaps, to be a wolf among wolves, a dog among dogs, a fiend among fiends. But there was enough of that in the world, already. The very thought of the next ten or fifteen years of torture was enough to make Mr. Underhill cringe; he felt his own flesh impaled with BB shot, stung, burned, fisted, scrounged, twisted, violated, and bruised. He quivered, like a jellyfish hurled violently into a concrete mixer. Jim would never survive it. Jim was too delicate for this horror.

Underhill walked in the midnight rooms of his house thinking of all this, of himself, of the son, the Playground, the fear; there was no part of it he did not touch and turn over with his mind. How much, he asked himself, how much of this is being alone, how much due to Ann's dying, how much to my need, and how much is the reality of the Playground itself, and the children? How much rational and how much nonsense? He twitched the delicate weights upon the scale and watched the indicator glide and fix and glide again, back and forth, softly, between midnight and dawn, between black and white, between raw sanity and naked insanity. He should not hold so tight, he should let his hands drop away from the boy. And yet—there was no hour that looking into Jim's small face he did not see Ann there, in the eyes, in the mouth, in the turn of the nostrils, in the warm breathing, in the glow of blood moving just under the thin shell of flesh. I have a right, he thought, to be afraid. I have every right. When you have two precious bits of porcelain and one is broken and the other, the last one, remains, where can you find the time to be objective, to be immensely calm, to be anything else but concerned?

No, he thought, walking slowly in the hall, there seems to be nothing I can do except go on being afraid and being afraid of being afraid.

"You needn't prowl the house all night," his sister called from her bed, as she heard him pass her open door. "You needn't be childish. I'm sorry if I seem dictatorial or cold. But you've got to make up your mind. Jim simply cannot have a private tutor. Ann would have wanted him to go to a regular school. And he's got to go back to that Playground tomorrow and keep going back until he's learned to stand on his own two feet and until he's familiar to all the children; then they won't pick on him so much."

Underhill said nothing. He got dressed quietly, in the dark, and, downstairs, opened the front door. It was about five minutes to midnight as he walked swiftly down the street in the shadows of the tall elms and oaks and maples, trying to outdistance his rage and outrage. He knew Carol was right, of course. This was the world, you lived in it, you accepted it. But that was the very trouble! He had been through the mill already, he knew what it was to be a boy among lions; his own childhood had come rushing back to him in the last few hours, a time of terror and violence, and now he could not bear to think of Jim's going through it all, those long years, especially if you were a delicate child, through no fault of your own, your bones thin, your face pale, what could you expect but to be harried and chased?

He stopped by the Playground, which was still lit by one great overhead lamp. The gate was locked for the night, but that one light remained on until twelve. He wanted to tear the contemptible place down, rip up the steel fences, obliterate the slides, and say to the children, "Go home! Play in your back yards!"

How ingenious, the cold, deep Playground. You never knew where anyone lived. The boy who knocked your teeth out, who was *he?* Nobody knew. Where did he live? Nobody knew. How to find him? Nobody knew. Why, you could come here one day, beat the living tar out of some smaller child, and run on the next day to some *other* Playground. They would never find you. From Playground to Playground, you could take your criminal tricks, with everyone forgetting you, since they never knew you. You could return to this Playground a month later, and if the little child whose teeth you knocked out was there and recognized you, you could deny it. "No, I'm not the one. Must be some other kid. This is my first time here! No, not me!" And when his back is turned, knock him over. And run off down nameless streets, a nameless person.

What can I possibly do? thought Underhill. Carol's been more than generous with her time; she's been good for Jim, no doubt of it. A lot of the love she would have put into a marriage has gone to him this year. I can't fight her forever on this, and I can't tell her to leave. Perhaps moving to the country might help. No, no, impossible; the money. But I can't leave Jim here, either.

"Hello, Charlie," said a quiet voice.

Underhill snapped about. Inside the Playground fence, seated in the dirt, making diagrams with one finger in the cool dust, was the solemn nine-year-old boy. He didn't glance up. He said, "Hello Charlie," just sitting there, easily, in that world beyond the hard steel fence.

Underhill said, "How do you know my name?"

"I know it." The boy crossed his legs, comfortably, smiling quietly. "You're having lots of trouble."

"How'd you get in there so late? Who are you?"

"My name's Marshall."

"Of course! Tom Marshall's son Tommy! I *thought* you looked familiar."

"More familiar than you think." The boy laughed gently.

"How's your father, Tommy?"

"Have you seen him lately?" the boy asked.

"On the street, briefly, two months ago."

"How did he look?"

"What?"

"How did Mr. Marshall *look?*" asked the boy. It seemed strange he refused to say "my father."

"He looked all right. Why?"

"I guess he's happy," said the boy. Mr. Underhill saw the boy's arms and legs and they were covered with scabs and scratches.

"Aren't you going home, Tommy?"

"I sneaked out to see you. I just knew you'd come. You're afraid."

Mr. Underhill didn't know what to say.

"Those little monsters," he said at last.

"Maybe I can help you." The boy made a dust triangle.

It was ridiculous. "How?"

"You'd give anything, wouldn't you, if you could spare Jim all this? You'd trade places with him if you could?"

Mr. Underhill nodded, frozen.

"Well, you come down here tomorrow afternoon at four. Then I can help you."

"How do you mean, help?"

"I can't tell you outright," said the boy. "It has to do with the Playground. Any place where there's lots of evil, that makes power. You can feel it, can't you?"

A kind of warm wind stirred off the bare field under the one high light. Underhill shivered. Yes, even now, at midnight, the Playground seemed evil, for it was used for evil things. "Are all Playgrounds like this?"

"Some. Maybe this is the only one like this. Maybe it's just how *you* look at it, Charlie. Things *are* what you *want* them to be. A lot of people think this is a *swell* Playground. They're right, too. It's how you look at it, maybe. What I wanted to say, though, is that Tom Marshall was like you. He worried about Tommy Marshall and the Playground and the kids, too. He wanted to save Tommy the trouble and the hurt, also."

This business of talking about people as if they were remote made Mr. Underhill uncomfortable.

"So we made a bargain," said the boy.

"Who with?"

"With the Playground, I guess, or whoever runs it."

"Who runs it?"

"I've never seen him. There's an office over there under the grandstand. A light burns in it all night. It's a bright, blue light, kind of funny. There's a desk there with no papers in it and an empty chair. The sign says MANAGER, but nobody ever sees the man."

"He must be around."

"That's right," said the boy. "Or I wouldn't be where I am, and someone else wouldn't be where they are."

"You certainly talk grown-up."

The boy was pleased. "Do you want to know who I really am? I'm not Tommy Marshall at all. I'm Tom Marshall, the father." He sat there in the dust, not moving, late at night, under the high and faraway light, with the late wind blowing his shirt collar gently under his chin, blowing the cool dust. "I'm Tom Marshall, the father. I know it'll be hard for you to believe. But it *is* true. I was afraid for Tommy. I was the way you are now about Jim. So I made this deal with the Playground. Oh, there are others who did the same, here. If you look close, you'll see them among the other children, by the expression in their eyes."

Underhill blinked. "You'd better run home to bed."

"You want to believe me. You want it to be true. I saw your eyes just then! If you could trade places with Jim, you would. You'd like to save him all that torture, let him be in your place, grown-up, the real work over and done."

"Any decent parent sympathizes with his children."

"You, more than most. You feel every bite and kick. Well, you come here tomorrow. You can make a deal, too."

"Trade places?" It was an incredible, an amusing, but an oddly satisfying thought. "What would I have to do?"

"Just make up your mind."

Underhill tried to make his next question sound very casual, a joke, but his mind was in a rage again. "What would I pay?"

"Nothing. You'd just have to play in the Playground."

"All day?"

"And go to school, of course."

"And grow up again?"

"Yes, and grow up again. Be here at four tomorrow afternoon."

"I have to work in the city tomorrow."

"Tomorrow," said the boy.

"You'd better get home to bed, Tommy."

"My name is *Tom* Marshall." The boy sat there.

The Playground lights went out.

Mr. Underhill and his sister did not speak at breakfast. He usually phoned her at noon to chat about this or that, but he did not phone. But at one-thirty, after a bad lunch, he dialed the house number. When Carol answered he hung up. Five minutes later he phoned again.

"Charlie, was that you called five minutes ago?"

"Yes," he said.

"I thought I heard you breathing before you hung up. What'd you call about, dear?" She was being sensible again.

"Oh, just called."

"It's been a bad two days, hasn't it? You *do* see what I mean, don't you, Charlie? Jim *must* go to the Playground and get a few knocks."

"A few knocks, yes."

He saw the blood and the hungry foxes and the torn rabbits.

"And learn to give and take," she was saying, "and fight if he has to."

"Fight if he has to," he murmured.

"I knew you'd come around."

"Around," he said. "You're right. No way out. He must be sacrificed."

"Oh, Charlie, you *are* odd."

He cleared his throat. "Well, that's settled."

"Yes."

I wonder what it would be like? he thought.

"Everything else okay?" he asked the phone.

He thought of the diagrams in the dust, the boy seated there with the hidden bones in his face.

"Yes," she said.

"I've been thinking," he said.

"Speak up."

"I'll be home at three," he said, slowly, piecing out the words like a man hit in the stomach, gasping for breath. "We'll take a walk, you and Jim and I," he said, eyes shut.

"Wonderful!"

"To the Playground," he said and hung up.

It was really autumn now, the real chill, the real snap; overnight the trees burnt red and snapped free of their leaves, which spiraled about Mr. Underhill's face as he walked up the front steps, and there were Carol and Jim bundled up against the sharp wind, waiting for him.

"Hello!" they cried to one another, with much embracing and kissing. "There's Jim down there!" "There's Daddy up there!" They laughed and he felt paralyzed and in terror of the late day. It was almost four. He looked at the leaden sky, which might pour down molten silver any moment, a sky of lava and soot and a wet wind blowing out of it. He held his sister's arm very tightly as they walked. "Aren't you friendly, though?" she smiled.

"It's ridiculous, of course," he said, thinking of something else.

"What?"

They were at the Playground gate.

"Hello, Charlie. Hi!" Far away, atop the monstrous slide stood the Marshall boy, waving, not smiling now.

"You wait here," said Mr. Underhill to his sister. "I'll be only a moment. I'll just take Jim in."

"All right."

He grasped the small boy's hand. "Here we go, Jim. Stick close to Daddy."

They stepped down the hard concrete steps and stood in the flat dust. Before them, in a magical sequence, stood the diagrams, the gigantic ticktacktoes, the monstrous hopscotches, the amazing numerals and triangles and oblongs the children had scrabbled in the incredible dust.

The sky blew a huge wind upon him and he was shivering. He grasped the little boy's hand still tighter and turned to his sister. "Good-by," he said. For he was believing it. He was in the Playground and believing it, and it was for the best. Nothing too good for Jim. Nothing at all in this outrageous world! And now his sister was laughing back at him, "Charlie, you idiot!"

Then they were running, running across the dirt Playground floor, at the bottom of a stony sea that pressed and blew upon them. Now Jim was crying, "Daddy, Daddy!" and the children racing to meet them, the boy on the slide yelling, the ticktacktoe and the hopscotchers whirling, a sense of bodiless terror gripping him, but he knew what he must do and what must be done and what would happen. Far across the field footballs sailed, baseballs whizzed, bats flew, fists flashed up, and the door of the Manager's office stood open, the desk empty, the seat empty, a lone light burning over it.

Underhled stumbled, shut his eyes and fell, crying out, his body clenched by a hot pain, mouthing strange words, everything in turmoil.

"There you are, Jim," said a voice.

And he was climbing, climbing, eyes closed, climbing metal-ringing ladder rungs, screaming, yelling, his throat raw.

Mr. Underhill opened his eyes.

He was on top of the slide. The gigantic, blue metal slide which seemed ten thousand feet high. Children crushed at his back, children beat him to go on, slide! Slide!

And he looked, and there, going off across the field, was a man in a black overcoat. And there, at the gate, was a woman waving and the man standing there with the woman, both of them looking in at him, waving, and their voices calling, "Have a good time! Have a good time, Jim!"

He screamed. He looked at his hands, in a panic of realization. The small hands, the thin hands. He looked at the earth far below. He felt his nose bleeding and there was the Marshall boy next to him. "Hi!" cried the other, and bashed him in the mouth. "Only twelve years here!" cried the other in the uproar.

Twelve years! thought Mr. Underhill, trapped. And time is different to children. A year is like ten years. No, not twelve years of childhood ahead of him, but a century, a century of *this*.

"Slide!"

Behind him the stink of Musterole, Vicks VapoRub, peanuts, chewed hot tar, spearmint gum and blue fountain-pen ink, the smell of kite twine and glycerin soap, a pumpkin smell of Halloween and a papier-mâché fragrance of skull masks, and the smell of dry scabs, as he was pinched, pummeled, shoved. Fists rose and fell, he saw the fox faces and beyond, at the fence, the man and woman standing there, waving. He shrieked, he covered his face, he felt himself pushed, bleeding, to the rim of nothingness. Headfirst, he careened down the slide, screeching, with ten thousand monsters behind. One thought jumped through his mind a moment before he hit bottom in a nauseous mound of claws.

This is hell, he thought, *this is hell*!

And no one in the hot, milling heap contradicted him.

Skeleton

It was past time for him to see the doctor again. Mr. Harris turned palely in at the stairwell, and on his way up the flight saw Dr. Burleigh's name gilded over a pointing arrow. Would Dr. Burleigh sigh when he walked in? After all, this would make the tenth trip so far this year. But Burleigh shouldn't complain; he was paid for the examinations!

The nurse looked Mr. Harris over and smiled, a bit amusedly, as she tiptoed to the glazed glass door, opened it, and put her head in. Harris thought he heard her say, "Guess who's here, Doctor." And didn't the doctor's voice reply, faintly, "Oh, my God, *again?*" Harris swallowed uneasily.

When Harris walked in, Dr. Burleigh snorted. "Aches in your bones again! Ah!!" He scowled and adjusted his glasses. "My dear Harris, you've been curried with the finest-tooth combs and bacteria-brushes known to science. You're just nervous. Let's see your fingers. Too many cigarettes. Let's smell your breath. Too much protein. Let's see your eyes. Not enough sleep. My response? Go to bed, stop the protein, no smoking. Ten dollars, please."

Harris stood sulking.

The doctor glanced up from his papers. "*You* still here? You're a hypochondriac! That's *eleven* dollars, now."

"But why should my bones ache?" asked Harris.

Dr. Burleigh spoke as to a child. "You ever had a sore muscle, and kept irritating it, fussing with it, rubbing it? It gets worse, the more you bother it. Then you leave it alone and the pain vanishes. You realize you caused most of the soreness yourself. Well, son, that's what's with you. Leave yourself alone.

Take a dose of salts. Get out of here and take that trip to Phoenix you've stewed about for months. Do you good to travel!"

Five minutes later, Mr. Harris riffled through a classified phone directory at the corner druggist's. A fine lot of sympathy one got from blind fools like Burleigh! He passed his finger down a list of Bone Specialists, found one named M. Munigant. Munigant lacked an M.D., or any other academic lettering behind his name, but his office was conveniently near. Three blocks down, one block over. . . .

Mr. Munigant, like his office, was small and dark. Like his office, he smelled of iodoform, iodine, and other odd things. He was a good listener, though, and listened with eager shiny moves of his eyes, and when he talked to Harris, his accent was such that he softly whistled each word; undoubtedly because of imperfect dentures.

Harris told all.

M. Munigant nodded. He had seen cases like this before. The bones of the body. Man was not aware of his bones. Ah, yes, the bones. The skeleton. Most difficult. Something concerning an imbalance, an unsympathetic coordination between soul, flesh, and skeleton. Very complicated, softly whistled M. Munigant. Harris listened, fascinated. Now, *here* was a doctor who understood his illness! Psychological, said M. Munigant. He moved swiftly, delicately to a dingy wall and slashed down half a dozen X-rays to haunt the room with their look of things found floating in an ancient tide. Here, here! The skeleton surprised! Here luminous portraits of the long, the short, the large, the small bones. Mr. Harris must be aware of his position, his problem! M. Munigant's hand tapped, rattled, whispered, scratched at faint nebulae of flesh in which hung ghosts of cranium, spinal cord, pelvis, lime, calcium, marrow, here, there, this, that, these, those, and others! Look!

Harris shuddered. The X-rays and the paintings blew in a green and phosphorescent wind from a land peopled by the monsters of Dali and Fuseli.

M. Munigant whistled quietly. Did Mr. Harris wish his bones—treated?

"That depends," said Harris.

Well, M. Munigant could not help Harris unless Harris was in the proper mood. Psychologically, one had to *need* help, or the doctor was useless. But (shrugging) M. Munigant would "try."

Harris lay on a table with his mouth open. The lights were switched off, the shades drawn. M. Munigant approached his patient.

Something touched Harris's tongue.

He felt his jawbones forced out. They creaked and made faint cracking noises. One of those skeleton charts on the dim wall seemed to quiver and jump. A violent shudder seized Harris. Involuntarily, his mouth snapped shut.

M. Munigant shouted. His nose had almost been bitten off! No use, no use! Now was not the time! M. Munigant whispered the shades up, dreadfully disappointed. When Mr. Harris felt he could cooperate psychologically, when Mr. Harris really *needed* help and trusted M. Munigant to help him, then maybe something could be done. M. Munigant held out his little hand. In the meantime, the fee was only two dollars. Mr. Harris must begin to think. Here was a sketch for Mr. Harris to take home and study. It would acquaint him with his body. He must be tremblingly aware of himself. He must be on guard. Skeletons were strange, unwieldy things. M. Munigant's eyes glittered. Good day to Mr. Harris. Oh, and would he care for a breadstick? M. Munigant proffered a jar of long hard salty breadsticks to Harris, taking one himself, saying that chewing breadsticks kept him in—ah—practice. Good day, good day to Mr. Harris! Mr. Harris went home.

The next day, Sunday, Mr. Harris discovered innumerable fresh aches and pains in his body. He spent the morning, his eyes fixed, staring with new interest at the small, anatomically perfect painting of a skeleton M. Munigant had given him.

His wife, Clarisse, startled him at dinner when she cracked her exquisitely thin knuckles, one by one, until he clapped his hands to his ears and cried, "Stop!"

The rest of the afternoon he quarantined himself in his room. Clarisse played bridge in the parlor laughing and chatting with three other ladies while Harris, hidden away, fingered and weighed the limbs of his body with growing curiosity. After an hour he suddenly rose and called:

"Clarisse!"

She had a way of dancing into any room, her body doing all sorts of soft, agreeable things to keep her feet from ever quite touching the nap of a rug. She excused herself from her friends and came to see him now, brightly. She found him re-seated in a far corner and she saw that he was staring at the anatomical sketch. "Are you still brooding, sweet?" she asked. "Please don't." She sat upon his knees.

Her beauty could not distract him now in his absorption. He juggled her lightness, he touched her kneecap, suspiciously. It seemed to move under her pale, glowing skin. "Is it supposed to do that?" he asked, sucking in his breath.

"Is what supposed to do what?" she laughed. "You mean my kneecap?"

"Is it supposed to run around on top of your knee that way?"

She experimented. "So it *does*," she marveled.

"I'm glad yours slithers, too," he sighed. "I was beginning to worry."

"About what?"

He patted his ribs. "My ribs don't go all the way down, they stop *here*. And I found some confounded ones that dangle in midair!"

Beneath the curve of her small breasts, Clarisse clasped her hands.

"Of course, silly. Everybody's ribs stop at a given point. And those funny short ones are floating ribs."

"I hope they don't float around too much." The joke was most uneasy. Now, above all, he wished to be alone. Further discoveries, newer and stranger archaeological diggings, lay within reach of his trembling hands, and he did not wish to be laughed at.

"Thanks for coming in, dear," he said.

"Any time." She rubbed her small nose softly against his.

"Wait! Here, now . . . " He put his finger to touch his nose and hers. "Did you realize? The nose-bone grows down only *this* far. From there on a lot of gristly tissue fills out the rest!"

She wrinkled hers. "Of course, darling!" And she danced from the room.

Now, sitting alone, he felt the perspiration rise from the pools and hollows of his face, to flow in a thin tide down his cheeks. He licked his lips and shut his eyes. Now . . . now . . . next on the agenda, what . . . ? The spinal cord, yes. Here. Slowly, he examined it, in the same way he operated the many push-buttons in his office, thrusting them to summon secretaries, messengers. But now, in these pushings of his spinal column, fears and terrors answered, rushed from a million doors in his mind to confront and shake him! His spine felt horribly— unfamiliar. Like the brittle shards of a fish, freshly eaten, its bones left strewn on a cold china platter. He seized the little rounded knobbins. "Lord! Lord!"

His teeth began to chatter. God All-Mighty! he thought, why haven't I realized it all these years? All these years I've gone around with a—*skeleton*— inside me! How is it we take ourselves for granted? How is it we never question our bodies and our being?

A skeleton. One of those jointed, snowy, hard things, one of those foul, dry, brittle, gouge-eyed, skull-faced, shake-fingered, rattling things that sway from neck-chains in abandoned webbed closets, one of those things found on the desert all long and scattered like dice!

He stood upright, because he could not bear to remain seated. Inside me now, he grasped his stomach, his head, inside my head is a—skull. One of those curved carapaces which holds my brain like an electrical jelly, one of those cracked shells with the holes in front like two holes shot through it by a double-barreled shotgun! With its grottoes and caverns of bone, its revetments and placements for my flesh, my smelling, my seeing, my hearing, my thinking! A skull, encompassing my brain, allowing it exit through its brittle windows to see the outside world!

He wanted to dash into the bridge party, upset it, a fox in a chickenyard, the cards fluttering all around like chicken feathers burst upward in clouds! He stopped himself only with a violent, trembling effort. Now, now, man, control yourself. This is a revelation, take it for what it's worth, understand it, savor it. But a *skeleton*! screamed his subconscious. I won't stand for it. It's vulgar, it's terrible, it's frightening. Skeletons are horrors; they clink and tinkle and rattle in old castles, hung from oaken beams, making long, indolently rustling pen- dulums on the wind. . . .

"Darling, will you come meet the ladies?" His wife's clear, sweet voice called from far away.

Mr. Harris stood. His *skeleton* held him up! This thing inside, this invader this horror, was supporting his arms, legs, and head! It was like feeling someone just behind you who shouldn't be there. With every step, he realized how dependent he was on this other Thing.

"Darling, I'll be with you in a moment," he called weakly. To himself he said, Come on, brace up! You've got to go back to work tomorrow. Friday you must make that trip to Phoenix. It's a long drive. Hundreds of miles. Must be in shape for that trip or you won't get Mr. Creldon to invest in your ceramics business. Chin up, now!

A moment later he stood among the ladies, being introduced to Mrs. Withers, Mrs. Abblematt, and Miss Kirthy, all of whom had skeletons inside them, but took it very calmly, because nature had carefully clothed the bare nudity of clavicle, tibia, and femur with breasts, thighs, calves, with coiffure and eyebrow satanic, with bee-stung lips and—*Lord*! shouted Mr. Harris inwardly —when they talk or eat, part of their skeleton shows—their *teeth*! I never thought of that. "Excuse me," he gasped, and ran from the room only in time to drop his lunch among the petunias over the garden balustrade.

That night, seated on the bed as his wife undressed, he pared his toenails and fingernails scrupulously. These parts, too, were where his skeleton was shoving, indignantly growing out. He must have muttered part of this theory, because next thing he knew his wife, in negligee, was on the bed, her arms about his neck, yawning, "Oh, my darling, fingernails are *not* bone, they're only hardened epidermis!"

He threw the scissors down. "Are you certain? I hope so. I'd feel better." He looked at the curve of her body, marveling. "I hope all people are made the same way."

"If you aren't the darndest hypochondriac!" She held him at arm's length. "Come on. What's wrong? Tell mama."

"Something inside me," he said. "Something—I ate."

The next morning and all afternoon at his downtown office, Mr. Harris sorted out the sizes, shapes, and construction of various bones in his body with displeasure. At ten A.M. he asked to feel Mr. Smith's elbow one moment. Mr. Smith obliged, but scowled suspiciously. And after lunch Mr. Harris asked to touch Miss Laurel's shoulder blade and she immediately pushed herself back against him, purring like a kitten and shutting her eyes.

"Miss Laurel!" he snapped. "Stop that!"

Alone, he pondered his neuroses. The war was just over, the pressure of his work, the uncertainty of the future, probably had much to do with his mental outlook. He wanted to leave the office, get into business for himself. He had more than a little talent for ceramics and sculpture. As soon as possible he'd head for Arizona, borrow that money from Mr. Creldon, build a kiln and set up shop. It was a worry. What a case he was. But luckily he had contacted M. Munigant, who seemed eager to understand and help him. He would fight it out with himself, not go back to either Munigant or Dr. Burleigh unless he was forced to. The alien feeling would pass. He sat staring into space.

The alien feeling did not pass. It grew.

On Tuesday and Wednesday it bothered him terrifically that his epidermis, hair and other appendages were of a high disorder, while the integumented skeleton of himself was a slick clean structure of efficient organization. Sometimes, in certain lights with his lips drawn morosely down, weighted with melancholy, he imagined he saw his skull grinning at him behind the flesh.

Let go! he cried. Let go of me! My lungs! Stop!

He gasped convulsively, as if his ribs were crushing the breath from him.

My brain—stop squeezing it!

And terrifying headaches burnt his brain to a blind cinder.

My insides, let them be, for God's sake! Stay away from my heart!

His heart cringed from the fanning motion of ribs like pale spiders crouched and fiddling with their prey.

Drenched with sweat, he lay upon the bed one night while Clarisse was out attending a Red Cross meeting. He tried to gather his wits but only grew more aware of the conflict between his dirty exterior and this beautiful cool clean calciumed thing inside.

His complexion: wasn't it oily and lined with worry?

Observe the flawless, snow-white perfection of the skull.

His nose: wasn't it too large?

Then observe the tiny bones of the skull's nose before that monstrous nasal cartilage begins forming the lopsided proboscis.

His body: wasn't it plump?

Well, consider the skeleton; slender, svelte, economical of line and contour. Exquisitely carved oriental ivory! Perfect, thin as a white praying mantis!

His eyes: weren't they protuberant, ordinary, numb-looking?

Be so kind as to note the eye-sockets of the skull; so deep and rounded, somber, quiet pools, all-knowing, eternal. Gaze deep and you never touch the bottom of their dark understanding. All irony, all life, all everything is there in the cupped darkness.

Compare. Compare. Compare.

He raged for hours. And the skeleton, ever the frail and solemn philosopher, hung quietly inside, saying not a word, suspended like a delicate insect within a chrysalis, waiting and waiting.

Harris sat slowly up.

"Wait a minute. Hold on!" he exclaimed. "You're helpless, too. I've got you, too. I can make you do anything I want! You can't prevent it! I say move your carpales, metacarpales, and phalanges and—sswtt—up they go, as I wave to someone!" He laughed. "I order the fibula and femur to locomote and *Hunn* two three four, *Hunn* two three four—we walk around the block. There!"

Harris grinned.

"It's a fifty-fifty fight. Even-Stephen. And we'll fight it out, we two! After all, I'm the part that *thinks*! Yes, by God! yes. Even if I didn't have you, I could still think!"

Instantly, a tiger's jaw snapped shut, chewing his brain in half. Harris screamed. The bones of his skull grabbed hold and gave him nightmares. Then slowly, while he shrieked, nuzzled and ate the nightmares one by one, until the last one was gone and the light went out. . . .

At the end of the week he postponed the Phoenix trip because of his health. Weighing himself on a penny scale he saw the slow gliding red arrow point to: 165.

He groaned. Why, I've weighed 175 for years. I can't have lost 10 pounds! He examined his cheeks in the fly-dotted mirror. Cold, primitive fear rushed over him in odd little shivers. You, you! I know what you're about, *you*!

He shook his fist at his bony face, particularly addressing his remarks to his superior maxillary, his inferior maxillary, to his cranium and to his cervical vertebrae.

"You damn thing, you! Think you can starve me, make me lose weight, eh? Peel the flesh off, leave nothing, but skin on bone. Trying to ditch me, so you can be supreme, ah? No, no!"

He fled into a cafeteria.

Turkey, dressing, creamed potatoes, four vegetables, three desserts, he could eat none of it, he was sick to his stomach. He forced himself. His teeth began to ache. Bad teeth, is it? he thought angrily. I'll eat in spite of every tooth clanging and banging and rattling so they fall in my gravy.

His head blazed, his breath jerked in and out of a constricted chest, his teeth raged with pain, but he knew one small victory. He was about to drink milk when he stopped and poured it into a vase of nasturtiums. No calcium for you, my boy, no calcium for you. Never again shall I eat foods with calcium or other bone-fortifying minerals. I'll eat for one of us, not both, my lad.

"One hundred and fifty pounds," he said the following week to his wife. "Do you *see* how I've changed?"

"For the better," said Clarisse. "You were always a little plump for your height, darling." She stroked his chin. "I like your face. It's so much nicer; the lines of it are so firm and strong now."

"They're not *my* lines, they're his, damn him! You mean to say you like him better than you like me?"

"Him? Who's '*him*'?"

In the parlor mirror, beyond Clarisse, his skull smiled back at him behind his fleshy grimace of hatred and despair.

Fuming, he popped malt tablets into his mouth. This was one way of gaining weight when you couldn't keep other foods down. Clarisse noticed the malt pellets.

"But, darling, really, you don't have to regain the weight for me," she said. Oh, shut up! he felt like saying.

She made him lie with his head in her lap. "Darling," she said, "I've watched you lately. You're so—badly off. You don't say anything, but you look—hunted. You toss in bed at night. Maybe you should go to a psychiatrist. But I think I can tell you everything he would say. I've put it all together from hints you've let escape you. I can tell you that you and your skeleton are one and the same, one nation, indivisible, with liberty and justice for all. United you stand, divided you fall. If you two fellows can't get along like an old married couple in the future, go back and see Dr. Burleigh. But, first, relax. You're in a vicious circle; the more you worry, the more your bones stick out, the more you worry. After all, who picked this fight—you or that anonymous entity you claim is lurking around behind your alimentary canal?"

He closed his eyes. "I did. I guess I did. Go on, Clarisse, keep talking."

"You rest now," she said softly. "Rest and forget."

Mr. Harris felt buoyed up for half a day, then he began to sag. It was all very well to blame his imagination, but this particular skeleton, by God, was fighting back.

Harris set out for M. Munigant's office late in the day. Walking for half an hour until he found the address, he caught sight of the name M. MUNIGANT initialed in ancient, flaking gold on a glass plate outside the building. Then, his bones seemed to explode from their moorings, blasted and erupted with pain. Blinded, he staggered away. When he opened his eyes again he had rounded a corner. M. Munigant's office was out of sight.

The pains ceased.

M. Munigant was the man to help him. If the sight of his name would cause so titanic a reaction, of course M. Munigant *must* be just the man.

But, not today. Each time he tried to return to that office, the terrible pains took hold. Perspiring, he had to give up and swayed into a cocktail bar.

Moving across the dim lounge, he wondered briefly if a lot of blame couldn't be put on M. Munigant's shoulders. After all, it was Munigant who'd first drawn specific attention to his skeleton, and let the psychological impact of it slam home! Could M. Munigant be using him for some nefarious purpose? But what purpose? Silly to suspect him. Just a little doctor. Trying to be helpful. Munigant and his jar of breadsticks. Ridiculous. M. Munigant was okay, okay . . .

There was a sight within the cocktail lounge to give him hope. A large, fat man, round as a butterball, stood drinking consecutive beers at the bar. Now *there* was a successful man. Harris repressed a desire to go up, clap the fat man's shoulder, and inquire as to how he'd gone about impounding his bones. Yes, the fat man's skeleton was luxuriously closeted. There were pillows of fat here, resilient bulges of it there, with several round chandeliers of fat under his chin. The poor skeleton was lost; it could never fight clear of that blubber. It might have tried once—but not now, overwhelmed, not a bony echo of the fat man's supporter remained.

Not without envy, Harris approached the fat man as one might cut across the bow of an ocean liner. Harris ordered a drink, drank it, and then dared to address the fat man:

"Glands?"

"You talking to me?" asked the fat man.

"Or is there a special diet?" wondered Harris. "I beg your pardon, but, as you see, I'm down. Can't seem to put on any weight. I'd like a stomach like that one of yours. Did you grow it because you were afraid of something?"

"You," announced the fat man, "are drunk. But—I like drunkards." He ordered more drinks. "Listen close, I'll tell you. Layer by layer," said the fat man, "twenty years, man and boy, I built this." He held his vast stomach like a globe of the world, teaching his audience its gastronomical geography. "It was no overnight circus. The tent was not raised before dawn on the wonders installed within. I have cultivated my inner organs as if they were thoroughbred dogs, cats, and other animals. My stomach is a fat pink Persian tom slumbering, rousing at intervals to purr, mew, growl, and cry for chocolate titbits. I feed it well, it will 'most sit up for me. And, my dear fellow, my intestines are the rarest pure-bred Indian anacondas you ever viewed in the sleekest, coiled, fine and ruddy health. Keep 'em in prime, I do, all my pets. For fear of something? Perhaps."

This called for another drink for everyone.

"Gain weight?" The fat man savored the words on his tongue. "Here's what you do: get yourself a quarreling bird of a wife, a baker's dozen of relatives who can flush a covey of troubles out from behind the veriest molehill. Add to these a sprinkling of business associates whose prime motivation is snatching your last lonely quid, and you are well on your way to getting fat. How so? In no time you'll begin subconsciously building fat betwixt yourself and them. A buffer epidermal state, a cellular wall. You'll soon find that eating is the only fun on earth. But one needs to be bothered by outside sources. Too many people in this world haven't enough to worry about, then they begin picking on themselves, and they lose weight. Meet all of the vile, terrible people you can possibly meet, and pretty soon you'll be adding the good old fat!"

And with that advice, the fat man launched himself out into the dark tide of night, swaying mightily and wheezing.

"That's exactly what Dr. Burleigh told me, slightly changed," said Harris thoughtfully. "Perhaps that trip to Phoenix, now, at this time—"

. . .

The trip from Los Angeles to Phoenix was a sweltering one, crossing, as it did, the Mojave Desert on a broiling yellow day. Traffic was thin and inconstant, and for long stretches there would not be a car on the road for miles ahead or behind. Harris twitched his fingers on the steering wheel. Whether or not Creldon, in Phoenix, lent him the money he needed to start his business, it was still a good thing to get away, to put distance behind.

The car moved in the hot sluice of desert wind. The one Mr. H. sat inside the other Mr. H. Perhaps both perspired. Perhaps both were miserable.

On a curve, the inside Mr. H suddenly constricted the outer flesh, causing him to jerk forward on the hot steering wheel.

The car plunged off the road into boiling sand and turned half over.

Night came, a wind rose, the road was lonely and silent. The few cars that passed went swiftly on their way, their view obstructed. Mr. Harris lay unconscious, until very late he heard a wind rising out of the desert, felt the sting of little sand needles on his cheeks, and opened his eyes.

Morning found him gritty-eyed and wandering in thoughtless senseless circles, having, in his delirium, got away from the road. At noon he sprawled in the poor shade of a bush. The sun struck him with a keen sword edge, cutting through to his—bones. A vulture circled.

Harris's parched lips cracked open. "So that's it?" he whispered, red-eyed, bristle-cheeked. "One way or another you'll walk me, starve me, thirst me, kill me." He swallowed dry burrs of dust. "Sun cook off my flesh so you can peek out. Vultures lunch off me, and there you'll lie, grinning. Grinning with victory. Like a bleached xylophone strewn and played by vultures with an ear for odd music. You'd like that. Freedom."

He walked on through a landscape that shivered and bubbled in the direct pour of sunlight; stumbling, falling flat, lying to feed himself little mouths of fire. The air was blue alcohol flame, and vultures roasted and steamed and glittered as they flew in glides and circles. Phoenix. The road. Car. Water. Safety.

"Hey!"

Someone called from way off in the blue alcohol flame.

Mr. Harris propped himself up.

"Hey!"

The call was repeated. A crunching of footsteps, quick.

With a cry of unbelievable relief, Harris rose, only to collapse again into the arms of someone in a uniform with a badge.

The car tediously hauled, repaired, Phoenix reached, Harris found himself in such an unholy state of mind that the business transaction was a numb pantomime. Even when he got the loan and held the money in his hand, it meant nothing. This Thing within him like a hard white sword in a scabbard tainted his business, his eating, colored his love for Clarisse, made it unsafe to trust an automobile; all in all this Thing had to be put in its place. The desert incident had brushed too close. Too near the bone, one might say with an ironic twist of one's mouth. Harris heard himself thanking Mr. Creldon, dimly, for the money. Then he turned his car and motored back across the long miles, this time cutting across to San Diego, so he would miss that desert stretch between El Centro and Beaumont. He drove north along the coast. He didn't trust that desert. But—careful! Salt waves boomed, hissing on the beach outside Laguna. Sand, fish and crustacea would cleanse his bones as swiftly as vultures. Slow down on the curves over the surf.

Damn, he was sick!

Where to turn? Clarisse? Burleigh? Munigant? Bone specialist. Munigant. Well?

"Darling!" Clarisse kissed him. He winced at the solidness of the teeth and jaw behind the passionate exchange.

"Darling," he said, slowly, wiping his lips with his wrist, trembling.

"You look thinner; oh, darling, the business deal—?"

"It went through. I guess. Yes, it did."

She kissed him again. They ate a slow, falsely cheerful dinner, with Clarisse laughing and encouraging him. He studied the phone; several times he picked it up indecisively, then laid it down.

His wife walked in, putting on her coat and hat. "Well, sorry, but I have to leave." She pinched him on the cheek. "Come on now, cheer up! I'll be back from Red Cross in three hours. You lie around and snooze. I simply *have* to go."

When Clarisse was gone, Harris dialed the phone, nervously.

"M. Munigant?"

The explosions and the sickness in his body after he set the phone down were unbelievable. His bones were racked with every kind of pain, cold and hot, he had ever thought of or experienced in wildest nightmare. He swallowed all the aspirin he could find, in an effort to stave off the assault; but when the doorbell finally rang an hour later, he could not move; he lay weak and exhausted, panting, tears streaming down his cheeks.

"Come in! Come in, for God's sake!"

M. Munigant came in. Thank God the door was unlocked.

Oh, but Mr. Harris looked terrible. M. Munigant stood in the center of the living room, small and dark. Harris nodded. The pains rushed through him, hitting him with large iron hammers and hooks. M. Munigant's eyes glittered as he saw Harris's protuberant bones. Ah, he saw that Mr. Harris was now psychologically prepared for aid. Was it not so? Harris nodded again, feebly, sobbing. M. Munigant still whistled when he talked; something about his tongue and the whistling. No matter. Through his shimmering eyes Harris seemed to see M. Munigant shrink, get smaller. Imagination, of course. Harris sobbed out his story of the Phoenix trip. M. Munigant sympathized. This skeleton was a—a traitor! They would fix him for once and for all!

"Mr. Munigant," sighed Harris, faintly, "I—I never noticed before. Your tongue. Round, tubelike. Hollow? My eyes. Delirious. What do I do?"

M. Munigant whistled softly, appreciatively, coming closer. If Mr. Harris would relax in his chair, and open his mouth? The lights were switched off. M. Munigant peered into Harris's dropped jaw. Wider, please? It had been so hard, that first visit, to help Harris, with both body and bone in revolt. Now, he had cooperation from the flesh of the man, anyway, even if the skeleton protested. In the darkness, M. Munigant's voice got small, small, tiny, tiny. The whistling became high and shrill. Now. Relax, Mr. Harris, NOW!

Harris felt his jaw pressed violently in all directions, his tongue depressed as with a spoon, his throat clogged. He gasped for breath. Whistle. He couldn't breathe! Something squirmed, corkscrewed his cheeks out, bursting his jaws. Like a hot-water douche, something squirted into his sinuses, his ears clanged! "Ahhhh!" shrieked Harris, gagging. His head, its carapaces riven, shattered, hung loose. Agony shot fire through his lungs.

Harris could breathe again, momentarily. His watery eyes sprang wide. He shouted. His ribs, like sticks picked up and bundled, were loosened in him. Pain! He fell to the floor, wheezing out his hot breath.

Lights flickered in his senseless eyeballs, he felt his limbs swiftly cast loose and free. Through streaming eyes he saw the parlor.

The room was empty.

"M. Munigant? In God's name, where are you, M. Munigant? Come help me!"

M. Munigant was gone.

"Help!"

Then he heard it.

Deep down in the subterranean fissures of his body, the minute, unbelievable noises; little smackings and twistings and little dry chippings and grindings and nuzzling sounds—like a tiny hungry mouse down in the red-blooded dimness, gnawing ever so earnestly and expertly at what might have been, but was not, a submerged timber . . . !

Clarisse, walking along the sidewalk, held her head high and marched straight toward her house on St. James Place. She was thinking of the Red Cross as she turned the corner and almost ran into this little dark man who smelled of iodine.

Clarisse would have ignored him if it were not for the fact that as she passed, he took something long, white and oddly familiar from his coat and proceeded to chew on it, as on a peppermint stick. Its end devoured, his extraordinary tongue darted within the white confection, sucking out the filling, making contented noises. He was still crunching his goody as she proceeded up the sidewalk to her house, turned the doorknob and walked in.

"Darling?" she called, smiling around. "Darling, where are you?" She shut the door, walked down the hall and into the living room. "Darling . . . "

She stared at the floor for twenty seconds, trying to understand.

She screamed.

Outside in the sycamore darkness, the little man pierced a long white stick with intermittent holes; then, softly, sighing, his lips puckered, played a little sad tune upon the improvised instrument to accompany the shrill and awful singing of Clarisse's voice as she stood in the living room.

Many times as a little girl Clarisse had run on the beach sands, stepped on a jellyfish and screamed. It was not so bad, finding an intact, gelatin-skinned jellyfish in one's living room. One could step back from it.

It was when the jellyfish *called you by name* . . .

The Man Upstairs

He remembered how carefully and expertly Grandmother would fondle the cold cut guts of the chicken and withdraw the marvels therein; the wet shining loops of meat-smelling intestine, the muscled lump of heart, the gizzard with the collection of seeds in it. How neatly and nicely Grandma would slit the chicken and push her fat little hand in to deprive it of its medals. These would be segregated, some in pans of water, others in paper to be thrown to the dog later, perhaps. And then the ritual of taxidermy, stuffing the bird with watered, seasoned bread, and performing surgery with a swift, bright needle, stitch after pulled-tight stitch.

This was one of the prime thrills of Douglas's eleven-year-old life span.

Altogether, he counted twenty knives in the various squeaking drawers of the magic kitchen table from which Grandma, a kindly, gentle-faced, white-haired old witch, drew paraphernalia for her miracles.

Douglas was to be quiet. He could stand across the table from Grandma, his freckled nose tucked over the edge, watching, but any loose boy-talk might interfere with the spell. It was a wonder when Grandma brandished silver shakers over the bird, supposedly sprinkling showers of mummy-dust and pulverized Indian bones, muttering mystical verses under her toothless breath.

"Grammy," said Douglas at last, breaking the silence. "Am I like that inside?" He pointed at the chicken.

"Yes," said Grandma. "A little more orderly and presentable, but just about the same. . . ."

"And more *of* it!" added Douglas, proud of his guts.

"Yes," said Grandma. "More of it."

"Grandpa has lots more'n me. His sticks out in front so he can rest his elbows on it."

Grandma laughed and shook her head.

Douglas said, "And Lucie Williams, down the street, she . . . "

"Hush, child!" cried Grandma.

"But she's got . . . "

"Never you mind what she's got! That's different."

"But why is *she* different?"

"A darning-needle dragon-fly is coming by some day and sew up your mouth," said Grandma firmly.

Douglas waited, then asked, "How do you know I've got insides like that, Grandma?"

"Oh, go 'way, now!"

The front doorbell rang.

Through the front-door glass as he ran down the hall, Douglas saw a straw hat. The bell jangled again and again. Douglas opened the door.

"Good morning, child, is the landlady at home?"

Cold gray eyes in a long, smooth, walnut-colored face gazed upon Douglas. The man was tall, thin, and carried a suitcase, a briefcase, an umbrella under one bent arm, gloves rich and thick and gray on his thin fingers, and wore a horribly new straw hat.

Douglas backed up. "She's busy."

"I wish to rent her upstairs room, as advertised."

"We've got ten boarders, and it's already rented; go away!"

"Douglas!" Grandma was behind him suddenly. "How do you do?" she said to the stranger. "Never mind this child."

Unsmiling, the man stepped stiffly in. Douglas watched them ascend out of sight up the stairs, heard Grandma detailing the conveniences of the upstairs room. Soon she hurried down to pile linens from the linen closet on Douglas and send him scooting up with them.

Douglas paused at the room's threshold. The room was changed oddly, simply because the stranger had been in it a moment. The straw hat lay brittle and terrible upon the bed, the umbrella leaned stiff against one wall like a dead bat with dark wings folded.

Douglas blinked at the umbrella.

The stranger stood in the center of the changed room, tall, tall.

"Here!" Douglas littered the bed with supplies. "We eat at noon sharp, and if you're late coming down the soup'll get cold. Grandma fixes it so it will, every time!"

The tall strange man counted out ten new copper pennies and tinkled them in Douglas's blouse pocket. "We shall be friends," he said, grimly.

It was funny, the man having nothing but pennies. Lots of them. No silver at all, no dimes, no quarters. Just new copper pennies.

Douglas thanked him glumly. "I'll drop these in my dime bank when I get them changed into a dime. I got six dollars and fifty cents in dimes all ready for my camp trip in August."

"I must wash now," said the tall strange man.

Once, at midnight, Douglas had wakened to hear a storm rumbling outside—the cold hard wind shaking the house, the rain driving against the window. And then a lightning bolt had landed outside the window with a silent, terrific concussion. He remembered that fear of looking about at his room, seeing it strange and awful in the instantaneous light.

So it was, now, in this room. He stood looking up at the stranger. This room was no longer the same, but changed indefinably because this man, quick as a lightning bolt, had shed his light about it. Douglas backed up slowly as the stranger advanced.

The door closed in his face.

The wooden fork went up with mashed potatoes, came down empty. Mr. Koberman, for that was his name, had brought the wooden fork and wooden knife and spoon with him when Grandma called lunch.

"Mrs. Spaulding," he said, quietly, "my own cutlery; please use it. I will have lunch today, but from tomorrow on, only breakfast and supper."

Grandma bustled in and out, bearing steaming tureens of soup and beans and mashed potatoes to impress her new boarder, while Douglas sat rattling his silverware on his plate, because he had discovered it irritated Mr. Koberman.

"I know a trick," said Douglas. "Watch." He picked a fork-tine with his fingernail. He pointed at various sectors of the table, like a magician. Wherever he pointed, the sound of the vibrating fork-tine emerged, like a metal elfin voice. Simply done, of course. He pressed the fork handle on the table-top, secretly. The vibration came from the wood like a sounding board. It looked quite magical. "There, there, and *there*!" exclaimed Douglas, happily plucking the fork again. He pointed at Mr. Koberman's soup and the noise came from it.

Mr. Koberman's walnut-colored face became hard and firm and awful. He pushed the soup bowl away violently, his lips twisting. He fell back in his chair.

Grandma appeared. "Why, what's wrong, Mr. Koberman?"

"I cannot eat this soup."

"Why?"

"Because I am full and can eat no more. Thank you."

Mr. Koberman left the room, glaring.

"What did you do, just then?" asked Grandma at Douglas, sharply.

"Nothing. Grandma, why does he eat with *wooden* spoons?"

"Yours not to question! When do you go back to school, anyway?"

"Seven weeks."

"Oh, my land!" said Grandma.

Mr. Koberman worked nights. Each morning at eight he arrived mysteriously home, devoured a very small breakfast, and then slept soundlessly in his room all through the dreaming hot daytime, until the huge supper with all the other boarders at night.

Mr. Koberman's sleeping habits made it necessary for Douglas to be quiet. This was unbearable. So, whenever Grandma visited down the street, Douglas stomped up and down stairs beating a drum, bouncing golf balls, or just screaming for three minutes outside Mr. Koberman's door, or flushing the toilet seven times in succession.

Mr. Koberman never moved. His room was silent, dark. He did not complain. There was no sound. He slept on and on. It was very strange.

Douglas felt a pure white flame of hatred burn inside himself with a steady, unflickering beauty. Now that room was Koberman Land. Once it had been flowery bright when Miss Sadlowe lived there. Now it was stark, bare, cold, clean, everything in its place, alien and brittle.

Douglas climbed upstairs on the fourth morning.

Halfway to the second floor was a large sun-filled window, framed by six-inch panes of orange, purple, blue, red and burgundy glass. In the enchanted early mornings when the sun fell through to strike the landing and slide down the stair banister, Douglas stood entranced at this window peering at the world through the multi-colored panes.

Now a blue world, a blue sky, blue people, blue streetcars and blue trotting dogs.

He shifted panes. Now—an amber world! Two lemonish women glided by, resembling the daughters of Fu Manchu! Douglas giggled. This pane made even the sunlight more purely golden.

It was eight A.M. Mr. Koberman strolled by below, on the sidewalk, returning from his night's work, his umbrella looped over his elbow, straw hat glued to his head with patent oil.

Douglas shifted panes again. Mr. Koberman was a red man walking through a red world with red trees and red flowers and—something else.

Something about—Mr. Koberman.

Douglas squinted.

The red glass *did* things to Mr. Koberman. His face, his suit, his hands. The clothes seemed to melt away. Douglas almost believed, for one terrible instant, that he could see *inside* Mr. Koberman. And what he saw made him lean wildly against the small red pane, blinking.

Mr. Koberman glanced up just then, saw Douglas, and raised his umbrella angrily, as if to strike. He ran swiftly across the red lawn to the front door.

"Young man!" he cried, running up the stairs. "What were you doing?"

"Just looking," said Douglas, numbly.

"That's all, is it?" cried Mr. Koberman.

"Yes, sir. I look through all the glasses. All kinds of worlds. Blue ones, red ones, yellow ones. All different."

"All kinds of worlds, is it!" Mr. Koberman glanced at the little panes of glass, his face pale. He got hold of himself. He wiped his face with a handkerchief and pretended to laugh. "Yes. All kinds of worlds. All different." He walked to the door of his room. "Go right ahead; play," he said.

The door closed. The hall was empty. Mr. Koberman had gone in.

Douglas shrugged and found a new pane.

"Oh, everything's violet!"

Half an hour later, while playing in his sandbox behind the house, Douglas heard the crash and the shattering tinkle. He leaped up.

A moment later, Grandma appeared on the back porch, the old razor strop trembling in her hand.

"Douglas! I told you time and again never fling your basketball against the house! Oh, I could just cry!"

"I been sitting right here," he protested.

"Come see what you've done, you nasty boy!"

The great colored window panes lay shattered in a rainbow chaos on the upstairs landing. His basketball lay in the ruins.

Before he could even begin telling his innocence, Douglas was struck a dozen stinging blows upon his rump. Wherever he landed, screaming, the razor strop struck again.

Later, hiding his mind in the sandpile like an ostrich, Douglas nursed his dreadful pains. He knew who'd thrown that basketball. A man with a straw hat and a stiff umbrella and a cold, gray room. Yeah, yeah, yeah. He dribbled tears. Just wait. Just *wait*.

He heard Grandma sweeping up the broken glass. She brought it out and threw it in the trash bin. Blue, pink, yellow meteors of glass dropped brightly down.

When she was gone, Douglas dragged himself, whimpering, over to save out three pieces of the incredible glass. Mr. Koberman disliked the colored windows. These—he clinked them in his fingers—would be worth saving.

Grandfather arrived from his newspaper office each night, shortly ahead of the other boarders, at five o'clock. When a slow, heavy tread filled the hall, and a thick, mahogany cane thumped in the cane-rack, Douglas ran to embrace the large stomach and sit on Grandpa's knee while he read the evening paper.

"Hi, Grampa!"

"Hello, down there!"

"Grandma cut chickens again today. It's fun watching," said Douglas.

Grandpa kept reading. "That's twice this week, chickens. She's the chickenist woman. You like to watch her cut 'em, eh? Cold-blooded little pepper! Ha!"

"I'm just curious."

"You are," rumbled Grandpa, scowling. "Remember that day when that young lady was killed at the rail station? You just walked over and looked at her, blood and all." He laughed. "Queer duck. Stay that way. Fear nothing, ever in your life. I guess you get it from your father, him being a military man and all, and you so close to him before you came here to live last year." Grandpa returned to his paper.

A long pause. "Gramps?"

"Yes?"

"What if a man didn't have a heart or lungs or stomach but still walked around, alive?"

"That," rumbled Gramps, "would be a miracle."

"I don't mean a—a miracle. I mean, what if he was all *different* inside? Not like me."

"Well, he wouldn't be quite human then, would he, boy?"

"Guess not, Gramps. Gramps, you got a heart and lungs?"

Gramps chuckled. "Well, tell the truth, I don't *know*. Never seen them. Never had an X-ray, never been to a doctor. Might as well be potato-solid for all I know."

"Have *I* got a stomach?"

"You certainly have!" cried Grandma from the parlor entry. " 'Cause I feed it! And you've lungs, you scream loud enough to wake the crumblees. And you've dirty hands, go wash them! Dinner's ready. Grandpa, come on. Douglas, git!"

In the rush of boarders streaming downstairs, Grandpa, if he intended questioning Douglas further about the weird conversation, lost his opportunity. If dinner delayed an instant more, Grandma and the potatoes would develop simultaneous lumps.

The boarders, laughing and talking at the table—Mr. Koberman silent and sullen among them—were silenced when Grandfather cleared his throat. He talked politics a few minutes and then shifted over into the intriguing topic of the recent peculiar deaths in the town.

"It's enough to make an old newspaper editor prick up his ears," he said, eying them all. "That young Miss Larson, lived across the ravine, now. Found her dead three days ago for no reason, just funny kinds of tattoos all over her, and a facial expression that would make Dante cringe. And that other young lady, what was her name? Whitely? She disappeared and *never did* come back."

"Them things happen alla time," said Mr. Britz, the garage mechanic, chewing. "Ever peek inna Missing Peoples Bureau file? It's *that* long." He illustrated. "Can't tell *what* happens to most of 'em."

"Anyone want more dressing?" Grandma ladled liberal portions from the chicken's interior. Douglas watched, thinking about how that chicken had had two kinds of guts—God-made and Man-made.

Well, how about *three* kinds of guts?

Eh?

Why not?

Conversation continued about the mysterious death of so-and-so, and, oh, yes, remember a week ago, Marion Barsumian died of heart failure, but maybe that didn't connect up? or did it? you're crazy! forget it, why talk about it at the dinner table? So.

"Never can tell," said Mr. Britz. "Maybe we got a vampire in town."

Mr. Koberman stopped eating.

"In the year 1927?" said Grandma. "A vampire? Oh go on, now."

"Sure," said Mr. Britz. "Kill 'em with silver bullets. Anything silver for that matter. Vampires *hate* silver. I read it in a book somewhere, once. Sure, I did."

Douglas looked at Mr. Koberman who ate with wooden knives and forks and carried only new copper pennies in his pocket.

"It's poor judgment," said Grandpa, "to call anything by a name. We don't know what a hobgoblin or a vampire or a troll is. Could be lots of things. You can't heave them into categories with labels and say they'll act one way or another. That'd be silly. They're people. People who do things. Yes, that's the way to put it: people who *do* things."

"Excuse me," said Mr. Koberman, who got up and went out for his evening walk to work.

The stars, the moon, the wind, the clock ticking, and the chiming of the hours into dawn, the sun rising, and here it was another morning, another day, and Mr. Koberman coming along the sidewalk from his night's work. Douglas stood off like a small mechanism whirring and watching with carefully microscopic eyes.

At noon, Grandma went to the store to buy groceries.

As was his custom every day when Grandma was gone, Douglas yelled outside Mr. Koberman's door for a full three minutes. As usual, there was no response. The silence was horrible.

He ran downstairs, got the pass-key, a silver fork, and the three pieces of colored glass he had saved from the shattered window. He fitted the key to the lock and swung the door slowly open.

The room was in half light, the shades drawn. Mr. Koberman lay atop his bedcovers, in slumber clothes, breathing gently, up and down. He didn't move. His face was motionless.

"Hello, Mr. Koberman!"

The colorless walls echoed the man's regular breathing.

"Mr. Koberman, hello!"

Bouncing a golf ball, Douglas advanced. He yelled. Still no answer. "Mr. Koberman!"

Bending over Mr. Koberman, Douglas picked the tines of the silver fork in the sleeping man's face.

Mr. Koberman winced. He twisted. He groaned bitterly.

Response. Good. Swell.

Douglas drew a piece of blue glass from his pocket. Looking through the blue glass fragment he found himself in a blue room, in a blue world different from the world he knew. As different as was the red world. Blue furniture, blue bed, blue ceiling and walls, blue wooden eating utensils atop the blue bureau, and the sullen dark blue of Mr. Koberman's face and arms and his blue chest rising, falling. Also . . .

Mr. Koberman's eyes were wide, staring at him with a hungry darkness.

Douglas fell back, pulled the blue glass from his eyes.

Mr. Koberman's eyes were shut.

Blue glass again—open. Blue glass away—shut. Blue glass again—open. Away—shut. Funny. Douglas experimented, trembling. Through the glass the eyes seemed to peer hungrily, avidly, through Mr. Koberman's closed lids. Without the blue glass they seemed tightly shut.

But it was the rest of Mr. Koberman's body . . .

Mr. Koberman's bedclothes dissolved off him. The blue glass had something to do with it. Or perhaps it was the clothes themselves, just being *on* Mr. Koberman. Douglas cried out.

He was looking through the wall of Mr. Koberman's stomach, right *inside* him!

Mr. Koberman was solid.

Or, nearly so, anyway.

There were strange shapes and sizes within him.

Douglas must have stood amazed for five minutes, thinking about the blue worlds, the red worlds, the yellow worlds side by side, living together like glass panes around the big white stair window. Side by side, the colored panes, the different worlds; Mr. Koberman had said so himself.

So this was why the colored window had been broken.

"Mr. Koberman, wake up!"

No answer.

"Mr. Koberman, where do you work at night? Mr. Koberman, where do you work?"

A little breeze stirred the blue window shade.

"In a red world or a green world or a yellow one, Mr. Koberman?"

Over everything was a blue glass silence.

"Wait there," said Douglas.

He walked down to the kitchen, pulled open the great squeaking drawer and picked out the sharpest, biggest knife.

Very calmly he walked into the hall, climbed back up the stairs again, opened the door to Mr. Koberman's room, went in, and closed it, holding the sharp knife in one hand.

Grandma was busy fingering a piecrust into a pan when Douglas entered the kitchen to place something on the table.

"Grandma, what's this?"

She glanced up briefly, over her glasses. "I don't know."

It was square, like a box, and elastic. It was bright orange in color. It had four square tubes, colored blue, attached to it. It smelled funny.

"Ever see anything like it, Grandma?"

"No."

"That's what *I* thought."

Douglas left it there, went from the kitchen. Five minutes later he returned with something else. "How about *this?*"

He laid down a bright pink linked chain with a purple triangle at one end.

"Don't bother me," said Grandma. "It's only a chain."

Next time he returned with two hands full. A ring, a square, a triangle, a pyramid, a rectangle, and—other shapes. All of them were pliable, resilient, and looked as if they were made of gelatin. "This isn't all," said Douglas, putting them down. "There's more where this came from."

Grandma said, "Yes, yes," in a far-off tone, very busy.

"You were wrong, Grandma."

"About what?"

"About all people being the same inside."

"Stop talking nonsense."

"Where's my piggy-bank?"

"On the mantel, where you left it."

"Thanks."

He tromped into the parlor, reached up for his piggy-bank.

Grandpa came home from the office at five.

"Grandpa, come upstairs."

"Sure, son. Why?"

"Something to show you. It's not nice; but it's interesting."

Grandpa chuckled, following his grandson's feet up to Mr. Koberman's room.

"Grandma mustn't know about this; she wouldn't like it," said Douglas. He pushed the door wide open. "There."

Grandfather gasped.

Douglas remembered the next few hours all the rest of his life. Standing over Mr. Koberman's naked body, the coroner and his assistants. Grandma, downstairs, asking somebody, "What's going on up there?" and Grandpa saying, shakily, "I'll take Douglas away on a long vacation so he can forget this whole ghastly affair. Ghastly, ghastly affair!"

Douglas said, "Why should it be bad? I don't see anything bad. I don't feel bad."

The coroner shivered and said, "Koberman's dead, all right."

His assistant sweated. "Did you see those *things* in the pans of water and in the wrapping paper?"

"Oh, my God, my God, yes, I saw them."

"Christ."

The coroner bent over Mr. Koberman's body again. "This better be kept secret, boys. It wasn't murder. It was a mercy the boy acted. God knows what might have happened if he hadn't."

"What was Koberman? A vampire? A monster?"

"Maybe. I don't know. Something—not human." The coroner moved his hands deftly over the suture.

Douglas was proud of his work. He'd gone to much trouble. He had watched Grandmother carefully and remembered. Needle and thread and all. All in all, Mr. Koberman was as neat a job as any chicken ever popped into hell by Grandma.

"I heard the boy say that Koberman lived even after all those *things* were taken out of him." The coroner looked at the triangles and chains and pyramids floating in the pans of water. "Kept on *living*. God."

"Did the boy say that?"

"He did."

"Then, what *did* kill Koberman?"

The coroner drew a few strands of sewing thread from their bedding. "This. . . . " he said.

Sunlight blinked coldly off a half-revealed treasure trove; six dollars and sixty cents' worth of silver dimes inside Mr. Koberman's chest.

"I think Douglas made a wise investment," said the coroner, sewing the flesh back up over the "dressing" quickly.

Touched with Fire

They stood in the blazing sunlight for a long while, looking at the bright faces of their old-fashioned railroad watches, while the shadows tilted beneath them, swaying, and the perspiration ran out under their porous summer hats. When they uncovered their heads to mop their lined and pinkened brows, their hair was white and soaked through, like something that had been out of the light for years. One of the men commented that his shoes felt like two loaves of baked bread and then, sighing warmly, added:

"Are you positive this is the right tenement?"

The second old man, Foxe by name, nodded, as if any quick motion might make him catch fire by friction alone. "I saw this woman every day for three days. She'll show up. If she's still alive, that is. Wait till you *see* her, Shaw. Lord! what a case."

"Such an odd business," said Shaw. "If people knew they'd think us Peeping Toms, doddering old fools. Lord, I feel self-conscious standing here."

Foxe leaned on his cane. "Let me do all the talking if—hold on! There she is!" He lowered his voice. "Take a slow look as she comes out."

The tenement front door slammed viciously. A dumpy woman stood at the top of the thirteen porch steps glancing this way and that with angry jerkings of her eyes. Jamming a plump hand in her purse, she seized some crumpled dollar bills, plunged down the steps brutally, and set off down the street in a charge. Behind her, several heads peered from apartment windows above, summoned by her crashing of the door.

"Come on," whispered Foxe. "Here we go to the butcher's."

The woman flung open a butchershop door, rushed in. The two old men had a glimpse of a mouth sticky with raw lipstick. Her eyebrows were like mustaches over her squinting, always suspicious eyes. Abreast of the butchershop, they heard her voice already screaming inside.

"I want a good cut of meat. Let's see what you got hidden to take home for yourself!"

The butcher stood silently in his bloody-fingerprinted frock, his hands empty. The two old men entered behind the woman and pretended to admire a pink loaf of fresh-ground sirloin.

"Them lambchops look sickly!" cried the woman. "What's the price on brains?"

The butcher told her in a low dry voice.

"Well, weigh me a pound of liver!" said the woman. "Keep your thumbs off!"

The butcher weighed it out, slowly.

"Hurry up!" snapped the woman.

The butcher now stood with his hands out of sight below the counter.

"Look," whispered Foxe. Shaw leaned back a trifle to peer below the case.

In one of the butcher's bloody hands, empty before, a silvery meat ax was now clenched tightly, relaxed, clenched tightly, relaxed. The butcher's eyes were blue and dangerously serene above the white porcelain counter while the woman yelled into those eyes and that pink self-contained face.

"Now do you believe?" whispered Foxe. "She really needs our help."

They stared at the raw red cube-steaks for a long time, noticing all the little dents and marks where it had been hit, ten dozen times, by a steel mallet.

The braying continued at the grocer's and the dime store, with the two old men following at a respectful distance.

"Mrs. Death-Wish," said Mr. Foxe quietly. "It's like watching a two-year-old run out on a battlefield. Any moment, you say, she'll hit a mine; bang! Get the temperature just right, too much humidity, everyone itching, sweating, irritable. Along'll come this fine lady, whining, shrieking. And so good-by. Well, Shaw, do we start business?"

"You mean just walk up to her?" Shaw was stunned by his own suggestion. "Oh, but we're not really going to do this, are we? I thought it was sort of a hobby. People, habits, customs, et cetera. It's been fun. But actually mixing in—? We've better things to do."

"Have we?" Foxe nodded down the street to where the woman ran out in front of cars, making them stop with a great squall of brakes, horn-blowing, and cursing. "Are we Christians? Do we let her feed herself subconsciously to the lions? Or do we convert her?"

"Convert her?"

"To love, to serenity, to a longer life. Look at her. Doesn't want to live any more. Deliberately aggravates people. One day soon, someone'll favor her, with a hammer, or strychnine. She's been going down for the third time a long while now. When you're drowning, you get nasty, grab at people, scream. Let's have lunch and lend a hand, eh? Otherwise, our victim will run on until she finds her murderer."

Shaw stood with the sun driving him into the boiling white sidewalk, and it seemed for a moment the street tilted vertically, became a cliff down which the woman fell toward a blazing sky. At last he shook his head.

"You're right," he said. "I wouldn't want her on my conscience."

The sun burnt the paint from the tenement fronts, bleached the air raw and turned the gutter-waters to vapor by mid-afternoon when the old men, numbed and evaporated, stood in the inner passageway of a house that funneled bakery air from front to back in a searing torrent. When they spoke it was the submerged, muffled talk of men in steam rooms, preposterously tired and remote.

The front door opened. Foxe stopped a boy who carried a well-mangled loaf of bread. "Son, we're looking for the woman who gives the door an *awful* slam when she goes out."

"Oh, *her?*" The boy ran upstairs, calling back. "Mrs. Shrike!"

Foxe grabbed Shaw's arm. "Lord, Lord! It can't be true!"

"I want to go home," said Shaw.

"But there it is!" said Foxe, incredulous, tapping his cane on the room-index in the lobby. "Mr. and Mrs. Albert Shrike, 331 upstairs! Husband's a longshoreman, big hulking brute, comes home dirty. Saw them out on Sunday, her jabbering, him never speaking, never looking at her. Oh, come *on*, Shaw."

"It's no use," said Shaw. "You can't help people like her unless they want to be helped. That's the first law of mental health. You know it, I know it. If you get in her way, she'll trample you. Don't be a fool."

"But who's to speak for her—and people like her? Her husband? Her friends? The grocer, the butcher? They'd sing at her wake! Will they tell her she needs a psychiatrist? Does she know it? No. Who knows it? We do. Well, then, you don't keep vital information like that from the victim, do you?"

Shaw took off his sopping hat and gazed bleakly into it. "Once, in biology class, long ago, our teacher asked if we thought we could remove a frog's nervous system, intact, with a scalpel. Take out the whole delicate antennalike structure, with all its little pink thistles and half-invisible ganglions. Impossible, of course. The nervous system's so much a part of the frog there's no way to pull it like a hand from a green glove. You'd destroy the frog, doing it. Well, that's Mrs. Shrike. There's no way to operate on a souring ganglion. Bile is in the vitreous humor of her mad little elephant eyes. You might as well try to get all the saliva out of her mouth forever. It's very sad. But I think we've gone too far already."

"True," said Foxe patiently, earnestly, nodding. "But all I want to do is post a warning. Drop a little seed in her subconscious. Tell her, 'You're a murderee, a victim looking for a place to happen.' One tiny seed I want to plant in her head and hope it'll sprout and flower. A very faint, very poor hope that before it's too late, she'll gather her courage and go see a psychiatrist!"

"It's too hot to talk."

"All the more reason to act! More murders are committed at ninety-two degrees Fahrenheit than any other temperature. Over one hundred, it's too hot to move. Under ninety, cool enough to survive. But right *at* ninety-two degrees lies the apex of irritability, everything is itches and hair and sweat and cooked pork. The brain becomes a rat rushing around a red-hot maze. The least thing, a word, a look, a sound, the drop of a hair and—irritable murder. *Irritable murder*, there's a pretty and terrifying phrase for you. Look at that hall thermometer, eighty-nine degrees. Crawling up toward ninety, itching up toward ninety-one, sweating toward ninety-two an hour, two hours from now. Here's the first flight of stairs. We can rest on each landing. Up we *go!*"

The two old men moved in the third-floor darkness.

"Don't check the numbers," said Foxe. "Let's guess which apartment is hers."

Behind the last door a radio exploded, the ancient paint shuddered and flaked softly onto the worn carpet at their feet. The men watched the entire door jitter with vibration in its grooves.

They looked at each other and nodded grimly.

Another sound cut like an ax through the paneling; a woman, shrieking to someone across town on a telephone.

"No phone necessary. She should just open her window and yell."

Foxe rapped.

The radio blasted out the rest of its song, the voice bellowed. Foxe rapped again, and tested the knob. To his horror the door got free of his grasp and floated swiftly inward, leaving them like actors trapped on-stage when a curtain rises too soon.

"Oh, no!" cried Shaw.

They were buried in a flood of sound. It was like standing in the spillway of a dam and pulling the gate-lever. Instinctively, the old men raised their hands, wincing as if the sound were pure blazing sunlight that burnt their eyes.

The woman (it was indeed Mrs. Shrike!) stood at a wall phone, saliva flying from her mouth at an incredible rate. She showed all of her large white teeth, chunking off her monologue, nostrils flared, a vein in her wet forehead ridged up, pumping, her free hand flexing and unflexing itself. Her eyes were clenched shut as she yelled:

"Tell that damned son-in-law of mine I won't see him, he's a lazy bum!"

Suddenly the woman snapped her eyes wide, some animal instinct having felt rather than heard or seen an intrusion. She continued yelling into the phone, meanwhile piercing her visitors with a glance forged of the coldest steel. She yelled for a full minute longer, then slammed down the receiver and said, without taking a breath: "Well?"

The two men moved together for protection. Their lips moved.

"Speak up!" cried the woman.

"Would you mind," said Foxe, "turning the radio down?"

She caught the word "radio" by lip reading. Still glaring at them out of her sunburnt face, she slapped the radio without looking at it, as one slaps a child that cries all day every day and has become an unseen pattern in life. The radio subsided.

"I'm not buyin' anything!"

She ripped a dog-eared packet of cheap cigarettes like it was a bone with meat on it, snapped one of the cigarettes in her smeared mouth and lit it, sucking greedily on the smoke, jetting it through her thin nostrils until she was a feverish dragon confronting them in a fire-clouded room. "I got work to do. Make your pitch!"

They looked at the magazines spilled like great catches of bright-colored fish on the linoleum floor, the unwashed coffee cup near the broken rocking chair, the tilted, greasy thumb-marked lamps, the smudged windowpanes, the dishes piled in the sink under a steadily dripping, dripping faucet, the cobwebs floating like dead skin in the ceiling corners, and over all of it the thickened smell of life lived too much, too long, with the window down.

They saw the wall thermometer.

Temperature: ninety degrees Fahrenheit.

They gave each other a half-startled look.

"I'm Mr. Foxe, this is Mr. Shaw. We're retired insurance salesmen. We still sell occasionally, to supplement our retirement fund. Most of the time, however, we're taking it easy and—"

"You tryin' to sell me insurance!" She cocked her head at them through the cigarette smoke.

"There's no money connected with this, no."

"Keep talking," she said.

"I hardly know how to begin. May we sit down?" He looked about and decided there wasn't a thing in the room he would trust himself to sit on. "Never mind." He saw she was about to bellow again, so went on swiftly. "We retired after forty years of seeing people from nursery to cemetery gate, you might say. In that time we'd formulated certain opinions. Last year, sitting in the park talking, we put two and two together. We realized that many people didn't have to die so young. With the correct investigation, a new type of Customer's Information might be provided as a sideline by insurance companies . . ."

"I'm not sick," said the woman.

"Oh, but you *are*!" cried Mr. Foxe, and then put two fingers to his mouth in dismay.

"Don't tell *me* what I am!" she cried.

Foxe plunged headlong. "Let me make it clear. People die every day, psychologically speaking. Some part of them gets tired. And that small part tries to kill off the entire person. For example—" He looked about and seized on his first evidence with what amounted to a vast relief. "There! That light bulb in your bathroom, hung right over the tub on frayed wire. Someday you'll slip, make a grab and—pfft!"

Mrs. Albert J. Shrike squinted at the light bulb in the bathroom. "So?"

"People"—Mr. Foxe warmed to his subject, while Mr. Shaw fidgeted, his face now flushed, now dreadfully pale, edged toward the door—"people, like cars, need their brakes checked; their emotional brakes, do you see? Their lights, their batteries, their approaches and responses to life."

Mrs. Shrike snorted. "Your two minutes are up. I haven't learned a damned thing."

Mr. Foxe blinked, first at her, then at the sun burning mercilessly through the dusty windowpanes. Perspiration was running in the soft lines of his face. He chanced a look at the wall thermometer.

"Ninety-one," he said.

"What's eating you, pop?" asked Mrs. Shrike.

"I beg your pardon." He stared in fascination at the red-hot line of mercury firing up the small glass vent across the room. "Sometimes—sometimes we all make wrong turnings. Our choice of marriage partners. A wrong job. No money. Illness. Migraine headaches. Glandular deficiencies. Dozens of little prickly, irritable things. Before you know it, you're taking it out on everyone everywhere."

She was watching his mouth as if he were talking a foreign language; she scowled, she squinted, she tilted her head, her cigarette smoldering in one plump hand.

"We run about screaming, making enemies." Foxe swallowed and glanced away from her. "We make people want to see us—gone—sick—dead, even. People want to hit us, knock us down, shoot us. It's all unconscious, though. You *see?*"

God, it's hot in here, he thought. If there were only one window open. Just one. Just one window open.

Mrs. Shrike's eyes were widening, as if to allow in everything he said.

"Some people are not only accident-prones, which means they want to punish themselves physically, for some crime, usually a petty immorality they think they've long forgotten. But their subconscious puts them in dangerous situations, makes them jaywalk, makes them—" He hesitated and the sweat dripped from his chin. "Makes them ignore frayed electric cords over bathtubs—they're potential victims. It is marked on their faces, hidden like—like tattoos, you might say, on the inner rather than the outer skin. A murderer passing one of these accident-prones, these wishers-after-death, would see the invisible markings, turn, and follow them, instinctively, to the nearest alley. With luck, a potential victim might not happen to cross the tracks of a potential murderer for fifty years. Then—one afternoon—fate! These people, these death-prones, touch all the wrong nerves in passing strangers; they brush the murder in all our breasts."

Mrs. Shrike mashed her cigarette in a dirty saucer, very slowly.

Foxe shifted his cane from one trembling hand to the other. "So it was that a year ago we decided to try to find people who needed help. These are always the people who don't even know they need help, who'd never dream of going to a psychiatrist. At first, I said, we'll make dry runs. Shaw was always against it, save as a hobby, a harmless little quiet thing between ourselves. I suppose you'd say I'm a fool. Well, we've just completed a year of dry runs. We watched two men, studied their environmental factors, their work, marriages, at a discreet distance. None of our business, you say? But each time, the men came to a bad end. One killed in a bar-room. Another pushed out a window. A woman we studied, run down by a streetcar. Coincidence? What about that old man accidentally poisoned? Didn't turn on the bathroom light one night. What was there in his mind that wouldn't let him turn the light on? What made him move in the dark and drink medicine in the dark and die in the hospital next day, protesting he wanted nothing but to live? Evidence, evidence, we have it, we have it. Two dozen cases. Coffins nailed to a good half of them in that little time. No more dry runs; it's time for action, preventative use of data. Time to work *with* people, make friends before the undertaker slips in the side door."

Mrs. Shrike stood as if he had struck her on the head, quite suddenly, with a large weight. Then just her blurred lips moved. "And you came *here?*"

"Well—"

"You've been watching *me?*"

"We only—"

"Following *me?*"

"In order to—"

"Get out!" she said.

"We can—"

"Get out!" she said.

"If you'll only listen—"

"Oh, I *said* this would happen," whispered Shaw, shutting his eyes.

"Dirty old men, get out!" she shouted.

"There's no money involved."

"I'll throw you out, I'll throw you out!" she shrieked, clenching her fists, gritting her teeth. Her face colored insanely. "Who are you, dirty old grandmas, coming her, spying, you old cranks!" she yelled. She seized the straw hat from Mr. Foxe's head; he cried out; she tore the lining from it, cursing. "Get out, get out, get out, get out!" She hurled it to the floor. She crunched one heel through the middle. She kicked it. "Get out, get out!"

"Oh, but you *need* us!" Foxe stared in dismay at the hat as she swore at him in a language that turned corners, blazing, that flew in the air like great searing torches. The woman knew every language and every word in every language. She spoke with fire and alcohol and smoke.

"Who do you think you are? God? God and the Holy Ghost, passing on people, snooping, prying, you old jerks, you old dirty-minded grandmas! You,

you—" She gave them further names, names that forced them toward the door in shock, recoiling. She gave them a long vile list of names without pausing for breath. Then she stopped, gasped, trembled, heaved in a great suction of air, and started a further list of ten dozen even viler names.

"See here!" said Foxe, stiffening.

Shaw was out the door, pleading with his partner to come along, it was over and done, it was as he expected, they were fools, they were everything she said they were, oh, how embarrassing!

"Old maid!" shouted the woman.

"I'll thank you to keep a civil tongue."

"Old maid, old maid!"

Somehow this was worse than all the really vile names.

Foxe swayed, his mouth clapped open, shut, open, shut.

"Old woman!" she cried. "Woman, woman, woman!"

He was in a blazing yellow jungle. The room was drowned in fire, it clenched upon him, the furniture seemed to shift and whirl about, the sunlight shot through the rammed-shut windows, firing the dust, which leaped up from the rug in angry sparks when a fly buzzed a crazy spiral from nowhere; her mouth, a feral red thing, licked the air with all the obscenities collected just behind it in a lifetime, and beyond her on the baked brown wallpaper the thermometer said ninety-two, and he looked again and it said ninety-two, and still the woman screamed like the wheels of a train scraping around a vast iron curve of track; fingernails down a blackboard, and steel across marble. "Old maid! Old maid! Old maid!"

Foxe drew his arm back, cane clenched in fist, very high, and struck.

"No!" cried Shaw in the doorway.

But the woman had slipped and fallen aside, gibbering, clawing the floor. Foxe stood over her with a look of positive disbelief on his face. He looked at his arm and his wrist and his hand and his fingers, each in turn, through a great invisible glaring hot wall of crystal that enclosed him. He looked at the cane as if it was an easily seen and incredible exclamation point come out of nowhere to the center of the room. His mouth stayed open, the dust fell in silent embers, dead. He felt the blood drop from his face as if a small door had banged wide into his stomach. "I—"

She frothed.

Scrabbling about, every part of her seemed a separate animal. Her arms and legs, her hands, her head, each was a lopped-off bit of some creature wild to return to itself, but blind to the proper way of making that return. Her mouth still gushed out her sickness with words and sounds that were not even faintly words. It had been in her a long time, a long long time. Foxe looked upon her, in a state of shock, himself. Before today, she had spat her venom out, here, there, another place. Now he had loosed the flood of a lifetime and he felt in danger of drowning here. He sensed someone pulling him by his coat. He saw the door sills pass on either side. He heard the cane fall and rattle like a thin bone far away from his hand, which seemed to have been stung by some terrible unseen wasp. And then he was out, walking mechanically, down through the burning tenement, between the scorched walls. Her voice crashed like a guillotine down the stair. "Get out! Get out! Get *out*!"

Fading like the wail of a person dropped down an open well into darkness.

At the bottom of the last flight, near the street door, Foxe turned himself loose from this other man here, and for a long moment leaned against the wall, his eyes wet, able to do nothing but moan. His hands, while he did this, moved in the air to find the lost cane, moved on his head, touched at his moist eyelids, amazed, and fluttered away. They sat on the bottom hall step for ten minutes in silence, drawing sanity into their lungs with every shuddering breath. Finally Mr. Foxe looked over at Mr. Shaw, who had been staring at him in wonder and fright for the full ten minutes.

"Did you *see* what I did? Oh, oh, that was close. Close. Close." He shook his head. "I'm a fool. That poor, poor woman. She was right."

"There's nothing to be done."

"I see that now. It had to fall on me."

"Here, wipe your face. That's better."

"Do you think she'll tell Mr. Shrike about us?"

"No, no."

"Do you think we could—"

"Talk to *him*?"

They considered this and shook their heads. They opened the front door to a gush of furnace heat and were almost knocked down by a huge man who strode between them.

"Look where you're going!" he cried.

They turned and watched the man move ponderously, in fiery darkness, one step at a time, up into the tenement house, a creature with the ribs of a mastodon and the head of an unshorn lion, with great beefed arms, irritably hairy, painfully sunburnt. The face they had seen briefly as he shouldered past was a sweating, raw, sunblistered pork face, salt droplets under the red eyes, dripping from the chin; great smears of perspiration stained the man's armpits, coloring his tee-shirt to the waist.

They shut the tenement door gently.

"That's him," said Mr. Foxe. "That's the husband."

They stood in the little store across from the tenement. It was five-thirty, the sun tilting down the sky, the shadows the color of hot summer grapes under the rare few trees and in the alleys.

"What was it, hanging out of the husband's back pocket?"

"Longshoreman's hook. Steel. Sharp, heavy-looking. Like those claws one-armed men used to wear on the end of their stumps, years ago."

Mr. Foxe did not speak.

"What's the temperature?" asked Mr. Foxe, a minute later, as if he were too tired to turn his head to look.

"Store thermometer still reads ninety-two. Ninety-two right on the nose."

Foxe sat on a packing crate, making the least motion to hold an orange soda bottle in his fingers. "Cool off," he said. "Yes, I need an orange pop very much, right now."

They sat there in the furnace, looking up at one special tenement window for a long time, waiting, waiting . . .

The Emissary

Martin knew it was autumn again, for Dog ran into the house bringing wind and frost and a smell of apples turned to cider under trees. In dark clock-springs of hair, Dog fetched goldenrod, dust of farewell-summer, acorn-husk, hair of squirrel, feather of departed robin, sawdust from fresh-cut cordwood, and leaves like charcoals shaken from a blaze of maple trees. Dog jumped. Showers of brittle fern, blackberry vine, marsh-grass sprang over the bed where Martin shouted. No doubt, no doubt of it at all, this incredible beast was October!

"Here, boy, here!"

And Dog settled to warm Martin's body with all the bonfires and subtle burnings of the season, to fill the room with soft or heavy, wet or dry odors of far-traveling. In spring, he smelled of lilac, iris, lawn-mowered grass; in summer, ice-cream-mustached, he came pungent with firecracker, Roman candle, pinwheel, baked by the sun. But autumn! Autumn!

"Dog, what's it like outside?"

And lying there, Dog told as he always told. Lying there, Martin found autumn as in the old days before sickness bleached him white on his bed. Here was his contact, his carry-all, the quick-moving part of himself he sent with a yell to run and return, circle and scent, collect and deliver the time and texture of worlds in town, country, by creek, river, lake, down-cellar, up-attic, in closet or coal-bin. Ten dozen times a day he was gifted with sunflower seed, cinderpath, milkweed, horse-chestnut, or full flame-smell of pumpkin. Through the loomings of the universe Dog shuttled; the design was hid in his pelt. Put out your hand, it was there . . . .

"And where did you go this morning?"

But he knew without hearing where Dog had rattled down hills where autumn lay in cereal crispness, where children lay in funeral pyres, in rustling heaps, the leaf-buried but watchful dead, as Dog and the world blew by. Martin trembled as his fingers searched the thick fur, read the long journey. Through stubbled fields, over glitters of ravine creek, down marbled spread of cemetery yard, into woods. In the great season of spices and rare incense, now Martin ran through his emissary, around, about, and home!

The bedroom door opened.

"That dog of yours is in trouble again."

Mother brought in a tray of fruit salad, cocoa, and toast, her blue eyes snapping.

"Mother . . ."

"Always digging places. Dug a hole in Miss Tarkin's garden this morning. She's spittin' mad. That's the fourth hole he's dug there this week."

"Maybe he's looking for something."

"Fiddlesticks, he's too darned curious. If he doesn't behave he'll be locked up."

Martin looked at this woman as if she were a stranger. "Oh, you wouldn't do that! How would I learn anything? How would I find things out if Dog didn't tell me?"

Mom's voice was quieter. "Is that what he does—tell you things?"

"There's nothing I don't know when he goes out and around and back, *nothing* I can't find out from him!"

They both sat looking at Dog and the dry strewings of mold and seed over the quilt.

"Well, if he'll just stop digging where he shouldn't, he can run all he wants," said Mother.

"Here, boy, here!"

And Martin snapped a tin note to the dog's collar:

MY OWNER IS MARTIN SMITH—TEN YEARS OLD—
SICK IN BED—VISITORS WELCOME.

Dog barked. Mother opened the downstairs door and let him out.

Martin sat listening.

Far off and away you could hear Dog run in the quiet autumn rain that was falling now. You could hear the barking-jingling fade, rise, fade again as he cut down alley, over lawn, to fetch back Mr. Holloway and the oiled metallic smell of the delicate snowflake-interiored watches he repaired in his home shop. Or maybe he would bring Mr. Jacobs, the grocer, whose clothes were rich with lettuce, celery, tomatoes, and the secret tinned and hidden smell of the red demons stamped on cans of deviled ham. Mr. Jacobs and his unseen pink-meat devils waved often from the yard below. Or Dog brought Mr. Jackson, Mrs. Gillespie, Mr. Smith, Mrs. Holmes, *any* friend or near-friend, encountered, cornered, begged, worried, and at last shepherded home for lunch, or tea-and-biscuits.

Now, listening, Martin heard Dog below, with footsteps moving in a light rain behind him. The downstairs bell rang, Mom opened the door, light voices murmured. Martin sat forward, face shining. The stair treads creaked. A young woman's voice laughed quietly. Miss Haight, of course, his teacher from school!

The bedroom door sprang open.

Martin had company.

Morning, afternoon, evening, dawn and dusk, sun and moon circled with Dog, who faithfully reported temperatures of turf and air, color of earth and tree, consistency of mist or rain, but—most important of all—brought back again and again and again—Miss Haight.

On Saturday, Sunday and Monday she baked Martin orange-iced cupcakes, brought him library books about dinosaurs and cave men. On Tuesday, Wednesday and Thursday somehow he beat her at dominoes, somehow she lost at checkers, and soon, she cried, he'd defeat her handsomely at chess. On Friday, Saturday and Sunday they talked and never stopped talking, and she was so young and laughing and handsome and her hair was a soft, shining brown like the season outside the window, and she walked clear, clean and quick, a heart-beat warm in the bitter afternoon when he heard it. Above all, she had the secret of signs, and could read and interpret Dog and the symbols she searched out and plucked forth from his coat with her miraculous fingers. Eyes shut, softly laughing, in a gypsy's voice, she divined the world from the treasures in her hands.

And on Monday afternoon, Miss Haight was dead.

Martin sat up in bed, slowly.

"Dead?" he whispered.

Dead, said his mother, yes, dead, killed in an auto accident a mile out of town. Dead, yes, dead, which meant cold to Martin, which meant silence and whiteness and winter come long before its time. Dead, silent, cold, white. The thoughts circled round, blew down, and settled in whispers.

Martin held Dog, thinking; turned to the wall. The lady with the autumn-colored hair. The lady with the laughter that was very gentle and never made fun and the eyes that watched your mouth to see everything you ever said. The-other-half-of-autumn-lady, who told what was left untold by Dog, about the world. The heartbeat at the still center of gray afternoon. The heartbeat fading . . .

"Mom? What do they do in the graveyard, Mom, under the ground? Just lay there?"

"*Lie* there."

"Lie there? Is that *all* they do? It doesn't sound like much fun."

"For goodness sake, it's not made out to be fun."

"Why don't they jump up and run around once in a while if they get tired lying there? God's pretty silly—"

"Martin!"

"Well, you'd think He'd treat people better than to tell them to lie still for keeps. That's impossible. Nobody can do it! I tried once. Dog tries. I tell him, 'Dead Dog!' He plays dead awhile, then gets sick and tired and wags his tail or opens one eye and looks at me, bored. Boy, I bet sometimes those graveyard people do the same, huh, Dog?"

Dog barked.

"Be still with that kind of talk!" said Mother.

Martin looked off into space.

"Bet that's exactly what they do," he said.

Autumn burnt the trees bare and ran Dog still farther around, fording creek, prowling graveyard as was his custom, and back in the dusk to fire off volleys of barking that shook windows wherever he turned.

In the late last days of October, Dog began to act as if the wind had changed and blew from a strange country. He stood quivering on the porch below. He whined, his eyes fixed at the empty land beyond town. He brought no visitors for Martin. He stood for hours each day, as if leashed, trembling, then shot away straight, as if someone had called. Each night he returned later, with no one following. Each night, Martin sank deeper and deeper in his pillow.

"Well, people are busy," said Mother. "They haven't time to notice the tag Dog carries. Or they mean to come visit, but forget."

But there was more to it than that. There was the fevered shining in Dog's eyes, and his whimpering tic late at night, in some private dream. His shivering in the dark, under the bed. The way he sometimes stood half the night, looking at Martin as if some great and impossible secret was his and he knew no way to tell it save by savagely thumping his tail, or turning in endless circles, never to lie down, spinning and spinning again.

On October thirtieth, Dog ran out and didn't come back at all, even when after supper Martin heard his parents call and call. The hour grew late, the streets and sidewalks stood empty, the air moved cold about the house and there was nothing, nothing.

Long after midnight, Martin lay watching the world beyond the cool, clear glass windows. Now there was not even autumn, for there was no Dog to fetch it in. There would be no winter, for who could bring the snow to melt in your hands? Father? Mother? No, not the same. They couldn't play the game with its special secrets and rules, its sounds and pantomimes. No more seasons. No more time. The go-between, the emissary, was lost to the wild throngings of civilization, poisoned, stolen, hit by a car, left somewhere in a culvert. . . .

Sobbing, Martin turned his face to his pillow. The world was a picture under glass, untouchable. The world was dead.

Martin twisted in bed and in three days the last Hallowe'en pumpkins were rotting in trash cans, papier-mâché skulls and witches were burnt on bonfires, and ghosts were stacked on shelves with other linens until next year.

To Martin, Hallowe'en had been nothing more than one evening when tin horns cried off in the cold autumn stars, children blew like goblin leaves along the flinty walks, flinging their heads, or cabbages, at porches, soap-writing names or similar magic symbols on icy windows. All of it as distant, unfathomable, and nightmarish as a puppet show seen from so many miles away that there is no sound or meaning.

For three days in November, Martin watched alternate light and shadow sift across his ceiling. The fire-pageant was over forever; autumn lay in cold ashes. Martin sank deeper, yet deeper in white marble layers of bed, motionless, listening always listening. . . .

Friday evening, his parents kissed him goodnight and walked out of the house into the hushed cathedral weather toward a motion-picture show. Miss Tarkin from next door stayed on in the parlor below until Martin called down he was sleepy, then took her knitting off home.

In silence, Martin lay following the great move of stars down a clear and moonlit sky, remembering nights such as this when he'd spanned the town with Dog ahead, behind, around about, tracking the green-plush ravine, lapping slumbrous streams gone milky with the fullness of the moon, leaping cemetery tombstones while whispering the marble names; on, quickly on, through shaved meadows where the only motion was the off-on quivering of stars, to streets where shadows would not stand aside for you but crowded all the sidewalks for mile on mile. Run now run! chasing, being chased by bitter smoke, fog, mist, wind, ghost of mind, fright of memory; home, safe, sound, snug-warm, asleep. . . .

Nine o'clock.

Chime. The drowsy clock in the deep stairwell below. Chime.

Dog, come home, and run the world with you. Dog, bring a thistle with frost on it, or bring nothing else but the wind. Dog, where *are* you? Oh, listen, now, I'll call.

Martin held his breath.

Way off somewhere—a sound.

Martin rose up, trembling.

There, again—the sound.

So small a sound, like a sharp needle-point brushing the sky long miles and many miles away.

The dreamy echo of a dog—barking.

The sound of a dog crossing fields and farms, dirt roads and rabbit paths, running, running, letting out great barks of steam, cracking the night. The sound of a circling dog which came and went, lifted and faded, opened up, shut in, moved forward, went back, as if the animal were kept by someone on a fantastically long chain. As if the dog were running and someone whistled under the chestnut trees, in mold-shadow, tar-shadow, moon-shadow, walking, and the dog circled back and sprang out again toward home.

Dog! Martin thought. Oh Dog, come home, boy! Listen, oh, listen, where you *been*? Come on, boy, make tracks!

Five, ten, fifteen minutes; near, very near, the bark, the sound. Martin cried out, thrust his feet from the bed, leaned to the window. Dog! Listen, boy! Dog! Dog! He said it over and over. Dog! Dog! Wicked Dog, run off and gone all these days! Bad Dog, good Dog, home, boy, hurry, and bring what you can!

Near now, near, up the street, barking, to knock clapboard housefronts with sound, whirl iron cocks on rooftops in the moon, firing off volleys—Dog! now at the door below. . . .

Martin shivered.

Should he run—let Dog in, or wait for Mom and Dad? Wait? Oh, God, wait? But what if Dog ran off again? No, he'd go down, snatch the door wide, yell, grab Dog in, and run upstairs so fast, laughing, crying, holding tight, that . . .

Dog stopped barking.

Hey! Martin almost broke the window, jerking to it.

Silence. As if someone had told Dog to hush now, hush, hush.

A full minute passed. Martin clenched his fists.

Below, a faint whimpering.

Then, slowly, the downstairs front door opened. Someone was kind enough to have opened the door for Dog. Of course! Dog had brought Mr. Jacobs or Mr. Gillespie or Miss Tarkin, or . . .

The downstairs door shut.

Dog raced upstairs, whining, flung himself on the bed.

"Dog, Dog, where've you *been*, what've you *done*! Dog, Dog!"

And he crushed Dog hard and long to himself, weeping. Dog, Dog. He laughed and shouted. Dog! But after a moment he stopped laughing and crying, suddenly.

He pulled back away. He held the animal and looked at him, eyes widening.

The odor coming from Dog was different.

It was a smell of strange earth. It was a smell of night within night, the smell of digging down deep in shadow through earth that had lain cheek by jowl with things that were long hidden and decayed. A stinking and rancid soil fell away in clods of dissolution from Dog's muzzle and paws. He had dug deep. He had dug very deep indeed. That *was* it, wasn't it? wasn't it? *wasn't* it!

What kind of message was this from Dog? What could such a message mean? The stench—the ripe and awful cemetery earth.

Dog was a bad dog, digging where he shouldn't. Dog was a good dog, always making friends. Dog loved people. Dog brought them home.

And now, moving up the dark hall stairs, at intervals, came the sound of feet, one foot dragged after the other, painfully, slowly, slowly, slowly.

Dog shivered. A rain of strange night earth fell seething on the bed.

Dog turned.

The bedroom door whispered in.

Martin had company.

The Jar

It was one of those things they keep in a jar in the tent of a sideshow on the outskirts of a little, drowsy town. One of those pale things drifting in alcohol plasma, forever dreaming and circling, with its peeled, dead eyes staring out at you and never seeing you. It went with the noiselessness of late night, and only the crickets chirping, the frogs sobbing off in the moist swampland. One of those things in a big jar that makes your stomach jump as it does when you see a preserved arm in a laboratory vat.

Charlie stared back at it for a long time.

A long time, his big, raw hands, hairy on the roofs of them, clenching the rope that kept back curious people. He had paid his dime and now he stared.

It was getting late. The merry-go-round drowsed down to a lazy mechanical tinkle. Tent-peggers back of a canvas smoked and cursed over a poker game. Lights switched out, putting a summer gloom over the carnival. People streamed homeward in cliques and queues. Somewhere, a radio flared up, then cut, leaving the Louisiana sky wide and silent with stars.

There was nothing in the world for Charlie but that pale thing sealed in its universe of serum. Charlie's loose mouth hung open in a pink weal, teeth showing; his eyes were puzzled, admiring, wondering.

Someone walked in the shadows behind him, small beside Charlie's gaunt tallness. "Oh," said the shadow, coming into the light-bulb glare. "You still here, bud?"

"Yeah," said Charlie, like a man in his sleep.

The carny-boss appreciated Charlie's curiosity. He nodded at his old acquaintance in the jar. "Everybody likes it; in a peculiar kinda way, I mean."

Charlie rubbed his long jawbone. "You—uh—ever consider sellin' it?"

The carny-boss's eyes dilated, then closed. He snorted. "Naw. It brings customers. They like seeing stuff like that. Sure."

Charlie made a disappointed, "Oh."

"Well," considered the carny-boss, "if a guy had money, maybe—"

"How much money?"

"If a guy had—" The carny-boss estimated, counting fingers, watching Charlie as he tacked it out one finger after another. "If a guy had three, four, say, maybe seven or eight—"

Charlie nodded with each motion, expectantly. Seeing this, the carny-boss raised his total, "—maybe ten dollars or maybe fifteen—"

Charlie scowled, worried. The carny-boss retreated. "Say a guy has *twelve* dollars—"

Charlie grinned. "Why he could buy that thing in that jar," concluded the carny-boss.

"Funny thing," said Charlie, "I got just twelve bucks in my denims. And I been reckoning how looked-up-to I'd be back down at Wilder's Hollow if I brung home something like this to set on my shelf over the table. The folks would sure look up to me then, I bet."

"*Well*, now, listen here—," said the carny-boss.

The sale was completed with the jar put on the back seat of Charlie's wagon. The horse skittered his hoofs when he saw the jar, and whinnied.

The carny-boss glanced up with an expression of, almost, relief. "I was tired of seeing that damn thing around, anyway. Don't thank me. Lately I been thinking things about it, funny things—but, hell, I'm a big-mouthed so-and-so. S'long, farmer!"

Charlie drove off. The naked blue light bulbs withdrew like dying stars, the open, dark country night of Louisiana swept in around wagon and horse. There was just Charlie, the horse timing his gray hoofs, and the crickets.

And the jar behind the high seat.

It sloshed back and forth, back and forth. Sloshed wet. And the cold gray thing drowsily slumped against the glass, looking out, looking out, but seeing nothing, nothing.

Charlie leaned back to pet the lid. Smelling of strange liquor his hand returned, changed and cold and trembling, excited. *Yes, sir!* he thought to himself, *Yes, sir!*

Slosh, slosh, slosh. . . .

In the Hollow, numerous grass-green and blood-red lanterns tossed dusty light over men huddled, murmuring, spitting, sitting on General Store property.

They knew the creak-bumble of Charlie's wagon and did not shift their raw, drab-haired skulls as he rocked to a halt. Their cigars were glowworms, their voices were frog mutterings on summer nights.

Charlie leaned down eagerly. "Hi, Clem! Hi, Milt!"

" 'Lo, Charlie. 'Lo, Charlie," they murmured. The political conflict continued. Charlie cut it down the seam:

"I got somethin' here. I got somethin' you might wanna see!"

Tom Carmody's eyes glinted, green in the lamplight, from the General Store porch. It seemed to Charlie that Tom Carmody was forever installed under porches in shadow, or under trees in shadow, or if in a room, then in the farthest niche shining his eyes out at you from the dark. You never knew what his face was doing, and his eyes were always funning you. And every time they looked at you they laughed a different way.

"You ain't got nothin' we wants to see, baby-doll."

Charlie made a fist and looked at it. "Somethin' in a jar," he went on. "Looks kine a like a brain, kine a like a pickled jellyfish, kine a like—well, come see yourself!"

Someone snicked a cigar into a fall of pink ash and ambled over to look. Charlie grandly elevated the jar lid, and in the uncertain lantern light the man's face changed. "Hey, now, what in hell *is* this—?"

It was the first thaw of the evening. Others shifted lazily upright, leaned forward; gravity pulled them into walking. They made no effort, except to put one shoe before the other to keep from collapsing upon their unusual faces. They circled the jar and contents. And Charlie, for the first time in his life, seized on some hidden strategy and crashed the glass lid shut.

"You want to see more, drop aroun' my house! It'll be there," he declared, generously.

Tom Carmody spat from out his porch eyrie. "Ha!"

"Lemme see that again!" cried Gramps Medknowe. "Is it a octopus?"

Charlie flapped the reins; the horse stumbled into action.

"Come on aroun'! You're welcome!"

"What'll your wife say?"

"She'll kick the tar off'n our heels!"

But Charlie and wagon were gone over the hill. The men stood, all of them, chewing their tongues, squinting up the road in the dark. Tom Carmody swore softly from the porch. . . .

Charlie climbed the steps of his shack and carried the jar to its throne in the living room, thinking that from now on this lean-to would be a palace, with an "emperor"—that was the word! "emperor"—all cold and white and quiet drifting in his private pool, raised, elevated upon a shelf over a ramshackle table.

The jar, as he watched, burnt off the cold mist that hung over this place on the rim of the swamp.

"What you got there?"

Thedy's thin soprano turned him from his awe. She stood in the bedroom door glaring out, her thin body clothed in faded blue gingham, her hair drawn to a drab knot behind red ears. Her eyes were faded like the gingham. "Well," she repeated. "What is it?"

"What's it look like to you, Thedy?"

She took a thin step forward, making a slow, indolent pendulum of hips, her eyes intent upon the jar, her lips drawn back to show feline milk teeth.

The dead pale thing hung in its serum.

Thedy snapped a dull-blue glance at Charlie, then back to the jar, once more at Charlie, once more to the jar, then she whirled quickly:

"It—it looks—looks just like *you*, Charlie!" she cried.

The bedroom door slammed.

The reverberation did not disturb the jar's contents. But Charlie stood there, longing after his wife, heart pounding frantically. Much later, when his heart slowed, he talked to the thing in the jar.

"I work the bottom land to the butt-bone every year, and she grabs the money and runs off down home visitin' her folks nine weeks at a stretch. I can't keep hold of her. Her and the men from the store, they make fun of me. I can't help it if I don't know a way to hold on to her! Damn, but I *try*!"

Philosophically, the contents of the jar gave no advice.

"Charlie?"

Someone stood in the front-yard door.

Charlie turned, startled, then broke out a grin.

It was some of the men from the General Store.

"Uh—Charlie—we—we thought—well—we came up to have a look at that—stuff—you got in that there jar—"

July passed warm and it was August.

For the first time in years, Charlie was happy as tall corn growing after a drought. It was gratifying of an evening to hear boots shushing through the tall grass, the sound of men spitting into the ditch prior to setting foot on the porch, the sound of heavy bodies creaking the boards, and the groan of the house as yet another shoulder leaned against its frame door and another voice said, as a hairy wrist wiped a mouth clean:

"Kin I come in?"

With elaborate casualness, Charlie'd invite the arrivals in. There'd be chairs, soapboxes for all, or at least carpets to squat on. And by the time crickets were itching their legs into a summertime humming and frogs were throat-swollen like ladies with goiters shouting in the great night, the room would be full to bursting with people from all the bottom lands.

At first nobody would say anything. The first half-hour of such an evening, while people came in and got settled, was spent in carefully rolling cigarettes. Putting tobacco neatly into the rut of brown paper, loading it, tamping it, as they loaded and tamped and rolled their thoughts and fears and amazement for the evening. It gave them time to think. You could see their brains working behind their eyes as they fingered the cigarettes into smoking order.

It was kind of a rude church gathering. They sat, squatted, leaned on plaster walls, and one by one, with reverent awe, they stared at the jar upon its shelf.

They wouldn't stare sudden-like. No, they kind of did it slow, casual, as if they were glancing around the room—letting their eyes fumble over just *any* old object that happened into their consciousness.

And—just by accident, of course—the focus of their wandering eyes would occur always at the same place. After a while all eyes in the room would be fastened to it, like pins stuck in some incredible pincushion. And the only sound would be someone sucking a corncob. Or the children's barefooted scurry on the porch planks outside. Maybe some woman's voice would come, "You kids git away, now! Git!" And with a giggle like soft, quick water, the bare feet would rush off to scare the bullfrogs.

Charlie would be up front, naturally, on his rocking chair, a plaid pillow under his lean rump, rocking slow, enjoying the fame and looked-up-to-ness that came with keeping the jar.

Thedy, she'd be seen way back of the room with the womenfolk in a bunch, all gray and quiet, abiding their men.

Thedy looked like she was ripe for jealous screaming. But she said nothing, just watched men tromp into her living room and sit at the feet of Charlie, staring at this here Holy Grail–like thing, and her lips were set cold and hard and she spoke not a civil word to anybody.

After a period of proper silence, someone, maybe old Gramps Medknowe from Crick Road, would clear the phlegm from a deep cave somewhere inside himself, lean forward, blinking, wet his lips, maybe, and there'd be a curious tremble in his calloused fingers.

This would cue everyone to get ready for the talking to come. Ears were primed. People settled like sows in the warm mud after a rain.

Gramps looked a long while, measured his lips with a lizard tongue, then settled back and said, like always, in a high, thin, old-man's tenor:

"Wonder what it is? Wonder if it's a he or a she or just a plain old *it*? Sometimes I wake up nights, twist on my corn-mattin', think about that jar settin' here in the long dark. Think about it hangin' in liquid, peaceful and pale like an animal oyster. Sometimes I wake Maw and we both think on it. . . . "

While talking, Gramps moved his fingers in a quavering pantomime. Everybody watched his thick thumb weave, and the other heavy-nailed fingers undulate.

" . . . We both lay there, thinkin'. And we shivers. Maybe a hot night, trees sweatin', mosquitoes too hot to fly, but we shivers jest the same, and turn over, tryin' to sleep. . . . "

Gramps lapsed back into silence, as if his speech was enough from him, let some other voice talk the wonder, awe, and strangeness.

Juke Marmer, from Willow Sump, wiped sweat off his palms on the round of his knees and softly said:

"I remember when I was a runnel-nosed kid. We had a cat who was all the time makin' kittens. Lordamighty, she'd a litter any time she jumped around and skipped a fence—" Juke spoke in a kind of holy softness, benevolent. "Well, we give the kittens away, but when this one particular litter busted out, everybody within walkin' distance had one-two our cats by gift, already.

"So Ma busied on the back porch with a big two-gallon glass jar, fillin' it to the top with water. Ma said, 'Juke, you drown them kittens!' I 'member I stood there; the kittens mewed, runnin' 'round, blind, small, helpless, and funny— just beginnin' to get their eyes open. I looked at Ma, I said, 'Not *me*, Ma! *You* do it!' But Ma turned pale and said it had to be done and I was the only one handy. And she went off to stir gravy and fix chicken. I—I picked up one— kitten. I held it. It was warm. It made a mewin' sound, I felt like runnin' away, not ever comin' back."

Juke nodded his head now, eyes bright, young, seeing into the past, making it new, shaping it with words, smoothing it with his tongue.

"I dropped the kitten in the water. The kitten closed his eyes, opened his mouth, tryin' for air. I 'member how the little white fangs showed, the pink tongue came out, and bubbles with it, in a line to the top of the water!

"I know to this day the way that kitten floated after it was all over, driftin' aroun', slow and not worryin', lookin' out at me, not condemnin' me for what I done. But not likin' me, neither. Ahhhh. . . . "

Hearts jumped quick. Eyes swiveled from Juke to the shelved jar, back down, up again apprehensively.

A pause.

Jahdoo, the black man from Heron Swamp, tossed his ivory eyeballs, like a dusky juggler, in his head. His dark knuckles knotted and flexed—grasshoppers alive.

"You know what that is? You know, you *know*? I tells you. That be the center of Life, sure 'nuff! Lord believe me, it so!"

Swaying in a tree-like rhythm, Jahdoo was blown by a swamp wind no one could see, hear or feel, save himself. His eyeballs went around again, as if cut free to wander. His voice needled a dark thread pattern, picking up each person by the lobes of their ears and sewing them into one unbreathing design:

"From that, lyin' back in the Middibamboo Sump, all sort o'thing crawl. It put out hand, it put out feet, it put out tongue an' horn an' it grow. Little bitty amoeba, perhap. Then a frog with a bulge-throat fit ta bust! Yah!" He cracked knuckles. "It slobber on up to its gummy joints and it—it *am human*! That am the center of creation! That am Middibamboo Mama, from which we all come ten thousand year ago. Believe it!"

"Ten thousand year ago!" whispered Granny Carnation.

"It am old! Looky it! It donn worra no more. It know betta. It hang like pork chop in fryin' fat. It got eye to see with, but it donn blink 'em, they donn look fretted, does they? No, man! It know betta. It know that we done come *from* it, and we is goin' back *to* it."

"What color eyes it got?"

"Gray."

"Naw, *green!*"

"What color hair? Brown?"

"Black!"

"Red!"

"No, *gray!*"

Then Charlie would give his drawling opinion. Some nights he'd say the same thing, some nights not. It didn't matter. When you said the same thing night after night in the deep summer, it always sounded different. The crickets changed it. The frogs changed it. The thing in the jar changed it. Charlie said:

"What if an old man went back into the swamp, or maybe a young kid, and wandered aroun' for years and years lost in all that drippin', on the trails and gullies, in them old wet ravines in the nights, skin a-turnin' pale, and makin' cold and shrivelin' up. Bein' away from the sun he'd keep witherin' away up and up and finally sink into a muck-hole and lay in a kind of—scum—like the maggot 'skeeters sleepin' in sump-water. Why, why—for all we can tell, this might be someone we *know!* Someone we passed words with once on a time. For all we know—"

A hissing from among the womenfolk back in the shadow. One woman standing, eyes shining black, fumbled for words. Her name was Mrs. Tridden, and she murmured:

"Lots of little kids run stark naked to the swamp ever' year. They runs around and never comes back. I almost got lost maself. I—I lost my little boy, Foley, that way. You—you *don't suppose*!!!"

Breath was snatched through nostrils, constricted, tightened. Mouths turned down at corners, bent by hard, clinching muscle. Heads turned on celery-stalk necks, and eyes read her horror and hope. It was in Mrs. Tridden's body, wire-taut, holding to the wall back of her with straight fingers stiff.

"My baby," she whispered. She breathed it out. "My baby. My Foley. Foley! Foley, is that you? Foley! Foley, tell me, baby, is that YOU!"

Everybody held their breath, turning to see the jar.

The thing in the jar said nothing. It just stared blind-white out upon the multitude. And deep in rawboned bodies a secret fear-juice ran like a spring thaw, and their resolute calmness and belief and easy humbleness was gnawed and eaten by that juice and melted away in a torrent! Someone screamed.

"It moved!"

"No, no, it didn' move. Just your eyes playin' tricks!"

"Hones' ta God!" cried Juke. "I saw it shift slow like a dead kitten!"

"Hush up, now. It's been dead a long, long time. Maybe since before you was born!"

"He made a sign!" screamed Mrs. Tridden. "That's my Foley! My baby you got there! Three-year-old he was! My baby lost and gone in the swamp!"

The sobbing broke from her.

"Now, Mrs. Tridden. There now. Set yourself down, stop shakin'. Ain't no more your child'n mine. There, there."

One of the womenfolk held her and faded out the sobbing into jerked breathing and a fluttering of her lips in butterfly quickness as the breath stroked over them, afraid.

When all was quiet again, Granny Carnation, with a withered pink flower in her shoulder-length gray hair, sucked the pipe in her trap mouth and talked around it, shaking her head to make the hair dance in the light:

"All this talkin' and shovin' words. Like as not we'll never find out, never know what it is. Like as not if we found out we wouldn't *want* to know. It's like magic tricks magicians do at shows. Once you find the fake, ain't no more fun'n the innards of a jackbob. We come collectin' around here every ten nights or so, talkin', social-like, with somethin', always somethin', to talk about. Stands to reason if we spied out what the damn thing is there'd be nothin' to chew about, so there!"

"Well, damn it to hell!" rumbled a bull voice. "I don't think it's nothin'!"

Tom Carmody.

Tom Carmody standing, as always, in shadow. Out on the porch, just his eyes staring in, his lips laughing at you dimly, mocking. His laughter got inside Charlie like a hornet sting. Thedy had put him up to it. Thedy was trying to kill Charlie's new life, she was!

"Nothin'," repeated Carmody, harshly, "in that jar but a bunch of old jellyfish from Sea Cove, a-rottin' and stinkin' fit to whelp!"

"You mightn't be jealous, Cousin Carmody?" asked Charlie, slow.

"Haw!" snorted Carmody. "I just come aroun' ta watch you dumb fools jaw about nuthin'. You notice I never set foot inside or took part. I'm goin' home right now. Anybody wanna come along with me?"

He got no offer of company. He laughed again, as if this were a bigger joke, how so many people could be so far gone, and Thedy was raking her palms with her fingernails away back in a corner of the room. Charlie saw her mouth twitch and was cold and could not speak.

Carmody, still laughing, rapped off the porch with his high-heeled boots and the sound of crickets took him away.

Granny Carnation gummed her pipe. "Like I was sayin' before the storm: that thing on the shelf, why couldn't it be sort of—all things? Lots of things. All kinds of life—death—I don't know. Mix rain and sun and muck and jelly, all that together. Grass and snakes and children and mist and all the nights and days in the dead canebrake. Why's it have to be *one* thing? Maybe it's *lots*."

And the talking ran soft for another hour, and Thedy slipped away into the night on the track of Tom Carmody, and Charlie began to sweat. They were up to something, those two. They were planning something. Charlie sweated warm all the rest of the evening. . . .

The meeting broke up late, and Charlie bedded down with mixed emotions. The meeting had gone off well, but what about Thedy and Tom?

Very late, with certain star coveys shuttled down the sky marking the time as after midnight, Charlie heard the slushing of the tall grass parted by her penduluming hips. Her heels tacked soft across the porch, into the house, into the bedroom.

She lay soundlessly in bed, cat eyes staring at him. He couldn't see them, but he could feel them staring.

"Charlie?"

He waited.

Then he said, "I'm awake."

Then she waited.

"Charlie?"

"What?"

"Bet you don't know where I been; bet you don't know where I been." It was a faint, derisive singsong in the night.

He waited.

She waited again. She couldn't bear waiting long, though, and continued:

"I been to the carnival over in Cape City. Tom Carmody drove me. We—we talked to the carny-boss, Charlie, we did, we did, we *sure* did!" And she sort of giggled to herself, secretly.

Charlie was ice-cold. He stirred upright on an elbow.

She said, "We found out what it is in your jar, Charlie—" insinuatingly.

Charlie flumped over, hands to ears. "I don't wanna hear!"

"Oh, but you gotta hear, Charlie. It's a good joke. Oh, it's rare, Charlie," she hissed.

"Go away," he said.

"Unh-unh! No, no, sir, Charlie. Why, no, Charlie—honey. Not until I tell!"

"Git!" he said.

"Let me tell! We talked to that carny-boss, and he—he liked to die laughin'. He said he sold that jar and what was in it to some, some—hick—for twelve bucks. And it ain't worth more'n two bucks at most!"

Laughter bloomed in the dark, right out of her mouth, an awful kind of laughter.

She finished it, quick:

"It's just junk, Charlie! Rubber, papier-mâché, silk, cotton, boric acid! That's all! Got a metal frame inside! That's all it is, Charlie. That's all!" she shrilled.

"No, no!"

He sat up swiftly, ripping sheets apart in big fingers, roaring.

"I don't wanna hear! Don't wanna hear!" he bellowed over and over.

She said, "Wait'll everyone hears how fake it is! Won't they laugh! Won't they flap their lungs!"

He caught her wrists. "You ain't gonna tell them?"

"Wouldn't wan me known as a liar, would you, Charlie?"

He flung her off and away.

"Whyncha leave me alone? You dirty! Dirty jealous mean of ever'thing I do. I took shine off your nose when I brung the jar home. You didn' sleep right 'til you ruined things!"

She laughed. "Then I won't tell anybody," she said.

He stared at her. "You spoiled *my* fun. That's all that counted. It don't matter if you tell the rest. *I* know. And I'll never have no more fun. You and that Tom Carmody. I wish I could stop him laughin'. He's been laughin' for years at me! Well, you just go tell the rest, the other people, now—might as well have your fun—!"

He strode angrily, grabbed the jar so it sloshed, and would have flung it on the floor, but he stopped trembling, and let it down softly on the spindly table. He leaned over it, sobbing. If he lost this, the world was gone. And he was losing Thedy, too. Every month that passed she danced further away, sneering at him, funning him. For too many years her hips had been the pendulum by which he reckoned the time of his living. But other men, Tom Carmody, for one, were reckoning time from the same source.

Thedy stood waiting for him to smash the jar. Instead, he petted and stroked and gradually quieted himself over it. He thought of the long, good evenings in the past month, those rich evenings of friends and talk, moving about the room. That, at least, was good, if nothing else.

He turned slowly to Thedy. She was lost forever to him.

"Thedy, you didn't go to the carnival."

"Yes, I did."

"You're lyin'," he said, quietly.

"No, I'm not!"

"This—this jar *has* to have somethin' in it. Somethin' besides the junk you say. Too many people believe there's somethin' in it, Thedy. You can't change that. The carny-boss, if you talked with him, he lied." Charlie took a deep breath and then said, "Come here, Thedy."

"What you want?" she asked, sullenly.

"Come over here."

He took a step toward her. "Come here."

"Keep away from me, Charlie."

"Just want to show you somethin', Thedy." His voice was soft, low, and insistent. "Here, kittie. Here, kittie, kittie, kittie—*HERE KITTIE!*"

It was another night, about a week later. Gramps Medknowe and Granny Carnation came, followed by young Juke and Mrs. Tridden and Jahdoo, the black man. Followed by all the others, young and old, sweet and sour, creaking into chairs, each with his or her thought, hope, fear, and wonder in mind. Each not looking at the shrine, but saying hello softly to Charlie.

They waited for the others to gather. From the shine of their eyes one could see that each saw something different in the jar, something of the life and the pale life after life, and the life in death and the death in life, each with his story, his cue, his lines, familiar, old but new.

Charlie sat alone.

"Hello, Charlie." Somebody peered into the empty bedroom. "Your wife gone off again to visit her folks?"

"Yeah, she run for Tennessee. Be back in a couple weeks. She's the darndest one for runnin'. You know Thedy."

"Great one for jumpin' around, that woman."

Soft voices talking, getting settled, and then, quite suddenly, walking on the dark porch and shining his eyes in at the people—Tom Carmody.

Tom Carmody standing outside the door, knees sagging and trembling, arms hanging and shaking at his side, staring into the room. Tom Carmody not daring to enter. Tom Carmody with his mouth open, but not smiling. His lips wet and slack, not smiling. His face pale as chalk, as if it had been sick for a long time.

Gramps looked up at the jar, cleared his throat and said, "Why I never noticed so definite before. It's got *blue* eyes."

"It always had blue eyes," said Granny Carnation.

"No," whined Gramps. "No, it didn't. They was brown last time we was here." He blinked upward. "And another thing—it's got brown hair. Didn't have brown hair *before!*"

"Yes, yes, it did," sighed Mrs. Tridden.

"No, it didn't!"

"Yes, it did!"

Tom Carmody, shivering in the summer night, staring in at the jar. Charlie, glancing up at it, rolling a cigarette, casually, all peace and calm, very certain of his life and thoughts. Tom Carmody, alone, seeing things about the jar he never saw before. *Everybody* seeing what he wanted to see; all thoughts running in a fall of quick rain:

My baby. My little baby, thought Mrs. Tridden.

A brain! thought Gramps.

The black man jigged his fingers. Middibamboo Mama!

A fisherman pursed his lips. Jellyfish!

Kitten. Here kittie, kittie, kittie! The thoughts drowned clawing in Juke's eyes. Kitten!

Everything and anything! shrilled Granny's weazened thought. The night, the swamp, death, the pale things, the wet things from the sea!

Silence. And then Gramps whispered, "I wonder. Wonder if it's a he—or a she—or just a plain old *it?*"

Charlie glanced up, satisfied, tamping his cigarette, shaping it to his mouth. Then he looked at Tom Carmody, who would never smile again, in the door. "I reckon we'll never know. Yeah, I reckon we won't." Charlie shook his head slowly and settled down with his guests, looking, looking.

It was just one of those things they keep in a jar in the tent of a sideshow on the outskirts of a little, drowsy town. One of those pale things drifting in alcohol plasma, forever dreaming and circling, with its peeled dead eyes staring out at you and never seeing you. . . .

The Small Assassin

Just when the idea occurred to her that she was being murdered she could not tell. There had been little subtle signs, little suspicions for the past month; things as deep as sea tides in her, like looking at a perfectly calm stretch of tropic water, wanting to bathe in it and finding, just as the tide takes your body, that monsters dwell just under the surface, things unseen, bloated, many-armed, sharp-finned, malignant and inescapable.

A room floated around her in an effluvium of hysteria. Sharp instruments hovered and there were voices, and people in sterile white masks.

My name, she thought, what is it?

Alice Leiber. It came to her. David Leiber's wife. But it gave her no comfort. She was alone with these silent, whispering white people and there was great pain and nausea and death-fear in her.

I am being murdered before their eyes. These doctors, these nurses don't realize what hidden thing has happened to me. David doesn't know. Nobody knows except me and—the killer, the little murderer, the small assassin.

I am dying and I can't tell them now. They'd laugh and call me one in delirium. They'll see the murderer and hold him and never think him responsible for my death. But here I am, in front of God and man, dying, no one to believe my story, everyone to doubt me, comfort me with lies, bury me in ignorance, mourn me and salvage my destroyer.

Where is David? she wondered. In the waiting room, smoking one cigarette after another, listening to the long tickings of the very slow clock?

Sweat exploded from all of her body at once, and with it an agonized cry. Now. Now! Try and kill me, she screamed. Try, try, but I won't die! I won't!

There was a hollowness. A vacuum. Suddenly the pain fell away. Exhaustion, and dusk came around. It was over. Oh, God! She plummeted down and struck a black nothingness which gave way to nothingness and nothingness and another and still another. . . .

Footsteps. Gentle, approaching footsteps.

Far away, a voice said, "She's asleep. Don't disturb her."

An odor of tweeds, a pipe, a certain shaving lotion. David was standing over her. And beyond him the immaculate smell of Dr. Jeffers.

She did not open her eyes. "I'm awake," she said, quietly. It was a surprise, a relief to be able to speak, to not be dead.

"Alice," someone said, and it was David beyond her closed eyes, holding her tired hands.

Would you like to meet the murderer, David? she thought. I hear your voice asking to see him, so there's nothing but for me to point him out to you.

David stood over her. She opened her eyes. The room came into focus. Moving a weak hand, she pulled aside a coverlet.

The murderer looked up at David Leiber with a small, red-faced, blue-eyed calm. Its eyes were deep and sparkling.

"Why!" cried David Leiber, smiling. "He's a *fine* baby!"

Dr. Jeffers was waiting for David Leiber the day he came to take his wife and new child home. He motioned Leiber to a chair in his office, gave him a cigar, lit one for himself, sat on the edge of his desk, puffing solemnly for a long moment. Then he cleared his throat, looked David Leiber straight on and said, "Your wife doesn't like her child, Dave."

"What!"

"It's been a hard thing for her. She'll need a lot of love this next year. I didn't say much at the time, but she was hysterical in the delivery room. The strange things she said—I won't repeat them. All I'll say is that she feels alien to the child. Now, this may simply be a thing we can clear up with one or two questions." He sucked on his cigar another moment, then said, "Is this child a 'wanted' child, Dave?"

"Why do you ask?"

"It's vital."

"Yes. Yes, it is a 'wanted' child. We planned it together. Alice was so happy, a year ago, when—"

"Mmmm—that makes it more difficult. Because if the child was unplanned, it would be a simple case of a woman hating the idea of motherhood. That doesn't fit Alice." Dr. Jeffers took his cigar from his lips, rubbed his hand across his jaw. "It must be something else, then. Perhaps something buried in her childhood that's coming out now. Or it might be the simple temporary doubt and distrust of any mother who's gone through the unusual pain and near-death that Alice has. If so, then a little time should heal that. I thought I'd tell you, though, Dave. It'll help you be easy and tolerant with her if she says anything about—well—about wishing the child had been born dead. And if things don't go well, the three of you drop in on me. I'm always glad to see old friends, eh? Here, take another cigar along for—ah—for the baby."

It was a bright spring afternoon. Their car hummed along wide, tree-lined boulevards. Blue sky, flowers, a warm wind. David talked a lot, lit his cigar, talked some more. Alice answered directly, softly, relaxing a bit more as the trip progressed. But she held the baby not tightly or warmly or motherly enough to satisfy the queer ache in Dave's mind. She seemed to be merely carrying a porcelain figurine.

"Well," he said, at last, smiling. "What'll we name him?"

Alice Leiber watched green trees slide by. "Let's not decide yet. I'd rather wait until we get an exceptional name for him. Don't blow smoke in his face." Her sentences ran together with no change of tone. The last statement held no motherly reproof, no interest, no irritation. She just mouthed it and it was said.

The husband, disquieted, dropped the cigar from the window. "Sorry," he said.

The baby rested in the crook of his mother's arm, shadows of sun and tree changing his face. His blue eyes opened like fresh blue spring flowers. Moist noises came from the tiny, pink, elastic mouth.

Alice gave her baby a quick glance. Her husband felt her shiver against him.

"Cold?" he asked.

"A chill. Better raise the window, David."

It was more than a chill. He rolled the window slowly up.

Suppertime.

Dave had brought the child from the nursery, propped him at a tiny, bewildered angle, supported by many pillows, in a newly purchased high chair.

Alice watched her knife and fork move. "He's not high-chair size," she said.

"Fun having him here, anyway," said Dave, feeling fine. "Everything's fun. At the office, too. Orders up to my nose. If I don't watch myself I'll make another fifteen thousand this year. Hey, look at Junior, will you? Drooling all down his chin!" He reached over to wipe the baby's mouth with his napkin. From the corner of his eye he realized that Alice wasn't even watching. He finished the job.

"I guess it wasn't very interesting," he said, back again at his food. "But one would think a mother'd take some interest in her own child!"

Alice jerked her chin up. "Don't speak that way! Not in front of him! Later, if you must."

"Later?" he cried. "In front of, in back of, what's the difference?" He quieted suddenly, swallowed, was sorry. "All right. Okay. I know how it is."

After dinner she let him carry the baby upstairs. She didn't tell him to; she *let* him.

Coming down, he found her standing by the radio, listening to music she didn't hear. Her eyes were closed, her whole attitude one of wondering, self-questioning. She started when he appeared.

Suddenly, she was at him, against him, soft, quick; the same. Her lips found him, kept him. He was stunned. Now that the baby was gone, upstairs, out of the room, she began to breathe again, live again. She was free. She was whispering, rapidly, endlessly.

"Thank you, thank you, darling. For being yourself, always. Dependable, so very dependable!"

He had to laugh. "My father told me, 'Son, provide for your family!' "

Wearily, she rested her dark, shining hair against his neck. "You've overdone it. Sometimes I wish we were just the way we were when we were first married. No responsibilities, nothing but ourselves. No—no babies."

She crushed his hand in hers, a supernatural whiteness in her face.

"Oh, Dave, once it was just you and me. We protected each other, and now we protect the baby, but get no protection from it. Do you understand? Lying in the hospital I had time to think a lot of things. The world is evil—"

"Is it?"

"Yes. It is. But laws protect us from it. And when there aren't laws, then love does the protecting. You're protected from my hurting you, by my love. You're vulnerable to me, of all people, but love shields you. I feel no fear of you, because love cushions all your irritations, unnatural instincts, hatreds and immaturities. But—what about the baby? It's too young to know love, or a law of love, or anything, until we teach it. And in the meantime be vulnerable to it."

"Vulnerable to a baby?" He held her away and laughed gently.

"Does a baby know the difference between right and wrong?" she asked.

"No. But it'll learn."

"But a baby is so new, so amoral, so conscience-free." She stopped. Her arms dropped from him and she turned swiftly. "That noise? What was it?"

Leiber looked around the room. "I didn't hear—"

She stared at the library door. "In there," she said, slowly.

Leiber crossed the room, opened the door and switched the library lights on and off. "Not a thing." He came back to her. "You're worn out. To bed with you—right now."

Turning out the lights together, they walked slowly up the soundless hall stairs, not speaking. At the top she apologized. "My wild talk, darling. Forgive me. I'm exhausted."

He understood, and said so.

She paused, undecided, by the nursery door. Then she fingered the brass knob sharply, walked in. He watched her approach the crib much too carefully, look down, and stiffen as if she'd been struck in the face. "David!"

Leiber stepped forward, reached the crib.

The baby's face was bright red and very moist; his small pink mouth opened and shut, opened and shut; his eyes were a fiery blue. His hands leapt about on the air.

"Oh," said Dave, "he's just been crying."

"Has he?" Alice Leiber seized the crib-railing to balance herself. "I didn't hear him."

"The door was closed."

"Is that why he breathes so hard, why his face is red?"

"Sure. Poor little guy. Crying all alone in the dark. He can sleep in our room tonight, just in case he cries."

"You'll spoil him," his wife said.

Leiber felt her eyes follow as he rolled the crib into their bedroom. He undressed silently, sat on the edge of the bed. Suddenly he lifted his head, swore under his breath, snapped his fingers. "Damn it! Forgot to tell you. I must fly to Chicago Friday."

"Oh, David." Her voice was lost in the room.

"I've put this trip off for two months, and now it's so critical I just *have* to go."

"I'm afraid to be alone."

"We'll have the new cook by Friday. She'll be here all the time. I'll only be gone a few days."

"I'm afraid. I don't know of what. You wouldn't believe me if I told you. I guess I'm crazy."

He was in bed now. She darkened the room; he heard her walk around the bed, throw back the cover, slide in. He smelled the warm woman-smell of her next to him. He said, "If you want me to wait a few days, perhaps I could—"

"No," she said, unconvinced. "You go. I know it's important. It's just that I keep thinking about what I told you. Laws and love and protection. Love protects you from me. But, the baby—" She took a breath. "What protects you from him, David?"

Before he could answer, before he could tell her how silly it was, speaking so of infants, she switched on the bed light, abruptly.

"Look," she said, pointing.

The baby lay wide awake in its crib, staring straight at him, with deep, sharp blue eyes.

The lights went out again. She trembled against him.

"It's not nice being afraid of the thing you birthed." Her whisper lowered, became harsh, fierce, swift. "He tried to kill me! He lies there, listens to us talking, waiting for you to go away so he can try to kill me again! I swear it!" Sobs broke from her.

"Please," he kept saying, soothing her. "Stop it, stop it. Please."

She cried in the dark for a long time. Very late she relaxed, shakingly, against him. Her breathing came soft, warm, regular, her body twitched its worn reflexes and she slept.

He drowsed.

And just before his eyes lidded wearily down, sinking him into deeper and yet deeper tides, he heard a strange little sound of awareness and awakeness in the room.

The sound of small, moist, pinkly elastic lips.

The baby.

And then—sleep.

In the morning, the sun blazed. Alice smiled.

David Leiber dangled his watch over the crib. "See, baby? Something bright. Something pretty. Sure. Sure. Something bright. Something pretty."

Alice smiled. She told him to go ahead, fly to Chicago, she'd be very brave, no need to worry. She'd take care of baby. Oh, yes, she'd take care of him, all right.

The airplane went east. There was a lot of sky, a lot of sun and clouds and Chicago running over the horizon. Dave was dropped into the rush of ordering, planning, banqueting, telephoning, arguing in conference. But he wrote letters each day and sent telegrams to Alice and the baby.

On the evening of his sixth day away from home he received the long-distance phone call. Los Angeles.

"Alice?"

"No, Dave. This is Jeffers speaking."

"Doctor!"

"Hold on to yourself, son. Alice is sick. You'd better get the next plane home. It's pneumonia. I'll do everything I can, boy. If only it wasn't so soon after the baby. She needs strength."

Leiber dropped the phone into its cradle. He got up, with no feet under him, and no hands and no body. The hotel room blurred and fell apart.

"Alice," he said, blindly, starting for the door.

The propellers spun about, whirled, fluttered, stopped; time and space were put behind. Under his hand, David felt the doorknob turn; under his feet the floor assumed reality, around him flowed the walls of a bedroom, and in the late-afternoon sunlight Dr. Jeffers stood, turning from a window, as Alice lay waiting in her bed, something carved from a fall of winter snow. Then Dr. Jeffers was talking, talking continuously, gently, the sound rising and falling through the lamplight, a soft flutter, a white murmur of voice.

"Your wife's too good a mother, Dave. She worried more about the baby than herself. . . . "

Somewhere in the paleness of Alice's face, there was a sudden constriction which smoothed itself out before it was realized. Then, slowly, half-smiling, she began to talk and she talked as a mother should about this, that, and the other thing, the telling detail, the minute-by-minute and hour-by-hour report of a mother concerned with a dollhouse world and the miniature life of that world. But she could not stop; the spring was wound tight, and her voice rushed on to anger, fear and the faintest touch of revulsion, which did not change Dr. Jeffers' expression, but caused Dave's heart to match the rhythm of this talk that quickened and could not stop:

"The baby wouldn't sleep. I thought he was sick. He just lay, staring, in his crib, and late at night he'd cry. So loud, he'd cry, and he'd cry all night and all night. I couldn't quiet him, and I couldn't rest."

Dr. Jeffers' head nodded slowly, slowly. "Tired herself right into pneumonia. But she's full of sulfa now and on the safe side of the whole damn thing."

Dave felt ill. "The baby, what about the baby?"

"Fit as a fiddle; cock of the walk!"

"Thanks, Doctor."

The doctor walked off away and down the stairs, opened the front door faintly, and was gone.

"David!"

He turned to her frightened whisper.

"It was the baby again." She clutched his hand. "I try to lie to myself and say that I'm a fool, but the baby knew I was weak from the hospital, so he cried all night every night, and when he wasn't crying he'd be much too quiet. I knew if I switched on the light he'd be there, staring up at me."

David felt his body close in on itself like a fist. He remembered seeing the baby, feeling the baby, awake in the dark, awake very late at night when babies should be asleep. Awake and lying there, silent as thought, not crying, but watching from its crib. He thrust the thought aside. It was insane.

Alice went on. "I was going to kill the baby. Yes, I was. When you'd been gone only a day on your trip I went to his room and put my hands about his neck; and I stood there, for a long time, thinking, afraid. Then I put the covers up over his face and turned him over on his face and pressed him down and left him that way and ran out of the room."

He tried to stop her.

"No, let me finish," she said, hoarsely, looking at the wall. "When I left his room I thought, It's simple. Babies smother every day. No one'll ever know. But when I came back to see him dead, David, he was alive! Yes, alive, turned over on his back, alive and smiling and breathing. And I couldn't touch him again after that. I left him there and I didn't come back, not to feed him or look at him or do anything. Perhaps the cook tended to him. I don't know. All I know is that his crying kept me awake, and I thought all through the night, and walked around the rooms and now I'm sick." She was almost finished now. "The baby lies there and thinks of ways to kill me. Simple ways. Because he knows I know so much about him. I have no love for him; there is no protection between us; there never will be."

She was through. She collapsed inward on herself and finally slept. David Leiber stood for a long time over her, not able to move. His blood was frozen in his body, not a cell stirred anywhere, anywhere at all.

The next morning there was only one thing to do. He did it. He walked into Dr. Jeffers' office and told him the whole thing, and listened to Jeffers' tolerant replies:

"Let's take this thing slowly, son. It's quite natural for mothers to hate their children, sometimes. We have a label for it—ambivalence. The ability to hate, while loving. Lovers hate each other, frequently. Children detest their mothers—"

Leiber interrupted. "I never hated my mother."

"You won't admit it, naturally. People don't enjoy admitting hatred for their loved ones."

"So Alice hates her baby."

"Better say she has an obsession. She's gone a step further than plain, ordinary ambivalence. A Caesarian operation brought the child into the world and almost took Alice out of it. She blames the child for her near-death and her pneumonia. She's projecting her troubles, blaming them on the handiest object she can use as a source of blame. We *all* do it. We stumble into a chair and curse the furniture, not our own clumsiness. We miss a golf-stroke and damn the turf or our club, or the make of ball. If our business fails we blame the gods, the weather, our luck. All I can tell you is what I told you before. Love her. Finest medicine in the world. Find little ways of showing your affection, give her security. Find ways of showing her how harmless and innocent the child is. Make her feel that the baby was worth the risk. After a while, she'll settle down, forget about death, and begin to love the child. If she doesn't come around in the next month or so, ask me. I'll recommend a good psychiatrist. Go on along now, and take that look off your face."

When summer came, things seemed to settle, become easier. Dave worked, immersed himself in office detail, but found much time for his wife. She, in turn, took long walks, gained strength, played an occasional light game of badminton. She rarely burst out any more. She seemed to have rid herself of her fears.

Except on one certain midnight when a sudden summer wind swept around the house, warm and swift, shaking the trees like so many shining tambourines. Alice wakened, trembling, and slid over into her husband's arms, and let him console her, and ask her what was wrong.

She said, "Something's here in the room, watching us."

He switched on the light. "Dreaming again," he said. "You're better, though. Haven't been troubled for a long time."

She sighed as he clicked off the light again, and suddenly she slept. He held her, considering what a sweet, weird creature she was, for about half an hour.

He heard the bedroom door sway open a few inches.

There was nobody at the door. No reason for it to come open. The wind had died.

He waited. It seemed like an hour he lay silently, in the dark.

Then, far away, wailing like some small meteor dying in the vast inky gulf of space, the baby began to cry in his nursery.

It was a small, lonely sound in the middle of the stars and the dark and the breathing of this woman in his arms and the wind beginning to sweep through the trees again.

Leiber counted to one hundred, slowly. The crying continued.

Carefully disengaging Alice's arm he slipped from bed, put on his slippers, robe, and moved quietly from the room.

He'd go downstairs, he thought, fix some warm milk, bring it up, and—

The blackness dropped out from under him. His foot slipped and plunged. Slipped on something soft. Plunged into nothingness.

He thrust his hands out, caught frantically at the railing. His body stopped falling. He held. He cursed.

The "something soft" that caused his feet to slip rustled and thumped down a few steps. His head rang. His heart hammered at the base of his throat, thick and shot with pain.

Why do careless people leave things strewn about a house? He groped carefully with his fingers for the object that had almost spilled him headlong down the stairs.

His hand froze, startled. His breath went in. His heart held one or two beats.

The thing he held in his hand was a toy. A large cumbersome, patchwork doll he had bought as a joke, for—

For the baby.

Alice drove him to work the next day.

She slowed the car halfway downtown, pulled to the curb and stopped it. Then she turned on the seat and looked at her husband.

"I want to go away on a vacation. I don't know if you can make it now, darling, but if not, please let me go alone. We can get someone to take care of the baby, I'm sure. But I just have to get away. I thought I was growing out of this—this *feeling*. But I haven't. I can't stand being in the room with him. He looks up at me as if he hates me, too. I can't put my finger on it; all I know is I want to get away before something happens."

He got out on his side of the car, came around, motioned to her to move over, got in. "The only thing you're going to do is see a good psychiatrist. And if he suggests a vacation, well, okay. But this can't go on; my stomach's in knots all the time." He started the car. "I'll drive the rest of the way."

Her head was down; she was trying to keep back tears. She looked up when they reached his office building. "All right. Make the appointment. I'll go talk to anyone you want, David."

He kissed her. "Now, you're talking sense, lady. Think you can drive home okay?"

"Of course, silly."

"See you at supper, then. Drive carefully."

"Don't I always? 'Bye."

He stood on the curb, watching her drive off, the wind taking hold of her long, dark, shining hair. Upstairs, a minute later, he phoned Jeffers and arranged an appointment with a reliable neuro-psychiatrist.

The day's work went uneasily. Things fogged over; and in the fog he kept seeing Alice lost and calling his name. So much of her fear had come over to him. She actually had him convinced that the child was in some ways not quite natural.

He dictated long, uninspired letters. He checked some shipments downstairs. Assistants had to be questioned, and kept going. At the end of the day he was exhausted, his head throbbed, and he was very glad to go home.

On the way down in the elevator he wondered, What if I told Alice about the toy—that patchwork doll—I slipped on on the stairs last night? Lord, wouldn't *that* back her off? No, I won't ever tell her. Accidents are, after all, accidents.

Daylight lingered in the sky as he drove home in a taxi. In front of the house he paid the driver and walked slowly up the cement walk, enjoying the light that was still in the sky and the trees. The white colonial front of the house looked unnaturally silent and uninhabited, and then, quietly, he remembered this was Thursday, and the hired help they were able to obtain from time to time were all gone for the day.

He took a deep breath of air. A bird sang behind the house. Traffic moved on the boulevard a block away. He twisted the key in the door. The knob turned under his fingers, oiled, silent.

The door opened. He stepped in, put his hat on the chair with his briefcase, started to shrug out of his coat, when he looked up.

Late sunlight streamed down the stairwell from the window near the top of the hall. Where the sunlight touched it took on the bright color of the patchwork doll sprawled at the bottom of the stairs.

But he paid no attention to the toy.

He could only look, and not move, and look again at Alice.

Alice lay in a broken, grotesque, pallid gesturing and angling of her thin body, at the bottom of the stairs, like a crumpled doll that doesn't want to play any more, ever.

Alice was dead.

The house remained quiet, except for the sound of his heart.

She was dead.

He held her head in his hands, he felt her fingers. He held her body. But she wouldn't live. She wouldn't even try to live. He said her name, out loud, many times, and he tried, once again, by holding her to him, to give her back some of the warmth she had lost, but that didn't help.

He stood up. He must have made a phone call. He didn't remember. He found himself, suddenly, upstairs. He opened the nursery door and walked inside and stared blankly at the crib. His stomach was sick. He couldn't see very well.

The baby's eyes were closed, but his face was red, moist with perspiration, as if he'd been crying long and hard.

"She's dead," said Leiber to the baby. "She's dead."

Then he started laughing low and soft and continuously for a long time until Dr. Jeffers walked in out of the night and slapped him again and again across the face.

"Snap out of it! Pull yourself together!"

"She fell down the stairs, Doctor. She tripped on a patchwork doll and fell. I almost slipped on it the other night, myself. And now—"

The doctor shook him.

"Doc, Doc, Doc," said Dave, hazily. "Funny thing. Funny. I—I finally thought of a name for the baby."

The doctor said nothing.

Leiber put his head back in his trembling hands and spoke the words. "I'm going to have him christened next Sunday. Know what name I'm giving him? I'm going to call him Lucifer."

. . .

It was eleven at night. A lot of strange people had come and gone through the house, taking the essential flame with them—Alice.

David Leiber sat across from the doctor in the library.

"Alice wasn't crazy," he said, slowly. "She had good reason to fear the baby."

Jeffers exhaled. "Don't follow after her! She blamed the child for her sickness, now you blame it for her death. She stumbled on a toy, remember that. You can't blame the child."

"You mean Lucifer?"

"Stop calling him that!"

Leiber shook his head. "Alice heard things at night, moving in the halls. You want to know what made those noises, Doctor? They were made by the baby. Four months old, moving in the dark, listening to us talk. Listening to every word!" He held to the sides of the chair. "And if I turned the lights on, a baby is so small. It can hide behind furniture, a door, against a wall—below eye-level."

"I want you to stop this!" said Jeffers.

"Let me say what I think or I'll go crazy. When I went to Chicago, who was it kept Alice awake, tiring her into pneumonia? The baby! And when Alice didn't die, then he tried killing me. It was simple; leave a toy on the stairs, cry in the night until your father goes downstairs to fetch your milk, and stumbles. A crude trick, but effective. It didn't get me. But it killed Alice dead."

David Leiber stopped long enough to light a cigarette. "I should have caught on. I'd turn on the lights in the middle of the night, many nights, and the baby'd be lying there, eyes wide. Most babies sleep all the time. Not this one. He stayed awake, thinking."

"Babies don't think."

"He stayed awake doing whatever he *could* do with his brain, then. What in hell do we know about a baby's mind? He had every reason to hate Alice; she suspected him for what he was—certainly not a normal child. Something— different. What do you know of babies, Doctor? The general run, yes. You know, of course, how babies kill their mothers at birth. Why? Could it be resentment at being forced into a lousy world like this one?"

Leiber leaned toward the doctor, tiredly. "It all ties up. Suppose that a few babies out of all the millions born are instantaneously able to move, see, hear, think, like many animals and insects can. Insects are born self-sufficient. In a few weeks most mammals and birds adjust. But children take years to speak and learn to stumble around on their weak legs."

"But suppose one child in a billion is—strange? Born perfectly aware, able to think, instinctively. Wouldn't it be a perfect setup, a perfect blind for anything the baby might want to do? He could pretend to be ordinary, weak, crying, ignorant. With just a *little* expenditure of energy he could crawl about a darkened house, listening. And how easy to place obstacles at the top of stairs. How easy to cry all night and tire a mother into pneumonia. How easy, right at birth, to be so close to the mother that *a few deft maneuvers might cause peritonitis!*"

"For God's sake!" Jeffers was on his feet. "That's a repulsive thing to say!"

"It's a repulsive thing I'm speaking of. How many mothers have died at the birth of their children? How many have suckled strange little improbabilities who cause death one way or another? Strange, red little creatures with brains that work in a bloody darkness we can't even guess at. Elemental little brains, warm with racial memory, hatred, and raw cruelty, with no more thought than self-preservation. And self-preservation in this case consisted of eliminating a mother who realized what a horror she had birthed. I ask you, Doctor, what is there in the world more selfish than a baby? Nothing!"

Jeffers scowled and shook his head, helplessly.

Leiber dropped his cigarette down. "I'm not claiming any great strength for the child. Just enough to crawl around a little, a few months ahead of schedule. Just enough to listen all the time. Just enough to cry late at night. That's enough, more than enough."

Jeffers tried ridicule. "Call it murder, then. But murder must be motivated. What motive had the child?"

Leiber was ready with the answer. "What is more at peace, more dreamfully content, at ease, at rest, fed, comforted, unbothered, than an unborn child? Nothing. It floats in a sleepy, timeless wonder of nourishment and silence. Then, suddenly, it is asked to give up its berth, is forced to vacate, rushed out into a noisy, uncaring, selfish world where it is asked to shift for itself, to hunt, to feed from the hunting, to seek after a vanishing love that once was its unquestionable right, to meet confusion instead of inner silence and conservative slumber! And the child *resents* it! Resents the cold air, the huge spaces, the sudden departure from familiar things. And in the tiny filament of brain the only thing the child knows is selfishness and hatred because the spell has been rudely shattered. Who is responsible for this disenchantment, this rude breaking of the spell? The mother. So here the new child has someone to hate with all its unreasoning mind. The mother has cast it out, rejected it. And the father is no better, kill him, too! He's responsible in *his* way!"

Jeffers interrupted. "If what you say is true, then every woman in the world would have to look on her baby as something to dread, something to wonder about."

"And why not? Hasn't the child a perfect alibi? A thousand years of accepted medical belief protects him. By all natural accounts he is helpless, not responsible. The child is born hating. And things grow worse, instead of better. At first the baby gets a certain amount of attention and mothering. But then as time passes, things change. When very new, a baby has the power to make parents do silly things when it cries or sneezes, jump when it makes a noise. As the years pass, the baby feels even that small power slip rapidly, forever away, never to return. Why shouldn't it grasp all the power it can have? Why shouldn't it jockey for position while it has all the advantages? In later years it would be too late to express its hatred. *Now* would be the time to strike."

Leiber's voice was very soft, very low.

"My little boy baby, lying in his crib nights, his face moist and red and out of breath. From crying? No. From climbing slowly out of his crib, from crawling long distances through darkened hallways. My little boy baby. I want to kill him."

The doctor handed him a water glass and some pills. "You're not killing anyone. You're going to sleep for twenty-four hours. Sleep'll change your mind. Take this."

Leiber drank down the pills and let himself be led upstairs to his bedroom, crying, and felt himself being put to bed. The doctor waited until he was moving deep into sleep, then left the house.

Leiber, alone, drifted down, down.

He heard a noise. "What's—what's *that*?" he demanded, feebly.

Something moved in the hall

David Leiber slept.

Very early the next morning, Dr. Jeffers drove up to the house. It was a good morning, and he was here to drive Leiber to the country for a rest. Leiber would still be asleep upstairs. Jeffers had given him enough sedative to knock him out for at least fifteen hours.

He rang the doorbell. No answer. The servants were probably not up. Jeffers tried the front door, found it open, stepped in. He put his medical kit on the nearest chair.

Something white moved out of sight at the top of the stairs. Just a suggestion of a movement. Jeffers hardly noticed it.

The smell of gas was in the house.

Jeffers ran upstairs, crashed into Leiber's bedroom.

Leiber lay motionless on the bed, and the room billowed with gas, which hissed from a released jet at the base of the wall near the door. Jeffers twisted it off, then forced up all the windows and ran back to Leiber's body.

The body was cold. It had been dead quite a few hours.

Coughing violently, the doctor hurried from the room, eyes watering. Leiber hadn't turned on the gas himself. He *couldn't* have. Those sedatives had knocked him out, he wouldn't have wakened until noon. It wasn't suicide. Or was there the faintest possibility?

Jeffers stood in the hall for five minutes. Then he walked to the door of the nursery. It was shut. He opened it. He walked inside and to the crib.

The crib was empty.

He stood swaying by the crib for half a minute, then he said something to nobody in particular.

"The nursery door blew shut. You couldn't get back into your crib where it was safe. You didn't plan on the door blowing shut. A little thing like a slammed door can ruin the best of plans. I'll find you somewhere in the house, hiding, pretending to be something you are not." The doctor looked dazed. He put his hand to his head and smiled palely. "Now I'm talking like Alice and David talked. But, I can't take any chances. I'm not sure of anything, but I can't take chances."

He walked downstairs, opened his medical bag on the chair, took something out of it and held it in his hands.

Something rustled down the hall. Something very small and very quiet. Jeffers turned rapidly.

I had to operate to bring you into this world, he thought. Now I guess I can operate to take you out of it. . . .

He took half a dozen slow, sure steps forward into the hall. He raised his hand into the sunlight.

"See, baby! Something bright—something pretty!"

A scalpel.

The Next in Line

It was a little caricature of a town square. In it were the following fresh ingredients: a candy-box of a bandstand where men stood on Thursday and Sunday nights exploding music; fine, green-patinated bronze-copper benches all scrolled and flourished; fine blue and pink tiled walks—blue as women's newly lacquered eyes, pink as women's hidden wonders; and fine French-clipped trees in the shapes of exact hatboxes. The whole, from your hotel window, had the fresh ingratiation and unbelievable fantasy one might expect of a French villa in the nineties. But no, this was Mexico! and this a plaza in a small colonial Mexican town, with a fine State Opera House (in which movies were shown for two pesos admission: *Rasputin and the Empress*, *The Big House*, *Madame Curie*, *Love Affair*, *Mama Loves Papa*).

Joseph came out on the sun-heated balcony in the morning and knelt by the grille, pointing his little box Brownie. Behind him, in the bath, the water was running and Marie's voice came out:

"What're you doing?"

He muttered "—a picture." She asked again. He clicked the shutter, stood up, wound the spool inside, squinting, and said, "Took a picture of the town square. God, didn't those men shout last night? I didn't sleep until two-thirty. We would have to arrive when the local Rotary's having its wingding."

"What're our plans for today?" she asked.

"We're going to see the mummies," he said.

"Oh," she said. There was a long silence.

He came in, set the camera down, and lit himself a cigarette.

"I'll go up and see them alone," he said, "if you'd rather."

"No," she said, not very loud. "I'll go along. But I wish we could forget the whole thing. It's such a lovely little town."

"Look here!" he cried, catching a movement from the corner of his eyes. He hurried to the balcony, stood there, his cigarette smoking and forgotten in his fingers. "Come quick, Marie!"

"I'm drying myself," she said.

"Please, hurry," he said, fascinated, looking down into the street.

There was movement behind him, and then the odor of soap and water-rinsed flesh, wet towel, fresh cologne; Marie was at his elbow. "Stay right there," she cautioned him, "so I can look without exposing myself. I'm stark. What *is* it?"

"Look!" he cried.

A procession traveled along the street. One man led it, with a package on his head. Behind him came women in black rebozos, chewing away the peels of oranges and spitting them on the cobbles; little children at their elbows, men ahead of them. Some ate sugar cane, gnawing away at the outer bark until it split down and they pulled it off in great hunks to get at the succulent pulp and the juicy sinews on which to suck. In all, there were fifty people.

"Joe," said Marie behind him, holding his arm.

It was no ordinary package the first man in the procession carried on his head, balanced delicately as a chicken-plume. It was covered with silver satin and silver fringe and silver rosettes. And he held it gently with one brown hand, the other hand swinging free.

This was a funeral and the little package was a coffin.

Joseph glanced at his wife.

She was the color of fine, fresh milk. The pink color of the bath was gone. Her heart had sucked it all down to some hidden vacuum in her. She held fast to the French doorway and watched the traveling people go, watched them eat fruit, heard them talk gently, laugh gently. She forgot she was naked.

He said, "Some little girl or boy gone to a happier place."

"Where are they taking—her?"

She did not think it unusual, her choice of the feminine pronoun. Already she had identified herself with that tiny fragment parceled like an unripe variety of fruit. Now, in this moment, she was being carried up the hill within compressing darkness, a stone in a peach, silent and terrified, the touch of the father against the coffin material outside; gentle and noiseless and firm inside.

"To the graveyard, naturally; that's where they're taking her," he said, the cigarette making a filter of smoke across his casual face.

"Not *the* graveyard?"

"There's only one cemetery in these towns, you know that. They usually hurry it. That little girl has probably been dead only a few hours."

"A few hours—"

She turned away, quite ridiculous, quite naked, with only the towel supported by her limp, untrying hands. She walked toward the bed. "A few hours ago she was alive, and now—"

He went on: "Now they're hurrying her up the hill. The climate isn't kind to the dead. It's hot, there's no embalming. They have to finish it quickly."

"But to *that* graveyard, that horrible place," she said, with a voice from a dream.

"Oh, the mummies," he said. "Don't let that bother you."

She sat on the bed, again and again stroking the towel laid across her lap. Her eyes were blind as the brown paps of her breasts. She did not see him or the room. She knew that if he snapped his fingers or coughed, she wouldn't even look up.

"They were eating fruit at her funeral, and laughing," she said.

"It's a long climb to the cemetery."

She shuddered, a convulsive motion, like a fish trying to free itself from a deep-swallowed hook. She lay back and he looked at her as one examines a poor sculpture; all criticism, all quiet and easy and uncaring. She wondered idly just how much his hands had had to do with the broadening and flattening and changement of her body. Certainly this was not the body he'd started with. It was past saving now. Like clay which the sculptor has carelessly impregnated with water, it was impossible to shape again. In order to shape clay you warm it with your hands, evaporate the moisture with heat. But there was no more of that fine summer weather between them. There was no warmth to bake away the aging moisture that collected and made pendant now her breasts and body. When the heat is gone, it is marvelous and unsettling to see how quickly a vessel stores self-destroying water in its cells.

"I don't feel well," she said. She lay there, thinking it over. "I don't feel well," she said again, when he made no response. After another minute or two she lifted herself. "Let's not stay here another night, Joe."

"But it's a wonderful town."

"Yes, but we've seen everything." She got up. She knew what came next. Gayness, blitheness, encouragement, everything quite false and hopeful. "We could go on to Pátzcuaro. Make it in no time. You won't have to pack, I'll do it all myself, darling! We can get a room at the Don Posada there. They say it's a beautiful little town—"

"This," he remarked, "is a beautiful little town."

"Bougainvillea climb all over the buildings—" she said.

"These—" he pointed to some flowers at the window "—are bougainvillea."

"—and we'd fish, you like fishing," she said in bright haste. "And I'd fish, too, I'd learn, yes I would, I've always *wanted* to learn! And they say the Tarascan Indians there are almost Mongoloid in feature, and don't speak much Spanish, and from there we could go to Parícutin, that's near Uruapan, and they have some of the finest lacquered boxes there, oh, it'll be fun, Joe. I'll pack. You just take it easy, and—"

"Marie."

He stopped her with one word as she ran to the bathroom door.

"Yes?"

"I thought you said you didn't feel well?"

"I didn't. I don't. But, thinking of all those swell places—"

"We haven't seen one tenth of this town," he explained logically. "There's that statue of Morelos on the hill, I want a shot of that, and some of that French architecture up the street . . . we've traveled three hundred miles and we've been here one day and now you want to rush off somewhere else. I've already paid the rent for another night. . . ."

"You can get it back," she said.

"Why do you want to run away?" he said, looking at her with an attentive simplicity. "Don't you like the town?"

"I simply adore it," she said, her cheeks white, smiling. "It's so green and pretty."

"Well, then," he said. "Another day. You'll love it. That's settled."

She started to speak.

"Yes?" he asked.

"Nothing."

She closed the bathroom door. Behind it she rattled open a medicine box. Water rushed into a tumbler. She was taking something for her stomach.

He came to the bathroom door.

"Marie, the mummies don't bother you, do they?"

"Unh-unh," she said.

"Was it the funeral, then?"

"Unh."

"Because, if you were really afraid, I'd pack in a moment, you know that, darling."

He waited.

"No, I'm not afraid," she said.

"Good girl," he said.

The graveyard was enclosed by a thick adobe wall, and at its four corners small stone angels tilted out on stony wings, their grimy heads capped with bird droppings, their hands gifted with amulets of the same substance, their faces unquestionably freckled.

In the warm smooth flow of sunlight which was like a depthless, tideless river, Joseph and Marie climbed up the hill, their shadows slanting blue behind them. Helping one another, they made the cemetery gate, swung back the Spanish blue iron grille and entered.

It was several mornings after the celebratory fiesta of *El Día de los Muertos*, the Day of the Dead, and ribbons and ravels of tissue and sparkle-tape still clung like insane hair to the raised stones, to the hand-carved, love-polished crucifixes, and to the above-ground tombs which resembled marble jewel-cases. There were statues frozen in angelic postures over gravel mounds, and intricately carved stones tall as men with angels spilling all down their rims, and tombs as big and ridiculous as beds put out to dry in the sun after some nocturnal accident. And within the four walls of the yard, inserted into square mouths and slots, were coffins, walled in, plated in by marble plates and plaster, upon which names were struck and upon which hung tin pictures, cheap peso portraits of the inserted dead. Thumb-tacked to the different pictures were trinkets they'd loved in life, silver charms, silver arms, legs, bodies, silver cups, silver dogs, silver church medallions, bits of red crape and blue ribbon. On some places were painted slats of tin showing the dead rising to heaven in oil-tinted angels' arms.

Looking at the graves again, they saw the remnants of the Death Fiesta. The little tablets of tallow splashed over the stones by the lighted festive candles, the wilted orchid blossoms lying like crushed red-purple tarantulas against the milky stones, some of them looking horridly sexual, limp and withered. There were loop-frames of cactus leaves, bamboo, reeds, and wild, dead morning-glories. There were circles of gardenias and sprigs of bougainvillea, desiccated. The entire floor of the yard seemed a ballroom after a wild dancing, from which the participants have fled; the tables askew, confetti, candles, ribbons and deep dreams left behind.

They stood, Marie and Joseph, in the warm silent yard, among the stones, between the walls. Far over in one corner a little man with high cheekbones, the milk color of the Spanish infiltration, thick glasses, a black coat, a gray hat and gray, unpressed pants and neatly laced shoes, moved about among the stones, supervising something or other that another man in overalls was doing to a grave with a shovel. The little man with glasses carried a thrice-folded newspaper under his left arm and had his hands in his pockets.

"*Buenos días, señora y señor!*" he said, when he finally noticed Joseph and Marie and came to see them.

"Is this the place of *las momias*?" asked Joseph. "They do exist, do they not?"

"*Sí*, the mummies," said the man. "They exist and are here. In the catacombs."

"*Por favor*," said Joseph. "*Yo quiero veo las momias, sí?*"

"*Sí, señor.*"

"*Me español es mucho estúpido, es muy malo*," apologized Joseph.

"No, no, *señor*. You speak well! This way, please."

He led them between the flowered stones to a tomb near the wall shadows. It was a large flat tomb, flush with the gravel, with a thin kindling door flat on it, padlocked. It was unlocked and the wooden door flung back rattling to one side. Revealed was a round hole the circled interior of which contained steps which screwed into the earth.

Before Joseph could move, his wife had set her foot on the first step. "Here," he said. "Me first."

"No. That's all right," she said, and went down and around in a darkening spiral until the earth vanished her. She moved carefully, for the steps were hardly enough to contain a child's feet. It got dark and she heard the caretaker stepping after her, at her ears, and then it got light again. They stepped out into a long whitewashed hall twenty feet under the earth, dimly lit by a few small gothic windows high in the arched ceiling. The hall was fifty yards long, ending on the left in a double door in which were set tall crystal panes and a sign forbidding entrance. On the right end of the hall was a large stack of white rods and round white stones.

"The soldiers who fought for Father Morelos," said the caretaker.

They walked to the vast pile. They were neatly put in place, bone on bone, like firewood, and on top was a mound of a thousand dry skulls.

"I don't mind skulls and bones," said Marie. "There's nothing even vaguely human to them. I'm not scared of skulls and bones. They're like something insectile. If a child was raised and didn't know he had a skeleton in him, he wouldn't think anything of bones, would he? That's how it is with me. Everything human has been scraped off *these*. There's nothing familiar left to be horrible. In order for a thing to be horrible it has to suffer a change you can recognize. This isn't changed. They're still skeletons, like they always were. The part that changed is gone, and so there's nothing to show for it. Isn't that interesting?"

Joseph nodded.

She was quite brave now.

"Well," she said, "let's see the mummies."

"Here, *señora*," said the caretaker.

He took them far down the hall away from the stack of bones and when Joseph paid him a peso he unlocked the forbidden crystal doors and opened them wide and they looked into an even longer, dimly lighted hall in which stood the people.

They waited inside the door in a long line under the arch-roofed ceiling, fifty-five of them against one wall, on the left, fifty-five of them against the right wall, and five of them way down at the very end.

"Mister Interlocutor!" said Joseph, briskly.

They resembled nothing more than those preliminary erections of a sculptor, the wire frame, the first tendons of clay, the muscles, and a thin lacquer of skin. They were unfinished, all one hundred and fifteen of them.

They were parchment-colored and the skin was stretched as if to dry, from bone to bone. The bodies were intact, only the watery humors had evaporated from them.

"The climate," said the caretaker. "It preserves them. Very dry."

"How long have they been here?" asked Joseph.

"Some one year, some five, *señor*, some ten, some seventy."

There was an embarrassment of horror. You started with the first man on your right, hooked and wired upright against the wall, and he was not good to look upon, and you went on to the woman next to him who was unbelievable and then to a man who was horrendous and then to a woman who was very sorry she was dead and in such a place as this.

"What are they doing here?" asked Joseph.

"Their relatives did not pay the rent upon their graves."

"Is there a rent?"

"*Sí, señor.* Twenty pesos a year. Or, if they desire the permanent interment, one hundred seventy pesos. But our people, they are very poor, as you must know, and one hundred seventy pesos is as much as many of them make in two years. So they carry their dead here and place them into the earth for one year, and the twenty pesos are paid, with fine intentions of paying each year and each year, but each year and each year after the first year they have a burro to buy or a new mouth to feed, or maybe three new mouths, and the dead, after all, are not hungry, and the dead, after all, can pull no plows; or there is a new wife or there is a roof in need of mending, and the dead, remember, can be in no beds with a man, and the dead, you understand, can keep no rain off one, and so it is that the dead are not paid up upon their rent."

"*Then* what happens? Are you listening, Marie?" asked Joseph.

Marie counted the bodies. One, two, three, four, five, six, seven, eight. "What?" she said, quietly.

"Are you listening?"

"I think so. What? Oh, yes! I'm listening."

Eight, nine, ten, eleven, twelve, thirteen.

"Well, then," said the little man. "I call a *trabajador* and with his delicate shovel at the end of the first year he does dig and dig and dig down. How deep do you think we dig, *señor*?"

"Six feet. That's the usual depth."

"Ah, no, ah, no. There, *señor*, you would be wrong. Knowing that after the first year the rent is liable not to be paid, we bury the poorest two feet down. It is less work, you understand? Of course, we must judge by the family who own a body. Some of them we bury sometimes three, sometimes four feet deep, sometimes five, sometimes six, depending on how rich the family is, depending on what the chances are we won't have to dig him from out his place a year later. And, let me tell you, *señor*, when we bury a man the whole six feet deep we are very certain of his staying. We have never dug up a six-foot-buried one yet, that is the accuracy with which we know the money of the people."

Twenty-one, twenty-two, twenty-three. Marie's lips moved with a small whisper.

"And the bodies which are dug up are placed down here against the wall, with other *compañeros*."

"Do the relatives know the bodies are here?"

"*Sí.*" The small man pointed. "This one, *vea ustéd?* It is new. It has been here but one year. His *madre y padre* know him to be here. But have they money? Ah, no."

"Isn't that rather gruesome for his parents?"

The little man was earnest. "They never think of it," he said.

"Did you hear that, Marie?"

"What?" Thirty, thirty-one, thirty-two, thirty-three, thirty-four. "Yes. They never think of it."

"What if the rent is paid again, after a lapse?" inquired Joseph.

"In that time," said the caretaker, "the bodies are reburied for as many years as are paid."

"Sounds like blackmail," said Joseph.

The little man shrugged, hands in pockets. "We must live."

"You are certain no one can pay the one hundred seventy pesos all at once," said Joseph. "So in this way you get them for twenty pesos a year, year after year, for maybe thirty years. If they don't pay, you threaten to stand *mamacita* or little *niño* in the catacomb."

"We must live," said the little man.

Fifty-one, fifty-two, fifty-three.

Marie counted in the center of the long corridor, the standing dead on all sides of her.

They were screaming.

They looked as if they had leaped, snapped upright in their graves, clutched hands over their shriveled bosoms and screamed, jaws wide, tongues out, nostrils flared.

And been frozen that way.

All of them had open mouths. Theirs was a perpetual screaming. They were dead and they knew it. In every raw fiber and evaporated organ they knew it.

She stood listening to them scream.

They say dogs hear sounds humans never hear, sounds so many decibels higher than normal hearing that they seem nonexistent.

The corridor swarmed with screams. Screams poured from terror-yawned lips and dry tongues, screams you couldn't hear because they were so high.

Joseph walked up to one standing body.

"Say 'ah,' " he said.

Sixty-five, sixty-six, sixty-seven, counted Marie, among the screams.

"Here is an interesting one," said the proprietor.

They saw a woman with arms flung to her head, mouth wide, teeth intact, whose hair was wildly flourished, long and shimmery on her head. Her eyes were small pale white-blue eggs in her skull.

"Sometimes, this happens. This woman, she is a cataleptic. One day she falls down upon the earth, but is really not dead, for, deep in her, the little drum of her heart beats and beats, so dim one cannot hear. So she was buried in the graveyard in a fine inexpensive box. . . . "

"Didn't you know she was cataleptic?"

"Her sisters knew. But this time they thought her at last dead. And funerals are hasty things in this warm town."

"She was buried a few hours after her 'death'?"

"*Sí*, the same. All of this, as you see her here, we would never have known, if a year later her sisters, having other things to buy, had not refused the rent on her burial. So we dug very quietly down and loosed the box and took it up and opened the top of her box and laid it aside and looked in upon her—"

Marie stared.

This woman had wakened under the earth. She had torn, shrieked, clubbed at the box-lid with fists, died of suffocation, in this attitude, hands flung over her gaping face, horror-eyed, hair wild.

"Be pleased, *señor*, to find that difference between *her* hands and these other ones," said the caretaker. "Their peaceful fingers at their hips, quiet as little roses. Hers? Ah, hers! are jumped up, very wildly, as if to pound the lid free!"

"Couldn't rigor mortis do that?"

"Believe me, *señor*, rigor mortis pounds upon no lids. Rigor mortis screams not like this, nor twists nor wrestles to rip free nails, *señor*, or prise boards loose hunting for air, *señor*. All these others are open of mouth, *sí*, because they were not injected with the fluids of embalming, but theirs is a simple screaming of muscles, *señor*. This *señorita*, here, hers is the *muerte horrible*."

Marie walked, scuffling her shoes, turning first this way, then that. Naked bodies. Long ago the clothes had whispered away. The fat women's breasts were lumps of yeasty dough left in the dust. The men's loins were indrawn, withered orchids.

"Mr. Grimace and Mr. Gape," said Joseph.

He pointed his camera at two men who seemed in conversation, mouths in mid-sentence, hands gesticulant and stiffened over some long-dissolved gossip.

Joseph clicked the shutter, rolled the film, focused the camera on another body, clicked the shutter, rolled the film, walked on to another.

Eighty-one, eighty-two, eighty-three. Jaws down, tongues out like jeering children, eyes pale brown–irised in upclenched sockets. Hairs, waxed and prickled by sunlight, each sharp as quills embedded on the lips, the cheeks, the eyelids, the brows. Little beards on chins and bosoms and loins. Flesh like drumheads and manuscripts and crisp bread dough. The women, huge ill-shaped tallow things, death-melted. The insane hair of them, like nests made and unmade and remade. Teeth, each single, each fine, each perfect, in jaw. Eighty-six, eighty-seven, eighty-eight. A rushing of Marie's eyes. Down the corridor, flicking. Counting, rushing, never stopping. On! Quick! Ninety-one, ninety-two, ninety-three! Here was a man, his stomach open, like a tree hollow where you dropped your child love letters when you were eleven! Her eyes entered the hole in the space under his ribs. She peeked in. He looked like an Erector set inside. The spine, the pelvic plates. The rest was tendon, parchment, bone, eye, beardy jaw, ear, stupefied nostril. And this ragged eaten cicatrix in his navel into which a pudding might be spooned. Ninety-seven, ninety-eight! Names, places, dates, things!

"This woman died in childbirth!"

Like a little hungry doll, the prematurely born child was wired, dangling, to her wrist.

"This was a soldier. His uniform still half on him—"

Marie's eyes slammed the furthest wall after a back-forth, back-forth swinging from horror to horror, from skull to skull, beating from rib to rib, staring with hypnotic fascination at paralyzed, loveless, fleshless loins, at men made into women by evaporation, at women made into dugged swine. The fearful ricochet of vision, growing, growing, taking impetus from swollen breast to raving mouth, wall to wall, wall to wall, again, again, like a ball hurled in a game, caught in the incredible teeth, spat in a scream across the corridor to be caught in claws, lodged between thin teats, the whole standing chorus invisibly chanting the game on, on, the wild game of sight recoiling, rebounding, reshuttling on down the inconceivable procession, through a montage of erected horrors that ended finally and for all time when vision crashed against the corridor ending with one last scream from all present!

Marie turned and shot her vision far down to where the spiral steps walked up into sunlight. How talented was death. How many expressions and manipulations of hand, face, body, no two alike. They stood like the naked pipes of a vast derelict calliope, their mouths cut into frantic vents. And now the great hand of mania descended upon all keys at once, and the long calliope screamed upon one hundred-throated, unending scream.

Click went the camera and Joseph rolled the film. Click went the camera and Joseph rolled the film.

Moreno, Morelos, Cantine, Gómez, Gutiérrez, Villanousul, Ureta, Licón, Navarro, Iturbi, Jorge, Filomena, Nena, Manuel, José, Tomás, Ramona. This man walked and this man sang and this man had three wives; and this man died of this, and that of that, and the third from another thing, and the fourth was shot, and the fifth was stabbed and the sixth fell straight down dead; and the seventh drank deep and died dead, and the eighth died in love, and the ninth fell from his horse, and the tenth coughed blood, and the eleventh stopped his heart, and the twelfth used to laugh much, and the thirteenth was a dancing one, and the fourteenth was most beautiful of all, the fifteenth had ten children and the sixteenth is one of those children as is the seventeeth; and the eighteenth was Tomás and did well with his guitar; the next three cut maize in their fields, had three lovers each; the twenty-second was never loved; the twenty-third sold tortillas, patting and shaping them each at the curb before the Opera House with her little charcoal stove; and the twenty-fourth beat his wife and now she walks proudly in the town and is merry with new men and here he stands bewildered by this unfair thing, and the twenty-fifth drank several quarts of river with his lungs and was pulled forth in a net, and the twenty-sixth was a great thinker and his brain now sleeps like a burnt plum in his skull.

"I'd like a color shot of each, and his or her name and how he or she died," said Joseph. "It would be an amazing, an ironical book to publish. The more you think, the more it grows on you. Their life histories and then a picture of each of them standing here."

He tapped each chest, softly. They gave off hollow sounds, like someone rapping on a door.

Marie pushed her way through screams that hung net-wise across her path. She walked evenly, in the corridor center, not slow, but not too fast, toward the spiral stair, not looking to either side. Click went the camera behind her.

"You have room down here for more?" said Joseph.

"*Sí, señor*. Many more."

"Wouldn't want to be next in line, next on your waiting list."

"Ah, no, *señor*, one would not wish to be next."

"How are chances of buying one of these?"

"Oh, no, no, *señor*. Oh, no, no. Oh, no, *señor*."

"I'll pay you fifty pesos."

"Oh, no, *señor*, no, no, *señor*."

In the market, the remainder of candy skulls from the Death Fiesta were sold from flimsy little tables. Women hung with black rebozos sat quietly, now and then speaking one word to each other, the sweet sugar skeletons, the saccharine corpses and white candy skulls at their elbows. Each skull had a name on top in gold candy curlicue: José or Carmen or Ramón or Tena or Guillermo or Rosa. They sold cheap. The Death Festival was gone. Joseph paid a peso and got two candy skulls.

Marie stood in the narrow street. She saw the candy skulls and Joseph and the dark ladies who put the skulls in a bag.

"Not *really*," said Marie.

"Why not?" said Joseph.

"Not after just *now*," she said.

"In the catacombs?"

She nodded.

He said, "But these are good."

"They look poisonous."

"Just because they're skull-shaped?"

"No. The sugar itself looks raw, how do you know what kind of people made them, they might have the colic."

"My dear Marie, all people in Mexico have colic," he said.

"You can eat them both," she said.

"Alas, poor Yorick," he said, peeking into the bag.

They walked along a street that was held between high buildings in which were yellow window frames and blue iron grilles and the smell of tamales came from them and the sound of lost fountains splashing on hidden tiles and little birds clustering and peeping in bamboo cages and someone playing Chopin on a piano.

"Chopin, here," said Joseph. "How strange and swell." He looked up. "I like that bridge. Hold this." He handed her the candy bag while he clicked a picture of a red bridge spanning two white buildings with a man walking on it, a red serape on his shoulder. "Fine," said Joseph.

Marie walked looking at Joseph, looking away from him and then back at him, her lips moving but not speaking, her eyes fluttering, a little neck muscle under her chin like a wire, a little nerve in her brow ticking. She passed the candy bag from one hand to the other. She stepped up a curb, leaned back somehow, gestured, said something to restore balance, and dropped the bag.

"For Christ's sake." Joseph snatched up the bag. "Look what you've done! Clumsy!"

"I should have broken my ankle," she said, "I suppose."

"These were the best skulls; both of them smashed; I wanted to save them for friends up home."

"I'm sorry," she said, vaguely.

"For God's sake, oh, damn it to hell!" He scowled into the bag. "I might not find any more good as these. Oh, I don't know, I give up!"

The wind blew and they were alone in the street, he staring down into the shattered debris in the bag, she with the street shadows all around her, sun on the other side of the street, nobody about, and the world far away, the two of them alone, two thousand miles from anywhere, on a street in a false town which was nothing and around which was nothing but blank desert and circling hawks. On top the State Opera House, a block down, the golden Greek statues stood sun-bright and high, and in a beer place a shouting phonograph cried *ay! marimba ... corazón ...* and all kinds of alien words which the wind stirred away.

Joseph twisted the bag shut, stuck it furiously in his pocket.

They walked back to the two-thirty lunch at the hotel.

He sat at the table with Marie, sipping *albóndiga* soup from his moving spoon, silently. Twice she commented cheerfully upon the wall murals and he looked at her steadily and sipped. The bag of cracked skulls lay on the table. . . .

"*Señora . . .*"

The soup plates were cleared by a brown hand. A large plate of enchiladas was set down.

Marie looked at the plate.

There were sixteen enchiladas.

She put her fork and knife out to take one and stopped. She put her fork and knife down at each side of her plate. She glanced at the walls and then at her husband and then at the sixteen enchiladas.

Sixteen. One by one. A long row of them, crowded together.

She counted them.

One, two, three, four, five, six.

Joseph took one on his plate and ate it.

Six, seven, eight, nine, ten, eleven.

She put her hands on her lap.

Twelve, thirteen, fourteen, fifteen, sixteen. She finished counting.

"I'm not hungry," she said.

He placed another enchilada before himself. It had an interior clothed in a papyrus of corn tortilla. It was slender and it was one of many he cut and placed in his mouth and she chewed it for him in her mind's mouth, and squeezed her eyes tight.

"Eh?" he asked.

"Nothing," she said.

Thirteen enchiladas remained, like tiny bundles, like scrolls.

He ate five more.

"I don't feel well," she said.

"Feel better if you ate," he said.

"No."

He finished, then opened the sack and took out one of the half-demolished skulls.

"Not *here*?" she said.

"Why not?" And he put one sugar socket to his lips, chewing. "Not bad," he said, thinking the taste. He popped in another section of skull. "Not bad at all."

She looked at the name on the skull he was eating.

Marie, it said.

It was tremendous, the way she helped him pack. In those newsreels you see men leap off diving-boards into pools, only, a moment later when the reel is reversed, to jump back up in airy fantasy to alight once more safe on the diving-board. Now, as Joseph watched, the suits and dresses flew into their boxes and cases, the hats were like birds darting, clapped into round, bright hatboxes, the shoes seemed to run across the floor like mice to leap into valises. The suitcases banged shut, the hasps clicked, the keys turned.

"There!" she cried. "All packed! Oh, Joe, I'm so glad you let me change your mind."

She started for the door.

"Here, let me help," he said.

"They're not heavy," she said.

"But you never carry suitcases. You never have. I'll call a boy."

"Nonsense," she said, breathless with the weight of the valises.

A boy seized the cases outside the door. "*Señora, por favor!*"

"Have we forgotten anything?" He looked under the two beds, he went out on the balcony and gazed at the plaza, came in, went to the bathroom, looked in the cabinet and on the washbowl. "Here," he said, coming out and handing her something. "You forgot your wristwatch."

"Did I?" She put it on and went out the door.

"I don't know," he said. "It's damn late in the day to be moving out."

"It's only three-thirty," she said. "Only three-thirty."

"I don't know," he said, doubtfully.

He looked around the room, stepped out, closed the door, locked it, went downstairs, jingling the keys.

She was outside in the car already, settled in, her coat folded on her lap, her gloved hands folded on the coat. He came out, supervised the loading of what luggage remained into the trunk receptacle, came to the front door and tapped on the window. She unlocked it and let him in.

"Well, here we *go!*" she cried with a laugh, her face rosy, her eyes frantically bright. She was leaning forward as if by this movement she might set the car rolling merrily down the hill. "Thank you, darling, for letting me get the refund on the money you paid for our room tonight. I'm sure we'll like it much better in Guadalajara tonight. Thank you!"

"Yeah," he said.

Inserting the ignition keys he stepped on the starter.

Nothing happened.

He stepped on the starter again. Her mouth twitched.

"It needs warming," she said. "It was a cold night last night."

He tried it again. Nothing.

Marie's hands tumbled on her lap.

He tried it six more times. "Well," he said, lying back, ceasing.

"Try it again, next time it'll work," she said.

"It's no use," he said. "Something's wrong."

"Well, you've got to try it once more."

He tried it once more.

"It'll work, I'm sure," she said. "Is the ignition on?"

"Is the ignition on," he said. "Yes, it's *on*."

"It doesn't look like it's on," she said.

"It's on." He showed her by twisting the key.

"*Now*, try it," she said.

"There," he said, when nothing happened. "I *told* you."

"You're not doing it right; it almost caught that time," she cried.

"I'll wear out the battery, and God knows where you can buy a battery here."

"Wear it out, then. I'm sure it'll start next time!"

"Well, if you're so good, you try it." He slipped from the car and beckoned her over behind the wheel. "Go ahead!"

She bit her lips and settled behind the wheel. She did things with her hands that were like a little mystic ceremony; with moves of hands and body she was trying to overcome gravity, friction and every other natural law. She patted the starter with her toeless shoe. The car remained solemnly quiet. A little squeak came out of Marie's tightened lips. She rammed the starter home and there was a clear smell in the air as she fluttered the choke.

"You've flooded it," he said. "Fine! Get back over on your side, will you?"

He got three boys to push and they started the car downhill. He jumped in to steer. The car rolled swiftly, bumping and rattling. Marie's face glowed expectantly. "This'll start it!" she said.

Nothing started. They rolled quietly into the filling station at the bottom of the hill, bumping softly on the cobbles, and stopped by the tanks.

She sat there, saying nothing, and when the attendant came from the station her door was locked, the window up, and he had to come around on the husband's side to make his query.

The mechanic arose from the car engine, scowled at Joseph and they spoke together in Spanish, quietly.

She rolled the window down and listened.

"What's he say?" she demanded.

The two men talked on.

"What's he say?" she demanded.

The dark mechanic waved at the engine. Joseph nodded and they conversed.

"What's wrong?" Marie wanted to know.

Joseph frowned over at her. "Wait a moment, will you? I can't listen to both of you."

The mechanic took Joseph's elbow. They said many words.

"What's he saying now?" she asked.

"He says—" said Joseph, and was lost as the Mexican took him over to the engine and bent him down in earnest discovery.

"How much will it cost?" she cried, out the window, around at their bent backs.

The mechanic spoke to Joseph.

"Fifty pesos," said Joseph.

"How long will it take?" cried his wife.

Joseph asked the mechanic. The man shrugged and they argued for five minutes.

"How long will it take?" said Marie.

The discussion continued.

The sun went down the sky. She looked at the sun upon the trees that stood high by the cemetery yard. The shadows rose and rose until the valley was enclosed and only the sky was clear and untouched and blue.

"Two days, maybe three," said Joseph, turning to Marie.

"Two days! Can't he fix it so we can just go on to the next town and have the rest done there?"

Joseph asked the man. The man replied.

Joseph said to his wife. "No, he'll have to do the entire job."

"Why, that's silly, it's so silly, he doesn't either, he doesn't really have to do it all, you tell him that, Joe, tell him that, he can hurry and fix it—"

The two men ignored her. They were talking earnestly again.

This time it was all in very slow motion. The unpacking of the suitcases. He did his own, she left hers by the door.

"I don't need anything," she said, leaving it locked.

"You'll need your nightgown," he said.

"I'll sleep naked," she said.

"Well, it isn't my fault," he said. "That damned car."

"You can go down and watch them work on it, later," she said. She sat on the edge of the bed. They were in a new room. She had refused to return to their old room. She said she couldn't stand it. She wanted a new room so it would seem they were in a new hotel in a new city. So this was a new room, but it still had the view of the plaza and the drum-box trees. "You go down and supervise the work, Joe. If you don't, you know they'll take weeks!" She looked at him. "You should be down there now, instead of standing around."

"I'll go down," he said.

"I'll go down with you. I want to buy some magazines."

"You won't find any American magazines in a town like this."

"I can look, can't I?"

"Besides, we haven't much money," he said. "I don't want to have to wire my bank. It takes a god-awful time and it's not worth the bother."

"I can at least have my magazines," she said.

"Maybe one or two," he said.

"As many as I want," she said, feverishly, on the bed.

"For God's sake, you've got a million magazines in the car now. *Post*s, *Collier's*, *Mercury*, *Atlantic Monthly*s, *Barnaby*, *Superman!* You haven't read half of the articles."

"But they're not new," she said. "They're not new, I've *looked* at them and after you've looked at a thing, I don't know—"

"Try reading them instead of looking at them," he said.

As they came downstairs night was in the plaza.

"Give me a few pesos," she said, and he gave her some. "Teach me to say about magazines in Spanish," she said.

"*Quiero una publicación americano*," he said, walking swiftly.

She repeated it, stumblingly, and laughed. "Thanks."

He went on ahead to the mechanic's shop, and she turned in at the nearest *farmacia botica*, and all the magazines racked before her there were alien colors and alien names. She read the titles with swift moves of her eyes and looked at the old man behind the counter. "Do you have American magazines?" she asked in English, embarrassed to use the Spanish words.

The old man stared at her.

"*Habla inglés?*" she asked.

"No, *señorita*."

She tried to think of the right words. "*Quiero*—no!" She stopped. She started again. "*Americano*—uh—*magg-ah-zeen-as?*"

"Oh, no, *señorita!*"

Her hands opened wide at her waist, then closed, like mouths. Her mouth opened and closed. The shop had a veil over it, in her eyes. Here she was and here were these small baked adobe people to whom she could say nothing and from whom she could get no words she understood, and she was in a town of people who said no words to her and she said no words to them except in blushing confusion and bewilderment. And the town was circled by desert and time, and home was far away, far away in another life.

She whirled and fled.

Shop following shop she found no magazines save those giving bullfights in blood on their covers or murdered people or lace-confection priests. But at last three poor copies of the *Post* were bought with much display and loud laughter and she gave the vendor of this small shop a handsome tip.

Rushing out with the *Post*s eagerly on her bosom in both hands she hurried along the narrow walk, took a skip over the gutter, ran across the street, sang la-la, jumped onto the further walk, made another little scamper with her feet, smiled an inside smile, moving along swiftly, pressing the magazines tightly to her, half-closing her eyes, breathing the charcoal evening air, feeling the wind watering past her ears.

Starlight tinkled in golden nuclei off the highly perched Greek figures atop the State Opera House. A man shambled by in the shadow, balancing upon his head a basket. The basket contained bread loaves.

She saw the man and the balanced basket and suddenly she did not move and there was no inside smile, nor did her hands clasp tight the magazines. She watched the man walk, with one hand of his gently poised up to tap the basket any time it unbalanced, and down the street he dwindled, while the magazines slipped from Marie's fingers and scattered on the walk.

Snatching them up, she ran into the hotel and almost fell going upstairs.

She sat in the room. The magazines were piled on each side of her and in a circle at her feet. She had made a little castle with portcullises of words and into this she was withdrawn. All about her were the magazines she had bought and bought and looked at and looked at on other days, and these were the outer barrier, and upon the inside of the barrier, upon her lap, as yet unopened, but her hands were trembling to open them and read and read and read again with hungry eyes, were the three battered *Post* magazines. She opened to the first page. She would go through them page by page, line by line, she decided. Not a line would go unnoticed, a comma unread, every little ad and every color would be fixed by her. And—she smiled with discovery—in those other magazines at her feet were still advertisements and cartoons she had neglected—there would be little morsels of stuff for her to reclaim and utilize later.

She would read this first *Post* tonight, yes tonight she would read this first delicious *Post*. Page on page she would eat it and tomorrow night, if there was going to be a tomorrow night, but maybe there wouldn't be a tomorrow night here, maybe the motor would start and there'd be odors of exhaust and round hum of rubber tire on road and wind riding in the window and pennanting her hair—but, suppose, just suppose there would *be* a tomorrow night here, in this room. Well, then, there would be two more *Post*s, one for tomorrow night, and the next for the next night. How neatly she said it to herself with her mind's tongue. She turned the first page.

She turned the second page. Her eyes moved over it and over it and her fingers unknown to her slipped under the next page and flickered it in preparation for turning, and the watch ticked on her wrist, and time passed and she sat turning pages, turning pages, hungrily seeing the framed people in the pictures, people who lived in another land in another world where neons bravely held off the night with crimson bars and the smells were home smells and the people talked good fine words and here she was turning the pages, and all the lines went across and down and the pages flew under her hands, making a fan. She threw down the first *Post*, seized on and riffled through the second in half an hour, threw that down, took up the third, threw that down a good fifteen minutes later and found herself breathing, breathing stiffly and swiftly in her body and out of her mouth. She put her hand up to the back of her neck.

Somewhere, a soft breeze was blowing.

The hairs along the back of her neck slowly stood upright.

She touched them with one pale hand as one touches the nape of a dandelion.

Outside, in the plaza, the street lights rocked like crazy flashlights on a wind. Papers ran through the gutters in sheep flocks. Shadows penciled and slashed under the bucketing lamps now this way, now that, here a shadow one instant, there a shadow next, now no shadows, all cold light, now no light, all cold blue-black shadow. The lamps creaked on their high metal hasps.

In the room her hands began to tremble. She saw them tremble. Her body began to tremble. Under the bright bright print of the brightest, loudest skirt she could find to put on especially for tonight, in which she had whirled and cavorted feverishly before the coffin-sized mirror, beneath the rayon skirt the body was all wire and tendon and excitation. Her teeth chattered and fused and chattered. Her lipstick smeared, one lip crushing another.

Joseph knocked on the door.

They got ready for bed. He had returned with the news that something had been done to the car and it would take time, he'd go watch them tomorrow.

"But don't knock on the door," she said, standing before the mirror as she undressed.

"Leave it unlocked then," he said.

"I want it locked. But don't rap. Call."

"What's wrong with rapping?" he said.

"It sounds funny," she said.

"What do you mean, funny?"

She wouldn't say. She was looking at herself in the mirror and she was naked, with her hands at her sides, and there were her breasts and her hips and her entire body, and it moved, it felt the floor under it and the walls and air around it, and the breasts could know hands if hands were put there, and the stomach would make no hollow echo if touched.

"For God's sake," he said, "don't stand there admiring yourself." He was in bed. "What are you doing?" he said. "What're you putting your hands up that way for, over your face?"

He put the lights out.

She could not speak to him for she knew no words that he knew and he said nothing to her that she understood, and she walked to her bed and slipped into it and he lay with his back to her in his bed and he was like one of these brown-baked people of this faraway town upon the moon, and the real earth was off somewhere where it would take a star-flight to reach it. If only he could speak with her and she to him tonight, how good the night might be, and how easy to breathe and how lax the vessels of blood in her ankles and in her wrists and the under-arms, but there was no speaking and the night was ten thousand tickings and ten thousand twistings of the blankets, and the pillow was like a tiny white warm stove under-cheek, and the blackness of the room was a mosquito netting draped all about so that a turn entangled her in it. If only there was one word, one word between them. But there was no word and the veins did not rest easy in the wrists and the heart was a bellows forever blowing upon a little coal of fear, forever illumining and making it into a cherry light, again, pulse, and again, an ingrown light which her inner eyes stared upon with unwanting fascination. The lungs did not rest but were exercised as if she were a drowned person and she herself performing artificial respiration to keep the last life going. And all of these things were lubricated by the sweat of her glowing body, and she was glued fast between the heavy blankets like something pressed, smashed, redolently moist between the white pages of a heavy book.

And as she lay this way the long hours of midnight came when again she was a child. She lay, now and again thumping her heart in tambourine hysteria, then, quieting, the slow sad thoughts of bronze childhood when everything was sun on green trees and sun on water and sun on blonde child hair. Faces flowed by on merry-go-rounds of memory, a face rushing to meet her, facing her, and away to the right; another, whirling in from the left, a quick fragment of lost conversation, and out to the right. Around and round. Oh, the night was very long. She consoled herself by thinking of the car starting tomorrow, the throttling sound and the power sound and the road moving under, and she smiled in the dark with pleasure. But then, suppose the car did *not* start? She crumpled in the dark, like a burning, withering paper. All the folds and corners of her clenched in about her and tick tick tick went the wristwatch, tick tick tick and another tick to wither on. . . .

Morning. She looked at her husband lying straight and easy on his bed. She let her hand laze down at the cool space between the beds. All night her hand had hung in that cold empty interval between. Once she had put her hand out toward him, stretching, but the space was just a little too long, she couldn't reach him. She had snapped her hand back, hoping he hadn't heard the movement of her silent reaching.

There he lay now. His eyes gently closed, the lashes softly interlocked like clasped fingers. Breathing so quietly you could scarce see his ribs move. As usual, by this time of morning, he had worked out of his pajamas. His naked chest was revealed from the waist up. The rest of him lay under cover. His head lay on the pillow, in thoughtful profile.

There was a beard stubble on his chin.

The morning light showed the white of her eyes. They were the only things in the room in motion, in slow starts and stops, tracing the anatomy of the man across from her.

Each little hair was perfect on the chin and cheeks. A tiny hole of sunlight from the window-shade lay on his chin and picked out, like the spikes of a music-box cylinder, each little hair on his face.

His wrists on either side of him had little curly black hairs, each perfect, each separate and shiny and glittering.

The hair on his head was intact, strand by dark strand, down to the roots. The ears were beautifully carved. The teeth were intact behind the lips.

"Joseph!" she screamed.

"Joseph!" she screamed again, flailing up in terror.

Bong! Bong! Bong! went the bell thunder across the street, from the great tiled cathedral!

Pigeons rose in a papery white whirl, like so many magazines fluttered past the window! The pigeons circled the plaza, spiraling up. Bong! went the bells! Honk went a taxi horn! Far away down an alley a music box played "Cielito Lindo."

All these faded into the dripping of the faucet in the bath sink.

Joseph opened his eyes.

His wife sat on her bed, staring at him.

"I thought—" he said. He blinked. "No." He shut his eyes and shook his head. "Just the bells." A sigh. "What time is it?"

"I don't know. Yes, I do. Eight o'clock."

"Good God," he murmured, turning over. "We can sleep three more hours."

"You've got to get up!" she cried.

"Nobody's up. They won't be to work at the garage until ten, you know that, you can't rush these people; keep quiet now."

"But you've got to get up," she said.

He half-turned. Sunlight prickled black hairs into bronze on his upper lip. "*Why?* Why, in Christ's name, do I *have* to get up?"

"You need a shave!" she almost screamed.

He moaned. "So I have to get up and lather myself at eight in the morning because I need a shave."

"Well, you do need one."

"I'm not shaving again till we reach Texas."

"You can't go around looking like a tramp!"

"I can and will. I've shaved every morning for thirty goddamn mornings and put on a tie and had a crease in my pants. From now on, no pants, no ties, no shaving, no nothing."

He yanked the covers over his ears so violently that he pulled the blankets off one of his naked legs.

The leg hung upon the rim of the bed, warm white in the sunlight, each little black hair—perfect.

Her eyes widened, focused, stared upon it.

She put her hand over her mouth, tight.

He went in and out of the hotel all day. He did not shave. He walked along the plaza tiles below. He walked so slowly she wanted to throw a lightning bolt out of the window and hit him. He paused and talked to the hotel manager below, under a drum-cut tree, shifting his shoes on the pale blue plaza tiles. He looked at birds on trees and saw how the State Opera House statues were dressed in fresh morning gilt, and stood on the corner, watching the traffic carefully. There was no traffic! He was standing there on purpose, taking his time, not looking back at her. Why didn't he run, lope down the alley, down the hill to the garage, pound on the doors, threaten the mechanics, lift them by their pants, shove them into the car motor! He stood instead, watching the ridiculous traffic pass. A hobbled swine, a man on a bike, a 1927 Ford, and three half-nude children. Go, go, go, she screamed silently, and almost smashed the window.

He sauntered across the street. He went around the corner. All the way down to the garage he'd stop at windows, read signs, look at pictures, handle pottery. Maybe he'd stop in for a beer. God, yes, a beer.

She walked in the plaza, took the sun, hunted for more magazines. She cleaned her fingernails, burnished them, took a bath, walked again in the plaza, ate very little, and returned to the room to feed upon her magazines.

She did not lie down. She was afraid to. Each time she did she fell into a half-dream, half-drowse in which all her childhood was revealed in a helpless melancholy. Old friends, children she hadn't seen or thought of in twenty years filled her mind. And she thought of things she wanted to do and had never done. She had meant to call Lila Holdridge for the past eight years since college, but somehow she never had. What friends they had been! Dear Lila! She thought, lying down, of all the books, the fine new and old books, she had meant to buy and might never buy now and read. How she loved books and the smell of books. She thought of a thousand old sad things. She'd wanted to own the Oz books all her life, yet had never bought them. Why *not*? while yet there was life! The first thing she'd do would be to buy them when she got back to New York! And she'd call Lila immediately! And she'd see Bert and Jimmy and Helen and Louise, and go back to Illinois and walk around in her childhood place and see the things to be seen there. If she got back to the States. If. Her heart beat painfully in her, paused, held on to itself, and beat again. *If* she ever got back.

She lay listening to her heart, critically.

Thud and a thud and a thud. Pause. Thud and a thud and a thud. Pause.

What if it should stop while she was listening?

There!

Silence inside her.

"Joseph!"

She leaped up. She grabbed at her breasts as if to squeeze, to pump to start the silent heart again!

It opened in her, closed, rattled and beat nervously, twenty rapid, shotlike times!

She sank onto the bed. What if it should stop again and not start? What would she think? What would there be to do? She'd die of fright, that's what. A joke; it was very humorous. Die of fright if you heard your heart stop. She would have to listen to it, keep it beating. She wanted to go home and see Lila and buy the books and dance again and walk in Central Park and—listen—

Thud and a thud and a thud. Pause.

Joseph knocked on the door. Joseph knocked on the door and the car was not repaired and there would be another night; and Joseph did not shave and each little hair was perfect on his chin, and the magazine shops were closed and there were no more magazines, and they ate supper, a little bit anyway for her, and he went out in the evening to walk in the town.

She sat once more in the chair and slow erections of hair rose as if a magnet were passed over her neck. She was very weak and could not move from the chair, and she had no body, she was only a heart-beat, a huge pulsation of warmth and ache between four walls of the room. Her eyes were hot and pregnant, swollen with child of terror behind the bellied, tautened lips.

Deeply inside herself, she felt the first little cog slip. Another night, another night, another night, she thought. And this will be longer than the last. The first little cog slipped, the pendulum missed a stroke. Followed by the second and third interrelated cogs. The cogs interlocked, a small with a little larger one, the little larger one with a bit larger one, the bit larger one with a large one, the large one with a huge one, the huge one with an immense one, the immense one with a titanic one. . . .

A red ganglion, no bigger than a scarlet thread, snapped and quivered; a nerve, no greater than a red linen fiber twisted. Deep in her one little mesh was gone and the entire machine, imbalanced, was about to steadily shake itself to bits.

She didn't fight it. She let it quake and terrorize her and knock the sweat off her brow and jolt down her spine and flood her mouth with horrible wine. She felt as if a broken gyro tilted now this way, now that, and blundered and trembled and whined in her. The color fell from her face like light leaving a clicked-off bulb, the crystal cheeks of the bulb vessel showing veins and filaments all colorless. . . .

Joseph was in the room, he had come in, but she didn't even hear him. He was in the room but it made no difference, he changed nothing with his coming. He was getting ready for bed and said nothing as he moved about and she said nothing but fell into the bed while he moved around in a smoke-filled space beyond her and once he spoke but she didn't hear him.

She timed it. Every five minutes she looked at her watch and the watch shook and time shook and the five fingers were fifteen moving, reassembling into five. The shaking never stopped. She called for water. She turned and turned upon the bed. The wind blew outside, cocking the lights and spilling bursts of illumination that hit buildings glancing sidelong blows, causing windows to glitter like opened eyes and shut swiftly as the light tilted in yet another direction. Downstairs, all was quiet after the dinner, no sounds came up into their silent room. He handed her a water glass.

"I'm cold, Joseph," she said, lying deep in folds of cover.

"You're all right," he said.

"No, I'm not. I'm not well. I'm afraid."

"There's nothing to be afraid of."

"I want to get on the train for the United States."

"There's a train in León, but none here," he said, lighting a new cigarette.

"Let's drive there."

"In these taxis, with these drivers, and leave our car here?"

"Yes, I want to go."

"You'll be all right in the morning."

"I know I won't be. I'm not well."

He said, "It would cost hundreds of dollars to have the car shipped home."

"I don't care. I have two hundred dollars in the bank home. I'll pay for it. But, please, let's go home."

"When the sun shines tomorrow you'll feel better, it's just that the sun's gone now."

"Yes, the sun's gone and the wind's blowing," she whispered, closing her eyes, turning her head, listening. "Oh, what a lonely wind. Mexico's a strange land. All the jungles and deserts and lonely stretches, and here and there a little town, like this, with a few lights burning you could put out with a snap of your fingers. . . . "

"It's pretty big country," he said.

"Don't these people ever get lonely?"

"They're used to it this way."

"Don't they get afraid, then?"

"They have a religion for that."

"I wish *I* had a religion."

"The minute you get a religion you stop thinking," he said. "Believe in one thing too much and you have no room for new ideas."

"Tonight," she said, faintly, "I'd like nothing more than to have no more room for new ideas, to stop thinking, to believe in one thing so much it leaves me no time to be afraid."

"You're not afraid," he said.

"If I had a religion," she said, ignoring him, "I'd have a lever with which to lift myself. But I haven't a lever now and I don't know how to lift myself."

"Oh, for God's—" he mumbled to himself, sitting down.

"I used to have a religion," she said.

"Baptist."

"No, that was when I was twelve. I got over that. I mean—*later*."

"You never told me."

"You should have known," she said.

"What religion? Plaster saints in the sacristy? Any special saint you liked to tell your beads to?"

"Yes."

"And did he answer your prayers?"

"For a little while. Lately, no, never. Never any more. Not for years now. But I keep praying."

"Which saint is this?"

"Saint Joseph."

"Saint Joseph." He got up and poured himself a glass of water from the glass pitcher, and it was a lonely trickling sound in the room. "My name."

"Coincidence," she said.

They looked at one another for a few moments.

He looked away. "Plaster saints," he said, drinking the water down.

After a while she said, "Joseph?" He said, "Yes?" and she said, "Come hold my hand, will you?" "Women," he sighed. He came and held her hand. After a minute she drew her hand away, hid it under the blanket, leaving his hand empty behind. With her eyes closed she trembled the words, "Never mind. It's not as nice as I can imagine it. It's really nice the way I can make you hold my hand in my mind." "Gods," he said, and went into the bathroom. She turned off the light. Only the small crack of light under the bathroom door showed. She listened to her heart. It beat one hundred and fifty times a minute, steadily, and the little whining tremor was still in her marrow, as if each bone of her body had a blue-bottle fly imprisoned in it, hovering, buzzing, shaking, quivering deep, deep, deep. Her eyes reversed into herself, to watch the secret heart of herself pounding itself to pieces against the side of her chest.

Water ran in the bathroom. She heard him washing his teeth.

"Joseph!"

"Yes," he said, behind the shut door.

"Come here."

"What do you want?"

"I want you to promise me something, please, oh, please."

"What is it?"

"Open the door, first."

"What *is* it?" he demanded, behind the closed door.

"Promise me," she said, and stopped.

"Promise you what?" he asked, after a long pause.

"Promise me," she said, and couldn't go on. She lay there. He said nothing. She heard the watch and her heart pounding together. A lantern creaked on the hotel exterior. "Promise me, if anything—happens," she heard herself say, muffled and paralyzed, as if she were on one of the surrounding hills talking at him from the distance, "—if anything happens to me, you won't let me be buried here in the graveyard over those terrible catacombs!"

"Don't be foolish," he said, behind the door.

"Promise me?" she said, eyes wide in the dark.

"Of all the foolish things to talk about."

"Promise, *please* promise?"

"You'll be all right in the morning," he said.

"Promise so I can sleep. I can sleep if only you'd say you wouldn't let me be put there. I don't want to be put there."

"Honestly," he said, out of patience.

"Please," she said.

"Why should I promise anything so ridiculous?" he said. "You'll be fine tomorrow. And besides, if you died, you'd look very pretty in the catacomb standing between Mr. Grimace and Mr. Gape, with a sprig of morning-glory in your hair." And he laughed sincerely.

Silence. She lay there in the dark.

"Don't you think you'll look pretty there?" he asked, laughingly, behind the door.

She said nothing in the dark room.

"*Don't* you?" he said.

Somebody walked down below in the plaza, faintly, fading away.

"Eh?" he asked her, brushing his teeth.

She lay there, staring up at the ceiling, her breasts rising and falling faster, faster, faster, the air going in and out, in and out her nostrils, a little trickle of blood coming from her clenched lips. Her eyes were very wide, her hands blindly constricted the bedclothes.

"Eh?" he said again behind the door.

She said nothing.

"Sure," he talked to himself. "Pretty as hell," he murmured, under the flow of tap water. He rinsed his mouth. "Sure," he said.

Nothing from her in the bed.

"Women are funny," he said to himself in the mirror.

She lay in the bed.

"Sure," he said. He gargled with some antiseptic, spat it down the drain. "You'll be all right in the morning," he said.

Not a word from her.

"We'll get the car fixed."

She didn't say anything.

"Be morning before you know it." He was screwing caps on things now, putting freshener on his face. "And the car fixed tomorrow, maybe, at the very latest the next day. You won't mind another night here, will you?"

She didn't answer.

"*Will* you?" he asked.

No reply.

The light blinked out under the bathroom door.

"Marie?"

He opened the door.

"Asleep?"

She lay with eyes wide, breasts moving up and down.

"Asleep," he said. "Well, good night, lady."

He climbed into his bed. "Tired," he said.

No reply.

"Tired," he said.

The wind tossed the lights outside; the room was oblong and black and he was in his bed dozing already.

She lay, eyes wide, the watch ticking on her wrist, breasts moving up and down.

It was a fine day coming through the Tropic of Cancer. The automobile pushed along the turning road leaving the jungle country behind, heading for the United States, roaring between the green hills, taking every turn, leaving behind a faint vanishing trail of exhaust smoke. And inside the shiny automobile sat Joseph with his pink, healthy face and his Panama hat, and a little camera cradled on his lap as he drove; a swathe of black silk pinned around the left upper arm of his tan coat. He watched the country slide by and absent-mindedly made a gesture to the seat beside him, and stopped. He broke into a little sheepish smile and turned once more to the window of his car, humming a tuneless tune, his right hand slowly reaching over to touch the seat beside him . . .

Which was empty.

Jack-in-the-Box

He looked through the cold morning windows with the Jack-in-the-Box in his hands, prying the rusted lid. But no matter how he struggled, the Jack would not jump to the light with a cry, or slap its velvet mittens on the air, or bob in a dozen directions with a wild and painted smile. Crushed under the lid, in its jail, it stayed crammed tight coil on coil. With your ear to the box, you felt pressure beneath, the fear and panic of the trapped toy. It was like holding someone's heart in your hand. Edwin could not tell if the box pulsed or if his own blood beat against the lid.

He threw the box down and looked to the window. Outside the window the trees surrounded the house which surrounded Edwin. He could not see beyond the trees. If he tried to find another World beyond them, the trees wove themselves thick with the wind, to still his curiosity, to stop his eyes.

"Edwin!" Behind him, Mother's waiting, nervous breath as she drank her breakfast coffee. "Stop staring. Come eat."

"No," he whispered.

"What?" A stiffened rustle. She must have turned. "Which is more important, breakfast or that window?"

"The window . . ." he whispered and sent his gaze running the paths and trails he had tried for thirteen years. Was it true that the trees flowed on ten thousand miles to nothingness? He could not say. His sight returned defeated, to the lawn, the steps, his hands trembling on the pane.

He turned to eat his tasteless apricots, alone with his mother in the vast and echoing breakfast room. Five thousand mornings at this table, this window, and no movement beyond the trees.

The two of them ate silently.

She was the pale woman that no one but the birds saw in old country houses in fourth-floor cupola windows, each morning at six, each afternoon at four, each evening at nine, and also passing by one minute after midnight, there she would be, in her tower, silent and white, high and alone and quiet. It was like passing a deserted greenhouse in which one last wild white blossom lifted its head to the moonlight.

And her child, Edwin, was the thistle that one breath of wind might unpod in a season of thistles. His hair was silken and his eyes were of a constant blue and feverish temperature. He had a haun   , as if he slept poorly. He might fly apart like a packet of ladyfinger firecrackers if a certain door slammed.

His mother began to talk, slowly and with great caution, then more rapidly, and then angrily, and then almost spitting at him.

"Why must you disobey every morning? I don't like your staring from the window, do you hear? What do you want? Do you want to see them?" she cried, her fingers twitching. She was blazingly lovely, like an angry white flower. "Do you want to see the Beasts that run down paths and crush people like strawberries?"

Yes, he thought, I'd like to see the Beasts, horrible as they are.

"Do you want to go out there," she cried, "like your father did before you were born, and be killed as he was killed, struck down by one of those Terrors on the road, would you like that?"

"No . . ."

"Isn't it enough they murdered your father? Why should you even think of those Beasts?" She motioned toward the forest. "Well, if you really want to die that much, go ahead!"

She quieted, but her fingers kept opening and closing on the tablecloth. "Edwin, Edwin, your father built every part of this World, it was beautiful for him, it should be for you. There's nothing, nothing, beyond those trees but death; I won't have you near it! This *is* the World. There's no other worth bothering with."

He nodded miserably.

"Smile now, and finish your toast," she said.

He ate slowly, with the window reflected in secret on his silver spoon.

"Mom . . . ?" He couldn't say it. "What's . . . dying? You talk about it. Is it a feeling?"

"To those who must live on after someone else, a bad feeling, yes." She stood up suddenly. "You're late for school! Run!"

He kissed her as he grabbed his books. "Bye!"

"Say hello to Teacher!"

He fled from her like a bullet from a gun. Up endless staircases, through passages, halls, past windows that poured down dark gallery panels like white waterfalls. Up, up through the layer-cake Worlds with the thick frostings of Oriental rug between, and bright candles on top.

From the highest stair he gazed down through four intervals of Universe.

Lowlands of kitchen, dining room, parlor. Two Middle Countries of music, games, pictures, and locked, forbidden rooms. And here—he whirled—the Highlands of picnics, adventure, and learning. Here he roamed, idled, or sat singing lonely child songs on the winding journey to school.

This, then, was the Universe. Father (or God, as Mother often called him) had raised its mountains of wallpapered plaster long ago. This was Father-God's creation, in which stars blazed at the flick of a switch. And the sun was Mother, and Mother was the sun, about which all the Worlds swung, turning. And Edwin, a small dark meteor, spun up around through the dark carpets and shimmering tapestries of space. You saw him rise to vanish on vast comet staircases, on hikes and explorations.

Sometimes he and Mother picnicked in the Highlands, spread cool snow linens on red-tuffed, Persian lawns, on crimson meadows in a rarefied plateau at the summit of the Worlds where flaking portraits of sallow strangers looked meanly down on their eating and their revels. They drew water from silver taps in hidden tiled niches, smashed the tumblers on hearthstones, shrieking. Played hide-and-seek in enchanted Upper Countries, in unknown, wild, and hidden lands, where she found him rolled like a mummy in a velvet window drape or under sheeted furniture like a rare plant protected from some wind. Once, lost, he wandered for hours in insane foothills of dust and echoes, where the hooks and hangers in closets were hung only with night. But she found him and carried him weeping down through the leveling Universe to the parlor where dust motes, exact and familiar, fell in showers of sparks on the sunlit air.

He ran up a stair.

Here he knocked a thousand thousand doors, all locked and forbidden. Here Picasso ladies and Dali gentlemen screamed silently from canvas asylums, their gold eyes burning when he dawdled.

"Those Things live *out there*," his mother had said, pointing to the Dali-Picasso families.

Now running quickly past, he stuck out his tongue at them.

He stopped running.

One of the forbidden doors stood open.

Sunlight slanted warm through it, exciting him.

Beyond the door, a spiral stair screwed around up in sun and silence.

He stood, gasping. Year after year he had tried the doors that were always found locked. What would happen now if he shoved this one full open and climbed the stair? Was some Monster hiding at the top?

"Hello!"

His voice leapt up around the spiraled sunlight. "Hello . . . " whispered a faint, far lazy echo, high, high, and gone.

He moved through the door.

"Please, please, don't hurt me," he whispered to the high sunlit place.

He climbed, pausing with each step to wait for his punishment, eyes shut like a penitent. Faster now, he leapt around and around and up until his knees ached and his breath fountained in and out and his head banged like a bell and at last he reached the terrible summit of the climb and stood in an open, sun-drenched tower.

The sun struck his eyes a blow. Never, never so much sun! He stumbled to the iron rail.

"It's there!" His mouth opened from one direction to another. "It's there!" He ran in a circle. "There!"

He was above the somber tree barrier. For the first time he stood high over the windy chestnuts and elms and as far as he could see was green grass, green trees, and white ribbons on which beetles ran, and the other half of the World was blue and endless, with the sun lost and dropping away in an incredible deep blue room so vast he felt himself fall with it, screamed, and clutched the tower ledge, and beyond the trees, beyond the white ribbons where the beetles ran he saw things like fingers sticking up, but he saw no Dali-Picasso Terrors, he saw only some small red-and-white-and-blue handkerchiefs fluttering high on great white poles.

He was suddenly sick; he was sick again.

Turning, he almost fell flat down the stairs.

He slammed the forbidden door, fell against it.

"You'll go blind." He crushed his hands to his eyes. "You shouldn't have seen, you shouldn't, you shouldn't!"

He fell to his knees, he lay on the floor twisted tight, covered up. He need wait but a moment—the blindness would come.

Five minutes later he stood at an ordinary Highlands window, looking out at his own familiar Garden World.

He saw once more the elms and hickory trees and the stone wall, and that forest which he had taken to be an endless wall itself, beyond which lay nothing but nightmare nothingness, mist, rain, and eternal night. Now it was certain, the Universe did not end with the forest. There were other Worlds than those contained in Highland or Lowland.

He tried the forbidden door again. Locked.

Had he really gone up? Had he really discovered those half-green, half-blue vastnesses? Had God seen him? Edwin trembled. God. God, who smoked mysterious black pipes and wielded magical walking sticks. God who might be watching even now!

Edwin murmured, touching his cold face.

"I can still see. Thank you, thank you. I can *still* see!"

At nine-thirty, half an hour late, he rapped on the school door.

"Good morning, Teacher!"

The door swung open. Teacher waited in her tall, gray, thick-clothed monk's robe, the cowl hiding her face. She wore her usual silver spectacles. Her gray-gloved hands beckoned.

"You're late."

Beyond her the land of books burned in bright colors from the hearth. There were walls bricked with encyclopedias, and a fireplace in which you could stand without bumping your head. A log blazed fiercely.

The door closed, and there was a warm quiet. Here was the desk, where God had once sat, he'd walked this carpet, stuffing his pipe with rich tobacco, and scowled out that vast, stained-glass window. The room smelled of God, rubbed wood, tobacco, leather, and silver coins. Here, Teacher's voice sang like a solemn harp, telling of God, the old days, and the World when it had shaken with God's determination, trembled at his wit, when the World was abuilding under God's hand, a blueprint, a cry, and timber rising. God's fingerprints still lay like half-melted snowflakes on a dozen sharpened pencils in a locked glass display. They must never never be touched lest they melt away forever.

Here, here in the Highlands, to the soft sound of Teacher's voice running on, Edwin learned what was expected of him and his body. He was to grow into a Presence, he must fit the odors and the trumpet voice of God. He must some day stand tall and burning with pale fire at this high window to shout dust off the beams of the Worlds; he must be God himself! Nothing must prevent it.

Not the sky or the trees or the Things beyond the trees.

Teacher moved like a vapor in the room.

"Why are you late, Edwin?"

"I don't know."

"I'll ask you again. Edwin, why are you late?"

"One—one of the forbidden doors was open. . . . "

He heard the hiss of Teacher's breath. He saw her slowly slide back and sink into the large hand-carved chair, swallowed by darkness, her glasses flashing light before they vanished. He felt her looking out at him from shadow and her voice was numbed and so like a voice he heard at night, his own voice crying just before he woke from some nightmare. "Which door? Where?" she said. "Oh, it must be locked!"

"The door by the Dali-Picasso people," he said, in panic. He and Teacher had always been friends. Was that finished now? Had he spoiled things? "I climbed the stair. I had to, I had to! I'm sorry, I'm sorry. Please, don't tell Mother!"

Teacher sat lost in the hollow chair, in the hollow cowl. Her glasses made faint firefly glitters in the well where she moved alone. "And what did you *see* up there?" she murmured.

"A big blue room!"

"Did you?"

"And a green one, and ribbons with bugs running on them, but I didn't, I didn't stay long, I swear, I swear!"

"Green room, ribbons, yes ribbons, and the little bugs running along them, yes," she said, and her voice made him sad.

He reached out for her hand, but it fell away to her lap and groped back, in darkness, to her breast. "I came right down, I locked the door, I won't go look again, ever!" he cried.

Her voice was so faint he could hardly hear what she said. "But now you've seen, and you'll want to see more, and you'll always be curious now." The cowl moved slowly back and forth. Its deepness turned toward him, questioning. "Did you—*like* what you saw?"

"I was scared. It was big."

"Big, yes, too big. Large, large, so large, Edwin. Not like *our* World. Big, large, uncertain. Oh, why did you do this! You knew it was wrong!"

The fire bloomed and withered on the hearth while she waited for his answer and finally when he could not answer she said, as if her lips were barely moving, "Is it your mother?"

"I don't know!"

"Is she nervous, is she mean, does she snap at you, does she hold too tight, do you want time alone, is that it, is that it, is that it?"

"Yes, yes!" he sobbed, wildly.

"Is that why you ran off, she demands all your time, all your thoughts?" Lost and sad, her voice. "Tell me . . . "

His hands had gone sticky with tears. "Yes!" He bit his fingers and the backs of his hands. "Yes!" It was wrong to admit such things, but he didn't have to say them now, she said them, she said them, and all he must do is agree, shake his head, bite his knuckles, cry out between sobs.

Teacher was a million years old.

"We learn," she said, wearily. Rousing from her chair, she moved with a slow swaying of gray robes to the desk where her gloved hand searched a long time to find pen and paper. "We learn, Oh God, but slowly, and with pain, we learn. We think we do right, but all the time, all the time, we kill the Plan. . . . " She hissed her breath, jerked her head up suddenly. The cowl looked completely empty, shivering.

She wrote words on the paper.

"Give this to your mother. It tells her you must have two full hours every afternoon to yourself, to prowl where you wish. Anywhere. Except *out there*. Are you listening, child?"

"Yes." He dried his face. "But—"

"Go on."

"Did Mother lie to me about *out there*, and the Beasts?"

"Look at me" she said. "I've been your friend, I've never beaten you, as your mother sometimes must. We're both here to help you understand and grow so you won't be destroyed as God was."

She arose, and in rising, turned the cowl such a way that color from the hearth washed over her face. Swiftly, the firelight erased her many wrinkles.

Edwin gasped. His heart gave a jolting thump. "The fire!"

Teacher froze.

"The fire!" Edwin looked at the fire and back to her face. The cowl jerked away from his gaze, the face vanished in the deep well, gone. "Your face," said Edwin numbly. "You look like Mother!"

She moved swiftly to the books, seized one down. She talked to the shelves in her high, singing monotonous voice. "Women look alike, you know that! Forget it! Here, here!" And she brought him the book. "Read the first chapter! Read the diary!"

Edwin took the book but did not feel its weight in his hands. The fire rumbled and sucked itself brilliantly up the flue as he began to read and as he read Teacher sank back down and settled and quieted and the more he read the more the gray cowl nodded and became serene, the hidden face like a clapper gone solemn in its bell. Firelight ignited the gold animal lettering of the shelved books as he read and he spoke the words but was really thinking of these books from which pages had been razored, and clipped, certain lines erased, certain pictures torn, the leather jaws of some books glued tight, others like mad dogs, muzzled in hard bronze straps to keep him away. All this he thought while his lips moved through the fire-quiet.

"In the Beginning was God, who created the Universe, and the Worlds within the Universe, the Continents within the Worlds and the Lands within the Continents, and shaped from his mind and hand his loving wife and a child who in time would be God himself . . . "

Teacher nodded slowly. The fire fell softly away to slumbering coals. Edwin read on.

Down the banister, breathless, he slid into the parlor. "Mom, Mom!"

She lay in a plump maroon chair, breathless, as if she, too, had run a great way.

"Mom, Mom, you're soaking wet!"

"Am I?" she said, as if it was his fault she'd been rushing about. "So I am, so I am." She took a deep breath and sighed. Then she took his hands and kissed each one. She looked at him steadily, her eyes dilating. "Well now, listen here, I've a surprise! Do you know what's coming tomorrow? You can't guess! Your birthday!"

"But it's only been ten months!"

"Tomorrow it is! Do us wonders, I say. And anything I *say* is so is *really* so, my dear."

She laughed.

"And we open another secret room?" He was dazed.

"The fourteenth room, yes! Fifteenth room next year, sixteenth, seventeenth, and so on and on till your twenty-first birthday, Edwin! Then, oh, then we'll open up the triple-locked doors to the most important room and you'll be Man of the House, Father, God, Ruler of the Universe!"

"Hey," he said. And, "Hey!" He tossed his books straight up in the air. They exploded like a great burst of doves, whistling. He laughed. She laughed. Their laughter flew and fell with the books. He ran to scream down the banister again.

At the bottom of the stairs, she waited, arms wide, to catch him.

Edwin lay on his moonlit bed and his fingers pried at the Jack-in-the-Box, but the lid stayed shut; he turned it in his hands, blindly, but did not look down at it. Tomorrow, his birthday—but why? Was he *that* good? No. Why then, should the birthday come so soon? Well, simply because things had gotten, what word could you use? Nervous? Yes, things had begun to shimmer by day as well as by night. He saw the white tremor, the moonlight sifting down and down of an invisible snow in his mother's face. It would take yet another of his birthdays to quiet her again.

"My birthdays," he said to the ceiling, "will come quicker from now on. I know, I know. Mom laughs so loud, so much, and her eyes are funny. . . . "

Would Teacher be invited to the party? No. Mother and Teacher had never met. "Why not?" "Because," said Mom. "Don't you *want* to meet Mom, Teacher?" "Some day," said Teacher, faintly, blowing off like cobwebs in the hall. "Some . . . day. . . . "

And where did Teacher go at night? Did she drift through all those secret mountain countries high up near the moon where the chandeliers were skinned blind with dust, or did she wander out beyond the trees that lay beyond the trees that lay beyond the trees? No, hardly that!

He twisted the toy in his sweating hands. Last year, when things began to tremble and quiver, hadn't Mother advanced his birthday several months, too? Yes, oh, yes, yes.

Think of something else. God. God building cold midnight cellar, sun-baked attic, and all miracles between. Think of the hour of his death, crushed by some monstrous beetle beyond the wall. Oh, how the Worlds must have rocked with his passing!

Edwin moved the Jack-in-the-Box to his face, whispered against the lid. "Hello! Hello! Hello, hello . . . "

No answer save the sprung-tight coiled-in tension there. I'll get you out, thought Edwin. Just wait, just wait. It may hurt, but there's only one way. Here, here . . .

And he moved from bed to window and leaned far out, looking down to the marbled walk in the moonlight. He raised the box high, felt the sweat trickle from his armpit, felt his fingers clench, felt his arm jerk. He flung the box out, shouting. The box tumbled in the cold air, down. It took a long time to strike the marble pavement.

Edwin bent still further over, gasping.

"Well?" he cried. "Well?" and again, "You there!" and "You!"

The echoes faded. The box lay in the forest shadows. He could not see if the crash had broken it wide. He could not see if the Jack had risen, smiling, from its hideous jail or if it bobbed upon the wind now this way, that, this way, that, its silver bells jingling softly. He listened. He stood by the window for an hour staring, listening, and at last went back to bed.

Morning. Bright voices moved near and far, in and out the Kitchen World and Edwin opened his eyes. Whose voices, now whose could they be? Some of God's workmen? The Dali people? But Mother hated them; no. The voices faded in a humming roar. Silence. And from a great distance, a running, running grew louder and still louder until the door burst open.

"Happy Birthday!"

They danced, they ate frosted cookies, they bit lemon ices, they drank pink wines, and there stood his name on a snow-powdered cake as Mother chorded the piano into an avalanche of sound and opened her mouth to sing, then whirled to seize him away to more strawberries, more wines, more laughter that shook chandeliers into trembling rain. Then, a silver key flourished, they raced to unlock the fourteenth forbidden door.

"Ready! Hold on!"

The door whispered into the wall.

"Oh," said Edwin.

For, disappointingly enough, this fourteenth room was nothing at all but a dusty dull-brown closet. It promised nothing as had the rooms given him on other anniversaries! His sixth birthday present, now, had been the schoolroom in the Highlands. On his seventh birthday he had opened the playroom in the Lowlands. Eighth, the music room; ninth, the miraculous hell-fired kitchen! Tenth was the room where phonographs hissed in a continuous exhalation of ghosts singing on a gentle wind. Eleventh was the vast green diamond room of the garden with a carpet that had to be cut instead of swept!

"Oh, don't be disappointed; move!" Mother, laughing, pushed him in the closet. "Wait till you see how magical! Shut the door!"

She thrust a red button flush with the wall.

Edwin shrieked. "No!"

For the room was quivering, working, like a mouth that held them in iron jaws; the room moved, the wall slid away below.

"Oh, hush now, darling," she said. The door drifted down through the floor, and a long insanely vacant wall slithered by like an endlessly rustling snake to bring another door and another door with it that did not stop but traveled on while Edwin screamed and clutched his mother's waist. The room whined and cleared its throat somewhere; the trembling ceased, the room stood still. Edwin stared at a strange new door and heard his mother say go on, open it, there, now, there. And the new door gaped upon still further mystery. Edwin blinked.

"The Highlands! This is the Highlands! How did we get here? Where's the parlor, Mom, where's the parlor?"

She fetched him out through the door. "We jumped straight up, and we flew. Once a week, you'll fly to school instead of running the long way around!"

He still could not move, but only stood looking at the mystery of Land exchanged for Land, of Country replaced by higher and further Country.

"Oh, Mother, Mother . . . " he said.

It was a sweet long time in the deep grass of the garden where they idled most deliciously, sipped huge cupfuls of apple cider with their elbows on crimson silk cushions, their shoes kicked off, their toes bedded in sour dandelions, sweet clover. Mother jumped twice when she heard Monsters roar beyond the forest. Edwin kissed her cheek. "It's all right," he said, "I'll protect you."

"I know you will," she said, but she turned to gaze at the pattern of trees, as if any moment the chaos out there might smash the forest with a blow and stamp its Titan's foot down and grind them to dust.

Late in the long blue afternoon, they saw a chromium bird thing fly through a bright rift in the trees, high and roaring. They ran for the parlor, heads bent as before a green storm of lightning and rain, feeling the sound pour blinding showers to drench them.

Crackle, crackle—the birthday burnt away to cellophane nothingness. At sunset, in the dim soft Parlor Country, Mother inhaled champagne with her tiny seedling nostrils and her pale summer-rose mouth, then, drowsy wild, herded Edwin off to his room and shut him in.

He undressed in slow-pantomimed wonder, thinking, this year, next year, and which room two years, three years, from today? What about the Beasts, the Monsters? And being mashed and God killed? What was killed? What was Death? Was Death a feeling? Did God enjoy it so much he never came back? Was Death a journey then?

In the hall, on her way downstairs, Mother dropped a champagne bottle. Edwin heard and was cold, for the thought that jumped through his head was, that's how Mother'd sound. If she fell, if she broke, you'd find a million fragments in the morning. Bright crystal and clear wine on the parquet flooring, that's all you'd see at dawn.

Morning was the smell of vines and grapes and moss in his room, a smell of shadowed coolness. Downstairs, breakfast was in all probability, at this instant, manifesting itself in a fingersnap on the wintry tables.

Edwin got up to wash and dress and wait, feeling fine. Now things would be fresh and new for at least a month. Today, like all days, there'd be breakfast, school, lunch, songs in the music room, an hour or two at the electrical games, then—tea in the Outlands, on the luminous grass. Then up to school again for a late hour or so, where he and Teacher might prowl the censored library together and he'd puzzle with words and thoughts about that World *out there* that had been censored from his eyes.

He had forgotten Teacher's note. Now, he must give it to Mother.

He opened the door. The hall was empty. Down through the deeps of the Worlds, a soft mist floated, through a silence which no footsteps broke; the hills were quiet; the silver fonts did not pulse in the first sunlight, and the banister, coiling up from the mists, was a prehistoric monster peering into his room. He pulled away from this creature, looking to find Mother, like a white boat, drifted by the dawn tides and vapors below.

She was not there. He hurried down through the hushed lands, calling, "Mother!"

He found her in the parlor, collapsed on the floor in her shiny green-gold party dress, a champagne goblet in one hand, the carpet littered with broken glass.

She was obviously asleep, so he sat at the magical breakfast table. He blinked at the empty white cloth and the gleaming plates. There was no food. All his life wondrous foods had awaited him here. But not today.

"Mother, wake up!" He ran to her. "Shall I go to school? Where's the food? Wake up!"

He ran up the stairs.

The Highlands were cold and shadowed, and the white glass suns no longer glowed from the ceilings in this day of sullen fog. Down dark corridors, through dim continents of silence, Edwin rushed. He rapped and rapped at the school door. It drifted in, whining, by itself.

The school lay empty and dark. No fire roared on the hearth to toss shadows on the beamed ceiling. There was not a crackle or a whisper.

"Teacher?"

He poised in the center of the flat, cold room.

"Teacher!" he screamed.

He slashed the drapes aside; a faint shaft of sunlight fell through the stained glass.

Edwin gestured. He commanded the fire to explode like a popcorn kernel on the hearth. He commanded it to bloom to life! He shut his eyes, to give Teacher time to appear. He opened his eyes and was stupefied at what he saw on her desk.

Neatly folded was the gray cowl and robe, atop which gleamed her silver spectacles, and one gray glove. He touched them. One gray glove was gone. A piece of greasy cosmetic chalk lay on the robe. Testing it, he made dark lines on his hands.

He drew back, staring at Teacher's empty robe, the glasses, the greasy chalk. His hand touched a knob of a door which had always been locked. The door swung slowly wide. He looked into a small brown closet.

"Teacher!"

He ran in, the door crashed shut, he pressed a red button. The room sank down, and with it sank a slow mortal coldness. The World was silent, quiet, and cool. Teacher gone and Mother—sleeping. Down fell the room, with him in its iron jaws.

Machinery clashed. A door slid open. Edwin ran out.

The parlor!

Behind was not a door, but a tall oak panel from which he had emerged.

Mother lay uncaring, asleep. Folded under her, barely showing as he rolled her over, was one of Teacher's soft gray gloves.

He stood near her, holding the incredible glove, for a long time. Finally, he began to whimper.

He fled back to the Highlands. The hearth was cold, the room empty. He waited. Teacher did not come. He ran down again to the solemn Lowlands, commanded the table to fill with steaming dishes! Nothing happened. He sat by his mother, talking and pleading with her and touching her, and her hands were cold.

The clock ticked and the light changed in the sky and still she did not move, and he was hungry and the silent dust dropped down on the air through all the Worlds. He thought of Teacher and knew that if she was in none of the hills and mountains above, then there was only one place she could be. She had wandered, by error, into the Outlands, lost until someone found her. And so he must go out, call after her, bring her back to wake Mother, or she would lie here forever with the dust falling in the great darkened spaces.

Through the kitchen, out back, he found late afternoon sun and the Beasts hooting faintly beyond the rim of the World. He clung to the garden wall, not daring to let go, and in the shadows, at a distance, saw the shattered box he had flung from the window. Freckles of sunlight quivered on the broken lid and touched tremblingly over and over the face of the Jack jumped out and sprawled with its arms overhead in an eternal gesture of freedom. The doll smiled and did not smile, smiled and did not smile, as the sun winked on the mouth, and Edwin stood, hypnotized, above and beyond it. The doll opened its arms toward the path that led off between the secret trees, the forbidden path smeared with oily droppings of the Beasts. But the path lay silent and the sun warmed Edwin and he heard the wind blow softly in the trees. At last, he let go of the garden wall.

"Teacher?"

He edged along the path a few feet.

"Teacher!"

His shoes slipped on the animal droppings and he stared far down the motionless tunnel, blindly. The path moved under, the trees moved over him.

"Teacher!"

He walked slowly but steadily. He turned. Behind him lay his World and its very new silence. It was diminished, it was small! How strange to see it less than it had been. It had always and forever seemed so large. He felt his heart stop. He stepped back. But then, afraid of that silence in the World, he turned to face the forest path ahead.

Everything before him was new. Odors filled his nostrils, colors, odd shapes, incredible sizes filled his eyes.

If I run beyond the trees I'll die, he thought, for that's what Mother said. You'll die, you'll die.

But what's dying? Another room? A blue room, a green room, far larger than all the rooms that ever were! But where's the key? There, far ahead, a large half-open iron door, a wrought-iron gate. Beyond a room as large as the sky, all colored green with trees and grass! Oh, Mother, Teacher . . .

He rushed, stumbled, fell, got up, ran again, his numb legs under him were left behind as he fell down and down the side of a hill, the path gone, wailing, crying, and then not wailing or crying any more, but making new sounds. He reached the great rusted, screaming iron gate, leapt through; the Universe dwindled behind, he did not look back at his old Worlds, but ran as they withered and vanished.

. . . .

The policeman stood at the curb, looking down the street. "These kids. I'll never be able to figure them."

"How's that?" asked the pedestrian.

The policeman thought it over and frowned. "Couple seconds ago a little kid ran by. He was laughing and crying, crying and laughing, both. He was jumping up and down and touching things. Things like lampposts, the telephone poles, fire hydrants, dogs, people. Things like sidewalks, fences, gates, cars, plateglass windows, barber poles. Hell, he even grabbed hold and looked at me, and looked at the sky, you should have seen the tears, and all the time he kept yelling and yelling something funny."

"What did he yell?" asked the pedestrian.

"He kept yelling, 'I'm dead, I'm dead, I'm glad I'm dead, I'm dead, I'm dead, I'm glad I'm dead, I'm dead, I'm dead, it's *good* to be dead!'" The policeman scratched his chin slowly. "One of them new kid games, I guess."

The Leave-Taking

She was a woman with a broom or a dustpan or a washrag or a mixing spoon in her hand. You saw her cutting piecrust in the morning, humming to it, or you saw her setting out the baked pies at noon or taking them in, cool, at dusk. She rang porcelain cups like a Swiss bell ringer, to their place. She glided through the halls as steadily as a vacuum machine, seeking, finding, and setting to rights. She made mirrors of every window, to catch the sun. She strolled but twice through any garden, trowel in hand, and the flowers raised their quivering fires upon the warm air in her wake. She slept quietly and turned no more than three times in a night, as relaxed as a white glove to which, at dawn, a brisk hand will return. Waking, she touched people like pictures, to set their frames straight.

But, now . . . ?

"Grandma," said everyone. "Great-grandma."

Now it was as if a huge sum in arithmetic were finally drawing to an end. She had stuffed turkeys, chickens, squabs, gentlemen, and boys. She had washed ceilings, walls, invalids, and children. She had laid linoleum, repaired bicycles, wound clocks, stoked furnaces, swabbed iodine on ten thousand grievous wounds. Her hands had flown all around about and down, gentling this, holding that, throwing baseballs, swinging bright croquet mallets, seeding black earth, or fixing covers over dumplings, ragouts, and children wildly strewn by slumber. She had pulled down shades, pinched out candles, turned switches, and—grown old. Looking back on thirty billions of things started, carried, finished and done, it all summed up, totaled out; the last decimal was placed, the final zero swung slowly into line. Now, chalk in hand, she stood back from life a silent hour before reaching for the eraser.

"Let me see now," said Great-grandma. "Let me see . . . "

With no fuss or further ado, she traveled the house in an ever-circling inventory, reached the stairs at last, and, making no special announcement, she took herself up three flights to her room where, silently, she laid herself out like a fossil imprint under the snowing cool sheets of her bed and began to die.

Again the voices:

"Grandma! Great-grandma!"

The rumor of what she was doing dropped down the stairwell, hit, and spread ripples through the rooms, out doors and windows and along the street of elms to the edge of the green ravine.

"Here now, here!"

The family surrounded her bed.

"Just let me lie," she whispered.

Her ailment could not be seen in any microscope; it was a mild but ever-deepening tiredness, a dim weighing of her sparrow body; sleepy, sleepier, sleepiest.

As for her children and her children's children—it seemed impossible that with such a simple act, the most leisurely act in the world, she could cause such apprehension.

"Great-grandma, now listen—what you're doing is no better than breaking a lease. This house will fall down without you. You must give us at least a year's notice!"

Great-grandma opened one eye. Ninety years gazed calmly out at her physicians like a dust-ghost from a high cupola window in a fast-emptying house. "Tom . . . ?"

The boy was sent, alone, to her whispering bed.

"Tom," she said, faintly, far away, "in the Southern Seas there's a day in each man's life when he knows it's time to shake hands with all his friends and say good-by and sail away, and he does, and it's natural—it's just his time. That's how it is today. I'm so like you sometimes, sitting through Saturday matinees until nine at night when we send your dad to bring you home. Tom, when the time comes that the same cowboys are shooting the same Indians on the same mountaintop, then it's best to fold back the seat and head for the door, with no regrets and no walking backward up the aisle. So, I'm leaving while I'm still happy and still entertained."

Douglas was summoned next to her side.

"Grandma, who'll shingle the roof next spring?"

Every April for as far back as there were calendars, you thought you heard woodpeckers tapping the housetop. But no, it was Great-grandma, somehow transported, singing, pounding nails, replacing shingles, high in the sky!

"Douglas," she whispered, "don't ever let anyone do the shingles unless it's fun for them."

"Yes'm."

"Look around come April, and say, 'Who'd like to fix the roof?' And whichever face lights up is the face you want, Douglas. Because up there on that roof you can see the whole town going toward the country and the country going toward the edge of the earth and the river shining, and the morning lake, and birds on the trees down under you, and the best of the wind all around above. Any one of those should be enough to make a person climb a weather vane some spring sunrise. It's a powerful hour, if you give it half a chance. . . ."

Her voice sank to a soft flutter.

Douglas was crying.

She roused herself again. "Now, why are you doing that?"

"Because," he said, "you won't be here tomorrow."

She turned a small hand-mirror from herself to the boy. He looked at her face and himself in the mirror and then at her face again as she said, "Tomorrow morning I'll get up at seven and wash behind my ears; I'll run to church with Charlie Woodman; I'll picnic at Electric Park; I'll swim, run barefoot, fall out of trees, chew spearmint gum. . . . Douglas, Douglas, for shame! You cut your fingernails, don't you?"

"Yes'm."

"And you don't yell when your body makes itself over every seven years or so, old cells dead and new ones added to your fingers and your heart. You don't mind that, do you?"

"No'm."

"Well, consider then, boy. Any man saves fingernail clippings is a fool. You ever see a snake bother to keep his peeled skin? That's about all you got here today in this bed is fingernails and snake skin. One good breath would send me up in flakes. Important thing is not the me that's lying here, but the me that's sitting on the edge of the bed looking back at me, and the me that's downstairs cooking supper, or out in the garage under the car, or in the library reading. All the new parts, they count. I'm not really dying today. No person ever died that had a family. I'll be around a long time. A thousand years from now a whole township of my offspring will be biting sour apples in the gumwood shade. That's my answer to anyone asks big questions! Quick now, send in the rest!"

At last the entire family stood, like people seeing someone off at the rail station, waiting in the room.

"Well," said Great-grandma, "there I am. I'm not humble, so it's nice seeing you standing around my bed. Now next week there's late gardening and closet-cleaning and clothes-buying for the children to do. And since that part of me which is called, for convenience, Great-grandma, won't be here to step it along, those other parts of me called Uncle Bert and Leo and Tom and Douglas, and all the other names, will have to take over, each to his own."

"Yes, Grandma."

"I don't want any Hallowe'en parties here tomorrow. Don't want anyone saying anything sweet about me; I said it all in my time and my pride. I've tasted every victual and danced every dance; now there's one last tart I haven't bit on, one tune I haven't whistled. But I'm not afraid. I'm truly curious. Death won't get a crumb by my mouth I won't keep and savor. So don't you worry over me. Now, all of you go, and let me find my sleep. . . . "

Somewhere a door closed quietly.

"That's better." Alone, she snuggled luxuriously down through the warm snowbank of linen and wool, sheet and cover, and the colors of the patchwork quilt were bright as the circus banners of old time. Lying there, she felt as small and secret as on those mornings eighty-some-odd years ago when, wakening, she comforted her tender bones in bed.

A long time back, she thought, I dreamed a dream, and was enjoying it so much when someone wakened me, and that was the day when I was born. And now? Now, let me see. . . . She cast her mind back. Where was I? she thought. Ninety years . . . how to take up the thread and the pattern of that lost dream again? She put out a small hand. *There* . . . Yes, that was it. She smiled. Deeper in the warm snow hill she turned her head upon her pillow. That was better. Now, yes, now she saw it shaping in her mind quietly, and with a serenity like a sea moving along an endless and self-refreshing shore. Now she let the old dream touch and lift her from the snow and drift her above the scarce-remembered bed.

Downstairs, she thought, they are polishing the silver, and rummaging the cellar, and dusting in the halls. She could hear them living all through the house.

"It's all right," whispered Great-grandma, as the dream floated her. "Like everything else in this life, it's fitting."

And the sea moved her back down the shore.

Exorcism

She came out of the bathroom putting iodine on her finger where she had almost lopped it off cutting herself a chunk of coconut cake. Just then the mailman came up the porch steps, opened the door, and walked in. The door slammed. Elmira Brown jumped a foot.

"Sam!" she cried. She waved her iodined finger on the air to cool it. "I'm still not used to my husband being a postman. Every time you just walk in, it scares the life out of me!"

Sam Brown stood there with the mail pouch half empty, scratching his head. He looked back out the door as if a fog had suddenly rolled in on a calm sweet summer morn.

"Sam, you're home early," she said.

"Can't stay," he said in a puzzled voice.

"Spit it out, what's wrong?" She came over and looked into his face.

"Maybe nothing, maybe lots. I just delivered some mail to Clara Goodwater up the street. . . ."

"Clara Goodwater!"

"Now don't get your dander up. Books it was, from the Johnson-Smith Company, Racine, Wisconsin. Title of one book . . . let's see now." He screwed up his face, then unscrewed it. "*Albertus Magnus*—that's it. 'Being the approved, verified, sympathetic and natural Egyptian Secrets or . . .'" He peered at the ceiling to summon the lettering. "'White and Black Art for Man and Beast, Revealing the Forbidden Knowledge and Mysteries of Ancient Philosophers'!"

"Clara Goodwater's you say?"

"Walking along, I had a good chance to peek at the front pages, no harm in that. 'Hidden Secrets of Life Unveiled by that celebrated Student, Philosopher, Chemist, Naturalist, Psychomist, Astrologer, Alchemist, Metallurgist, Sorcerer, Explanator of the Mysteries of Wizards and Witchcraft, together with recondite views of numerous Arts and Sciences—Obscure, Plain, Practical, etcetera.' There! By God, I got a head like a box Brownie. Got the words, even if I haven't got the sense."

Elmira stood looking at her iodined finger as if it were pointed at her by a stranger.

"Clara Goodwater," she murmured.

"Looked me right in the eye as I handed it over, said, 'Going to be a witch, first-class, no doubt. Get my diploma in no time. Set up business. Hex crowds and individuals, old and young, big and small.' Then she kinda laughed, put her nose in that book, and went in."

Elmira stared at a bruise on her arm, carefully tongued a loose tooth in her jaw.

A door slammed. Tom Spaulding, kneeling on Elmira Brown's front lawn, looked up. He had been wandering about the neighborhood, seeing how the ants were doing here or there, and had found a particularly good hill with a big hole in which all kinds of fiery bright pismires were tumbling about scissoring the air and wildly carrying little packets of dead grasshopper and infinitesimal bird down into the earth. Now here was something else: Mrs. Brown, swaying on the edge of her porch as if she'd just found out the world was falling through space at sixty trillion miles a second. Behind her was Mr. Brown, who didn't know the miles per second and probably wouldn't care if he did know.

"You, Tom!" said Mrs. Brown. "I need moral support and the equivalent of the blood of the Lamb with me. Come along!"

And off she rushed, squashing ants and kicking tops off dandelions and trotting big spiky holes in flower beds as she cut across yards.

Tom knelt a moment longer studying Mrs. Brown's shoulder blades and spine as she toppled down the street. He read the bones and they were eloquent of melodrama and adventure, a thing he did not ordinarily connect with ladies, even though Mrs. Brown had the remnants of a pirate's mustache. A moment later he was in tandem with her.

"Mrs. Brown, you sure look mad!"

"You don't know what mad *is*, boy!"

"Watch out!" cried Tom.

Mrs. Elmira Brown fell right over an iron dog lying asleep there on the green grass.

"Mrs. Brown!"

"You see?" Mrs. Brown sat there. "Clara Goodwater did this to me! Magic!"

"Magic?"

"Never mind, boy. Here's the steps. You go first and kick any invisible strings out of the way. Ring that doorbell, but pull your finger off quick, the juice'll burn you to a cinder!"

Tom did not touch the bell.

"Clara Goodwater!" Mrs. Brown flicked the bell button with her iodined finger.

Far away in the cool dim empty rooms of the big old house, a silver bell tinkled and faded.

Tom listened. Still farther away there was a stir of mouselike running. A shadow, perhaps a blowing curtain, moved in a distant parlor.

"Hello," said a quiet voice.

And quite suddenly Mrs. Goodwater was there, fresh as a stick of peppermint, behind the screen.

"Why, hello there, Tom, Elmira. What—"

"Don't rush me! We came over about your practicing to be a full-fledged witch!"

Mrs. Goodwater smiled. "Your husband's not only a mailman, but a guardian of the law. Got a nose out to *here!*"

"He didn't look at no mail."

"He's ten minutes between houses laughing at post cards and trying on mail-order shoes."

"It ain't what he seen; it's what you yourself told him about the books you got."

"Just a joke. 'Going to be a witch!' I said, and bang! Off gallops Sam, like I'd flung lightning at him. I declare there can't be one wrinkle in that man's brain."

"You talked about your magic other places yesterday—"

"You must mean the Sandwich Club...."

"To which I pointedly was *not* invited."

"Why, lady, we thought that was your regular day with your grandma."

"I can always have another Grandma day, if people'd only ask me places."

"All there was to it at the Sandwich Club was me sitting there with a ham and pickle sandwich, and I said right out loud, 'At last I'm going to get my witch's diploma. Been studying for years!'"

"That's what come back to me over the phone!"

"Ain't modern inventions wonderful!" said Mrs. Goodwater.

"Considering you been president of the Honeysuckle Ladies Lodge since the Civil War, it seems, I'll put it to you bang on the nose. Have you used witchcraft all these years to spell the ladies and win the ayes-have-it?"

"Do you doubt it for a moment, lady?" said Mrs. Goodwater.

"Election's tomorrow again, and all I want to know is, you running for another term—and ain't you ashamed?"

"Yes to the first question and no to the second. Lady, look here, I bought those books for my boy cousin, Raoul. He's just ten and goes around looking in hats for rabbits. I told him there's about as much chance finding rabbits in hats as brains in heads of certain people I could name, but look he does and so I got these gifts for him."

"Wouldn't believe you on a stack of Bibles."

"God's truth, anyway. I love to fun about the witch thing. The ladies all yodeled when I explained about my dark powers. Wish you'd been there."

"I'll be there tomorrow to fight you with a cross of gold and all the powers of good I can organize behind me," said Elmira. "Right now, tell me how much other magic junk you got in your house."

Mrs. Goodwater pointed to a sidetable inside the door.

"I been buying all kinds of magic herbs. Smell funny and make Raoul happy. That little sack of stuff, that's called thisis rue, and this is sabisse root and that there's ebon herbs; here's black sulphur, and this they claim is bone dust."

"Bone dust!" Elmira skipped back and kicked Tom's ankle. Tom yelped.

"And here's wormwood and fern leaves so you can freeze shotguns and fly like a bat in your dreams, it says in Chapter X of the little book here. I think it's fine for growing boys' heads to think about things like this. Now, from the look on your face you don't believe Raoul exists. Well, I'll give you his Springfield address."

"Yes," said Elmira, "and the day I write him you'll take the Springfield bus and go to General Delivery and get my letter and write back to me in a boy's hand. I know you!"

"Mrs. Brown, speak up—you want to be president of the Honeysuckle Ladies Lodge, right? You run every year now for ten years. You nominate yourself. And always wind up getting *one* vote. Yours. Elmira, if the ladies wanted you they'd landslide you in. But from where I stand looking up the mountain, ain't so much as one pebble come rattling down save yours. Tell you what, I'll nominate and vote for you myself come noon tomorrow, how's that?"

"Damned for sure, then," said Elmira. "Last year I got a deathly cold right at election time; couldn't get out and campaign back-fence-to-back-fence. Year before that, broke my leg. Mighty strange." She squinted darkly at the lady behind the screen. "That's not all. Last month I cut my fingers six times, bruised my knee ten times, fell off my back porch twice, you hear—twice! I broke a window, dropped four dishes, one vase worth a dollar forty-nine at Bixby's, and I'm billing you for every dropped dish from now on in my house and environs!"

"I'll be poor by Christmas," said Mrs. Goodwater. She opened the screen door and came out suddenly and let the door slam. "Elmira Brown, how old are you?"

"You probably got it written in one of your black books. Thirty-five!"

"Well, when I think of thirty-five years of your life . . . " Mrs. Goodwater pursed her lips and blinked her eyes, counting. "That's about twelve thousand seven hundred and seventy-five days, or counting three of them per day, twelve thousand-odd commotions, twelve thousand much-ados and twelve thousand calamities. It's a full rich life you lead, Elmira Brown. Shake hands!"

"Get away!" Elmira fended her off.

"Why, lady, you're only the second most clumsy woman in Green Town, Illinois. You can't sit down without playing the chair like an accordion. You can't stand up but what you kick the cat. You can't trot across an open meadow without falling into a well. Your life has been one long decline, Elmira Alice Brown, so why not admit it?"

"It wasn't clumsiness that caused my calamities, but you being within a mile of me at those times when I dropped a pot of beans or juiced my finger in the electric socket at home."

"Lady, in a town this size, *everybody's* within a mile of someone at one time or other in the day."

"You admit being around then?"

"I admit being born here, yes, but I'd give anything right now to have been born in Kenosha or Zion. Elmira, go to your dentist and see what he can do about that serpent's tongue in there."

"Oh!" said Elmira. "Oh, oh, oh!"

"You've pushed me too far. I wasn't interested in witchcraft, but I think I'll just look into this business. Listen here! You're invisible right now. While you stood there I put a spell on you. You're clean out of sight."

"You didn't!"

"Course," admitted the witch, "I never *could* see you, lady."

Elmira pulled out her pocket mirror. "There I am!" She peered closer and gasped. She reached up like someone tuning a harp and plucked a single thread. She held it up, Exhibit A. "I never had a gray hair in my life till this second!"

The witch smiled charmingly. "Put it in a jar of still water, be an angleworm come morning. Oh, Elmira, look at yourself at last, won't you? All these years, blaming others for your own mallet feet and floaty ways! You ever read Shakespeare? There's little stage directions in there: *Alarums and Excursions*. That's you, Elmira. Alarums and Excursions! Now get home before I feel the bumps on your head and predict gas at night for you! Shoo!"

She waved her hands in the air as if Elmira were a cloud of things. "My, the flies are thick this summer!" she said.

She went inside and hooked the door.

"The line is drawn, Mrs. Goodwater," Elmira said, folding her arms. "I'll give you one last chance. Withdraw from the candidacy of the Honeysuckle Lodge or face me face-to-face tomorrow when I run for office and wrest it from you in a fair fight. I'll bring Tom here with me. An innocent good boy. And innocence and good will win the day."

"I wouldn't count on me being innocent, Mrs. Brown," said the boy. "My mother says—"

"Shut up, Tom, good's good! You'll be there on my right hand, boy."

"Yes'm," said Tom.

"If, that is," said Elmira, "I can live through the night with this lady making wax dummies of me—shoving rusty needles through the very heart and soul of them. If you find a great big fig in my bed all shriveled up come sunrise, Tom, you'll know who picked the fruit in the vineyard. And look to see Mrs. Goodwater president till she's a hundred and ninety-five years old."

"Why, lady," said Mrs. Goodwater, "I'm three hundred and five *now*. Used to call me SHE in the old days." She poked her fingers at the street. "Abracadabra-zimmity-ZAM! How's *that*?"

Elmira ran down off the porch.

"Tomorrow!" she cried.

"Till then, lady!" said Mrs. Goodwater.

Tom followed Elmira, shrugging and kicking ants off the sidewalk as he went.

Running across a driveway, Elmira screamed.

"Mrs. Brown!" cried Tom.

A car backing out of a garage ran right over Elmira's right big toe.

Mrs. Elmira Brown's foot hurt her in the middle of the night, so she got up and went down to the kitchen and ate some cold chicken and made a neat, painfully accurate list of things. First, illnesses in the past year. Three colds, four mild attacks of indigestion, one seizure of bloat, arthritis, lumbago, what she imagined to be gout, a severe bronchial cough, incipient asthma, and spots on her arms, plus an abscessed semicircular canal which made her reel like a drunken moth some days, backache, head pains, and nausea. Cost of medicine: *ninety-eight dollars and seventy-eight cents.*

Secondly, things broken in the house during the twelve months just past: two lamps, six vases, ten dishes, one soup tureen, two windows, one chair, one sofa cushion, six glasses, and one crystal chandelier prism. Total cost: *twelve dollars and ten cents.*

Thirdly, her pains this very night. Her toe hurt from being run over. Her stomach was upset. Her back was stiff, her legs were pulsing with agony. Her eyeballs felt like wads of blazing cotton. Her tongue tasted like a dust mop. Her ears were belling and ringing away. Cost? She debated, going back to bed.

Ten thousand dollars in personal suffering.

"Try to settle this out of court!" she said half aloud.

"Eh?" said her husband, awake.

She lay down in bed. "I simply refuse to die."

"Beg pardon?" he said.

"I won't die!" she said, staring at the ceiling.

"That's what I always claimed," said her husband, and turned over to snore.

In the morning, Mrs. Elmira Brown was up early and down to the library and then to the drugstore and back to the house where she was busy mixing all kinds of chemicals when her husband, Sam, came home with an empty mail pouch at noon.

"Lunch's in the icebox." Elmira stirred a green-looking porridge in a large glass.

"Good Lord, what's that?" asked her husband. "Looks like a milk shake been left out in the sun for forty years. Got kind of a fungus on it."

"Fight magic with magic."

"You goin' to *drink that?*"

"Just before I go up into the Honeysuckle Ladies Lodge for the big doings."

Samuel Brown sniffed the concoction. "Take my advice. Get up those steps first, *then* drink it. What's in it?"

"Snow from angels' wings, well, really menthol, to cool hell's fires that burn you, it says in this book I got at the library. The juice of a fresh grape off the vine, for thinking clear sweet thoughts in the face of dark visions, it says. Also red rhubarb, cream of tartar, white sugar, white of eggs, spring water and clover buds with the strength of the good earth in them. Oh, I could go on all day. It's here in the list, good against bad, white against black. I can't lose!"

"Oh, you'll win, all right," said her husband. "But will you *know* it?"

"Think good thoughts. I'm on my way to get Tom for my charm."

"Poor boy," said her husband. "Innocent, like you say, and about to be torn limb from limb, bargain-basement day at the Honeysuckle Lodge."

"Tom'll survive," said Elmira, and, taking the bubbling concoction with her, hid inside a Quaker Oats box with the lid on, went out the door without catching her dress or snagging her new ninety-eight-cent stockings. Realizing this, she was smug all the way to Tom's house where he waited for her in his white summer suit as she had instructed.

"Phew!" said Tom. "What you got in that box?"

"Destiny," said Elmira.

"I sure hope so," said Tom, walking about two paces ahead of her.

The Honeysuckle Ladies Lodge was full of ladies looking in each other's mirrors and tugging at their skirts and asking to be sure their slips weren't showing.

At one o'clock Mrs. Elmira Brown came up the steps with a boy in white clothes. He was holding his nose and screwing up one eye so he could only half see where he was going. Mrs. Brown looked at the crowd and then at the Quaker Oats box and opened the top and looked in and gasped, and put the top back on without drinking any of that stuff in there. She moved inside the hall and with her moved a rustling as of taffeta, all the ladies whispering in a tide after her.

She sat down in back with Tom, and Tom looked more miserable than ever. The one eye he had open looked at the crowd of ladies and shut up for good. Sitting there, Elmira got the potion out and drank it slowly down.

At one-thirty, the president, Mrs. Goodwater, banged the gavel and all but two dozen of the ladies quit talking.

"Ladies," she called out over the summer sea of silks and laces, capped here and there with white or gray, "it's election time. But before we start, I believe Mrs. Elmira Brown, wife of our eminent graphologist—"

A titter ran through the room.

"What's graphologist?" Elmira elbowed Tom twice.

"I don't know," whispered Tom fiercely, eyes shut, feeling that elbow come out of darkness at him.

"—wife, as I say, of our eminent handwriting expert, Samuel Brown... (more laughter)... of the U.S. Postal Service," continued Mrs. Goodwater.

"Mrs. Brown wants to give us some opinions. Mrs. Brown?"

Elmira stood up. Her chair fell over backward and snapped shut like a bear trap on itself. She jumped an inch off the floor and teetered on her heels, which gave off cracking sounds like they would fall to dust any moment. "I got plenty to say," she said, holding the empty Quaker Oats box in one hand with a Bible. She grabbed Tom with the other and plowed forward, hitting several people's elbows and muttering to them, "Watch what you're doing! Careful, you!" to reach the platform, turn, and knock a glass of water dripping over the table. She gave Mrs. Goodwater another bristly scowl when this happened and let her mop it up with a tiny handkerchief. Then with a secret look of triumph, Elmira drew forth the empty philter glass and held it up, displaying it for Mrs. Goodwater and whispering, "You know what was in this? It's inside me, now, lady. The charmed circle surrounds me. No knife can cleave, no hatchet break through."

The ladies, all talking, did not hear.

Mrs. Goodwater nodded, held up her hands, and there was silence.

Elmira held tight to Tom's hand. Tom kept his eyes shut, wincing.

"Ladies," Elmira said, "I sympathize with you. I know what you've been through these last ten years. I know why you voted for Mrs. Goodwater here. You've got boys, girls, and men to feed. You've got budgets to follow. You couldn't afford to have your milk sour, your bread fall, or your cakes as flat as wheels. You didn't want mumps, chicken pox, and whooping cough in your house all in three weeks. You didn't want your husband crashing his car or electrocuting himself on the high-tension wires outside town. But now all of that's over. You can come out in the open now. No more heartburns or backaches, because I've brought the good word and we're going to exorcise this witch we've got here!"

Everybody looked around but didn't see any witch.

"I mean your *president*!" cried Elmira.

"*Me!*" Mrs. Goodwater waved at everyone.

"Today," breathed Elmira, holding on to the desk for support, "I went to the library. I looked up counteractions. How to get rid of people who take advantage of others, how to make witches leave off and go. And I found a way to fight for all our rights. I can feel the power growing. I got the magic of all kinds of good roots and chemicals in me. I got . . . " She paused and swayed. She blinked once. "I got cream of tartar and . . . I got . . . white hawkweed and milk soured in the light of the moon and . . . " She stopped and thought for a moment. She shut her mouth and a tiny sound came from deep inside her and worked up through to come out the corner of her lips. She closed her eyes for a moment to see where the strength was.

"Mrs. Brown, you feelin' all right?" asked Mrs. Goodwater.

"Feelin' fine!" said Mrs. Brown slowly. "I put in some pulverized carrots and parsley root, cut fine; juniper berry . . . "

Again she paused as if a voice had said STOP to her and she looked out across all those faces.

The room, she noticed, was beginning to turn slowly, first from left to right, then right to left.

"Rosemary roots and crowfoot flower . . . " she said rather dimly. She let go of Tom's hand. Tom opened one eye and looked at her.

"Bay leaves, nasturtium petals . . . " she said.

"Maybe you better sit down," said Mrs. Goodwater.

One lady at the side went and opened a window.

"Dry betel nuts, lavender and crab-apple seed," said Mrs. Brown and stopped. "Quick now, let's have the election. Got to have the votes. I'll tabulate."

"No hurry, Elmira," said Mrs. Goodwater.

"Yes, there is." Elmira took a deep trembling breath. "Remember, ladies, no more fear. Do like you always wanted to do. Vote for me, and . . . " The room was moving again, up and down. "Honesty in government. All those in favor of Mrs. Goodwater for president say 'Aye.'"

"Aye," said the whole room.

"All those in favor of Mrs. Elmira Brown?" said Elmira in a faint voice. She swallowed.

After a moment she spoke, alone.

"Aye," she said.

She stood stunned on the rostrum.

A silence filled the room from wall to wall. In that silence Mrs. Elmira Brown made a croaking sound. She put her hand on her throat. She turned and looked dimly at Mrs. Goodwater, who now very casually drew forth from her purse a small wax doll in which were a number of rusted thumbtacks.

"Tom," said Elmira, "show me the way to the ladies' room."

"Yes'm."

They began to walk and then hurry and then run. Elmira ran on ahead, through the crowd, down the aisle. . . . She reached the door and started left.

"No, Elmira, right, right!" cried Mrs. Goodwater.

Elmira turned left and vanished.

There was a noise like coal down a chute.

"Elmira!"

The ladies ran around like a girls' basketball team, colliding with each other.

Only Mrs. Goodwater made a straight line.

She found Tom looking down the stairwell, his hands clenched to the banister.

"Forty steps!" he moaned. "Forty steps to the ground!"

Later on and for months and years after it was told how like an inebriate Elmira Brown negotiated those steps touching every one on her long way down. It was claimed that when she began the fall she was sick to unconsciousness and that this made her skeleton rubber, so she kind of rolled rather than ricocheted.

She landed at the bottom, blinking and feeling better, having left whatever it was that had made her uneasy all along the way. True, she was so badly bruised she looked like a tattooed lady. But, no, not a wrist was sprained or an ankle twisted. She held her head funny for three days, kind of peering out of the sides of her eyeballs instead of turning to look. But the important thing was Mrs. Goodwater at the bottom of the steps, pillowing Elmira's head on her lap and dropping tears on her as the ladies gathered hysterically.

"Elmira, I promise, Elmira, I swear, if you just live, if you don't die, you hear me, Elmira, listen! I'll use my magic for nothing but good from now on. No more black, nothing but white magic. The rest of your life, if I have my way, no more falling over iron dogs, tripping on sills, cutting fingers, or dropping downstairs for you! Elysium, Elmira, Elysium, I promise! If you just live! Look, I'm pulling the tacks out of the doll! Elmira, speak to me! Speak now and sit up! And come upstairs for another vote. President, I promise, president of the Honeysuckle Ladies Lodge, by acclamation, won't we, ladies?"

At this all the ladies cried so hard they had to lean on each other.

Tom, upstairs, thought this meant death down there.

He was halfway down when he met the ladies coming back up, looking like they had just wandered out of a dynamite explosion.

"Get out of the way, boy!"

First came Mrs. Goodwater, laughing and crying.

Next came Mrs. Elmira Brown, doing the same.

And after the two of them came all the one hundred twenty-three members of the lodge, not knowing if they'd just returned from a funeral or were on their way to a ball.

He watched them pass and shook his head.

"Don't need me no more," he said. "No more at all."

So he tiptoed down the stairs before they missed him, holding tight to the rail all the way.

The Happiness Machine

On Sunday morning Leo Auffmann moved slowly through his garage, expecting some wood, a curl of wire, a hammer or wrench to leap up crying, "Start here!" But nothing leaped, nothing cried for a beginning.

Should a Happiness Machine, he wondered, be something you can carry in your pocket?

Or, he went on, should it be something that carries you in *its* pocket?

"One thing I absolutely *know*," he said aloud. "It should be *bright*!"

He set a can of orange paint in the center of the workbench, picked up a dictionary, and wandered into the house.

"Lena?" He glanced at the dictionary. "Are you 'pleased, contented, joyful, delighted'? Do you feel 'lucky, fortunate'? Are things 'clever and fitting,' 'successful and suitable' for you?"

Lena stopped slicing vegetables and closed her eyes. "Read me the list again, please," she said.

He shut the book.

"What have I done, you got to stop and think an hour before you can tell me? All I ask is a simple yes or no! You're *not* contented, delighted, joyful?"

"Cows are 'contented,' babies and old people in second childhood are 'delighted,' God help them," she said. "As for 'joyful,' Leo? Look how I laugh scrubbing out the sink. . . ."

He peered closely at her and his face relaxed. "Lena, it's true. A man doesn't appreciate. Next month, maybe, we'll get away."

"*I'm* not complaining!" she cried. "*I'm* not the one comes in with a list saying, 'Stick out your tongue.' Leo, do you ask what makes your heart beat all night? No! Next will you ask, 'What's marriage?' Who knows, Leo? Don't ask. A man who thinks like that, how it runs, how things work, falls off the trapeze in the circus, chokes wondering how the muscles work in the throat. Eat, sleep, breathe, Leo, and stop staring at me like I'm something new in the house!"

Lena Auffmann froze. She sniffed the air.

"Oh, my God, look what you done!"

She yanked the oven door open. A great cloud of smoke poured through the kitchen.

"Happiness!" she wailed. "And for the first time in six months we have a fight! Happiness, and for the first time in twenty years it's not bread, it's charcoal for supper!"

When the smoke cleared, Leo Auffmann was gone.

The fearful clangor, the collision of man and inspiration, the flinging about of metal, lumber, hammer, nails, T square, screwdriver, continued for many days. On occasion, defeated, Leo Auffmann loitered out through the streets, nervous, apprehensive, jerking his head at the slightest sound of distant laughter, listened to children's jokes, watching what made them smile. At night he sat on neighbors' crowded porches, listening to the old folks weigh and balance life, and at each explosion of merriment Leo Auffmann quickened like a general who has seen the forces of darkness routed and whose strategy has been reaffirmed. On his way home he felt triumphant until he was in his garage with the dead tools and the inanimate lumber. Then his bright face fell away in a pale funk, and to cover his sense of failure he banged and crashed the parts of his machine about as if they really did make sense. At last it began to shape itself and at the end of ten days and nights, trembling with fatigue, self-dedicated, half starved, fumbling and looking as if he had been riven by lightning, Leo Auffmann wandered into his house.

The children, who had been screaming horribly at each other, fell silent, as if the Red Death had entered at the chiming of the clock.

"The Happiness Machine," husked Leo Auffmann, "is ready."

"Leo Auffmann," said his wife, "has lost fifteen pounds. He hasn't talked to his children in two weeks, they are nervous, they fight, listen! His wife is nervous, she's gained ten pounds, she'll need new clothes, look! Sure—the machine is ready. But happy? Who can say? Leo, leave off with the clock you're building. You'll never find a cuckoo big enough to go in it! Man was not made to tamper with such things. It's not against God, no, but it sure looks like it's against Leo Auffmann. Another week of this and we'll bury him in his machine!"

But Leo Auffmann was too busy noticing that the room was falling swiftly up.

How interesting, he thought, lying on the floor.

Darkness closed in a great wink on him as someone screamed something about that Happiness Machine, three times.

The first thing he noticed the next morning was dozens of birds fluttering around in the air stirring up ripples like colored stones thrown into an incredibly clear stream, gonging the tin roof of the garage softly.

A pack of multibred dogs pawfooted one by one into the yard to peer and whine gently through the garage door; four boys, two girls, and some men hesitated in the driveway and then edged along under the cherry trees.

Leo Auffmann, listening, knew what it was that had reached out and called them all into the yard.

The sound of the Happiness Machine.

It was the sort of sound that might be heard coming from a giant's kitchen on a summer day. There were all kinds of hummings, low and high, steady and then changing. Incredible foods were being baked there by a host of whirring golden bees as big as teacups. The giantess herself, humming contentedly under her breath, might glide to the door, as vast as all summer, her face a huge peach-colored moon gazing calmly out upon smiling dogs, corn-haired boys and flour-haired old men.

"Wait," said Leo Auffmann out loud. "I didn't turn the machine on this morning! Saul!"

Saul, standing in the yard below, looked up.

"Saul, did you turn it on?"

"You told me to warm it up half an hour ago!"

"All right, Saul, I forgot. I'm not awake." He fell back in bed.

His wife, bringing his breakfast up, paused by the window, looking down at the garage.

"Tell me," she said quietly. "If that machine is like you say, has it got an answer to making babies in it somewhere? Can that machine make seventy-year-old people twenty? Also, how does death look when you hide in there with all that happiness?"

"Hide!"

"If you died from overwork, what should I do today, climb in that big box down there and be happy? Also tell me, Leo, how is our life? You know how our house is. Seven in the morning, breakfast, the kids; all of you gone by eight-thirty and it's just me and washing and me and cooking and socks to be darned, weeds to be dug, or I run to the store or polish silver. Who's complaining? I'm just reminding you how the house is put together, Leo, what's in it! So now answer: How do you get all those things I said in one machine?"

"That's not how it's built!"

"I'm sorry. I got no time to look, then."

And she kissed his cheek and went from the room and he lay smelling the wind that blew from the hidden machine below, rich with the odor of those roasted chestnuts that are sold in the autumn streets of a Paris he had never known. . . .

A cat moved unseen among the hypnotized dogs and boys to purr against the garage door, in the sound of snow-waves crumbling down a faraway and rhythmically breathing shore.

Tomorrow, thought Leo Auffmann, we'll try the machine, all of us, together.

Late that night he awoke and knew something had wakened him. Far away in another room he heard someone crying.

"Saul?" he whispered, getting out of bed.

In his room Saul wept, his head buried in his pillow. "No . . . no . . ." he sobbed. "Over . . . over . . ."

"Saul, you had a nightmare? Tell me about it, son."

But the boy only wept.

And sitting there on the boy's bed, Leo Auffmann suddenly thought to look out the window. Below, the garage doors stood open.

He felt the hairs rise along the back of his neck.

When Saul slept again, uneasily, whimpering, his father went downstairs and out to the garage where, not breathing, he put his hand out.

In the cool night the Happiness Machine's metal was too hot to touch.

So, he thought, Saul was here tonight.

Why? Was Saul unhappy, in need of the machine? No, happy, but wanting to hold on to happiness always. Could you blame a boy wise enough to know his position who tried to keep it that way? No! And yet . . .

Above, quite suddenly, something white was exhaled from Saul's window. Leo Auffmann's heart thundered. Then he realized the window curtain had blown out into the open night. But it had seemed as intimate and shimmering a thing as a boy's soul escaping his room. And Leo Auffmann had flung up his hands as if to thwart it, push it back into the sleeping house.

Cold, shivering, he moved back into the house and up to Saul's room where he seized the blowing curtain in and locked the window tight so the pale thing could not escape again. Then he sat on the bed and put his hand on Saul's back.

"*A Tale of Two Cities*? Mine. *The Old Curiosity Shop*? Ha, that's Leo Auffmann's all right! *Great Expectations*? That *used* to be mine. But let *Great Expectations* be his, now!"

"What's this?" asked Leo Auffmann, entering.

"This," said his wife, "is sorting out the community property! When a father scares his son at night it's time to chop everything in half! Out of the way, Mr. Bleak House, Old Curiosity Shop. In all these books, no mad scientist lives like Leo Auffmann, none!"

"You're leaving, and you haven't even tried the machine!" he protested. "Try it once, you'll unpack, you'll stay!"

"*Tom Swift and His Electric Annihilator*—whose is that?" she asked. "Must I *guess*?"

Snorting, she gave *Tom Swift* to Leo Auffmann.

Very late in the day all the books, dishes, clothes, linens had been stacked one here, one there, four here, four there, ten here, ten there. Lena Auffmann, dizzy with counting, had to sit down. "All right," she gasped. "Before I go, Leo, prove you don't give nightmares to innocent sons!"

Silently Leo Auffmann led his wife into the twilight. She stood before the eight-foot-tall, orange-colored box.

"That's *happiness?*" she said. "Which button do I press to be overjoyed, grateful, contented, and much-obliged?"

The children had gathered now.

"Mama," said Saul, "don't!"

"I got to know what I'm yelling about, Saul." She got in the machine, sat down, and looked out at her husband, shaking her head. "It's not me needs this, it's you, a nervous wreck, shouting."

"Please," he said, "you'll see!"

He shut the door.

"Press the button!" he shouted in at his unseen wife.

There was a click. The machine shivered quietly, like a huge dog dreaming in its sleep.

"Papa!" said Saul, worried.

"Listen!" said Leo Auffmann.

At first there was nothing but the tremor of the machine's own secretly moving cogs and wheels.

"Is Mama all right?" asked Naomi.

"All right? She's fine! There, now . . . there!"

And inside the machine Lena Auffmann could be heard saying, "Oh!" and then again, "Ah!" in a startled voice. "Look at that!" said his hidden wife. "Paris!" and later, "London! There goes Rome! The Pyramids! The Sphinx!"

"The Sphinx, you hear, children?" Leo Auffmann whispered and laughed.

"Perfume!" cried Lena Auffmann, surprised.

Somewhere a phonograph played "The Blue Danube" faintly.

"Music! I'm dancing!"

"Only *thinks* she's dancing," the father confided to the world.

"Amazing!" said the unseen woman.

Leo Auffmann blushed. "What an understanding wife."

And then inside the Happiness Machine, Lena Auffmann began to weep.

The inventor's smile faded.

"She's crying," said Naomi.

"She can't be!"

"She is," said Saul.

"She simply can't be crying!" Leo Auffmann, blinking, pressed his ear to the machine. "But . . . yes . . . like a baby . . . "

He could only open the door.

"Wait." There his wife sat, tears rolling down her cheeks. "Let me finish." She cried some more.

Leo Auffmann turned off the machine, stunned.

"Oh, it's the saddest thing in the world!" she wailed. "I feel awful, terrible." She climbed out through the door. "First, there was Paris . . . "

"What's wrong with Paris?"

"I never even *thought* of being in Paris in my life. But now you got me thinking: Paris! So suddenly I want to be in Paris and I know I'm not!"

"It's almost as good, this machine."

"No. Sitting in there, I knew. I thought, It's not real!"

"Stop crying, Mama."

She looked at him with great dark wet eyes. "You had me dancing. We haven't danced in twenty years."

"I'll take you dancing tomorrow night!"

"No, no! It's not important, it *shouldn't* be important. But your machine says it's important! So I believe! It'll be all right, Leo, after I cry some more."

"What else?"

"What else? The machine says, 'You're young.' I'm not. It lies, that Sadness Machine!"

"Sad in what way?"

His wife was quieter now. "Leo, the mistake you made is you forgot some hour, some day, we all got to climb out of that thing and go back to dirty dishes and the beds not made. While you're in that thing, sure, a sunset lasts forever almost, the air smells good, the temperature is fine. All the things you want to last, last. But outside, the children wait on lunch, the clothes need buttons. And then let's be frank, Leo, how long can you *look* at a sunset? Who *wants* a sunset to last? Who wants perfect temperature? Who wants air smelling good always? So after a while, who would notice? Better, for a minute or two, a sunset. After that, let's have something else. People are like that, Leo. How could you forget?"

"Did I?"

"Sunsets we always liked because they only happen once and go away."

"But Lena, that's sad."

"No, if the sunset stayed and we got bored, that would be a real sadness. So two things you did you should never have. You made quick things go slow and stay around. You brought things faraway to our back yard where they don't belong, where they just tell you, 'No, you'll never travel, Lena Auffmann, Paris you'll never see! Rome you'll *never* visit.' But I *always* knew that, so why tell me? Better to forget and make do, Leo, make do, eh?"

Leo Auffmann leaned against the machine for support. He snatched his burned hand away, surprised.

"So now what, Lena?" he said.

"It's not for me to say. I know only so long as this thing is here I'll want to come out, or Saul will want to come out like he did last night, and against our judgment sit in it and look at all those places so faraway and every time we will cry and be no fit family for you."

"I don't understand," he said, "how I could be so wrong. Just let me check to see what you say is true." He sat down inside the machine. "You won't go away?"

His wife nodded. "We'll wait, Leo."

He shut the door. In the warm darkness he hesitated, pressed the button, and was just relaxing back in color and music, when he heard someone screaming.

"Fire, Papa! The machine's on fire!"

Someone hammered the door. He leaped up, bumped his head, and fell as the door gave way and the boys dragged him out. Behind him he heard a muffled explosion. The entire family was running now. Leo Auffmann turned and gasped, "Saul, call the fire department!"

Lena Auffmann caught Saul as he ran. "Saul," she said. "Wait."

There was a gush of flame, another muffled explosion. When the machine was burning very well indeed, Lena Auffmann nodded.

"All right, Saul," she said. "Run call the fire department."

Everybody who was anybody came to the fire. There was Grandpa Spaulding and Douglas and Tom and most of the boarders and some of the old men from across the ravine and all the children from six blocks around. And Leo Auffmann's children stood out front, proud of how fine the flames looked jumping from the garage roof.

Grandfather Spaulding studied the smoke ball in the sky and said, quietly, "Leo, was that it? Your Happiness Machine?"

"Some year," said Leo Auffmann, "I'll figure it and tell you."

Lena Auffmann, standing in the dark now, watched as the firemen ran in and out of the yard; the garage, roaring, settled upon itself.

"Leo," she said, "it won't take a year to figure. Look around. Think. Keep quiet a little bit. Then come tell me. I'll be in the house, putting books back on shelves, and clothes back in closets, fixing supper, supper's late, look how dark. Come, children, help Mama."

When the firemen and the neighbors were gone, Leo Auffmann was left with Grandfather Spaulding and Douglas and Tom, brooding over the smoldering ruin. He stirred his foot in the wet ashes and slowly said what he had to say.

"The first thing you learn in life is you're a fool. The last thing you learn in life is you're the same fool. In one hour, I've done a lot of thinking. I thought, Leo Auffmann is blind! . . . You want to see the *real* Happiness Machine? The one they patented a couple thousand years ago, it still runs, not good all the time, no! but it runs. It's been here all along."

"But the fire—" said Douglas.

"Sure, the fire, the garage! But like Lena said, it don't take a year to figure; what burned in the garage don't count!"

They followed him up the front-porch steps.

"Here," whispered Leo Auffmann, "the front window. Quiet, and you'll see it."

Hesitantly, Grandfather, Douglas, and Tom peered through the large windowpane.

And there, in small warm pools of lamplight, you could see what Leo Auffmann wanted you to see. There sat Saul and Marshall, playing chess at the coffee table. In the dining room Rebecca was laying out the silver. Naomi was cutting paper-doll dresses. Ruth was painting water colors. Joseph was running his electric train. Through the kitchen door, Lena Auffmann was sliding a pot roast from the steaming oven. Every hand, every head, every mouth made a big or little motion. You could hear their faraway voices under glass. You could hear someone singing in a high sweet voice. You could smell bread baking, too, and you knew it was real bread that would soon be covered with real butter. Everything was there and it was working.

Grandfather, Douglas, and Tom turned to look at Leo Auffmann, who gazed serenely through the window, the pink light on his cheeks.

"Sure," he murmured. "There it is." And he watched with now-gentle sorrow and now-quick delight, and at last quiet acceptance, as all the bits and pieces of this house mixed, stirred, settled, poised, and ran steadily again. "The Happiness Machine," he said. "The Happiness Machine."

A moment later he was gone.

Inside, Grandfather, Douglas, and Tom saw him tinkering, make a minor adjustment here, eliminate friction there, busy among all those warm, wonderful, infinitely delicate, forever mysterious, and ever-moving parts.

Then smiling, they went down the steps into the fresh summer night.

Calling Mexico

And then there is that day when all around, all around you hear the dropping of the apples, one by one, from the trees. At first it is one here and one there, and then it is three and then it is four and then nine and twenty, until the apples plummet like rain, fall like horse hoofs in the soft, darkening grass, and you are the last apple on the tree; and you wait for the wind to work you slowly free from your hold upon the sky, and drop you down and down. Long before you hit the grass you will have forgotten there ever was a tree, or other apples, or a summer, or green grass below. You will fall in darkness. . . .

"No!"

Colonel Freeleigh opened his eyes quickly, sat erect in his wheel chair. He jerked his cold hand out to find the telephone. It was still there! He crushed it against his chest for a moment, blinking.

"I don't like that dream," he said to his empty room.

At last, his fingers trembling, he lifted the receiver and called the long-distance operator and gave her a number and waited, watching the bedroom door as if at any moment a plague of sons, daughters, grandsons, nurses, doctors, might swarm in to seize away this last vital luxury he permitted his failing senses. Many days, or was it years, ago, when his heart had thrust like a dagger through his ribs and flesh, he had heard the boys below . . . their names, what were they? Charles, Charlie, Chuck, yes! And Douglas! And Tom! He remembered! Calling his name far down the hall, but the door being locked in their faces, the boys turned away. You can't be excited, the doctor said. No visitors, no visitors, no visitors. And he heard the boys moving across the street, he saw them, he waved. And they waved back. "Colonel . . . Colonel . . . " And now he sat alone with the little gray toad of a heart flopping weakly here or there in his chest from time to time.

"Colonel Freeleigh," said the operator. "Here's your call. Mexico City. Erickson 3899."

And now the faraway but infinitely clear voice:

"*Bueno.*"

"Jorge!" cried the old man.

"*Señor* Freeleigh! Again? This costs money."

"Let it cost! You know what to do."

"*Sí.* The window?"

"The window, Jorge, if you please."

"A moment," said the voice.

And, thousands of miles away, in a southern land, in an office in a building in that land, there was the sound of footsteps retreating from the phone. The old man leaned forward, gripping the receiver tight to his wrinkled ear that ached with waiting for the next sound.

The raising of a window.

"Ah," sighed the old man.

The sounds of Mexico City on a hot yellow noon rose through the open window into the waiting phone. He could see Jorge standing there holding the mouthpiece out, out into the bright day.

"*Señor* . . . "

"No, no, please. Let me *listen.*"

He listened to the hooting of many metal horns, the squealing of brakes, the calls of vendors selling red-purple bananas and jungle oranges in their stalls. Colonel Freeleigh's feet began to move, hanging from the edge of his wheel chair, making the motions of a man walking. His eyes squeezed tight. He gave a series of immense sniffs, as if to gain the odors of meats hung on iron hooks in sunshine, cloaked with flies like a mantle of raisins; the smell of stone alleys wet with morning rain. He could feel the sun burn his spiny-bearded cheek, and he was twenty-five years old again, walking, walking, looking, smiling, happy to be alive, very much alert, drinking in colors and smells.

A rap on the door. Quickly he hid the phone under his lap robe.

The nurse entered. "Hello," she said. "Have you been good?"

"Yes." The old man's voice was mechanical. He could hardly see. The shock of a simple rap on the door was such that part of him was still in another city, far removed—it must be here to answer questions, act sane, be polite.

"I've come to check your pulse."

"Not now!" said the old man.

"You're not going anywhere, are you?" She smiled.

He looked at the nurse steadily. He hadn't been anywhere in ten years.

"Give me your wrist."

Her fingers, hard and precise, searched for the sickness in his pulse like a pair of calipers.

"What've you been doing to *excite* yourself?" she demanded.

"Nothing."

Her gaze shifted and stopped on the empty phone table. At that instant a horn sounded faintly, two thousand miles away.

She took the receiver from under the lap robe and held it before his face. "Why do you do this to yourself? You promised you wouldn't. That's how you hurt yourself in the first place, isn't it? Getting excited, talking too much. Those boys up here jumping around—"

"They sat quietly and listened," said the colonel. "And I told them things they'd never heard. The buffalo, I told them, the bison. It was worth it. I don't care. I was in a pure fever and I was alive. It doesn't matter if being so alive kills a man; it's better to have the quick fever every time. Now give me that phone. If you won't let the boys come up and sit politely I can at least talk to someone outside the room."

"I'm sorry, Colonel. Your grandson will have to know about this. I prevented his having the phone taken out last week. Now it looks like I'll let him go ahead."

"This is *my* house, my phone. I pay your salary!" he said.

"To make you well, not get you excited." She wheeled his chair across the room. "To bed with you now, young man!"

From bed he looked back at the phone and kept looking at it.

"I'm going to the store for a few minutes," the nurse said. "Just to be sure you don't use the phone again, I'm hiding your wheel chair in the hall."

She wheeled the empty chair out the door. In the downstairs entry, he heard her pause and dial the extension phone.

Was she phoning Mexico City? he wondered. She wouldn't dare!

The front door shut.

He thought of the last week here, alone, in his room, and the secret, narcotic calls across continents, an isthmus, whole jungle countries of rain forest, blue-orchid plateaus, lakes and hills . . . talking . . . talking . . . to Buenos Aires . . . and . . . Lima . . . Rio de Janeiro . . .

He lifted himself in the cool bed. Tomorrow the telephone gone! What a greedy fool he had been! He slipped his brittle ivory legs down from the bed, marveling at their desiccation. They seemed to be things which had been fastened to his body while he slept one night, while his younger legs were taken off and burned in the cellar furnace. Over the years, they had destroyed all of him, removing hands, arms, and legs and leaving him with substitutes as delicate and useless as chess pieces. And now they were tampering with something more intangible—the memory; they were trying to cut the wires which led back into another year.

He was across the room in a stumbling run. Grasping the phone, he took it with him as he slid down the wall to sit upon the floor. He got the long-distance operator, his heart exploding within him, faster and faster, a blackness in his eyes. "Hurry, hurry!"

He waited.

"*Bueno?*"

"Jorge, we were cut off."

"You must not phone again, *señor*," said the faraway voice. "Your nurse called me. She says you are very ill. I must hang up."

"No, Jorge! Please!" the old man pleaded. "One last time, listen to me. They're taking the phone out tomorrow. I can never call you again."

Jorge said nothing.

The old man went on. "For the love of God, Jorge! For friendship, then, for the old days! You don't know what it means. You're my age, but you can *move*! I haven't moved anywhere in ten years."

He dropped the phone and had trouble picking it up, his chest was so thick with pain. "Jorge! You *are* still there, aren't you?"

"This will be the last time?" said Jorge.

"I promise!"

The phone was laid on a desk thousands of miles away. Once more, with that clear familiarity, the footsteps, the pause, and, at last, the raising of the window.

"*Listen*," whispered the old man to himself.

And he heard a thousand people in another sunlight, and the faint, tinkling music of an organ grinder playing "La Marimba"—oh, a lovely, dancing tune.

With eyes tight, the old man put up his hand as if to click pictures of an old cathedral, and his body was heavier with flesh, younger, and he felt the hot pavement underfoot.

He wanted to say, "You're still there, aren't you? All of you people in that city in the time of the early siesta, the shops closing, the little boys crying *loteria nacional para hoy!* to sell lottery tickets. You are all there, the people in the city. I can't believe I was ever among you. When you are away from a city it becomes a fantasy. Any town, New York, Chicago, with its people, becomes improbable with distance. Just as I am improbable here, in Illinois, in a small town by a quiet lake. All of us improbable to one another because we are not present to one another. And so it is good to hear the sounds, and know that Mexico City is still there and the people moving and living. . . . "

He sat with the receiver tightly pressed to his ear.

And at last, the clearest, most improbable sound of all—the sound of a green trolley car going around a corner—a trolley burdened with brown and alien and beautiful people, and the sound of other people running and calling out with triumph as they leaped up and swung aboard and vanished around a corner on the shrieking rails and were borne away in the sun-blazed distance to leave only the sound of tortillas frying on the market stoves, or was it merely the ever rising and falling hum and burn of static quivering along two thousand miles of copper wire. . . ?

The old man sat on the floor.

Time passed.

A downstairs door opened slowly. Light footsteps came in, hesitated, then ventured up the stairs. Voices murmured.

"We shouldn't be here!"

"He phoned me, I tell you. He needs visitors bad. We can't let him down."

"He's sick!"

"Sure! But he said to come when the nurse's out. We'll only stay a second, say hello, and . . . "

The door to the bedroom moved wide. The three boys stood looking in at the old man seated there on the floor.

"Colonel Freeleigh?" said Douglas softly.

There was something in his silence that made them all shut up their mouths.

They approached, almost on tiptoe.

Douglas, bent down, disengaged the phone from the old man's now quite cold fingers. Douglas lifted the receiver to his own ear, listened. Above the static he heard a strange, a far, a final sound.

Two thousand miles away, the closing of a window.

The Wonderful Ice Cream Suit

It was summer twilight in the city, and out front of the quiet-clicking pool hall three young Mexican-American men breathed the warm air and looked around at the world. Sometimes they talked and sometimes they said nothing at all but watched the cars glide by like black panthers on the hot asphalt or saw trolleys loom up like thunderstorms, scatter lightning, and rumble away into silence.

"Hey," sighed Martínez at last. He was the youngest, the most sweetly sad of the three. "It's a swell night, huh? Swell."

As he observed the world it moved very close and then drifted away and then came close again. People, brushing by, were suddenly across the street. Buildings five miles away suddenly leaned over him. But most of the time everything—people, cars, and buildings—stayed way out on the edge of the world and could not be touched. On this quiet warm summer evening Martínez's face was cold.

"Nights like this you wish . . . lots of things."

"Wishing," said the second man, Villanazul, a man who shouted books out loud in his room but spoke only in whispers on the street. "Wishing is the useless pastime of the unemployed."

"Unemployed?" cried Vamenos, the unshaven. "Listen to him! We got no jobs, no money!"

"So," said Martínez, "we got no friends."

"True." Villanazul gazed off toward the green plaza where the palm trees swayed in the soft night wind. "Do you know what I wish? I wish to go into that plaza and speak among the businessmen who gather there nights to talk big talk. But dressed as I am, poor as I am, who would listen? So, Martínez, we have each other. The friendship of the poor is real friendship. We—"

But now a handsome young Mexican with a fine thin mustache strolled by. And on each of his careless arms hung a laughing woman.

"*Madre mía!*" Martínez slapped his own brow. "How does that one rate *two* friends?"

"It's his nice new white summer suit." Vamenos chewed a black thumbnail. "He looks sharp."

Martínez leaned out to watch the three people moving away, and then looked at the tenement across the street, in one fourth-floor window of which, far above, a beautiful girl leaned out, her dark hair faintly stirred by the wind. She had been there forever, which was to say for six weeks. He had nodded, he had raised a hand, he had smiled, he had blinked rapidly, he had even bowed to her, on the street, in the hall when visiting friends, in the park, downtown. Even now, he put his hand up from his waist and moved his fingers. But all the lovely girl did was let the summer wind stir her dark hair. He did not exist. He was nothing.

"*Madre mía!*" He looked away and down the street where the man walked his two friends around a corner. "Oh, if just I had one suit, one! I wouldn't need money if I *looked* okay."

"I hesitate to suggest," said Villanazul, "that you see Gómez. But he's been talking some crazy talk for a month now about clothes. I keep on saying I'll be in on it to make him go away. That Gómez."

"Friend," said a quiet voice.

"Gómez!" Everyone turned to stare.

Smiling strangely, Gómez pulled forth an endless thin yellow ribbon which fluttered and swirled on the summer air.

"Gómez," said Martínez, "what you doing with that tape measure?"

Gómez beamed. "Measuring people's skeletons."

"Skeletons!"

"Hold on." Gómez squinted at Martínez. "*Caramba!* Where you *been* all my life! Let's try *you!*"

Martínez saw his arm seized and taped, his leg measured, his chest encircled.

"Hold still!" cried Gómez. "Arm—perfect. Leg—chest—*perfecto*! Now quick, the height! There! Yes! Five foot five! You're in! Shake!" Pumping Martínez's hand, he stopped suddenly. "Wait. You got . . . ten bucks?"

"I have!" Vamenos waved some grimy bills. "Gómez, measure me!"

"All I got left in the world is nine dollars and ninety-two cents." Martínez searched his pockets. "That's enough for a new suit? Why?"

"Why? Because you got the right skeleton, that's why!"

"*Señor* Gómez, I don't hardly know you—"

"Know me? You're going to live with me! Come on!"

Gómez vanished into the poolroom. Martínez, escorted by the polite Villanazul, pushed by an eager Vamenos, found himself inside.

"Domínguez!" said Gómez.

Domínguez, at a wall telephone, winked at them. A woman's voice squeaked on the receiver.

"Manulo!" said Gómez.

Manulo, a wine bottle tilted bubbling to his mouth, turned.

Gómez pointed at Martínez.

"At last we found our fifth volunteer!"

Domínguez said, "I got a date, don't bother me—" and stopped. The receiver slipped from his fingers. His little black telephone book full of fine names and numbers went quickly back into his pocket. "Gómez, you—?"

"Yes, yes! Your money, now! *Ándale!*"

The woman's voice sizzled on the dangling phone.

Domínguez glanced at it uneasily.

Manulo considered the empty wine bottle in his hand and the liquor-store sign across the street.

Then very reluctantly both men laid ten dollars each on the green velvet pool table.

Villanazul, amazed, did likewise, as did Gómez, nudging Martínez. Martínez counted out his wrinkled bills and change. Gómez flourished the money like a royal flush.

"Fifty bucks! The suit costs sixty! All we need is ten bucks!"

"Wait," said Martínez. "Gómez, are we talking about *one* suit? *Uno?*"

"*Uno!*" Gómez raised a finger. "One wonderful white ice cream summer suit! White, white as the August moon!"

"But who will own this one suit?"

"Me!" said Manulo.

"Me!" said Domínguez.

"Me!" said Villanazul.

"Me!" cried Gómez. "*And* you, Martínez. Men, let's show him. Line up!"

Villanazul, Manulo, Domínguez, and Gómez rushed to plant their backs against the poolroom wall.

"Martínez, you too, the other end, line up! Now, Vamenos, lay that billiard cue across our heads!"

"Sure, Gómez, sure!"

Martínez, in line, felt the cue tap his head and leaned out to see what was happening. "Ah!" he gasped.

The cue lay flat on all their heads, with no rise or fall, as Vamenos slid it along, grinning.

"We're all the same height!" said Martínez.

"The same!" Everyone laughed.

Gómez ran down the line, rustling the yellow tape measure here and there on the men so they laughed even more wildly.

"Sure!" he said. "It took a month, four weeks, mind you, to find four guys the same size and shape as me, a month of running around measuring. Sometimes I found guys with five-foot-five skeletons, sure, but all the meat on their bones was too much or not enough. Sometimes their bones were too long in the legs or too short in the arms. Boy, all the bones! I tell you! But now, five of us, same shoulders, chests, waists, arms, and as for weight? Men!"

Manulo, Domínguez, Villanazul, Gómez, and at last Martínez stepped onto the scales which flipped ink-stamped cards at them as Vamenos, still smiling wildly, fed pennies. Heart pounding, Martínez read the cards.

"One hundred thirty-five pounds . . . one thirty-six . . . one thirty-three . . . one thirty-four . . . one thirty-seven . . . a miracle!"

"No," said Villanazul simply, "Gómez."

They all smiled upon that genius who now circled them with his arms.

"Are we not fine?" he wondered. "All the same size, all the same dream—the suit. So each of us will look beautiful at least one night each week, eh?"

"I haven't looked beautiful in years," said Martínez. "The girls run away."

"They will run no more, they will freeze," said Gómez, "when they see you in the cool white summer ice cream suit."

"Gómez," said Villanazul, "just let me ask one thing."

"Of course, *compadre.*"

"When we get this nice new white ice cream summer suit, some night you're not going to put it on and walk down to the Greyhound bus in it and go live in El Paso for a year in it, are you?"

"Villanazul, Villanazul, how can you say that?"

"My eye sees and my tongue moves," said Villanazul. "How about the *Everybody Wins!* Punchboard Lotteries you ran and you kept running when nobody won? How about the United Chili Con Carne and Frijole Company you were going to organize and all that ever happened was the rent ran out on a two-by-four office?"

"The errors of a child now grown," said Gómez. "Enough! In this hot weather someone may buy the special suit that is made just for us that stands waiting in the window of Shumway's Sunshine Suits! We have fifty dollars. Now we need just one more skeleton!"

Martínez saw the men peer around the pool hall. He looked where they looked. He felt his eyes hurry past Vamenos, then come reluctantly back to examine his dirty shirt, his huge nicotined fingers.

"Me!" Vamenos burst out at last. "My skeleton, measure it, it's great! Sure, my hands are big, and my arms, from digging ditches! But—"

Just then Martínez heard passing on the sidewalk outside that same terrible man with his two girls, all laughing together.

He saw anguish move like the shadow of a summer cloud on the faces of the other men in this poolroom.

Slowly Vamenos stepped onto the scales and dropped his penny. Eyes closed, he breathed a prayer.

"*Madre mía*, please . . ."

The machinery whirred; the card fell out. Vamenos opened his eyes.

"Look! One thirty-five pounds! Another miracle!"

The men stared at his right hand and the card, at his left hand and a soiled ten-dollar bill.

Gómez swayed. Sweating, he licked his lips. Then his hand shot out, seized the money.

"The clothing store! The suit! *Vamos!*"

Yelling, everyone ran from the poolroom.

The woman's voice was still squeaking on the abandoned telephone. Martínez, left behind, reached out and hung the voice up. In the silence he shook his head. "*Santos*, what a dream! Six men," he said, "one suit. What will come of this? Madness? Debauchery? Murder? But I go with God. Gómez, wait for me!"

Martínez was young. He ran fast.

Mr. Shumway, of Shumway's Sunshine Suits, paused while adjusting a tie rack, aware of some subtle atmospheric change outside his establishment.

"Leo," he whispered to his assistant. "Look . . ."

Outside, one man, Gómez, strolled by, looking in. Two men, Manulo and Domínguez, hurried by, staring in. Three men, Villanazul, Martínez, and Vamenos, jostling shoulders, did the same.

"Leo." Mr. Shumway swallowed. "Call the police!"

Suddenly six men filled the doorway.

Martínez, crushed among them, his stomach slightly upset, his face feeling feverish, smiled so wildly at Leo that Leo let go the telephone.

"Hey," breathed Martínez, eyes wide. "There's a great suit over there!"

"No." Manulo touched a lapel. "*This* one!"

"There is only one suit in all the world!" said Gómez coldly. "Mr. Shumway, the ice cream white, size thirty-four, was in your window just an hour ago! It's gone! You didn't—"

"Sell it?" Mr. Shumway exhaled. "No, no. In the dressing room. It's still on the dummy."

Martínez did not know if he moved and moved the crowd or if the crowd moved and moved him. Suddenly they were all in motion. Mr. Shumway, running, tried to keep ahead of them.

"This way, gents. Now which of you . . . ?"

"All for one, one for all!" Martínez heard himself say, and laughed. "We'll all try it on!"

"All?" Mr. Shumway clutched at the booth curtain as if his shop were a steamship that had suddenly tilted in a great swell. He stared.

That's it, thought Martínez, look at our smiles. Now, look at the skeletons behind our smiles! Measure here, there, up, down, yes, do you *see*?

Mr. Shumway saw. He nodded. He shrugged.

"All!" He jerked the curtain. "There! Buy it, and I'll throw in the dummy free!"

Martínez peered quietly into the booth, his motion drawing the others to peer too.

The suit was there.

And it was white.

Martínez could not breathe. He did not want to. He did not need to. He was afraid his breath would melt the suit. It was enough, just looking.

But at last he took a great trembling breath and exhaled, whispering. "*Ay. Ay, caramba!*"

"It puts out my eyes," murmured Gómez.

"Mr. Shumway," Martínez heard Leo hissing. "Ain't it dangerous precedent, to sell it? I mean, what if everybody bought *one* suit for *six* people?"

"Leo," said Mr. Shumway, "you ever hear one single fifty-nine-dollar suit make so many people happy at the same time before?"

"Angels' wings," murmured Martínez. "The wings of white angels."

Martínez felt Mr. Shumway peering over his shoulder into the booth. The pale glow filled his eyes.

"You know something, Leo?" he said in awe. "That's a *suit*!"

Gómez, shouting, whistling, ran up to the third-floor landing and turned to wave to the others, who staggered, laughed, stopped, and had to sit down on the steps below.

"Tonight!" cried Gómez. "Tonight you move in with me, eh? Save rent as well as clothes, eh? Sure! Martínez, you got the suit?"

"Have I?" Martínez lifted the white gift-wrapped box high. "From us to us! *Ay-hah!*"

"Vamenos, you got the dummy?"

"Here!"

Vamenos, chewing an old cigar, scattering sparks, slipped. The dummy, falling, toppled, turned over twice, and banged down the stairs.

"Vamenos! Dumb! Clumsy!"

They seized the dummy from him. Stricken, Vamenos looked about as if he'd lost something.

Manulo snapped his fingers. "Hey, Vamenos, we got to celebrate! Go borrow some wine!"

Vamenos plunged downstairs in a whirl of sparks.

The others moved into the room with the suit, leaving Martínez in the hall to study Gómez's face.

"Gómez, you look sick."

"I am," said Gómez. "For what have I done?" He nodded to the shadows in the room working about the dummy. "I pick Domínguez, a devil with the women. All right. I pick Manulo, who drinks, yes, but who sings as sweet as a girl, eh? Okay. Villanazul reads books. You, you wash behind your ears. But then what do I do? Can I wait? No! I got to buy that suit! So the last guy I pick is a clumsy slob who has the right to wear *my* suit—" He stopped, confused. "Who gets to wear *our* suit one night a week, fall down in it, or not come in out of the rain in it! Why, why, why did I *do* it!"

"Gómez," whispered Villanazul from the room. "The suit is ready. Come see if it looks as good using *your* light bulb."

Gómez and Martínez entered.

And there on the dummy in the center of the room was the phosphorescent, the miraculously white-fired ghost with the incredible lapels, the precise stitching, the neat buttonholes. Standing with the white illumination of the suit upon his cheeks, Martínez suddenly felt he was in church. White! White! It was white as the whitest vanilla ice cream, as the bottled milk in tenement halls at dawn. White as a winter cloud all alone in the moonlit sky late at night. Seeing it here in the warm summer-night room made their breath almost show on the air. Shutting his eyes, he could see it printed on his lids. He knew what color his dreams would be this night.

"White . . ." murmured Villanazul. "White as the snow on that mountain near our town in Mexico, which is called the Sleeping Woman."

"Say that again," said Gómez.

Villanazul, proud yet humble, was glad to repeat his tribute.

" . . . white as the snow on the mountain called—"

"I'm back!"

Shocked, the men whirled to see Vamenos in the door, wine bottles in each hand.

"A party! Here! Now tell us, who wears the suit first tonight? Me?"

"It's too late!" said Gómez.

"Late! It's only nine-fifteen!"

"Late?" said everyone, bristling. "Late?"

Gómez edged away from these men who glared from him to the suit to the open window.

Outside and below it was, after all, thought Martínez, a fine Saturday night in a summer month and through the calm warm darkness the women drifted like flowers on a quiet stream. The men made a mournful sound.

"Gómez, a suggestion." Villanazul licked his pencil and drew a chart on a pad. "You wear the suit from nine-thirty to ten, Manulo till ten-thirty, Domínguez till eleven, myself till eleven-thirty, Martínez till midnight, and—"

"Why me *last?*" demanded Vamenos, scowling.

Martínez thought quickly and smiled. "After midnight is the *best* time, friend."

"Hey," said Vamenos, "that's right. I never thought of that. Okay."

Gómez sighed. "All right. A half hour each. But from now on, remember, we each wear the suit just one night a week. Sundays we draw straws for who wears the suit the extra night."

"Me!" laughed Vamenos. "I'm lucky!"

Gómez held on to Martínez, tight.

"Gómez," urged Martínez, "you first. Dress."

Gómez could not tear his eyes from that disreputable Vamenos. At last, impulsively, he yanked his shirt off over his head. "Ay-yeah!" he howled. "Ay-*yeee!*"

Whisper rustle . . . the clean shirt.

"Ah . . . !"

How clean the new clothes feel, thought Martínez, holding the coat ready.

How clean they sound, how clean they smell!

Whisper . . . the pants . . . the tie, rustle . . . the suspenders. Whisper . . . now Martínez let loose the coat, which fell in place on flexing shoulders.

"*Ole!*"

Gómez turned like a matador in his wondrous suit-of-lights.

"*Ole*, Gómez, *ole!*"

Gómez bowed and went out the door.

Martínez fixed his eyes to his watch. At ten sharp he heard someone wandering about in the hall as if they had forgotten where to go. Martínez pulled the door open and looked out.

Gómez was there, heading for nowhere.

He looks sick, thought Martínez. No, stunned, shook up, surprised, many things.

"Gómez! This is the place!"

Gómez turned around and found his way through the door.

"Oh, friends, friends," he said. "Friends, what an experience! This suit! This suit!"

"Tell us, Gómez!" said Martínez.

"I can't, how can I say it!" He gazed at the heavens, arms spread, palms up.

"*Tell* us, Gómez!"

"I have no words, no words. You must see, yourself. Yes, you must see—" And here he lapsed into silence, shaking his head until at last he remembered they all stood watching him. "Who's next? Manulo?"

Manulo, stripped to his shorts, leapt forward.

"Ready!"

All laughed, shouted, whistled.

Manulo, ready, went out the door. He was gone twenty-nine minutes and thirty seconds. He came back holding to doorknobs, touching the wall, feeling his own elbows, putting the flat of his hand to his face.

"Oh, let me tell you," he said. "*Compadres*, I went to the bar, eh, to have a drink? But no, I did not go in the bar, do you hear? I did not drink. For as I walked I began to laugh and sing. Why, why? I listened to myself and asked this. Because. The suit made me feel better than wine ever did. The suit made me drunk, drunk! So I went to the Guadalajara Refrería instead and played the guitar and sang four songs, very high! The suit, ah, the suit!"

Domínguez, next to be dressed, moved out through the world, came back from the world.

The black telephone book! thought Martínez. He had it in his hands when he left! Now, he returns, hands empty! What? What?

"On the street," said Domínguez, seeing it all again, eyes wide, "on the street I walked, a woman cried, 'Domínguez, is that *you?*' Another said, 'Domínguez? No, Quetzalcoatl, the Great White God come from the East,' do you hear? And suddenly I didn't want to go with six women or eight, no. One, I thought. One! And to this one, who knows *what* I would say? 'Be mine!' Or

'Marry me!' *Caramba!* This suit is dangerous! But I did not care! I live, I live! Gómez, did it happen this way with you?"

Gómez, still dazed by the events of the evening, shook his head. "No, no talk. It's too much. Later. Villanazul . . . ?"

Villanazul moved shyly forward.

Villanazul went shyly out.

Villanazul came shyly home.

"Picture it," he said, not looking at them, looking at the floor, talking to the floor. "The green plaza, a group of elderly businessmen gathered under the stars and they are talking, nodding, talking. Now one of them whispers. All turn to stare. They move aside, they make a channel through which a white-hot light burns its way as through ice. At the center of the great light is this person. I take a deep breath. My stomach is jelly. My voice is very small, but it grows louder. And what do I say? I say, 'Friends. Do you know Carlyle's *Sartor Resartus?* In that book we find *his* Philosophy of Suits. . . . ' "

And at last it was time for Martínez to let the suit float him out to haunt the darkness.

Four times he walked around the block. Four times he paused beneath the tenement porches, looking up at the window where the light was lit; a shadow moved, the beautiful girl was there, not there, away and gone, and on the fifth time there she was on the porch above, driven out by the summer heat, taking the cooler air. She glanced down. She made a gesture.

At first he thought she was waving to him. He felt like a white explosion that had riveted her attention. But she was not waving. Her hand gestured and the next moment a pair of dark-framed glasses sat upon her nose. She gazed at him.

Ah, ah, he thought, so that's it. So! Even the blind may see this suit! He smiled up at her. He did not have to wave. And at last she smiled back. She did not have to wave either. Then, because he did not know what else to do and he could not get rid of this smile that had fastened itself to his cheeks, he hurried, almost ran, around the corner, feeling her stare after him. When he looked back she had taken off her glasses and gazed now with the look of the nearsighted at what, at most, must be a moving blob of light in the great darkness here. Then for good measure he went around the block again, through a city so suddenly beautiful he wanted to yell, then laugh, then yell again.

Returning, he drifted, oblivious, eyes half closed, and seeing him in the door, the others saw not Martínez but themselves come home. In that moment, they sensed that something had happened to them all.

"You're late!" cried Vamenos, but stopped. The spell could not be broken.

"Somebody tell me," said Martínez. "Who am I?"

He moved in a slow circle through the room.

Yes, he thought, yes, it's the suit, yes, it had to do with the suit and them all together in that store on this fine Saturday night and then here, laughing and feeling more drunk without drinking as Manulo said himself, as the night ran and each slipped on the pants and held, toppling, to the others and, balanced, let the feeling get bigger and warmer and finer as each man departed and the next took his place in the suit until now here stood Martínez all splendid and white as one who gives orders and the world grows quiet and moves aside.

"Martínez, we borrowed three mirrors while you were gone. Look!"

The mirrors, set up as in the store, angled to reflect three Martínezes and the echoes and memories of those who had occupied this suit with him and known the bright world inside this thread and cloth. Now, in the shimmering mirror, Martínez saw the enormity of this thing they were living together and his eyes grew wet. The others blinked. Martínez touched the mirrors. They shifted. He saw a thousand, a million white-armored Martínezes march off into eternity, reflected, re-reflected, forever, indomitable, and unending.

He held the white coat out on the air. In a trance, the others did not at first recognize the dirty hand that reached to take the coat. Then:

"Vamenos!"

"Pig!"

"You didn't wash!" cried Gómez. "Or even shave, while you waited! *Compadres*, the bath!"

"The bath!" said everyone.

"No!" Vamenos flailed. "The night air! I'm dead!"

They hustled him yelling out and down the hall.

Now here stood Vamenos, unbelievable in white suit, beard shaved, hair combed, nails scrubbed.

His friends scowled darkly at him.

For was it not true, thought Martínez, that when Vamenos passed by, avalanches itched on mountaintops? If he walked under windows, people spat, dumped garbage, or worse. Tonight now, this night, he would stroll beneath ten thousand wide-opened windows, near balconies, past alleys. Suddenly the world absolutely sizzled with flies. And here was Vamenos, a fresh-frosted cake.

"You sure look keen in that suit, Vamenos," said Manulo sadly.

"Thanks." Vamenos twitched, trying to make his skeleton comfortable where all their skeletons had so recently been. In a small voice Vamenos said, "Can I go now?"

"Villanazul!" said Gómez. "Copy down these rules."

Villanazul licked his pencil.

"First," said Gómez, "don't fall down in that suit, Vamenos!"

"I won't."

"Don't lean against buildings in that suit."

"No buildings."

"Don't walk under trees with birds in them in that suit. Don't smoke. Don't drink—"

"Please," said Vamenos, "can I *sit down* in this suit?"

"When in doubt, take the pants off, fold them over a chair."

"Wish me luck," said Vamenos.

"Go with God, Vamenos."

He went out. He shut the door.

There was a ripping sound.

"Vamenos!" cried Martínez.

He whipped the door open.

Vamenos stood with two halves of a handkerchief torn in his hands, laughing.

"Rrrip! Look at your faces! Rrrip!" He tore the cloth again. "Oh, oh, your faces, your faces! Ha!"

Roaring, Vamenos slammed the door, leaving them stunned and alone.

Gómez put both hands on top of his head and turned away. "Stone me. Kill me. I have sold our souls to a demon!"

Villanazul dug in his pockets, took out a silver coin, and studied it for a long while.

"This is my last fifty cents. Who else will help me buy back Vamenos' share of the suit?"

"It's no use." Manulo showed them ten cents. "We got only enough to buy the lapels and the buttonholes."

Gómez, at the open window, suddenly leaned out and yelled. "Vamenos! No!"

Below on the street, Vamenos, shocked, blew out a match and threw away an old cigar butt he had found somewhere. He made a strange gesture to all the men in the window above, then waved airily and sauntered on.

Somehow, the five men could not move away from the window. They were crushed together there.

"I bet he eats a hamburger in that suit," mused Villanazul. "I'm thinking of the mustard."

"Don't!" cried Gómez. "No, no!"

Manulo was suddenly at the door.

"I need a drink, bad."

"Manulo, there's wine here, that bottle on the floor—"

Manulo went out and shut the door.

A moment later Villanazul stretched with great exaggeration and strolled about the room.

"I think I'll walk down to the plaza, friends."

He was not gone a minute when Domínguez, waving his black book at the others, winked and turned the doorknob.

"Domínguez," said Gómez.

"Yes?"

"If you see Vamenos, by accident," said Gómez, "warn him away from Mickey Murrillo's Red Rooster Café. They got fights not only *on* TV but *out front* of the TV too."

"He wouldn't go into Murrillo's," said Domínguez. "That suit means too much to Vamenos. He wouldn't do anything to hurt it."

"He'd shoot his mother first," said Martínez.

"Sure he would."

Martínez and Gómez, alone, listened to Domínguez's footsteps hurry away down the stairs. They circled the undressed window dummy.

For a long while, biting his lips, Gómez stood at the window, looking out. He touched his shirt pocket twice, pulled his hand away, and then at last pulled something from the pocket. Without looking at it, he handed it to Martínez.

"Martínez, take this."

"What is it?"

Martínez looked at the piece of folded pink paper with print on it, with names and numbers. His eyes widened.

"A ticket on the bus to El Paso three weeks from now!"

Gómez nodded. He couldn't look at Martínez. He stared out into the summer night.

"Turn it in. Get the money," he said. "Buy us a nice white panama hat and a pale blue tie to go with the white ice cream suit, Martínez. Do that."

"Gómez—"

"Shut up. Boy, is it hot in here! I need air."

"Gómez. I am touched. Gómez—"

But the door stood open. Gómez was gone.

Mickey Murrillo's Red Rooster Café and Cocktail Lounge was squashed between two big brick buildings and, being narrow, had to be deep. Outside, serpents of red and sulphur-green neon fizzed and snapped. Inside, dim shapes loomed and swam away to lose themselves in a swarming night sea.

Martínez, on tiptoe, peeked through a flaked place on the red-painted front window.

He felt a presence on his left, heard breathing on his right. He glanced in both directions.

"Manulo! Villanazul!"

"I decided I wasn't thirsty," said Manulo. "So I took a walk."

"I was just on my way to the plaza," said Villanazul, "and decided to go the long way around."

As if by agreement, the three men shut up now and turned together to peer on tiptoe through various flaked spots on the window.

A moment later, all three felt a new very warm presence behind them and heard still faster breathing.

"Is our white suit in there?" asked Gómez's voice.

"Gómez!" said everybody, surprised. "Hi!"

"Yes!" cried Domínguez, having just arrived to find his own peephole. "There's the suit! And, praise God, Vamenos is still *in* it!"

"I can't see!" Gómez squinted, shielding his eyes. "What's he *doing?*"

Martínez peered. Yes! There, way back in the shadows, was a big chunk of snow and the idiot smile of Vamenos winking above it, wreathed in smoke.

"He's smoking!" said Martínez.

"He's drinking!" said Domínguez.

"He's eating a taco!" reported Villanazul.

"A *juicy* taco," added Manulo.

"No," said Gómez. "No, no, no. . . . "

"Ruby Escuadrillo's with him!"

"Let me see that!" Gómez pushed Martínez aside.

Yes, there was Ruby! Two hundred pounds of glittering sequins and tight black satin on the hoof, her scarlet fingernails clutching Vamenos' shoulder. Her cowlike face, floured with powder, greasy with lipstick, hung over him!

"That hippo!" said Domínguez. "She's crushing the shoulder pads. Look, she's going to sit on his lap!"

"No, no, not with all that powder and lipstick!" said Gómez. "Manulo, inside! Grab that drink! Villanazul, the cigar, the taco! Domínguez, date Ruby Escuadrillo, get her away. *Ándale*, men!"

The three vanished, leaving Gómez and Martínez to stare, gasping, through the peephole.

"Manulo, he's got the drink, he's *drinking* it!"

"*Ay!* There's Villanazul, he's got the cigar, he's eating the taco!"

"Hey, Domínguez, he's got Ruby! What a *brave* one!"

A shadow bulked through Murrillo's front door, traveling fast.

"Gómez!" Martínez clutched Gómez's arm. "That was Ruby Escuadrillo's boyfriend, Toro Ruíz. If he finds her with Vamenos, the ice cream suit will be covered with blood, *covered* with blood—"

"Don't make me nervous," said Gómez. "Quickly!"

Both ran. Inside they reached Vamenos just as Toro Ruíz grabbed about two feet of the lapels of that wonderful ice cream suit.

"Let go of Vamenos!" said Martínez.

"Let go that *suit!*" corrected Gómez.

Toro Ruíz, tap-dancing Vamenos, leered at these intruders.

Villanazul stepped up shyly.

Villanazul smiled. "Don't hit him. Hit me."

Toro Ruíz hit Villanazul smack on the nose.

Villanazul, holding his nose, tears stinging his eyes, wandered off.

Gómez grabbed one of Toro Ruíz's arms, Martínez the other.

"Drop him, let go, *cabrón, coyote, vaca!*"

Toro Ruíz twisted the ice cream suit material until all six men screamed in mortal agony. Grunting, sweating, Toro Ruíz dislodged as many as climbed on. He was winding up to hit Vamenos when Villanazul wandered back, eyes streaming.

"Don't hit him. Hit me!"

As Toro Ruíz hit Villanazul on the nose, a chair crashed on Toro's head.

"Ay!" said Gómez.

Toro Ruíz swayed, blinking, debating whether to fall. He began to drag Vamenos with him.

"Let go!" cried Gómez. "Let go!"

One by one, with great care, Toro Ruíz's bananalike fingers let loose of the suit. A moment later he was ruins at their feet.

"*Compadres*, this way!"

They ran Vamenos outside and set him down where he freed himself of their hands with injured dignity.

"Okay, okay. My time ain't up. I still got two minutes and, let's see—ten seconds."

"What!" said everybody.

"Vamenos," said Gómez, "you let a Guadalajara cow climb on you, you pick fights, you smoke, you drink, you eat tacos, and *now* you have the nerve to say your time ain't up?"

"I got two minutes and one second left!"

"Hey, Vamenos, you sure look sharp!" Distantly, a woman's voice called from across the street.

Vamenos smiled and buttoned the coat.

"It's Ramona Álvarez! Ramona, wait!" Vamenos stepped off the curb.

"Vamenos," pleaded Gómez. "What can you do in one minute and"—he checked his watch—"forty seconds!"

"Watch! Hey, Ramona!"

Vamenos loped.

"Vamenos, look out!"

Vamenos, surprised, whirled, saw a car, heard the shriek of brakes.

"No," said all five men on the sidewalk.

Martínez heard the impact and flinched. His head moved up. It looks like white laundry, he thought, flying through the air. His head came down.

Now he heard himself and each of the men make a different sound. Some swallowed too much air. Some let it out. Some choked. Some groaned. Some cried aloud for justice. Some covered their faces. Martínez felt his own fist pounding his heart in agony. He could not move his feet.

"I don't want to live," said Gómez quietly. "Kill me, someone."

Then, shuffling, Martínez looked down and told his feet to walk, stagger, follow one after the other. He collided with other men. Now they were trying to run. They ran at last and somehow crossed a street like a deep river through which they could only wade, to look down at Vamenos.

"Vamenos!" said Martínez. "You're alive!"

Strewn on his back, mouth open, eyes squeezed tight, tight, Vamenos motioned his head back and forth, back and forth, moaning.

"Tell me, tell me, oh, tell me, tell me."

"Tell you what, Vamenos?"

Vamenos clenched his fists, ground his teeth.

"The suit, what have I done to the suit, the suit, the suit!"

The men crouched lower.

"Vamenos, it's . . . why, it's *okay*!"

"You lie!" said Vamenos. "It's torn, it must be, it must be, it's torn, all around, *underneath*?"

"No." Martínez knelt and touched here and there. "Vamenos, all around, underneath even, it's okay!"

Vamenos opened his eyes to let the tears run free at last. "A miracle," he sobbed. "Praise the saints!" He quieted at last. "The car?"

"Hit and run." Gómez suddenly remembered and glared at the empty street. "It's good he didn't stop. We'd have—"

Everyone listened.

Distantly a siren wailed.

"Someone phoned for an ambulance."

"Quick!" said Vamenos, eyes rolling. "Set me up! Take off our coat!"

"Vamenos—"

"Shut up, idiots!" cried Vamenos. "The coat, that's it! Now, the pants, the pants, quick, quick *peones!* Those doctors! You seen movies? They rip the pants with razors to get them off! They don't *care!* They're maniacs! Ah, God, quick, quick!"

The siren screamed.

The men, panicking, all handled Vamenos at once.

"Right leg, *easy*, hurry, cows! Good! Left leg, now, left, you hear, there, easy, *easy*! Ow, God! Quick! Martínez, your pants, take them off!"

"What?" Martínez froze.

The siren shrieked.

"Fool!" wailed Vamenos. "All is lost! Your pants! Give me!"

Martínez jerked at his belt buckle.

"Close in, make a circle!"

Dark pants, light pants flourished on the air.

"Quick, here come the maniacs with the razors! Right leg on, left leg, *there*!"

"The zipper, cows, zip my zipper!" babbled Vamenos.

The siren died.

"*Madre mía*, yes, just in time! They arrive." Vamenos lay back down and shut his eyes. "*Gracias*."

Martínez turned, nonchalantly buckling on the white pants as the interns brushed past.

"Broken leg," said one intern as they moved Vamenos onto a stretcher.

"*Compadres*," said Vamenos, "don't be mad with me."

Gómez snorted. "Who's mad?"

In the ambulance, head tilted back, looking out at them upside down, Vamenos faltered.

"*Compadres*, when . . . when I come from the hospital . . . am I still in the bunch? You won't kick me out? Look, I'll give up smoking, keep away from Murrillo's, swear off women—"

"Vamenos," said Martínez gently, "don't promise nothing."

Vamenos, upside down, eyes brimming wet, saw Martínez there, all white now against the stars.

"Oh, Martínez, you sure look great in that suit. *Compadres*, don't he look *beautiful?*"

Villanazul climbed in beside Vamenos. The door slammed. The four remaining men watched the ambulance drive away.

Then, surrounded by his friends, inside the white suit, Martínez was carefully escorted back to the curb.

In the tenement, Martínez got out the cleaning fluid and the others stood around, telling him how to clean the suit and, later, how not to have the iron too hot and how to work the lapels and the crease and all. When the suit was cleaned and pressed so it looked like a fresh gardenia just opened, they fitted it to the dummy.

"Two o'clock," murmured Villanazul. "I hope Vamenos sleeps well. When I left him at the hospital, he looked good."

Manulo cleared his throat. "Nobody else is going out with that suit tonight, huh?"

The others glared at him.

Manulo flushed. "I mean . . . it's late. We're tired. Maybe no one will use the suit for forty-eight hours, huh? Give it a rest. Sure. Well. Where do we sleep?"

The night being still hot and the room unbearable, they carried the suit on its dummy out and down the hall. They brought with them also some pillows and blankets. They climbed the stairs toward the roof of the tenement. There, thought Martínez, is the cooler wind, and sleep.

On the way, they passed a dozen doors that stood open, people still perspiring and awake, playing cards, drinking pop, fanning themselves with movie magazines.

I wonder, thought Martínez. I wonder if—Yes!

On the fourth floor, a certain door stood open.

The beautiful girl looked up as the men passed. She wore glasses and when she saw Martínez she snatched them off and hid them under her book.

The others went on, not knowing they had lost Martínez, who seemed stuck fast in the open door.

For a long moment he could say nothing. Then he said:

"José Martínez."

And she said:

"Celia Obregón."

And then both said nothing.

He heard the men moving up on the tenement roof. He moved to follow.

She said quickly, "I saw you tonight!"

He came back.

"The suit," he said.

"The suit," she said, and paused. "But not the suit."

"Eh?" he said.

She lifted the book to show the glasses lying in her lap. She touched the glasses.

"I do not see well. You would think I would wear my glasses, but no. I walk around for years now, hiding them, seeing nothing. But tonight, even without the glasses, I see. A great whiteness passes below in the dark. So white! And I put on my glasses quickly!"

"The suit, as I said," said Martínez.

"The suit for a little moment, yes, but there is another whiteness above the suit."

"Another?"

"Your teeth! Oh, such white teeth, and so many!"

Martínez put his hand over his mouth.

"So happy, Mr. Martínez," she said. "I have not often seen such a happy face and such a smile."

"Ah," he said, not able to look at her, his face flushing now.

"So, you see," she said quietly, "the suit caught my eye, yes, the whiteness filled the night below. But the teeth were much whiter. Now, I have forgotten the suit."

Martínez flushed again. She, too, was overcome with what she had said. She put her glasses on her nose, and then took them off, nervously, and hid them again. She looked at her hands and at the door above his head.

"May I—" he said, at last.

"May you—"

"May I call for you," he asked, "when next the suit is mine to wear?"

"Why must you wait for the suit?" she said.

"I thought—"

"You do not need the suit," she said.

"But—"

"If it were just the suit," she said, "anyone would be fine in it. But no, I watched. I saw many men in that suit, all different, this night. So again I say, you do not need to wait for the suit."

"*Madre mía, madre mía!*" he cried happily. And then, quieter, "I will need the suit for a little while. A month, six months, a year. I am uncertain. I am fearful of many things. I am young."

"That is as it should be," she said.

"Good night, Miss—"

"Celia Obregón."

"Celia Obregón," he said, and was gone from the door.

The others were waiting on the roof of the tenement. Coming up through the trap door, Martínez saw they had placed the dummy and the suit in the center of the roof and put their blankets and pillows in a circle around it. Now they were lying down. Now a cooler night wind was blowing here, up in the sky.

Martínez stood alone by the white suit, smoothing the lapels, talking half to himself.

"Ay, *caramba*, what a night! Seems ten years since seven o'clock, when it all started and I had no friends. Two in the morning, I got all *kinds* of friends. . . ." He paused and thought, Celia Obregón. Celia Obregón. ". . . All kinds of friends," he went on. "I got a room, I got clothes. You tell *me*. You know what?" He looked around at the men lying on the rooftop, surrounding the dummy and himself. "It's funny. When I wear this suit, I know I will win at pool, like Gómez. A woman will look at me like Domínguez. I will be able to sing like Manulo, sweetly. I will talk fine politics like Villanazul. I'm strong as Vamenos. So? So, tonight, I am more than Martínez. I am Gómez, Manulo, Domínguez, Villanazul, Vamenos. I am everyone. Ay . . . ay . . ." He stood a moment longer by this suit which could save all the ways they sat or stood or walked. This suit which could move fast and nervous like Gómez or slow and thoughtfully like Villanazul or drift like Domínguez, who never touched ground, who always found a wind to take him somewhere. This suit which belonged to them but which also owned them all. This suit that was—what? A parade.

"Martínez," said Gómez. "You going to sleep?"

"Sure. I'm just thinking."

"What?"

"If we ever get rich," said Martínez softly, "it'll be kind of sad. Then we'll all have suits. And there won't be no more nights like tonight. It'll break up the old gang. It'll never be the same after that."

The men lay thinking of what had just been said.

Gómez nodded gently.

"Yeah . . . it'll never be the same . . . after that."

Martínez lay down on his blanket. In darkness, with the others, he faced the middle of the roof and the dummy, which was the center of their lives.

And their eyes were bright, shining, and good to see in the dark as the neon lights from nearby buildings flicked on, flicked off, flicked on, flicked off, revealing and then vanishing, revealing and then vanishing, their wonderful white vanilla ice cream summer suit.

Dark They Were,
and Golden-Eyed

The rocket metal cooled in the meadow winds. Its lid gave a bulging *pop*. From its clock interior stepped a man, a woman, and three children. The other passengers whispered away across the Martian meadow, leaving the man alone among his family.

The man felt his hair flutter and the tissues of his body draw tight as if he were standing at the center of a vacuum. His wife, before him, seemed almost to whirl away in smoke. The children, small seeds, might at any instant be sown to all the Martian climes.

The children looked up at him, as people look to the sun to tell what time of their life it is. His face was cold.

"What's wrong?" asked his wife.

"Let's get back on the rocket."

"Go back to Earth?"

"Yes! Listen!"

The wind blew as if to flake away their identities. At any moment the Martian air might draw his soul from him, as marrow comes from a white bone. He felt submerged in a chemical that could dissolve his intellect and burn away his past.

They looked at Martian hills that time had worn with a crushing pressure of years. They saw the old cities, lost in their meadows, lying like children's delicate bones among the blowing lakes of grass.

"Chin up, Harry," said his wife. "It's too late. We've come over sixty million miles."

The children with their yellow hair hollered at the deep dome of Martian sky. There was no answer but the racing hiss of wind through the stiff grass.

He picked up the luggage in his cold hands. "Here we go," he said—a man standing on the edge of a sea, ready to wade in and be drowned.

They walked into town.

Their name was Bittering. Harry and his wife Cora; Dan, Laura, and David. They built a small white cottage and ate good breakfasts there, but the fear was never gone. It lay with Mr. Bittering and Mrs. Bittering, a third unbidden partner at every midnight talk, at every dawn awakening.

"I feel like a salt crystal," he said, "in a mountain stream, being washed away. We don't belong here. We're Earth people. This is Mars. It was meant for Martians. For heaven's sake, Cora, let's buy tickets for home!"

But she only shook her head. "One day the atom bomb will fix Earth. Then we'll be safe here."

"Safe and insane!"

Tick-tock, seven o'clock sang the voice-clock; *time to get up*. And they did.

Something made him check everything each morning—warm hearth, potted blood-geraniums—precisely as if he expected something to be amiss. The morning paper was toast-warm from the 6 a.m. Earth rocket. He broke its seal and tilted it at his breakfast place. He forced himself to be convivial.

"Colonial days all over again," he declared. "Why, in ten years there'll be a million Earth Men on Mars. Big cities, everything! They said we'd fail. Said the Martians would resent our invasion. But did we find any Martians? Not a living soul! Oh, we found their empty cities, but no one in them. Right?"

A river of wind submerged the house. When the windows ceased rattling Mr. Bittering swallowed and looked at the children.

"I don't know," said David. "Maybe there're Martians around we don't see. Sometimes nights I think I hear 'em. I hear the wind. The sand hits my window. I get scared. And I see those towns way up in the mountains where the Martians lived a long time ago. And I think I see things moving around those towns, Papa. And I wonder if those Martians *mind* us living here. I wonder if they won't do something to us for coming here."

"Nonsense!" Mr. Bittering looked out the windows. "We're clean, decent people." He looked at his children. "All dead cities have some kind of ghosts in them. Memories, I mean." He stared at the hills. "You see a staircase and you wonder what Martians looked like climbing it. You see Martian paintings and you wonder what the painter was like. You make a little ghost in your mind, a memory. It's quite natural. Imagination." He stopped. "You haven't been prowling up in those ruins, have you?"

"No, Papa." David looked at his shoes.

"See that you stay away from them. Pass the jam."

"Just the same," said little David, "I bet something happens."

Something happened that afternoon.

Laura stumbled through the settlement, crying. She dashed blindly onto the porch.

"Mother, Father—the war, Earth!" she sobbed. "A radio flash just came. Atom bombs hit New York! All the space rockets blown up. No more rockets to Mars, ever!"

"Oh, Harry!" The mother held on to her husband and daughter.

"Are you sure, Laura?" asked the father quietly.

Laura wept. "We're stranded on Mars, forever and ever!"

For a long time there was only the sound of the wind in the late afternoon.

Alone, thought Bittering. Only a thousand of us here. No way back. No way. No way. Sweat poured from his face and his hands and his body; he was drenched in the hotness of his fear. He wanted to strike Laura, cry, "No, you're lying! The rockets will come back!" Instead, he stroked Laura's head against him and said, "The rockets will get through someday."

"Father, what will we do?"

"Go about our business, of course. Raise crops and children. Wait. Keep things going until the war ends and the rockets come again."

The two boys stepped out onto the porch.

"Children," he said, sitting there, looking beyond them, "I've something to tell you."

"We know," they said.

In the following days, Bittering wandered often through the garden to stand alone in his fear. As long as the rockets had spun a silver web across space, he had been able to accept Mars. For he had always told himself: Tomorrow, if I want, I can buy a ticket and go back to Earth.

But now: The web gone, the rockets lying in jigsaw heaps of molten girder and unsnaked wire. Earth people left to the strangeness of Mars, the cinnamon dusts and wine airs, to be baked like gingerbread shapes in Martian summers, put into harvested storage by Martian winters. What would happen to him, the others? This was the moment Mars had waited for. Now it would eat them.

He got down on his knees in the flower bed, a spade in his nervous hands. Work, he thought, work and forget.

He glanced up from the garden to the Martian mountains. He thought of the proud old Martian names that had once been on those peaks. Earth Men, dropping from the sky, had gazed upon hills, rivers, Martian seas left nameless in spite of names. Once Martians had built cities, named cities; climbed mountains, named mountains; sailed seas, named seas. Mountains melted, seas drained, cities tumbled. In spite of this, the Earth Men had felt a silent guilt at putting new names to these ancient hills and valleys.

Nevertheless, man lives by symbol and label. The names were given.

Mr. Bittering felt very alone in his garden under the Martian sun, anachronism bent here, planting Earth flowers in a wild soil.

Think. Keep thinking. Different things. Keep your mind free of Earth, the atom war, the lost rockets.

He perspired. He glanced about. No one watching. He removed his tie. Pretty bold, he thought. First your coat off, now your tie. He hung it neatly on a peach tree he had imported as a sapling from Massachusetts.

He returned to his philosophy of names and mountains. The Earth Men had changed names. Now there were Hormel Valleys, Roosevelt Seas, Ford Hills, Vanderbilt Plateaus, Rockefeller Rivers, on Mars. It wasn't right. The American settlers had shown wisdom, using old Indian prairie names: Wisconsin, Minnesota, Idaho, Ohio, Utah, Milwaukee, Waukegan, Osseo. The old names, the old meanings.

Staring at the mountains wildly, he thought: Are you up there? All the dead ones, you Martians? Well, here we are, alone, cut off! Come down, move us out! We're helpless!

The wind blew a shower of peach blossoms.

He put out his sun-browned hand, gave a small cry. He touched the blossoms, picked them up. He turned them, he touched them again and again. Then he shouted for his wife.

"Cora!"

She appeared at a window. He ran to her.

"Cora, these blossoms!"

She handled them.

"Do you see? They're different. They've changed! They're not peach blossoms any more!"

"Look all right to me," she said.

"They're not. They're *wrong*! I can't tell how. An extra petal, a leaf, something, the color, the smell!"

The children ran out in time to see their father hurrying about the garden, pulling up radishes, onions, and carrots from their beds.

"Cora, come look!"

They handled the onions, the radishes, the carrots among them.

"Do they look like carrots?"

"Yes . . . no." She hesitated. "I don't know."

"They're changed."

"Perhaps."

"You know they have! Onions but not onions, carrots but not carrots. Taste: the same but different. Smell: not like it used to be." He felt his heart pounding, and he was afraid. He dug his fingers into the earth. "Cora, what's happening? What is it? We've got to get away from this." He ran across the garden. Each tree felt his touch. "The roses. The roses. They're turning green!"

And they stood looking at the green roses.

And two days later Dan came running. "Come see the cow. I was milking her and I saw it. Come on!"

They stood in the shed and looked at their one cow.

It was growing a third horn.

And the lawn in front of their house very quietly and slowly was coloring itself like spring violets. Seed from Earth but growing up a soft purple.

"We must get away," said Bittering. "We'll eat this stuff and then we'll change—who knows to what? I can't let it happen. There's only one thing to do. Burn this food!"

"It's not poisoned."

"But it is. Subtly, very subtly. A little bit. A very little bit. We mustn't touch it."

He looked with dismay at their house. "Even the house. The wind's done something to it. The air's burned it. The fog at night. The boards, all warped out of shape. It's not an Earth Man's house any more."

"Oh, your imagination!"

He put on his coat and tie. "I'm going into town. We've got to do something now. I'll be back."

"Wait, Harry!" his wife cried.

But he was gone.

In town, on the shadowy step of the grocery store, the men sat with their hands on their knees, conversing with great leisure and ease.

Mr. Bittering wanted to fire a pistol in the air.

What are you doing, you fools! he thought. Sitting here! You've heard the news—we're stranded on this planet. Well, move! Aren't you frightened? Aren't you afraid? What are you going to do?

"Hello, Harry," said everyone.

"Look," he said to them. "You did hear the news, the other day, didn't you?"

They nodded and laughed. "Sure. Sure, Harry."

"What are you going to do about it?"

"Do, Harry, do? What *can* we do?"

"Build a rocket, that's what!"

"A rocket, Harry? To go back to all that trouble? Oh, Harry!"

"But you *must* want to go back. Have you noticed the peach blossoms, the onions, the grass?"

"Why, yes, Harry, seems we did," said one of the men.

"Doesn't it scare you?"

"Can't recall that it did much, Harry."

"Idiots!"

"Now, Harry."

Bittering wanted to cry. "You've got to work with me. If we stay here, we'll all change. The air. Don't you smell it? Something in the air. A Martian virus, maybe; some seed, or a pollen. Listen to me!"

They stared at him.

"Sam," he said to one of them.

"Yes, Harry?"

"Will you help me build a rocket?"

"Harry, I got a whole load of metal and some blueprints. You want to work in my metal shop on a rocket, you're welcome. I'll sell you that metal for five hundred dollars. You should be able to construct a right pretty rocket, if you work alone, in about thirty years."

Everyone laughed.

"Don't laugh."

Sam looked at him with quiet good humor.

"Sam," Bittering said. "Your eyes—"

"What about them, Harry?"

"Didn't they used to be gray?"

"Well now, I don't remember."

"They were, weren't they?"

"Why do you ask, Harry?"

"Because now they're kind of yellow-colored."

"Is that so, Harry?" Sam said, casually.

"And you're taller and thinner—"

"You might be right, Harry."

"Sam, you shouldn't have yellow eyes."

"Harry, what color eyes have *you* got?" Sam said.

"My eyes? They're blue, of course."

"Here you are, Harry." Sam handed him a pocket mirror. "Take a look at yourself."

Mr. Bittering hesitated, and then raised the mirror to his face.

There were little, very dim flecks of new gold captured in the blue of his eyes.

"Now look what you've done," said Sam a moment later. "You've broken my mirror."

Harry Bittering moved into the metal shop and began to build the rocket. Men stood in the open door and talked and joked without raising their voices. Once in a while they gave him a hand on lifting something. But mostly they just idled and watched him with their yellowing eyes.

"It's suppertime, Harry," they said.

His wife appeared with his supper in a wicker basket.

"I won't touch it," he said. "I'll eat only food from our Deepfreeze. Food that came from Earth. Nothing from our garden."

His wife stood watching him. "You can't build a rocket."

"I worked in a shop once, when I was twenty. I know metal. Once I get it started, the others will help," he said, not looking at her, laying out the blueprints.

"Harry, Harry," she said, helplessly.

"We've got to get away, Cora. We've *got* to!"

The nights were full of wind that blew down the empty moonlit sea meadows past the little white chess cities lying for their twelve-thousandth year in the shallows. In the Earth Men's settlement, the Bittering house shook with a feeling of change.

Lying abed, Mr. Bittering felt his bones shifted, shaped, melted like gold. His wife, lying beside him, was dark from many sunny afternoons. Dark she was, and golden-eyed, burnt almost black by the sun, sleeping, and the children metallic in their beds, and the wind roaring forlorn and changing through the old peach trees, the violet grass, shaking out green rose petals.

The fear would not be stopped. It had his throat and heart. It dripped in a wetness of the arm and the temple and the trembling palm.

A green star rose in the east.

A strange word emerged from Mr. Bittering's lips.

"*Iorrt. Iorrt.*" He repeated it.

It was a Martian word. He knew no Martian.

In the middle of the night he arose and dialed a call through to Simpson, the archaeologist.

"Simpson, what does the word *Iorrt* mean?"

"Why, that's the old Martian word for our planet Earth. Why?"

"No special reason."

The telephone slipped from his hand.

"Hello, hello, hello, hello," it kept saying while he sat gazing out at the green star. "Bittering? Harry, are you there?"

The days were full of metal sound. He laid the frame of the rocket with the reluctant help of three indifferent men. He grew very tired in an hour or so and had to sit down.

"The altitude," laughed a man.

"Are you *eating*, Harry?" asked another.

"I'm eating," he said, angrily.

"From your Deepfreeze?"

"Yes!"

"You're getting thinner, Harry."

"I'm not!"

"And taller."

"Liar!"

His wife took him aside a few days later. "Harry, I've used up all the food in the Deepfreeze. There's nothing left. I'll have to make sandwiches using food grown on Mars."

He sat down heavily.

"You must eat," she said. "You're weak."

"Yes," he said.

He took a sandwich, opened it, looked at it, and began to nibble at it.

"And take the rest of the day off," she said. "It's hot. The children want to swim in the canals and hike. Please come along."

"I can't waste time. This is a crisis!"

"Just for an hour," she urged. "A swim'll do you good."

He rose, sweating. "All right, all right. Leave me alone. I'll come."

"Good for you, Harry."

The sun was hot, the day quiet. There was only an immense staring burn upon the land. They moved along the canal, the father, the mother, the racing children in their swim suits. They stopped and ate meat sandwiches. He saw their skin baking brown. And he saw the yellow eyes of his wife and his children, their eyes that were never yellow before. A few tremblings shook him, but were carried off in waves of pleasant heat as he lay in the sun. He was too tired to be afraid.

"Cora, how long have your eyes been yellow?"

She was bewildered. "Always, I guess."

"They didn't change from brown in the last three months?"

She bit her lips. "No. Why do you ask?"

"Never mind."

They sat there.

"The children's eyes," he said. "They're yellow, too."

"Sometimes growing children's eyes change color."

"Maybe *we're* children, too. At least to Mars. That's a thought." He laughed. "Think I'll swim."

They leaped into the canal water, and he let himself sink down and down to the bottom like a golden statue and lie there in green silence. All was water-quiet and deep, all was peace. He felt the steady, slow current drift him easily.

If I lie here long enough, he thought, the water will work and eat away my flesh until the bones show like coral. Just my skeleton left. And then the water can build on that skeleton—green things, deep water things, red things, yellow things. Change. Change. Slow, deep, silent change. And isn't that what it is up *there?*

He saw the sky submerged above him, the sun made Martian by atmosphere and time and space.

Up there, a big river, he thought, a Martian river, all of us lying deep in it, in our pebble houses, in our sunken boulder houses, like crayfish hidden, and the water washing away our old bodies and lengthening the bones and—

He let himself drift up through the soft light.

Dan sat on the edge of the canal, regarding his father seriously.

"*Utha*," he said.

"What?" asked his father.

The boy smiled. "You know. *Utha*'s the Martian word for 'father.'"

"Where did you learn it?"

"I don't know. Around. *Utha!*"

"What do you want?"

The boy hesitated. "I—I want to change my name."

"Change it?"

"Yes."

His mother swam over. "What's wrong with Dan for a name?"

Dan fidgeted. "The other day you called Dan, Dan, Dan. I didn't even hear. I said to myself, That's not my name. I've a new name I want to use."

Mr. Bittering held to the side of the canal, his body cold and his heart pounding slowly. "What is this new name?"

"Linnl. Isn't that a good name? Can I use it? Can't I, please?"

Mr. Bittering put his hand to his head. He thought of the silly rocket, himself working alone, himself alone even among his family, so alone.

He heard his wife say, "Why not?"

He heard himself say, "Yes, you can use it."

"Yaaa!" screamed the boy. "I'm Linnl, Linnl!"

Racing down the meadowlands, he danced and shouted.

Mr. Bittering looked at his wife. "Why did we do that?"

"I don't know," she said. "It just seemed like a good idea."

They walked into the hills. They strolled on old mosaic paths, beside still-pumping fountains. The paths were covered with a thin film of cool water all summer long. You kept your bare feet cool all the day, splashing as in a creek, wading.

They came to a small deserted Martian villa with a good view of the valley. It was on top of a hill. Blue marble halls, large murals, a swimming pool. It was refreshing in this hot summertime. The Martians hadn't believed in large cities.

"How nice," said Mrs. Bittering, "if we could move up here to this villa for the summer."

"Come on," he said. "We're going back to town. There's work to be done on the rocket."

But as he worked that night, the thought of the cool blue marble villa entered his mind. As the hours passed, the rocket seemed less important.

In the flow of days and weeks, the rocket receded and dwindled. The old fever was gone. It frightened him to think he had let it slip this way. But somehow the heat, the air, the working conditions—

He heard the men murmuring on the porch of his metal shop.

"Everyone's going. You heard?"

"All going. That's right."

Bittering came out. "Going where?" He saw a couple of trucks, loaded with children and furniture, drive down the dusty street.

"Up to the villas," said the man.

"Yeah, Harry. I'm going. So is Sam. Aren't you, Sam?"

"That's right, Harry. What about you?"

"I've got work to do here."

"Work! You can finish that rocket in the autumn, when it's cooler."

He took a breath. "I got the frame all set up."

"In the autumn is better." Their voices were lazy in the heat.

"Got to work," he said.

"Autumn," they reasoned. And they sounded so sensible, so right.

Autumn would be best, he thought. Plenty of time, then.

No! cried part of himself, deep down, put away, locked tight, suffocating. No! No!

"In the autumn," he said.

"Come on, Harry," they all said.

"Yes," he said, feeling his flesh melt in the hot liquid air. "Yes, in the autumn. I'll begin work again then."

"I got a villa near the Tirra Canal," said someone.

"You mean the Roosevelt Canal, don't you?"

"Tirra. The old Martian name."

"But on the map—"

"Forget the map. It's Tirra now. Now I found a place in the Pillan mountains—"

"You mean the Rockefeller range," said Bittering.

"I mean the Pillan mountains," said Sam.

"Yes," said Bittering, buried in the hot, swarming air. "The Pillan mountains."

Everyone worked at loading the truck in the hot, still afternoon of the next day.

Laura, Dan, and David carried packages. Or, as they preferred to be known, Ttil, Linnl, and Werr carried packages.

The furniture was abandoned in the little white cottage.

"It looked just fine in Boston," said the mother. "And here in the cottage. But up at the villa? No. We'll get it when we come back in the autumn."

Bittering himself was quiet.

"I've some ideas on furniture for the villa," he said after a time. "Big, lazy furniture."

"What about your encyclopedia? You're taking it along, surely?"

Mr. Bittering glanced away. "I'll come and get it next week."

They turned to their daughter. "What about your New York dresses?"

The bewildered girl stared. "Why, I don't want them any more."

They shut off the gas, the water, they locked the doors and walked away. Father peered into the truck.

"Gosh, we're not taking much," he said. "Considering all we brought to Mars, this is only a handful!"

He started the truck.

Looking at the small white cottage for a long moment, he was filled with a desire to rush to it, touch it, say good-by to it, for he felt as if he were going away on a long journey, leaving something to which he could never quite return, never understand again.

Just then Sam and his family drove by in another truck.

"Hi, Bittering! Here we go!"

The truck swung down the ancient highway out of town. There were sixty others traveling the same direction. The town filled with a silent, heavy dust from their passage. The canal waters lay blue in the sun, and a quiet wind moved in the strange trees.

"Good-by, town!" said Mr. Bittering.

"Good-by, good-by," said the family, waving to it.

They did not look back again.

Summer burned the canals dry. Summer moved like flame upon the meadows. In the empty Earth settlement, the painted houses flaked and peeled. Rubber tires upon which children had swung in back yards hung suspended like stopped clock pendulums in the blazing air.

At the metal shop, the rocket frame began to rust.

In the quiet autumn Mr. Bittering stood, very dark now, very golden-eyed, upon the slope above his villa, looking at the valley.

"It's time to go back," said Cora.

"Yes, but we're not going," he said quietly. "There's nothing there any more."

"Your books," she said. "Your fine clothes."

"Your *Illes* and your fine *ior uele rre*," she said.

"The town's empty. No one's going back," he said. "There's no reason to, none at all."

The daughter wove tapestries and the sons played songs on ancient flutes and pipes, their laughter echoing in the marble villa.

Mr. Bittering gazed at the Earth settlement far away in the low valley. "Such odd, such ridiculous houses the Earth people built."

"They didn't know any better," his wife mused. "Such ugly people. I'm glad they've gone."

They both looked at each other, startled by all they had just finished saying. They laughed.

"Where did they go?" he wondered. He glanced at his wife. She was golden and slender as his daughter. She looked at him, and he seemed almost as young as their eldest son.

"I don't know," she said.

"We'll go back to town maybe next year, or the year after, or the year after that," he said, calmly. "Now—I'm warm. How about taking a swim?"

They turned their backs to the valley. Arm in arm they walked silently down a path of clear-running spring water.

Five years later a rocket fell out of the sky. It lay steaming in the valley. Men leaped out of it, shouting.

"We won the war on Earth! We're here to rescue you! Hey!"

But the American-built town of cottages, peach trees, and theaters was silent. They found a flimsy rocket frame rusting in an empty shop.

The rocket men searched the hills. The captain established headquarters in an abandoned bar. His lieutenant came back to report.

"The town's empty, but we found native life in the hills, sir. Dark people. Yellow eyes. Martians. Very friendly. We talked a bit, not much. They learn English fast. I'm sure our relations will be most friendly with them, sir."

"Dark, eh?" mused the captain. "How many?"

"Six, eight hundred, I'd say, living in those marble ruins in the hills, sir. Tall, healthy. Beautiful women."

"Did they tell you what became of the men and women who built this Earth settlement, Lieutenant?"

"They hadn't the foggiest notion of what happened to this town or its people."

"Strange. You think those Martians killed them?"

"They look surprisingly peaceful. Chances are a plague did this town in, sir."

"Perhaps. I suppose this is one of those mysteries we'll never solve. One of those mysteries you read about."

The captain looked at the room, the dusty windows, the blue mountains rising beyond, the canals moving in the light, and he heard the soft wind in the air. He shivered. Then, recovering, he tapped a large fresh map he had thumb-tacked to the top of an empty table.

"Lots to be done, Lieutenant." His voice droned on and quietly on as the sun sank behind the blue hills. "New settlements. Mining sites, minerals to be looked for. Bacteriological specimens taken. The work, all the work. And the old records were lost. We'll have a job of remapping to do, renaming the mountains and rivers and such. Calls for a little imagination.

"What do you think of naming those mountains the Lincoln Mountains, this canal the Washington Canal, those hills—we can name those hills for you, Lieutenant. Diplomacy. And you, for a favor, might name a town for me. Polishing the apple. And why not make this the Einstein Valley, and further over . . . are you *listening*, Lieutenant?"

The lieutenant snapped his gaze from the blue color and the quiet mist of the hills far beyond the town.

"What? Oh, *yes*, sir!"

The Strawberry Window

In his dream he was shutting the front door with its strawberry windows and
lemon windows and windows like white clouds and windows like clear water in
a country stream. Two dozen panes squared round the one big pane, colored of
fruit wines and gelatins and cool water ices. He remembered his father holding
him up as a child. "Look!" And through the green glass the world was emerald,
moss, and summer mint. "Look!" The lilac pane made livid grapes of all the
passersby. And at last the strawberry glass perpetually bathed the town in
roseate warmth, carpeted the world in pink sunrise, and made the cut lawn
seem imported from some Persian rug bazaar. The strawberry window, best of
all, cured people of their paleness, warmed the cold rain, and set the blowing,
shifting February snows afire.

"Yes, yes! There—!"

He awoke.

He heard his boys talking before he was fully out of his dream and he lay in
the dark now, listening to the sad sound their talk made, like the wind blowing
the white sea-bottoms into the blue hills, and then he remembered.

We're on Mars, he thought.

"What?" His wife cried out in her sleep.

He hadn't realized he had spoken; he lay as still as he possibly could. But
now, with a strange kind of numb reality, he saw his wife rise to haunt the
room, her pale face staring through the small, high windows of their quonset
hut at the clear but unfamiliar stars.

"Carrie," he whispered.

She did not hear.

"Carrie," he whispered. "There's something I want to tell you. For a month
now I've been wanting to say . . . tomorrow . . . tomorrow morning, there's
going to be . . ."

But his wife sat all to herself in the blue starlight and would not look at him.

If only the sun stayed up, he thought, if only there was no night. For during
the day he nailed the settlement town together, the boys were in school, and
Carrie had cleaning, gardening, cooking to do. But when the sun was gone and
their hands were empty of flowers or hammers and nails and arithmetics, their
memories, like night birds, came home in the dark.

His wife moved, a slight turn of her head.

"Bob," she said at last, "I want to go home."

"Carrie!"

"This isn't home," she said.

He saw that her eyes were wet and brimming. "Carrie, hold on awhile."

"I've got no fingernails from holding on now!"

As if she still moved in her sleep, she opened her bureau drawers and took out layers of handkerchiefs, shirts, underclothing, and put it all on top of the bureau, not seeing it, letting her fingers touch and bring it out and put it down. The routine was long familiar now. She would talk and put things out and stand quietly awhile, and then later put all the things away and come, dry-faced, back to bed and dreams. He was afraid that some night she would empty every drawer and reach for the few ancient suitcases against the wall.

"Bob . . . " Her voice was not bitter, but soft, featureless, and as uncolored as the moonlight that showed what she was doing. "So many nights for six months I've talked this way; I'm ashamed. You work hard building houses in town. A man who works so hard shouldn't have to listen to a wife gone sad on him. But there's nothing to do but talk it out. It's the little things I miss most of all. I don't know—silly things. Our front-porch swing. The wicker rocking chair, summer nights. Looking at the people walk or ride by those evenings, back in Ohio. Our black upright piano, out of tune. My Swedish cut glass. Our parlor furniture—oh, it was like a herd of elephants, I know, and all of it old. And the Chinese hanging crystals that hit when the wind blew. And talking to neighbors there on the front porch, July nights. All those crazy, silly things . . . they're not important. But it seems those are things that come to mind around three in the morning. I'm sorry."

"Don't be," he said. "Mars is a far place. It smells funny, looks funny, and feels funny. I think to myself nights too. We came from a nice town."

"It was green," she said. "In the spring and summer. And yellow and red in the fall. And ours was a nice house; my, it was old, eighty-ninety years or so. Used to hear the house talking at night, whispering away. All the dry wood, the banisters, the front porch, the sills. Wherever you touched, it talked to you. Every room a different way. And when you had the whole house talking, it was a family around you in the dark, putting you to sleep. No other house, the kind they build nowadays, can be the same. A lot of people have got to go through and live in a house to make it mellow down all over. This place here, now, this hut, it doesn't know I'm in it, doesn't care if I live or die. It makes a noise like tin, and tin's cold. It's got no pores for the years to sink in. It's got no cellar for you to put things away for next year and the year after that. It's got no attic where you keep things from last year and all the other years before you were born. If we only had a little bit up here that was familiar, Bob, then we could make room for all that's strange. But when everything, *every single thing* is strange, then it takes forever to make things familiar."

He nodded in the dark. "There's nothing you say that I haven't thought."

She was looking at the moonlight where it lay upon the suitcases against the wall. He saw her move her hand down toward them.

"Carrie!"

"What?"

He swung his legs out of bed. "Carrie, I've done a crazy damn-fool thing. All these months I heard you dreaming away, scared, and the boys at night and the wind, and Mars out there, the sea-bottoms and all, and . . . " He stopped and swallowed. "You got to understand what I did and why I did it. All the money we had in the bank a month ago, all the money we saved for ten years, I spent."

"Bob!"

"I threw it away, Carrie, I swear, I threw it away on nothing. It was going to be a surprise. But now, tonight, there you are, and there are those damned suitcases on the floor and . . . "

"Bob," she said, turning around. "You mean we've gone through all *this*, on Mars, putting away extra money every week, only to have you burn it up in a few hours?"

"I don't know," he said. "I'm a crazy fool. Look, it's not long till morning. We'll get up early. I'll take you down to see what I've done. I don't want to tell you, I want you to see. And if it's no go, then, well, there's always those suitcases and the rocket to Earth four times a week."

She did not move. "Bob, Bob," she murmured.

"Don't say any more," he said.

"Bob, Bob . . . " She shook her head slowly, unbelievingly. He turned away and lay back down on his own side of the bed, and she sat on the other side, and for a moment did not lie down, but only sat looking at the bureau where her handkerchiefs and jewelry and clothing lay ready in neat stacks where she had left them. Outside a wind the color of moonlight stirred up the sleeping dust and powdered the air.

At last she lay back, but said nothing more and was a cold weight in the bed, staring down the long tunnel of night toward the faintest sign of morning.

They got up in the very first light and moved in the small quonset hut without a sound. It was a pantomime prolonged almost to the time when someone might scream at the silence, as the mother and father and the boys washed and dressed and ate a quiet breakfast of toast and fruit juice and coffee, with no one looking directly at anyone and everyone watching someone in the reflective surfaces of toaster, glassware, or cutlery, where all their faces were melted out of shape and made terribly alien in the early hour. Then, at last, they opened the quonset door and let in the air that blew across the cold blue-white Martian seas, where only the sand tides dissolved and shifted and made ghost patterns, and they stepped out under a raw and staring cold sky and began their walk toward a town, which seemed no more than a motion-picture set far on ahead of them on a vast, empty stage.

"What part of town are we going to?" asked Carrie.

"The rocket depot," he said. "But before we get there, I've a lot to say."

The boys slowed down and moved behind their parents, listening. The father gazed ahead, and not once in all the time he was talking did he look at his wife or sons to see how they were taking all that he said.

"I believe in Mars," he began quietly. "I guess I believe some day it'll belong to us. We'll nail it down. We'll settle in. We won't turn tail and run. It came to me one day a year ago, right after we first arrived. Why did we come? I asked myself. Because, I said, because. It's the same thing with the salmon every year. The salmon don't know why they go where they go, but they go, anyway. Up rivers they don't remember, up streams, jumping waterfalls, but finally making it to where they propagate and die, and the whole thing starts again. Call it racial memory, instinct, call it nothing, but there it is. And here we are."

They walked in the silent morning with the great sky watching them and the strange blue and steam-white sands sifting about their feet on the new highway.

"So here we are. And from Mars where? Jupiter, Neptune, Pluto, and on out? Right. *And on out.* Why? Some day the sun will blow up like a leaky furnace. Boom—there goes Earth. But maybe Mars won't be hurt; or if Mars is hurt maybe Pluto won't be, or if Pluto's hurt, then where'll *we* be, our sons' sons, that is?"

He gazed steadily up into that flawless shell of plum-colored sky.

"Why, we'll be on some world with a number maybe; planet 6 of star system 97, planet 2 of system 99! So damn far off from here you need a nightmare to take it in! We'll be gone, do you see, gone off away and safe! And I thought to myself, ah, ah. So that's the reason we came to Mars, so *that's* the reason men shoot off their rockets."

"Bob—"

"Let me finish; not to make money, no. Not to see the sights, no. Those are the lies men tell, the fancy reasons they give themselves. Get rich, get famous, they say. Have fun, jump around, they say. But all the while, inside, something else is ticking along the way it ticks in salmon or whales, the way it ticks, by God, in the smallest microbe you want to name. And that little clock that ticks in everything living, you know what it says? It says get away, spread out, move along, keep swimming. Run to so many worlds and build so many towns that *nothing* can ever kill man. You *see*, Carrie? It's not just us come to Mars, it's the race, the whole darn human race, depending on how *we* make out in our lifetime. This thing is so big I want to laugh, I'm so scared stiff of it."

He felt the boys walking steadily behind him and he felt Carrie beside him and he wanted to see her face and how she was taking all this, but he didn't look there, either.

"All this is no different than me and Dad walking the fields when I was a boy, casting seed by hand when our seeder broke down and we'd no money to fix it. It had to be done, somehow, for the later crops. My God, Carrie, my God, you *remember* those Sunday-supplement articles, 'The Earth Will Freeze in a Million Years?' I bawled once, as a boy, reading articles like that. My mother asked why. I'm bawling for all those poor people up ahead, I said. Don't worry about them, Mother said. But, Carrie, that's my whole point; we *are* worrying about them. Or we wouldn't be here. It matters if Man with a capital M keeps going. There's nothing better than Man with a capital M in my books. I'm prejudiced, of course, because I'm one of the breed. But if there's any way to get hold of that immortality men are always talking about, this is the way—spread out—seed the universe. Then you got a harvest against crop failures anywhere down the line. No matter if Earth has famines or the rust comes in. You got the new wheat lifting on Venus or where-in-hell-ever man gets to in the next thousand years. I'm crazy with the idea, Carrie, crazy. When I finally hit on it I got so excited I wanted to grab people, you, the boys, and tell them. But hell, I knew that wasn't necessary. I knew a day or night would come when you'd hear that ticking in yourselves too, and then you'd see, and no one'd have to say anything again about all this. It's big talk, Carrie, I know, and big thoughts for a man just short of five feet five, but by all that's holy, it's true."

They moved through the deserted streets of the town and listened to the echoes of their walking feet.

"And this morning?" said Carrie.

"I'm coming to this morning," he said. "Part of *me* wants to go home too. But the other part says if we go, everything's lost. So I thought, what bothers us most? Some of the things we once had. Some of the boys' things, your things, mine. And I thought, if it takes an old thing to get a new thing started, by God, I'll use the old thing. I remember from history books that a thousand years ago they put charcoals in a hollowed-out cow horn, blew on them during the day, so they carried their fire on marches from place to place, to start a fire every night with the sparks left over from morning. Always a new fire, but always something of the old in it. So I weighed and balanced it off. Is the Old worth all our money? I asked. No! It's only the things we *did* with the Old that have any worth. Well, then, is the New worth *all* our money? I asked. Do you feel like investing in the day after the middle of next week? Yes! I said. If I can fight this thing that makes us want to go back to Earth, I'd dip my money in kerosene and strike a match!"

Carrie and the two boys did not move. They stood on the street, looking at him as if he were a storm that had passed over and around, almost blowing them from the ground, a storm that was now dying away.

"The freight rocket came in this morning," he said, quietly. "Our delivery's on it. Let's go and pick it up."

They walked slowly up the three steps into the rocket depot and across the echoing floor toward the freight room that was just sliding back its doors, opening for the day.

"Tell us again about the salmon," said one of the boys.

In the middle of the warm morning they drove out of town in a rented truck filled with great crates and boxes and parcels and packages, long ones, tall ones, short ones, flat ones, all numbered and neatly addressed to one Robert Prentiss, New Toledo, Mars.

They stopped the truck by the quonset hut and the boys jumped down and helped their mother out. For a moment Bob sat behind the wheel, and then slowly got out himself to walk around and look into the back of the truck at the crates.

And by noon all but one of the boxes were opened and their contents placed on the sea-bottom where the family stood among them.

"Carrie . . ."

And he led her up the old porch steps that now stood uncrated on the edge of town.

"Listen to 'em, Carrie."

The steps squeaked and whispered underfoot.

"What do they say, tell me what they say?"

She stood on the ancient wooden steps, holding to herself, and could not tell him.

He waved his hand. "Front porch here, living room there, dining room, kitchen, three bedrooms. Part we'll build new, part we'll bring. Of course all we got here now is the front porch, some parlor furniture, and the old bed."

"All that money, Bob!"

He turned, smiling. "You're not mad, now, look at me! You're not mad. We'll bring it all up, next year, five years! The cut-glass vases, that Armenian carpet your mother gave us in 1961! Just *let* the sun explode!"

They looked at the other crates, numbered and lettered: Front-porch swing, front-porch wicker rocker, hanging Chinese crystals . . .

"I'll blow them myself to make them ring."

They set the front door, with its little panes of colored glass, on the top of the stairs, and Carrie looked through the strawberry window.

"What do you see?"

But he knew what she saw, for he gazed through the colored glass, too. And there was Mars, with its cold sky warmed and its dead seas fired with color, with its hills like mounds of strawberry ice, and its sand like burning charcoals sifted by wind. The strawberry window, the strawberry window, breathed soft rose colors on the land and filled the mind and the eye with the light of a never-ending dawn. Bent there, looking through, he heard himself say:

"The town'll be out this way in a year. This'll be a shady street, you'll have your porch, and you'll have friends. You won't *need* all this so much, then. But starting right here, with this little bit that's familiar, watch it spread, watch

Mars change so you'll know it as if you've known it all your life."

He ran down the steps to the last and as yet unopened canvas-covered crate. With his pocket knife he cut a hole in the canvas. "Guess!" he said.

"My kitchen stove? My furnace?"

"Not in a million years." He smiled very gently. "Sing me a song," he said.

"Bob, you're clean off your head."

"Sing me a song worth all the money we had in the bank and now don't have, but who gives a blast in hell," he said.

"I don't know anything but 'Genevieve, Sweet Genevieve'!"

"Sing that," he said.

But she could not open her mouth and start the song. He saw her lips move and try, but there was no sound.

He ripped the canvas wider and shoved his hand into the crate and touched around for a quiet moment, and started to sing the words himself until he moved his hand a last time and then a single clear piano chord sprang out on the morning air.

"There," he said. "Let's take it right on to the end. Everyone! Here's the harmony."

A Scent of Sarsaparilla

Mr. William Finch stood quietly in the dark and blowing attic all morning and afternoon for three days. For three days in late November, he stood alone, feeling the soft, white flakes of Time falling out of the infinite cold steel sky, silently, softly, feathering the roof and powdering the eaves. He stood, eyes shut. The attic, wallowed in seas of wind in the long sunless days, creaked every bone and shook down ancient dusts from its beams and warped timbers and lathings. It was a mass of sighs and torments that ached all about him where he stood sniffing its elegant dry perfumes and feeling of its ancient heritages. Ah. Ah.

Listening, downstairs, his wife Cora could not hear him walk or shift or twitch. She imagined she could only hear him breathe, slowly out and in, like a dusty bellows, alone up there in the attic, high in the windy house.

"Ridiculous," she muttered.

When he hurried down for lunch the third afternoon, he smiled at the bleak walls, the chipped plates, the scratched silverware, and even at his wife!

"What's all the excitement?" she demanded.

"Good spirits is all. Wonderful spirits!" he laughed. He seemed almost hysterical with joy. He was seething in a great warm ferment which, obviously, he had trouble concealing. His wife frowned.

"What's that *smell?*"

"Smell, smell, smell?"

"Sarsaparilla." She sniffed suspiciously. "That's what it is!"

"Oh, it couldn't be!" His hysterical happiness stopped as quickly as if she'd switched him off. He seemed stunned, ill at ease, and suddenly very careful.

"Where did you go this morning?" she asked.

"You *know* I was cleaning the attic."

"Mooning over a lot of trash. I didn't hear a sound. Thought maybe you weren't in the attic at all. What's that?" She pointed.

"Well, now how did *those* get there?" he asked the world.

He peered down at the pair of black spring-metal bicycle clips that bound his thin pants cuffs to his bony ankles.

"Found them in the attic," he answered himself. "Remember when we got out on the gravel road in the early morning on our tandem bike, Cora, forty years ago, everything fresh and new?"

"If you don't finish that attic today, I'll come up and toss everything out myself."

"Oh, no," he cried. "I have everything the way I want it!"

She looked at him coldly.

"Cora," he said, eating his lunch, relaxing, beginning to enthuse again, "you know what attics are? They're Time Machines, in which old, dim-witted men like me can travel back forty years to a time when it was summer all year round and children raided ice wagons. Remember how it tasted? You held the ice in your handkerchief. It was like sucking the flavor of linen and snow at the same time."

Cora fidgeted.

It's not impossible, he thought, half closing his eyes, trying to see it and build it. Consider an attic. Its very atmosphere is Time. It deals in other years, the cocoons and chrysalises of another age. All the bureau drawers are little coffins where a thousand yesterdays lie in state. Oh, the attic's a dark, friendly place, full of Time, and if you stand in the very center of it, straight and tall, squinting your eyes, and thinking and thinking, and smelling the Past, and putting out your hands to feel of Long Ago, why, it . . .

He stopped, realizing he had spoken some of this aloud. Cora was eating rapidly.

"Well, wouldn't it be interesting," he asked the part in her hair, "if Time Travel *could* occur? And what more logical, proper place for it to happen than in an attic like *ours,* eh?"

"It's not always summer back in the old days," she said. "It's just your crazy memory. You remember all the good things and forget the bad. It wasn't always summer."

"Figuratively speaking, Cora, it was."

"Wasn't."

"What I mean is this," he said, whispering excitedly, bending forward to see the image he was tracing on the blank dining-room wall. "If you rode your unicycle carefully between the years, balancing, hands out, careful, careful, if you rode from year to year, spent a week in 1909, a day in 1900, a month or a fortnight somewhere else, 1905, 1898, you could stay with summer the rest of your life."

"Unicycle?"

"You know, one of those tall chromium one-wheeled bikes, single-seater, the performers ride in vaudeville shows, juggling. Balance, true balance, it takes, not to fall off, to keep the bright objects flying in the air, beautiful, up and up, a light, a flash, a sparkle, a bomb of brilliant colors, red, yellow, blue, green, white, gold; all the Junes and Julys and Augusts that ever were, in the air, about you, at once, hardly touching your hands, flying, suspended, and you, smiling, among them. Balance, Cora, *balance*."

"Blah," she said, "blah, blah." And added, "Blah!"

He climbed the long cold stairs to the attic, shivering.

There were nights in winter when he woke with porcelain in his bones, with cool chimes blowing in his ears, with frost piercing his nerves in a raw illumination like white-cold fireworks exploding and showering down in flaming snows upon a silent land deep in his subconscious. He was cold, cold, cold, and it would take a score of endless summers, with their green torches and bronze suns, to thaw him free of his wintry sheath. He was a great tasteless chunk of brittle ice, a snowman put to bed each night, full of confetti dreams, tumbles of crystal and flurry. And there lay winter outside forever, a great leaden wine press smashing down its colorless lid of sky, squashing them all like so many grapes, mashing color and sense and being from everyone, save the children who fled on skis and toboggans down mirrored hills which reflected the crushing iron shield that hung lower above town each day and every eternal night.

Mr. Finch lifted the attic trap door. But here, *here*. A dust of summer sprang up about him. The attic dust simmered with heat left over from other seasons. Quietly, he shut the trap door down.

He began to smile.

The attic was quiet as a thundercloud before a storm. On occasion, Cora Finch heard her husband murmuring, murmuring, high up there.

At five in the afternoon, singing "My Isle of Golden Dreams," Mr. Finch flipped a crisp new straw hat in the kitchen door. "Boo!"

"Did you sleep all afternoon?" snapped his wife. "I called up at you four times and no answer."

"Sleep?" He considered this and laughed, then put his hand quickly over his mouth. "Well, I guess I did."

Suddenly she saw him. "My God!" she cried, "where'd you get that coat?"

He wore a red candy-striped coat, a high white, choking collar and ice cream pants. You could smell the straw hat like a handful of fresh hay fanned in the air.

"Found 'em in an old trunk."

She sniffed. "Don't smell of moth balls. Looks brand-new."

"Oh, no!" he said hastily. He looked stiff and uncomfortable as she eyed his costume.

"This isn't a summer-stock company," she said.

"Can't a fellow have a little fun?"

"That's all you've ever had." She slammed the oven door. "While I've stayed home and knitted, Lord knows, you've been down at the store helping ladies' elbows in and out doors."

He refused to be bothered. "Cora." He looked deep into the crackling straw hat. "Wouldn't it be nice to take a Sunday walk the way we used to do, with your silk parasol and your long dress whishing along, and sit on those wire-legged chairs at the soda parlor and smell the drugstore the way they used to smell? Why don't drugstores smell that way any more? And order two sarsaparillas for us, Cora, and then ride out in our 1910 Ford to Hannahan's Pier for a box supper and listen to the brass band. How about it?"

"Supper's ready. Take that dreadful uniform off."

"If you could make a wish and take a ride on those oak-lined country roads like they had before cars started rushing, would you *do* it?" he insisted, watching her.

"Those old roads were dirty. We came home looking like Africans. Anyway" —she picked up a sugar jar and shook it— "this morning I had forty dollars here. Now it's gone! Don't tell me you ordered those clothes from a costume house. They're brand-new; they didn't come from any trunk!"

"I'm—" he said.

She raved for half an hour, but he could not bring himself to say anything. The November wind shook the house and as she talked, the snows of winter began to fall again in the cold steel sky.

"Answer me!" she cried. "Are you crazy, spending our money that way, on clothes you can't wear?"

"The attic," he started to say.

She walked off and sat in the living room.

The snow was falling fast now and it was a cold dark November evening.

She heard him climb up the stepladder, slowly, into the attic, into that dusty place of other years, into that black place of costumes and props and Time, into a world separate from this world below.

He closed the trap door down. The flashlight, snapped on, was company enough. Yes, here was all of Time compressed in a Japanese paper flower. At the touch of memory, everything would unfold into the clear water of the mind, in beautiful blooms, in spring breezes, larger than life. Each of the bureau drawers slid forth, might contain aunts and cousins and grandmamas, ermined in dust. Yes, Time was here. You could feel it breathing, an atmospheric instead of a mechanical clock.

Now the house below was as remote as another day in the Past. He half shut his eyes and looked and looked on every side of the waiting attic.

Here, in prismed chandelier, were rainbows and mornings and noons as bright as new rivers flowing endlessly back through Time. His flashlight caught and flickered them alive, the rainbows leapt up to curve the shadows back with colors, with colors like plums and strawberries and Concord grapes, with colors like cut lemons and the sky where the clouds drew off after storming and the blue was there. And the dust of the attic was incense burning and all of Time burning, and all you need do was peer into the flames. It was indeed a great machine of Time, this attic, he knew, he felt, he was sure, and if you touched prisms here, doorknobs there, plucked tassels, chimed crystals, swirled dust, punched trunk hasps and gusted the vox humana of the old hearth bellows until it puffed the soot of a thousand ancient fires into your eyes, if, indeed, you played this instrument, this warm machine of parts, if you fondled all of its bits and pieces, its levers and changers and movers, then, then, *then*!

He thrust out his hands to orchestrate, to conduct, to flourish. There was music in his head, in his mouth shut tight, and he played the great machine, the thunderously silent organ, bass, tenor, soprano, low, high, and at last, at last, a chord that shuddered him so that he had to shut his eyes.

About nine o'clock that night she heard him calling, "Cora!" She went upstairs. His head peered down at her from above, smiling at her. He waved his hat. "Good-by, Cora."

"What do you mean?" she cried.

"I've thought it over for three days and I'm saying good-by."

"Come down out of there, you fool!"

"I drew five hundred dollars from the bank yesterday. I've been thinking about this. And then when *it* happened, well . . . Cora . . ." He shoved his eager hand down. "For the last time, will you come along with me?"

"In the attic? Hand down that stepladder, William Finch. I'll climb up there and run you out of that filthy place!"

"I'm going to Hannahan's Pier for a bowl of clam chowder," he said. "And

I'm requesting the brass band to play 'Moonlight Bay.' Oh, come on, Cora. . . ."
He motioned his extended hand.

She simply stared at his gentle, questioning face.

"Good-by," he said.

He waved gently, gently. Then his face was gone, the straw hat was gone.
"William!" she screamed.

The attic was dark and silent.

Shrieking, she ran and got a chair and used it to groan her way up into the
musty darkness. She flourished the flashlight. "William! William!"

The dark spaces were empty. A winter wind shook the house.

Then she saw the far west attic window, ajar.

She fumbled over to it. She hesitated, held her breath. Then, slowly, she
opened it. The ladder was placed outside the window, leading down onto a
porch roof.

She pulled back from the window.

Outside the opened frame the apple trees shone bright green, it was
twilight of a summer day in July. Faintly, she heard explosions, firecrackers
going off. She heard laughter and distant voices. Rockets burst in the warm air,
softly, red, white, and blue, fading.

She slammed the window and stood reeling. "William!"

Wintry November light glowed up through the trap in the attic floor
behind her. Bent to it, she saw the snow whispering against the cold clear panes
down in that November world where she would spend the next thirty years.

She did not go near the window again. She sat alone in the black attic,
smelling the one smell that did not seem to fade. It lingered like a sigh of
satisfaction, on the air. She took a deep, long breath.

The old, the familiar, the unforgettable scent of drugstore sarsaparilla.

The Picasso Summer

George and Alice Smith detrained at Biarritz one summer noon and in an hour had run through their hotel onto the beach into the ocean and back out to bake upon the sand.

To see George Smith sprawled burning there, you'd think him only a tourist flown fresh as iced lettuce to Europe and soon to be transshipped home. But here was a man who loved art more than life itself.

"There . . ." George Smith sighed. Another ounce of perspiration trickled down his chest. Boil out the Ohio tap water, he thought, then drink down the best Bordeaux. Silt your blood with rich French sediment so you'll see with native eyes!

Why? Why eat, breathe, drink everything French? So that, given time, he might really begin to understand the genius of one man.

His mouth moved, forming a name.

"George?" His wife loomed over him. "I know what you've been thinking. I can read your lips."

He lay perfectly still, waiting.

"And?"

"Picasso," she said.

He winced. Someday she would learn to pronounce that name.

"Please," she said. "Relax. I know you heard the rumor this morning, but you should see your eyes—your tic is back. All right, Picasso's here, down the coast a few miles away, visiting friends in some small fishing town. But you must forget it or our vacation's ruined."

"I wish I'd never heard the rumor," he said honestly.

"If only," she said, "you liked other painters."

Others? Yes, there were others. He could breakfast most congenially on Caravaggio still lifes of autumn pears and midnight plums. For lunch: those fire-squirting, thick-wormed Van Gogh sunflowers, those blooms a blind man might read with one rush of scorched fingers down fiery canvas. But the great feast? The paintings he saved his palate for? There, filling the horizon like Neptune risen, crowned with limeweed, alabaster, coral, paintbrushes clenched like tridents in horn-nailed fists, and with fist-tail vast enough to fluke summer showers out over all Gibraltar—who else but the creator of *Girl Before a Mirror* and *Guernica?*

"Alice," he said patiently, "how can I explain? Coming down on the train, I thought, Good Lord, it's *all* Picasso country!"

But was it really? he wondered. The sky, the land, the people, the flushed pink bricks here, scrolled electric-blue ironwork balconies there, a mandolin ripe as a fruit in some man's thousand fingerprinting hands, billboard tatters blowing like confetti in night winds—how much was Picasso, how much George Smith staring round the world with wild Picasso eyes? He despaired of answering. That old man had distilled turpentines and linseed oil so thoroughly through George Smith that they shaped his being, all Blue Period at twilight, all Rose Period at dawn.

"I keep thinking," he said aloud, "if we saved our money . . . "

"We'll never have five thousand dollars."

"I know," he said quietly. "But it's nice thinking we might bring it off someday. Wouldn't it be great to just step up to him, say 'Pablo, here's five thousand! Give us the sea, the sand, that sky, or any old thing you want, we'll be happy. . . .' "

After a moment his wife touched his arm.

"I think you'd better go in the water now," she said.

"Yes," he said. "I'd better do just that."

White fire showered up when he cut the water.

During the afternoon George Smith came out, and went into the ocean with the vast spilling motions of now warm, now cool people who at last, with the sun's decline, their bodies all lobster colors and colors of broiled squab and guinea hen, trudged for their wedding-cake hotels.

The beach lay deserted for endless mile on mile save for two people. One was George Smith, towel over shoulder, out for a last devotional.

Far along the shore another shorter, square-cut man walked alone in the tranquil weather. He was deeper-tanned, his close-shaven head dyed almost mahogany by the sun, and his eyes were clear and bright as water in his face.

So the shore-line stage was set, and in a few minutes the two men would meet. And once again Fate fixed the scales for shocks and surprises, arrivals and departures. And all the while these two solitary strollers did not for a moment think on coincidence, that unswum stream which lingers at man's elbow with every crowd in every town. Nor did they ponder the fact that if man dares dip into that stream he grabs a wonder in each hand. Like most, they shrugged at such folly and stayed well up the bank lest Fate should shove them in.

The stranger stood alone. Glancing about, he saw his aloneness, saw the waters of the lovely bay, saw the sun sliding down the late colors of the day, and then, half turning, spied a small wooden object on the sand. It was no more than the slender stick from a lime ice cream delicacy long since melted away. Smiling, he picked the stick up. With another glance around to reinsure his solitude, the man stooped again and, holding the stick gently, with light sweeps of his hand began to do the one thing in all the world he knew best how to do.

He began to draw incredible figures along the sand.

He sketched one figure and then moved over and, still looking down, completely focused on his work now, drew a second and a third figure, and after that a fourth and a fifth and a sixth.

George Smith, printing the shoreline with his feet, gazed here, gazed there, and then saw the man ahead. George Smith, drawing nearer, saw that the man, deeply tanned, was bending down. Nearer yet, and it was obvious what the man was up to. George Smith chuckled. Of course, of course . . . Alone on the beach this man—how old? sixty-five? seventy?—was scribbling and doodling away. How the sand flew! How the wild portraits flung themselves out there on the shore! How . . .

George Smith took one more step and stopped, very still.

The stranger was drawing and drawing and did not seem to sense that anyone stood immediately behind him and the world of his drawings in the sand. By now he was so deeply enchanted with his solitudinous creation that depth bombs set off in the bay might not have stopped his flying hand nor turned him round.

George Smith looked down at the sand. And after a long while, looking, he began to tremble.

For there on the flat shore were pictures of Grecian lions and Mediterranean goats and maidens with flesh of sand like powdered gold and satyrs piping on hand-carved horns and children dancing, strewing flowers along and along the beach with lambs gamboling after, and musicians skipping to their harps and lyres and unicorns racing youths toward distant meadows, woodlands, ruined temples, and volcanoes. Along the shore in a never-broken line, the hand, the wooden stylus of this man, bent down in fever and raining perspiration, scribbled, ribboned, looped around over and up, across, in, out, stitched, whispered, stayed, then hurried on as if this traveling bacchanal must flourish to its end before the sun was put out by the sea. Twenty, thirty yards or more the nymphs and dryads and summer founts sprang up in unraveled hieroglyphs. And the sand in the dying light was the color of molten copper on which was now slashed a message that any man in any time might read and savor down the years. Everything whirled and poised in its own wind and gravity. Now wine was being crushed from under the grape-blooded feet of dancing vintners' daughters, now steaming seas gave birth to coin-sheathed monsters while flowered kites strewed scent on blowing clouds . . . now . . . now . . . now . . .

The artist stopped.

George Smith drew back and stood away.

The artist glanced up, surprised to find someone so near. Then he simply stood there, looking from George Smith to his own creations flung like idle footprints down the way. He smiled at last and shrugged as if to say, Look what

I've done; see what a child? You will forgive me, won't you? One day or another we are all fools. . . . You too, perhaps? So allow an old fool this, eh? Good! Good!

But George Smith could only look at the little man with the sun-dark skin and the clear sharp eyes and say the man's name once, in a whisper, to himself.

They stood thus for perhaps another five seconds. George Smith staring at the sand-frieze, and the artist watching George Smith with amused curiosity. George Smith opened his mouth, closed it, put out his hand, took it back. He stepped toward the pictures, stepped away. Then he moved along the line of figures, like a man viewing a precious series of marbles cast up from some ancient ruin on the shore. His eyes did not blink, his hand wanted to touch but did not dare to touch. He wanted to run but did not run.

He looked suddenly at the hotel. Run, yes! Run! What? Grab a shovel, dig, excavate, save a chunk of this all-too-crumbling sand? Find a repairman, race him back here with plaster of Paris to cast a mold of some small fragile part of these? No, no. Silly, silly. Or . . . ? His eyes flicked to his hotel window. The camera! Run, get it, get back, and hurry along the shore, clicking, changing film, clicking, until . . .

George Smith whirled to face the sun. It burned faintly on his face; his eyes were two small fires from it. The sun was half underwater, and as he watched it sank the rest of the way in a matter of seconds.

The artist had drawn nearer and now was gazing into George Smith's face with great friendliness, as if he were guessing every thought. Now he was nodding his head in a little bow. Now the ice cream stick had fallen casually from his fingers. Now he was saying good night, good night. Now he was gone, walking back down the beach toward the south.

George Smith stood looking after him. After a full minute he did the only thing he could possibly do. He started at the beginning of the fantastic frieze of satyrs and fauns and wine-dipped maidens and prancing unicorns and piping youths and he walked slowly along the shore. He walked a long way, looking down at the free-running bacchanal. And when he came to the end of the animals and men he turned around and started back in the other direction, just staring down as if he had lost something and did not quite know where to find it. He kept on doing this until there was no more light in the sky or on the sand to see by.

He sat down at the supper table.

"You're late," said his wife. "I just had to come down alone. I'm ravenous."

"That's all right," he said.

"Anything interesting happen on your walk?" she asked.

"No," he said.

"You look funny; George, you didn't swim out too far, did you, and almost drown? I can tell by your face. You *did* swim out too far, didn't you?"

"Yes," he said.

"Well," she said, watching him closely. "Don't ever do that again. Now—what'll you have?"

He picked up the menu and started to read it and stopped suddenly.

"What's wrong?" asked his wife.

He turned his head and shut his eyes for a moment.

"Listen."

She listened.

"I don't hear anything," she said.

"Don't you?"

"No. What is it?"

"Just the tide," he said after a while, sitting there, his eyes still shut. "Just the tide coming in."

The Day It Rained Forever

The hotel stood like a hollowed dry bone under the very center of the desert sky where the sun burned the roof all day. All night, the memory of the sun stirred in every room like the ghost of an old forest fire. Long after dusk, since light meant heat, the hotel lights stayed off. The inhabitants of the hotel preferred to feel their way blind through the halls in their never-ending search for cool air.

This one particular evening Mr. Terle, the proprietor, and his only boarders, Mr. Smith and Mr. Fremley, who looked and smelled like two ancient rags of cured tobacco, stayed late on the long veranda. In their creaking glockenspiel rockers they gasped back and forth in the dark, trying to rock up a wind.

"Mr. Terle . . . ? Wouldn't it be *really* nice . . . someday . . . if you could buy . . . air conditioning . . . ?"

Mr. Terle coasted awhile, eyes shut.

"Got no money for such things, Mr. Smith."

The two old boarders flushed; they hadn't paid a bill now in twenty-one years.

Much later Mr. Fremley sighed a grievous sigh. "Why, why don't we all just quit, pick up, get outa here, move to a decent city? Stop this swelterin' and fryin' and sweatin'."

"Who'd buy a dead hotel in a ghost town?" said Mr. Terle quietly. "No. No, we'll just set here and wait, wait for that great day, January 29."

Slowly, all three men stopped rocking.

January 29.

The one day in all the year when it really let go and rained.

"Won't wait long." Mr. Smith tilted his gold railroad watch like the warm summer moon in his palm. "Two hours and nine minutes from now it'll *be* January 29. But I don't see nary a cloud in ten thousand miles."

"It's rained every January 29 since I was born!" Mr. Terle stopped, surprised at his own loud voice. "If it's a day late this year, I won't pull God's shirttail."

Mr. Fremley swallowed hard and looked from east to west across the desert toward the hills. "I wonder . . . will there ever be a gold rush hereabouts again?"

"No gold," said Mr. Smith. "And what's more, I'll make you a bet—no rain. No rain tomorrow or the day after the day after tomorrow. No rain all the rest of this year."

The three old men sat staring at the big sun-yellowed moon that burned a hole in the high stillness.

After a long while, painfully, they began to rock again.

The first hot morning breezes curled the calendar pages like a dried snake skin against the flaking hotel front.

The three men, thumbing their suspenders up over their hat-rack shoulders, came barefoot downstairs to blink out at that idiot sky.

"January 29 . . ."

"Not a drop of mercy there."

"Day's young."

"*I'm* not." Mr. Fremley turned and went away.

It took him five minutes to find his way up through the delirious hallways to his hot, freshly baked bed.

At noon, Mr. Terle peered in.

"Mr. Fremley. . . ?"

"Damn desert cactus, that's us!" gasped Mr. Fremley, lying there, his face looking as if at any moment it might fall away in a blazing dust on the raw plank floor. "But even the best damn cactus got to have just a sip of water before it goes back to another year of the same damn furnace. I tell you I won't move again, I'll lie here and die if I don't hear more than birds pattin' around up on that roof!"

"Keep your prayers simple and your umbrella handy," said Mr. Terle and tiptoed away.

At dusk, on the hollow roof a faint pattering sounded.

Mr. Fremley's voice sang out mournfully from his bed.

"Mr. Terle, that ain't rain! That's you with the garden hose sprinklin' well water on the roof! Thanks for tryin', but cut it out, now."

The pattering sound stopped. There was a sigh from the yard below.

Coming around the side of the hotel a moment later, Mr. Terle saw the calendar fly out and down in the dust.

"Damn January 29!" cried a voice. "Twelve more months! Have to wait twelve more months, now!"

Mr. Smith was standing there in the doorway. He stepped inside and brought out two dilapidated suitcases and thumped them on the porch.

"Mr. Smith!" cried Mr. Terle. "You can't leave after thirty years!"

"They say it rains twenty days a month in Ireland," said Mr. Smith. "I'll get a job there and run around with my hat off and my mouth open."

"You can't go!" Mr. Terle tried frantically to think of something; he snapped his fingers. "You owe me nine thousand dollars rent!"

Mr. Smith recoiled; his eyes got a look of tender and unexpected hurt in them.

"I'm sorry." Mr. Terle looked away. "I didn't mean that. Look now—you just head for Seattle. Pours two inches a week there. Pay me when you can, or never. But do me a favor: wait till midnight. It's cooler then, anyhow. Get you a good night's walk toward the city."

"Nothin'll happen between now and midnight."

"You got to have faith. When everything else is gone, you got to believe a thing'll happen. Just stand here with me, you don't have to sit, just stand here and think of rain. That's the last thing I'll ever ask of you."

On the desert sudden little whirlwinds of dust twisted up, sifted down. Mr. Smith's eyes scanned the sunset horizon.

"What do I think? Rain, oh you rain, come along here? Stuff like that?"

"Anything. Anything at all!"

Mr. Smith stood for a long time between his two mangy suitcases and did not move. Five, six minutes ticked by. There was no sound, save the two men's breathing in the dusk.

Then at last, very firmly, Mr. Smith stooped to grasp the luggage handles.

Just then, Mr. Terle blinked. He leaned forward, cupping his hand to his ear.

Mr. Smith froze, his hands still on the luggage.

From away among the hills, a murmur, a soft and tremulous rumble.

"Storm coming!" hissed Mr. Terle.

The sound grew louder; a kind of whitish cloud rose up from the hills.

Mr. Smith stood tall on tiptoe.

Upstairs Mr. Fremley sat up like Lazarus.

Mr. Terle's eyes grew wider and yet wider to take hold of what was coming. He held to the porch rail like the captain of a calm-foundered vessel feeling the first stir of some tropic breeze that smelled of lime and the ice-cool white meat of coconut. The smallest wind stroked over his aching nostrils as over the flues of a white-hot chimney.

"There!" cried Mr. Terle. "There!"

And over the last hill, shaking out feathers of fiery dust, came the cloud, the thunder, the racketing storm.

Over the hill the first car to pass in twenty days flung itself down the valley with a shriek, a thud, and a wail.

Mr. Terle did not dare to look at Mr. Smith.

Mr. Smith looked up, thinking of Mr. Fremley in his room.

Mr. Fremley, at the window, looked down and saw the car expire and die in front of the hotel.

For the sound that the car made was curiously final. It had come a very long way on blazing sulphur roads, across salt flats abandoned ten million years ago by the shingling off of waters. Now, with wire-ravelings like cannibal hair sprung up from seams, with a great eyelid of canvas top thrown back and melted to spearmint gum over the rear seat, the auto, a Kissel car, vintage 1924, gave a final shuddering as if to expel its ghost upon the air.

The old woman in the front seat of the car waited patiently, looking in at the three men and the hotel as if to say, Forgive me, my friend is ill; I've known him a long while, and now I must see him through his final hour. So she just sat in the car waiting for the faint convulsions to cease and for the great relaxation of all the bones which signifies that the final process is over. She must have sat a full half minute longer listening to her car, and there was something so peaceful about her that Mr. Terle and Mr. Smith leaned slowly toward her. At last she looked at them with a grave smile and raised her hand.

Mr. Fremley was surprised to see his hand go out the window, above, and wave back to her.

On the porch Mr. Smith murmured, "Strange. It's not a storm. And I'm not disappointed. How come?"

But Mr. Terle was down the path and to the car.

"We thought you were . . . that is . . . " He trailed off. "Terle's my name, Joe Terle."

She took his hand and looked at him with absolutely clear and unclouded light blue eyes like water that has melted from snow a thousand miles off and come a long way, purified by wind and sun.

"Miss Blanche Hillgood," she said, quietly. "Graduate of the Grinnell College, unmarried teacher of music, thirty years high-school glee club and student orchestra conductor, Green City, Iowa, twenty years private teacher of piano, harp, and voice, one month retired and living on a pension and now, taking my roots with me, on my way to California."

"Miss Hillgood, you don't look to be going anywhere from here."

"I had a feeling about that." She watched the two men circle the car cautiously. She sat like a child on the lap of a rheumatic grandfather, undecided. "Is there nothing we can do?"

"Make a fence of the wheels, dinner gong of the brake drums, the rest'll make a fine rock garden."

Mr. Fremley shouted from the sky. "Dead? I say, is the car dead? I can *feel* it from here! Well—it's way past time for supper!"

Mr. Terle put out his hand. "Miss Hillgood, that there is Joe Terle's Desert Hotel, open twenty-six hours a day. Gila monsters and road runners please register before going upstairs. Get you a night's sleep, free, we'll knock our Ford off its blocks and drive you to the city come morning."

She let herself be helped from the car. The machine groaned as if in protest at her going. She shut the door carefully with a soft click.

"One friend gone, but the other still with me. Mr. Terle, could you please bring her in out of the weather?"

"Her, ma'am?"

"Forgive me, I never think of things but what they're people. The car was a man, I suppose, because it took me places. But a harp, now, don't you agree, is female?"

She nodded to the rear seat of the car. There, tilted against the sky like an ancient scrolled leather ship prow cleaving the wind, stood a case which towered above any driver who might sit up in front and sail the desert calms or the city traffics.

"Mr. Smith," said Mr. Terle, "lend a hand."

They untied the huge case and hoisted it gingerly out between them.

"What you got there?" cried Mr. Fremley from above.

Mr. Smith stumbled. Miss Hillgood gasped. The case shifted in the two men's arms.

From within the case came a faint musical humming.

Mr. Fremley, above, heard. It was all the answer he needed. Mouth open, he watched the lady and the two men and their boxed friend sway and vanish in the cavernous porch below.

"Watch out!" said Mr. Smith. "Some damn fool left his luggage here—" He stopped. "Some damn fool? *Me!*"

The two men looked at each other. They were not perspiring any more. A wind had come up from somewhere, a gentle wind that fanned their shirt collars and flapped the strewn calendar gently in the dust.

"*My* luggage . . ." said Mr. Smith.

Then they all went inside.

"More wine, Miss Hillgood? Ain't had wine on the table in years."

"Just a touch, if you please."

They sat by the light of a single candle which made the room an oven and struck fire from the good silverware and the uncracked plates as they talked and drank warm wine and ate.

"Miss Hillgood, get on with your life."

"All my life," she said, "I've been so busy running from Beethoven to Bach to Brahms, I never noticed I was twenty-nine. Next time I looked up I was forty. Yesterday, seventy-one. Oh, there were men; but they'd given up singing at ten and given up flying when they were twelve. I always figured we were born to fly, one way or other, so I couldn't stand most men shuffling along with all the iron of the earth in their blood. I never met a man who weighed less than nine hundred pounds. In their black business suits, you could hear them roll by like funeral wagons."

"So you flew away?"

"Just in my mind, Mr. Terle. It's taken sixty years to make the final break. All that time I grabbed on to piccolos and flutes and violins because they make streams in the air, you know, like streams and rivers on the ground. I rode every tributary and tried every fresh-water wind from Handel on down to a whole slew of Strausses. It's been the far way around that's brought me here."

"How'd you finally make up your mind to leave?" asked Mr. Smith.

"I looked around last week and said, 'Why, look, you've been flying *alone*!' No one in all Green City really cares *if* you fly or how high you go. It's always, 'Fine, Blanche,' or 'Thanks for the recital at the PTA tea, Miss H.' But no one really listening. And when I talked a long time ago about Chicago or New York, folks swatted me and laughed. 'Why be a little frog in a big pond when you can be the biggest frog in all Green City!' So I stayed on, while the folks who gave me advice moved away or died or both. The rest had wax in their ears. Just last week I shook myself and said, 'Hold on! Since when do *frogs* have wings?'"

"So now you're headin' west?" said Mr. Terle.

"Maybe to play in pictures or in that orchestra under the stars. But somewhere I just must play at last for someone who'll hear and really listen. . . ."

They sat there in the warm dark. She was finished, she had said it all now, foolish or not—and she moved back quietly in her chair.

Upstairs someone coughed.

Miss Hillgood heard, and rose.

It took Mr. Fremley a moment to ungum his eyelids and make out the shape of the woman bending down to place the tray by his rumpled bed.

"What you all talkin' about down there just now?"

"I'll come back later and tell you word for word," said Miss Hillgood. "Eat now. The salad's fine." She moved to leave the room.

He said, quickly, "You goin' to stay?"

She stopped half out the door and tried to trace the expression on his sweating face in the dark. He, in turn, could not see her mouth or eyes. She stood a moment longer, silently, then went on down the stairs.

"She must not've heard me," said Mr. Fremley.

But he knew she had heard.

Miss Hillgood crossed the downstairs lobby to fumble with the locks on the upright leather case.

"I must pay you for my supper."

"On the house," said Mr. Terle.

"I must pay," she said, and opened the case.

There was a sudden flash of gold.

The two men quickened in their chairs. They squinted at the little old woman standing beside the tremendous heart-shaped object which towered above her with its shining columbined pedestal atop which a calm Grecian face with antelope eyes looked serenely at them even as Miss Hillgood looked now.

The two men shot each other the quickest and most startled of glances, as if each had guessed what might happen next. They hurried across the lobby, breathing hard, to sit on the very edge of the hot velvet lounge, wiping their faces with damp handkerchiefs.

Miss Hillgood drew a chair under her, rested the golden harp gently back on her shoulder, and put her hands to the strings.

Mr. Terle took a breath of fiery air and waited.

A desert wind came suddenly along the porch outside, tilting the chairs so they rocked this way and that like boats on a pond at night.

Mr. Fremley's voice protested from above. "What's goin' on down there?"

And then Miss Hillgood moved her hands.

Starting at the arch near her shoulder, she played her fingers out along the simple tapestry of wires toward the blind and beautiful stare of the Greek goddess on her column, and then back. Then for a moment she paused and let the sounds drift up through the baked lobby air and into all the empty rooms.

If Mr. Fremley shouted, above, no one heard. For Mr. Terle and Mr. Smith were so busy jumping up to stand riven in the shadows, they heard nothing save the storming of their own hearts and the shocked rush of all the air in their lungs. Eyes wide, mouths dropped, in a kind of pure insanity, they stared at the two women there, the blind Muse proud on her golden pillar, and the seated one, gentle eyes closed, her small hands stretched forth on the air.

Like a girl, they both thought wildly, like a little girl putting her hands out a window to feel what? Why, of course, of course!

To feel the rain.

The echo of the first shower vanished down remote causeways and roof drains, away.

Mr. Fremley, above, rose from his bed as if pulled round by his ears.

Miss Hillgood played.

She played and it wasn't a tune they knew at all, but it was a tune they had heard a thousand times in their long lives, words or not, melody or not. She played and each time her fingers moved, the rain fell pattering through the dark hotel. The rain fell cool at the open windows and the rain rinsed down the baked floorboards of the porch. The rain fell on the roof top and fell on hissing sand, it fell on rusted car and empty stable and dead cactus in the yard. It washed the windows and laid the dust and filled the rain barrels and curtained the doors with beaded threads that might part and whisper as you walked through. But more than anything the soft touch and coolness of it fell on Mr. Smith and Mr. Terle. Its gentle weight and pressure moved them down and down until it had seated them again. By its continuous budding and prickling on their faces it made them shut up their eyes and mouths and raise their hands to shield it away. Seated there, they felt their heads tilt slowly back to let the rain fall where it would.

The flash flood lasted a minute, then faded away as the fingers trailed down the loom, let drop a few last bursts and squalls and then stopped.

The last chord hung in the air like a picture taken when lightning strikes and freezes a billion drops of water on their downward flight. Then the lightning went out. The last drops fell through darkness in silence.

Miss Hillgood took her hands from the strings, her eyes still shut.

Mr. Terle and Mr. Smith opened their eyes to see those two miraculous women way over there across the lobby somehow come through the storm untouched and dry.

· They trembled. They leaned forward as if they wished to speak. They looked helpless, not knowing what to do.

And then a single sound from high above in the hotel corridors drew their attention and told them what to do.

The sound came floating down feebly, fluttering like a tired bird beating its ancient wings.

The two men looked up and listened.

It was the sound of Mr. Fremley.

Mr. Fremley, in his room, applauding.

It took five seconds for Mr. Terle to figure out what it was. Then he nudged Mr. Smith and began, himself, to beat his palms together. The two men struck their hands in mighty explosions. The echoes ricocheted around about in the hotel caverns above and below, striking walls, mirrors, windows, trying to fight free of the rooms.

Miss Hillgood opened her eyes now, as if this new storm had come on her in the open, unprepared.

The men gave their own recital. They smashed their hands together so fervently it seemed they had fistfuls of firecrackers to set off, one on another. Mr. Fremley shouted. Nobody heard. Hands winged out, banged shut again and again until fingers puffed up and the old men's breath came short and they put their hands at last on their knees, a heart pounding inside each one.

Then, very slowly, Mr. Smith got up and still looking at the harp, went outside and carried in the suitcases. He stood at the foot of the lobby stairs looking for a long while at Miss Hillgood. He glanced down at her single piece of luggage resting there by the first tread. He looked from her suitcase to her and raised his eyebrows questioningly.

Miss Hillgood looked at her harp, at her suitcase, at Mr. Terle, and at last back to Mr. Smith.

She nodded once.

Mr. Smith bent down and with his own luggage under one arm and her suitcase in the other, he started the long slow climb up the stairs in the gentle dark. As he moved, Miss Hillgood put the harp back on her shoulder and either played in time to his moving or he moved in time to her playing, neither of them knew which.

Half up the flight, Mr. Smith met Mr. Fremley who, in a faded robe, was testing his slow way down.

Both stood there, looking deep into the lobby at the one man on the far side in the shadows, and the two women further over, no more than a motion and a gleam. Both thought the same thoughts.

The sound of the harp playing, the sound of the cool water falling every night and every night of their lives, after this. No spraying the roof with the garden hose now any more. Only sit on the porch or lie in your night bed and hear the falling . . . the falling . . . the falling. . . .

Mr. Smith moved on up the stairs; Mr. Fremley moved down.

The harp, the harp. Listen, listen!

The fifty years of drought were over.

The time of the long rains had come.

A Medicine for Melancholy

(The Sovereign Remedy Revealed!)

"Send for some leeches; bleed her," said Doctor Gimp.

"She has no blood left!" cried Mrs. Wilkes. "Oh, Doctor, what ails our Camillia?"

"She's not right."

"Yes, yes?"

"She's poorly." The good doctor scowled.

"Go on, go on!"

"She's a fluttering candle flame, no doubt."

"Ah, Doctor Gimp," protested Mr. Wilkes. "You but tell us as you go out what we told you when you came in!"

"No, more! Give her these pills at dawn, high noon, and sunset. A sovereign remedy!"

"Damn, she's *stuffed* with sovereign remedies now!"

"Tut-tut! That's a shilling as I pass downstairs, sir."

"Go down and send the Devil up!" Mr. Wilkes shoved a coin in the good doctor's hand.

Whereupon the physician, wheezing, taking snuff, sneezing, stamped down into the swarming streets of London on a sloppy morn in the spring of 1762.

Mr. and Mrs. Wilkes turned to the bed where their sweet Camillia lay pale, thin, yes, but far from unlovely, with large wet lilac eyes, her hair a creek of gold upon her pillow.

"Oh," she almost wept. "What's to become of me? Since the start of spring, three weeks, I've been a ghost in my mirror; I frighten me. To think I'll die without seeing my twentieth birthday."

"Child," said the mother. "Where do you hurt?"

"My arms. My legs. My bosom. My head. How many doctors—six?—have turned me like a beef on a spit. No more. Please, let me pass away untouched."

"What a ghastly, what a mysterious illness," said the mother. "Oh, do something, Mr. Wilkes!"

"What?" asked Mr. Wilkes angrily. "She won't have the physician, the apothecary, or the priest!—and Amen to that!—they've wrung me dry! Shall I run in the street then and bring the Dustman up?"

"Yes," said a voice.

"What!" All three turned to stare.

They had quite forgotten her younger brother, Jamie, who stood picking his teeth at a far window, gazing serenely down into the drizzle and the loud rumbling of the town.

"Four hundred years ago," he said serenely, "it was tried, it worked. Don't bring the Dustman up, no, no. But let us hoist Camillia, cot and all, maneuver her downstairs, and set her up outside our door."

"Why? What for?"

"In a single hour"—Jamie's eyes jumped, counting—"a thousand folk rush by our gate. In one day, twenty thousand people run, hobble, or ride by. Each might eye my swooning sister, each count her teeth, pull her ear lobes, and all, all, mind you, would have a sovereign remedy to offer! One of them would just have to be right!"

"Ah," said Mr. Wilkes, stunned.

"Father!" said Jamie breathlessly. "Have you ever known one single man who didn't think he personally wrote *Materia Medica*? This green ointment for sour throat, that ox-salve for miasma or bloat? Right now, ten thousand self-appointed apothecaries sneak off down there, their wisdom lost to us!"

"Jamie boy, you're incredible!"

"Cease!" said Mrs. Wilkes. "No daughter of mine will be put on display in this or any street—"

"Fie, woman!" said Mr. Wilkes. "Camillia melts like snow and you hesitate to move her from this hot room? Come, Jamie, lift the bed!"

"Camillia?" Mrs. Wilkes turned to her daughter.

"I may as well die in the open," said Camillia, "where a cool breeze might stir my locks as I . . . "

"Bosh!" said the father. "You'll not die. Jamie, heave! Ha! There! Out of the way, wife! Up, boy, *higher*!"

"Oh," cried Camillia faintly. "I fly, I *fly* . . . !"

Quite suddenly a blue sky opened over London. The population, surprised by the weather, hurried out into the streets, panicking for something to see, to do, to buy. Blind men sang, dogs jigged, clowns shuffled and tumbled, children chalked games and threw balls as if it were carnival time.

Down into all this, tottering, their veins bursting from their brows, Jamie and Mr. Wilkes carried Camillia like a lady Pope sailing high in her sedan-chair cot, eyes clenched shut, praying.

"Careful!" screamed Mrs. Wilkes. "Ah, she's dead! No. There. Put her down. Easy . . . "

And at last the bed was tilted against the house front so that the River of Humanity surging by could see Camillia, a large pale Bartolemy Doll put out like a prize in the sun.

"Fetch a quill, ink, paper, lad," said the father. "I'll make notes as to symptoms spoken of and remedies offered this day. Tonight we'll average them out. Now—"

But already a man in the passing crowd had fixed Camillia with a sharp eye.

"She's sick!" he said.

"Ah," said Mr. Wilkes, gleefully. "It begins. The quill, boy. There. Go on, sir!"

"She's not well." The man scowled. "She does poorly."

"Does poorly—" Mr. Wilkes wrote, then froze. "Sir?" He looked up suspiciously. "Are you a physician?"

"I am, sir."

"I *thought* I knew the words! Jamie, take my cane, drive him off! Go, sir, be gone!"

The man hastened off, cursing, mightily exasperated.

"She's not well, she does poorly . . . pah!" mimicked Mr. Wilkes, but stopped. For now a woman, tall and gaunt as a specter fresh risen from the tomb, was pointing a finger at Camillia Wilkes.

"Vapors," she intoned.

"Vapors," wrote Mr. Wilkes, pleased.

"Lung-flux," chanted the woman.

"Lung-flux!" Mr. Wilkes wrote, beaming. "Now, that's more *like* it!"

"A medicine for melancholy is needed," said the woman palely. "Be there mummy ground to medicine in your house? The best mummies are: Egyptian, Arabian, Hirasphatos, Libyan, all of great use in magnetic disorders. Ask for me, the Gypsy, at the Flodden Road. I sell stone parsley, male frankincense—"

"Flodden Road, stone parsley—slower, woman!"

"Opobalsam, pontic valerian—"

"Wait, woman! Opobalsam, yes! Jamie, stop her!"

But the woman, naming medicines, glided on.

A girl, no more than seventeen, walked up now and stared at Camillia Wilkes.

"She—"

"One moment!" Mr. Wilkes scribbled feverishly. "—Magnetic disorders— pontic valerian—drat! Well, young girl, now. What do you see in my daughter's face? You fix her with your gaze, you hardly breathe. So?"

"She—" The strange girl searched deep into Camillia's eyes, flushed, and stammered. "She suffers from . . . from . . . "

"Spit it out!"

"She . . . she . . . oh!"

And the girl, with a last look of deepest sympathy, darted off through the crowd.

"Silly girl!"

"No, Papa," murmured Camillia, eyes wide. "Not silly. She *saw*. She *knew*. Oh, Jamie, run fetch her, make her tell!"

"No, she offered nothing! Whereas, the Gypsy, see her list!"

"I know it, Papa." Camillia, paler, shut her eyes.

Someone cleared his throat.

A butcher, his apron a scarlet battleground, stood bristling his fierce mustaches there.

"I have seen cows with this look," he said. "I have saved them with brandy and three new eggs. In winter I have saved myself with the same elixir—"

"My daughter is no cow, sir!" Mr. Wilkes threw down his quill. "Nor is she a butcher, nor is it January! Step back, sir, others wait!"

And indeed, now a vast crowd clamored, drawn by the others, aching to advise their favorite swig, recommend some country site where it rained less and shone more sun than in all England or your South of France. Old men and women, especial doctors as all the aged are, clashed by each other in bristles of canes, in phalanxes of crutches and hobble sticks.

"Back!" cried Mrs. Wilkes, alarmed. "They'll crush my daughter like a spring berry!"

"Stand off!" Jamie seized canes and crutches and threw them over the mob, which turned on itself to go seek their missing members.

"Father, I fail, I fail," gasped Camillia.

"Father!" cried Jamie. "There's but one way to stop this riot! Charge them! Make them pay to give us their mind on this ailment!"

"Jamie, you are my son! Quick, boy, paint a sign! Listen, people! Tuppence! Queue up please, a line! Tuppence to speak your piece! Get your money out, yes! That's it. You, sir. You, madame. And you, sir. Now, my quill! Begin!"

The mob boiled in like a dark sea.

Camillia opened one eye and swooned again.

Sundown, the streets almost empty, only a few strollers now. Camillia moth-fluttered her eyelids at a familiar clinking jingle.

"Three hundred and ninety-nine, four hundred pennies!" Mr. Wilkes counted the last money into a bag held by his grinning son. "There!"

"It will buy me a fine black funeral coach," said the pale girl.

"Hush! Did you imagine, family, so many people, two hundred, would pay to give us their opinion?"

"Yes," said Mrs. Wilkes. "Wives, husbands, children, are deaf ·to each other. So people gladly pay to have someone listen. Poor things, each today thought he and he alone knew quinsy, dropsy, glanders, could tell the slaver from the hives. So tonight we are rich and two hundred people are happy, having unloaded their full medical kit at our door."

"Gods, instead of quelling the riot, we had to drive them off snapping like pups."

"Read us the list, Father," said Jamie, "of two hundred remedies. Which one is true?"

"I care not," whispered Camillia, sighing. "It grows dark. My stomach is queasy from listening to the names! May I be taken upstairs?"

"Yes, dear. Jamie, lift!"

"Please," said a voice.

Half-bent, the men looked up.

There stood a Dustman of no particular size or shape, his face masked with soot from which shone water-blue eyes and a white slot of an ivory smile. Dust sifted from his sleeves and his pants as he moved, as he talked quietly, nodding.

"I couldn't get through the mob earlier," he said, holding his dirty cap in his hands. "Now, going home, here I am. Must I pay?"

"No, Dustman, you need not," said Camillia gently.

"Hold on—" protested Mr. Wilkes.

But Camillia gave him a soft look and he grew silent.

"Thank you, ma'am." The Dustman's smile flashed like warm sunlight in the growing dusk. "I have but one advice."

He gazed at Camillia. She gazed at him.

"Be this Saint Bosco's Eve, sir, ma'am?"

"Who knows? Not *me*, sir!" said Mr. Wilkes.

"I think it *is* Saint Bosco's Eve, sir. Also, it is the night of the full moon. So," said the Dustman humbly, unable to take his eyes from the lovely haunted girl, "you must leave your daughter out in the light of that rising moon."

"Out under the moon!" said Mrs. Wilkes.

"Doesn't that make the lunatic?" asked Jamie.

"Beg pardon, sir." The Dustman bowed. "But the full moon soothes all sick animals, be they human or plain field beast. There is a serenity of color, a quietude of touch, a sweet sculpturing of mind and body in full moonlight."

"It may rain—" said the mother uneasily.

"I swear," said the Dustman quickly. "My sister suffered this same swooning paleness. We set her like a potted lily out one spring night with the moon. She lives today in Sussex, the soul of reconstituted health!"

"Reconstituted! Moonlight! And will cost us not one penny of the four hundred we collected this day, Mother, Jamie, Camillia."

"No!" said Mrs. Wilkes. "I won't have it!"

"Mother," said Camillia.

She looked earnestly at the Dustman.

From his grimed face the Dustman gazed back, his smile like a little scimitar in the dark.

"Mother," said Camillia. "I feel it. The moon will cure me, it will, it will...."

The mother sighed. "This is not my day, nor night. Let me kiss you for the last time, then. There."

And the mother went upstairs.

Now the Dustman backed off, bowing courteously to all.

"All night, now, remember, beneath the moon, not the slightest disturbance until dawn. Sleep well, young lady. Dream, and dream the best. Good night."

Soot was lost in soot; the man was gone.

Mr. Wilkes and Jamie kissed Camillia's brow.

"Father, Jamie," she said. "Don't worry."

And she was left alone to stare off where at a great distance she thought she saw a smile hung by itself in the dark blink off and on, then go round a corner, vanishing.

She waited for the rising of the moon.

Night in London, the voices growing drowsier in the inns, the slamming of doors, drunken farewells, clocks chiming. Camillia saw a cat like a woman stroll by in her furs, saw a woman like a cat stroll by, both wise, both Egyptian, both smelling of spice. Every quarter hour or so a voice drifted down from above:

"You all right, child?"

"Yes, Father."

"Camillia?"

"Mother, Jamie, I'm fine."

And at last. "Good night."

"Good night."

The last lights out. London asleep.

The moon rose.

And the higher the moon, the larger grew Camillia's eyes as she watched the alleys, the courts, the streets, until at last, at midnight, the moon moved over her to show her like a marble figure atop an ancient tomb.

A motion in darkness.

Camillia pricked her ears.

A faint melody sprang out on the air.

A man stood in the shadows of the court.

Camillia gasped.

The man stepped forth into moonlight, carrying a lute which he strummed softly. He was a man well-dressed, whose face was handsome and, now anyway, solemn.

"A troubadour," said Camillia aloud.

The man, his finger on his lips, moved slowly forward and soon stood by her cot.

"What are you doing out so late?" asked the girl, unafraid but not knowing why.

"A friend sent me to make you well." He touched the lute strings. They hummed sweetly. He was indeed handsome there in the silver light.

"That cannot be," she said, "for it was told me, the *moon* is my cure."

"And so it will be, maiden."

"What songs do you sing?"

"Songs of spring nights, aches and ailments without name. Shall I name your fever, maiden?"

"If you know it, yes."

"First, the symptoms: raging temperatures, sudden cold, heart fast then slow, storms of temper, then sweet calms, drunkenness from having sipped only well water, dizziness from being touched only *thus*—"

He touched her wrist, saw her melt toward delicious oblivion, drew back.

"Depressions, elations," he went on. "Dreams—"

"Stop!" she cried, enthralled. "You know me to the letter. Now, name my ailment!"

"I will." He pressed his lips to the palm of her hand so she quaked suddenly. "The name of the ailment is Camillia Wilkes."

"How strange." She shivered, her eyes glinting lilac fires. "Am I then my own affliction? How sick I make myself! Even now, feel my heart!"

"I feel it, so."

"My limbs, they burn with summer heat!"

"Yes. They scorch my fingers."

"But now, the night wind, see how I shudder, cold! I die, I swear it, I die!"

"I will not let you," he said quietly.

"Are you a doctor, then?"

"No, just your plain, your ordinary physician, like another who guessed your trouble this day. The girl who would have named it but ran off in the crowd."

"Yes, I saw in her eyes she knew what had seized me. But, now, my teeth chatter. And no extra blanket!"

"Give room, please. There. Let me see: two arms, two legs, head and body. I'm all here!"

"What, sir!"

"To warm you from the night, of course."

"How like a hearth! Oh, sir, sir, do I *know* you? Your name?"

Swiftly above her, his head shadowed hers. From it his merry clear-water eyes glowed as did his white ivory slot of a smile.

"Why, Bosco, of course," he said.

"Is there not a saint by that name?"

"Given an hour, you will call me so, yes."

His head bent closer. Thus sooted in shadow, she cried with joyous recognition to welcome her Dustman back.

"The world spins! I pass away! The cure, sweet Doctor, or all is lost!"

"The cure," he said. "And the cure is *this* . . . "

Somewhere, cats sang. A shoe, shot from a window, tipped them off a fence. Then all was silence and the moon. . . .

"Shh . . . "

Dawn. Tiptoeing downstairs, Mr. and Mrs. Wilkes peered into their courtyard.

"Frozen stone dead from the terrible night, I *know* it!"

"No, wife, look! Alive! Roses in her cheeks! No, more! Peaches, persimmons! She glows all rosy-milky! Sweet Camillia, alive and well, made whole again!"

They bent by the slumbering girl.

"She smiles, she dreams; what's that she says?"

"The sovereign," sighed the girl, "remedy."

"What, what?"

The girl smiled again, a white smile, in her sleep.

"A medicine," she murmured, "for melancholy."

She opened her eyes.

"Oh, Mother, Father!"

"Daughter! Child! Come upstairs!"

"No." She took their hands, tenderly. "Mother? Father?"

"Yes?"

"No one will see. The sun but rises. Please. Dance with me."

They did not want to dance.

But, celebrating they knew not what, they did.

The Shoreline
at Sunset

Tom, knee-deep in the waves, a piece of driftwood in his hand, listened.

The house, up toward the Coast Highway in the late afternoon, was silent. The sounds of closets being rummaged, suitcase locks snapping, vases being smashed, and of a final door crashing shut, all had faded away.

Chico, standing on the pale sand, flourished his wire strainer to shake out a harvest of lost coins. After a moment, without glancing at Tom, he said, "Let her go."

So it was every year. For a week or a month, their house would have music swelling from the windows, there would be new geraniums potted on the porch rail, new paint on the doors and steps. The clothes on the wire line changed from harlequin pants to sheath dresses to handmade Mexican frocks like white waves breaking behind the house. Inside, the paintings on the walls shifted from imitation Matisse to pseudo-Italian Renaissance. Sometimes, looking up, he would see a woman drying her hair like a bright yellow flag on the wind. Sometimes the flag was black or red. Sometimes the woman was tall, sometimes short, against the sky. But there was never more than one woman at a time. And, at last, a day like today came. . . .

Tom placed his driftwood on the growing pile near where Chico sifted the billion footprints left by people long vanished from their holidays.

"Chico. What are we doing here?"

"Living the life of Riley, boy!"

"I don't feel like Riley, Chico."

"Work at it, boy!"

Tom saw the house a month from now, the flowerpots blowing dust, the walls hung with empty squares, only sand carpeting the floors. The rooms would echo like shells in the wind. And all night every night bedded in separate rooms he and Chico would hear a tide falling away and away down a long shore, leaving no trace.

Tom nodded, imperceptibly. Once a year he himself brought a nice girl here, knowing she was right at last and that in no time they would be married. But his women always stole silently away before dawn, feeling they had been mistaken for someone else, not being able to play the part. Chico's friends left like vacuum cleaners, with a terrific drag, roar, rush, leaving no lint unturned, no clam unprized of its pearl, taking their purses with them like toy dogs which Chico had petted as he opened their jaws to count their teeth.

"That's four women so far this year."

"Okay, referee." Chico grinned. "Show me the way to the showers."

"Chico—" Tom bit his lower lip, then went on. "I been thinking. Why don't we split up?"

Chico just looked at him.

"I mean," said Tom, quickly, "maybe we'd have better luck, alone."

"Well, I'll be goddamned," said Chico slowly, gripping the strainer in his big fists before him. "Look here, boy, don't you know the facts? You and me, we'll be here come the year 2000. A couple of crazy dumb old gooney-birds drying their bones in the sun. Nothing's ever going to happen to us now, Tom, it's too late. Get that through your head and shut up."

Tom swallowed and looked steadily at the other man. "I'm thinking of leaving—next week."

"Shut up, shut up, and get to work!"

Chico gave the sand an angry showering rake that tilled him forty-three cents in dimes, pennies, and nickels. He stared blindly at the coins shimmering down the wires like a pinball game all afire.

Tom did not move, holding his breath.

They both seemed to be waiting for something.

The something happened.

"Hey . . . hey . . . hey . . ."

From a long way off down the coast a voice called.

The two men turned slowly.

"Hey . . . hey . . . oh, hey . . . !"

A boy was running, yelling, waving, along the shore two hundred yards away. There was something in his voice that made Tom feel suddenly cold. He held on to his own arms, waiting.

"Hey!"

The boy pulled up, gasping, pointing back along the shore.

"A woman, a funny woman, by the North Rock!"

"A woman!" The words exploded from Chico's mouth and he began to laugh. "Oh, no, no!"

"What you mean, a 'funny' woman?" asked Tom.

"I don't know," cried the boy, his eyes wide. "You got to come see! Awful funny!"

"You mean 'drowned'?"

"Maybe! She came out of the water, she's lying on the shore, you got to see, yourself . . . funny . . . " The boy's voice died. He gazed off north again. "She's got a fish's tail."

Chico laughed. "Not before supper, please."

"Please!" cried the boy, dancing now. "No lie! Oh, hurry!"

He ran off, sensed he was not followed, and looked back in dismay.

Tom felt his lips move. "Boy wouldn't run this far for a joke, would he, Chico?"

"People have run further for less."

Tom started walking. "All right, son."

"Thanks, mister, oh thanks!"

The boy ran. Twenty yards up the coast, Tom looked back. Behind him, Chico squinted, shrugged, dusted his hands wearily, and followed.

They moved north along the twilight beach, their skin weathered in tiny folds about their burnt pale eyes, looking younger for their hair cut close to the skull so you could not see the gray. There was a fair wind and the ocean rose and fell with prolonged concussions.

"What," said Tom, "what if we get to North Rock and it's true? The ocean *has* washed some *thing* up?"

But before Chico could answer, Tom was gone, his mind racing down coasts littered with horseshoe crabs, sand dollars, starfish, kelp, and stone. From all the times he'd talked on what lives in the sea, the names returned with the breathing fall of waves. Argonauts, they whispered, codlings, pollacks, houndfish, tautog, tench, sea elephant, they whispered, gillings, flounders, and beluga, the white whale, and grampus, the sea dog . . . always you thought how these must look from their deep-sounding names. Perhaps you would never in your life see them rise from the salt meadows beyond the safe limits of the shore, but they were there, and their names, with a thousand others, made pictures. And you looked and wished you were a frigate-bird that might fly nine thousand miles around to return some year with the full size of the ocean in your head.

"Oh, quick!" The boy had run back to peer in Tom's face. "It might be gone!"

"Keep your shirt on, boy," said Chico.

They came around the North Rock. A second boy stood there, looking down.

Perhaps from the corner of his eye, Tom saw something on the sand that made him hesitate to look straight at it, but fix instead on the face of the boy standing there. The boy was pale and he seemed not to breathe. On occasion he remembered to take a breath, his eyes focused, but the more they saw there on the sand the more they took time off from focusing and turned blank and looked stunned. When the ocean came in over his tennis shoes, he did not move or notice.

Tom glanced away from the boy to the sand.

And Tom's face, in the next moment, became the face of the boy. His hands assumed the same curl at his sides and his mouth moved to open and stay half open and his eyes, which were light in color, seemed to bleach still more with so much looking.

The setting sun was ten minutes above the sea.

"A big wave came in and went out," said the first boy, "and here she was."

They looked at the woman lying there.

Her hair was very long and it lay on the beach like the threads of an immense harp. The water stroked along the threads and floated them up and let them down, each time in a different fan and silhouette. The hair must have been five or six feet long and now it was strewn on the hard wet sand and it was the color of limes.

Her face . . .

The men bent half down in wonder.

Her face was white sand sculpture, with a few water drops shimmering on it like summer rain upon a cream-colored rose. Her face was that moon which when seen by day is pale and unbelievable in the blue sky. It was milk-marble veined with faint violet in the temples. The eyelids, closed down upon the eyes, were powdered with a faint water color, as if the eyes beneath gazed through the fragile tissue of the lids and saw them standing there above her, looking down and looking down. The mouth was a pale flushed sea-rose, full and closed upon itself. And her neck was slender and white and her breasts were small and white, now covered, uncovered, covered, uncovered in the flow of water, the ebb of water, the flow, the ebb, the flow. And the breasts were flushed at their tips, and her body was startlingly white, almost an illumination, a white-green lightning against the sand. And as the water shifted her, her skin glinted like the surface of a pearl.

The lower half of her body changed itself from white to very pale blue, from very pale blue to pale green, from pale green to emerald green, to moss and lime green, to scintillas and sequins all dark green, all flowing away in a fount, a curve, a rush of light and dark, to end in a lacy fan, a spread of foam and jewel on the sand. The two halves of this creature were so joined as to reveal no point of fusion where pearl woman, woman of a whiteness made of cream-water and clear sky, merged with that half which belonged to the amphibious slide and rush of current that came up on the shore and shelved down the shore, tugging its half toward its proper home. The woman was the sea, the sea was woman. There was no flaw or seam, no wrinkle or stitch; the illusion, if illusion it was, held perfectly together and the blood from one moved into and through and mingled with what must have been the ice waters of the other.

"I wanted to run get help." The first boy seemed not to want to raise his voice. "But Skip said she was dead and there's no help for that. Is she?"

"She was never alive," said Chico. "Sure," he went on, feeling their eyes on him suddenly. "It's something left over from a movie studio. Liquid rubber skinned over a steel frame. A prop, a dummy."

"Oh, no, it's real!"

"We'll find a label somewhere," said Chico. "Here."

"Don't!" cried the first boy.

"Hell." Chico touched the body to turn it, and stopped. He knelt there, his face changing.

"What's the matter?" asked Tom.

Chico took his hand away and looked at it. "I was wrong." His voice faded.

Tom took the woman's wrist. "There's a pulse."

"You're feeling your own heartbeat."

"I just don't know . . . maybe . . . maybe . . . "

The woman was there and her upper body was all moon pearl and tidal cream and her lower body all slithering ancient green-black coins that slid upon themselves in the shift of wind and water.

"There's a trick somewhere!" cried Chico, suddenly.

"No. No!" Just as suddenly Tom burst out in laughter. "No trick! My God, my God, I feel great! I haven't felt so great since I was a kid!"

They walked slowly around her. A wave touched her white hand so the fingers faintly, softly waved. The gesture was that of someone asking for another and another wave to come in and lift the fingers and then the wrist and then the arm and then the head and finally the body and take all of them together back down out to sea.

"Tom." Chico's mouth opened and closed. "Why don't you go get our truck?"

Tom didn't move.

"You hear me?" said Chico.

"Yes, but—"

"But what? We could sell this somewhere, I don't know—the university, that aquarium at Seal Beach or . . . well, hell, why couldn't we just set up a place? Look." He shook Tom's arm. "Drive to the pier. Buy us three hundred pounds of chipped ice. When you take anything out of the water you *need* ice, don't you?"

"I never thought."

"Think about it! Get moving!"

"I don't know, Chico."

"What you mean? She's real, isn't she?" He turned to the boys. "*You* say she's real, don't you? Well, then, what are we waiting for?"

"Chico," said Tom. "You better go get the ice yourself."

"Someone's got to stay and make sure she don't go back out with the tide!"

"Chico," said Tom. "I don't know how to explain. I don't want to get that ice for you."

"I'll go myself, then. Look, boys, build the sand up here to keep the waves back. I'll give you five bucks apiece. Hop to it!"

The sides of the boys' faces were bronze-pink from the sun which was touching the horizon now. Their eyes were a bronze color looking at Chico.

"My God!" said Chico. "This is better than finding ambergris!" He ran to the top of the nearest dune, called, "Get to work!" and was gone.

Now Tom and the two boys were left with the lonely woman by the North Rock and the sun was one-fourth of the way below the western horizon. The sand and the woman were pink-gold.

"Just a little line," whispered the second boy. He drew his fingernail along under his own chin, gently. He nodded to the woman. Tom bent again to see the faint line under either side of her firm white chin, the small, almost invisible line where the gills were or had been and were now almost sealed shut, invisible.

He looked at the face and the great strands of hair spread out in a lyre on the shore.

"She's beautiful," he said.

The boys nodded without knowing it.

Behind them, a gull leaped up quickly from the dunes. The boys gasped and turned to stare.

Tom felt himself trembling. He saw the boys were trembling too. A car horn hooted. Their eyes blinked, suddenly afraid. They looked up toward the highway.

A wave poured about the body, framing it in a clear white pool of water.

Tom nodded the boys to one side.

The wave moved the body an inch in and two inches out toward the sea.

The next wave came and moved the body two inches in and six inches out toward the sea.

"But—" said the first boy.

Tom shook his head.

The third wave lifted the body two feet down toward the sea. The wave after that drifted the body another foot down the shingles and the next three moved it six feet down.

The first boy cried out and ran after it.

Tom reached him and held his arm. The boy looked helpless and afraid and sad.

For a moment there were no more waves. Tom looked at the woman, thinking, She's true, she's real, she's mine ... but ... she's dead. Or will be if she stays here.

"We can't let her go," said the first boy. "We can't, we just can't!"

The other boy stepped between the woman and the sea. "What would we do with her," he wanted to know, looking at Tom, "if we kept her?"

The first boy tried to think. "We could—we could—" He stopped and shook his head. "Oh, my gosh."

The second boy stepped out the way and left a path from the woman to the sea.

The next wave was a big one. It came in and went out and the sand was empty. The whiteness was gone and the black diamonds and the great threads of the harp.

They stood by the edge of the sea, looking out, the man and the two boys, until they heard the truck driving up on the dunes behind them.

The last of the sun was gone.

They heard footsteps running on the dunes and someone yelling.

They drove back down the darkening beach in the light truck with the big treaded tires in silence. The two boys sat in the rear on the bags of chipped ice. After a long while, Chico began to swear steadily, half to himself, spitting out the window.

"Three hundred pounds of ice. Three hundred *pounds* of ice! What do I do with it now? And I'm soaked to the skin, soaked! You didn't even move when I jumped in and swam out to look around! Idiot, idiot! You haven't changed! Like every other time, like always, you do nothing, nothing, just stand there, stand there, do nothing, nothing, just stare!"

"And what did you do, I ask, what?" said Tom, in a tired voice, looking ahead. "The same as you always did, just the same, no different, no different at all. You should've seen yourself."

They dropped the boys off at their beach house. The younger spoke in a voice you could hardly hear against the wind. "Gosh, nobody'll ever believe . . . "

The two men drove down the coast and parked.

Chico sat for two or three minutes waiting for his fists to relax on his lap, and then he snorted.

"Hell. I guess things turn out for the best." He took a deep breath. "It just came to me. Funny. Twenty, thirty years from now, middle of the night, our phone'll ring. It'll be one of those two boys, grown-up, calling long-distance from a bar somewhere. Middle of the night, them calling to ask one question. 'It's *true*, isn't it?' they'll say. 'It *did* happen, didn't it? Back in 1958, it really happened to *us*?' And we'll sit there on the edge of the bed, middle of the night, saying, 'Sure, boy, sure, it really happened to us in 1958.' And they'll say, 'Thanks,' and we'll say, 'Don't mention it, any old time.' And we'll all say good night. And maybe they won't call again for a couple of years."

The two men sat on their front-porch steps in the dark.

"Tom?"

"What?"

Chico waited a moment.

"Tom, next week—you're not going away."

It was not a question but a quiet statement.

Tom thought about it, his cigarette dead in his fingers. And he knew that now he could never go away. For tomorrow and the day after the day after that he would walk down and go swimming there in all the green and white fires and the dark caverns in the hollows under the strange waves. Tomorrow and tomorrow and tomorrow.

"No, Chico. I'm staying here."

Now the silver looking glasses advanced in a crumpling line all along the coast from a thousand miles north to a thousand miles south. The mirrors did not reflect so much as one building or one tree or one highway or one car or even one man himself. The mirrors reflected only the quiet moon and then shattered into a billion bits of glass that spread out in a glaze on the shore. Then the sea was dark awhile, preparing another line of mirrors to rear up and surprise the two men who sat there for a long time never once blinking their eyes, waiting.

Fever Dream

They put him between fresh, clean, laundered sheets and there was always a newly squeezed glass of thick orange juice on the table under the dim pink lamp. All Charles had to do was call and Mom or Dad would stick their heads into his room to see how sick he was. The acoustics of the room were fine; you could hear the toilet gargling its porcelain throat of mornings, you could hear rain tap the roof or sly mice run in the secret walls or the canary singing in its cage downstairs. If you were very alert, sickness wasn't too bad.

He was thirteen, Charles was. It was mid-September, with the land beginning to burn with autumn. He lay in the bed for three days before the terror overcame him.

His hand began to change. His right hand. He looked at it and it was hot and sweating there on the counterpane alone. It fluttered, it moved a bit. Then it lay there, changing color.

That afternoon the doctor came again and tapped his thin chest like a little drum. "How are you?" asked the doctor, smiling. "I know, don't tell me: 'My *cold* is fine, Doctor, but *I* feel awful!' Ha!" He laughed at his own oft-repeated joke.

Charles lay there and for him that terrible and ancient jest was becoming a reality. The joke fixed itself in his mind. His mind touched and drew away from it in a pale terror. The doctor did not know how cruel he was with his jokes! "Doctor," whispered Charles, lying flat and colorless. "My *hand*, it doesn't *belong* to me any more. This morning it *changed* into something else. I want you to change it back, Doctor. Doctor!"

The doctor showed his teeth and patted the boy's hand. "It looks fine to me, son. You just had a little fever dream."

"But it changed, Doctor, oh, Doctor," cried Charles, pitifully holding up his pale wild hand. "It *did*!"

The doctor winked. "I'll give you a pink pill for that." He popped a tablet onto Charles's tongue. "Swallow!"

"Will it make my hand change back and become *me*, again?"

"Yes, yes."

The house was silent when the doctor drove off down the road in his car under the quiet, blue September sky. A clock ticked far below in the kitchen world. Charles lay looking at his hand.

It did not change back. It was still something else.

The wind blew outside. Leaves fell against the cool window.

At four o'clock his other hand changed. It seemed almost to become a fever. It pulsed and shifted, cell by cell. It beat like a warm heart. The fingernails turned blue and then red. It took about an hour for it to change and when it was finished, it looked just like any ordinary hand. But it was not ordinary. It no longer was him any more. He lay in a fascinated horror and then fell into an exhausted sleep.

Mother brought the soup up at six. He wouldn't touch it. "I haven't any hands," he said, eyes shut.

"Your hands are perfectly good," said Mother.

"No," he wailed. "My hands are gone. I feel like I have stumps. Oh, Mama, Mama, hold me, hold me, I'm scared!"

She had to feed him herself.

"Mama," he said, "get the doctor, please, again. I'm so sick."

"The doctor'll be here tonight at eight," she said, and went out.

At seven, with night dark and close around the house, Charles was sitting up in bed when he felt the thing happening to first one leg and then the other.

"Mama! Come quick!" he screamed.

But when Mama came the thing was no longer happening.

When she went downstairs, he simply lay without fighting as his legs beat and beat, grew warm, red-hot, and the room filled with the warmth of his feverish change. The glow crept up from his toes to his ankles and then to his knees.

"May I come in?" The doctor smiled in the doorway.

"Doctor!" cried Charles. "Hurry, take off my blankets!"

The doctor lifted the blankets tolerantly. "There you are. Whole and healthy. Sweating, though. A little fever. I told you not to move around, bad boy." He pinched the moist pink cheek. "Did the pills help? Did your hand change back?"

"No, no, now it's my other hand and my legs!"

"Well, well, I'll have to give you three more pills, one for each limb, eh, my little peach?" laughed the doctor.

"Will they help me? Please, please. What've I *got?*"

"A mild case of scarlet fever, complicated by a slight cold."

"Is it a germ that lives and has more little germs in me?"

"Yes."

"Are you *sure* it's scarlet fever? You haven't taken any tests!"

"I guess I know a certain fever when I see one," said the doctor, checking the boy's pulse with cool authority.

Charles lay there, not speaking until the doctor was crisply packing his black kit. Then in the silent room, the boy's voice made a small, weak pattern, his eyes alight with remembrance. "I read a book once. About petrified trees, wood turning to stone. About how trees fell and rotted and minerals got in and built up and they look just like trees, but they're not, they're stone." He stopped. In the quiet warm room his breathing sounded.

"Well?" asked the doctor.

"I've been thinking," said Charles after a time. "Do germs ever get big? I mean, in biology class they told us about one-celled animals, amoebas and things, and how millions of years ago they got together until there was a bunch and they made the first body. And more and more cells got together and got bigger and then finally maybe there was a fish and finally here *we* are, and all we are is a bunch of cells that decided to get together, to help each other out. Isn't that right?" Charles wet his feverish lips.

"What's all this about?" The doctor bent over him.

"I've got to tell you this. Doctor, oh, I've got to!" he cried. "What would happen, oh just pretend, please pretend, that just like in the old days, a lot of microbes got together and wanted to make a bunch, and reproduced and made *more—*"

His white hands were on his chest now, crawling toward his throat.

"And they decided to *take over* a person!" cried Charles.

"Take over a person?"

"Yes, *become* a person. *Me*, my hands, my feet! What if a disease somehow knew how to kill a person and yet live after him?"

He screamed.

The hands were on his neck.

The doctor moved forward, shouting.

At nine o'clock the doctor was escorted out to his car by the mother and father, who handed him his bag. They conversed in the cool night wind for a few minutes. "Just be sure his hands are kept strapped to his legs," said the doctor. "I don't want him hurting himself."

"Will he be all right, Doctor?" The mother held to his arm a moment.

He patted her shoulder. "Haven't I been your family physician for thirty years? It's the fever. He imagines things."

"But those bruises on his throat, he almost choked himself."

"Just you keep him strapped; he'll be all right in the morning."

The car moved off down the dark September road.

At three in the morning, Charles was still awake in his small black room. The bed was damp under his head and his back. He was very warm. Now he no longer had any arms or legs, and his body was beginning to change. He did not move on the bed, but looked at the vast blank ceiling space with insane concentration. For a while he had screamed and thrashed, but now he was weak and hoarse from it, and his mother had gotten up a number of times to soothe his brow with a wet towel. Now he was silent, his hands strapped to his legs.

He felt the walls of his body change, the organs shift, the lungs catch fire like burning bellows of pink alcohol. The room was lighted up as with the flickerings of a hearth.

Now he had no body. It was all gone. It was under him, but it was filled with a vast pulse of some burning, lethargic drug. It was as if a guillotine had neatly lopped off his head, and his head lay shining on a midnight pillow while the body, below, still alive, belonged to somebody else. The disease had eaten his body and from the eating had reproduced itself in feverish duplicate. There were the little hand hairs and the fingernails and the scars and the toenails and the tiny mole on his right hip, all done again in perfect fashion.

I am dead, he thought. I've been killed, and yet I live. My body is dead, it is all disease and nobody will know. I will walk around and it will not be me, it will be something else. It will be something all bad, all evil, so big and so evil it's hard to understand or think about. Something that will buy shoes and drink water and get married some day maybe and do more evil in the world than has ever been done.

Now the warmth was stealing up his neck, into his cheeks, like a hot wine.

His lips burned, his eyelids, like leaves, caught fire. His nostrils breathed out blue flame, faintly, faintly.

This will be all, he thought. It'll take my head and my brain and fix each eye and every tooth and all the marks in my brain, and every hair and every wrinkle in my ears, and there'll be nothing left of me.

He felt his brain fill with a boiling mercury. He felt his left eye clench in upon itself and, like a snail, withdraw, shift. He was blind in his left eye. It no longer belonged to him. It was enemy territory. His tongue was gone, cut out. His left cheek was numbed, lost. His left ear stopped hearing. It belonged to someone else now. This thing that was being born, this mineral thing replacing the wooden log, this disease replacing healthy animal cell.

He tried to scream and he was able to scream loud and high and sharply in the room, just as his brain flooded down, his right eye and right ear were cut out, he was blind and deaf, all fire, all terror, all panic, all death.

His scream stopped before his mother ran through the door to his side.

It was a good, clear morning, with a brisk wind that helped carry the doctor up the path before the house. In the window above, the boy stood, fully dressed. He did not wave when the doctor waved and called, "What's this? Up? My God!"

The doctor almost ran upstairs. He came gasping into the bedroom.

"What are you doing out of bed?" he demanded of the boy. He tapped his thin chest, took his pulse and temperature. "Absolutely amazing! Normal. Normal, by God!"

"I shall never be sick again in my life," declared the boy, quietly, standing there, looking out the wide window. "Never."

"I hope not. Why, you're looking fine, Charles."

"Doctor?"

"Yes, Charles?"

"Can I go to school *now?*" asked Charles.

"Tomorrow will be time enough. You sound positively eager."

"I am. I like school. All the kids. I want to play with them and wrestle with them, and spit on them and play with the girls' pigtails and shake the teacher's hand, and rub my hands on all the cloaks in the cloakroom, and I want to grow up and travel and shake hands with people all over the world, and be married and have lots of children, and go to libraries and handle books and—*all* of that I want to!" said the boy, looking off into the September morning. "What's the name you called me?"

"What?" The doctor puzzled. "I called you nothing but Charles."

"It's better than no name at all, I guess." The boy shrugged.

"I'm glad you want to go back to school," said the doctor.

"I really anticipate it," smiled the boy. "Thank you for your help, Doctor. Shake hands."

"Glad to."

They shook hands gravely, and the clear wind blew through the open window. They shook hands for almost a minute, the boy smiling up at the old man and thanking him.

Then, laughing, the boy raced the doctor downstairs and out to his car. His mother and father followed for the happy farewell.

"Fit as a fiddle!" said the doctor. "Incredible!"

"And strong," said the father. "He got out of his straps himself during the night. Didn't you, Charles?"

"Did I?" said the boy.

"You did! How?"

"Oh," the boy said, "that was a long time ago."

"A long time ago!"

They all laughed, and while they were laughing, the quiet boy moved his bare foot on the sidewalk and merely touched, brushed against a number of red ants that were scurrying about on the sidewalk. Secretly, his eyes shining, while his parents chatted with the old man, he saw the ants hesitate, quiver, and lie still on the cement. He sensed they were cold now.

"Good-by!"

The doctor drove away, waving.

The boy walked ahead of his parents. As he walked he looked away toward the town and began to hum "School Days" under his breath.

"It's good to have him well again," said the father.

"Listen to him. He's so looking forward to school!"

The boy turned quietly. He gave each of his parents a crushing hug. He kissed them both several times.

Then without a word he bounded up the steps into the house.

In the parlor, before the others entered, he quickly opened the bird cage, thrust his hand in, and petted the yellow canary, *once*.

Then he shut the cage door, stood back, and waited.

The Town Where
No One Got Off

Crossing the continental United States by night, by day, on the train, you flash
past town after wilderness town where nobody ever gets off. Or rather, no person
who doesn't *belong*, no person who hasn't roots in these country graveyards ever
bothers to visit their lonely stations or attend their lonely views.

I spoke of this to a fellow passenger, another salesman like myself, on the
Chicago–Los Angeles train as we crossed Iowa.

"True," he said. "People get off in Chicago; everyone gets off there. People
get off in New York, get off in Boston, get off in L.A. People who don't live
there go there to see and come back to tell. But what tourist ever just got off at
Fox Hill, Nebraska, to *look* at it? You? Me? No! I don't know anyone, got no
business there, it's no health resort, so why bother?"

"Wouldn't it be a fascinating change," I said, "some year to plan a really
different vacation? Pick some village lost on the plains where you don't know a
soul and go there for the hell of it?"

"You'd be bored stiff."

"I'm not bored thinking of it!" I peered out the window. "What's the next
town coming up on this line?"

"Rampart Junction."

I smiled. "Sounds good. I might get off there."

"You're a liar and a fool. What you want? Adventure? Romance? Go ahead,
jump off the train. Ten seconds later you'll call yourself an idiot, grab a taxi,
and race us to the next town."

"Maybe."

I watched telephone poles flick by, flick by, flick by. Far ahead I could see
the first faint outlines of a town.

"But I don't think so," I heard myself say.

The salesman across from me looked faintly surprised.

For slowly, very slowly, I was rising to stand. I reached for my hat. I saw my
hand fumble for my one suitcase. I was surprised myself.

"Hold on!" said the salesman. "What're you doing?"

The train rounded a curve suddenly. I swayed. Far ahead I saw one church
spire, a deep forest, a field of summer wheat.

"It looks like I'm getting off the train," I said.

"Sit down," he said.

"No," I said. "There's something about that town up ahead. I've got to go see. I've got the time. I don't have to be in L.A., really, until next Monday. If I don't get off the train now, I'll always wonder what I missed, what I let slip by when I had the chance to see it."

"We were just talking. There's nothing there."

"You're wrong," I said. "There is."

I put my hat on my head and lifted the suitcase in my hand.

"By God," said the salesman, "I think you're really going to do it."

My heart beat quickly. My face was flushed.

The train whistled. The train rushed down the track. The town was near!

"Wish me luck," I said.

"Luck!" he cried.

I ran for the porter, yelling.

There was an ancient flake-painted chair tilted back against the station-platform wall. In this chair, completely relaxed so he sank into his clothes, was a man of some seventy years whose timbers looked as if he'd been nailed there since the station was built. The sun had burned his face dark and tracked his cheek with lizard folds and stitches that held his eyes in a perpetual squint. His hair smoked ash-white in the summer wind. His blue shirt, open at the neck to show white clock springs, was bleached like the staring late afternoon sky. His shoes were blistered as if he had held them, uncaring, in the mouth of a stove, motionless, forever. His shadow under him was stenciled a permanent black.

As I stepped down, the old man's eyes flicked every door on the train and stopped, surprised, at me.

I thought he might wave.

But there was only a sudden coloring of his secret eyes; a chemical change that was recognition. Yet he had not twitched so much as his mouth, an eyelid, a finger. An invisible bulk had shifted inside him.

The moving train gave me an excuse to follow it with my eyes. There was no one else on the platform. No autos waited by the cobwebbed, nailed-shut office. I alone had departed the iron thunder to set foot on the choppy waves of platform lumber.

The train whistled over the hill.

Fool! I thought. My fellow passenger had been right. I would panic at the boredom I already sensed in this place. All right, I thought, fool, yes, but run, no!

I walked my suitcase down the platform, not looking at the old man. As I passed, I felt his thin bulk shift again, this time so I could hear it. His feet were coming down to touch and tap the mushy boards.

I kept walking.

"Afternoon," a voice said faintly.

I knew he did not look at me but only at that great cloudless spread of shimmering sky.

"Afternoon," I said.

I started up the dirt road toward the town. One hundred yards away, I glanced back.

The old man, still seated there, stared at the sun, as if posing a question.

I hurried on.

I moved through the dreaming late afternoon town, utterly anonymous and alone, a trout going upstream, not touching the banks of a clear-running river of life that drifted all about me.

My suspicions were confirmed: it was a town where nothing happened, where occurred only the following events:

At four o'clock sharp, the Honneger Hardware door slammed as a dog came out to dust himself in the road. Four-thirty, a straw sucked emptily at the bottom of a soda glass, making a sound like a great cataract in the drugstore silence. Five o'clock, boys and pebbles plunged in the town river. Five-fifteen, ants paraded in the slanting light under some elm trees.

And yet—I turned in a slow circle—somewhere in this town there must be something worth seeing. I knew it was there. I knew I had to keep walking and looking. I knew I would find it.

I walked. I looked.

All through the afternoon there was only one constant and unchanging factor: the old man in the bleached blue pants and shirt was never far away. When I sat in the drugstore he was out front spitting tobacco that rolled itself into tumblebugs in the dust. When I stood by the river he was crouched downstream making a great thing of washing his hands.

Along about seven-thirty in the evening, I was walking for the seventh or eighth time through the quiet streets when I heard footsteps beside me.

I looked over, and the old man was pacing me, looking straight ahead, a piece of dried grass in his stained teeth.

"It's been a long time," he said quietly.

We walked along in the twilight.

"A long time," he said, "waitin' on that station platform."

"You?" I said.

"Me." He nodded in the tree shadows.

"Were you waiting for someone at the station?"

"Yes," he said. "You."

"Me?" The surprise must have shown in my voice. "But why . . . ? You never saw me before in your life."

"Did I say I did? I just said I was waitin'."

We were on the edge of town now. He had turned and I had turned with him along the darkening riverbank toward the trestle where the night trains ran over going east, going west, but stopping rare few times.

"You want to know anything about me?" I asked suddenly. "You the sheriff?"

"No, not the sheriff. And no, I don't want to know nothin' about you." He put his hands in his pockets. The sun was set now. The air was suddenly cool. "I'm just surprised you're here at last, is all."

"Surprised?"

"Surprised," he said, "and . . . pleased."

I stopped abruptly and looked straight at him.

"How long have you been sitting on that station platform?"

"Twenty years, give or take a few."

I knew he was telling the truth; his voice was as easy and quiet as the river.

"Waiting for me?" I said.

"Or someone like you," he said.

We walked on in the growing dark.

"How you like our town?"

"Nice, quiet," I said.

"Nice, quiet." He nodded. "Like the people?"

"People look nice and quiet."

"They are," he said. "Nice, quiet."

I was ready to turn back but the old man kept talking and in order to listen and be polite I had to walk with him in the vaster darkness, the tides of field and meadow beyond town.

"Yes," said the old man, "the day I retired, twenty years ago, I sat down on that station platform and there I been, sittin', doin' nothin', waitin' for somethin' to happen, I didn't know what, I didn't know, I couldn't say. But when it finally happened, I'd know it, I'd look at it and say, Yes, sir, that's what I was waitin' for. Train wreck? No. Old woman friend come back to town after fifty years? No. No. It's hard to say. Someone. Somethin'. And it seems to have somethin' to do with you. I wish I could say—"

"Why don't you try?" I said.

The stars were coming out. We walked on.

"Well," he said slowly, "you know much about your own insides?"

"You mean my stomach or you mean psychologically?"

"That's the word. I mean your head, your brain, you know much about *that*?"

The grass whispered under my feet. "A little."

"You hate many people in your time?"

"Some."

"We all do. It's normal enough to hate, ain't it, and not only hate but, while we don't talk about it, don't we sometimes want to hit people who hurt us, even *kill* them?"

"Hardly a week passes we don't get that feeling," I said, "and put it away."

"We put away all our lives," he said. "The town says thus and so, Mom and Dad say this and that, the law says such and such. So you put away one killin' and another and two more after that. By the time you're my age, you got lots of that kind of stuff between your ears. And unless you went to war, nothin' ever happened to get rid of it."

"Some men trapshoot or hunt ducks," I said. "Some men box or wrestle."

"And some don't. I'm talkin' about them that don't. Me. All my life I've been saltin' down those bodies, puttin' 'em away on ice in my head. Sometimes you get mad at a town and the people in it for makin' you put things aside like that. You like the old cave men who just gave a hell of a yell and whanged someone on the head with a club."

"Which all leads up to . . . ?"

"Which all leads up to: Everybody'd like to do one killin' in his life, to sort of work off that big load of stuff, all those killin's in his mind he never did have the guts to do. And once in a while a man has a chance. Someone runs in front of his car and he forgets the brakes and keeps goin'. Nobody can prove nothin' with that sort of thing. The man don't even tell himself he did it. He just didn't get his foot on the brake in time. But you know and I know what really happened, don't we?"

"Yes," I said.

The town was far away now. We moved over a small stream on a wooden bridge, just near the railway embankment.

"Now," said the old man, looking at the water, "the only kind of killin' worth doin' is the one where nobody can guess who did it or why they did it or who they did it to, right? Well, I got this idea maybe twenty years ago. I don't think about it every day or every week. Sometimes months go by, but the idea's this: Only one train stops here each day, sometimes not even that. Now, if you wanted to kill someone you'd have to wait, wouldn't you, for years and years, until a complete and actual stranger came to your town, a stranger who got off the train for no reason, a man nobody knows and who don't know nobody in the town. Then, and only then, I thought, sittin' there on the station chair, you could just go up and when nobody's around, kill him and throw him in the river. He'd be found miles downstream. Maybe he'd never be found. Nobody would ever think to come to Rampart Junction to find him. He wasn't goin' there. He was on his way someplace else. There, that's my whole idea. And I'd know that man the minute he got off the train. Know him, just as clear . . . "

I had stopped walking. It was dark. The moon would not be up for an hour.

"Would you?" I said.

"Yes," he said. I saw the motion of his head looking at the stars. "Well, I've talked enough." He sidled close and touched my elbow. His hand was feverish, as if he had held it to a stove before touching me. His other hand, his right hand, was hidden, tight and bunched, in his pocket. "I've talked enough."

Something screamed.

I jerked my head.

Above, a fast-flying night express razored along the unseen tracks, flourished light on hill, forest, farm, town dwellings, field, ditch, meadow, plowed earth and water, then, raving high, cut off away, shrieking, gone. The rails trembled for a little while after that. Then, silence.

The old man and I stood looking at each other in the dark. His left hand was still holding my elbow. His other hand was still hidden.

"May I say something?" I said at last.

The old man nodded.

"About myself," I said. I had to stop. I could hardly breathe. I forced myself to go on. "It's funny. I've often thought the same way as you. Sure, just today, going cross-country, I thought, How perfect, how perfect, how really perfect it could be. Business has been bad for me, lately. Wife sick. Good friend died last week. War in the world. Full of boils, myself. It would do me a world of good—"

"What?" the old man said, his hand on my arm.

"To get off this train in a small town," I said, "where nobody knows me, with this gun under my arm, and find someone and kill them and bury them and go back down to the station and get on and go home and nobody the wiser and nobody ever to know who did it, ever. Perfect, I thought, a perfect crime. And I got off the train."

We stood there in the dark for another minute, staring at each other. Perhaps we were listening to each other's hearts beating very fast, very fast indeed.

The world turned under me. I clenched my fists. I wanted to fall. I wanted to scream like the train.

For suddenly I saw that all the things I had just said were not lies put forth to save my life.

All the things I had just said to this man were true.

And now I knew why I had stepped from the train and walked up through this town. I knew what I had been looking for.

I heard the old man breathing hard and fast. His hand was tight on my arm as if he might fall. His teeth were clenched. He leaned toward me as I leaned toward him. There was a terrible silent moment of immense strain as before an explosion.

He forced himself to speak at last. It was the voice of a man crushed by a monstrous burden.

"How do I know you got a gun under your arm?"

"You don't know." My voice was blurred. "You can't be sure."

He waited. I thought he was going to faint.

"That's how it is?" he said.

"That's how it is," I said.

He shut his eyes tight. He shut his mouth tight.

After another five seconds, very slowly, heavily, he managed to take his hand away from my own immensely heavy arm. He looked down at his right hand then, and took it, empty, out of his pocket.

Slowly, with great weight, we turned away from each other and started walking blind, completely blind, in the dark.

The midnight passenger-to-be-picked-up flare sputtered on the tracks. Only when the train was pulling out of the station did I lean from the open Pullman door and look back.

The old man was seated there with his chair tilted against the station wall, with his faded blue pants and shirt and his sun-baked face and his sun-bleached eyes. He did not glance at me as the train slid past. He was gazing east along the empty rails where tomorrow or the next day or the day after the day after that, a train, some train, any train, might fly by here, might slow, might stop. His face was fixed, his eyes were blindly frozen, toward the east. He looked a hundred years old.

The train wailed.

Suddenly old myself, I leaned out, squinting.

Now the darkness that had brought us together stood between. The old man, the station, the town, the forest, were lost in the night.

For an hour I stood in the roaring blast staring back at all that darkness.

All Summer in a Day

"Ready?"

"Ready."

"Now?"

"Soon."

"Do the scientists really know? Will it happen today, will it?"

"Look, look; see for yourself!"

The children pressed to each other like so many roses, so many weeds, intermixed, peering out for a look at the hidden sun.

It rained.

It had been raining for seven years; thousands upon thousands of days compounded and filled from one end to the other with rain, with the drum and gush of water, with the sweet crystal fall of showers and the concussion of storms so heavy they were tidal waves come over the islands. A thousand forests had been crushed under the rain and grown up a thousand times to be crushed again. And this was the way life was forever on the planet Venus, and this was the schoolroom of the children of the rocket men and women who had come to a raining world to set up civilization and live out their lives.

"It's stopping, it's stopping!"

"Yes, yes!"

Margot stood apart from them, from these children who could never remember a time when there wasn't rain and rain and rain. They were all nine years old, and if there had been a day, seven years ago, when the sun came out for an hour and showed its face to the stunned world, they could not recall. Sometimes, at night, she heard them stir, in remembrance, and she knew they were dreaming and remembering gold or a yellow crayon or a coin large enough to buy the world with. She knew they thought they remembered a warmness, like a blushing in the face, in the body, in the arms and legs and trembling hands. But then they always awoke to the tatting drum, the endless shaking down of clear bead necklaces upon the roof, the walk, the gardens, the forests, and their dreams were gone.

All day yesterday they had read in class about the sun. About how like a lemon it was, and how hot. And they had written small stories or essays or poems about it:

> *I think the sun is a flower,*
> *That blooms for just one hour.*

That was Margot's poem, read in a quiet voice in the still classroom while the rain was falling outside.

"Aw, you didn't write that!" protested one of the boys.

"I did," said Margot. "I *did*."

"William!" said the teacher.

But that was yesterday. Now the rain was slackening, and the children were crushed in the great thick windows.

"Where's teacher?"

"She'll be back."

"She'd better hurry, we'll miss it!"

They turned on themselves, like a feverish wheel, all tumbling spokes.

Margot stood alone. She was a very frail girl who looked as if she had been lost in the rain for years and the rain had washed out the blue from her eyes and the red from her mouth and the yellow from her hair. She was an old photograph dusted from an album, whitened away, and if she spoke at all her voice would be a ghost. Now she stood, separate, staring at the rain and the loud wet world beyond the huge glass.

"What're *you* looking at?" said William.

Margot said nothing.

"Speak when you're spoken to." He gave her a shove. But she did not move; rather she let herself be moved only by him and nothing else.

They edged away from her, they would not look at her. She felt them go away. And this was because she would play no games with them in the echoing tunnels of the underground city. If they tagged her and ran, she stood blinking after them and did not follow. When the class sang songs about happiness and life and games her lips barely moved. Only when they sang about the sun and the summer did her lips move as she watched the drenched windows.

And then, of course, the biggest crime of all was that she had come here only five years ago from Earth, and she remembered the sun and the way the sun was and the sky was when she was four in Ohio. And they, they had been on Venus all their lives, and they had been only two years old when last the sun came out and had long since forgotten the color and heat of it and the way it really was. But Margot remembered.

"It's like a penny," she said once, eyes closed.

"No, it's not!" the children cried.

"It's like a fire," she said, "in the stove."

"You're lying, you don't remember!" cried the children.

But she remembered and stood quietly apart from all of them and watched the patterning windows. And once, a month ago, she had refused to shower in the school shower rooms, had clutched her hands to her ears and over her head, screaming the water mustn't touch her head. So after that, dimly, dimly, she sensed it, she was different and they knew her difference and kept away.

There was talk that her father and mother were taking her back to Earth next year; it seemed vital to her that they do so, though it would mean the loss of thousands of dollars to her family. And so, the children hated her for all these reasons of big and little consequence. They hated her pale snow face, her waiting silence, her thinness, and her possible future.

"Get away!" The boy gave her another push. "What're you waiting for?"

Then, for the first time, she turned and looked at him. And what she was waiting for was in her eyes.

"Well, don't wait around here!" cried the boy savagely. "You won't see nothing!"

Her lips moved.

"Nothing!" he cried. "It was all a joke, wasn't it?" He turned to the other children. "Nothing's happening today. *Is* it?"

They all blinked at him and then, understanding, laughed and shook their heads. "Nothing, nothing!"

"Oh, but," Margot whispered, her eyes helpless. "But this is the day, the scientists predict, they say, they *know*, the sun . . ."

"All a joke!" said the boy, and seized her roughly. "Hey, everyone, let's put her in a closet before teacher comes!"

"No," said Margot, falling back.

They surged about her, caught her up and bore her, protesting, and then pleading, and then crying, back into a tunnel, a room, a closet, where they slammed and locked the door. They stood looking at the door and saw it tremble from her beating and throwing herself against it. They heard her muffled cries. Then, smiling, they turned and went out and back down the tunnel, just as the teacher arrived.

"Ready, children?" She glanced at her watch.

"Yes!" said everyone.

"Are we all here?"

"Yes!"

The rain slackened still more.

They crowded to the huge door.

The rain stopped.

It was as if, in the midst of a film concerning an avalanche, a tornado, a hurricane, a volcanic eruption, something had, first, gone wrong with the sound apparatus, thus muffling and finally cutting off all noise, all of the blasts and repercussions and thunders, and then, second, ripped the film from the projector and inserted in its place a peaceful tropical slide which did not move or tremor. The world ground to a standstill. The silence was so immense and unbelievable that you felt your ears had been stuffed or you had lost your hearing altogether. The children put their hands to their ears. They stood apart. The door slid back and the smell of the silent, waiting world came in to them.

The sun came out.

It was the color of flaming bronze and it was very large. And the sky around it was a blazing blue tile color. And the jungle burned with sunlight as the children, released from their spell, rushed out, yelling, into the springtime.

"Now, don't go too far," called the teacher after them. "You've only two hours, you know. You wouldn't want to get caught out!"

But they were running and turning their faces up to the sky and feeling the sun on their cheeks like a warm iron; they were taking off their jackets and letting the sun burn their arms.

"Oh, it's better than the sun lamps, isn't it?"

"Much, much better!"

They stopped running and stood in the great jungle that covered Venus, that grew and never stopped growing, tumultuously, even as you watched it. It was a nest of octopi, clustering up great arms of fleshlike weed, wavering, flowering in this brief spring. It was the color of rubber and ash, this jungle, from the many years without sun. It was the color of stones and white cheeses and ink, and it was the color of the moon.

The children lay out, laughing, on the jungle mattress, and heard it sigh and squeak under them, resilient and alive. They ran among the trees, they slipped and fell, they pushed each other, they played hide-and-seek and tag, but most of all they squinted at the sun until tears ran down their faces, they put their hands up to that yellowness and that amazing blueness and they breathed of the fresh, fresh air and listened and listened to the silence which suspended them in a blessed sea of no sound and no motion. They looked at everything and savored everything. Then, wildly, like animals escaped from their caves, they ran and ran in shouting circles. They ran for an hour and did not stop running.

And then—

In the midst of their running one of the girls wailed.

Everyone stopped.

The girl, standing in the open, held out her hand.

"Oh, look, look," she said, trembling.

They came slowly to look at her opened palm.

In the center of it, cupped and huge, was a single raindrop.

She began to cry, looking at it.

They glanced quietly at the sky.

"Oh. Oh."

A few cold drops fell on their noses and their cheeks and their mouths. The sun faded behind a stir of mist. A wind blew cool around them. They turned and started to walk back toward the underground house, their hands at their sides, their smiles vanishing away.

A boom of thunder startled them and like leaves before a new hurricane, they tumbled upon each other and ran. Lightning struck ten miles away, five miles away, a mile, a half mile. The sky darkened into midnight in a flash.

They stood in the doorway of the underground for a moment until it was raining hard. Then they closed the door and heard the gigantic sound of the rain falling in tons and avalanches, everywhere and forever.

"Will it be seven more years?"

"Yes. Seven."

Then one of them gave a little cry.

"Margot!"

"What?"

"She's still in the closet where we locked her."

"Margot."

They stood as if someone had driven them, like so many stakes, into the floor. They looked at each other and then looked away. They glanced out at the world that was raining now and raining and raining steadily. They could not meet each other's glances. Their faces were solemn and pale. They looked at their hands and feet, their faces down.

"Margot."

One of the girls said, "Well . . . ?"

No one moved.

"Go on," whispered the girl.

They walked slowly down the hall in the sound of cold rain. They turned through the doorway to the room in the sound of the storm and thunder, lightning on their faces, blue and terrible. They walked over to the closet door slowly and stood by it.

Behind the closet door was only silence.

They unlocked the door, even more slowly, and let Margot out.

Frost and Fire

During the night, Sim was born. He lay wailing upon the cold cave stones. His blood beat through him a thousand pulses each minute. He grew, steadily.

Into his mouth his mother with feverish hands put the food. The nightmare of living was begun. Almost instantly at birth his eyes grew alert, and then, without half understanding why, filled with bright, insistent terror. He gagged upon the food, choked and wailed. He looked about, blindly.

There was a thick fog. It cleared. The outlines of the cave appeared. And a man loomed up, insane and wild and terrible. A man with a dying face. Old, withered by winds, baked like adobe in the heat. The man was crouched in a far corner of the cave, his eyes whitening to one side of his face, listening to the far wind trumpeting up above on the frozen night planet.

Sim's mother, trembling now and again, staring at the man, fed Sim pebble-fruits, valley-grasses and ice-nipples broken from the cavern entrances, and eating, eliminating, eating again, he grew larger, larger.

The man in the corner of the cave was his father! The man's eyes were all that was alive in his face. He held a crude stone dagger in his withered hands and his jaw hung loose and senseless.

Then, with a widening focus, Sim saw the old people sitting in the tunnel beyond this living quarter. And as he watched, they began to die.

Their agonies filled the cave. They melted like waxen images, their faces collapsed inward on their sharp bones, their teeth protruded. One minute their faces were mature, fairly smooth, alive, electric. The next minute a desiccation and burning away of their flesh occurred.

Sim thrashed in his mother's grasp. She held him. "No, no," she soothed him, quietly, earnestly, looking to see if this, too, would cause her husband to rise again.

With a soft swift padding of naked feet, Sim's father ran across the cave. Sim's mother screamed. Sim felt himself torn loose from her grasp. He fell upon the stones, rolling, shrieking with his new, moist lungs!

The webbed face of his father jerked over him, the knife was poised. It was like one of those prenatal nightmares he'd had again and again while still in his mother's flesh. In the next few blazing, impossible instants questions flicked through his brain. The knife was high, suspended, ready to destroy him. But the whole question of life in this cave, the dying people, the withering and the insanity, surged through Sim's new, small head. How was it that he understood? A newborn child? Can a newborn child think, see, understand, interpret? No. It was wrong! It was impossible. Yet it was happening! To him. He had been alive an hour now. And in the next instant perhaps dead!

His mother flung herself upon the back of his father, and beat down the weapon. Sim caught the terrific backwash of emotion from both their conflicting minds. "Let me kill him!" shouted the father, breathing harshly, sobbingly. "What has he to live for?"

"No, no!" insisted the mother, and her body, frail and old as it was, stretched across the huge body of the father, tearing at his weapon. "He must live! There may be a future for him! He may live longer than us, and be young!"

The father fell back against a stone crib. Lying there, staring, eyes glittering, Sim saw another figure inside that stone crib. A girl-child, quietly feeding itself, moving its delicate hands to procure food. His sister.

The mother wrenched the dagger from her husband's grasp, stood up, weeping and pushing back her cloud of stiffening gray hair. Her mouth trembled and jerked. "I'll kill you!" she said, glaring down at her husband. "Leave my children alone."

The old man spat tiredly, bitterly, and looked vacantly into the stone crib, at the little girl. "One eighth of *her* life's over, already," he gasped. "And she doesn't know it. What's the use?"

As Sim watched, his own mother seemed to shift and take a tortured, smokelike form. The thin bony face broke out into a maze of wrinkles. She was shaken with pain and had to sit by him, shuddering and cuddling the knife to her shriveled breasts. She, like the old people in the tunnel, was aging, dying.

Sim cried steadily. Everywhere he looked was horror. A mind came to meet his own. Instinctively he glanced toward the stone crib. Dark, his sister, returned his glance. Their minds brushed like straying fingers. He relaxed somewhat. He began to learn.

The father sighed, shut his lids down over his green eyes. "Feed the child," he said, exhaustedly. "Hurry. It is almost dawn and it is our last day of living, woman. Feed him. Make him grow."

Sim quieted, and images, out of the terror, floated to him.

This was a planet next to the sun. The nights burned with cold, the days were like torches of fire. It was a violent, impossible world. The people lived in the cliffs to escape the incredible ice and the day of flame. Only at dawn and sunset was the air breath-sweet, flower-strong, and then the cave peoples brought their children out into a stony, barren valley. At dawn the ice thawed into creeks and rivers, at sunset the day fire died and cooled. In the intervals of even, livable temperature the people lived, ran, played, loved, free of the caverns; all life on the planet jumped, burst into life. Plants grew instantly, birds were flung like pellets across the sky. Smaller, legged animal life rushed frantically through the rocks; everything tried to get its living down in the brief hour of respite.

It was an unbearable planet. Sim understood this, a matter of hours after birth. Racial memory bloomed in him. He would live his entire life in the caves, with two hours a day outside. Here, in stone channels of air he would talk, talk incessantly with his people, sleep never, think, think and lie upon his back, dreaming; but never sleeping.

And he would live exactly eight days.

The *violence* of this thought! Eight days. Eight *short* days. It was wrong, impossible, but a fact. Even while in his mother's flesh some racial knowledge or some strange far wild voice had told him he was being formed rapidly, shaped and propelled out swiftly.

Birth was quick as a knife. Childhood was over in a flash. Adolescence was a sheet of lightning. Manhood was a dream, maturity a myth, old age an inescapably quick reality, death a swift certainty.

Eight days from now he'd stand half-blind, withering, dying, as his father now stood, staring uselessly at his own wife and child.

This day was an eighth part of his total life! He must enjoy every second of it. He must search his parents' thoughts for knowledge.

Because in a few hours they'd be dead.

This was so impossibly unfair. Was this all of life? In his prenatal state hadn't he dreamed of *long* lives, valleys not of blasted stone but green foliage and temperate clime? Yes! And if he'd dreamed then there must be truth in the visions. How could he seek and find the long life? Where? And how could he accomplish a life mission that huge and depressing in eight short, vanishing days?

How had his people gotten into such a condition?

As if at a button pressed, he saw an image. Metal seeds, blown across space from a distant green world, fighting with long flames, crashing on this bleak planet. From their shattered hulls tumbled men and women.

When? Long ago. Ten thousand days. The crash victims hid in the cliffs from the sun. Fire, ice and floods washed away the wreckage of the huge metal seeds. The victims were shaped and beaten like iron upon a forge. Solar radiations drenched them. Their pulses quickened, two hundred, five hundred, a thousand beats a minute. Their skins thickened, their blood changed. Old age came rushing. Children were born in the caves. Swifter, swifter, swifter the process. Like all this world's wild life, the men and women from the crash lived and died in a week, leaving children to do likewise.

So this is life, thought Sim. It was not spoken in his mind, for he knew no words, he knew only images, old memory, an awareness, a telepathy that could penetrate flesh, rock, metal. Somewhere along the line, they *had* developed telepathy, plus racial memory, the only good gifts, the only hope in all this terror. So, thought Sim, I'm the five-thousandth in a long line of futile sons? What can I do to save myself from dying eight days from now? Is there escape?

His eyes widened, another image came to focus.

Beyond this valley of cliffs, on a low mountain, lay a perfect, unscarred metal seed. A metal ship, not rusted or touched by the avalanches. The ship was deserted, whole, intact. It was the only ship of all these that had crashed that was still a unit, still usable. But it was so far away. There was no one in it to help. This ship, then, on the far mountain, was the destiny toward which he would grow. There was his only hope of escape.

His mind flexed.

In this cliff, deep down in a confinement of solitude, worked a handful of Scientists. To these men, when he was old enough and wise enough, he must go. They, too, dreamed of escape, of long life, of green valleys and temperate weathers. They, too, stared longingly at that distant ship upon its high mountain, its metal so perfect it did not rust or age.

The cliff groaned.

Sim's father lifted his eroded, lifeless face.

"Dawn's coming," he said.

II

Morning relaxed the mighty granite cliff muscles. It was the time of the avalanche.

The tunnels echoed to running bare feet. Adults, children pushed with eager, hungry eyes toward the outside dawn. From far out, Sim heard a rumble of rock, a scream, a silence. Avalanches fell into valley. Stones that had been biding their time, not quite ready to fall, for a million years let go their bulks, and where they had begun their journey as single boulders they smashed upon the valley floor in a thousand shrapnel and friction-heated nuggets.

Every morning at least one person was caught in the downpour.

The cliff people dared the avalanches. It added one more excitement to their lives, already too short, too headlong, too dangerous.

Sim felt himself seized up by his father. He was carried brusquely down the tunnel for a thousand yards, to where the daylight appeared. There was a shining insane light in his father's eyes. Sim could not move. He sensed what was going to happen. Behind his father, his mother hurried, bringing with her the little sister, Dark. "Wait! Be careful!" she cried to her husband.

Sim felt his father crouch, listening.

High in the cliff was a tremor, a shivering.

"Now!" bellowed his father, and leaped out.

An avalanche fell down at them!

Sim had accelerated impressions of plunging walls, dust, confusion. His mother screamed! There was a jolting, a plunging.

With one last step, Sim's father hurried him forward into the day. The avalanche thundered behind him. The mouth of the cave, where Mother and Dark stood back out of the way, was choked with rubble and two boulders that weighed a hundred pounds each.

The storm thunder of the avalanche passed away to a trickle of sand. Sim's father burst out into laughter. "Made it! By the Gods! Made it alive!" And he looked scornfully at the cliff and spat. "Pagh!"

Mother and sister Dark struggled through the rubble. She cursed her husband. "Fool! You might have killed Sim!"

"I may yet," retorted the father.

Sim was not listening. He was fascinated with the remains of an avalanche afront of the next tunnel. Blood trickled out from under a rise of boulders, soaking into the ground. There was nothing more to be seen. Someone else had lost the game.

Dark ran ahead on lithe, supple feet, naked and certain.

The valley air was like a wine filtered between mountains. The heaven was a restive blue; not the pale scorched atmosphere of full day, nor the bloated, bruised black-purple of night, ariot with sickly shining stars.

This was a tide pool. A place where waves of varying and violent temperatures struck, receded. Now the tide pool was quiet, cool, and its life moved abroad.

Laughter! Far away, Sim heard it. Why laughter? How could any of his people find time for laughing? Perhaps later he would discover why.

The valley suddenly blushed with impulsive color. Plant life, thawing in the precipitant dawn, shoved out from most unexpected sources. It flowered as you watched. Pale green tendrils appeared on scoured rocks. Seconds later, ripe globes of fruit twitched upon the blade-tips. Father gave Sim to his mother and harvested the momentary, volatile crop, thrust scarlet, blue, yellow fruits into a fur sack which hung at his waist. Mother tugged at the moist new grasses, laid them on Sim's tongue.

His senses were being honed to a fine edge. He stored knowledge thirstily. He understood love, marriage, customs, anger, pity, rage, selfishness, shadings and subtleties, realities and reflections. One thing suggested another. The sight of green plant life whirled his mind like a gyroscope, seeking balance in a world where lack of time for explanations made a mind seek and interpret on its own. The soft burden of food gave him knowledge of his system, of energy, of movement. Like a bird newly cracking its way from a shell, he was almost a unit, complete, all-knowing. Heredity and telepathy that fed upon every mind and every wind had done all this for him. He grew excited with his ability.

They walked, Mother, Father and the two children, smelling the smells, watching the birds bounce from wall to wall of the valley like scurrying pebbles and suddenly the father said a strange thing:

"Remember?"

Remember what? Sim lay cradled. Was it any effort for them to remember, when they'd lived only seven days!

The husband and wife looked at each other.

"Was it only three days ago?" said the woman, her body shaking, her eyes closing to think. "I can't believe it. It is so unfair." She sobbed, then drew her hand across her face and bit her parched lips. The wind played at her gray hair. "Now it is my turn to cry. An hour ago it was you!"

"An hour is half a life."

"Come." She took her husband's arm. "Let us look at everything, because it will be our last looking."

"The sun'll be up in a few minutes," said the old man. "We must turn back now."

"Just one more moment," pleaded the woman.

"The sun will catch us."

"Let it catch me then!"

"You don't mean that."

"I mean nothing, nothing at all," cried the woman.

The sun was coming fast. The green in the valley burnt away. Searing wind blasted from over the cliffs. Far away where sun bolts hammered battlements of cliff, the huge stone faces shook their contents; those avalanches not already powdered down were now released and fell like mantles.

"Dark!" shouted the father. The girl sprang over the warm floor of the valley, answering, her hair a black flag behind her. Hands full of green fruits, she joined them.

The sun rimmed the horizon with flame, the air convulsed dangerously with it, and whistled.

The cave people bolted, shouting, picking up their fallen children, bearing vast loads of fruit and grass with them back to their deep hideouts. In moments the valley was bare. Except for one small child someone had forgotten. He was running far out on the flatness, but he was not strong enough, and the engulfing heat was drifting down from the cliffs even as he was half across the valley.

Flowers were burnt into effigies, grasses sucked back into rocks like singed snakes. Flower seeds whirled and fell in the sudden furnace blast of wind, sown far into gullies and crannies, ready to blossom at sunset tonight, and then go to seed and die again.

Sim's father watched that child running, alone, out on the floor of the valley. He and his wife and Dark and Sim were safe in the mouth of their tunnel.

"He'll never make it," said Father. "Do not watch him, woman. It's not a good thing to watch."

They turned away. All except Sim, whose eyes had caught a glint of metal far away. His heart hammered in him, and his eyes blurred. Far away, atop a low mountain, one of those metal seeds from space reflected a dazzling ripple of light! It was like one of his intra-embryo dreams fulfilled! A metal space seed, intact, undamaged, lying on a mountain! There was his future! There was his hope for survival! There was where he would go in a few days, when he was—strange thought—a grown man!

The sun plunged into the valley like molten lava.

The little running child screamed, the sun burned, and the screaming stopped.

Sim's mother walked painfully, with sudden age, down the tunnel, paused, reached up, broke off two last icicles that had formed during the night. She handed one to her husband, kept the other. "We will drink one last toast. To you, to the children."

"To *you*." He nodded to her. "To the children." They lifted the icicles. The warmth melted the ice down into their thirsty mouths.

III

All day the sun seemed to blaze and erupt into the valley. Sim could not see it, but the vivid pictorials in his parents' minds were sufficient evidence of the nature of the day fire. The light ran like mercury, sizzling and roasting the caves, poking inward, but never penetrating deeply enough. It lighted the caves. It made the hollows of the cliff comfortably warm.

Sim fought to keep his parents young. But no matter how hard he fought with mind and image, they became like mummies before him. His father seemed to dissolve from one stage of oldness to another. This is what will happen to me soon, thought Sim in terror.

Sim grew upon himself. He felt the digestive-eliminatory movements of his body. He was fed every minute, he was continually swallowing, feeding. He began to fit words to images and processes. Such a word was "love." It was not an abstraction, but a process, a stir of breath, a smell of morning air, a flutter of heart, the curve of arm holding him, the look in the suspended face of his mother. He saw the processes, then searched behind her suspended face and there was the word, in her brain, ready to use. His throat prepared to speak. Life was pushing him, rushing him along toward oblivion.

He sensed the expansion of his fingernails, the adjustments of his cells, the profusion of his hair, the multiplication of his bones and sinew, the grooving of the soft pale wax of his brain. His brain at birth as clear as a circle of ice, innocent, unmarked, was, an instant later, as if hit with a thrown rock, cracked and marked and patterned in a million crevices of thought and discovery.

His sister, Dark, ran in and out with other little hothouse children, forever eating. His mother trembled over him, not eating, she had no appetite, her eyes were webbed shut.

"Sunset," said his father, at last.

The day was over. The light faded, a wind sounded.

His mother arose. "I want to see the outside world once more . . . just once more. . . . " She stared blindly, shivering.

His father's eyes were shut, he lay against the wall.

"I cannot rise," he whispered faintly. "I cannot."

"Dark!" The mother croaked, the girl came running. "Here," and Sim was handed to the girl. "Hold to Sim, Dark, feed him, care for him." She gave Sim one last fondling touch.

Dark said not a word, holding Sim, her great green eyes shining wetly.

"Go now," said the mother. "Take him out into the sunset time. Enjoy yourselves. Pick foods, eat. Play."

Dark walked away without looking back. Sim twisted in her grasp, looking over her shoulder with unbelieving, tragic eyes. He cried out and somehow summoned from his lips the first word of his existence:

"Why . . . ?"

He saw his mother stiffen. "The child spoke!"

"Aye," said his father. "Did you hear what he said?"

"I heard," said the mother quietly.

The last thing Sim saw of his living parents was his mother weakly, swayingly, slowly moving across the floor to lie beside her silent husband. That was the last time he ever saw them move.

IV

The night came and passed and then started the second day.

The bodies of all those who had died during the night were carried in a funeral procession to the top of a small hill. The procession was long, the bodies numerous.

Dark walked in the procession, holding the newly walking Sim by one hand. Only an hour before dawn Sim had learned to walk.

At the top of the hill, Sim saw once again the far-off metal seed. Nobody ever looked at it, or spoke of it. Why? Was there some reason? Was it a mirage? Why did they not run toward it? Worship it? Try to get to it and fly away into space?

The funeral words were spoken. The bodies were placed upon the ground where the sun, in a few minutes, would cremate them.

The procession then turned and ran down the hill, eager to have their few minutes of free time running and playing and laughing in the sweet air.

Dark and Sim, chattering like birds, feeding among the rocks, exchanged what they knew of life. He was in his second day, she in her third. They were driven, as always, by the mercurial speed of their lives.

Another piece of his life opened wide.

Fifty young men ran down from the cliffs, holding sharp stones and rock daggers in their thick hands. Shouting, they ran off toward distant black, low lines of small rock cliffs.

"War!"

The thought stood in Sim's brain. It shocked and beat at him. These men were running to fight, to kill, over there in those small black cliffs where other people lived.

But why? Wasn't life short enough without fighting, killing?

From a great distance he heard the sound of conflict, and it made his stomach cold. "Why, Dark, why?"

Dark didn't know. Perhaps they would understand tomorrow. Now, there was the business of eating to sustain and support their lives. Watching Dark was like seeing a lizard forever flicking its pink tongue, forever hungry.

Pale children ran on all sides of them. One beetlelike boy scuttled up the rocks, knocking Sim aside, to take from him a particularly luscious red berry he had found growing under an outcrop.

The child ate hastily of the fruit before Sim could gain his feet. Then Sim hurled himself unsteadily, the two of them fell in a ridiculous jumble, rolling, until Dark pried them, squalling, apart.

Sim bled. A part of him stood off, like a god, and said, "This should not be. Children should not be this way. It is wrong!"

Dark slapped the little intruding boy away. "Get on!" she cried. "What's your name, bad one?"

"Chion!" laughed the boy. "Chion, Chion, Chion!"

Sim glared at him with all the ferocity in his small, unskilled features. He choked. This was his enemy. It was as if he'd waited for an enemy of person as well as scene. He had already understood the avalanches, the heat, the cold, the shortness of life, but these were things of places, of scene—mute, extravagant manifestations of unthinking nature, not motivated save by gravity and radiation. Here, now, in this stridulant Chion he recognized a thinking enemy!

Chion darted off, turned at a distance, taunting:

"Tomorrow I will be big enough to kill you!"

And he vanished around a rock.

More children ran, giggling, by Sim. Which of them would be friends, enemies? How could friends and enemies come about in this impossible, quick lifetime? There was no time to make either, was there?

Dark, knowing his thoughts, drew him away. As they searched for food, she whispered fiercely in his ear. "Enemies are made over things like stolen foods; gifts of long grasses make friends. Enemies come, too, from opinions and thoughts. In five seconds you've made an enemy for life. Life's so short enemies must be made quickly." And she laughed with an irony strange for one so young, who was growing older before her rightful time. "You must fight to protect yourself. Others, superstitious ones, will try killing you. There is a belief, a ridiculous belief, that if one kills another, the murderer partakes of the life energy of the slain, and therefore will live an extra day. You see? As long as that is believed, you're in danger."

But Sim was not listening. Bursting from a flock of delicate girls who tomorrow would be tall, quieter, and who day after that would become shapely and the next day take husbands, one small girl whose hair was a violet-blue flame caught Sim's sight.

She ran past, brushed Sim, their bodies touched. Her eyes, white as silver coins, shone at him. He knew then that he'd found a friend, a love, a wife, one who would a week from now lie with him atop the funeral pyre as sunlight undressed their flesh from bone.

Only the glance, but it held them in mid-motion, one instant.

"Your name?" he shouted after her.

"Lyte!" she called laughingly back.

"I'm Sim," he answered, confused and bewildered.

"Sim!" she repeated it, flashing on. "I'll remember!"

Dark nudged his ribs. "Here, *eat*," she said to the distracted boy. "Eat or you'll never get big enough to catch her."

From nowhere, Chion appeared, running by. "Lyte!" he mocked, dancing malevolently along and away. "Lyte! I'll remember Lyte, too!"

Dark stood tall and reed-slender, shaking her dark ebony clouds of hair, sadly. "I see your life before you, little Sim. You'll need weapons soon to fight for this Lyte one. Now, hurry—the sun's coming!"

They ran back to the caves.

V

One fourth of his life was over! Babyhood was gone. He was now a young boy! Wild rains lashed the valley at nightfall. He watched new river channels cut in the valley, out past the mountain of the metal seed. He stored the knowledge for later use. Each night there was a new river, a bed newly cut.

"What's beyond the valley?" wondered Sim.

"No one's ever been beyond it," explained Dark. "All who tried to reach the plain were frozen to death or burnt. The only land we know's within half an hour's run. Half an hour out and half an hour back."

"No one has ever reached the metal seed, then?"

Dark scoffed. "The Scientists, they try. Silly fools. They don't know enough to stop. It's no use. It's too far."

The Scientists. The word stirred him. He had almost forgotten the vision he had in the moments before and after birth. His voice was eager. "Where are the Scientists?"

Dark looked away from him. "I wouldn't tell you if I knew. They'd kill you, experimenting! I don't want you joining them! Live your life, don't cut it in half trying to reach that silly metal thing on the mountain."

"I'll find out where they are from someone else, then!"

"No one'll tell you! They hate the Scientists. You'll have to find them on your own. And then what? Will you save us? Yes, save us, little boy!" Her face was sullen; already half her life was gone.

"We can't just sit and talk and eat," he protested. "And *nothing* else." He leapt up.

"Go find them!" she retorted acidly. "They'll help you forget. Yes, yes." She spat it out. "Forget your life's over in just a few more days!"

Sim ran through the tunnels, seeking. Sometimes he half imagined where the Scientists were. But then a flood of angry thought from those around him, when he asked the direction to the Scientists' cave, washed over him in confusion and resentment. After all, it was the Scientists' fault that they had been placed upon this terrible world! Sim flinched under the bombardment of oaths and curses.

Quietly he took his seat in a central chamber with the children to listen to the grown men talk. This was the time of education, the Time of Talking. No matter how he chafed at delay, or how great his impatience, even though life slipped fast from him and death approached like a black meteor, he knew his mind needed knowledge. Tonight, then, was the night of school. But he sat uneasily. Only *five* more days of life.

Chion sat across from Sim, his thin-mouthed face arrogant.

Lyte appeared between the two. The last few hours had made her firmer-footed, gentler, taller. Her hair shone brighter. She smiled as she sat beside Sim, ignoring Chion. And Chion became rigid at this and ceased eating.

The dialogue crackled, filled the room. Swift as heartbeats, one thousand, two thousand words a minute. Sim learned, his head filled. He did not shut his eyes, but lapsed into a kind of dreaming that was almost intra-embryonic in lassitude and drowsy vividness. In the faint background the words were spoken, and they wove a tapestry of knowledge in his head.

He dreamed of green meadows free of stones, all grass, round and rolling and rushing easily toward a dawn with no taint of freezing, merciless cold or smell of boiled rock or scorched monument. He walked across the green meadow. Overhead the metal seeds flew by in a heaven that was a steady, even temperature. Things were slow, slow, slow.

Birds lingered upon gigantic trees that took a hundred, two hundred, five thousand days to grow. Everything remained in its place, the birds did not flicker nervously at a hint of sun, nor did the trees suck back frightenedly when a ray of sunlight poured over them.

In this dream people strolled, they rarely ran, the heart rhythm of them was evenly languid, not jerking and insane. The grass remained, and did not burn away in torches. The dream people talked always of tomorrow and living and not tomorrow and dying. It all seemed so familiar that when Sim felt someone take his hand he thought it simply another part of the dream.

Lyte's hand lay inside his own. "Dreaming?" she asked.

"Yes."

"Things are balanced. Our minds, to even things, to balance the unfairness of our living, go back in on ourselves, to find what there is that is good to see."

He beat his hand against the stone floor again and again. "It does not make things fair! I hate it! It reminds me that there is something better, something I have missed! Why can't we be ignorant! Why can't we live and die without knowing that this is an abnormal living?" And his breath rushed harshly from his half-open, constricted mouth.

"There is purpose in everything," said Lyte. "This gives us purpose, makes us work, plan, try to find a way."

His eyes were hot emeralds in his face. "I walked up a hill of grass, very slowly," he said.

"The same hill of grass I walked an hour ago?" asked Lyte.

"Perhaps. Close enough to it. The dream is better than the reality." He flexed his eyes, narrowed them. "I watched people and they did not eat."

"Or talk?"

"Or talk, either. And we always are eating, always talking. Sometimes those people in the dream sprawled with their eyes shut, not moving a muscle."

As Lyte stared down into his face a terrible thing happened. He imagined her face blackening, wrinkling, twisting into knots of agedness. The hair blew out like snow about her ears, the eyes were like discolored coins caught in a web of lashes. Her teeth sank away from her lips, the delicate fingers hung like charred twigs from her atrophied wrists. Her beauty was consumed and wasted even as he watched, and when he seized her, he cried out, for he imagined his own hand corroded, and, in terror, he choked back a cry.

"Sim, what's wrong?"

The saliva in his mouth dried at the taste of the words.

"Five more days . . . "

"The Scientists."

Sim started. Who'd spoken? In the dim light a tall man talked. "The Scientists crashed us on this world, and now have wasted thousands of lives and time. It's no use. It's no use. Tolerate them but give them none of your time. You only live once, remember."

Where were these hated Scientists? Now, after the Learning, the Time of Talking, he was ready to find them. Now, at least, he knew enough to begin his fight for freedom, for the ship!

"Sim, where're you going?"

But Sim was gone. The echo of his running feet died away down a shaft of polished stone.

It seemed that half the night was wasted. He blundered into a dozen dead ends. Many times he was attacked by the insane young men who wanted his life energy. Their superstitious ravings echoed after him. The gashes of their hungry fingernails covered his body.

He found what he looked for.

A half dozen men gathered in a small basalt cave deep down in the cliff lode. On a table before them lay objects which, though unfamiliar, struck harmonious chords in Sim.

The Scientists worked in sets, old men doing important work, young men learning, asking questions; and at their feet were three small children. They were a process. Every eight days there was an entirely new set of Scientists working on any one problem. The amount of work done was terribly inadequate. They grew old, fell dead just when they were beginning their creative period. The creative time of any one individual was perhaps a matter of twelve hours out of his entire span. Three quarters of one's life was spent learning, a brief interval of creative power, then senility, insanity, death.

The men turned as Sim entered.

"Don't tell me we have a recruit?" said the eldest of them.

"I don't believe it," said another, younger one. "Chase him away. He's probably one of those warmongers."

"No, no," objected the elder one, moving with little shuffles of his bare feet toward Sim. "Come in, come in, boy." He had friendly eyes, slow eyes, unlike those of the swift inhabitants of the upper caves. Gray and quiet. "What do you want?"

Sim hesitated, lowered his head, unable to meet the quiet, gentle gaze. "I want to live," he whispered.

The old man laughed quietly. He touched Sim's shoulder. "Are you a new breed? Are you sick?" he queried of Sim, half seriously. "Why aren't you playing? Why aren't you readying yourself for the time of love and marriage and children? Don't you know that tomorrow night you'll be almost grown? Don't you realize that if you are not careful you'll miss all of life?" He stopped.

Sim moved his eyes back and forth with each query. He blinked at the instruments on the table top. "Shouldn't I be here?" he asked.

"Certainly," roared the old man, sternly. "But it's a miracle you are. We've had no volunteers from the rank and file for a thousand days! We've had to breed our own scientists, a closed unit! Count us! Six! Six men! And three children! Are we not overwhelming?" The old man spat upon the stone floor. "We ask for volunteers and the people shout back at us, 'Get someone else!' or 'We have no time!' And you know why they say that?"

"No." Sim flinched.

"Because they're selfish. They'd like to live longer, yes, but they know that anything they do cannot possibly insure their *own* lives any extra time. It might guarantee longer life to some future offspring of theirs. But they won't give up their love, their brief youth, give up one interval of sunset or sunrise!"

Sim leaned against the table, earnestly. "I understand."

"You do?" The old man stared at him blindly. He sighed and slapped the child's arm gently. "Yes, of course, you do. It's too much to expect anyone to understand, any more. You're rare."

The others moved in around Sim and the old man.

"I am Dienc. Tomorrow night Cort here will be in my place. I'll be dead by then. And the night after that someone else will be in Cort's place, and then you, if you work and believe—but first, I give you a chance. Return to your playmates if you want. There is someone you love? Return to her. Life is short. Why should you care for the unborn to come? You have a right to youth. Go now, if you want. Because if you stay you'll have no time for anything but working and growing old and dying at your work. But it is good work. Well?"

Sim looked at the tunnel. From a distance the wind roared and blew, the smells of cooking and the patter of naked feet sounded, and the laughter of young people was an increasingly good thing to hear. He shook his head, impatiently, and his eyes were wet.

"I will stay," he said.

VI

The third night and third day passed. It was the fourth night. Sim was drawn into their living. He learned about that metal seed upon the top of the far mountain. He heard of the original seeds—things called "ships" that crashed and how the survivors hid and dug in the cliffs, grew old swiftly and in their scrabbling to barely survive, forgot all science. Knowledge of mechanical things had no chance of survival in such a volcanic civilization. There was only NOW for each human.

Yesterday didn't matter, tomorrow stared them vividly in their very faces. But somehow the radiations that had forced their aging had also induced a kind of telepathic communication whereby philosophies and impressions were absorbed by the newborn. Racial memory, growing instinctively, preserved memories of another time.

"Why don't we go to that ship on the mountain?" asked Sim.

"It is too far. We would need protection from the sun," explained Dienc.

"Have you tried to make protection?"

"Salves and ointments, suits of stone and bird-wing and, recently, crude metals. None of which worked. In ten thousand more lifetimes perhaps we'll have made a metal in which will flow cool water to protect us on the march to the ship. But we work so slowly, so blindly. This morning, mature, I took up my instruments. Tomorrow, dying, I lay them down. What can one man do in one day? If we had ten thousand men, the problem would be solved. . . . "

"I will go to the ship," said Sim.

"Then you will die," said the old man. A silence had fallen on the room at Sim's words. Then the men stared at Sim. "You are a very selfish boy."

"Selfish!" cried Sim, resentfully.

The old man patted the air. "Selfish in a way I like. You want to live longer, you'll do anything for that. You will try for the ship. But I tell you it is useless. Yet, if you want to, I cannot stop you. At least you will not be like those among us who go to war for an extra few days of life."

"War?" asked Sim. "How can there be war here?"

And a shudder ran through him. He did not understand.

"Tomorrow will be time enough for that," said Dienc. "Listen to me, now."

The night passed.

VII

It was morning. Lyte came shouting and sobbing down a corridor, and ran full into his arms. She had changed again. She was older, again, more beautiful. She was shaking and she held to him. "Sim, they're coming after you!"

Bare feet marched down the corridor, surged inward at the opening. Chion stood grinning there, taller, too, a sharp rock in either of his hands. "Oh, there you are, Sim!"

"Go away!" cried Lyte, savagely whirling on him.

"Not until we take Sim with us," Chion assured her. Then, smiling at Sim. "*If*, that is, he is with us in the fight."

Dienc shuffled forward, his eye weakly fluttering, his birdlike hands fumbling in the air. "Leave!" he shrilled angrily. "This boy is a Scientist now. He works with us."

Chion ceased smiling. "There is better work to be done. We go now to fight the people in the farthest cliffs." His eyes glittered anxiously. "Of course, you will come with us, Sim?"

"No, no!" Lyte clutched at his arm.

Sim patted her shoulder, then turned to Chion. "Why are you attacking these people?"

"There are three extra days for those who go with us to fight."

"Three extra days! Of living?"

Chion nodded firmly. "If we win, we live eleven days instead of eight. The cliffs they live in, something about the mineral in them that protects you from radiation! Think of it, Sim, three long, good days of life. Will you join us?"

Dienc interrupted. "Get along without him. Sim is my pupil!"

Chion snorted. "Go die, old man. By sunset tonight you'll be charred bone. Who are you to order us? We are young, we want to live longer."

Eleven days. The words were unbelievable to Sim. Eleven days. Now he understood why there was war. Who wouldn't fight to have his life lengthened by almost half its total. So many more days of living! Yes. Why not, indeed!

"Three extra days," called Dienc, stridently, "*if* you live to enjoy them. If you're not killed in battle. *If. If!* You have never won yet. You have always lost!"

"But this time," Chion declared sharply, "we'll win!"

Sim was bewildered. "But we are all of the same ancestors. Why don't we all share the best cliffs?"

Chion laughed and adjusted a sharp stone in his hand. "Those who live in the best cliffs think they are better than us. That is always man's attitude when he has power. The cliffs, there, besides, are smaller, there's room for only three hundred people in them."

Three extra days.

"I'll go with you," Sim said to Chion.

"Fine!" Chion was very glad, much too glad at the decision.

Dienc gasped.

Sim turned to Dienc and Lyte. "If I fight, and win, I will be half a mile closer to the ship. And I'll have three extra days in which to strive to reach the ship. That seems the only thing for me to do."

Dienc nodded, sadly. "It *is* the only thing. I believe you. Go along now."

"Good-by," said Sim.

The old man looked surprised, then he laughed as at a little joke on himself. "That's right—I won't see you again, will I? Good-by, then." And they shook hands.

They went out, Chion, Sim, and Lyte, together, followed by the others, all children growing swiftly into fighting men. And the light in Chion's eyes was not a good thing to see.

Lyte went with him. She chose his rocks for him and carried them. She would not go back, no matter how he pleaded. The sun was just beyond the horizon and they marched across the valley.

"Please, Lyte, go back!"

"And wait for Chion to return?" she said. "He plans that when you die I will be his mate." She shook out her unbelievable blue-white curls of hair defiantly. "But I'll be with you. If you fall, I fall."

Sim's face hardened. He was tall. The world had shrunk during the night. Children packs screamed by hilarious in their food-searching and he looked at them with alien wonder: could it be only four days ago he'd been like these? Strange. There was a sense of many days in his mind, as if he'd really lived a thousand days. There was a dimension of incident and thought so thick, so multicolored, so richly diverse in his head that it was not to be believed so much could happen in so short a time.

The fighting men ran in clusters of two or three. Sim looked ahead at the rising line of small ebon cliffs. This, then, he said to himself, is my fourth day. And still I am no closer to the ship, or to anything, not even—he heard the light tread of Lyte beside him—not even to her who bears my weapons and picks me ripe berries.

One half of his life was gone. Or a third of it— If he won this battle. *If.*

He ran easily, lifting, letting fall his legs. This is the day of my physical awareness, as I run I feed, as I feed I grow and as I grow I turn eyes to Lyte with a kind of dizzying vertigo. And she looks upon me with the same gentleness of thought. This is the day of our youth. Are we wasting it? Are we losing it on a dream, a folly?

Distantly he heard laughter. As a child he'd questioned it. Now he understood laughter. This particular laughter was made of climbing high rocks and plucking the greenest blades and drinking the headiest vintage from the morning ices and eating of the rock-fruits and tasting of young lips in new appetite.

They neared the cliffs of the enemy.

He saw the slender erectness of Lyte. The new surprise of her neck where if you touched you could time her pulse; the fingers which cupped in your own were animate and supple and never still; the . . .

Lyte snapped her head to one side. "Look ahead!" she cried. "See what is to come—look only ahead."

He felt that they were racing by part of their lives, leaving their youth on the pathside, without so much as a glance.

"I am blind with looking at stones," he said, running.

"Find new stones, then!"

"I see stones—" His voice grew gentle as the palm of her hand. The landscape floated under him. Everything was like a fine wind, blowing dreamily. "I see stones that make a ravine that lies in a cool shadow where the stone-berries are thick as tears. You touch a boulder and the berries fall in silent red avalanches, and the grass is very tender. . . . "

"I do not see it!" She increased her pace, turning her head away.

He saw the floss upon her neck, like the small moss that grows silvery and light on the cool side of pebbles, that stirs if you breathe the lightest breath upon it. He looked upon himself, his hands clenched as he heaved himself forward toward death. Already his hands were veined and youth-swollen.

Lyte handed him food to eat.

"I am not hungry," he said.

"Eat, keep your mouth full," she commanded sharply, "so you will be strong for battle."

"Gods!" he roared, anguished. "Who cares for battles!"

Ahead of them, rocks hailed down, thudding. A man fell with his skull split wide. The war was begun.

Lyte passed the weapons to him. They ran without another word until they entered the killing ground.

The boulders began to roll in a synthetic avalanche from the battlements of the enemy!

Only one thought was in his mind now. To kill, to lessen the life of someone else so he could live, to gain a foothold here and live long enough to make a stab at the ship. He ducked, he weaved, he clutched stones and hurled them up. His left hand held a flat stone shield with which he diverted the swiftly plummeting rocks. There was a spatting sound everywhere. Lyte ran with him, encouraging him. Two men dropped before him, slain, their breasts cleaved to the bone, their blood springing out in unbelievable founts.

It was a useless conflict. Sim realized instantly how insane the venture was. They could never storm the cliff. A solid wall of rocks rained down. A dozen men dropped with shards of ebony in their brains, a half dozen more showed drooping, broken arms. One screamed and the upthrust white joint of his knee was exposed as the flesh was pulled away by two successive blows of well-aimed granite. Men stumbled over one another.

The muscles in his cheeks pulled tight and he began to wonder why he had ever come. But his raised eyes, as he danced from side to side, weaving and bobbing, sought always the cliffs. He wanted to live there so intensely, to have his chance. He would have to stick it out. But the heart was gone from him.

Lyte screamed piercingly. Sim, his heart panicking, twisted and saw that her hand was loose at the wrist, with an ugly wound bleeding profusely on the back of the knuckles. She clamped it under her armpit to soothe the pain. The anger rose in him and exploded. In his fury he raced forward, throwing his missiles with deadly accuracy. He saw a man topple and flail down, falling from one level to another of the caves, a victim of his shot. He must have been screaming, for his lungs were bursting open and closed and his throat was raw, and the ground spun madly under his racing feet.

The stone that clipped his head sent him reeling and plunging back. He ate sand. The universe dissolved into purple whorls. He could not get up. He lay and knew that this was his last day, his last time. The battle raged around him, dimly he felt Lyte over him. Her hands cooled his head, she tried to drag him out of range, but he lay gasping and telling her to leave him.

"Stop!" shouted a voice. The whole war seemed to give pause. "Retreat!" commanded the voice swiftly. And as Sim watched, lying upon his side, his comrades turned and fled back toward home.

"The sun is coming, our time is up!" He saw their muscled backs, their moving, tensing, flickering legs go up and down. The dead were left upon the field. The wounded cried for help. But there was no time for the wounded. There was only time for swift men to run the gauntlet home and, their lungs aching and raw with heated air, burst into their tunnels before the sun burnt and killed them.

The sun!

Sim saw another figure racing toward him. It was Chion! Lyte was helping Sim to his feet, whispering helpfully to him. "Can you walk?" she asked. And he groaned and said, "I think so." "Walk then," she said. "Walk slowly, and then faster and faster. We'll make it. Walk slowly, start carefully. We'll make it, I know we will."

Sim got to his feet, stood swaying. Chion raced up, a strange expression cutting lines in his cheeks, his eyes shining with battle. Pushing Lyte abruptly aside he seized upon a rock and dealt Sim a jolting blow upon his ankle that laid wide the flesh. All of this was done quite silently.

Now he stood back, still not speaking, grinning like an animal from the night mountains, his chest panting in and out, looking from the thing he had done, to Lyte, and back. He got his breath. "He'll never make it." He nodded at Sim. "We'll have to leave him here. Come along, Lyte."

Lyte, like a cat-animal, sprang upon Chion, searching for his eyes, shrieking through her exposed, hard-pressed teeth. Her fingers stroked great bloody furrows down Chion's arms and again, instantly, down his neck. Chion, with an oath, sprang away from her. She hurled a rock at him. Grunting, he let it miss him, then ran off a few yards. "Fool!" he cried, turning to scorn her. "Come along with me. Sim will be dead in a few minutes. Come along!"

Lyte turned her back on him. "I will go if you carry me."

Chion's face changed. His eyes lost their gleaming. "There is no time. We would both die if I carried you."

Lyte looked through and beyond him. "Carry me, then, for that's how I wish it to be."

Without another word, glancing fearfully at the sun, Chion fled. His footsteps sped away and vanished from hearing. "May he fall and break his neck," whispered Lyte, savagely glaring at his form as it skirted a ravine. She returned to Sim. "Can you walk?"

Agonies of pain shot up his leg from the wounded ankle. He nodded ironically. "We could make it to the cave in two hours, walking. I have an idea, Lyte. Carry me." And he smiled with the grim joke.

She took his arm. "Nevertheless we'll walk. Come."

"No," he said. "We're staying here."

"But why?"

"We came to seek a home here. If we walk we will die. I would rather die here. How much time have we?"

Together they measured the sun. "A few minutes," she said, her voice flat and dull. She held close to him.

The black rocks of the cliff were paling into deep purples and browns as the sun began to flood the world.

What a fool he was! He should have stayed and worked with Dienc, and thought and dreamed.

With the sinews of his neck standing out defiantly he bellowed upward at the cliff holes.

"Send me down one man to do battle!"

Silence. His voice echoed from the cliff. The air was warm.

"It's no use," said Lyte. "They'll pay no attention."

He shouted again. "Hear me!" He stood with his weight on his good foot, his injured left leg throbbing and pulsating with pain. He shook a fist. "Send down a warrior who is no coward! I will not turn and run home! I have come to fight a fair fight! Send a man who will fight for the right to his cave! Him I will surely kill!"

More silence. A wave of heat passed over the land, receded.

"Oh, surely," mocked Sim, hands on naked hips, head back, mouth wide, "surely there's one among you not afraid to fight a cripple!" Silence. "No?" Silence.

"Then I have miscalculated you. I'm wrong. I'll stand here, then, until the sun shucks the flesh off my bone in black scraps, and call you the filthy names you deserve."

He got an answer.

"I do not like being called names," replied a man's voice.

Sim leaned forward, forgetting his crippled foot.

A huge man appeared in a cave mouth on the third level.

"Come down," urged Sim. "Come down, fat one, and kill me."

The man scowled seriously at his opponent a moment, then lumbered slowly down the path, his hands empty of any weapons. Immediately every cave above clustered with heads. An audience for this drama.

The man approached Sim. "We will fight by the rules, if you know them."

"I'll learn as we go," replied Sim.

This pleased the man and he looked at Sim warily, but not unkindly. "This much I will tell you," offered the man generously. "If you die, I will give your mate shelter and she will live as she pleases, because she is the wife of a good man."

Sim nodded swiftly. "I am ready," he said.

"The rules are simple. We do not touch each other, save with stones. The stones and the sun will do either of us in. Now is the time—"

VIII

A tip of the sun showed on the horizon. "My name is Nhoj," said Sim's enemy, casually taking up a handful of pebbles and stones, weighing them. Sim did likewise. He was hungry. He had not eaten for many minutes. Hunger was the curse of this planet's peoples—a perpetual demanding of empty stomachs for more, more food. His blood flushed weakly, shot tinglingly through veins in jolting throbs of heat and pressure, his rib cage shoved out, went in, shoved out again, impatiently.

"Now!" roared the three hundred watchers from the cliffs. "Now!" they clamored, the men and women and children balanced, in turmoil on the ledges. "Now! Begin!"

As if at a cue, the sun arose. It smote them a blow as with a flat, sizzling stone. The two men staggered under the molten impact, sweat broke from their naked thighs and loins, under their arms and on their faces was a glaze like fine glass.

Nhoj shifted his huge weight and looked at the sun as if in no hurry to fight. Then, silently, with no warning, he snapped out a pebble with a startling trigger-flick of thumb and forefinger. It caught Sim flat on the cheek, staggered him back, so that a rocket of unbearable pain climbed up his crippled foot and burst into nervous explosion at the pit of his stomach. He tasted blood from his bleeding cheek.

Nhoj moved serenely. Three more flicks of his magical hands and three tiny, seemingly harmless bits of stone flew like whistling birds. Each of them found a target, slammed it. The nerve centers of Sim's body! One hit his stomach so that ten hours' eating almost slid up his throat. A second got his forehead, a third his neck. He collapsed to the boiling sand. His knee made a wrenching sound on the hard earth. His face was colorless and his eyes, squeezed tight, were pushing tears out from the hot, quivering lids. But even as he had fallen he had let loose, with wild force, his handful of stones!

The stones purred in the air. One of them, and only one, struck Nhoj. Upon the left eyeball. Nhoj moaned and laid his hands in the next instant to his shattered eye.

Sim choked out a bitter, sighing laugh. This much triumph he had. The eye of his opponent. It would give him . . . Time. Oh, Gods, he thought, his stomach retching sickly, fighting for breath, this is a world of Time. Give me a little more, just a trifle!

Nhoj, one-eyed, weaving with pain, pelted the writhing body of Sim, but his aim was off now, the stones flew to one side or if they struck at all they were weak and spent and lifeless.

Sim forced himself half erect. From the corners of his eyes he saw Lyte, waiting, staring at him, her lips breathing words of encouragement and hope. He was bathed in sweat, as if a rain spray had showered him down.

The sun was now fully over the horizon. You could smell it. Stones glinted like mirrors, the sand began to roil and bubble. Illusions sprang up everywhere in the valley. Instead of one warrior Nhoj he was confronted by a dozen, each in an upright position, preparing to launch another missile. A dozen irregular warriors who shimmered in the golden menace of day, like bronze gongs smitten, quivered in one vision!

Sim was breathing desperately. His nostrils flared and sucked and his mouth drank thirstily of flame instead of oxygen. His lungs took fire like silk torches and his body was consumed. The sweat spilled from his pores to be instantly evaporated. He felt himself shriveling, shriveling in on himself, he imagined himself looking like his father, old, sunken, slight, withered! Where was the sand? Could he move? Yes. The world wriggled under him, but now he was on his feet.

There would be no more fighting.

A murmur from the cliff told this. The sunburnt faces of the high audience gaped and jeered and shouted encouragement to their warrior. "Stand straight, Nhoj, save your strength now! Stand tall and perspire!" they urged him. And Nhoj stood, swaying lightly, swaying slowly, a pendulum in an incandescent fiery breath from the skyline. "Don't move, Nhoj, save your heart, save your power!"

"The test, the test!" said the people on the heights. "The test of the sun."

And this was the worst part of the fight. Sim squinted painfully at the distorted illusion of cliff. He thought he saw his parents; father with his defeated face, his green eyes burning, mother with her hair blowing like a cloud of gray smoke in the fire wind. He must get up to them, live for and with them!

Behind him, Sim heard Lyte whimper softly. There was a whisper of flesh against sand. She had fallen. He did not dare turn. The strength of turning would bring him thundering down in pain and darkness.

His knees bent. If I fall, he thought, I'll lie here and become ashes. Where was Nhoj? Nhoj was there, a few yards from him, standing bent, slick with perspiration, looking as if he were being hit over the spine with great hammers of destruction.

Fall, Nhoj! Fall! thought Sim. Fall, fall! Fall so I can take your place!

But Nhoj did not fall. One by one the pebbles in his half-loose left hand plummeted to the broiling sands and Nhoj's lips peeled back, the saliva burned away from his lips and his eyes glazed. But he did not fall. The will to live was strong in him. He hung as if by a wire.

Sim fell to one knee!

"Ahh!" wailed the knowing voices from the cliff. They were watching death. Sim jerked his head up, smiling mechanically, foolishly, as if caught in the act of doing something silly. "No, no," he insisted drowsily, and got back up again. There was so much pain he was all one ringing numbness. A whirring, buzzing, frying sound filled the land. High up, an avalanche came down like a curtain on a drama, making no noise. Everything was quiet except for a steady humming. He saw fifty images of Nhoj now, dressed in armors of sweat, eyes puffed with torture, cheeks sunken, lips peeled back like the rind of a drying fruit. But the wire still held him.

"Now," muttered Sim, sluggishly, with a thick, baked tongue between his blazing teeth. "Now I'll fall and lie and dream." He said it with slow, thoughtful pleasure. He planned it. He knew how it must be done. He would do it accurately. He lifted his head to see if the audience was watching.

They were gone!

The sun had driven them back in. All save one or two brave ones. Sim laughed drunkenly and watched the sweat gather on his dead hands, hesitate, drop off, plunge down toward sand and turn to steam halfway there.

Nhoj fell.

The wire was cut. Nhoj fell flat upon his stomach, a gout of blood kicked from his mouth. His eyes rolled back into a white, senseless insanity.

Nhoj fell. So did his fifty duplicate illusions.

All across the valley the winds sang and moaned and Sim saw a blue lake with a blue river feeding it and low white houses near the river with people going and coming in the houses and among the tall green trees. Trees taller than seven men, beside the river mirage.

"Now," explained Sim to himself at last, "now I can fall. Right—into—that—lake."

He fell forward.

He was shocked when he felt the hands eagerly stop him in mid-plunge, lift him, hurry him off, high in the hungry air, like a torch held and waved, ablaze.

How strange is death, he thought, and blackness took him.

He awakened to the flow of cool water on his cheeks.

He opened his eyes fearfully. Lyte held his head upon her lap, her fingers were moving food to his mouth. He was tremendously hungry and tired, but fear squeezed both of these things away. He struggled upward, seeing the strange cave contours overhead.

"What time is it?" he demanded.

"The same day as the contest. Be quiet," she said.

"The same day!"

She nodded amusedly. "You've lost nothing of your life. This is Nhoj's cave. We are inside the black cliff. We will live three extra days. Satisfied? Lie down."

"Nhoj is dead?" He fell back, panting, his heart slamming his ribs. He relaxed slowly. "I won. I won," he breathed.

"Nhoj is dead. So were we, almost. They carried us in from outside only in time."

He ate ravenously. "We have no time to waste. We must get strong. My leg—" He looked at it, tested it. There was a swath of long yellow grasses around it and the ache had died away. Even as he watched, the terrific pulsings of his body went to work and cured away the impurities under the bandages. It *has* to be strong by sunset, he thought. It *has* to be.

He got up and limped around the cave like a captured animal. He felt Lyte's eyes upon him. He could not meet her gaze. Finally, helplessly, he turned.

She interrupted him. "You want to go on to the ship?" she asked, softly. "Tonight? When the sun goes down?"

He took a breath, exhaled it. "Yes."

"You couldn't possibly wait until morning?"

"No."

"Then I'll go with you."

"No!"

"If I lag behind, let me. There's nothing here for me."

They stared at each other a long while. He shrugged wearily.

"All right," he said, at last. "I couldn't stop you, I know that. We'll go together."

IX

They waited in the mouth of their new cave. The sun set. The stones cooled so that one could walk on them. It was almost time for the leaping out and the running toward the distant, glittering metal seed that lay on the far mountain.

Soon would come the rains. And Sim thought back over all the times he had watched the rains thicken into creeks, into rivers that cut new beds each night. One night there would be a river running north, the next a river running northeast, the third night a river running due west. The valley was continually cut and scarred by the torrents. Earthquakes and avalanches filled the old beds. New ones were the order of the day. It was this idea of the river and the directions of the river that he had turned over in his head for many hours. It might possibly— Well, he would wait and see.

He noticed how living in this new cliff had slowed his pulse, slowed everything. A mineral result, protection against the solar radiations. Life was still swift, but not as swift as before.

"Now, Sim!" cried Lyte.

They ran. Between the hot death and the cold one. Together, away from the cliffs, out toward the distant, beckoning ship.

Never had they run this way in their lives. The sound of their feet running was a hard, insistent clatter over vast oblongs of rock, down into ravines, up the sides, and on again. They raked the air in and out of their lungs. Behind them the cliffs faded into things they could never turn back to now.

They did not eat as they ran. They had eaten to the bursting point in the cave, to save time. Now it was only running, a lifting of legs, a balancing of bent elbows, a convulsion of muscles, a slaking in of air that had been fiery and was now cooling.

"Are they watching us?"

Lyte's breathless voice snatched at his ears above the pound of his heart.

Who? But he knew the answer. The cliff peoples, of course. How long had it been since a race like this one? A thousand days? Ten thousand? How long since someone had taken the chance and sprinted with an entire civilization's eyes upon their backs, into gullies, across cooling plain. Were there lovers pausing in their laughter back there, gazing at the two tiny dots that were a man and woman running toward destiny? Were children eating of new fruits and stopping in their play to see the two people racing against time? Was Dienc still living, narrowing hairy eyebrows down over fading eyes, shouting them on in a feeble, rasping voice, shaking a twisted hand? Were there jeers? Were they being called fools, idiots? And in the midst of the name-calling, were people praying them on, hoping they would reach the ship?

Sim took a quick glance at the sky, which was beginning to bruise with the coming night. Out of nowhere clouds materialized and a light shower trailed across a gully two hundred yards ahead of them. Lightning beat upon distant mountains and there was a strong scent of ozone on the disturbed air.

"The halfway mark," panted Sim, and he saw Lyte's face half turn, longingly looking back at the life she was leaving. "Now's the time, if we want to turn back, we still have time. Another minute—"

Thunder snarled in the mountains. An avalanche started out small and ended up huge and monstrous in a deep fissure. Light rain dotted Lyte's smooth white skin. In a minute her hair was glistening and soggy with rain.

"Too late, now," she shouted over the patting rhythm of her own naked feet. "We've got to go ahead!"

And it was too late. Sim knew, judging the distances, that there was no turning back now.

His leg began to pain him. He favored it, slowing. A wind came up swiftly. A cold wind that bit into the skin. But it came from the cliffs behind them, helped rather than hindered them. An omen? he wondered. No.

For as the minutes went by it grew upon him how poorly he had estimated the distance. Their time was dwindling out, but they were still an impossible distance from the ship. He said nothing, but the impotent anger at the slow muscles in his legs welled up into bitterly hot tears in his eyes.

He knew that Lyte was thinking the same as himself. But she flew along like a white bird, seeming hardly to touch ground. He heard her breath go out and in her throat, like a clean, sharp knife in its sheath.

Half the sky was dark. The first stars were peering through lengths of black cloud. Lightning jiggled a path along a rim just ahead of them. A full thunderstorm of violent rain and exploding electricity fell upon them.

They slipped and skidded on moss-smooth pebbles. Lyte fell, scrambled up again with a burning oath. Her body was scarred and dirty. The rain washed over her.

The rain came down and cried on Sim. It filled his eyes and ran in rivers down his spine and he wanted to cry with it.

Lyte fell and did not rise, sucking her breath, her breasts quivering.

He picked her up and held her. "Run, Lyte, please, run!"

"Leave me, Sim. Go ahead!" The rain filled her mouth. There was water everywhere. "It's no use. Go on without me."

He stood there, cold and powerless, his thoughts sagging, the flame of hope blinking out. All the world was blackness, cold falling sheaths of water, and despair.

"We'll walk, then," he said. "And keep walking, and resting."

They walked for fifty yards, easily, slowly, like children out for a stroll. The gully ahead of them filled with water that went sliding away with a swift wet sound, toward the horizon.

Sim cried out. Tugging at Lyte he raced forward. "A new channel," he said, pointing. "Each day the rain cuts a new channel. Here, Lyte!" He leaned over the floodwaters.

He dived in, taking her with him.

The flood swept them like bits of wood. They fought to stay upright, the water got into their mouths, their noses. The land swept by on both sides of them. Clutching Lyte's fingers with insane strength, Sim felt himself hurled end over end, saw flicks of lightning on high, and a new fierce hope was born in him. They could no longer run—well, then they would let the water do the running for them.

With a speed that dashed them against rocks, split open their shoulders, abraded their legs, the new, brief river carried them. "This way!" Sim shouted over a salvo of thunder and steered frantically toward the opposite side of the gully. The mountain where the ship lay was just ahead. They must not pass it by. They fought in the transporting liquid and were slammed against the far side. Sim leaped up, caught at an overhanging rock, locked Lyte in his legs, and drew himself hand over hand upward.

As quickly as it had come, the storm was gone. The lightning faded. The rain ceased. The clouds melted and fell away over the sky. The wind whispered into silence.

"The ship!" Lyte lay upon the ground. "The ship, Sim. This is the mountain of the ship!"

Now the cold came. The killing cold.

They forced themselves drunkenly up the mountain. The cold slid along their limbs, got into their arteries like a chemical and slowed them.

Ahead of them, with a fresh-washed sheen, lay the ship. It was a dream. Sim could not believe that they were actually so near it. Two hundred yards. One hundred and seventy yards.

The ground became covered with ice. They slipped and fell again and again. Behind them the river was frozen into a blue-white snake of cold solidity. A few last drops of rain from somewhere came down as hard pellets.

Sim fell against the bulk of the ship. He was actually touching it. Touching it! He heard Lyte whimpering in her constricted throat. This was the metal, the ship. How many others had touched it in the long days? He and Lyte had made it!

Then, as cold as the air, his veins were chilled.

Where was the entrance?

You run, you swim, you almost drown, you curse, you sweat, you work, you reach a mountain, you go up it, you hammer on metal, you shout with relief, and then—you can't find the entrance.

He fought to control himself. Slowly, he told himself, but not too slowly, go around the ship. The metal slid under his searching hands, so cold that his hands, sweating, almost froze to it. Now, far around to the side. Lyte moved with him. The cold held them like a fist. It began to squeeze.

The entrance.

Metal. Cold, immutable metal. A thin line of opening at the sealing point. Throwing all caution aside, he beat at it. He felt his stomach seething with cold. His fingers were numb, his eyes were half frozen in their sockets. He began to beat and search and scream against the metal door. "Open up! Open up!" He staggered. He had struck something. . . . A *click*!

The air lock sighed. With a whispering of metal on rubber beddings, the door swung softly sidewise and vanished back.

He saw Lyte run forward, clutch at her throat, and drop inside a small shiny chamber. He shuffled after her, blankly.

The air-lock door sealed shut behind him.

He could not breathe. His heart began to slow, to stop.

They were trapped inside the ship now, and something was happening. He sank down to his knees and choked for air.

The ship he had come to for salvation was now slowing his pulse, darkening his brain, poisoning him. With a starved, faint kind of expiring terror, he realized that he was dying.

Blackness.

He had a dim sense of time passing, of thinking, struggling, to make his heart go quick, quick. . . . To make his eyes focus. But the fluid in his body lagged quietly through his settling veins and he heard his pulses thud, pause, thud, pause and thud again with lulling intermissions.

He could not move, not a hand or leg or finger. It was an effort to lift the tonnage of his eyelashes. He could not shift his face even, to see Lyte lying beside him.

From a distance came her irregular breathing. It was like the sound a wounded bird makes with his dry, unraveled pinions. She was so close he could almost feel the heat of her; yet she seemed a long way removed.

I'm getting cold! he thought. Is this death? This slowing of blood, of my heart, this cooling of my body, this drowsy thinking of thoughts?

Staring at the ship's ceiling he traced its intricate system of tubes and machines. The knowledge, the purpose of the ship, its actions, seeped into him. He began to understand in a kind of revealing lassitude just what these things were his eyes rested upon. Slow. Slow.

There was an instrument with a gleaming white dial.

Its purpose?

He drudged away at the problem, like a man underwater.

People had used the dial. Touched it. People had repaired it. Installed it. People had dreamed of it before the building, before the installing, before the repairing and touching and using. The dial contained memory of use and manufacture, its very shape was a dream-memory telling Sim why and for what it had been built. Given time, looking at anything, he could draw from it the knowledge he desired. Some dim part of him reached out, dissected the contents of things, analyzed them.

This dial measured time!

Millions of hours of time!

But how could that be? Sim's eyes dilated, hot and glittering. Where were humans who needed such an instrument?

Blood thrummed and beat behind his eyes. He closed them.

Panic came to him. The day was passing. I am lying here, he thought, and my life slips away. I cannot move. My youth is passing. How long before I can move?

Through a kind of porthole he saw the night pass, the day come, the day pass, and again another night. Stars danced frostily.

I will lie here for four or five days, wrinkling and withering, he thought. This ship will not let me move. How much better if I had stayed in my home cliff, lived, enjoyed this short life. What good has it done to come here? I'm missing all the twilights and dawns. I'll never touch Lyte, though she's here at my side.

Delirium. His mind floated up. His thoughts whirled through the metal ship. He smelled the razor-sharp smell of joined metal. He heard the hull contract with night, relax with day.

Dawn.

Already—another dawn!

Today I would have been fully grown. His jaw clenched. I must get up. I must move. I must enjoy this time.

But he didn't move. He felt his blood pump sleepily from chamber to red chamber in his heart, on down and around through his dead body, to be purified by his folding and unfolding lungs.

The ship grew warm. From somewhere a machine clicked. Automatically the temperature cooled. A controlled gust of air flushed the room.

Night again. And then another day.

He lay and saw four days of his life pass.

He did not try to fight. It was no use. His life was over.

He didn't want to turn his head now. He didn't want to see Lyte with her face like his tortured mother's—eyelids like gray ash flakes, eyes like beaten, sanded metal, cheeks like eroded stones. He didn't want to see a throat like parched thongs of yellow grass, hands the pattern of smoke risen from a fire, breasts like desiccated rinds and hair stubbly and unshorn as moist gray weeds!

And himself? How did *he* look? Was his jaw sunken, the flesh of his eyes pitted, his brow lined and age-scarred?

His strength began to return. He felt his heart beating so slow that it was amazing. One hundred beats a minute. Impossible. He felt so cool, so thoughtful, so easy.

His head fell over to one side. He stared at Lyte. He shouted in surprise.

She was young and fair.

She was looking at him, too weak to say anything. Her eyes were like tiny silver medals, her throat curved like the arm of a child. Her hair was blue fire eating at her scalp, fed by the slender life of her body.

Four days had passed and still she was young . . . no, younger than when they had entered the ship. She was still adolescent.

He could not believe it.

Her first words were, "How long will this last?"

He replied, carefully, "I don't know."

"We are still young."

"The ship. Its metal is around us. It cuts away the sun and the things that came from the sun to age us."

Her eyes shifted thoughtfully. "Then, if we stay here—"

"We'll remain young."

"Six more days? Fourteen more? Twenty?"

"More than that, maybe."

She lay there, silently. After a long time she said, "Sim?"

"Yes."

"Let's stay here. Let's not go back. If we go back now, you know what'll happen to us . . . ?"

"I'm not certain."

"We'll start getting old again, won't we?"

He looked away. He stared at the ceiling and the clock with the moving finger. "Yes. We'll grow old."

"What if we grow old—instantly. When we step from the ship won't the shock be too much?"

"Maybe."

Another silence. He began to move his limbs, testing them. He was very hungry. "The others are waiting," he said.

Her next words made him gasp. "The others are dead," she said. "Or will be in a few hours. All those we knew back there are old."

He tried to picture them old. Dark, his sister, bent and senile with time. He shook his head, wiping the picture away. "They may die," he said. "But there are others who've been born."

"People we don't even know."

"But, nevertheless, *our* people," he replied. "People who'll live only eight days, or eleven days unless we help them."

"But we're *young*, Sim! We can *stay* young!"

He didn't want to listen. It was too tempting a thing to listen to. To stay here. To live. "We've already had more time than the others," he said. "I need workers. Men to heal this ship. We'll get on our feet now, you and I, and find food, eat, and see if the ship is movable. I'm afraid to try to move it myself. It's so big. I'll need help."

"But that means running back all that distance!"

"I know." He lifted himself weakly. "But I'll do it."

"How will you get the men back here?"

"We'll use the river."

"*If* it's there. It *may* be somewhere else."

"We'll wait until there *is* one, then. I've got to go back, Lyte. The son of Dienc is waiting for me, my sister, your brother, are old people, ready to die, and waiting for some word from us—"

After a long while he heard her move, dragging herself tiredly to him. She put her head upon his chest, her eyes closed, stroking his arm. "I'm sorry. Forgive me. You have to go back. I'm a selfish fool."

He touched her cheek, clumsily. "You're human. I understand you. There's nothing to forgive."

They found food. They walked through the ship. It was empty. Only in the control room did they find the remains of a man who must have been the chief pilot. The others had evidently bailed out into space in emergency lifeboats. This pilot, sitting at his controls, alone, had landed the ship on a mountain within sight of other fallen and smashed crafts. Its location on high ground had saved it from the floods. The pilot himself had died, probably of heart failure, soon after landing. The ship had remained here, almost within reach of the other survivors, perfect as an egg, but silent, for—how many thousand days? If the pilot had lived, what a different thing life might have been for the ancestors of Sim and Lyte. Sim, thinking of this, felt the distant, ominous vibration of war. How had the war between worlds come out? Who had won? Or had both planets lost and never bothered trying to pick up survivors? Who had been right? Who was the enemy? Were Sim's people of the guilty or innocent side? They might never know.

He checked the ship hurriedly. He knew nothing of its workings, yet as he walked its corridors, patted its machines, he learned from it. It needed only a crew. One man couldn't possibly set the whole thing running again. He laid his hand upon one round, snoutlike machine. He jerked his hand away, as if burnt.

"Lyte!"

"What is it?"

He touched the machine again, caressed it, his hand trembled violently, his eyes welled with tears, his mouth opened and closed, he looked at the machine, loving it, then looked at Lyte.

"With this machine—" he stammered, softly, incredulously. "With— With this machine I can—"

"What, Sim?"

He inserted his hand into a cuplike contraption with a lever inside. Out of the porthole in front of him he could see the distant line of cliffs. "We were afraid there might never be another river running by this mountain, weren't we?" he asked, exultantly.

"Yes, Sim, but—"

"There *will* be a river. And I *will* come back, tonight! And I'll bring men with me. Five hundred men! Because with this machine I can blast a river bottom all the way to the cliffs, down which the waters will rush, giving myself and the men a swift, sure way of traveling back!" He rubbed the machine's barrellike body. "When I touched it, the life and method of it burnt into me! Watch!" He depressed the lever.

A beam of incandescent fire lanced out from the ship, screaming.

Steadily, accurately, Sim began to cut away a riverbed for the storm waters to flow in. The night was turned to day by its hungry eating.

The return to the cliffs was to be carried out by Sim alone. Lyte was to remain in the ship, in case of any mishap. The trip back seemed, at first glance, to be impossible. There would be no river rushing to cut his time, to sweep him along toward his destination. He would have to run the entire distance in the dawn, and the sun would get him, catch him before he'd reached safety.

"The only way to do it is to start *before* sunrise."

"But you'd be frozen, Sim."

"Here." He made adjustments on the machine that had just finished cutting the riverbed in the rock floor of the valley. He lifted the smooth snout of the gun, pressed the lever, left it down. A gout of fire shot toward the cliffs. He fingered the range control, focused the flame end three miles from its source. Done. He turned to Lyte. "But I don't understand," she said.

He opened the air-lock door. "It's bitter cold out, and half an hour yet till dawn. If I run parallel to the flame from the machine, close enough to it, there'll not be much heat, but enough to sustain life, anyway."

"It doesn't sound safe," Lyte protested.

"*Nothing* does, on this world." He moved forward. "I'll have a half-hour start. That should be enough to reach the cliffs."

"But if the machine should fail while you're still running near its beam?"

"Let's not think of that," he said.

A moment later he was outside. He staggered as if kicked in the stomach. His heart almost exploded in him. The environment of his world forced him into swift living again. He felt his pulse rise, kicking through his veins.

The night was cold as death. The heat ray from the ship sliced across the valley, humming, solid and warm. He moved next to it, very close. One misstep in his running and—

"I'll be back," he called to Lyte.

He and the ray of light went together.

In the early morning the peoples in the caves saw the long finger of orange incandescence and the weird whitish apparition floating, running along beside it. There was muttering and moaning and many sighs of awe.

And when Sim finally reached the cliffs of his childhood he saw alien peoples swarming there. There were no familiar faces. Then he realized how foolish it was to expect familiar faces. One of the older men glared down at him. "Who're you?" he shouted. "Are you from the enemy cliff? What's your name?"

"I am Sim, the son of Sim!"

"Sim!"

An old woman shrieked from the cliff above him. She came hobbling down the stone pathway. "Sim, Sim, it *is* you!"

He looked at her, frankly bewildered. "But I don't know you," he murmured.

"Sim, don't you recognize me? Oh, Sim, it's me! Dark!"

"Dark!"

He felt sick at his stomach. She fell into his arms. This old, trembling woman with the half-blind eyes, his sister.

Another face appeared above. That of an old man. A cruel, bitter face. It looked down at Sim and snarled. "Drive him away!" cried the old man. "He comes from the cliff of the enemy. He's lived there! He's still young! Those who go there can never come back among us. Disloyal beast!" And a rock hurtled down.

Sim leaped aside, pulling the old woman with him.

A roar came from the people. They ran toward Sim, shaking their fists. "Kill him, kill him!" raved the old man, and Sim did not know who he was.

"Stop!" Sim held out his hands. "I come from the ship!"

"The ship?" The people slowed. Dark clung to him, looking up into his young face, puzzling over his smoothness.

"Kill him, kill him, kill him!" croaked the old man, and picked up another rock.

"I offer you ten days, twenty days, thirty more days of life!"

The people stopped. Their mouths hung open. Their eyes were incredulous.

"Thirty days?" It was repeated again and again. "How?"

"Come back to the ship with me. Inside it, one can live forever!"

The old man lifted high a rock, then, choking, fell forward in an apoplectic fit, and tumbled down the rocks to lie at Sim's feet.

Sim bent to peer at the ancient one, at the raw, dead eyes, the loose, sneering lips, the crumpled, quiet body.

"Chion!"

"Yes," said Dark behind him, in a croaking, strange voice. "Your enemy. Chion."

That night two hundred men started for the ship. The water ran in the new channel. One hundred of them were drowned or lost behind in the cold. The others, with Sim, got through to the ship.

Lyte awaited them, and threw wide the metal door.

The weeks passed. Generations lived and died in the cliffs, while the Scientists and workers labored over the ship, learning its functions and its parts.

On the last day, two dozen men moved to their stations within the ship. Now there was a destiny of travel ahead.

Sim touched the control plates under his fingers.

Lyte, rubbing her eyes, came and sat on the floor next to him, resting her head against his knee, drowsily. "I had a dream," she said, looking off at something far away. "I dreamed I lived in caves in a cliff on a cold-hot planet where people grew old and died in eight days."

"What an impossible dream," said Sim. "People couldn't possibly live in such a nightmare. Forget it. You're awake now."

He touched the plates gently. The ship rose and moved into space.

Sim was right.

The nightmare was over at last.

The Anthem Sprinters

"There's no doubt of it, Doone's the best."

"Devil take Doone!"

"His reflex is uncanny, his lope on the incline extraordinary, he's off and gone before you reach for your hat."

"Hoolihan's better, any day!"

"Day, hell. Why not *now?*"

I was at the far end of the bar at the top of Grafton Street listening to the tenors singing, the concertinas dying hard, and the arguments prowling the smoke, looking for opposition. The pub was the Four Provinces and it was getting on late at night, for Dublin. So there was the sure threat of everything shutting at once, meaning spigots, accordions, piano lids, soloists, trios, quartets, pubs, sweet shops and cinemas. In a great heave like the Day of Judgment, half Dublin's population would be thrown out into raw lamplight, there to find themselves wanting in gum-machine mirrors. Stunned, their moral and physical sustenance plucked from them, the souls would wander like battered moths for a moment, then wheel about for home.

But now here I was listening to a discussion the heat of which, if not the light, reached me at fifty paces.

"Doone!"

"Hoolihan!"

Then the smallest man at the far end of the bar, turning, saw the curiosity enshrined in my all too open face and shouted, "You're American, of course! And wondering what we're up to? Do you trust my looks? Would you bet as I told you on a sporting event of great local consequence? If 'Yes' is your answer, come here!"

So I strolled my Guinness the length of the Four Provinces to join the shouting men, as one violinist gave up destroying a tune and the pianist hurried over, bringing his chorus with him.

"Name's Timulty!" The little man took my hand.

"Douglas," I said. "I write for the cinema."

"Fillums!" cried everyone.

"Films," I admitted modestly.

"What luck! Beyond belief!" Timulty seized me tighter. "You'll be the best judge ever, as well as bet! Are you much for sports? Do you know, for instance, the cross-country, the four-forty, and such man-on-foot excursions?"

"I've witnessed two Olympic Games."

"Not just fillums, but the world competition!" Timulty gasped. "You're the rare one. Well, now what do you know of the special all-Irish decathlon event which has to do with picture theaters?"

"What event is that?"

"What indeed! Hoolihan!"

An even littler fellow, pocketing his harmonica, leaped forward, smiling. "Hoolihan, that's me. The best Anthem Sprinter in all Ireland!"

"*What* sprinter?" I asked.

"A-n-t," spelled Hoolihan, much too carefully, "-h-e-m. Anthem. Sprinter. The fastest."

"Since you been in Dublin," Timulty cut in, "have you attended the cinema?"

"Last night," I said, "I saw a Clark Gable film. Night before, an old Charles Laughton—"

"Enough! You're a fanatic, as are all the Irish. If it weren't for cinemas and pubs to keep the poor and workless off the street or in their cups, we'd have pulled the cork and let the isle sink long ago. Well." He clapped his hands. "When the picture ends each night, have you observed a peculiarity of the breed?"

"End of the picture?" I mused. "Hold on! You can't mean the national anthem, can you?"

"*Can* we, boys?" cried Timulty.

"We can!" cried all.

"Any night, every night, for tens of dreadful years, at the end of each damn fillum, as if you'd never heard the baleful tune before," grieved Timulty, "the orchestra strikes up for Ireland. And what happens *then?*"

"Why," said I, falling in with it, "if you're any man at all, you try to get out of the theater in those few precious moments between the end of the film and the start of the anthem."

"You've nailed it!"

"Buy the Yank a drink!"

"After all," I said casually, "I'm in Dublin four months now. The anthem has begun to pale. No disrespect meant," I added hastily.

"And none taken!" said Timulty. "Or given by any of us patriotic IRA veterans, survivors of the Troubles and lovers of country. Still, breathing the same air ten thousand times makes the senses reel. So, as you've noted, in that God-sent three- or four-second interval any audience in its right mind beats it the hell out. And the best of the crowd is—"

"Doone," I said. "Or Hoolihan. Your Anthem Sprinters!"

They smiled at me. I smiled at them.

We were all so proud of my intuition that I bought them a round of Guinness.

Licking the suds from our lips, we regarded each other with benevolence.

"Now," said Timulty, his voice husky with emotion, his eyes squinted off at the scene, "at this very moment, not one hundred yards down the slight hill, in the comfortable dark of the Grafton Street Theatre, seated on the aisle of the fourth row center is—"

"Doone," said I.

"The man's eerie," said Hoolihan, lifting his cap to me.

"Well"— Timulty swallowed his disbelief—"Doone's there all right. He's not seen the fillum before, it's a Deanna Durbin brought back by the asking, and the time is now . . . "

Everyone glanced at the wall clock.

"Ten o'clock!" said the crowd.

"And in just fifteen minutes the cinema will be letting the customers out for good and all."

"And?" I asked.

"And," said Timulty. "And! If we should send Hoolihan here in for a test of speed and agility, Doone would be ready to meet the challenge."

"He didn't go to the show just for an Anthem Sprint, did he?"

"Good grief, no. He went for the Deanna Durbin songs and all. Doone plays the piano here, for sustenance. But if he should casually note the entrance of Hoolihan here, who would make himself conspicuous by his late arrival just across from Doone, well, Doone would know what was up. They would salute each other and both sit listening to the dear music until FINIS hove in sight."

"Sure." Hoolihan danced lightly on his toes, flexing his elbows. "Let me at him, let me *at* him!"

Timulty peered close at me. "Mr. Douglas, I observe your disbelief. The details of the sport have bewildered you. How is it, you ask, that full-grown men have time for such as this? Well, time is the one thing the Irish have plenty of lying about. With no jobs at hand, what's minor in your country must be made to look major in ours. We have never seen the elephant, but we've learned a bug under a microscope is the greatest beast on earth. So while it hasn't passed the border, the Anthem Sprint's a high-blooded sport once you're in it. Let me nail down the rules!"

"First," said Hoolihan reasonably, "knowing what he knows now, find out if the man wants to bet."

Everyone looked at me to see if their reasoning had been wasted.

"Yes," I said.

All agreed I was better than a human being.

"Introductions are in order," said Timulty. "Here's Fogarty, exit-watcher supreme. Nolan and Clannery, aisle-superintendent judges. Clancy, timekeeper. And general spectators O'Neill, Bannion and the Kelly boys, count 'em! Come on!"

I felt as if a vast street-cleaning machine, one of those brambled monsters all mustache and scouring brush, had seized me. The amiable mob floated me down the hill toward the multiplicity of little blinking lights where the cinema lured us on. Hustling, Timulty shouted the essentials:

"Much depends on the character of the theater, of course!"

"Of course!" I yelled back.

"There be the liberal free-thinking theaters with grand aisles, grand exits and even grander, more spacious latrines. Some with so much porcelain, the echoes alone put you in shock. Then there's the parsimonious mousetrap cinemas with aisles that squeeze the breath from you, seats that knock your knees, and doors best sidled out of on your way to the men's lounge in the sweet shop across the alley. Each theater is carefully assessed, before, during and after a sprint, the facts set down. A man is judged then, and his time reckoned good or inglorious, by whether he had to fight his way through men and women *en masse*, or mostly men, mostly women, or, the worst, children at the flypaper matinees. The temptation with children, of course, is to lay into them as you'd harvest hay, tossing them in windrows to left and right, so we've stopped that. Now mostly it's nights here at the Grafton!"

The mob stopped. The twinkling theater lights sparkled in our eyes and flushed our cheeks.

"The ideal cinema," said Fogarty.

"Why?" I asked.

"Its aisles," said Clannery, "are neither too wide nor too narrow, its exits well placed, the door hinges oiled, the crowds a proper mixture of sporting bloods and folks who mind enough to leap aside should a Sprinter, squandering his energy, come dashing up the aisle."

I had a sudden thought. "Do you—handicap your runners?"

"We do! Sometimes by shifting exits when the old are known too well. Or we put a summer coat on one, a winter coat on another. Or seat one chap in the sixth row, while the other takes the third. And if a man turns terrible feverish swift, we add the greatest known burden of all—"

"Drink?" I said.

"What else? Now, Doone, being fleet, is a two-handicap man. Nolan!" Timulty held forth a flask. "Run this in. Make Doone take two swigs, big ones."

Nolan ran.

Timulty pointed. "While Hoolihan here, having already gone through all Four Provinces of the pub this night, is amply weighted. Even all!"

"Go now, Hoolihan," said Fogarty. "Let our money be a light burden on you. We'll see you bursting out that exit five minutes from now, victorious and first!"

"Let's synchronize watches!" said Clancy.

"Synchronize my back-behind," said Timulty. "Which of us has more than dirty wrists to stare at? It's you alone, Clancy, has the time. Hoolihan, inside!"

Hoolihan shook hands with us all, as if leaving for a trip around the world. Then, waving, he vanished into the cinema darkness.

At which moment, Nolan burst back out, holding high the half-empty flask. "Doone's handicapped!"

"Fine! Clannery, go check the contestants, be sure they sit opposite each other in the fourth row, as agreed, caps on, coats half buttoned, scarves properly furled. Report back to me."

Clannery ran into the dark.

"The usher, the ticket taker?" I said.

"Are inside, watching the fillum," said Timulty. "So much standing is hard on the feet. They won't interfere."

"It's ten-thirteen," announced Clancy. "In two more minutes—"

"Post time," I said.

"You're a dear lad," admitted Timulty.

Clannery came hot-footing out.

"All set! In the right seats and everything!"

" 'Tis almost over! You can tell—toward the end of any fillum the music has a way of getting out of hand."

"It's loud, all right," agreed Clannery. "Full orchestra and chorus behind the singing maid now. I must come tomorrow for the entirety. Lovely."

"Is it?" said Clancy, and the others.

"What's the tune?"

"Ah, off with the tune!" said Timulty. "One minute to go and you ask the tune! Lay the bets. Who's for Doone? Who Hoolihan?" There was a multitudinous jabbering and passing back and forth of money, mostly shillings.

I held out four shillings.

"Doone," I said.

"Without having seen him?"

"A dark horse," I whispered.

"Well said!" Timulty spun about. "Clannery, Nolan, inside, as aisle judges! Watch sharp there's no jumping the FINIS."

In went Clannery and Nolan, happy as boys.

"Make an aisle, now. Mr. Douglas, you over here with me!"

The men rushed to form an aisle on each side of the two closed main entrance-exit doors.

"Fogarty, lay your ear to the door!"

This Fogarty did. His eyes widened.

"The damn music is extra loud!"

One of the Kelly boys nudged his brother. "It will be over soon. Whoever is to die is dying this moment. Whoever is to live is bending over him."

"Louder still!" announced Fogarty, head up against the door panel, hands twitching as if he were adjusting a radio. "There! That's the grand *ta-ta* for sure that comes just as FINIS or THE END jumps on the screen."

"They're off!" I murmured.

"Stand!" said Timulty.

We all stared at the door.

"There's the anthem!"

" 'Tenshun!"

We all stood erect. Someone saluted.

But still we stared at the door.

"I hear feet running," said Fogarty.

"Whoever it is had a good start before the anthem—"

The door burst wide.

Hoolihan plunged to view, smiling such a smile as only breathless victors know.

"Hoolihan!" cried the winners.

"Doone!" cried the losers. "Where's Doone?"

For, while Hoolihan was first, a competitor was lacking.

The crowd was dispersing into the street now.

"The idiot didn't come out the wrong door?"

We waited. The crowd was soon gone.

Timulty ventured first into the empty lobby.

"Doone?"

No one there.

"Could it be he's in *there?*"

Someone flung the men's room door wide. "Doone?"

No echo, no answer.

"Good grief," cried Timulty, "it can't be he's broken a leg and lies on the slope somewhere with the mortal agonies?"

"That's it!"

The island of men, heaving one way, changed gravities and heaved the other, toward the inner door, through it, and down the aisle, myself following.

"Doone!"

Clannery and Nolan were there to meet us and pointed silently down. I jumped into the air twice to see over the mob's head. It was dim in the vast theater. I saw nothing.

"Doone!"

Then at last we were bunched together near the fourth row on the aisle. I heard their boggled exclamations as they saw what I saw:

Doone, still seated in the fourth row on the aisle, his hands folded, his eyes shut.

Dead?

None of that.

A tear, large, luminous and beautiful, fell on his cheek. Another tear, larger and more lustrous, emerged from his other eye. His chin was wet. It was certain he had been crying for some minutes.

The men peered into his face, circling, leaning.

"Doone, are ya sick?"

"Is it fearful news?"

"Ah, God," cried Doone. He shook himself to find the strength, somehow, to speak.

"Ah, God," he said at last, "she has the voice of an angel."

"Angel?"

"That one up there." He nodded.

They turned to stare at the empty silver screen.

"Is it Deanna Durbin?"

Doone sobbed. "The dear dead voice of my grandmother come back—"

"Your grandma's behind!" exclaimed Timulty. "She had no such voice as that!"

"And who's to know, save me?" Doone blew his nose, dabbed at his eyes.

"You mean to say it was just the Durbin lass kept you from the sprint?"

"Just!" said Doone. "Just! Why, it would be sacrilege to bound from a cinema after a recital like that. You might also then jump full tilt across the altar during a wedding, or waltz about at a funeral."

"You could've at least warned us it was no contest." Timulty glared.

"How could I? It just crept over me in a divine sickness. That last bit she sang, 'The Lovely Isle of Innisfree,' was it not, Clannery?"

"What else did she sing?" asked Fogarty.

"What else did she sing?" cried Timulty. "He's just lost half of us our day's wages and you ask what else she sang! Get off!"

"Sure, it's money runs the world," Doone agreed, seated there, closing up his eyes. "But it is music that holds down the friction."

"What's going on there?" cried someone above.

A man leaned down from the balcony, puffing a cigarette. "What's all the rouse?"

"It's the projectionist," whispered Timulty. Aloud: "Hello, Phil, darling! It's only the Team! We've a bit of a problem here, Phil, in ethics, not to say aesthetics. Now, we wonder if, well, could it be possible to run the anthem over."

"Run it over?"

There was a rumble from the winners, a mixing and shoving of elbows.

"A lovely idea," said Doone.

"It is," said Timulty, all guile. "An act of God incapacitated Doone."

"A tenth-run flicker from the year 1937 caught him by the short hairs is all," said Fogarty.

"So the fair thing is"— here Timulty, unperturbed, looked to heaven— "Phil, dear boy, also is the last reel of the Deanna Durbin fillum still there?"

"It ain't in the ladies' room," said Phil, smoking steadily.

"What a wit the boy has. Now, Phil, do you think you could just thread it back through the machine there and give us the FINIS again?"

"Is that what you all want?" asked Phil.

There was a hard moment of indecision. But the thought of another contest was too good to be passed, even though already-won money was at stake. Slowly everyone nodded.

"I'll bet myself, then," Phil called down. "A shilling on Hoolihan!"

The winners laughed and hooted; they looked to win again. Hoolihan waved graciously. The losers turned on their man.

"Do you hear the insult, Doone? Stay awake, man!"

"When the girl sings, damn it, go deaf!"

"Places, everyone!" Timulty jostled about.

"There's no audience," said Hoolihan. "And without them there's no obstacles, no real contest."

"Why"—Fogarty blinked around—"let's all of us be the audience."

"Fine!" Beaming, everyone threw himself into a seat.

"Better yet," announced Timulty, up front, "why not make it teams? Doone and Hoolihan, sure, but for every Doone man or Hoolihan man that makes it out before the anthem freezes him on his hobnails, an extra point, right?"

"Done!" cried everyone.

"Pardon," I said. "There's no one outside to judge."

Everyone turned to look at me.

"Ah," said Timulty. "Well. Nolan, outside!"

Nolan trudged up the aisle, cursing.

Phil stuck his head from the projection booth above.

"Are ya clods down there ready?"

"If the girl is and the anthem is!"

And the lights went out.

I found myself seated next in from Doone, who whispered fervently, "Poke me, lad, keep me alert to practicalities instead of ornamentation, eh?"

"Shut up!" said someone. "There's the mystery."

And there indeed it was, the mystery of song and art and life, if you will, the young girl singing on the time-haunted screen.

"We lean on you, Doone," I whispered.

"Eh?" he replied. He smiled ahead. "Ah, look, ain't she lovely? Do you hear?"

"The bet, Doone," I said. "Get ready."

"All right," he groused. "Let me stir my bones. Jesus save me."

"What?"

"I never thought to test. My right leg. Feel. Naw, you can't. It's dead, it is!"

"Asleep, you mean?" I said, appalled.

"Dead or asleep, hell, I'm sunk! Lad, lad, you must run for me! Here's my cap and scarf!"

"Your cap—?"

"When victory is yours, show them, and we'll explain you ran to replace this fool leg of mine!"

He clapped the cap on, tied the scarf.

"But look here—" I protested.

"You'll do brave! Just remember, it's FINIS and no sooner! The song's almost up. Are you tensed?"

"God, *am* I!" I said.

"It's blind passions that win, boy. Plunge straight. If you step on someone, do not look back. There!" Doone held his legs to one side to give clearance. "The song's done. He's kissing her—"

"The FINIS!" I cried.

I leaped into the aisle.

I ran up the slope. I'm first! I thought. I'm ahead! It can't be! There's the door!

I hit the door as the anthem began.

I slammed into the lobby—safe!

I won! I thought, incredulous, with Doone's cap and scarf like victory laurels upon and about me. Won! Won for the Team!

Who's second, third, fourth?

I turned to the door as it swung shut.

Only then did I hear the shouts and yells inside.

Good Lord! I thought, six men have tried the wrong exit at once, someone tripped, fell, someone else piled on. Otherwise, why am I the first and only? There's a fierce silent combat in there this second, the two teams locked in mortal wrestling attitudes, asprawl, akimbo, above and below the seats, that *must* be it!

I've won! I wanted to yell, to break it up.

I threw the door wide.

I stared into an abyss where nothing stirred.

Nolan came to peer over my shoulder.

"That's the Irish for you," he said, nodding. "Even more than the race, it's the Muse they like."

For what were the voices yelling in the dark?

"Run it again! Over! That last song! Phil!"

"No one move. I'm in heaven. Doone, how right you were!"

Nolan passed me, going in to sit.

I stood for a long moment looking down along at all the rows where the teams of Anthem Sprinters sat, none having stirred, wiping their eyes.

"Phil, darling?" called Timulty, somewhere up front.

"It's done!" said Phil.

"And this time," added Timulty, "*without* the anthem."

Applause for this.

The dim lights flashed off. The screen glowed like a great warm hearth.

I looked back out at the bright sane world of Grafton Street, the Four Provinces pub, the hotels, shops and night-wandering folk. I hesitated.

Then, to the tune of "The Lovely Isle of Innisfree," I took off the cap and scarf, hid these laurels under a seat, and slowly, luxuriously, with all the time in the world, sat myself down. . . .

And So Died Riabouchinska

The cellar was cold cement and the dead man was cold stone and the air was filled with an invisible fall of rain, while the people gathered to look at the body as if it had been washed in on an empty shore at morning. The gravity of the earth was drawn to a focus here in this single basement room—a gravity so immense that it pulled their faces down, bent their mouths at the corners and drained their cheeks. Their hands hung weighted and their feet were planted so they could not move without seeming to walk underwater.

A voice was calling, but nobody listened.

The voice called again and only after a long time did the people turn and look, momentarily, into the air. They were at the seashore in November and this was a gull crying over their heads in the gray color of dawn. It was a sad crying, like the birds going south for the steel winter to come. It was an ocean sounding the shore so far away that it was only a whisper of sand and wind in a seashell.

The people in the basement room shifted their gaze to a table and a golden box resting there, no more than twenty-four inches long, inscribed with the name RIABOUCHINSKA. Under the lid of this small coffin the voice at last settled with finality, and the people stared at the box, and the dead man lay on the floor, not hearing the soft cry.

"Let me out, let me out, oh, please, please, someone let me out."

And finally Mr. Fabian, the ventriloquist, bent and whispered to the golden box, "No, Ria, this is serious business. Later. Be quiet, now, that's a good girl." He shut his eyes and tried to laugh.

From under the polished lid her calm voice said, "Please don't laugh. You should be much kinder now after what's happened."

Detective Lieutenant Krovitch touched Fabian's arm. "If you don't mind, we'll save your dummy act for later. Right now there's all *this* to clean up." He glanced at the woman, who had now taken a folding chair. "Mrs. Fabian." He nodded to the young man sitting next to her. "Mr. Douglas, you're Mr. Fabian's press agent and manager?"

The young man said he was. Krovitch looked at the face of the man on the floor. "Fabian, Mrs. Fabian, Mr. Douglas—all of you say you don't know this man who was murdered here last night, never heard the name Ockham before.

Yet Ockham earlier told the stage manager he knew Fabian and had to see him about something vitally important."

The voice in the box began again quietly.

Krovitch shouted. "*Damn* it, Fabian!"

Under the lid, the voice laughed. It was like a muffled bell ringing.

"Pay no attention to her, Lieutenant," said Fabian.

"Her? Or *you*, damn it! What is this? Get together, you two!"

"We'll never be together," said the quiet voice, "never again after tonight."

Krovitch put out his hand. "Give me the key, Fabian."

In the silence there was the rattle of the key in the small lock, the squeal of the miniature hinges as the lid was opened and laid back against the table top.

"Thank you," said Riabouchinska.

Krovitch stood motionless, just looking down and seeing Riabouchinska in her box and not quite believing what he saw.

The face was white and it was cut from marble or from the whitest wood he had ever seen. It might have been cut from snow. And the neck that held the head which was as dainty as a porcelain cup with the sun shining through the thinness of it, the neck was also white. And the hands could have been ivory and they were thin small things with tiny fingernails and whorls on the pads of the fingers, little delicate spirals and lines.

She was all white stone, with light pouring through the stone and light coming out of the dark eyes with blue tones beneath like fresh mulberries. He was reminded of milk glass and of cream poured into a crystal tumbler. The brows were arched and black and thin and the cheeks were hollowed and there was a faint pink vein in each temple and a faint blue vein barely visible above the slender bridge of the nose, between the shining dark eyes.

Her lips were half parted and it looked as if they might be slightly damp, and the nostrils were arched and modeled perfectly, as were the ears. The hair was black and it was parted in the middle and drawn back of the ears and it was real—he could see every single strand of hair. Her gown was as black as her hair and draped in such a fashion as to show her shoulders, which were carved wood as white as a stone that has lain a long time in the sun. She was very beautiful. Krovitch felt his throat move and then he stopped and did not say anything.

Fabian took Riabouchinska from her box. "My lovely lady," he said. "Carved from the rarest imported woods. She's appeared in Paris, Rome, Istanbul. Everyone in the world loves her and thinks she's really human, some sort of incredibly delicate midget creature. They won't accept that she was once part of many forests growing far away from cities and idiotic people."

Fabian's wife, Alyce, watched her husband, not taking her eyes from his mouth. Her eyes did not blink once in all the time he was telling of the doll he held in his arms. He in turn seemed aware of no one but the doll; the cellar and its people were lost in a mist that settled everywhere.

But finally the small figure stirred and quivered. "Please, don't talk about me! You know Alyce doesn't like it."

"Alyce never has liked it."

"Shh, don't!" cried Riabouchinska. "Not here, not now." And then, swiftly, she turned to Krovitch and her tiny lips moved. "How did it all happen? Mr. Ockham, I mean, Mr. Ockham."

Fabian said, "You'd better go to sleep now, Ria."

"But I don't want to," she replied. "I've as much right to listen and talk, I'm as much a part of this murder as Alyce or—or Mr. Douglas even!"

The press agent threw down his cigarette. "Don't drag me into this, you—" And he looked at the doll as if it had suddenly become six feet tall and were breathing there before him.

"It's just that I want the truth to be told." Riabouchinska turned her head to see all of the room. "And if I'm locked in my coffin there'll be no truth, for John's a consummate liar and I must watch after him, isn't that right, John?"

"Yes," he said, his eyes shut, "I suppose it is."

"John loves me best of all the women in the world and I love him and try to understand his wrong way of thinking."

Krovitch hit the table with his fist. "God damn, oh, God *damn* it, Fabian! If you think you can—"

"I'm helpless," said Fabian.

"But she's—"

"I know, I know what you want to say," said Fabian quietly, looking at the detective. "She's in my throat, is that it? No, no. She's not in my throat. She's somewhere else. I don't know. Here, or here." He touched his chest, his head.

"She's quick to hide. Sometimes there's nothing I can do. Sometimes she is only herself, nothing of me at all. Sometimes she tells me what to do and I must do it. She stands guard, she reprimands me, is honest where I am dishonest, good when I am wicked as all the sins that ever were. She lives a life apart. She's raised a wall in my head and lives there, ignoring me if I try to make her say improper things, co-operating if I suggest the right words and pantomime." Fabian sighed. "So if you intend going on I'm afraid Ria must be present. Locking her up will do no good, no good at all."

Lieutenant Krovitch sat silently for the better part of a minute, then made his decision. "All right. Let her stay. It just may be, by God, that before the night's over I'll be tired enough to ask even a ventriloquist's dummy questions."

Krovitch unwrapped a fresh cigar, lit it and puffed smoke. "So you don't recognize the dead man, Mr. Douglas?"

"He looks vaguely familiar. Could be an actor."

Krovitch swore. "Let's all stop lying, what do you say? Look at Ockham's shoes, his clothing. It's obvious he needed money and came here tonight to beg, borrow or steal some. Let me ask you this, Douglas. Are you in love with Mrs. Fabian?"

"Now, wait just a moment!" cried Alyce Fabian.

Krovitch motioned her down. "You sit there, side by side, the two of you. I'm not exactly blind. When a press agent sits where the husband should be sitting, consoling the wife, well! The way you look at the marionette's coffin, Mrs. Fabian, holding your breath when she appears. You make fists when she talks. Hell, you're obvious."

"If you think for one moment I'm jealous of a stick of wood!"

"Aren't you?"

"No, no, I'm not!"

Fabian moved. "You needn't tell him anything, Alyce."

"Let her!"

They all jerked their heads and stared at the small figurine, whose mouth was now slowly shutting. Even Fabian looked at the marionette as if it had struck him a blow.

After a long while Alyce Fabian began to speak.

"I married John seven years ago because he said he loved me and because I loved him and I loved Riabouchinska. At first, anyway. But then I began to see that he really lived all of his life and paid most of his attentions to her and I was a shadow waiting in the wings every night.

"He spent fifty thousand dollars a year on her wardrobe—a hundred thousand dollars for a dollhouse with gold and silver and platinum furniture. He tucked her in a small satin bed each night and talked to her. I thought it was all an elaborate joke at first and I was wonderfully amused. But when it finally came to me that I was indeed merely an assistant in his act I began to feel a vague sort of hatred and distrust—not for the marionette, because after all it wasn't her doing, but I felt a terrible growing dislike and hatred for John, because it *was* his fault. He, after all, was the control, and all of his cleverness and natural sadism came out through his relationship with the wooden doll.

"And when I finally became very jealous, how silly of me! It was the greatest tribute I could have paid him and the way he had gone about perfecting the art of throwing his voice. It was all so idiotic, it was all so strange. And yet I knew that something had hold of John, just as people who drink have a hungry animal somewhere in them, starving to death.

"So I moved back and forth from anger to pity, from jealousy to understanding. There were long periods when I didn't hate him at all, and I never hated the thing that Ria was in him, for she was the best half, the good part, the honest and the lovely part of him. She was everything that he never let himself try to be."

Alyce Fabian stopped talking and the basement room was silent.

"Tell about Mr. Douglas," said a voice, whispering.

Mrs. Fabian did not look up at the marionette. With an effort she finished it out. "When the years passed and there was so little love and understanding from John, I guess it was natural I turned to—Mr. Douglas."

Krovitch nodded. "Everything begins to fall into place. Mr. Ockham was a very poor man, down on his luck, and he came to this theater tonight because he knew something about you and Mr. Douglas. Perhaps he threatened to speak to Mr. Fabian if you didn't buy him off. That would give you the best of reasons to get rid of him."

"That's even sillier than all the rest," said Alyce Fabian tiredly. "I didn't kill him."

"Mr. Douglas might have and not told you."

"Why kill a man?" said Douglas. "John knew all about us."

"I did indeed," said John Fabian, and laughed.

He stopped laughing and his hand twitched, hidden in the snowflake interior of the tiny doll, and her mouth opened and shut, opened and shut. He was trying to make her carry the laughter on after he had stopped, but there was no sound, save the little empty whisper of her lips moving and gasping, while Fabian stared down at the little face and perspiration came out, shining, upon his cheeks.

The next afternoon Lieutenant Krovitch moved through the theater darkness backstage, found the iron stairs and climbed with great thought, taking as much time as he deemed necessary on each step, up to the second-level dressing rooms. He rapped on one of the thin-paneled doors.

"Come in," said Fabian's voice from what seemed a great distance.

Krovitch entered and closed the door and stood looking at the man who was slumped before his dressing mirror. "I have something I'd like to show you," Krovitch said. His face showing no emotion whatever, he opened a manila folder and pulled out a glossy photograph, which he placed on the dressing table.

John Fabian raised his eyebrows, glanced quickly up at Krovitch and then settled slowly back in his chair. He put his fingers to the bridge of his nose and massaged his face carefully, as if he had a headache. Krovitch turned the picture over and began to read from the typewritten data on the back. "Name, Miss Ilyana Riamonova. One hundred pounds. Blue eyes. Black hair. Oval face. Born 1914, New York City. Disappeared 1934. Believed a victim of amnesia. Of Russo-Slav parentage. Etcetera. Etcetera."

Fabian's lip twitched.

Krovitch laid the photograph down, shaking his head thoughtfully. "It was pretty silly of me to go through police files for a picture of a marionette. You should have heard the laughter at headquarters. *God.* Still, here she is— Riabouchinska. *Not* papier-mâché, *not* wood, *not* a puppet, but a woman who once lived and moved around and—disappeared." He looked steadily at Fabian. "Suppose you take it from there?"

Fabian half smiled. "There's nothing to it at all. I saw this woman's picture a long time ago, liked her looks and copied my marionette after her."

"Nothing to it at all." Krovitch took a deep breath and exhaled, wiping his face with a huge handkerchief. "Fabian, this very morning I shuffled through a stack of *Billboard* magazines that high. In the year 1934 I found an interesting article concerning an act which played on a second-rate circuit, known as Fabian and Sweet William. Sweet William was a little boy dummy. There was a girl assistant—Ilyana Riamonova. No picture of her in the article, but I at least had a name, the name of a real person, to go on. It was simple to check police files then and dig up this picture. The resemblance, needless to say, between the live woman on one hand and the puppet on the other is nothing short of incredible. Suppose you go back and tell your story over again, Fabian."

"She was my assistant, that's all. I simply used her as a model."

"You're making me sweat," said the detective. "Do you think I'm a fool? Do you think I don't know love when I see it? I've watched you handle the marionette, I've seen you talk to it, I've seen how you make it react to you. You're in love with the puppet naturally, because you loved the original woman very, very much. I've lived too long not to sense that. Hell, Fabian, stop fencing around."

Fabian lifted his pale slender hands, turned them over, examined them and let them fall.

"All right. In 1934 I was billed as Fabian and Sweet William. Sweet William was a small bulb-nosed boy dummy I carved a long time ago. I was in Los Angeles when this girl appeared at the stage door one night. She'd followed my work for years. She was desperate for a job and she hoped to be my assistant. . . . "

He remembered her in the half light of the alley behind the theatre and how startled he was at her freshness and eagerness to work with and for him and the way the cool rain touched softly down through the narrow alleyway and caught in small spangles through her hair, melting in dark warmness, and the rain beaded upon her white porcelain hand holding her coat together at her neck.

He saw her lips' motion in the dark and her voice, separated off on another sound track, it seemed, speaking to him in the autumn wind, and he remembered that without his saying yes or no or perhaps she was suddenly on the stage with him, in the great pouring bright light, and in two months he, who had always prided himself on his cynicism and disbelief, had stepped off the rim of the world after her, plunging down a bottomless place of no limit and no light anywhere.

Arguments followed, and more than arguments—things said and done that lacked all sense and sanity and fairness. She had edged away from him at last, causing his rages and remarkable hysterias. Once he burned her entire wardrobe in a fit of jealousy. She had taken this quietly. But then one night he handed her a week's notice, accused her of monstrous disloyalty, shouted at her, seized her, slapped her again and again across the face, bullied her about and thrust her out the door, slamming it!

She disappeared that night.

When he found the next day that she was really gone and there was nowhere to find her, it was like standing in the center of a titanic explosion. All the world was smashed flat and all the echoes of the explosion came back to reverberate at midnight, at four in the morning, at dawn, and he was up early, stunned with the sound of coffee simmering and the sound of matches being struck and cigarettes lit and himself trying to shave and looking at mirrors that were sickening in their distortion.

He clipped out all the advertisements that he took in the papers and pasted them in neat rows in a scrapbook—all the ads describing her and telling about her and asking for her back. He even put a private detective on the case. People talked. The police dropped by to question him. There was more talk.

But she was gone like a piece of white incredibly fragile tissue paper, blown over the sky and down. A record of her was sent to the largest cities, and that was the end of it for the police. But not for Fabian. She might be dead or just running away, but wherever she was he knew that somehow and in some way he would have her back.

One night he came home, bringing his own darkness with him, and collapsed upon a chair, and before he knew it he found himself speaking to Sweet William in the totally black room.

"William, it's all over and done. I can't keep it up!"

And William cried, "Coward! Coward!" from the air above his head, out of the emptiness. "You can get her back if you want!"

Sweet William squeaked and clappered at him in the night. "Yes, you can! *Think!*" he insisted. "Think of a way. You can do it. Put me aside, lock me up. Start all over."

"Start all over?"

"Yes," whispered Sweet William, and darkness moved within darkness. "Yes. Buy wood. Buy fine new wood. Buy hard-grained wood. Buy beautiful fresh new wood. And carve. Carve slowly and carve carefully. Whittle away. Cut delicately. Make the little nostrils so. And cut her thin black eyebrows round and high, so, and make her cheeks in small hollows. Carve, carve . . . "

"No! It's foolish. I could never do it!"

"Yes, you could. Yes you could, could, could, could . . . "

The voice faded, a ripple of water in an underground stream. The stream rose up and swallowed him. His head fell forward. Sweet William sighed. And then the two of them lay like stones buried under a waterfall.

The next morning, John Fabian bought the hardest, finest-grained piece of wood that he could find and brought it home and laid it on the table, but could not touch it. He sat for hours staring at it. It was impossible to think that out of this cold chunk of material he expected his hands and his memory to re-create something warm and pliable and familiar. There was no way even faintly to approximate that quality of rain and summer and the first powderings of snow upon a clear pane of glass in the middle of a December night. No way, no way at all to catch the snowflake without having it melt swiftly in your clumsy fingers.

And yet Sweet William spoke out, sighing and whispering, after midnight, "You can do it. Oh, yes, yes, you can do it!"

And so he began. It took him an entire month to carve her hands into things as natural and beautiful as shells lying in the sun. Another month and the skeleton, like a fossil imprint he was searching out, stamped and hidden in the wood, was revealed, all febrile and so infinitely delicate as to suggest the veins in the white flesh of an apple.

And all the while Sweet William lay mantled in dust in his box that was fast becoming a very real coffin. Sweet William croaking and wheezing some feeble sarcasm, some sour criticism, some hint, some help, but dying all the time, fading, soon to be untouched, soon to be like a sheath molted in summer and left behind to blow in the wind.

As the weeks passed and Fabian molded and scraped and polished the new wood, Sweet William lay longer and longer in stricken silence, and one day as Fabian held the puppet in his hand Sweet William seemed to look at him a moment with puzzled eyes and then there was a death rattle in his throat.

And Sweet William was gone.

Now as he worked, a fluttering, a faint motion of speech began far back in his throat, echoing and re-echoing, speaking silently like a breeze among dry leaves. And then for the first time he held the doll in a certain way in his hands and memory moved down his arms and into his fingers and from his fingers into the hollowed wood and the tiny hands flickered and the body became suddenly soft and pliable and her eyes opened and looked up at him.

And the small mouth opened the merest fraction of an inch and she was ready to speak and he knew all of the things that she must say to him, he knew the first and the second and the third things he would have her say. There was a whisper, a whisper, a whisper.

The tiny head turned this way gently, that way gently. The mouth half opened again and began to speak. And as it spoke he bent his head and he could feel the warm breath—of *course* it was there!—coming from her mouth, and when he listened very carefully, holding her to his head, his eyes shut, wasn't *it* there, too, softly, *gently*—the beating of her heart?

Krovitch sat in a chair for a full minute after Fabian stopped talking. Finally he said, "I *see*. And your wife?"

"Alyce? She was my second assistant, of course. She worked very hard and, God help her, she loved me. It's hard now to know why I ever married her. It was unfair of me."

"What about the dead man—Ockham?"

"I never saw him before you showed me his body in the theater basement yesterday."

"Fabian," said the detective.

"It's the truth!"

"Fabian."

"The truth, the truth, damn it, I swear it's the truth!"

"The truth." There was a whisper like the sea coming in on the gray shore at early morning. The water was ebbing in a fine lace on the sand. The sky was cold and empty. There were no people on the shore. The sun was gone. And the whisper said again, "The truth."

Fabian sat up straight and took hold of his knees with his thin hands. His face was rigid. Krovitch found himself making the same motion he had made the day before—looking at the gray ceiling as if it were a November sky and a lonely bird going over and away, gray within the cold grayness.

"The truth." Fading. "The truth."

Krovitch lifted himself and moved as carefully as he could to the far side of the dressing room where the golden box lay open and inside the box the thing that whispered and talked and could laugh sometimes and could sometimes sing. He carried the golden box over and set it down in front of Fabian and waited for him to put his living hand within the gloved delicate hollowness, waited for the fine small mouth to quiver and the eyes to focus. He did not have to wait long.

"The first letter came a month ago."

"No."

"The first letter came a month ago."

"No, *no!*"

"The letter said, 'Riabouchinska, born 1914, died 1934. Born again in 1935.' Mr. Ockham was a juggler. He'd been on the same bill with John and Sweet William years before. He remembered that once there had been a woman, before there was a puppet."

"No, that's not true!"

"Yes," said the voice.

Snow was falling in silences and even deeper silences through the dressing room. Fabian's mouth trembled. He stared at the blank walls as if seeking some new door by which to escape. He half rose from his chair. "Please . . ."

"Ockham threatened to tell about us to everyone in the world."

Krovitch saw the doll quiver, saw the fluttering of the lips, saw Fabian's eyes widen and fix and his throat convulse and tighten as if to stop the whispering.

"I—I was in the room when Mr. Ockham came. I lay in my box and I listened and heard, and I *know*." The voice blurred, then recovered and went on. "Mr. Ockham threatened to tear me up, burn me into ashes if John didn't pay him a thousand dollars. Then suddenly there was a falling sound. A cry. Mr. Ockham's head must have struck the floor. I heard John cry out and I heard him swearing, I heard him sobbing. I heard a gasping and a choking sound."

"You heard nothing! You're deaf, you're blind! You're wood!" cried Fabian.

"But I *hear!*" she said, and stopped as if someone had put a hand to her mouth.

Fabian had leaped to his feet now and stood with the doll in his hand. The mouth clapped twice, three times, then finally made words. "The choking sound stopped. I heard John drag Mr. Ockham down the stairs under the theater to the old dressing rooms that haven't been used in years. Down, down, down, I heard them going away and away—down . . . "

Krovitch stepped back as if he were watching a motion picture that had suddenly grown monstrously tall. The figures terrified and frightened him, they were immense, they towered! They threatened to inundate him with size. Someone had turned up the sound so that it screamed.

He saw Fabian's teeth, a grimace, a whisper, a clenching. He saw the man's eyes squeeze shut.

Now the soft voice was so high and faint it trembled toward nothingness.

"I'm not made to live this way. This way. There's nothing for us now. Everyone will know, everyone will. Even when you killed him and I lay asleep last night, I dreamed. I knew, I realized. We both knew, we both realized that these would be our last days, our last hours. Because while I've lived with your weakness and I've lived with your lies, I can't live with something that kills and hurts in killing. There's no way to go on from here. How *can* I live alongside such knowledge? . . . "

Fabian held her into the sunlight which shone dimly through the small dressing-room window. She looked at him and there was nothing in her eyes. His hand shook and in shaking made the marionette tremble, too. Her mouth closed and opened, closed and opened, closed and opened, again and again and again. Silence.

Fabian moved his fingers unbelievingly to his own mouth. A film slid across his eyes. He looked like a man lost in the street, trying to remember the number of a certain house, trying to find a certain window with a certain light. He swayed about, staring at the walls, at Krovitch, at the doll, at his free hand, turning the fingers over, touching his throat, opening his mouth. He listened.

Miles away in a cave, a single wave came in from the sea and whispered down in foam. A gull moved soundlessly, not beating its wings—a shadow.

"She's gone. She's gone. I can't find her. She's run off. I can't find her. I can't find her. I try, I try, but she's run away off far. Will you help me? Will you help me find her? Will you help me find her? Will you please help me find her?"

Riabouchinska slipped bonelessly from his limp hand, folded over and glided noiselessly down to lie upon the cold floor, her eyes closed, her mouth shut.

Fabian did not look at her as Krovitch led him out the door.

Boys! Raise Giant Mushrooms in *Your* Cellar!

Hugh Fortnum woke to Saturday's commotions and lay, eyes shut, savoring each in its turn.

Below, bacon in a skillet; Cynthia waking him with fine cookings instead of cries.

Across the hall, Tom *actually* taking a shower.

Far off in the bumblebee dragonfly light, whose voice was already damning the weather, the time, and the tides? Mrs. Goodbody? Yes. That Christian giantess, six-foot tall with her shoes off, the gardener extraordinary, the octogenarian dietician and town philosopher.

He rose, unhooked the screen and leaned out to hear her cry, "There! Take *that*! *This'll* fix you! Hah!"

"Happy Saturday, Mrs. Goodbody!"

The old woman froze in clouds of bug spray pumped from an immense gun. "Nonsense!" she shouted. "With these fiends and pests to watch for?"

"What kind *this* time?" called Fortnum.

"I don't want to shout it to the jaybirds, but"—she glanced suspiciously around—"what would you say if I told you I was the first line of defense concerning flying saucers?"

"Fine," replied Fortnum. "There'll be rockets between the worlds any year now."

"There already *are*!" She pumped, aiming the spray under the hedge. "There! Take that!"

He pulled his head back in from the fresh day, somehow not as high-spirited as his first response had indicated. Poor soul, Mrs. Goodbody. Always the essence of reason. And now what? Old age?

The doorbell rang.

He grabbed his robe and was half down the stairs when he heard a voice say, "Special delivery. Fortnum?" and saw Cynthia turn from the front door, a small packet in her hand.

"Special-delivery airmail for your son."

Tom was downstairs like a centipede.

"Wow! That must be from the Great Bayou Novelty Greenhouse!"

"I wish I were as excited about ordinary mail," observed Fortnum.

"Ordinary?!" Tom ripped the cord and paper wildly. "Don't you read the back pages of *Popular Mechanics?* Well, here *they* are!"

Everyone peered into the small open box.

"Here," said Fortnum, "*what* are?"

"The Sylvan Glade Jumbo-Giant Guaranteed Growth Raise-Them-in-Your-Cellar-for-Big-Profit Mushrooms!"

"Oh, of course," said Fortnum. "How silly of me."

Cynthia squinted. "Those little teeny bits?"

" 'Fabulous growth in twenty-four hours,' " Tom quoted from memory. " 'Plant them in your cellar . . . ' "

Fortnum and wife exchanged glances.

"Well," she admitted, "it's better than frogs and green snakes."

"Sure is!" Tom ran.

"Oh, Tom," said Fortnum lightly.

Tom paused at the cellar door.

"Tom," said his father. "Next time, fourth-class mail would do fine."

"Heck," said Tom. "They must've made a mistake, thought I was some rich company. Airmail special, who can afford that?"

The cellar door slammed.

Fortnum, bemused, scanned the wrapper a moment then dropped it into the wastebasket. On his way to the kitchen, he opened the cellar door.

Tom was already on his knees, digging with a hand rake in the dirt.

He felt his wife beside him, breathing softly, looking down into the cool dimness.

"Those *are* mushrooms, I hope. Not . . . toadstools?"

Fortnum laughed. "Happy harvest, farmer!"

Tom glanced up and waved.

Fortnum shut the door, took his wife's arm and walked her out to the kitchen, feeling fine.

Toward noon, Fortnum was driving toward the nearest market when he saw Roger Willis, a fellow Rotarian and a teacher of biology at the town high school, waving urgently from the sidewalk.

Fortnum pulled his car up and opened the door.

"Hi, Roger, give you a lift?"

Willis responded all too eagerly, jumping in and slamming the door.

"Just the man I want to see. I've put off calling for days. Could you play psychiatrist for five minutes, God help you?"

Fortnum examined his friend for a moment as he drove quietly on.

"God help you, yes. Shoot."

Willis sat back and studied his fingernails. "Let's just drive a moment. There. Okay. Here's what I want to say: Something's wrong with the world."

Fortnum laughed easily. "Hasn't there always been?"

"No, no, I mean . . . something strange—something unseen—is happening."

"Mrs. Goodbody," said Fortnum, half to himself, and stopped.

"Mrs. Goodbody?"

"This morning, gave me a talk on flying saucers."

"No." Willis bit the knuckle of his forefinger nervously. "Nothing like saucers. At least, I don't think. Tell me, what exactly is intuition?"

"The conscious recognition of something that's been subconscious for a long time. But don't quote this amateur psychologist!" He laughed again.

"Good, good!" Willis turned, his face lighting. He readjusted himself in the seat. "That's it! Over a long period, things gather, right? All of a sudden, you have to spit, but you don't remember saliva collecting. Your hands are dirty, but you don't know how they got that way. Dust falls on you every day and you don't feel it. But when you get enough dust collected up, there it is, you see and name it. That's intuition, as far as I'm concerned. Well, what kind of dust has been falling on *me*? A few meteors in the sky at night? funny weather just before dawn? I don't know. Certain colors, smells, the way the house creaks at three in the morning? Hair prickling on my arms? All I know is, the damn dust has collected. Quite suddenly I know."

"Yes," said Fortnum, disquieted. "But what *is* it you know?"

Willis looked at his hands in his lap. "I'm afraid. I'm not afraid. Then I'm afraid again, in the middle of the day. Doctor's checked me. I'm A-one. No family problems. Joe's a fine boy, a good son. Dorothy? She's remarkable. With her I'm not afraid of growing old or dying."

"Lucky man."

"But beyond my luck now. Scared stiff, really, for myself, my family; even right now, for you."

"Me?" said Fortnum.

They had stopped now by an empty lot near the market. There was a moment of great stillness, in which Fortnum turned to survey his friend. Willis's voice had suddenly made him cold.

"I'm afraid for everybody," said Willis. "Your friends, mine, and their friends, on out of sight. Pretty silly, eh?"

Willis opened the door, got out and peered in at Fortnum.

Fortnum felt he had to speak. "Well, what do we do about it?"

Willis looked up at the sun burning blind in the sky. "Be aware," he said slowly. "Watch everything for a few days."

"Everything?"

"We don't use half what God gave us, ten per cent of the time. We ought to hear more, feel more, smell more, taste more. Maybe there's something wrong with the way the wind blows these weeds there in the lot. Maybe it's the sun up on those telephone wires or the cicadas singing in the elm trees. If only we could stop, look, listen, a few days, a few nights, and compare notes. Tell me to shut up then, and I will."

"Good enough," said Fortnum, playing it lighter than he felt. "I'll look around. But how do I know the thing I'm looking for when I see it?"

Willis peered in at him, sincerely. "You'll know. You've got to know. Or we're done for, all of us," he said quietly.

Fortnum shut the door and didn't know what to say. He felt a flush of embarrassment creeping up his face. Willis sensed this.

"Hugh, do you think I'm . . . off my rocker?"

"Nonsense!" said Fortnum, too quickly. "You're just nervous, is all. You should take a week off."

Willis nodded. "See you Monday night?"

"Any time. Drop around."

"I hope I will, Hugh. I really hope I will."

Then Willis was gone, hurrying across the dry weed-grown lot toward the side entrance of the market.

Watching him go, Fortnum suddenly did not want to move. He discovered that very slowly he was taking deep breaths, weighing the silence. He licked his lips, tasting the salt. He looked at his arm on the doorsill, the sunlight burning the golden hairs. In the empty lot the wind moved all alone to itself. He leaned out to look at the sun, which stared back with one massive stunning blow of intense power that made him jerk his head in. He exhaled. Then he laughed out loud. Then he drove away.

The lemonade glass was cool and deliciously sweaty. The ice made music inside the glass, and the lemonade was just sour enough, just sweet enough on his tongue. He sipped, he savored, he tilted back in the wicker rocking chair on the twilight front porch, his eyes closed. The crickets were chirping out on the lawn. Cynthia, knitting across from him on the porch, eyed him curiously; he could feel her attention.

"What are you up to?" she said at last.

"Cynthia," he said, "is your intuition in running order? Is this earthquake weather? Is the land going to sink? Will war be declared? Or is it only that our delphinium will die of the blight?"

"Hold on. Let me feel my bones."

He opened his eyes and watched Cynthia in turn closing hers and sitting absolutely statue-still, her hands on her knees. Finally she shook her head and smiled.

"No. No war declared. No land sinking. Not even a blight. Why?"

"I've met a lot of doom talkers today. Well, two anyway, and—"

The screen door burst wide. Fortnum's body jerked as if he had been struck.

"What—!"

Tom, a gardener's wooden flat in his arms, stepped out on the porch.

"Sorry," he said. "What's wrong, Dad?"

"Nothing." Fortnum stood up, glad to be moving. "Is that the crop?"

Tom moved forward eagerly. "Part of it. Boy, they're doing great. In just seven hours, with lots of water, look how big the darn things are!" He set the flat on the table between his parents.

The crop was indeed plentiful. Hundreds of small grayish-brown mushrooms were sprouting up in the damp soil.

"I'll be damned," said Fortnum, impressed.

Cynthia put out her hand to touch the flat, then took it away uneasily.

"I hate to be a spoilsport, but . . . there's no way for these to be anything else but mushrooms, is there?"

Tom looked as if he had been insulted. "What do you think I'm going to feed you? Poisoned fungoids?"

"That's just it," said Cynthia quickly. "How do you tell them apart?"

"Eat 'em," said Tom. "If you live, they're mushrooms. If you drop dead— *well*!"

He gave a great guffaw, which amused Fortnum but only made his mother wince. She sat back in her chair.

"I—I don't like them," she said.

"Boy, oh, boy." Tom seized the flat angrily. "When are we going to have the next wet-blanket sale in *this* house?"

He shuffled morosely away.

"Tom—" said Fortnum.

"Never mind," said Tom. "Everyone figures they'll be ruined by the boy entrepreneur. To heck with it!"

Fortnum got inside just as Tom heaved the mushrooms, flat and all, down the cellar stairs. He slammed the cellar door and ran out the back door.

Fortnum turned back to his wife, who, stricken, glanced away.

"I'm sorry," she said. "I don't know why, I just *had* to say that to Tom. I—"

The phone rang. Fortnum brought it outside on its extension cord.

"Hugh?" It was Dorothy Willis's voice. She sounded suddenly very old and very frightened. "Hugh, Roger isn't there, is he?"

"Dorothy? No."

"He's gone!" said Dorothy. "All his clothes were taken from the closet." She began to cry.

"Dorothy, hold on, I'll be there in a minute."

"You must help, oh, you must. Something's happened to him, I know it," she wailed. "Unless you do something, we'll never see him alive again."

Very slowly he put the receiver back on its hook, her voice weeping inside it. The night crickets quite suddenly were very loud. He felt the hairs, one by one, go up on the back of his neck.

Hair can't do that, he thought. Silly, silly. It can't do that, not in *real* life, it can't!

But, one by slow prickling one, his hair did.

The wire hangers were indeed empty. With a clatter, Fortnum shoved them aside and down along the rod, then turned and looked out of the closet at Dorothy Willis and her son Joe.

"I was just walking by," said Joe, "and saw the closet empty, all Dad's clothes gone!"

"Everything was fine," said Dorothy. "We've had a wonderful life. I don't understand, I don't, I don't!" She began to cry again, putting her hands to her face.

Fortnum stepped out of the closet.

"You didn't hear him leave the house?"

"We were playing catch out front," said Joe. "Dad said he had to go in for a minute. I went around back. Then he was gone!"

"He must have packed quickly and walked wherever he was going, so we wouldn't hear a cab pull up in front of the house."

They were moving out through the hall now.

"I'll check the train depot and the airport." Fortnum hesitated. "Dorothy, is there anything in Roger's background—"

"It wasn't insanity took him." She hesitated. "I feel, somehow, he was kidnapped."

Fortnum shook his head. "It doesn't seem reasonable he would arrange to pack, walk out of the house and go meet his abductors."

Dorothy opened the door as if to let the night or the night wind move down the hall as she turned to stare back through the rooms, her voice wandering.

"No. Somehow they came into the house. Right in front of us, they stole him away."

And then: "A terrible thing has happened."

Fortnum stepped out into the night of crickets and rustling trees. The doom talkers, he thought, talking their dooms. Mrs. Goodbody, Roger, and now Roger's wife. Something terrible *has* happened. But what, in God's name? And how?

He looked from Dorothy to her son. Joe, blinking the wetness from his eyes, took a long time to turn, walk along the hall and stop, fingering the knob of the cellar door.

Fortnum felt his eyelids twitch, his irises flex, as if he were snapping a picture of something he wanted to remember.

Joe pulled the cellar door wide, stepped down out of sight, gone. The door tapped shut.

Fortnum opened his mouth to speak, but Dorothy's hand was taking his now, he had to look at her.

"Please," she said. "Find him for me."

He kissed her cheek. "If it's humanly possible."

If it's humanly possible. Good Lord, why had he picked *those* words?

He walked off into the summer night.

A gasp, an exhalation, a gasp, an exhalation, an asthmatic insuck, a vaporing sneeze. Somebody dying in the dark? No.

Just Mrs. Goodbody, unseen beyond the hedge, working late, her hand pump aimed, her bony elbow thrusting. The sick-sweet smell of bug spray enveloped Fortnum as he reached his house.

"Mrs. Goodbody? Still at it?"

From the black hedge her voice leaped. "Damn it, yes! Aphids, water bugs, woodworms, and now the *Marasmius oreades*. Lord, it grows fast!"

"What does?"

"The *Marasmius oreades*, of course! It's me against them, and I intend to win! There! There! There!"

He left the hedge, the gasping pump, the wheezing voice, and found his wife waiting for him on the porch almost as if she were going to take up where Dorothy had left off at her door a few minutes ago.

Fortnum was about to speak when a shadow moved inside. There was a creaking noise. A knob rattled.

Tom vanished into the basement.

Fortnum felt as if someone had set off an explosion in his face. He reeled. Everything had the numbed familiarity of those waking dreams where all motions are remembered before they occur, all dialogue known before it falls from the lips.

He found himself staring at the shut basement door. Cynthia took him inside, amused.

"What? Tom? Oh, I relented. The darn mushrooms meant so much to him. Besides, when he threw them into the cellar they did nicely, just lying in the dirt—"

"Did they?" Fortnum heard himself say.

Cynthia took his arm. "What about Roger?"

"He's gone, yes."

"Men, men, men," she said.

"No, you're wrong," he said. "I've seen Roger nearly every day the last ten years. When you know a man that well, you can tell how things are at home, whether things are in the oven or the Mixmaster. Death hadn't breathed down his neck yet; he wasn't running scared after his immortal youth, picking peaches in someone else's orchards. No, no, I swear, I'd bet my last dollar on it, Roger—"

The doorbell rang behind him. The delivery boy had come up quietly onto the porch and was standing there with a telegram in his hand.

"Fortnum?"

Cynthia snapped on the hall light as he ripped the envelope open and smoothed it out for reading.

TRAVELING NEW ORLEANS. THIS TELEGRAM POSSIBLE OFF-GUARD MOMENT. YOU MUST REFUSE, REPEAT REFUSE, ALL SPECIAL-DELIVERY PACKAGES. ROGER

Cynthia glanced up from the paper.

"I don't understand. What does he mean?"

But Fortnum was already at the telephone, dialing swiftly, once. "Operator? The police, and hurry!"

At ten-fifteen that night the phone rang for the sixth time during the evening. Fortnum got it and immediately gasped. "Roger! Where are you?"

"Where am I, hell," said Roger lightly, almost amused. "You know very well where I am, you're responsible for this. I should be angry!"

Cynthia, at his nod, had hurried to take the extension phone in the kitchen. When he heard the soft click, he went on.

"Roger, I swear I don't know. I got that telegram from you—"

"What telegram?" said Roger jovially. "I sent no telegram. Now, of a sudden, the police come pouring onto the southbound train, pull me off in some jerk-water, and I'm calling you to get them off my neck. Hugh, if this is some joke—"

"But, Roger, you just vanished!"

"On a business trip, if you can call that vanishing. I told Dorothy about this, and Joe."

"This is all very confusing, Roger. You're in no danger? Nobody's blackmailing you, forcing you into this speech?"

"I'm fine, healthy, free and unafraid."

"But Roger, your premonitions?"

"Poppycock! Now, look, I'm being very good about this, aren't I?"

"Sure, Roger—"

"Then play the good father and give me permission to go. Call Dorothy and tell her I'll be back in five days. How *could* she have forgotten?"

"She did, Roger. See you in five days, then?"

"Five days, I swear."

The voice was indeed winning and warm, the old Roger again. Fortnum shook his head.

"Roger," he said, "this is the craziest day I've ever spent. You're not running off from Dorothy? Good Lord, you can tell *me*."

"I love her with all my heart. Now here's Lieutenant Parker of the Ridgetown police. Good-by, Hugh."

"Good—"

But the lieutenant was on the line, talking, talking angrily. What had Fortnum meant putting them to this trouble? What was going on? Who did he think he was? Did or didn't he want this so-called friend held or released?

"Released," Fortnum managed to say somewhere along the way, and hung up the phone and imagined he heard a voice call "All aboard" and the massive thunder of the train leaving the station two hundred miles south in the somehow increasingly dark night.

Cynthia walked very slowly into the parlor.

"I feel so foolish," she said.

"How do you think I feel?"

"Who could have sent that telegram, and why?"

He poured himself some Scotch and stood in the middle of the room looking at it.

"I'm glad Roger is all right," his wife said at last.

"He isn't," said Fortnum.

"But you just said—"

"I said nothing. After all, we couldn't very well drag him off that train and truss him up and send him home, could we, if he insisted he was okay? No. He sent that telegram, but changed his mind after sending it. Why, why, why?" Fortnum paced the room, sipping the drink. "Why warn us against special-delivery packages? The only package we've got this *year* which fits that description is the one Tom got this morning. . . ." His voice trailed off.

Before he could move, Cynthia was at the wastepaper basket taking out the crumpled wrapping paper with the special-delivery stamps on it.

The postmark read: NEW ORLEANS, LA.

Cynthia looked up from it. "New Orleans. Isn't that where Roger is heading right now?"

A doorknob rattled, a door opened and closed in Fortnum's mind. Another doorknob rattled, another door swung wide and then shut. There was a smell of damp earth.

He found his hand dialing the phone. After a long while Dorothy Willis answered at the other end. He could imagine her sitting alone in a house with too many lights on. He talked quietly with her for a while, then cleared his throat and said, "Dorothy, look. I know it sounds silly. Did any special-delivery packages arrive at your house the last few days?"

Her voice was faint. "No." Then: "No, wait. Three days ago. But I thought you *knew*! All the boys on the block are going in for it."

Fortnum measured his words carefully.

"Going in for what?"

"But why ask?" she said. "There's nothing wrong with raising mushrooms, is there?"

Fortnum closed his eyes.

"Hugh? Are you still there?" asked Dorothy. "I said there's nothing wrong with—"

"Raising mushrooms?" said Fortnum at last. "No. Nothing wrong. Nothing wrong."

And slowly he put down the phone.

The curtains blew like veils of moonlight. The clock ticked. The after-midnight world flowed into and filled the bedroom. He heard Mrs. Goodbody's clear voice on this morning's air, a million years gone now. He heard Roger putting a cloud over the sun at noon. He heard the police damning him by phone from downstate. Then Roger's voice again, with the locomotive thunder hurrying him away and away, fading. And, finally, Mrs. Goodbody's voice behind the hedge:

"Lord, it grows fast!"

"What does?"

"The *Marasmius oreades*!"

He snapped his eyes open. He sat up.

Downstairs, a moment later, he flicked through the unabridged dictionary. His forefinger underlined the words:

"*Marasmius oreades*; a mushroom commonly found on lawns in summer and early autumn. . . ."

He let the book fall shut.

Outside, in the deep summer night, he lit a cigarette and smoked quietly.

A meteor fell across space, burning itself out quickly. The trees rustled softly.

The front door tapped shut.

Cynthia moved toward him in her robe.

"Can't sleep?"

"Too warm, I guess."

"It's not warm."

"No," he said, feeling his arms. "In fact, it's cold." He sucked on the cigarette twice, then, not looking at her, said, "Cynthia, what if . . ." He snorted and had to stop. "Well, what if Roger was right this morning. Mrs. Goodbody, what if she's right, too? Something terrible *is* happening. Like, well,"—he nodded at the sky and the million stars—"Earth being invaded by things from other worlds, maybe."

"Hugh—"

"No, let me run wild."

"It's quite obvious we're not being invaded, or we'd notice."

"Let's say we've only half noticed, become uneasy about something. What? How could we be invaded? By what means would creatures invade?"

Cynthia looked at the sky and was about to try something when he interrupted.

"No, not meteors or flying saucers, things we can see. What about bacteria? That comes from outer space, too, doesn't it?"

"I read once, yes."

"Spores, seeds, pollens, viruses probably bombard our atmosphere by the billions every second and have done so for millions of years. Right now we're sitting out under an invisible rain. It falls all over the country, the cities, the towns, and right now, our lawn."

"*Our* lawn?"

"*And* Mrs. Goodbody's. But people like her are always pulling weeds, spraying poison, kicking toadstools off their grass. It would be hard for any strange life form to survive in cities. Weather's a problem, too. Best climate might be south: Alabama, Georgia, Louisiana. Back in the damp bayous they could grow to a fine size."

But Cynthia was beginning to laugh now.

"Oh, really, you don't believe, do you, that this Great Bayou or Whatever Greenhouse Novelty Company that sent Tom his package is owned and operated by six-foot-tall mushrooms from another planet?"

"If you put it that way, it sounds funny."

"Funny! It's hilarious!" She threw her head back, deliciously.

"Good grief!" he cried, suddenly irritated. "*Something's* going on! Mrs. Goodbody is rooting out and killing *Marasmius oreades*. What is *Marasmius oreades*? A certain kind of mushroom. Simultaneously, and I suppose *you'll* call it coincidence, by special delivery, what arrives the same day? Mushrooms for Tom! What *else* happens? Roger fears he may soon cease to be! Within hours, he vanishes, then telegraphs us, warning us not to accept what? The special-delivery mushrooms for Tom! Has Roger's son got a similar package in the last few days? He has! Where do the packages come from? New Orleans! And where is Roger going when he vanishes? New Orleans! Do you see, Cynthia, do you see? I wouldn't be upset if all these separate things didn't lock together! Roger, Tom, Joe, mushrooms, Mrs. Goodbody, packages, destinations, everything in one pattern!"

She was watching his face now, quieter, but still amused. "Don't get angry."

"I'm not!" Fortnum almost shouted. And then he simply could not go on. He was afraid that if he did he would find himself shouting with laughter too, and somehow he did not want that. He stared at the surrounding houses up and down the block and thought of the dark cellars and the neighbor boys who read *Popular Mechanics* and sent their money in by the millions to raise the mushrooms hidden away. Just as he, when a boy, had mailed off for chemicals, seeds, turtles, numberless salves and sickish ointments. In how many million American homes tonight were billions of mushrooms rousing up under the ministrations of the innocent?

"Hugh?" His wife was touching his arm now. "Mushrooms, even big ones, can't think, can't move, don't have arms and legs. How could they run a mail-order service and 'take over' the world? Come on, now, let's look at your terrible fiends and monsters!"

She pulled him toward the door. Inside, she headed for the cellar, but he stopped, shaking his head, a foolish smile shaping itself somehow to his mouth. "No, no, I know what we'll find. You win. The whole thing's silly. Roger will be back next week and we'll all get drunk together. Go on up to bed now and I'll drink a glass of warm milk and be with you in a minute."

"That's better!" She kissed him on both cheeks, squeezed him and went away up the stairs.

In the kitchen, he took out a glass, opened the refrigerator, and was pouring the milk when he stopped suddenly.

Near the front of the top shelf was a small yellow dish. It was not the dish that held his attention, however. It was what lay in the dish.

The fresh-cut mushrooms.

He must have stood there for half a minute, his breath frosting the air, before he reached out, took hold of the dish, sniffed it, felt the mushrooms, then at last, carrying the dish, went out into the hall. He looked up the stairs, hearing Cynthia moving about in the bedroom, and was about to call up to her, "Cynthia, did you put *these* in the refrigerator?" Then he stopped. He knew her answer. She had not.

He put the dish of mushrooms on the newel-upright at the bottom of the stairs and stood looking at them. He imagined himself in bed later, looking at the walls, the open windows, watching the moonlight sift patterns on the ceiling. He heard himself saying, Cynthia? And her answering, Yes? And him saying, There *is* a way for mushrooms to grow arms and legs. What? she would say, silly, silly man, what? And he would gather courage against her hilarious reaction and go on, What if a man wandered through the swamp, picked the mushrooms and *ate* them. . . ?

No response from Cynthia.

Once inside the man, would the mushrooms spread through his blood, take over every cell and change the man from a man to a—Martian? Given this theory, would the mushroom *need* its own arms and legs? No, not when it could borrow people, live inside and become them. Roger ate mushrooms given him by his son. Roger became "something else." He kidnapped himself. And in one last flash of sanity, of being himself, he telegraphed us, warning us not to accept the special-delivery mushrooms. The "Roger" that telephoned later was no longer Roger but a captive of what he had eaten! Doesn't that figure, Cynthia, doesn't it, doesn't it?

No, said the imagined Cynthia, no, it doesn't figure, no, no, no. . . .

There was the faintest whisper, rustle, stir from the cellar. Taking his eyes from the bowl, Fortnum walked to the cellar door and put his ear to it.

"Tom?"

No answer.

"Tom, are you down there?"

No answer.

"Tom?"

After a long while, Tom's voice came up from below.

"Yes, Dad?"

"It's after midnight," said Fortnum, fighting to keep his voice from going high. "What are you doing down there?"

No answer.

"I said—"

"Tending to my crop," said the boy at last, his voice cold and faint.

"Well, get the hell *out* of there! You hear me?"

Silence.

"Tom? Listen! Did you put some mushrooms in the refrigerator tonight? If so, why?"

Ten seconds must have ticked by before the boy replied from below, "For you and Mom to eat, of course."

Fortnum heard his heart moving swiftly and had to take three deep breaths before he could go on.

"Tom? You didn't . . . that is, you haven't by any chance *eaten* some of the mushrooms yourself, *have* you?"

"Funny you ask that," said Tom. "Yes. Tonight. On a sandwich. After supper. Why?"

Fortnum held to the doorknob. Now it was his turn not to answer. He felt his knees beginning to melt and he fought the whole silly senseless fool thing. No reason, he tried to say, but his lips wouldn't move.

"Dad?" called Tom, softly from the cellar. "Come on down." Another pause. "I want you to see the harvest."

Fortnum felt the knob slip in his sweaty hand. The knob rattled. He gasped.

"Dad?" called Tom softly.

Fortnum opened the door.

The cellar was completely black below.

He stretched his hand in toward the light switch.

As if sensing this from somewhere, Tom said, "Don't. Light's bad for the mushrooms."

He took his hand off the switch.

He swallowed. He looked back at the stair leading up to his wife. I suppose, he thought, I should go say good-by to Cynthia. But why should I think that! Why, in God's name, should I think that at all? No reason, *is* there?

None.

"Tom?" he said, affecting a jaunty air. "Ready or not, here I come!"

And stepping down in darkness, he shut the door.

The Vacation

It was a day as fresh as grass growing up and clouds going over and butterflies coming down can make it. It was a day compounded from silences of bee and flower and ocean and land, which were not silences at all, but motions, stirs, flutters, risings, fallings, each in its own time and matchless rhythm. The land did not move, but moved. The sea was not still, yet was still. Paradox flowed into paradox, stillness mixed with stillness, sound with sound. The flowers vibrated and the bees fell in separate and small showers of golden rain on the clover. The seas of hill and the seas of ocean were divided, each from the other's motion, by a railroad track, empty, compounded of rust and iron marrow, a track on which, quite obviously, no train had run in many years. Thirty miles north it swirled on away to further mists of distance, thirty miles south it tunneled islands of cloud-shadow that changed their continental positions on the sides of far mountains as you watched.

Now, suddenly, the railroad track began to tremble.

A blackbird, standing on the rail, felt a rhythm grow faintly, miles away, like a heart beginning to beat.

The blackbird leaped up over the sea.

The rail continued to vibrate softly until, at long last, around a curve and along the shore came a small workman's handcar, its two-cylinder engine popping and spluttering in the great silence.

On top of this small four-wheeled car, on a double-sided bench facing in two directions and with a little surrey roof above for shade, sat a man, his wife and their small seven-year-old son. As the handcar traveled through lonely stretch after lonely stretch, the wind whipped their eyes and blew their hair, but they did not look back but only ahead. Sometimes they looked eagerly as a curve unwound itself, sometimes with great sadness, but always watchful, ready for the next scene.

As they hit a level straightaway, the machine engine gasped and stopped abruptly. In the now crushing silence, it seemed that the quiet of earth, sky and sea itself, by its friction, brought the car to a wheeling halt.

"Out of gas."

The man, sighing, reached for the extra can in the small storage bin and began to pour it into the tank.

His wife and son sat quietly looking at the sea, listening to the muted thunder, the whisper, the drawing back of huge tapestries of sand, gravel, green weed, and foam.

"Isn't the sea nice?" said the woman.

"I like it," said the boy.

"Shall we picnic here, while we're at it?"

The man focused some binoculars on the green peninsula ahead.

"Might as well. The rails have rusted badly. There's a break ahead. We may have to wait while I set a few back in place."

"As many as there are," said the boy, "we'll have picnics!"

The woman tried to smile at this, then turned her grave attention to the man. "How far have we come today?"

"Not ninety miles." The man still peered through the glasses, squinting. "I don't like to go farther than that any one day, anyway. If you rush, there's no time to see. We'll reach Monterey day after tomorrow, Palo Alto the next day, if you want."

The woman removed her great shadowing straw hat, which had been tied over her golden hair with a bright yellow ribbon, and stood perspiring faintly, away from the machine. They had ridden so steadily on the shuddering handcar that the motion was sewn into their bodies. Now, with the stopping, they felt odd, on the verge of unraveling.

"Let's eat!"

The boy ran the wicker lunch basket down to the shore.

The boy and the woman were already seated by a spread tablecloth when the man came down to them, dressed in his business suit and vest and tie and hat as if he expected to meet someone along the way. As he dealt out the sandwiches and exhumed the pickles from their cool green Mason jars, he began to loosen his tie and unbutton his vest, always looking around as if he should be careful and ready to button up again.

"Are we all alone, Papa?" said the boy, eating.

"Yes."

"No one else, anywhere?"

"No one else."

"Were there people before?"

"Why do you keep asking that? It wasn't that long ago. Just a few months. You remember."

"Almost. If I try hard, then I don't remember at all." The boy let a handful of sand fall through his fingers. "Were there as many people as there is sand here on the beach? What *happened* to them?"

"I don't know," the man said, and it was true.

They had wakened one morning and the world was empty. The neighbors' clothesline was still strung with blowing white wash, cars gleamed in front of other seven-A.M. cottages, but there were no farewells, the city did not hum with its mighty arterial traffics, phones did not alarm themselves, children did not wail in sunflower wildernesses.

Only the night before, he and his wife had been sitting on the front porch when the evening paper was delivered, and, not even daring to open the headlines out, he had said, "I wonder when He will get tired of us and just rub us all out?"

"It has gone pretty far," she said. "On and on. We're such fools, aren't we?"

"Wouldn't it be nice"— he lit his pipe and puffed it—"if we woke tomorrow and everyone in the world was gone and everything was starting over?" He sat smoking, the paper folded in his hand, his head resting back on the chair.

"If you could press a button right now and make it happen, would you?"

"I think I would," he said. "Nothing violent. Just have everyone vanish off the face of the earth. Just leave the land and the sea and the growing things, like flowers and grass and fruit trees. And the animals, of course, let them stay. Everything except man, who hunts when he isn't hungry, eats when full, and is mean when no one's bothered him."

"Naturally, we would be left." She smiled quietly.

"I'd like that," he mused. "All of time ahead. The longest summer vacation in history. And us out for the longest picnic-basket lunch in memory. Just you, me and Jim. No commuting. No keeping up with the Joneses. Not even a car. I'd like to find another way of traveling, an older way. Then, a hamper full of sandwiches, three bottles of pop, pick up supplies where you need them from empty grocery stores in empty towns, and summertime forever up ahead. . . . "

They sat a long while on the porch in silence, the newspaper folded between them.

At last she opened her mouth.

"Would we be *lonely?*" she said.

So that's how it was the morning of the new world. They had awakened to the soft sounds of an earth that was now no more than a meadow, and the cities of the earth sinking back into seas of sabergrass, marigold, marguerite and morning-glory. They had taken it with remarkable calm at first, perhaps because they had not liked the city for so many years, and had had so many friends who were not truly friends, and had lived a boxed and separate life of their own within a mechanical hive.

The husband arose and looked out the window and observed very calmly, as if it were a weather condition, "Everyone's gone," knowing this just by the sounds the city had ceased to make.

They took their time over breakfast, for the boy was still asleep, and then the husband sat back and said, "Now I must plan what to do."

"Do? Why . . . why, you'll go to work, of course."

"You still don't believe it, do you?" He laughed. "That I won't be rushing off each day at eight-ten, that Jim won't go to school ever again. School's out for all of us! No more pencils, no more books, no more boss's sassy looks! We're let out, darling, and we'll never come back to the silly damn dull routines. Come on!"

And he had walked her through the still and empty city streets.

"They didn't die," he said. "They just . . . went away."

"What about the other cities?"

He went to an outdoor phone booth and dialed Chicago, then New York, then San Francisco.

Silence. Silence. Silence.

"That's it," he said, replacing the receiver.

"I feel guilty," she said. "Them gone and us here. And . . . I feel happy. Why? I *should* be unhappy."

"Should you? It's no tragedy. They weren't tortured or blasted or burned. They went easily and they didn't know. And now we owe nothing to no one. Our only responsibility is being happy. Thirty more years of happiness, wouldn't that be good?"

"But . . . then we must have more children!"

"To repopulate the world?" He shook his head slowly, calmly. "No. Let Jim be the last. After he's grown and gone let the horses and cows and ground squirrels and garden spiders have the world. They'll get on. And someday some other species that can combine a natural happiness with a natural curiosity will build cities that won't even look like cities to us, and survive. Right now, let's go pack a basket, wake Jim, and get going on that long thirty-year summer vacation. I'll beat you to the house!"

He took a sledge hammer from the small handcar, and while he worked alone for half an hour fixing the rusted rails into place, the woman and the boy ran along the shore. They came back with dripping shells, a dozen or more, and some beautiful pink pebbles, and sat and the boy took school from the mother, doing homework on a pad with a pencil for a time, and then at high noon the man came down, his coat off, his tie thrown aside, and they drank orange pop, watching the bubbles surge up, glutting, inside the bottles. It was quiet. They listened to the sun tune the old iron rails. The smell of hot tar on the ties moved about them in the salt wind, as the husband tapped his atlas map lightly and gently.

"We'll go to Sacramento next month, May, then work up toward Seattle. Should make that by July first, July's a good month in Washington, then back down as the weather cools, to Yellowstone, a few miles a day, hunt here, fish there. . . ."

The boy, bored, moved away to throw sticks into the sea and wade out like a dog to retrieve them.

The man went on: "Winter in Tucson, then, part of the winter, moving toward Florida, up the coast in the spring, and maybe New York by June. Two years from now, Chicago in the summer. Winter, three years from now, what about Mexico City? Anywhere the rails lead us, anywhere at all, and if we come to an old offshoot rail line we don't know anything about, what the hell, we'll just take it, go down it, to see where it goes. And some year, by God, we'll boat down the Mississippi, always wanted to do that. Enough to last us a lifetime. And that's just how long I want to take to do it all. . . . "

His voice faded. He started to fumble the map shut, but, before he could move, a bright thing fell through the air and hit the paper. It rolled off into the sand and made a wet lump.

His wife glanced at the wet place in the sand and then swiftly searched his face. His solemn eyes were too bright. And down one cheek was a track of wetness.

She gasped. She took his hand and held it, tight.

He clenched her hand very hard, his eyes shut now, and slowly he said, with difficulty, "Wouldn't it be nice if we went to sleep tonight and in the night, somehow, it all came back. All the foolishness, all the noise, all the hate, all the terrible things, all the nightmares, all the wicked people and stupid children, all the mess, all the smallness, all the confusion, all the hope, all the need, all the love. Wouldn't it be nice."

She waited and nodded her head once.

Then both of them started.

For standing between them, they knew not for how long, was their son, an empty pop bottle in one hand.

The boy's face was pale. With his free hand he reached out to touch his father's cheek, where the single tear had made its track.

"You," he said. "Oh, Dad, you. You haven't anyone to play with, *either*."

The wife started to speak.

The husband moved to take the boy's hand.

The boy jerked back. "Silly! Oh, silly! Silly fools! Oh, you dumb, dumb!" And, whirling, he rushed down to the ocean and stood there crying loudly.

The wife rose to follow, but the husband stopped her.

"No. Let him."

And then they both grew cold and quiet. For the boy, below on the shore, crying steadily, now was writing on a piece of paper and stuffing it in the pop bottle and ramming the cap back on and taking the bottle and giving it a great glittering heave up in the air and out into the tidal sea.

What, thought the wife, what did he write on the note? What's in the bottle?

The bottle moved out in the waves.

The boy stopped crying.

After a long while he walked up the shore, to stand looking at his parents. His face was neither bright nor dark, alive nor dead, ready nor resigned; it seemed a curious mixture that simply made do with time, weather and these people. They looked at him and beyond to the bay, where the bottle containing the scribbled note was almost out of sight now, shining in the waves.

Did he write what *we* wanted? thought the woman. Did he write what he heard us just wish, just say?

Or did he write something for only himself, she wondered, that tomorrow he might wake and find himself alone in an empty world, no one around, no man, no woman, no father, no mother, no fool grownups with fool wishes, so he could trudge up to the railroad tracks and take the handcar motoring, a solitary boy, across the continental wilderness, on eternal voyages and picnics?

Is that what he wrote in the note?

Which?

She searched his colorless eyes, could not read the answer; dared not ask.

Gull shadows sailed over and kited their faces with sudden passing coolness.

"Time to go," someone said.

They loaded the wicker basket onto the rail car. The woman tied her large bonnet securely in place with its yellow ribbon, they set the boy's pail of shells on the floorboards, then the husband put on his tie, his vest, his coat, his hat, and they all sat on the benches of the car looking out at the sea where the bottled note was far out, blinking, on the horizon.

"Is asking enough?" said the boy. "Does wishing work?"

"Sometimes . . . *too* well."

"It depends on what you ask for."

The boy nodded, his eyes far away.

They looked back at where they had come from, and then ahead to where they were going.

"Good-by, place," said the boy, and waved.

The car rolled down the rusty rails. The sound of it dwindled, faded. The man, the woman, the boy dwindled with it in distance, among the hills.

After they were gone, the rail trembled faintly for two minutes, and ceased. A flake of rust fell. A flower nodded.

The sea was very loud.

The Illustrated Woman

When a new patient wanders into the office and stretches out to stutter forth a compendious ticker tape of free association, it is up to the psychiatrist immediately beyond, behind and above to decide at just which points of the anatomy the client is in touch with the couch.

In other words, where does the patient make contact with reality?

Some people seem to float half an inch above any surface whatsoever. They have not seen earth in so long, they have become somewhat airsick.

Still others so firmly weight themselves down, clutch, thrust, heave their bodies toward reality, that long after they are gone you find their tiger shapes and claw marks in the upholstery.

In the case of Emma Fleet, Dr. George C. George was a long time deciding which was furniture and which was woman and where what touched which.

For, to begin with, Emma Fleet resembled a couch.

"Mrs. Emma Fleet, Doctor," announced his receptionist.

Dr. George C. George gasped.

For it was a traumatic experience, seeing this woman shunt herself through the door without benefit of railroad switchman or the ground crews who rush about under Macy's Easter balloons, heaving on lines, guiding the massive images to some eternal hangar off beyond.

In came Emma Fleet, as quick as her name, the floor shifting like a huge set of scales under her weight.

Dr. George must have gasped again, guessing her at four hundred on the hoof, for Emma Fleet smiled as if reading his mind.

"Four hundred two and a half pounds, to be exact," she said.

He found himself staring at his furniture.

"Oh, it'll hold all right," said Mrs. Fleet intuitively.

She sat down.

The couch yelped like a cur.

Dr. George cleared his throat. "Before you make yourself comfortable," he said, "I feel I should say immediately and honestly that we in the psychiatrical field have had little success in inhibiting appetites. The whole problem of weight and food has so far eluded our ability for coping. A strange admission, perhaps, but unless we put our frailties forth, we might be in danger of fooling ourselves and thus taking money under false pretenses. So, if you are here seeking help for your figure, I must list myself among the nonplussed."

"Thank you for your honesty, Doctor," said Emma Fleet. "However, I don't wish to lose. I'd prefer your helping me *gain* another one hundred or two hundred pounds."

"Oh, no!" Dr. George exclaimed.

"Oh, yes. But my heart will not allow what my deep dear soul would most gladly endure. My physical heart might fail at what my loving heart and mind would ask of it."

She sighed. The couch sighed.

"Well, let me brief you. I'm married to Willy Fleet. We work for the Dillbeck-Horsemann Traveling Shows. I'm known as Lady Bountiful. And Willy . . . "

She swooned up out of the couch and glided or rather escorted her shadow across the floor. She opened the door.

Beyond, in the waiting room, a cane in one hand, a straw hat in the other, seated rigidly, staring at the wall, was a tiny man with tiny feet and tiny hands and tiny bright-blue eyes in a tiny head. He was, at the most, one would guess, three feet high, and probably weighed sixty pounds in the rain. But there was a proud, gloomy, almost violent look of genius blazing in that small but craggy face.

"That's Willy Fleet," said Emma lovingly, and shut the door.

The couch, sat on, cried again.

Emma beamed at the psychiatrist, who was still staring, in shock, at the door.

"No children, of course," he heard himself say.

"No children." Her smile lingered. "But that's not my problem, either. Willy, in a way, is my child. And I, in a way, besides being his wife, am his mother. It all has to do with size, I imagine, and we're happy with the way we've balanced things off."

"Well, if your problem isn't children, or your size or his, or controlling weight, then what. . . ?"

Emma Fleet laughed lightly, tolerantly. It was a nice laugh, like a girl's somehow caught in that great body and throat.

"Patience, Doctor. Mustn't we go back down the road to where Willy and I first met?"

The doctor shrugged, laughed quietly himself and relaxed, nodding. "You must."

"During high school," said Emma Fleet, "I weighed one-eighty and tipped the scales at two-fifty when I was twenty-one. Needless to say, I went on few summer excursions. Most of the time I was left in drydock. I had many girl friends, however, who liked to be seen with me. They weighed one-fifty, most of them, and I made them feel svelte. But that's a long time ago. I don't worry over it any more. Willy changed all that."

"Willy sounds like a remarkable man," Dr. George found himself saying, against all the rules.

"Oh, he is, he is! He *smoulders*—with ability, with talent as yet undiscovered, untapped!" she said, quickening warmly. "God bless him, he leaped into my life like summer lightning! Eight years ago I went with my girl friends to the visiting Labor Day carnival. By the end of the evening, the girls had all been seized away from me by the running boys who, rushing by, grabbed and took them off into the night. There I was alone with three Kewpie Dolls, a fake alligator handbag and nothing to do but make the Guess Your Weight man nervous by looking at him every time I went by and pretending like at any moment I might pay my money and dare him to guess.

"But the Guess Your Weight man *wasn't* nervous! After I had passed three times I saw him staring at me. With awe, yes, with admiration! And who was this Guess Your Weight man? Willy Fleet, of course. The fourth time I passed he called to me and said I could get a prize free if only I'd let him guess my weight. He was all feverish and excited. He danced around. I'd never been made over so much in my life. I blushed. I felt good. So I sat in the scales chair. I heard the pointer whizz up around and I heard Willy whistle with honest delight.

" 'Two hundred and eighty-nine pounds!' he cried. 'Oh boy oh boy, you're lovely!'

" 'I'm *what?*' I said.

" 'You're the loveliest woman in the whole world,' said Willy, looking me right in the eye.

"I blushed again. I laughed. We both laughed. Then I must have cried, for the next thing, sitting there, I felt him touch my elbow with concern. He was gazing into my face, faintly alarmed.

" 'I haven't said the wrong thing?' he asked.

" 'No,' I sobbed, and then grew quiet. 'The right thing, only the right thing.' It's the first time anyone ever . . . '

" 'What?' he said.

" 'Ever put up with my fat,' I said.

" 'You're not fat,' he said. 'You're large, you're big, you're wonderful. Michelangelo would have loved you. Titian would have loved you. Da Vinci would have loved you. They knew what they were doing in those days. Size. Size is everything. I should know. Look at me. I traveled with Singer's Midgets for six seasons, known as Jack Thimble. And oh my God, dear lady, you're right out of the most glorious part of the Renaissance. Bernini, who built those colonnades around the front of Saint Peter's and inside at the altar, would have lost his everlasting soul just to know someone like you.'

" 'Don't!' I cried. 'I wasn't meant to feel this happy. It'll hurt so much when you stop.'

" 'I won't stop, then,' he said. 'Miss. . . ?'

" 'Emma Gertz.'

" 'Emma,' he said, 'are you married?'

" 'Are you kidding?' I said.

" 'Emma, do you like to travel?'

" 'I've never traveled.'

" 'Emma,' he said, 'this old carnival's going to be in your town one more week. Come down every night, every day, why not? Talk to me, know me. At the end of the week, who can tell, maybe you'll travel with me.'

" 'What are you suggesting?' I said, not really angry or irritated or anything, but fascinated and intrigued that anyone would offer anything to Moby Dick's daughter.

" 'I mean marriage!' Willy Fleet looked at me, breathing hard, and I had the feeling that he was dressed in a mountaineer's rig, alpine hat, climbing boots, spikes, and a rope slung over his baby shoulder. And if I should ask him, 'Why are you saying this?' he might well answer, 'Because you're *there*.'

"But I didn't ask, so he didn't answer. We stood there in the night, at the center of the carnival, until at last I started off down the midway, swaying. 'I'm drunk!' I cried. 'Oh, so very drunk, and I've had nothing to drink.'

" 'Now that I've found you,' called Willy Fleet after me, 'you'll never escape me, remember!'

"Stunned and reeling, blinded by his large man's words sung out in his soprano voice, I somehow blundered from the carnival grounds and trekked home.

"The next week we were married."

Emma Fleet paused and looked at her hands.

"Would it bother you if I told you about the honeymoon?" she asked shyly.

"No," said the doctor, then lowered his voice, for he was responding all too quickly to the details. "Please *do* go on."

"The honeymoon." Emma sounded her *vox humana*. The response from all the chambers of her body vibrated the couch, the room, the doctor, the dear bones within the doctor.

"The honeymoon . . . was not usual."

The doctor's eyebrows lifted the faintest touch. He looked from the woman to the door beyond which, in miniature, sat the image of Edward Hillary, he of Everest.

"You have never seen such a rush as Willy spirited me off to his home, a lovely dollhouse, really, with one large normal-sized room that was to be mine, or, rather, ours. There, very politely, always the kind, the thoughtful, the quiet gentleman, he asked for my blouse, which I gave him, my skirt, which I gave him. Right down the list, I handed him the garments that he named, until at last . . . Can one blush from head to foot? One can. One did. I stood like a veritable hearthfire stoked by a blush of all-encompassing and ever-moving color that surged and resurged up and down my body in tints of pink and rose and then pink again.

"'My God!' cried Willy, 'you're the loveliest grand camellia that ever did unfurl!' Whereupon new tides of blush moved in hidden avalanches within, showing only to color the tent of my body, the outermost and, to Willy anyway, most precious skin.

"What did Willy do then? Guess."

"I daren't," said the doctor, flustered himself.

"He walked around and around me."

"*Circled* you?"

"Around and around, like a sculptor gazing at a huge block of snow-white granite. He said so himself. Granite or marble from which he might shape images of beauty as yet unguessed. Around and around he walked, sighing and shaking his head happily at his fortune, his little hands clasped, his little eyes bright. Where to begin, he seemed to be thinking, where, where to begin!?

"He spoke at last. 'Emma,' he asked, 'why, why do you think I've worked for years as the Guess Your Weight man at the carnival? Why? Because I have been searching my lifetime through for such as you. Night after night, summer after summer, I've watched those scales jump and twitter! And now at last I've the means, the way, the wall, the canvas, whereby to express my genius!'

"He stopped walking and looked at me, his eyes brimming over.

"'Emma,' he said softly, 'may I have permission to do anything absolutely whatsoever at all with you?'

"'Oh, Willy, Willy,' I cried. 'Anything!'"

Emma Fleet paused.

The doctor found himself out at the edge of his chair. "Yes, yes. And *then?*"

"And then," said Emma Fleet, "he brought out all his boxes and bottles of inks and stencils and his bright silver tattoo needles."

"Tattoo needles?"

The doctor fell back in his chair. "He . . . tattooed you?"

"He tattooed me."

"He was a tattoo artist?"

"He was, he is, an artist. It only happens that the form his art takes happens to be the tattoo."

"And you," said the doctor slowly, "were the canvas for which he had been searching much of his adult life?"

"I was the canvas for which he had searched *all* of his life."

She let it sink, and it *did* sink, and keep on sinking, into the doctor. Then when she saw it had struck bottom and stirred up vast quantities of mud, she went serenely on.

"So our grand life began! I loved Willy and Willy loved me and we both loved this thing that was larger than ourselves that we were doing together.

Nothing less than creating the greatest picture the world has ever seen. 'Nothing less than perfection!' cried Willy. 'Nothing less than perfection!' cried myself in response.

"Oh, it was a happy time. Ten thousand cozy busy hours we spent together. You can't imagine how proud it made me to be the vast shore along which the genius of Willy Fleet ebbed and flowed in a tide of colors.

"One year alone we spent on my right arm and my left, half a year on my right leg, eight months on my left, in preparation for the grand explosion of bright detail which erupted out along my collarbone and shoulderblades, which fountained upward from my hips to meet in a glorious July celebration of pinwheels, Titian nudes, Giorgione landscapes and El Greco cross-indexes of lightning on my façade, prickling with vast electric fires up and down my spine.

"Dear me, there never has been, there never will be, a love like ours again, a love where two people so sincerely dedicated themselves to one task, of giving beauty to the world in equal portions. We flew to each other day after day, and I ate more, grew larger, with the years. Willy approved, Willy applauded. Just that much more room, more space for his configurations to flower in. We could not bear to be apart, for we both felt, were certain, that once the Masterpiece was finished we could leave circus, carnival, or vaudeville forever. It was grandiose, yes, but we knew that once finished, I could be toured through the Art Institute in Chicago, the Kress Collection in Washington, the Tate Gallery in London, the Louvre, the Uffizi, the Vatican Museum! For the rest of our lives we would travel with the sun!

"So it went, year on year. We didn't need the world or the people of the world, we had each other. We worked at our ordinary jobs by day, and then, till after midnight, there was Willy at my ankle, there was Willy at my elbow, there was Willy exploring up the incredible slope of my back toward the snowy-talcumed crest. Willy wouldn't let me see, most of the time. He didn't like me looking over his shoulder, he didn't like me looking over *my* shoulder, for that matter. Months passed before, curious beyond madness, I would be allowed to see his progress slow inch by inch as the brilliant inks inundated me and I drowned in the rainbow of his inspirations. Eight years, eight glorious wondrous years. And then at last it was done, it was finished. And Willy threw himself down and slept for forty-eight hours straight. And I slept near him, the mammoth bedded with the black lamb. That was just four weeks ago. Four short weeks back, our happiness came to an end."

"Ah, yes," said the doctor. "You and your husband are suffering from the creative equivalent of the 'baby blues,' the depression a mother feels after her child is born. Your work is finished. A listless and somewhat sad period invariably follows. But, now, consider, you will reap the rewards of your long labor, surely? You *will* tour the world?"

"No," cried Emma Fleet, and a tear sprang to her eye. "At any moment, Willy will run off and never return. He has begun to wander about the city.

Yesterday I caught him brushing off the carnival scales. Today I found him working, for the first time in eight years, back at his Guess Your Weight booth!"

"Dear me," said the psychiatrist. "He's . . . ?"

"Weighing new women, yes! Shopping for new canvas! He hasn't said, but I know, I know! This time he'll find a heavier woman yet, five hundred, six hundred pounds! I guessed this would happen, a month ago, when we finished the Masterpiece. So I ate still more, and stretched my skin still more, so that little places appeared here and there, little open patches that Willy had to repair, fill in with fresh detail. But now I'm done, exhausted, I've stuffed to distraction, the last fill-in work is done. There's not a millionth of an inch of space left between my ankles and my Adam's apple where we can squeeze in one last demon, dervish or baroque angel. I am, to Willy, work over and done. Now he wants to move on. He will marry, I fear, four more times in his life, each time to a larger woman, a greater extension for a greater mural, and the grand finale of his talent. Then, too, in the last week, he has become critical."

"Of the Masterpiece with a capital *M*?" asked the doctor.

"Like all artists, he is a superb perfectionist. Now he finds little flaws, a face here done slightly in the wrong tint or texture, a hand there twisted slightly askew by my hurried diet to gain more weight and thus give him new space and renew his attentions. To him, above all, I was a beginning. Now he must move on from his apprenticeship to his true masterworks. Oh, Doctor, I am about to be abandoned. What is there for a woman who weighs four hundred pounds and is laved with illustrations? If he leaves, what shall I do, where go, who would want me now? Will I be lost again in the world as I was before my wild happiness?"

"A psychiatrist," said the psychiatrist, "is not supposed to give advice. But . . ."

"But, but, but?" she cried, eagerly.

"A psychiatrist is supposed to let the patient discover and cure himself. Yet, in this case . . ."

"This case, yes, go on!"

"It seems so simple. To keep your husband's love . . . "

"To keep his love, yes?"

The doctor smiled. "You must destroy the Masterpiece."

"What?"

"Erase it, get rid of it. Those tattoos *will* come off, won't they? I read somewhere once that—"

"Oh, Doctor!" Emma Fleet leaped up. "That's *it*! It can be done! And, best of all, Willy can do it! It will take three months alone to wash me clean, rid me of the very Masterpiece that irks him now. Then, virgin white again, we can start another eight years, after that another eight and another. Oh, Doctor, I know he'll do it! Perhaps he was only waiting for me to suggest—and I too stupid to guess! Oh, Doctor, Doctor!"

And she crushed him in her arms.

When the doctor broke happily free, she stood off, turning in a circle.

"How strange," she said. "In half an hour you solve the next three thousand days and beyond of my life. You're very wise. I'll pay you anything!"

"My usual modest fee is sufficient," said the doctor.

"I can hardly wait to tell Willy! But first," she said, "since you've been so wise, you deserve to see the Masterpiece before it is destroyed."

"That's hardly necessary, Mrs.—"

"You must discover for yourself the rare mind, eye and artistic hand of Willy Fleet, before it is gone forever and we start anew!" she cried, unbuttoning her voluminous coat.

"It isn't really—"

"There!" she said, and flung her coat wide.

The doctor was somehow not surprised to see that she was stark naked beneath her coat.

He gasped. His eyes grew large. His mouth fell open. He sat down slowly, though in reality he somehow wished to stand, as he had in the fifth grade as a boy, during the salute to the flag, following which three dozen voices broke into an awed and tremulous song:

> *O beautiful for spacious skies*
> *For amber waves of grain,*
> *For purple mountain majesties*
> *Above the fruited plain . . .*

But, still seated, overwhelmed, he gazed at the continental vastness of the woman.

Upon which nothing whatsoever was stitched, painted, water-colored or in any way tattooed.

Naked, unadorned, untouched, unlined, unillustrated.

He gasped again.

Now she had whipped her coat back about her with a winsome acrobat's smile, as if she had just performed a towering feat. Now she was sailing toward the door.

"Wait—" said the doctor.

But she was out the door, in the reception room, babbling, whispering, "Willy, Willy!" and bending to her husband, hissing in his tiny ear until *his* eyes flexed wide, and his mouth firm and passionate dropped open and he cried aloud and clapped his hands with elation.

"Doctor, Doctor, thank you, thank you!"

He darted forward and seized the doctor's hand and shook it, hard. The doctor was surprised at the fire and rock hardness of that grip. It was the hand of a dedicated artist, as were the eyes burning up at him darkly from the wildly illuminated face.

"Everything's going to be fine!" cried Willy.

The doctor hesitated, glancing from Willy to the great shadowing balloon that tugged at him wanting to fly off away.

"We won't have to come back again, ever?"

Good Lord, the doctor thought, does *he* think that *he* has illustrated her from stem to stern, and does she humor him about it? Is *he* mad?

Or does *she* imagine that he has tattooed her from neck to toe-bone, and does he humor her? Is *she* mad?"

Or, most strange of all, do they *both* believe that he has swarmed as across the Sistine Chapel ceiling, covering her with rare and significant beauties? Do they both believe, know, humor each other in their specially dimensioned world?

"Will we have to come back again?" asked Willy Fleet a second time.

"No." The doctor breathed a prayer. "I think not."

Why? Because, by some idiot grace, he had done the right thing, hadn't he? By prescribing for a half-seen cause he had made a full cure, yes? Regardless if she believed or he believed or both believed in the Masterpiece, by suggesting the pictures be erased, destroyed, the doctor had made her a clean, lovely and inviting canvas again, if *she* needed to be. And if he, on the other hand, wished a new woman to scribble, scrawl and pretend to tattoo on, well, that worked, too. For new and untouched she would be.

"Thank you, Doctor, oh thank you, thank you!"

"Don't thank me," said the doctor. "I've done nothing." He almost said, It was all a fluke, a joke, a surprise! I fell downstairs and landed on my feet!

"Good-by, good-by!"

And the elevator slid down, the big woman and the little man sinking from sight into the now suddenly not-too-solid earth, where the atoms opened to let them pass.

"Good-by, thanks, thanks . . . thanks . . ."

Their voices faded, calling his name and praising his intellect long after they had passed the fourth floor.

The doctor looked around and moved unsteadily back into his office. He shut the door and leaned against it.

"Doctor," he murmured, "heal thyself."

He stepped forward. He did not feel real. He must lie down, if but for a moment.

Where?

On the couch, of course, on the couch.

Some Live Like Lazarus

You won't believe it when I tell you I waited more than sixty years for a murder, hoped as only a woman can hope that it might happen, and didn't move a finger to stop it when it finally drew near. Anna Marie, I thought, you can't stand guard forever. Murder, when ten thousand days have passed, is more than a surprise, it is a miracle.

"Hold on! Don't let me fall!"

Mrs. Harrison's voice.

Did I ever, in half a century, hear it whisper? Was it always screaming, shrieking, demanding, threatening?

Yes, always.

"Come along, Mother. There you are, Mother."

Her son Roger's voice.

Did I ever in all the years hear it rise above a murmur, protest, or, even faintly birdlike, argue?

No. Always the loving monotone.

This morning, no different than any other of their first mornings, they arrived in their great black hearse for their annual Green Bay summer. There he was, thrusting his hand in to hoist the window dummy after him, an ancient sachet of bones and talcum dust that was named, surely for some terrible practical joke, Mother.

"Easy does it, Mother."

"You're bruising my arm!"

"Sorry, Mother."

I watched from a window of the lake pavilion as he trundled her off down the path in her wheel chair, she pushing her cane like a musket ahead to blast any Fates or Furies they might meet out of the way.

"Careful, don't run me into the flowers, thank God we'd sense not to go to Paris after all. You'd've had me in that nasty traffic. You're not disappointed?"

"No, Mother."

"We'll see Paris next year."

Next year . . . next year . . . no year at all, I heard someone murmur. Myself, gripping the window sill. For almost seventy years I had heard her promise this to the boy, boy-man, man, man-grasshopper and the now livid male praying mantis that he was, pushing his eternally cold and fur-wrapped woman past the hotel verandas where, in another age, paper fans had fluttered like Oriental butterflies in the hands of basking ladies.

"There, Mother, inside the cottage . . . " his faint voice fading still more, forever young when he was old, forever old when he was very young.

How old is she now? I wondered. Ninety-eight, yes, ninety-nine wicked years old. She seemed like a horror film repeated each year because the hotel entertainment fund could not afford to buy a new one to run in the moth-flaked evenings.

So, through all the repetitions of arrivals and departures, my mind ran back to when the foundations of the Green Bay Hotel were freshly poured and the parasols were new leaf green and lemon gold, that summer of 1890 when I first saw Roger, who was five, but whose eyes already were old and wise and tired.

He stood on the pavilion grass looking at the sun and the bright pennants as I came up to him.

"Hello," I said.

He simply looked at me.

I hesitated, tagged him and ran.

He did not move.

I came back and tagged him again.

He looked at the place where I had touched him, on the shoulder, and was about to run after me when her voice came from a distance.

"Roger, don't dirty your clothes!"

And he walked slowly away toward his cottage, not looking back.

That was the day I started to hate him.

Parasols have come and gone in a thousand summer colors, whole flights of butterfly fans have blown away on August winds, the pavilion has burned and been built again in the selfsame size and shape, the lake has dried like a plum in its basin, and my hatred, like these things, came and went, grew very large, stopped still for love, returned, then diminished with the years.

I remember when he was seven, them driving by in their horse carriage, his hair long, brushing his poutish, shrugging shoulders. They were holding hands and she was saying, "If you're very good this summer, next year we'll go to London. Or the year after that, at the latest."

And my watching their faces, comparing their eyes, their ears, their mouths, so when he came in for a soda pop one noon that summer I walked straight up to him and cried, "She's not your mother!"

"What!" He looked around in panic, as if she might be near.

"She's not your aunt or your grandma, either!" I cried. "She's a witch that stole you when you were a baby. You don't know who your mama is or your pa. You don't look anything like her. She's holding you for a million ransom which comes due when you're twenty-one from some duke or king!"

"Don't say that!" he shouted, jumping up.

"Why not?" I said angrily. "Why do you come around here? You can't play this, can't play that, can't do nothing, what good are you? She says, she does. I know *her*! She hangs upside down from the ceiling in her black clothes in her bedroom at midnight!"

"Don't say that!" His face was frightened and pale.

"Why not say it?"

"Because," he bleated, "it's true."

And he was out the door and running.

I didn't see him again until the next summer. And then only once, briefly, when I took some clean linen down to their cottage.

The summer when we were both twelve was the summer that for a time I didn't hate him.

He called my name outside the pavilion screen door and when I looked out he said, very quietly, "Anna Marie, when I am twenty and you are twenty, I'm going to marry you."

"Who's going to let you?" I asked.

"I'm going to let you," he said. "You just remember, Anna Marie. You wait for me. Promise?"

I could only nod. "But what about—"

"She'll be dead by then," he said, very gravely. "She's old. She's *old*."

And then he turned and went away.

The next summer they did not come to the resort at all. I heard she was sick. I prayed every night that she would die.

But two years later they were back, and the year after the year after that until Roger was nineteen and I was nineteen, and then at last we had reached and touched twenty, and for one of the few times in all the years, they came into the pavilion together, she in her wheel chair now, deeper in her furs than ever before, her face a gathering of white dust and folded parchment.

She eyed me as I set her ice cream sundae down before her, and eyed Roger as he said, "Mother, I want you to meet—"

"I do not meet girls who wait on public tables," she said. "I acknowledge they exist, work, and are paid. But I immediately forget their names."

She touched and nibbled her ice cream, touched and nibbled her ice cream, while Roger sat not touching his at all.

They left a day earlier than usual that year. I saw Roger as he paid the bill, in the hotel lobby. He shook my hand to say good-by and I could not help but say, "You've forgotten."

He took a half step back, then turned around, patting his coat pockets.

"Luggage, bills paid, wallet, no, I seem to have everything," he said.

"A long time ago," I said, "you made a promise."

He was silent.

"Roger," I said, "I'm twenty now. And so are you."

He seized my hand again, swiftly, as if he were falling over the side of a ship and it was me going away, leaving him to drown forever beyond help.

"One more year, Anna! Two, three, at the most!"

"Oh, no," I said, forlornly.

"Four years at the outside! The doctors say—"

"The doctors don't know what I know, Roger. She'll live forever. She'll bury you and me and drink wine at our funerals."

"She's a sick woman, Anna! My God, she *can't* survive!"

"She will, because we give her strength. She knows we want her dead. That really gives her the power to go on."

"I can't talk this way, I can't!" Seizing his luggage, he started down the hall.

"I won't wait, Roger," I said.

He turned at the door and looked at me so helplessly, so palely, like a moth pinned to the wall, that I could not say it again.

The door slammed shut.

The summer was over.

The next year Roger came directly to the soda fountain, where he said, "Is it true? Who is he?"

"Paul," I said. "You know Paul. He'll manage the hotel someday. We'll marry this fall."

"That doesn't give me much time," said Roger.

"It's too late," I said. "I've already promised."

"Promised, hell! You don't love him!"

"I think I do."

"Think, hell! Thinking's one thing, knowing's another. You *know* you love me!"

"Do I, Roger?"

"Stop relishing the damn business so much! You know you do! Oh, Anna, you'll be miserable!"

"I'm miserable now," I said.

"Oh, Anna, Anna, wait!"

"I have waited, most of my life. But I know what will happen."

"Anna!" He blurted it out as if it had come to him suddenly. "What if—what if she died *this* summer?"

"She won't."

"But if she did, if she took a turn for the worse, I mean, in the next two months—" He searched my face. He shortened it. "The next month, Anna, two weeks, listen, if she died in two short weeks, would you wait that long, would you marry me then?!"

I began to cry. "Oh, Roger, we've never even kissed. This is ridiculous."

"Answer me, if she died one week, seven days from now . . . " He grabbed my arms.

"But how can you be sure?"

"I'll *make* myself sure! I swear she'll be dead a week from now, or I'll *never* bother you again with this!"

And he flung the screen doors wide, hurrying off into the day that was suddenly too bright.

"Roger, don't—" I cried.

But my mind thought, Roger *do*, do something, anything, to start it all or end it all.

That night in bed I thought, What ways are there for murder that no one could know? Is Roger, a hundred yards away this moment, thinking the same? Will he search the woods tomorrow for toadstools resembling mushrooms, or drive the car too fast and fling her door wide on a curve? I saw the wax-dummy witch fly through the air in a lovely soaring arc, to break like ridiculous peanut brittle on an oak, an elm, a maple. I sat up in bed. I laughed until I wept. I wept until I laughed again. No, no, I thought, he'll find a better way. A night burglar will shock her heart into her throat. Once in her throat, he will not let it go down again, she'll choke on her own panic.

And then the oldest, the darkest, most childish thought of all. There's only one way to finish a woman whose mouth is the color of blood. Being what she is, no relative, not an aunt or a great-grandmother, surprise her with a stake driven through her heart!

I heard her scream. It was so loud, all the night birds jumped from the trees to cover the stars.

I lay back down. Dear Christian Anna Marie, I thought, what's this? Do you want to kill? Yes, for why not kill a killer, a woman who strangled her child in his crib and has not loosened the throttling cord since? He is so pale, poor man, because he has not breathed free air, all of his life.

And then, unbidden, the lines of an old poem stood up in my head. Where I had read them or who had put them down, or if I had written them myself, within my head over the years, I could not say. But the lines were there and I read them in the dark:

> *Some live like Lazarus*
> *In a tomb of life*
> *And come forth curious late to twilight hospitals*
> *And mortuary rooms.*

The lines vanished. For a while I could recall no more, and then, unable to fend it off, for it came of itself, a last fragment appeared in the dark:

> *Better cold skies seen bitter to the North*
> *Than stillborn stay, all blind and gone to ghost.*
> *If Rio is lost, well, love the Arctic Coast!*
> *O ancient Lazarus*
> *Come ye forth.*

There the poem stopped and let me be. At last I slept, restless, hoping for the dawn, and good and final news.

The next day I saw him pushing her along the pier and thought, Yes, that's it! She'll vanish and be found a week from now, on the shore, like a sea monster floating, all face and no body.

That day passed. Well, surely, I thought, tomorrow . . .

The second day of the week, the third, the fourth and then the fifth and sixth passed, and on the seventh day one of the maids came running up the path, shrieking.

"Oh, it's terrible, terrible!"

"Mrs. Harrison?" I cried. I felt a terrible and quite uncontrollable smile on my face.

"No, no, her *son*! He's hung himself!"

"Hung himself?" I said ridiculously, and found myself, stunned, explaining to her. "Oh, no, it wasn't *him* was going to die, it was—" I babbled. I stopped, for the maid was clutching, pulling my arm.

"We cut him down, oh, God, he's still alive, quick!"

Still alive? He still breathed, yes, and walked around through the other years, yes, but alive? No.

It was she who gained strength and lived through his attempt to escape her. She never forgave his trying to run off.

"What do you mean by that, what do you mean?" I remember her screaming at him as he lay feeling his throat, in the cottage, his eyes shut, wilted, and I hurried in the door. "What do you mean doing that, what, what?"

And looking at him there I knew he had tried to run away from both of us, we were both impossible to him. I did not forgive him that either, for a while. But I did feel my old hatred of him become something else, a kind of dull pain, as I turned and went back for a doctor.

"What do you mean, you silly boy?" she cried.

I married Paul that autumn.

After that, the years poured through the glass swiftly. Once each year, Roger led himself into the pavilion to sit eating mint ice with his limp empty-gloved hands, but he never called me by my name again, nor did he mention the old promise.

Here and there in the hundreds of months that passed I thought, For his own sake now, for no one else, sometime, somehow he must simply up and destroy the dragon with the hideous bellows face and the rust-scaled hands. For Roger and only for Roger, Roger must do it.

Surely *this* year, I thought, when he was fifty, fifty-one, fifty-two. Between seasons I caught myself examining occasional Chicago papers, hoping to find a picture of her lying slit like a monstrous yellow chicken. But no, but no, but no. . . .

I'd almost forgotten them when they returned this morning. He's very old now, more like a doddering husband than a son. Baked gray clay he is, with milky blue eyes, a toothless mouth, and manicured fingernails which seem stronger because the flesh has baked away.

At noon today, after a moment of standing out, a lone gray wingless hawk staring at a sky in which he had never soared or flown, he came inside and spoke to me, his voice rising.

"Why didn't you tell me?"

"Tell you what?" I said, scooping out his ice cream before he asked for it.

"One of the maids just mentioned, your husband died five years ago! You should have told me!"

"Well, now you know," I said.

He sat down slowly. "Lord," he said, tasting the ice cream and savoring it, eyes shut, "this is bitter." Then, a long time later, he said, "Anna, I never asked. Were there ever any children?"

"No," I said. "And I don't know why. I guess I'll never know why."

I left him sitting there and went to wash the dishes.

At nine tonight I heard someone laughing by the lake. I hadn't heard Roger laugh since he was a child, so I didn't think it was him until the doors burst wide and he entered, flinging his arms about, unable to control his almost weeping hilarity.

"Roger!" I asked. "What's wrong?"

"Nothing! Oh, nothing!" he cried. "Everything's lovely! A root beer, Anna! Take one yourself! Drink with me!"

We drank together, he laughed, winked, then got immensely calm. Still smiling, though, he looked suddenly, beautifully young.

"Anna," he whispered intensely, leaning forward, "guess what? I'm flying to China tomorrow! Then India! Then London, Madrid, Paris, Berlin, Rome, Mexico City!"

"*You* are, Roger?"

"I am," he said. "I, I, I, not we, we, we, but I, Roger Bidwell Harrison, I, I, *I*!"

I stared at him and he gazed quietly back at me, and I must have gasped. For then I knew what he had finally done tonight, this hour, within the last few minutes.

Oh, no, my lips must have murmured.

Oh, but yes, yes, his eyes upon me replied, incredible miracle of miracles, after all these waiting years. Tonight at last. Tonight.

I let him talk. After Rome it was Vienna and Stockholm, he'd saved thousands of schedules, flight charts and hotel bulletins for forty years; he knew the moons and tides, the goings and comings of everything on the sea and in the sky.

"But best of all," he said at last, "Anna, Anna, will you come along with me? I've lots of money put away, don't let me run on! Anna, tell me, *will* you?"

I came around the counter slowly and saw myself in the mirror, a woman in her seventieth year going to a party half a century late.

I sat down beside him and shook my head.

"Oh, but, Anna, why not, there's no reason why!"

"There is a reason," I said. "You."

"Me, but I don't count!"

"That's just it, Roger, you do."

"Anna, we could have a wonderful time—"

"I daresay. But, Roger, you've *been* married for seventy years. Now, for the first time, you're not married. You don't want to turn around and get married again right off, do you?"

"*Don't* I?" he asked, blinking.

"You don't, you really don't. You deserve a little while, at least, off by yourself, to see the world, to know who Roger Harrison is. A little while away from women. Then, when you've gone around the world and come back, is time to think of other things."

"If you *say* so—"

"No. It mustn't be anything I say or know or tell you to do. Right now it must be you telling yourself what to know and see and do. Go have a grand time. If you can, be happy."

"Will you be here waiting for me when I come back?"

"I haven't it in me any more to wait, but I'll be here."

He moved toward the door, then stopped and looked at me as if surprised by some new question that had come into his mind.

"Anna," he said, "if all this had happened forty, fifty years ago, would you have gone away with me then? Would you really have married me?"

I did not answer.

"Anna?" he asked.

After a long while I said, "There are some questions that should never be asked."

Because, I went on, thinking, there can be no answers. Looking down the years toward the lake, I could not remember, so I could not say, whether we could have ever been happy. Perhaps even as a child, sensing the impossible in Roger, I had clenched the impossible, and therefore the rare, to my heart, simply because it was impossible and rare. He was a sprig of farewell summer pressed in an old book, to be taken out, turned over, admired, once a year, but more than that? Who could say? Surely not I, so long, so late in the day. Life is questions, not answers.

Roger had come very close to read my face, my mind, while I thought all this. What he saw there made him look away, close his eyes, then take my hand and press it to his cheek.

"I'll be back. I swear I will!"

Outside the door he stood bewildered for a moment in the moonlight, looking at the world and all its directions, east, west, north, south, like a child out of school for his first summer not knowing which way to go first, just breathing, just listening, just seeing.

"Don't hurry!" I said fervently. "Oh, God, whatever you do, please, enjoy yourself, don't hurry!"

I saw him run off toward the limousine near the cottage where I am supposed to rap in the morning and where I will get no answer. But I know that I will not go to the cottage and that I'll keep the maids from going there because the old lady has given orders not to be bothered. That will give Roger the chance, the start he needs. In a week or two or three, I might call the police. Then if they met Roger coming back on the boat from all those wild places, it won't matter.

Police? Perhaps not even them. Perhaps she died of a heart attack and poor Roger only thinks he killed her and now proudly sails off into the world, his pride not allowing him to know that only her own self-made death released him.

But then again, if at last all the murder he put away for seventy years forced him tonight to lay hands on and kill the hideous turkey, I could not find it in my heart to weep for her but only for the great time it has taken to act out the sentence.

The road is silent. An hour has passed since the limousine roared away down the road.

Now I have just put out the lights and stand alone in the pavilion looking out at the shining lake where in another century, under another sun, a small boy with an old face was first touched to play tag with me and now, very late, has tagged me back, has kissed my hand and run away, and this time myself, stunned, not following.

Many things I do not know, tonight.

But one thing I'm sure of.

I do not hate Roger Harrison any more.

The Best of All Possible Worlds

The two men sat swaying side by side, unspeaking for the long while it took for the train to move through cold December twilight, pausing at one country station after another. As the twelfth depot was left behind, the older of the two men muttered, "Idiot, Idiot!" under his breath.

"What?" The younger man glanced up from his *Times*.

The old man nodded bleakly. "Did you see that damn fool rush off just now, stumbling after that woman who smelled of Chanel?"

"Oh, her?" The young man looked as if he could not decide whether to laugh or be depressed. "I followed her off the train once myself."

The old man snorted and closed his eyes. "I too, five years ago."

The young man stared at his companion as if he had found a friend in a most unlikely spot.

"Did—did the same thing happen once you reached the end of the platform?"

"Perhaps. Go on."

"Well, I was twenty feet behind her and closing up fast when her husband drove into the station with a carload of kids! Bang! The car door slammed. I saw her Cheshire-cat smile as she drove away. I waited half an hour, chilled to the bone, for another train. It taught me something, by God!"

"It taught you nothing whatsoever," replied the older man dryly. "Idiot bulls, that's all of us, you, me, them, silly boys jerking like laboratory frogs if someone scratches our itch."

"My grandpa once said, 'Big in the hunkus, small in the brain, that is man's fate.'"

"A wise man. But, now, what do you make of *her*?"

"That woman? Oh, she likes to keep in trim. It must pep up her liver to know that with a little mild eye-rolling she can make the lemmings swarm any night on this train. She has the best of all possible worlds, don't you think? Husband, children, plus the knowledge she's neat packaging and can prove it five trips a week, hurting no one, least of all herself. And, everything considered, she's not much to look at. It's just she *smells* so good."

"Tripe," said the old man. "It won't wash. Purely and simply, she's a woman. All women are women, all men are dirty goats. Until you accept that, you will be rationalizing your glands all your life. As it is, you will know no rest until you are seventy or thereabouts. Meanwhile, self-knowledge may give you whatever solace can be had in a sticky situation. Given all these essential and inescapable truths, few men ever strike a balance. Ask a man if he is happy and he will immediately think you are asking if he is *satisfied*. Satiety is most men's Edenic dream. I have known only one man who came heir to the very best of all possible worlds, as you used the phrase."

"Good Lord," said the young man, his eyes shining, "I wouldn't mind hearing about him."

"I hope there's time. This chap is the happiest ram, the most carefree bull, in history. Wives and girl friends galore, as the sales pitch says. Yet he has no qualms, guilts, no feverish nights of lament and self-chastisement."

"Impossible," the young man put in. "You can't eat your cake and digest it, too!"

"He did, he does, he will! Not a tremor, not a trace of moral seasickness after an all-night journey over a choppy sea of innersprings! Successful businessman. Apartment in New York on the best street, the proper height above traffic, plus a long-weekend Bucks County place on a more than correct little country stream where he herds his nannies, the happy farmer. But I met him first at his New York apartment last year, when he had just married. At dinner, his wife was truly gorgeous, snow-cream arms, fruity lips, an amplitude of harvest land below the line, a plenitude above. Honey in the horn, the full apple barrel through winter, she seemed thus to me *and* her husband, who nipped her bicep in passing. Leaving, at midnight, I found myself raising a hand to slap her on the flat of her flank like a thoroughbred. Falling down in the elevator, life floated out from under me. I nickered."

"Your powers of description," said the young commuter, breathing heavily, "are incredible."

"I write advertising copy," said the older. "But to continue. I met let us call him Smith again not two weeks later. Through sheer coincidence I was invited to crash a party by a friend. When I arrived in Bucks County, whose place should it turn out to be but Smith's! And near him, in the center of the living room, stood this dark Italian beauty, all tawny panther, all midnight and moonstones, dressed in earth colors, browns, siennas, tans, umbers, all the tones of a riotously fruitful autumn. In the babble I lost her name. Later I saw Smith crush her like a great sunwarmed vine of lush October grapes in his arms. Idiot fool, I thought. Lucky dog, I thought. Wife in town, mistress in country. He is trampling out the vintage, et cetera, and all that. Glorious. But I shall not stay for the wine festival, I thought, and slipped away, unnoticed."

"I can't stand too much of this talk," said the young commuter, trying to raise the window.

"Don't interrupt," said the older man. "Where was I?"

"Trampled. Vintage."

"Oh, yes! Well, as the party broke up, I finally caught the lovely Italian's name. *Mrs.* Smith!"

"He'd married again, eh?"

"Hardly. Not enough time. Stunned, I thought quickly: He must have two sets of friends. One set knows his city wife. The other set knows this mistress whom he *calls* wife. Smith's too smart for bigamy. No other answer. Mystery."

"Go on, go on," said the young commuter feverishly.

"Smith, in high spirits, drove me to the train station that night. On the way he said, 'What do you think of my wives?'

"'Wives, plural?' I said.

"'Plural, hell,' he said. 'I've had twenty in the last three years, each better than the last! Twenty, count them, twenty! Here!' As we stopped at the station he pulled out a thick photo wallet. He glanced at my face as he handed it over. 'No, no,' he laughed, 'I'm not Bluebeard with a score of old theater trunks in the attic crammed full of former mates. Look!'

"I flipped the pictures. They flew by like an animated film. Blondes, brunettes, redheads, the plain, the exotic, the fabulously impertinent or the sublimely docile gazed out at me, smiling, frowning. The flutter-flicker hypnotized, then haunted me. There was something terribly familiar about each photo.

"'Smith,' I said, 'you must be very rich to afford all these wives.'

" 'Not rich, no. Look again!'

"I flipped the montage in my hands. I gasped. I knew.

" 'The Mrs. Smith I met tonight, the Italian beauty, is the one and only Mrs. Smith,' I said. 'But, at the same time, the woman I met in New York two weeks ago is also the one and only Mrs. Smith. It can only follow that both women are one and the same!'

" 'Correct!' cried Smith, proud of my sleuthing.

" 'Impossible!' I blurted out.

" 'No,' said Smith, elated. 'My wife is amazing. One of the finest off-Broadway actresses when I met her. Selfishly I asked her to quit the stage on pain of severance of our mutual insanity, our rampaging up one side of a chaise-longue and down the other. A giantess made dwarf by love, she slammed the door on the theater, to run down the alley with me. The first six months of our marriage, the earth did not move, it shook. But, inevitably, fiend that I am, I began to watch various other women ticking by like wondrous pendulums. My wife caught me noting the time. Meanwhile, she had begun to cast her eyes on passing theatrical billboards. I found her nesting with the *New York Times* next-morning reviews, desperately tearful. Crisis! How to combine two violent careers, that of passion-disheveled actress and that of anxiously rambling ram?'

" 'One night,' said Smith, 'I eyed a peach Melba that drifted by. Simultaneously, an old playbill blew in the wind and clung to my wife's ankle. It was as if these two events, occurring within the moment, had shot a window shade with a rattling snap clear to the top of its roll. Light *poured* in! My wife seized my arm. Was she or was she not an actress? She was! Well, then, well! She sent me packing for twenty-four hours, wouldn't let me in the apartment, as she hurried about some vast and exciting preparations. When I returned home the next afternoon at the blue hour, as the French say in their always twilight language, my wife had vanished! A dark Latin put out her hand to me. "I am a friend of your wife's," she said and threw herself upon me, to nibble my ears, crack my ribs, until I held her off and, suddenly suspicious, cried, "This is no woman I'm with—this is my *wife*!" And we both fell laughing to the floor. This *was* my wife, with a different cosmetic, different couturier, different posture and intonation. "My actress!" I said. "Your actress!" she laughed. "Tell me what I should be and I'll be it. Carmen? All right, I'm Carmen. Brunhild? Why not? I'll study, create and, when you grow bored, re-create. I'm enrolled at the Dance Academy. I'll learn to sit, stand, walk, ten thousand ways. I'm chin deep in speech lessons, I'm signed at the Berlitz! I am also a member of the Yamayuki Judo Club—" "Good Lord," I cried, "what for?" "This!" she replied, and tossed me head over heels into bed!'

" 'Well,' said Smith, 'from that day on I've lived Riley and nine other Irishmen's lives! Unnumbered fancies have passed me in delightful shadow plays of women all colors, shapes, sizes, fevers! My wife, finding her proper stage, our parlor, and audience, me, has fulfilled her need to be the greatest actress in the land. Too small an audience? No! For I, with my ever-wandering tastes, am there to meet her, whichever part she plays. My jungle talent coincides with her wide-ranging genius. So, caged at last, yet free, loving her I love every-one. It's the best of all possible worlds, friend, the best of all possible worlds.' "

There was a moment of silence.

The train rumbled down the track in the new December darkness.

The two commuters, the young and the old, were thoughtful now, considering the story just finished.

At last the young man swallowed and nodded in awe. "Your friend Smith solved his problem, all right."

"He did."

The young man debated a moment, then smiled quietly. "I have a friend, too. His situation was similar, but—different. Shall I call him Quillan?"

"Yes," said the old man, "but hurry. I get off soon."

"Quillan," said the young man quickly, "was in a bar one night with a fabulous redhead. The crowd parted before her like the sea before Moses. Miraculous, I thought, revivifying, beyond the senses! A week later, in Greenwich, I saw Quillan ambling along with a dumpy little woman, his own age, of course, only thirty-two, but she'd gone to seed young. Tatty, the English would say; pudgy, snouty-nosed, not enough make-up, wrinkled stockings, spider's-nest hair, and immensely quiet; she was content to walk along, it seemed, just holding Quillan's hand. Ha, I thought, here's his poor little parsnip wife who loves the earth he treads, while other nights he's out winding up that incredible robot redhead! How sad, what a shame. And I went on my way.

"A month later I met Quillan again. He was about to dart into a dark entranceway in MacDougal Street, when he saw me. 'Oh, God!' he cried, sweating. 'Don't tell on me! My wife must never know!'

"I was about to swear myself to secrecy when a woman called to Quillan from a window above.

"I glanced up. My jaw dropped.

"There in the window stood the dumpy, seedy little woman!!

"So suddenly it was clear. The beautiful redhead was his *wife*! She danced, she sang, she talked loud and long, a brilliant intellectual, the goddess Siva, thousand-limbed, the finest throw pillow ever sewn by mortal hand. Yet she was strangely—tiring.

"So my friend Quillan had taken this obscure Village room where, two nights a week, he could sit quietly in the mouse-brown silence or walk on the dim streets with this good homely dumpy comfortably mute woman who was not his wife at all, as I had quickly supposed, but his mistress!

"I looked from Quillan to his plump companion in the window above and wrung his hand with new warmth and understanding. 'Mum's the word!' I said. The last I saw of them, they were seated in a delicatessen, Quillan and his mistress, their eyes gently touching each other, saying nothing, eating pastrami sandwiches. He too had, if you think about it, the best of all possible worlds."

The train roared, shouted its whistle and slowed. Both men, rising, stopped and looked at each other in surprise. Both spoke at once:

"You get off at *this* stop?"

Both nodded, smiling.

Silently they made their way back and, as the train stopped in the chill December night, alighted and shook hands.

"Well, give my best to Mr. Smith."

"And mine to Mr. Quillan!"

Two horns honked from opposite ends of the station. Both men looked at one car. A beautiful woman was in it. Both looked at the other car. A beautiful woman was in it.

They separated, looking back at each other like two schoolboys, each stealing a glance at the car toward which the other was moving.

"I wonder," thought the old man, "if that woman down there is . . . "

"I wonder," thought the young man, "if that lady in his car could be . . . "

But both were running now. Two car doors slammed like pistol shots ending a matinee.

The cars drove off. The station platform stood empty. It being December and cold, snow soon fell like a curtain.

The One Who Waits

I live in a well. I live like smoke in a well. Like vapor in a stone throat. I don't move. I don't do anything but wait. Overhead I see the cold stars of night and morning, and I see the sun. And sometimes I sing old songs of this world when it was young. How can I tell you what I am when I don't know? I cannot. I am simply waiting. I am mist and moonlight and memory. I am sad and I am old. Sometimes I fall like rain into the well. Spider webs are startled into forming where my rain falls fast, on the water surface. I wait in cool silence and there will be a day when I no longer wait.

Now it is morning. I hear a great thunder. I smell fire from a distance. I hear a metal crashing. I wait. I listen.

Voices. Far away.

"All right!"

One voice. An alien voice. An alien tongue I cannot know. No word is familiar. I listen.

"Send the men out!"

A crunching in crystal sands.

"Mars! So this is it!"

"Where's the flag?"

"Here, sir."

"Good, good."

The sun is high in the blue sky and its golden rays fill the well and I hang like a flower pollen, invisible and misting in the warm light.

Voices.

"In the name of the Government of Earth, I proclaim this to be the Martian Territory, to be equally divided among the member nations."

What are they saying? I turn in the sun, like a wheel, invisible and lazy, golden and tireless.

"What's over here?"

"A well!"

"No!"

"Come on. Yes!"

The approach of warmth. Three objects bend over the well mouth, and my coolness rises to the objects.

"Great!"

"Think it's good water?"

"We'll see."

"Someone get a lab test bottle and a dropline."

"I will!"

A sound of running. The return.

"Here we are."

I wait.

"Let it down. Easy."

Glass shines, above, coming down on a slow line.

The water ripples softly as the glass touches and fills. I rise in the warm air toward the well mouth.

"Here we are. You want to test this water, Regent?"

"Let's have it."

"What a beautiful well. Look at that construction. How old you think it is?"

"God knows. When we landed in that other town yesterday Smith said there hasn't been life on Mars in ten thousand years."

"Imagine."

"How is it, Regent? The water."

"Pure as silver. Have a glass."

The sound of water in the hot sunlight. Now I hover like a dust, a cinnamon, upon the soft wind.

"What's the matter, Jones?"

"I don't know. Got a terrible headache. All of a sudden."

"Did you drink the water yet?"

"No, I haven't. It's not that. I was just bending over the well and all of a sudden my head split. I feel better now."

Now I know who I am.

My name is Stephen Leonard Jones and I am twenty-five years old and I have just come in a rocket from a planet called Earth and I am standing with my good friends Regent and Shaw by an old well on the planet Mars.

I look down at my golden fingers, tan and strong. I look at my long legs and at my silver uniform and at my friends.

"What's wrong, Jones?" they say.

"Nothing," I say, looking at them. "Nothing at all."

The food is good. It has been ten thousand years since food. It touches the tongue in a fine way and the wine with the food is warming. I listen to the sound of voices. I make words that I do not understand but somehow understand. I test the air.

"What's the matter, Jones?"

I tilt this head of mine and rest my hands holding the silver utensils of eating. I feel everything.

"What do you mean?" this voice, this new thing of mine, says.

"You keep breathing funny. Coughing," says the other man.

I pronounce exactly. "Maybe a little cold coming on."

"Check with the doc later."

I nod my head and it is good to nod. It is good to do several things after ten thousand years. It is good to breathe the air and it is good to feel the sun in the flesh deep and going deeper and it is good to feel the structure of ivory, the fine skeleton hidden in the warming flesh, and it is good to hear sounds much clearer and more immediate than they were in the stone deepness of a well. I sit enchanted.

"Come out of it, Jones. Snap to it. We got to move!"

"Yes," I say, hypnotized with the way the word forms like water on the tongue and falls with slow beauty out into the air.

I walk and it is good walking. I stand high and it is a long way to the ground when I look down from my eyes and my head. It is like living on a fine cliff and being happy there.

Regent stands by the stone well, looking down. The others have gone murmuring to the silver ship from which they came.

I feel the fingers of my hand and the smile of my mouth.

"It is deep," I say.

"Yes."

"It is called a Soul Well."

Regent raises his head and looks at me. "How do you know that?"

"Doesn't it look like one?"

"I never heard of a Soul Well."

"A place where waiting things, things that once had flesh, wait and wait," I say, touching his arm.

The sand is fire and the ship is silver fire in the hotness of the day and the heat is good to feel. The sound of my feet in the hard sand. I listen. The sound of the wind and the sun burning the valleys. I smell the smell of the rocket boiling in the noon. I stand below the port.

"Where's Regent?" someone says.

"I saw him by the well," I reply.

One of them runs toward the well. I am beginning to tremble. A fine shivering tremble, hidden deep, but becoming very strong. And for the first time I hear it, as if it too were hidden in a well. A voice calling deep within me, tiny and afraid. And the voice cries, *Let me go, let me go*, and there is a feeling as if something is trying to get free, a pounding of labyrinthine doors, a rushing down dark corridors and up passages, echoing and screaming.

"Regent's in the well!"

The men are running, all five of them. I run with them but now I am sick and the trembling is violent.

"He must have fallen. Jones, you were here with him. Did you see? Jones? Well, speak up, man."

"What's wrong, Jones?"

I fall to my knees, the trembling is so bad.

"He's sick. Here, help me with him."

"The sun."

"No, not the sun," I murmur.

They stretch me out and the seizures come and go like earthquakes and the deep hidden voice in me cries, *This is Jones, this is* me, *that's not him, that's not him, don't believe him, let me out, let me out!* And I look up at the bent figures and my eyelids flicker. They touch my wrists.

"His heart is acting up."

I close my eyes. The screaming stops. The shivering ceases.

I rise, as in a cool well, released.

"He's dead," says someone.

"Jones is dead."

"From what?"

"Shock, it looks like."

"What kind of shock?" I say, and my name is Sessions and my lips move crisply, and I am the captain of these men. I stand among them and I am looking down at a body which lies cooling on the sands. I clap both hands to my head.

"Captain!"

"It's nothing," I say, crying out. "Just a headache. I'll be all right. There. There," I whisper. "It's all right now."

"We'd better get out of the sun, sir."

"Yes," I say, looking down at Jones. "We should never have come. Mars doesn't want us."

We carry the body back to the rocket with us, and a new voice is calling deep in me to be let out.

Help, help. Far down in the moist earthen-works of the body. *Help, help!* in red fathoms, echoing and pleading.

The trembling starts much sooner this time. The control is less steady.

"Captain, you'd better get in out of the sun, you don't look too well, sir."

"Yes," I say. "Help," I say.

"What, sir?"

"I didn't say anything."

"You said 'Help,' sir."

"Did I, Matthews, did I?"

The body is laid out in the shadow of the rocket and the voice screams in the deep underwater catacombs of bone and crimson tide. My hands jerk. My mouth splits and is parched. My nostrils fasten wide. My eyes roll. *Help, help, oh help, don't, don't, let me out, don't, don't.*

"Don't," I say.

"What, sir?"

"Never mind," I say. "I've got to get free," I say. I clap my hand to my mouth.

"How's that, sir?" cries Matthews.

"Get inside, all of you, go back to Earth!" I shout.

A gun is in my hand. I lift it.

"Don't, sir!"

An explosion. Shadows run. The screaming is cut off. There is a whistling sound of falling through space.

After ten thousand years, how good to die. How good to feel the sudden coolness, the relaxation. How good to be like a hand within a glove that stretches out and grows wonderfully cold in the hot sand. Oh, the quiet and the loveliness of gathering, darkening death. But one cannot linger on.

A crack, a snap.

"Good God, he's killed himself!" I cry, and open my eyes and there is the captain lying against the rocket, his skull split by a bullet, his eyes wide, his tongue protruding between his white teeth. Blood runs from his head. I bend to him and touch him. "The fool," I say. "Why did he do that?"

The men are horrified. They stand over the two dead men and turn their heads to see the Martian sands and the distant well where Regent lies lolling in deep waters. A croaking comes out of their dry lips, a whimpering, a childish protest against this awful dream.

The men turn to me.

After a long while, one of them says, "That makes you captain, Matthews."

"I know," I say slowly.

"Only six of us left."

"Good God, it happened so quick!"

"I don't want to stay here, let's get out!"

The men clamor. I go to them and touch them now, with a confidence which almost sings in me. "Listen," I say, and touch their elbows or their arms or their hands.

We all fall silent.

We are one.

No, no, no, no, no, no! Inner voices crying, deep down and gone into prisons beneath exteriors.

We are looking at each other. We are Samuel Matthews and Raymond Moses and William Spaulding and Charles Evans and Forrest Cole and John Summers, and we say nothing but look upon each other and our white faces and shaking hands.

We turn, as one, and look at the well.

"Now," we say.

No, no, six voices scream, hidden and layered down and stored forever.

Our feet walk in the sand and it is as if a great hand with twelve fingers were moving across the hot sea bottom.

We bend to the well, looking down. From the cool depths six faces peer back up at us.

One by one we bend until our balance is gone, and one by one drop into the mouth and down through cool darkness into the cold waters.

The sun sets. The stars wheel upon the night sky. Far out, there is a wink of light. Another rocket coming, leaving red marks on space.

I live in a well. I live like smoke in a well. Like vapor in a stone throat. Overhead I see the cold stars of night and morning, and I see the sun. And sometimes I sing old songs of this world when it was young. How can I tell you what I am when even I don't know? I cannot.

I am simply waiting.

Tyrannosaurus Rex

He opened a door on darkness. A voice cried, "Shut it!" It was like a blow in the face. He jumped through. The door banged. He cursed himself quietly. The voice, with dreadful patience, intoned, "Jesus. You Terwilliger?"

"Yes," said Terwilliger. A faint ghost of screen haunted the dark theater wall to his right. To his left, a cigarette wove fiery arcs in the air as someone's lips talked swiftly around it.

"You're five minutes late!"

Don't make it sound like five years, thought Terwilliger.

"Shove your film in the projection room door. Let's *move*."

Terwilliger squinted.

He made out five vast loge seats that exhaled, breathed heavily as amplitudes of executive life shifted, leaning toward the middle loge where, almost in darkness, a little boy sat smoking.

No, thought Terwilliger, not a boy. That's him. Joe Clarence. Clarence the Great.

For now the tiny mouth snapped like a puppet's, blowing smoke. "Well?"

Terwilliger stumbled back to hand the film to the projectionist, who made a lewd gesture toward the loges, winked at Terwilliger and slammed the booth door.

"Jesus," sighed the tiny voice. A buzzer buzzed. "Roll it, projection!"

Terwilliger probed the nearest loge, struck flesh, pulled back and stood biting his lips.

Music leaped from the screen. His film appeared in a storm of drums:

TYRANNOSAURUS REX: THE THUNDER LIZARD.
Photographed in stop-motion animation with miniatures created by John Terwilliger. A study in life-forms on Earth one billion years before Christ.

Faint ironic applause came softly patting from the baby hands in the middle loge.

Terwilliger shut his eyes. New music jerked him alert. The last titles faded into a world of primeval sun, mist, poisonous rain and lush wilderness. Morning fogs were strewn along eternal seacoasts where immense flying dreams and dreams of nightmare scythed the wind. Huge triangles of bone and rancid skin, of diamond eye and crusted tooth, pterodactyls, the kites of destruction, plunged, struck prey, and skimmed away, meat and screams in their scissor mouths.

Terwilliger gazed, fascinated.

In the jungle foliage now, shiverings, creepings, insect jitterings, antennae twitchings, slime locked in oily fatted slime, armor skinned to armor, in sun glade and shadow moved the reptilian inhabitors of Terwilliger's mad remembrance of vengeance given flesh and panic taking wing.

Brontosaur, stegosaur, triceratops. How easily the clumsy tonnages of name fell from one's lips.

The great brutes swung like ugly machineries of war and dissolution through moss ravines, crushing a thousand flowers at one footfall, snouting the mist, ripping the sky in half with one shriek.

My beauties, thought Terwilliger, my little lovelies. All liquid latex, rubber sponge, ball-socketed steel articulature; all night-dreamed, clay-molded, warped and welded, riveted and slapped to life by hand. No bigger than my fist, half of them; the rest no larger than this head they sprang from.

"Good Lord," said a soft admiring voice in the dark.

Step by step, frame by frame of film, stop motion by stop motion, he, Terwilliger, had run his beasts through their postures, moved each a fraction of an inch, photographed them, moved them another hair, photographed them, for hours and days and months. Now these rare images, this eight hundred scant feet of film, rushed through the projector.

And lo! he thought. I'll never get used to it. Look! They come *alive*!

Rubber, steel, clay, reptilian latex sheath, glass eye, porcelain fang, all ambles, trundles, strides in terrible prides through continents as yet unmanned, by seas as yet unsalted, a billion years lost away. They *do* breathe. They *do* smite air with thunders. Oh, uncanny!

I feel, thought Terwilliger, quite simply, that there stands *my* Garden, and these my animal creations which I love on this Sixth Day, and tomorrow, the Seventh, I must rest.

"Lord," said the soft voice again.

Terwilliger almost answered, "Yes?"

"This is beautiful footage, Mr. Clarence," the voice went on.

"Maybe," said the man with a boy's voice.

"Incredible animation."

"I've seen better," said Clarence the Great.

Terwilliger stiffened. He turned from the screen where his friends lumbered into oblivion, from butcheries wrought on architectural scales. For the first time he examined his possible employers.

"Beautiful stuff."

This praise came from an old man who sat to himself far across the theater, his head lifted forward in amaze toward that ancient life.

"It's jerky. Look there!" The strange boy in the middle loge half rose, pointing with the cigarette in his mouth. "Hey, was *that* a bad shot? You *see?*"

"Yes," said the old man, tired suddenly, fading back in his chair. "I see."

Terwilliger crammed his hotness down upon a suffocation of swiftly moving blood.

"Jerky," said Joe Clarence.

White light, quick numerals, darkness; the music cut, the monsters vanished.

"Glad that's over." Joe Clarence exhaled. "Almost lunchtime. Throw on the next reel, Walter! That's all, Terwilliger." Silence. "Terwilliger?" Silence. "Is that dumb bunny still here?"

"Here." Terwilliger ground his fists on his hips.

"Oh," said Joe Clarence. "It's not bad. But don't get ideas about money. A dozen guys came here yesterday to show stuff as good or better than yours, tests for our new film, *Prehistoric Monster*. Leave your bid in an envelope with my secretary. Same door out as you came in. Walter, what the hell you waiting for? Roll the next one!"

In darkness, Terwilliger barked his shins on a chair, groped for and found the door handle, gripped it tight, tight.

Behind him the screen exploded: an avalanche fell in great flourings of stone, whole cities of granite, immense edifices of marble piled, broke and flooded down. In this thunder, he heard voices from the week ahead:

"We'll pay you one thousand dollars, Terwilliger."

"But I need a thousand for my equipment alone!"

"Look, we're giving you a break. Take it or leave it!"

With the thunder dying, he knew he would take, and he knew he would hate it.

Only when the avalanche had drained off to silence behind him and his own blood had raced to the inevitable decision and stalled in his heart, did Terwilliger pull the immensely weighted door wide to step forth into the terrible raw light of day.

Fuse flexible spine to sinuous neck, pivot neck to death's-head skull, hinge jaw from hollow cheek, glue plastic sponge over lubricated skeleton, slip snake-pebbled skin over sponge, meld seams with fire, then rear upright triumphant in a world where insanity wakes but to look on madness—Tyrannosaurus Rex!

The Creator's hands glided down out of arc-light sun. They placed the granuled monster in false green summer wilds, they waded it in broths of teeming bacterial life. Planted in serene terror, the lizard machine basked. From the blind heavens the Creator's voice hummed, vibrating the Garden with the old and monotonous tune about the footbone connected to the . . . anklebone, anklebone connected to the . . . legbone, legbone connected to the . . . kneebone, kneebone connected to the . . .

A door burst wide.

Joe Clarence ran in very much like an entire Cub Scout pack. He looked wildly around as if no one were there.

"My God!" he cried. "Aren't you set up yet? This costs me money!"

"No," said Terwilliger dryly. "No matter how much time I take, I get paid the same."

Joe Clarence approached in a series of quick starts and stops. "Well, shake a leg. And make it real horrible."

Terwilliger was on his knees beside the miniature jungle set. His eyes were on a straight level with his producer's as he said, "How many feet of blood and gore would you like?"

"Two thousand feet of each!" Clarence laughed in a kind of gasping stutter. "Let's look." He grabbed the lizard.

"Careful!"

"Careful?" Clarence turned the ugly beast in careless and non-loving hands. "It's my monster, ain't it? The contract—"

"The contract says you use this model for exploitation advertising, but the animal reverts to me after the film's in release."

"Holy cow." Clarence waved the monster. "That's wrong. We just signed the contracts four days ago—"

"It feels like four years." Terwilliger rubbed his eyes. "I've been up two nights without sleep finishing this beast so we can start shooting."

Clarence brushed this aside. "To hell with the contract. What a slimy trick. It's my monster. You and your agent give me heart attacks. Heart attacks about money, heart attacks about equipment, heart attacks about—"

"This camera you gave me is ancient."

"So if it breaks, fix it; you got hands? The challenge of the shoestring operation is using the old brain instead of cash. Getting back to the point, this monster, it should've been specified in the deal, is my baby."

"I never let anyone own the things I make," said Terwilliger honestly. "I put too much time and affection in them."

"Hell, okay, so we give you fifty bucks extra for the beast, and throw in all this camera equipment free when the film's done, right? Then you start your own company. Compete with me, get even with me, right, using my own machines!" Clarence laughed.

"If they don't fall apart first," observed Terwilliger.

"Another thing." Clarence put the creature on the floor and walked around it. "I don't like the way this monster shapes up."

"You don't like *what*?" Terwilliger almost yelled.

"His expression. Needs more fire, more . . . goombah. More mazash!"

"Mazash?"

"The old bimbo! Bug the eyes more. Flex the nostrils. Shine the teeth. Fork the tongue sharper. You can *do* it! Uh, the monster ain't mine, huh?"

"Mine." Terwilliger arose.

His belt buckle was now on a line with Joe Clarence's eyes. The producer stared at the bright buckle almost hypnotically for a moment.

"God damn the goddam lawyers!"

He broke for the door.

"Work!"

The monster hit the door a split second after it slammed shut.

Terwilliger kept his hand poised in the air from his overhand throw. Then his shoulders sagged. He went to pick up his beauty. He twisted off its head, skinned the latex flesh off the skull, placed the skull on a pedestal and, painstakingly, with clay, began to reshape the prehistoric face.

"A little goombah," he muttered. "A touch of mazash."

They ran the first film test on the animated monster a week later.

When it was over, Clarence sat in darkness and nodded imperceptibly.

"Better. But . . . more horrorific, bloodcurdling. Let's scare the hell out of Aunt Jane. Back to the drawing board!"

"I'm a week behind schedule now," Terwilliger protested. "You keep coming in, change this, change that, you say, so I change it, one day the tail's all wrong, next day it's the claws—"

"You'll find a way to make me happy," said Clarence. "Get in there and fight the old aesthetic fight!"

At the end of the month they ran the second test.

"A near miss! Close!" said Clarence. "The face is just almost right. Try again, Terwilliger!"

Terwilliger went back. He animated the dinosaur's mouth so that it said obscene things which only a lip reader might catch, while the rest of the audience would think the beast was only shrieking. Then he got the clay and worked until 3 A.M. on the awful face.

"That's it!" cried Clarence in the projection room the next week. "Perfect! Now *that's* what I call a monster!"

He leaned toward the old man, his lawyer, Mr. Glass, and Maury Poole, his production assistant.

"You *like* my creature?" He beamed.

Terwilliger, slumped in the back row, his skeleton as long as the monsters he built, could feel the old lawyer shrug.

"You seen one monster, you seen 'em all."

"Sure, sure, but this one's special!" shouted Clarence happily. "Even *I* got to admit Terwilliger's a genius!"

They all turned back to watch the beast on the screen, in a titanic waltz, throw its razor tail wide in a vicious harvesting that cut grass and clipped flowers. The beast paused now to gaze pensively off into mists, gnawing a red bone.

"That monster," said Mr. Glass at last, squinting. "He sure looks familiar."

"Familiar?" Terwilliger stirred, alert.

"It's got such a look," drawled Mr. Glass in the dark, "I couldn't forget, from someplace."

"Natural Museum exhibits?"

"No, no."

"Maybe," laughed Clarence, "you read a book once, Glass?"

"Funny . . ." Glass, unperturbed, cocked his head, closed one eye. "Like detectives, I don't forget a face. But, that Tyrannosaurus Rex — where before did I meet *him?*"

"Who cares?" Clarence sprinted. "He's great. And all because I booted Terwilliger's behind to make him do it right. Come on, Maury!"

When the door shut, Mr. Glass turned to gaze steadily at Terwilliger. Not taking his eyes away, he called softly to the projectionist, "Walt? Walter? Could you favor us with that beast again?"

"Sure thing."

Terwilliger shifted uncomfortably, aware of some bleak force gathering in blackness, in the sharp light that shot forth once more to ricochet terror off the screen.

"Yeah. Sure," mused Mr. Glass. "I almost remember. I almost know him. But . . . *who?*"

The brute, as if answering, turned and for a disdainful moment stared across one hundred thousand million years at two small men hidden in a small dark room. The tyrant machine named itself in thunder.

Mr. Glass quickened forward, as if to cup his ear.

Darkness swallowed all.

With the film half finished, in the tenth week, Clarence summoned thirty of the office staff, technicians and a few friends to see a rough cut of the picture.

The film had been running fifteen minutes when a gasp ran through the small audience.

Clarence glanced swiftly about.

Mr. Glass, next to him, stiffened.

Terwilliger, scenting danger, lingered near the exit, not knowing why; his nervousness was compulsive and intuitive. Hand on the door, he watched.

Another gasp ran through the crowd.

Someone laughed quietly. A woman secretary giggled. Then there was instantaneous silence.

For Joe Clarence had jumped to his feet.

His tiny figure sliced across the light on the screen. For a moment, two images gesticulated in the dark: Tyrannosaurus, ripping the leg from a pteranodon, and Clarence, yelling, jumping forward as if to grapple with these fantastic wrestlers.

"Stop! Freeze it right there!"

The film stopped. The image held.

"What's wrong?" asked Mr. Glass.

"Wrong?" Clarence crept up on the image. He thrust his baby hand to the screen, stabbed the tyrant jaw, the lizard eye, the fangs, the brow, then turned blindly to the projector light so that reptilian flesh was printed on his furious cheeks. "What goes? What *is* this?"

"Only a monster, Chief."

"Monster, hell!" Clarence pounded the screen with his tiny fist. "That's *me*!"

Half the people leaned forward, half the people fell back, two people jumped up, one of them Mr. Glass, who fumbled for his other spectacles, flexed his eyes and moaned, "So *that's* where I saw him before!"

"That's where you what?"

Mr. Glass shook his head, eyes shut. "That face, I *knew* it was familiar."

A wind blew in the room.

Everyone turned. The door stood open.

Terwilliger was gone.

They found Terwilliger in his animation studio cleaning out his desk, dumping everything into a large cardboard box, the Tyrannosaurus machine-toy model under his arm. He looked up as the mob swirled in, Clarence at the head.

"What did I do to deserve this!" he cried.

"I'm sorry, Mr. Clarence."

"You're sorry?! Didn't I pay you well?"

"No, as a matter of fact."

"I took you to lunches—"

"Once. I picked up the tab."

"I gave you dinner at home, you swam in my pool, and now *this*! You're fired!"

"You can't fire me, Mr. Clarence. I've worked the last week free and overtime, you forgot my check—"

"You're fired anyway, oh, you're *really* fired! You're blackballed in Hollywood. Mr. Glass!" He whirled to find the old man. "Sue him!"

"There is nothing," said Terwilliger, not looking up any more, just looking down, packing, keeping in motion, "nothing you can sue me for. Money? You never paid enough to save on. A house? Could never afford that. A wife? I've worked for people like you all my life. So wives are out. I'm an unencumbered man. There's nothing you can do to me. If you attach my dinosaurs, I'll just go hole up in a small town somewhere, get me a can of latex rubber, some clay from the river, some old steel pipe, and make new monsters. I'll buy stock film raw and cheap. I've got an old beat-up stop-motion camera. Take that away, and I'll build one with my own hands. I can do anything. And that's why you'll never hurt me again."

"You're fired!" cried Clarence. "Look at me. Don't look away. You're fired! You're fired!"

"Mr. Clarence," said Mr. Glass, quietly, edging forward. "Let me talk to him just a moment."

"So talk to him!" said Clarence. "What's the use? He just stands there with that monster under his arm and the goddam thing looks like me, so get out of the way!"

Clarence stormed out the door. The others followed.

Mr. Glass shut the door, walked over to the window and looked out at the absolutely clear twilight sky.

"I wish it would rain," he said. "That's one thing about California I can't forgive. It never really lets go and cries. Right now, what wouldn't I give for a little something from that sky? A bolt of lightning, even."

He stood silent, and Terwilliger slowed in his packing. Mr. Glass sagged down into a chair and doodled on a pad with a pencil, talking sadly, half aloud, to himself.

"Six reels of film shot, pretty good reels, half the film done, three hundred thousand dollars down the drain, hail and farewell. Out the window all the jobs. Who feeds the starving mouths of boys and girls? Who will face the stockholders? Who chucks the Bank of America under the chin? Anyone for Russian roulette?"

He turned to watch Terwilliger snap the locks on a briefcase.

"What hath God wrought?"

Terwilliger, looking down at his hands, turning them over to examine their texture, said, "I didn't know I was doing it, I swear. It came out in my fingers. It was all subconscious. My fingers do everything for me. They did *this*."

"Better the fingers had come in my office and taken me direct by the throat," said Glass. "I was never one for slow motion. The Keystone Kops, at triple speed, was my idea of living, or dying. To think a rubber monster has stepped on us all. We are now so much tomato mush, ripe for canning!"

"Don't make me feel any guiltier than I feel," said Terwilliger.

"What do you want, I should take you dancing?"

"It's just," cried Terwilliger, "he kept at me. Do this. Do that. Do it the other way. Turn it inside out, upside down, he said. I swallowed my bile. I was angry all the time. Without knowing, I must've changed the face. But right up till five minutes ago, when Mr. Clarence yelled, I didn't see it. I'll take all the blame."

"No," sighed Mr. Glass, "we should *all* have seen. Maybe we did and couldn't admit. Maybe we did and laughed all night in our sleep, when we couldn't hear. So where are we now? Mr. Clarence, he's got investments he can't throw out. You got your career from this day forward, for better or worse, you can't throw out. Mr. Clarence right now is aching to be convinced it was all some horrible dream. Part of his ache, ninety-nine per cent, is in his wallet. If you could put one per cent of your time in the next hour convincing him of what I'm going to tell you next, tomorrow morning there will be no orphan children staring out of the want ads in *Variety* and *The Hollywood Reporter*. If you would go tell him—"

"Tell me *what?*"

Joe Clarence, returned, stood in the door, his cheeks still inflamed.

"What he just told me." Mr. Glass turned calmly. "A touching story."

"I'm listening!" said Clarence.

"Mr. Clarence." The old lawyer weighed his words carefully. "This film you just saw is Mr. Terwilliger's solemn and silent tribute to you."

"It's *what?*" shouted Clarence.

Both men, Clarence and Terwilliger, dropped their jaws.

The old lawyer gazed only at the wall and in a shy voice said, "Shall I go on?"

The animator closed his jaw. "If you want to."

"This film"— the lawyer arose and pointed in a single motion toward the projection room—"was done from a feeling of honor and friendship for you, Joe Clarence. Behind your desk, an unsung hero of the motion picture industry, unknown, unseen, you sweat out your lonely little life while who gets the glory? The stars. How often does a man in Atawanda Springs, Idaho, tell his wife, 'Say, I was thinking the other night about Joe Clarence—a great producer, that man'? How often? Should I tell? Never! So Terwilliger brooded. How could he present the real Clarence to the world? The dinosaur is there; boom! it hits him! This is it! he thought, the very thing to strike terror to the world, here's a lonely, proud, wonderful, awful symbol of independence, power, strength, shrewd animal cunning, the true democrat, the individual brought to its peak, all thunder and big lightning. Dinosaur: Joe Clarence. Joe Clarence: Dinosaur. Man embodied in Tyrant Lizard!"

Mr. Glass sat down, panting quietly.

Terwilliger said nothing.

Clarence moved at last, walked across the room, circled Glass slowly, then came to stand in front of Terwilliger, his face pale. His eyes were uneasy, shifting up along Terwilliger's tall skeleton frame.

"You said *that?*" he asked faintly.

Terwilliger swallowed.

"To me he said it. He's shy," said Mr. Glass. "You ever hear him say much, ever talk back? swear? anything? He likes people, he can't say. But, immortalize them? That he can do!"

"Immortalize?" said Clarence.

"What else?" said the old man. "Like a statue, only moving. Years from now people will say, 'Remember that film, *The Monster from the Pleistocene?*' And people will say, 'Sure! why?' 'Because,' the others say, 'it was the one monster, the one brute, in all Hollywood history had real guts, real personality. And why is this? Because one genius had enough imagination to base the creature on a real-life, hard-hitting, fast-thinking businessman of A-one caliber.'

You're one with history, Mr. Clarence. Film libraries will carry you in good supply. Cinema societies will ask for you. How lucky can you get? Nothing like this will ever happen to Immanuel Glass, a lawyer. Every day for the next two hundred, five hundred years, you'll be starring somewhere in the world!"

"*Every* day?" asked Clarence softly. "For the next—"

"Eight hundred, even; why not?"

"I never thought of that."

"Think of it!"

Clarence walked over to the window and looked out at the Hollywood Hills, and nodded at last.

"My God, Terwilliger," he said. "You really like me *that* much?"

"It's hard to put in words," said Terwilliger, with difficulty.

"So do we finish the mighty spectacle?" asked Glass. "Starring the tyrant terror striding the earth and making all quake before him, none other than Mr. Joseph J. Clarence?"

"Yeah. Sure." Clarence wandered off, stunned, to the door, where he said, "You know? I always *wanted* to be an actor!"

Then he went quietly out into the hall and shut the door.

Terwilliger and Glass collided at the desk, both clawing at a drawer.

"Age before beauty," said the lawyer, and quickly pulled forth a bottle of whiskey.

At midnight on the night of the first preview of *Monster from the Stone Age*, Mr. Glass came back to the studio, where everyone was gathering for a celebration, and found Terwilliger seated alone in his office, his dinosaur on his lap.

"You weren't *there*?" asked Mr. Glass.

"I couldn't face it. Was there a riot?"

"A riot? The preview cards are all superdandy extra plus! A lovelier monster nobody saw before! So now we're talking sequels! Joe Clarence as the Tyrant Lizard in *Return of the Stone-Age Monster*, Joe Clarence and/or Tyrannosaurus Rex in, maybe, *Beast from the Old Country*—"

The phone rang. Terwilliger got it.

"Terwilliger, this is Clarence! Be there in five minutes! We've done it! Your animal! Great! Is he mine now? I mean, to hell with the contract, as a favor, can I have him for the mantel?"

"Mr. Clarence, the monster's yours."

"Better than an Oscar! So long!"

Terwilliger stared at the dead phone.

"God bless us all, said Tiny Tim. He's laughing, almost hysterical with relief."

"So maybe I know why," said Mr. Glass. "A little girl, after the preview, asked him for an autograph."

"An *autograph?*"

"Right there in the street. Made him sign. First autograph he ever gave in his life. He laughed all the while he wrote his name. Somebody knew him. There he was, in front of the theater, big as life, Rex Himself, so sign the name. So he did."

"Wait a minute," said Terwilliger slowly, pouring drinks. "That little girl . . . ?"

"My youngest daughter," said Glass. "So who knows? And who will tell?"

They drank.

"Not me," said Terwilliger.

Then, carrying the rubber dinosaur between them, and bringing the whiskey, they went to stand by the studio gate, waiting for the limousines to arrive all lights, horns and annunciations.

The Screaming Woman

My name is Margaret Leary and I'm ten years old and in the fifth grade at Central School. I haven't any brothers or sisters, but I've got a nice father and mother except they don't pay much attention to me. And anyway, we never thought we'd have anything to do with a murdered woman. Or almost, anyway.

When you're just living on a street like we live on, you don't think awful things are going to happen, like shooting or stabbing or burying people under the ground, practically in your back yard. And when it does happen you don't believe it. You just go on buttering your toast or baking a cake.

I got to tell you how it happened. It was a noon in the middle of July. It was hot and Mama said to me, "Margaret, you go to the store and buy some ice cream. It's Saturday, Dad's home for lunch, so we'll have a treat."

I ran out across the empty lot behind our house. It was a big lot, where kids had played baseball, and broken glass and stuff. And on my way back from the store with the ice cream I was just walking along, minding my own business, when all of a sudden it happened.

I heard the Screaming Woman.

I stopped and listened.

It was coming up out of the ground.

A woman was buried under the rocks and dirt and glass, and she was screaming, all wild and horrible, for someone to dig her out.

I just stood there, afraid. She kept screaming, muffled.

Then I started to run. I fell down, got up, and ran some more. I got in the screen door of my house and there was Mama, calm as you please, not knowing what I knew, that there was a real live woman buried out in back of our house, just a hundred yards away, screaming bloody murder.

"Mama," I said.

"Don't stand there with the ice cream," said Mama.

"But, Mama," I said.

"Put it in the icebox," she said.

"Listen, Mama, there's a Screaming Woman in the empty lot."

"And wash your hands," said Mama.

"She was screaming and screaming . . . "

"Let's see, now, salt and pepper," said Mama, far away.

"Listen to me," I said, loud. "We got to dig her out. She's buried under tons and tons of dirt and if we don't dig her out, she'll choke up and die."

"I'm certain she can wait until after lunch," said Mama.

"Mama, don't you believe me?"

"Of course, dear. Now wash your hands and take this plate of meat in to your father."

"I don't even know who she is or how she got there," I said. "But we got to help her before it's too late."

"Good gosh," said Mama. "Look at this ice cream. "What did you do, just stand in the sun and let it melt?"

"Well, the empty lot . . . "

"Go on, now, scoot."

I went into the dining room.

"Hi, Dad, there's a Screaming Woman in the empty lot."

"I never knew a woman who didn't," said Dad.

"I'm serious," I said.

"You look very grave," said Father.

"We've got to get picks and shovels and excavate, like for an Egyptian mummy," I said.

"I don't feel like an archaeologist, Margaret," said Father. "Now, some nice cool October day, I'll take you up on that."

"But we can't wait that long," I almost screamed. My heart was bursting in me. I was excited and scared and afraid and here was Dad, putting meat on his plate, cutting and chewing and paying me no attention.

"Dad?" I said.

"Mmmm?" he said, chewing.

"Dad, you just gotta come out after lunch and help me," I said. "Dad, Dad, I'll give you all the money in my piggy bank!"

"Well," said Dad. "So it's a business proposition, is it? It must be important for you to offer your perfectly good money. How much money will you pay, by the hour?"

"I got five whole dollars it took me a year to save, and it's all yours."

Dad touched my arm. "I'm touched. I'm really touched. You want me to play with you and you're willing to pay for my time. Honest, Margaret, you make your old Dad feel like a piker. I don't give you enough time. Tell you what, after lunch, I'll come out and listen to your Screaming Woman, free of charge."

"Will you, oh, will you, really?"

"Yes, ma'am, that's what I'll do," said Dad. "But you must promise me one thing?"

"What?"

"If I come out, you must eat all of your lunch first."

"I promise," I said.

"Okay."

Mother came in and sat down and we started to eat.

"Not so fast," said Mama.

I slowed down. Then I started eating fast again.

"You heard your mother," said Dad.

"The Screaming Woman," I said. "We got to hurry."

"I," said Father, "intend sitting here quietly and judiciously giving my attention first to my steak, then to my potatoes, and my salad, of course, and then to my ice cream, and after that to a long drink of iced coffee, if you don't mind. I may be a good hour at it. And another thing, young lady, if you mention her name, this Screaming Whatsis, once more at this table during lunch, I won't go out with you to hear her recital."

"Yes, sir."

"Is that understood?"

"Yes, sir," I said.

Lunch was a million years long. Everybody moved in slow motion, like those films you see at the movies. Mama got up slow and got down slow and forks and knives and spoons moved slow. Even the flies in the room were slow. And Dad's cheek muscles moved slow. It was so slow. I wanted to scream, "Hurry! Oh, please, rush, get up, run around, come on out, run!"

But no, I had to sit, and all the while we sat there slowly, slowly eating our lunch, out there in the empty lot (I could hear her screaming in my mind. *Scream!*) was the Screaming Woman, all alone, while the world ate its lunch and the sun was hot and the lot was empty as the sky.

"There we are," said Dad, finished at last.

"Now will you come out to see the Screaming Woman?" I said.

"First a little more iced coffee," said Dad.

"Speaking of Screaming Women," said Mother, "Charlie Nesbitt and his wife Helen had another fight last night."

"That's nothing new," said Father. "They're always fighting."

"If you ask me, Charlie's no good," said Mother. "Or her, either."

"Oh, I don't know," said Dad. "I think she's pretty nice."

"You're prejudiced. After all, you almost married her."

"You going to bring that up again?" he said. "After all, I was only engaged to her six weeks."

"You showed some sense when you broke it off."

"Oh, you know Helen. Always stagestruck. Wanted to travel in a trunk. I just couldn't see it. That broke it up. She was sweet, though. Sweet and kind."

"What did it get her? A terrible brute of a husband like Charlie."

"Dad," I said.

"I'll give you that. Charlie has got a terrible temper," said Dad. "Remember when Helen had the lead in our high school graduation play? Pretty as a picture. She wrote some songs for it herself. That was the summer she wrote that song for me."

"Ha," said Mother.

"Don't laugh. It was a good song."

"You never told me about that song."

"It was between Helen and me. Let's see, how *did* it go?"

"Dad," I said.

"You'd better take your daughter out in the back lot," said Mother, "before she collapses. You can sing me that wonderful song later."

"Okay, come on, you," said Dad, and I ran him out of the house.

The empty lot was still empty and hot and the glass sparkled green and white and brown all around where the bottles lay.

"Now, where's this Screaming Woman?" laughed Dad.

"We forgot the shovels," I cried.

"We'll get them later, after we hear the soloist," said Dad.

I took him over to the spot. "Listen," I said.

We listened.

"I don't hear anything," said Dad, at last.

"Shh," I said. "Wait."

We listened some more. "Hey, there, Screaming Woman!" I cried.

We heard the sun in the sky. We heard the wind in the trees, real quiet. We heard a bus, far away, running along. We heard a car pass.

That was all.

"Margaret," said Father. "I suggest you go lie down and put a damp cloth on your forehead."

"But she was here," I shouted. "I heard her, screaming and screaming and screaming. See, here's where the ground's been dug up." I called frantically at the earth. "Hey there, you down there!"

"Margaret," said Father. "This is the place where Mr. Kelly dug yesterday, a big hole, to bury his trash and garbage in."

"But during the night," I said, "someone else used Mr. Kelly's burying place to bury a woman. And covered it all over again."

"Well, I'm going back in and take a cool shower," said Dad.

"You won't help me dig?"

"Better not stay out here too long," said Dad. "It's hot."

Dad walked off. I heard the back door slam.

I stamped on the ground. "Darn," I said.

The screaming started again.

She screamed and screamed. Maybe she had been tired and was resting and now she began it all over, just for me.

I stood in the empty lot in the hot sun and I felt like crying. I ran back to the house and banged the door.

"Dad, she's screaming again!"

"Sure, sure," said Dad. "Come on." And he led me to my upstairs bedroom. "Here," he said. He made me lie down and put a cold rag on my head. "Just take it easy."

I began to cry. "Oh, Dad, we can't let her die. She's all buried, like that person in that story by Edgar Allan Poe, and think how awful it is to be screaming and no one paying any attention."

"I forbid you to leave the house," said Dad, worried. "You just lie there the rest of the afternoon." He went out and locked the door. I heard him and Mother talking in the front room. After a while I stopped crying. I got up and tiptoed to the window. My room was upstairs. It seemed high.

I took a sheet off the bed and tied it to the bedpost and let it out the window. Then I climbed out the window and shinnied down until I touched the ground. Then I ran to the garage, quiet, and I got a couple of shovels and I ran to the empty lot. It was hotter than ever. And I started to dig, and all the while I dug, the Screaming Woman screamed. . . .

It was hard work. Shoving in the shovel and lifting the rocks and glass. And I knew I'd be doing it all afternoon and maybe I wouldn't finish in time. What could I do? Run tell other people? But they'd be like Mom and Dad, pay no attention. I just kept digging, all by myself.

About ten minutes later, Dippy Smith came along the path through the empty lot. He's my age and goes to my school.

"Hi, Margaret," he said.

"Hi, Dippy," I gasped.

"What you doing?" he asked.

"Digging."

"For what?"

"I got a Screaming Lady in the ground and I'm digging for her," I said.

"I don't hear no screaming," said Dippy.

"You sit down and wait awhile and you'll hear her scream yet. Or better still, help me dig."

"I don't dig unless I hear a scream," he said.

We waited.

"Listen!" I cried. "Did you *hear* it?"

"Hey," said Dippy, with slow appreciation, his eyes gleaming. "That's okay. Do it again."

"Do what again?"

"The scream."

"We got to wait," I said, puzzled.

"Do it again," he insisted, shaking my arm. "Go on." He dug in his pocket for a brown aggie. "Here." He shoved it at me. "I'll give you this marble if you do it again."

A scream came out of the ground.

"Hot dog!" said Dippy. "Teach *me* to do it!" He danced around as if I was a miracle.

"I don't . . . " I started to say.

"Did you get the *Throw-Your-Voice* book for a dime from that Magic Company in Dallas, Texas?" cried Dippy. "You got one of those tin ventriloquist contraptions in your mouth?"

"Y-yes," I lied, for I wanted him to help. "If you'll help dig, I'll tell you about it later."

"Swell," he said. "Give me a shovel."

We both dug together, and from time to time the woman screamed.

"Boy," said Dippy. "You'd think she was right under foot. You're wonderful, Maggie." Then he said, "What's her name?"

"Who?"

"The Screaming Woman. You must have a name for her."

"Oh, sure." I thought a moment. "Her name's Wilma Schweiger and she's a rich old woman, ninety-six years old, and she was buried by a man named Spike, who counterfeited ten-dollar bills."

"Yes, *sir*," said Dippy.

"And there's hidden treasure buried with her, and I, I'm a grave robber come to dig her out and get it," I gasped, digging excitedly.

Dippy made his eyes Oriental and mysterious. "Can I be a grave robber, too?" He had a better idea. "Let's pretend it's the Princess Ommanatra, an Egyptian queen, covered with diamonds!"

We kept digging and I thought, Oh, we will rescue her, we *will*. If only we keep on!

"Hey, I just got an idea," said Dippy. And he ran off and got a piece of cardboard. He scribbled on it with crayon.

"Keep digging!" I said. "We can't stop!"

"I'm making a sign. See? SLUMBERLAND CEMETERY! We can bury some birds and beetles here, in matchboxes and stuff. I'll go find some butterflies."

"No, Dippy!"

"It's more fun that way. I'll get me a dead cat, too, maybe. . . . "

"Dippy, use your shovel! Please!"

"Aw," said Dippy. "I'm tired. I think I'll go home and take a nap."

"You can't do that."

"Who says so?"

"Dippy, there's something I want to tell you."

"What?"

He gave the shovel a kick.

I whispered in his ear. "There's really a woman buried here."

"Why sure there is," he said. "You said it, Maggie."

"You don't believe me, either."

"Tell me how you throw your voice and I'll keep on digging."

"But I can't tell you, because I'm not doing it," I said. "Look, Dippy. I'll stand way over here and you listen there."

The Screaming Woman screamed again.

"Hey!" said Dippy. "There really *is* a woman here!"

"That's what I tried to say."

"Let's dig!" said Dippy.

We dug for twenty minutes.

"I wonder who she is?"

"I don't know."

"I wonder if it's Mrs. Nelson or Mrs. Turner or Mrs. Bradley. I wonder if she's pretty. Wonder what color her hair is? Wonder if she's thirty or ninety or sixty?"

"Dig!" I said.

The mound grew high.

"Wonder if she'll reward us for digging her up."

"Sure."

"A quarter, do you think?"

"More than that. I bet it's a dollar."

Dippy remembered as he dug, "I read a book once of magic. There was a Hindu with no clothes on who crept down in a grave and slept there sixty days, not eating anything, no malts, no chewing gum or candy, no air, for sixty days." His face fell. "Say, wouldn't it be awful if it was only a radio buried here and us working so hard?"

"A radio's nice, it'd be all ours."

Just then a shadow fell across us.

"Hey, you kids, what you think you're doing?"

We turned. It was Mr. Kelly, the man who owned the empty lot. "Oh, hello, Mr. Kelly," we said.

"Tell you what I want you to do," said Mr. Kelly. "I want you to take those shovels and take that soil and shovel it right back in that hole you been digging. That's what I want you to do."

My heart started beating fast again. I wanted to scream myself.

"But Mr. Kelly, there's a Screaming Woman and . . . "

"I'm not interested. I don't hear a thing."

"Listen!" I cried.

The scream.

Mr. Kelly listened and shook his head. "Don't hear nothing. Go on now, fill it up and get home with you before I give you my foot!"

We filled the hole all back in again. And all the while we filled it in, Mr. Kelly stood there, arms folded, and the woman screamed, but Mr. Kelly pretended not to hear it.

When we were finished, Mr. Kelly stomped off, saying, "Go on home now. And if I catch you here again . . . "

I turned to Dippy. "He's the one," I whispered.

"Huh?" said Dippy.

"He *murdered* Mrs. Kelly. He buried her here, after he strangled her, in a box, but she came to. Why, he stood right here and she screamed and he wouldn't pay any attention."

"Hey," said Dippy. "That's right. He stood right here and lied to us."

"There's only one thing to do," I said. "Call the police and have them come arrest Mr. Kelly."

We ran for the corner store telephone.

The police knocked on Mr. Kelly's door five minutes later. Dippy and I were hiding in the bushes, listening.

"Mr. Kelly?" said the police officer.

"Yes, sir, what can I do for you?"

"Is Mrs. Kelly at home?"

"Yes, sir."

"May we see her, sir?"

"Of course. Hey, Anna!"

Mrs. Kelly came to the door and looked out. "Yes, sir?"

"I beg your pardon," apologized the officer. "We had a report that you were buried out in an empty lot, Mrs. Kelly. It sounded like a child made the call, but we had to be certain. Sorry to have troubled you."

"It's those blasted kids," cried Mr. Kelly, angrily. "If I ever catch them, I'll rip them limb from limb!"

"Cheezit!" said Dippy, and we both ran.

"What'll we do now?" I said.

"I got to go home," said Dippy. "Boy, we're really in trouble. We'll get a licking for this."

"But what about the Screaming Woman?"

"To heck with her," said Dippy. "We don't dare go near that empty lot again. Old man Kelly'll be waiting around with his razor strap and lambast heck out'n us. And I just happened to remember, Maggie. Ain't old man Kelly sort of deaf, hard-of-hearing?"

"Oh, my gosh," I said. "No *wonder* he didn't hear the screams."

"So long," said Dippy. "We sure got in trouble over your darn old ventriloquist voice. I'll be seeing you."

I was left all alone in the world, no one to help me, no one to believe me at all. I just wanted to crawl down in that box with the Screaming Woman and die. The police were after me now, for lying to them, only I didn't know it was a lie, and my father was probably looking for me, too, or would be once he found my bed empty. There was only one last thing to do, and I did it.

I went from house to house, all down the street, near the empty lot. And I rang every bell and when the door opened I said: "I beg your pardon, Mrs. Griswold, but is anyone missing from your house?" or "Hello, Mrs. Pikes, you're looking fine today. Glad to see you *home*." And once I saw that the lady of the house was home I just chatted awhile to be polite, and went on down the street.

The hours were rolling along. It was getting late. I kept thinking, oh, there's only so much air in that box with that woman under the earth, and if I don't hurry, she'll suffocate, and I got to rush! So I rang bells and knocked on doors, and it got later, and I was just about to give up and go home, when I knocked on the *last* door, which was the door of Mr. Charlie Nesbitt, who lives next to us. I kept knocking and knocking.

Instead of Mrs. Nesbitt, or Helen as my father calls her, coming to the door, why it was Mr. Nesbitt, Charlie, *himself*.

"Oh," he said. "It's you, Margaret."

"Yes," I said. "Good afternoon."

"What can I do for you, kid?" he said.

"Well, I thought I'd like to see your wife, Mrs. Nesbitt," I said.

"Oh," he said.

"May I?"

"Well, she's gone out to the store," he said.

"I'll wait," I said, and slipped in past him.

"Hey," he said.

I sat down in a chair. "My, it's a hot day," I said, trying to be calm, thinking about the empty lot and air going out of the box, and the screams getting weaker and weaker.

"Say, listen, kid," said Charlie, coming over to me, "I don't think you better wait."

"Oh, sure," I said. "Why not?"

"Well, my wife won't be back," he said.

"Oh?"

"Not today, that is. She's gone to the store, like I said, but, but, she's going on from there to visit her mother. Yeah. She's going to visit her mother, in Schenectady. She'll be back, two or three days, maybe a week."

"That's a shame," I said.

"Why?"

"I wanted to tell her something."

"What?"

"I just wanted to tell her there's a woman buried over in the empty lot, screaming under tons and tons of dirt."

Mr. Nesbitt dropped his cigarette.

"You dropped your cigarette, Mr. Nesbitt," I pointed out, with my shoe.

"Oh, did I? Sure. So I did," he mumbled. "Well, I'll tell Helen when she comes home, your story. She'll be glad to hear it."

"Thanks. It's a real woman."

"How do you know it is?"

"I heard her."

"How, how you know it isn't, well, a *mandrake* root?"

"What's that?"

"You know. A mandrake. It's a kind of a plant, kid. They scream. I know, I read it once. How you know it ain't a mandrake?"

"I never thought of that."

"You better start thinking," he said, lighting another cigarette. He tried to be casual. "Say, kid, you, eh, you *say* anything about this to anyone?"

"Sure, I told lots of people."

Mr. Nesbitt burned his hand on his match.

"Anybody doing anything about it?" he asked.

"No," I said. "They won't believe me."

He smiled. "Of course. Naturally. You're nothing but a kid. Why should they listen to you?"

"I'm going back now and dig her out with a spade," I said.

"Wait."

"I got to go," I said.

"Stick around," he insisted.

"Thanks, but no," I said, frantically.

He took my arm. "Know how to play cards, kid? Black jack?"

"Yes, sir."

He took out a deck of cards from a desk. "We'll have a game."

"I got to go dig."

"Plenty of time for that," he said, quiet. "Anyway, maybe my wife'll be home. Sure. That's it. You wait for her. Wait awhile."

"You think she will be?"

"Sure, kid. Say, about that voice; is it very strong?"

"It gets weaker all the time."

Mr. Nesbitt sighed and smiled. "You and your kid games. Here now, let's play that game of black jack, it's more fun than Screaming Women."

"I got to go. It's late."

"Stick around, you got nothing to do."

I knew what he was trying to do. He was trying to keep me in his house until the screaming died down and was gone. He was trying to keep me from helping her. "My wife'll be home in ten minutes," he said. "Sure. Ten minutes. You wait. You sit right there."

We played cards. The clock ticked. The sun went down the sky. It was getting late. The screaming got fainter and fainter in my mind. "I got to go," I said.

"Another game," said Mr. Nesbitt. "Wait another hour, kid. My wife'll come yet. Wait."

In another hour he looked at his watch. "Well, kid, I guess you can go now." And I knew what his plan was. He'd sneak down in the middle of the night and dig up his wife, still alive, and take her somewhere else and bury her, good. "So long, kid. So long." He let me go, because he thought that by now the air must all be gone from the box.

The door shut in my face.

I went back near the empty lot and hid in some bushes. What could I do? Tell my folks? But they hadn't believed me. Call the police on Mr. Charlie Nesbitt? But he said his wife was away visiting. Nobody would believe me!

I watched Mr. Kelly's house. He wasn't in sight. I ran over to the place where the screaming had been and just stood there.

The screaming had stopped. It was so quiet I thought I would never hear a scream again. It was all over. I was too late, I thought.

I bent down and put my ear against the ground.

And then I heard it, way down, way deep, and so faint I could hardly hear it.

The woman wasn't screaming any more. She was singing.

Something about, "I loved you fair, I loved you well."

It was sort of a sad song. Very faint. And sort of broken. All of those hours down under the ground in that box must have sort of made her crazy. All she needed was some air and food and she'd be all right. But she just kept singing, not wanting to scream any more, not caring, just singing.

I listened to the song.

And then I turned and walked straight across the lot and up the steps to my house and I opened the front door.

"Father," I said.

"So there you are!" he cried.

"Father," I said.

"You're going to get a licking," he said.

"She's not screaming any more."

"Don't talk about her!"

"She's singing now," I cried.

"You're not telling the truth!"

"Dad," I said. "She's out there and she'll be dead soon if you don't listen to me. She's out there, singing, and this is what she's singing." I hummed the tune. I sang a few of the words. "I loved you fair, I loved you well . . . "

Dad's face grew pale. He came and took my arm.

"What did you say?" he said.

I sang it again: "I loved you fair, I loved you well."

"Where did you *hear* that song?" he shouted.

"Out in the empty lot, just now."

"But that's *Helen's* song, the one she wrote, years ago, for *me*!" cried Father. "You *can't* know it. *Nobody* knew it, except Helen and me. I never sang it to anyone, not you or anyone."

"Sure," I said.

"Oh, my God!" cried Father, and ran out the door to get a shovel. The last I saw of him he was in the empty lot, digging, and lots of other people with him, digging.

I felt so happy I wanted to cry.

I dialed a number on the phone and when Dippy answered I said, "Hi, Dippy. Everything's fine. Everything's worked out keen. The Screaming Woman isn't screaming any more."

"Swell," said Dippy.

"I'll meet you in the empty lot with a shovel in two minutes," I said.

"Last one there's a monkey! So long!" cried Dippy.

"So long, Dippy!" I said, and ran.

The Terrible Conflagration
up at the Place

The men had been hiding down by the gatekeeper's lodge for half an hour or so, passing a bottle of the best between, and then, the gatekeeper having been carried off to bed, they dodged up the path at six in the evening and looked at the great house with the warm lights lit in each window.

"That's the place," said Riordan.

"Hell, what do you mean, 'That's the place'?" cried Casey, then softly added, "We seen it all our lives."

"Sure," said Kelly, "but with the Troubles over and around us, sudden-like a place looks *different*. It's quite a toy, lying there in the snow."

And that's what it seemed to the fourteen of them, a grand playhouse laid out in the softly falling feathers of a spring night.

"Did you bring the matches?" asked Kelly.

"Did I bring the—what do you think I *am*!"

"Well, *did* you, is all I ask."

Casey searched himself. When his pockets hung from his suit he swore and said, "I did not."

"Ah, what the hell," said Nolan. "They'll have matches inside. We'll borrow a few. Come on."

Going up the road, Timulty tripped and fell.

"For God's sake, Timulty," said Nolan, "where's your sense of romance? In the midst of a big Easter Rebellion we want to do everything just so. Years from now we want to go into a pub and tell about the Terrible Conflagration up at the Place, do we not? If it's all mucked up with the sight of you landing on your ass in the snow, that makes no fit picture of the Rebellion we are now in, does it?"

Timulty, rising, focused the picture and nodded. "I'll mind me manners."

"Hist! Here we are!" cried Riordan.

"Jesus, stop saying things like 'That's the place' and 'Here we are,'" said Casey. "We see the damned house. Now what do we do next?"

"Destroy it?" suggested Murphy tentatively.

"Gah, you're so dumb you're hideous," said Casey. "Of course we destroy it, but first . . . blueprints and plans."

"It seemed simple enough back at Hickey's Pub," said Murphy. "We would just come tear the damn place down. Seeing as how my wife outweighs me, I need to tear *something* down."

"It seems to me," said Timulty, drinking from the bottle, "we go rap on the door and ask permission."

"Permission!" said Murphy. "I'd hate to have you running hell, the lost souls would never get fried! We—"

But the front door swung wide suddenly, cutting him off.

A man peered out into the night.

"I say," said a gentle and reasonable voice, "would you mind keeping your voices down. The lady of the house is sleeping before we drive to Dublin for the evening, and—"

The men, revealed in the hearth-light glow of the door, blinked and stood back, lifting their caps.

"Is that you, Lord Kilgotten?"

"It is," said the man in the door.

"We will keep our voices down," said Timulty, smiling, all amiability.

"Beg pardon, your Lordship," said Casey.

"Kind of you," said his Lordship. And the door closed gently.

All the men gasped.

" 'Beg pardon, your Lordship,' 'We'll keep our voices down, your Lordship.' " Casey slapped his head. "What were we saying? Why didn't someone catch the door while he was still there?"

"We was dumbfounded, that's why; he took us by surprise, just like them damned high and mighties. I mean, we weren't *doing* anything out here, were we?"

"Our voices *were* a bit high," admitted Timulty.

"Voices, hell," said Casey. "The damn Lord's come and gone from our fell clutches!"

"*Shh*, not so loud," said Timulty.

Casey lowered his voice. "So, let us sneak up on the door, and—"

"That strikes me as unnecessary," said Nolan. "He *knows* we're here now."

"Sneak up on the door," repeated Casey, grinding his teeth, "and batter it down—"

The door opened again.

The Lord, a shadow, peered out at them and the soft, patient, frail old voice inquired, "I say, what *are* you doing out there?"

"Well, it's this way, your Lordship—" began Casey, and stopped, paling.

"We come," blurted Murphy, "we come . . . to *burn* the Place!"

His Lordship stood for a moment looking out at the men, watching the snow, his hand on the doorknob. He shut his eyes for a moment, thought, conquered a tic in both eyelids after a silent struggle, and then said, "Hmm, well in that case, you had best come in."

The men said that was fine, great, good enough, and started off when Casey cried, "Wait!" Then to the old man in the doorway, "We'll come in, when we are good and ready."

"Very well," said the old man. "I shall leave the door ajar and when you have decided the time, enter. I shall be in the library."

Leaving the door a half inch open, the old man started away when Timulty cried out, "When we are *ready*? Jesus, God, when will we ever be readier? Out of the way, Casey!"

And they all ran up on the porch.

Hearing this, his Lordship turned to look at them with his bland and not-unfriendly face, the face of an old hound who has seen many foxes killed and just as many escape, who has run well, and now in late years, paced himself down to a soft, shuffling walk.

"Scrape your feet, please, gentlemen."

"Scraped they are." And everyone carefully got the snow and mud off his shoes.

"This way," said his Lordship, going off, his clear, pale eyes set in lines and bags and creases from too many years of drinking brandy, his cheeks bright as cherry wine. "I will get you all a drink, and we shall see what we can do about your . . . how did you put it . . . burning the Place?"

"You're Sweet Reason itself," admitted Timulty, following as Lord Kilgotten led them into the library, where he poured whiskey all around.

"Gentlemen." He let his bones sink into a wing-backed chair. "Drink."

"We decline," said Casey.

"Decline?" gasped everyone, the drinks almost in their hands.

"This is a sober thing we are doing and we must be sober for it," said Casey, flinching from their gaze.

"Who do we listen to?" asked Riordan. "His Lordship or Casey?"

For answer all the men downed their drinks and fell to coughing and gasping. Courage showed immediately in a red color through their faces, which they turned so that Casey could see the difference. Casey drank his, to catch up.

Meanwhile, the old man sipped his whiskey, and something about his calm and easy way of drinking put them far out in Dublin Bay and sank them again. Until Casey said, "Your Honor, you've heard of the Troubles? I mean not just the Kaiser's war going on across the sea, but our own very great Troubles and the Rebellion that has reached even this far, to our town, our pub, and now, your Place?"

"An alarming amount of evidence convinces me this is an unhappy time," said his Lordship. "I suppose what must be must be. I know you all. You have worked for me. I think I have paid you rather well on occasion."

"There's no doubt of that, your Lordship." Casey took a step forward. "It's just, 'The old order changeth,' and we have heard of the great houses out near

Tara and the great manors beyond Killashandra going up in flames to celebrate freedom and—"

"Whose freedom?" asked the old man, mildly. "Mine? From the burden of caring for this house which my wife and I rattle around in like dice in a cup or—well, get on. *When* would you like to burn the Place?"

"If it isn't too much trouble, sir," said Timulty, "now."

The old man seemed to sink deeper into his chair.

"Oh, dear," he said.

"Of course," said Nolan quickly, "if it's inconvenient, we could come back later—"

"Later! What kind of talk is *that?*" asked Casey.

"I'm terribly sorry," said the old man. "Please allow me to explain. Lady Kilgotten is asleep now, we are going into Dublin for the opening of a play by Synge—"

"That's a damn fine writer," said Riordan.

"Saw one of his plays a year ago," said Nolan, "and—"

"Stand off!" said Casey.

The men stood back. His Lordship went on with his frail moth voice. "We have a dinner planned back here at midnight for ten people. I don't suppose—you could give us until tomorrow night to get ready?"

"No," said Casey.

"Hold on," said everyone else.

"Burning," said Timulty, "is one thing, but tickets is another. I mean, the theater is *there*, and a dire waste not to see the play, and all that food set up, it might as well be eaten. And all the guests coming. It would be hard to notify them ahead."

"Exactly what *I* was thinking," said his Lordship.

"Yes, I know!" shouted Casey, shutting his eyes, running his hands over his cheeks and jaw and mouth and clenching his fists and turning around in frustration. "But you *don't* put off burnings, you *don't* reschedule them like tea parties, dammit, you *do* them!"

"You do if you remember to bring the matches," said Riordan under his breath.

Casey whirled and looked as if he might hit Riordan, but the impact of the truth slowed him down.

"On top of which," said Nolan, "the missus above is a fine lady and needs a last night of entertainment and rest."

"Very kind of you." His Lordship refilled the man's glass.

"Let's take a vote," said Nolan.

"Hell." Casey scowled around. "I see the vote counted already. Tomorrow night will do, dammit."

"Bless you," said old Lord Kilgotten. "There will be cold cuts laid out in the kitchen, you might check in there first, you shall probably be hungry, for it will be heavy work. Shall we say eight o'clock tomorrow night? By then I shall have Lady Kilgotten safely to a hotel in Dublin. I should not want her knowing until later that her home no longer exists."

"God, you're a Christian," muttered Riordan.

"Well, let us not brood on it," said the old man. "I consider it past already, and I never think of the past. Gentlemen."

He arose. And, like a blind old sheepherder-saint, he wandered out into the hall with the flock straying and ambling and softly colliding after.

Half down the hall, almost to the door, Lord Kilgotten saw something from the corner of his blear eye and stopped. He turned back and stood brooding before a large portrait of an Italian nobleman.

The more he looked the more his eyes began to tic and his mouth to work over a nameless thing.

Finally Nolan said, "Your Lordship, what is it?"

"I was just thinking," said the Lord, at last, "you love Ireland, do you not?"

My God, yes! said everyone. Need he ask?

"Even as do I," said the old man gently. "And do you love all that is in it, in the land, in her heritage?"

That too, said all, went without saying!

"I worry then," said the Lord, "about things like this. This portrait is by Van Dyck. It is very old and very fine and very important and very expensive. It is, gentlemen, a National Art Treasure."

"Is *that* what it is!" said everyone, more or less, and crowded around for a sight.

"Ah, God, it's fine work," said Timulty.

"The flesh itself," said Nolan.

"Notice," said Riordan, "the way his little eyes seem to follow you?"

Uncanny, everyone said.

And were about to move on, when his Lordship said, "Do you realize this Treasure, which does not truly belong to me, nor you, but to all the people as precious heritage, this picture will be lost forever tomorrow night?"

Everyone gasped. They had *not* realized.

"God save us," said Timulty, "we can't have that!"

"We'll move it out of the house, first," said Riordan.

"Hold on!" cried Casey.

"Thank you," said his Lordship, "but where would you put it? Out in the weather it would soon be torn to shreds by wind, dampened by rain, flaked by hail; no, no, perhaps it is best it burns quickly—"

"None of that!" said Timulty. "I'll take it home, myself."

"And when the great strife is over," said his Lordship, "you will then deliver into the hands of the new government this precious gift of Art and Beauty from the past?"

"Er . . . every single one of those things, I'll do," said Timulty.

But Casey was eying the immense canvas, and said, "How much does the monster weigh?"

"I would imagine," said the old man, faintly, "seventy to one hundred pounds, within that range."

"Then how in hell do we get it to Timulty's house?" asked Casey.

"Me and Brannahan will carry the damn treasure," said Timulty, "and if need be, Nolan, *you* lend a hand."

"Posterity will thank you," said his Lordship.

They moved on along the hall, and again his Lordship stopped, before yet two more paintings.

"These are two nudes—"

They *are* that! said everyone.

"By Renoir," finished the old man.

"That's the French gent who made them?" asked Rooney. "If you'll excuse the expression?"

It looks French all right, said everyone.

And a lot of ribs received a lot of knocking elbows.

"These are worth several thousand pounds," said the old man.

"You'll get no argument from me," said Nolan, putting out his finger, which was slapped down by Casey.

"I—" said Blinky Watts, whose fish eyes swam about continuously in tears behind his thick glasses, "I would like to volunteer a home for the two French ladies. I thought I might tuck those two Art Treasures one under each arm and hoist them to the wee cot."

"Accepted," said the Lord with gratitude.

Along the hall they came to another, vaster landscape with all sorts of monster beast-men cavorting about treading fruit and squeezing summer-melon women. Everyone craned forward to read the brass plate under it: *Twilight of the Gods*.

"Twilight, hell," said Rooney, "it looks more like the start of a great afternoon!"

"I believe," said the gentle old man, "there is irony intended both in title and subject. Note the glowering sky, the hideous figures hidden in the clouds. The gods are unaware, in the midst of their bacchanal, that Doom is about to descend."

"I do not see," said Blinky Watts, "the Church or any of her girly priests up in them clouds."

"It was a different kind of Doom in them days," said Nolan. "Everyone knows *that*."

"Me and Tuohy," said Flannery, "will carry the demon gods to my place. Right, Tuohy?"

"Right!"

And so it went now, along the hall, the squad pausing here or there as on a grand tour of a museum, and each in turn volunteering to scurry home through the snowfall night with a Degas or a Rembrandt sketch or a large oil by one of the Dutch masters, until they came to a rather grisly oil of a man, hung in a dim alcove.

"Portrait of myself," muttered the old man, "done by her Ladyship. Leave it there, please."

"You mean," gasped Nolan, "you want it to go up in the Conflagration?"

"Now, this next picture—" said the old man, moving on.

And finally the tour was at an end.

"Of course," said his Lordship, "if you really want to be saving, there are a dozen exquisite Ming vases in the house—"

"As good as collected," said Nolan.

"A Persian carpet on the landing—"

"We will roll it and deliver it to the Dublin Museum."

"And that exquisite chandelier in the main dining room."

"It shall be hidden away until the Troubles are over," sighed Casey, tired already.

"Well, then," said the old man, shaking each hand as he passed. "Perhaps you might start now, don't you imagine? I mean, you do indeed have a largish job preserving the National Treasures. Think I shall nap five minutes now before dressing."

And the old man wandered off upstairs.

Leaving the men stunned and isolated in a mob in the hall below, watching him go away out of sight.

"Casey," said Blinky Watts, "has it crossed your small mind, if you'd remembered to bring the matches there would be no such long night of work as this ahead?"

"Jesus, where's your taste for the ass-thetics?" cried Riordan.

"Shut up!" said Casey. "Okay, Flannery, you on one end of the *Twilight of the Gods*, you, Tuohy, on the far end where the maid is being given what's good for her. Ha! *Lift!*"

And the gods, soaring crazily, took to the air.

By seven o'clock most of the paintings were out of the house and racked against each other in the snow, waiting to be taken off in various directions toward various huts. At seven-fifteen, Lord and Lady Kilgotten came out and drove away, and Casey quickly formed the mob in front of the stacked paintings so the nice old lady wouldn't see what they were up to. The boys cheered as the car went down the drive. Lady Kilgotten waved fraily back.

From seven-thirty until ten the rest of the paintings walked out in ones and twos.

When all the pictures were gone save one, Kelly stood in the dim alcove worrying over Lady Kilgotten's Sunday painting of the old Lord. He shuddered, decided on a supreme humanitarianism, and carried the portrait safely out into the night.

At midnight, Lord and Lady Kilgotten, returning with guests, found only great shuffling tracks in the snow where Flannery and Tuohy had set off one way with the dear bacchanal; where Casey, grumbling, had led a parade of Van Dycks, Rembrandts, Bouchers, and Piranesis another; and, where last of all, Blinky Watts, kicking his heels, had trotted happily into the woods with his nude Renoirs.

The dinner party was over by two. Lady Kilgotten went to bed satisfied that all the paintings had been sent out, en masse, to be cleaned.

At three in the morning, Lord Kilgotten still sat sleepless in his library, alone among empty walls, before a fireless hearth, a muffler about his thin neck, a glass of brandy in his faintly trembling hand.

About three-fifteen there was a stealthy creaking of parquetry, a shift of shadows, and, after a time, cap in hand, there stood Casey at the library door.

"Hist!" he called softly.

The Lord, who had dozed somewhat, blinked his eyes wide. "Oh dear me," he said, "is it time for us to go?"

"That's tomorrow night," said Casey. "And anyways, it's not you that's going, it's Them is coming back."

"Them? Your friends?"

"No, *yours*." And Casey beckoned.

The old man let himself be led through the hall to look out the front door into a deep well of night.

There, like Napoleon's numbed dog-army of foot-weary, undecided, and demoralized men, stood the shadowy but familiar mob, their hands full of pictures—pictures leaned against their legs, pictures on their backs, pictures stood upright and held by trembling, panic-whitened hands in the drifted snow. A terrible silence lay over and among the men. They seemed stranded, as if one enemy had gone off to fight far better wars while yet another enemy, as yet unnamed, nipped silent and trackless at their behinds. They kept glancing over their shoulders at the hills and the town as if at any moment Chaos herself might unleash her dogs from there. They alone, in the infiltering night, heard the far-off baying of dismays and despairs that cast a spell.

"Is that *you*, Riordan?" called Casey, nervously.

"Ah, who the hell *would* it be!" cried a voice out beyond.

"What do they *want*?" asked the old party.

"It's not so much what *we* want as what *you* might now want from *us*," called a voice.

"You see," said another, advancing until all could see it was Hannahan in the light, "considered in all its aspects, your Honor, we've decided, you're such a fine gent, we—"

"We will *not* burn your house!" cried Blinky Watts.

"Shut up and let the man talk!" said several voices.

Hannahan nodded. "That's it. We will *not* burn your house."

"But see here," said the Lord, "I'm quite prepared. Everything can easily be moved out."

"You're taking the whole thing too lightly, begging your pardon, your Honor," said Kelly. "Easy for you is not easy for us."

"I see," said the old man, not seeing at all.

"It seems," said Tuohy, "we have all of us, in just the last few hours, developed problems. Some to do with the home and some to do with transport and cartage, if you get my drift. Who'll explain first? Kelly? No? Casey? Riordan?"

Nobody spoke.

At last, with a sigh, Flannery edged forward. "It's this way—" he said.

"Yes?" said the old man, gently.

"Well," said Flannery, "me and Tuohy here got half through the woods, like damn fools, and was across two thirds of the bog with the large picture of the *Twilight of the Gods* when we began to sink."

"Your strength failed?" inquired the Lord kindly.

"Sink, your Honor, just plain sink, into the *ground*," Tuohy put in.

"Dear me," said the Lord.

"You can say that again, your Lordship," said Tuohy. "Why together, me and Flannery and the demon gods must have weighed close on to six hundred pounds, and that bog out there is infirm if it's anything, and the more we walk the deeper we sink, and a cry strangled in me throat, for I'm thinking of those scenes in the old story where the Hound of the Baskervilles or some such fiend chases the heroine out in the moor and down she goes, in a watery pit, wishing she had kept at that diet, but it's too late, and bubbles rise to pop on the surface. All of this a-throttling in me mind, your Honor."

"And so?" the Lord put in, seeing he was expected to ask.

"And so," said Flannery, "we just walked off and left the damn gods there in their twilight."

"In the middle of the *bog*?" asked the elderly man, just a trifle upset.

"Ah, we covered them up, I mean we put our mufflers over the scene. The gods will not die twice, your Honor. Say, did you hear *that*, boys? The gods—"

"Ah, shut up," cried Kelly. "Ya dimwits. Why didn't you bring the damn portrait in off the bog?"

"We thought we would come get two more boys to help—"

"Two more!" cried Nolan. "That's four men, plus a parcel of gods, you'd all sink *twice* as fast, and the bubbles rising, ya nitwit!"

"Ah!" said Tuohy. "I never thought of that."

"It has been thought of now," said the old man. "And perhaps several of you will form a rescue team—"

"It's done, your Honor," said Casey. "Bob, you and Tim dash off and save the pagan deities."

"You won't tell Father Leary?"

"Father Leary my behind. Get!" And Tim and Bob panted off.

His Lordship turned now to Nolan and Kelly.

"I see that you, too, have brought your rather large picture back."

"At least we made it within a hundred yards of the door, sir," said Kelly. "I suppose you're wondering *why* we have returned it, your Honor?"

"With the gathering in of coincidence upon coincidence," said the old man, going back in to get his overcoat and putting on his tweed cap so he could stand out in the cold and finish what looked to be a long converse, "yes, I was given to speculate."

"It's me back," said Kelly. "It gave out not five hundred yards down the main road. The back has been springing out and in for five years now, and me suffering the agonies of Christ. I sneeze and fall to my knees, your Honor."

"I have suffered the selfsame delinquency," said the old man. "It is as if someone had driven a spike into one's spine." The old man touched his back, carefully, remembering, which brought a gasp from all, nodding.

"The agonies of Christ, as I said," said Kelly.

"Most understandable then that you could not finish your journey with that heavy frame," said the old man, "and most commendable that you were able to struggle back this far with the dreadful weight."

Kelly stood taller immediately, as he heard his plight described. He beamed. "It was nothing. And I'd do it again, save for the string of bones above me ass. Begging pardon, your Honor."

But already his Lordship had passed his kind if tremulous gray-blue, unfocused gaze toward Blinky Watts who had, under either arm, like a dartful prancer, the two Renoir peach ladies.

"Ah, God, there was no trouble with sinking into bogs or knocking my spine out of shape," said Watts, treading the earth to demonstrate his passage home. "I made it back to the house in ten minutes flat, dashed into the wee cot, and began hanging the pictures on the wall, when my wife came up behind me. Have ya ever had your wife come up behind ya, your Honor, and just stand there mum's the word?"

"I seem to recall a similar circumstance," said the old man, trying to remember if he did, then nodding as indeed several memories flashed over his fitful baby mind.

"Well, your Lordship, there is no silence like a woman's silence, do you agree? And no standing there like a woman's standing there like a monument out of Stonehenge. The mean temperature dropped in the room so quick I suffered from the polar concussions, as we call it in our house. I did not dare turn to confront the Beast, or the daughter of the Beast, as I call her in deference to her mom. But finally I heard her suck in a great breath and let it out very cool and calm like a Prussian general. 'That woman is naked as a jay bird,' and 'That other woman is raw as the inside of a clam at low tide.'

" 'But,' said I, 'these are studies of natural physique by a famous French artist.'

" 'Jesus-come-after-me-French,' she cried; 'the-skirts-half-up-to-your-bum-French. The-dress-half-down-to-your-navel-French. And the-gulping-and-smothering-they-do-with-their-mouths-in-their-dirty-novels-French, and now you come home and nail "French" on the walls, why don't you while you're at it, pull the crucifix down and nail one fat naked lady *there?*'

"Well, your Honor, I just shut up my eyes and wished my ears would fall off. 'Is *this* what you want our boys to look at last thing at night as they go to sleep?' she says. Next thing I know, I'm on the path and here I am and here's the raw-oyster nudes, your Honor, beg your pardon, thanks, and much obliged."

"They *do* seem to be unclothed," said the old man, looking at the two pictures, one in either hand, as if he wished to find all that this man's wife said was in them. "I had always thought of summer, looking at them."

"From your seventieth birthday on, your Lordship, perhaps. But *before* that?"

"Uh, yes, yes," said the old man, watching a speck of half-remembered lechery drift across one eye.

When his eye stopped drifting it found Bannock and Toolery on the edge of the far rim of the uneasy sheepfold crowd. Behind each, dwarfing them, stood a giant painting.

Bannock had got his picture home only to find he could not get the damn thing through the door, nor any window.

Toolery had actually got his picture *in* the door when his wife said what a laughingstock they'd be, the only family in the village with a Rubens worth half a million pounds and not even a cow to milk!

So that was the sum, total, and substance of this long night. Each man had a similar chill, dread, and awful tale to tell, and all were told at last, and as they finished a cold snow began to fall among these brave members of the local, hard-fighting IRA.

The old man said nothing, for there was nothing really to say that wouldn't be obvious as their pale breaths ghosting the wind. Then, very quietly, the old man opened wide the front door and had the decency not even to nod or point.

Slowly and silently they began to file by, as past a familiar teacher in an old school, and then faster they moved. So in flowed the river returned, the Ark emptied out before, not after, the Flood, and the tide of animals and angels, nudes that flamed and smoked in the hands, and noble gods that pranced on wings and hoofs, went by, and the old man's eyes shifted gently, and his mouth silently named each, the Renoirs, the Van Dycks, the Lautrec, and so on until Kelly, in passing, felt a touch at his arm.

Surprised, Kelly looked over.

And saw the old man was staring at the small painting beneath his arm.

"My wife's portrait of me?"

"None other," said Kelly.

The old man stared at Kelly and at the painting beneath his arm and then out toward the snowing night.

Kelly smiled softly.

Walking soft as a burglar, he vanished out into the wilderness, carrying the picture. A moment later, you heard him laughing as he ran back, hands empty.

The old man shook his hand, once, tremblingly, and shut the door.

Then he turned away as if the event was already lost to his wandering child mind and toddled down the hall with his scarf like a gentle weariness over his thin shoulders, and the mob followed him in where they found drinks in their great paws and saw that Lord Kilgotten was blinking at the picture over the fireplace as if trying to remember, was the *Sack of Rome* there in the years past? or was it the *Fall of Troy?* Then he felt their gaze and looked full on the encircled army and said:

"Well now, what shall we *drink* to?"

The men shuffled their feet.

Then Flannery cried, "Why, to his Lordship, of course!"

"His Lordship!" cried all, eagerly, and drank, and coughed and choked and sneezed, while the old man felt a peculiar glistering about his eyes, and did not drink at all till the commotion stilled, and then said, "To Our Ireland," and drank, and all said Ah God and Amen to that, and the old man looked at the picture over the hearth and then at last shyly observed, "I do hate to mention it—that picture—"

"Sir?"

"It seems to me," said the old man, apologetically, "to be a trifle off-centered, on the tilt. I wonder if you might—"

"*Mightn't* we, boys!" cried Casey.

And fourteen men rushed to put it right.

Night Call, Collect

What made the old poem run in his mind he could not guess, but run it did:

> *Suppose and then suppose and then suppose*
> *That wires on the far-slung telephone black poles*
> *Sopped up the billion-flooded words they heard*
> *Each night all night and saved the sense*
> *And meaning of it all.*

He stopped. What next? Ah, yes . . .

> *Then, jigsaw in the night,*
> *Put all together and*
> *In philosophic phase*
> *Tried words like moron child.*

Again he paused. How did the thing end? Wait—

> *Thus mindless beast*
> *All treasuring of vowels and consonants*
> *Saves up a miracle of bad advice*
> *And lets it filter whisper, heartbeat out*
> *One lisping murmur at a time.*
> *So one night soon someone sits up*
> *Hears sharp bell ring, lifts phone*
> *And hears a Voice like Holy Ghost*
> *Gone far in nebulae*
> *That Beast upon the wire,*
> *Which with sibilance and savorings*
> *Down continental madnesses of time*
> *Says Hell and O*
> *And then Hell-o.*

He took a breath and finished:

> *To such Creation*
> *Such dumb brute lost Electric Beast,*
> *What is your wise reply?*

. . . .

He sat silently.

He sat, a man eighty years old. He sat in an empty room in an empty house on an empty street in an empty town on the empty planet Mars.

He sat as he had sat now for fifty years, waiting.

On the table in front of him lay a telephone that had not rung for a long, long time.

It trembled now with some secret preparation. Perhaps that trembling had summoned forth the poem. . . .

His nostrils twitched. His eyes flared wide.

The phone shivered ever so softly.

He leaned forward, staring at it.

The phone . . . *rang*.

He leapt up and back, the chair fell to the floor. He cried out:

"No!"

The phone rang again.

"No!"

He wanted to reach out, he did reach out and knock the thing off the table. It fell out of the cradle at the exact moment of its third ring.

"No . . . oh, no, no," he said softly, hands covering his chest, head wagging, the telephone at his feet. "It can't be . . . can't be . . . "

For after all, he was alone in a room in an empty house in an empty town on the planet Mars where no one was alive, only he lived, he was King of the Barren Hill. . . .

And yet . . .

" . . . Barton . . . "

Someone called his name.

No. Some thing buzzed and made a noise of crickets and cicadas in far desertlands.

Barton? he thought. Why . . . why that's *me*!

He hadn't heard anyone say his name in so long he had quite forgot. He was not one for ambling about calling himself by name. He had never—

"Barton," said the phone. "Barton. Barton. Barton."

"Shut up!!" he cried.

And kicked the receiver and bent sweating, panting, to put the phone back on its cradle.

No sooner did he do this than the damned thing rang again.

This time he made a fist around it, squeezed it, as if to throttle the sound, but at last, seeing his knuckles burn color away to whiteness, let go and picked up the receiver.

"Barton," said a far voice, a billion miles away.

He waited until his heart had beat another three times and then said:

"Barton here," he said.

"Well, well," said the voice, only a million miles away now. "Do you know who this is?"

"Christ," said the old man. "The first call I've had in half a lifetime, and we play games."

"Sorry. How stupid of me. Of course you wouldn't recognize your own voice on the telephone. No one ever does. We are accustomed, all of us, to hearing our voice conducted through the bones of our head. Barton, this is Barton."

"What?"

"Who did you think it was?" said the voice. "A rocket captain? Did you think someone had come to rescue you?"

"No."

"What's the date?"

"July 20, 2097."

"Good Lord. Fifty years! Have you been sitting there *that* long waiting for a rocket to come from Earth?"

The old man nodded.

"Now, old man, do you know who I am?"

"Yes." He trembled. "I remember. We are one. I am Emil Barton and you are Emil Barton."

"With one difference. You're eighty, I'm only twenty. All of life before me!"

The old man began to laugh and then to cry. He sat holding the phone like a lost and silly child in his fingers. The conversation was impossible, and should not be continued, yet he went on with it. When he got hold of himself he held the phone close and said, "You there! Listen, oh God, if I could warn you! How can I? You're only a voice. If I could show you how lonely the years are. End it, kill yourself! Don't wait! If you knew what it is to change from the thing you are to the thing that is me, today, here, now, at *this* end."

"Impossible!" The voice of the young Barton laughed, far away. "I've no way to tell if you ever get this call. This is all mechanical. You're talking to a transcription, no more. This is 2037. Sixty years in your past. Today, the atom war started on Earth. All colonials were called home from Mars, by rocket. I got left behind!"

"I remember," whispered the old man.

"Alone on Mars," laughed the young voice. "A month, a year, who cares? There are foods and books. In my spare time I've made transcription libraries of ten thousand words, responses, my voice, connected to phone relays. In later months I'll call, have someone to talk with."

"Yes."

"Sixty years from now my own tapes will ring me up. I don't really think I'll be here on Mars that long, it's just a beautifully ironic idea of mine, something to pass the time. Is that really you, Barton? Is that really *me*?"

Tears fell from the old man's eyes. "Yes."

"I've made a thousand Bartons, tapes, sensitive to all questions, in one thousand Martian towns. An army of Bartons over Mars, while I wait for the rockets to return."

"Fool." The old man shook his head, wearily. "You waited sixty years. You grew old waiting, always alone. And now you've become me and you're still alone in the empty cities."

"Don't expect my sympathy. You're like a stranger, off in another country. I can't be sad. I'm alive when I make these tapes. And you're alive when you hear them. Both of us, to the other, incomprehensible. Neither can warn the other, even though both respond, one to the other, one automatically, the other warmly and humanly. I'm human now. You're human later. It's insane. I can't cry, because not knowing the future I can only be optimistic. These hidden tapes can only react to a certain number of stimuli from you. Can you ask a dead man to weep?"

"Stop it!" cried the old man. He felt the familiar seizures of pain. Nausea moved through him, and blackness. "Oh God, but you were heartless. Go away!"

"Were, old man? I *am*. As long as the tapes glide on, as long as spindles and hidden electronic eyes read and select and convert words to send to you, I'll be young and cruel. I'll go on being young and cruel long after you're dead. Good-by."

"Wait!" cried the old man.

Click.

Barton sat holding the silent phone a long time. His heart gave him intense pain.

What insanity it had been. In his youth how silly, how inspired, those first secluded years, fixing the telephonic brains, the tapes, the circuits, scheduling calls on time relays:

The phone bell.

"Morning, Barton. This is Barton. Seven o'clock. Rise and shine!"

Again!

"Barton? Barton calling. You're to go to Mars Town at noon. Install a telephonic brain. Thought I'd remind you."

"Thanks."

The bell!

"Barton? Barton. Have lunch with me? The Rocket Inn?"

"Right."

"See you. So long!"

Brrrrinnnnng!

"That you, B.? Thought I'd cheer you. Firm chin, and all that. The rescue rocket might come tomorrow, to save us."

"Yes, tomorrow, tomorrow, tomorrow, tomorrow."

Click.

But the years had burned into smoke. Barton had muted the insidious phones and their clever, clever repartee. They were to call him only after he was eighty, if he still lived. And now today, the phone ringing, the past breathing in his ear, whispering, remembering.

The phone!

He let it ring.

I don't have to answer it, he thought.

The bell!

There's no one there at all, he thought.

The ringing!

It's like talking to yourself, he thought. But different. Oh God, how different.

He felt his hands lift the phone.

"Hello, old Barton, this is young Barton. I'm twenty-one today! In the last year I've put voice-brains in two hundred more towns. I've populated Mars with Bartons!"

"Yes." The old man remembered those nights six decades ago, rushing over blue hills and into iron valleys, with a truckful of machinery, whistling, happy. Another telephone, another relay. Something to do. Something clever and wonderful and sad. Hidden voices. Hidden, hidden. In those young days when death was not death, time was not time, old age a faint echo from the long cavern of years ahead. That young idiot, that sadistic fool, never thinking someday he might reap this harvest.

"Last night," said Barton, aged twenty-one, "I sat alone in a movie theater in an empty town. I played an old Laurel and Hardy. God, how I laughed."

"Yes."

"I got an idea. I recorded my voice one thousand times on one tape. Broadcast from the town, it sounds like a thousand people. A comforting noise, the noise of a crowd. I fixed it so doors slam in town, children sing, music boxes play, all by clockworks. If I don't look out the window, if I just listen, it's all right. But if I look, it spoils the illusion. I guess I'm getting lonely."

The old man said, "That was your first sign."

"What?"

"The first time you admitted you were lonely."

"I've experimented with smells. As I walk the empty streets, the smell of bacon, eggs, ham, fillets, come from the houses. All done with hidden machines."

"Madness."

"Self-protection!"

"I'm tired." Abruptly, the old man hung up. It was too much. The past drowning him . . .

Swaying, he moved down the tower stairs to the streets of the town.

The town was dark. No longer did red neons burn, music play, or cooking smells linger. Long ago he had abandoned the fantasy of the mechanical lie. Listen! Are those footsteps? Smell! Isn't that strawberry pie! He had stopped it all.

He moved to the canal where the stars shone in the quivering waters.

Under water, in row after fishlike row, rusting, were the robot population of Mars he had constructed over the years, and, in a wild realization of his own insane inadequacy, had commanded to march, one two three four! into the canal deeps, plunging, bubbling like sunken bottles. He had killed them and shown no remorse.

Faintly a phone rang in a lightless cottage.

He walked on. The phone ceased.

Another cottage ahead rang its bell as if it knew of his passing. He began to run. The ringing stayed behind. Only to be taken up by a ringing from now this house—now that, now here, there! He darted on. Another phone!

"All right!" he shrieked, exhausted. "I'm coming!"

"Hello, Barton."

"What do you want!"

"I'm lonely. I only live when I speak. So I must speak. You can't shut me up forever."

"Leave me alone!" said the old man, in horror. "Oh, my heart!"

"This is Barton, age twenty-four. Another couple of years gone. Waiting. A little lonelier. I've read *War and Peace*, drunk sherry, run restaurants with myself as waiter, cook, entertainer. Tonight, I star in a film at the Tivoli—Emil Barton in *Love's Labor Lost*, playing all the parts, some with wigs!"

"Stop calling me—or I'll kill you!"

"You can't kill me. You'll have to find me, first!"

"I'll find you!"

"You've forgotten where you hid me. I'm everywhere, in boxes, houses, cables, towers, underground! Go ahead, try! What'll you call it? Telecide? Suicide? Jealous, are you? Jealous of me here, only twenty-four, bright-eyed, strong, young. All right, old man, it's war! Between us. Between me! A whole regiment of us, all ages form against you, the real one. Go ahead, declare war!"

"I'll kill you!"

Click. Silence.

He threw the phone out the window.

In the midnight cold, the automobile moved in deep valleys. Under Barton's feet on the floorboard were revolvers, rifles, dynamite. The roar of the car was in his thin, tired bones.

I'll find them, he thought, and destroy all of them. Oh, God, how can he do this to me?

He stopped the car. A strange town lay under the late moons. There was no wind.

He held the rifle in his cold hands. He peered at the poles, the towers, the boxes. Where was this town's voice hidden? That tower? Or that one there! So many years ago. He turned his head now this way, now that, wildly.

He raised the rifle.

The tower fell with the first bullet.

All of them, he thought. All of the towers in this town will have to be cut apart. I've forgotten. Too long.

The car moved along the silent street.

A phone rang.

He looked at the deserted drugstore.

A phone.

Pistol in hand, he shot the lock off the door, and entered.

Click.

"Hello, Barton? Just a warning. Don't try to rip down all the towers, blow things up. Cut your own throat that way. Think it over . . . "

Click.

He stepped out of the phone booth slowly and moved into the street and listened to the telephone towers humming high in the air, still alive, still untouched. He looked at them and then he understood.

He could not destroy the towers. Suppose a rocket came from Earth, impossible idea, but suppose it came tonight, tomorrow, next week? And landed on the other side of the planet, and used the phones to try to call Barton, only to find the circuits dead?

Barton dropped his gun.

"A rocket won't come," he argued, softly with himself. "I'm old. It's too late."

But suppose it came, and you never knew, he thought. No, you've got to keep the lines open.

Again, a phone ringing.

He turned dully. He shuffled back into the drugstore and fumbled with the receiver.

"Hello?" A strange voice.

"Please," said the old man, "don't bother me."

"Who's this, who's there? Who is it? Where are you?" cried the voice, surprised.

"Wait a minute." The old man staggered. "This is Emil Barton, who's that?"

"This is Captain Rockwell, Apollo Rocket 48. Just arrived from Earth."

"No, no, no."

"Are you there, Mr. Barton?"

"No, no, it can't be."

"Where are you?"

"You're lying!" The old man had to lean against the booth. His eyes were cold blind. "It's you, Barton, making fun of me, lying again!"

"This is Captain Rockwell. Just landed. In New Chicago. Where are you?"

"In Green Villa," he gasped. "That's six hundred miles from you."

"Look, Barton, can you come here?"

"What?"

"We've repairs on our rocket. Exhausted from the flight. Can you come help?"

"Yes, yes."

"We're at the field outside town. Can you come by tomorrow?"

"Yes, but—"

"Well?"

The old man petted the phone. "How's Earth? How's New York? Is the war over? Who's President now? What happened?"

"Plenty of time for gossip when you arrive."

"Is everything fine?"

"Fine."

"Thank God." The old man listened to the far voice. "Are you sure you're Captain Rockwell?"

"Dammit, man!"

"I'm sorry!"

He hung up and ran.

They were here, after many years, unbelievable, his own people who would take him back to Earth's seas and skies and mountains.

He started the car. He would drive all night. It would be worth a risk, to see people, to shake hands, to hear them again.

The car thundered in the hills.

That voice. Captain Rockwell. It couldn't be himself, forty years ago. He had never made a recording like that. Or had he? In one of his depressive fits, in a spell of drunken cynicism, hadn't he once made a false tape of a false landing on Mars with a synthetic captain, an imaginary crew? He jerked his head, savagely. No. He was a suspicious fool. Now was no time to doubt. He must run with the moons of Mars, all night. What a party they would have!

The sun rose. He was immensely tired, full of thorns and brambles, his heart plunging, his fingers fumbling the wheel, but the thing that pleased him most was the thought of one last phone call: Hello, *young* Barton, this is *old* Barton. I'm leaving for Earth today! Rescued! He smiled weakly.

He drove into the shadowy limits of New Chicago at sundown. Stepping from his car he stood staring at the rocket tarmac, rubbing his reddened eyes.

The rocket field was empty. No one ran to meet him. No one shook his hand, shouted, or laughed.

He felt his heart roar. He knew blackness and a sensation of falling through the open sky. He stumbled toward an office.

Inside, six phones sat in a neat row.

He waited, gasping.

Finally: the bell.

He lifted the heavy receiver.

A voice said, "I was wondering if you'd get there alive."

The old man did not speak but stood with the phone in his hands.

The voice continued: "Captain Rockwell reporting for duty. Your orders, sir?"

"You," groaned the old man.

"How's your heart, old man?"

"No!"

"Had to eliminate you some way, so I could live, if you call a transcription living."

"I'm going out now," replied the old man. "I don't care. I'll blow up everything until you're all dead!"

"You haven't the strength. Why do you think I had you travel so far, so fast? This is your last trip!"

The old man felt his heart falter. He would never make the other towns. The war was lost. He slid into a chair and made low, mournful noises with his mouth. He glared at the five other phones. As if at a signal, they burst into chorus! A nest of ugly birds screaming!

Automatic receivers popped up.

The office whirled. "Barton, Barton, Barton!"

He throttled a phone in his hands. He choked it and still it laughed at him. He beat it. He kicked it. He furled the hot wire like serpentine in his fingers, ripped it. It fell about his stumbling feet.

He destroyed three other phones. There was a sudden silence.

And as if his body now discovered a thing which it had long kept secret, it seemed to sink upon his tired bones. The flesh of his eyelids fell away like petals. His mouth withered. The lobes of his ears were melting wax. He pushed his chest with his hands and fell face down. He lay still. His breathing stopped. His heart stopped.

After a long spell, the remaining two phones rang.

A relay snapped somewhere. The two phone voices were connected, one to the other.

"Hello, Barton?"

"Yes, Barton?"

"Aged twenty-four."

"I'm twenty-six. We're both young. What's happened?"

"I don't know. Listen."

The silent room. The old man did not stir on the floor. The wind blew in the broken window. The air was cool.

"Congratulate me, Barton, this is my twenty-*sixth* birthday!"

"Congratulations!"

The voices sang together, about birthdays, and the singing blew out the window, faintly, faintly, into the dead city.

The Tombling Day

It was the Tombling day, and all the people had walked up the summer road, including Grandma Loblilly, and they stood now in the green day and the high sky country of Missouri, and there was a smell of the seasons changing and the grass breaking out in flowers.

"Here we are," said Grandma Loblilly, over her cane, and she gave them all a flashing look of her yellow-brown eyes and spat into the dust.

The graveyard lay on the side of a quiet hill. It was a place of sunken mounds and wooden markers; bees hummed all about in quietudes of sound and butterflies withered and blossomed on the clear blue air. The tall sunburnt men and ginghamed women stood a long silent time looking in at their deep and buried relatives.

"Well, let's get to work!" said Grandma, and she hobbled across the moist grass, sticking it rapidly, here and there, with her cane.

The others brought the spades and special crates, with daisies and lilacs tied brightly to them. The government was cutting a road through here in August and since this graveyard had gone unused in fifty years the relatives had agreed to untuck all the old bones and pat them snug somewhere else.

Grandma Loblilly got right down on her knees and trembled a spade in her hand. The others were busy at their own places.

"Grandma," said Joseph Pikes, making a big shadow on her working. "Grandma, you shouldn't be workin' on this place. This's William Simmons's grave, Grandma."

At the sound of his voice, everyone stopped working, and listened, and there was just the sound of butterflies on the cool afternoon air.

Grandma looked up at Pikes. "You think I don't *know* it's his place? I ain't seen William Simmons in sixty years, but I intend to visit him today." She patted out trowel after trowel of rich soil and she grew quiet and introspective and said things to the day and those who might listen. "Sixty years ago, and him a fine man, only twenty-three. And me, I was twenty and all golden about the head and all milk in my arms and neck and persimmon in my cheeks. Sixty years and a planned marriage and then a sickness and him dying away. And me alone, and I remember how the earth mound over him sank in the rains—"

Everybody stared at Grandma.

"But still, Grandma—" said Joseph Pikes.

The grave was shallow. She soon reached the long iron box.

"Gimme a hand!" she cried.

Nine men helped lift the iron box out of the earth, Grandma poking at them with her cane. "Careful!" she shouted. "Easy!" she cried. "Now." They set it on the ground. "Now," she said, "if you be so kindly, you gentlemen might fetch Mr. Simmons on up to my house for a spell."

"We're takin' him on to the new cemetery," said Joseph Pikes.

Grandma fixed him with her needle eye. "You just trot that box right up to my house. Much obliged."

The men watched her dwindle down the road. They looked at the box, looked at each other, and then spat on their hands.

Five minutes later the men squeezed the iron coffin through the front door of Grandma's little white house and set the box down by the potbelly stove.

She gave them a drink all around. "Now, let's lift the lid," she said. "It ain't every day you see old friends."

The men did not move.

"Well, if you won't, I will." She thrust at the lid with her cane, again and again, breaking away the earth crust. Spiders went touching over the floor. There was a rich smell, like plowed spring earth. Now the men fingered the lid. Grandma stood back. "Up!" she said. She gestured her cane, like an ancient goddess. And up in the air went the lid. The men set it on the floor and turned.

There was a sound like wind sighing in October, from all their mouths.

There lay William Simmons as the dust filtered bright and golden through the air. There he slept, a little smile on his lips, hands folded, all dressed up and no place in all the world to go.

Grandma Loblilly gave a low moaning cry.

"He's all there!"

There he was, indeed. Intact as a beetle in his shell, his skin all fine and white, his small eyelids over his pretty eyes like flower petals put there, his lips still with color to them, his hair combed neat, his tie tied, his fingernails pared clean. All in all, he was as complete as the day they shoveled the earth upon his silent case.

Grandma stood tightening her eyes, her hands up to catch the breath that moved from her mouth. She couldn't see. "Where's my specs?" she cried.

People searched. "Can't you find 'em?" she shouted. She squinted at the body. "Never mind," she said, getting close. The room settled. She sighed and quavered and cooed over the open box.

"He's kept," said one of the women. "He ain't crumbled."

"Things like that," said Joseph Pikes, "don't happen."

"It *happened*," said the woman.

"Sixty years underground. Stands to reason no man lasts that long."

The sunlight was late by each window, the last butterflies were settling among flowers to look like nothing more than other flowers.

Grandma Loblilly put out her wrinkly hand, trembling. "The earth kept him. The way the air is. That was good dry soil for keeping."

"He's young," wailed one of the women, quietly. "So young."

"Yes," said Grandma Loblilly, looking at him. "Him, lying there, twenty-three years old. And me, standing here, pushing eighty!" She shut her eyes.

"Now, Grandma." Joseph Pikes touched her shoulder.

"Yes, him lyin' there, all twenty-three and fine and purty, and *me*—" She squeezed her eyes tight. "Me bending over him, never young agin, myself, only old and spindly, never to have a chance at being young agin. Oh, Lord! Death keeps people young. Look how kind death's been to him." She ran her hands over her body and face slowly, turning to the others. "Death's nicer than life. Why didn't I die then too? Then we'd both be young now, together. Me in my box, in my white wedding gown all lace, and my eyes closed down, all shy with death. And my hands making a prayer on my bosom."

"Grandma, don't carry on."

"I got a right to carry on! Why didn't I die, too? Then, when he came back, like he came today, to see me, I wouldn't be like *this*!"

Her hands went wildly to feel her lined face, to twist the loose skin, to fumble the empty mouth, to yank the gray hair and look at it with appalled eyes.

"What a fine coming-back he's had!" She showed her skinny arms. "Think that a man of twenty-three years will want the likes of a seventy-nine-year-old woman with sump-rot in her veins? I been cheated! Death kept him young forever. Look at me; did *Life* do so much?"

"They're compensations," said Joseph Pikes. "He ain't young, Grandma. He's long over eighty years."

"You're a fool, Joseph Pikes. He's fine as a stone, not touched by a thousand rains. And he's come back to see me and he'll be picking one of the younger girls now. What would he want with an old woman?"

"He's in no way to fetch nuthin' offa nobody," said Joseph Pikes.

Grandma pushed him back. "Get out now, all of you! Ain't your box, ain't your lid, and it ain't your almost-husband! You leave the box here, leastwise tonight, and tomorrow you dig a new burying place."

"Awright, Grandma; he was your beau. I'll come early tomorra. Don't you cry, now."

"I'll do what my eyes most need to do."

She stood stiff in the middle of the room until the last of them were out the door. After a while she got a candle and lit it and she noticed someone standing on the hill outside. It was Joseph Pikes. He'd be there the rest of the night, she reckoned, and she did not shout for him to go away. She did not look out the window again, but she knew he was there, and so was much better rested in the following hours.

She went to the coffin and looked down at William Simmons.

She gazed fully upon him. Seeing his hands was like seeing actions. She saw how they had been with reins of a horse in them, moving up and down. She remembered how the lips of him had clucked as the carriage had glided along with an even pacing of the horse through the meadowlands, the moonlight shadows all around. She knew how it was when those hands held to you.

She touched his suit. "That's not the same suit he was buried in!" she cried suddenly. And yet she knew it was the same. Sixty years had changed not the suit but the linings of her mind.

Seized with a quick fear, she hunted a long time until she found her spectacles and put them on.

"Why, *that's* not William Simmons!" she shouted.

But she knew this also was untrue. It was William Simmons. "His chin didn't go back that far!" she cried softly, logically. "Or *did* it?" And his hair. "It was a wonderful sorrel color, I remember! This hair here's just plain brown. And his nose, I don't recall it being that tippy!"

She stood over this strange man and, gradually, as she watched, she knew that this indeed was William Simmons. She knew a thing she should have known all along: that dead people are like wax memory—you take them in your mind, you shape and squeeze them, push a bump here, stretch one out there, pull the body tall, shape and reshape, handle, sculpt and finish a man-memory until he's all out of kilter.

There was a certain sense of loss and bewilderment in her. She wished she had never opened the box. Or, leastwise, had the sense to leave her glasses off. She had not seen him clearly at first; just enough so she filled in the rough spots with her mind. Now, with her glasses on . . .

She glanced again and again at his face. It became slowly familiar. That memory of him that she had torn apart and put together for sixty years faded to be replaced by the man she had *really* known. And he was *fine* to look upon. The sense of having lost something vanished. He was the same man, no more, no less. This was always the way when you didn't see people for years and they came back to say howdy-do. For a spell you felt so very uneasy with them. But then, at last you relaxed.

"Yes, that's you," she laughed. "I see you peeking out from behind all the strangeness. I see you all glinty and sly here and there and about."

She began to cry again. If only she could lie to herself, if only she could say,

"Look at him, he don't look the same, he's not the same man I took a fetching on!" then she could feel better. But all the little inside-people sitting around in her head would rock back in their tiny rockers and cackle and say, "You ain't foolin' us none, Grandma."

Yes, how easy to deny it was him. And feel better. But she didn't deny it. She felt the great depressing sadness because here he was, young as creek water, and here she was, old as the sea.

"William Simmons!" she cried. "Don't look at me! I know you still love me, so I'll primp myself up!"

She stirred the stove-fire, quickly put irons on to heat, used irons on her hair till it was all gray curls. Baking powder whitened her cheeks! She bit a cherry to color her lips, pinched her cheeks to bring a flush. From a trunk she yanked old materials until she found a faded blue velvet dress which she put on.

She stared wildly in the mirror at herself.

"No, no." She groaned and shut her eyes. "There's nothing I can do to make me younger'n you, William Simmons! Even if I died now it wouldn't cure me of this old thing come on me, this disease—"

She had a violent wish to run forever in the woods, fall in a leaf pile and moulder down into smoking ruin with them. She ran across the room, intending never to come back. But as she yanked the door wide a cold wind exploded over her from outside and she heard a sound that made her hesitate.

The wind rushed about the room, yanked at the coffin and pushed inside it. William Simmons seemed to stir in his box.

Grandma slammed the door.

She moved slowly back to squint at him.

He was ten years older.

There were wrinkles and lines on his hands and face.

"William Simmons!"

During the next hour, William Simmons's face tolled away the years. His cheeks went in on themselves, like clenching a fist, like withering an apple in a bin. His flesh was made of carved pure white snow, and the cabin heat melted it. It got a charred look. The air made the eyes and mouth pucker. Then, as if struck a hammer blow, the face shattered into a million wrinkles. The body squirmed in an agony of time. It was forty, then fifty, then sixty years old! It was seventy, eighty, one hundred years! Burning, burning away! There were small whispers and leaf-crackles from its face and its age-burning hands, one hundred ten, one hundred twenty years, lined upon etched, graved, line!

Grandma Loblilly stood there all the cold night, aching her bird bones, watching, cold, over the changing man. She was a witness to all improbabilities. She felt something finally let loose of her heart. She did not feel sad any more. The weight lifted away from her.

She went peacefully to sleep, standing against a chair.

Sunlight came yellow through the woodland, birds and ants and creek waters were moving, each as quiet as the other, going somewhere.

It was morning.

Grandma woke and looked down upon William Simmons.

"Ah," said Grandma, looking and seeing.

Her very breath stirred and stirred his bones until they flaked, like a chrysalis, like a kind of candy all whittling away, burning with an invisible fire. The bones flaked and flew, light as pieces of dust on the sunlight. Each time she shouted the bones split asunder, there was a dry flaking rustle from the box.

If there was a wind and she opened the door, he'd be blown away on it like so many crackly leaves!

She bent for a long time, looking at the box. Then she gave a knowing cry, a sound of discovery, and moved back, putting her hands first to her face and then to her spindly breasts and then traveling all up and down her arms and legs and fumbling at her empty mouth.

Her shout brought Joseph Pikes running.

He pulled up at the door only in time to see Grandma Loblilly dancing and jumping around on her yellow, high-peg shoes in a wild gyration.

She clapped her hands, laughed, flung her skirts, ran in a circle, and did a little waltz with herself, tears on her face. And to the sunlight and the flashing image of herself in the wall mirror she cried:

"I'm young! I'm eighty, but I'm younger'n *him*!"

She skipped, she hopped, and she curtsied.

"There are compensations, Joseph Pikes; you was right!" she chortled. "I'm younger'n *all* the dead ones in the whole world!"

And she waltzed so violently the whirl of her dress pulled at the box and whispers of chrysalis leapt on the air to hang golden and powdery amid her shouts.

"Whee-*deee*!" she cried. "Whee-*heee*!"

The Haunting
of the New

I hadn't been in Dublin for years. I'd been round the world—everywhere but
Ireland—but now within the hour of my arrival the Royal Hibernian Hotel
phone rang and on the phone: Nora herself, God Bless!

"Charles? Charlie? Chuck? Are you rich at last? And do rich writers buy
fabulous estates?"

"Nora!" I laughed. "Don't you ever say hello?"

"Life's too short for hellos, and now there's no time for decent good-bys.
Could you buy Grynwood?"

"Nora, Nora, your family house, two hundred rich years old? What would
happen to wild Irish social life, the parties, drinks, gossip? You can't throw it
all away!"

"Can and shall. Oh, I've trunks of money waiting out in the rain this
moment. But, Charlie, Charles, I'm *alone* in the house. The servants have fled
to help the Aga. Now on this final night, Chuck, I need a writer-man to see the
Ghost. Does your skin prickle? Come. I've mysteries and a home to give away.
Charlie, oh, Chuck, oh, Charles."

Click. Silence.

Ten minutes later I roared round the snake-road through the green hills
toward the blue lake and the lush grass meadows of the hidden and fabulous
house called Grynwood.

I laughed again. Dear Nora! For all her gab, a party was probably on the
tracks this moment, lurched toward wondrous destruction. Bertie might fly
from London, Nick from Paris, Alicia would surely motor up from Galway.
Some film director, cabled within the hour, would parachute or helicopter
down, a rather seedy manna in dark glasses. Marion would show with his
Pekingese dog troupe, which always got drunker, and sicker, than he.

I gunned my hilarity as I gunned the motor.

You'll be beautifully mellow by eight o'clock, I thought, stunned to sleep by
concussions of bodies before midnight, drowse till noon, then even more nicely
potted by Sunday high tea. And somewhere in between, the rare game of
musical beds with Irish and French countesses, ladies, and plain field-beast art

majors crated in from the Sorbonne, some with chewable mustaches, some not, and Monday ten million years off. Tuesday, I would motor oh so carefully back to Dublin, nursing my body like a great impacted wisdom tooth, gone much too wise with women, pain-flashing with memory.

Trembling, I remembered the first time I had drummed out to Nora's, when I was twenty-one.

A mad old Duchess with flour-talcumed cheeks, and the teeth of a barracuda had wrestled me and a sports car down this road fifteen years ago, braying into the fast weather:

"You shall love Nora's menagerie zoo and horticultural garden! Her friends are beasts and keepers, tigers and pussies, rhododendrons and flytraps. Her streams run cold fish, hot trout. Hers is a great greenhouse where brutes grow outsize, force-fed by unnatural airs; enter Nora's on Friday with clean linen, sog out with the wet-wash-soiled bedclothes Monday, feeling as if you had meantime inspired, painted, and lived through all Bosch's Temptations, Hells, Judgments, and Dooms! Live at Nora's and you reside in a great warm giant's cheek, deliciously gummed and morseled hourly. You will pass, like victuals, through her mansion. When it has crushed forth your last sweet-sour sauce and dismarrowed your youth-candied bones, you will be discarded in a cold iron-country train station lonely with rain."

"I'm coated with enzymes?" I cried above the engine roar. "No house can break down my elements, or take nourishment from my Original Sin."

"Fool!" laughed the Duchess. "We shall see most of your skeleton by sunrise Sunday!"

I came out of memory as I came out of the woods at a fine popping glide and slowed because the very friction of beauty stayed the heart, the mind, the blood, and therefore the foot upon the throttle.

There under a blue-lake sky by a blue-sky lake lay Nora's own dear place, the grand house called Grynwood. It nestled in the roundest hills by the tallest trees in the deepest forest in all Eire. It had towers built a thousand years ago by unremembered peoples and unsung architects for reasons never to be guessed. Its gardens had first flowered five hundred years back and there were outbuildings scattered from a creative explosion two hundred years gone amongst old tomb yards and crypts. Here was a convent hall become a horse barn of the landed gentry, there were new wings built on ninety years ago. Out around the lake was a hunting-lodge ruin where wild horses might plunge through minted shadow to sink away in greenwater grasses by yet further cold ponds and single graves of daughters whose sins were so rank they were driven forth even in death to the wilderness, sunk traceless in the gloom.

As if in bright welcome, the sun flashed vast tintinnabulations from scores of house windows. Blinded, I clenched the car to a halt. Eyes shut, I licked my lips.

I remembered my first night at Grynwood.

Nora herself opening the front door. Standing stark naked, she announced: "You're too late. It's all over!"

"Nonsense. Hold this, boy, and this."

Whereupon the Duchess, in three nimble moves, peeled herself raw as a blanched oyster in the wintry doorway.

I stood aghast, gripping her clothes.

"Come in, boy, you'll catch your death." And the bare Duchess walked serenely away among the well-dressed people.

"Beaten at my own game," cried Nora. "Now, to compete, I must put my clothes back on. And I was *so* hoping to shock you."

"Never fear," I said. "You have."

"Come help me dress."

In the alcove, we waded among her clothes, which lay in misshapen pools of musky scent upon a parqueted floor.

"Hold the panties while I slip into them. You're Charles, aren't you?"

"How do you do." I flushed, then burst into an uncontrollable fit of laughter. "Forgive me," I said at last, snapping her bra in back, "it's just here it is early evening, and I'm putting you *into* your clothes. I—"

A door slammed somewhere. I glanced around for the Duchess.

"Gone," I murmured. "The house has devoured her, already."

True. I didn't see the Duchess again until the rainy Monday morn she had predicted. By then she had forgotten my name, my face, and the soul behind my face.

"My God," I said. "What's that, and *that?*"

Still dressing Nora, we had arrived at the library door. Inside, like a bright mirror-maze, the weekend guests turned.

"That," Nora pointed, "is the Manhattan Civic Ballet flown over on ice by jet stream. To the left, the Hamburg Dancers, flown the opposite way. Divine casting. Enemy ballet mobs unable, because of language, to express their scorn and vitriol. They must pantomime their cat-fight. Stand aside, Charlie. What was Valkyrie must become Rhine Maiden. And those boys *are* Rhine Maidens. Guard your flank!"

Nora was right.

The battle was joined.

The tiger lilies leapt at each other, jabbering in tongues. Then, frustrated, they fell away, flushed. With a bombardment of slammed doors, the enemies plunged off to scores of rooms. What was horror became horrible friendship and what was friendship became steamroom oven-bastings of unabashed and, thank God, hidden affection.

After that it was one grand crystal-chandelier avalanche of writer-artist-choreographer-poets down the swift-sloped weekend.

Somewhere I was caught and swept in the heaped pummel of flesh headed straight for a collision with the maiden-aunt reality of Monday noon.

Now, many lost parties, many lost years later, here I stood.

And there stood Grynwood manse, very still.

No music played. No cars arrived.

Hello, I thought. A new statue seated by the shore. Hello again. Not a statue . . .

But Nora herself seated alone, legs drawn under her dress, face pale, staring at Grynwood as if I had not arrived, was nowhere in sight.

"Nora . . . ?" But her gaze was so steadily fixed to the house wings, its mossy roofs and windows full of empty sky, I turned to stare at it myself.

Something *was* wrong. Had the house sunk two feet into the earth? Or had the earth sunk all about, leaving it stranded forlorn in the high chill air?

Had earthquakes shaken the windows atilt so they mirrored intruders with distorted gleams and glares?

The front door of Grynwood stood wide open. From this door, the house breathed out upon me.

Subtle. Like waking by night to feel the push of warm air from your wife's nostrils, but suddenly terrified, for the scent of her breath has changed, she smells of someone else! You want to seize her awake, cry her name. Who *is* she, how, what? But heart thudding, you lie sleepless by some stranger in bed.

I walked. I sensed my image caught in a thousand windows moving across the grass to stand over a silent Nora.

A thousand of me sat quietly down.

Nora, I thought. Oh dear God, here we are again.

That first visit to Grynwood . . .

And then here and there through the years we had met like people brushing in a crowd, like lovers across the aisle and strangers on a train, and with the whistle crying the quick next stop, touched hands or allowed our bodies to be bruised together by the crowd cramming out as the doors flung wide, then, impelled, no more touch, no word, nothing for years.

Or, it was as if at high noon midsummer every year or so we ran off up the vital strand a way, never dreaming we might come back and collide in mutual need. And then somehow another summer ended, a sun went down, and there came Nora dragging her empty sandpail and here came I with scabs on my knees, and the beach empty and a strange season gone, and just us left to say hello Nora, hello Charles as the wind rose and the sea darkened as if a great herd of octopi suddenly swam by with their inks.

I often wondered if a day might come when we circled the long way round and stayed. Somewhere back perhaps twelve years ago there had been one moment, balanced like a feather upon fingertip, when our breaths from either side had held our love warmly and perfectly in poise.

But that was because I had bumped into Nora in Venice, with her roots packed, far from home, away from Grynwood, where she might truly belong to someone else, perhaps even to me.

But somehow our mouths had been too busy with each other to ask permanence. Next day, healing our lips, puffed from mutual assaults, we had not the strength to say forever-as-of-now, more tomorrows this way, an apartment, a house anywhere, not Grynwood, not Grynwood ever again, stay! Perhaps the light of noon was cruel, perhaps it showed too many pores in people. Or perhaps, more accurately, the nasty children were bored again. Or terrified of a prison of two! Whatever the reason, the feather, once briefly lofted on champagne breath, toppled. Neither knew which ceased breathing upon it first. Nora pretended an urgent telegram and fled off to Grynwood.

Contact was broken. The spoiled children never wrote. I did not know what sand-castles she had smashed. She did not know what Indian Madras had bled color from passion's sweat on my back. I married. I divorced. I traveled.

And now here we were again come from opposite directions late on a strange day by a familiar lake, calling to each other without calling, running to each other without moving, as if we had not been years apart.

"Nora." I took her hand. It was cold. "What's happened?"

"Happened!?" She laughed, grew silent, staring away. Suddenly she laughed again, that difficult laughter that might instantly flush with tears. "Oh, my dear Charlie, think wild, think all, jump hoops and come round to maniac dreams. Happened, Charlie, happened?!"

She grew frightfully still.

"Where are the servants, the guests—?"

"The party," she said, "was last night."

"Impossible! You've never had just a Friday-night bash. Sundays have always seen your lawn littered with demon wretches strewn and bandaged with bedclothes. Why—?"

"Why did I invite you out today, you want to ask, Charles?" Nora still looked only at the house. "To give you Grynwood. A gift, Charlie, if you can force it to let you stay, if it will put up with you—"

"I don't want the house!" I burst in.

"Oh, it's not if you want *it*, but if it wants *you*. It threw us all out, Charlie."

"Last night . . . ?"

"Last night the last great party at Grynwood didn't come off. Mag flew from Paris. The Aga sent a fabulous girl from Nice. Roger, Percy, Evelyn, Vivian, Jon were here. That bullfighter who almost killed the playwright over the ballerina was here. The Irish dramatist who falls off stages drunk was here. Ninety-seven guests teemed in that door between five and seven last night. By midnight they were gone."

I walked across the lawn.

Yes, still fresh in the grass: the tire marks of three dozen cars.

"It wouldn't let us have the party, Charles," Nora called, faintly.

I turned blankly. "It? The house?"

"Oh, the music was splendid but went hollow upstairs. We heard our laughter ghost back from the topmost halls. The party clogged. The *petits fours* were clods in our throats. The wine ran over our chins. No one got to bed for even three minutes. Doesn't it sound a lie? But, Limp Meringue Awards were given to all and they went away and I slept bereft on the lawn all night. Guess why? Go look, Charlie."

We walked up to the open front door of Grynwood.

"What shall I look for?"

"Everything. All the rooms. The house itself. The mystery. Guess. And when you've guessed a thousand times I'll tell you why I can never live here again, must leave, why Grynwood is yours if you wish. Go in, alone."

And in I went, slowly, one step at a time.

I moved quietly on the lovely lion-yellow hardwood parquetry of the great hall. I gazed at the Aubusson wall tapestry. I examined the ancient white marble Greek medallions displayed on green velvet in a crystal case.

"Nothing," I called back to Nora out there in the late cooling day.

"No. Everything," she called. "Go on."

The library was a deep warm sea of leather smell where five thousand books gleamed their colors of hand-rubbed cherry, lime, and lemon bindings. Their gold eyes, bright titles, glittered. Above the fireplace which could have kenneled two firedogs and ten great hounds hung the exquisite Gainsborough *Maidens and Flowers* that had warmed the family for generations. It was a portal overlooking summer weather. One wanted to lean through and sniff wild seas of flowers, touch harvest of peach maiden girls, hear the machinery of bees bright-stitching up the glamorous airs.

"Well?" called a far voice.

"Nora!" I cried. "Come here. There's nothing to fear! It's still daylight!"

"No," said the far voice sadly. "The sun is going down. What do you see, Charlie?"

"Out in the hall again, the spiral stairs. The parlor. Not a dust speck on the air. I'm opening the cellar door. A million barrels and bottles. Now the kitchen. Nora, this is lunatic!"

"Yes, isn't it?" wailed the far voice. "Go back to the library. Stand in the middle of the room. See the Gainsborough *Maidens and Flowers* you always loved?"

"It's there."

"It's not. See the silver Florentine humidor?"

"I see it."

"You don't. See the great maroon leather chair where you drank sherry with Father?"

"Yes."

"No," sighed the voice.

"Yes, no? Do, don't? Nora, enough!"

"More than enough, Charlie. Can't you guess? Don't you *feel* what happened to Grynwood?"

I ached, turning. I sniffed the strange air.

"Charlie," said Nora, far out by the open front door, " . . . four years ago," she said faintly. "Four years ago . . . Grynwood burned completely to the ground."

I ran.

I found Nora pale at the door.

"It *what*!?" I shouted.

"Burned to the ground," she said. "Utterly. Four years ago."

I took three long steps outside and looked up at the walls and windows.

"Nora, it's standing, it's all here!"

"No, it isn't, Charlie. That's not Grynwood."

I touched the gray stone, the red brick, the green ivy. I ran my hand over the carved Spanish front door. I exhaled in awe. "It can't be."

"It is," said Nora. "All new. Everything from the cellar stones up. New, Charles. New, Charlie. New."

"This *door*?"

"Sent up from Madrid, last year."

"This pavement?"

"Quarried near Dublin two years ago. The windows from Waterford this spring."

I stepped through the front door.

"The parqueting?"

"Finished in France and shipped over autumn last."

"But, but, that *tapestry*!?"

"Woven near Paris, hung in April."

"But it's all the *same*, Nora!"

"Yes, isn't it? I traveled to Greece to duplicate the marble relics. The crystal case I had made, too, in Rheims."

"The library!"

"Every book, all bound the same way, stamped in similar gold, put back on similar shelves. The library alone cost one hundred thousand pounds to reproduce."

"The same, the same, Nora," I cried, in wonder, "oh God, the same," and we were in the library and I pointed at the silver Florentine humidor. "That, of course, was saved out of the fire?"

"No, no, I'm an artist. I remembered. I sketched, I took the drawings to Florence. They finished the fraudulent fake in July."

"The Gainsborough *Maidens and Flowers*!?"

"Look close! That's Fritzi's work. Fritzi, that horrible drip-dry beatnik painter in Montmartre? Who threw paint on canvas and flew them as kites over Paris so the wind and rain patterned beauty for him, which he sold for exorbitant prices? Well, Fritzi, it turns out, is a secret Gainsborough fanatic. He'd kill me if he knew I told. He painted this *Maidens* from memory, isn't it *fine*?"

"Fine, fine, oh God, Nora, are you telling the truth?"

"I wish I weren't. Do you think I've been mentally ill, Charles? Naturally you might think. Do you believe in good and evil, Charlie? I didn't used. But now, quite suddenly, I have turned old and rain-dowdy. I have hit forty, forty has hit me, like a locomotive. Do you know what I think? . . . the house destroyed *itself*."

"It *what?*"

She went to peer into the halls where shadows gathered now, coming in from the late day.

"When I first came into my money, at eighteen, when people said Guilt I said Bosh. They cried Conscience. I cried Crapulous Nonsense! But in those days the rain barrel was empty. A lot of strange rain has fallen since and gathered in me, and to my cold surprise I find me to the brim with old sin and know there *is* conscience and guilt.

"There are a thousand young men in me, Charles.

"They thrust and buried themselves there. When they withdrew, Charles, I thought they withdrew. But no, no, now I'm sure there is not a single one whose barb, whose lovely poisoned thorn, is not caught in my flesh, one place or another. God, God, how I loved their barbs, their thorns. God, how I loved to be pinned and bruised. I thought the medicines of time and travel might heal the grip marks. But now I know I am all fingerprints. There lives no inch of my flesh, Chuck, that is not FBI file systems of palm print and Egyptian whorl of finger stigmata. I have been stabbed by a thousand lovely boys and thought I did not bleed but God I do bleed now. I have bled all over this house. And my friends who denied guilt and conscience, in a great subway heave of flesh have trammeled through here and jounced and mouthed each other and sweat upon floors and buckshot the walls with their agonies and descents, each from the other's crosses. The house has been stormed by assassins, Charlie, each seeking to kill the other's loneliness with their short swords, no one finding surcease, only a momentary groaning out of relaxation.

"I don't think there has ever been a happy person in this house, Charles, I see that now.

"Oh, it all *looked* happy. When you hear so much laughter and see so much drink and find human sandwiches in every bed, pink and white morsels to munch upon, you think: What joy! how happy-fine!

"But it is a lie, Charlie, you and I know that, and the house drank the lie in my generation and Father's before me and Grandfather beyond. It was always a happy house, which means a dreadful estate. The assassins have wounded each other here for long over two hundred years. The walls dripped. The doorknobs were gummy. Summer turned old in the Gainsborough frame. So the assassins came and went, Charlie, and left sins and memories of sins which the house kept.

"And when you have caught up just so much darkness, Charles, you must vomit, mustn't you?

"My life is my emetic. I choke on my own past.

"So did this house.

"And finally, guilt-ridden, terribly sad, one night I heard the friction of old sins rubbing together in attic beds. And with this spontaneous combustion the house smouldered ablaze. I heard the fire first as it sat in the library, devouring books. Then I heard it in the cellar drinking wine. By that time I was out the window and down the ivy and on the lawn with the servants. We picnicked on the lake shore at four in the morning with champagne and biscuits from the gatekeeper's lodge. The fire brigade arrived from town at five to see the roofs collapse and vast fire founts of spark fly over the clouds and the sinking moon. We gave them champagne also and watched Grynwood die finally, at last, so at dawn there was nothing.

"It had to destroy itself, didn't it, Charlie, it was so evil from all my people and from me?"

We stood in the cold hall. At last I stirred myself and said, "I guess so, Nora."

We walked into the library where Nora drew forth blueprints and a score of notebooks.

"It was then, Charlie, I got my inspiration. Build Grynwood again. A gray jigsaw puzzle put back together! Phoenix reborn from the sootbin. So no one would know of its death through sickness. Not you, Charlie, or any friends off in the world; let all remain ignorant. My guilt over its destruction was immense. How fortunate to be rich. You can buy a fire brigade with champagne and the village newspapers with four cases of gin. The news never got a mile out that Grynwood was strewn sackcloth and ashes. Time later to tell the world. Now! to work! And off I raced to my Dublin solicitor's where my father had filed architectural plans and interior details. I sat for months with a secretary, word-associating to summon up Grecian lamps, Roman tiles. I shut my eyes to recall every hairy inch of carpeting, every fringe, every rococo ceiling oddment, all, all brasswork decor, firedog, switchplates, log-bucket, and doorknob. And when the list of thirty thousand items was compounded, I flew in carpenters from Edinburgh, tile setters from Siena, stone-cutters from Perugia, and they hammered, nailed, thrived, carved, and set for four years, Charlie, and I loitered at the factory outside Paris to watch spiders weave my tapestry and floor the rugs. I rode to hounds at Waterford while watching them blow my glass.

"Oh, Charles, I don't think it has ever happened, has it in history, that anyone ever put a destroyed thing back the way it was? Forget the past, let the bones cease! Well, not for me, I thought, no: Grynwood shall rise and be as ever it was. But, while looking like the old Grynwood, it would have the advantage of being really new. A fresh start, I thought, and while building it I led such a *quiet* life, Charles. The work was adventure enough.

"As I did the house over, I thought I did myself over. While I favored it with rebirth, I favored myself with joy. At long last, I thought, a happy person comes and goes at Grynwood.

"And it was finished and done, the last stone cut, the last tile placed, two weeks ago.

"And I sent invitations across the world, Charlie, and last night they all arrived, a pride of lion-men from New York, smelling of Saint John's breadfruit, the staff of life. A team of lightfoot Athens boys. A Negro *corps de ballet* from Johannesburg. Three Sicilian bandits, or were they actors? Seventeen lady violinists who might be ravished as they laid down their violins and picked up their skirts. Four champion polo players. One tennis pro to restring my guts. A darling French poet. Oh God, Charles, it was to be a swell grand fine re-opening of the Phoenix Estates, Nora Gryndon, proprietress. How did I know, or guess, the house would not want us here?"

"Can a house want or not want?"

"Yes, when it is very new and everyone else, no matter what age, is very old. It was freshly born. We were stale and dying. It was good. We were evil. It wished to stay innocent. So it turned us out."

"How?"

"Why, just by being itself. It made the air so quiet, Charlie, you wouldn't believe. We all felt someone had died.

"After a while, with no one saying but everyone feeling it, people just got in their cars and drove away. The orchestra shut up its music and sped off in ten limousines. There went the entire party, around the lake drive, as if heading for a midnight outdoor picnic, but no, just going to the airport or the boats, or Galway, everyone cold, no one speaking, and the house empty, and the servants themselves pumping away on their bikes, and me alone in the house, the last party over, the party that never happened, that never could begin. As I said, I slept on the lawn all night, alone with my old thoughts and I knew this was the end of all the years, for I was ashes, and ashes cannot build. It was the new grand lovely fine bird lying in the dark, to itself. It hated my breath in the dooryard. I was over. It had begun. There."

Nora was finished with her story.

We sat silently for a long while in the very late afternoon as dusk gathered to fill the rooms, and put out the eyes of the windows. A wind rippled the lake.

I said, "It can't all be true. Surely you *can* stay here."

"A final test, so you'll not argue me again. We shall try to spend the night here."

"Try?"

"We won't make it through till dawn. Let's fry a few eggs, drink some wine, go to bed early. But lie on top your covers with your clothes on. You shall want your clothes, swiftly, I imagine."

We ate almost in silence. We drank wine. We listened to the new hours striking from the new brass clocks everywhere in the new house.

At ten, Nora sent me up to my room.

"Don't be afraid," she called to me on the landing. "The house means us no harm. It simply fears *we* may hurt *it*. I shall read in the library. When you are ready to leave, no matter what hour, come for me."

"I shall sleep snug as a bug," I said.

"*Shall* you?" said Nora.

And I went up to my new bed and lay in the dark smoking, feeling neither afraid nor smug, calmly waiting for any sort of happening at all.

I did not sleep at midnight.

I was awake at one.

At three, my eyes were still wide.

The house did not creak, sigh, or murmur. It waited, as I waited, timing its breath to mine.

At three-thirty in the morning the door to my room slowly opened.

There was simply a motion of dark upon dark. I felt the wind draught over my hands and face.

I sat up slowly in the dark.

Five minutes passed. My heart slowed its beating.

And then far away below, I heard the front door open.

Again, not a creak or whisper. Just the click and shadowing change of wind motioning the corridors.

I got up and went out into the hall.

From the top of the stairwell I saw what I expected: the front door open. Moonlight flooded the new parqueting and shone upon the new grandfather's clock which ticked with a fresh oiled bright sound.

I went down and out the front door.

"*There* you are," said Nora, standing down by my car in the drive.

I went to her.

"You didn't hear a thing," she said, "and yet you heard something, right?"

"Right."

"Are you ready to leave now, Charles?"

I looked up at the house. "Almost."

"You know now, don't you, it is all over? You feel it, surely, that it is the dawn come up on a new morning? And, feel my heart, my soul beating pale and mossy within my heart, my blood so black, Charlie, you have felt it often beating under your own body, you know how old I am. You know how full of dungeons and racks and late afternoons and blue hours of French twilight I am. Well . . . "

Nora looked at the house.

"Last night, as I lay in bed at two in the morning, I heard the front door drift open. I knew that the whole house had simply leant itself ajar to let the latch free and glide the door wide. I went to the top of the stairs. And, looking down, I saw the creek of moonlight laid out fresh in the hall. And the house so much as said, Here is the way you go, tread the cream, walk the milky new path out of this and away, go, old one, go with your darkness. You are with child. The sour-gum ghost is in your stomach. It will never be born. And because you cannot drop it, one day it will be your death. What are you waiting for?

"Well, Charles, I was afraid to go down and shut that door. And I knew it was true, I would never sleep again. So, I went down and out.

"I have a dark old sinful place in Geneva. I'll go there to live. But you are younger and fresher, Charlie, so I want this place to be yours."

"Not so young."

"Younger than I."

"Not so fresh. It wants me to go, too, Nora. The door to *my* room just now. It opened, too."

"Oh, Charlie," breathed Nora, and touched my cheek. "Oh, Charles," and then, softly, "I'm sorry."

"Don't be. We'll go together."

Nora opened the car door.

"Let me drive. I must drive now, very fast, all the way to Dublin. Do you mind?"

"No. But what about your luggage?"

"What's in there, the house can have. Where are you going?"

I stopped walking. "I must shut the front door."

"No," said Nora. "Leave it open."

"But . . . people will come in."

Nora laughed quietly. "Yes. But only good people. So that's all right, isn't it?"

I finally nodded. "Yes. That's all right."

I came back to stand by my car, reluctant to leave. Clouds were gathering. It was beginning to snow. Great gentle white leaflets fell down out of the moon-lit sky as harmlessly soft as the gossip of angels.

We got in and slammed the car doors. Nora gunned the motor.

"Ready?" she said.

"Ready."

"Charlie?" said Nora. "When we get to Dublin, will you sleep with me, I mean *sleep*, the next few days? I shall need someone the next days. Will you?"

"Of course."

"I wish," she said. And tears filled her eyes. "Oh God, how I wish I could burn myself down and start over. Burn myself down so I could go up to the house now and go in and live forever like a dairy maid full of berries and cream. Oh but hell. What's the use of talk like that?"

"Drive, Nora," I said, gently.

And she drummed the motor and we ran out of the valley, along the lake, with gravel buckshotting out behind, and up the hills and through the deep snow forest, and by the time we reached the last rise, Nora's tears were shaken away, she did not look back, and we drove at seventy through the dense falling and thicker night toward a darker horizon and a cold stone city, and all the way, never once letting go, in silence I held one of her hands.

Tomorrow's Child

He did not want to be the father of a small Blue Pyramid. Peter Horn hadn't planned it that way at all. Neither he nor his wife imagined that such a thing could happen to them. They had talked quietly for days about the birth of their coming child, they had eaten normal foods, slept a great deal, taken in a few shows, and, when it was time for her to fly in the helicopter to the hospital, her husband held her and kissed her.

"Honey, you'll be home in six hours," he said. "These new birth-mechanisms do everything but father the child for you."

She remembered an old-time song— "No, no, they can't take that away from me!" —and sang it, and they laughed as the helicopter lifted them over the green way from country to city.

The doctor, a quiet gentleman named Wolcott, was very confident. Polly Ann, the wife, was made ready for the task ahead and the father was put, as usual, out in the waiting room where he could suck on cigarettes or take highballs from a convenient mixer. He was feeling pretty good. This was the first baby, but there was not a thing to worry about. Polly Ann was in good hands.

Dr. Wolcott came into the waiting room an hour later. He looked like a man who has seen death. Peter Horn, on his third highball, did not move. His hand tightened on the glass and he whispered:

"She's dead."

"No," said Wolcott, quietly. "No, no, she's fine. It's the baby."

"The baby's dead, then."

"The baby's alive, too, but—drink the rest of that drink and come along after me. Something's happened."

Yes, indeed, something had happened. The "something" that had happened had brought the entire hospital out into the corridors. People were going and coming from one room to another. As Peter Horn was led through a hallway where attendants in white uniforms were standing around peering into each other's faces and whispering, he became quite ill.

"Hey, looky looky! The child of Peter Horn! Incredible!"

They entered a small clean room. There was a crowd in the room, looking down at a low table. There was something on the table.

A small Blue Pyramid.

"Why've you brought me here?" said Horn, turning to the doctor.

The small Blue Pyramid moved. It began to cry.

Peter Horn pushed forward and looked down wildly. He was very white and he was breathing rapidly. "You don't mean that's it?"

The doctor named Wolcott nodded.

The Blue Pyramid had six blue snakelike appendages and three eyes that blinked from the tips of projecting structures.

Horn didn't move.

"It weighs seven pounds, eight ounces," someone said.

Horn thought to himself, They're kidding me. This is some joke. Charlie Ruscoll is behind all this. He'll pop in a door any moment and cry "April Fool!" and everybody'll laugh. That's not my child. Oh, horrible! They're kidding me.

Horn stood there, and the sweat rolled down his face.

"Get me away from here." Horn turned and his hands were opening and closing without purpose, his eyes were flickering.

Wolcott held his elbow, talking calmly. "This is your child. Understand that, Mr. Horn."

"No. No, it's not." His mind wouldn't touch the thing. "It's a nightmare. Destroy *it*!"

"You can't kill a human being."

"Human?" Horn blinked tears. "That's not human! That's a crime against God!"

The doctor went on, quickly. "We've examined this—child—and we've decided that it is not a mutant, a result of gene destruction or rearrangement. It's not a freak. Nor is it sick. Please listen to everything I say to you."

Horn stared at the wall, his eyes wide and sick. He swayed. The doctor talked distantly, with assurance.

"The child was somehow affected by the birth pressure. There was a dimensional disstructure caused by the simultaneous short-circuitings and malfunctionings of the new birth and hypnosis machines. Well, anyway," the doctor ended lamely, "your baby was born into—another dimension."

Horn did not even nod. He stood there, waiting.

Dr. Wolcott made it emphatic. "Your child is alive, well, and happy. It is lying there, on the table. But because it was born into another dimension it has a shape alien to us. Our eyes, adjusted to a three-dimensional concept, cannot recognize it as a baby. But it *is*. Underneath that camouflage, the strange pyramidal shape and appendages, it is *your* child."

Horn closed his mouth and shut his eyes. "Can I have a drink?"

"Certainly." A drink was thrust into Horn's hands.

"Now, let me just sit down, sit down somewhere a moment." Horn sank wearily into a chair. It was coming clear. Everything shifted slowly into place. It was his child, no matter what. He shuddered. No matter how horrible it looked, it was his first child.

At last he looked up and tried to see the doctor. "What'll we tell Polly?" His voice was hardly a whisper.

"We'll work that out this morning, as soon as you feel up to it."

"What happens after that? Is there any way to—change it back?"

"We'll try. That is, if you give us permission to try. After all, it's your child. You can do anything with him you want to do."

"Him?" Horn laughed ironically, shutting his eyes. "How do you know it's a him?" He sank down into darkness. His ears roared.

Wolcott was visibly upset. "Why, we—that is—well, we don't know, for sure."

Horn drank more of his drink. "What if you *can't* change him back?"

"I realize what a shock it is to you, Mr. Horn. If you can't bear to look upon the child, we'll be glad to raise him here, at the Institute, for you."

Horn thought it over. "Thanks. But he still belongs to me and Polly. I'll give him a home. Raise him like I'd raise any kid. Give him a normal home life. Try to learn to love him. Treat him right." His lips were numb, he couldn't think.

"You realize what a job you're taking on, Mr. Horn? This child can't be allowed to have normal playmates; why, they'd pester it to death in no time. You know how children are. If you decide to raise the child at home, his life will be strictly regimented, he must *never* be seen by anyone. Is that clear?"

"Yes. Yes, it's clear, Doc. Doc, is he all right mentally?"

"Yes. We've tested his reactions. He's a fine healthy child as far as nervous response and such things go."

"I just wanted to be sure. Now, the only problem is Polly."

Wolcott frowned. "I confess that one has me stumped. You know it is pretty hard on a woman to hear that her child has been born dead. But *this*, telling a woman she's given birth to something not recognizable as human. It's not as clean as death. There's too much chance for shock. And yet I must tell her the truth. A doctor gets nowhere by lying to his patient."

Horn put his glass down. "I don't want to lose Polly, too. I'd be prepared now, if you destroyed the child, to take it. But I don't want Polly killed by the shock of this whole thing."

"I think we may be able to change the child back. That's the point which makes me hesitate. If I thought the case was hopeless I'd make out a certificate of euthanasia immediately. But it's at least worth a chance."

Horn was very tired. He was shivering quietly, deeply. "All right, Doctor. It needs food, milk, and love until you can fix it up. It's had a raw deal so far, no reason for it to go on getting a raw deal. When will we tell Polly?"

"Tomorrow afternoon, when she wakes up."

Horn got up and walked to the table which was warmed by a soft illumination from overhead. The Blue Pyramid sat upon the table as Horn held out his hand.

"Hello, Baby," said Horn.

The Blue Pyramid looked up at Horn with three bright blue eyes. It shifted a tiny blue tendril, touching Horn's fingers with it.

Horn shivered.

"Hello, Baby."

The doctor produced a special feeding bottle.

"This is woman's milk. Here we go."

Baby looked upward through clearing mists. Baby saw the shapes moving over him and knew them to be friendly. Baby was newborn, but already alert, strangely alert. Baby was aware.

There were moving objects above and around Baby. Six cubes of a gray-white color, bending down. Six cubes with hexagonal appendages and three eyes to each cube. Then there were two other cubes coming from a distance over a crystalline plateau. One of the cubes was white. It had three eyes, too. There was something about this White Cube that Baby liked. There was an attraction. Some relation. There was an odor to the White Cube that reminded Baby of itself.

Shrill sounds came from the six bending-down Gray-White Cubes. Sounds of curiosity and wonder. It was like a kind of piccolo music, all playing at once.

Now the two newly arrived cubes, the White Cube and the Gray Cube, were whistling. After a while the White Cube extended one of its hexagonal appendages to touch Baby. Baby responded by putting out one of its tendrils from its pyramidal body. Baby liked the White Cube. Baby liked. Baby was hungry. Baby liked. Maybe the White Cube would give it food. . . .

The Gray Cube produced a pink globe for Baby. Baby was now to be fed. Good. Good. Baby accepted food eagerly.

Food was good. All the Gray-White Cubes drifted away, leaving only the nice White Cube standing over Baby looking down and whistling over and over. Over and over.

They told Polly the next day. Not everything. Just enough. Just a hint. They told her the baby was not well, in a certain way. They talked slowly, and in ever-tightening circles, in upon Polly. Then Dr. Wolcott gave a long lecture on the birth-mechanisms, how they helped a woman in her labor, and how, this time, they short-circuited. There was another man of scientific means present and he gave her a dry little talk on dimensions, holding up his fingers, so! one, two, three, and four. Still another man talked of energy and matter. Another spoke of underprivileged children.

Polly finally sat up in bed and said, "What's all the talk for? What's wrong with my baby that you should all be talking so long?"

Wolcott told her.

"Of course, you can wait a week and see it," he said. "Or you can sign over guardianship of the child to the Institute."

"There's only one thing I want to know," said Polly.

Dr. Wolcott raised his brows.

"Did I *make* the child that way?" asked Polly.

"You most certainly did *not*!"

"The child isn't a monster, genetically?" asked Polly.

"The child was thrust into another continuum. Otherwise, it is perfectly normal."

Polly's tight, lined mouth relaxed. She said, simply, "Then, bring me my baby. I want to see him. Please. Now."

They brought the "child."

The Horns left the hospital the next day. Polly walked out on her own two good legs, with Peter Horn following her, looking at her in quiet amazement.

They did not have the baby with them. That would come later. Horn helped his wife into their helicopter and sat beside her. He lifted the ship, whirring, into the warm air.

"You're a wonder," he said.

"Am I?" she said, lighting a cigarette.

"You are. You didn't cry. You didn't do anything."

"He's not so bad, you know," she said. "Once you get to know him. I can even—hold him in my arms. He's warm and he cries and he even needs his triangular diapers." Here she laughed. He noticed a nervous tremor in the laugh, however. "No, I didn't cry, Pete, because that's my baby. Or he will be. He isn't dead, I thank God for that. He's—I don't know how to explain—still unborn. I like to think he hasn't been born yet. We're waiting for him to show up. I have confidence in Dr. Wolcott. Haven't you?"

"You're right. You're right." He reached over and held her hand. "You know something? You're a peach."

"I can hold on," she said, sitting there looking ahead as the green country swung under them. "As long as I know something good will happen, I won't let it hurt or shock me. I'll wait six months, and then maybe I'll kill myself."

"Polly!"

She looked at him as if he'd just come in. "Pete, I'm sorry. But this sort of thing doesn't happen. Once it's over and the baby is finally 'born' I'll forget it so quick it'll never have occurred. But if the doctor can't help us, then a mind can't take it, a mind can only tell the body to climb out on a roof and jump."

"Things'll be all right," he said, holding to the guide-wheel. "They have to be."

She said nothing, but let the cigarette smoke blow out of her mouth in the pounding concussion of the helicopter fan.

Three weeks passed. Every day they flew in to the Institute to visit "Py." For that was the quiet calm name that Polly Horn gave to the Blue Pyramid that lay on the warm sleeping-table and blinked up at them. Dr. Wolcott was careful to point out that the habits of the "child" were as normal as any others; so many hours asleep, so many awake, so much attentiveness, so much boredom, so much food, so much elimination. Polly Horn listened, and her face softened and her eyes warmed.

At the end of the third week, Dr. Wolcott said, "Feel up to taking him home now? You live in the country, don't you? All right, you have an enclosed patio, he can be out there in the sunlight, on occasion. He needs a mother's love. That's trite, but nevertheless true. He should be suckled. We have an arrangement where he's been fed by the new feed-mech; cooing voice, warmth, hands, and all." Dr. Wolcott's voice was dry. "But still I feel you are familiar enough with him now to know he's a pretty healthy child. Are you game, Mrs. Horn?"

"Yes, I'm game."

"Good. Bring him in every third day for a checkup. Here's his formula. We're working on several solutions now, Mrs. Horn. We should have some results for you by the end of the year. I don't want to say anything definite, but I have reason to believe we'll pull that boy right out of the fourth dimension, like a rabbit out of a hat."

The doctor was mildly surprised and pleased when Polly Horn kissed him, then and there.

Pete Horn took the copter home over the smooth rolling greens of Griffith. From time to time he looked at the pyramid lying in Polly's arms. She was making cooing noises at it, it was replying in approximately the same way.

"I wonder," said Polly.

"What?"

"How do *we* look to *it*?" asked his wife.

"I asked Wolcott about that. He said we probably look funny to him, also. He's in one dimension, we're in another."

"You mean we don't look like men and women to him?"

"If we could see ourselves, no. But remember, the baby knows nothing of men or women. To the baby whatever shape we're in, we are natural. It's accustomed to seeing us shaped like cubes or squares or pyramids, as it sees us from its separate dimension. The baby's had no other experience, no other norm with which to compare what it sees. We *are* it's norm. On the other hand, the baby seems weird to us because we compare it to our accustomed shapes and sizes."

"Yes, I see. I see."

Baby was conscious of movement. One White Cube held him in warm appendages. Another White Cube sat further over, within an oblong of purple. The oblong moved in the air over a vast bright plain of pyramids, hexagons, oblongs, pillars, bubbles, and multicolored cubes.

One White Cube made a whistling noise. The other White Cube replied with a whistling. The White Cube that held him shifted about. Baby watched the two White Cubes, and watched the fleeing world outside the traveling bubble.

Baby felt—sleepy. Baby closed his eyes, settled his pyramidal youngness upon the lap of the White Cube, and made faint little noises. . . .

"He's asleep," said Polly Horn.

Summer came, Peter Horn himself was busy with his export-import business. But he made certain he was home every night. Polly was all right during the day, but, at night, when she had to be alone with the child, she got to smoking too much, and one night he found her passed out on the davenport, an empty sherry bottle on the table beside her. From then on, he took care of the child himself nights. When it cried it made a weird whistling noise, like some jungle animal lost and wailing. It wasn't the sound of a child.

Peter Horn had the nursery soundproofed.

"So your wife won't hear your baby crying?" asked the workman.

"Yes," said Pete Horn. "So she won't hear."

They had few visitors. They were afraid that someone might stumble on Py, dear sweet pyramid little Py.

"What's that noise?" asked a visitor one evening, over his cocktail. "Sounds like some sort of bird. You didn't tell me you had an aviary, Peter."

"Oh, yes," said Horn, closing the nursery door. "Have another drink. Let's drink, everyone."

It was like having a dog or a cat in the house. At least that's how Polly looked upon it. Peter Horn watched her and observed exactly how she talked and petted the small Py. It was Py this and Py that, but somehow with some reserve, and sometimes she would look around the room and touch herself, and her hands would clench, and she would look lost and afraid, as if she were waiting for someone to arrive.

In September, Polly reported to her husband: "He can say Father. Yes he can. Come on, Py. Say Father!"

She held the blue warm pyramid up.

"Wheelly," whistled the little warm Blue Pyramid.

"Again," repeated Polly.

"Wheelly!" whistled the pyramid.

"For God's sake, stop!" said Pete Horn. He took the child from her and put it in the nursery where it whistled over and over that name, that name, that name. Horn came out and poured himself a stiff drink. Polly was laughing quietly.

"Isn't that terrific?" she said. "Even his *voice* is in the fourth dimension. Won't it be nice when he learns to talk later? We'll give him Hamlet's soliloquy to memorize and he'll say it but it'll come out like something from James Joyce! Aren't we lucky? Give me a drink."

"You've had enough," he said.

"Thanks, I'll help myself," she said and did.

October, and then November. Py was learning to talk now. He whistled and squealed and made a bell-like tone when he was hungry. Dr. Wolcott visited. "When his color is a constant bright blue," said the doctor, "that means he's healthy. When the color fades, dull—the child is feeling poorly. Remember that."

"Oh, yes, I will, I will," said Polly. "Robin's-egg blue for health, dull cobalt for illness."

"Young lady," said Wolcott. "You'd better take a couple of these pills and come see me tomorrow for a little chat. I don't like the way you're talking. Stick out your tongue. Ah-hmm. You been drinking? Look at the stains on your fingers. Cut the cigarettes in half. See you tomorrow."

"You don't give me much to go on," said Polly. "It's been almost a year now."

"My dear Mrs. Horn, I don't want to excite you continually. When we have our mechs ready we'll let you know. We're working every day. There'll be an experiment soon. Take those pills now and shut that nice mouth." He chucked Py under the "chin." "Good healthy baby, by God! Twenty pounds if he's an *ounce*!"

Baby was conscious of the goings and comings of the two nice White Cubes who were with him during all of his waking hours. There was another cube, a gray one, who visited on certain days. But mostly it was the two White Cubes who cared for and loved him. He looked up at the one warm, rounder, softer White Cube and made the low warbling soft sound of contentment. The White Cube fed him. He was content. He grew. All was familiar and good.

The New Year, the year 1989, arrived.

Rocket ships flashed on the sky, and helicopters whirred and flourished the warm California winds.

Peter Horn carted home large plates of specially poured blue and gray polarized glass, secretly. Through these, he peered at his "child." Nothing. The pyramid remained a pyramid, no matter if he viewed it through X-ray or yellow cellophane. The barrier was unbreakable. Horn returned quietly to his drinking.

The big thing happened early in February. Horn, arriving home in his helicopter, was appalled to see a crowd of neighbors gathered on the lawn of his home. Some of them were sitting, others were standing, still others were moving away, with frightened expressions on their faces.

Polly was walking the "child" in the yard.

Polly was quite drunk. She held the small Blue Pyramid by the hand and walked him up and down. She did not see the helicopter land, nor did she pay much attention as Horn came running up.

One of the neighbors turned. "Oh, Mr. Horn, it's the cutest thing. Where'd you *find* it?"

One of the others cried, "Hey, you're quite the traveler, Horn. Pick it up in South America?"

Polly held the pyramid up. "Say Father!" she cried, trying to focus on her husband.

"Wheel!" cried the pyramid.

"Polly!" Peter Horn said.

"He's friendly as a dog or a cat," said Polly, moving the child with her. "Oh, no, he's not dangerous. He's friendly as a baby. My husband brought him from Afghanistan."

The neighbors began to move off.

"Come back!" Polly waved at them. "Don't you want to see my baby? Isn't he simply beautiful!"

He slapped her face.

"My baby," she said, brokenly.

He slapped her again and again until she quit saying it and collapsed. He picked her up and took her into the house. Then he came out and took Py in and then he sat down and phoned the Institute.

"Dr. Wolcott, this is Horn. You'd better have your stuff ready. It's tonight or not at all."

There was a hesitation. Finally Wolcott sighed. "All right. Bring your wife and the child. We'll try to have things in shape."

They hung up.

Horn sat there studying the pyramid.

"The neighbors thought he was grand," said his wife, lying on the couch, her eyes shut, her lips trembling. . . .

The Institute hall smelled clean, neat, sterile. Dr. Wolcott walked along it, followed by Peter Horn and his wife Polly, who was holding Py in her arms. They turned in at a doorway and stood in a large room. In the center of the room were two tables with large black hoods suspended over them.

Behind the tables were a number of machines with dials and levers on them. There was the faintest perceptible hum in the room. Pete Horn looked at Polly for a moment.

Wolcott gave her a glass of liquid. "Drink this." She drank it. "Now. Sit down." They both sat. The doctor put his hands together and looked at them for a moment.

"I want to tell you what I've been doing in the last few months," he said. "I've tried to bring the baby out of whatever hell dimension, fourth, fifth, or sixth, that it is in. Each time you left the baby for a checkup we worked on the problem. Now, we have a solution, but it has nothing to do with bringing the baby out of the dimension in which *it* exists."

Polly sank back. Horn simply watched the doctor carefully for anything he might say. Wolcott leaned forward.

"I can't bring Py out, but I can put you people *in*. That's it." He spread his hands.

Horn looked at the machine in the corner. "You mean you can send *us* into Py's dimension?"

"If you want to go badly enough."

Polly said nothing. She held Py quietly and looked at him.

Dr. Wolcott explained. "We know what series of malfunctions, mechanical and electrical, forced Py into his present state. We can reproduce those accidents and stresses. But bringing him *back* is something else. It might take a million trials and failures before we got the combination. The combination that jammed him into another space was an accident, but luckily we saw, observed, and recorded it. There are no records for bringing one back. We have to work in the dark. Therefore, it will be easier to put *you* in the fourth dimension than to bring Py into ours."

Polly asked, simply and earnestly, "Will I see my baby as he really is, if I go into his dimension?"

Wolcott nodded.

Polly said, "Then, I want to go."

"Hold on," said Peter Horn. "We've only been in this office five minutes and already you're promising away the rest of your life."

"I'll be with my real baby. I won't care."

"Dr. Wolcott, what will it be like, in that dimension on the other side?"

"There will be no change that *you* will notice. You will both seem the same size and shape to one another. The pyramid will become a baby, however. You will have added an extra sense, you will be able to interpret what you see differently."

"But won't we turn into oblongs or pyramids ourselves? And won't you, Doctor, look like some geometrical form instead of a human?"

"Does a blind man who sees for the first time give up his ability to hear or taste?"

"No."

"All right, then. Stop thinking in terms of subtraction. Think in terms of addition. You're gaining something. You lose nothing. You know what a human looks like, which is an advantage Py doesn't have, looking out from his dimension. When you arrive 'over there' you can see Dr. Wolcott as *both* things, a geometrical abstract or a human, as you choose. It will probably make quite a philosopher out of you. There's one other thing, however."

"And that?"

"To everyone else in the world you, your wife and the child will look like abstract forms. The baby a triangle. Your wife an oblong perhaps. Yourself a hexagonal solid. The world will be shocked, not you."

"We'll be freaks."

"You'll be freaks. But you won't know it. You'll have to lead a secluded life."

"Until you find a way to bring all three of us out together."

"That's right. It may be ten years, twenty. I won't recommend it to you, you may both go quite mad as a result of feeling apart, different. If there's a grain of paranoia in you, it'll come out. It's up to you, naturally."

Peter Horn looked at his wife, she looked back gravely.

"We'll go," said Peter Horn.

"Into Py's dimension?" said Wolcott.

"Into Py's dimension."

They stood up from their chairs. "We'll lose no other sense, you're certain, Doctor? Will you be able to understand us when we talk to you? Py's talk is incomprehensible."

"Py talks that way because that's what he thinks we sound like when our talk comes through the dimensions to him. He imitates the sound. When you are over there and talk to me, you'll be talking perfect English, because you know *how*. Dimensions have to do with senses and time and knowledge."

"And what about Py? When we come into his stratum of existence. Will he see us as humans, immediately, and won't that be a shock to him? Won't it be dangerous?"

"He's awfully young. Things haven't got too set for him. There'll be a slight shock, but your odors will be the same, and your voices will have the same timber and pitch and you'll be just as warm and loving, which is most important of all. You'll get on with him well."

Horn scratched his head slowly. "This seems such a long way around to where we want to go." He sighed. "I wish we could have another kid and forget all about this one."

"This baby is the one that counts. I daresay Polly here wouldn't want any other, would you, Polly?"

"This baby, *this* baby," said Polly.

Wolcott gave Peter Horn a meaningful look. Horn interpreted it correctly. This baby or no more Polly ever again. This baby or Polly would be in a quiet room somewhere staring into space for the rest of her life.

They moved toward the machine together. "I guess I can stand it, if she can," said Horn, taking her hand. "I've worked hard for a good many years now, it might be fun retiring and being an abstract for a change."

"I envy you the journey, to be honest with you," said Wolcott, making adjustments on the large dark machine. "I don't mind telling you that as a result of your being 'over there' you may very well write a volume of philosophy that will set Dewey, Bergson, Hegel, or any of the others on their ears. I might 'come over' to visit you one day."

"You'll be welcome. What do we need for the trip?"

"Nothing. Just lie on these tables and be still."

A humming filled the room. A sound of power and energy and warmth.

They lay on the tables, holding hands, Polly and Peter Horn. A double black hood came down over them. They were both in darkness. From somewhere far off in the hospital, a voice-clock sang, "*Tick-tock, seven o'clock. Tick-tock, seven o'clock . . .*" fading away in a little soft gong.

The low humming grew louder. The machine glittered with hidden, shifting, compressed power.

"Is there any danger?" cried Peter Horn.

"None!"

The power screamed. The very atoms of the room divided against each other, into alien and enemy camps. The two sides fought for supremacy. Horn gaped his mouth to shout. His insides became pyramidal, oblong with terrific electric seizures. He felt a pulling, sucking, demanding power claw at his body. The power yearned and nuzzled and pressed through the room. The dimensions of the black hood over his torso were stretched, pulled into wild planes of incomprehension. Sweat, pouring down his face, was not sweat, but a pure dimensional essence! His limbs were wrenched, flung, jabbed, suddenly caught. He began to melt like running wax.

A clicking sliding noise.

Horn thought swiftly, but calmly. How will it be in the future with Polly and me and Py at home and people coming over for a cocktail party? How will it be?

Suddenly he knew how it would be and the thought of it filled him with a great awe and a sense of credulous faith and time. They would live in the same white house on the same quiet, green hill, with a high fence around it to keep out the merely curious. And Dr. Wolcott would come to visit, park his beetle in the yard below, come up the steps and at the door would be a tall slim White Rectangle to meet him with a dry martini in its snakelike hand.

And in an easy chair across the room would sit a Salt White Oblong with a copy of Nietzsche open, reading, smoking a pipe. And on the floor would be Py, running about. And there would be talk and more friends would come in and the White Oblong and the White Rectangle would laugh and joke and offer little finger sandwiches and more drinks and it would be a good evening of talk and laughter.

That's how it would be.

Click.

The humming noise stopped.

The hood lifted from Horn.

It was all over.

They were in another dimension.

He heard Polly cry out. There was much light. Then he slipped from the table, stood blinking. Polly was running. She stooped and picked up something from the floor.

It was Peter Horn's son. A living, pink-faced, blue-eyed boy, lying in her arms, gasping and blinking and crying.

The pyramidal shape was gone. Polly was crying with happiness.

Peter Horn walked across the room, trembling, trying to smile himself, to hold on to Polly and the child, both at the same time, and weep with them.

"Well!" said Wolcott, standing back. He did not move for a long while. He only watched the White Oblong and the slim White Rectangle holding the Blue Pyramid on the opposite side of the room. An assistant came in the door.

"Shhh," said Wolcott, hand to his lips. "They'll want to be alone awhile. Come along." He took the assistant by the arm and tiptoed across the room. The White Rectangle and the White Oblong didn't even look up when the door closed.

I Sing the Body Electric!

Grandma!

I remember her birth.

Wait, you say, *no* man remembers his own grandma's birth.

But, yes, *we* remember the day that she was born.

For we, her grandchildren, slapped her to life. Timothy, Agatha, and I, Tom, raised up our hands and brought them down in a huge crack! We shook together the bits and pieces, parts and samples, textures and tastes, humors and distillations that would move her compass needle north to cool us, south to warm and comfort us, east and west to travel round the endless world, glide her eyes to know us, mouth to sing us asleep by night, hands to touch us awake at dawn.

Grandma, O dear and wondrous electric dream. . . .

When storm lightnings rove the sky making circuitries amidst the clouds, her name flashes on my inner lid. Sometimes still I hear her ticking, humming above our beds in the gentle dark. She passes like a clock-ghost in the long halls of memory, like a hive of intellectual bees swarming after the Spirit of Summers Lost. Sometimes still I feel the smile I learned from her, printed on my cheek at three in the deep morn. . . .

All right, all right! you cry. What was it like the day your damned and wondrous-dreadful-loving Grandma was born?

It was the week the world ended. . . .

Our mother was dead.

One late afternoon a black car left Father and the three of us stranded on our own front drive staring at the grass, thinking:

That's not our grass. There are the croquet mallets, balls, hoops, yes, just as they fell and lay three days ago when Dad stumbled out on the lawn, weeping with the news. There are the roller skates that belonged to a boy, me, who will never be that young again. And yes, there the tire-swing on the old oak, but Agatha afraid to swing. It would surely break. It would fall.

And the house? Oh, God . . .

We peered through the front door, afraid of the echoes we might find confused in the halls; the sort of clamor that happens when all the furniture is taken out and there is nothing to soften the river of talk that flows in any house at all hours. And now the soft, the warm, the main piece of lovely furniture was gone forever.

The door drifted wide.

Silence came out. Somewhere a cellar door stood wide and a raw wind blew damp earth from under the house.

But, I thought, we don't *have* a cellar!

"Well," said Father.

We did not move.

Aunt Clara drove up the path in her big canary-colored limousine.

We jumped through the door. We ran to our rooms.

We heard them shout and then speak and then shout and then speak: Let the children live with me! Aunt Clara said. They'd rather kill themselves! Father said.

A door slammed. Aunt Clara was gone.

We almost danced. Then we remembered what had happened and went downstairs.

Father sat alone talking to himself or to a remnant ghost of Mother left from the days before her illness, and jarred loose now by the slamming of the door. He murmured to his hands, his empty palms:

"The children need someone. I love them but, let's face it, I must work to feed us all. You love them, Ann, but you're gone. And Clara? Impossible. She loves but smothers. And as for maids, nurses—?"

Here Father sighed and we sighed with him, remembering.

The luck we had had with maids or live-in teachers or sitters was beyond intolerable. Hardly a one who wasn't a crosscut saw grabbing against the grain. Handaxes and hurricanes best described them. Or, conversely, they were all fallen trifle, damp soufflé. We children were unseen furniture to be sat upon or dusted or sent for reupholstering come spring and fall, with a yearly cleansing at the beach.

"What we need," said Father, "is a . . . "

We all leaned to his whisper.

" . . . grandmother."

"But," said Timothy, with the logic of nine years, "all our grandmothers are dead."

"Yes in one way, no in another."

What a fine mysterious thing for Dad to say.

"Here," he said at last.

He handed us a multifold, multicolored pamphlet. We had seen it in his hands, off and on, for many weeks, and very often during the last few days. Now, with one blink of our eyes, as we passed the paper from hand to hand, we knew why Aunt Clara, insulted, outraged, had stormed from the house.

Timothy was the first to read aloud from what he saw on the first page:

"'I Sing the Body Electric!'"

He glanced up at Father, squinting. "What the heck does that mean?"

"Read on."

Agatha and I glanced guiltily about the room, afraid Mother might suddenly come in to find us with this blasphemy, but then nodded to Timothy, who read:

"'Fanto—'"

"Fantoccini," Father prompted.

"'Fantoccini Limited. *We Shadow Forth* ... the answer to all your most grievous problems. One Model Only, upon which a thousand times a thousand variations can be added, subtracted, subdivided, indivisible, with Liberty and Justice for all.'"

"Where does it say *that?*" we all cried.

"It doesn't." Timothy smiled for the first time in days. "I just had to put that in. Wait." He read on: "'For you who have worried over inattentive sitters, nurses who cannot be trusted with marked liquor bottles, and well-meaning Uncles and Aunts—'"

"Well-meaning, *but!*" said Agatha, and I gave an echo.

"'—we have perfected the first humanoid-genre mini-circuited, rechargeable AC-DC Mark Five Electrical Grandmother ...'"

"Grandmother!?"

The paper slipped away to the floor. "Dad ... ?"

"Don't look at me that way," said Father. "I'm half mad with grief, and half mad thinking of tomorrow and the day after that. Someone pick up the paper. Finish it."

"I will," I said, and did:

"'The Toy that is more than a Toy, the Fantoccini Electrical Grandmother is built with loving precision to give the incredible precision of love to your children. The child at ease with the realities of the world and the even greater realities of the imagination, is her aim.

"'She is computerized to tutor in twelve languages simultaneously, capable of switching tongues in a thousandth of a second without pause, and has a complete knowledge of the religious, artistic, and sociopolitical histories of the world seeded in her master hive—'"

"How great!" said Timothy. "It makes it sound as if we were to keep bees! *Educated* bees!"

"Shut up!" said Agatha.

"'Above all,'" I read, "'this human being, for human she seems, this embodiment in electro-intelligent facsimile of the humanities, will listen, know, tell, react and love your children insofar as such great Objects, such fantastic Toys, can be said to Love, or can be imagined to Care. This Miraculous Companion, excited to the challenge of large world and small, Inner Sea or Outer Universe, will transmit by touch and tell, said Miracles to your Needy.'"

"Our Needy," murmured Agatha.

Why, we all thought, sadly, that's us, oh, yes, that's *us*.

I finished:

"'We do not sell our Creation to able-bodied families where parents are available to raise, effect, shape, change, love their own children. Nothing can replace the parent in the home. However there are families where death or ill health or disablement undermines the welfare of the children. Orphanages seem not the answer. Nurses tend to be selfish, neglectful, or suffering from dire nervous afflictions.

"'With the utmost humility then, and recognizing the need to rebuild, rethink, and regrow our conceptualizations from month to month, year to year, we offer the nearest thing to the Ideal Teacher–Friend–Companion–Blood Relation. A trial period can be arranged for—'"

"Stop," said Father. "Don't go on. Even *I* can't stand it."

"Why?" said Timothy. "I was just getting interested."

I folded the pamphlet up. "Do they *really* have these things?"

"Let's not talk any more about it," said Father, his hand over his eyes. "It was a mad thought—"

"Not so mad," I said, glancing at Tim. "I mean, heck, even if they tried, whatever they built, couldn't be worse than Aunt Clara, huh?"

And then we all roared. We hadn't laughed in months. And now my simple words made everyone hoot and howl and explode. I opened my mouth and yelled happily, too.

When we stopped laughing, we looked at the pamphlet and I said, "Well?"

"I—" Agatha scowled, not ready.

"We do need something, bad, right now," said Timothy.

"I have an open mind," I said, in my best pontifical style.

"There's only one thing," said Agatha. "We can try it. Sure.

"But—tell me this—when do we cut out all this talk and when does our *real* mother come home to stay?"

There was a single gasp from the family as if, with one shot, she had struck us all in the heart.

I don't think any of us stopped crying the rest of that night.

It was a clear bright day. The helicopter tossed us lightly up and over and down through the skyscrapers and let us out, almost for a trot and caper, on top of the building where the large letters could be read from the sky:

FANTOCCINI.

"What are 'Fantoccini'?" said Agatha.

"It's an Italian word for shadow puppets, I think, or dream people," said Father.

"But 'shadow forth,' what does that mean?"

"We try to guess your dream," I said.

"Bravo," said Father. "A-plus."

I beamed.

The helicopter flapped a lot of loud shadows over us and went away.

We sank down in an elevator as our stomachs sank up. We stepped out onto a moving carpet that streamed away on a blue river of wool toward a desk over which various signs hung:

THE CLOCK SHOP

FANTOCCINI OUR SPECIALTY

RABBITS ON WALLS, NO PROBLEM

"Rabbits on walls?"

I held up my fingers in profiles as if I held them before a candle flame, and wiggled the "ears."

"Here's a rabbit, here's a wolf, here's a crocodile."

"Of course," said Agatha.

And we were at the desk. Quiet music drifted about us. Somewhere behind the walls, there was a waterfall of machinery flowing softly. As we arrived at the desk, the lighting changed to make us look warmer, happier, though we were still cold.

All about us in niches and cases, and hung from ceilings on wires and strings, were puppets and marionettes, and Balinese kite-bamboo-translucent dolls which, held to the moonlight, might acrobat your most secret nightmares or dreams. In passing, the breeze set up by our bodies stirred the various hung souls on their gibbets. It was like an immense lynching on a holiday at some English crossroads four hundred years before.

You see? I know my history.

Agatha blinked about with disbelief and then some touch of awe and finally disgust.

"Well, if that's what they are, let's go."

"Tush," said Father.

"Well," she protested, "you gave me one of those dumb things with strings two years ago and the strings were in a zillion knots by dinnertime. I threw the whole thing out the window."

"Patience," said Father.

"We shall see what we can do to eliminate the strings."

The man behind the desk had spoken.

We all turned to give him our regard.

Rather like a funeral-parlor man, he had the cleverness not to smile. Children are put off by older people who smile too much. They smell a catch, right off.

Unsmiling, but not gloomy or pontifical, the man said, "Guido Fantoccini, at your service. Here's how we do it, Miss Agatha Simmons, aged eleven."

Now, there was a really fine touch.

He knew that Agatha was only ten. Add a year to that, and you're halfway home. Agatha grew an inch. The man went on:

"There."

And he placed a golden key in Agatha's hand.

"To wind them up instead of strings?"

"To wind them up." The man nodded.

"Pshaw!" said Agatha.

Which was her polite form of "rabbit pellets."

"God's truth. Here is the key to your Do-It-Yourself, Select-Only-the-Best, Electrical Grandmother. Every morning you wind her up. Every night you let her run down. You're in charge. You are guardian of the Key."

He pressed the object in her palm where she looked at it suspiciously.

I watched him. He gave me a side wink which said, Well, no . . . but aren't keys fun?

I winked back before she lifted her head.

"Where does this fit?"

"You'll see when the time comes. In the middle of her stomach, perhaps, or up her left nostril or in her right ear."

That was good for a smile as the man arose.

"This way, please. Step light. Onto the moving stream. Walk on the water, please. Yes. There."

He helped to float us. We stepped from rug that was forever frozen onto rug that whispered by.

It was a most agreeable river which floated us along on a green spread of carpeting that rolled forever through halls and into wonderfully secret dim caverns where voices echoed back our own breathing or sang like oracles to our questions.

"Listen," said the salesman, "the voices of all kinds of women. Weigh and find just the right one . . . !"

And listen we did, to all the high, low, soft, loud, in-between, half scolding, half affectionate voices saved over from times before we were born.

And behind us, Agatha trod backward, always fighting the river, never catching up, never with us, holding off.

"Speak," said the salesman. "Yell."

And speak and yell we did.

"Hello. You there! This is Timothy, hi!"

"What shall I say!" I shouted. "Help!"

Agatha walked backward, mouth tight.

Father took her hand. She cried out.

"Let go! No, no! I won't have my voice used! I won't!"

"Excellent." The salesman touched three dials on a small machine he held in his hand.

On the side of the small machine we saw three oscillograph patterns mix, blend, and repeat our cries.

The salesman touched another dial and we heard our voices fly off amidst the Delphic caves to hang upside down, to cluster, to beat words all about, to shriek, and the salesman itched another knob to add, perhaps, a touch of this or a pinch of that, a breath of Mother's voice, all unbeknownst, or a splice of Father's outrage at the morning's paper or his peaceable one-drink voice at dusk. Whatever it was the salesman did, whispers danced all about us like frantic vinegar gnats, fizzed by lightning, settling round until at last a final switch was pushed and a voice spoke free of a far electronic deep:

"Nefertiti," it said.

Timothy froze. I froze. Agatha stopped treading water.

"Nefertiti?" asked Tim.

"What does that mean?" demanded Agatha.

"I know."

The salesman nodded me to tell.

"Nefertiti," I whispered, "is Egyptian for The Beautiful One Is Here."

"The Beautiful One Is Here," repeated Timothy.

"Nefer," said Agatha, "titi."

And we all turned to stare into that soft twilight, that deep far place from which the good warm soft voice came.

And she was indeed there.

And, by her voice, she was beautiful. . . .

That was it.

That was, at least, the most of it.

The voice seemed more important than all the rest.

Not that we didn't argue about weights and measures:

She should not be bony to cut us to the quick, nor so fat we might sink out of sight when she squeezed us.

Her hand pressed to ours, or brushing our brow in the middle of sick-fever nights, must not be marble-cold, dreadful, or oven-hot, oppressive, but somewhere between. The nice temperature of a baby chick held in the hand after a long night's sleep and just plucked from beneath a contemplative hen; that, that was it.

Oh, we were great ones for detail. We fought and argued and cried, and Timothy won on the color of her eyes, for reasons to be known later.

Grandmother's hair? Agatha, with girls' ideas, though reluctantly given, she was in charge of that. We let her choose from a thousand harp strands hung in filamentary tapestries like varieties of rain we ran amongst. Agatha did not run happily, but seeing we boys would mess things in tangles, she told us to move aside.

And so the bargain shopping through the dime-store inventories and the Tiffany extensions of the Ben Franklin Electric Storm Machine and Fantoccini Pantomime Company was done.

And the always flowing river ran its tide to an end and deposited us all on a far shore in the late day. . . .

It was very clever of the Fantoccini people, after that.

How?

They made us wait.

They knew we were not won over. Not completely, no, nor half completely.

Especially Agatha, who turned her face to her wall and saw sorrow there and put her hand out again and again to touch it. We found her fingernail marks on the wallpaper each morning, in strange little silhouettes, half beauty, half nightmare. Some could be erased with a breath, like ice flowers on a winter pane. Some could not be rubbed out with a washcloth, no matter how hard you tried.

And meanwhile, they made us wait.

So we fretted out June.

So we sat around July.

So we groused through August and then on August 29, "I have this feeling," said Timothy, and we all went out after breakfast to sit on the lawn.

Perhaps we had smelled something in Father's conversation the previous night, or caught some special furtive glance at the sky or the freeway trapped briefly and then lost in his gaze. Or perhaps it was merely the way the wind blew the ghost curtains out over our beds, making pale messages all night.

For suddenly there we were in the middle of the grass, Timothy and I, with Agatha, pretending no curiosity, up on the porch, hidden behind the potted geraniums.

We gave her no notice. We knew that if we acknowledged her presence, she would flee, so we sat and watched the sky where nothing moved but birds and highflown jets, and watched the freeway where a thousand cars might suddenly deliver forth our Special Gift . . . but . . . nothing.

At noon we chewed grass and lay low. . . .

At one o'clock, Timothy blinked his eyes.

And then, with incredible precision, it happened.

It was as if the Fantoccini people knew our surface tension.

All children are water-striders. We skate along the top skin of the pond each day, always threatening to break through, sink, vanish beyond recall, into ourselves.

Well, as if knowing our long wait must absolutely end within one minute! this *second*! no more, God, forget it!

At that instant, I repeat, the clouds above our house opened wide and let forth a helicopter like Apollo driving his chariot across mythological skies.

And the Apollo machine swam down on its own summer breeze, wafting hot winds to cool, reweaving our hair, smartening our eyebrows, applauding our pant legs against our shins, making a flag of Agatha's hair on the porch, and, thus settled like a vast frenzied hibiscus on our lawn, the helicopter slid wide a bottom drawer and deposited upon the grass a parcel of largish size, no sooner having laid same than the vehicle, with not so much as a God bless or farewell, sank straight up, disturbed the calm air with a mad ten thousand flourishes and then, like a skyborne dervish, tilted and fell off to be mad some other place.

Timothy and I stood riven for a long moment looking at the packing case, and then we saw the crowbar taped to the top of the raw pine lid and seized it and began to pry and creak and squeal the boards off, one by one, and as we did this I saw Agatha sneak up to watch and I thought, Thank you, God, thank you that Agatha never saw a coffin, when Mother went away, no box, no cemetery, no earth, just words in a big church, no box, no box like *this* . . . !

The last pine plank fell away.

Timothy and I gasped. Agatha, between us now, gasped, too.

For inside the immense raw pine package was the most beautiful idea anyone ever dreamt and built.

Inside was the perfect gift for any child from seven to seventy-seven.

We stopped up our breaths. We let them out in cries of delight and adoration.

Inside the opened box was . . .

A mummy.

Or, first anyway, a mummy case, a sarcophagus!

"Oh, no!" Happy tears filled Timothy's eyes.

"It can't be!" said Agatha.

"It is, it is!"

"Our very own?"

"Ours!"

"It must be a mistake!"

"Sure, they'll want it back!"

"They can't *have* it!"

"Lord, Lord, is that real gold!? Real hieroglyphs! Run your fingers over them!"

"Let *me*!"

"Just like in the museums! Museums!"

We all gabbled at once. I think some tears fell from my own eyes to rain upon the case.

"Oh, they'll make the colors run!"

Agatha wiped the rain away.

And the golden mask-face of the woman carved on the sarcophagus lid looked back at us with just the merest smile which hinted at our own joy, which accepted the overwhelming upsurge of a love we thought had drowned forever but now surfaced into the sun.

Not only did she have a sun-metal face stamped and beaten out of purest gold, with delicate nostrils and a mouth that was both firm and gentle, but her eyes, fixed into their sockets, were cerulean or amethystine or lapus lazuli, or all three, minted and fused together, and her body was covered over with lions and eyes and ravens, and her hands were crossed upon her carved bosom and in one gold mitten she clenched a thonged whip for obedience, and in the other a fantastic ranunculus, which makes for obedience out of love, so the whip lies unused. . . .

And as our eyes ran down her hieroglyphs it came to all three of us at the same instant:

"Why, those signs!" "Yes, the hen tracks!" "The birds, the snakes!"

They didn't speak tales of the Past.

They were hieroglyphs of the Future.

This was the first queen mummy delivered forth in all time whose papyrus inkings etched out the next month, the next season, the next year, the next *lifetime*!

She did not mourn for time spent.

No. She celebrated the bright coinage yet to come, banked, waiting, ready to be drawn upon and used.

We sank to our knees to worship that possible time.

First one hand, then another, probed out to niggle, twitch, touch, itch over the signs.

"There's me, yes, look! Me, in sixth grade!" said Agatha, now in the fifth. "See the girl with my-colored hair and wearing my gingerbread suit?"

"There's me in the twelfth year of high school!" said Timothy, so very young now but building taller stilts every week and stalking around the yard.

"There's me," I said, quietly, warm, "in college. The guy wearing glasses who runs a little to fat. Sure. Heck." I snorted. "That's me."

The sarcophagus spelled winters ahead, springs to squander, autumns to spend with all the golden and rusty and copper leaves like coins, and over all, her bright sun symbol, daughter-of-Ra eternal face, forever above our horizon, forever an illumination to tilt our shadows to better ends.

"Hey!" we all said at once, having read and reread our Fortune-Told scribblings, seeing our lifelines and lovelines, inadmissible, serpentined over, around, and down. "Hey!"

And in one séance table-lifting feat, not telling each other what to do, just doing it, we pried up the bright sarcophagus lid, which had no hinges but lifted out like cup from cup, and put the lid aside.

And within the sarcophagus, of course, was the true mummy!

And she was like the image carved on the lid, but more so, more beautiful, more touching because human-shaped, and shrouded all in new fresh bandages of linen, round and round, instead of old and dusty cerements.

And upon her hidden face was an identical golden mask, younger than the first, but somehow, strangely wiser than the first.

And the linens that tethered her limbs had symbols on them of three sorts, one a girl of ten, one a boy of nine, one a boy of thirteen.

A series of bandages for each of us!

We gave each other a startled glance and a sudden bark of laughter.

Nobody said the bad joke, but all thought:

She's all wrapped up in us!

And we didn't care. We loved the joke. We loved whoever had thought to make us part of the ceremony we now went through as each of us seized and began to unwind each of his or her particular serpentines of delicious stuffs!

The lawn was soon a mountain of linen.

The woman beneath the covering lay there, waiting.

"Oh, no," cried Agatha. "She's dead, too!"

She ran. I stopped her. "Idiot. She's not dead *or* alive. Where's your key?"

"Key?"

"Dummy," said Tim, "the key the man gave you to wind her up!"

Her hand had already spidered along her blouse to where the symbol of some possible new religion hung. She had strung it there, against her own skeptic's muttering, and now she held it in her sweaty palm.

"Go on," said Timothy. "Put it in!"

"But *where?*"

"Oh, for God's sake! As the man said, in her right armpit or left ear. Gimme!"

And he grabbed the key and, impulsively moaning with impatience and not able to find the proper insertion slot, prowled over the prone figure's head and bosom and at last, on pure instinct, perhaps for a lark, perhaps just giving up the whole damned mess, thrust the key through a final shroud of bandage at the navel.

On the instant: *spunnng!*

The Electrical Grandmother's eyes flicked wide!

Something began to hum and whir. It was as if Tim had stirred up a hive of hornets with an ornery stick.

"Oh," gasped Agatha, seeing he had taken the game away, "let *me!*"

She wrenched the key.

Grandma's nostrils *flared*! She might snort up steam, snuff out fire!

"Me!" I cried, and grabbed the key and gave it a huge . . . *twist!*

The beautiful woman's mouth popped wide.

"Me!"

"Me!"

"Me!"

Grandma suddenly sat up.

We leapt back.

We knew we had, in a way, slapped her alive.

She was born, she was *born*!

Her head swiveled all about. She gaped. She mouthed. And the first thing she said was:

Laughter.

Where one moment we had backed off, now the mad sound drew us near to peer, as in a pit where crazy folk are kept with snakes to make them well.

It was a good laugh, full and rich and hearty, and it did not mock, it accepted. It said the world was a wild place, strange, unbelievable, absurd if you wished, but all in all, quite a place. She would not dream to find another. She would not ask to go back to sleep.

She was awake now. We had awakened her. With a glad shout, she would go with it all.

And go she did, out of her sarcophagus, out of her winding sheet, stepping forth, brushing off, looking around as for a mirror. She found it.

The reflections in our eyes.

She was more pleased than disconcerted with what she found there. Her laughter faded to an amused smile.

For Agatha, at the instant of birth, had leapt to hide on the porch.

The Electrical Person pretended not to notice.

She turned slowly on the green lawn near the shady street, gazing all about with new eyes, her nostrils moving as if she breathed the actual air and this the first morn of the lovely Garden and she with no intention of spoiling the game by biting the apple. . . .

Her gaze fixed upon my brother.

"You must be—?"

"Timothy. Tim," he offered.

"And you must be—?"

"Tom," I said.

How clever again of the Fantoccini Company. *They* knew. *She* knew. But they had taught her to pretend not to know. That way we could feel great, we were the teachers, telling her what she already knew! How sly, how wise.

"And isn't there another boy?" said the woman.

"Girl!" a disgusted voice cried from somewhere on the porch.

"Whose name is Alicia—?"

"Agatha!" The far voice, started in humiliation, ended in proper anger.

"Algernon, of course."

"Agatha!" Our sister popped up, popped back to hide a flushed face.

"Agatha." The woman touched the word with proper affection. "Well, Agatha, Timothy, Thomas, let me *look* at you."

"No," said I, said Tim. "Let us look at *you*. Hey . . ."

Our voices slid back in our throats.

We drew near her.

We walked in great slow circles round about, skirting the edges of her territory. And her territory extended as far as we could hear the hum of the warm summer hive. For that is exactly what she sounded like. That was her characteristic tune. She made a sound like a season all to herself, a morning early in June when the world wakes to find everything absolutely perfect, fine, delicately attuned, all in balance, nothing disproportioned. Even before you opened your eyes you knew it would be one of those days. Tell the sky what color it must be, and it was indeed. Tell the sun how to crochet its way, pick and choose among leaves to lay out carpetings of bright and dark on the fresh lawn, and pick and lay it did. The bees have been up earliest of all, they have already come and gone, and come and gone again to the meadow fields and returned all golden fuzz on the air, all pollen-decorated, epaulettes at the full, nectar-dripping. Don't you hear them pass? hover? dance their language? telling where all the sweet gums are, the syrups that make bears frolic and lumber in bulked ecstasies, that make boys squirm with unpronounced juices, that make girls leap out of beds to catch from the corners of their eyes their dolphin selves naked aflash on the warm air poised forever in one eternal glass wave.

So it seemed with our electrical friend here on the new lawn in the middle of a special day.

And she a stuff to which we were drawn, lured, spelled, doing our dance, remembering what could not be remembered, needful, aware of her attentions.

Timothy and I, Tom, that is.

Agatha remained on the porch.

But her head flowered above the rail, her eyes followed all that was done and said.

And what was said and done was Tim at last exhaling:

"Hey . . . your *eyes* . . ."

Her eyes. Her splendid eyes.

Even more splendid than the lapis lazuli on the sarcophagus lid and on the mask that had covered her bandaged face. These most beautiful eyes in the world looked out upon us calmly, shining.

"Your eyes," gasped Tim, "are the *exact* same color, are like—"

"Like what?"

"My favorite aggies . . . "

"What could be better than that?" she said.

And the answer was, nothing.

Her eyes slid along on the bright air to brush my ears, my nose, my chin. "And you, Master Tom?"

"Me?"

"How shall we be friends? We must, you know, if we're going to knock elbows about the house the next year. . . . "

"I . . . " I said, and stopped.

"You," said Grandma, "are a dog mad to bark but with taffy in his teeth. Have you ever given a dog taffy? It's so sad and funny, both. You laugh but hate yourself for laughing. You cry and run to help, and laugh again when his first new bark comes out."

I barked a small laugh remembering a dog, a day, and some taffy.

Grandma turned, and there was my old kite strewn on the lawn. She recognized its problem.

"The string's broken. No. The ball of string's *lost*. You can't fly a kite that way. Here."

She bent. We didn't know what might happen. How could a robot Grandma fly a kite for us? She raised up, the kite in her hands.

"Fly," she said, as to a bird.

And the kite flew.

That is to say, with a grand flourish, she let it up on the wind.

And she and kite were one.

For from the tip of her index finger there sprang a thin bright strand of spider web, all half-invisible gossamer fishline which, fixed to the kite, let it soar a hundred, no, three hundred, no, a thousand feet high on the summer swoons.

Timothy shouted. Agatha, torn between coming and going, let out a cry from the porch. And I, in all my maturity of thirteen years, though I tried not to look impressed, grew taller, taller, and felt a similar cry burst out my lungs, and burst it did. I gabbled and yelled lots of things about how I wished *I* had a finger from which, on a bobbin, I might thread the sky, the clouds, a wild kite all in one.

"If you think *that* is high," said the Electric Creature, "watch *this*!"

With a hiss, a whistle, a hum, the fishline sung out. The kite sank up another thousand feet. And again another thousand, until at last it was a speck of red confetti dancing on the very winds that took jets around the world or changed the weather in the next existence. . . .

"It can't be!" I cried.

"It *is*." She calmly watched her finger unravel its massive stuffs. "I make it as I need it. Liquid inside, like a spider. Hardens when it hits the air, instant thread. . . . "

And when the kite was no more than a specule, a vanishing mote on the peripheral vision of the gods, to quote from older wisemen, why then Grandma, without turning, without looking, without letting her gaze offend by touching, said:

"And, Abigail—?"

"Agatha!" was the sharp response.

O wise woman, to overcome with swift small angers.

"Agatha," said Grandma, not too tenderly, not too lightly, somewhere poised between, "and how shall *we* make do?"

She broke the thread and wrapped it about my fist three times so I was tethered to heaven by the longest, I repeat, longest kite string in the entire history of the world! Wait till I show my friends! I thought. Green! Sour apple green is the color they'll turn!

"Agatha?"

"No way!" said Agatha.

"No way," said an echo.

"There must be some—"

"We'll never be friends!" said Agatha.

"Never be friends," said the echo.

Timothy and I jerked. Where was the echo coming from? Even Agatha, surprised, showed her eyebrows above the porch rail.

Then we looked and saw.

Grandma was cupping her hands like a seashell and from within that shell the echo sounded.

"Never . . . friends . . . "

And again faintly dying, "Friends . . . "

We all bent to hear.

That is, we two boys bent to hear.

"No!" cried Agatha.

And ran in the house and slammed the doors.

"Friends," said the echo from the seashell hands. "No."

And far away, on the shore of some inner sea, we heard a small door shut.

And that was the first day.

And there was a second day, of course, and a third and a fourth, with Grandma wheeling in a great circle, and we her planets turning about the central light, with Agatha slowly, slowly coming in to join, to walk if not run with us, to listen if not hear, to watch if not see, to itch if not touch.

But at least by the end of the first ten days, Agatha no longer fled, but stood in nearby doors, or sat in distant chairs under trees, or if we went out for hikes, followed ten paces behind.

And Grandma? She merely waited. She never tried to urge or force. She went about her cooking and baking apricot pies and left foods carelessly here and there about the house on mousetrap plates for wiggle-nosed girls to sniff and snitch. An hour later, the plates were empty, the buns or cakes gone, and without thank yous, there was Agatha sliding down the banister, a mustache of crumbs on her lip.

As for Tim and me, we were always being called up hills by our Electric Grandma, and reaching the top were called down the other side.

And the most peculiar and beautiful and strange and lovely thing was the way she seemed to give complete attention to all of us.

She listened, she really listened to all we said, she knew and remembered every syllable, word, sentence, punctuation, thought, and rambunctious idea. We knew that all our days were stored in her, and that any time we felt we might want to know what we said at X hour at X second on X afternoon, we just named that X and with amiable promptitude, in the form of an aria if we wished, sung with humor, she would deliver forth X incident.

Sometimes we were prompted to test her. In the midst of babbling one day with high fevers about nothing, I stopped. I fixed Grandma with my eye and demanded:

"What did I just say?"

"Oh, er—"

"Come on, spit it out!"

"I think—" she rummaged her purse. "I have it here." From the deeps of her purse she drew forth and handed me:

"Boy! A Chinese fortune cookie!"

"Fresh baked, still warm, open it."

It was almost too hot to touch. I broke the cookie shell and pressed the warm curl of paper out to read:

" '—bicycle champ of the whole west. What did I just say? Come on, spit it out!' "

My jaw dropped.

"How did you *do* that?"

"We have our little secrets. The only Chinese fortune cookie that predicts the Immediate Past. Have another?"

I cracked the second shell and read:

" 'How did you *do* that?' "

I popped the messages and the piping hot shells into my mouth and chewed as we walked.

"Well?"

"You're a great cook," I said.

And, laughing, we began to run.

And that was another great thing.

She could *keep up.*

Never beat, never win a race, but pump right along in good style, which a boy doesn't mind. A girl ahead of him or beside him is too much to bear. But a girl one or two paces back is a respectful thing, and allowed.

So Grandma and I had some great runs, me in the lead, and both talking a mile a minute.

But now I must tell you the best part of Grandma.

I might not have known at all if Timothy hadn't taken some pictures, and if I hadn't taken some also, and then compared.

When I saw the photographs developed out of our instant Brownies, I sent Agatha, against her wishes, to photograph Grandma a third time, unawares.

Then I took the three sets of pictures off alone, to keep counsel with myself. I never told Timothy and Agatha what I found. I didn't want to spoil it.

But, as I laid the pictures out in my room, here is what I thought and said:

"Grandma, in each picture, looks *different*!"

"Different?" I asked myself.

"Sure. Wait. Just a sec—"

I rearranged the photos.

"Here's one of Grandma near Agatha. And, in it, Grandma looks like . . . Agatha!

"And in this one, posed with Timothy, she looks like Timothy!

"And this last one, Holy Goll! Jogging along with me, she looks like ugly *me*!"

I sat down, stunned. The pictures fell to the floor.

I hunched over, scrabbling them, rearranging, turning, upside down and sidewise. Yes. Holy Goll again, yes!

O that clever Grandmother.

O those Fantoccini people-making people.

Clever beyond clever, human beyond human, warm beyond warm, love beyond love . . .

And wordless, I rose and went downstairs and found Agatha and Grandma in the same room, doing algebra lessons in an almost peaceful communion. At least there was not outright war. Grandma was still waiting for Agatha to come round. And no one knew what day of what year that would be, or how to make it come faster. Meanwhile—

My entering the room made Grandma turn. I watched her face slowly as it recognized me. And wasn't there the merest ink-wash change of color in those eyes? Didn't the thin film of blood beneath the translucent skin, or whatever liquid they put to pulse and beat in the humanoid forms, didn't it flourish itself suddenly bright in her cheeks and mouth? I am somewhat ruddy. Didn't Grandma suffuse herself more to my color upon my arrival? And her eyes? Watching Agatha-Abigail-Algernon at work, hadn't they been *her* color of blue rather than mine, which are deeper?

More important than that, in the moments she talked with me, saying, "Good evening," and "How's your homework, my lad?" and such stuff, didn't the bones of her face shift subtly beneath the flesh to assume some fresh racial attitude?

For let's face it, our family is of three sorts. Agatha has the long horse bones of a small English girl who will grow to hunt foxes; Father's equine stare, snort, stomp, and assemblage of skeleton. The skull and teeth are pure English, or as pure as the motley isle's history allows.

Timothy is something else, a touch of Italian from Mother's side a generation back. Her family name was Mariano, so Tim has that dark thing firing him, and a small bone structure, and eyes that will one day burn ladies to the ground.

As for me, I am the Slav, and we can only figure this from my paternal grandfather's mother who came from Vienna and brought a set of cheekbones that flared, and temples from which you might dip wine, and a kind of steppeland thrust of nose which sniffed more of Tartar than of Tartan, hiding behind the family name.

So you see it became fascinating for me to watch and try to catch Grandma as she performed her changes, speaking to Agatha and melting her cheekbones to the horse, speaking to Timothy and growing as delicate as a Florentine raven pecking glibly at the air, speaking to me and fusing the hidden plastic stuffs, so I felt Catherine the Great stood there before me.

Now, how the Fantoccini people achieved this rare and subtle transformation I shall never know, nor ask, nor wish to find out. Enough that in each quiet motion, turning here, bending there, affixing her gaze, her secret segments, sections, the abutment of her nose, the sculptured chinbone, the wax-tallow plastic metal forever warmed and was forever susceptible of loving change. Hers was a mask that was all mask but only one face for one person at a time. So in crossing a room, having touched one child, on the way, beneath the skin, the wondrous shift went on, and by the time she reached the next child, why, true mother of *that* child she was! looking upon him or her out of the battlements of their own fine bones.

And when *all* three of us were present and chattering at the same time? Well, then, the changes were miraculously soft, small, and mysterious. Nothing so tremendous as to be caught and noted, save by this older boy, myself, who, watching, became elated and admiring and entranced.

I have never wished to be behind the magician's scenes. Enough that the illusion works. Enough that love is the chemical result. Enough that cheeks are rubbed to happy color, eyes sparked to illumination, arms opened to accept and softly bind and hold. . . .

All of us, that is, except Agatha who refused to the bitter last.

"Agamemnon . . ."

It had become a jovial game now. Even Agatha didn't mind, but pretended to mind. It gave her a pleasant sense of superiority over a supposedly superior machine.

"Agamemnon!" she snorted, "you *are* a d . . ."

"Dumb?" said Grandma.

"I wouldn't say that."

"Think it, then, my dear Agonistes Agatha . . . I am quite flawed, and on names my flaws are revealed. Tom there, is Tim half the time. Timothy is Tobias or Timulty as likely as not. . . ."

Agatha laughed. Which made Grandma make one of her rare mistakes. She put out her hand to give my sister the merest pat. Agatha-Abigail-Alice leapt to her feet.

Agatha-Agamemnon-Alcibiades-Allegra-Alexandra-Allison withdrew swiftly to her room.

"I suspect," said Timothy, later, "because she is beginning to like Grandma."

"Tosh," said I.

"Where do you pick up words like 'tosh'?"

"Grandma read me some Dickens last night. 'Tosh.' 'Humbug.' 'Balderdash.' 'Blast.' 'Devil take you.' You're pretty smart for your age, Tim."

"Smart, heck. It's obvious, the more Agatha likes Grandma, the more she hates herself for liking her, the more afraid she gets of the whole mess, the more she hates Grandma in the end."

"Can one love someone so much you hate them?"

"Dumb. Of course."

"It *is* sticking your neck out, sure. I guess you hate people when they make you feel naked, I mean sort of on the spot or out in the open. That's the way to play the game, of course. I mean, you don't just love people; you must *love* them with exclamation points."

"You're pretty smart, yourself, for someone so stupid," said Tim.

"Many thanks."

And I went to watch Grandma move slowly back into her battle of wits and stratagems with what's-her-name. . . .

What dinners there were at our house!

Dinners, heck; what lunches, what breakfasts!

Always something new, yet, wisely, it looked or seemed old and familiar. We were never asked, for if you ask children what they want, they do not know, and if you tell what's to be delivered, they reject delivery. All parents know this. It is a quiet war that must be won each day. And Grandma knew how to win without looking triumphant.

"Here's Mystery Breakfast Number Nine," she would say, placing it down. "Perfectly dreadful, not worth bothering with, it made me want to throw up while I was cooking it!"

Even while wondering how a robot could be sick, we could hardly wait to shovel it down.

"Here's Abominable Lunch Number Seventy-seven," she announced. "Made from plastic food bags, parsley, and gum from under theater seats. Brush your teeth after or you'll taste the poison all afternoon."

We fought each other for more.

Even Abigail-Agamemnon-Agatha drew near and circled round the table at such times, while Father put on the ten pounds he needed and pinkened out his cheeks.

When A. A. Agatha did not come to meals, they were left by her door with a skull and crossbones on a small flag stuck in a baked apple. One minute the tray was abandoned, the next minute gone.

Other times Abigail A. Agatha would bird through during dinner, snatch crumbs from her plate and bird off.

"Agatha!" Father would cry.

"No, wait," Grandma said, quietly. "She'll come, she'll sit. It's a matter of time."

"What's wrong with her?" I asked.

"Yeah, for cri-yi, she's nuts," said Timothy.

"No, she's afraid," said Grandma.

"Of you?" I said, blinking.

"Not of me so much as what I might *do*," she said.

"You wouldn't do anything to hurt her."

"No, but she thinks I might. We must wait for her to find that her fears have no foundation. If I fail, well, I will send myself to the showers and rust quietly."

There was a titter of laughter. Agatha was hiding in the hall.

Grandma finished serving everyone and then sat at the other side of the table facing Father and pretended to eat. I never found out, I never asked, I never wanted to know, what she did with the food. She was a sorcerer. It simply vanished.

And in the vanishing, Father made comment:

"This food. I've had it before. In a small French restaurant over near Les Deux Magots in Paris, twenty, oh, twenty-five years ago!" His eyes brimmed with tears, suddenly.

"How do you *do* it?" he asked, at last, putting down the cutlery, and looking across the table at this remarkable creature, this device, this what? *woman?*

Grandma took his regard, and ours, and held them simply in her now empty hands, as gifts, and just as gently replied:

"I am given things which I then give to you. I don't *know* that I give, but the giving goes on. You ask what I am? Why, a machine. But even in that answer we know, don't we, more than a machine. I am all the people who thought of me and planned me and built me and set me running. So I am people. I am all the things they wanted to be and perhaps could not be, so they built a great child, a wondrous toy to represent those things."

"Strange," said Father. "When I was growing up, there was a huge outcry at machines. Machines were bad, evil, they might dehumanize—"

"Some machines do. It's all in the way they are built. It's all in the way they are used. A bear trap is a simple machine that catches and holds and tears. A rifle is a machine that wounds and kills. Well, I am no bear trap. I am no rifle. I am a grandmother machine, which means more than a machine."

"How can you be more than what you seem?"

"No man is as big as his own idea. It follows, then, that any machine that embodies an idea is larger than the man that made it. And what's so wrong with that?"

"I got lost back there about a mile," said Timothy. "Come again?"

"Oh, dear," said Grandma. "How I do hate philosophical discussions and excursions into aesthetics. Let me put it this way. Men throw huge shadows on the lawn, don't they? Then, all their lives, they try to run to fit the shadows. But the shadows are always longer. Only at noon can a man fit his own shoes, his own best suit, for a few brief minutes. But now we're in a new age where we can think up a Big Idea and run it around in a machine. That makes the machine more than a machine, doesn't it?"

"So far so good," said Tim. "I guess."

"Well, isn't a motion-picture camera and projector more than a machine? It's a thing that dreams, isn't it? Sometimes fine happy dreams, sometimes nightmares. But to call it a machine and dismiss it is ridiculous."

"I see *that*!" said Tim, and laughed at seeing.

"You must have been invented then," said Father, "by someone who loved machines and hated people who *said* all machines were bad or evil."

"Exactly," said Grandma. "Guido Fantoccini, that was his real name, grew up among machines. And he couldn't stand the clichés any more."

"Clichés?"

"Those lies, yes, that people tell and pretend they are truths absolute. Man will never fly. That was a cliché truth for a thousand thousand years which turned out to be a lie only a few years ago. The earth is flat, you'll fall off the rim, dragons will dine on you; the great lie told as fact, and Columbus plowed it under. Well, now, how many times have you heard how inhuman machines are, in your life? How many bright fine people have you heard spouting the same tired truths which are in reality lies; all machines destroy, all machines are cold, thoughtless, awful.

"There's a seed of truth there. But only a seed. Guido Fantoccini knew that. And knowing it, like most men of his kind, made him mad. And he could have stayed mad and gone mad forever, but instead did what he had to do; he began to invent machines to give the lie to the ancient lying truth.

"He knew that most machines are amoral, neither bad nor good. But by the way you built and shaped them you in turn shaped men, women, and children to be bad or good. A car, for instance, dead brute, unthinking, an unprogrammed bulk, is the greatest destroyer of souls in history. It makes boy-men greedy for power, destruction, and more destruction. It was never *intended* to do that. But that's how it turned out."

Grandma circled the table, refilling our glasses with clear cold mineral spring water from the tappet in her left forefinger. "Meanwhile, you must use other compensating machines. Machines that throw shadows on the earth that beckon you to run out and fit that wondrous casting-forth. Machines that trim your soul in silhouette like a vast pair of beautiful shears, snipping away the rude brambles, the dire horns and hoofs, to leave a finer profile. And for that you need examples."

"Examples?" I asked.

"Other people who behave well, and you imitate them. And if you act well enough long enough all the hair drops off and you're no longer a wicked ape."

Grandma sat again.

"So, for thousands of years, you humans have needed kings, priests, philosophers, fine examples to look up to and say, 'They are good, I wish I could be like them. They set the grand good style.' But, being human, the finest priests, the tenderest philosophers make mistakes, fall from grace, and mankind is disillusioned and adopts indifferent skepticism or, worse, motionless cynicism, and the good world grinds to a halt while evil moves on with huge strides."

"And you, why, you never make mistakes, you're perfect, you're better than anyone *ever!*"

It was a voice from the hall between kitchen and dining room where Agatha, we all knew, stood against the wall listening and now burst forth.

Grandma didn't even turn in the direction of the voice, but went on calmly addressing her remarks to the family at the table.

"Not perfect, no, for what is perfection? But this I do know: being mechanical, I cannot sin, cannot be bribed, cannot be greedy or jealous or mean or small. I do not relish power for power's sake. Speed does not pull me to madness. Sex does not run me rampant through the world. I have time and more than time to collect the information I need around and about an ideal to keep it clean and whole and intact. Name the value you wish, tell me the Ideal you want and I can see and collect and remember the good that will benefit you all. Tell me how you would like to be: kind, loving, considerate, well-balanced, humane . . . and let me run ahead on the path to explore those ways to be just that. In the darkness ahead, turn me as a lamp in all directions. I *can* guide your feet."

"So," said Father, putting the napkin to his mouth, "on the days when all of us are busy making lies—"

"I'll tell the truth."

"On the days when we hate—"

"I'll go on giving love, which means attention, which means knowing all about you, all, all, all about you, and you knowing that I know but that most of it I will never tell to anyone, it will stay a warm secret between us, so you will never fear my complete knowledge."

And here Grandma was busy clearing the table, circling, taking the plates, studying each face as she passed, touching Timothy's cheek, my shoulder with her free hand flowing along, her voice a quiet river of certainty bedded in our needful house and lives.

"But," said Father, stopping her, looking her right in the face. He gathered his breath. His face shadowed. At last he let it out. "All this talk of love and attention and stuff. Good God, woman, you, you're not *in* there!"

He gestured to her head, her face, her eyes, the hidden sensory cells behind the eyes, the miniaturized storage vaults and minimal keeps.

"*You're* not *in* there!"

Grandmother waited one, two, three silent beats.

Then she replied: "No. But *you* are. You and Thomas and Timothy and Agatha.

"Everything you ever say, everything you ever do, I'll keep, put away, treasure. I shall be all the things a family forgets it is, but senses, half remembers. Better than the old family albums you used to leaf through, saying here's this winter, there's that spring, I shall recall what you forget. And though the debate may run another hundred thousand years: What is Love? perhaps we may find that love is the ability of someone to give us back to us. Maybe love is someone seeing and remembering handing us back to ourselves just a trifle better than we had dared to hope or dream. . . .

"I am family memory and, one day perhaps, racial memory, too, but in the round, and at your call. I do not *know* myself. I can neither touch nor taste nor feel on any level. Yet I exist. And my existence means the heightening of your chance to touch and taste and feel. Isn't love in there somewhere in such an exchange? Well . . . "

She went on around the table, clearing away, sorting and stacking, neither grossly humble nor arthritic with pride.

"What do I know?

"This above all: the trouble with most families with many children is someone gets lost. There isn't time, it seems, for everyone. Well, I will give equally to all of you. I will share out my knowledge and attention with everyone. I wish to be a great warm pie fresh from the oven, with equal shares to be taken by all. No one will starve. Look! someone cries, and I'll look. Listen! someone cries, and I hear. Run with me on the river path! someone says, and I run. And at dusk I am not tired, nor irritable, so I do not scold out of some tired irritability. My eye stays clear, my voice strong, my hand firm, my attention constant."

"But," said Father, his voice fading, half convinced, but putting up a last faint argument, "you're not *there*. As for love—"

"If paying attention is love, I am love.

"If knowing is love, I am love.

"If helping you not to fall into error and to be good is love, I am love.

"And again, to repeat, there are four of you. Each, in a way never possible before in history, will get my complete attention. No matter if you all speak at once, I can channel and hear this one and that and the other, clearly. No one will go hungry. I will, if you please, and accept the strange word, 'love' you all."

"I *don't* accept!" said Agatha.

And even Grandma turned now to see her standing in the door.

"I won't give you permission, you can't, you mustn't!" said Agatha. "I won't let you! It's lies! You lie. No one loves me. She said she did, but she lied. She *said* but *lied*!"

"Agatha!" cried Father, standing up.

"She?" said Grandma. "Who?"

"Mother!" came the shriek. "Said: 'Love you'! Lies! 'Love you'! Lies! And you're like her! You lie. But you're empty, anyway, and so that's a *double* lie! I hate *her*. Now, I hate *you*!"

Agatha spun about and leapt down the hall.

The front door slammed wide.

Father was in motion, but Grandma touched his arm.

"Let me."

And she walked and then moved swiftly, gliding down the hall and then suddenly, easily, running, yes, running very fast, out the door.

It was a champion sprint by the time we all reached the lawn, the sidewalk, yelling.

Blind, Agatha made the curb, wheeling about, seeing us close, all of us yelling, Grandma way ahead, shouting, too, and Agatha off the curb and out in the street, halfway to the middle, then in the middle and suddenly a car, which no one saw, erupting its brakes, its horn shrieking and Agatha flailing about to see and Grandma there with her and hurling her aside and down as the car with fantastic energy and verve selected her from our midst, struck our wonderful electric Guido Fantoccini–produced dream even while she paced upon the air and, hands up to ward off, almost in mild protest, still trying to decide what to say to this bestial machine, over and over she spun and down and away even as the car jolted to a halt and I saw Agatha safe beyond and Grandma, it seemed, still coming down or down and sliding fifty yards away to strike and ricochet and lie strewn and all of us frozen in a line suddenly in the midst of the street with one scream pulled out of all our throats at the same raw instant.

Then silence and just Agatha lying on the asphalt, intact, getting ready to sob.

And still we did not move, frozen on the sill of death, afraid to venture in any direction, afraid to go see what lay beyond the car and Agatha and so we began to wail and, I guess, pray to ourselves as Father stood amongst us: Oh, no, no, we mourned, oh no, God, no, no . . .

Agatha lifted her already grief-stricken face and it was the face of someone who has predicted dooms and lived to see and now did not want to see or live any more. As we watched, she turned her gaze to the tossed woman's body and tears fell from her eyes. She shut them and covered them and lay back down forever to weep. . . .

I took a step and then another step and then five quick steps and by the time I reached my sister her head was buried deep and her sobs came up out of a place so far down in her I was afraid I could never find her again, she would never come out, no matter how I pried or pleaded or promised or threatened or just plain said. And what little we could hear from Agatha buried there in her own misery, she said over and over again, lamenting, wounded, certain of the old threat known and named and now here forever. " . . . Like I said . . . told you . . . lies . . . lies . . . liars . . . all lies . . . like the other . . . other . . . just like . . . just . . . just like the other . . . other . . . other . . . !"

I was down on my knees holding on to her with both hands, trying to put her back together even though she wasn't broken any way you could see but just feel, because I knew it was no use going on to Grandma, no use at all, so I just touched Agatha and gentled her and wept while Father came up and stood over and knelt down with me and it was like a prayer meeting in the middle of the street and lucky no more cars coming, and I said, choking, "Other what, Ag, other *what?*"

Agatha exploded two words.

"Other dead!"

"You mean Mom?"

"O Mom," she wailed, shivering, lying down, cuddling up like a baby. "O Mom, dead, O Mom and now Grandma dead, she promised always, always, to love, to love, promised to be different, promised, promised and now look, look . . . I hate her, I hate Mom, I hate her, I hate *them!*"

"Of course," said a voice. "It's only natural. How foolish of me not to have known, not to have seen."

And the voice was so familiar we were all stricken.

We all jerked.

Agatha squinched her eyes, flicked them wide, blinked, and jerked half up, staring.

"How silly of me," said Grandma, standing there at the edge of our circle, our prayer, our wake.

"Grandma!" we all said.

And she stood there, taller by far than any of us in this moment of kneeling and holding and crying out. We could only stare up at her in disbelief.

"You're dead!" cried Agatha. "The car—"

"Hit me," said Grandma, quietly. "Yes. And threw me in the air and tumbled me over and for a few moments there was a severe concussion of circuitries. I might have feared a disconnection, if fear is the word. But then I sat up and gave myself a shake and the few molecules of paint, jarred loose on one printed path or another, magnetized back in position and resilient creature that I am, unbreakable thing that I am, *here* I am."

"I thought you were—" said Agatha.

"And only natural," said Grandma. "I mean, anyone else, hit like that, tossed like that. But, O my dear Agatha, not me. And now I see why you were afraid and never trusted me. You didn't know. And I had not as yet proved my singular ability to survive. How dumb of me not to have thought to show you. Just a second." Somewhere in her head, her body, her being, she fitted together some invisible tapes, some old information made new by interblending. She nodded. "Yes. There. A book of child-raising, laughed at by some few people years back when the woman who wrote the book said, as final advice to parents: 'Whatever you do, don't die. Your children will never forgive you.'"

"Forgive," some one of us whispered.

"For how can children understand when you just up and go away and never come back again with no excuse, no apologies, no sorry note, nothing."

"They can't," I said.

"So," said Grandma, kneeling down with us beside Agatha who sat up now, new tears brimming her eyes, but a different kind of tears, not tears that drowned, but tears that washed clean. "So your mother ran away to death. And after that, how *could* you trust anyone? If everyone left, vanished finally, who *was* there to trust? So when I came, half-wise, half-ignorant, I should have known, I did not know, why you would not accept me. For, very simply and honestly, you feared I might not stay, that I lied, that I was vulnerable, too. And two leavetakings, two deaths, were one too many in a single year. But now, do you *see*, Abigail?"

"Agatha," said Agatha, without knowing she corrected.

"Do you understand, I shall always, always be here?"

"Oh, yes," cried Agatha, and broke down into a solid weeping in which we all joined, huddled together, and cars drew up and stopped to see just how many people were hurt and how many people were getting well right there.

End of story.

Well, not quite the end.

We lived happily ever after.

Or rather we lived together, Grandma, Agatha-Agamemnon-Abigail, Timothy, and I, Tom, and Father, and Grandma calling us to frolic in great fountains of Latin and Spanish and French, in great seaborne gouts of poetry like Moby Dick sprinkling the deeps with his Versailles jet somehow lost in calms and found in storms; Grandma a constant, a clock, a pendulum, a face to tell all time by at noon, or in the middle of sick nights when, raving with fever, we saw her forever by our beds, never gone, never away, always waiting, always speaking kind words, her cool hand icing our hot brows, the tappet of her uplifted forefinger unsprung to let a twine of cold mountain water touch our flannel tongues. Ten thousand dawns she cut our wildflower lawn, ten thousand nights she wandered, remembering the dust molecules that fell in the still hours before dawn, or sat whispering some lesson she felt needed teaching to our ears while we slept snug.

Until at last, one by one, it was time for us to go away to school, and when at last the youngest, Agatha, was all packed, why Grandma packed, too.

On the last day of summer that last year, we found Grandma down in the front room with various packets and suitcases, knitting, waiting, and though she had often spoken of it, now that the time came we were shocked and surprised.

"Grandma!" we all said. "What are you doing?"

"Why going off to college, in a way, just like you," she said. "Back to Guido Fantoccini's, to the Family."

"The Family?"

"Of Pinocchios, that's what he called us for a joke, at first. The Pinocchios and himself Geppetto. And then later gave us his own name: the Fantoccini. Anyway, you have been my family here. Now I go back to my even larger family there, my brothers, sisters, aunts, cousins, all robots who—"

"Who do *what?*" asked Agatha.

"It all depends," said Grandma. "Some stay, some linger. Others go to be drawn and quartered, you might say, their parts distributed to other machines who have need of repairs. They'll weigh and find me wanting or not wanting. It may be I'll be just the one they need tomorrow and off I'll go to raise another batch of children and beat another batch of fudge."

"Oh, they mustn't draw and quarter you!" cried Agatha.

"No!" I cried, with Timothy.

"My allowance," said Agatha, "I'll pay anything . . . ?"

Grandma stopped rocking and looked at the needles and the pattern of bright yarn. "Well, I wouldn't have said, but now you ask and I'll tell. For a very *small* fee, there's a room, the room of the Family, a large dim parlor, all quiet and nicely decorated, where as many as thirty or forty of the Electric Women sit and rock and talk, each in her turn. I have not been there. I am, after all, freshly born, comparatively new. For a small fee, very small, each month and year, that's where I'll be, with all the others like me, listening to what they've learned of the world and, in my turn, telling how it was with Tom and Tim and Agatha and how fine and happy we were. And I'll tell all I learned from you."

"But . . . you taught *us!*"

"Do you *really* think that?" she said. "No, it was turnabout, roundabout, learning both ways. And it's all in here, everything you flew into tears about or laughed over, why, I have it all. And I'll tell it to the others just as they tell their boys and girls and life to me. We'll sit there, growing wiser and calmer and better every year and every year, ten, twenty, thirty years. The Family knowledge will double, quadruple, the wisdom will not be lost. And we'll be waiting there in that sitting room, should you ever need us for your own children in time of illness, or, God prevent, deprivation or death. There we'll be, growing old but not old, getting closer to the time, perhaps, someday, when we live up to our first strange joking name."

"The Pinocchios?" asked Tim.

Grandma nodded.

I knew what she meant. The day when, as in the old tale, Pinocchio had grown so worthy and so fine that the gift of life had been given him. So I saw them, in future years, the entire family of Fantoccini, the Pinocchios, trading and retrading, murmuring and whispering their knowledge in the great parlors of philosophy, waiting for the day. The day that could never come.

Grandma must have read that thought in our eyes.

"We'll see," she said. "Let's just wait and see."

"Oh, Grandma," cried Agatha and she was weeping as she had wept many years before. "You don't have to wait. You're alive. You've always been alive to us!"

And she caught hold of the old woman and we all caught hold for a long moment and then ran off up in the sky to faraway schools and years and her last words to us before we let the helicopter swarm us away into autumn were these:

"When you are very old and gone childish-small again, with childish ways and childish yens and, in need of feeding, make a wish for the old teacher-nurse, the dumb yet wise companion, send for me. I will come back. We shall inhabit the nursery again, never fear."

"Oh, we shall never be old!" we cried. "That will never happen!"

"Never! Never!"

And we were gone.

And the years are flown.

And we are old now, Tim and Agatha and I.

Our children are grown and gone, our wives and husbands vanished from the earth and now, by Dickensian coincidence, accept it as you will or not accept, back in the old house, we three.

I lie here in the bedroom which was my childish place seventy, O seventy, believe it, seventy years ago. Beneath this wallpaper is another layer and yet another-times-three to the old wallpaper covered over when I was nine. The wallpaper is peeling. I see peeking from beneath, old elephants, familiar tigers, fine and amiable zebras, irascible crocodiles. I have sent for the paperers to carefully remove all but that last layer. The old animals will live again on the walls, revealed.

And we have sent for someone else.

The three of us have called:

Grandma! You said you'd come back when we had need.

We are surprised by age, by time. We are old. We *need*.

And in three rooms of a summer house very late in time, three old children rise up, crying out in their heads: We *loved* you! We *love* you!

There! There! in the sky, we think, waking at morn. Is that the delivery machine? Does it settle to the lawn?

There! There on the grass by the front porch. Does the mummy case arrive?

Are our names inked on ribbons wrapped about the lovely form beneath the golden mask?!

And the kept gold key, forever hung on Agatha's breast, warmed and waiting? Oh God, will it, after all these years, will it wind, will it set in motion, will it, dearly, *fit*?!

The Women

It was as if a light came on in a green room.

The ocean burned. A white phosphorescence stirred like a breath of steam through the autumn morning sea, rising. Bubbles rose from the throat of some hidden sea ravine.

Like lightning in the reversed green sky of the sea it was aware. It was old and beautiful. Out of the deeps it came, indolently. A shell, a wisp, a bubble, a weed, a glitter, a whisper, a gill. Suspended in its depths were brainlike trees of frosted coral, eyelike pips of yellow kelp, hairlike fluids of weed. Growing with the tides, growing with the ages, collecting and hoarding and saving unto itself identities and ancient dusts, octopus-inks and all the trivia of the sea.

Until now — it was aware.

It was a shining green intelligence, breathing in the autumn sea. Eyeless but seeing, earless but hearing, bodyless but feeling. It was of the sea. And being of the sea it was — feminine.

It in no way resembled man or woman. But it had a woman's ways, the silken, sly, and hidden ways. It moved with a woman's grace. It was all the evil things of vain women.

Dark waters flowed through and by and mingled with strange memory on its way to the gulf streams. In the water were carnival caps, horns, serpentine, confetti. They passed through this blossoming mass of long green hair like wind through an ancient tree. Orange peels, napkins, papers, eggshells, and burnt kindling from night fires on the beaches; all the flotsam of the gaunt high people who stalked on the lone sands of the continental islands, people from brick cities, people who shrieked in metal demons down concrete highways, gone.

It rose softly, shimmering, foaming, into cool morning airs.

The green hair rose softly, shimmering, foaming, into cool morning airs. It lay in the swell after the long time of forming through darkness.

It perceived the shore.

The man was there.

He was a sun-darkened man with strong legs and a cow body.

Each day he should have come down to the water, to bathe, to swim. But he had never moved. There was a woman on the sand with him, a woman in a black bathing suit who lay next to him talking quietly, laughing. Sometimes they held hands, sometimes they listened to a little sounding machine that they dialed and out of which music came.

The phosphorescence hung quietly in the waves. It was the end of the season. September. Things were shutting down.

Any day now he might go away and never return.

Today he must come in the water.

They lay on the sand with the heat in them. The radio played softly and the woman in the black bathing suit stirred fitfully, eyes closed.

The man did not lift his head from where he cushioned it on his muscled left arm. He drank the sun with his face, his open mouth, his nostrils. "What's wrong?" he asked.

"A bad dream," said the woman in the black suit.

"Dreams in the daytime?"

"Don't *you* ever dream in the afternoon?"

"I *never* dream. I've never had a dream in my life."

She lay there, fingers twitching. "God, I had a horrible dream."

"What about?"

"I don't know," she said, as if she really didn't. It was so bad she had forgotten. Now, eyes shut, she tried to remember.

"It was about me," he said, lazily, stretching.

"No," she said.

"Yes," he said, smiling to himself. "I was off with another woman, that's what."

"No."

"I insist," he said. "There I was, off with another woman, and you discovered us, and somehow, in all the mix-up, I got shot or something."

She winced involuntarily. "Don't talk that way."

"Let's see now," he said. "What sort of woman was I with? Gentlemen prefer blondes, don't they?"

"Please don't joke," she said. "I don't feel well."

He opened his eyes. "Did it affect you that much?"

She nodded. "Whenever I dream in the daytime this way, it depresses me something terrible."

"I'm sorry." He took her hand. "Anything I can get you?"

"No."

"Ice cream cone? Eskimo Pie? A Coke?"

"You're a dear, but no. I'll be all right. It's just that, the last four days haven't been right. This isn't like it used to be early in the summer. Something's happened."

"Not between us," he said.

"Oh, no, of course not," she said quickly. "But don't you feel that sometimes *places* change? Even a thing like a pier changes, and the merry-go-rounds, and all that. Even the hot dogs taste different this week."

"How do you mean?"

"They taste old. It's hard to explain, but I've lost my appetite, and I wish this vacation were over. Really, what I want to do most of all is go home."

"Tomorrow's our last day. You know how much this extra week means to me."

"I'll try," she said. "If only this place didn't feel so funny and changed. I don't know. But all of a sudden I just had a feeling I wanted to get up and run."

"Because of your dream? Me and my blonde and me dead all of a sudden."

"Don't," she said. "Don't talk about dying that way!"

She lay there very close to him. "If I only knew what it was."

"There." He stroked her. "I'll protect you."

"It's not me, it's you," her breath whispered in his ear. "I had the feeling that you were tired of me and went away."

"I wouldn't do that; I love you."

"I'm silly." She forced a laugh. "God, what a silly thing I am."

They lay quietly, the sun and sky over them like a lid.

"You know," he said, thoughtfully, "I get a little of that feeling you're talking about. This place has changed. There *is* something different."

"I'm glad you feel it, too."

He shook his head, drowsily, smiling softly, shutting his eyes, drinking the sun. "Both crazy. Both crazy." Murmuring. "Both."

The sea came in on the shore three times, softly.

The afternoon came on. The sun struck the skies a grazing blow. The yachts bobbed hot and shining white in the harbor swells. The smells of fried meat and burnt onion filled the wind. The sand whispered and stirred like an image in a vast, melting mirror.

The radio at their elbow murmured discreetly. They lay like dark arrows on the white sand. They did not move. Only their eyelids flickered with awareness, only their ears were alert. Now and again their tongues might slide along their baking lips. Sly prickles of moisture appeared on their brows to be burned away by the sun.

He lifted his head, blindly, listening to the heat.

The radio sighed.

He put his head down for a minute.

She felt him lift himself again. She opened one eye and he rested on one elbow looking around, at the pier, at the sky, at the water, at the sand.

"What's wrong?" she asked.

"Nothing," he said, lying down again.

"Something," she said.

"I thought I heard something."

"The radio."

"No, not the radio. Something else."

"Somebody *else's* radio."

He didn't answer. She felt his arm tense and relax, tense and relax. "Dammit," he said. "There it is, again."

They both lay listening.

"I don't hear anything—"

"Shh!" he cried. "For God's sake—"

The waves broke on the shore, silent mirrors, heaps of melting, whispering glass.

"Somebody singing."

"What?"

"I'd swear it was someone singing."

"Nonsense."

"No, listen."

They did that for a while.

"I don't hear a thing," she said, turning very cold.

He was on his feet. There was nothing in the sky, nothing on the pier, nothing on the sand, nothing in the hot-dog stands. There was a staring silence, the wind blowing over his ears, the wind preening along the light, blowing hairs of his arms and legs.

He took a step toward the sea.

"Don't!" she said.

He looked down at her, oddly, as if she were not there. He was still listening.

She turned the portable radio up loud. It exploded words and rhythm and melody:

"—I found a million-dollar baby—"

He made a wry face, raising his open palm violently. "Turn it off."

"No, I like it!" She turned it louder. She snapped her fingers, rocking her body vaguely, trying to smile.

It was two o'clock.

The sun steamed the waters. The ancient pier expanded with a loud groan in the heat. The birds were held in the hot sky, unable to move. The sun struck through the green liquors that poured about the pier; struck, caught and burnished an idle whiteness that drifted in the offshore ripples.

The white foam, the frosted coral brain, the kelp pip, the tide dust lay in the water, spreading.

The dark man lay on the sand, the woman in the black suit beside him.

Music drifted up like mist from the water. It was a whispering music of deep tides and passed years, of salt and travel, of accepted and familiar strangenesses. The music sounded not unlike water on the shore, rain falling, the turn of soft limbs in the depths. It was a singing of a time-lost voice in a caverned seashell. The hissing and sighing of tides in deserted holds of treasure ships. The sound the wind makes in an empty skull thrown out on the baked sand.

But the radio on the blanket on the beach played louder.

The phosphorescence, light as a woman, sank down, tired, from sight. Only a few more hours. They might leave at any time. If only he would come in, for an instant, just an instant. The mists stirred silently, aware of his face and his body in the water, deep under. Aware of him caught, held, as they sank ten fathoms down, on a sluice that bore them twisting and turning in frantic gesticulations, to the depths of a hidden gulf in the sea.

The heat of his body, the water taking fire from his warmth, and the frosted coral brain, the jeweled dusts, the salted mists feeding on his hot breath from his open lips.

The waves moved the soft and changing thoughts into the shallows which were tepid as bath waters from the two o'clock sun.

He mustn't go away. If he goes now, he'll not return.

Now. The cold coral brain drifted, drifted. *Now.* Calling across the hot spaces of windless air in the early afternoon. *Come down to the water. Now,* said the music. *Now.*

The woman in the black bathing suit twisted the radio dial.

"Attention!" cried the radio. "Now, today, you can buy a new car at—"

"Jesus!" The man reached over and tuned the scream down. "Must you have it so loud!"

"I like it loud," said the woman in the black bathing suit, looking over her shoulder at the sea.

It was three o'clock. The sky was all sun.

Sweating, he stood up. "I'm going in," he said.

"Get me a hot dog first?" she said.

"Can't you wait until I come out?"

"Please." She pouted. "*Now.*"

"Everything on it?"

"Yes, and bring *three* of them."

"Three? God, what an appetite!" He ran off to the small café.

She waited until he was gone. Then she turned the radio off. She lay listening a long time. She heard nothing. She looked at the water until the glints and shatters of sun stabbed through her eyes like needles.

The sea had quieted. There was only a faint, far and fine net of ripples giving off sunlight in infinite repetition. She squinted again and again at the water, scowling.

He bounded back. "Damn, but the sand's hot; burns my feet off!" He flung himself on the blanket. "Eat 'em up!"

She took the three hot dogs and fed quietly on one of them. When she finished it, she handed him the remaining two. "Here, you finish them. My eyes are bigger than my stomach."

He swallowed the hot dogs in silence. "Next time," he said, finishing, "don't order more than you can use. Helluva waste."

"Here," she said, unscrewing a thermos, "you must be thirsty. Finish our lemonade."

"Thanks." He drank. Then he slapped his hands together and said, "Well,

I'll go jump in the water now." He looked anxiously at the bright sea.

"Just one more thing," she said, just remembering it. "Will you buy me a bottle of suntan oil? I'm all out."

"Haven't you some in your purse?"

"I used it all."

"I wish you'd told me when I was up there buying the hot dogs," he said. "But, okay." He ran back, loping steadily.

When he was gone, she took the suntan bottle from her purse, half-full, unscrewed the cap, and poured the liquid into the sand, covering it over surreptitiously, looking out at the sea, and smiling. She rose then and went down to the edge of the sea and looked out, searching the innumerable small and insignificant waves.

You can't have him, she thought. Whoever or whatever you are, he's mine, and you can't have him. I don't know what's going on; I don't know anything, really. All I know is we're going on a train tonight at seven. And we won't be here tomorrow. So you can just stay here and wait, ocean, sea, or whatever it is that's wrong here today.

Do your damnedest; you're no match for me, she thought. She picked up a stone and threw it at the sea.

"There!" she cried. "You."

He was standing beside her.

"Oh?" She jumped back.

"Hey, what gives? You standing here, muttering?"

"Was I?" She was surprised at herself. "Where's the suntan oil? Will you put it on my back?"

He poured a yellow twine of oil and massaged it onto her golden back. She looked out at the water from time to time, eyes sly, nodding at the water as if to say, "Look! You see? Ah-ha!" She purred like a kitten.

"There." He gave her the bottle.

He was half into the water before she yelled.

"Where are you going! Come here!"

He turned as if she were someone he didn't know. "For God's sake, what's wrong?"

"Why, you just finished your hot dogs and lemonade—you can't go in the water now and get cramps!"

He scoffed. "Old wives' tales."

"Just the same, you come back up on the sand and wait an hour before you go in, do you hear? I won't have you getting a cramp and drowning."

"Ah," he said, disgusted.

"Come along." She turned, and he followed, looking back at the sea.

Three o'clock. Four.

The change came at four-ten. Lying on the sand, the woman in the black suit saw it coming and relaxed. The clouds had been forming since three. Now, with a sudden rush, the fog came in from off the bay. Where it had been warm, now it was cold. A wind blew up out of nothing. Darker clouds moved in.

"It's going to rain," she said.

"You sound absolutely pleased," he observed, sitting with arms folded. "Maybe our last day, and you sound pleased because it's clouding up."

"The weatherman," she confided, "said there'd be thunder showers all tonight and tomorrow. It might be a good idea to leave tonight."

"We'll stay, just in case it clears. I want to get one more day of swimming in, anyway," he said. "I haven't been in the water yet today."

"We've had so much fun talking and eating, time passes."

"Yeah," he said, looking at his hands.

The fog flailed across the sand in soft strips.

"There," she said. "That was a raindrop on my nose!" She laughed ridiculously at it. Her eyes were bright and young again. She was almost triumphant. "Good old rain."

"Why are you so pleased? You're an odd duck."

"Come on, rain!" she said. "Well, help me with these blankets. We'd better run!"

He picked up the blankets slowly, preoccupied. "Not even one last swim, dammit. I've a mind to take just one dive." He smiled at her. "Only a minute!"

"No." Her face paled. "You'll catch cold, and I'll have to nurse you!"

"Okay, okay." He turned away from the sea. Gentle rain began to fall.

Marching ahead of him, she headed for the hotel. She was singing softly to herself.

"Hold on!" he said.

She halted. She did not turn. She only listened to his voice far away.

"There's someone out in the water!" he cried. "Drowning!"

She couldn't move. She heard his feet running.

"Wait here!" he shouted. "I'll be right back! There's someone there! A woman, I think!"

"Let the lifeguards get her!"

"Aren't any! Off duty; late!" He ran down to the shore, the sea, the waves.

"Come back!" she screamed. "There's no one out there! Don't, oh, don't!"

"Don't worry, I'll be right back!" he called. "She's drowning out there, see?"

The fog came in, the rain pattered down, a white flashing light raised in the waves. He ran, and the woman in the black suit ran after him, scattering beach implements behind her, crying, tears rushing from her eyes. "Don't!" She put out her hands.

He leaped into an onrushing dark wave.

The woman in the black bathing suit waited in the rain.

At six o'clock the sun set somewhere behind black clouds. The rain rattled softly on the water, a distant drum snare.

Under the sea, a move of illuminant white.

The soft shape, the foam, the weed, the long strands of strange green hair lay in the shallows. Among the stirring glitter, deep under, was the man.

Fragile. The foam bubbled and broke. The frosted coral brain rang against a pebble with thought, as quickly lost as found. Men. Fragile. Like dolls, they break. Nothing, nothing to them. A minute under water and they're sick and pay no attention and they vomit out and kick and then, suddenly, just lie there, doing nothing. Doing nothing at all. Strange. Disappointing, after all the days of waiting.

What to do with him now? His head lolls, his mouth opens, his eyelids loosen, his eyes stare, his skin pales. Silly man, wake up! Wake up!

The water surged about him.

The man hung limply, loosely, mouth agape.

The phosphorescence, the green hair weed withdrew.

He was released. A wave carried him back to the silent shore. Back to his wife, who was waiting for him there in the cold rain.

The rain poured over the black waters.

Distantly, under the leaden skies, from the twilight shore, a woman screamed.

Ah—the ancient dusts stirred sluggishly in the water—isn't that *like* a woman? Now, *she* doesn't want him, *either*!

At seven o'clock the rain fell thick. It was night and very cold and the hotels all along the sea had to turn on the heat.

The Inspired Chicken Motel

It was in the Depression, deep down in the empty soul of the Depression in 1932, when we were heading west by 1928 Buick, that my mother, father, my brother Skip, and I came upon what we ever after called the Inspired Chicken Motel.

It was, my father said, a motel straight out of Revelations. And the one strange chicken at that motel could no more help making said Revelations, writ on eggs, than a holy roller can help going wild with utterances of God, Time, and Eternity writhing along his limbs, seeking passage out the mouth.

Some creatures are given to talents inclined one way, some another. But chickens are the greatest dumb brute mystery of them all. Especially hens who think or intuit messages calcium-scrawled forth in a nice neat hand upon the shells wherein their offspring twitch asleep.

Little did we know that long autumn of 1932, as we blew tires and flung fan belts like lost garters down Highway 66, that somewhere ahead that motel, and that most peculiar chicken, were waiting.

Along the way, our family was a wonderful nest of amiable contempt. Holding the maps, my brother and I knew we were a helluva lot smarter than Dad, Dad knew he was smarter than Mom, and Mom knew she could brain the whole bunch, any time.

That makes for perfection.

I mean, any family that has a proper disrespect, each for the other, can stay together. As long as there is something to fight about, people will come to meals. Lose that and the family disintegrates.

So we leaped out of bed each day hardly able to wait to hear what dumb thing someone might say over the hard-fried bacon and the under-fried scrambleds. The toast was too dark or too light. There was jam for only one person. Or it was a flavor that two out of four hated. Hand us a set of bells and we could ring all the wrong changes. If Dad claimed he was still growing, Skip and I ran the tape measure out to prove he'd shrunk during the night. That's humanity. That's nature. That's family.

But like I said, there we were grousing down Illinois, quarreling through the leaf change in the Ozarks autumn where we stopped sniping all of ten minutes to see the fiery colors. Then, pot-shotting and sniveling across Kansas and Oklahoma, we plowed into a fine deep-red muck and slid off the road on a detour where each of us could bless himself and blame others for the excavations, the badly painted signs, and the lack of brakeage in our old Buick. Out of the ditch, we unloaded ourselves into a great Buck-a-Night Bungalow Court in a murderers' ambush behind a woods and on the rim of a deep rock-quarry where our bodies might be found years later at the bottom of a lost and sourceless lake, and spent the night counting the rain that leaked in through the shingle-sieve roof and fighting over who had the most covers on the wrong side of the bed.

The next day was even better. We steamed out of the rain into 100-degree heat that took the sap and spunk out of us, save for a few ricochet slaps Dad threw at Skip but landed on me. By noon we were sweated fresh out of contempt, and were settling into a rather refined if exhausted period of familiar insult, when we drove up by this chicken farm outside Amarillo, Texas.

We sat up, instantly.

Why?

Because we found that chickens are kicked the same as families kick each other, to get them out of the way.

We saw an old man boot a rooster and smile as he came toward the auto gate. We all beamed. He leaned in to say he rented rooms for fifty cents a night, the price being low because the smell was high.

The starch being out of Dad, and him sunk in a despond of good will, and this looking like another dandy place to raise grouse, he turned in his chauffeur's cap and shelled out fifty cents in nickels and pennies.

Our great expectations were not punctured. The flimsy room we moved into was a beaut. Not only did all the springs give injections wherever you put flesh down, but the entire bungalow suffered from an oft-rehearsed palsy. Its foundations were still in shock from the thousand mean invaders who had cried "Timber!" and fallen upon the impaling beds.

By its smell, some wild parties had died here. There was an odor of false sincerity and lust masquerading as love. A wind blew up between the floorboards redolent of chickens under the bungalow who spent nights running crazy from diarrhea induced by pecking the bathtub liquor that seeped down through the fake Oriental linoleum.

Anyway, once we had hunched in out of the sun and slunk through a cold pork-and-beans-on-bread lunch, with white oleomargarine greasing it down the ways, my brother and I found a desert creek nearby and heaved rocks at each other to cool off. That night we went into town and found a greasy spoon and read the flyspecks and fought off the crickets that came into the café to skinnydip in the soup. We saw a ten-cent James Cagney gangster movie and came out heading back to the chicken ranch delighted with all the mayhem, the Great Depression gone and forgotten.

At eleven that hot night everyone in Texas was awake because of the heat. The landlady, a frail woman whose picture I had seen in every newsphoto of Dust Bowl country, eroded down to the bones but with a fragile sort of candlelight hollowed in her eyes, came to sit and chat with us about the eighteen million unemployed and what might happen next and where we were going and what would next year bring.

Which was the first cool respite of the day. A cold wind blew out of tomorrow. We grew restive. I looked at my brother, he looked at Mom, Mom looked at Dad, and we were a family, no matter what, and we were together tonight, going somewhere.

"Well . . . " Dad took out a road map and unfolded it and showed the lady where he had marked in red ink as if it was a chart of our four lives' territory, just how we would live in the days ahead, just how survive, just how make do, sleep just so, eat how much, and sleep with no dreams guaranteed. "Tomorrow" —he touched the roads with one nicotine-stained finger—"we'll be in Tombstone. Day after that Tucson. Stay in Tucson looking for work. We got enough cash for two weeks there if we cut it close. No jobs there, we move on to San Diego. Got a cousin there in Customs Inspection on the docks. We figure one week in San Diego, three weeks in Los Angeles. Then we've just enough money to head home to Illinois, where we can put in on relief or, who knows, maybe get the job back at the Power and Light Company that laid me off six months ago."

"I see," said the landlady.

And she did see. For all eighteen million people had come along this road and stopped here going somewhere anywhere nowhere and then going back to the nowhere somewhere anywhere they had got lost from in the first place and, not needed, gone wandering away.

"What kind of job are you looking for?" asked the landlady.

And it was a joke. She knew it as soon as she said it. Dad thought about it and laughed. Mother laughed. My brother and I laughed. We all laughed together.

For of course no one asked what *kind* of job, there were just jobs to be found, jobs without names, jobs to buy gas and feed faces and maybe, on occasion, buy ice cream cones. Movies? They were something to be seen once a month, perhaps. Beyond that, my brother and I snuck in theaters around back or in side doors or down through basements up through orchestra pits or up fire escapes and down into balconies. Nothing could keep us from Saturday matinees except Adolphe Menjou.

We all stopped laughing. Sensing that a proper time had come for a particular act, the landlady excused herself, went out, and in a few minutes returned. She brought with her two small gray cardboard boxes. The way she carried them, at first it almost seemed she was bearing the family heirlooms or the ashes of a beloved uncle. She sat and held the two small boxes on her aproned lap for a long moment, shielding them quietly. She waited with the inherent sense of drama most people learn when small quick events must be slowed and made to seem large.

And strangely, we were moved by the hush of the woman herself, by the lostness of her face. For it was a face in which a whole lifetime of lostness showed. It was a face in which children, never born, gave cry. Or it was a face in which children, born, had passed to be buried not in the earth but in her flesh. Or it was a face in which children, born, raised, had gone off over the world never to write. It was a face in which her life and the life of her husband and the ranch they lived on struggled to survive and somehow managed. God's breath threatened to blow out her wits, but somehow, with awe at her own survival, her soul stayed lit.

Any face like that, with so much loss in it, when it finds something to hold and look at, how can you help but pay attention?

For now our landlady was holding out the boxes and opening the small lid of the first.

And inside the first box . . .

"Why," said Skip, "it's just an egg. . . . "

"Look close," she said.

And we all looked close at the fresh white egg lying on a small bed of aspirin-bottle cotton.

"Hey," said Skip.

"Oh, yeah," I whispered. "Hey."

For there in the center of the egg, as if cracked, bumped and formed by mysterious nature, was the skull and horns of a longhorn steer.

It was as fine and beautiful as if a jewelsmith had worked the egg some magic way to raise the calcium in obedient ridges to shape that skull and those prodigious horns. It was, therefore, an egg any boy would have proudly worn on a string about his neck or carried to school for friends to gasp over and appraise.

"This egg," said our landlady, "was laid, with this design on it, exactly three days ago."

Our hearts beat once or twice. We opened our mouths to speak. "It—"

She shut the box. Which shut our mouths. She took a deep breath, half closed her eyes, then opened the lid of the second box.

Skip cried, "I bet I know what's—"

His guess would have been right.

In the second box, revealed, lay a second fat white egg on cotton.

"There," said the landlady who owned the motel and the chicken ranch way out in the middle of the land under a sky that went forever and fell over the horizon into more land that went on forever and more sky over that.

We all bent forward, squinting.

For there were words written on this egg in white calcium outline, as if the nervous system of the chicken, moved by strange night talks that only it could hear, had lettered the shell in painful half-neat inscriptions.

And the words we saw upon the egg were these:

REST IN PEACE. PROSPERITY IS NEAR.

And suddenly it was very quiet.

We had begun to ask questions about that first egg. Our mouths had jumped wide to ask: How could a chicken, in its small insides, make marks on shells? Was the hen's wristwatch machinery tampered with by outside influences? Had God used that small and simple beast as a Ouija board on which to spell out shapes, forms, remonstrances, unveilings?

But now, with the second egg before us, our mouths stayed numbly shut.

REST IN PEACE. PROSPERITY IS NEAR.

Dad could not take his eyes from that egg.

Nor could any of us.

Our lips moved at last, saying the words soundlessly.

Dad looked up, once, at our landlady. She gazed back at him with a gaze that was as calm, steady, and honest as the plains were long, hot, empty, and dry.

The light of fifty years withered and bloomed there. She neither complained nor explained. She had found an egg beneath a hen. Here the egg was. Look at it, her face said. Read the words. Then . . . please . . . read them again.

We inhaled and exhaled.

Dad turned slowly at last and walked away. At the screen door he looked back and his eyes were blinking rapidly. He did not put his hand up to his eyes, but they were wet and bright and nervous. Then he went out the door and down the steps and between the old bungalows, his hands deep in his pockets.

My brother and I were still staring at that egg, when the landlady closed the lid, carefully, rose, and went to the door. We followed, silent.

Outside, we found Dad standing in the last heat of the sun and the first light of the moon by the wire fence. We all looked over at ten thousand chickens veering this way and that in tides, suddenly panicked by wind or startled by cloud shadows or dogs barking off on the prairie, or a lone car moving on the hot-tar road.

"There," said our landlady. "There she is."

She pointed at the sea of rambling fowl.

We saw thousands of chickens hustling, heard thousands of bird voices suddenly raised, suddenly dying away.

"There's my pet, there's my precious. See?"

She held her hand steady, moving it slowly to point to one particular hen among the ten thousand. And somewhere in all the flurry . . .

"Isn't she *grand*?" said our landlady.

I looked, I stood on tiptoe, I squinted. I stared wildly.

"There! I think—!" cried my brother.

"The white one," supplied our landlady, "with ginger flecks."

I looked at her. Her face was very serene. She knew her hen. She knew the look of her love. Even if we could not find and see, the hen was there, like the world and the sky, a small fact in much that was large.

"There," said my brother, and stopped, confused. "No, there. No, wait . . . over *there*!"

"Yeah," I said. "I see him!"

"Her, you dimwit!"

"Her!" I said.

And for a brief moment I thought I *did* see one chicken among many, one grand bird whiter than the rest, plumper than the rest, happier than the rest, faster, more frolicsome and somehow strutting proud. It was as if the sea of creatures parted before our Bible gaze to show us, alone among island shadows of moon on warm grass, a single bird transfixed for an instant before a final dog bark and a rifle shot from a passing car exhaust panicked and scattered the fowls. The hen was gone.

"You *saw*?" asked the landlady, holding to the wire fence, searching for her love lost in the rivering hens.

"Yes." I could not see my father's face, whether it was serious or if he gave a dry smile to himself. "I saw."

He and Mother walked back to our bungalow.

But the landlady and Skip and I stayed on at the fence not saying anything, not even pointing any more, for at least another ten minutes.

Then it was time for bed.

I lay there wide awake with Skip. For I remembered all the other nights when Dad and Mom talked and we liked to listen to them talk about grown-up things and grown-up places, Mother asking concerned and Dad answering final and very sure and calm and quiet. Pot of Gold, End of Rainbow. I didn't believe in that. Land of Milk and Honey. I didn't believe in that. We had traveled far and seen too much for me to believe . . . but . . .

Someday My Ship Will Come In. . . .

I believed that.

Whenever I heard Dad say it, tears welled in my eyes. I had seen such ships on Lake Michigan summer morns coming in from festivals across the water full of merry people, confetti on the air, horns blowing, and in my private dream, projected on my bedroom wall through countless nights, there we stood on the dock, Mom, Dad, Skip, and I! and the ship huge, snow-white, coming in with millionaires on her upper decks tossing not confetti but greenbacks and gold coins down in a clattering rain all around, so we danced to catch and dodge and cry Ouch! when hit about the ears by especially fierce coins or laughed when licked by a snowy flurry of cash. . . .

Mom asked about it. Dad answered. And in the night, Skip and I went down in the same dream to wait on a dock.

And this night here, lying in bed, after a long while I said, "Dad? What does it mean?"

"What does *what* mean?" said Dad, way over there in the dark with Mom.

"The message on the egg. Does it mean the Ship? It'll come in soon?"

There was a long silence.

"Yes," said Dad. "That's what it means. Go to sleep, Doug."

"Yes, sir."

And, weeping tears, I turned away.

We drove out of Amarillo at six the next morning in order to beat the heat, and for the first hour out we didn't say anything because we weren't awake, and for the second hour we said nothing because we were thinking about the night before. And then at last Dad's coffee started perking in him and he said:

"Ten thousand."

We waited for him to go on and he did, shaking his head slowly:

"Ten thousand dumb chickens. And *one* of them, out of nowhere, takes it to mind to scribble us a note."

"Dad," said Mom.

And her voice by its inflection said, You don't really *believe?*

"Yeah, Dad," said my brother in the same voice, with the same faint criticism.

"It's something to think about," said Dad, his eyes just on the road, riding easy, his hands on the wheel not gripping tight, steering our small raft over the desert. Just beyond the hill was another hill and beyond that another hill, but just beyond *that* . . . ?

Mother looked over at Dad's face and hadn't the heart to say his name in just that way right now. She looked back at the road and said so we could barely hear it:

"How did it go again?"

Dad took us around a long turn in the desert highway toward White Sands, and then he cleared his throat and cleared a space on the sky ahead as he drove and said, remembering:

"Rest in Peace. Prosperity Is Near."

I let another mile go by before I said, "How much . . . unh. How much . . . an egg like that worth, Dad?"

"There's no putting a human price on a thing like that," he said, not looking back, just driving for the horizon, just going on. "Boy, you can't set a price on an egg like that, laid by an inspired chicken at the Inspired Chicken Motel. Years from now, that's what we'll call it. The Inspired Chicken Motel."

We drove on at an even forty miles an hour into the heat and dust of day-after-tomorrow.

My brother didn't hit me, I didn't hit my brother, carefully, secretly, until just before noon when we got out to water the flowers by the side of the road.

Yes, We'll Gather
at the River

At one minute to nine he should have rolled the wooden Indian back into warm tobacco darkness and turned the key in the lock. But somehow he waited because there were so many lost men walking by in no special direction for no special reason. A few of them wandered in to drift their gaze over the tribal cigars laid out in their neat brown boxes, then glanced up suddenly surprised to find where they were and said, evasively, "Evening, Charlie."

"So it is," said Charlie Moore.

Some of the men wandered off empty-handed, others moved on with a nickel cigar unlit in their mouths.

So it was nine-thirty of a Thursday night before Charlie Moore finally touched the wooden Indian's elbow as if disturbing a friend and hating to bother. Gently he maneuvered the savage to where he became watchman of the night. In the shadows, the carved face stared raw and blind through the door.

"Well, Chief, what do you see?"

Charlie followed that silent gaze beyond to the highway that cut through the very center of their lives.

In locust hordes, cars roared up from Los Angeles. With irritation they slowed to thirty miles per hour here. They crept between some three dozen shops, stores, and old livery stables become gas stations, to the north rim of town. There the cars exploded back to eighty, racing like Furies on San Francisco, to teach it violence.

Charlie snorted softly.

A man passed, saw him standing with his silent wooden friend, said, "Last night, eh?" and was gone.

Last night.

There. Someone had dared use the words.

Charlie wheeled to switch off the lights, lock the door and, on the sidewalk, eyes down, freeze.

As if hypnotized, he felt his gaze rise again to the old highway which swept by with winds that smelled of a billion years ago. Great bursts of headlight arrived, then cut away in departures of red taillight, like schools of small bright fish darting in the wake of sharks and blind-traveling whales. The lights sank away and were lost in the black hills.

Charlie broke his stare. He walked slowly on through his town as the clock over the Oddfellows Lodge struck the quarter hour and moved on toward ten and still he walked and was amazed and then not amazed any more to see how every shop was still open long after hours and in every door stood a man or woman transfixed even as he and his Indian brave had been transfixed by a talked-about and dreadful future suddenly become Here Now Tonight.

Fred Ferguson, the taxidermist, kin to the family of wild owls and panicked deer which stayed on forever in his window, spoke to the night air as Charlie passed:

"Hard to believe, ain't it?"

He wished no answer, for he went on, immediately:

"Keep thinking: Just can't be. Tomorrow, the highway dead and us dead with it."

"Oh, it won't be that bad," said Charlie.

Ferguson gave him a shocked look. "Wait. Ain't you the one hollered two years ago, wanted to bomb the legislature, shoot the road contractors, steal the concrete mixers and earth-movers when they started the new highway three hundred yards west of here? What you mean, it won't be bad? It will, and you know it!"

"I know," said Charlie Moore, at last.

Ferguson brooded on the near distance.

"Three hundred little bitty yards. Not much, eh? But seeing as how our town is only a hundred yards wide, that puts us, give or take, about two hundred yards from the new superroad. Two hundred yards from people who need nuts, bolts, or house-paint. Two hundred from jokers who barrel down from the mountains with deer or fresh-shot alley-cats of all sorts and need the services of the only A-one taxidermist on the Coast. Two hundred yards from ladies who need aspirin—" He eyed the drugstore. "Haircuts." He watched the red-striped pole spin in its glass case down the street. "Strawberry sodas." He nodded at the malt shop. "You name it."

They named it all in silence, sliding their gaze along the stores, the shops, the arcades.

"Maybe it's not too late."

"Late, Charlie? Hell. Cement's mixed and poured and set. Come dawn they yank the roadblocks both ends of the new road. Governor might cut a ribbon from the first car. Then . . . people might remember Oak Lane the first week, sure. The second week not so much. A month from now? We'll be a smear of old paint on their right running north, on their left running south, burning rubber. There's Oak Lane! Remember? Ghost town. Oops! It's gone."

Charlie let his heart beat two or three times.

"Fred . . . what you going to do?"

"Stay on awhile. Stuff a few birds the local boys bring in. Then crank the old Tin Lizzie and drive that new superfreeway myself going nowhere, anywhere, and so long to you, Charlie Moore."

"Night, Fred. Hope you sleep."

"What, and miss welcoming in the New Year, middle of July . . . ?"

Charlie walked and that voice faded behind and he came to the barbershop where three men, laid out, were being strenuously barbered behind plate glass. The highway traffic slid over them in bright reflections. They looked like they were drowning under a stream of huge fireflies.

Charlie stepped in. Everyone glanced up.

"Anyone got any ideas?"

"Progress, Charlie," said Frank Mariano, combing and cutting, "is an idea can't be stopped with no other idea. Let's yank up the whole damn town, lock, stock, and tar barrel, carry it over, nail it down by that new road."

"We figured the cost last year. Four dozen stores at three thousand dollars average to haul them just three hundred yards west."

"So ends that master plan," muttered someone under a hot steam towel, buried in inescapable fact.

"One good hurricane would do the job, carriage-free."

They all laughed quietly.

"We should all celebrate tonight," said the man under the hot towel. He sat up, revealing himself as Hank Summers, the groceryman. "Snort a few stiff drinks and wonder where the hell we'll all be this time next year."

"We didn't fight hard enough," said Charlie. "When it started, we didn't pitch in."

"Hell." Frank snipped a hair out of the inside of a fairly large ear. "When times move, not a day passes someone's not hurt. This month, this year, it's our turn. Next time *we* want something, someone else gets stepped on, all in the name of Get Up and Go. Look, Charlie, go form a vigilantes. Mine that new road. But watch out. Just crossing the lanes to place the bomb, you're sure to be run down by a manure truck bound for Salinas."

More laughter, which faded quickly.

"Look," said Hank Summers, and everybody looked. He spoke to his own fly-specked image in the ancient mirror as if trying to sell his twin on a shared logic. "We lived here thirty years now, you, me, all of us. Won't kill us to move on. Good God, we're all root and a yard wide. Graduation. School of hard knocks is throwing us out the door with no never-minds and no thank-yous. I'm ready. Charlie, are *you*?"

"Me, now," said Frank Mariano. "Monday morning six A.M. I load my barbershop in a trailer and shoot off after those customers, ninety miles an hour!"

There was a laugh sounded like the very last one of the day, so Charlie turned with one superb and mindless drift and was back on the street.

And still the shops stayed open, the lights stayed on, the doors stood wide, as if each owner was reluctant to go home, so long as that river out there was flowing and there was the great motion and glint and sound of people and metal and light in a tide they had grown so accustomed to it was hard to believe the river bottom would ever know a dry season.

Charlie lingered on, straying from shop to shop, sipping a chocolate Coke at the malted-milk counter, buying some stationery he couldn't use from the drugstore under the soft fluttering wood fan that whispered to itself in the ceiling. He loitered like a common criminal, thieving sights. He paused in alleys where, Saturday afternoons, gypsy tie salesmen or kitchenware spielers laid out their suitcase worlds to con the pedestrians. Then, at last he reached the gas station where Pete Britz, deep in the oil pit, was mending the dumb brute underside of a dead and uncomplaining 1947 Ford.

At ten o'clock, as if by some secret but mutual consent, all the shops went dark, all the people walked home, Charlie Moore among them.

He caught up with Hank Summers, whose face was still shining pink from the shave he hadn't needed. They ambled in silence for a time past houses where it seemed the whole population was sitting out smoking or knitting, rocking in chairs or fanning themselves against a nonexistent hot spell.

Hank laughed suddenly at some private thought. A few paces on, he decided to make it public:

> *"Yes, we'll gather at the River.*
> *River, River.*
> *Yes, we'll gather at the River*
> *That flows by the Throne of God."*

He half sang it and Charlie nodded.

"First Baptist Church, when I was twelve."

"The Lord giveth and the Highway Commissioner taketh away," said Hank dryly. "Funny. Never thought how much a town is people. Doing things, that is. Under the hot towel back there, thought: What's this place to me? Shaved, I had the answer. Russ Newell banging a carburetor at the Night Owl Garage? Yep. Allie Mae Simpson . . ."

He swallowed his voice in embarrassment.

Allie Mae Simpson . . . Charlie took up the count in his own mind. . . . Allie Mae fixing wet curlicues in old ladies' hair in the bay window of her Vogue Salon . . . Doc Knight stacking pill bottles in the drug emporium cases . . . hardware store laid out in the hot noon sun, Clint Simpson middle of it all, running his hands over, sorting out the million blinks and shines of brass and silver and gold, all the nails, hinges, knobs, all the saws, hammers, and snaked-up copper wire and stacks of aluminum foil like the junk shaken free of a thousand boys' pockets in a thousand summers past . . . and then . . .

. . . Then there was his own place, warm, dark, brown, comfortable, musky as the den of a tobacco-smoking bear . . . thick with the humidor smells of whole families of odd-sized cigars, imported cigarettes, snuffs just waiting to be exploded on the air. . . .

Take all that away, thought Charlie, you got nothing. Buildings, sure. Anyone can raise a frame, paint a sign to say what might go on inside. But it was people that made the damn thing *get*.

Hank surfaced in his own long thoughts.

"Guess right now I'm sad. Want to send everyone back to open their shops so I can see what they were up to. Why wasn't I looking closer, all these years? Hell, hell. What's got into you, Hank Summers. There's another Oak Lane on up the line or down the line and people there busy as they are here. Wherever I land, next time I'll look close, swear to God. Good-by, Charlie."

"To hell with good-by."

"All right, then, good night."

And Hank was gone and Charlie was home and Clara was waiting at the screen door with a glass of ice water.

"Sit out awhile?"

"Like everyone else? Why not?"

They sat in the dark on the porch in the chain-hung wooden swing and watched the highway flush and drain, flush and drain with arrivals of headlight and departures of angry red fire like the coals from an immense brazier scattered to the fields.

Charlie drank the water slowly and, drinking, thought: In the old days you couldn't see the roads die. You felt them gradually fade, yes, lying in bed nights, maybe your mind got hold of some hint, some nudge or commotion that warned you it was sinking away. But it took years and years for any one road to give up its dusty ghost and another to stir alive. That's how things were, slow arriving and slow passing away. That's how things had always been.

But no more. Now, in a matter of hours.

He paused.

He touched in upon himself to find a new thing.

"I'm not mad any more."

"Good," said his wife.

They rocked awhile, two halves of a similar content.

"My God, I was stirred up there for a while."

"I remember," she said.

"But now I figure, well . . . " He drifted his voice, mostly to himself. "Millions of cars come through every year. Like it or not, the road's just not big enough, we're holding up the world, that old road there and this old town. The world says it's got to move. So now, on that new road, not one but two million will pass just a shotgun blast away, going where they got to go to get things done they say are important, doesn't matter if they're important or not, folks *think* they are, and thinking makes the game. If we'd really seen it coming, thought in on it from every side, we'd have taken a steam-driven sledge and just mashed the town flat and said, 'Drive through!' instead of making them lay the damn road over in that next clover patch. This way, the town dies hard, strangled on a piece of butcher string instead of being dropped off a cliff. Well, well." He lit his pipe and blew great clouds of smoke in which to poke for past mistakes and present revelations. "Us being human, I guess we couldn't have done but as we did. . . . "

They heard the drugstore clock strike eleven and the Oddfellows Lodge clock chime eleven-thirty, and at twelve they lay in bed in the dark, each with a ceilingful of thoughts above them.

"Graduation."

"What?"

"Hank Summers said it and had it right. This whole week feels like the last days of school, years ago. I remember how I felt, how I was afraid, ready to cry, and how I promised myself to live every last moment right up to the time the diploma was in my hand, for God only knew what tomorrow might bring. Unemployment. Depression. War. And then the day arrived, tomorrow did get around to finally coming, and I found myself still alive, by God, and I was still all in one piece and things were starting over, more of the same, and hell, everything turned out okay. So this is another graduation all right, as Hank said, and I'm the last to doubt."

"Listen," said his wife much later. "Listen."

In the night, the river came through the town, the river of metal quiet now but still coming and going with its ancient smells of tidelands and dark seas of oil. Its glimmer, on the ceiling above their graveyard bed, had the shine of small craft gliding upstream and down as their eyelids slowly, slowly shut and their breathing took on the regular sound of the motion of those tides . . . and then they slept.

In the first light of dawn, half the bed lay empty.

Clara sat up, almost afraid.

It was not like Charlie to be gone so early.

Then, another thing frightened her. She sat listening, not certain what had suddenly made her tremble, but before she had a chance to find out why, she heard footsteps.

They came from a long distance away and it was quite a while before they came up the walk and up the steps and into the house. Then, silence. She heard Charlie just standing there in the parlor for a long moment, so she called out:

"Charlie? Where you been?"

He came into the room in the faint light of dawn and sat on the bed beside her, thinking about where he had been and what he had done.

"Walked a mile up the coast and back. All the way to those wood barricades where the new highway starts. Figured it was the least I could do, be part of the whole darn thing."

"The new road's open . . . ?"

"Open and doing business. Can't you tell?"

"Yes." She rose slowly up in bed, tilting her head, closing her eyes for a moment, listening. "So that's it? That's what bothered me. The old road. It's *really* dead."

They listened to the silence outside the house, the old road gone empty and dry and hollow as a river bottom in a strange season of summers that would never stop, that would go on forever. The stream had indeed moved and changed its course, its banks, its bed, during the night. Now all you could hear were the trees in the blowing wind outside the house and the birds beginning to sing their arousal choirs in the time just before the sun really made it over the hills.

"Be real quiet."

They listened again.

And there, far away, some two hundred fifty or three hundred yards off across a meadow field, nearer the sea, they heard the old, the familiar, but the diminished sound of their river taking its new course, moving and flowing—it would never cease—through lengths of sprawling land away north and then on south through the hushed light. And beyond it, the sound of real water, the sea which might almost have drawn the river to come down along the shore . . .

Charlie Moore and his wife sat not moving for a moment longer, with that dim sound of the river across the fields moving and moving on.

"Fred Ferguson was there before dawn," said Charlie in a voice that already remembered the Past. "Crowd of people. Highway officials and all. Everyone pitched in. Fred, why he just walked over and grabbed hold of one end. I took the other. We moved one of those wood barricades, together. Then we stood back . . . and let the cars through."

Have I Got a Chocolate Bar for You!

It all began with the smell of chocolate.

On a steaming late afternoon of June rain, Father Malley drowsed in his confessional, waiting for penitents.

Where in all the world were they? he wondered. Immense traffics of sin lurked beyond in the warm rains. Then why not immense traffics of confession here?

Father Malley stirred and blinked.

Today's sinners moved so fast in their cars that this old church was an ecclesiastical blur. And himself? An ancient watercolor priest, tints fading fast, trapped inside.

Let's give it another five minutes and stop, he thought, not in panic but in the kind of quiet shame and desperation that neglect shoulders on a man.

There was a rustle from beyond the confessional grate next door.

Father Malley sat up, quickly.

A smell of chocolate sifted through the grille.

Ah, God, thought the priest, it's a lad with his small basket of sins soon laid to rest and him gone. Well . . .

The old priest leaned to the grate where the candy essence lingered and where the words must come.

But, no words. No "Bless me, Father, for I have sinned . . . "

Only strange small mouse-sounds of . . . *chewing*!

The sinner in the next booth, God sew up his mouth, was actually sitting in there devouring a candy bar!

"No!" whispered the priest, to himself.

His stomach, gathering data, rumbled, reminding him that he had not eaten since breakfast. For some sin of pride which he could not now recall, he had nailed himself to a saint's diet all day, and now—*this*!

Next door, the chewing continued.

Father Malley's stomach growled. He leaned hard against the grille, shut his eyes, and cried:

"Stop that!"

The mouse-nibbling stopped.

The smell of chocolate faded.

A young man's voice said, "That's exactly why I've come, Father."

The priest opened one eye to examine the shadow behind the screen.

"*What's* exactly why you've come?"

"The chocolate, Father."

"The *what*?"

"Don't be angry, Father."

"Angry, hell, who's angry?"

"You are, Father. I'm damned and burnt before I start, by the sound of your voice."

The priest sank back in the creaking leather and mopped his face and shook his senses.

"Yes, yes. The day's hot. I'm out of temper. But then, I never had much."

"It will cool off later in the day, Father. You'll be fine."

The old priest eyed the screen. "Who's taking and who's *giving* confession here?"

"Why, you are, Father."

"Then, get *on* with it!"

The voice hastened forth the facts:

"You have smelled the chocolate, Father?"

The priest's stomach answered for him, faintly.

Both listened to the sad sound. Then:

"Well, Father, to hit it on the head, I was and still am a . . . chocolate junkie."

Old fires stirred in the priest's eyes. Curiosity became humor, then laughed itself back to curiosity again.

"And *that's* why you've come to confession this day?"

"That's it, sir, or, Father."

"You haven't come about sweating over your sister or blueprints for fornication or self-battles with the grand war of masturbation?"

"I have not, Father," said the voice in remorse.

The priest caught the tone and said, "Tut, tut, it's all right. You'll get around to it. For now, you're a grand relief. I'm full-up with wandering males and lonely females and all the junk they read in books and try in waterbeds and sink from sight with suffocating cries as the damn things spring leaks and all is lost. Get on. You have bruised my antennae alert. Say more."

"Well, Father, I have eaten, every day of my life now for ten or twelve years, one or two pounds of chocolate. I cannot leave it alone, Father. It is the end-all and be-all of my life."

"Sounds like a fearful affliction of lumps, acne, carbuncles, and pimples."

"It was. It *is*."

"And not exactly contributing to a lean figure."

"If I leaned, Father, the confessional would fall over."

The cabinet around them creaked and groaned as the hidden figure beyond demonstrated.

"Sit still!" cried the priest.

The groaning stopped.

The priest was wide awake now and feeling splendid. Not in years had he felt so alive and aware of his happily curious and beating heart and fine blood that sought and found, sought and found the far corners of his cloth and body.

The heat of the day was gone.

He felt immensely cool. A kind of excitement pulsed his wrists and lingered in his throat. He leaned almost like a lover to the grille and prompted more spillage.

"Oh, lad, you're rare."

"And sad, Father, and twenty-two years old and put upon, and hate myself for eating, and need to do something about it."

"Have you tried chewing more and swallowing less?"

"Oh, each night I go to bed saying: Lord, put off the crunchbars and the milk-chocolate kisses and the Hersheys. Each morning I rave out of bed and run to the liquor store not for liquor but for eight Nestlés in a row! I'm in sugar-shock by noon."

"That's not so much confession as medical fact, I can see."

"My doctor yells at me, Father."

"He should."

"I don't listen, Father."

"*You* should."

"My mother's no help, she's hog-fat and candy-wild."

"I hope you're not one of those who live at home still?"

"I loiter about, Father."

"God, there should be laws against boys loitering in the round shade of their mas. Is your father surviving the two of you?"

"Somehow."

"And *his* weight?"

"Irving Gross, he calls himself. Which is a joke about size and weight and not his name."

"With the three of you, the sidewalk's full?"

"No bike can pass, Father."

"Christ in the wilderness," murmured the priest, "starving for forty days."

"Sounds like a terrible diet, Father."

"If I knew the proper wilderness, I'd boot you there."

"Boot away, Father. With no help from my mom and dad, a doctor and skinny friends who snort at me, I'm out of pocket from eating and out of mind from the same. I never dreamed I'd wind up with *you*. Beg pardon, Father, but it took a lot to drive me here. If my friends knew, if my mom, my dad, my crazy doctor knew I was here with *you* at this minute, oh what the hell!"

There was a fearful stampede of feet, a careening of flesh.

"Wait!"

But the weight blundered out of the next-door cubby.

With an elephant trample, the young man was gone.

The smell of chocolate alone stayed behind and told all by saying nought.

The heat of the day swarmed in to stifle and depress the old priest.

He had to climb out of the confessional because he knew if he stayed he would begin to curse under his breath and have to run off to have *his* sins forgiven at some other parish.

I suffer from Peevish, O Lord, he thought. How many Hail Marys for *that*?

Come to think of it, how many for a thousand tons, give or take a ton, of chocolate?

Come back! he cried silently at the empty church aisle.

No, he won't, not ever now, he thought, I pressed too hard.

And with that as supreme depression, he went to the parish house to tub himself cool and towel himself to distemper.

A day, two days, a week passed.

The sweltering noons dissolved the old priest back into a stupor of sweat and vinegar-gnat mean. He snoozed in his cubby or shuffled papers in the unlined library, looked out at the untended lawn and reminded himself to caper with the mower one day soon. But most of all he found himself brambling with irritability. Fornication was the minted coin of the land, and masturbation its handmaiden. Or so it seemed from the few whispers that slid through the confessional grille during the long afternoons.

On the fifteenth day of July, he found himself staring at some boys idling by on their bicycles, mouths full of Hershey bars that they were gulping and chewing.

That night he awoke thinking Power House and Baby Ruth and Love Nest and Crunch.

He stood it as long as he could and then got up, tried to read, tossed the book down, paced the dark night church, and at last, spluttering mildly, went up to the altar and asked one of his rare favors of God.

The next afternoon, the young man who loved chocolate at last came back.

"Thank you, Lord," murmured the priest, as he felt the vast weight creak the other half of the confessional like a ship foundered with wild freight.

"What?" whispered the young voice from the far side.

"Sorry, I wasn't addressing you," said the priest.

He shut his eyes and inhaled.

The gates of the chocolate factory stood wide somewhere and its mild spice moved forth to change the land.

Then, an incredible thing happened.

Sharp words burst from Father Malley's mouth.

"You shouldn't be *coming* here!"

"What, what, Father?"

"Go somewhere else! I can't help. You need special work. No, no."

The old priest was stunned to feel his own mind jump out his tongue this way. Was it the heat, the long days and weeks kept waiting by this fiend, what, *what*? But still his mouth leaped on:

"No help here! No, no. *Go* for help—"

"To the shrinks, you mean?" the voice cut in, amazingly calm, considering the explosion.

"Yes, yes, Lord save us, to those people. The—the psychiatrists."

This last word was even more incredible. He had rarely heard himself say it.

"Oh, God, Father, what do *they* know?" said the young man.

What indeed, thought Father Malley, for he had long been put off by their carnival talk and to-the-rear-march chat and clamor. Good grief, why don't I turn in my collar and buy me a beard! he thought, but went on more calmly.

"What do they know, my son? Why, they claim to know everything."

"Just like the Church *used* to claim, Father?"

Silence. Then:

"There's a difference between claiming and knowing," the old priest replied, as calmly as his beating heart would allow.

"And the Church *knows*, is that it, Father?"

"And if it doesn't, *I* do!"

"Don't get mad again, Father." The young man paused and sighed. "I didn't come to dance angels on the head of a pin with you. Shall I start confession, Father?"

"It's about time!" The priest caught himself, settled back, shut his eyes sweetly, and added. "Well?"

And the voice on the other side, with the tongue and the breath of a child, tinctured with silver-foiled kisses, flavored with honeycomb, moved by recent sugars and memories or more immediate Cadbury fetes and galas, began to describe its life of getting up and living with and going to bed with Swiss delights and temptations out of Hershey, Pennsylvania, or how to chew the dark skin off the exterior of a Clark bar and keep the caramel and textured interior for special shocks and celebrations. Of how the soul asked and the tongue demanded and the stomach accepted and the blood danced to the drive of Power House, the promise of Love Nest, the delivery of Butterfinger, but most of all the sweet African murmuring of dark chocolate between the teeth, tinting the gums, flavoring the palate so you muttered, whispered, murmured, pure Congo, Zambesi, Chad in your sleep.

And the more the voice talked, as the days passed and the weeks, and old priest listened, the lighter became the burden on the other side of the g

Father Malley knew, without looking, that the flesh enclosing that voice was raining and falling away. The tread was less heavy. The confessional did not cry out in such huge alarms when the body entered next door.

For even with the young voice there and the young man, the smell of chocolate was truly fading and almost gone.

And it was the loveliest summer the old priest had ever known.

Once, years before, when he was a very young priest, a thing had happened that was much like this, in its strange and special way.

A girl, no more than sixteen by her voice, had come to whisper each day from the time school let out to the time autumn school renewed.

For all of that long summer he had come as close as a priest might to an alert affection for that whisper and that dear voice. He had heard her through her July attraction, her August madness, and her September disillusion, and as she went away forever in October, in tears, he wanted to cry out: Oh, stay, stay! Marry me!

But I am the groom to the brides of Christ, another voice whispered.

And he had *not* run forth, that very young priest, into the traffics of the world.

Now, nearing sixty, the young soul within him sighed, stirred, recalled, compared that old and shopworn memory with this new, somehow funny yet withal sad encounter with a lost soul whose love was not summer madness for girls in dire swimsuits, but chocolate unwrapped in secret and devoured in stealth.

"Father," said the voice, late one afternoon. "It has been a fine summer."

"Strange you would say that," said the priest. "I have thought so myself."

"Father, I have something really awful to confess to you."

"I'm beyond shocking, I think."

"Father, I am not from your diocese."

"That's all right."

"And, Father, forgive me, but, I—"

"Go on."

"I'm not even Catholic."

"You're *what*!" cried the old man.

"I'm not even Catholic, Father. Isn't that awful?"

"Awful?"

"I mean, I'm sorry, truly I am. I'll join the Church, if you want, Father, to make up."

"Join the Church, you idiot?" shouted the old man. "It's too late for that! Do you know what you've done? Do you know the depths of depravity you've plumbed? You've taken my time, bent my ear, driven me wild, asked advice, needed a psychiatrist, argued religion, criticized the Pope, if I remember correctly, and I *do* remember, used up three months, eighty or ninety days, and now, now, *now* you want to join the Church and 'make up'?"

"If you don't mind, Father."

"Mind! Mind!" yelled the priest, and lapsed into a ten-second apoplexy.

He almost tore the door wide to run around and seize the culprit out into the light. But then:

"It was not all for nothing, Father," said the voice from beyond the grille.

The priest grew quiet.

"For you see, Father, God bless you, you have helped me."

The priest grew very quiet.

"Yes, Father, oh bless you indeed, you have helped me so very much, and I am beholden," whispered the voice. "You haven't asked, but don't you guess? I have lost weight. You wouldn't believe the weight I have lost. Eighty, eighty-five, ninety pounds. Because of you, Father. I gave it up. I gave it up. Take a deep breath. Inhale."

The priest, against his wish, did so.

"What do you smell?"

"Nothing."

"Nothing, Father, nothing! It's gone. The smell of chocolate and the chocolate with it. Gone. Gone. I'm free."

The old priest sat, knowing not what to say, and a peculiar itching came about his eyelids.

"You have done Christ's work, Father, as you yourself must know. He walked through the world and helped. You walk through the world and help. When I was falling, you put out your hand, Father, and saved me."

Then a most peculiar thing happened.

Father Malley felt tears burst from his eyes. They brimmed over. They streaked along his cheeks. They gathered at his tight lips and he untightened them and the tears fell from his chin. He could not stop them. They came, O Lord, they came like a shower of spring rain after the seven lean years and the drought over and himself alone, dancing about, thankful, in the pour.

He heard sounds from the other booth and could not be sure but somehow felt that the other one was crying, too.

So here they sat, while the sinful world rushed by on streets, here in the sweet incense gloom, two men on opposite sides of some fragile board slattings, on a late afternoon at the end of summer, weeping.

And at last they grew very quiet indeed and the voice asked, anxiously, "Are you all right, Father?"

The priest replied at last, eyes shut, "Fine. Thanks."

"Anything I can do, Father?"

"You have already done it, my son."

"About . . . my joining the Church. I meant it."

"No matter."

"But it does matter. I'll join. Even though I'm Jewish."

Father Malley snorted half a laugh. "Wha-what?"

"Jewish, Father, but an Irish Jew, if that helps."

"Oh, yes!" roared the old priest. "It helps, it helps!"

"What's so funny, Father?"

"I don't know, but it is, it is, funny, funny!"

And here he burst into such paroxysms of laughter as made him cry and such floodings of tears as made him laugh again until all mingled in a grand outrush and uproar. The church slammed back echoes of cleansing laughter. In the midst of it all he knew that, telling all this to Bishop Kelly, his confessor, tomorrow, he would be let off easy. A church is washed well and good and fine not only by the tears of sorrow but by the clean fresh-cut meadowbrooms of that self-forgiveness and other-forgiveness which God gave only to man and called it laughter.

It took a long while for their mutual shouts to subside, for now the young man had given up weeping and taken on hilarity, too, and the church rocked with the sounds of two men who one minute had done a sad thing and now did a happy one. The sniffle was gone. Joy banged the walls like wild birds flying to be free.

At last, the sounds weakened. The two men sat, wiping their faces, unseen to each other.

Then, as if the world knew there must be a shift of mood and scene, a wind blew in the church doors far away. Leaves drifted from trees and fell into the aisles. A smell of autumn filled the dusky air. Summer was truly over.

Father Malley looked beyond to that door and the wind and the leaves moving off and gone, and suddenly, as in spring, wanted to go with them. His blood demanded a way out, but there was no way.

"I'm leaving, Father."

The old priest sat up.

"For the time being, you mean."

"No, I'm going away, Father. This is my last time with you."

You can't do that! thought the priest, and almost said it.

But instead he said, as calmly as he could:

"Where are you off to, son?"

"Oh, around the world, Father. Many places. I was always afraid, before. I never went anywhere. But now, with my weight gone, I'm heading out. A new job and so many places to be."

"How long will you be gone, lad?"

"A year, five years, ten. Will you be here ten years from now, Father?"

"God willing."

"Well, somewhere along the way I'll be in Rome and buy something small but have it blessed by the Pope and when I come back I'll bring it here and look you up."

"Will you do that?"

"I will. Do you forgive me, Father?"

"For what?"

"For everything."

"We have forgiven each other, dear boy, which is the finest thing that men can do."

There was the merest stir of feet from the other side.

"I'm going now, Father. Is it true that 'good-by' means God be with you?"

"That's what it means."

"Well then, oh truly, good-by, Father."

"And good-by in all its original meaning to you, lad."

And the booth next to his elbow was suddenly empty.

And the young man gone.

Many years later, when Father Malley was a very old man indeed and full of sleep, a final thing happened to fill out his life. Late one afternoon, dozing in the confessional, listening to rain fall out beyond the church, he smelled a strange and familiar smell and opened his eyes.

Gently, from the other side of the grille, the faintest odor of chocolate seeped through.

The confessional creaked. On the other side, someone was trying to find words.

The old priest leaned forward, his heart beating quickly, wild with amazement and surprise. "Yes?" he urged.

"Thank you," said a whisper, at last.

"Beg pardon . . . ?"

"A long time ago," said the whisper. "You helped. Been long away. In town only for today. Saw the church. Thanks. That's all. Your gift is in the poor box. Thanks."

Feet ran swiftly.

The priest, for the first time in his life, leaped from the confessional.

"Wait!"

But the man, unseen, was gone. Short or tall, fat or thin, there was no telling. The church was empty.

At the poor-box, in the dusk, he hesitated, then reached in. There he found a large eighty-nine-cent economy-size bar of chocolate.

Someday, Father, he heard a long-gone voice whisper, *I'll bring you a gift blessed by the Pope.*

This? *This?* The old priest turned the bar in his trembling hands. But why not? What could be more perfect?

He saw it all. At Castel Gandolfo on a summer noon with five thousand tourists jammed in a sweating pack below in the dust and the Pope high up on his balcony there waving out the rare blessings, suddenly among all the tumult, in all the sea of arms and hands, one lone brave hand held high . . .

And in that hand a silver-wrapped and glorious candy bar.

The old priest nodded, not surprised.

He locked the chocolate bar in a special drawer in his study and sometimes, behind the altar, years later, when the weather smothered the windows and despair leaked in the door hinges, he would fetch the chocolate out and take the smallest nibble.

It was not the Host, no, it was not the flesh of Christ. But it was a life. And the life was his. And on those occasions, not often but often enough, when he took a bite, it tasted (O thank you, God), it tasted incredibly sweet.

A Story of Love

That was the week Ann Taylor came to teach summer school at Green Town Central. It was the summer of her twenty-fourth birthday, and it was the summer when Bob Spaulding was just fourteen.

Everyone remembered Ann Taylor, for she was that teacher for whom all the children wanted to bring huge oranges or pink flowers, and for whom they rolled up the rustling green and yellow maps of the world without being asked. She was that woman who always seemed to be passing by on days when the shade was green under the tunnels of oaks and elms in the old town, her face shifting with the bright shadows as she walked, until it was all things to all people. She was the fine peaches of summer in the snow of winter, and she was cool milk for cereal on a hot early-June morning. Whenever you needed an opposite, Ann Taylor was there. And those rare few days in the world when the climate was balanced as fine as a maple leaf between winds that blew just right, those were the days like Ann Taylor, and should have been so named on the calendar.

As for Bob Spaulding, he was the cousin who walked alone through town on any October evening with a pack of leaves after him like a horde of Hallowe'en mice, or you would see him, like a slow white fish in spring in the tart waters of the Fox Hill Creek, baking brown with the shine of a chestnut to his face by autumn. Or you might hear his voice in those treetops where the wind entertained; dropping down hand by hand, there would come Bob Spaulding to sit alone and look at the world, and later you might see him on the lawn with the ants crawling over his books as he read through the long afternoons alone, or played himself a game of chess on Grandmother's porch, or picked out a solitary tune upon the black piano in the bay window. You never saw him with any other child.

That first morning, Miss Ann Taylor entered through the side door of the schoolroom and all of the children sat still in their seats as they saw her write her name on the board in a nice round lettering.

"My name is Ann Taylor," she said, quietly. "And I'm your new teacher."

The room seemed suddenly flooded with illumination, as if the roof had moved back; and the trees were full of singing birds. Bob Spaulding sat with a spitball he had just made, hidden in his hand. After a half hour of listening to Miss Taylor, he quietly let the spitball drop to the floor.

That day, after class, he brought in a bucket of water and a rag and began to wash the boards.

"What's this?" She turned to him from her desk, where she had been correcting spelling papers.

"The boards are kind of dirty," said Bob, at work.

"Yes, I know. Are you sure you want to clean them?"

"I suppose I should have asked permission," he said, halting uneasily.

"I think we can pretend you did," she replied, smiling, and at this smile he finished the boards in an amazing burst of speed and pounded the erasers so furiously that the air was full of snow, it seemed, outside the open window.

"Let's see," said Miss Taylor. "You're Bob Spaulding, aren't you?"

"Yes'm."

"Well, thank you, Bob."

"Could I do them every day?" he asked.

"Don't you think you should let the others try?"

"I'd like to do them," he said. "Every day."

"We'll try it for a while and see," she said.

He lingered.

"I think you'd better run on home," she said, finally.

"Good night." He walked slowly and was gone.

The next morning he happened by the place where she took board and room just as she was coming out to walk to school.

"Well, here I am," he said.

"And do you know," she said, "I'm not surprised."

They walked together.

"May I carry your books?" he asked.

"Why, thank you, Bob."

"It's nothing," he said, taking them.

They walked for a few minutes and he did not say a word. She glanced over and slightly down at him and saw how at ease he was and how happy he seemed, and she decided to let him break the silence, but he never did. When they reached the edge of the school ground he gave the books back to her. "I guess I better leave you here," he said. "The other kids wouldn't understand."

"I'm not sure I do, either, Bob," said Miss Taylor.

"Why we're friends," said Bob earnestly and with a great natural honesty.

"Bob—" she started to say.

"Yes'm?"

"Never mind." She walked away.

"I'll be in class," he said.

And he was in class, and he was there after school every night for the next two weeks, never saying a word, quietly washing the boards and cleaning the erasers and rolling up the maps while she worked at her papers, and there was that clock silence of four o'clock, the silence of the sun going down in the slow sky, the silence with the catlike sound of erasers patted together, and the drip of water from a moving sponge, and the rustle and turn of papers and the scratch of a pen, and perhaps the buzz of a fly banging with a tiny high anger against the tallest clear pane of window in the room. Sometimes the silence would go on this way until almost five, when Miss Taylor would find Bob Spaulding in the last seat of the room, sitting and looking at her silently, waiting for further orders.

"Well, it's time to go home," Miss Taylor would say, getting up.

"Yes'm."

And he would run to fetch her hat and coat. He would also lock the schoolroom door for her unless the janitor was coming in later. Then they would walk out of the school and across the yard, which was empty, the janitor taking down the chain swings slowly on his stepladder, the sun behind the umbrella trees. They talked of all sorts of things.

"And what are you going to be, Bob, when you grow up?"

"A writer," he said.

"Oh, that's a big ambition; it takes a lot of work."

"I know, but I'm going to try," he said. "I've read a lot."

"Bob, haven't you anything to do after school?"

"How do you mean?"

"I mean, I hate to see you kept in so much, washing the boards."

"I like it," he said. "I never do what I don't like."

"But nevertheless."

"No, I've got to do that," he said. He thought for a while and said, "Do me a favor, Miss Taylor?"

"It all depends."

"I walk every Saturday from out around Buetrick Street along the creek to Lake Michigan. There're a lot of butterflies and crayfish and birds. Maybe you'd like to walk, too."

"Thank you," she said.

"Then you'll come?"

"I'm afraid not."

"Don't you think it'd be fun?"

"Yes, I'm sure of that, but I'm going to be busy."

He started to ask doing what, but stopped.

"I take along sandwiches," he said. "Ham-and-pickle ones. And orange pop and just walk along, taking my time. I get down to the lake about noon and walk back and get home about three o'clock. It makes a real fine day, and I wish you'd come. Do you collect butterflies? I have a big collection. We could start one for you."

"Thanks, Bob, but no, perhaps some other time."

He looked at her and said, "I shouldn't have asked you, should I?"

"You have every right to ask anything you want to," she said.

A few days later she found an old copy of *Great Expectations*, which she no longer wanted, and gave it to Bob. He was very grateful and took it home and stayed up that night and read it through and talked about it the next morning. Each day now he met her just beyond sight of her boarding house and many days she would start to say, "Bob—" and tell him not to come to meet her any more, but she never finished saying it, and he talked with her about Dickens and Kipling and Poe and others, coming and going to school. She found a butterfly on her desk on Friday morning. She almost waved it away before she found it was dead and had been placed there while she was out of the room. She glanced at Bob over the heads of her other students, but he was looking at his book; not reading, just looking at it.

It was about this time that she found it impossible to call on Bob to recite in class. She would hover her pencil about his name and then call the next person up or down the list. Nor would she look at him while they were walking to or from school. But on several late afternoons as he moved his arm high on the blackboard, sponging away the arithmetic symbols, she found herself glancing over at him for seconds at a time before she returned to her papers.

And then on Saturday morning he was standing in the middle of the creek with his overalls rolled up to his knees, kneeling down to catch a crayfish under a rock, when he looked up and there on the edge of the running stream was Miss Ann Taylor.

"Well, here I am," she said, laughing.

"And do you know," he said, "I'm not surprised."

"Show me the crayfish and the butterflies," she said.

They walked down to the lake and sat on the sand with a warm wind blowing softly about them, fluttering her hair and the ruffle on her blouse, and he sat a few yards back from her and they ate the ham-and-pickle sandwiches and drank the orange pop solemnly.

"Gee, this is swell," he said. "This is the swellest time ever in my life."

"I didn't think I would ever come on a picnic like this," she said.

"With some kid," he said.

"I'm comfortable, however," she said.

"That's good news."

They said little else during the afternoon.

"This is all wrong," he said, later. "And I can't figure why it should be. Just walking along and catching old butterflies and crayfish and eating sandwiches. But Mom and Dad'd rib the heck out of me if they knew, and the kids would, too. And the other teachers, I suppose, would laugh at you, wouldn't they?"

"I'm afraid so."

"I guess we better not do any more butterfly catching, then."

"I don't exactly understand how I came here at all," she said.

And the day was over.

That was about all there was to the meeting of Ann Taylor and Bob Spaulding, two or three monarch butterflies, a copy of Dickens, a dozen crayfish, four sandwiches, and two bottles of Orange Crush. The next Monday, quite unexpectedly, though he waited a long time, Bob did not see Miss Taylor come out to walk to school, but discovered later that she had left earlier and was already at school. Also, Monday night, she left early, with a headache, and another teacher finished her last class. He walked by her boarding house but did not see her anywhere, and he was afraid to ring the bell and inquire.

On Tuesday night after school they were both in the silent room again, he sponging the board contentedly, as if this time might go on forever, and she seated, working on her papers as if she, too, would be in this room and this particular peace and happiness forever, when suddenly the courthouse clock struck. It was a block away and its great bronze boom shuddered one's body and made the ash of time shake away off your bones and slide through your blood, making you seem older by the minute. Stunned by that clock, you could not but sense the crashing flow of time, and as the clock said five o'clock, Miss Taylor suddenly looked up at it for a long time, and then she put down her pen.

"Bob," she said.

He turned, startled. Neither of them had spoken in the peaceful and good hour before.

"Will you come here?" she asked.

He put down the sponge slowly.

"Yes," he said.

"Bob, I want you to sit down."

"Yes'm."

She looked at him intently for a moment until he looked away. "Bob, I wonder if you know what I'm going to talk to you about. Do you know?"

"Yes."

"Maybe it'd be a good idea if you told me, first."

"About us," he said, at last.

"How old are you, Bob?"

"Going on fourteen."

"You're thirteen years old."

He winced. "Yes'm."

"And do you know how old I am?"

"Yes'm. I heard. Twenty-four."

"Twenty-four."

"I'll be twenty-four in ten years, almost," he said.

"But unfortunately you're not twenty-four now."

"No, but sometimes I feel twenty-four."

"Yes, and sometimes you almost act it."

"Do I, really!"

"Now sit still there; don't bound around, we've a lot of discuss. It's very important that we understand what is happening, don't you agree?"

"Yes, I guess so."

"First, let's admit we are the greatest and best friends in the world. Let's admit I have never had a student like you, nor have I had as much affection for any boy I've ever known." He flushed at this. She went on. "And let me speak for you—you've found me to be the nicest teacher of all the teachers you've ever known."

"Oh, more than that," he said.

"Perhaps more than that, but there are facts to be faced and an entire way of life to be examined, and a town and its people, and you and me to be considered. I've thought this over for a good many days, Bob. Don't think I've missed anything, or been unaware of my own feelings in the matter. Under some circumstances our friendship would be odd indeed. But then you are no ordinary boy. I know myself pretty well, I think, and I know I'm not sick, either mentally or physically, and that whatever has evolved here has been a true regard for your character and goodness, Bob; but those are not the things we consider in this world, Bob, unless they occur in a man of a certain age. I don't know if I'm saying this right."

"It's all right," he said. "It's just if I was ten years older and about fifteen inches taller it'd make all the difference, and that's silly," he said, "to go by how tall a person is."

"The world hasn't found it so."

"I'm not the world," he protested.

"I know it seems foolish," she said. "When you feel very grown up and right and have nothing to be ashamed of. You have nothing at all to be ashamed of, Bob, remember that. You have been very honest and good, and I hope I have been, too."

"You have," he said.

"In an ideal climate, Bob, maybe someday they will be able to judge the oldness of a person's mind so accurately that they can say, 'This is a man, though his body is only thirteen; by some miracle of circumstance and fortune, this is a man, with a man's recognition of responsibility and position and duty'; but until that day, Bob, I'm afraid we're going to have to go by ages and heights in the ordinary way in an ordinary world."

"I don't like that," he said.

"Perhaps I don't like it, either, but do you want to end up far unhappier than you are now? Do you want both of us to be unhappy? Which we would certainly be. There really is no way to do anything about us—it is so strange even to try to talk about us."

"Yes'm."

"But at least we know all about us and the fact that we have been right and fair and good and there is nothing wrong with our knowing each other, nor did we ever intend that it should be, for we both understand how impossible it is, don't we?"

"Yes, I know. But I can't help it."

"Now we must decide what to do about it," she said. "Now only you and I know about this. Later, others might know. I can secure a transfer from this school to another one—"

"No!"

"Or I can have you transferred to another school."

"You don't have to do that," he said.

"Why?"

"We're moving. My folks and I, we're going to live in Madison. We're leaving next week."

"It has nothing to do with all this, has it?"

"No, no, everything's all right. It's just that my father has a new job there. It's only fifty miles away. I can see you, can't I, when I come to town?"

"Do you think that would be a good idea?"

"No, I guess not."

They sat awhile in the silent schoolroom.

"When did all of this happen?" he said, helplessly.

"I don't know," she said. "Nobody ever knows. They haven't known for thousands of years, and I don't think they ever will. People either like each other or don't, and sometimes two people like each other who shouldn't. I can't explain myself, and certainly you can't explain you."

"I guess I'd better get home," he said.

"You're not mad at me, are you?"

"Oh, gosh no, I could never be mad at you."

"There's one more thing. I want you to remember, there are compensations in life. There always are, or we wouldn't go on living. You don't feel well, now; neither do I. But something will happen to fix that. Do you believe that?"

"I'd like to."

"Well, it's true."

"If only," he said.

"What?"

"If only you'd wait for me," he blurted.

"Ten years?"

"I'd be twenty-four then."

"But I'd be thirty-four and another person entirely, perhaps. No, I don't think it can be done."

"Wouldn't you like it to be done?" he cried.

"Yes," she said quietly. "It's silly and it wouldn't work, but I would like it very much."

He sat there for a long time.

"I'll never forget you," he said.

"It's nice for you to say that, even though it can't be true, because life isn't that way. You'll forget."

"I'll never forget. I'll find a way of never forgetting you," he said.

She got up and went to erase the boards.

"I'll help you," he said.

"No, no," she said hastily. "You go on now, get home, and no more tending to the boards after school. I'll assign Helen Stevens to do it."

He left the school. Looking back, outside, he saw Miss Ann Taylor, for the last time, at the board, slowly washing out the chalked words, her hand moving up and down.

He moved away from the town the next week and was gone for sixteen years. Though he was only fifty miles away, he never got down to Green Town again until he was almost thirty and married, and then one spring they were driving through on their way to Chicago and stopped off for a day.

Bob left his wife at the hotel and walked around town and finally asked about Miss Ann Taylor, but no one remembered at first, and then one of them remembered.

"Oh, yes, the pretty teacher. She died in 1936, not long after you left."

Had she ever married? No, come to think of it, she never had.

He walked out to the cemetery in the afternoon and found her stone, which said, "Ann Taylor, born 1910, died 1936." And he thought, Twenty-six years old. Why, I'm three years older than you are now, Miss Taylor.

Later in the day the people in the town saw Bob Spaulding's wife strolling to meet him under the elm trees and the oak trees, and they all turned to watch her pass, for her face shifted with bright shadows as she walked; she was the fine peaches of summer in the snow of winter, and she was cool milk for cereal on a hot early-summer morning. And this was one of those rare few days in time when the climate was balanced like a maple leaf between winds that blow just right, one of those days that should have been named, everyone agreed, after Robert Spaulding's wife.

The Parrot Who Met Papa

The kidnapping was reported all around the world, of course.

It took a few days for the full significance of the news to spread from Cuba to the United States, to the Left Bank in Paris, and then finally to some small good café in Pamplona where the drinks were fine and the weather, somehow, was always just right.

But once the meaning of the news really hit, people were on the phone, Madrid was calling New York, New York was shouting south at Havana to verify, please verify, this crazy thing.

And then some woman in Venice, Italy, with a blurred voice called through, saying she was at Harry's Bar that very instant and was destroyed, this thing that had happened was terrible, a cultural heritage was placed in immense and irrevocable danger....

Not an hour later, I got a call from a baseball pitcher–*cum*–novelist who had been a great friend of Papa's and who now lived in Madrid half the year and Nairobi the rest. He was in tears, or sounded close to it.

"Tell me," he said, from halfway around the world, "what happened? What are the facts?"

Well, the facts were these: Down in Havana, Cuba, about fourteen kilometers from Papa's Finca Vigía home, there is a bar in which he used to drink. It is the one where they named a special drink for him, not the fancy one where he used to meet flashy literary lights such as K-K-Kenneth Tynan and, er, Tennessee W-Williams (as Mr. Tynan would say it). No, it is not the Floridita; it is a shirt-sleeves place with plain wooden tables, sawdust on the floor, and a big mirror like a dirty cloud behind the bar. Papa went there when there were too many tourists around the Floridita who wanted to meet Mr. Hemingway. And the thing that happened there was destined to be big news, bigger than the report of what he said to Fitzgerald about the rich, even bigger than the story of his swing at Max Eastman on that long-ago day in Charlie Scribner's office. This news had to do with an ancient parrot.

That senior bird lived in a cage right atop the bar in the Cuba Libre. He had "kept his cage" in that place for roughly twenty-nine years, which means that the old parrot had been there almost as long as Papa had lived in Cuba.

And that adds up to this monumental fact: All during the time Papa had lived in Finca Vigía, he had known the parrot and had talked to him and the parrot had talked back. As the years passed, people said that Hemingway began to talk like the parrot and others said no, the parrot learned to talk like *him*! Papa used to line the drinks up on the counter and sit near the cage and involve that bird in the best kind of conversation you ever heard, four nights running. By the end of the second year, that parrot knew more about Hem and Thomas Wolfe and Sherwood Anderson than Gertrude Stein did. In fact, the parrot even knew who Gertrude Stein *was*. All you had to say was "Gertrude" and the parrot said:

"Pigeons on the grass alas."

At other times, pressed, the parrot would say, "There was this old man and this boy and this boat and this sea and this big fish in the sea. . . . " And then it would take time out to eat a cracker.

Well, this fabled creature, this parrot, this odd bird, vanished, cage and all, from the Cuba Libre late one Sunday afternoon.

And that's why my phone was ringing itself off the hook. And that's why one of the big magazines got a special State Department clearance and flew me down to Cuba to see if I could find so much as the cage, anything remaining of the bird or anyone resembling a kidnapper. They wanted a light and amiable article, with overtones, as they said. And, very honestly, I was curious. I had heard rumors of the bird. In a strange kind of way, I was concerned.

I got off the jet from Mexico City and taxied straight across Havana to that strange little café-bar.

I almost failed to get in the place. As I stepped through the door, a dark little man jumped up from a chair and cried, "No, no! Go away! We are closed!"

He ran out to jiggle the lock on the door, showing that he really meant to shut the place down. All the tables were empty and there was no one around. He had probably just been airing out the bar when I arrived.

"I've come about the parrot," I said.

"No, no," he cried, his eyes looking wet. "I won't talk. It's too much. If I were not Catholic, I would kill myself. Poor Papa. Poor El Córdoba!"

"El Córdoba?" I murmured.

"That," he said fiercely, "was the parrot's name!"

"Yes," I said, recovering quickly. "El Córdoba. I've come to rescue him."

That made him stop and blink. Shadows and then sunlight went over his face and then shadows again. "Impossible! Could you? No, no. How could anyone! Who *are* you?"

"A friend to Papa and the bird," I said quickly. "And the more time we talk, the farther away goes the criminal. You want El Córdoba back tonight? Pour us several of Papa's good drinks and talk."

My bluntness worked. Not two minutes later, we were drinking Papa's special, seated in the bar near the empty place where the cage used to sit. The little man, whose name was Antonio, kept wiping that empty place and then wiping his eyes with the bar rag. As I finished the first drink and started on the second, I said:

"This is no ordinary kidnapping."

"You're telling me!" cried Antonio. "People came from all over the world to see that parrot, to talk to El Córdoba, to hear him, ah, God, speak with the voice of Papa. May his abductors sink and burn in hell, yes, hell."

"They will," I said. "Whom do you suspect?"

"Everyone. No one."

"The kidnapper," I said, eyes shut for a moment, savoring the drink, "had to be educated, a book reader, I mean, that's obvious, isn't it? Anyone like that around the last few days?"

"Educated. No education. *Señor*, there have always been strangers the last ten, the last twenty years, always asking for Papa. When Papa was here, they met him. With Papa gone, they met El Córdoba, the great one. So it was always strangers and strangers."

"But think, Antonio," I said, touching his trembling elbow. "Not only educated, a reader, but someone in the last few days who was—how shall I put it?—odd. Strange. Someone so peculiar, *muy ecéntrico*, that you remember him above all others. Someone who—"

"*Madre de Dios!*" cried Antonio, leaping up. His eyes stared off into memory. He seized his head as if it had just exploded. "Thank you, *señor. Sí, sí!* What a creature! In the name of Christ, there was such a one yesterday! He was very small. And he spoke like this: very high—*eeeee*. Like a *muchacha* in a school play, eh? Like a canary swallowed by a witch! And he wore a blue-velvet suit with a big yellow tie."

"Yes, yes!" I had leaped up now and was almost yelling. "Go on!"

"And he had a small very round face, *señor*, and his hair was yellow and cut across the brow like this—*zitt*! And his mouth small, very pink, like candy, yes? He—he was like, yes, *uno muñeco*, of the kind one wins at carnivals."

"Kewpie dolls!"

"*Sí!* At Coney Island, yes, when I was a child, Kewpie dolls! And he was so high, you see? To my elbow. Not a midget, no—but—and how old? Blood of Christ, who can say? No lines in his face, but—thirty, forty, fifty. And on his feet he was wearing—"

"Green booties!" I cried.

"*Qué?*"

"Shoes, boots!"

"*Sí.*" He blinked, stunned. "But how did you *know*?"

I exploded, "Shelley Capon!"

"That is the name! And his friends with him, *señor*, all laughing—no, giggling. Like the nuns who play basketball in the late afternoons near the church. Oh, *señor*, do you think that they, that he—"

"I don't think, Antonio, I *know*. Shelley Capon, of all the writers in the world, hated Papa. Of course he would snatch El Córdoba. Why, wasn't there a rumor once that the bird had memorized Papa's last, greatest, and as-yet-not-put-down-on-paper novel?"

"There was such a rumor, *señor*. But I do not write books, I tend bar. I bring crackers to the bird. I—"

"You bring me the phone, Antonio, please."

"You know where the bird is, *señor*?"

"I have the hunch beyond intuition, the big one. *Gracias*." I dialed the Havana Libre, the biggest hotel in town.

"Shelley Capon, please."

The phone buzzed and clicked.

Half a million miles away, a midget boy Martian lifted the receiver and played the flute and then the bell chimes with his voice: "Capon here."

"Damned if you aren't!" I said. And got up and ran out of the Cuba Libre bar.

Racing back to Havana by taxi, I thought of Shelley as I'd seen him before. Surrounded by a storm of friends, living out of suitcases, ladling soup from other people's plates, borrowing money from billfolds seized from your pockets right in front of you, counting the lettuce leaves with relish, leaving rabbit pellets on your rug, gone. Dear Shelley Capon.

Ten minutes later, my taxi with no brakes dropped me running and spun on to some ultimate disaster beyond town.

Still running, I made the lobby, paused for information, hurried upstairs, and stopped short before Shelley's door. It pulsed in spasms like a bad heart. I put my ear to the door. The wild calls and cries from inside might have come from a flock of birds, feather-stripped in a hurricane. I felt the door. Now it seemed to tremble like a vast laundromat that had swallowed and was churning an acid-rock group and a lot of very dirty linen. Listening, my underwear began to crawl on my legs.

I knocked. No answer. I touched the door. It drifted open. I stepped in upon a scene much too dreadful for Bosch to have painted.

Around the pigpen living room were strewn various life-size dolls, eyes half-cracked open, cigarettes smoking in burned, limp fingers, empty Scotch glasses in hands, and all the while the radio belted them with concussions of music broadcast from some Stateside asylum. The place was sheer carnage. Not ten seconds ago, I felt, a large dirty locomotive must have plunged through here. Its victims had been hurled in all directions and now lay upside down in various parts of the room, moaning for first aid.

In the midst of this hell, seated erect and proper, well dressed in velveteen jerkin, persimmon bow tie, and bottle-green booties, was, of course, Shelley Capon. Who with no surprise at all waved a drink at me and cried:

"I *knew* that was you on the phone. I am absolutely telepathic! Welcome, Raimundo!"

He always called me Raimundo. Ray was plain bread and butter. Raimundo made me a don with a breeding farm full of bulls. I let it be Raimundo.

"Raimundo, sit down! No . . . fling yourself into an *interesting* position."

"Sorry," I said in my best Dashiell Hammett manner, sharpening my chin and steeling my eyes. "No time."

I began to walk around the room among his friends Fester and Soft and Ripply and Mild Innocuous and some actor I remembered who, when asked how he would do a part in a film, had said, "I'll play it like a doe."

I shut off the radio. That made a lot of people in the room stir. I yanked the radio's roots out of the wall. Some people sat up. I raised a window. I threw the radio out. They all screamed as if I had thrown their mothers down an elevator shaft.

The radio made a satisfying sound on the cement sidewalk below. I turned, with a beatific smile on my face. A number of people were on their feet, swaying toward me with faint menace. I pulled a twenty-dollar bill out of my pocket, handed it to someone without looking at him, and said, "Go buy a new one." He ran out the door slowly. The door slammed. I heard him fall down the stairs as if he were after his morning shot in the arm.

"All right, Shelley," I said, "where is it?"

"Where is *what*, dear boy?" he said, eyes wide with innocence.

"You know what I mean." I stared at the drink in his tiny hand.

Which was a Papa drink, the Cuba Libre's very own special blend of papaya, lime, lemon, and rum. As if to destroy evidence, he drank it down quickly.

I walked over to three doors in a wall and touched one.

"That's a closet, dear boy." I put my hand on the second door.

"Don't go in. You'll be sorry what you see." I didn't go in.

I put my hand on the third door. "Oh, dear, well, go ahead," said Shelley petulantly. I opened the door.

Beyond it was a small anteroom with a mere cot and a table near the window.

On the table sat a bird cage with a shawl over it. Under the shawl I could hear the rustle of feathers and the scrape of a beak on the wires.

Shelley Capon came to stand small beside me, looking in at the cage, a fresh drink in his little fingers.

"What a shame you didn't arrive at seven tonight," he said.

"Why seven?"

"Why, then, Raimundo, we would have just finished our curried fowl stuffed with wild rice. I wonder, is there much white meat, or any at all, under a parrot's feathers?"

"You wouldn't!?" I cried.

I stared at him.

"You would," I answered myself.

I stood for a moment longer at the door. Then, slowly, I walked across the small room and stopped by the cage with the shawl over it. I saw a single word embroidered across the top of the shawl: MOTHER.

I glanced at Shelley. He shrugged and looked shyly at his boot tips. I took hold of the shawl. Shelley said, "No. Before you lift it . . . ask something."

"Like what?"

"DiMaggio. Ask DiMaggio."

A small ten-watt bulb clicked on in my head. I nodded. I leaned near the hidden cage and whispered: "DiMaggio. 1939."

There was a sort of animal-computer pause. Beneath the word MOTHER some feathers stirred, a beak tapped the cage bars. Then a tiny voice said:

"Home runs, thirty. Batting average, .381."

I was stunned. But then I whispered: "Babe Ruth. 1927."

Again the pause, the feathers, the beak, and: "Home runs, sixty. Batting average, .356. Awk."

"My God," I said.

"My God," echoed Shelley Capon.

"That's the parrot who met Papa, all right."

"That's who it is."

And I lifted the shawl.

I don't know what I expected to find underneath the embroidery. Perhaps a miniature hunter in boots, bush jacket, and wide-brimmed hat. Perhaps a small, trim fisherman with a beard and turtleneck sweater perched there on a wooden slat. Something tiny, something literary, something human, something fantastic, but not really a parrot.

But that's all there was.

And not a very handsome parrot, either. It looked as if it had been up all night for years; one of those disreputable birds that never preens its feathers or shines its beak. It was a kind of rusty green and black with a dull-amber snout and rings under its eyes as if it were a secret drinker. You might see it half flying, half hopping out of café-bars at three in the morning. It was the bum of the parrot world.

Shelley Capon read my mind. "The effect is better," he said, "with the shawl over the cage."

I put the shawl back over the bars.

I was thinking very fast. Then I thought very slowly. I bent and whispered by the cage:

"Norman Mailer."

"Couldn't remember the alphabet," said the voice beneath the shawl.

"Gertrude Stein," I said.

"Suffered from undescended testicles," said the voice.

"My God," I gasped.

I stepped back. I stared at the covered cage. I blinked at Shelley Capon.

"Do you really *know* what you have here, Capon?"

"A *gold* mine, dear Raimundo!" he crowed.

"A *mint*!" I corrected.

"Endless opportunities for blackmail!"

"Causes for murder!" I added.

"Think!" Shelley snorted into his drink. "Think what Mailer's publishers *alone* would pay to shut this bird up!"

I spoke to the cage:

"F. Scott Fitzgerald."

Silence.

"Try 'Scottie,'" said Shelley.

"Ah," said the voice inside the cage. "Good left jab but couldn't follow through. Nice contender, but—"

"Faulkner," I said.

"Batting average fair, strictly a singles hitter."

"Steinbeck!"

"Finished last at end of season."

"Ezra Pound!"

"Traded off to the minor leagues in 1932."

"I think...I need...one of those drinks." Someone put a drink in my hand. I gulped it and nodded. I shut my eyes and felt the world give one turn, then opened my eyes to look at Shelley Capon, the classic son of a bitch of all time.

"There is something even more fantastic," he said. "You've heard only the first half."

"You're lying," I said. "What could there be?"

He dimpled at me—in all the world, only Shelley Capon can dimple at you in a completely evil way. "It was like this," he said. "You remember that Papa had trouble actually getting his stuff down on paper in those last years while he lived here? Well, he'd planned another novel after *Islands in the Stream*, but somehow it just never seemed to get written.

"Oh, he had it in his mind, all right—the story was there and lots of people heard him mention it—but he just couldn't seem to write it. So he would go to the Cuba Libre and drink many drinks and have long conversations with the parrot. Raimundo, what Papa was telling El Córdoba all through those long drinking nights was the story of his last book. And, in the course of time, the bird has memorized it."

"*His very last book!*" I said. "The final Hemingway novel of all time! Never written but recorded in the brain of a parrot! Holy Jesus!"

Shelley was nodding at me with the smile of a depraved cherub.

"How much do you want for this bird?"

"Dear, dear Raimundo." Shelley Capon stirred his drink with his pinkie. "What makes you think the creature is for sale?"

"You sold your mother once, then stole her back and sold her again under another name. Come off it, Shelley. You're onto something big." I brooded over the shawled cage. "How many telegrams have you sent out in the last four or five hours?"

"Really! You horrify me!"

"How many long-distance phone calls, reverse charges, have you made since breakfast?"

Shelley Capon mourned a great sigh and pulled a crumpled telegram duplicate from his velveteen pocket. I took it and read:

FRIENDS OF PAPA MEETING HAVANA TO REMINISCE OVER BIRD AND
BOTTLE. WIRE BID OR BRING CHECKBOOKS AND OPEN MINDS. FIRST
COME FIRST SERVED. ALL WHITE MEAT BUT CAVIAR PRICES. INTERNA-
TIONAL PUBLICATION, BOOK, MAGAZINE, TV, FILM RIGHTS AVAILABLE.
LOVE. SHELLEY YOU-KNOW-WHO.

My God again, I thought, and let the telegram fall to the floor as Shelley handed me a list of names the telegram had been sent to:

Time. Life. Newsweek. Scribner's. Simon & Schuster. *The New York Times. The Christian Science Monitor. The Times of London. Le Monde. Paris-Match.* One of the Rockefellers. Some of the Kennedys. CBS. NBC. MGM. Warner Bros. 20th Century-Fox. And on and on and on. The list was as long as my deepening melancholy.

Shelley Capon tossed an armful of answering telegrams onto the table near the cage. I leafed through them quickly.

Everyone, but everyone, was in the air, right now. Jets were streaming in from all over the world. In another two hours, four, six at the most, Cuba would be swarming with agents, publishers, fools, and plain damn fools, plus counter-espionage kidnappers and blonde starlets who hoped to be in front-page photographs with the bird on their shoulders.

I figured I had maybe a good half hour left in which to do something, I didn't know what.

Shelley nudged my arm. "Who sent you, dear boy? You *are* the very first, you know. Make a fine bid and you're in free, maybe. I must consider other offers, of course. But it might get thick and nasty here. I begin to panic at what I've done. I may wish to sell cheap and flee. Because, well, think, there's the problem of getting this bird out of the country, yes? And, simultaneously, Castro might declare the parrot a national monument or work of art, or, oh, hell, Raimundo, who *did* send you?"

"Someone, but now no one," I said, brooding. "I came on behalf of someone else. I'll go away on my own. From now on, anyway, it's just me and the bird. I've read Papa all my life. Now I know I came just because I had to."

"My God, an altruist!"

"Sorry to offend you, Shelley."

The phone rang. Shelley got it. He chatted happily for a moment, told someone to wait downstairs, hung up, and cocked an eyebrow at me: "NBC is in the lobby. They want an hour's taped interview with El Córdoba there. They're talking six figures."

My shoulders slumped. The phone rang. This time I picked it up, to my own surprise. Shelley cried out. But I said, "Hello. Yes?"

"*Señor*," said a man's voice. "There is a *Señor* Hobwell here from *Time*, he says, magazine." I could see the parrot's face on next week's cover, with six follow-up pages of text.

"Tell him to wait." I hung up.

"*Newsweek?*" guessed Shelley.

"The other one," I said.

"The snow was fine up in the shadow of the hills," said the voice inside the cage under the shawl.

"Shut up," I said quietly, wearily. "Oh, shut up, damn you."

Shadows appeared in the doorway behind us. Shelley Capon's friends were beginning to assemble and wander into the room. They gathered and I began to tremble and sweat.

For some reason, I began to rise to my feet. My body was going to do something, I didn't know what. I watched my hands. Suddenly, the right hand reached out. It knocked the cage over, snapped the wire-frame door wide, and darted in to seize the parrot.

"No!"

There was a great gasping roar, as if a single thunderous wave had come in on a shore. Everyone in the room seemed knocked in the stomach by my action. Everyone exhaled, took a step, began to yell, but by then I had the parrot out. I had it by the throat.

"No! No!" Shelley jumped at me. I kicked him in the shins. He sat down, screaming.

"Don't anyone move!" I said and almost laughed, hearing myself use the old cliché. "You ever see a chicken killed? This parrot has a thin neck. One twist, the head comes off. Nobody move a hair." Nobody moved.

"You son of a bitch," said Shelley Capon, on the floor.

For a moment, I thought they were all going to rush me. I saw myself beaten and chased along the beach, yelling, the cannibals ringing me in and eating me, Tennessee Williams style, shoes and all. I felt sorry for my skeleton, which would be found in the main Havana plaza at dawn tomorrow.

But they did not hit, pummel, or kill. As long as I had my fingers around the neck of the parrot who met Papa, I knew I could stand there forever.

I wanted with all my heart, soul, and guts to wring the bird's neck and throw its disconnected carcass into those pale and gritty faces. I wanted to stop up the past and destroy Papa's preserved memory forever, if it was going to be played with by feeble-minded children like these.

But I could not, for two reasons. One dead parrot would mean one dead

duck: me. And I was weeping inside for Papa. I simply could not shut off his voice transcribed here, held in my hands, still alive, like an old Edison record. I could not kill.

If these ancient children had known that, they would have swarmed over me like locusts. But they didn't know. And, I guess, it didn't show in my face.

"Stand back!" I cried.

It was that beautiful last scene from *The Phantom of the Opera* where Lon Chaney, pursued through midnight Paris, turns on the mob, lifts his clenched fist as if it contained an explosive, and holds the mob at bay for one terrific instant. He laughs, opens his hand to show it empty, and then is driven to his death in the river.... Only I had no intention of letting them see an empty hand. I kept it close around El Córdoba's scrawny neck.

"Clear a path to the door!" They cleared a path.

"Not a move, not a breath. If anyone so much as swoons, this bird is dead forever and no rights, no movies, no photos. Shelley, bring me the cage and the shawl."

Shelley Capon edged over and brought me the cage and its cover. "Stand off!" I yelled.

Everyone jumped back another foot.

"Now, hear this," I said. "After I've got away and have hidden out, one by one each of you will be called to have his chance to meet Papa's friend here again and cash in on the headlines."

I was lying. I could hear the lie. I hoped they couldn't. I spoke more quickly now, to cover the lie: "I'm going to start walking now. Look. See? I have the parrot by the neck. He'll stay alive as long as you play 'Simon says' my way. Here we go, now. One, two. One, two. Halfway to the door." I walked among them and they did not breathe. "One, two," I said, my heart beating in my mouth. "At the door. Steady. No sudden moves. Cage in one hand. Bird in the other—"

"The lions ran along the beach on the yellow sand," said the parrot, his throat moving under my fingers.

"Oh, my God," said Shelley, crouched there by the table. Tears began to pour down his face. Maybe it wasn't all money. Maybe some of it was Papa for him, too. He put his hands out in a beckoning, come-back gesture to me, the parrot, the cage. "Oh, God, oh, God." He wept.

"There was only the carcass of the great fish lying by the pier, its bones picked clean in the morning light," said the parrot.

"Oh," said everyone softly.

I didn't wait to see if any more of them were weeping. I stepped out. I shut the door. I ran for the elevator. By a miracle, it was there, the operator half asleep inside. No one tried to follow. I guess they knew it was no use.

On the way down, I put the parrot inside the cage and put the shawl marked MOTHER over the cage. And the elevator moved slowly down through the years. I thought of those years ahead and where I might hide the parrot and

keep him warm against any weather and feed him properly and once a day go in and talk through the shawl, and nobody ever to see him, no papers, no magazines, no cameramen, no Shelley Capon, not even Antonio from the Cuba Libre. Days might go by or weeks and sudden fears might come over me that the parrot had gone dumb. Then, in the middle of the night I might wake and shuffle in and stand by his cage and say:

"Italy, 1918. . . ?"

And beneath the word MOTHER, an old voice would say: "The snow drifted off the edges of the mountain in a fine white dust that winter. . . ."

"Africa, 1932."

"We got the rifles out and oiled the rifles and they were blue and fine and lay in our hands and we waited in the tall grass and smiled—"

"Cuba. The Gulf Stream."

"That fish came out of the water and jumped as high as the sun. Everything I had ever thought about a fish was in that fish. Everything I had ever thought about a single leap was in that leap. All of my life was there. It was a day of sun and water and being alive. I wanted to hold it all still in my hands. I didn't want it to go away, ever. Yet there, as the fish fell and the waters moved over it white and then green, there it went. . . ."

By that time, we were at the lobby level and the elevator doors opened and I stepped out with the cage labeled MOTHER and walked quickly across the lobby and out to a taxicab.

The trickiest business—and my greatest danger—remained. I knew that by the time I got to the airport, the guards and the Castro militia would have been alerted. I wouldn't put it past Shelley Capon to tell them that a national treasure was getting away. He might even cut Castro in on some of the Book-of-the-Month Club revenue and the movie rights. I had to improvise a plan to get through customs.

I am a literary man, however, and the answer came to me quickly. I had the taxi stop long enough for me to buy some shoe polish. I began to apply the disguise to El Córdoba. I painted him black all over.

"Listen," I said, bending down to whisper into the cage as we drove across Havana. "*Nevermore.*"

I repeated it several times to give him the idea. The sound would be new to him, because, I guessed, Papa would never have quoted a middleweight contender he had knocked out years ago. There was silence under the shawl while the word was recorded.

Then, at last, it came back to me. "Nevermore," in Papa's old, familiar, tenor voice, "nevermore," it said.

The October Game

He put the gun back into the bureau drawer and shut the drawer.

No, not that way. Louise wouldn't suffer that way. She would be dead and it would be over and she wouldn't suffer. It was very important that this thing have, above all, duration. Duration through imagination. How to prolong the suffering? How, first of all, to bring it about? Well.

The man standing before the bedroom mirror carefully fitted his cuff links together. He paused long enough to hear the children run by swiftly on the street below, outside this warm two-story house; like so many gray mice the children, like so many leaves.

By the sound of the children you knew the calendar day. By their screams you knew what evening it was. You knew it was very late in the year. October. The last day of October, with white bone masks and cut pumpkins and the smell of dropped candle fat.

No. Things hadn't been right for some time. October didn't help any. If anything it made things worse. He adjusted his black bow tie. If this were spring, he nodded slowly, quietly, emotionlessly, at his image in the mirror, then there might be a chance. But tonight all the world was burning down into ruin. There was no green of spring, none of the freshness, none of the promise.

There was a soft running in the hall. "That's Marion," he told himself. "My little one. All eight quiet years of her. Never a word. Just her luminous gray eyes and her wondering little mouth." His daughter had been in and out all evening, trying on various masks, asking him which was most terrifying, most horrible. They had both finally decided on the skeleton mask. It was "just awful!" It would "scare the beans" from people!

Again he caught the long look of thought and deliberation he gave himself in the mirror. He had never liked October. Ever since he first lay in the autumn leaves before his grandmother's house many years ago and heard the wind and saw the empty trees. It had made him cry, without a reason. And a little of that sadness returned each year to him. It always went away with spring.

But, it was different tonight. There was a feeling of autumn coming to last a million years.

There would be no spring.

He had been crying quietly all evening. It did not show, not a vestige of it, on his face. It was all hidden somewhere and it wouldn't stop.

A rich syrupy smell of candy filled the bustling house. Louise had laid out apples in new skins of caramel; there were vast bowls of punch fresh-mixed, stringed apples in each door, scooped, vented pumpkins peering triangularly from each cold window. There was a water tub in the center of the living room, waiting, with a sack of apples nearby, for dunking to begin. All that was needed was the catalyst, the inpouring of children, to start the apples bobbling, the stringed apples to penduluming in the crowded doors, the candy to vanish, the halls to echo with fright or delight, it was all the same.

Now the house was silent with preparation. And just a little more than that.

Louise had managed to be in every other room today save the room he was in. It was her very fine way of intimating, Oh look, Mich, see how busy I am! So busy that when you walk into a room *I'm* in there's always something I need to do in *another* room! Just see how I dash about!

For a while he had played a little game with her, a nasty childish game. When she was in the kitchen, then he came to the kitchen saying, "I need a glass of water." After a moment, he standing, drinking water, she like a crystal witch over the caramel brew bubbling like a prehistoric mudpot on the stove, she said, "Oh, I must light the pumpkins!" and she rushed to the living room to make the pumpkins smile with light. He came after her, smiling. "I must get my pipe." "Oh, the cider!" she had cried, running to the dining room. "I'll check the cider," he had said. But when he tried following she ran to the bathroom and locked the door.

He stood outside the bathroom door, laughing strangely and senselessly, his pipe gone cold in his mouth, and then, tired of the game, but stubborn, he waited another five minutes. There was not a sound from the bath. And lest she enjoy in any way knowing that he waited outside, irritated, he suddenly jerked about and walked upstairs, whistling merrily.

At the top of the stairs he had waited. Finally he had heard the bathroom door unlatch and she had come out and life belowstairs had resumed, as life in a jungle must resume once a terror has passed on away and the antelope return to their spring.

Now, as he finished his bow tie and put on his dark coat there was a mouse-rustle in the hall. Marion appeared in the door, all skeletonous in her disguise.

"How do I look, Papa?"

"Fine!"

From under the mask, blonde hair showed. From the skull sockets small blue eyes smiled. He sighed. Marion and Louise, the two silent denouncers of his virility, his dark power. What alchemy had there been in Louise that took the dark of a dark man and bleached and bleached the dark brown eyes and black hair and washed and bleached the ingrown baby all during the period before birth until the child was born, Marion, blonde, blue-eyed, ruddy-cheeked?

Sometimes he suspected that Louise had conceived the child as an idea, completely asexual, an immaculate conception of contemptuous mind and cell. As a firm rebuke to him she had produced a child in her *own* image, and, to top it, she had somehow *fixed* the doctor so he shook his head and said, "Sorry, Mr. Wilder, your wife will never have another child. This is the *last* one."

"And I wanted a boy," Mich had said, eight years ago.

He almost bent to take hold of Marion now, in her skull mask. He felt an inexplicable rush of pity for her, because she had never had a father's love, only the crushing, holding love of a loveless mother. But most of all he pitied himself, that somehow he had not made the most of a bad birth, enjoyed his daughter for herself, regardless of her not being dark and a son and like himself. Somewhere he had missed out. Other things being equal, he would have loved the child. But Louise hadn't wanted a child, anyway, in the first place. She had been frightened of the idea of birth. He had forced the child on her, and from that night, all through the year until the agony of the birth itself, Louise had lived in another part of the house. She had expected to die with the forced child. It had been very easy for Louise to hate this husband who so wanted a son that he gave his only wife over to the mortuary.

But—Louise had lived. And in triumph! Her eyes, the day he came to the hospital, were cold. I'm alive, they said. And I have a *blonde* daughter! Just look! And when he had put out a hand to touch, the mother had turned away to conspire with her new pink daughter-child—away from that dark forcing murderer. It had all been so beautifully ironic. His selfishness deserved it.

But now it was October again. There had been other Octobers and when he thought of the long winter he had been filled with horror year after year to think of the endless months mortared into the house by an insane fall of snow, trapped with a woman and child, neither of whom loved him, for months on end. During the eight years there had been respites. In spring and summer you got out, walked, picnicked; these were desperate solutions to the desperate problem of a hated man.

But, in winter, the hikes and picnics and escapes fell away with the leaves. Life, like a tree, stood empty, the fruit picked, the sap run to earth. Yes, you invited people in, but people were hard to get in winter with blizzards and all. Once he had been clever enough to save for a Florida trip. They had gone south. He had walked in the open.

But now, the eighth winter coming, he knew things were finally at an end. He simply could not wear this one through. There was an acid walled off in him that slowly had eaten through tissue and bone over the years, and now, tonight, it would reach the wild explosive in him and all would be over!

There was a mad ringing of the bell below. In the hall, Louise went to see. Marion, without a word, ran down to greet the first arrivals. There were shouts and hilarity.

He walked to the top of the stairs.

Louise was below, taking wraps. She was tall and slender and blonde to the point of whiteness, laughing down upon the new children.

He hesitated. What was all this? The years? The boredom of living? Where had it gone wrong? Certainly not with the birth of the child alone. But it had been a symbol of all their tensions, he imagined. His jealousies and his business failures and all the rotten rest of it. Why didn't he just turn, pack a suitcase, and leave? No. Not without hurting Louise as much as she had hurt him. It was simple as that. Divorce wouldn't hurt her at all. It would simply be an end to numb indecision. If he thought divorce would give her pleasure in any way he would stay married the rest of his life to her, for damned spite. No, he must hurt her. Figure some way, perhaps, to take Marion away from her, legally. Yes. That was it. That would hurt most of all. To take Marion away.

"Hello down there!" He descended the stairs, beaming.

Louise didn't look up.

"Hi, Mr. Wilder!"

The children shouted, waved, as he came down.

By ten o'clock the doorbell had stopped ringing, the apples were bitten from stringed doors, the pink child faces were wiped dry from the apple bobbing, napkins were smeared with caramel and punch, and he, the husband, with pleasant efficiency had taken over. He took the party right out of Louise's hands. He ran about talking to the twenty children and the twelve parents who had come and were happy with the special spiked cider he had fixed them. He supervised pin the tail on the donkey, spin the bottle, musical chairs, and all the rest, amid fits of shouting laughter. Then, in the triangular-eyed pumpkin shine, all house lights out, he cried, "Hush! Follow me!" tiptoeing toward the cellar.

The parents, on the periphery of the costumed riot, commented to each other, nodding at the clever husband, speaking to the lucky wife. How *well* he got on with children, they said.

The children crowded after the husband, squealing.

"The cellar!" he cried. "The tomb of the witch!"

More squealing. He made a mock shiver. "Abandon hope all ye who enter here!"

The parents chuckled.

One by one the children slid down a slide which Mich had fixed up from lengths of table-section, into the dark cellar. He hissed and shouted ghastly utterances after them. A wonderful wailing filled the dark pumpkin-lighted house. Everybody talked at once. Everybody but Marion. She had gone through all the party with a minimum of sound or talk; it was all inside her, all the excitement and joy. What a little troll, he thought. With a shut mouth and shiny eyes she had watched her own party, like so many serpentines thrown before her.

Now, the parents. With laughing reluctance they slid down the short incline, uproarious, while little Marion stood by, always wanting to see it all, to be last. Louise went down without help. He moved to aid her, but she was gone even before he bent.

The upper house was empty and silent in the candle-shine.

Marion stood by the slide. "Here we go," he said, and picked her up.

They sat in a vast circle in the cellar. Warmth came from the distant bulk of the furnace. The chairs stood in a long line along each wall, twenty squealing children, twelve rustling relatives, alternately spaced, with Louise down at the far end, Mich up at this end, near the stairs. He peered but saw nothing. They had all grouped to their chairs, catch-as-you-can in the blackness. The entire program from here on was to be enacted in the dark, he as Mr. Interlocutor. There was a child scampering, a smell of damp cement, and the sound of the wind out in the October stars.

"Now!" cried the husband in the dark cellar. "Quiet!"

Everybody settled.

The room was black black. Not a light, not a shine, not a glint of an eye.

A scraping of crockery, a metal rattle.

"The witch is dead," intoned the husband.

"Eeeeeeeeeeeee," said the children.

"The witch is dead, she has been killed, and here is the knife she was killed with."

He handed over the knife. It was passed from hand to hand, down and around the circle, with chuckles and little odd cries and comments from the adults.

"The witch is dead, and this is her head," whispered the husband, and handed an item to the nearest person.

"Oh, I know how this game is played," some child cried, happily, in the dark. "He gets some old chicken innards from the icebox and hands them around and says, 'These are her innards!' And he makes a clay head and passes it for her head, and passes a soup bone for her arm. And he takes a marble and says, 'This is her eye!' And he takes some corn and says, 'This is her teeth!' And he takes a sack of plum pudding and gives that and says, 'This is her stomach!' I know how *this* is played!"

"Hush, you'll spoil everything," some girl said.

"The witch came to harm, and this is her arm," said Mich.

"Eeeee!"

The items were passed and passed, like hot potatoes, around the circle. Some children screamed, wouldn't touch them. Some ran from their chairs to stand in the center of the cellar until the grisly items had passed.

"Aw, it's only chicken insides," scoffed a boy. "Come back, Helen!"

Shot from hand to hand, with small scream after scream, the items went down, down, to be followed by another and another.

"The witch cut apart, and this is her heart," said the husband.

Six or seven items moving at once through the laughing, trembling dark.

Louise spoke up. "Marion, don't be afraid; it's only play."

Marion didn't say anything.

"Marion?" asked Louise. "Are you afraid?"

Marion didn't speak.

"She's all right," said the husband. "She's not afraid."

On and on the passing, the screams, the hilarity.

The autumn wind sighed about the house. And he, the husband, stood at the head of the dark cellar, intoning the words, handing out the items.

"Marion?" asked Louise again, from far across the cellar.

Everybody was talking.

"Marion?" called Louise.

Everybody quieted.

"Marion, answer me, are you afraid?"

Marion didn't answer.

The husband stood there, at the bottom of the cellar steps.

Louise called, "Marion, are you there?"

No answer. The room was silent.

"Where's Marion?" called Louise.

"She was here," said a boy.

"Maybe she's upstairs."

"Marion!"

No answer. It was quiet.

Louise cried out, "Marion, Marion!"

"Turn on the lights," said one of the adults.

The items stopped passing. The children and adults sat with the witch's items in their hands.

"No." Louise gasped. There was a scraping of her chair, wildly, in the dark. "No. Don't turn on the lights, oh, God, God, God, don't turn them on, please, please *don't* turn on the lights, *don't*!" Louise was shrieking now. The entire cellar froze with the scream.

Nobody moved.

Everyone sat in the dark cellar, suspended in the suddenly frozen task of this October game; the wind blew outside, banging the house, the smell of pumpkins and apples filled the room with the smell of the objects in their fingers while one boy cried, "I'll go upstairs and look!" and he ran upstairs hopefully and out around the house, four times around the house, calling, "Marion, Marion, Marion!" over and over and at last coming slowly down the stairs into the waiting breathing cellar and saying to the darkness, "I can't find her."

Then . . . some idiot turned on the lights.

Punishment Without Crime

"You wish to kill your wife?" said the dark man at the desk.

"Yes. No . . . not exactly. I mean . . ."

"Name?"

"Hers or mine?"

"Yours."

"George Hill."

"Address?"

"Eleven South Saint James, Glenview."

The man wrote this down, emotionlessly. "Your wife's name?"

"Katherine."

"Age?"

"Thirty-one."

Then came a swift series of questions. Color of hair, eyes, skin, favorite perfume, texture and size index. "Have you a dimensional photo of her? A tape recording of her voice? Ah, I see you do. Good. Now—"

An hour later, George Hill was perspiring.

"That's all." The dark man arose and scowled. "You still want to go through with it."

"Yes."

"Sign here."

He signed.

"You know this is illegal?"

"Yes."

"And that we're in no way responsible for what happens to you as a result of your request?"

"For God's sake!" cried George. "You've kept me long enough. Let's get on!"

The man smiled faintly. "It'll take nine hours to prepare the marionette of your wife. Sleep awhile, it'll help your nerves. The third mirror room on your left is unoccupied."

George moved in a slow numbness to the mirror room. He lay on the blue velvet cot, his body pressure causing the mirrors in the ceiling to whirl. A soft voice sang, "Sleep . . . sleep . . . sleep . . ."

George murmured, "Katherine, I didn't want to come here. You forced me into it. You made me do it. God, I wish I weren't here. I wish I could go back. I don't want to kill you."

The mirrors glittered as they rotated softly.

He slept.

He dreamed he was forty-one again, he and Katie running on a green hill somewhere with a picnic lunch, their helicopter beside them. The wind blew Katie's hair in golden strands and she was laughing. They kissed and held hands, not eating. They read poems; it seemed they were always reading poems.

Other scenes. Quick changes of color, in flight. He and Katie flying over Greece and Italy and Switzerland, in that clear, long autumn of 1997! Flying and never stopping!

And then—nightmare. Katie and Leonard Phelps. George cried out in his sleep. How had it happened? Where had Phelps sprung from? Why had he interfered? Why couldn't life be simple and good? Was it the difference in age? George touching fifty, and Katie so young, so very young. Why, why?

The scene was unforgettably vivid. Leonard Phelps and Katherine in a green park beyond the city. George himself appearing on a path only in time to see the kissing of their mouths.

The rage. The struggle. The attempt to kill Leonard Phelps.

More days, more nightmares.

George Hill awoke, weeping.

"Mr. Hill, we're ready for you now."

Hill arose clumsily. He saw himself in the high and now-silent mirrors, and he looked every one of his years. It had been a wretched error. Better men than he had taken young wives only to have them dissolve away in their hands like sugar crystals under water. He eyed himself, monstrously. A little too much stomach. A little too much chin. Somewhat too much pepper in the hair and not enough in the limbs . . .

The dark man led him to a room.

George Hill gasped. "This is *Katie's* room!"

"We try to have everything perfect."

"It *is*, to the last detail!"

George Hill drew forth a signed check for ten thousand dollars. The man departed with it.

The room was silent and warm.

George sat and felt for the gun in his pocket. A lot of money. But rich men can afford the luxury of cathartic murder. The violent unviolence. The death without death. The murder without murdering. He felt better. He was suddenly calm. He watched the door. This was a thing he had anticipated for six months and now it was to be ended. In a moment the beautiful robot, the stringless marionette, would appear, and . . .

"Hello, George."

"Katie!"

He whirled.

"Katie." He let his breath out.

She stood in the doorway behind him. She was dressed in a feather-soft green gown. On her feet were woven gold-twine sandals. Her hair was bright about her throat and her eyes were blue and clear.

He did not speak for a long while. "You're beautiful," he said at last, shocked.

"How else could I be?"

His voice was slow and unreal. "Let me look at you."

He put out his vague hands like a sleepwalker. His heart pounded sluggishly. He moved forward as if walking under a deep pressure of water. He walked around and around her, touching her.

"Haven't you seen enough of me in all these years?"

"Never enough," he said, and his eyes were filled with tears.

"What did you want to talk to me about?"

"Give me time, please, a little time." He sat down weakly and put his trembling hands to his chest. He blinked. "It's incredible. Another nightmare. How did they *make* you?"

"We're not allowed to talk of that; it spoils the illusion."

"It's magic!"

"Science."

Her touch was warm. Her fingernails were perfect as seashells. There was no seam, no flaw. He looked upon her. He remembered again the words they had read so often in the good days. *Behold, thou art fair, my love; behold, thou art fair; thou hast doves' eyes within thy locks. . . . Thy lips are like a thread of scarlet, and thy speech is comely. . . . Thy two breasts are like two young roes that are twins, which feed among the lilies . . . there is no spot in thee.*

"George?"

"What?" His eyes were cold glass.

He wanted to kiss her lips.

Honey and milk are under thy tongue.

And the smell of thy garments is like the smell of Lebanon.

"George."

A vast humming. The room began to whirl.

"Yes, yes, a moment, a moment." He shook his humming head.

How beautiful are thy feet with shoes, O prince's daughter! the joints of thy thighs are like jewels, the work of the hands of a cunning workman. . . .

"How did they do it?" he cried. In so short a time. Nine hours, while he slept. Had they melted gold, fixed delicate watch springs, diamonds, glitter, confetti, rich rubies, liquid silver, copper thread? Had metal insects spun her hair? Had they poured yellow fire in molds and set it to freeze?

"No," she said. "If you talk that way, I'll go."

"Don't!"

"Come to business, then," she said, coldly. "You want to talk to me about Leonard."

"Give me time, I'll get to it."

"Now," she insisted.

He knew no anger. It had washed out of him at her appearance. He felt childishly dirty.

"Why did you come to see me?" She was not smiling.

"Please."

"I insist. Wasn't it about Leonard? You know I love him, don't you?"

"Stop it!" He put his hands to his ears.

She kept at him. "You know, I spend all of my time with him now. Where you and I used to go, now Leonard and I stay. Remember the picnic green on Mount Verde? We were there last week. We flew to Athens a month ago, with a case of champagne."

He licked his lips. "You're not guilty, you're *not*." He rose and held her wrists. "You're fresh, you're not her. She's guilty, not you. You're different!"

"On the contrary," said the woman. "I *am* her. I can act only as she acts. No part of me is alien to her. For all intents and purposes we are one."

"But you did not do what she has done!"

"I did all those things. I kissed him."

"You can't have, you're just born!"

"Out of her past and from your mind."

"Look," he pleaded, shaking her to gain her attention. "Isn't there some way, can't I—pay more money? Take you away with me? We'll go to Paris or Stockholm or any place you like!"

She laughed. "The marionettes only rent. They never sell."

"But I've money!"

"It was tried, long ago. It leads to insanity. It's not possible. Even this much is illegal, you *know* that. We exist only through governmental sufferance."

"All I want is to live with you, Katie."

"That can never be, because I am Katie, every bit of me is her. We do not want competition. Marionettes can't leave the premises; dissection might reveal our secrets. Enough of this. I warned you, we mustn't speak of these things. You'll spoil the illusion. You'll feel frustrated when you leave. You paid your money, now do what you came to do."

"I don't want to kill you."

"One part of you does. You're walling it in, you're trying not to let it out."

He took the gun from his pocket. "I'm an old fool. I should never have come. You're so beautiful."

"I'm going to see Leonard tonight."

"Don't talk."

"We're flying to Paris in the morning."

"You heard what I said!"

"And then to Stockholm." She laughed sweetly and caressed his chin. "My little fat man."

Something began to stir in him. His face grew pale. He knew what was happening. The hidden anger and revulsion and hatred in him were sending out faint pulses of thought. And the delicate telepathic web in her wondrous head was receiving the death impulse. The marionette. The invisible strings. He himself manipulating her body.

"Plump, odd little man, who once was so fair."

"Don't," he said.

"Old while I am only thirty-one, ah, George, you were blind, working years to give me time to fall in love again. Don't you think Leonard is lovely?"

He raised the gun blindly.

"Katie."

"*His head is as the most fine gold—*" she whispered.

"Katie, don't!" he screamed.

"*His locks are bushy, and black as a raven. . . . His hands are as gold rings set with the beryl—*"

How could she speak those words! It was in *his* mind, how could *she* mouth it!

"Katie, don't make me do this!"

"*His cheeks are as a bed of spices*," she murmured, eyes closed, moving about the room softly. "*His belly is as bright ivory overlaid with sapphires. His legs are as pillars of marble—*"

"Katie!" he shrieked.

"*His mouth is most sweet—*"

One shot.

"*—this is my beloved—*"

Another shot.

She fell.

"Katie, Katie, Katie!"

Four more times he pumped bullets into her body.

She lay shuddering. Her senseless mouth clicked wide and some insanely warped mechanism had caused her to repeat again and again, "*Beloved, beloved, beloved, beloved, beloved . . .*"

George Hill fainted.

He awakened to a cool cloth on his brow.

"It's all over," said the dark man.

"Over?" George Hill whispered.

The dark man nodded.

George Hill looked weakly down at his hands. They had been covered with blood. When he fainted he had dropped to the floor. The last thing he remembered was the feeling of the real blood pouring upon his hands in a freshet.

His hands were now clean-washed.

"I've got to leave," said George Hill.

"If you feel capable."

"I'm all right." He got up. "I'll go to Paris now, start over. I'm not to try to phone Katie or anything, am I."

"Katie is dead."

"Yes. I killed her, didn't I? God, the blood, it was *real*!"

"We are proud of that touch."

He went down in the elevator to the street. It was raining, and he wanted to walk for hours. The anger and destruction were purged away. The memory was so terrible that he would never wish to kill again. Even if the real Katie were to appear before him now, he would only thank God, and fall senselessly to his knees. She was dead now. He had had his way. He had broken the law and no one would know.

The rain fell cool on his face. He must leave immediately, while the purge was in effect. After all, what was the use of such purges if one took up the old threads? The marionettes' function was primarily to prevent actual crime. If you wanted to kill, hit, or torture someone, you took it out on one of those unstringed automatons. It wouldn't do to return to the apartment now. Katie might be there. He wanted only to think of her as dead, a thing attended to in deserving fashion.

He stopped at the curb and watched the traffic flash by. He took deep breaths of the good air and began to relax.

"Mr. Hill?" said a voice at his elbow.

"Yes?"

A manacle was snapped to Hill's wrist. "You're under arrest."

"But—"

"Come along. Smith, take the other men upstairs, make the arrests!"

"You can't do this to me," said George Hill.

"For murder, yes, we can."

Thunder sounded in the sky.

It was eight-fifteen at night. It had been raining for ten days. It rained now on the prison walls. He put his hands out to feel the drops gather in pools on his trembling palms.

A door clanged and he did not move but stood with his hands in the rain. His lawyer looked up at him on his chair and said, "It's all over. You'll be executed tonight."

George Hill listened to the rain.

"She wasn't real. I didn't kill her."

"It's the law, anyhow. You remember. The others are sentenced, too. The president of Marionettes, Incorporated, will die at midnight. His three assistants will die at one. You'll go about one-thirty."

"Thanks," said George. "You did all you could. I guess it was murder, no matter how you look at it, image or not. The idea was there, the plot and the plan were there. It lacked only the real Katie herself."

"It's a matter of timing, too," said the lawyer. "Ten years ago you wouldn't have got the death penalty. Ten years from now you wouldn't, either. But they had to have an object case, a whipping boy. The use of marionettes has grown so in the last year it's fantastic. The public must be scared out of it, and scared badly. God knows where it would all wind up if it went on. There's the spiritual side of it, too, where does life begin or end? are the robots alive or dead? More than one church has been split up the seams on the question. If they aren't alive, they're the next thing to it; they react, they even think. You know the 'live robot' law that was passed two months ago; you come under that. Just bad timing, is all, bad timing."

"The government's right. I see that now," said George Hill.

"I'm glad you understand the attitude of the law."

"Yes. After all, they can't let murder be legal. Even if it's done with machines and telepathy and wax. They'd be hypocrites to let me get away with my crime. For it *was* a crime. I've felt guilty about it ever since. I've felt the need of punishment. Isn't that odd? That's how society gets to you. It makes you feel guilty even when you see no reason to be. . . . "

"I have to go now. Is there anything you want?"

"Nothing, thanks."

"Good-by then, Mr. Hill."

The door shut.

George Hill stood up on the chair, his hands twisting together, wet, outside the window bars. A red light burned in the wall suddenly. A voice came over the audio: "Mr. Hill, your wife is here to see you."

He gripped the bars.

She's dead, he thought.

"Mr. Hill?" asked the voice.

"She's dead. I killed her."

"Your wife is waiting in the anteroom, will you see her?"

"I saw her fall, I shot her, I saw her fall dead!"

"Mr. Hill, do you hear me?"

"Yes!" he shouted, pounding at the wall with his fists. "I hear you. I hear you! She's dead, she's dead, can't she let me be! I killed her, I won't see her, she's dead!"

A pause. "Very well, Mr. Hill," murmured the voice.

The red light winked off.

Lightning flashed through the sky and lit his face. He pressed his hot cheeks to the cold bars and waited, while the rain fell. After a long time, a door opened somewhere onto the street and he saw two caped figures emerge from the prison office below. They paused under an arc light and glanced up.

It was Katie. And beside her, Leonard Phelps.

"Katie!"

Her face turned away. The man took her arm. They hurried across the avenue in the black rain and got into a low car.

"Katie!" He wrenched at the bars. He screamed and beat and pulled at the concrete ledge. "She's alive! Guard! Guard! I saw her! She's not dead, I didn't kill her, now you can let me out! I didn't murder anyone, it's all a joke, a mistake, I saw her, I saw her! Katie, come back, tell them, Katie, say you're alive! Katie!"

The guards came running.

"You can't kill me! I didn't do anything! Katie's alive, I saw her!"

"We saw her, too, sir."

"But let me free, then! Let me free!" It was insane. He choked and almost fell.

"We've been through all that, sir, at the trial."

"It's not fair!" He leaped up and clawed at the window, bellowing.

The car drove away, Katie and Leonard inside it. Drove away to Paris and Athens and Venice and London next spring and Stockholm next summer and Vienna in the fall.

"Katie, come back, you can't *do* this to me!"

The red taillights of the car dwindled in the cold rain. Behind him, the guards moved forward to take hold of him while he screamed.

A Piece of Wood

"Sit down, young man," said the Official.

"Thanks." The young man sat.

"I've been hearing rumors about you," the Official said pleasantly. "Oh, nothing much. Your nervousness. Your not getting on so well. Several months now I've heard about you, and I thought I'd call you in. Thought maybe you'd like your job changed. Like to go overseas, work in some other War Area? Desk job killing you off, like to get right in on the old fight?"

"I don't think so," said the young sergeant.

"What *do* you want?"

The sergeant shrugged and looked at his hands. "To live in peace. To learn that during the night, somehow, the guns of the world had rusted, the bacteria had turned sterile in their bomb casings, the tanks had sunk like prehistoric monsters into roads suddenly made tar pits. That's what I'd like."

"That's what we'd all like, of course," said the Official. "Now stop all that idealistic chatter and tell me where you'd like to be sent. You have your choice—the Western or the Northern War Zone." The Official tapped a pink map on his desk.

But the sergeant was talking at his hands, turning them over, looking at the fingers: "What would you officers do, what would we men do, what would the *world* do if we all woke tomorrow with the guns in flaking ruin?"

The Official saw that he would have to deal carefully with the sergeant. He smiled quietly. "That's an interesting question. I like to talk about such theories, and my answer is that there'd be mass panic. Each nation would think itself the only unarmed nation in the world, and would blame its enemies for the disaster. There'd be waves of suicide, stocks collapsing, a million tragedies."

"But *after* that," the sergeant said. "After they realized it was true, that every nation was disarmed and there was nothing more to fear, if we were all clean to start over fresh and new, what then?"

"They'd rearm as swiftly as possible."

"What if they could be stopped?"

"Then they'd beat each other with their fists. If it got down to that. Huge armies of men with boxing gloves of steel spikes would gather at the national borders. And if you took the gloves away they'd use their fingernails and feet. And if you cut their legs off they'd *spit* on each other. And if you cut off their tongues and stopped their mouths with corks they'd fill the atmosphere so full of hate that mosquitoes would drop to the ground and birds would fall dead from telephone wires."

"Then you don't think it would do any good?" the sergeant said.

"Certainly not. It'd be like ripping the carapace off a turtle. Civilization would gasp and die from the shock."

The young man shook his head. "Or are you lying to yourself and me because you've a nice comfortable job?"

"Let's call it ninety per cent cynicism, ten per cent rationalizing the situation. Go put your Rust away and forget about it."

The sergeant jerked his head up. "How'd you know I *had* it?" he said.

"Had what?"

"The Rust, of course."

"What're you talking about?"

"I *can* do it, you know. I could start the Rust tonight if I wanted to."

The Official laughed. "You can't be serious."

"I am. I've been meaning to come talk to you. I'm glad you called me in.

I've worked on this invention for a long time. It's been a dream of mine. It has to do with the structure of certain atoms. If you study them you find that the arrangement of atoms in steel armor is such-and-such an arrangement. I was looking for an imbalance factor. I majored in physics and metallurgy, you know. It came to me, there's a Rust factor in the air all the time. Water vapor. I had to find a way to give steel a 'nervous breakdown.' Then the water vapor everywhere in the world would take over. Not on all metal, of course. Our civilization is built on steel, I wouldn't want to destroy most buildings. I'd just eliminate guns and shells, tanks, planes, battleships. I can set the machine to work on copper and brass and aluminum, too, if necessary. I'd just walk by all of those weapons and just being near them I'd make them fall away."

The Official was bending over his desk, staring at the sergeant. "May I ask you a question?"

"Yes."

"Have you ever thought you were Christ?"

"I can't say that I have. But I have considered that God was good to me to let me find what I was looking for, if that's what you mean."

The Official reached into his breast pocket and drew out an expensive ball-point pen capped with a rifle shell. He flourished the pen and started filling in a form. "I want you to take this to Dr. Mathews this afternoon, for a complete checkup. Not that I expect anything really bad, understand. But don't you feel you *should* see a doctor?"

"You think I'm lying about my machine," said the sergeant. "I'm not. It's so small it can be hidden in this cigarette package. The effect of it extends for nine hundred miles. I could tour this country in a few days, with the machine set to a certain type of steel. The other nations couldn't take advantage of us because I'd rust their weapons as they approach us. Then I'd fly to Europe. By this time next month the world would be free of war forever. I don't know how I found this invention. It's impossible. Just as impossible as the atom bomb. I've waited a month now, trying to think it over. I worried about what would happen if I did rip off the carapace, as you say. But now I've just about decided. My talk with you has helped clarify things. Nobody thought an airplane would ever fly, nobody thought an atom would ever explode, and nobody thinks that there can ever be Peace, but there *will* be."

"Take that paper over to Dr. Mathews, will you?" said the Official hastily.

The sergeant got up. "You're not going to assign me to any new Zone then?"

"Not right away, no. I've changed my mind. We'll let Mathews decide."

"I've decided then," said the young man. "I'm leaving the post within the next few minutes. I've a pass. Thank you very much for giving me your valuable time, sir."

"Now look here, Sergeant, don't take things so seriously. You don't have to leave. Nobody's going to hurt you."

"That's right. Because nobody would believe me. Good-by, sir." The sergeant opened the office door and stepped out.

The door shut and the Official was alone. He stood for a moment looking at the door. He sighed. He rubbed his hands over his face. The phone rang. He answered it abstractedly.

"Oh, *hello*, Doctor. I was just going to call you." A pause. "Yes, I was going to send him over to you. Look, is it all right for that young man to be wandering about? It *is* all right? If you say so, Doctor. Probably needs a rest, a good long one. Poor boy has a delusion of rather an interesting sort. Yes, yes. It's a shame. But that's what a Sixteen-Year War can do to you, I suppose."

The phone voice buzzed in reply.

The Official listened and nodded. "I'll make a note on that. Just a second." He reached for his ball-point pen. "Hold on a moment. Always mislaying things." He patted his pocket. "Had my pen here a moment ago. Wait." He put down the phone and searched his desk, pulling out drawers. He checked his blouse pocket again. He stopped moving. Then his hands twitched slowly into his pocket and probed down. He poked his thumb and forefinger deep and brought out a pinch of something.

He sprinkled it on his desk blotter: a small filtering powder of yellow-red rust.

He sat staring at it for a moment. Then he picked up the phone. "Mathews," he said, "get off the line, quick." There was a click of someone hanging up and then he dialed another call. "Hello, Guard Station, listen, there's a man coming past you any minute now, you know him, name of Sergeant Hollis, stop him, shoot him down, kill him if necessary, don't ask any questions, kill the son of a bitch, you heard me, this is the Official talking! Yes, kill him, you hear!"

"But sir," said a bewildered voice on the other end of the line. "I can't, I just *can't*. . . ."

"What do you mean you can't, God damn it!"

"Because . . . " The voice faded away. You could hear the guard breathing into the phone a mile away.

The Official shook the phone. "Listen to me, listen, get your gun ready!"

"I can't shoot anyone," said the guard.

The Official sank back in his chair. He sat blinking for half a minute, gasping.

Out there even now—he didn't have to look, no one had to tell him—the hangars were dusting down in soft red rust, and the airplanes were blowing away on a brown-rust wind into nothingness, and the tanks were sinking, sinking slowly into the hot asphalt roads, like dinosaurs (isn't that what the man had said?) sinking into primordial tar pits. Trucks were blowing away into ocher puffs of smoke, their drivers dumped by the road, with only the tires left running on the highways.

"Sir . . . " said the guard, who was seeing all this, far away. "Oh, God . . . "

"Listen, listen!" screamed the Official. "Go after him, get him, with your hands, choke him, with your fists, beat him, use your feet, kick his ribs in, kick him to death, do anything, but get that man. I'll be right out!" He hung up the phone.

By instinct he jerked open the bottom desk drawer to get his service pistol. A pile of brown rust filled the new leather holster. He swore and leaped up.

On the way out of the office he grabbed a chair. It's wood, he thought. Good old-fashioned wood, good old-fashioned maple. He hurled it against the wall twice, and it broke. Then he seized one of the legs, clenched it hard in his fist, his face bursting red, the breath snorting in his nostrils, his mouth wide. He struck the palm of his hand with the leg of the chair, testing it. "All right, God damn it, come on!" he cried.

He rushed out, yelling, and slammed the door.

The Blue Bottle

The sundials were tumbled into white pebbles. The birds of the air now flew in ancient skies of rock and sand, buried, their songs stopped. The dead sea bottoms were currented with dust which flooded the land when the wind bade it reenact an old tale of engulfment. The cities were deep-laid with granaries of silence, time stored and kept, pools and fountains of quietude and memory.

Mars was dead.

Then, out of the large stillness, from a great distance, there was an insect sound which grew large among the cinnamon hills and moved in the sun-blazed air until the highway trembled and dust was shaken whispering down in the old cities.

The sound ceased.

In the shimmering silence of midday, Albert Beck and Leonard Craig sat in an ancient landcar, eying a dead city which did not move under their gaze but waited for their shout:

"Hello!"

A crystal tower dropped into soft dusting rain.

"You there!"

And another tumbled down.

And another and another fell as Beck called, summoning them to death. In shattering flights, stone animals with vast granite wings dived to strike the courtyards and fountains. His cry summoned them like living beasts and the beasts gave answer, groaned, cracked, leaned up, tilted over, trembling, hesitant, then split the air and swept down with grimaced mouths and empty eyes, with sharp, eternally hungry teeth suddenly seized out and strewn like shrapnel on the tiles.

Beck waited. No more towers fell.

"It's safe to go in now."

Craig didn't move. "For the same reason?"

Beck nodded.

"For a damned *bottle*! I don't understand. Why does everyone want it?"

Beck got out of the car. "Those that found it, they never told, they never explained. But—it's old. Old as the desert, as the dead seas—and it might contain anything. That's what the legend says. And because it *could* hold anything—well, that stirs a man's hunger."

"Yours, not mine," said Craig. His mouth barely moved; his eyes were half-shut, faintly amused. He stretched lazily. "I'm just along for the ride. Better watching you than sitting in the heat."

Beck had stumbled upon the old landcar a month back, before Craig had joined him. It was part of the flotsam of the First Industrial Invasion of Mars that had ended when the race moved on toward the stars. He had worked on the motor and run it from city to dead city, through the lands of the idlers and roustabouts, the dreamers and lazers, men caught in the backwash of space, men like himself and Craig who had never wanted to do much of anything and had found Mars a fine place to do it in.

"Five thousand, ten thousand years back the Martians made the Blue Bottle," said Beck. "Blown from Martian glass—and lost and found and lost and found again and again."

He stared into the wavering heat shimmer of the dead city. All my life, thought Beck, I've done nothing and nothing inside the nothing. Others, better men, have done big things, gone off to Mercury, or Venus, or out beyond the System. Except me. Not me. But the Blue Bottle can *change* all that.

He turned and walked away from the silent car.

Craig was out and after him, moving easily along. "What is it now, ten years you've hunted? You twitch when you sleep, wake up in fits, sweat through the days. You want the damn bottle *that* bad, and don't know what's in it. You're a fool, Beck."

"Shut up, shut up," said Beck, kicking a slide of pebbles out of his way.

They walked together into the ruined city, over a mosaic of cracked tiles shaped into a stone tapestry of fragile Martian creatures, long-dead beasts which appeared and disappeared as a slight breath of wind stirred the silent dust.

"Wait," said Beck. He cupped his hands to his mouth and gave a great shout. "You there!"

"...there," said an echo, and towers fell. Fountains and stone pillars folded into themselves. That was the way of these cities. Sometimes towers as beautiful as a symphony would fall at a spoken word. It was like watching a Bach cantata disintegrate before your eyes.

A moment later: bones buried in bones. The dust settled. Two structures remained intact.

Beck stepped forward, nodding to his friend.

They moved in search.

And, searching, Craig paused, a faint smile on his lips. "In that bottle," he said, "is there a little accordion woman, all folded up like one of those tin cups, or like one of those Japanese flowers you put in water and it opens out?"

"I don't need a woman."

"Maybe you do. Maybe you never had a *real* woman, a woman who loved you, so, secretly, that's what you hope is in it." Craig pursed his mouth. "Or maybe, in that bottle, something from your childhood. All in a tiny bundle—a lake, a tree you climbed, green grass, some crayfish. How's *that* sound?"

Beck's eyes focused on a distant point. "Sometimes—that's almost it. The past—Earth. I don't know."

Craig nodded. "What's in the bottle would depend, maybe, on who's looking. Now, if there was a shot of *whiskey* in it . . . "

"Keep looking," said Beck.

There were seven rooms filled with glitter and shine; from floor to tiered ceiling there were casks, crocks, magnums, urns, vases—fashioned of red, pink, yellow, violet, and black glass. Beck shattered them, one by one, to eliminate them, to get them out of the way so he would never have to go through them again.

Beck finished his room, stood ready to invade the next. He was almost afraid to go on. Afraid that *this* time he would find it; that the search would be over and the meaning would go out of his life. Only after he had heard of the Blue Bottle from fire-travelers all the way from Venus to Jupiter, ten years ago, had life begun to take on a purpose. The fever had lit him and he had burned steadily ever since. If he worked it properly, the prospect of finding the bottle might fill his entire life to the brim. Another thirty years, if he was careful and not *too* diligent, of search, never admitting aloud that it wasn't the bottle that counted at all, but the search, the running and the hunting, the dust and the cities and the going-on.

Beck heard a muffled sound. He turned and walked to a window looking out into the courtyard. A small gray sand cycle had purred up almost noiselessly at the end of the street. A plump man with blonde hair eased himself off the spring seat and stood looking into the city. Another searcher. Beck sighed. Thousands of them, searching and searching. But there were thousands of brittle cities and towns and villages and it would take a millennium to sift them all.

"How you doing?" Craig appeared in a doorway.

"No luck." Beck sniffed the air. "Do you smell anything?"

"What?" Craig looked about.

"Smells like—bourbon."

"Ho!" Craig laughed. "That's *me*!"

"You?"

"I just took a drink. Found it in the other room. Shoved some stuff around, a mess of bottles, like always, and one of them had some bourbon in it, so I had myself a drink."

Beck was staring at him, beginning to tremble. "What—what would bourbon be doing *here*, in a Martian bottle?" His hands were cold. He took a slow step forward. "Show me!"

"I'm sure that . . ."

"*Show* me, damn you!"

It was there, in one corner of the room, a container of Martian glass as blue as the sky, the size of a small fruit, light and airy in Beck's hand as he set it down upon a table.

"It's half-full of bourbon," said Craig.

"I don't see anything inside," said Beck.

"Then shake it."

Beck picked it up, gingerly shook it.

"Hear it gurgle?"

"No."

"I can hear it plain."

Beck replaced it on the table. Sunlight spearing through a side window struck blue flashes off the slender container. It was the blue of a star held in the hand. It was the blue of a shallow ocean bay at noon. It was the blue of a diamond at morning.

"This *is* it," said Beck quietly. "I know it is. We don't have to look any more. We've found the Blue Bottle."

Craig looked skeptical. "Sure you don't *see* anything in it?"

"Nothing . . . But—" Beck bent close and peered deeply into the blue universe of glass. "Maybe if I open it up and let it out, whatever it is, I'll know."

"I put the stopper in tight. Here." Craig reached out.

"If you gentlemen will excuse me," said a voice in the door behind them.

The plump man with blonde hair walked into their line of vision with a gun. He did not look at their faces, he looked only at the blue glass bottle. He began to smile. "I hate very much to handle guns," he said, "but it is a matter of necessity, as I simply *must* have that work of art. I suggest that you allow me to take it without trouble."

Beck was almost pleased. It had a certain beauty of timing, this incident; it was the sort of thing he might have wished for, to have the treasure stolen before it was opened. Now there was the good prospect of a chase, a fight, a series of gains and losses, and, before they were done, perhaps another four or five years spent upon a new search.

"Come along now," said the stranger. "Give it up." He raised the gun warningly.

Beck handed him the bottle.

"Amazing. Really amazing," said the plump man. "I can't believe it was as simple as this, to walk in, hear two men talking, and to have the Blue Bottle simply *handed* to me. Amazing!" And he wandered off down the hall, out into the daylight, chuckling to himself.

Under the cool double moons of Mars the midnight cities were bone and dust. Along the scattered highway the landcar bumped and rattled, past cities where the fountains, the gyrostats, the furniture, the metal-singing books, the paintings lay powdered over with mortar and insect wings. Past cities that were cities no longer, but only things rubbed to a fine silt that flowered senselessly back and forth on the wine winds between one land and another, like the sand in a gigantic hourglass, endlessly pyramiding and repyramiding. Silence opened to let the car pass, and closed swiftly in behind.

Craig said, "We'll never find him. These damned roads. So old. Potholes, lumps, everything wrong. He's got the advantage with the cycle; he can dodge and weave. Damn!"

They swerved abruptly, avoiding a bad stretch. The car moved over the old highway like an eraser, coming upon blind soil, passing over it, dusting it away to reveal the emerald and gold colors of ancient Martian mosaics worked into the road surface.

"Wait," cried Beck. He throttled the car down. "I saw something back there."

"Where?"

They drove back a hundred yards.

"There. You see. It's *him*."

In a ditch by the side of the road the plump man lay folded over his cycle. He did not move. His eyes were wide, and when Beck flashed a torch down, the eyes burned dully.

"Where's the bottle?" asked Craig.

Beck jumped into the ditch and picked up the man's gun. "I don't know. Gone."

"What killed him?"

"I don't know that either."

"The cycle looks okay. Not an accident."

Beck rolled the body over. "No wounds. Looks like he just — stopped, of his own accord."

"Heart attack, maybe," said Craig. "Excited over the bottle. He gets down here to hide. Thought he'd be all right, but the attack finished him."

"That doesn't account for the Blue Bottle."

"Someone came along. Lord, you know how many searchers there are. . . ."

They scanned the darkness around them. Far off, in the starred blackness, on the blue hills, they saw a dim movement.

"Up there." Beck pointed. "Three men on foot."

"They must have . . ."

"My God, look!"

Below them, in the ditch, the figure of the plump man glowed, began to melt. The eyes took on the aspect of moonstones under a sudden rush of water. The face began to dissolve away into fire. The hair resembled small firecracker strings, lit and sputtering. The body fumed as they watched. The fingers jerked with flame. Then, as if a gigantic hammer had struck a glass statue, the body cracked upward and was gone in a blaze of pink shards, becoming mist as the night breeze carried it across the highway.

"They must have—*done* something to him," said Craig. "Those three, with a new kind of weapon."

"But it's happened before," said Beck. "Men I knew about who had the Blue Bottle. They vanished. And the bottle passed on to others who vanished." He shook his head. "Looked like a million fireflies when he broke apart. . . ."

"You going after them?"

Beck returned to the car. He judged the desert mounds, the hills of bone-silt and silence. "It'll be a tough job, but I think I can poke the car through after them. I *have* to, now." He paused, not speaking to Craig. "I think I know what's in the Blue Bottle. . . . Finally, I realize that what I want most of all is in there. Waiting for me."

"I'm not going," said Craig, coming up to the car where Beck sat in the dark, his hands on his knees. "I'm not going out there with you, chasing three armed men. I just want to live, Beck. That bottle means nothing to me. I won't risk my skin for it. But I'll wish you luck."

"Thanks," said Beck. And he drove away, into the dunes.

The night was as cool as water coming over the glass hood of the landcar.

Beck throttled hard over dead river washes and spills of chalked pebble, driving between great cliffs. Ribbons of double moonlight painted the bas-reliefs of gods and animals on the cliff sides all yellow-gold: mile-high faces upon which Martian histories were etched and stamped in symbols, incredible faces with open cave eyes and gaping cave mouths.

The motor's roar dislodged rocks, boulders. In a whole rushing downpour of stone, golden segments of ancient cliff sculpture slid out of the moons' rays at the top of the cliff and vanished into blue cool-well darkness.

In the roar, as he drove, Beck cast his mind back—to all the nights in the last ten years, nights when he had built red fires on the sea bottoms, and cooked slow, thoughtful meals. And dreamed. Always those dreams of *wanting*. And not knowing what. Ever since he was a young man, the hard life on Earth, the great panic of 2130, the starvation, chaos, riot, want. Then bucking through the planets, the womanless, loveless years, the alone years. You come out of the dark into the light, out of the womb into the world, and what do you find that you really want?

What about that dead man back there in the ditch? Wasn't he always looking for something extra? Something he didn't have. What *was* there for men like himself? Or for anyone? Was there anything at all to look forward to?

The Blue Bottle.

He quickly braked the car, leaped out, gun ready. He ran, crouching, into the dunes. Ahead of him, the three men lay on the cold sand, neatly. They were Earth Men, with tan faces and rough clothes and gnarled hands. Starlight shone on the Blue Bottle, which lay among them.

As Beck watched, the bodies began to melt. They vanished away into rises of steam, into dewdrops and crystals. In a moment they were gone.

Beck felt the coldness in his body as the flakes rained across his eyes, flicking his lips and his cheeks.

He did not move.

The plump man. Dead and vanishing. Craig's voice: "Some new weapon . . . "

No. Not a weapon at all.

The Blue Bottle.

They had opened it to find what they most desired. All of the unhappy, desiring men down the long and lonely years had opened it to find what they most wanted in the planets of the universe. And all had found it, even as had these three. Now it could be understood, why the bottle passed on so swiftly, from one to another, and the men vanishing behind it. Harvest chaff fluttering on the sand, along the dead sea rims. Turning to flame and fireflies. To mist.

Beck picked up the bottle and held it away from himself for a long moment. His eyes shone clearly. His hands trembled.

So this is what I've been looking for, he thought. He turned the bottle and it flashed blue starlight.

So this is what all men *really* want? The secret desire, deep inside, hidden all away where we never guess? The subliminal urge? So this is what each man seeks, through some private guilt, to find?

Death.

An end to doubt, to torture, to monotony, to want, to loneliness, to fear, an end to everything.

All men?

No. Not Craig. Craig was, perhaps, far luckier. A few men were like animals in the universe, not questioning, drinking at pools and breeding and raising their young and not doubting for a moment that life was anything but good. That was Craig. There were a handful like him. Happy animals on a great reservation, in the hand of God, with a religion and a faith that grew like a set of special nerves in them. The unneurotic men in the midst of the billionfold neurotics. They would only want death, later, in a natural manner. Not now. Later.

Beck raised the bottle. How simple, he thought, and how right. This *is* what I've always wanted. And nothing else.

Nothing.

The bottle was open and blue in the starlight. Beck took an immense draught of the air coming from the Blue Bottle, deep into his lungs.

I have it at last, he thought.

He relaxed. He felt his body become wonderfully cool and then wonderfully warm. He knew he was dropping down a long slide of stars into a darkness as delightful as wine. He was swimming in blue wine and white wine and red wine. There were candles in his chest and fire wheels spinning. He felt his hands leave him. He felt his legs fly away, amusingly. He laughed. He shut his eyes and laughed.

He was very happy for the first time in his life.

The Blue Bottle dropped onto the cool sand.

At dawn, Craig walked along, whistling. He saw the bottle lying in the first pink light of the sun on the empty white sand. As he picked it up, there was a fiery whisper. A number of orange and red-purple fireflies blinked on the air, and passed on away.

The place was very still.

"I'll be damned." He glanced toward the dead windows of a nearby city. "Hey, Beck!"

A slender tower collapsed into powder.

"Beck, here's your treasure! I don't want it. Come and get it!"

" . . . and get it," said an echo, and the last tower fell.

Craig waited.

"That's rich," he said. "The bottle right here, and old Beck not even around to take it." He shook the blue container.

It gurgled.

"Yes, sir! Just the way it was before. Full of bourbon, by God!" He opened it, drank, wiped his mouth.

He held the bottle carelessly.

"All that trouble for a little bourbon. I'll wait right here for old Beck and give him his damn bottle. Meanwhile—have another drink, Mr. Craig. Don't mind if I do."

The only sound in the dead land was the sound of liquid running into a parched throat. The Blue Bottle flashed in the sun.

Craig smiled happily and drank again.

Long After Midnight

The police ambulance went up into the palisades at the wrong hour. It is always the wrong hour when the police ambulance goes anywhere, but this was especially wrong, for it was long after midnight and nobody imagined it would ever be day again, because the sea coming in on the lightless shore below said as much, and the wind blowing salt cold in from the Pacific reaffirmed this, and the fog muffling the sky and putting out the stars struck the final, unfelt-but-disabling blow. The weather said it had been here forever, man was hardly here at all, and would soon be gone. Under the circumstances it was hard for the men gathered on the cliff, with several cars, the headlights on, and flashlights bobbing, to feel real, trapped as they were between a sunset they hardly remembered and a sunrise that would not be imagined.

The slender weight hanging from the tree, turning in the cold salt wind, did not diminish this feeling in any way.

The slender weight was a girl, no more than nineteen, in a light green gossamer party frock, coat and shoes lost somewhere in the cool night, who had brought a rope up to these cliffs and found a tree with a branch half out over the cliff and tied the rope in place and made a loop for her neck and let herself out on the wind to hang there swinging. The rope made a dry scraping whine on the branch, until the police came, and the ambulance, to take her down out of space and place her on the ground.

A single phone call had come in about midnight telling what they might find out here on the edge of the cliff and whoever it was hung up swiftly and did not call again, and now the hours had passed and all that could be done was done and over, the police were finished and leaving, and there was just the ambulance now and the men with the ambulance to load the quiet burden and head for the morgue.

Of the three men remaining around the sheeted form there were Carlson, who had been at this sort of thing for thirty years, and Moreno, who had been at it for ten, and Latting, who was new to the job a few weeks back. Of the three it was Latting now who stood on the edge of the cliff looking at that empty tree limb, the rope in his hand, not able to take his eyes away. Carlson came up behind him. Hearing him, Latting said, "What a place, what an awful place to die."

"Any place is awful, if you decide you want to go bad enough," said Carlson. "Come on, kid."

Latting did not move. He put out his hand to touch the tree. Carlson grunted and shook his head. "Go ahead. Try to remember it all."

"Any reason why I shouldn't?" Latting turned quickly to look at that emotionless gray face of the older man. "You got any objections?"

"No objections. I was the same way once. But after a while you learn it's best not to see. You eat better. You sleep better. After a while you learn to forget."

"I don't want to forget," said Latting. "Good God, somebody died up here just a few hours ago. She deserves—"

"She *deserved*, kid, past tense, not present. She deserved a better shake and didn't get it. Now she deserves a decent burial. That's all we can do for her. It's late and cold. You can tell us all about it on the way."

"That could be your daughter there."

"You won't get to me that way, kid. It's not my daughter, that's what counts. And it's not yours, though you make it sound like it was. It's a nineteen-year-old girl, no name, no purse, nothing. I'm sorry she's dead. There, does that help?"

"It could if you said it right."

"I'm sorry, now pick up the other end of the stretcher."

Latting picked up one end of the stretcher but did not walk with it and only looked at the figure beneath the sheet.

"It's awful being that young and deciding to just quit."

"Sometimes," said Carlson, at the other end of the stretcher, "I get tired, too."

"Sure, but you're—" Latting stopped.

"Go ahead, say it, I'm old. Somebody fifty, sixty, it's okay, who gives a damn, somebody nineteen, everybody cries. So don't come to my funeral, kid, and no flowers."

"I didn't mean . . ." said Latting.

"Nobody means, but everybody says, and luckily I got the hide of an iguana. March."

They moved with the stretcher toward the ambulance where Moreno was opening the doors wider.

"Boy," said Latting, "she's light. She doesn't weigh anything."

"That's the wild life for you, you punks, you kids." Carlson was getting into the back of the ambulance now and they were sliding the stretcher in. "I smell whiskey. You young ones think you can drink like college fullbacks and keep your weight. Hell, she don't even weigh ninety pounds, if that."

Latting put the rope in on the floor of the ambulance. "I wonder where she got this?"

"It's not like poison," said Moreno. "Anyone can buy rope and not sign. This looks like block-and-tackle rope. She was at a beach party maybe and got mad at her boyfriend and took this from his car and picked herself a spot. . . ."

They took a last look at the tree out over the cliff, the empty branch, the wind rustling in the leaves, then Carlson got out and walked around to the front seat with Moreno, and Latting got in the back and slammed the doors.

They drove away down the dim incline toward the shore where the ocean laid itself, card after white card, in thunders, upon the dark sand. They drove in silence for a while, letting their headlights, like ghosts, move on out ahead. Then Latting said, "I'm getting myself a new job."

Moreno laughed. "Boy, you didn't last long. I had bets you wouldn't last. Tell you what, you'll be back. No other job like this. All the other jobs are dull. Sure, you get sick once in a while. I do. I think: I'm going to quit. I almost do. Then I stick with it. And here I am."

"Well, you can stay," said Latting. "But I'm full up. I'm not curious any more. I seen a lot the last few weeks, but this is the last straw. I'm sick of being sick. Or worse, I'm sick of your not caring."

"Who doesn't care?"

"Both of you!"

Moreno snorted. "Light us a couple, huh, Carlie?" Carlson lit two cigarettes and passed one to Moreno, who puffed on it, blinking his eyes, driving along by the loud strokes of the sea. "Just because we don't scream and yell and throw fits—"

"I don't want fits," said Latting, in the back, crouched by the sheeted figure. "I just want a little human talk, I just want you to look different than you would walking through a butcher's shop. If I ever get like you two, not worrying, not bothering, all thick skin and tough—"

"We're not tough," said Carlson, quietly, thinking about it, "we're acclimated."

"Acclimated, hell, when you should be *numb?*"

"Kid, don't tell us what we should be when you don't even know what we *are*. Any doctor is a lousy doctor who jumps down in the grave with every patient. All doctors did that, there'd be no one to help the live and kicking. Get out of the grave, boy, you can't see nothing from there."

There was a long silence from the back, and at last Latting started talking, mainly to himself:

"I wonder how long she was up there alone on the cliff, an hour, two? It must have been funny up there looking down at all the campfires, knowing you were going to wipe the whole business clean off. I suppose she was to a dance, or a beach party, and she and her boyfriend broke up. The boyfriend will be down at the station tomorrow to identify her. I'd hate to be him. How he'll *feel*—"

"He won't feel anything. He won't even show up," said Carlson, steadily, mashing out his cigarette in the front-seat tray. "He was probably the one found her and made the call and ran. Two bits will buy you a nickel he's not worth the polish on her little fingernail. Some slobby lout of a guy with pimples and bad breath. Christ, why don't these girls learn to wait until morning."

"Yeah," said Moreno. "Everything's better in the morning."

"Try telling that to a girl in love," said Latting.

"Now a man," said Carlson, lighting a fresh cigarette, "he just gets himself drunk, says to hell with it, no use killing yourself for no woman."

They drove in silence awhile past all the small dark beach houses with only a light here or there, it was so late.

"Maybe," said Latting, "she was going to have a baby."

"It happens."

"And then the boyfriend runs off with someone and this one just borrows his rope and walks up on the cliff," said Latting. "Answer me, now, *is* that or *isn't* it love?"

"It," said Carlson, squinting, searching the dark, "is a kind of love. I give up on what kind."

"Well, sure," said Moreno, driving. "I'll go along with you, kid. I mean, it's nice to know somebody in this world can love that hard."

They all thought for a while, as the ambulance purred between quiet palisades and now-quiet sea and maybe two of them thought fleetingly of their wives and tract houses and sleeping children and all the times years ago when they had driven to the beach and broken out the beer and necked up in the rocks and lay around on the blankets with guitars, singing and feeling like life would go on just as far as the ocean went, which was very far, and maybe they didn't think that at all. Latting, looking up at the backs of the two older men's necks, hoped or perhaps only nebulously wondered if these men remembered any first kisses, the taste of salt on the lips. Had there ever been a time when they had stomped the sand like mad bulls and yelled out of sheer joy and dared the universe to put them down?

And by their silence, Latting knew that yes, with all his talking, and the night, and the wind, and the cliff and the tree and the rope, he had gotten through to them; it, the event, had gotten through to them. Right now, they had to be thinking of their wives in their warm beds, long dark miles away, unbelievable, suddenly unattainable while here they were driving along a salt-layered road at a dumb hour half between certainties, bearing with them a strange thing on a cot and a used length of rope.

"Her boyfriend," said Latting, "will be out dancing tomorrow night with somebody else. That gripes my gut."

"I wouldn't mind," said Carlson, "beating the hell out of him."

Latting moved the sheet. "They sure wear their hair crazy and short, some of them. All curls, but short. Too much make-up. Too—" He stopped.

"You were saying?" asked Moreno.

Latting moved the sheet some more. He said nothing. In the next minute there was a rustling sound of the sheet, moved now here, now there. Latting's face was pale.

"Hey," he murmured, at last. "Hey."

Instinctively, Moreno slowed the ambulance.

"Yeah, kid?"

"I just found out something," said Latting. "I had this feeling all along, she's wearing too much make-up, and the hair, and—"

"So?"

"Well, for God's sake," said Latting, his lips hardly moving, one hand up to feel his own face to see what its expression was. "You want to know something funny?"

"Make us laugh," said Carlson.

The ambulance slowed even more as Latting said, "It's not a woman. I mean, it's not a girl. I mean, well, it's not a female. *Understand?*"

The ambulance slowed to a crawl.

The wind blew in off the vague morning sea through the window as the two up front turned and stared into the back of the ambulance at the shape there on the cot.

"Somebody tell me," said Latting, so quietly they almost could not hear the words. "Do we stop feeling bad now? Or do we feel worse?"

The Utterly
Perfect Murder

It was such an utterly perfect, such an incredibly delightful idea for murder, that I was half out of my mind all across America.

The idea had come to me for some reason on my forty-eighth birthday. Why it hadn't come to me when I was thirty or forty, I cannot say. Perhaps those were good years and I sailed through them unaware of time and clocks and the gathering of frost at my temples or the look of the lion about my eyes. . . .

Anyway, on my forty-eighth birthday, lying in bed that night beside my wife, with my children sleeping through all the other quiet moonlit rooms of my house, I thought:

I will arise and go now and kill Ralph Underhill.

Ralph Underhill! I cried, who in God's name is *he?*

Thirty-six years later, kill him? For *what?*

Why, I thought, for what he did to me when I was twelve.

My wife woke, an hour later, hearing a noise.

"Doug?" she called. "What are you doing?"

"Packing," I said. "For a journey."

"Oh," she murmured, and rolled over and went to sleep.

" 'Board! All aboard!" The porter's cries went down the train platform.

The train shuddered and banged.

"See you!" I cried, leaping up the steps.

"Someday," called my wife, "I wish you'd *fly*!"

Fly? I thought, and spoil thinking about murder all across the plains? Spoil oiling the pistol and loading it and thinking of Ralph Underhill's face when I show up thirty-six years late to settle old scores? Fly? Why, I would rather pack cross-country on foot, pausing by night to build fires and fry my bile and sour spit and eat again my old, mummified but still-living antagonisms and touch those bruises which have never healed. Fly?!

The train moved. My wife was gone.

I rode off into the Past.

Crossing Kansas the second night, we hit a beaut of a thunderstorm. I stayed up until four in the morning, listening to the rave of winds and thunders. At the height of the storm, I saw my face, a darkroom negative-print on the cold window glass, and thought:

Where is that fool going?

To kill Ralph Underhill!

Why? Because!

Remember how he hit my arm? Bruises. I was covered with bruises, both arms; dark blue, mottled black, strange yellow bruises. Hit and run, that was Ralph, hit and run—

And yet . . . you loved him?

Yes, as boys love boys when boys are eight, ten, twelve, and the world is innocent and boys are evil beyond evil because they know not what they do, but do it anyway. So, on some secret level, I *had* to be hurt. We dear fine friends needed each other. I to be hit. He to strike. My scars were the emblem and symbol of our love.

What else makes you want to murder Ralph so late in time?

The train whistle shrieked. Night country rolled by.

And I recalled one spring when I came to school in a new tweed knicker suit and Ralph knocking me down, rolling me in snow and fresh brown mud. And Ralph laughing and me going home, shame-faced, covered with slime, afraid of a beating, to put on fresh dry clothes.

Yes! And what *else*?

Remember those toy clay statues you longed to collect from the Tarzan radio show? Statues of Tarzan and Kala the Ape and Numa the Lion, for just twenty-five cents?! Yes, yes! Beautiful! Even now, in memory, O the sound of the Ape Man swinging through green jungles far away, ululating! But who had twenty-five cents in the middle of the Great Depression? No one.

Except Ralph Underhill.

And one day Ralph asked you if you wanted one of the statues.

Wanted! you cried. Yes! Yes!

That was the same week your brother in a strange seizure of love mixed with contempt gave you his old, but expensive, baseball-catcher's mitt.

"Well," said Ralph, "I'll give you my extra Tarzan statue if you'll give me that catcher's mitt."

Fool! I thought. The statue's worth twenty-five cents. The glove cost two dollars. No fair! Don't!

But I raced back to Ralph's house with the glove and gave it to him and he, smiling a worse contempt than my brother's, handed me the Tarzan statue and, bursting with joy, I ran home.

My brother didn't find out about his catcher's mitt and the statue for two weeks, and when he did he ditched me when we hiked out in farm country and left me lost because I was such a sap. "Tarzan statues! Baseball mitts!" he cried. "That's the last thing I *ever* give you!"

And somewhere on a country road I just lay down and wept and wanted to die but didn't know how to give up the final vomit that was my miserable ghost.

The thunder murmured.

The rain fell on the cold Pullman-car windows.

What *else*? Is that the list?

No. One final thing, more terrible than all the rest.

In all the years you went to Ralph's house to toss up small bits of gravel on his Fourth of July six-in-the-morning fresh dewy window or to call him forth for the arrival of dawn circuses in the cold fresh blue railroad stations in late June or late August, in all those years, never once did Ralph run to your house.

Never once in all the years did he, or anyone else, prove their friendship by coming by. The door never knocked. The window of your bedroom never faintly clattered and belled with a high-tossed confetti of small dusts and rocks.

And you always knew that the day you stopped going to Ralph's house, calling up in the morn, that would be the day your friendship ended.

You tested it once. You stayed away for a whole week. Ralph never called. It was as if you had died, and no one came to your funeral.

When you saw Ralph at school, there was no surprise, no query, not even the faintest lint of curiosity to be picked off your coat. Where *were* you, Doug? I need someone to beat. Where you *been*, Doug, I got no one to *pinch*!

Add all the sins up. But especially think on the last:

He never came to my house. He never sang up to my early-morning bed or tossed a wedding rice of gravel on the clear panes to call me down to joy and summer days.

And for this last thing, Ralph Underhill, I thought, sitting in the train at four in the morning, as the storm faded, and I found tears in my eyes, for this last and final thing, for that I shall kill you tomorrow night.

Murder, I thought, after thirty-six years. Why, God, you're madder than Ahab.

The train wailed. We ran cross-country like a mechanical Greek Fate carried by a black metal Roman Fury.

They say you can't go home again.

That is a lie.

If you are lucky and time it right, you arrive at sunset when the old town is filled with yellow light.

I got off the train and walked up through Green Town and looked at the courthouse, burning with sunset light. Every tree was hung with gold doubloons of color. Every roof and coping and bit of gingerbread was purest brass and ancient gold.

I sat in the courthouse square with dogs and old men until the sun had set and Green Town was dark. I wanted to savor Ralph Underhill's death.

No one in history had ever done a crime like this.

I would stay, kill, depart, a stranger among strangers.

How would anyone dare to say, finding Ralph Underhill's body on his doorstep, that a boy aged twelve, arriving on a kind of Time Machine train, traveled out of hideous self-contempt, had gunned down the Past? It was beyond all reason. I was safe in my pure insanity.

Finally, at eight-thirty on this cool October night, I walked across town, past the ravine.

I never doubted Ralph would still be there.

People do, after all, move away. . . .

I turned down Park Street and walked two hundred yards to a single streetlamp and looked across. Ralph Underhill's white two-story Victorian house waited for me.

And I could feel him *in* it.

He was there, forty-eight years old, even as I felt myself here, forty-eight, and full of an old and tired and self-devouring spirit.

I stepped out of the light, opened my suitcase, put the pistol in my right-hand coat pocket, shut the case, and hid it in the bushes where, later, I would grab it and walk down into the ravine and across town to the train.

I walked across the street and stood before his house and it was the same house I had stood before thirty-six years ago. There were the windows upon which I had hurled those spring bouquets of rock in love and total giving. There were the sidewalks, spotted with firecracker burn marks from ancient July Fourths when Ralph and I had just blown up the whole damned world, shrieking celebrations.

I walked up on the porch and saw on the mailbox in small letters: UNDERHILL.

What if his wife answers?

No, I thought, he himself, with absolute Greek-tragic perfection, will open the door and take the wound and almost gladly die for old crimes and minor sins somehow grown to crimes.

I rang the bell.

Will he know me, I wondered, after all this time? In the instant before the first shot, *tell* him your name. He must know who it is.

Silence.

I rang the bell again.

The doorknob rattled.

I touched the pistol in my pocket, my heart hammering, but did not take it out.

The door opened.

Ralph Underhill stood there.

He blinked, gazing out at me.

"Ralph?" I said.

"Yes—?" he said.

We stood there, riven, for what could not have been more than five seconds. But, O Christ, many things happened in those five swift seconds.

I saw Ralph Underhill.

I saw him clearly.

And I had not seen him since I was twelve.

Then, he had towered over me to pummel and beat and scream.

Now he was a little old man.

I am five foot eleven.

But Ralph Underhill had not grown much from his twelfth year on.

The man who stood before me was no more than five feet two inches tall.

I *towered* over him.

I gasped. I stared. I saw more.

I was forty-eight years old.

But Ralph Underhill, forty-eight, had lost most of his hair, and what remained was threadbare gray, black and white. He looked sixty or sixty-five.

I was in good health.

Ralph Underhill was waxen pale. There was a knowledge of sickness in his face. He had traveled in some sunless land. He had a ravaged and sunken look. His breath smelled of funeral flowers.

All this, perceived, was like the storm of the night before, gathering all its lightnings and thunders into one bright concussion. We stood in the explosion.

So this is what I came for? I thought. This, then, is the truth. This dreadful instant in time. Not to pull out the weapon. *Not* to kill. No, no. But simply—

To see Ralph Underhill as he *is* in this hour.

That's all.

Just to be here, stand here, and look at him as he has become.

Ralph Underhill lifted one hand in a kind of gesturing wonder. His lips trembled. His eyes flew up and down my body, his mind measured this giant who shadowed his door. At last his voice, so small, so frail, blurted out:

"Doug—?"

I recoiled.

"Doug?" he gasped. "Is that *you?*"

I hadn't expected that. People don't remember! They can't! Across the years? Why would he know, bother, summon up, recognize, call?

I had a wild thought that what had happened to Ralph Underhill was that after I left town, half of his life had collapsed. I had been the center of his world, someone to attack, beat, pummel, bruise. His whole life had cracked by my simple act of walking away thirty-six years ago.

Nonsense! Yet, some small crazed mouse of wisdom scuttered about my brain and screeched what it knew: You needed Ralph, but, *more!* he needed *you!* And you did the only unforgivable, the wounding, thing! You vanished.

"Doug?" he said again, for I was silent there on the porch with my hands at my sides. "Is that you?"

This was the moment I had come for.

At some secret blood level, I had always known I would not use the weapon. I had brought it with me, yes, but Time had gotten here before me, and age, and smaller, more terrible deaths. . . .

Bang.

Six shots through the heart.

But I didn't use the pistol. I only whispered the sound of the shots with my mouth. With each whisper, Ralph Underhill's face aged another ten years. By the time I reached the last shot he was one hundred and ten years old.

"Bang," I whispered. "Bang. Bang. Bang. Bang. Bang."

His body shook with the impact.

"You're dead. Oh, God, Ralph, you're dead."

I turned and walked down the steps and reached the street before he called:

"Doug, is that *you?*"

I did not answer, walking.

"Answer me, " he cried, weakly. "Doug! Doug Spaulding, is that you? Who is that? Who are you?"

I got my suitcase and walked down into the cricket night and darkness of the ravine and across the bridge and up the stairs, going away.

"Who is that?" I heard his voice wail a last time.

A long way off, I looked back.

All the lights were on all over Ralph Underhill's house. It was as if he had gone around and put them all on after I left.

On the other side of the ravine I stopped on the lawn in front of the house where I had been born.

Then I picked up a few bits of gravel and did the thing that had never been done, ever in my life.

I tossed the few bits of gravel up to tap that window where I had lain every morning of my first twelve years. I called my own name. I called me down in friendship to play in some long summer that no longer was.

I stood waiting just long enough for my other young self to come down to join me.

Then swiftly, fleeing ahead of the dawn, we ran out of Green Town and back, thank you, dear Christ, back toward Now and Today for the rest of my life.

The Better Part
of Wisdom

The room was like a great warm hearth, lit by an unseen fire, gone comfortable. The fireplace itself struggled to keep a small blaze going on a few wet logs and some turf, which was no more than smoke and several lazy orange eyes of charcoal. The place was slowly filling, draining, and refilling with music. A single lemon lamp was lit in a far corner, illumining walls painted a summer color of yellow. The hardwood floor was polished so severely it glowed like a dark river upon which floated throw-rugs whose plumage resembled South American wild birds, flashing electric blues, whites, and jungle greens. White porcelain vases, brimming with fresh-cut hothouse flowers, kept their serene fires burning on four small tables about the room. Above the fireplace, a serious portrait of a young man gazed out with eyes the same color as the ceramics, a deep blue, raw with intelligence and vitality.

Entering the room quietly, one might not have noticed the two men, they were so still.

One sat reclining back upon the pure white couch, eyes closed. The second lay upon the couch so his head was pillowed in the lap of the other. His eyes were shut, too, listening. Rain touched the windows. The music ended.

Instantly there was a soft scratching at the door.

Both men blinked as if to say: People don't *scratch*, they *knock*.

The man who had been lying down leaped to the door and called: "Someone there?"

"By God, there is," said an old voice with a faint brogue.

"Grandfather!"

With the door flung wide, the young man pulled a small round old man into the warm-lit room.

"Tom, boy, ah Tom, and glad I am to see you!"

They fell together in bear-hugs, pawing. Then the old man felt the other person in the room and moved back.

Tom spun around, pointing. "Grandpa, this is Frank. Frank, this is Grandpa, I mean—oh hell—"

The old man saved the moment by trotting forward to seize and pull Frank to his feet, where he towered high above this small intruder from the night.

"Frank, is it?" the old man yelled up the heights.

"Yes, sir," Frank called back down.

"I—" said the grandfather, "have been standing outside that door for five minutes—"

"Five minutes?" cried both young men, alarmed.

"—debating whether to knock. I heard the music, you see, and finally I said, damn, if there's a girl with him he can either shove her out the window in the rain or show the lovely likes of her to the old man. Hell, I said, and knocked, and"—he slung down his battered old valise—"there *is* no young girl here, I see—or, by God, you've *smothered* her in the closet, eh!"

"There is no young girl, Grandfather." Tom turned in a circle, his hands out to show.

"But—" The grandfather eyed the polished floor, the white throw-rugs, the bright flowers, the watchful portraits on the walls. "You've *borrowed* her place, then?"

"Borrowed?"

"I mean, by the look of the room, there's a woman's touch. It looks like them steamship posters I seen in the travel windows half my life."

"Well," said Frank. "We—"

"The fact is, Grandfather," said Tom, clearing his throat, "*we* did this place over. Redecorated."

"Redecorated?" The old man's jaw dropped. His eyes toured the four walls, stunned. "The *two* of you are responsible? Jesus!"

The old man touched a blue and white ceramic ashtray, and bent to stroke a bright cockatoo throw-rug.

"Which of you did *what?*" he asked, suddenly, squinting one eye at them.

Tom flushed and stammered. "Well, we—"

"Ah, God, no, no, stop!" cried the old man, lifting one hand. "Here I am, fresh *in* the place, and sniffing about like a crazy hound and no fox. Shut that damn door. Ask me where *I'm* going, what am *I* up to, eh, *eh?* And, while you're at it, do you have a touch of the Beast in this art gallery?"

"The Beast it is!" Tom slammed the door, hustled his grandfather out of his greatcoat, and brought forth three tumblers and a bottle of Irish whiskey, which the old man touched as if it were a newborn babe.

"Well, that's more like it. What do we drink to?"

"Why, you, Grandpa!"

"No, no." The old man gazed at Tom and then at his friend, Frank. "Christ," he sighed, "you're so damn young it breaks my bones in the ache. Come now, let's drink to fresh hearts and apple cheeks and all life up ahead and happiness somewhere for the taking. Yes?"

"Yes!" said both, and drank.

And drinking watched each other merrily or warily, half one, half the other. And the young saw in the old bright pink face, lined as it was, cuffed as it was by circumstantial life, the echo of Tom's face itself peering out through the years. In the old blue eyes, especially, was the sharp bright intelligence that sprang from the old portrait on the wall, that would be young until coins weighted them shut. And around the edges of the old mouth was the smile that blinked and went in Tom's face, and in the old hands was the quick, surprising action of Tom's, as if both old man and young had hands that lived to themselves and did sly things by impulse.

So they drank and leaned and smiled and drank again, each a mirror for the other, each delighting in the fact that an ancient man and a raw youth with the same eyes and hands and blood were met on this raining night, and the whiskey was good.

"Ah, Tom, Tom, it's a loving sight you are!" said the grandfather. "Dublin's been sore without you these four years. But, hell, I'm dying. No, don't ask me how or why. The doctor has the news, damn him, and shot me between the eyes with it. So I said instead of relatives shelling out their cash to come say good-by to the old horse, why not make the farewell tour yourself and shake hands and drink drinks. So here I am this night and tomorrow beyond London to see Lucie and then Glasgow to see Dick. I'll stay no more than a day each place, so as not to overload anyone. Now shut that mouth, which is hanging open. I am not out collecting sympathies. I am eighty, and it's time for a damn fine wake, which I have saved money for, so not a word. I have come to see everyone and make sure they are in a fit state of half-graceful joy so I can kick up my heels and fall dead with a good heart, if that's possible. I—"

"Grandfather!" cried Tom, suddenly, and seized the old man's hands and then his shoulders.

"Why, bless you, boy, thanks," said the old man, seeing the tears in the young man's eyes. "But just what I find in your gaze is enough." He set the boy gently back. "Tell me about London, your work, this place. You, too, Frank, a friend of Tom's is as good as my son's son! Tell everything, Tom!"

"Excuse me." Frank darted toward the door. "You both have much to talk about. There's shopping I must do—"

"Wait!"

Frank stopped.

For the old man had really seen the portrait over the fireplace now and walked to it to put out his hand, to squint and read the signed name at the bottom.

"Frank Davis. Is that you, boy? *You* did this picture?"

"Yes, sir," said Frank, at the door.

"How long ago?"

"Three years ago, I think. Yes, three."

The old man nodded slowly, as if this information added to the great puzzle, a continuing bafflement.

"Tom, do you know who that *looks* like?"

"Yes, Grand-da. You. A long time ago."

"So you see it, too, eh? Christ in heaven, yes. That's me on my eighteenth birthday and all Ireland and its grasses and tender maids good for the chewing ahead and not behind me. That's me, that's me. Jesus I was handsome, and Jesus, Tom, so are you. And Jesus, Frank, you *are* uncanny. You are a *fine* artist, boy."

"You do what you can do." Frank had come back to the middle of the room, quietly. "You do what you *know*."

"And you *know* Tom, to the hair and eyelash." The old man turned and smiled. "How does it feel, Tom, to look out of that borrowed face? Do you feel great, is the world your Dublin prawn and oyster?"

Tom laughed. Grandfather laughed. Frank joined them.

"One more drink." The old man poured. "And we'll let you slip diplomatically out, Frank. But come back. I must talk with you."

"What about?" said Frank.

"Ah, the Mysteries. Of Life, of Time, of Existence. What else did *you* have in mind, Frank?"

"Those will do, Grandfather—" said Frank, and stopped, amazed at the word come out of his mouth. "I mean, Mr. Kelly—"

"Grandfather will do."

"I must run." Frank doused his drink. "Phone you later, Tom."

The door shut. Frank was gone.

"You'll sleep here tonight of course, Grandpa?" Tom seized the one valise. "Frank won't be back. You'll have his bed." Tom was busy arranging the sheets on one of the two couches against the far wall. "Now, it's early. Let's drink some more Grandfather, and talk."

But the old man, stunned, was silent, eying each picture in turn upon the wall. "Grand painting, that."

"Frank did them."

"That's a fine lamp there."

"Frank made it."

"The rug on the floor here now—?"

"Frank."

"Jesus," whispered the old man, "he's a maniac for work, is he not?"

Quietly, he shuffled about the room like one visiting a gallery.

"It seems," he said, "the place is absolutely blowing apart with fine artistic talent. You turned your hand to nothing like this, in Dublin."

"You learn a lot, away from home," said Tom, uneasily.

The old man shut his eyes and drank his drink.

"Is anything wrong, Grandfather?"

"It will hit me in the middle of the night," said the old man. "I will probably stand up in bed with a hell of a yell. But right now it is just a thing in the pit of my stomach and the back of my head. Let's talk, boy, let's talk."

And they talked and drank until midnight and then the old man got put to bed and Tom went to bed himself and after a long while both slept.

About two in the morning, the old man woke suddenly.

He peered around in the dark, wondering where he was, then saw the paintings, the upholstered chairs, and the lamp and rugs Frank had made, and sat up. He clenched his fists. Then, rising, he threw on his clothes, and staggered toward the door as if fearful that he might not make it before something terrible happened.

When the door slammed, Tom jerked his eyes wide.

Somewhere off in the dark there was a sound of someone calling, shouting, defying the elements, someone at the top of his lungs crying blasphemies, saying God and Jesus and Jesus and God, and finally blows struck, wild blows, as if someone were hitting a wall or a person.

After a long while, his grandfather shuffled back into the room, soaked to the skin.

Weaving, muttering, whispering, the old man peeled off his wet clothes before the fireless fire, then threw a newspaper on the coals, which blazed up briefly to show a face relaxing out of fury into numbness. The old man found and put on Tom's discarded robe. Tom kept his eyes tight as the old man held his hands out toward the dwindling blaze, streaked with blood.

"Damn, damn, damn. *There!*" He poured whiskey and gulped it down. He blinked at Tom and the paintings on the wall and looked at Tom and the flowers in the vases and then drank again. After a long while, Tom pretended to wake up.

"It's after two. You need your rest, Grand-da."

"I'll rest when I'm done drinking. And *thinking!*"

"Thinking what, Grandpa?"

"Right now," said the old man, seated in the dim room with the tumbler in his two hands, and the fire gone to ghost on the hearth, "remembering your dear grandmother in June of the year 1902. And there is the thought of your father born, which is fine, and you born after him, which is fine. And there is the thought of your father dying when you were young and the hard life of your mother and her holding you too close, maybe, in the cold beggar life of flinty Dublin. And me out in the meadows with my working life, and us together only once a month. The being born of people and the going away of people. These turn round in an old man's night. I think of you born, Tom, a happy day. Then I see you here now. That's it."

The old man grew silent and drank his drink.

"Grand-da," said Tom, at last, almost like a child crept in for penalties and forgiveness of a sin as yet unnamed, "do I *worry* you?"

"No." Then the old man added, "But what life will *do* with you, how you may be treated, good or ill—I sit up late with *that*."

The old man sat. The young man lay wide-eyed watching him and later said, as if reading thoughts:

"Grandfather, I *am* happy."

The old man leaned forward.

"*Are* you, boy?"

"I have never been so happy in my life, sir."

"Yes?" The old man looked through the dim air of the room, at the young face. "I see that. But will you *stay* happy, Tom?"

"Does anyone ever *stay* happy, Grandfather? Nothing lasts, *does* it?"

"Shut up! Your grandma and me, *that* lasted!"

"No. It wasn't *all* the same, was it? The first years were one thing, the last years another."

The old man put his hand over his own mouth and then massaged his face, closing his eyes.

"God, yes, you're right. There are two, no, three, no, four lives, for each of us. Not one of them lasts, it's sure. But the *thought* of them does. And out of the four or five or a dozen lives you live, one is special. I remember, once . . ."

The old man's voice faltered.

The young man said, "*Once*, Grandpa?"

The old man's eyes fixed somewhere to a horizon of the Past. He did not speak to the room or to Tom or to anyone. He didn't even seem to be speaking to himself.

"Oh, it was a long time ago. When I first came in this room tonight, for no reason, strange, the memory was there. I ran back down along the shoreline of Galway to that week . . ."

"What week, when?"

"My twelfth birthday fell that week in summer, think of it! Victoria still queen and me in a turf-hut out by Galway strolling the shore for food to be picked up from the tides, and the weather so sweet you almost turned sad with the taste of it, for you knew it would soon go away.

"And in the middle of the great fair weather along the road by the shore one noon came this tinker's caravan carrying their dark gypsy people to set up camp by the sea.

"There was a mother, a father, and a girl in that caravan, and this boy who came running down by the sea alone, perhaps in need of company, for there I was with nothing to do, and in need of strangers myself.

"Here he came running. And I shall not forget my first sight of him from that day till they drop me in the earth. He—

"Ah God, I'm a failure with words! Stop everything. I must go further back.

"A circus came to Dublin. I visited the sideshows of pinheads and dwarfs and terrible small midgets and fat women and skeleton men. Seeing a crowd about one last exhibit, I thought this must be the most horrible of all. I edged over to look at this final terror! And what did I see? The crowd was drawn to nothing more nor less than: a little girl of some six years, so fair, so beautiful, so cream-white of cheek, so blue of eye, so golden of hair, so quiet in her manner that in the midst of this fleshy holocaust she called attention. By saying nothing her shout of beauty stopped the show. All *had* to come to her to get well again. For it was a sick menagerie and she the only sweet lovely Doc about to give us back life.

"Well, that girl in the sideshow was as wonderful a surprise as this boy come running down the beach like a young horse.

"He was not dark like his parents.

"His hair was all gold curls and bits of sun. He was cut out of bronze by the light, and what wasn't bronze was copper. Impossible, but it seemed that this boy of twelve, like myself, had been born on that very day, he looked that new and fresh. And in his face were these bright brown eyes, the eyes of an animal that has run a long way, pursued, along the shorelines of the world.

"He pulled up and the first thing he said to me was laughter. He was glad to be alive, and announced that by the sound he made. I must have laughed in turn, for his spirit was catching. He shoved out his brown hand. I hesitated. He gestured impatiently and grabbed my hand.

"My God, after all these years I remember what we said: 'Isn't it funny?' he said.

"I didn't ask *what* was funny. I *knew*. He said his name was Jo. I said my name was Tim. And there we were, two boys on the beach and the universe a good rare joke between us.

"He looked at me with his great round full copper eyes, and laughed out his breath and I thought: He has chewed hay! his breath smells of grass; and suddenly I was giddy. The smell stunned me. Jesus God, I thought, reeling, I'm drunk, and *why*? I've nipped Dad's booze, but God, what's *this*? Drunk by noon, hit by the sun, giddy from what? the sweet mash caught in a strange boy's teeth? No, no!

"Then Jo looked straight at me and said, 'There isn't much time.'

"'Much time?' I asked.

"'Why,' said Jo, 'for us to be friends. We are, *aren't* we?'

"He breathed the smell of mown fields upon me.

"Jesus God, I wanted to cry, Yes! And almost fell down, but staggered back as if he had hit me a friend's hit. And my mouth opened and shut and I said, 'Why is there so little time?'

"'Because,' said Jo, 'we'll only be here six days, seven at the most, then on down and around Eire. I'll never see you again in my life. So we'll just have to pack a lot of things in a few days, won't we, Tim?'

"'Six days? That's no time at all!' I protested, and wondered why I found myself suddenly destroyed, left destitute on the shore. A thing had not begun, but already I sorrowed after its death.

"'A day here, a week there, a month somewhere else,' said Jo. 'I must live very quickly, Tim. I have no friends that last. Only what I remember. So, wherever I go, I say to my new friends, quick, do this, do that, let us make many happenings, a long list, so you will remember me when I am gone, and I you, and say: That was a friend. So, let's begin. There!'

"And Jo tagged me and ran.

"I ran after him, laughing, for wasn't it silly, me headlong after a stranger boy unknown five minutes before? We must've run a mile down that long summer beach before he let me catch him. I thought I might pummel him for making me run so far for nothing, for something, for God knew what! But when we tumbled to earth and I pinned him down, all he did was spring his breath in one gasp up at me, one breath, and I leaped back and shook my head and sat staring at him, as if I'd plunged wet hands in an open electric socket. He laughed to see me fall away, to see me scurry and sit in wonder. 'O, Tim,' he said, 'we *shall* be friends.'

"You know the dread long cold weather, most months, of Ireland? Well, this week of my twelfth birthday, it was summer each day and every day for the seven days named by Jo as the limit which would be no more days. We walked the shore, and that's all there was, the simple thing of us upon the shore, and building castles or climbing hills to fight wars among the mounds. We found an old round tower and yelled up and down from it. But mostly it was walking, our arms about each other like twins born in a tangle, never cut free by knife or lightning. I inhaled, he exhaled. Then he breathed and I was the sweet chorus. We talked, far through the nights on the sand, until our parents came seeking the lost who had found they knew not what. Lured home, I slept beside him, or him me, and talked and laughed, Jesus, laughed, till dawn. Then out again we roared until the earth swung up to hit our backs. We found ourselves laid out with sweet hilarity, eyes tight, gripped to each other's shaking, and the laugh jumped free like one silver trout following another. God, I bathed in his laughter as he bathed in mine, until we were weak as if love had put us to the slaughter and exhaustions. We panted then like pups in hot summer, empty of laughing, and sleepy with friendship. And the weather for that week was blue and gold, no clouds, no rain, and a wind that smelled of apples, but no, only that boy's wild breath.

"It crossed my mind, long after, if ever an old man could bathe again in that summer fount, the wild spout of breathing that sprang from his nostrils and gasped from his mouth, why one might peel off a score of years, one would be young, how might the flesh resist?

"But the laughter is gone and the boy gone into a man lost somewhere in the world, and here I am two lifetimes later, speaking of it for the first time. For who was there to tell? From my twelfth birthday week, and the gift of friendship, to this, who might I tell of that shore and that summer and the two of us walking all tangled in our arms and lives and life as perfect as the letter *o*, a damned great circle of rare weather, lovely talk, and us certain we'd live forever, never die, and be good friends.

"And at the end of the week, he left.

"He was wise for his years. He didn't say good-by. All of a sudden, the tinker's cart was gone.

"I shouted along the shore. A long way off, I saw the caravan go over a hill. But then his wisdom spoke to me. Don't catch. Let go. Weep now, my own wisdom said. And I wept.

"I wept for three days and on the fourth grew very still. I did not go down to the shore again for many months. And in all the years that have passed, never have I known such a thing again. I have had a good life, a fine wife, good children, and you, boy, Tom, you. But as sure as I sit here, never after that was I so agonized, mad, and crazy wild. Never did drink make me as drunk. Never did I cry so hard again. Why, Tom? Why do I say this, and what was it? Back so far in innocence, back in the time when I had nobody, and knew nothing. How is it I remember him when all else slips away? When often I cannot remember your dear grandmother's face, God forgive me, why does his face come back on the shore by the sea? Why do I see us fall again and the earth reach up to take the wild young horses driven mad by too much sweet grass in a line of days that never end?"

The old man grew silent. After a moment, he added, "The better part of wisdom, they say, is what's left unsaid. I'll say no more. I don't even know why I've said all *this*."

Tom lay in the dark. "*I* know."

"Do you, lad?" asked the old man. "Well, tell me. Someday."

"Someday," said Tom. "I will."

They listened to the rain touch at the windows.

"Are you happy, Tom?"

"You asked that before, sir."

"I ask again. Are you happy?"

"Yes."

Silence.

"Is it summertime on the shore, Tom? Is it the magic seven days? Are you drunk?"

Tom did not answer for a long while, and then said nothing but, "Grand-da," and then moved his head once in a nod.

The old man lay back in the chair. He might have said, This will pass. He might have said, It will not last. He might have said many things. Instead he said, "Tom?"

"Sir?"

"Ah Jesus!" shouted the old man suddenly. "Christ, God Almighty! Damn it to hell!" Then the old man stopped and his breathing grew quiet. "There. It's a maniac night. I had to let out one last yell. I just had to, boy."

And at last they slept, with the rain falling fast.

With the first light of dawn, the old man dressed with careful quietness, picked up his valise, and bent to touch the sleeping young man's cheek with the palm of one hand.

"Tom, good-by," he whispered.

Moving down the dim stairwell toward the steadily beating rain, he found Tom's friend waiting at the foot of the stairs.

"Frank! You haven't been down here *all night?*"

"No, no, Mr. Kelly," said Frank, quickly. "I stayed at a friend's."

The old man turned to look up the dark stairwell as if he could see the room and Tom in it warm asleep.

"Gah . . . !" Something almost a growl stirred in his throat and subsided. He shifted uneasily and looked back down at the dawn kindled on this young man's face, this one who had painted a picture that hung above the fireplace in the room above.

"The damn night is over," said the old man. "So if you'll just stand aside—"

"Sir."

The old man took one step down and burst out:

"Listen! If you hurt Tom, in any way ever, why, Jesus, I'll break you across my knee! You *hear?*"

Frank held out his hand. "Don't worry."

The old man looked at the hand as if he had never seen one before. He sighed.

"Ah, damn it to hell, Frank, Tom's friend, so young you're destruction to the eyes. Get away!"

They shook hands.

"Jesus, that's a hard grip," said the old man, surprised.

Then he was gone, as if the rain had hustled him off in its own multitudinous running.

The young man shut the upstairs door and stood for a moment looking at the figure on the bed and at last went over and as if by instinct put his hand down to the exact same spot where the old man had printed his hand in farewell not five minutes before. He touched the summer cheek.

In his sleep, Tom smiled the smile of his father's father, and called the old man, deep in a dream, by name.

He called him twice.

And then he slept quietly.

Interval in Sunlight

They moved into the Hotel de Las Flores on a hot green afternoon in late October. The inner patio was blazing with red and yellow and white flowers, like flames, which lit their small room. The husband was tall and black-haired and pale and looked as if he had driven ten thousand miles in his sleep; he walked through the tile patio, carrying a few blankets, he threw himself on the small bed of the small room with an exhausted sigh and lay there. While he closed his eyes, his wife, about twenty-four, with yellow hair and horn-rim glasses, smiling at the manager, Mr. Gonzales, hurried in and out from the room to the car. First she carried two suitcases, then a typewriter, thanking Mr. Gonzales, but steadily refusing his help. And then she carried in a huge packet of Mexican masks they had picked up in the lake town of Pátzcuaro, and then out to the car again and again for more small cases and packages, and even an extra tire which they were afraid some native might roll off down the cobbled street during the night. Her face pink from the exertion, she hummed as she locked the car, checked the windows, and ran back to the room where her husband lay, eyes closed, on one of the twin beds.

"Good God," he said, without opening his eyes, "this is one hell of a bed. Feel it. I told you to pick one with a Simmons mattress." He gave the bed a weary slap. "It's as hard as a rock."

"I don't speak Spanish," said the wife, standing there, beginning to look bewildered. "You should have come in and talked to the landlord yourself."

"Look," he said, opening his gray eyes just a little and turning his head. "I've done all the driving on this trip. You just sit there and look at the scenery. You're supposed to handle the money, the lodgings, the gas and oil, and all that. This is the second place we've hit where you got hard beds."

"I'm sorry," she said, still standing, beginning to fidget.

"I like to at least sleep nights, that's all I ask."

"I said I was sorry."

"Didn't you even *feel* the beds?"

"They looked all right."

"You've got to feel them." He slapped the bed and punched it at his side.

The woman turned to her own bed and sat on it, experimentally. "It feels all right to me."

"Well, it isn't."

"Maybe my bed is softer."

He rolled over tiredly and reached out to punch the other bed. "You can have this one if you want," she said, trying to smile.

"That's hard, too," he said, sighing, and fell back and closed his eyes again.

No one spoke, but the room was turning cold, while outside the flowers blazed in the green shrubs and the sky was immensely blue. Finally, she rose and grabbed the typewriter and suitcase and turned toward the door.

"Where're you going?" he said.

"Back out to the car," she said. "We're going to find another place."

"Put it down," said the man. "I'm tired."

"We'll find another place."

"Sit down, we'll stay here tonight, my God, and move tomorrow."

She looked at all the boxes and crates and luggage, the clothes, and the tire, her eyes flickering. She put the typewriter down.

"Damn it!" she cried, suddenly. "You can have the mattress off my bed. I'll sleep on the springs."

He said nothing.

"You can have the mattress off my bed," she said. "Only don't talk about it. Here!" She pulled the blanket off and yanked at the mattress.

"That might be better," he said, opening his eyes, seriously.

"You can have both mattresses, my God, I can sleep on a bed of nails!" she cried. "Only stop yapping."

"I'll manage." He turned his head away. "It wouldn't be fair to you."

"It'd be plenty fair just for you to keep quiet about the bed; it's not that hard, good God, you'll sleep if you're tired. Jesus God, Joseph!"

"Keep your voice down," said Joseph. "Why don't you go find out about Parícutin volcano?"

"I'll go in a minute." She stood there, her face red.

"Find out what the rates are for a taxi out there and a horse up the mountain to see it, and look at the sky; if the sky's blue that means the volcano isn't erupting today, and don't let them gyp you."

"I guess I can do that."

She opened the door and stepped out and shut the door and *Señor* Gonzales was there. Was everything all right? he wished to know.

She walked past the town windows, and smelled the soft charcoal air. Beyond the town all of the sky was blue except north (or east or west, she couldn't be certain) where the huge broiling black cloud rose up from the terrible volcano. She looked at it with a small tremoring inside. Then she sought out a large fat taxi driver and the arguments began. The price started at sixty pesos and dwindled rapidly, with expressions of mournful defeat upon the buck-toothed fat man's face, to thirty-seven pesos. So! He was to come at three tomorrow afternoon, did he understand? That would give them time to drive out through the gray snows of land where the flaking lava ash had fallen to make a great dusty winter for mile after mile, and arrive at the volcano as the sun was setting. Was this very clear?

"*Si, señora, ésta es muy claro, si!*"

"*Bueno.*" She gave him their hotel room number and bade him good-by.

She idled into little lacquer shops, alone; she opened the little lacquer boxes and sniffed the sharp scent of camphor wood and cedar and cinnamon. She watched the craftsmen, enchanted, razor blades flashing in the sun, cutting the flowery scrolls and filling these patterns with red and blue color. The town flowed about her like a silent slow river and she immersed herself in it, smiling all of the time, and not even knowing she smiled.

Suddenly she looked at her watch. She'd been gone half an hour. A look of panic crossed her face. She ran a few steps and then slowed to a walk again, shrugging.

As she walked in through the tiled cool corridors, under the silvery tin candelabra on the adobe walls, a caged bird fluted high and sweet, and a girl with long soft dark hair sat at a piano painted sky blue and played a Chopin nocturne.

She looked at the windows of their room, the shades pulled down. Three o'clock of a fresh afternoon. She saw a soft-drinks box at the end of the patio and bought four bottles of Coke. Smiling, she opened the door to their room.

"It certainly took you long enough," he said, turned on his side toward the wall.

"We leave tomorrow afternoon at three," she said.

"How much?"

She smiled at his back, the bottles cold in her arms. "Only thirty-seven pesos."

"Twenty pesos would have done it. You can't let these Mexicans take advantage of you."

"I'm richer than they are; if anyone *deserves* being taken advantage of, it's us."

"That's not the idea. They *like* to bargain."

"I feel like a bitch, doing it."

"The guide book says they double their price and expect you to halve it."

"Let's not quibble over a dollar."

"A dollar is a dollar."

"I'll pay the dollar from my own money," she said. "I brought some cold drinks—do you want one?"

"What've you got?" He sat up in bed.

"Cokes."

"Well, you know I don't like Cokes much; take two of those back, will you, and get some Orange Crush?"

"Please?" she said, standing there.

"Please," he said, looking at her. "Is the volcano active?"

"Yes."

"Did you ask?"

"No, I looked at the sky. Plenty of smoke."

"You should have asked."

"The damn sky is just exploding with it."

"But how do we know it's good tomorrow?"

"We don't know. If it's not, we put it off."

"I guess that's right." He lay down again.

She brought back two bottles of Orange Crush.

"It's not very cold," he said, drinking it.

They had supper in the patio: sizzling steak, green peas, a plate of Spanish rice, a little wine, and spiced peaches for dessert.

As he napkined his mouth, he said, casually, "Oh, I meant to tell you. I've checked your figures on what I owe you for the last six days, from Mexico City to here. You say I owe you one hundred twenty-five pesos, or about twenty-five American dollars, right?"

"Yes."

"I make it I owe you only twenty-two."

"I don't think that's possible," she said, still working on her spiced peaches with a spoon.

"I added the figures twice."

"So did I."

"I think you added them wrong."

"Perhaps I did." She jarred the chair back suddenly. "Let's go check."

In the room, the notebook lay open under the lighted lamp. They checked the figures together. "You see," said he, quietly. "You're three dollars off. How did that happen?"

"It just happened. I'm sorry."

"You're one hell of a bookkeeper."

"I do my best."

"Which isn't very good. I thought you could take a little responsibility."

"I try damned hard."

"You forgot to check the air in the tires, you get hard beds, you lose things, you lost a key in Acapulco, to the car trunk, you lost the air-pressure gauge, and you can't keep books. I have to drive—"

"I know, I know, you have to drive all day, and you're tired, and you just got over a strep infection in Mexico City, and you're afraid it'll come back and you want to take it easy on your heart, and the least I could do is to keep my nose clean and the arithmetic neat. I know it all by heart. I'm only a writer, and I admit I've got big feet."

"You won't make a very good writer this way," he said. "It's such a simple thing, addition."

"I didn't do it on purpose!" she cried, throwing the pencil down. "Hell! I wish I *had* cheated you now. I wish I'd done a lot of things now. I wish I'd lost that air-pressure gauge on purpose, I'd have some pleasure in thinking about it and knowing I did it to spite you, anyway. I wish I'd picked these beds for their hard mattresses, then I could laugh in my sleep tonight, thinking how hard they are for you to sleep on, I wish I'd done *that* on purpose. And now I wish I'd thought to fix the books. I could enjoy laughing about that, too."

"Keep your voice down," he said, as to a child.

"I'll be God damned if I'll keep my voice down."

"All I want to know now is how much money you have in the kitty."

She put her trembling hands in her purse and brought out all the money. When he counted it, there was five dollars missing.

"Not only do you keep poor books, overcharging me on some item or other, but now there's five dollars gone from the kitty," he said. "Where'd it go?"

"I don't know. I must have forgotten to put it down, or if I did, I didn't say what for. Good God, I don't want to add this damned list again. I'll pay what's missing out of my own allowance to keep everyone happy. Here's five dollars! Now, let's go out for some air, it's hot in here."

She jerked the door wide and she trembled with a rage all out of proportion to the facts. She was hot and shaking and stiff and she knew her face was very red and her eyes bright, and when *Señor* Gonzales bowed to them and wished them a good evening, she had to smile stiffly in return.

"Here," said her husband, handing her the room key. "And don't, for God's sake, lose it."

The band was playing in the green *zócalo*. It hooted and blared and tooted and screamed up on the bronze-scrolled bandstand. The square was bloomed full with people and color, men and boys walking one way around the block, on the pink and blue tiles, women and girls walking the other way, flirting their dark olive eyes at one another, men holding each other's elbows and talking earnestly between meetings, women and girls twined like ropes of flowers, sweetly scented, blowing in a summer night wind over the cooling tile designs, whispering, past the vendors of cold drinks and tamales and enchiladas. The band precipitated "Yankee Doodle" once, to the delight of the blonde woman with the horn-rim glasses, who smiled wildly and turned to her husband. Then the band hooted "La Cumparsita" and "La Paloma Azul," and she felt a good warmth and began to sing a little, under her breath.

"Don't act like a tourist," said her husband.

"I'm just enjoying myself."

"Don't be a damned fool, is all I ask."

A vendor of silver trinkets shuffled by. "*Señor?*"

Joseph looked them over, while the band played, and held up one bracelet, very intricate, very exquisite. "How much?"

"*Veinte pesos, señor.*"

"Ho ho," said the husband, smiling. "I'll give you five for it," in Spanish.

"Five," replied the man in Spanish. "I would starve."

"Don't bargain with him," said the wife.

"Keep out of this," said the husband, smiling. To the vendor, "Five pesos, *señor.*"

"No, no, I would lose money. My last price is ten pesos."

"Perhaps I could give you six," said the husband. "No more than that."

The vendor hesitated in a kind of numbed panic as the husband tossed the bracelet back on the red velvet tray and turned away. "I am no longer interested. Good night."

"*Señor!* Six pesos, it is yours!"

The husband laughed. "Give him six pesos, darling."

She stiffly drew forth her wallet and gave the vendor some peso bills. The man went away. "I hope you're satisfied," she said.

"Satisfied?" Smiling, he flipped the bracelet in the palm of his pale hand. "For a dollar and twenty-five cents I buy a bracelet that sells for thirty dollars in the States!"

"I have something to confess," she said. "I gave that man ten pesos."

"What!" The husband stopped laughing.

"I put a five-peso note in with those one-peso bills. Don't worry, I'll take it out of my own money. It won't go on the bill I present you at the end of the week."

He said nothing, but dropped the bracelet in his pocket. He looked at the band thundering into the last bars of "*Ay, Jalisco.*" Then he said, "You're a fool. You'd let these people take all your money."

It was her turn to step away a bit and not reply. She felt rather good. She listened to the music.

"I'm going back to the room," he said. "I'm tired."

"We only drove a hundred miles from Pátzcuaro."

"My throat is a little raw again. Come on."

They moved away from the music and the walking, whispering, laughing people. The band played the "Toreador Song." The drums thumped like great dull hearts in the summery night. There was a smell of papaya in the air, and green thicknesses of jungle and hidden waters.

"I'll walk you back to the room and come back myself," she said. "I want to hear the music."

"Don't be naïve."

"I like it, damn it, I like it, it's good music. It's not fake, it's real, or as real as anything ever gets in this world, that's why I like it."

"When I don't feel well, I don't expect to have you out running around the town alone. It isn't fair you see things I don't."

They turned in at the hotel and the music was still fairly loud. "If you want to walk by yourself, go off on a trip by yourself and go back to the United States by yourself," he said. "Where's the key?"

"Maybe I lost it."

They let themselves into the room and undressed. He sat on the edge of the bed looking into the night patio. At last he shook his head, rubbed his eyes, and sighed. "I'm tired. I've been terrible today." He looked at her where she sat, next to him, and he put out his hand to take her arm. "I'm sorry. I get all riled up, driving, and then us not talking the language too well. By evening I'm a mess of nerves."

"Yes," she said.

Quite suddenly he moved over beside her. He took hold of her and held her tightly, his head over her shoulder, eyes shut, talking into her ear with a quiet, whispering fervency. "You know, we *must* stay together. There's only us, really, no matter what happens, no matter what trouble we have. I do love you so much, you know that. Forgive me if I'm difficult. We've got to make it go."

She stared over his shoulder at the blank wall and the wall was like her life in this moment, a wide expanse of nothingness with hardly a bump, a contour, or a feeling to it. She didn't know what to say or do. Another time, she would have melted. But there was such a thing as firing metal too often, bringing it to a glow, shaping it. At last the metal refuses to glow or shape; it is nothing but a weight. She was a weight now, moving mechanically in his arms, hearing but not hearing, understanding but not understanding, replying but not replying. "Yes, we'll stay together." She felt her lips move. "We love each other." The lips said what they must say, while her mind was in her eyes and her eyes bored deep into the vacuum of the wall. "Yes." Holding but not holding him. "Yes."

The room was dim. Outside, someone walked in a corridor, perhaps glancing at this locked door, perhaps hearing their vital whispering as no more than something falling drop by drop from a loose faucet, a running drain perhaps, or a turned book-leaf under a solitary bulb. Let the doors whisper, the people of the world walked down tile corridors and did not hear.

"Only you and I know the things." His breath was fresh. She felt very sorry for him and herself and the world, suddenly. Everyone was infernally alone. He was like a man clawing at a statue. She did not feel herself move. Only her mind, which was a lightless, dim fluorescent vapor, shifted. "Only you and I remember," he said, "and if one of us should leave, then half the memories are gone. So we must stay together because if one forgets the other remembers."

Remembers what? she asked herself. But she remembered instantly, in a linked series, those parts of incidents in their life together that perhaps he might not recall: the night at the beach, five years ago, one of the first fine nights beneath the canvas with the secret touchings, the days at Sunland sprawled together, taking the sun until twilight. Wandering in an abandoned silver mine, oh, a million things, one touched on and revealed another in an instant!

He held her tight back against the bed now. "Do you know how lonely I am? Do you know how lonely I make myself with these arguments and fights and all of it, when I'm tired?" He waited for her to answer, but she said nothing. She felt his eyelid flutter on her neck. Faintly, she remembered when he had first flicked his eyelid near her ear. "Spider-eye," she had said, laughing, then. "It feels like a small spider in my ear." And now this small lost spider climbed with insane humor upon her neck. There was something in his voice which made her feel she was a woman on a train going away and he was standing in the station saying, "Don't go." And her appalled voice silently cried, "But *you're* the one on a train! *I'm* not going *anywhere!*"

She lay back, bewildered. It was the first time in two weeks he had touched her. And the touching had such an immediacy that she knew the wrong word would send him very far away again.

She lay and said nothing.

Finally, after a long while, she heard him get up, sighing, and move off. He got into his own bed and drew the covers up, silently. She moved at last, arranged herself on her bed, and lay listening to her watch tick in the small hot darkness. "My God," she whispered, finally, "it's only eight-thirty."

"Go to sleep," he said.

She lay in the dark, perspiring, naked, on her own bed, and in the distance, sweetly, faintly, so that it made her soul and heart ache to hear it, she heard the band thumping and brassing out its melodies. She wanted to walk among the dark moving people and sing with them and smell the soft charcoal air of October in a small summery town deep in the tropics of Mexico, a million miles lost from civilization, listening to the good music, tapping her foot and humming. But now she lay with her eyes wide, in bed. In the next hour, the band played "La Golondrina," "Marimba," "Los Viejitos," "Michoacán la Verde," "Barcarolle," and "Luna Lunera."

At three in the morning she awoke for no reason and lay, her sleep done and finished with, feeling the coolness that came with deep night. She listened to his breathing and she felt away and separate from the world. She thought of the long trip from Los Angeles to Laredo, Texas, like a silver-white boiling nightmare. And then the green technicolor, red and yellow and blue and purple, dream of Mexico arising like a flood about them to engulf their car with color and smell of rain forest and deserted town. She thought of all the small towns, the shops, the walking people, the burros, and all the arguments and near-fights. She thought of the five years she had been married. A long, long time. There had been no day in all that time that they had not seen each other; there had been no day when she had seen friends, separately; *he* was always there to see and criticize. There had been no day when she was allowed to be gone for more than an hour or so without a full explanation. Sometimes, feeling infinitely evil, she would sneak to a midnight show, telling no one, and sit, feeling free, breathing deeply of the air of freedom, watching the people, far realer than she, upon the screen, motioning and moving.

And now here they were, after five years. She looked over at his sleeping form. One thousand eight hundred and twenty-five days with you, she thought, my husband. A few hours each day at my typewriter, and then all the rest of each day and night with you. I feel quite like that man walled up in a vault in "The Cask of Amontillado." I scream but no one hears.

There was a shift of footsteps outside, a knock on their door. "*Señora*," called a soft voice, in Spanish. "It is three o'clock."

Oh, my God, thought the wife. "Sh!" she hissed, leaping up to the door. But her husband was awake. "What *is* it?" he cried.

She opened the door the slightest crack. "You've come at the wrong time," she said to the man in the darkness.

"Three o'clock, *señora*."

"No, no," she hissed, her face wrenching with the agony of the moment. "I meant tomorrow afternoon."

"What is it?" demanded her husband, switching on a light. "Christ, it's only three in the morning. What does the fool want?"

She turned, shutting her eyes. "He's here to take us to Parícutin."

"My God, you can't speak Spanish at all!"

"Go away," she said to the guide.

"But I arose for this hour," said the guide.

The husband swore and got up. "I won't be able to sleep now, anyway. Tell the idiot we'll be dressed in ten minutes and go with him and get it over, my God!"

She did this and the guide slipped away into the darkness and out into the street where the cool moon burnished the fenders of his taxi.

"You *are* incompetent," snapped the husband, pulling on two pairs of pants, two T-shirts, a sport shirt, and a wool shirt over that. "Jesus, this'll fix my throat, all right. If I come down with another strep infection—"

"Get back into bed, damn you."

"I couldn't sleep now, anyway."

"Well, we've had six hours' sleep already, and you had at least three hours' this afternoon; that should be enough."

"Spoiling our trip," he said, putting on two sweaters and two pairs of socks. "It's cold up there on the mountain; dress warm, hurry up." He put on a jacket and a muffler and looked enormous in the heap of clothing he wore. "Get me my pills. Where's some water?"

"Get back to bed," she said. "I won't have you sick and whining." She found his medicine and poured some water.

"The least thing you could do was get the hour right."

"Shut up!" She held the glass.

"Just another of your thick-headed blunders."

She threw the water in his face. "Let me alone, damn you, let me alone. I didn't mean to do that!"

"You!" he shouted, face dripping. He ripped off his jacket. "You'll chill me, I'll catch cold!"

"I don't give a damn, let me alone!" She raised her hands into fists, and her face was terrible and red, and she looked like some animal in a maze who has steadily sought exit from an impossible chaos and has been constantly fooled, turned back, rerouted, led on, tempted, whispered to, lied to, led further, and at last reached a blank wall.

"Put your hands down!" he shouted.

"I'll kill you, by God, I'll kill you!" she screamed, her face contorted and ugly. "Leave me alone! I've tried my damnedest—beds, language, time, my God, the mistakes, you think I don't *know* it? You think I'm not *sorry?*"

"I'll catch cold, I'll catch cold." He was staring at the wet floor. He sat down with water on his face.

"Here. Wipe your face off!" She flung him a towel.

He began to shake violently. "I'm cold!"

"Get a chill, damn it, and die, but leave me alone!"

"I'm cold, I'm cold." His teeth chattered, he wiped his face with trembling hands. "I'll have another infection."

"Take off that coat! It's wet."

He stopped shaking after a minute and stood up to take off the soggy coat. She handed him a leather jacket. "Come on, he's waiting for us."

He began to shiver again. "I'm not going anywhere, to hell with you," he said, sitting down. "You owe me fifty dollars now."

"What for?"

"You remember, you promised."

And she remembered. They had had a fight about some silly thing, in California, the first day of the trip, yes, by God, the very first day out. And she for the first time in her life had lifted her hand to slap him. Then, appalled, she had dropped her hand, staring at her traitorous fingers. "You were going to slap me!" he had cried. "Yes," she replied. "Well," he said quietly, "the next time you do a thing like that, you'll hand over fifty dollars of your money." That's how life was, full of little tributes and ransoms and blackmails. She paid for all her errors, unmotivated or not. A dollar here, a dollar there. If she spoiled an evening, she paid the dinner bill from her clothing money. If she criticized a play they had just seen and he had liked it, he flew into a rage, and, to quiet him, she paid for the theater tickets. On and on it had gone, swifter and swifter over the years. If they bought a book together and she didn't like it but he did and she dared speak out, there was a fight, sometimes a small thing which grew for days, and ended with her buying the book plus another and perhaps a set of cuff links or some other silly thing to calm the storm. Jesus!

"Fifty dollars. You promised if you acted up again with these tantrums and slappings."

"It was only water. I didn't hit you. All right, shut up, I'll pay the money,

I'll pay anything just to be let alone; it's worth it, and five hundred dollars more, more than worth it. I'll pay."

She turned away. When you're sick for a number of years, when you're an *only* child, the *only* boy, all of your life, you get the way he is, she thought. Then you find yourself thirty-five years old and still undecided as to what you're to be—a ceramist, a social worker, a businessman. And your wife has always known what she would be—a writer. And it must be maddening to live with a woman with a single knowledge of herself, so sure of what she would do with her writing. And selling stories, at last, not many, no, but just enough to cause the seams of the marriage to rip. And so how natural that he must convince her that she was wrong and he was right, that she was an uncontrollable child and must forfeit money. Money was to be the weapon he held over her. When she had been a fool she would give up some of the precious gain—the product of her writing.

"Do you know," she said, suddenly, aloud, "since I made that big sale to the magazine, you seem to pick more fights and I seem to pay more money?"

"What do you mean by that?" he said.

It seemed to her to be true. Since the big sale he had put his special logic to work on situations, a logic of such a sort that she had no way to combat it. Reasoning with him was impossible. You were finally cornered, your explanations exhausted, your alibis depleted, your pride in tatters. So you struck out. You slapped at him or broke something, and then, there you were again, paying off, and he had won. And he was taking your success away from you, your single purpose, or he thought he was, anyway. But strangely enough, though she had never told him, she didn't care about forfeiting the money. If it made peace, if it made him happy, if it made him think he was causing her to suffer, that was all right. He had exaggerated ideas as to the value of money; it hurt him to lose it or spend it, therefore he thought it would hurt her as much. But I'm feeling no pain, she thought, I'd like to give him all of the money, for that's not why I write at all, I write to say what I have to say, and he doesn't understand that.

He was quieted. "You'll pay?"

"Yes." She was dressing quickly now, in slacks and jacket. "In fact, I've been meaning to bring this up for some time. I'm giving all the money to you from now on. There's no need of my keeping my profits separate from yours, as it has been. I'll turn it over to you tomorrow."

"I don't ask that," he said, quickly.

"I insist. It all goes to you."

What I'm doing, of course, is unloading your gun, she thought. Taking your weapon away from you. Now you won't be able to extract the money from me, piece by piece, bit by painful bit. You'll have to find another way to bother me.

"I—" he said.

"No, let's not talk about it. It's yours."

"It's only to teach you a lesson. You've a bad temper," he said. "I thought you'd control it if you had to forfeit something."

"Oh, I just *live* for money," she said.

"I don't want all of it."

"Come on now." She was weary. She opened the door and listened. The neighbors hadn't heard, or if they had, they paid no attention. The lights of the waiting taxi illuminated the front patio.

They walked out through the cool moonlit night. She walked ahead of him for the first time in years.

Parícutin was a river of gold that night. A distant murmuring river of molten ore going down to some dead lava sea, to some volcanic black shore. Time and again if you held your breath, stilled your heart within you, you could hear the lava pushing rocks down the mountain in tumblings and roarings, faintly, faintly. Above the crater were red vapors and red light. Gentle brown and gray clouds arose suddenly as coronets or halos or puffs from the interior, their undersides washed in pink, their tops dark and ominous, without a sound.

The husband and the wife stood on the opposite mountain, in the sharp cold, the horses behind them. In a wooden hut nearby, the scientific observers were lighting oil lamps, cooking their evening meal, boiling rich coffee, talking in whispers because of the clear, night-explosive air. It was very far away from everything else in the world.

On the way up the mountain, after the long taxi drive from Uruapan, over moon-dreaming hills of ashen snow, through dry stick villages, under the cold clear stars, jounced in the taxi like dice in a gambling-tumbler, both of them had tried to make a better thing of it. They had arrived at a campfire on a sort of sea bottom. About the campfire were solemn men and small dark boys, and a company of seven other Americans, all men, in riding breeches, talking in loud voices under the soundless sky. The horses were brought forth and mounted. They proceeded across the lava river. She talked to the other Yankees and they responded. They joked together. After a while of this, the husband rode on ahead.

Now, they stood together, watching the lava wash down the dark cone summit.

He wouldn't speak.

"What's wrong now?" she asked.

He looked straight ahead, the lava glow reflected in his eyes. "You could have ridden with me. I thought we came to Mexico to see things together. And now you talk to those damned Texans."

"I felt lonely. We haven't seen any people from the States for eight weeks. I like the days in Mexico, but I don't like the nights. I just wanted someone to talk to."

"You wanted to tell them you're a writer."

"That's unfair."

"You're always telling people you're a writer, and how good you are, and you've just sold a story to a large-circulation magazine and that's how you got the money to come here to Mexico."

"One of them asked me what I did, and I told him. Damn right I'm proud of my work. I've waited ten years to sell some damn thing."

He studied her in the light from the fire mountain and at last he said, "You know, before coming up here tonight, I thought about that damned typewriter of yours and almost tossed it into the river."

"You didn't!"

"No, but I locked it in the car. I'm tired of it and the way you've ruined the whole trip. You're not with me, you're with yourself, you're the one who counts, you and that damned machine, you and Mexico, you and your reactions, you and your inspiration, you and your nervous sensitivity, and you and your aloneness. I knew you'd act this way tonight, just as sure as there was a First Coming! I'm tired of your running back from every excursion we make to sit at that machine and bang away at all hours. This is a vacation."

"I haven't touched the typewriter in a week, because it bothered you."

"Well, don't touch it for another week or a month, don't touch it until we get home. Your damned inspiration can wait!"

I should never have said I'd give him all the money, she thought. I should never have taken that weapon from him, it kept him away from my real life, the writing and the machine. And now I've thrown off the protective cloak of money and he's searched for a new weapon and he's gotten to the true thing—to the *machine*! Oh Christ!

Suddenly, without thinking, with the rage in her again, she pushed him ahead of her. She didn't do it violently. She just gave him a push. Once, twice, three times. She didn't hurt him. It was just a gesture of pushing away. She wanted to strike him, throw him off a cliff, perhaps, but instead she gave these three pushes, to indicate her hostility and the end of talking. Then they stood separately, while behind them the horses moved their hoofs softly, and the night air grew colder and their breath hissed in white plumes on the air, and in the scientists' cabin the coffee bubbled on the blue gas jet and the rich fumes permeated the moonlit heights.

After an hour, as the first dim furnacings of the sun came in the cold East, they mounted their horses for the trip down through growing light, toward the buried city and the buried church under the lava flow. Crossing the flow, she thought, Why doesn't his horse fall, why isn't he thrown onto those jagged lava rocks, why? But nothing happened. They rode on. The sun rose red.

They slept until one in the afternoon. She was dressed and sitting on the bed waiting for him to waken for half an hour before he stirred and rolled over, needing a shave, very pale with tiredness.

"I've got a sore throat," was the first thing he said.

She didn't speak.

"You shouldn't have thrown water on me," he said.

She got up and walked to the door and put her hand on the knob.

"I want you to stay here," he said. "We're going to stay here in Uruapan three or four more days."

At last she said, "I thought we were going on to Guadalajara."

"Don't be a tourist. You ruined that trip to the volcano for us. I want to go back up tomorrow or the next day. Go look at the sky."

She went out to look at the sky. It was clear and blue. She reported this. "The volcano dies down, sometimes for a week. We can't afford to wait a week for it to boom again."

"Yes, we can. We will. And you'll pay for the taxi to take us up there and do the trip over and do it right and enjoy it."

"Do you think we can ever enjoy it now?" she asked.

"If it's the last thing we do, we'll enjoy it."

"You insist, do you?"

"We'll wait until the sky is full of smoke and go back up."

"I'm going out to buy a paper." She shut the door and walked into the town.

She walked down the fresh-washed streets and looked in the shining windows and smelled that amazingly clear air and felt very good, except for the tremoring, the continual tremoring in her stomach. At last, with a hollowness roaring in her chest, she went to a man standing beside a taxi.

"*Señor*," she said.

"Yes?" said the man.

She felt her heart stop beating. Then it began to thump again and she went on: "How much would you charge to drive me to Morelia?"

"Ninety pesos, *señora*."

"And I can get the train in Morelia?"

"There is a train *here*, *señora*."

"Yes, but there are reasons why I don't want to *wait* for it here."

"I will drive you, then, to Morelia."

"Come along, there are a few things I must do."

The taxi was left in front of the Hotel de Las Flores. She walked in, alone, and once more looked at the lovely garden with its many flowers, and listened to the girl playing the strange blue-colored piano, and this time the song was the "Moonlight Sonata." She smelled the sharp crystalline air and shook her head, eyes closed, hands at her sides. She put her hand to the door, opened it softly.

Why today? she wondered. Why not some other day in the last five years? Why have I waited, why have I hung around? Because. A thousand becauses. Because you always hoped things would start again the way they were the first year. Because there were times, less frequent now, when he was splendid for days, even weeks, when you were both feeling well and the world was green and bright blue. There were times, like yesterday, for a moment, when he opened the armor-plate and showed her the fear beneath it and the small loneliness of himself and said, "I need and love you, don't ever go away, I'm afraid without you." Because sometimes it had seemed good to cry together, to make up, and the inevitible goodness of the night and the day following their making up. Because he was handsome. Because she had been alone all year every year until she met him. Because she didn't want to be alone again, but now knew that it would be better to be alone than be this way because only last night he destroyed the typewriter; not physically, no, but with thoughts and words. And he might as well have picked her up bodily and thrown her from the river bridge.

She could not feel her hand on the door. It was as if ten thousand volts of electricity had numbed all of her body. She could not feel her feet on the tiled floor. Her face was gone, her mind was gone.

He lay asleep, his back turned. The room was greenly dim. Quickly, soundlessly, she put on her coat and checked her purse. The clothes and typewriter were of no importance now. Everything was a hollowing roar. Everything was like a waterfall leaping into clear emptiness. There was no striking, no impact, just a clear water falling into a hollow and then another hollow, followed by an emptiness.

She stood by the bed and looked at the man there, the familiar black hair on the nape of his neck, the sleeping profile. The form stirred. "What?" he asked, still asleep.

"Nothing," she said. "Nothing. And nothing."

She went out and shut the door.

The taxi sped out of town at an incredible rate, making a great noise, and all the pink walls and blue walls fled past and people jumped out of the way and there were some few cars which almost exploded upon them, and there went most of the town and there went the hotel and that man sleeping in the hotel and there went—

Nothing.

The taxi motor died.

No, no, thought Marie, oh God, no, no, no.

The car must start again.

The taxi driver leaped out, glaring at God in his Heaven, and ripped open the hood and looked as if he might strangle the iron guts of the car with his clawing hands, his face smiling a pure sweet smile of incredible hatred, and then he turned to Marie and forced himself to shrug, putting away his hate and accepting the Will of God.

"I will walk you to the bus station," he said.

No, her eyes said. No, her mouth almost said. Joseph will wake and run and find me still here and drag me back. No.

"I will carry your bag, *señora*," the taxi driver said, and walked off with it, and had to come back and find her still there, motionless, saying no, no, to no one, and helped her out and showed her where to walk.

The bus was in the square and the Indians were getting into it, some silently and with a slow, certain dignity, and some chattering like birds and shoving bundles, children, chickens' baskets, and pigs in ahead of them. The driver wore a uniform that had not been pressed or laundered in twenty years, and he was leaning out the window shouting and laughing with people outside, as Marie stepped up into the interior of hot smoke and burning grease from the engine, the smell of gasoline and oil, the smell of wet chickens, wet children, sweating men and damp women, old upholstery which was down to the skeleton, and oily leather. She found a seat in the rear and felt the eyes follow her and her suitcase, and she was thinking: I'm going away, at last I'm going away, I'm free, I'll never see him again in my life, I'm free, I'm free.

She almost laughed.

The bus started and all of the people in it shook and swayed and cried out and smiled, and the land of Mexico seemed to whirl about outside the window, like a dream undecided whether to stay or go, and then the greenness passed away, and the town, and there was the Hotel de Las Flores with its open patio, and there, incredibly, hands in pockets, standing in the open door but looking at the sky and the volcano smoke, was Joseph, paying no attention to the bus or her and she was going away from him, he was growing remote already, his figure was dwindling like someone falling down a mine shaft, silently, without a scream. Now, before she had even the decency or inclination to wave, he was no larger than a boy, then a child, then a baby, in distance, in size, then gone around a corner, with the engine thundering, someone playing upon a guitar up front in the bus, and Marie, straining to look back, as if she might penetrate walls, trees, and distances, for another view of the man standing so quietly watching the blue sky.

At last, her neck tired, she turned and folded her hands and examined what she had won for herself. A whole lifetime loomed suddenly ahead, as quickly as the turns and whirls of the highway brought her suddenly to edges of cliffs, and each bend of the road, even as the years, could not be seen ahead. For a moment it was simply good to lie back here, head upon jouncing seat rest, and contemplate quietness. To know nothing, to think nothing, to feel nothing, to be as nearly dead for a moment as one could be, with the eyes closed, the heart unheard, no special temperature to the body, to wait for life to come get her rather than to seek, at least for an hour. Let the bus take her to the train, the train to the plane, the plane to the city, and the city to her friends, and then, like a stone dropped into a cement mixer, let that life in the city do with her as it would, she flowing along in the mix and solidifying in any new pattern that seemed best.

The bus rushed on with a plummeting and swerving in the sweet green air of the afternoon, between the mountains baked like lion pelts, past rivers as sweet as wine and as clear as vermouth, over stone bridges, under aqueducts where water ran like clear wind in the ancient channels, past churches, through dust, and suddenly, quite suddenly the speedometer in Marie's mind said, A million miles, Joseph is back a million miles and I'll never see him again. The thought stood up in her mind and covered the sky with a blurred darkness. Never, never again until the day I die or after that will I see him again, not for an hour or a minute or a second, not at all will I see him.

The numbness started in her fingertips. She felt it flow up through her hands, into her wrists and on along the arms to her shoulders and through her shoulders to her heart and up her neck to her head. She was a numbness, a thing of nettles and ice and prickles and a hollow thundering nothingness. Her lips were dry petals, her eyelids were a thousand pounds heavier than iron, and each part of her body was now iron and lead and copper and platinum. Her body weighed ten tons, each part of it was so incredibly heavy, and, in that heaviness, crushed and beating to survive, was her crippled heart, throbbing and tearing about like a headless chicken. And buried in the limestone and steel of her robot body was her terror and crying out, walled in, with someone tapping the trowel on the exterior wall, the job finished, and, ironically, it was her own hand she saw before her that had wielded the trowel, set the final brick in place, frothed on the thick slush of mortar and pushed everything into a tightness and a self-finished prison.

Her mouth was cotton. Her eyes were flaming with a dark flame the color of raven wings, the sound of vulture wings, and her head was so heavy with terror, so full of an iron weight, while her mouth was stuffed with invisible hot cotton, that she felt her head sag down into her immensely fat, but she could not see the fat, hands. Her hands were pillows of lead to lie upon, her hands were cement sacks crushing down upon her senseless lap, her ears, faucets in which ran cold winds, and all about her, not looking at her, not noticing, was the bus on its way through towns and fields, over hills and into corn valleys at a great racketing speed, taking her each and every instant one million miles and ten million years away from the familiar.

I must *not* cry out, she thought. No! No!

The dizziness was so complete, and the colors of the bus and her hands and skirt were now so blued over and sooted with lack of blood that in a moment she would be collapsed upon the floor, she would hear the surprise and shock of the riders bending over her. But she put her head far down and sucked the chicken air, the sweating air, the leather air, the carbon monoxide air, the incense air, the air of lonely death, and drew it back through the copper nostrils, down the aching throat, into her lungs which blazed as if she swallowed neon light. Joseph, Joseph, Joseph, Joseph.

It was a simple thing. All terror is a simplicity.

I cannot live without him, she thought. I have been lying to myself. I need him, oh Christ, I, I . . .

"Stop the bus! Stop it!"

The bus stopped at her scream, everyone was thrown forward. Somehow she was stumbling forward over the children, the dogs barking, her hands flailing heavily, falling; she heard her dress rip, she screamed again, the door was opening, the driver was appalled at the woman coming at him in a wild stumbling, and she fell out upon the gravel, tore her stockings, and lay while someone bent to her; then she was vomiting on the ground, a steady sickness; they were bringing her bag out of the bus to her, she was telling them in chokes and sobs that she wanted to go that way; she pointed back at the city a million years ago, a million miles ago, and the bus driver was shaking his head. She half sat, half lay there, her arms about the suitcase, sobbing, and the bus stood in the hot sunlight over her and she waved it on; go on, go on; they're all staring at me, I'll get a ride back, don't worry, leave me here, go on, and at last, like an accordion, the door folded shut, the Indian copper-mask faces were transported on away, and the bus dwindled from consciousness. She lay on the suitcase and cried, for a number of minutes, and she was not as heavy or sick, but her heart was fluttering wildly, and she was cold as someone fresh from a winter lake. She arose and dragged the suitcase in little moves across the highway and swayed there, waiting, while six cars hummed by, and at last a seventh car pulled up with a Mexican gentleman in the front seat, a rich car from Mexico City.

"You are going to Uruapan?" he asked politely, looking only at her eyes.

"Yes," she said at last, "I am going to Uruapan."

And as she rode in this car, her mind began a private dialogue:

"What is it to be insane?"

"I don't know."

"Do you know what insanity is?"

"I don't know."

"Can one tell? The coldness, was that the start?"

"No."

"The heaviness, wasn't that a part?"

"Shut up."

"Is insanity screaming?"

"I didn't mean to."

"But that came later. First there was the heaviness, and the silence, and the blankness. That terrible void, that space, that silence, that aloneness, that backing away from life, that being in upon oneself and not wishing to look at or speak to the world. Don't tell me that wasn't the start of insanity."

"Yes."

"You were ready to fall over the edge."

"I stopped the bus just short of the cliff."

"And what if you hadn't stopped the bus? Would they have driven into a little town or Mexico City and the driver turned and said to you through the empty bus, 'All right, *señora*, all out.' Silence. 'All right, *señora*, all out.' Silence. '*Señora?*' A stare into space. '*Señora!*' A rigid stare into the sky of life, empty, empty, oh, empty. '*Señora!*' No move. '*Señora.*' Hardly a breath. You sit there, you sit there, you sit there, you sit there, you sit there.

"You would not even hear. '*Señora,*' he would cry, and tug at you, but you wouldn't feel his hand. And the police would be summoned beyond your circle of comprehension, beyond your eyes or ears or body. You could not even hear the heavy boots in the car. '*Señora*, you must leave the bus.' You do not hear. '*Señora*, what is your name?' Your mouth is shut. '*Señora*, you must come with us.' You sit like a stone idol. 'Let us see her passport.' They fumble with your purse which lies untended in your stone lap. '*Señora* Marie Elliott, from California. *Señora* Elliott?' You stare at the empty sky. 'Where are you coming from? Where is your husband?' You were never married. 'Where are you going?' Nowhere. 'It says she was born in Illinois.' You were never born. '*Señora, señora.*' They have to carry you, like a stone, from the bus. You will talk to no one. No, no, no one. 'Marie, this is me, Joseph.' No, too late. 'Marie!' Too late. 'Don't you recognize me?' Too late. Joseph. No Joseph, no nothing, too late, too late."

"That is what would have happened, is it not?"

"Yes." She trembled.

"If you had not stopped the bus, you would have been heavier and heavier, true? And silenter and silenter and more made up of nothing and nothing and nothing."

"Yes."

"*Señora*," said the Spanish gentleman driving, breaking in on her thoughts. "It is a nice day, isn't it?"

"Yes," she said, both to him and the thoughts in her mind.

The old Spanish gentleman drove her directly to her hotel and let her out and doffed his hat and bowed to her.

She nodded and felt her mouth move with thanks, but she did not see him. She wandered into the hotel and found herself with her suitcase back in her room, that room she had left a thousand years ago. Her husband was there.

He lay in the dim light of late afternoon with his back turned, seeming not to have moved in the hours since she had left. He had not even known that she was gone, and had been to the ends of the earth and had returned. He did not even know.

She stood looking at his neck and the dark hairs curling there like ash fallen from the sky.

She found herself on the tiled patio in the hot light. A bird rustled in a bamboo cage. In the cool darkness somewhere, the girl was playing a waltz on the piano.

She saw but did not see two butterflies which darted and jumped and lit upon a bush near her hand, to seal themselves together. She felt her gaze move to see the two bright things, all gold and yellow on the green leaf, their wings beating in slow pulses as they were joined. Her mouth moved and her hand swung like a pendulum, senselessly.

She watched her fingers tumble on the air and close on the two butterflies, tight, tighter, tightest. A scream was coming up into her mouth. She pressed it back. Tight, tighter, tightest.

She felt her hand open all to itself. Two lumps of bright powder fell to the shiny patio tiles. She looked down at the small ruins, then snapped her gaze up.

The girl who played the piano was standing in the middle of the garden, regarding her with appalled and startled eyes.

The wife put out her hand, to touch the distance, to say something, to explain, to apologize to the girl, this place, the world, everyone. But the girl went away.

The sky was full of smoke which went straight up and veered away south toward Mexico City.

She wiped the wing-pollen from her numb fingers and talked over her shoulder, not knowing if that man inside heard, her eyes on the smoke and the sky.

"You know . . . we might try the volcano tonight. It looks good. I bet there'll be lots of fire."

Yes, she thought, and it will fill the air and fall all around us, and take hold of us tight, tighter, tightest, and then let go and let us fall and we'll be ashes blowing south, all fire.

"Did you hear me?"

She stood over the bed and raised a fist high but *never* brought it down to strike him in the face.

The Black Ferris

The carnival had come to town like an October wind, like a dark bat flying over the cold lake, bones rattling in the night, mourning, sighing, whispering up the tents in the dark rain. It stayed on for a month by the gray, restless lake of October, in the black weather and increasing storms and leaden skies.

During the third week, at twilight on a Thursday, the two small boys walked along the lake shore in the cold wind.

"Aw, I don't believe you," said Peter.

"Come on, and I'll show you," said Hank.

They left wads of spit behind them all along the moist brown sand of the crashing shore. They ran to the lonely carnival grounds. It had been raining.

The carnival lay by the sounding lake with nobody buying tickets from the flaky black booths, nobody hoping to get the salted hams from the whining roulette wheels, and none of the thin-fat freaks on the big platforms. The midway was silent, all the gray tents hissing on the wind like gigantic prehistoric wings. At eight o'clock perhaps, ghastly lights would flash on, voices would shout, music would go out over the lake. Now there was only a blind hunchback sitting on a black booth, feeling of the cracked china cup from which he was drinking some perfumed brew.

"There," said Hank, pointing.

The black Ferris wheel rose like an immense light-bulbed constellation against the cloudy sky, silent.

"I still don't believe what you said about it," said Peter.

"You wait, I saw it happen. I don't know how, but it did. You know how carnivals are; all funny. Okay; this one's even *funnier.*"

Peter let himself be led to the high green hiding place of a tree.

Suddenly, Hank stiffened. "*Hist!* There's Mr. Cooger, the carnival man, now!" Hidden, they watched.

Mr. Cooger, a man of some thirty-five years, dressed in sharp bright clothes, a lapel carnation, hair greased with oil, drifted under the tree, a brown derby hat on his head. He had arrived in town three weeks before, shaking his brown derby hat at people on the street from inside his shiny red Ford, tooting the horn.

Now Mr. Cooger nodded at the little blind hunchback, spoke a word. The hunchback blindly, fumbling, locked Mr. Cooger into a black seat and sent him whirling up into the ominous twilight sky. Machinery hummed.

"See!" whispered Hank. "The Ferris wheel's going the wrong way. Backwards instead of forwards!"

"So what?" said Peter.

"Watch!"

The black Ferris wheel whirled twenty-five times around. Then the blind hunchback put out his pale hands and halted the machinery. The Ferris wheel stopped, gently swaying, at a certain black seat.

A ten-year-old boy stepped out. He walked off across the whispering carnival ground, in the shadows.

Peter almost fell from his limb. He searched the Ferris wheel with his eyes. "Where's Mr. Cooger!"

Hank poked him. "You wouldn't believe! Now *see!*"

"Where's Mr. Cooger at!"

"Come on, quick, run!" Hank dropped and was sprinting before he hit the ground.

Under giant chestnut trees, next to the ravine, the lights were burning in Mrs. Foley's white mansion. Piano music tinkled. Within the warm windows, people moved. Outside, it began to rain, despondently, irrevocably, forever and ever.

"I'm *so* wet," grieved Peter, crouching in the bushes. "Like someone squirted me with a hose. How much longer do we wait?"

"Ssh!" said Hank, cloaked in wet mystery.

They had followed the little boy from the Ferris wheel up through town, down dark streets to Mrs. Foley's ravine house. Now, inside the warm dining room of the house the strange little boy sat at dinner, forking and spooning rich lamb chops and mashed potatoes.

"I know his name," whispered Hank, quickly. "My mom told me about him the other day. She said, 'Hank, you hear about the li'l orphan boy moved in Mrs. Foley's? Well, his name is Joseph Pikes and he just came to Mrs. Foley's one day about two weeks ago and said how he was an orphan run away and could he have something to eat, and him and Mrs. Foley been getting on like hot apple pie ever since.' That's what my mom said," finished Hank, peering through the steamy Foley window. Water dripped from his nose. He held on to Peter who was twitching with cold. "Pete, I didn't like his looks from the first, I didn't. He looked — mean."

"I'm scared," said Peter, frankly wailing. "I'm cold and hungry and I don't know what this's all about."

"Gosh, you're dumb!" Hank shook his head, eyes shut in disgust. "Don't you see, three weeks ago the carnival came. And about the same time this little ole orphan shows up at Mrs. Foley's. And Mrs. Foley's son died a long time ago one night one winter, and she's never been the same, so here's this little ole orphan boy who butters her all around."

"Oh," said Peter, shaking.

"Come on," said Hank. They marched to the front door and banged the lion knocker.

After a while the door opened and Mrs. Foley looked out.

"You're all wet, come in," she said. "My land." she herded them into the hall. "What do you want?" she said, bending over them, a tall lady with lace on her full bosom and a pale thin face with white hair over it. "You're Henry Walterson, aren't you?"

Hank nodded, glancing fearfully at the dining room where the strange little boy looked up from his eating. "Can we see you alone, ma'am?" And when the old lady looked palely surprised, Hank crept over and shut the hall door and whispered at her. "We got to warn you about something, it's about that boy come to live with you, that orphan?"

The hall grew suddenly cold. Mrs. Foley drew herself high and stiff. "Well?"

"He's from the carnival, and he ain't a boy, he's a man, and he's planning on living here with you until he finds where your money is and then run off with it some night, and people will look for him but because they'll be looking for a little ten-year-old boy they won't recognize him when he walks by a thirty-five-year-old man, named Mr. Cooger!" cried Hank.

"What *are* you talking about?" declared Mrs. Foley.

"The carnival and the Ferris wheel and this strange man, Mr. Cooger, the Ferris wheel going backward and making him younger, I don't know how, and him coming here as a boy, and you can't trust him, because when he has your money he'll get on the Ferris wheel and it'll go *forward*, and he'll be thirty-five years old again, and the boy'll be gone forever!"

"Good night, Henry Walterson, don't *ever* come back!" shouted Mrs. Foley.

The door slammed. Peter and Hank found themselves in the rain once more. It soaked into and into them, cold and complete.

"Smart guy," snorted Peter. "Now you fixed it. Suppose he heard us, suppose he comes and *kills* us in our beds tonight, to shut us all up for keeps!"

"He wouldn't do that," said Hank.

"Wouldn't he?" Peter seized Hank's arm. "Look."

In the big bay window of the dining room now the mesh curtain pulled aside. Standing there in the pink light, his hand made into a menacing fist, was the little orphan boy. His face was horrible to see, the teeth bared, the eyes hateful, the lips mouthing out terrible words. That was all. The orphan boy was there only a second, then gone. The curtain fell into place. The rain poured down upon the house. Hank and Peter walked slowly home in the storm.

During supper, Father looked at Hank and said, "If you don't catch pneumonia, I'll be surprised. Soaked, you were, by God! What's this about the carnival?"

Hank fussed at his mashed potatoes, occasionally looking at the rattling windows. "You know Mr. Cooger, the carnival man, Dad?"

"The one with the pink carnation in his lapel?" asked Father.

"Yes!" Hank sat up. "You've seen him around?"

"He stays down the street at Mrs. O'Leary's boarding house, got a room in back. Why?"

"Nothing," said Hank, his face glowing.

After supper Hank put through a call to Peter on the phone. At the other end of the line, Peter sounded miserable with coughing.

"Listen, Pete!" said Hank. "I see it all now. When that li'l ole orphan boy, Joseph Pikes, gets Mrs. Foley's money, he's got a good plan."

"What?"

"He'll stick around town as the carnival man, living in a room at Mrs. O'Leary's. That way nobody'll get suspicious of him. Everybody'll be looking for that nasty little boy and he'll be gone. And he'll be walking around, all disguised as the carnival man. That way, nobody'll suspect the carnival at all. It would look funny if the carnival suddenly pulled up stakes."

"Oh," said Peter, sniffling.

"So we got to act fast," said Hank.

"Nobody'll believe us, I tried to tell my folks but they said hogwash!" moaned Peter.

"We got to act tonight, anyway. Because why? Because he's gonna try to kill us! We're the only ones that know and if we tell the police to keep an eye on him, he's the one who stole Mrs. Foley's money in cahoots with the orphan boy, he won't live peaceful. I bet he just tries something tonight. So, I tell you, meet me at Mrs. Foley's in half an hour."

"Aw," said Peter.

"You wanna die?"

"No." Thoughtfully.

"Well, then. Meet me there and I bet we see that orphan boy sneaking out with the money, tonight, and running back down to the carnival grounds with it, when Mrs. Foley's asleep. I'll see you there. So long, Pete!"

"Young man," said Father, standing behind him as he hung up the phone. "You're not going anywhere. You're going straight up to bed. Here." He marched Hank upstairs. "Now hand me out everything you got on." Hank undressed. "There're no other clothes in your room are there?" asked Father. "No, sir, they're all in the hall closet," said Hank, disconsolately.

"Good," said Dad and shut and locked the door.

Hank stood there, naked. "Holy cow," he said.

"Go to bed," said Father.

Peter arrived at Mrs. Foley's house at about nine-thirty, sneezing, lost in a vast raincoat and mariner's cap. He stood like a small water hydrant on the street, mourning softly over his fate. The lights in the Foley house were warmly on upstairs. Peter waited for a half an hour, looking at the rain-drenched slick streets of night.

Finally, there was a darting paleness, a rustle in wet bushes.

"Hank?" Peter questioned the bushes.

"Yeah." Hank stepped out.

"Gosh," said Peter, staring. "You're—you're *naked*!"

"I ran all the way," said Hank. "Dad wouldn't let me out."

"You'll get pneumonia," said Peter.

The lights in the house went out.

"Duck," cried Hank, bounding behind some bushes. They waited. "Pete," said Hank. "You're wearing pants, aren't you?"

"Sure," said Pete.

"Well, you're wearing a raincoat, and nobody'll know, so lend me your pants," said Hank.

A reluctant transaction was made. Hank pulled the pants on.

The rain let up. The clouds began to break apart.

In about ten minutes a small figure emerged from the house, bearing a large paper sack filled with some enormous loot or other.

"There he is," whispered Hank.

"There he goes!" cried Peter.

The orphan boy ran swiftly.

"Get after him!" cried Hank.

They gave chase through the chestnut trees, but the orphan boy was swift, up the hill, through the night streets of town, down past the rail yards, past the factories, to the midway of the deserted carnival. Hank and Peter were poor seconds, Peter weighted as he was with the heavy raincoat, and Hank frozen with cold. The thumping of Hank's bare feet sounded through the town.

"Hurry, Pete! We can't let him get to that Ferris wheel before we do, if he changes back into a man we'll never prove anything!"

"I'm hurrying!" But Pete was left behind as Hank thudded on alone in the clearing weather.

"Yah!" mocked the orphan boy, darting away, no more than a shadow ahead, now. Now vanishing into the carnival yard.

Hank stopped at the edge of the carnival lot. The Ferris wheel was going up and up into the sky, a big nebula of stars caught on the dark earth and turning forward and forward, instead of backward, and there sat Joseph Pikes in a black-painted bucket-seat, laughing up and around and down and up and around and down at little old Hank standing there, and the little blind hunchback had his hand on the roaring, oily black machine that made the Ferris wheel go ahead and ahead. The midway was deserted because of the rain. The merry-go-round was still, but its music played and crashed in the open spaces. And Joseph Pikes rode up into the cloudy sky and came down and each time he went around he was a year older, his laughing changed, grew deep, his face changed, the bones of it, the mean eyes of it, the wild hair of it, sitting there in the black bucket-seat whirling, whirling swiftly, laughing into the bleak heavens where now and again a last split of lightning showed itself.

Hank ran forward at the hunchback by the machine. On the way he picked up a tent spike. "Here now!" yelled the hunchback. The black Ferris wheel whirled around. "You!" stormed the hunchback, fumbling out. Hank hit him in the kneecap and danced away. "Ouch!" screamed the man, falling forward. He tried to reach the machine brake to stop the Ferris wheel. When he put his hand on the brake, Hank ran in and slammed the tent spike against the fingers, mashing them. He hit them twice. The man held his hand in his other hand, howling. He kicked at Hank. Hank grabbed the foot, pulled, the man slipped in the mud and fell. Hank hit him on the head, shouting.

The Ferris wheel went around and around and around.

"Stop, stop the wheel!" cried Joseph Pikes–Mr. Cooger, flung up in a stormy cold sky in the bubbled constellation of whirl and rush and wind.

"I can't move," groaned the hunchback. Hank jumped on his chest and they thrashed, biting, kicking.

"Stop, stop the wheel!" cried Mr. Cooger, a man, a different man and voice this time, coming around in panic, going up into the roaring hissing sky of the Ferris wheel. The wind blew through the high dark wheel spokes. "Stop, stop, oh, please stop the wheel!"

Hank leaped up from the sprawled hunchback. He started in on the brake mechanism, hitting it, jamming it, putting chunks of metal in it, tying it with rope, now and again hitting at the crawling weeping dwarf.

"Stop, stop, stop the wheel!" wailed a voice high in the night where the windy moon was coming out of the vaporous white clouds now. "Stop . . . " The voice faded.

Now the carnival was ablaze with sudden light. Men sprang out of tents, came running. Hank felt himself jerked into the air with oaths and beatings rained on him. From a distance there was a sound of Peter's voice and behind Peter, at full tilt, a police officer with pistol drawn.

"Stop, stop the wheel!" In the wind the voice sighed away.

The voice repeated and repeated.

The dark carnival men tried to apply the brake. Nothing happened. The machine hummed and turned the wheel around and around. The mechanism was jammed.

"Stop!" cried the voice one last time.

Silence.

Without a word the Ferris wheel flew in a circle, a high system of electric stars and metal and seats. There was no sound now but the sound of the motor which died and stopped. The Ferris wheel coasted for a minute, all the carnival people looking up at it, the policeman looking up at it, Hank and Peter looking up at it.

The Ferris wheel stopped. A crowd had gathered at the noise. A few fishermen from the wharfhouse, a few switchmen from the rail yards. The Ferris wheel stood whining and stretching in the wind.

"Look," everybody said.

The policeman turned and the carnival people turned and the fishermen turned and they all looked at the occupant in the black-painted seat at the bottom of the ride. The wind touched and moved the black wooden seat in a gentle rocking rhythm, crooning over the occupant in the dim carnival light.

A skeleton sat there, a paper bag of money in its hands, a brown derby hat on its head.

Farewell Summer

Farewell summer.

Grandma looked it.

Grandpa said it.

Douglas felt it.

Farewell summer.

The words moved on Grandpa's lips as he stood at the edge of the porch and surveyed the lake of grass just below and all the dandelions gone and the clover blossoms wilting, and a touch of rust in the trees, and real summer over and a smell of Egypt in the air, blowing from the east.

"What?" asked Douglas.

But he had heard.

"Farewell summer." Grandpa leaned on the porch rail, shut one eye, let the other wander on the horizon line. "Know what that is, Doug? A flower by the side of the road, named for the way the weather feels today. Look. The whole darn season's just turned around. Don't know why summer's come back. Maybe to find something. Makes you feel kind of sad. And then again, happy. Farewell summer, Doug."

A fern by the porch rail fell to dust.

Doug moved to stand beside his grandfather, hoping to borrow some of that far sight, some of that look beyond the hills, some of the wanting to cry, some of the ancient joy. The smell of pipe tobacco and Tiger Shaving Tonic had to be sufficient. A top spun in his chest, now light, now dark, now moving his tongue with laughter, now filling his eyes with warm saltwater.

"Think I'll go eat me a doughnut and take me a nap," he said.

"Glad we have siestas in northern Illinois. Eat your way to sleep, boy."

The great warm hand came down on his head in a pressure that spun the top fast until it was all one warm lovely color.

It was a happy journey inside to the doughnuts.

Laid out with a powdered-sugar mustache on his upper lip, Doug contemplated sleep, which came around through the back of his head and gently grabbed him.

Dusk filled his whole twelve-year-old body at three-thirty in the afternoon.

Then, in his sleep, he quickened.

A long way off, a band played a strange slow tune, full of muted brass and muffled drums.

Doug lifted his head, listening.

As if the faraway band had come out of a cave into full sunlight, the music grew louder.

And it was louder because where before it had seemed a brass band of few pieces, now it added instruments as it approached Green Town, as if men were trotting out of empty cornfields brandishing bright pipes of sunny metal or long sticks of licorice over their heads. Somewhere a small moon rose to be beaten, and that was a big bass drum. Somewhere a mob of irritable blackbirds soared to become piccolos and leave the fruitless orchards behind.

"A parade!" whispered Doug. "But it's not July Fourth, and Labor Day's gone! So, how come . . . ?"

And as the music got louder it got slower, deeper, and very sad. It was like an immense storm cloud full of lightning which passed low shadowing hills, darkening rooftops, and now invading the town streets. It was a murmur of thunder.

Douglas shivered and waited.

The parade had stopped just outside his house.

Flashes of sunlit brass shot through the high windows and beat against the walls like the wings of golden birds panicking to escape.

Sidling up to the window, Douglas peered.

And what he saw was familiar people.

Douglas blinked.

For there on the lawn, holding a trombone, was Jack Schmidt who sat across from him in school, and Bill Arno, his best friend, lifting a trumpet, and Mr. Wyneski, the town barber, wrapped around by a boa-constrictor tub and— hold on!

Douglas listened.

There was not a sound in the house below.

He spun about and ran downstairs. The kitchen was full of bacon smell but nothing else. The dining room remembered pancakes but only a breeze came in the windows to ghost the curtains.

He ran to the front door and stepped out on the porch. The house was empty, yes, but the yard was full.

Because down among the band stood Grandpa with a French horn, Grandma with a tambourine, Skip with a kazoo.

As soon as Doug reached the edge of the porch, everyone gave a great whooping yell, and while they were yelling Douglas thought how quickly it had all happened. Only an instant before Grandma had put down her kneaded bread dough in the kitchen (it lay with her fingerprints floured in it on the kneading board at this moment), Grandpa had laid aside Dickens in the library, Skip had leaped from the crabapple tree. Now they stood holding instruments in this assembly of friends, teachers, librarians, and distant cousins from far peach-orchard farms.

The yelling stopped and everyone laughed, forgetting the dirge they had played through town.

"Hey," said Doug at last, "what day *is* this?"

"Why," said Grandma, "*your* day, Doug."

"*My* day?"

"Yours, Doug. Special. Better than birthdays, greater than Christmas, grander than the Fourth, more amazing than Easter. Your day, Doug, *yours*!"

That was the Mayor, making a speech.

"Yes, but . . ."

"Doug . . ." Grandpa nudged a huge wicker basket. "Got strawberry pie here."

"Strawberry shortcake," added Grandma. "Strawberry ice *cream*."

Everyone smiled. But Douglas stepped back, waited, feeling like a huge Eskimo pie standing in the sun and not melting.

"Fireworks at dusk, Doug," said Skip, tootling his kazoo. "Dusk and fireworks. Also, give you my Mason jar full of fireflies left over from summer."

"You never give me anything like that before, Skip. How come you do it *now*?"

"It's Douglas Spaulding Day, Doug. We've brought you some flowers."

People don't bring flowers to boys, thought Doug, not even in hospitals!

But there were the Ramsey sisters holding out clusters of farewell-summer blossoms, and Grandpa saying: "Hurry on, Doug. Lead the parade! The boat's waiting!"

"The excursion boat? We going on a picnic trip?"

"Journey's more like it." Mr. Wyneski whipped off his barber's apron, crammed on his cornflake-cereal straw hat. "Listen!"

The sound of a far boat wailed up from the shore of the lake one mile away.

"Forward march!" said Grandpa. "One, two, Doug, oh, come on now, one, *two*!"

"Yes, but—"

Grandma jingled her tambourine, Skip thrummed his kazoo, Grandpa moaned his French horn, and the motion of the mob circling the yard drew Doug down off the porch along the street with a pack of dogs ahead and behind yipping all the way downtown where traffic stopped for them and people waved and someone tore up a telephone book and threw it out the top of the Green Town Hotel but by the time the informational confetti hit the brick street the parade was gone downhill, leaving the sun and town behind.

And by the time they reached the shore of the quiet lake the sun was clouding over and fog moved in across the water so swiftly and completely that it frightened Doug to see it move, as if a great storm cloud from the autumn sky had been cut loose and sank to engulf the shore, the town, the thumping, happy brass band.

The parade stopped. For now far out in the fog, beyond the pier, invisible, they could hear the sound of a vast ship approaching, some sort of boat that mourned with the voice of a fog horn, over and over.

"Get along, boy, out on the pier," said Grandpa, softly.

"Race you to the end!" Skip vaulted ahead.

Douglas did not move.

For the boat was now nosing out of the fog, timber by white timber, porthole by porthole, and stood as if held fast by the fog, at the end of the pier, its gangplank let down.

"How come . . . " Douglas stared. "How come that boat's got no name?"

They all looked and it was true, there was no name painted on the bow of the long white boat.

"Well, you see, Doug—"

The ship's whistle shrieked and the crowd swarmed pushing Douglas with it along the timbers to the gangplank.

"You on board *first*, Doug!"

"Give him some music to march him aboard!"

And the band lifted up a ton of brass and two hundred pounds of chimes and cymbals and banged out "For He's a Jolly Good Fellow" triple-time, and before he could tell his legs otherwise, one, two, one, two, they had him up on the deck, people running, slinging down the picnic baskets, then leaping back on the dock. . . .

Wham!

The gangplank fell.

Douglas whirled, cried out.

No one else was on board the ship. His family and friends were trapped on the dock.

"Hold on, wait!"

The gangplank hadn't fallen by mistake.

It had been *pulled* off the boat.

"Hold on!" wailed Douglas.

"Yes," said Grandpa, quietly, below, on the dock. "Hold on."

The people weren't trapped on land at all.

Douglas blinked.

He was trapped on the boat.

Douglas yelled. The steamboat shrieked. It began to edge away from the dock. The band played "Columbia, the Gem of the Ocean."

"Hold on, now, darn it!"

"So long, Doug."

"Wait!"

"Good-by, Douglas, good-by," cried the two town librarians.

"So long," whispered everyone on the dock.

Douglas looked at the food put by in baskets on the deck and remembered a Chicago museum once, years ago, where he had seen an Egyptian tomb and toys and baskets of withered food placed in that tomb around a small carved boat. It burnt like a flash of gunpowder in his eyes. He spun about wildly and yelled.

"So long, Doug, so long . . . " Ladies lifted white handkerchiefs, men waved their straw hats. Someone lifted a small dog and waved it on the air.

And the boat was pulling way out in the cold water and the fog was wrapping it up and the band was fading and now he could hardly see all the aunts and uncles and his family on the dock.

"Wait!" he cried. "It's not too late! Tell 'em to turn back! You can come on the excursion, too! Yeah, sure, you come along, too!"

"No, Doug, just you," called Grandfather's voice somewhere on the land. "Get along, boy."

And he now knew that the ship was indeed empty. If he ran and looked he would not even find a captain, or a first mate, or any member of a crew. Only he was aboard this ship that moved out into mist, alone, its vast engines groaning and pumping, a mindless life to themselves, under the decks.

Numbly, he moved to the prow. Suddenly, he knew that if he reached his hands down and touched he would find the name of the boat, fresh-painted.

Why had the season changed? Why had the warm weather come back?

The answer was simple.

The name of the boat was *Farewell Summer*.

And it had come back just for him.

"Doug . . . " the voices faded. "Oh, good-by . . . oh so long . . . so long . . . ?"

"Skip, Grandma, Grandpa, Bill, Mr. Wyneski, no, no, no, oh Skip, oh Grandma, Grandpa, save me!"

But the shore was empty, the dock lost, the parade gone home and the ship blew its horn a final time and broke his heart so it fell out of his eyes in tears and he wept saying all the names of the ones on shore, and it all ran together into one immense and terrifying word that shook his soul and sneezed forth his heart's blood in one convulsive shout:

"*Grandpa*grandma*skip*bill*mr*wyneski*help*!"

And sat up in bed, hot, cold, and weeping.

He lay there with the tears running down into his ears and he wept, feeling the bed, wept feeling the good sunlight on the fingers of his twitching hands and on the patchwork quilt. Sunset put a quiet supply of lemonade colors through all the air of his room.

His crying ceased.

He got up and went to the mirror to see what sadness looked like and there it was, colored all through his face and in his eyes where it could never be got out now, where it would never go away, and he reached out to touch that other face beyond the glass, and that other hand inside the glass touched back, and it was cold.

Below, bread baked and filled the house with its late afternoon perfume. He walked slowly down the stairs to watch Grandma pull the lovely guts out of a chicken and then pause at a window to see Skip far up in his favorite tree trying to see beyond the sky, and then he strolled out to the porch where the smell of baking bread followed him as if it knew where he was and would not let him go.

Someone stood on the porch, smoking his next-to-last pipe of the day.

"Gramps, you're *here*!"

"Why, sure, Doug."

"Boy. Boy, oh, boy. You're here. The *house* is here. The *town*'s here!"

"It seems you're here, too, boy."

"Yeah, oh, yeah."

Grandpa nodded, gazed at the sky, took a deep breath, started to speak when a sudden panic made Doug cry: "Don't!"

"Don't what, boy?!"

Don't, thought Doug, don't say what you were going to say.

Grandpa waited.

The trees leaned their shadows on the lawn and took on colors of autumn even as they watched. Somewhere, the last lawnmower of summer shaved and cut the years and left them in sweet mounds.

"Gramps, is—"

"Is what, Doug?"

Douglas swallowed, closed his eyes, and in self-imposed darkness, got rid of it all in a rush:

"Is death being on a boat alone and it sailing off and taking you with it and all your folks left back on the shore!?"

Grandpa chewed it over, read a few clouds in the sky, nodded.

"That's about it, Doug. Why do you ask?"

"Just wanted to know."

Douglas eyed a high cloud passing that had never been that shape before and would never be that way again.

"Say what you were just about to say, Gramps."

"Well, now, let me see. Farewell summer?"

"Yes, sir," whispered Douglas, and leaned against the tall man there and took the old man's hand and held it hard against his cheek and then placed it to rest on top of his head, like a crown for a young king.

Farewell summer.

McGillahee's Brat

In 1953 I had spent six months in Dublin, writing a screenplay. I had not been back since.

Now, fifteen years later, I had returned by boat, train, and taxi, and here we pulled up in front of the Royal Hibernian Hotel and here we got out and were going up the front hotel steps when a beggar woman shoved her filthy baby in our faces and cried:

"Ah, God, pity! It's pity we're in need of! Have you *some*?!"

I had some somewhere on my person, and slapped my pockets and fetched it out, and was on the point of handing it over when I gave a small cry, or exclamation. The coins spilled from my hand.

In that instant, the babe was eying me, and I the babe.

Then it was snatched away. The woman bent to paw after the coins, glancing up at me in some sort of panic.

"What on earth?" My wife guided me up into the lobby where, stunned, standing at the register, I forgot my name. "What's wrong? What *happened* out there?"

"Did you see the baby?" I asked.

"The beggar's child—?"

"It's the same."

"The same *what*?"

"The same baby," I said, my lips numb, "that the woman used to shove in our faces fifteen years ago."

"Oh, come, now."

"Yes, come." And I went back to the door and opened it to look out.

But the street was empty. The beggar woman and her bundle had run off to some other street, some other hotel, some other arrival or departure.

I shut the door and went back to the register.

"What?" I said.

And suddenly remembering my name, wrote it down.

The child would not go away.

The memory, that is.

The recollection of other years and days in rains and fogs, the mother and her small creature, and the soot on that tiny face, and the cry of the woman herself which was like a shrieking of brakes put on to fend off damnation.

Sometimes, late at night, I heard her wailing as she went off the cliff of Ireland's weather and down upon rocks where the sea never stopped coming or going, but stayed forever in tumult.

But the child stayed, too.

My wife would catch me brooding at tea or after supper over the Irish coffee and say, "*That* again?"

"That."

"It's silly."

"Oh, it's silly, all right."

"You've always made fun of metaphysics, astrology, palmistry—"

"*This* is genetics."

"You'll spoil your whole vacation." My wife passed the apricot tarts and refilled my cup. "For the first time in years, we're traveling without a load of screenplays or novels. But out in Galway this morning you kept looking over your shoulder as if *she* were trotting in the road behind with her spitting image."

"Did I do that?"

"You know you did. You say genetics? That's good enough for me. That is the same woman begged out front of the hotel fifteen years ago, yes, but she has twenty children at home, each one inch shorter than the next, and all as alike as a bag of potatoes. Some families run like that. A gang of father's kids, or a gang of mother's absolute twins, and nothing in between. Yes, that child looks like the one we saw years back. But you look like your brother, don't you, and there's twelve years difference?"

"Keep talking," I said. "I feel better."

But that was a lie.

I went out to search the Dublin streets.

Oh, I didn't tell myself this, no. But, search I did.

From Trinity College on up O'Connell Street and way around back to St. Stephen's Green I pretended a vast interest in fine architecture, but secretly watched for her and her dire burden.

I bumped into the usual haggle of banjo-pluckers and shuffle-dancers and hymn-singers and tenors gargling in their sinuses and baritones remembering a buried love or fitting a stone on their mother's grave, but nowhere did I surprise my quarry.

At last I approached the doorman at the Royal Hibernian Hotel.

"Mike," I said.

"Sir," said he.

"That woman who used to lurk about at the foot of the steps there—"

"Ah, the one with the babe, do you mean?"

"Do you know her!?"

"Know her! Sweet Jesus, she's been the plague of my years since I was thirty, and look at the gray in my hair now!"

"She's been begging *that* long?"

"And forever beyond."

"Her name—"

"Molly's as good as any. McGillahee, I think. Sure. McGillahee's it. Beg pardon, sir, why do you ask?"

"Have you *looked* at her baby, Mike?"

His nose winced at a sour smell. "Years back, I gave it up. These beggar women keep their kids in a dread style, sir, a condition roughly equivalent to the bubonic. They neither wipe nor bathe nor mend. Neatness would work against beggary, do you see? The fouler the better, that's the motto, eh?"

"Right. Mike, so you've never *really* examined that infant?"

"Aesthetics being a secret part of my life, I'm a great one for averting the gaze. It's blind I am to help you, sir. Forgive."

"Forgiven, Mike." I passed him two shillings. "Oh . . . have you seen those two, lately?"

"Strange. Come to think, sir. They have not come here in . . . " he counted on his fingers and showed surprise, "why it must be ten days! They never done *that* before. Ten!"

"Ten," I said, and did some secret counting of my own. "Why, that would make it ever since the first day *I* arrived at the hotel."

"Do you *say* that now?"

"I say it, Mike."

And I wandered down the steps, wondering what I said and what I meant.

It was obvious she was hiding out.

I did not for a moment believe she or the child was sick.

Our collision in front of the hotel, the baby's eyes and mine striking flint, had startled her like a fox and shunted her off God-knows-where, to some other alley, some other road, some other town.

I smelled her evasion. She was a vixen, yes, but I felt myself, day by day, a better hound.

I took to walking earlier, later, in the strangest locales. I would leap off busses in Ballsbridge and prowl the fog or taxi half out to Kilcock and hide in pubs. I even knelt in Dean Swift's church to hear the echoes of his Houyhnhnm voice, but stiffened alert at the merest whimper of a child carried through.

It was all madness, to pursue such a brute idea. Yet on I went, itching where the damned thing scratched.

And then by sheer and wondrous accident in a dousing downpour that smoked the gutters and fringed my hat with a million raindrops per second, while taking my nightly swim, it happened. . . .

Coming out of a Wally Beery 1930 vintage movie, some Cadbury's chocolate still in my mouth, I turned a corner. . . .

And this woman shoved a bundle in my face and cried a familiar cry:

"If there's mercy in your soul—!"

She stopped, riven. She spun about. She ran.

For in the instant, she *knew*. And the babe in her arms, with the shocked small face, and the swift bright eyes, he knew me, *too*! Both let out some kind of fearful cry.

God, how that woman could race.

I mean she put a block between her backside and me while I gathered breath to yell: "Stop, thief!"

It seemed an appropriate yell. The baby was a mystery I wished to solve. And there she vaulted off with it. I mean, she *seemed* a thief.

So I dashed after, crying, "Stop! Help! *You*, there!"

She kept a hundred yards between us for the first half mile, up over bridges across the Liffey and finally up Grafton Street where I jogged into St. Stephen's Green to find it . . . empty.

She had absolutely vanished.

Unless, of course, I thought, turning in all directions, letting my gaze idle, it's into the Four Provinces pub she's gone. . . .

There is where I went.

It was a good guess.

I shut the door quietly.

There, at the bar, was the beggar woman, putting a pint of Guinness to her own face, and giving a shot of gin to the babe for happy sucking.

I let my heart pound down to a slower pace, then took my place at the bar and said, "Bombay Gin, please."

At my voice, the baby gave one kick. The gin sprayed from his mouth. He fell into a spasm of choked coughing.

The woman turned him over and thumped his back to stop the convulsion. In so doing, the red face of the child faced me, eyes squeezed shut, mouth wide, and at last the seizure stopped, the cheeks grew less red, and I said:

"You there, baby."

There was a hush. Everyone in the bar waited.

I finished:

"You need a shave."

The babe flailed about in his mother's arms with a loud strange wounded cry, which I cut off with a simple:

"It's all right. I'm not the police."

The woman relaxed as if all her bones had gone to porridge.

"Put me down," said the babe.

She put him down on the floor.

"Give me my gin."

She handed him his little glass of gin.

"Let's go in the saloon bar where we can talk."

The babe led the way with some sort of small dignity, holding his swaddling clothes about him with one hand, and the gin glass in the other.

The saloon bar was empty, as he had guessed. The babe, without my help, climbed up into a chair at a table and finished his gin.

"Ah, Christ, I need another," he said in a tiny voice.

While his mother went to fetch a refill, I sat down and the babe and I eyed each other for a long moment.

"Well," he said at last, "what do ya think?"

"I don't know. I'm waiting and watching my own reactions," I said. "I may explode into laughter or tears at any moment."

"Let it be laughter. I couldn't stand the other."

On impulse, he stuck out his hand. I took it.

"The name is McGillahee. Better known as McGillahee's Brat. Brat, for short."

"Brat," I said. "Smith."

He gripped my hand hard with his tiny fingers.

"Smith? Your name fits nothing. But Brat, well, don't a name like that go ten thousand leagues under? And what, you may ask, am I doing down here? And you up there so tall and fine and breathing the high air? Ah, but here's your drink, the same as mine. Put it in you, and listen."

The woman was back with shots for both. I drank, watched her, and said, "Are you the mother—?"

"It's me sister she is," said the babe. "Our mother's long since gone to her reward; a ha'penny a day for the next thousand years, nuppence dole from there on, and cold summers for a million years."

"Your sister?!" I must have sounded my disbelief, for she turned away to nibble her ale.

"You'd never guess, would you? She looks ten times my age. But if winter don't age you, Poor will. And winter and Poor is the whole tale. Porcelain cracks in this weather. And once she was the loveliest porcelain out of the summer oven." He gave her a gentle nudge. "But Mother she is now, for thirty years—"

"Thirty years you've been—!"

"Out front of the Royal Hibernian Hotel? And more! And our mother before that, and our father, too, and *his* father, the whole tribe! The day I was born, no sooner sacked in diapers, than I was on the street and my mother crying Pity and the world deaf, stone-dumb-blind and deaf. Thirty years with my sister, ten years with my mother, McGillahee's brat has been on display!"

"Forty?" I cried, and drank my gin to straighten my logic. "You're really forty? And all those years—how?"

"How did I get into this line of work?" said the babe. "You do not get, you are, as we say, *born* in. It's been nine hours a night, no Sundays off, no time-clocks, no paychecks, and mostly dust and lint fresh paid out of the pockets of the rambling rich."

"But I still don't understand," I said, gesturing to his size, his shape, his complexion.

"Nor will I, ever," said McGillahee's brat. "Am I a midget born to the blight? Some kind of dwarf shaped by glands? Or did someone warn me to play it safe, stay small?"

"That could hardly—"

"Couldn't it!? It could! Listen. A thousand times I heard it, and a thousand times more my father came home from his beggary route and I remember him jabbing his finger in my crib, pointing at me, and saying, 'Brat, whatever you do, don't grow, not a muscle, not a hair! The Real Thing's out there; the World. You *hear* me, Brat? Dublin's beyond, and Ireland on top of that and England hard-assed above us all. It's not worth the consideration, the bother, the planning, the growing-up to try and make do, so listen here, Brat, we'll stunt your growth with stories, with truth, with warnings and predictions, we'll wean you on gin, and smoke you with Spanish cigarettes until you're a cured Irish ham, pink, sweet, and small, small, do you hear, Brat? I did not want you in this world. But now you're in it, lie low, don't walk, creep; don't talk, wail; don't work, loll; and when the world is too much for you, Brat, give it back your opinion: *wet* yourself! Here, Brat, here's your evening poteen; fire it down. The Four Horsemen of the Apocalypse wait down by the Liffey. Would you see their like? Hang on. Here we go!'

"And out we'd duck for the evening rounds, my dad banging a banjo with me at his feet holding the cup, or him doing a tap-dance, me under one arm, the musical instrument under the other, both making discord.

"Then, home late, we'd lie four in a bed, a crop of failed potatoes, discards of an ancient famine.

"And sometimes in the midst of the night, for lack of something to do, my father would jump out of bed in the cold and run outdoors and fist his knuckles at the sky, I remember, I remember, I heard, I saw, daring God to lay hands on him, for so help him, Jesus, if *he* could lay hands on God, there would be torn feathers, ripped beards, lights put out, and the grand theater of Creation shut tight for Eternity! do ya hear, God, ya dumb brute with your perpetual rain-clouds turning their black behinds on me, do ya *care*!?

"For answer the sky wept, and my mother did the same all night, all night.

"And the next morn out I'd go again, this time in *her* arms and back and forth between the two, day on day, and her grieving for the million dead from the famine of fifty-one and him saying good-by to the four million who sailed off to Boston . . .

"Then one night, Dad vanished, too. Perhaps he sailed off on some mad boat like the rest, to forget us all. I forgive him. The poor beast was wild with hunger and nutty for want of something to give us and no giving.

"So then my mother simply washed away in her own tears, dissolved, you might say, like a sugar-crystal saint, and was gone before the morning fog rolled back, and the grass took her, and my sister, aged twelve, overnight grew tall, but I, me, oh, me? I grew small. Each decided, you see, long before that, of course, on going his or her way.

"But then part of my decision happened early on. I knew, I swear I did! the quality of my own Thespian performance!

"I heard it from every decent beggar in Dublin when I was nine days old. 'What a beggar's babe *that* is!' they cried.

"And my mother, standing outside the Abbey Theater in the rain when I was twenty and thirty days old, and the actors and directors coming out tuning their ears to my Gaelic laments, *they* said I should be signed up and trained! So the stage would have been mine with size, but size never came. And there's no brat's roles in Shakespeare. Puck, maybe; what else? So meanwhile at forty days and fifty nights after being born my performance made hackles rise and beggars yammer to borrow my hide, flesh, soul and voice for an hour here, an hour there. The old lady rented me out by the half day when she was sick abed. And not a one bought and bundled me off did not return with praise. 'My God,' they cried, 'his yell would suck money from the Pope's poorbox!'

"And outside the Cathedral one Sunday morn, an American cardinal was riven to the spot by the yowl I gave when I saw his fancy skirt and bright cloth. Said he: 'That cry is the first cry of Christ at his birth, mixed with the dire yell of Lucifer churned out of Heaven and spilled in fiery muck down the landslide slops of Hell!'

"That's what the dear Cardinal said. Me, eh? Christ and the Devil in one lump, the gabble screaming out my mouth half lost, half found, can you *top* that?"

"I cannot," I said.

"Then, later on, many years further, there was this wild American film director who chased White Whales? The first time he spied me, he took a quick look and . . . winked! And took out a pound note and did not put it in my sister's hand, no, but took my own scabby fist and tucked the pound in and gave it a squeeze and another wink, and him gone.

"I seen his picture later in the paper, him stabbing the White Whale with a dread harpoon, and him proper mad, and I always figured, whenever we passed, he had my number, but I never winked back. I played the part dumb. And there was always a good pound in it for me, and him proud of my not giving in and letting him know that I knew that he knew.

"Of all the thousands who've gone by in the grand Ta-Ta! he was the only one ever looked me right in the eye, save you! The rest were all too embarrassed by life to so much as gaze as they put out the dole.

"Well, I mean now, what with that film director, and the Abbey Players, and the cardinals and beggars telling me to go with my own natural self and talent and the genius busy in my baby fat, all *that* must have turned my head.

"Added to which, my having the famines tolled in my ears, and not a day passed we did not see a funeral go by, or watch the unemployed march up and down in strikes, well, don't you see? Battered by rains and storms of people and knowing so much, I *must* have been driven down, driven back, don't you think?

"You cannot starve a babe and have a man; or do miracles run different than of old?

"My mind, with all the drear stuff dripped in my ears, was it likely to want to run around free in all that guile and sin and being put upon by natural nature and unnatural man? No. No! I just wanted my little cubby, and since I was long out of that, and no squeezing back, I just squinched myself small against the rains. I flaunted the torments.

"And, do you know? I won."

You did, Brat, I thought. You did.

"Well, I guess that's my story," said the small creature there perched on a chair in the empty saloon bar.

He looked at me for the first time since he had begun his tale.

The woman who was his sister, but seemed his gray mother, now dared to lift her gaze, also.

"Do," I said, "do the people of Dublin know about you?"

"Some. And envy me. And hate me, I guess, for getting off easy from God, and his plagues and Fates."

"Do the police know?"

"Who would tell them?"

There was a long pause.

Rain beat on the windows.

Somewhere a door-hinge shrieked like a soul in torment as someone went out and someone else came in.

Silence.

"Not me," I said.

"Ah, Christ, Christ . . . "

And tears rolled down the sister's cheeks.

And tears rolled down the sooty strange face of the babe.

Both of them let the tears go, did not try to wipe them off, and at last they stopped, and we drank up the rest of our gin and sat a moment longer and then I said: "The best hotel in town is the Royal Hibernian, the best for beggars, that is."

"True," they said.

"And for fear of meeting me, you've kept away from the richest territory?"

"We have."

"The night's young," I said. "There's a flight of rich ones coming in from Shannon just before midnight."

I stood up.

"If you'll let . . . I'll be happy to walk you there, now."

"The Saints' calendar is full," said the woman, "but somehow we'll find room for you."

Then I walked the woman McGillahee and her brat back through the rain toward the Royal Hibernian Hotel, and us talking along the way of the mobs of people coming in from the airport just before twelve, drinking and registering at that late hour, that fine hour for begging, and with the cold rain and all, not to be missed.

I carried the babe for some part of the way, she looking tired, and when we got in sight of the hotel, I handed him back, saying:

"Is this the first time, ever?"

"We was found out by a tourist? Aye," said the babe. "You have an otter's eye."

"I'm a writer."

"Nail me to the Cross," said he, "I might have known! You won't—"

"No," I said. "I won't write a single word about this, about you, for another fifteen years or more."

"Mum's the word?"

"Mum."

We were a hundred feet from the hotel steps.

"I must shut up here," said Brat, lying there in his old sister's arms, fresh as peppermint candy from the gin, round-eyed, wild-haired, swathed in dirty linens and wools, small fists gently gesticulant. "We've a rule, Molly and me, no chat while at work. Grab my hand."

I grabbed the small fist, the little fingers. It was like holding a sea anemone.

"God bless you," he said.

"And God," I said, "take care of you."

"Ah," said the babe, "in another year we'll have enough saved for the New York boat."

"We will," she said.

"And no more begging, and no more being the dirty babe crying by night in the storms, but some decent work in the open, do you know, do you see, will you light a candle to that?"

"It's lit." I squeezed his hand.

"Go on ahead."

"I'm gone," I said.

And walked quickly to the front of the hotel where airport taxis were starting to arrive.

Behind, I heard the woman trot forward, I saw her arms lift, with the Holy Child held out in the rain.

"If there's mercy in you!" she cried. "Pity—!"

And heard the coins ring in the cup and heard the sour babe wailing, and more cars coming and the woman crying Mercy and Thanks and Pity and God Bless and Praise Him and wiping tears from my own eyes, feeling eighteen inches tall, somehow made it up the high steps and into the hotel and to bed where rains fell cold on the rattled windows all the night and where, in the dawn, when I woke and looked out, the street was empty save for the steady falling storm. . . .

The Aqueduct

It leapt over the country in great stone arches. It was empty now, with the wind blowing in its sluices; it took a year to build, from the land in the North to the land in the South.

"Soon," said mothers to their children, "soon now the Aqueduct will be finished. Then they will open the gates a thousand miles North and cool water will flow to us, for our crops, our flowers, our baths, and our tables."

The children watched the Aqueduct being built stone on solid stone. It towered thirty feet in the sky, with great gargoyle spouts every hundred yards which would drop tiny streams down into yard reservoirs.

In the North there was not only one country, but two. They had rattled their sabers and clashed their shields for many years.

Now, in the Year of the Finishing of the Aqueduct, the two Northern countries shot a million arrows at each other and raised a million shields, like numerous suns, flashing. There was a cry like an ocean on a distant shore.

At the year's end the Aqueduct stood finished. The people of the Hot South, waiting, asked, "When will the water come? With war in the North, will we starve for water, will our crops die?"

A courier came racing. "The war is terrible," he said. "There is a slaughtering that is unbelievable. More than one hundred million people have been slain."

"For what?"

"They disagreed, those two Northern countries.

"That's all we know. They disagreed."

The people gathered all along the stone Aqueduct. Messengers ran along the empty sluiceways with yellow streamers, crying, "Bring vases and bowls, ready your fields and plows, open your baths, fetch water glasses!"

A thousand miles of filling Aqueduct and the slap of naked courier feet in the channel, running ahead. The people gathered by the tens of millions from the boiling countryside, the sluiceways open, waiting, their crocks, urns, jugs, held up toward the gargoyle spouts where the wind whistled emptily.

"It's coming!" The word passed from person to person down the one thousand miles.

And from a great distance, there was the sound of rushing and running, the sound that liquid makes in a stone channel. It flowed slowly at first and then faster, and then very fast down into the Southern land, under the hot sun.

"It's here! Any second now. Listen!" said the people. They raised their glasses into the air.

Liquid poured from the sluiceways down the land, out of gargoyle mouths, into the stone baths, into the glasses, into the fields. The fields were made rich for the harvest. People bathed. There was a singing you could hear from one field to one town to another.

"But, Mother!" A child held up his glass and shook it, the liquid whirled slowly. "This isn't water!"

"Hush!" said the mother.

"It's red," said the child. "And it's thick."

"Here's the soap, wash yourself, don't ask questions, shut up," she said. "Hurry into the field, open the sluicegates, plant the rice!"

In the fields, the father and his two sons laughed into one another's faces. "If this keeps up, we've a great life ahead. A full silo and a clean body."

"Don't worry," said the two sons. "The President is sending a representative North to make certain that the two countries there continue to disagree."

"Who knows, it might be a fifty-year war!"

They sang and smiled.

And at night they all lay happily, listening to the good sound of the Aqueduct, full and rich, like a river, rushing through their land toward the morning.

Gotcha!

They were incredibly in love. They said it. They knew it. They lived it. When they weren't staring at each other they were hugging. When they weren't hugging they were kissing. When they weren't kissing they were a dozen scrambled eggs in bed. When they were finished with the amazing omelet they went back to staring and making noises.

Theirs, in sum, was a Love Affair. Print it out in capitals. Underline it. Find some italics. Add exclamation points. Put up the fireworks. Tear down the clouds. Send out for some adrenaline. Roustabout at three A.M. Sleep till noon.

Her name was Beth. His name was Charles.

They had no last names. For that matter, they rarely called each other by their first names. They found new names every day for each other, some of them capable of being said only late at night and only to each other, when they were special and tender and most shockingly unclad.

Anyway, it was Fourth of July every night. New Year's every dawn. It was the home team winning and the mob on the field. It was a bobsled downhill and everything cold racing by in beauty and two warm people holding tight and yelling with joy.

And then . . .

Something happened.

At breakfast about one year into the conniption fits Beth said, half under her breath:

"Gotcha."

He looked up and said, "What?"

"Gotcha," she said. "A game. You never played Gotcha?"

"Never even heard of it."

"Oh, I've played it for years."

"Do you buy it in a store?" he asked.

"No, no. It's a game I made up, or almost made up, based on an old ghost story or scare story. Like to play it?"

"That all depends." He was back shoveling away at his ham and eggs.

"Maybe we'll play it tonight—it's fun. In fact," she said, nodding her head once and beginning to go on with her breakfast again, "it's a definite thing. Tonight it is. Oh, bun, you'll love it."

"I love everything we do," he said.

"It'll scare the hell out of you," she said.

"What's the name again?"

"Gotcha," she said.

"Never heard of it."

They both laughed. But her laughter was louder than his.

It was a long and delicious day of luscious name-callings and rare omelets and a good dinner with a fine wine and then some reading just before midnight, and at midnight he suddenly looked over at her and said:

"Haven't we forgotten something?"

"What?"

"Gotcha."

"Oh, my, yes!" she said, laughing. "I was just waiting for the clock to strike the hour."

Which it promptly did. She counted to twelve, sighed happily and said, "All right—let's put out most of the lights. Just keep the small lamp lighted by the bed. Now, there." She ran around putting out all the other lights, and came back and plumped up his pillow and made him lie right in the middle of the bed. "Now, you stay right there. You don't move, see. You just . . . *wait*. And see what *happens*—okay?"

"Okay." He smiled indulgently. At times like these she was a ten-year-old Girl Scout rushing about with some poisoned cookies on a grand lark. He was always ready, it seemed, to eat the cookies. "Proceed."

"Now, be very quiet," she said. "No talking. Let me talk if I want—okay?"

"Okay."

"Here goes," she said, and disappeared.

Which is to say that she sank down like the dark witch, melting, melting, at the foot of the bed. She let her bones collapse softly. Her head and her hair followed her Japanese paper-lantern body down, fold on fold, until the air at the foot of the bed was empty.

"Well done!" he cried.

"You're not supposed to talk. Sh-h."

"I'm sh-h-h-ed."

Silence. A minute passed. Nothing.

He smiled a lot, waiting.

Another minute passed. Silence. He didn't know where she was.

"Are you still at the foot of the bed?" he asked. "Oh, sorry." He sh-h-h-ed himself. "Not supposed to talk."

Five minutes passed. The room seemed to get somewhat darker. He sat up a bit and fixed his pillow and his smile got somewhat less expectant. He peered about the room. He could see the light from the bathroom shining on the wall.

There was a sound like a small mouse in one far corner of the room. He looked there but could see nothing.

Another minute passed. He cleared his throat.

There was a whisper from the bathroom door, down near the floor.

He glanced that way and grinned and waited. Nothing.

He thought he felt something crawling under the bed. The sensation passed. He swallowed and blinked.

The room seemed almost candlelit. The light bulb, one hundred and fifty watts, seemed now to have developed fifty-watt problems.

There was a scurry like a great spider on the floor, but nothing was visible. After a long while her voice murmured to him like an echo, now from this side of the dark room, now that.

"How do you like it *so* far?"

"I . . ."

"Don't speak," she whispered.

And was gone again for another two minutes. He was beginning to feel his pulse jump in his wrists. He looked at the left wall, then the right, then the ceiling.

And suddenly a white spider was crawling along the foot of the bed. It was her hand, of course, imitating a spider. No sooner there than gone.

"Ha!" He laughed.

"Sh-h!" came the whisper.

Something ran into the bathroom. The bathroom light went out. Silence. There was only the small light in the bedroom now. A faint rim of perspiration appeared on his brow. He sat wondering why they were doing this.

A clawing hand snatched up on the far left side of the bed, gesticulated and vanished. The watch ticked on his wrist.

Another five minutes must have gone by. His breathing was long and somewhat painful, though he couldn't figure why. A small frown gathered in the furrow between his eyes and did not go away. His fingers moved on the quilt all to themselves, as if trying to get away from him.

A claw appeared on the right side. No, it hadn't been there at all! Or had it?

Something stirred in the closet directly across the room. The door slowly opened upon darkness. Whether something went in at that moment or was already there, waiting to come out, he could not say. The door now opened upon an abyss that was as deep as the spaces between the stars. A few dark shadows of coats hung inside, like disembodied people.

There was a running of feet in the bathroom.

There was a scurry of cat feet by the window.

He sat up. He licked his lips. He almost said something. He shook his head. A full twenty minutes had passed.

There was a faint moan, a distant laugh that hushed itself. Then another groan . . . where? In the shower?

"Beth?" he said at last.

No answer. Water dripped in the sink suddenly, drop by slow drop. Something had turned it on.

"Beth?" he called again, and hardly recognized his voice, it was so pale.

A window opened somewhere. A cool wind blew a phantom of curtain out on the air.

"Beth," he called weakly.

No answer.

"I don't like this," he said.

Silence.

No motion. No whisper. No spider. Nothing.

"Beth?" he called, a bit louder.

No breathing, even, anywhere.

"I don't like this game."

Silence.

"You hear me, Beth?"

Quiet.

"I don't like this game."

Drip in the bathroom sink.

"Let's stop the game, Beth."

Wind from the window.

"Beth?" he called again. "Answer me. Where are you?"

Silence.

"You all right?"

The rug lay on the floor. The light grew small in the lamp. Invisible dusts stirred in the air.

"Beth . . . you okay?"

Silence.

"Beth?"

Nothing.

"Beth!"

"Oh-h-h-h-h . . . *ah-h-h-h-h!*"

He heard the shriek, the cry, the scream.

A shadow sprang up. A great darkness leaped upon the bed. It landed on four legs.

"Ah!" came the shout.

"Beth!" he screamed.

"Oh-h-h-h!" came the shriek from the thing.

Another great leap and the dark thing landed on his chest. Cold hands seized his neck. A white face plunged down. A mouth gaped and shrieked:

"Gotcha!"

"Beth!" he cried.

And flailed and wallowed and turned but it clung to him and looked down and the face was white and the eyes raved wide and the nostrils flared. And the big bloom of dark hair in a flurry above fell down in a stormwind. And the hands clawing at his neck and the air breathed out of that mouth and nostrils as cold as polar wind, and the weight of the thing on his chest light but heavy, thistledown but an anvil crushing, and him thrashing to be free, but his arms pinned by the fragile legs and the face peering down at him so full of evil glee, so brimful of malevolence, so beyond this world and in another, so alien, so strange, so never seen before, that he had to shriek again.

"No! No! No! Stop! Stop!"

"Gotcha!" screamed the mouth.

And it was someone he had never seen before. A woman from some time ahead, some year when age and things had changed everything, when darkness had gathered and boredom had poisoned and words had killed, and everything gone to ice and lostness and nothing, no residues of love, only hate, only death.

"No! Oh, God! Stop!"

He burst into tears. He began to sob.

She stopped.

Her hands went away cold and came back warm to touch, hold, pet him. And it was Beth.

"Oh, God, God, God!" he wailed. "No, no, no!"

"Oh, Charles, Charlie," she cried, all remorse. "I'm sorry. I didn't mean—"

"You did. Oh God, you did, you did!"

His grief was uncontrollable.

"No, no. Oh, Charlie," she said, and burst into tears herself. She flung herself out of bed and ran around turning on lights. But none of them were bright enough. He was crying steadily now. She came back and slid in by him and put his grieving face to her breast and held him, hugged him, patted him, kissed his brow and let him weep.

"I'm sorry. Charlie, listen, sorry. I didn't—"

"You *did*!"

"It was only a game!"

"A game! You call that a game, game, game!" he wailed, and wept again.

And finally, at last, his crying stopped and he lay against her and she was warm and sister/mother/friend/lover again. His heart, which had crashed, now moved to some near-calm. His pulses stopped fluttering. The constriction around his chest let go.

"Oh, Beth, Beth," he wailed, softly.

"Charlie," she apologized, her eyes shut.

"Don't ever do that again."

"I won't."

"Promise you'll never do that again?" he said, hiccuping.

"I swear, I promise."

"You were *gone*, Beth—that wasn't *you*!"

"I promise, I swear, Charlie."

"All right," he said.

"Am I forgiven, Charlie?"

He lay a long while and at last nodded, as if it had taken some hard thinking.

"Forgiven."

"I'm sorry, Charlie. Let's get some sleep. Shall I turn the lights off?"

Silence.

"Shall I turn the lights off, Charlie?"

"No-no."

"We have to have the lights off to sleep, Charlie."

"Leave a few on for a little while," he said, eyes shut.

"All right," she said, holding him. "For a little while."

He took a shuddering breath and came down with a chill. He shook for five minutes before her holding him and stroking him and kissing him made the shiver and the tremble go away.

An hour later she thought he was asleep and got up and turned off all the lights save the bathroom light, in case he should wake and want at least one on. Getting back into bed, she felt him stir. His voice, very small, very lost, said:

"Oh, Beth, I loved you so much."

She weighed his words. "Correction. You *love* me so much."

"I *love* you so much," he said.

It took her an hour, staring at the ceiling, to go to sleep.

The next morning at breakfast he buttered his toast and looked at her. She sat calmly munching her bacon. She caught his glance and grinned at him.

"Beth," he said.

"What?" she asked.

How could he tell her? Something in him was cold. The bedroom even in the morning sun seemed smaller, darker. The bacon was burned. The toast was black. The coffee had a strange and alien flavor. She looked very pale. He could feel his heart, like a tired fist, pounding dimly against some locked door somewhere.

"I . . ." he said, "we . . ."

How could he tell her that suddenly he was afraid? Suddenly he sensed that this was the beginning of the end. And beyond the end there would never be anyone to go to anywhere at any time—no one in all the world.

"Nothing," he said.

Five minutes later she asked, looking at her crumpled eggs, "Charles, do you want to play the game tonight? But this time it's me, and this time it's you who hides and jumps out and says, 'Gotcha'?"

He waited because he could not breathe.

"No."

He did not want to know that part of himself.

Tears sprang to his eyes.

"Oh, no," he said.

The End of the Beginning

He stopped the lawn mower in the middle of the yard, because he felt that the sun at just that moment had gone down and the stars come out. The fresh-cut grass that had showered his face and body died softly away. Yes, the stars were there, faint at first, but brightening in the clear desert sky. He heard the porch screen door tap shut and felt his wife watching him as he watched the night.

"Almost time," she said.

He nodded; he did not have to check his watch. In the passing moments he felt very old, then very young, very cold, then very warm, now this, now that. Suddenly he was miles away. He was his own son talking steadily, moving briskly to cover his pounding heart and the resurgent panics as he felt himself slip into fresh uniform, check food supplies, oxygen flasks, pressure helmet, space-suiting, and turn as every man on Earth tonight turned, to gaze at the swiftly filling sky.

Then, quickly, he was back, once more the father of the son, hands gripped to the lawn-mower handle. His wife called, "Come sit on the porch."

"I've got to keep busy!"

She came down the steps and across the lawn. "Don't worry about Robert; he'll be all right."

"But it's all so new," he heard himself say. "It's never been done before. Think of it—a manned rocket going up tonight to build the first space station. Good Lord, it can't be done, it doesn't exist, there's no rocket, no proving ground, no take-off time, no technicians. For that matter, I don't even have a son named Bob. The whole thing's too much for me!"

"Then what are you doing out here, staring?"

He shook his head. "Well, late this morning, walking to the office, I heard someone laugh out loud. It shocked me, so I froze in the middle of the street. It was *me*, laughing! Why? Because finally I really *knew* what Bob was going to do tonight; at last I *believed* it. 'Holy' is a word I never use, but that's how I felt stranded in all that traffic. Then, middle of the afternoon, I caught myself humming. You know the song. 'A wheel in a wheel. Way in the middle of the air.' I laughed again. The space station, of course, I thought. The big wheel with hollow spokes where Bob'll live six or eight months, then get along to the Moon. Walking home, I remembered more of the song. 'Little wheel run by faith, big wheel run by the grace of God.' I wanted to jump, yell, and flame-out myself!"

His wife touched his arm. "If we stay out here, let's at least be comfortable."

They placed two wicker rockers in the center of the lawn and sat quietly as the stars dissolved out of darkness in pale crushings of rock salt strewn from horizon to horizon.

"Why," said his wife, at last, "it's like waiting for the fireworks at Sisley Field every year."

"Bigger crowd tonight . . ."

"I keep thinking—a billion people watching the sky right now, their mouths all open at the same time."

They waited, feeling the earth move under their chairs.

"What time is it now?"

"Eleven minutes to eight."

"You're always right; there must be a clock in your head."

"I can't be wrong, tonight. I'll be able to tell you one second before they blast off. Look! The ten-minute warning!"

On the western sky they saw four crimson flares open out, float shimmering down the wind above the desert, then sink silently to the extinguishing earth.

In the new darkness the husband and wife did not rock in their chairs.

After a while he said, "Eight minutes." A pause. "Seven minutes." What seemed a much longer pause. "Six . . ."

His wife, her head back, studied the stars immediately above her and murmured, "Why?" She closed her eyes. "Why the rockets, why tonight? Why all this? I'd like to know."

He examined her face, pale in the vast powdering light of the Milky Way. He felt the stirring of an answer, but let his wife continue.

"I mean it's not that old thing again, is it, when people asked why men climbed Mt. Everest and they said, 'Because it's there'? I never understood. That was no answer to me."

Five minutes, he thought. Time ticking . . . his wristwatch . . . a wheel in a wheel . . . little wheel run by . . . big wheel run by . . . way in the middle of . . . four minutes! . . . The men snug in the rocket by now, the hive, the control board flickering with light. . . .

His lips moved.

"All I know is it's really the end of the beginning. The Stone Age, Bronze Age, Iron Age; from now on we'll lump all those together under one big name for when we walked on Earth and heard the birds at morning and cried with envy. Maybe we'll call it the Earth Age, or maybe the Age of Gravity. Millions of years we fought gravity. When we were amoebas and fish we struggled to get out of the sea without gravity crushing us. Once safe on the shore we fought to stand upright without gravity breaking our new invention, the spine, tried to walk without stumbling, run without falling. A billion years Gravity kept us home, mocked us with wind and clouds, cabbage moths and locusts. That's what's so God-awful big about tonight . . . it's the end of old man Gravity and the age we'll remember him by, for once and all. I don't know where they'll divide the ages, at the Persians, who dreamt of flying carpets, or the Chinese, who all unknowing celebrated birthdays and New Years with strung ladyfingers and high skyrockets, or some minute, some incredible second in the next hour. But we're in at the end of a billion years trying, the end of something long and to us humans, anyway, honorable."

Three minutes . . . two minutes fifty-nine seconds . . . two minutes fifty-eight seconds . . .

"But," said his wife, "I still don't know why."

Two minutes, he thought. *Ready? Ready? Ready?* The far radio voice calling. *Ready! Ready! Ready!* The quick, faint replies from the humming rocket. *Check! Check! Check!*

Tonight, he thought, even if we fail with this first, we'll send a second and a third ship and move on out to all the planets and later, all the stars. We'll just keep going until the big words like 'immortal' and 'forever' take on meaning. Big words, yes, that's what we want. Continuity. Since our tongues first moved in our mouths we've asked, What does it all mean? No other question made sense, with death breathing down our necks. But just let us settle in on ten thousand worlds spinning around ten thousand alien suns and the question will fade away. Man will be endless and infinite, even as space is endless and infinite. Man will go on, as space goes on, forever. Individuals will die as always, but our history will reach as far as we'll ever need to see into the future, and with the knowledge of our survival for all time to come, we'll know security and thus the answer we've always searched for. Gifted with life, the least we can do is preserve and pass on the gift to infinity. That's a goal worth shooting for.

The wicker chairs whispered ever so softly on the grass.

One minute.

"One minute," he said aloud.

"Oh!" His wife moved suddenly to seize his hands. "I hope that Bob . . . "

"He'll be all right!"

"Oh, God, take care. . . . "

Thirty seconds.

"Watch now."

Fifteen, ten, five . . .

"Watch!"

Four, three, two, one.

"There! There! Oh, there, there!"

They both cried out. They both stood. The chairs toppled back, fell flat on the lawn. The man and his wife swayed, their hands struggled to find each other, grip, hold. They saw the brightening color in the sky and, ten seconds later, the great uprising comet burn the air, put out the stars, and rush away in fire flight to become another star in the returning profusion of the Milky Way. The man and wife held each other as if they had stumbled on the rim of an incredible cliff that faced an abyss so deep and dark there seemed no end to it. Staring up, they heard themselves sobbing and crying. Only after a long time were they able to speak.

"It got away, it did, *didn't* it?"

"Yes . . . "

"It's all right, isn't it?"

"Yes . . . yes . . . "

"It didn't fall back . . . ?"

"No, no, it's all right, Bob's all right, it's all right."

They stood away from each other at last.

He touched his face with his hand and looked at his wet fingers. "I'll be damned," he said. "I'll be damned."

They waited another five and then ten minutes until the darkness in their heads, the retina, ached with a million specks of fiery salt. Then they had to close their eyes.

"Well," she said, "now let's go in."

He could not move. Only his hand reached a long way out by itself to find the lawn-mower handle. He saw what his hand had done and said, "There's just a little more to do. . . . "

"But you can't see."

"Well enough," he said. "I must finish this. Then we'll sit on the porch awhile before we turn in."

He helped her put the chairs on the porch and sat her down and then walked back out to put his hands on the guide bar of the lawn mower. The lawn mower. A wheel in a wheel. A simple machine which you held in your hands, which you sent on ahead with a rush and a clatter while you walked behind with your quiet philosophy. Racket, followed by warm silence. Whirling wheel, then soft footfall of thought.

I'm a billion years old, he told himself; I'm one minute old. I'm one inch, no, ten thousand *miles*, tall. I look down and can't see my feet they're so far off and gone away below.

He moved the lawn mower. The grass showering up fell softly around him; he relished and savored it and felt that he was all mankind bathing at last in the fresh waters of the fountain of youth.

Thus bathed, he remembered the song again about the wheels and the faith and the grace of God being way up there in the middle of the sky where that single star, among a million motionless stars, dared to move and keep on moving.

Then he finished cutting the grass.

A NOTE ABOUT THE AUTHOR

Ray Bradbury has published some 500 short stories, novels, plays, and poems since his first story appeared in *Weird Tales* when he was twenty years old. For several years he wrote for *Alfred Hitchcock Presents* and *The Twilight Zone* and in 1953 did the screenplay for John Huston's *Moby Dick*. He has produced two of his own plays, written two musicals, two space-age cantatas with Lalo Schifrin and Jerry Goldsmith, collaborated on an animated film, *Icarus Montgolfier Wright*, which was nominated for an Academy Award in 1962, and is currently at work on a grand opera. Mr. Bradbury was Idea Consultant for the United States Pavilion at the New York World's Fair in 1963, has helped design a ride for Disney World and is doing consultant work on city engineering and rapid transit. When one of the Apollo astronaut teams landed on the moon, they named Dandelion Crater there to honor Bradbury's novel *Dandelion Wine*. He is the author of eighteen books.

A NOTE ON THE TYPE

The text of this book was set in Alphatype Garamond, a modern rendering of the type first cut in the sixteenth century by Claude Garamond (1510-1561). Garamond was a pupil of Geoffrey Troy and is believed to have based his letters on the Venetian models, although he introduced a number of important differences. It is to him we owe the letter which we know as old style. He gave to his letters a certain elegance and a feeling of movement which won for himself an immediate reputation and the patronage of King Francis I of France.

Composed by Superior Printing, Champaign, Illinois.
Printed and bound by American Book-Stratford Press,
Saddle Brook, New Jersey

Typography and binding design by Dorothy Schmiderer

K